F

RLAN CHONTAE MHUI

ook m   oe kept for two weeks. It ma
ewed   it required by another borrow
atest   ntered is the date by which th
should be returned.

THE WEDDING SUIT

JUDI JAMES

THE
WEDDING SUIT

HarperCollins*Publishers*

This novel is entirely a work of fiction. The names,
characters and incidents portrayed in it are the work of the
author's imagination. Any resemblance to actual persons,
living or dead, events or localities is entirely coincidental.

HarperCollins*Publishers*
77–85 Fulham Palace Road,
Hammersmith, London W6 8JB

Published by HarperCollins*Publishers* 1997
1 3 5 7 9 8 6 4 2

A catalogue record for this book
is available from the British Library

ISBN 0 00 225463 8

Set in Sabon by
Rowland Phototypesetting Limited, Bury St Edmunds, Suffolk

Printed in Great Britain by
HarperCollinsManufacturing Glasgow

CHAPTER ONE

ZG

LONDON 1998

VICUNA
On tall mist-shrouded mountains, high above the
clouds in Peru, live small goats with fleeces so fine
and delicate the fabric spun from them is known as
The King of All Cloths. Softer than cashmere and
therefore six times as expensive, it will take as many
as forty fleeces to make one vicuna overcoat. In its
natural state vicuna is either fawn in colour or a rich
cinnamon brown, and wearing it must always be
considered a privilege.

THE MURDER

Abusing that privilege through neglect or misuse should rate
as a criminal offence – though that was not the reason why
the police had been called out on this particular evening.

The suit must always fit the man – the man must never
be expected to fit the suit. This suit fitted like bespoke
rattlesnake skin. All the best suits reflect the character of
their wearer, and this garment – both cut and finished
by hand with a minimum of five hours' work in the
buttonholes alone – delineated an exacting perfectionist,

traditionalist and consummate purist who was, above all else, outstandingly, overwhelmingly and nauseatingly rich.

Even a detective swathed in a high-static blend of Bri-nylon and crease-resistant polyester could bend to pay homage at this altar of style and expert workmanship and, as he fingered the cloth reverently, he felt a twinge of resent-ment for the suit's wearer – even though the man was obviously dead.

The corpse was clad in a double-vented jacket with notched lapels and working cuff buttons. The stain was a shame, though, running as it did from chest to crotch with a particularly dense concentration around the stomach and the waist. The blotch would have been crimson, edged with a pie-crust frill of dull rust where the blood had dried, but it was night and so it lay dark and saturating, like wet ink.

He was a once-handsome man, though not young, tall and well-built in the Armani manner, with a meringue of dove-white hair crowning a face of nicotine-coloured, Continental skin. It was impossible to tell the shade of his eyes because the eyeballs had been removed by the murderer and the lids carefully stitched, along with the mouth.

'Gimp,' the SOCO noted. 'A special thread used for stitching buttonholes.' He turned to the young policeman beside him. 'My grandfather was a tailor,' he explained. 'Those stitches are professional, see?'

The policeman began to careen slightly.

'Tell me what's in the bag,' the detective-in-charge asked, dusting his knees as he rose from an unsteady crouch. The tone of his voice told the others they should guess rather than look. A great, waddling, whale-bellied man in an edge-

2

to-edge shirt and Roadrunner socks, Malcolm Abberline was noted for the large black-and-white picture of Robbie Coltrane he had tacked to the cork-board behind his desk, alongside the snap of his dead collie Roy, and he didn't care who bloody saw it. As he pointed towards the ground a Man. United solid silver memento cufflink slithered slyly out from beneath the sleeve of his Hugo Boss jacket.

Beside the corpse lay a Gucci handbag – a six-hundred-dollar job, brand new and fresh off the catwalks, puffball-shaped in gleaming mint-green patent. The bag appeared to be heavily full. The policemen made bets on its contents:

'Money. The guy was a mugger who took off with some rich tart's coffer – maybe her bodyguard caught up with him and took a little revenge.'

'In that suit? No fucking way, José. No way is a suit like that going round on a fucking bag-snatch, no siree.'

'So how come a suit like that in an area like this, then?'

They all straightened together like a pack of meerkats and looked around, sniffing the air. The question was valid. The body did look poetically misplaced in that turbid, crap-carpeted street. Off to their left somewhere lay the dreaming spires of Spitalfields. To their right a small army of Japanese on a walking tour of 'The Undiscovered London' gawped from behind a length of fluttering blue-and-white tape.

Six pairs of policemen's eyeballs glinted suddenly in fanciful unison – for it was at that precise moment that the first whiff of a major scandal rounded the corner and doffed its cap by way of introduction. They scented big-league. A spread in the *Screws* at the very least. At best a *Crimewatch* reconstruction: '. . . and in tonight's show actors replace the victim and his family, but the police involved will be playing themselves . . .' A line of looping smiles spread across their faces like bunting.

'Heroin?' one of them asked, looking back at the bag.

'Leather-gear, pervie-wear. Thongs and stuff.' A nervous laugh ran round the group.

'Intestines,' said Detective Abberline finally, silencing the sniggers in an instant.

And as it happened he was right; glistening greasily in the spanking-new Gucci bag lay a fat wine- and elderberry-coloured mound that appeared almost to writhe with life as it lay pinned in the lights from their torches once the faux-gold, logo-bearing zipper was gingerly pulled back.

THE PARTY

Imagine this: an abandoned urban tower-block earmarked for demolition, standing ghastly black and cavernous on a howling bitter night. Raddled and scarred by scorchmarks and sun-bleached graffiti, partially blinded by nailed-up chipboard hoarding, the place retains a strange gothic dignity while at the same time scaring you shitless.

Packs of mongrel dogs race and skitter around the building's shabby, urine-marinated legs. Your taxi abandoned you at the perimeter of the estate, refusing all inducement to venture further. The wind whips around the hem of your snazzy Versace and you realize you are gripped in the gruesome bowels of your own worst nightmare, clutching nothing more substantial than a gilt-edged invitation to ward off the terrors that lie beyond.

At this point you wish to be anywhere else on this planet,

but sweet-Jesus, there is no multiple choice involved here. This very venue on this particular night is the hippest place in London – and you are aware that if you aren't hip then you may as well be dead.

And so you teeter on your heels across meadows of undulating tarmac, past rusted, char-grilled Vauxhalls, through dripping dark alleys where green lights gutter over a sorry line of wind-blasted plaques erected in the memory of various policemen who fell in countless age-old battles.

There is the scent of Special Brew and cat's pee in the air. You come to a dead end and you feel the muscles of your heart begin to pucker in genuine fear.

There is a lift. The doors part noiselessly and, pulse pounding a gay rhumba beat, you step inside on gelatine legs. There is no apparent motion, but when the doors slide open again you are blinded by light so white that you feel actual heat from it and have to shield your eyes before you can begin to advance.

You are in the very crotch of the tower-block, then, but you are also somehow in a gilded and scented cathedral to style and chic. Someone has gutted out twenty floors above you so that there is no apparent ceiling, only row upon sick-inducing row of walls and balconies, all swathed in lengths of shimmering opal fabric.

When you look up the roof is so high you get vertigo and you pitch like a drunk. There is music so violently loud it slaps against your eardrums, making them smart. Others swarm around you; beautiful people or uglies, you can't really tell – A-list guests, anyway, bug-eyed with chemical mood-enhancers, all gazing opaquely while French-kissing the king prawns-en-croûte they have lifted from the finger buffet, while the roar of Bach's 'Toccata' buzzes busily about their lacquered heads.

There is womb-like warmth and there is the smell of a thousand hot scents. A white catwalk descends slowly from the heavens in clouds of dry ice and suddenly there are stilt-legged models upon it, around twenty or thirty of the most emaciated British faces, plus a couple of pouting celebs and ex-royals prancing ridiculously among them for good measure.

The theme of the show is evasive, though its title is 'The Divine Comedy', but the audience roars anyway because the alcohol quota has erred on the comatose side of adequate.

Laser lights cut through the dazzle overhead as the music builds to a crescendo. They spell out initials: ZG entwined. There is applause and you laugh, near-hysterical with relief. You have made it. You thought you might die en route but instead you are here, at the party of the season, held in honour of Gabriel Zigo's triumphant return to British Fashion Week after four years of showing in Paris or Milan.

Voices crow nearby: '. . . there are few things worse than sleeping alone and Michael is definitely one of them.'

'. . . if you enjoyed Tarantino then you absolutely *must* hoof it down to Camden to see the little Mongolian pic we caught last week . . . very arthouse and so minimalist it reads like a home movie . . . all hand-held and everything . . . Jean Paul swore the murders were real but it was in *Time Out*, after all, and I can't see them giving a rating to a snuff movie . . .'

'. . . would somebody please find out if this is soya in the pastry, only I'm on gluten-free and I already carry a

6

loaded syringe in my bag in case I catch as much as a sniff of a peanut . . .'

'. . . did you say Paul McCartney? Who? Oh, *Linda's* husband. I seeeee . . .'

'. . . and you know one bee sting can put me into a fucking coma – remember that shoot in Provence where I had that complete collapse in that field and it was only because the stylist had studied basic first-aid on his aromatherapy course that I'm here to tell the tale today, so I have numbers always in my bag here where people can get help. I can never travel alone, never . . . shit, I brought the wrong bag out tonight, anyway, just ring this chap at the allergy clinic in Harley Street if I begin to turn blue. Where are you going? . . .'

There is a surge around the buffet. Hester Zigofsky pushes past, lost in a fog of Givenchy and utter confusion. Her children are vanished and her ears pop and sizzle from the speed of the lift. Only the very young are tolerant of such things. She peers at someone's heaped plate and clicks her tongue: marinated cheese-hearts, egg-size truffles and wild mushrooms in vine leaves, braised sweetbreads and fresh beetroot meringues – nothing kosher, she notices. Was this worth such a scrum?

Her son Burgess hares past but fails to stop when she hails him. Or perhaps he just doesn't hear. All the rest of her brood are there somewhere, of course – China, Kitty, Nula and, of course, Chloe, who organized the whole ghastly event.

There is a life-size Hockney portrait of them all in one of the anterooms. It took ten men or more to carry the vast canvas into the building at dawn that morning and then the frame had broken, which sent Chloe off into a spontaneously-combusted breakdown, not just for the glass, which could be replaced, but for the very occurrence itself, which she claimed was an omen of impending disaster.

The portrait is good – weirdly surreal but good. What is wrong is the way the whole group looks. Functional, that is the word that springs into Hester's mind, they look functional. A functioning family. She smiles, but more to air her teeth than from any genuine pleasure.

Gabriel is seated in the middle of the portrait, of course, his face no more than a few swipes with the palette knife, but very alive for all that. He appears god-like among them, as he does in real life, his prematurely whitened hair a halo around his strong, broad, classical head. Kitty is shyly but adoringly at his side as always, her well-honed features a virtual mirror of her father's. Burgess is smiling, which is deeply unlikely. He is behind his father, straight-backed and in awe, with his eyes fixed on Gabriel's head. The son and heir, so ambitious and yet so painfully in need of praise and approval from the parent who eclipses him. Chloe is sprawled in an effort to attract maximum attention, while China's leaden-featured face is turned slightly away. She wanted her husband in the portrait but Gabriel said not, and his word is law and always will be.

Hester peers at her own portrait – a blur beside the others, like a shadow dressed in yellow – smudged and indistinct as a thumbprint, as though the artist had not really seen her there at all.

She touches the picture with her finger. The paint of her husband's suit still feels wet. She gasps and draws her digit back quickly. There is a crimson stain on the tip. Mesmerized, she stares at it in some horror.

A camera crew appears alongside and she is momentarily confused by the lights in her face.

'A success?' a voice asks her. She turns, alarmed, her expression distraught.

'The party?' the interviewer prompts. 'A success?' He is young and he is nodding encouragingly. Hurry. Speak. They are wasting good film.

Hester straightens and smiles the smile of the Sphinx. The smile she uses for *Hello*! and *Harpers*. 'Of course a success!' she trills, her eyes sparkling. She puts her hand to her face and a fistful of diamonds glints like a glitterball.

'Is your husband here? We don't seem to find him.'

Hester shrugs and her smile widens. 'You know Gabriel!' she laughs. 'Always the workaholic. He's bound to be in his cutting-room right now, putting the finishing touches to a new design. He forgets what hour it is when he's in a creative mood – I'm sure he'll turn up later.'

The scorching light disappears as quickly as it arrived, leaving her feeling like a cooling, fresh-baked roll. A woman clutches at her hands and she is air-kissed, solemnly and ceremoniously.

'Wonderful, magnificent!'

'*Marie-Claire*,' a voice whispers in her ear. It is Deeta, the company PR, a minuscule but muscular girl who looks no older than twelve in a Minnie Mouse dress. She's been circling Hester all night. Her hair is citrus-yellow with orange tips to the knotted peaks.

'Italian *Vogue*,' the girl adds, as a woman in gleaming pvc looms.

Hester feels a shriek forming somewhere inside. Mumbling apologies, she finds a door marked 'Exit' and thrusts herself through it, waving blindly, then up some stairs, like a mole towards the air of the lawn. The atmosphere outside is shockingly cold, like a vapour of iced water. She has tinnitus from all the noise. Where is her husband? She needs him. She can't handle all this on her own. She slips a Prozac from bag to mouth and swallows it dry. The outside world smells funny; musty old smells of her childhood – boiled food and the pungent smoke from burning coal.

She turns her face to the east and sees the shimmering tower at Canary Wharf flashing like a lighthouse in the darkness. Maybe there are still ships out there to be warned off the rocks – the same ships that brought her family and her husband's family to this country many years before. What had their thoughts been, those wretched souls? Did they see this party from hell mapped out in their future ambitions?

Between there and here lay ancient streets: Commercial Road, Radcliffe Highway, Brick Lane. Lost in a dream, Hester feels the heat from the pressing irons and hears the zip of French chalk making deft marks down a yard of navy suiting; the hum of ancient machines and a stench of old oil and cloth-dust; the phantoms of old noises ring in her ears. She shudders suddenly and rubs her pimple-chilled fat arms twice over with her hot hands.

A car approaches warily across the tarmac. She has never seen a police car drive so slowly, only when . . . Maybe someone has complained about the noise. She fumbles for cigarettes, glancing back at the tower-block. Only it has been soundproofed – no noise, no trouble. Maybe a form of lowlife still haunts the old estate. Perhaps there has been some disturbance. Heroin-hawking. Window-smashing. But she is aware at the same time that that's not it.

Hester knows before she hears the car doors thud and she knows before she sees the expression on the policemen's faces what it is they have come to say to her.

'He's dead,' she tells them helpfully, once they are standing before her. It really is the only option. Her mind is suddenly totally lucid and logical. Strange that – the police thought they'd come to break the news to her, not the other way round. Sixth sense perhaps, or maybe the look of gravitas they put onto their youthful, kebab-fattened faces. They wonder at the sight of such a rich-looking woman, standing in this steaming piss-pit.

'My husband.' Hester's voice sounds patient.

'Mrs Zigo?'

'Zigofsky,' she corrects them. 'Zigo is a trade name. It is from the old family name, Zigofsky. My husband's family emigrated here many years ago. Like many Jews with names that were too complicated for the English ear and tongue, they found it was abbreviated on the immigration lists, hence Zigo. Zigofsky – Zigo, it sounds so much better, don't you think? So English? Ha!'

And then they tell her what she already knows, almost as though she had never spoken. No one offers her a chair, no one asks if she would like to go inside.

'I'm afraid Mr Zigo . . . Zigofsky . . . has been found dead,' they tell her. They don't say it was murder, not yet.

11

It even crosses their minds that she might have done it. It could explain the way she already knew, before they'd told her.

Then Hester slides to the ground before they can stop her, a great buttery mountain of slithering embarrassment, laddering her eight-pounds-ninety-five-pence Harvey Nichols stockings at the knee as she does so. And they think that maybe she didn't do it after all, or if she did she's a bloody good actress, what with all that snot coming out of her nose all of a sudden and the way all that screaming suddenly starts emerging from her Chanel-painted mouth. Very Helen Mirren, that – or maybe Diana Rigg *après The Avengers*, after she went all arty.

They look at the woman lying shrieking at their feet like a run-over rat and as it starts very suddenly to rain – and rain hard at that – the policemen realize reluctantly that, despite her considerable size, they have little option but to carry her inside.

1889

We are a million miles from anywhere and sick with all the delay. I miss Papa so badly that each night I cry until the others complain angrily.

The sea makes a terrible sight – pitching and grey by day, while in the crimson skies of sunset it becomes boiling sulphur – so that I would not be surprised to see the devil himself rise from its bowels and take us all to hell with him in his fist.

It is a miserable thing to be frightened and alone, and the stories I am told of the country we are travelling to for

12

our stop-over make me wonder whether I should ever have left The Pale of Settlement.

We are saving the meagre candles for *Pesach*, so at night we sit in the dark, and Kaspar the cutter's wife – a huge, dark-eyed peasant from the Ukraine – has taken it upon herself to tell us stories. There is much shrieking at what she has to say and last night four women swooned right away and had to be carried up on deck to recover.

According to the presser's wife there has been a murderous fiend stalking the streets of London preying on young women, cutting out their entrails before they are even killed, and cooking and eating them once they are dead. They call him The Ripper, she says, and he guts the women just as cleanly as a fishmonger guts a fish.

The picture she paints is so vivid that it has me quaking beneath my blanket, though I will not scream out as I want to, for fear that it will give her even greater satisfaction.

She tells me his victims are whores so I had better beware. I catch her staring strangely at my belly and pull my shawl tighter. I reply haughtily that I am certainly no whore and never will be, but then she laughs, saying I might not be so full of myself once I am on the streets without money and my gut is growling for food.

I fear now that I have left bad for worse and that I shall be killed for certain, if not by the Ripper then by the sea itself, for we have lost twelve to the sickness already and more will die daily if we do not reach land soon.

At dawn I stand hidden by fog so dense it plasters my hair to my face, and watch the sailors slipping corpses over the side of the boat and down into the pitching grey water. In my silent terror I imagine one of the shapes cries out as it falls but the men mock me, saying it was a gull that screamed. I count five bodies altogether – one of them a child, by the size of the sack.

Then tonight I think my time has come to join the dead. I wake in such pain that I have to bite my lip to avoid crying out. I dreamt that I was being butchered by the Ripper and that he was cutting at my vitals. When I wake I feel wetness beneath me on my little straw mattress and I am more scared than ever before in my life.

'I am killed!' I cry out at last. 'He has butchered me in my sleep!'

The women gather around, hissing and shushing, stuffing cloth into my mouth to silence me, so that I now fear suffocation more than the pain that tears through my belly. In my head I scream for my mother, though God knows she is too far away to hear and would be little enough help even if she were.

Many hours go by in this way as, full of pain and terror, I slip in and out of strange dreams. Then one of the women whispers angrily into my ear: 'You have a child, girl. A baby.'

She takes the gag from my mouth and mops my brow with it. I look at her ugly old face in disbelief at such a strange miracle.

'Let me see it,' I say, for I still imagine that she must be lying to me.

They hold the bloody little package up by its hind legs like a skinned hare for my inspection and I can see very little of it in the dark, apart from its face, which catches some of the yellow light from the candle they shield with their hoary old hands.

I see one thing, though. I see the mark on its face – the tiny red, thumbnail-shaped impression between its minute brows. In an instant the pain and hot aches leave my body and I am chilled like ice through my veins, instead. I fall to quaking then, and the shakes become so violent that even the old crab at my side looks alarmed.

'Stop that, now,' she says.

'Why doesn't it cry?' I ask. 'The child – it makes no sound.'

'It's dead,' the woman tells me, 'and better off, too, the bastard.'

I cry bitterly then, though no one gives comfort for they all think me damned for the shame of my terrible situation.

'Forget the baby,' they tell me, 'forget you ever gave birth. Lead your life. Do the best you can.'

At dawn I am discovered again shivering at the side of the ship, only this time I watch as my own child is dropped into the sea. She is wrapped in my vest, which I have stitched quickly but carefully into a suitable shroud, for I could not stand to look at even such a poor thing put out to sea in a filthy sack.

As I sat stitching by the light of the one meagre candle they allowed me, I was reminded of my father stitching my wedding suit, and how joyous it was to watch him, and I saw what a miserable sight I must make now as I sew for my own child.

I wish I had time to embroider a little message onto the fabric. I think of my father in his workroom, sewing delicate flowers in Indian-dyed silks onto the waistcoat of the wedding suit.

15

I am thirteen years old. The following day will be my fourteenth birthday. The sun is so beautiful as it rises, swollen huge and blood-red from the sea-mists. I watch the spot where my dead child was swallowed by the water. My eyes ache but they will not leave that point, even long after it is gone on the distant horizon.

CHAPTER TWO

ZG

LONDON 1998

ZEPHYR
A fine, lightweight woollen fabric.

The room was dark, apart from a candle that burnt day and night, filling the room with the warm, rich scents of tallow and beeswax.

Murmuring visitors materialized and evaporated and Kitty barely knew who they were, for their whispered regrets all sounded so similar; but after they were gone, like the tide, the family alone remained as stubborn as pebbles on the beach, sitting face-to-face in silence, though not one of them could look into the eyes of another.

Who did it? The low chairs made their legs ache. Who was it? Kitty rubbed at her temples in an attempt to separate overwhelming grief from suspicion and revenge. Her father had been murdered. When she looked in the mirror she saw his face merged with her own. Of them all it was she who most resembled him. 'Who killed me, Kitty? Who did it?'

They observed the traditions at that time: a family

17

then for the seven days of *shiva*, not a board meeting or collective. A mother, four daughters and a son, all mourning the passing of their famous husband and father, a proudly dominating man who had them all reined in so tight they had scattered like drops of oil on water at his death.

What they had in that room was the end of an era, for as they sat in silence they were aware that out there somewhere a business empire was crumbling. It could never have survived the death of Gabriel. A principled, honourable and – to them – heroic man, he was central to their very existence and, in their view, the rays of the sun literally shone from his arse.

What a group they made! You would have known their faces, each of them, for they had stalked the pages of the press for a decade, slithering from Fashion to Gossip, to Finance and on to Reportage and Crime with all the óily ease of a butterpat on a hot plate.

They were the Family Zigofsky, but you would have known them only by the name Zigo, which was the brand-name of the fashion group and had been for many years. You would also have known their trademark: Z_G. If you were a person of substance, style and taste you would have it etched on your luggage, while the children of the family had it tattooed wittily on their ankles, each of them branded with the corporate logo long before they were old enough to complain.

There was the mother, made quite mad by her grief, but struck with such a quiet and polite type of insanity that the only outward symptom was that her stockings didn't match. One leg was tan and the other the colour of putty, but nobody dared mention this in case other, uglier crazinesses should well up from inside somewhere and start to spill out.

Hester Lucille. Her face was never terribly well known to you for, like her son, she was eternally eclipsed by her husband's dazzle. She was a large woman but appeared small. Her skin was the colour of marmalade and her hair treacle-black. Her husband had told the children so many times that she was beautiful it was only once he was gone and the magic spell broken that they discovered that she was merely unremarkable.

Chloe, however, had beauty to an inordinate degree. Gorgon-haired and flame-eyed, she was the bogeyman of Kitty's childhood and still capable of terrifying. Sparks had been known to fly from her; Kitty would flinch when she spoke and become paralysed with terror when she moved. The inactivity of the *shiva* threatened to prove fatal to her. Kitty sat in readiness, aware that her sister would combust spontaneously sooner or later.

There was no continuity with Chloe, apart from her height. She was thin but strong and had had three noses in the previous two years. She picked up accents and buzzwords faster than she picked up her men, but through each and every sea-change she had always found a place on the published list of the world's most beautiful people.

Her hair was currently dyed chartreuse and her skin had been laminated against wrinkles or ageing. Her eyes were like dragonfly eyes and her mouth was stained tangerine. She appeared to survive on a diet of lychees and breadsticks and so the kosher food was causing great internal anguish.

Chloe had bullied Kitty remorselessly as a child. Ghosts

19

of long-faded bruises rose up to haunt the younger sister with pains again when she walked by.

Burgess was Lizard Man – the brother who never blinked, farted or fucked. An ex-alcoholic who dried out via cocaine to discover a loathing for any abusable substance short of pure oxygen, Burgess looked like the most un-hip man in the universe as he pursued his eternal crusade to disprove the theory about still waters always running deep.

Kitty carried a photo in her wallet of Burgess at his Bar mitzvah and would pull it out every time she needed reassurance that he was in fact of human extraction. She used to love the boy in the photo, with his geeky grin and his skinny legs in the long pants, but that was before the drugs ate away the cute part and left just a smile in a suit. Then he became Corporate Man, a virtual reality of what used to be, with his pink, pinned-back ears and his helmet of cropped black hair.

'Who killed me, Kitty?'

She had that childhood photograph with her now. She needed it badly. She needed to remind herself that Burgess, with all his impatience and his cold calculations that made business a boardgame, could never have wanted his father removed from the field of play.

The timelessness of the *shiva* was anathema to her brother as well. God created the world in seven days, but Burgess would personally have done it in four and sold it knock-down to the Japanese by the fifth. He had glanced at his watch forty-three times before the first hour was over. Then he discovered some internal focus and sat hunched in the dark, dank womb of his family instead, his eyes glazed in corporate contemplation as his mind grazed through the pastures of exotic far-off lands like Hang Seng and Dow Jones.

China, the eldest sister, was the most like their mother and was married to Stephano, who would bite the heads off babies for fun. On the day that she married China shaved off her hair, following ancient traditions, and ceased to speak – allowing Stephano to do the communicating for her via some form of advanced telepathy. When asked a direct question she would turn mutely to her husband, and signals would seem to come out of her head, which Stephano was capable of translating into answers of such indifference and arrogance that you would have thought they had emanated from his brain in the first place.

Nula, the youngest, was perfection: pretty, shy and talented, she was as sweet as Chloe could be sour and they all cherished the very bones of her for being what they couldn't be – sensitive, modest and quiet.

Nula had the round face of an overstuffed cherub and an earthy, herbal smell. Her hair was short like soft fuzzy moleskin and she wore cellophane fabrics and hand-knits.

China, Chloe, Burgess and Nula – and not forgetting Kitty, of course. And their ages? Twenty-two, nineteen, twenty, fifteen and eighteen respectively. Fashion is a young business, at least that's what their Uncle Leonard kept saying and he should have known, for he was the greater side of ninety.

Kitty looked around at the circle of shocked faces that were frozen in grief, like masks of a Greek chorus. Ghosts spoke to her via voices in her head. 'Who was it?' She heard

21

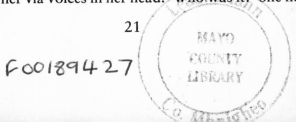

Gabriel, his voice coming in snippets and half-remembered phrases; it was like flicking through the pages of a talking-book photo-album.

His face had already slipped from her mental grasp. Did this happen? Would she start to forget how he looked? And so soon? How little had she dared to stare at him when he was alive – even she, who was his own cherished darling. Sometimes when he worked she would watch. She concentrated on his frown as he spent time on his sketches. A black cashmere roll-neck. The glasses with the half-rimmed frames that he never wore outside the studio. Music. She could hear the stuff he would play while he drew. Ella Fitzgerald. Billie Holliday. She would stuff her fingers into her ears and howl like a dog because to her it was off-key, and he would laugh – though he didn't laugh now in her memory, she had lost sight of his face altogether . . .

She saw his back as he bent over the cutting-table. Why was he being so elusive? Why was he turned away from her? She wanted to call out, to make him show her his face again.

'Kitty.' She heard his whisper in her head, along with other, unfamiliar voices. 'Who was it?' She opened her eyes quickly. Was he to be turned away from her until she discovered his murderer? Was that her task? Was this shunning to be her punishment if she failed him?

Time and again she looked across at the other members of her family. Their misery should have united them, but a sense of fear held them apart. They were wealthy – powerful even – but most of all they were terrified, each in their own way.

When God created Gabriel he must have made Kitty from the off-cuts. She too was darkly handsome with the same graphite eyes and hair thick enough to make even regular combing painful. To her father she was a peach of a child; quiet and sunny, with the same disposition as the family dog – loyal to the point of stupidity, ferociously loving to anyone dumb enough to show a kindness, and effortlessly comical.

Now she was none of those things. Since his death she had become humourless, simmering in the darkness, waiting for the fan of air that would cause her to burst into flames of anger and resentment.

This was her own family, her blood. And she believed one of them might be a murderer. Her father had been killed and his death was symbolic. They had stitched his eyes and they had stitched his mouth, using tailor's thread to do it. It was a planned slaying, full of hatred and irony.

'Inevitable,' a voice whispered in Kitty's head. 'His death was inevitable.' She blew her nose hard to make the voice go away.

'Watch me, Kitty.' Her father was teaching her to sew. 'Watch the needle. See the way my hands work. Don't let your fingers stiffen, keep them strong but supple. The smaller and sharper the needle the less the mark it will leave on the fabric and these are the finest cloths, Kitty. Feel them against your cheek. Angel's breath, eh?'

He had designed less in recent years, as the job had become more a desperately-salvaged business than an adored obsession. Yet as a child she had watched him

23

pinning fabric onto a dummy, marvelling as it took shape, guessing at his thoughts, trying to follow his creative path and maybe sometimes jump ahead, although she never could. She was not an artist.

The only tragedy of Kitty's young life until now had been that she had shared Gabriel's passion for the business, but not his talent – at least not for design. She could be a useful spectator, though. As she grew older she would be allowed to sip at the brandy her father always drank prior to launching a new collection, making useful comments, keeping the day-to-day problems of running the place off his shoulders when he was busy.

The voice was right; her father had had to die, there was no question of it. The wheels of evolution and development must grind on relentlessly, and anyone who stands in the way will fall and be crushed.

Despite herself, Kitty loved them all – Chloe, Nula, China and Burgess. How could it have been otherwise, for they were of the same blood and they were her family, and there lay the two lynch-pins of her very existence: Family and Business. Blood ties and the clothing industry. They were all that was important in life, it had been drummed into her from birth.

She chewed at her fingernails. Soon she would have a new family. She was marrying Freddy. Starting a new life. Leaving the business, except for retaining a place on the sidelines. Her cuticle started to bleed. She could have managed a glass of her father's brandy right now.

'Who *was* it, Kitty?' The voice was becoming insistent, angry even.

'Okay, Daddy, okay.'

'Who will run the business now, Kitty? Who will take over from me?'

'What you worked at was dying too, Daddy. You saw the figures. We were going under. Let it go.'

'It's family, Kitty, a family firm. It has a history. It must be inherited, not bought.'

Her culture, her birthright. Tradition. Continuity. How many times had she and Chloe groaned or laughed at all that crap?

Family – her family.

'*Kitty*!'

'Okay.'

The wedding would have to be postponed.

THE BUSINESS

The real heart of the British rag trade is not sited – as many would believe – in the swanky climes of Chelsea and Mayfair, but in the busy, dusty network of narrow roads around Great Portland Street in the West End, and the rather more feisty area around Mile End Road, in the East. These are the places where the work gets done, from the orders being taken in the wholesale showrooms of Great Portland and Great Titchfield Streets, to the sweatshops of the East End, where many of the garments get made.

There is very little glamour in either of these locations and they are not the haunts of top models or wealthy clients.

Immigrant labour is exploited to full capacity in the sweatshops to keep the making costs of each garment down. This tradition has a long history and is the main reason why so many of the businesses are sited

25

around the docks in the East End, because the immi-
grants set up business almost at the point where they
stepped off the ships.

The four greatest memories of Kitty's childhood were:

1. Being towed, screaming, up a Milan catwalk aged two years and five months, by a model with hands so pallid and cold she could have been made out of frozen pastry. Until the time of her father's death this was still Kitty's most *awful* and *traumatic* memory, too.

This had been *rehearsed* terror – before the show had started she had been trawled the length of the runway many times, just in case, and each time her screams and yelps had been enough to drown out the music.

Look at Chloe's face, though. Wreathed in dimpled smiles she is the all-perfect model infant. Her baby hair is sculpted into a neat chignon, her tiny legs move in time to the beat with immaculate precision, and her eyes! She is loving it, just adoring the whole whorey nature of the event, being stared at and photographed; this is her moment.

2. The faces around her cot. Real or imagined, they are there in her mind. What expectation shone from all their eyes! What did they want? Swaddled in French silk with a huge Chanel velvet bow stuck to her bald little head, Kitty would lie there for ages trying to work this one out. Her father wanted an ally. Her mother wanted peace from her nanny's demands. Her uncles wanted cute. Her sister Chloe wanted a toy. Each day she would reach out and squeeze Kitty's arm, just to see how she was coming along,

staring at her, sizing her up, seeing if she would bounce.

One day she painted lipstick on Kitty's mouth – three months old and with a port-wine pout. This was Chloe's disappointment, then, because Kitty never wore make-up in the rest of her life. Neither did she dye her hair. Nor resculpt herself with plastic surgery. This Chloe could never understand. Even now she would paint Kitty's toenails with varnish while she was sleeping.

3. The day she realized her father was *somebody*. This was not a gradual realization, but sudden. This was the day of her fifth birthday, when her father had booked a table at the Ritz for a whole dozen of her little friends, and when they had walked in dressed up like the cast from *Les Miserables* the maitre d' had pointed them towards a large table – a beautiful table, dressed in fashion fabrics and trimmings – laid with party gifts and crackers and balloons, and Kitty's father had just said, 'No,' in a quiet voice.

'No,' he had told the maitre d', 'that one.' And he had nodded towards a larger table, an even more beautiful one right next to the fountain. Kitty had nearly peed her little Swiss-lace-trimmed knickers right there on the spot for fear the maitre d' was going to throw them all out onto the street, dressed as they were, in the middle of Piccadilly on a cold afternoon.

But he hadn't. Instead he had smiled and said, 'Naturally,' and they had been given free fizzy orange, while the changes had been made like magic. Even so, being the sort of child she was, Kitty had still felt the need to say a whispered, 'I'm sorry,' to the maitre d' and gave him her

27

party gift to make up for the aggravation when they were leaving.

4. Then there was the moment – only this wasn't early in her life, but later – about *now*, in fact – when Kitty had first been given the wedding suit.

As soon as Kitty was grown-up enough to walk, her father took her to work with him like a sweet little mascot, teaching her every aspect of the industry: couture, ready-to-wear, the high street short-order, and even the cabbage. She saw samples being pinned, shaped and sewn, and jumped like a flea as the steam rose when the final garments were being finished.

Gabriel focused his expectations for her like this: what he needed from her he saw in her. Our earliest self-belief is founded by our parents' opinions and perceptions. What Gabriel perceived in Kitty was something that passed for genuine talent – an honest interest that mirrored his own – and he took it upon himself to nurture that imagined spark until it became reality.

His passion for exquisite fabrics, therefore, was her birthright, and his eye for design and cut came to exemplify all she ever wanted in life. Uncle Louie, Uncle Benjamin, Uncle Leonard and her father – the Business was their Family and their Family was the Business.

It was Gabriel who saw the Dream Merchants appear on the horizon long before most people; that smiling army of grey financiers and suited money men – polite, quietly-spoken hordes – who were to hold out the hand of assistance only to take the rag trade businesses by the throat once they were within grip, and choke the vital essence out of them.

Or maybe the great houses would have destroyed themselves eventually anyway, for the internecine scraps between Kitty's family members were savage and relentless – and had been since long before Kitty was born.

When the seven days of *shiva* were ended, right down to the very exact minute, if not the second that they were finished, there was a banging downstairs and all action resumed in uproar as limousines arrived at the door of their mother's vast mausoleum of a house and they were shrouded in coats and spirited away from St John's Wood to the new heart of the ancient city and the magical Palace of Chrome.

Kitty travelled with Chloe, noting that her sister's foot had become a metronome, tapping out each second and minute that had passed since their father's death. Did she still remember Gabriel? It had been a whole two weeks since he died. Chloe's attention-span was as fleeting as a gnat's. Time heals all and Kitty expected Chloe's wounds would mend much faster than most.

Chloe excelled at excess. It is what she was best at and she used it to great advantage in the business. What the big names did, she would have to do better. If Versace hosted a party then she would outdo him. When Lacroix dressed actors for the Oscars, she would sniff out the winners and bribe them with wardrobes both larger and more extravagant. When she saw the Armani Wall in the via Broletto – the five-storey-high painting of his newest collection – she would not rest until the cream of their own

29

designs were displayed in laser along fifty floors of the tower at Canary Wharf.

Hence the party on the night of their father's death. Hence the codfish-cold shutters that had slithered across Chloe's eyes like a third lid when the police had staggered in carrying their mother clumsily between them, signalling a premature halt to the evening's activities.

To get her own way Chloe would cajole, flirt, bribe and, ultimately, threaten. She was an acknowledged diva of the fashion circuit, a celebrity sans cause. Their father loved her too, of course.

To reach the Palace of Chrome it was necessary to travel via the East and hence the Streets-That-Throng-With-Poor. Chloe had the door-locks on sharply – urgently – before the dispossessed rose up to prise the car wide open like a sardine can and have the Rolex off her wrist.

'Don't look,' she insisted to her sister, as though skewering the oppressed with eye contact would inspire serious insurrection.

For maximum irritation Kitty let her window down an inch, savouring the patchouli and cardamom and dust smells that were a fragrant relief to her sister's fifty-pound-a-squirt scent. She didn't want a conversation, she didn't want to set her sister off talking, because Chloe currently had a fad for peppering her speech-patterns with unspeakably aggravating New-Age words. She would say wrong things and then they would argue in the sort of hissy, spitty, snake-style language that sisters often indulge in. Kitty desperately wanted silence. Her brain had turned to mush in the heat.

They rode to the twenty-first floor of the Palace of Chrome in a lift made of molasses-tinted glass that treated all on the bustling mezzanine to a view of Kitty's Calvin Klein knickers. Chloe still scorched and sizzled with suppressed urgency. The lift was so speedy their faces contorted with G-force, but still it was too slow for Chloe and she pummelled the controls like an astronaut set for Warp Nine. The button for the third floor had no number, just the logo ZG, on its dial.

There was ZG on the glass doors that they passed through and ZG on the gum wrapper that Nula was flicking into the ZG aluminium waste-bin. Household goods was one of the newer additions to the Zigo Empire, acquired in a blind panic after Versace and Ralph Lauren had made lucrative forays into that end of the market.

The boardroom had been transformed. No longer a place of minimalist sterility, it hummed and glowed with electronic life like the Harrods gift hall at Christmas. A dozen small desks had been strategically scattered and on each desk winked the eye of an ever-vigilant VDU screen. Nula gawped at the magical effect; it was an Aladdin's cave of on-line digital technology.

Stephano and China came up behind the others so fast they almost forgot to brake.

'Fucking shit!' Was that from Stephano or did China's words come out of his mouth? And who was the magician in charge of all that wizardry? Burgess appeared on cue, arms akimbo, Master of Ceremonies, the Unsmiling Host of the afternoon's celebrations.

Behind him, half-concealed in the slatted shadows by the Venetian blind-draped windows, a figure rocked back and

31

forward gently in a grey leather chair. It was Nicky Kofteros, Burgess's own little superhero, the western face of giant-size eastern corporations; polite, well-mannered and handsome.

His suit fitted too perfectly, Kitty noted. Pretension. It was a class thing – ghastly, but a fact of life. A way of telling real earthlings from alien invaders. Kofteros looked like a being with a human outer skin that he would shed at night. Underneath would be a grinning Robert De Niro shelling hard-boiled eggs with long fingernails, like he did in *Angel Heart*. Kitty felt Nula shudder beside her.

'Where are they?' Chloe asked Burgess. 'Where are the others?' Her brother snapped his fingers and the dozen VDUs speckled about the room flickered with life.

At first each screen seemed to display an identical image: a gleaming, bland, oriental face in a suit, beaming and full-frontal. Mesmerized, Nula bent to peer.

'He blinked,' she whispered in awe, 'this one's alive! It blinked!'

'We are on-line live,' Burgess told her with a sidelong glance at Kofteros and a voice as flat from embarrassment as a stale, unbuttered croissant. 'We are video-conferencing on the global network. Take seats, please. You are watching and you are both watched and heard. Translation will be instantaneous. Please reserve questions until the end, when you will be expected to register a voting tendency.' One of the identical screen faces fell to chattering on cue and a virtual-reality oriental woman of air-hostess proportions and garb appeared in their midst to umpire the verbal ping-pong.

'Mr Hutchai of the Korean Waika Retail Group wishes

to bid you all welcome and to beg your kind attention while he outlines the proposed intensive globalization programme for the esteemed Zigo International Fashion and Wholesale Group,' she began. Burgess beamed.

Fazed as she was by all the technology, Kitty was still able to recognize the name of the woman's masters. Gabriel had sold certain merchandizing and licensing rights to Waika long ago in the Days Of Darkness, when liquidation loomed and injected capital was vital plasma.

Since then Waika had bought up the rest of the world, stamping desperate-looking, poor-quality tack from here to Timbuktu with their once-prestigious ZG logo.

'In an initial three-point-five million pound expansion programme,' the woman continued, 'Mr Hutchai and his board envisage the current twelve per cent year-on-year rise in first quarter sales to be raised a minimum thirty per cent, with margins up forty per cent from their current seventeen per cent position.'

With this tempting *hors d'oeuvre* on the table the translator began to assail them with details of the main course. Kitty watched the face on the screen in front of her in fascination as it flickered and chattered amicably. The face on Nula's screen just blinked, and not often at that. The face on China's screen was so still it might have been that of a hologrammed corpse. Stephano cracked about looking for knobs as though chasing horizontal hold on his ancient television set at home.

'. . . pre-tax losses for the group in the year to December totalled three-point-nine million pounds and the current forecast for the following year stands at seven-point-four million . . .'

Burgess gasped politely like a netted guppy. His etiquette always was impeccable, even when he was drunk, and it was appropriate to feign shock at hearing they were so totally and completely up to their necks in debt.

The Zigo empire was a lumbering, complex creature, founded financially on its mail-order business – which had since been sold – and currently consisting of three main segments: Couture, which is where the company made its name but lost its money; Ready-to-wear, and Diffusion. It was the couture side that was dearest to Gabriel's heart and – therefore – to Kitty's.

The couture name had been lent to various items of upmarket merchandise throughout the fifties and sixties, but always under licence. Gabriel's own name was also applied to a range of shoes and – for a brief while – cosmetics. But it was the perfume and handbag market that proved the most lucrative, and it was this that Gabriel sold to Waika to keep the salon afloat during the late seventies.

The Ready-to-wear and Diffusion ranges were marketed from the showroom. These garments sold to a world-wide market, both in small boutiques and the better class stores.

In the eighties the trend for concessions within stores became rife and Gabriel was forced to open several of these 'shops within shops' to avoid losing business. He was further encouraged to open half a dozen small retail outlets of his own in Britain – a move that proved to be a costly mistake.

The boutique in Beauchamp Place was expensive to rent, and for much of the year, even though business was good, the rental and overheads far exceeded the sales. The shop in Bond Street was only bought after pressure from Chloe, who concluded that they could not afford *not* to be seen there. Clients expected personal attention and pampering. Chloe's bill for champagne for one famous customer outstripped the cost of their purchase by three pounds. Most celebrities treated the place as a lending library, borrowing frocks for big events and then returning them the following day.

The wholesale showroom in the West End handled what Gabriel had called the '*schmutter* trade', which was the cheapest, and therefore most accessible and also most lucrative side of their business. For Chloe this side did not exist, yet it supported their largest factory, a state-of-the-art place in Wales where fabric was cut by laser and designs logged into computers.

The business as a whole had also supported many other outworkers – until Gabriel had been forced to make cutbacks, that was . . .

'. . . with an initial injection of up to thirty million into the parent company, the Korean Waika Retail Group envisages a massive reorganization programme to ensure Zigo are at the forefront of the market as we move towards the Millennium . . .'

Kitty began to twitch in her seat. Her acute allergy to techno-speak was making her itch.

'. . . the constant utilization of International Trend Forecast Consultants to keep us abreast of trends, styles and market intelligence . . . the deployment of the current market and showroom methods of sales presentation and a turn to 3D CAD images in fashion runway mode to display on a local or global scale, with the potential for virtual reality as a point-of-sale technique . . .'

35

In a moment of great sanity and enlightenment Kitty leant forward and pressed the button to the right of her screen, banishing Mr Hutchai to the dark outerspace of the Internet hinterlands.

'That was wonderful.' Kitty had been forced to take the great ride back down to the ground floor in the flying glass coffin with her youngest sister, Nula the gum-chewer.

'Did you understand any of it?' she asked her sister. In the silent void that constituted Nula's answer Kitty took it upon herself as a kind of sibling duty to explain.

'No more fashion shows, Nula, no more clothes in shops, no more sitting at the board designing a new model, no more trying garments on and – later – no more shops,' she said in a flat voice. 'In future you just plug in and go. Throw a 3D model of yourself on screen and dress it up before ordering up. Swap a virtual reality helmet for the shopping mall. Hell, who even needs to wear the damn things? Programme your little 3D image in the chosen outfit and watch it go off to the party instead of you!'

Kitty was fulfilling a sorely-felt need to see someone else as hacked off as herself with all this blasphemy. She started punching the lift buttons for dramatic effect, much in the aggressive style of Chloe.

Nula stared out from the lift in gummy silence. A little puffball of mist appeared where her breath met the cold glass. She wiped the condensation with her sleeve and then Kitty could see in the reflection that there were tears coursing down her small pudgy cheeks, and she turned her and hugged her while they both wept.

'It's a lot of fucking money, though, Kit,' Nula croaked between tears. Kitty nodded because there was no arguing with that statement.

'But you voted *for* . . .' Nula began, 'when Burgess asked you said yes . . .'

'I voted to think about it,' Kitty corrected her. She had voted to live. She had voted not to wake up to find her guts in a Gucci bag. 'It's okay, Nule,' she whispered.

'No.' Her sister's voice sounded weird. 'No, it's not okay, Kit,' she said, 'don't tell me it ever can be, not now, not again.'

They clasped one another in an embrace that was nothing less than pure unadulterated schmaltz. Kitty had voted not to stand in front of the wheels, like her dead father had done. She'd voted not to make the same mistake. She'd voted not to get killed. She was getting married. Soon. Despite the voices in her head. She was out of it. Safe, not dead, like Gabriel.

Kitty had popped into the off-licence on the way back from the city. A new experience, she discovered, standing at the counter, pointing to a stylish-looking bottle of Hine. The brown paper bag it came in made her feel guilty. She couldn't even find the right glass in her father's office, she had had to use a tumbler. The first sip was so full of nostalgia it made her head spin.

The workroom was empty and dark. The police had been through the entire place, inch by inch, but they had been amazingly careful and – apart from small patches of white powder around the safe door and desk drawers – very little looked different.

Kitty's feet made a padding noise on the thick wool carpet of the salon and then tapped across the bare boards of the studio one floor above. She wasn't ready for this yet. She would go home right now and forget about anger and revenge. This wasn't *The Godfather*. She wasn't about to go out blowing people's heads off until family honour was satisfied. Yet the voices were still there in her mind: 'Find out, Kitty. No one else can.'

The police will, she thought as she snapped on a desk lamp. They'll find out who did it.

She'd phoned them three times. What she got each time was patience, sympathy and weary politeness; an offer of victim support; counselling. She wanted to know what they knew, to find out how far they'd got. She'd tried to sound rational, intelligent and intensely sane on the phone. There was someone coming to interview her: Detective Abberline. He'd already spoken to Burgess and her mother. Maybe they worked in some sort of dynastic pecking order: her mother, Burgess, China, Chloe. What was she? Fifth in line to the throne?

She sat at her father's computer, staring at the blank screen for a full five minutes before she could summon up the courage to switch it on. The tears had been a problem, starting as they did the moment the screen lit up and her father's codes appeared, but she had wiped them scruffily out of the way with the back of her hand and she could see enough to get the information she wanted.

Gabriel had kept files on everyone. A compulsively tidy man, he had liked his friends, family and colleagues to appear in some type of order, even if they ran a disorganized lifestyle. He had told Kitty that his records were the secret of his social success; when he was introduced to anyone new he would always be sure to open a file on them, containing all that he'd discovered, even in a short space of time. Tastes, family, interests. If they met again they would be charmed by his recollected knowledge of them.

Kitty had laughed inwardly about this habit, but never to her father's face. He even had photos to go with most of the files. It was an unusual hobby but her Gabriel was an unusual man. He had been called a genius during his lifetime and so occasional lapses into eccentricity were always indulged.

Kitty saw her own face come up on the screen – a smiling shot, curiously dated and taken when she was still at school, but she beat the temptation to stop at that page. Instead she pulled up all the other major players in Gabriel's life and printed each sheet, one at a time. In the end she had a fair-sized bundle on the desk in front of her.

When she got home the apartment was empty – Freddy was working late at a trade fair – and she was able to sort the papers into two piles, excluding passing acquaintances and lost contacts and bundling the rest into one stack for 'close' and the other for 'unlikely'.

She pulled on her reading glasses and poured herself some more brandy. There were noises from the apartment upstairs. Freddy said the block – she'd bought new – reminded him of Japan, with paper-thin walls. The couple above were having sex. Kitty yawned and slid off her glasses to massage the bridge of her nose.

'Oh, dear God,' she sighed as the squealing and pet-name-calling started. She slipped a CD onto the player: Manic Street Preachers – one of Freddy's. She'd thought it might shame her neighbours into silence, but instead they barely paused a beat before picking up the rhythm with gusto. Kitty forced a smile and took a large slug of brandy before focusing again on her task.

She laid each sheet out in front of her: family first, then close friends, enemies and other business acquaintances.

About thirty in all. She had created a circle of paper around herself. She rotated slowly, the drink making her dizzy.

'Who?'

'*Who*?'

She pulled out the ones she wanted it to be.

Business rivals.

People he blocked.

People he sacked.

People who wanted him out of the way. The whole of the buy-out corporation. An Italian designer her father had slagged off in Rome last season. The press had made a thing of it but it was all hype and publicity. A chauffeur he had sacked last year for being drunk at the wheel. These were the ones she didn't mind hating.

But there were others.

Burgess: washed and scrubbed, with his hair plastered down like a little boy's. He wanted the buy-out so badly, but would never have stood against Gabriel while he was alive.

Stephano? But he was a joke baddy. And China never left his side, which would mean she was in cahoots . . .

She stared at Chloe's face. Gabriel was running the

business into the ground through his own stubborn pride and sense of history. A family-run business, as it was and as it had always been. A dinosaur in the fashion world.

'Your family suffered to create this empire, Kitty.' That was her mother's voice now. Generations on and she was still harping on about what they owed to the past.

'So if our ancestors were coalmen you'd still expect us to be humping sacks of the stuff around?' Chloe would joke. You couldn't joke about the past with their parents, though. The suffering that had gone was sacrosanct.

Freddy had found her sitting clutched into a miserable ball in the middle of her paper circle.

'Rogues' gallery?' he'd asked.

'Something like that,' she'd replied.

He'd hugged her and fed her coffee until the tears stopped. She loved him. Of course she loved him. She was marrying him. Only not yet.

'You know this has to stop, Kitty.' His eyes were large, sane and sensible. 'Right now. Before you hit paranoia.'

But because he said that, she just started to suspect him, too. Why else would he want her to stop hunting down her father's murderer? Was he scared she might guess? He'd been so keen for her to see a doctor, too. Did he want to see her drugged up and out of it?

Then she smelt his normal, lucid smell and felt his lips on the side of her face and knew she had to hold on or she would be losing it. Freddy? Kill her father? She drank more of the strong coffee he'd given her.

'*Caffe latte*. Double shot. The Seattle Coffee Company,' she said. Freddy grinned, nodding.

'You looked at the paper cup.'

41

'No. Absolutely not. Not even a peek.'

It was a game they played. Guess the take-away coffee. Freddy was good but she was better.

And then he'd given her the package. 'It came this morning,' he told her.

It was a photograph, taken from an old newspaper. A wedding shot. Her parents' wedding. Gabriel was smiling. Hester looked nervous and very very young.

'I hadn't seen this before,' Freddy said, looking over Kitty's shoulder.

There was no letter with the picture.

'Jesus, look at those outfits,' Freddy whispered.

Hester was in ankle-length crushed velvet with ribbons around the neck. Gabriel wore a suit from what looked like the same fabric, with an elaborate waistcoat underneath. Kitty had seen the shot before, of course. But not properly. Parents' wedding shots are something you see but don't look at, like your own face in the mirror each morning – familiar but unstudied. Until one of your parents dies, of course. Then you start scanning in properly.

Anonymous photos. Kitty's hands went white. Was this supposed to be a message? Was it some kind of a warning? Was it from the killer? Did they already know she was trying to piece things together? Did they see her as some sort of threat, like her father?

Kitty had been brought up to be happy, not brave. Her father would not have wanted her put in any danger. But even as she restacked the computer print-outs with shaking hands and placed the wedding shot carefully on top, prior to throwing the lot into the rubbish, she heard the voices again in her head.

42

'Who, Kitty? Who killed me?'

And another voice now – a woman's voice, old and heavily accented: 'Two things, Kitty, two things, dearest. Never be poor and never grow old. Learn from your past. And never, ever forget.'

CHAPTER THREE

ᴢG

LONDON 1954

BOMBAZINE
*Bombazine is a twilled fabric of silk and worsted, and
its name is said to derive from the Greek word for
silkworm. Dyed black, it became very popular years
ago as a fabric for mourning clothes. In Victorian
times the Jews called death 'God's kiss', while to the
Gentiles it was known as 'The Great Secret'.*

ROSA'S STORY

Dearest Kitty,

When I was dead they bore my coffin the entire length
of the Commercial Road and there was much wailing and
gnashing as I passed, though in truth I doubt there was
one Jew present not secretly relieved that I had gone. 'She
was dead three days when they found her,' Rabbi Fleish-
man whispered, sucking the moustache of his yellowing
beard. 'I saw her with my own eyes, face bloated and white
as the belly of a toad. The skin flaked so much you could
have pared it off yourself with the nail of your smallest
finger.'

'I could never eat fish again in my life because of the

way she smelt,' Leon Bloomberg muttered into his chest, and old Ada Markovitz at his side overheard and passed out cold.

Kitty, they were wrong, of course. I am beautiful in death, not plain as I have been all my life. My skin is iridescent and fine-veined, like the petals of lilies, and my blind eyes are milk-white, like rare opals. My lips are the colour of irises. When I was discovered my hair lay spread and webbed with dew and hung with spangles of frost. There is no ugliness now. I am transformed.

I chose three woods for my casket: pine for its sweet fragrant scent, oak for its strength to see me against the worms, and mahogany for its richness of colour. The lining came from a bolt of silk spun by the old Huguenot in Whitechapel. Not mere China silk, either, but the finest faille, dyed a regal scarlet by a gentleman in Bow and then stitched into a thousand pin-tucks in my own workshop.

How those same machines must have hummed each night to ensure the quantity of new costumes that are displayed today. A sea of seal-black bombazine parts before my coffin. All the mourners bought new, supposing death cancels all debts. They reckoned without my employees though, who have a detailed and accurate list of each penny that is owed. Your father is there, Kitty – a young child, dressed smartly in black. He is bored by the event and why not? Old women are daunting creatures. He called me Bubba but I doubt he understands that I have gone at last.

For my shroud I have the finest outfit I ever wore or made. I stitched it myself in secret, a black marocain

45

tea-dress in the old-fashioned style. It has a ruby georgette bodice with long circular ruffles that fall in soft folds at my bare wrists, and a beaded jacket of the best rayon faille.

Next to my skin is a foundation bodice lined with heavy taffeta that rustled like leaves as I was lifted into my casket. There are bust pads made of soft black crepe padded with cotton wool, and a zip fastener stab-stitched into position by my own hand runs from the bodice to the narrow Petersham waistband.

How can I describe the perfume that each fabric has always had for me, Kitty? The faintest acrid, metallic tang of the taffeta; the sharp-edged aroma from the Petersham; the soft fat muskiness of the crepe? What of the scent that flies screaming from the outfit as its seams are steamed? Or the delicate sweetness that hangs over the swatch of fresh rayon when it first arrives?

Did you ever in your life smell a garment before it has hung in a shop or been perfumed by its owner? I could always select fabrics blind by scent alone; maybe even tell colour by sucking at the taste of the dye.

If you know of cut and seam you will already see the old-fashioned skill in my death-dress, but even a novice would find much to wonder at in the more showy detail of the elaborate revers. There could be less work on a cardinal's robe: gold and silver embroidery in twisted wire braid; ruby glass beads forming delicate, gleaming flowers, with diamante on a raised twist of silver between each bloom; and precious hanging pearls along the edge of each lapel, with gold bobbles sewn top and bottom to gleam and sparkle in the unseen light.

You may laugh at me for my vanity now, dear, for I was an old and ugly woman. I would take pleasure in your humour, though, and even welcome it. The *Chevra kaddisha* may have me later to wrap in their plain linen and seal in a bare box; until then I will travel in style, and the grander the better!

There are those who would say that a life spent on the creation of garments is a wasted life, Kitty, and yet where would society be without clothes to define its parameters? Where would rich or poor stand if both dressed alike? Who could tell judge from criminal or duchess from whore if all bought from the same source? I am proud of my grand obsession. I know of no more worthwhile occupation.

So what of my life, now that I am discovered in death? Who are my mourners to arrive at my home and sit on their low chairs burning a candle and reciting Kaddish through the *shiva*? How many heads will be bowed for me? Or shall my soul wait alone, listening for its prayers in an empty room?

My tale is simple to tell, but full of lies and secrets. We are each of us the hero of our own life story, but my story is not my own. I share it with millions and it is therefore without ending. I am the ghost of my ancestors and will haunt the generations of the future.

I am *your* ghost, Kitty. You cannot hear me or see me but I am here nevertheless, watching you and your destiny. You are like my own child, for even though more than one generation separates us my blood still runs in your veins. I beg you to remember that, dear. You are *my* future and my own destiny, just as much as I am your past.

We were all of us the children of history, blown like

smoke across many oceans to strange lands: moving spirits, drifting and homeless.

Seventy-nine years old at my death I was, and yet now in my dreams I am a child again, studying the sulphurous clouds that amass daily in the purple skies above our steamship that will bring us to England. How many of us have left Russia for the new country? We stand there on deck, miserable and grief-stricken but at the same time aching with such hope for the new lands. When we arrive in England, our eyes brimming with dreams, we are called, 'The offal of the earth'. Such a welcome!

1889 is the year, Kitty. I am fourteen years old and have left Russia for America, and my only ambition right now is to stay alive. Can you imagine that, dear? I have no beauty, either; if your taste is for elegant heroines such as yourself you had best turn away. My face is full of bitterness at what has been my misfortune and my legs as thin and bent as a wishbone. The clouds have grown the colour of albumen and the snow has begun to fall . . .

I am three years old when I catch my first snowflake. It falls into my lap, surprising me immensely and filling me with wonder, and I fold it carefully into my apron like a precious gift and trot into the house to show it to my mamma. She, of course, laughs at my tears when I see it has vanished. She is an astonishing woman: tall and strong and, for the most part, insane.

Papa – your great-great-grandpapa – is a fine-looking man, and a master tailor, which is to say he can make a suit complete from start to end. At home we speak only Yiddish, but Papa is fluent in the master tongue, which is

48

Russian, as well as having a little English, too. Papa is an intellectual while Mamma is illiterate, for she cannot read Russian, only Yiddish that is written phonetically in Hebrew characters.

Papa spends his evenings locked alone in his study poring over the Talmud like a scholar, to discover the meaning of life. So far he has uncovered two things for me:

'Never be poor, Rosa,' he tells me, 'and never grow old.' I swear solemnly to obey him. Wealth and youth throughout my life, such easy things for a child to promise. My father calls me Rosa, even though my name is Bertha. Bertha Cecilia Zigofsky. Thank God for simple Rosa.

A lifetime ago we lived well in Moscow, in a great house that I loved. Papa was originally a travelling tailor before the business expanded, and would often work for goods in lieu of money, so that the cellar at our house was full of cheeses and salamis that his grateful clients had paid him with. The smell as you stood on the basement stairs! He was a generous man, too, and often gave much of the produce to the needy.

But then we were moved on to our new home here in Vilna, in The Pale of Settlement, to live alongside our grandmother, who we call Bubba, and the other Jews, and it was then that Mother began to plan the terrible thing and Papa started his quest for the truth.

I am happy enough in Vilna. Bubba has seven children other than Papa and we all visit together at her home and she bakes *kichels* to eat with the sweet wine and I sit with the aunts while they talk, though they all become quiet when it is my mother's turn to speak.

Our mother's name is Ernestine but she answers only to

49

Rintzi, which was her mother's family name. Rintzi has views on many things, and most of them angry. When she speaks her face becomes flushed and the aunts smile strangely and turn their eyes to their feet.

'Where is the history of Jewish women written?' Rintzi shouts. And, 'Why are we the nameless ones? Eh? Why should we be segregated in the synagogues and why are we ineligible to be counted in *minyan*? Who can tell me? Why?'

Rintzi has large pink hands and smells of the sour vinegar she sprinkles about to rid us of the scent of Bubba's many cats. Her face is large and handsome with thick brows set over wild, darting eyes. Those eyes miss nothing. Sometimes they see what is not even there. Before she married her hair was black and long enough to sit upon and she tied it into two long plaits that she bound across the top of her skull. Now her head is shaven and she covers it with scarves, which is the custom.

Rintzi is the best-dressed woman in the *shtetle* because my father makes her clothes. There is an old Yiddish saying, *Ale shuste geyn borves*, or, 'All shoemakers go barefoot', but that was never true in our house, for we are all dressed well. There are more tailors and shoemakers in Vilna than there could ever be buyers, and yet still people come from miles to purchase my father's suits.

I hide happily in the fabrics in his workroom and Papa pretends to have lost me. He is a thick-built man with a fine set of whiskers that ice up in the cold. His business in Moscow employed ten other workers but here the room is small and here there is just Papa. At night he nails wooden

50

boards to the windows in case they get smashed. Some nights he will sleep here, on guard.

The great rolls of cloth are more home to me than my own house. It is gentlemen's cloth; dark flannels and gabardines, soft undyed cottons and rough gluey calico for the stiffening and interfacings. I wrap myself in the end of the roll. The room buzzes like a hive and the steam makes my little nest warm. I hear the hiss and thud as the hot iron hits the padded sleeveboard. Sometimes I sleep here, knowing that I am safe. I know you love fabrics every bit as much as I, Kitty. Close your eyes now and imagine the scene.

Gregory is Rintzi's favourite. He is her son and her eldest and her love for him is intense and exclusive. She adores him and she fears for him. Her life revolves around him as the moon revolves around the earth. That is the way of the world and also the way it has always been, therefore Papa and I cannot mind.

I love Gregory, too – it is impossible not to. He is quiet and earnest and pale and very beautiful. His speech is slow, like his thoughts, and next to him I am like an ugly little monkey with a flea in its fur.

Gregory should be studious, like Papa, but he does not have the mind for study. His hair is brown, like mine though a little lighter, but his eyes are paler and have a dreaminess that mine do not. When he smiles you can see that his teeth are crooked.

Bubba takes us to the store to buy us pickles and the old woman who was Bubba's friend in Odessa rolls up the sleeve of her dress and plunges her fat arm into the barrel of cucumbers. The sourness of the pickle makes Gregory's eyes water with tears but he always eats it all because he knows it makes Bubba happy.

When Rintzi was a child herself her beloved brother Isaac was kidnapped for the army. She never saw him again, though for years she lived in hope. Jewish boys were taken at the age of twelve, though some were younger, and they served twenty-five years each.

One day ten years later, when she and Papa had just married, Rintzi was hurrying through snows outside the town when she saw a long crocodile of small children making its way somewhere off to the east. She stopped to watch as they passed; tiny, whey-faced Jewish boys, some as young as eight, all in too-large uniforms and all with faces of such misery and terror and despair that she was on her knees, trembling and shaking from pity, before half of them had stumbled by.

There was a guard with them, a man with a face as round as a loaf and icicles on his moustache.

'Where are you taking them?' Rintzi shouted out, wringing her hands in anguish.

'To Kazan,' came the reply, and then Rintzi knew that the boys she watched were mostly doomed, because Kazan was miles and miles away and they would never survive in all that snow.

'Isaac,' was all she could think, for she had now at last realized her poor brother's fate. Papa searched for her when it became dark and found her by the woods and carried her home, more dead than alive. The rabbi even tried to make her recite the Shema, but for two days she was unable to speak.

Rintzi recovered from the exposure but her mind never really did. When Gregory was born she became happy again, but the happiness turned slowly to terror with each year of his life as it passed. Now she often argues with Papa in his study, begging him to pay the authorities to watch her to keep her son at home and out of the army. I listen at the keyhole and always it is the same thing: 'Pay them the money, Dovid! Three hundred roubles! It's not so much – find it, find it, I beg you . . . look, I am begging!' She always falls to the floor then, and clutches at my father's knees. Papa is crying too, and it would be a cruel hard man who could not, for her voice is so full of sadness and desperation.

'I don't have the money, Rintzi,' he tells her.

'He'll die,' she says, her voice full of hatred. 'Gregory will die like all the others, like all those other little boys!'

Papa tries to hold her but she scuttles away from him across the floor.

Gregory is twelve and I am seven when Rintzi decides at last to do the terrible thing. There has been a burning of the shops the night before and Papa has left early to see to his workroom. Outside is a swirling tangled mist of snow, and a hammering echoes through the small house as Uncle Levin nails planks to the windowframe to protect us from the gangs that night.

There is one window still bare. I press my tongue against it to taste the ice that has formed on the inside.

I am wearing an overall Papa made for me: plain blue ratine with my initial, 'R', embroidered in pink silk on the handkerchief pocket. Rintzi is in the kitchen crying and she has been there for the entire morning. Gregory pretends to be bored, but in fact he is full of fear, we both are.

Rintzi is quiet suddenly and that is somehow worse than the crying. We hear her boots on the bare wooden floor and then suddenly she is inside the doorway. She must have washed her face because it looks dry and calm now.

'Put on your coat, dearest,' she tells Gregory, and he rushes off to fetch it obediently. She appears not to have noticed me. While Gregory is gone she paces the room, pressing her scarf to her head with her hands, and when he returns she smiles. She takes his arm when he is dressed. I see they are prepared to leave and so I run for my cape too, because Uncle Levin is finished now and I don't care to be left alone in a boarded house.

Rintzi pulls Gregory across the street and his legs are going two steps for her one. The road bends towards the left but she strides out towards the open country as though hurrying off to the shops. I follow but I cannot catch up and neither do I wish to. Afraid as I am of the forest and the snow, the expression on Rintzi's face fills me with a far deeper dread. Also, I have noticed what Gregory has not, that she has the knife from the kitchen – the biggest one that we are always told never to touch – tucked into the back of her belt, so that the silver tip of it peeks beneath the fur lining of her grey wool jacket.

I lose them now in the whiteness. When the flakes clear again they appear miles away, like two scurrying beetles in the distance, one grey and one black. Gregory's coat is whipped up by the wind and lifts out behind him like dark, shiny wings.

I run behind them, following their footprints, envying

54

my brother his cap because my own head is so cold now.

'Mamma!' I see her turn and Gregory turns with her. He is smiling, he thinks it is a game. He is just happy to be with his beloved mother after all her tears of the morning. His britches are wet to the knee but he is still happy. They turn and walk again, only now I am nearer.

Are there wolves in the wood? Papa said so and we sometimes hear them howling at night. Perhaps Rintzi has the knife to kill a wolf. I run without appearing to move. My legs are tired. I am pleased when I see them halt.

Gregory is standing still now, his arms and legs rigid with indecision. I am close enough to see his face, so I stop running. I can't go any closer. The snow has eased a little and I look around for wild animals.

Rintzi takes Gregory gently by the hand again and at first I think they will walk some more, but she removes his glove before clutching him to her body and kissing his head. She pulls him down until they are sitting right there in the snow and then she pushes his bare hand into the ice and holds it down, staring at his face all the time.

Gregory doesn't squirm at all, which is peculiar to say the least. I push a fingertip into the snow to see just how it feels for him. After a few seconds it becomes unbearable, but still Gregory is obedient and doesn't move one inch. Rintzi is his mother and what she does is right.

Which is why he sits, still and upright, as she lifts his now-blue hand from the ice and pulls the knife out from her belt. Maybe he is even smiling because he trusts his besotted mother and knows she would never harm him.

She splays his fingers carefully and then uses the knife quickly, like an axe. Chop. Nothing happens. I stuff my hands into my mouth and the sky begins to spin about me. Rintzi looks at Gregory's face but it holds no expression, unlike her own, which is a mask of agony. She looks down at his little hand. And then she lifts it slowly and Gregory's fingers remain in the snow.

Four little pink-blue-and-white sticks, all in a neat row.

Gregory moves now, at last. His legs kick out frantically, like a beheaded turkey's. His feet find the ground and somehow he stands up. His mouth is smiling but then the smile splits wide and his whole face falls apart and his mouth is now open larger than I knew a mouth could go. He is silent, though; the scream I hear comes from my mother, followed by a louder scream from me. We set off crows which rise, flapping, from the bare black trees, shrieking their own mad cries. And then the blood comes at last, trickling in four sad little ribbons onto the white ground.

Rintzi forces the hand back into the snow to freeze the pain and then binds it quickly with some cloth. Gregory's legs kick and twitch but he does not make a noise. Rintzi takes off her scarf and ties it about his head, which would normally have been a treat, and she tries to embrace him and kiss him again, but he struggles to get away from her, so she folds him under the wing of her cloak and drags him back towards the house once again.

I walk to where they were. My teeth chatter and I make a noise with my mouth: 'Zee-zeee-zeee-zeee.' It is a noise of cold and fear and shock. The fingers are still there on the ground. They are Gregory's fingers, I know them, I recognize each one. His nails were dirty. Rintzi was always telling him to wash them. I kick snow over them and I say a short prayer, but I don't cry because I can't, because my tears will freeze my face.

The army won't want Gregory now. Rintzi did it to save him. She is the bravest woman I know. I pray that Papa will agree.

CHAPTER FOUR

ZG

THE SEASON

*Seasons are meagre in the fashion trade: four weeks in
spring, when the winter orders are taken, and four
more in autumn, when the summer styles are sold.
A range of sample garments is hawked about to the
buyers from home and abroad, first at the fashion
exhibitions and later at the showrooms themselves. Unlike
the couture ranges, which will be modelled professionally in front of wine-swilling clients, the business in
showrooms is often done on the rails by buyers
clutching tea and a biscuit.*

Everybody in the business knew that couture was dead; a
lost leader at best, a dinosaur at worst. Which was why
Kitty sat in the Zigo-owned wholesale – or 'down-market',
as Burgess would call it – showroom in Newman Street
watching the buyer from The House of Fraser tapping on
a laptop before calling out her order to the showroom
manager. Kitty didn't mind downmarket. Kitty didn't mind
any of it – up, down, cabbage, *prêt-à-porter*, diffusion,
couture – it was all the same business and it was all part
of her life.

It was difficult not to hover. Kitty had never learnt the
art of diplomacy in the way most of her siblings had. Also,

people were looking at her as though she was some sort of freak because of her bereavement. Things were leaking into the newspapers; every day a new fact – it was like a simmering pot waiting to boil over. Death is embarrassing enough, people run out of conversation after the initial condolences, but murder? She walked about the business in a miasma of self-conscious hush. She knew she was like the Ancient Mariner to the business right now, haunting the showrooms with her grim-faced presence, but it was hard to keep away at such a vital time.

She checked her watch. The buyers were onto their third lemon tea and looking about for sandwiches. If the girl was sent out to the little Italian place on the corner it would mean she'd be unavailable to model the range. There was silence – plus the muffled tap-tap-tap of the laptop keyboard.

The buyer paused for thought and air. There was an expectant rustle of pure silk dupion suiting. Kitty leant across. 'Would you like some lunch?' Food meant a pause, a respite. Kitty had to be at the Chelsea barracks for a show in fifty minutes. Lunch spelt disaster. Small triangles of granary interleaved with cos and smoked salmon signalled the end of all hope.

The buyer shook her head. Oh joy – she must be on a diet.

The Chelsea show was high-class crap. The models were quite blatantly smoking something-or-other backstage, and were subsequently turned out by a new stylist to look like tramps. Many were pale, starved and bruised, like elderly fruit. They contrasted painfully with the gleaming, fit and sporty types that Ralph Lauren had been parading the week before in the US. Or the older and quietly elegant models that had been so well-acclaimed in Milan.

This was the opening show of British Design Week. The silent groans from contributors reached a vacuum-like crescendo during the retro sequence, where students from the leading art colleges had been asked to participate as a come-on to new talent of the future.

In a moment of supposedly highest camp satire one of the students had dressed a live cow in a kilt and sent it out on stage. They'd sprayed it liberally with Chanel to get rid of the farmyard smell and the result was an intriguing bouquet that had fashion hacks in the stalls fishing into their Prada bags for hankies to press to their noses like Regency fops.

As the placid, pongy animal lumbered past, Kitty peered through the spotlights to the faces seated opposite her. Once reserved for the top journalists from *Vogue* and *Elle*, the little gilt seats that made up the front-row now tended to be filled with bemused-looking sponsors in flat-arsed suits. These were the same dull faces that occupied other front-row seats at all the top sporting events and concerts. Nervously poised and silent, eyes glazed and fully aware that they had barely a nut-size speck of knowledge or interest in the event they were attending, they smiled politely and clapped as the cow was led round and, udders swinging, made its way back up the runway.

Kitty glanced at the press photographers, who were penned in like battery hens on tottering tiers of lightweight, aluminium ladders, at the far end of the stage. Hadn't they lost the will to live yet? Did they honestly want to clamour for shots of a heifer clad in tartan lycra?

'This is a fucking travesty!' someone said next to her, but not with enough feeling or pitch to constitute a 'scene' that might make the front pages the following day, and Kitty noticed that the hacks continued sketching and scribbling in their notebooks regardless.

Kitty had notes of her own, but they weren't about the show. She was busy compiling a list of names. At the top of the list was one name that had been underlined several times – Nicky Kofteros, one of the major players in the financial market. One of the Dream Merchants, henchman of the Waika corporation. One of the men-in-suits who sat opposite her right now. She wanted him dematerialized. She looked across at him. He smiled back. She underlined his name one more time. He was poised to take all that was important in her life. She wanted him gone.

There was a crush in the reception area as journalists fought to be the first out to file their copy. Kitty moved to the side of the tent, closing her eyes to the hum of the voices. Maybe what she had just seen had all been a dream – a nightmare. Maybe she would wake up any minute and take herself off to the real show, where fabrics would hang like liquid around the sylph-like shapes of smiling, healthy models. Maybe she'd see bias cuts and faultless seams and shapes that flattered and styles so innovative she would wonder why no designer had conceived them before.

The photographers found her leaning up against the ropes and, judging her expression to be one of unutterable personal grief, started snapping mercilessly. Kitty opened her eyes in mild surprise. Ten paparazzi. No matter. She'd

61

lived with them for years now. Two were currently camped outside her apartment, tailing her since her father's murder. She'd got into the habit of buying take-away coffee for them, too. In fact, she'd miss them if they weren't there. They rarely used the shots they took, anyway. Kitty was attractive but hers wasn't the sort of beauty that worked in print. Chloe was the one the cameras fell for. Subtlety didn't exactly pan out in newsprint.

'Miss Zigofsky?' She opened her eyes onto Kofteros's wide, smiling, clean-featured face. Almost humanoid. Maybe a little too chisled. He took her hand and shook it. His flesh felt amazingly life-like. The photographers continued to snap away. Oh joy, a chummy shot for the city to brood over.

There was not a trace of a crease on the man's suit, despite the cramped heat of the fashion theatre. Not a linen man, then.

'We met in your brother's office,' he said. His handshake was just right – not too strong, not too weak. His eye contact was straight out of the training manuals – focused but not overpowering, forceful but with the hint of a twinkle to imply an underlying sense of irony.

His tie told of Pall Mall clubs and his suit was pure Jermyn Street, although the narrow leather wrist-thong, just visible below the sleeve of the Turnbull and Asser shirt, smacked of a sense of native, ethnic cunning. He was slobber-inducingly good-looking. The sort of looks that had moral standards tripping off down the street with a wave of adieu. The kind of man that made you realize you were wearing tights and knickers *plus* a lycra bodysuit that joined at the crotch with noisy velcro – and that you'd

62

somehow pulled them all up in the wrong order on your last trip to the loo.

Kitty found him nauseating.

'Might I buy you a drink?' he asked.

She looked at her watch. 'I have to be at the factory by three-twenty,' she told him.

'Then perhaps I can accompany you?'

Kitty smiled then. 'Oh yes,' she said. Why not? Dressed as he was he'd go down a storm in Mile End.

When they got to the car park she discovered he had a brand new, virginal Bentley and her happiness was complete. She could hear them sharpening sticks and coins even now in the Commercial Road. With a bit of luck the wheel-removers might be on duty – or even the gangs who liked to pee through the sun roofs of flash cars.

Her mood was good, then, as they hit the Marylebone Road. Maybe it was time for Mr Kofteros to see the less prestigious side of the business that he was so keen to buy into.

CHAPTER FIVE

ℤG

RUSSIA

Fashionable Parisian society responded to the blood-shed of the Russian Revolution by developing a taste for Russian embroidery on its dress designs. The demand was so great that Grand Duchess Marie Pavlovna, daughter of Grand Duke Paul, started a lucrative business employing ex-patriate women to embroider traditional peasant designs onto clothes. The houses of both Chanel and Patou were customers of this business.

Kitty,

It is wonderful to see the whole family assembled in Bubba's house. Grandmother is, of course, the oldest person present and therefore is allotted the great wooden chair in the centre of the room. The chair is huge and Bubba is tiny, but she more than fills the space through presence and bearing alone.

The room is small and lit by flickering candles, in whose warm and golden light I watch the stony faces of my bear-like uncles and their cheerfully-gossiping wives. When I look from the small, wood-framed window I see the peasants walking home across the fields in the scarlet light of the dusk. They sing as they walk, great booming Russian harmonies that I will remember the whole of my life.

We eat before business is done. There is no table big enough and so planks have been found and laid with white cloths. We sit in lines with the planks resting on our knees. The women are on one side and the men facing them, so that the planks tip unevenly, but that is how it has to be, according to Bubba. When someone moves the 'table' rocks and we all grab at the bowls to save them, and Bubba lectures the unfortunate person who moved about the sin of fidgeting while the rest of us laugh out loud.

Uncle Leopold is the youngest of Bubba's eight sons, yet his moustache is the longest. Uncle Sergei has hands as big as anvils and can eat a whole loaf at one sitting. Uncle Reuben repairs watches for a living, and Uncle Levin makes cabinets when not nailing boards over the windows of our houses.

This is the last time we will all be present in one house, for soon four of the brothers will be leaving to make great lives for themselves in America. The room is as warm as an oven, apart from a knife-like draught from beneath the kitchen door, which makes me wish I had worn boots. When the wind blows I lift my feet, careful not to make the planks wobble.

We eat hot beetroot soup that leaves pink-purple stains on all the beards, and pickled fish with potato. Bubba's house is bare in style, but full of fine things from the old days. Grandpa's picture hangs on the wall in a painted wooden frame behind his sons' heads. He looks small, like his wife, and yet he would terrorize his strapping boys and beat them with logs of wood if they misbehaved.

When the food is finished and the planks cleared and

put away the chairs are pushed into a circle and I am banished to the kitchen to eat sweet cakes while the business of the evening commences. I nibble at one cake and then kneel to peer through the crack in the door.

Papa sits with his hands on his knees and tells the tale of Gregory's fingers simply and with as little anger as possible. Bubba listens but her eyes do not leave Rintzi's face. My mother sits beside my father, her back as straight as a soldier's and her eyes fixed on a spot somewhere close to the ceiling.

When Papa has told of the terrible thing that Rintzi did there is silence and then Uncle Andrei, the eldest brother, clears his throat to speak. His job is a difficult one because, although he is the eldest brother, he is far from being the cleverest, and he is aware of the fact that his judgment of the problem will require more wisdom than he is able to muster, even with three beakers of vodka inside his belly.

'Is the boy well again now?' he asks. The aunts nod approval. He has things in the right order of priority. He smiles broadly with relief.

My father looks at my mother. 'He is well again now,' he says. He loves his wife and he pities her, but he will never forgive her for cutting the fingers from his only son's right hand. Gregory was to be a tailor too, Papa was training him for the trade. They would have worked together, and Gregory would have taken over the business once he was old enough and Papa's eyes too worn from all the fine stitching . . .

Bubba interrupts. 'Ernestine, why did you do this thing?' she asks. Mother's eyes are like lakes, full of water and far

66

away. Gregory will no longer approach her. When she enters a room he scuttles out in fear. When she attempts to touch him he screams. Her hands are pale and composed in her lap. She did this thing to keep her son, yet now she has lost him anyway. She has been outrageously selfless. I admire her more now than ever before in my life, but she scares me, too. Her courage and single-mindedness are terrifying.

Bubba sits back in her chair and folds her arms across her chest. She nods as though she has had an answer, although my mother has not yet spoken one word.

'Gregory should come here to live with me,' Bubba says, quietly. Her face is perfectly round and there is not an inch of unlined skin on it. Her nut-brown eyes peep out from two cracks among a sea of tanned leather crinkles.

Rintzi's fixed gaze drops down from the ceiling. 'No,' she says, clearly.

There is a pause that hangs around this one word, trapping it in empty air like a bird in a cage.

'Well then!' Uncle Andrei claps his hands on his thighs and then shrugs a little, beaming around the room as though something has been settled.

Perhaps it has. Gregory will remain at our house where he will continue to refuse to even look at the mother he once adored so much. Papa will try to teach me the tailoring trade instead of his son – at least until his patience runs out – and the aunts will take turns to smother us with care and concern.

And, most importantly, no one ever tries to tell poor deluded Rintzi that the cruel policy of child recruitment had died along with the old Czar many years before.

67

CHAPTER SIX

Z̶G

LINEN
*Taken from flax, which is widely thought of as one of
the oldest fibres known to man, linen is famous for its
natural, uneven look. For many years a sign of wealth
has been the well-pressed, uncreased suit, but recently,
in a trend of reverse psychology following the glut of
cheap, crease-resistant man-made fibres, linen and all
its wrinkles has come to signify money and taste.*

I am thirteen years old now, Kitty, almost a woman. Rintzi
has employed a marriage broker to match me with a husband and we are to ride out of the *shtetle* to the town on
a borrowed sleigh to meet the man she has found. If all is
well Papa says he will begin to make the wedding suit for
my husband-to-be.

The boy's name is Aaron and we first met as children,
when the snowdrift cut off the *shtetle* and his brothers
bravely brought fabrics in by cart for Papa to sew. I have
not seen him since, but I know he is handsome and clever
because Papa says so, and I am happier than ever before
in my life.

The uncles are all gone away now, and Bubba died last
spring when her stovepipe blocked in the night and the
smoke filled her room and killed her in her sleep.

Rintzi plaits my hair like her own used to be and we all don our best coats and take thick blankets for the ride into town. When I look in the mirror I would like to be prettier, but perhaps I am not too bad, and Aaron will be pleased anyway.

My skin is my best feature; it is pale but not white and I swear it will never have wrinkles like Bubba's, no matter how long I shall live. My eyes are like Rintzi's, dark and never still, and I believe that if you could find Papa's mouth beneath his whiskers, it would be thin-lipped and curved, like my own.

My forehead is too short and my hair too thick to lay flat. My ears are peculiarly large, like a boy's, so that other children at school would sometimes nickname me 'Rabbit', but Rintzi has combed my hair in such a way as to take care of that.

What else is there to say of myself? I am small but, like Bubba, I put up a good fight. I am thin just now, but there are signs that I might inherit my grandmother's figure, which was round with a tiny waist. My legs are more peculiar than my ears but long skirts solve that problem for me. If Aaron likes lively girls with a quick mind and strange looks, then I am the one for him.

That evening we ride back to the *shtetle* again and, whereas we travelled out noisily, with much excitement, the return journey is taken in silence. I watch the frost glittering like diamonds in the moonlight. Rintzi goes home but Papa takes us on to the workshop, where he sits me down on a bentwood chair.

I watch him go round the room, measuring cloth, picking up scissors. Putting them down again.

'Well, Rosa?' he says at last.

'Well, Papa?' I ask him. He picks up his chalk now and studies it like a precious stone.

'I thought maybe Aaron was a little quiet,' he says. In fact Aaron said not one word all evening.

'Yes, Papa,' I agree. He puts his spectacles onto the bridge of his nose and studies some patterns.

'Maybe I was a little optimistic when I described him as handsome, Rosa,' he says quietly, stroking his beard.

'I think he looks very well, Papa,' I say. My father looks surprised and perhaps relieved. In fact Aaron is not at all handsome but then neither am I, so we should make a suitable pair. 'I think he is very dignified,' I continue, and this is what I have told myself on the journey home: when he speaks it will be worth waiting for. Only fools talk when there is nothing to say. I have decided Aaron will make the perfect husband. I smile with excitement while Papa kisses me on the cheek.

Papa spends every spare hour on the wedding suit. He works without measurements for he has a good eye for such things and can even tell how much Aaron will grow by the time we are married. I watch him in the workshop and I can see this is the best suit he will ever make. The fabric took two months to arrive because he ordered it from special weavers.

'Feel it,' he says. It is too soft and fine to feel properly with my fingertips so I press it against my cheek, instead. It smells buttery. When I touch a little against my tongue it has a beautiful, sour-almond flavour.

'Can you smell the spices, too, Rosa?' Papa asks. When I try again I can. The fabric has been made in the East. It is black enough to be invisible.

He cuts the first pattern from bleached calico and pins it to the dummy, spinning the thing around quickly many times to tell shape and fit. I wonder if he will swallow any pins, for he has so many in his mouth, but he never does, although I once saw him lose one in his beard.

He lays out the dark wool on the cutting-table and marks it with his chalk before slicing it with a pair of the sharpest scissors ever seen. If they were not so sharp the fabric would move, but as it is he doesn't even have to rest his hand on it to keep it still as he cuts.

I love the noise the scissors make. Small fringes of black fluff fall from the cutting-table to the floor and I sweep them up quickly, being careful to keep out of Papa's way as I do so.

I will not speak while I watch, for fear he will lose concentration and make a mistake. Sometimes I fall asleep with my head on the tailor's ham, but when I wake Papa is still working as before, quickly and deftly. His hands are skilful and swift, like a conjurer's. If I studied for a thousand years I could never create such magic.

In the corner of the workroom is a large copper urn filled with constantly boiling water heated by a charcoal fire. On top of the urn is a teapot and there is a small dripping tap at the bottom. I fetch glasses and pour tea from this samovar, which I press my father to drink. When he finally pauses for a break we sit on either side of the urn and sip the strong tea through lumps of sugar which we suck in our mouths.

When the suit is on the dummy Papa starts work on the waistcoat, which will be worn underneath. The suit itself is a masterpiece, but the waistcoat is little short of miraculous. Papa is an artist when it comes to embroidery and this waistcoat is to be a sample of the finest work he can create. He spends weeks on the intricate designs alone. The silks must be dyed by hand to get a certain depth and richness of colour, even though the overall effect is to be a subtle blend of rouge and maroon.

I forget how many weeks or months pass before the suit nears completion, but when it is I am banished from the workroom because Papa wishes to surprise me with the finished garment. I am so excited I can barely wait. Rintzi tries to share my excitement but I know she is sad, too, because the wedding suit should have been made for Gregory, not Aaron. We all know Gregory will never marry, though, because he has grown a child's heart – his mind seemed to stop maturing after the shock of the thing Rintzi did to him.

Papa works all night to get the suit finished. I am up with the dawn, full of excitement and, when I can stand the waiting no longer, when I am making poor Rintzi's head ache with my continual questioning: 'When? Now? Yet?', I set out to walk from home to the workroom to surprise him.

It is a cold, sun-lit morning and I see people hurrying down the street, away from me. I take large, quick steps, like a man. If my legs would move faster then I would make them. But I don't wish to run. Walking is the nearest thing to patience that I can muster. The air puffs from my hot mouth like steam from a samovar. I feel nine-foot tall and smile at my neighbours as they pass. Don't run, Rosa. Walk. Run and the suit will not be finished when you get there. Only patience gets its reward. My muscles ache from all the effort.

Someone grabs me by the arm, making me spin round in surprise.

'Rosa Zigofsky?' It's the old woman from the laundry. I wonder why she asks my name since she has known me well all my life.

'They burnt the shops last night,' she says. I stare at her face. Suddenly we are strangers. I try to think but nothing comes. I am stupid and dull, suddenly. Shock has made my wits as blunt as Gregory's.

I have my legs, though, if not my brain. Now I begin to run until the stamping of my feet begins to rattle my little brain within its own skull. Run and you will find there is nothing, no problem. Walk now and all may be lost. I can smell the first oily sweet aroma of burnt wood now, and my eyes begin to sting from the drifting pall of smoke.

When I turn the corner I think things don't look so bad, and stop to draw breath into my lungs, bending double with my hands resting on my thighs. Waiting until my ribs stop heaving. A couple of the buildings have windows that are broken but Papa's place appears to be untouched. I have been stupid, racing about like an old horse. My fingers fly to cover my mouth and I let out a laugh. Papa will be waiting to tell me how stupid I am to have galloped about in such a way. I hope he did not see me. He tells me I am a woman, nearly, and I know he would like me to act like one at last.

73

When I get to his doorway there are three men sheltering inside.

'Rosa,' the biggest man says. I know him, of course, as I know all who live in our village. He worked with Uncle Reuben sometimes. I smile at him but he doesn't smile back.

'They tried to burn the workroom, Rosa,' he says. I think at once of the wedding suit. Papa's best work, all gone in the flames. 'Your father stopped them, though,' he continues. I have never seen him before without a smile on his face. I would barely have recognized him with this solemn expression. 'They got angry, Rosa. They were only kids, but a couple of them were drunk. They nailed your father into one of Lucien Binstock's huge barrels and then they rolled him down the street for a joke. When we opened the barrel your father was dead, Rosa. It broke his bones. I'm sorry. It's a terrible thing.'

I push past them suddenly and run up the stairs, two at a time. Papa will be working there, as usual, and he will smile at me and take off his glasses and rub at his eyes, because he has been working all night . . .

The suit is there, on the stand. It is almost finished. I inspect it carefully, turning it, barely wanting to touch it, and it is so beautiful that it makes me sad. The waistcoat is the most wonderful garment I have ever seen in my life. It makes me realize how little beauty there is here in our poor *shtetle*, where things are drab and bare.

The embroidery is so intricate it seems impossible to think it could have been done by a human hand. Papa's glasses lie on the cutting-table. Perhaps he took them off

74

when he heard so much noise outside. His first thought must have been for this suit. Maybe he smelt the burning as I did and ran out, scared that his life's best work might go up in the flames.

I put his abandoned spectacles on and peer, and every detail of the pattern of stitches is instantly magnified. I inspect it carefully and slowly. Now I can see my name stitched among the flowers and exotic creatures there: *Rosa, the daughter I love*. He has stitched the words there, right amidst the pattern, all but invisible to the human eye. I am so proud my eyes well with tears. The copper samovar lies on its side in the corner of the room. Did Papa knock it over in his struggles with the boys? Tea has stained the bare boards like blood.

'Papa,' I whisper. The suit is not quite finished. There are buttons lying, waiting to be sewn on, and then the whole delicate garment must be pressed.

I thread up a needle, even though my eyes are too wet to see properly and I have to blink hard to make them clear enough to see the silks.

I sew the buttons carefully by hand, using the best stitches I can, so that Papa will be proud of me. The fabric is so soft that I know there must be no mistakes – if I unpick bad stitching the needle will have left holes and the entire garment will be ruined by my clumsiness.

Papa worked quickly but I am as slow as a snail. When the buttons are done I heat the iron and carry the suit, one piece at a time, across to the board. My hands shake from the grave importance of the job that I have to do. To make a mistake would be unthinkable. I pray that I will not burn the delicate cloth, telling God that I will do anything –

anything! If only the suit can be pressed without mistake . . .

When every crease is gone, and every seam flattened into its rightful place, I hang the suit carefully back onto the dummy and then I am so relieved and pleased that I begin to speak to it.

'You are to be my husband's wedding suit,' I tell it, 'my Papa made you. You are the finest outfit in the world.' I reach out and touch the special place on the embroidery: *Rosa, the daughter I love.* Papa guarded this suit with his life.

Only then, when the precious thing is finished, do I sink back onto my little bentwood chair and allow myself to weep for my dreadful loss.

We can't exist here, the three of us. Rintzi barely speaks and the shock of Papa's death has left her exhausted, so I have to fetch and carry for her all day. Gregory is terrified that there will be another pogrom, and that we will all be killed in barrels, like Papa. There are no men here to look out for us. Gregory would be hopeless in a fight, because although he is tall enough in stature his mind is as useless as a child's.

At night I feel that the wolves from the wood are circling closer and closer to the house. I look out into the darkness for the sight of their yellow eyes, that Bubba used to say would be lit up like coach lamps, and my ears ache from listening for their howls.

We each sit at windows, waiting. Rintzi waits for Papa to return, Gregory for the men with the barrels, and I wait for Aaron, for I believe he will get to hear of our plight and somehow come to save us, as he saved Papa's business in the time of the great snowdrifts.

We live like this for many months before I make an important decision: I will ride instead to the town and fetch Aaron for myself. We must have a man in the house again. Once I have decided I know I must go at once, while I have the courage, even though the weather is bad. I am so scared and excited it is as though I have a fever.

We can marry earlier than planned – no one will mind.

I hire a sleigh from the local school, and then have to pay double when they complain that the snows are too bad and there is a risk that the pony could be injured. Rintzi tries to stop me packing but then she suddenly gives up and sits down on the bed instead, with her face in her apron. Even she understands the sense of this thing. She knows this journey has to be done.

I leave at midday, when there is a little pale sun in the sky and the snows have eased to a delightful sprinkling, as though flour were being sifted from above. The pony is as keen to reach town as I am and we are several hours out of the *shtetle* before I realize this is the furthest I have been on my own in my life. I whistle a bit, like Papa used to do, but when we finally see the first shacks of the town I am dearly relieved.

Aaron's house is a two-storey wooden building with a green tiled roof. I wonder if he has seen me from the window and I pat my hair into place, in case he is watching. Now I will hear him speak at last: 'What on earth brings you here alone, Bertha Zigofsky? Don't you know the danger involved, riding alone?' I will tell him our troubles and he will arrange things. When his mother's face appears at the door I am a little disappointed.

'Bertha?' She looks shocked. She is a small thin woman and her hair is wrapped in a black shawl. I wipe my nose on my hand in case it is running and step up to greet her.

'I've come to get married,' I say, smiling politely, holding out the square leather case for her to see. Inside is Aaron's wedding suit. I packed it carefully in the workroom, with paper and lavender between each fold. Aaron will be delighted with it and I will be more proud than I can say when he wears it.

His mother looks confused. 'The wedding has not been planned yet, Bertha,' she says. So far she has not invited me into her house, despite the fact that the wind is making our cheeks pinched and our noses blue.

'I know,' I say, 'but Papa has been killed and we cannot manage. We need to start the plans right away. Aaron must come and care for us.'

Her eyes drop to the floor at my sad news. She turns at last and walks into the house. I follow her inside and she offers me a seat in the parlour. When she disappears I think she has gone to fetch her son, but she comes back with tea. My hands are so cold I can barely hold the cup and I'm embarrassed when my clothes begin to steam in the heat from the stove.

'Bertha, you are so young, still,' she says. I laugh, a little nervously. Of course I am young but then these are exceptional circumstances and I feel she should understand that. Who can wait for the niceties of age when death is a reasonable option? If I do not marry her son now there will be nothing for him to wed but a corpse. But surely she is not stupid? I look at her again.

'Aaron isn't here, Bertha,' she says, after a while. At first I think he is dead, but then I see she looks nervous, not sad. 'He left two months ago, before *Pesach*.'

'When is he coming back?' I ask. I sip some tea and it burns my mouth.

'He left to go to America,' she replies simply. I can only stare. After a while I remember to shut my mouth. The room seems too hot now – the tea has made me giddy.

'We are going to be married,' I whisper.

She shrugs and looks at her feet. 'Maybe,' she says. 'Aaron is a clever boy. He wanted to do well. It was his decision, Bertha, he wouldn't have his mind changed. I would have written to your parents. I'm sorry about your father.'

'When did he decide to emigrate?' I ask.

'Soon after you came,' she says, blushing despite the cold. So he left after he had seen me. Aaron's mother is an honest woman, but I would rather she had lied. I can feel my mouth begin to tremble. I don't want to cry, it wouldn't be dignified. I straighten my back and rub my chin with my finger, pretending to be thinking.

'So he'll send for me once he's made his mark?' I ask her. I have to put the cup down before I break it with my shaking.

She shrugs again and tries to smile at me. 'I'm sorry, Bertha. Who knows? Young men these days – ach!'

Anger and distress fall upon me on the journey home. Aaron's mother begs me to stop when she sees the snows begin again, but I would rather drive to hell and back than stay a night in that house. The pony snorts and complains when I turn him around in the darkness but I shout and yell so much that he takes off like a shot from a gun.

I am the stupid one, and ugly, too. I will never marry now, that is for sure. My face drove Aaron off to America! I spare a hand from the reins to run a finger over my features. Can anyone be that plain? No – Aaron must have gone to make our fortune. He will send for me, I know it! Not all women are beautiful yet all women I know of are wives. I have a quick mind, too – Aaron would know that my conversation would never have bored him and that is more than most husbands can claim! Papa was always entertained by my talk, even when he was working. At the thought of my father a new pain slices me through to the bone.

I am too angry to be afraid, even when the sleet begins to blind me and the wind screams about my ears. The sleigh rolls down off the path. For a moment I think it will tip but it slowly straightens and I jump out to pull it back onto the track, complaining bitterly to the wind for blowing us there.

Despite all that I have said to myself inside my head, though – all the time I am shouting and jabbering to myself – I think of Rintzi and Gregory and wonder why I am even going home, when all I want to do is lay down there in the snow and die of shame and self-pity.

My skirt tears when the sleigh lurches and lands on top of the hem. I am wet through, and dirty, and now my clothes are torn, which makes me thoroughly miserable. We start off again, more slowly and carefully this time, and I promise the pony I will not scream at him again, if only he will get us back to the *shtetle* in one piece.

We ride on a little way with peace restored, and are only half an hour from the village when I first see the dark shapes of a small troupe of men and boys on the road.

The snow has cleared and I can count around half a dozen of them. At first I think they are men from the village, and that I must therefore know them, but when I pull nearer I can see they are strangers. Their faces are wrapped in mufflers, from which their breath rises on either side like steam from a samovar.

I try to pass in silence but one of them puts a hand out quickly and the pony rears, and another catches the reins and we are pulled to a stop.

I climb down from the cart with a mixture of fear and anger, clutching my case with the wedding suit in it to my chest. The men circle me and it appears they have little idea what to do next. Then one walks nearer.

'Are you a Jew?' he asks. I can tell from his voice that he is older than the others. He pulls his muffler down, and his face looks as harsh as his words.

'I asked if you are a Jew,' he insists. His lips are blue and there are spots of yellow pus dotted around his chin. He has the sulphurous eyes of a wolf and a scar in between the brows, like the mark of a thumbnail.

I look round at the others with him, who appear happy to let this older man do all the questioning, and then I stare back at him with what I hope looks like arrogance. He spits at me, which is shocking.

The younger boys laugh.

I spit back noisily, and there is a loud gasp from the

81

group. The pony rears up and its eyes roll in terror. What did you do, Rosa? You spat back! You should be on your knees begging for your life, but instead you spat back!

The man in front of me stares in disbelief. 'Jews can't spit!' he sneers. He hates me deeply now, I can see it in his eyes. He has lost face in front of his friends. A girl and a Jew has dared to spit at him. I wonder whether he is the one. I wonder whether he killed my father.

They are peasants, I can tell from their clothes. The man looks round at the others but they make no move to help him. He is going to hurt me now – he has to, I know that, I'm not completely stupid, only a little mad.

He takes a step towards me and he grabs me by the arm, staring into my face. He tries to kiss me. I pull away and this time he snatches me harder. I turn to run and manage to drag him with me a few steps up the track. He swears at me in Russian but the circle of friends parts to let us through.

When he slaps me round the face I am shocked, because it is the first time in my life that anyone has hit me. He has cut my lip, but I am so frozen I barely feel the pain. We begin to struggle together and I fall onto a large drift of snow. I look up and a boy is staring at me, his eyes as wide as coach lamps.

'Gunter,' the man calls to the boy, 'get on with things, lad.'

The boy is young – maybe younger even than me. He tries to smile at the older man who holds me, but his eyes are full of terror.

82

'Move, son!' the man growls. 'It's colder than a witch's teat out here!'

The boy moves to his side dutifully. His features are similar though less unpleasant and when he raises his cap I see he has the same birthmark between his eyes.

The man pulls the boy down to his knees and pushes him onto the ground between my legs. I try to move but he has me pegged out like a pelt drying in the sun. I stare into the boy's eyes. He begins to unbutton his little trousers and the other men watching laugh.

'Come on, son, she's a Jew – you don't have to woo her!'

'Where is all this time going? Didn't your father teach you what you have to do? Hurry up, for God's sake, at this rate she'll be too old before you get started!'

'You were the same at *your* first, remember? That whore charged your father twice for all the time you took snuffling about!'

The boy looks scared. He starts to push at my skirts and petticoats and I struggle so hard I hurt myself with my twisting.

'Ah, he has the scent of her now! That's it, son. Look, now he's got the idea! Like a hound after a rabbit, eh?'

All is quiet while the boy lies on top of me. I close my eyes, awaiting the worst, listening to the groans and whistles of disappointment that slowly build up. After a while I feel his weight leave me and when I look up he is lifted in mid-air by his father, his lifeless little member still dangling from the flap of his britches.

The father curses and throws the sobbing boy into the snow. The other men pick him out, dusting his clothes down and slapping him jovially about the face. I laugh to shame him more but a vile smack on the cheek takes the wind out of me for a while.

'Look at her, she's a whore!' the father says. He is a tall man and heavily built. He would kill me right now, but he has the honour of the family to restore. Instead his hand is upon his trousers and I begin to say my prayers.

My legs are exposed like two bare pink pegs in the snow but I barely feel the cold. I am terrified and full of shame to be seen in such a way. I fill my lungs with air and scream so loud that it would seem the sky could shatter with the noise.

When I can scream no more, when I am gasping to breathe, the man stretches my legs apart again with his hands and falls onto me like an ox, and I feel burning and a tearing inside as he pushes and finally enters me. I am silent with shock at such a thing. My eyes bulge and a line of spittle runs down the side of my chin. There is a pain inside me, like fire, but I will not scream again.

The man makes plenty of noise as he works away: 'Umph! Ungh!' He works so long the others get bored again.

'Hey, Jaspar, it is freezing out here, you know!'

'Let's move! Hurry, hurry!'

'He's no better than his son, you know! No wonder his wife always has such a sour face!'

'It's *her* face, the girl's,' another laughs, 'a face that ugly would put a ram off its stride! Shall I cover it with my coat for you, Jaspar? Would that help, eh?' And my head is suddenly covered by a sweat-smelling jacket. I am in darkness now, blind and in pain.

With their shouts goading him on the father reaches a point where his body is twitching like a dying horse. He lets out a cry of victory that would shame the armies of Peter The Great and then, as he rolls back with a groan I pull away suddenly from the one that is holding me and his coat comes away from my head and he falls back in surprise.

In my terror I am onto my feet like a cat, grabbing my suitcase and thrusting it up at the weapon that still hangs between the father's legs, like an axeman felling a tree.

His scream sounds greater even than my own. He curls up in agony, clutching at himself and vomiting, his feet kicking out in his pain.

I stare round at the others.

'Well?' I scream. 'Is there anyone else that wants me?'

They stare at me in silence.

'Please,' I shout, 'take your turn. After all, what does it matter, I am only a Jew!'

I spin in a circle, my suitcase catching some of them on the hands and the knees. One boy studies his grazed knuckles and another looks at his companion on the ground and shrugs. The others look away. Most of them are just boys, I realize. Perhaps Gunter's father brought them into the woods to learn how to hunt.

Maybe they are too drunk or stupid, or maybe they are a little scared now that their protector is felled. Either way, I watch, panting, as they walk off slowly. A mad girl, that is what they are thinking, and they are right.

I look at the father who has raped me.

'I know your name!' I scream. 'Remember that, I know it! My father will have you killed! He will come with my fiancé and you will be a dead man! Jaspar! See, I have it in my head!' I look at the expression on his face and I can see my madness scares even him.

There is blood on the snow – my blood, from between my legs. I ache inside and out but the shame hurts worse. I am alive, though, I am not killed. I tell myself this many times on the journey home: 'You are alive, Rosa, you are still alive. Alive. It is a miracle. That is all that is important.' I know I am lying, though. My father is dead and somehow I wish I, too, had been killed.

When I get home Rintzi looks at my torn dress and begins to cry. I say nothing of what happened on the road, for fear she will do something terrible. When I tell her Aaron isn't coming her tears get profuse enough.

I watch a while from the window, terrified at my own stupidity of threatening the man with revenge, but mercifully no one comes for me, and I say a long prayer of thanks in my bed that night for that. I must be strong, it is the only way.

Terrible thoughts start to scratch at my head. My shame is unbearable. What has happened is the finish of me. I have been taken before my marriage, and by a non-Jewish man, at that. Does it matter that I was taken without consent? There are teachings on these matters. I quake with fear at the thought that my entire life may have been ruined by the attack. If I marry Aaron now I will be thoroughly wicked. Yet how else can we survive? Should we all die from this one vile act? Should I never be married because I have been touched by that man?

*   *   *

86

A month has passed, Kitty, and I begin to make plans now. When the snows have gone I will take myself off to America and I will find Aaron and bring him back. It's the only possible thing if we are all to stay alive. I have his wedding suit. No one else knows what has taken place. The terrible thing lives only in my memory and I know I can forget it if I try hard enough. When each snow of winter is melted it is gone – and so can this be, too. When I have forgotten it will melt and vanish. Is this so bad? Aaron and I were matched to one another. I will find him wherever he has gone, and one day he will wear Papa's suit, I promise myself.

No one knows. No one *will* know. We will be married, and then everything will be all right once again.

CHAPTER SEVEN

ZG

LONDON 1998

VELVET
*A soft, rich fabric that has been used in Europe since
the Middle Ages, velvet would have originally been
made from silk, though more recently it will more
likely be made from a less costly blend of acetate and
rayon. The name is taken from the Latin vellus,
meaning 'tufted hair'. Some of the more exotic forms of
velvet carry the beautiful names of: cisele, panne
and nacre.*

The sex was neither good nor bad. It was satisfying in the
way that anything ending in orgasm has to be by definition
– but he knew at the same time that it was not the end of
his search, merely a stop-off point on his hunt for the Holy
Grail.

Everything that needed to be sucked had been sucked
and every kissable niche had received unstinting attention
from her lips. There had been damp shuddering moments
and wet gasping bits, and even one fleeting, unpursuable
split second when he had found himself on the brink of
crying out – but what? A name? Her name? (Now that

would have been ludicrous!) A word? Something from the dimmest reaches of his childhood, perhaps?

The woman had been – what? Beautiful? Of course. He had selected her from his own ideal. Good company? She had said what needed saying at all the appropriate moments. Innovative? A lot of what she had done to him had been pre-selected by the manufacturer. This added, of course, a rather hit-and-miss spin to the whole procedure, but there had been more hits than misses, so nothing to question there.

The name she had given was crass in the extreme: Vanessa Velvet. Whore-sounding. The sort of stuff you saw printed on cards in telephone boxes. The kind of pseudonym that meant a girl – and even a hooker, at that – would have to be either dangerously witless or desperately tired of the whole bother of the life-thing to assume.

Vanessa had not been a whore, though. Her names had been chosen for storage and filing purposes, rather than cheaply-manufactured thrill. She had emphatically instructed him, in fact, to call her whatever he pleased. This was part of the deal, along with her eye colour and hair length. If he had asked she would have arrived with a cleanly-shaven scalp.

In the event she had arrived wearing a brilliantly-engineered swathe of Yamamoto silk. He always found Japanese designs seductively sterile and deceptively simple. In fact he had been rather disappointed when she had taken the outfit off, and there were a few moments of dull, throbbing temptation when he had found himself torn between bending to examine the garment in more intimate, lingering detail, or allowing Vanessa to perform her first act of oral stimulation on his cock.

Burgess removed the visor from his head with a sigh of boredom and threw it down onto the chair beside him. Cybersex with Vanessa Velvet. Until the program was right he could see no point in making the kind of investment the software house was suggesting.

Maybe if a new strain of virulent sexually transmitted virus escaped from some laboratory or other . . . he tapped his fingers against his chin. And, of course, it would mean the sensory-immersive program would have to come to long-awaited fruition.

What if the whole set-up could be marketed as a health item? He inspected the Vanessa Velvet program notes. Then his eye hit upon some hand-labelled software that lay beside it. His father's name was written in his own, neat print.

Burgess pulled the head visor on once again. There was darkness around him. A huge black void. A glimpse of space as empty and vast as death itself. Emptiness so profound that its infinity made him fearful. Then someone appeared in the distance, walking towards him. And that sight made him more fearful than the emptiness. The figure headed towards him at speed, walking purposefully. Gabriel. His father. Only he was smiling, which had not been his usual expression when he was alive – not when he regarded his son, at least.

Burgess had programmed the smile himself, to see how it would have looked. He smiled back. The two men smiled at one another. Burgess's face felt strange with all the effort. Gabriel strode up beside him and clapped a hand on his back. 'Well done, Burgess,' the anthropomorphic image said, 'well done, son. That was a great deal. I'm proud of you. You make me happy. Where shall we go to celebrate? I think you have earned a glass or two of malt.'

Enough. Burgess ripped the visor off this time. His face and body were drenched in sweat. He checked his pulse with his own fingers and leant back in the seat while its rhumba subsided. Then he rose shakily to his feet and went off in search of a shower.

CHAPTER EIGHT

ZG

AFTER THE POGROM
*In 1881 massacres in Russia led to mass immigration
of Jews from that country. Many of them came to
Whitechapel. The Spitalfields ghetto was acclaimed as
the site of 'solid, sodden poverty', with three thousand
poor souls to an acre.*

Rintzi is excited. After all the wailing that first accompanied my announcement that I would be going to America she has finally realized the sanity of my decision and has set about making plans for my departure.

She leaves the house many times a day and I wonder where she goes off to, in her tired brown coat with the sleeves that she has left torn, now that Papa is no longer here to mend them for her. Her madness appears to gather force and builds like a whirlwind, with Gregory and myself at the eye of the storm.

For many days after Papa's murder Rintzi would barely move. Now it is difficult for her to sit still for a split second. Every morning she is up before dawn, cleaning the house. I ask if she expects visitors but she just taps the side of her nose and her eyes look like the eyes of a bird.

All the activity frightens Gregory so much that he scarcely eats. He watches Rintzi constantly with the fingers of his good hand shoved into his mouth, and I wonder if he worries that she will set about him with the knife again one day. It is as though we are both holding our breath, Gregory and I, waiting for something to happen. And all the while Rintzi darts about hither and thither, throwing buckets of foul, lye-smelling water over the floors and scrubbing the wood until her knuckles bleed.

Then one day there is noise outside the house. Rintzi is up like a colt and I am at the window, peering through the snow. The sudden movement makes my head spin and I clutch at the doorframe. There is a man outside, tall and dark. I think maybe it is Jaspar come for his revenge at last and the fear is like an explosion inside my head. Everything becomes black and I fall to the floor.

When I wake again I find Rintzi bending over me, clucking like a demented hen, and a large man pulling at my arms, trying to get me upright. They sit me in a chair. Rintzi is smiling now, wiping her hands on her apron.

'Rosa,' she announces, 'this is Menachem Kluchersky. We are very fortunate. Menachem has agreed to be your landsman.'

She looks so proud of her own achievement. Her eyes gleam and there is a smile that threatens to split her face. I look at Menachem Kluchersky. Of course I know him, he is the son of the local butcher. Only today he looks like a clown, with that expression of haughty self-importance painted all over his great red face.

'Well,' Rintzi says, almost bursting with conceit, 'what do you say?'

I say nothing and she looks across at Menachem. 'My

clever daughter,' she sighs, rolling her eyes in mock disgust, 'lost for words. Not even a thank you.'

Menachem clears his throat in a noisy process that involves the use of his hand and two grey linen handkerchiefs.

'Are you sure she is strong enough for the journey?' he enquires finally. He looks at my mother. He has not yet looked at me. 'She fainted,' he says.

Rintzi flaps her hands about as though to say the whole event was nothing.

'You understand the role of a landsman, Rosa?' she asks me. 'Menachem is making the same trip as you and he will look out for you on the way. You will be safe with his protection, Rosa. Your poor mother can sleep at night now, knowing you will not be killed en route. Then when you get to America, Uncle Reuben will take care of you. So now I can rest a little in my mind, eh?'

I look up at the butcher's son, whose eyes have returned to the well-scrubbed floor. 'I don't need a landsman,' I tell my mother. Rintzi laughs.

Menachem rises to his feet. There is not much to see of him, he is so wrapped against the cold, but his eyebrows meet in the middle and the skin around his eyes looks raw.

'I'll be here for her in twenty days,' he says, addressing my mother. 'Teach her to lie about her age. Tell her to say she is twenty if anyone stops us. No one will look close enough to notice.'

Rintzi is angry with me once he has gone.

'You don't know how hard it was for me to find you a landsman!' she cries. 'I had to meet with him many times before he would agree. Then you are so rude I would not

94

be surprised if he left without you! How can you go alone, Rosa? You would get no further than the next village! The journey is dangerous – there are guards to bribe and the threat of attack! I had to tell the landsman you are seventeen years, by the way, so act like a young woman, Rosa, for pity's sake!'

I scoff at this. 'Menachem has a sister at my school,' I tell her, 'he would have seen through that little lie straightaway.'

Baile Kluchersky is, in fact, two years above me in school, and much hated by me for all her gracious airs, but Rintzi no longer listens, her agitation is too great. Her large hands flap about before alighting on a broom that is lying near the doorway. She throws the door open and attacks the snow on the step with great energy, sending clouds of the stuff billowing into the house. She now believes the butcher's son will abandon me and that I will be left to the mercy of the Jew-baiters and bandits.

I am more worried at being left to the mercy of the butcher's son's stupidity.

When I have packed my belongings I find Rintzi staring at the bags. She picks them up herself, judging the weight by pacing up and down the room with them.

'If I give you string you can tie this smaller one to your back,' she tells me. 'But this leather one looks too good. What is in it? It will attract robbers from miles around.'

I take the case from her. 'It's the suit,' I tell her quietly, 'the suit Papa made.'

She is on the floor in an instant, kneeling before the case, fiddling with the clasps. 'It's locked, Rosa.'

I give her the small key that I have on some cord around my neck. I watch as she opens the lid and I nearly cry as she rips at the tissue that I have taken so long packing.

Shards of dried lavender fall to her well-scrubbed floor. 'The wedding suit,' she says. She has to be pretending. She could never have forgotten Papa's greatest work.

'It's for Aaron,' I tell her.

She has the waistcoat in her hands. The embroidery is so fine and so beautiful in such an ugly setting as this that I feel like weeping. I can see the back of Papa's head as he bent over his table, sewing it. His neck was pale and clean. He was stitching my name in silks, to surprise me. Of course it is the wedding suit. Like Papa, I would die before I would be parted from it.

'For when you find him,' Rintzi says.

'Who?' I am confused.

'Aaron,' Rintzi says gently, 'it is for when you find Aaron.'

'Yes.'

'Rosa,' she says, 'how will you find him in America? I'm scared for you. You don't know where he is.'

I smile, even though I know she is right. 'They'll have records,' I tell her. 'There will be authorities, like here. Everyone will be monitored and I will only have to ask. Besides, I have the address of one of his cousins, who went there three years before. Aaron is bound to have looked him up. You know how things are. I will have no trouble. When word reaches him that I have arrived I dare say it will be he who contacts me first! I'm sure I will find him, with or without a search.'

'Of course,' Rintzi says, smiling.

And something in her voice tells me that she doesn't
believe I ever will. I watch her fold the suit again, as softly
as if she were covering a sleeping child with its blanket,
and I watch two tears fall from her face onto the tissue.

CHAPTER NINE

ℤG

LONDON

PEAU DE SOIE
*This heavy satin is popular for wedding dresses and
ornate evening gowns. The word 'satin' is taken from
Zaytoun, in China – the place where it was first made.
Satin is still considered a luxurious fabric, despite the
fact that these days it is more likely to be made from
rayon and other synthetics than from its original silk.*

Kitty sat in her parents' vast, polish-scented lounge, trying
hard not to look at the brigade of gilt-framed photographs
displayed on top of the grand piano. 'Dead Man's Gulch'
was what Nula had once labelled this ghastly array of
long-gone smiling faces that Hester so cherished. Even the
cleaner was not allowed to touch them, and sully their
memory with her can of Pledge. No, Hester would dust
these herself, lovingly. Like the TV, which was also cleaned
by her, these things were sacrosanct.

It was a strictly posthumous Hall of Fame. To get onto
the lid of the piano you had to die first – that was an
acknowledged fact. Grandmothers, second cousins, uncles,
rabbis, stars, royalty – rank didn't matter, but the death-

rattle did. Kitty didn't want to look. Not now – not today. She was too afraid of seeing her father's photo there, smiling out with all the other ghosts.

When she did look, which *had* to happen, as sure as eggs is eggs – no brain can avoid the stimulation of being told *not* to look at something for very long without being forced to take a peek – it was worse than she'd imagined, and that was bad enough. All the old platoon had been removed. Nothing had been cleaned, so their previous positions remained obvious from the thin rectangular holes left in the dust. In the middle of this greying landscape sat a particularly obnoxiously-posed and formal portrait of Gabriel, with a large vase of white funereal lilies looming over it.

When had this shot been taken? It was the sort of thing high street photographers who knew no better did: blue, out-of-focus background, foreground so fogged to be flattering that it looked as though he was smiling through a muslin-like hue. He wore a god-awful suit which Kitty had never seen before and a grin that was completely alien to his features. Was it taken after death, or something? Surely Gabriel would never have permitted it otherwise.

Hester entered the room, followed by a servant with a tea-tray. There was cake on the tray, as well as tea; good, home-made vanilla cake that would forever remain untouched. Hester was diabetic and Kitty had no sweet tooth. The cake was therapeutic, though. Mother and cake. This was how Hester liked to be thought of.

'I phoned the Savoy.' Kitty watched her mother smooth her skirt as she sat down. Today her clothing was especially idiosyncratic: dress, jacket, hat and socks. No shoes. The socks, like the stockings before them, did not match. In fact they were Gabriel's socks – one grey and one russet.

'Ah . . . I . . . phoned the Savoy, Kitty. *Not* to *cancel*, I told them, but to *postpone*. They understood, of course. They read the newspapers like the rest of us. In fact I believe they were *expecting* my call? Perhaps they had already put us on *provisional*?'

Hester's speech-patterns had changed. She spoke slowly now, accentuating certain words carefully, like a drunk.

Mother and daughter looked across at one another. Of course the Savoy had been expecting the cancellation of the wedding reception. Hester had phoned them three times about it already, only her depression made her forgetful. Kitty hoped the sales team were people of enormous tact and patience, for she felt sure it was not the last call her mother would make.

Kitty's head ached. She felt bone tired. Her afternoon with Kofteros had not gone well. He had maintained a polite, cheerful expression during the entire visit to the East End. He had cheerfully drunk three cups of the disgusting, evaporated-milk tea that they made in the factory – and which Kitty herself loved – and he had spoken fluent Turkish and Bangladeshi to the workers there. Even his car had been left untouched by the local miscreants, who must have been on some council-sponsored awayday to Clacton-on-sea.

'How is Freddy?' Hester asked, licking the tip of one finger and dabbing at an imaginary stain on her skirt.

'Fine,' Kitty told her, 'he's fine.'

'He should have been in touch.' Hester's voice sounded reproachful.

'He has been,' Kitty said quietly, 'he was there at the funeral and he has phoned you each day since. Remember? Look – these are his flowers.' She pointed, not to the lilies, with their overpowering scent, but to a bucketful of hybrid blooms that was acting as a doorstop.

'He's always so busy.' Hester sighed.

'He has his own business,' Kitty reminded her. Freddy Jacobs was the young heir-apparent to Jaycee Outerwear, owners of the Right O! and Muira labels. Their marriage was to be the merging of the two fashion dynasties. Only now it had to wait. Kitty felt a shiver, as though a breeze had just passed through the huge room.

'Time, Kitty, you're wasting time,' the voices murmured, 'don't dither, dearest. Things are moving so very quickly without you.'

She thought of Freddy. He had been everything he should have been about their loss. He had held Kitty while she wept and comforted her daily with gifts, calls and food.

She had noticed something lacking in his father's eyes, though. A certain shuttering against the on-coming tornado. Murder. It was an indigestible word. 'Murder in the business' could cause mild heartburn. 'Murder in the family' would be responsible for acute colic and colitis.

'I have something for you, Kitty,' Hester was smiling now. A secret. A secret gift. She left the room, as regal and sweeping as a galleon. Kitty did not want to be left alone. She badly needed company there, in her parents' house, even for the few minutes that her mother was gone. While Hester was not there Kitty was forced to forget Gabriel

101

was dead and her mother made half-deranged. While she was alone she started to imagine that none of it had happened. That she could smell her father's cologne and hear Hester talking sanely. It was too much to bear, like the photograph. Too sad.

When her mother returned she was carrying what looked like an ancient attaché case. Rotted with age, it left a powdering of leather across the top of the piano, where she placed it. Something placed on the piano. This act was unheard of. Gabriel's photograph got knocked aside by the case but Hester did not even move to right it and Kitty could not bring herself to touch it.

The object had a smell about it. Mould? Not unpleasant. Maybe even evocative. But of what? Kitty sniffed lightly. Age: it smelt of old things. She looked at her mother.

Hester was smiling – the first broad smile since Gabriel's death. Not a 'Thank you for your concern' smile of the sort she had pulled during the *shiva*. Or a 'What else can you expect from life such as this?' smile, of the sort she had pulled when friends and business colleagues put a hand on her arm and told her how tragic it all was. This was a mysterious smile. A 'Wait till you see this' smile. It also, to Kitty's eyes, at least, looked like a broken smile. A wrong-in-the-head sort of smile. Like something vital was missing inside.

There was a lock on the case, ochre with rust. Hester had a key, though. Its metal was as thin as a pin but she still worried the clasp until it opened.

Kitty leant across to study the contents. There was tissue – new-looking tissue, and inside that was some clothing.

'The wedding suit,' Hester said in a whisper. Her fat

hands riffled among the paper and pulled the top garment out.

It was a jacket. Dark wool, faded in parts with age. Very old. Incredibly old, maybe. Something for a museum or flea-market. Kitty winced as her mother flapped it about like a sand-covered towel on the beach.

'Look!' she said. 'Look at that fabric!'

Kitty fingered the stuff gingerly. It was soft. She rubbed it between thumb and forefinger. Soft and deceptively light. Quality stuff. She bent her head to smell it.

'Well?' Hester asked.

'What is it?'

Her mother rooted once more in the case. There were trousers first, and then a waistcoat. 'Look at that stitching!' she said.

The embroidery was well-preserved and most of the colour was still left in the silks. Kitty took the waistcoat from her mother and sat back down on her chair, squinting her eyes against the minute detail of the designs, turning her head one way and then another, holding the garment first at arm's length and then closer, to see.

'It was Gabriel's,' Hester told her, 'and now it's yours. Your father kept it in its own little wardrobe but this is the case it came in and I put it back in there so you could see it as Gabriel did on the day it was handed down to him. It was made by your great-great-grandfather in Russia, Kitty. It is for your husband to wear at your wedding. That is tradition. Each generation has worn it once. Apart from . . .' her voice trailed.

Kitty found herself starting melt-down, and oozing inwardly, too.

103

'I've seen it before,' she said quietly, 'I've seen this waist-coat. In the wedding photo . . .' she nearly mentioned the photograph that had been sent to her in the post. For that was where she had seen it. Gabriel had been wearing it beneath a different suit. It was the first time she had noticed it. Fear: the emotion returned in a rush.

'Of course,' Hester told her, 'you saw the waistcoat in our wedding pictures. I never thought you paid them too much attention, either. You and Chloe were always too busy screaming with laughter at my own outfit. You would groan when I got the album out. Gabriel would have worn the entire suit but it was too small for him, of course. So he settled for the waistcoat instead. I believe it was only ever worn once before, by your grand-father, although it's so old. Gabriel always claimed his own grandfather hadn't worn it at his wedding – I believe he was a huge man, much too big, even for the waistcoat.'

'But China should have it,' Kitty said, 'or Burgess?'

'No,' Hester told her. 'This is yours. Gabriel always said so. Could he have seen Stephano in it? Do you think Bur-gess would ever wear it? Your father always knew it was you who inherited his love for the business. You all have equal shares now, Kitty, but it is you who must carry the business on.'

Kitty shook her head slowly.

'It's yours,' Hester continued, 'like the suit. He knew you would be the only one to truly understand and value them both. You might laugh and sneer, Kitty – you're young, I remember how that feels – but I know you under-stand the importance of family traditions.' She looked back at the suit. 'Freddy is slimmer than your father was. Perhaps you could alter it to fit?'

Kitty had no words to speak. Hester's eyes looked full of pleading. 'Of course,' she managed to get out. 'Of course I can fix it.'

Hester nodded, relieved and pleased. Kitty watched her mother as she folded the suit again lovingly and placed it back in the case. One last embrace of the waistcoat. Perhaps it smelt still of Gabriel on his wedding day. How could Hester think it would ever fit Freddy? It had been made for someone a very different shape. Even the fabric looked too frail to wear. Choked with emotion, Kitty took the case from her beaming mother and placed it beside her chair. It was like the vanilla cake, really – a comfort gesture from mother to daughter. One would never get eaten and the other would never be worn.

CHAPTER TEN

ZG

RUSSIA 1889

CABBAGE

A long-established perk of the rag trade, 'cabbage' is the name given to any surplus garments created when a cutter, who has been asked to get, say, fifteen items from a roll of cloth, will lay the pattern up in such a way as to create seventeen. The extra two garments will be made up and often sold on to street-market traders.

I tell Gregory that I am leaving. His reaction is astonishing. His eyes fill with more terror than I have seen in a face before.

'NO,' he tells me. What good does he think I can do staying there with them? Does he imagine I can fight like a man when the time comes? Does he think I could save him from the sort of fighters that killed Papa? I touch his hand – his good hand – but he pulls away.

'Take me too, Rosa,' he says.

'No, Gregory,' I tell him, 'I can't. It's impossible.' He starts to cry then, and I am glad Rintzi is out of the house.

'Gregory,' I whisper, 'you have to look after Mamma.

You are all she has when I am gone. Besides, I will be back once I am married and then Aaron will take care of us all. It's the only way, Gregory, can't you see that?' His crying becomes louder and I try not to listen. He has to stop. When he clings to me I think of the boy in the forest and push him away, staring at the ceiling to avoid his beautiful, cabbage-white, shocked face.

I feel ill and angry and as old as Bubba.

When Menachem Kluchersky finally calls – and call he does, for Rintzi is paying him, of course – the old women of the *shtetle* turn out to see me off.

I am wearing a full black coat of Bubba's and my hair is plaited and hidden beneath a large cap of Papa's. This is Rintzi's game plan – if men attack us on the way they will take me for a boy and shoot me instead of rape me. How could anyone but my mother be so devious! I would share in her delight at this cleverness, but unfortunately for her I really have no wish to die. And what if she knew that the worst had already occurred? What if she knew that I am already defiled? What of her poor, innocent little Rosa then?

So I stand in my hat and coat with my tears forming ice on my raw pink cheeks and the old women hand me presents that load me until my knees begin to buckle.

There are dried meats for us, and dried meats and jars of pickles to use as bribes for the *grenitz* who guard the borders en route. Then just as I think I can carry no more, one of Bubba's oldest friends, a blind woman who must be over one hundred years, is led up and, with shaking hands, presents me with my grandmother's samovar – a glorious brass object at least twice as old as the woman who holds it and which, to my utter dismay, weighs about as much as four large cats.

Weeping profusely now, Rintzi wraps the thing in brown paper and ties it with string, which she ropes around my neck. I smile but I can barely breathe. My face turns red as beet and my poor eyes water with the effort. Can't she see the string is choking me?

I turn then, gasping like a landed fish, and who do I find myself staring at? None other than Baile Kluchersky, sister of my able-bodied landsman. (I will tell you now that Baile was an extremely beautiful girl, though it has taken me sixty-odd years to admit it.)

'Bertha Zigofsky?' she asks, though she knows that is my name. I wonder how she can look so well in this weather. Her light-brown hair looks polished like the brass of the samovar and her eyes gleam with a perky confidence.

Did I tell you how much I hated this girl at school, Kitty? Not for her face or her figure, of course. While the boys watched Baile with codfish eyes we girls considered her face too white-cheeked and her figure a little too vulgar – a fault she tended to exaggerate with a rather affected-looking walk. No, it was Baile's priggishness that generally made her unpopular with her colleagues. Like her brother, she seemed to think she was a little above the rest of us. I just hope Menachem has informed her that I am to marry Aaron in America.

Baile smiles, showing her white teeth to perfection. She holds her hand out towards me. 'Hello Rabbit,' she says, 'I hear you are coming with us on our journey.'

The train journey to the coast is a kind of enforced hell because the seats are hard and Baile has not stopped complaining from the moment we left the *shtetle*. Had I known she was to accompany us I believe I would have defied Mamma and insisted on travelling alone.

Can I describe the terror I felt when I saw my first train, Kitty? I thought it a steam-belching monster come to kill us all. The sight of it on the track filled me with dread enough, but watching it come to a halt! Sparks flew from its wheels just as a scream flew from my mouth! It skidded and slithered to a standstill on the iced tracks, Kitty, *right alongside where I stood*! Fortunately its whistle drowned my yells and Baile did not hear me, and neither did her precious brother. For then I would never have heard an end to it, for all the dry comments they would have made.

Baile is a bad traveller – the motion of the train makes her sick. Menachem, meanwhile, has spoken not one word, either to me or his beloved sister. His eyes remain fixed on the view from the window, which is, in the main, only of snow – though I feel him looking at me when I pretend to sleep.

Baile insists on calling me 'Rabbit', which was my hated name from school. I warn her many times, nicely at first, but she is deaf to my words and will not stop. When she is finished being sick I remind myself that I will kick her.

My buttocks ache and my ears are ringing from the sound of Baile's voice. Did I mention her mouth has a pink, pursed look, like the end of a small pig's snout? Her features appear painted onto her face and her eyes register permanent surprise. She looks like a doll but is less stupid than she appears. Why did all the boys at school blush so much when she was around? Are men such idiots that they can see no further than all this primping and head-tossing?

The view bores me. I decide to stretch my poor legs by walking down through the carriage. There is a queue for the water-closet and the stench is so bad that I walk on further, rubbing my aching back.

There is an empty mail carriage near the front of the train and, although the place rattles me about like a dried pea in a tin and the noise of the engine is deafening, I am relieved to be alone for once and sit down upon my leather case.

I am desperate now for the water-closet and regret not joining the sorry-looking queue that waited outside. Maybe I can relieve myself here. After all, there is no one about. No sooner do I begin to adjust my coat, though, than I believe I hear footsteps coming my way and so am forced to sit rocking in agony instead. To divert my own attention from the subject I pull off my gloves and blow onto my frozen fingers before stuffing them beneath my armpits to thaw them.

The sight of my own reflection in the window amuses me. There outside, flashing by on the endless drifts of snow, goes Papa's big black cap and underneath it the sorriest-looking young monster you could ever hope to see! My face is white, apart from the nose, which is bright crimson. With my hair hidden under the cap my ears stick out like the handles of the samovar. Would I pass for a boy? Only a sickly and idiotic one, I decide. Perhaps I should pass myself off to the other travellers as Baile's young beau – now that would be enough to silence her mouth, for sure.

Laughing, I pinch at my cheeks to pinken them and rub

my nose furiously to get rid of the red. When I look up again in the glass there is another face behind my own – huge and red with raw-looking eyes.

'Menachem!' I gasp. What a fool he is! I all but pissed in my clothes at the sight of him!

The idiot just gawps at my reflection. This is the first time he has deigned to look at me and even now that is just via the glass. His silent staring irritates me. If he is comparing my beauty to that of his sister then he had better wait until we pass through a tunnel and the glass is black!

I listen to his breathing and tooth-rattling and wonder what it is that makes men's noses incapable of taking a silent inhale. They snuffle and snort like great boars while women breathe silently, like cats. Then I feel Menachem fingering the cloth of Bubba's coat and I freeze. He says nothing, neither of us does.

I know Menachem of old, and not just from the synagogue. When I was younger and with the other girls in the *bod*, which is the communal Turkish bath in the *shtetle* that we all used once a week, we would hear the men's laughter from behind the wooden partition that separated us. Anna Klowinski and I climbed the partition to see who was peeping and guess who? Menachem Kluchersky, the butcher's son, no less.

He was naked, what's more. When we squawked and fell down Anna was shaking her head from side to side. 'If that great lump of meat is what it's like, then I will never ever marry,' she said. 'The thing was as big as any donkey's.' We have never spoken about it since. And now here is Menachem Kluchersky the landsman and he is fingering my grandmother's coat.

111

I can stand it no longer. I rise to my feet as suddenly as is possible with two legs frozen by the cold, and turn to face the oaf. He looks away quickly but still his hand rises again and this time it is making its way to my face.

I grab my case and, in a lather of spiralling arms and shaking legs, make my way out of the carriage and back towards the water-closet. Menachem shouts something after me. I cannot hear it exactly, for the steam engine is too loud, but it sounds something like: 'Aaron will never marry you, you are far too ugly.' So be it. But Aaron has something that Menachem has never possessed, and that is a brain. He is clever and quick, and recognizing those same qualities in me he will find them more valuable than a mere sugar-face, like Baile's.

I am so irritable by the time I have returned to my seat that I begin to bicker with Baile and we do not stop, even when the train journey is over and we are marching through the snow on the way to the border.

Menachem has been walking in silence but suddenly he halts and when he turns we see he has a snow-covered beard. I laugh at this and even Baile lets out a snort.

'You will stop these arguments!' Menachem shouts. His voice is incredible when he is angry, it rises to the pitch of an hysterical girl's. I open my mouth to argue and so does Baile, which surprises me, for I didn't think she had the backbone.

'Stop!' Menachem yells, raising a hand in the air. He is close enough now for us to smell the breath that issues in steam-clouds from his mouth.

'You go alone from here,' he says. I feel my insides turn to water.

Baile looks at me and then back at her brother. 'You can't leave her here,' she says.

'Both of you,' Menachem tells us, and I almost laugh again, despite my personal fear. Baile's face must be a picture.

Menachem waits, hands on hips. 'You will stop this ridiculous gibbering, then?' he asks. Baile nods and I join her. I don't believe Menachem would abandon us both, but he is stupid enough for anything and I do not want to push him. 'Come on then,' he says, and I hear Baile sob with relief.

She is still crying when we reach the border which annoys me, though I say nothing, just in case. Menachem talks to the *grenitz* and there is much arm-waving. Then he comes across to me.

'Give them the meats and the pickles – all of them,' he says. I do not consider this the best way to barter but I hand the precious packages over anyway, for I am tired of carrying them.

The *grenitz* look at the bribes and begin to laugh. One of them spits tobacco onto the ground by Menachem's feet.

'It's not enough,' the butcher's son says, and I note that this is the first time he has looked me in the eye, which tells me how desperate he must be.

Smiling hard, I turn to his sister. 'Baile,' I whisper, 'I know you have money. Give it to him.'

Baile's eyes widen but she is not a good liar. 'I have no money,' she tells me.

I move closer. 'I know you have money,' I say, 'it is stuffed into your boot. Don't pretend it isn't, I saw you

113

put it there when you thought I was asleep. It is the reason why you keep limping.'

Her eyes meet mine and I see a stubbornness there to match my own. 'I have no money,' she says. Her little pink hands have formed fists. We would have fought there and then and I would have had the boot off her foot, had Menachem not been watching.

'Give them your samovar,' she says.

'While you have the cash?' I ask. We are forced to whisper. If the *grenitz* hear they will take the samovar and the money.

Baile grins. 'Give them the old thing,' she says, 'you know you didn't want it, I saw the look on your face when it was given to you. It's been hanging around your neck choking you and now's your chance to get rid of it. It's money we'll need when we reach the ship, not cups of tea.'

I grit my teeth and narrow my eyes, but Baile is not intimidated and, in a way, I know she is right. With slow, reluctant steps I approach the *grenitz* and hand over the precious object that has been in my family for generations.

By the time Baile and I have jostled our way through the border and found the road to the docks we are fighting again and Menachem, thank God, is no longer within earshot.

There is a pitiful-looking queue waiting to board the ship. When we stand in line an old man in a threadbare suit takes our tickets and pins labels to our chests with our names chalked on them. I look at Baile and she looks at me and we both think the other looks ridiculous.

'How long do you think we'll have to wait out here?' she asks. I shrug.

114

'Until we have died from the cold,' I tell her. Her teeth are chattering. Women in the queue ahead are crying and children they carry have started to scream. I can't see Menachem but he must be in the men's queue somewhere.

We wait for an hour. A sailor comes down the line, counting us.

'How long?' Baile asks him. His reply is a curse, which shocks her.

Another hour passes. I think perhaps I was right, that maybe they will leave us all to die here – after all they have our ticket money, so why should they take us?

Baile nudges me in the ribs. A tall young man in expensive clothes walks past us, making his way to the top of the queue. All eyes are upon him as he approaches one of the sailors. We, miserable wretches that we have become, watch as he pulls a wad of notes out of the pocket of his overcoat. The sailor smiles and waves him onto the ship. There is a collective groan from the queue. Money. That is what it is all about. I look at Baile's boot but she turns her head away. How much must we suffer before she undoes those brown laces and hands over the cash?

'Who do you think that was?' a woman beside me asks. I study her face. There is no resentment there for the man, only admiration. 'Maybe he is an actor, or a businessman.'

'Maybe he is a crook,' I tell her harshly. 'The money was probably thieved.'

To my horror I hear the woman take this tale as the truth and I listen as it is told and repeated all the way down the line. I think of stopping her but wonder why I should bother. So they think the man's a crook? Good.

115

Perhaps he will be less inclined to bribe his way in front of honest folk again in the future.

After another two hours the queue begins to move and there is much wailing as people try to move their frozen limbs. The sailors shout at us to hurry, now. Baile's name is called first and then mine. We hear nothing of Menachem and Baile begins to fret.

We huddle on deck like cattle and eventually the gang-plank is drawn up and steam belches from the funnel and we are on our way to America, at last!

CHAPTER ELEVEN

ZG

RUSSIA

NANKEEN
Originally woven by hand in Nanking, China,
this yellow-coloured cotton cloth was popular for
lightweight summer wear during the mid- to late-
nineteenth century.

The boat is so crowded that half a day has passed before
we realize Menachem is not on it with us. Baile turns
hysterical: 'He has been killed! They must have shot him
on the shore! How many grown men do you see here,
Rosa? They must have rounded them all up while we
queued and murdered them! What will become of us now,
eh? What hope can we have without my brother to guide
us? We are young girls, Rosa! We will die now for sure!'
Suddenly she is clinging to my arm. 'Don't leave me, Rosa!
Promise me we will never be split up!'

So now I am 'Rosa' all of a sudden, and not 'Rabbit'! I
watch her in silence. I have my own ideas about Menachem's disappearance, for with him has gone some of our
belongings and most of our cash. He took our things before
we reached the dock, saying they were less likely to be

thieved from a grown man than two whey-faced girls, despite my boy's disguise. He even persuaded Baile to part with her boot-cash, on the grounds that he might need it to get us comfortable cabins for the journey.

The anger in me surfaces during the terrible journey. 'You should know your brother is a thief!' I tell Baile. She looks at me with shocked eyes. 'He has run off with our money, Baile – look, he would even cheat his own sister.'

Baile makes a few noises of disagreement, but even those noises begin to lose conviction once she has had time to think the whole situation through. Then she comes up with a new plan of attack.

'You were rude to my brother,' she tells me on the second day. 'You shamed him, Rosa, that is why he left us. He couldn't bear to spend the journey in your company.'

'And just how did that happen?' I ask her quietly.

Her face puckers like a child's. 'He told me he paid you attention,' she whispers, 'but that you insulted him with your arrogance. Menachem took pity on you, Rosa Zigofsky, he would have proposed had you played your hand right! It's your fault we are in this predicament, you should learn your place in life and know when to be grateful!'

I turn on this spoilt child like a cat. 'I am marrying Aaron!' I tell her, noting that crowds are beginning to gather now. 'What do I have to be grateful to your brother for?'

'Hah!' I watch the spite build in her face now, making it ugly. 'Everyone in the *shtetle* knows Aaron left Russia to avoid marrying you, Rosa, it was the talk of the place for days. "Poor Bertha Zigofsky," they would say, "it is her face that has driven young Aaron out of the country."

He ran off to America to get away from you, Rosa – only a fool would not have realized that!'

I catch Baile by the hair and she screams. The crowd parts suddenly and I see the tall young man in the good clothes who bribed his way aboard pushing through with some authority. He takes my wrist and holds it so hard I am forced to let go of Baile's hair.

'What's this about?' he asks. He has straight, light-brown hair and large, gleaming eyes. Angry as I am, I notice his clothes are not of such good quality as I first thought, though they fit him well enough and are clean and pressed. He looks at me and his eyes narrow.

'A young lad attacking a beautiful young lady?' he asks. 'Where's your manners, boy?'

Baile was all set to fight back, but the sight of this man's handsome face has her patting her hair back in place and fluttering her lashes.

I pull off my father's cap quickly, tugging at my hair as it falls so that it goes part-way to covering my rabbity ears.

The young man sees his mistake and begins to laugh.

'My apologies, miss,' he says, when he can talk again. 'I thought this fight was too one-sided but now I realize my mistake. Please, continue. I'm sorry for the interruption.' His eyes are mocking me. I don't imagine he has ever looked serious for too long in his life. I stare across at Baile. The crowd begins to get restless at the delay. It had been looking forward to a good show. We begin to square up to one another but I know our hearts are no longer in the fight.

Baile raises an arm gingerly and makes to punch me on the shoulder.

119

'What if . . .' the man begins, interrupting once again. 'What if we make the fight more interesting? Eh? After all, no one likes to watch a bloody scrap, especially between two well-mannered young ladies. What if we follow a tradition from my part of the country? A way of fighting that ensures neither woman gets hurt?'

I can see this appeals to Baile and the crowd is so keen at this new suggestion of fun it can hardly wait for it to get started.

I watch as the man calls to an amused sailor to bring us some rope, then he pulls us back to back and binds us together around the waist.

'There,' he says, smiling, 'that should do it.'

The ship pitches and we stagger together to keep our balance. The crowd moves obligingly and the sniggering begins.

Being mocked in such a way makes me mad again. I pull at the rope but the man has tied it too firmly. The audience sees my struggle as the prelude to a scrap and begins to shout encouragement. Some old crone has remembered all the insults we traded and starts to yell them out loud. This sets Baile off, and I feel her arms flail as she tries to land a punch. I begin to retaliate, knocking her on the side of the ribs while she kicks at me backwards, like a mule. The audience roars approval, but within minutes of all this squirming we are both panting and exhausted, with neither of us having landed any damaging blows.

'Wait, Baile,' I shout at her. 'We look ridiculous, don't you see?' I can feel she is pleased to stop.

'Finished, then?' the young man asks. His teeth are white as he grins at us. 'Honour settled? Friends again?'

Baile nods. I feel too sick to reply. The rope is cutting into my belly and I would agree to anything to get it untied.

'You must shake like true ladies,' the man announces once we are free of our shackles and face-to-face once more. Baile holds out her lily-white hand and I take it, though I would prefer to break her arm. The audience's reaction is one of acute disappointment. Then the smell of cooked food wafts up from the galley and people begin to disperse quickly.

'So,' the young man says, smiling at us both, 'you must allow me to invite you to tea. You must be thirsty after such a show.'

His idea makes me laugh. Tea? You'd think he was on a pleasure trip instead of crushed in with a hundred other poor unfortunates. I decide to hate him at this moment. His arrogance and *joie de vivre* are quite unbearable under the circumstances.

He sees my face. 'Anything is possible,' he smiles, 'you should learn that in life, if nothing else.'

'I mean to learn a good deal more than that,' I tell him, 'and I suppose you mean that anything is possible if you only have the money to pay for it.'

He nods. 'Of course,' he says, ushering us away from the main mass of hungry peasants, 'money is a key, that's all, so what's the harm? Just don't ask where I acquired my stash, that's all. I may have to confess to my villainous habits that are the talk of the ship.'

He looks at me as he says this and I am childish enough to blush. So he knows who put the rumour around about his thieving.

The young man's name is Max Warkofski and he is

journeying to London to start up business as a photographer. This impresses Baile, I can see – as does the tea-tray he has somehow bribed a sailor to have delivered to our table.

The smell of the tea calms us down and the taste of it is so good and fresh on my tongue that I nearly weep, for our food has been poor since we left the *shtetle*.

'Do you two sisters really hate one another?' Max asks as he pours a second cup.

Baile is offended and shocked by the idea that anyone might take us for sisters.

'We aren't related,' she tells Max. 'We might have been sisters but she refused my brother Menachem, who is known to be a great catch. It is because of that we fell out. I felt obliged to defend the family honour.'

Max looks across at me but I can only stare at Baile's face.

'The best cure for an argument is time spent apart,' Max says, seeing our expressions. 'What if I arrange for you to switch berths so that you don't have to live in one another's pockets – for the duration of the voyage, at least? Are you both off in England?'

I shake my head. 'No. I'm going to America,' I tell him.

'By yourself?' He looks surprised.

'Since her brother changed his mind, yes,' I tell him.

'So that's it, then,' he says.

We return to our cramped berth and Baile packs to move because my journey is the longer. I am pleased to see her go, but then frightened once she is gone.

*　　*　　*

122

I was delivered of the dead child some three days after this. How amazing that I could not have known! Yet my body is still skinny and what weight I put on around the waist I put down to the fact that Rintzi was mad to fill me up with as much fatty food as possible prior to the journey, to stave off the cold and other deprivations.

I am still sickly from the birth when our ship sails from sea into river and we are travelling up the Thames on our way into London.

There is much excitement, of course, though I cannot see cause for any celebration, save to mark the fact that we are all still alive. Youth has strange priorities, though. Hard as I try to remain groaning in my little bunk I cannot help but grow curious when I hear all the shouting and excitement from up on deck and eventually, wrapping a blanket about my body to keep off any cold, I walk feebly down the passage to join the others.

Baile, of course, is up there waiting with a smile. She knows nothing of my situation and shows no alarm when she sees me, despite my white, haggard little face.

'Rabbit!' she exclaims, as though surprised to see me.

'Don't you wish your journey were ending here too?'

I look around at the grey buildings looming out of the fog like ghosts. 'With the Ripper waiting to pick you all off?' I say. 'I should think not, Baile.'

I watch her expression turn to one of shock and fear and find myself feeling sorry for my own unpleasantness. The rivalry can end now – we will never see one another again.

'Wait there,' I tell her, 'I'll get dressed and see you off properly.'

*   *   *

Pulling on my grandmother's coat I find I am in better spirits than I had thought. I splash some water on my face and comb my hair for the first time in many days and, even though the experience is difficult and painful, I am pleased that my body feels whole again and that I can button my skirt now that my stomach is no longer swollen. If I had been older and wiser I would have known I was with child, but I am still just a child myself and Rintzi had told me very little of such things.

When I reach the deck again the fog has cleared a little and people are leaning over the rail, stretching their eyesight to make sense out of all the gloom. Baile has met up with Max Warkofski and she is smoking a cigarette that she must have been given by him. Max smiles as I approach.

'How are you, Rosa?' he asks, lifting his hat. I start to pick at my hair with my fingers but I see Baile watching me and my arm falls to my side, instead. 'Are you going to Liverpool?' Max continues. I regard him with as blank an expression as I can muster.

'Max says you will have to change ships,' Baile tells me, her eyes watering from the smoke. She has taken a glove off to avoid staining it with the nicotine. 'You have to get off in London and travel north to get the ship to America,' she tells me, quoting her companion, 'so you may meet with the Ripper after all, Rabbit – won't that be exciting?'

I look around me in a panic. Everyone is disembarking.

'You didn't think you could travel west from the east side of England, did you Rabbit?' Baile asks. She throws her head back and laughs for Max's benefit. I look at her thin, pale throat and know I would have contemplated

124

throttling it had I not been consumed with terror at what she had said.

Forgetting my recent infirmity completely, I push my way through the crowds and run back to my billet for my things. The day is cold but I am sweating as I sink to my knees and scrabble on the wooden floor to find the case with the wedding suit inside. I had hidden it at the foot of the bunk for safety and it is wedged so hard I cry out with the effort of lifting it.

By the time I am back on deck the ship has docked and Baile is a white dot on a lower deck, waiting her turn to be name-tagged by immigration. I call out to her but my voice gets lost in all the clatter of feet and cases. I clutch my own bag to my chest.

'Baile!' I am sadly in need of her, now she is going. Without this irritating girl I am alone in the world; I realize that with a start.

'Baile!' I would even be grateful for Menachem's company right now.

It is an hour before I reach the steps to the lower deck and by then people are pushing and jostling with irritation that comes from exhaustion. Their children are screaming and it is that sound I can bear least of all. I stand tall in my grandmother's coat, denying the desire to join in the wailing and falling to the floor in a welter of wretched self-pity.

I have never seen so many shadows as those I see on the shore. Everywhere is the colour of wet grey flannel and every wall throws a shadow that envelops the next.

There is a stench of sulphur in the air. The river slaps against the hull and looks like black treacle. I clamber down dank wooden steps with the aid of a rusting chain handrail and at the foot of the steps I slip on sea-slime, clinging so hard to the wet rail that I graze my face. I think I might tumble into the sea and I cry out, 'Papa!'. When I regain my balance I am deeply ashamed of myself. I must be stronger. I clutch my case to my chest again and lift my chin. There is no sky here in England. No sky to see and no air to breathe. The shadows are enveloping us all. I cannot wait to see what I imagine will be the cleaner skies of America.

CHAPTER TWELVE

Z_G

GREENERS

*Immigrants to Britain were nicknamed 'greeners' by
the local population. When they arrived at the docks
many fell prey to the organized bands of robbers,
known as 'crimps', who set themselves up to defraud
them of any cash they might have brought into the
country. Many of the greeners were afraid to report
the crimes, as they feared the British police would be
as bad as the dreaded Objescik, which they had left
behind in their own country.*

We are at Irongate Stairs, Kitty – do you know it? I overheard one of the sailors telling another, and this charming
place is the point where Baile is to set dainty foot upon
her new homeland for the first time. How excited she must
be to find herself the guest of so much stink and soot!

We sit on the lower deck now, exhausted and bewildered, each clutching baskets or bags to our chests while
various officials board the ship to check out our suitability
for integration into this shadowy land.

Most of us have not changed clothes since the day we
boarded ship and many have existed on stale food brought
from the homeland. What must these officials think as they
gaze on us? I do not need to ask, though, I can read the
contempt in their eyes.

They are, in the most part, wearing suits, as are the relatives who wait miserably on the quayside, stamping their feet with the cold and waving sullenly at any face that is visible on the upper deck. Their clothing fascinates me. Their British style of dress may appear vastly superior to the peasant styles sported by most of those aboard, but I am proud to note that nowhere do I see handiwork close to the standards of that produced by my own father.

An elderly gentleman is helped on board and we are told he is a doctor, and that we must all prepare for an examination. This sets off much caterwauling among the women, who are appalled at the prospect of being examined in the raw air. In the event the man's disgust at our state is so acute that he barely touches us. By the time it comes to my turn he has a cologne-soaked handkerchief tied around his chin. He looks into my eyes and feels the side of my throat before declaring me 'fit'.

A younger man carrying a ledger walks behind him asking us each how much money we have. He speaks Yiddish, but with such a poor accent that many find it hard to answer. I reply that I have nothing, which is almost true, since Baile's wonderful brother now has most of my money tucked into the seat of his pants and what little I do have left I intend to keep to myself. I make sure to reply in English, carefully pronouncing some of the words I learnt before leaving Russia, which seems to surprise the man.

'I am bound for America,' I tell him. 'Could you please tell me which line I should join?' Amazed, he walks away without answering.

The queue moves on. I can see now that they have rigged a makeshift desk up on the deck and a man sitting behind it is examining everyone's tickets. As I draw close I notice his cuffs are frayed and that he has skin as pink as a pig's. Do all Englishmen have this same soft pink skin? As I approach the desk he looks up at me through a fringe of thick white lashes.

At least Menachem left us with our tickets. I place mine on the desk in front of the pig-man, then watch as he stamps a word onto the front of it before laying it on top of a large pile to his left. I smile pleasantly.

'I need the ticket back,' I tell him.

'Why?' he asks.

'I need it to take me to America. I can't travel without it.'

I watch as he pulls the ticket from the pile and pretends to read it slowly.

'This ticket terminates here,' he says. He looks at my face for a while before turning to his interpreter, a middle-aged Jewish man dressed in an expensive black astrakhan coat.

'Your ticket is for England,' he tells me in Yiddish. 'Look, it says here . . .' He points to some words on the front of the paper, speaking slowly, as though I am stupid.

'I *paid* for America,' I tell him. He is wrong, they both are. There has been some mistake.

The men look at one another and the pig-man shrugs. 'Where did you buy this ticket?' he asks, and the second man interprets.

'From an agent back at home,' I reply. I am beginning to feel sick. Apart from my weakness after giving birth, I have been sitting still for hours without food or drink inside me.

'You paid fifteen shillings for this ticket?'

129

'What?' I ask. I do not understand the currency. When it is translated for me I shake my head. 'More than that,' I tell them. Rintzi and I were sewing many nights to make up the money.

The man sighs and throws my ticket back onto the pile. 'Then you were taken for a ride,' he tells me. 'You paid for a through ticket but bought steerage to London only. It happens all the time. One day someone will have enough wit to check before paying and I will call myself a China-man when he does.'

So Menachem has feathered even more of his little nest than I had imagined, and from the sweat of my family! If only I had inherited one half of Papa's wits! He would weep if he were alive to see how stupidly his beloved little Rosa is behaving! To think I was always known for my cleverness! I need time to stop and plan but the queue behind me is naturally impatient.

'How old are you?' the interpreter asks.

'Eighteen,' is my lie. He shrugs and they let me through.

Fear and hunger are making my head spin so that I cannot see what I should do. The money I have on me would never buy a ticket to America. There is so much noise around me I can barely know my own name. I look about for Baile but I am shorter than most of the crowd and so can see little, even when I stretch onto my toes.

I see a space near a wall and head for it, sinking down onto my case beside an old woman who, by her colour, expression and smell, could well be dead. I close my eyes and press my hands against my ears to concentrate my thoughts. What would Papa have done? Be clever! Be clever!

Someone touches my arm and I let out a cry. There is a man in front of me, wearing striped trousers and a faded *yamulkh* on his head.

'Do you have relatives here?' he asks. His teeth are yellow, like singed kindling. I look around for help but the crowd has moved to another part of the quay. I must have been asleep. I look to the old woman beside me but even she has either moved or been dragged away.

'Are you waiting for family?' the man asks again in Yiddish. 'If you are alone and penniless there is the Jews' Temporary Shelter, in Leman Street. Would you like me to take you? They will give you shelter for several days.'

Could this be the famous Ripper? If it is then he is smaller than in my imagination because when I scramble to my feet I find I am a good inch taller than him. He still scares me, though.

I pick up my case and push unsteadily past him. 'There will be a hot meal each day and water for bathing,' he calls after me. My feet echo as I run up a sooty alley and out into a narrow cobbled street. To my relief there is a man with a small black carriage waiting beneath one of the gas lamps.

'Cab?' he asks. When I make no answer he repeats the word in Russian.

'Could you take me to the Jews' Shelter?' I ask him, almost crying with relief as he touches his hat and smiles.

'Get inside,' he tells me.

The interior of the cab is dark but it is warmer than the streets and I feel safe enough inside its confining walls. I pull Bubba's coat around my body like a blanket and lean back against the grease-stained headrest. The streets are so

131

narrow I could stretch my arms out of the windows and touch the houses on either side. Do the English hate light so much that they have built everything in shadow?

I am tired right through to my bones but too excited and fearful to sleep. We drive through dank streets for an hour before the road starts to widen and the houses fall away to either side, revealing what I take to be fields or even marshes. The shelter must be in another town, for we pass by many barren stretches before the landscape becomes spotted with dwellings again.

I am so tired my eyes are rolling in their sockets before the cab ceases its rocking and we pull up outside a large, two-storey house.

The cab driver calls out, 'Leman Street,' and jumps down to help me with my case, but I refuse to part with it, a little rudely, I think afterwards.

When my feet are safe on the pavement in front of him he smiles again and touches his hat.

'Two hundred and thirty miles in total,' he says, 'that will be two pounds and fifteen shillings.'

I stare at him dumbly. 'But that is far more money than I have,' I tell him.

His smile fades a little. I watch him studying my clothes and my case. Perhaps he thought I was one of the wealthier immigrants.

'So how much are you carrying on you?' he asks. I turn out all the coins in my right pocket, praying he will not ask me to empty the left one as well. The coins are Russian, of course. The cab driver holds one of them up in the light. I think it looks rather handsome but his expression becomes angry and he says a word I do not understand.

'You owe me twice this much,' he tells me.

'It's all I have,' I say, trying to keep my voice calm. Will he have me arrested for a thief?

As we stand staring eye-to-eye the door to the shelter opens and a shaft of golden light envelops us, making us both jump.

'Is there trouble out there?' a voice calls out. It is an elderly woman with hips as wide as the flanks of the gelding that pulls the man's cab. I watch as she emerges from the doorway, wheezing at every cumbersome step her slipper-clad feet are forced to take. 'Did you pay him?' she asks me, pointing a thumb towards the cab driver.

'I gave him all I have . . .' I begin. 'I owe him double, though. I'm not a thief. I will pay him back if he will wait a few days.'

'How far did he take you?' the woman asks. 'One hundred, two hundred yards? Eh?'

'Two hundred and thirty miles,' I tell her, 'all the way from the docks.'

'The docks?' she says, laughing. 'You mean *those* docks?' She turns me around to face the other end of the street. In a gap between the houses I see the tall iron gates that led out of the quayside. When I turn back, my mouth open in disbelief, I see the cab driver climbing back into his seat and flipping his reins to get the gelding moving.

'I don't understand . . .' I say, 'we drove for two hours, maybe more . . .'

'Two hours going round in a circle.' The woman laughs. 'They try it all the time with you greeners. Lucky you didn't have more on you, or he'd have had it all.'

I drop my bag and run towards the cab as it pulls away,

but Bubba's coat wraps around my ankles and I am forced to stop before I end up sprawled across the cobbles. Frustrated and angry I pick up a stone instead, hurling it with all my strength towards the driver. I hear a shout and to my great satisfaction, watch as his hat flies into the air and goes tumbling off down the street.

Barely has the smile of victory crossed my face, though, than a smaller stone hits the back of my coat, followed by a second stone and a third. I spin round, thinking the old lady is attacking me, but find myself confronted by a group of young boys not much older than I am.

'Greener!' they shout in unison. 'Jew!'

Mad as hell and still buoyed up by my victory with the cab driver's hat, I run straight towards them with arms circling and such a blood-curdling cry issuing from my mouth that they disperse in a rush, dissolving back to the shadows that spawned them.

The old woman watches them hurtling about like chickens, then looks back at me. 'Don't be too smart,' she says, 'they don't mean no harm.'

'They threw stones at me,' I tell her.

She sighs. 'They think the greeners steal their jobs.'

'What's a greener?' I ask her.

'You are,' she says, simply.

CHAPTER THIRTEEN

ZG

MOIRE
Watered silk was popular during the late nineteenth century and is currently used almost exclusively for evening wear. The effect, called moire, is achieved by applying heated, engraved copper rollers onto the delicate fabric.

Hester telephoned her daughter in the middle of the night. Three o'clock. It is a magic hour. A time when sleepers can no longer discern dream from reality. Her voice had a scratchy quality to it – not tired, not at all drowsily hushed and night-timey, but full of mid-afternoon impatience.

'They're saying it was suicide,' she yelled. Kitty cupped her hand around the earpiece of her phone but it was too late, the ringing alone had been enough to wake Freddy. She watched him rise silently from the bed and walk out of the room, arse-naked, like a sleepy child. When he returned he was clutching a bottle of iced water and two mugs. One mug said 'Dick' and the other 'Head'. For an intelligent, sophisticated man Freddy suffered from a severely under-developed sense of humour. He thought the mugs were funny. He had bought them himself on his last

135

trip to New York. Every time he used them he laughed – in fact he was smiling now, but then he didn't know who it was on the phone yet. There were other things Freddy didn't know yet, too. One of them was about the wedding. She hadn't told him she had postponed already.

Kitty laughed at different things to Freddy. He would split himself apart over someone walking into a lamppost on the street. His favourite comic was Jim Carey and he laughed so much at the burglars in *Home Alone* that he had to be taken out of the cinema to recover. And that had been on their first date, when Kitty was still at school.

Kitty laughed at cleverer stuff, like satire. Fortunately she also laughed at Freddy laughing, or they would probably never have got engaged. Only she didn't laugh in bed at that moment because her mother's tone was worrying.

'Suicide!' Hester repeated. 'How can they say such things?' She sounded angry, not upset.

Kitty sighed. There had been very little information passed to the press about Gabriel's death, and so they had had to resort to speculation, which gave them much better sport. Kitty had tried to keep the papers away from her mother.

At first they had guessed a heart attack. Then it was suicide. The news that he had been disembowelled put paid to that theory quite quickly in all but one of the tabloids. This particular one was made of sterner stuff, though. Their showbiz hack had been quoted in print as saying Gabriel had killed himself over the failing family business – and so suicide it still had to be in the minds of at least a third of the public. The current issue even contained an interview

136

with a 'leading exponent of Eastern martial arts', explaining the technique of Hara Kiri.

'Kitty, you have to take over,' Hester said, her voice dropping.

'What?' Kitty asked. She'd forgotten to recharge her pone batteries and the line was breaking up into hiccups. Hester sounded as though she was talking under water. 'You . . . have . . . tooo . . . take-overrrr.' It had a ghostly quality in the darkened room, at that time of night. Kitty shivered and rubbed her arm. She preferred the scratchy tone.

Freddy stared at her when the call was finished. 'What is it, possum?' he asked.

'My mother says I should save the business for us. She thinks I'm some sort of anointed, chosen one. She says it's what Gabriel would have wanted.' She looked away. 'I expect she's been saying the same things to Burgess and Chloe. She's desperate, Freddy.'

Freddy whistled through his teeth. 'Do you have to save the business tonight or can it wait until the morning?' he asked.

Kitty shook her head and her hair shone burnished silver in the moonlight. 'She means it, Freddo, even though she's confused,' she said. 'Please,' she begged, the smile fading from her face, 'I have to talk. My head's so full of terrible stuff.' Stuff like murder and violence and who would run the business. Stuff like revenge.

Freddy put down the mugs and looked at her. Kitty was silent. When her fiancé went quiet he was thinking business. Like Burgess he had a computer-compartment in his brain that could be activated at will. Thank God he was most-part human, too. His flesh smelt good, like freshly washed socks. He ran a hand through Kitty's hair as he thought.

'*If* your season is a blow-your-pants-off success you *might* find another investor willing to pick up the tab,' he said, slowly, 'although the likelihood of discovering anyone willing to part with the sort of financial injection you must be needing to stay intact, *and* willing to keep on the little lost leaders like your father's precious dream of *haute couture*, could well be as rare as hen's teeth –' Kitty stopped him by placing a hand over his mouth.

'I couldn't do it, Freddy,' she said. 'Even with all that. Burgess wants to sell. Let him pick the bones out of it if he likes.'

'How strong is your current collection?' Freddy asked her. Kitty shrugged. Of course she wouldn't tell him. He was her fiancé but he was also a competitor of sorts.

And anyway, there was a problem – a *huge* problem. Insurmountable. A labour that even Hercules would have balked at. There *was* no finished collection so far. Things had sort of naturally ground to a halt after Gabriel's murder. They had been tied up with mourning. Burgess was too busy selling the whole package. Chloe was solid with PR, milking every opportunity to turn negative press into positive publicity. Hester was in another world of her own creation. Perhaps Raphael, Gabriel's designer, had been getting on with the job. Who knew? The reins lay slack on the ground right then. Gabriel had always taken care of business. What nobody had realized was that he'd trained no one to run it properly when he was gone.

Kitty felt sick and cold. Too many chiefs, all of a sudden. Her head was too focused on the horror of her father's death to bother. Every day brought something more. New little details, leaking like a rusty tub. Murder. Mutilation. Suicide? Revenge killing. Her mind was still on that pavement, alongside her father's corpse. Who could do such a thing? How much more was there to emerge about the death?

Freddy kissed her hot forehead. Kitty realized that now she had his attention she could no more confide in him than slice off her own hand. Her thoughts were too dark and obsessional. She wished he could kiss them away altogether, like a mother can kiss pain away when her child has a small graze. Perspectives had changed. Her whole life was out of kilter. There was nothing that was right or normal now – not one single solitary thing.

Until Gabriel's death Kitty had had roles. She had been a bride-to-be. She had been hands-on in the business, taking over the bits of real work that Burgess rarely saw and Chloe tried to ignore. Helping her father. Not figures on a screen or cuttings in a book, but manufacture. Chloe thought work ended once the collections were over. She hated the factory and the outworkers. Kitty loved them. It was the part of the business she would miss the most once she and Freddy got married.

She rubbed her temples. 'The collection is great,' she said. Why was Freddy so interested, all of a sudden? Did he have some sort of hidden agenda behind all of this? Did he have some part in her father's death? And since when did crappy, paranoid thoughts like that start filling her scrambled-egg-for-brains head?

Up until Gabriel's death there had been so many of them – family and friends, a thick, suffocating duck-down quilt-load of relatives and people. Now she felt isolated and lonely. Distrust was completely alienating. Who had killed Gabriel? She would be alone forever if she did not find out. Even her father would not turn to face her. When she tried to picture him now he was further away than before, his back totally hunched over his work. It was him she needed to confide in, not Freddy. Yet the conversations with Gabriel were strictly one-way.

'Who, Kitty? *Who*?'

Later, in her uncannily quiet apartment, with only herself for company – and in this little relief, for her head-full of dark nonsense could not be left outside the door like the rubbish – Kitty lay alone in the shadowy silence, sifting through her thoughts, tidying them into piles. Things to do. Things to think about. Things that can wait. Things that can't. Things too goddamn awful to think about until your brain heals a little.

She phoned Nula.

'Nule?' Her sister sounded tired and sleep-sodden.

'Are you okay?' Gabriel would have looked after Nula. He would have looked after Kitty, too. The tears began again, tears of loneliness and self-pity, not worthy emotions at all. The pecking order had changed now. The top name in the whole flaming set-up was struck off the list. Kitty searched in her own mind for the next in line, the family member who would stand up to be counted now that the big cheese was gone. The one to do a little looking-after of the others. A rock strong enough to shoulder the business as well as the sorry mess of a family. Unfortunately no name came to mind.

140

Who was looking after Hester? Would China bother? A large felt-tip had just been applied to the list of those above her in the natural, hierarchical line of succession of authority and responsibility. Suddenly there was no one there to look after *her* – Kitty – yet there were many other things and people in urgent need of her care and attention *themselves*.

'Are you okay, Nules?' she asked her sister again. There was a series of grunts and then a yawn.

'I was asleep, Kit.' Not complaining, just telling. Nula had never been a complainer or a whiner. Nula was quiet. She just got on with life.

'How's Mother?'

Another yawn. 'Okay, I guess. She's sort of out of it too. She has a jab of something. She doesn't come up again until noon.'

'What kind of jab?'

'A doctor-sort-of-jab, Kit. It's okay. He doesn't want to leave her tablets, in case . . . you know, in case she gets greedy, or anything. He calls at night like Doctor Death with his leetle syringe . . .' Her voice broke suddenly. 'Kit, you know what she's done? Did you see the piano? Can you come and live here, Kit? Can I come and stay over with you? Burgess got a nurse in but it's gone like a fucking mausoleum here, and now China's threatening to stay, too.'

'China?' This was new.

'She's pregnant, Kit, did you know?' There was a pause. Both started to laugh, despite their misery. *Because* of their misery. The sort of incredibly against-the-odds, unbidden, hysterically huge type of laughter that only occurs when it really shouldn't. When tears get diverted and come bubbling up through your nose instead of your eyes, making you whoop and choke.

Stephano *avec bébé*. Stephano in Mothercare. Stephano at antenatal classes . . .

But Nula's laugh went on just too long. 'Nule?'

Eventually the girl stopped abruptly, as though she had been garotted. 'I'll phone you when China gets here,' she told Kitty. 'Maybe I can come and stay then, eh?' And then she was gone.

Suddenly the loneliness became unbearable. Kitty pulled on an old, fleece-lined tracksuit and woolly hat, with which to fool the doorstepping press, and took a cab for a second trip to the studio.

It was the nearest she could get to Gabriel, standing in his deserted office. Being in there after his death was not the same as being in there while he was alive. He was a formal man. She was there again without permission. She clutched the edge of the massive desk with her palms as a wave of vertigo ran over her. When had she last eaten? Hester would have nagged her endlessly. But it didn't matter. She could buy a sandwich from the all-nighter on the way home.

Moving carefully, almost like a burglar, she began to open drawers and cupboards. She didn't know what she was looking for, but felt there would be answers there for her somewhere.

'Who, Kitty? *Why?*' The question had changed recently. Why was he murdered? What was the reason for her father's death? She loved him so much she could have forgiven him anything, but her view was biased. She'd spent hours trying to think herself outside that love – to see Gabriel as others would have seen him. To examine his faults. To view his imperfections.

Vain? He was a meticulous man, a perfectionist – in his own image as well as that of his business. But then Gabriel *was* the business.

Ruthless? He could never suffer fools gladly. If something or someone didn't work he would dismiss it without hesitation. What was wrong was wrong. But surely that was admirable?

Arrogant? But he had been at the top of his profession for too long to be anything else. The business thrived on arrogance. Any designer who was not also a dictator was a failure. Hesitancy and indecision were anathema to the craft. People had to be *told* what they wanted to wear, not *asked*.

A family man? Gabriel's values were as firm at home as they were at work. He set the example and the rest of them were expected to follow. He was an adoring husband and father and expected the same in return.

Kitty was the only child he ever indulged. Burgess had suffered the most. It was easy to find favour with Gabriel – all you had to do was copy him. Anyone failing to do so would meet terrible tempers or absolute coldness. It was this coldness that had destroyed Burgess, but then it had been his own fault.

She pulled out business diaries and notebooks. Many of them contained entries in her own hand. There was one cupboard with more personal effects: some cloth from his first sold design; a couple of precious press cuttings; a designer of the year award that was faultlessly polished but never displayed; a child's shoe – a baby shoe, hand crafted in pale lemon kid.

Kitty pulled it from the cupboard and examined it. She hoped it was her own – she so wanted it to be hers. *Her* baby shoe, not one of the others'. Selfish, selfish girl, wanting to be the favourite, even after all this time. Even after his death. She turned the small memento over. There was a tiny initial embroidered on the bottom: 'B'. Not her shoe, then. Burgess's shoe. Her eyes stung with childish disappointment. Like a stupid, jealous child. Why her brother's, though? Why, when they had such a difficult relationship? Why not hers? She put the shoe carefully back into its place.

Apart from that the cupboard was disappointingly empty. Kitty sighed and looked around the office. Then she stopped. Next to the Krupts coffee machine that she had bought Gabriel for his last birthday lay what looked like a small pile of picture frames. Had they been there before? She had no memory of seeing them there the last time she had paid a visit. And she was sure she had made herself a coffee then, to take some of the sting out of the brandy. But she had been misty-eyed with grief. Perhaps the police had just moved them. She walked across to examine the pile.

Some of the frames were large and quite heavy. They were stacked in careful order, not a speck of dust on them. Gabriel had planned to have the office re-decorated after this next collection and the pictures all had notes stuck to them, telling exactly where they should be hung.

The top frame held a portrait photograph of Hester, taken recently, as Kitty remembered, by Terry O'Neill. It was flattering enough to embarrass her mother, but Gabriel had loved it, for it was how he saw his wife. Then there was a shot of her father himself, accepting an award from a smiling Princess Diana. One more portrait of them all as children – a telling shot in retrospect. It showed China in the days before she had no identity, smiling at the camera while keeping a watchful hand on Chloe's shoulder; Burgess, grinning playfully in the days before drugs took the playfulness away; Nula trying to totter out of shot while Kitty held her back lovingly – had they all looked so much alike in those days? They could have been in training to become one of those ghastly all–American family pop groups, with their cute bobbed hair and their matching white-toothed grins.

There was a much older picture beneath that one, a black-and-white shot of a Victorian workshop, with all the staff scrubbed up and posed for the camera. Kitty pulled it closer to the desk-lamp. Had she seen it before? She had no memory of it, though it could have hung on a wall in the studio for years beneath patterns and swatches.

The original must have been sepia. Gabriel must have had it re-shot and re-framed. Kitty peered closer and smiled. The age of the picture meant the people in it were posed rigidly and self-consciously, but it was still possible to spot an expression or two of utter amusement. Kitty felt the assembled staff would have all collapsed with laughter once the shot was taken. There were three women seated in the foreground, all in aprons and caps, and six men lined up behind them, all with their arms folded and beards down to their chests. Behind the men stood two young boys, both also aproned and with caps on their heads. In

145

the distance Kitty could make out the workroom itself, with the blocks and steam irons.

'Who, Kitty? And why?'

She put the picture carefully to one side and looked at the last one in the pile. It was as old as the previous one – maybe older. A formal studio shot. A wedding photograph, the bride seated, clutching a huge bouquet that covered her legs and the groom standing warily behind her.

'Who?'

Smiling, Kitty turned the shot over to see how it was labelled. To her intense disappointment there was no information on the back, apart from the photographer's mark: 'Max Warkofski, Society Photographer' it read, and there was an address underneath.

Kitty turned the shot right-side up again. She looked hopefully at the groom's outfit, but her stomach dropped with disappointment when she saw he was not wearing the wedding suit that Hester had given her. So who were these two?

The bride was beautiful, and apparently quite comfortable in front of the camera, to judge by her tilted head and smile. Even her pose was quite artful, with her back held straight but her shoulders turned slightly away to flatter the neckline of the dress.

The groom appeared far more fazed. His pose was wooden and his expression nothing more than a blank stare. Even so, it was easy to see that he must have been a good-looking man.

'Who, Kitty, who?'

'Look at your birthright, dearest. Discover your past.'

146

Kitty shuddered suddenly. The room felt cold. She hadn't noticed before. She considered taking the pictures but felt she would be grave-robbing. If her father had put them there then that was where he must have wanted them. Placing them carefully back onto the table she pulled her coat about her shoulders and picked up the phone to call for a taxi.

CHAPTER FOURTEEN

ZG

LONDON 1889

BROADCLOTH
*The original broadcloth was a fine woollen fabric, cut
wider than most other cloths so that it could be used
for the voluminous shirts that were once the fashion.
It is also the name of close-weave woollen suiting,
which has a smooth, lustrous nap.*

Kitty,

The old lady at the hostel is Mrs Sourdean, known as
'Queer Tess' because of the severe squint she has in one
eye. She is the cleaner of this shelter where I am arrived,
though she takes me through to the superintendent with
an air that would imply she is the owner of the place.

I am told I can stay here fourteen days, though most
residents will leave before that time. They will help trace
relatives, though when I tell them I am bound for America
they say they cannot search outside the capital unless I
have an address, which of course I do not. I am informed
I should leave my money with the superintendent and when
I say I have none a nought is penned into a large ledger
and I am led away to a bath, instead.

'You should give him your dosh,' Queer Tess tells me.

'It could be stolen otherwise. You can trust the staff here, you know.' Her speech is an odd mixture of English and Yiddish.

My clothes are taken away to be disinfected and I am left with just my case, which I will not allow out of my sight. When my garments are returned their smell makes me cough and my skin begins to itch. By the time I am led down into the dining hall I am all but famished, though cough and retch too much to eat all but a few meagre mouthfuls. We sit in rows at long tables and there is much talking and laughter, which surprises me, for I had thought all the women would be wretched and miserable creatures like myself.

My bed is on the top floor of the ancient building, in a dormitory so overcrowded that it has hammocks slung between the rows of small metal beds. I take off my clothes, folding them into a pile and buckling my belt around them to keep them together in one package with my case. I then sleep in my underwear and boots, tying the end of the belt to my wrist and pulling the scratchy grey blanket provided above my head to drown out the noise, for the women are still talking. I hear them laughing at my security arrangements.

Someone lays a hand on my shoulder and says, quite kindly, '*Schwer und bitter ist das Leben.*' Hard and bitter is life. My mother's lament, and that of many Jewish women before her. I remain beneath my little blanket for I do not want the shame of being caught crying. The room becomes quieter. Then one of the women begins to sing. Her voice is unexpectedly beautiful, and all the more so in contrast to the ugliness of our surroundings. It flies and soars

149

around the room like a trapped bird. The song she sings is an old one from my home town. How I miss Papa and the clean whiteness of the snow and the warmth of Bubba's old room when all the family were there!

I have been in this country for several hours now but I still do not have a plan formed in my mind! How to get to America when I have neither money nor friends? How will I live once fourteen days have passed in this place? I try to think but once again my wits let me down and I am soon asleep.

I wake before dawn, my stomach groaning with hunger. Few of the women are stirring and some still snore. I dress in the dark, nose running and arms and legs shivering with the cold, and tip-toe downstairs to the communal privy in the yard. Queer Tess is about and rattling her buckets loud enough to raise the dead.

'Up to take a stroll in the morning air?' she asks. I believe she thinks I am a little too grand for my situation.

'You're early, too,' I tell her.

'We're toshers,' she says. 'Toshers always rise before everyone else. That way we don't have to see the looks on their faces when we set about our work.'

'Toshers?' I ask.

She places her hands on her enormous hips and I believe she stares at me, though her squint is so severe it is difficult to tell the precise direction of her gaze. I notice that she has only one tooth in her head. She is not altogether a pleasant sight.

'Toshers are professional men,' she smiles proudly. 'You want to see a tosher going about his business? Run for your coat then, angel, you're about to get your first sight of a London tradesman going about his honest day's trade.'

Despite her size, Tess can move at quite a rate and I am forced into a trot to keep up with her, which is difficult on an empty stomach. Fortunately we are only round a couple of corners before she stops, panting.

'Caught them,' she says with some relief, 'I thought we might be too late.'

In front of us, down the narrow alley and pitched into strange silhouette by the first glint of the sun, are a thin, ragged-looking man and four young boys – very similar in height and shape to the boys who stoned me in the street. I can make out little of their appearance as they are mere shapes in the gloom, but assume from Tess's tone that this is her husband and sons.

It seems the mother is sole treasurer of the Sourdean family blubber, for her sons are as lean as Tess is fat. In the guttering light the boys appear as sticks clad in rags, though I am impressed at the relative speed and grace of their movements as they teem about a spot on the gleaming cobbles. When they sense our presence they spring up like hares, looking as alarmed at my appearance as I do at theirs.

'Don't worry,' Tess tells me, 'they're toshers. They don't know how to speak to decent folk.'

She waves to her husband and the man nods back. Even from this distance I am assailed by a stench so potent that it makes my poor stomach contract again with nausea. I pinch my nose with my fingers and Tess laughs.

'Sweet, isn't it?' she asks.

Her clan re-groups around the spot in the road. The smell intensifies, and becomes so unbearable that I heave and retch like a spewing cat. There is a scraping of metal and suddenly the boys vanish into the ground, one at a time.

Tess laughs at the astonishment on my face. 'They work down the sewers,' she says. 'They go down at dawn and come up after dusk. We make our living off things people lose down there – buttons, rags, the odd piece of jewellery if you're lucky.'

The smell is so foul that, now I have the cause of it in my mind too, I have to walk away. This seems to amuse Queer Tess for some reason.

'Do they make much money?' I ask through my hands, when I have voice to speak again, and this convulses her. Her laughter echoes horribly as we make our way up the narrow alleys that lead back to the shelter.

'Tess,' I say, once she is quieter, 'it's money that I need if I am to get out of this place. How can I make some? Where can I earn the fare to get to America?'

'You're plain, but not ugly,' she tells me. 'You could earn quite a bit as a bride.' She is walking slowly now, having used up all her breath on her laughing.

'A bride?' I say. 'But I already have a fiancé waiting for me in America.'

Tess is chuckling again. 'Oh, I don't think the sailors will mind that much, angel,' she says, 'most brides are long married. The punters aren't that fussy, you know.'

I would ask her what she means, for either her Yiddish is poorer than I thought or she has ceased talking sense. Then I begin to wonder if she is a little deranged, as her laughter has an hysterical ring to it, and I decide merely to smile and nod agreement politely.

That evening I approach a group of rather more kindly-looking women in the shelter and ask them how one can become wealthy in this city. Like Queer Tess they appear amused by my question. Eventually one woman – a tall, bony-looking peasant from the east of my country – tells me that the most money to be made locally is from one of the three Jewish trades: shoe-making, cabinet-making or tailoring.

One of the wealthiest men around is Israel Bloom, she tells me. This gentleman has a business in the Commercial Road and a sweatshop employing sixty souls in Fieldgate Street, off Whitechapel. Bloom's is known best for its coat manufacture.

'It sells to large retail outlets in the West End,' one woman tells me. Her uncle is an employee of Israel Bloom and she will be working for him herself once her family come for her.

I am both excited and peeved by this information. Excited, because this is the very business I carry some skill in, and peeved because I remember Baile telling me her relations in London were engaged in the same occupation.

The women seem pleasant enough and the conversation continues.

'What is a greener?' I ask them, remembering my conversations with Queer Tess.

'It's the name they give immigrants when we first arrive,' one woman explains. She pulls a face, as though the word is an insult.

'And how may I earn money as a bride?' I ask. This time

all their expressions change at once. They rise together, clutching their knitting to their chests, and I find myself abandoned yet again.

'And we thought you were a good girl, from a nice Russian family,' one of them whispers as she takes her leave.

It is Friday evening – tomorrow will be Sabbath. I walk a little way from the shelter, hoping to chance upon Fieldgate Street and see Israel Bloom's vast empire for myself. I have it into my head that I too can make money in this trade.

I remember how we used to live in Russia before we were banished to The Pale of Settlement. We too were wealthy. Papa and Rintzi lived well – Rintzi reminded me of this many times.

'We dressed you in finest furs, little Rosa,' she would say. 'Other wives and mothers would stop to stare in the street when we walked by. You looked so enchanting, you were spoilt by everyone.' The fur must have covered my rabbit's ears for anyone with half a wit to be so impressed by my poor face.

My ramble takes me up Angel Alley and along Fashion Street to a wider road, called Brick Lane. The small strip of sky overhead turns indigo at dusk but there are people everywhere, so I have no need to feel afraid. I scurry past houses so grey with crumbling filth that they could barely be described as shelter, yet outside each one of these dwellings is placed a chair made of rusted iron or splintered wood, and upon each chair sits a character so advanced in years you would think them already dead and awaiting removal by the funeral cart.

These folk have the look of farmers or peasants from

my childhood. Amid the clatter of Yiddish I hear Russian and Polish words used. I see chickens peck around their feet and peas and beans growing from boxes on their windowsills.

My legs begin to ache. The whole world appears to be covered with a layer of grime, yet everywhere there are yellow candles flickering in parlour windows to see in the Sabbath. I smell butter and honeycakes above the bitter aromas of soot and burning coal, and my stomach growls when it thinks of the *challah* bread that will be eaten during the sacred meal that night.

Somehow I reach Fieldgate Street and wander the length of it, looking for signs of great wealth and hope. Eventually, when I have all but given up my search, I notice a gloomy doorway and a faded, painted sign outside that reads: 'I. BLOOM. OUTERWEAR MANUFACTURER.'

This is no empire, though. The building I stand in front of is large but not huge. Its black bricks look as sturdy as cake-crumbs. The only windows are small, high and barred, and as impenetrable with filth as the walls themselves. The place is still there today if you look, Kitty. Is this how wealth appears in this country? I think of the vast ivory mansions and palaces of my birthplace and the sugary stucco townhouse we inhabited before we left for the *shtetle*. How clean things were there!

Hunched with depression I stare shrewdly at the place. The doors part and a group of whey-faced workers spew out, smelling sour as vinegar from the oil they use on their machines. I place myself in their path.

'Are there jobs in this place?' I ask. One of the men looks at me and spits onto the ground.

'Greener,' he says, speaking in English.

I try my Yiddish on the others, but none of them appears to understand. Alarmed by their aggressive expressions, though, I walk away at speed.

The streets are becoming quieter and I yearn for the protection of the shelter. Attempting to retrace my steps I become momentarily lost in a maze of streets and, by the time I reach Leman Street I am in a welter of terror and sick with relief.

A small band of well-dressed women waits outside the hostel. Nearly fainting with exhaustion, I take the gloved hand one of them offers me and she holds my arm to steady me while the others all smile and click their tongues.

'Are you hungry, my dear?' one of them asks in faltering Yiddish.

I nod and she hands me some bread.

'Do you need money?' asks another. I wonder if I am dreaming, or whether these women are angels, come to escort me to Papa.

Nodding again, I hold out my hand, but it appears that no coins are forthcoming.

'You will receive both money and succour as soon as you convert,' the eldest woman tells me. She has such a pleasant face and her coat, though ill-fitting, has been well crafted from emerald velvet.

'Money to get me to America?' I ask. They look at one another before resuming their smiles.

'You are in England now, my dear,' the first one tells me, 'all we ask is that you become Anglicized.'

I smile politely enough, though I have no idea what it is they are talking about.

'You will find us in Bethnal Green,' the older woman says, handing me a pamphlet. 'If you want good kosher food and money for yourself then come for conversion and let us save your soul.'

At that moment two of the women from my dormitory walk past us on their way into the shelter. Seeing me caught in conversation they push me – rather rudely, I consider – in through the doorway before I can even take my leave.

'Taking the penny for conversion now, are you?' one of them asks me when we are inside. I now conclude I am more unpopular than before with my fellow inmates, and not through any doing of my own.

Regardless of this, on the Sabbath I fall in with the other women from the shelter and we walk in a large noisy group to Brick Lane, to the Great Synagogue. The building is packed with worshippers. To my enormous humiliation and to the deep embarrassment of the other women I find myself shaking throughout the entire service.

On the way back to the hostel the women walk quickly and in silence, afraid, it seems, of the very shadows themselves. As the street widens I look up and the grey smog parts a little and all at once I see the stars – the same stars that twinkled overhead when I walked in the snow in Russia. I am still Rosa, then, and must be like those stars – unchangeable. My courage returning, I walk to the front of the timid little group and march ahead, quoting an old Jewish prayer. This brings gasps from the women and some would try to keep me quiet, though a strange-looking girl I have heard is called Hannah comes up to join me both in step and in prayer, and I am pleased to hear her voice is more pleasant than my own, which sounds like a saw against tree-bark.

We are no further than maybe a hundred paces before a stone hits the side of my face and I know from Hannah's scream that she has been struck too. I turn, expecting the same ragged group that greeted me on my arrival to this country, but instead find a crowd of women, each one with a face more ghastly than the next. To my horror one of the ugliest walks straight up to poor little Hannah and butts her square in the head.

'Jew!' the woman screeches at me. I find myself laughing into her face. We stare full-on and I see a pink circle on her forehead where she butted Hannah like a goat.

'Tosher!' I shout to her in English, and I pinch my nose with my fingers as though I can smell the sewer about her. Who would have imagined that one of my first words in the new language would be such a fine insult to hold me in such stead?

There is an expression of eruption behind the woman's eyes and her cheeks begin to wobble.

'Tosher,' I repeat, making as if to retch. This is splendid. For a moment I feel more like my old self again. I laugh delightedly as the woman backs away in shock and shame. Clearly no whey-faced Jew has dared to stand her ground before.

Helping Hannah to her feet, I pull my group on and we join hands, and this time they all walk together.

What a line we make as we march back to the shelter! At last I am Rosa the heroine, rather than Rosa the tearful cry-baby. All will be well now, I know it.

When I lie in my bed one of the women places a second

blanket over me, patting the edges in like a mother would do to a small child. This brings the hated tears back into my eyes, but I manage to squeeze them back in, which makes me very proud.

CHAPTER FIFTEEN

Z͞G

BUSK
*In the late-nineteenth century, long, knife-shaped
strips of whalebone or shell were inserted into corsets
or stays to give women the S-bend silhouette shape
that was popular at the time. In 1881 the Rational
Dress Society was founded, in a bid to resist these
fashions which restricted or deformed the body. Via
its mouthpiece, the* Gazette, *the RDS advocated bone-
less stays and the wearing of no more than seven
pounds of underwear, and made a stand against the
fashion for high heels.*

Kitty,
   My life has much improved. I have now left the shelter
for another establishment in the Mile End Road called the
Young Jewish Girls' Association. I must say that this place
is still not the sort of home Papa would have wished to
see me inhabiting, but it is eminently more suitable than
Leman Street, and the twenty or so inmates much younger
and less likely to be caught dribbling over their broth-bowls
at night. I am told this place is for friendless but respectable
foreign girls. The building leaves much to be desired but
in two weeks we will be re-housed in new premises in

Tenter Street, Aldgate, which sounds prettier to my ears than Mile End.

The regime here is strict, and the place run by a matron who has more pairs of eyes in her head than a floor-bug, but I am not in the least sorry to have left the shelter. I had thought Queer Tess befriended me out of pity, but was told by a fellow inmate of the establishment that the old witch had found me, 'a strange sort, and a great deal too full of myself, too'. She had been using the story of my visit to her verminous family to amuse the other women of an evening.

At the Girls' Association we are kept clean and taught to speak in English. I am given a navy pinafore to wear, made of simple serge that holds its dye so poorly that a single boil reduces it to a fade. I notice this immediately and send mine to be washed, which at least reduces the smell and stiffness of the fabric. When the others undress at night I notice the dye has left dark stains on their underclothes.

I have decided I must track down Baile. She told me she had an uncle who owned a high-class dressmaker's, and much as it galls me to beg from her I feel I must find a job if I am to save up the fare for New York. Besides, she owes me this at least, as it is her brother whom I have to thank for my current predicament.

I remember how much Baile spoke about the wealth and class of her English relatives. They own vast factories that would make Bloom's sweatshop look like a cottage by comparison. If Baile is already married there may be no need for me to see her at all. Perhaps I could beg a job or some money from her family and be on my way before she pays a visit. Maybe they will be so full of shame when I

161

relate how much was stolen from me by Baile's precious brother they will reimburse me immediately. I am so full of hope at this thought that my hands shake. In a few weeks I could be away from this grey place and on a boat bound for America.

I take to roaming the streets in search of the Kluchersky name above a manufacturer's doorway. The weather is improved now, although the sun does little to penetrate the gloom of the streets. I am so determined to be of an optimistic nature, though, that the minute it appears I run to where I can feel its pale heat upon my cheek. There are small patches of clear ground in this city, surrounded by metal railings and laid to unhealthy, patchy grass. I spend some time in one of these areas, along with many other local residents. We sit on painted wooden benches and turn our grateful faces to the sun.

Eventually, after several exhausting days' search, I am forced to lie to the benefactors of the home and claim Baile as a long-lost relative, in the hope that they will discover her for me.

There is no news for several days. Then the matron presents me with an envelope containing a list of families with the name 'Kluchersky' and their addresses. I devour the list greedily, though there appears to be no way of telling if any have a young greener called Baile, just arrived in this country.

None of the addresses is commercial and only three of them are in London. With closed eyes I place a pin in the page and allow it to pick out the right address for me. This was Rintzi's way of bringing luck wherever a choice was to be involved.

My mother's luck has followed me. The house, when I find it, is home to Baile's uncle and his family. Far from being the mansion I had imagined, though, the place is a small room in a tenement block near the Mile End Road. Any joy I might have felt at discovering the very place I have searched for so close to my own doorstep evaporates at the sight of it.

I am viewed warily and not invited to cross the threshold, though behind Baile's aunt's skirts I espy a dull-looking room that I could hardly describe as clean. When I ask about her niece's whereabouts I am directed to a factory less than a mile from the tenements.

The walk is easy enough, for I have a good memory for streets and am beginning to know the area well. When I reach the factory, though, the shock I feel on viewing it leaves me weak and exhausted.

The place is an eighth of the size of Bloom's – a tiny sweatshop on the fifth floor of a grimy warehouse near the docks. Can it really be owned by relatives of the wondrous Baile? If so she will never have graced the premises with her presence for fear of grubbying her expensive kid gloves.

When I push through the painted double doors I am immediately assailed by nostalgic smells – so much so that I am forced to steady myself on the wall and close my eyes to recover. The heat in the room is unbearable, and so is the smell of labouring flesh. To most visitors the stench would be overpowering, but my nose has been trained to seek out sweeter scents. There is cheap, rough fabric here, but quality cloths, too.

The room is less than twelve paces in length and six in

163

width. Its walls are barely visible, hung as they are with brown paper patterns of all shapes and fit, strung on large metal hooks of the type used by butchers to hang a carcass. What wall can be seen consists of fetid and stained plaster, crumbling with damp and filth and covered in parts with peeling, dark-green paint.

In the centre of this room are six seamstresses, two working on sewing machines that create so much noise as to render any attempt at speech worthless, and the other four working by hand, their backs bent so low that their faces are hidden.

A tailor in a dark jacket and skull-cap sits cross-legged on a high stool, sewing buttons with a long thread, and beside him the finisher and steamers with their press irons are lost in a haze of scorching steam.

Behind this cloud I catch glimpses of a small and very elderly cutter unrolling a bale of dull-looking fabric on a long wooden table. There are blocks and dummies behind him and behind them a small mountain of cloth waste and off-cuts.

There is no floor in this place, just a carpet of fluff and dust. The only light comes from hissing gas mantles on the walls as the only window is too covered with grime to allow natural light to penetrate. At a desk near the door sits a young Jewish boy, smoking a pipe that adds to the fetid air and scratching into a ledger with a quill pen.

Beneath his desk I spot pelts of finer quality flannel, some light China silk linings and some woollen broadcloth dyed for gentlemen's suits. Above him hangs strips and rolls of Petersham ribbon and Russian braid for trimmings. Near my elbow as I turn is a rickety table upon which lie a sleeve-board and a tailor's ham for pressing darts. My father had these things in his own workroom. His were clean but these are so shabby the fabric is worn right through. Nevertheless, I remove my glove and reach to touch them, for they remind me so of home.

My movement disturbs the boy, who looks up at me through the thickest spectacles I have ever seen.

'My name is Bertha Cecilia Zigofsky,' I tell him. 'I am the daughter of Zigofsky the Master Tailor from Moscow. I am an acquaintance of Baile Kluchersky, whose family own this business. I have come here for a job. I need temporary employment.'

The boy's laughter rings cruelly in my ears. I consider shouting at him for his rudeness, but then notice that he is pointing down the workroom. I look in the direction of his finger and see one of the pressers peering in our direction.

'Israel!' the boy calls with some mirth. 'Israel Kluchersky! You forgot to tell us this is your business, you old rogue! Why did you keep us in the dark all this time? Eh? Did you think we'd be after your money if you admitted to such wealth? Eh? Now we have another greener here from the old country, keen to cash in on the Kluchersky fortune. What did you say your name was, miss?'

'Bertha,' I tell him, confused, 'Bertha Zigofsky.'

'Miss Zigofsky is here for an appointment, sir,' the boy yells across to the old presser. 'Shall I tell her to wait?'

The old man waves his hands about in agitation and shakes his head many times in apparent confusion.

'He works here too?' I ask, equally confused.

'Oh yes,' the boy says, exploding into laughter again.

165

'Oh you could say Israel's job is his life. He even sleeps right here in the workroom, along with his employees, did you know that?'

'Stop it!' I hear a woman's voice shout above the racket of the machines. One of the sewers is standing up.

'Baile?' I cannot believe it is the same girl I left at the docks. Baile is either heavier or her posture is no longer upright enough to give shape to her figure. Her hair is concealed beneath a scarf and her face looks grimy.

'Baile?' I repeat. 'You work here in the family sweat-shop?' I had no idea she could even thread a needle. When I look down at her hands she is quick to conceal them behind her back, but not before I notice that they are stained with dye and dotted with pin-pricks.

Suddenly I feel sorry for the girl. She arrived in London to stay with wealthy relatives, only to discover Israel Kluchersky is mean enough to sleep on his own workroom floor. No wonder she has been enlisted to graft here, too. What a shock it must have been! I almost join in with the boy's unsuppressed laughter.

Baile hurries down past the sewing machines, tucking stray hair into her scarf as she does so. 'What are you doing here, Rosa?' she asks, angrily.

'Baile,' I begin, 'I am stranded here in London. Your brother took my money and then bought the wrong ticket. I need a job to earn money to get to America. It is the least your family can do for me.'

'Menachem is dead,' Baile said, her face pinched into a frown. 'The guards killed him. That is why he never got on the ship. You shouldn't speak so of him any more, Rosa. You have no right.'

166

'I have a right to my money,' I tell her, for I doubt Menachem is anywhere other than a smart town in Russia, with a decent house to live in and a full belly. 'But I'll earn it, Baile. Tell your family to give me a job. Please. I'm desperate.'

Baile's face puckers further.

'You're standing here on paid time, Miss Kluchersky,' the boy tells her, 'there will be no breaks for the privy this afternoon now.'

I see fear cross Baile's face and it is then that the true extent of my own stupidity begins to occur to me.

'This place isn't owned by your family, is it?' I ask her. Her head drops. I would have paid to see such shame on her face while we were travelling together, but in my present predicament it brings me dread, rather than pleasure.

'My uncle Israel works here, Rabbit,' she tells me, 'we don't own it. I didn't think you'd find out. I'm working here until I am married, then it will all be over. This is just temporary, just to pay my uncle back for my keep.'

'But you sleep on the floor!' I tell her.

She shakes her head. 'No, Rabbit, we sleep on benches. It's not so bad.' But there are tears in her eyes, nevertheless.

I look about, feeling sick. 'I still need a job,' I tell the boy. Baile's head pops up again in surprise.

'No more greeners,' the boy replies, grinning. 'Jobs are to go to locals or those who have lived here one generation or more. Didn't you hear about the *Judenhetz*? The natives are getting upset, Miss Zigofsky. Do you want pogroms here too, eh?'

I match his gaze. 'I need a job,' I say.

He looks across at Baile. She tosses her head and I see

167

something of the old haughtiness there. I also see that the boy has an eye for her.

'Can you sew?' he asks me.

'Better than her,' I answer. 'Didn't you hear? My father was a master tailor. He taught me all he knew. Tell him, Baile.'

Baile nods, quickly.

'Can you operate a Singer?' the boy asks.

'Of course,' I lie. What can be so difficult about a machine like that?

'We can only take you on as a general hand,' he says. I know enough from listening to other girls in my hostel to know what this means. 'That's the lowest grade,' I tell him, 'I'm skilled.'

He laughs again. 'Israel has slept on these floors for twenty-two years and has only achieved middle grade,' he says. 'Look at him work – do you think you could do better?' Israel's hands move so quickly across the cloth they are almost rendered invisible. Even my father could not work with such speed. I shake my head reluctantly.

The boy slaps the top of his ledger. 'Agreed, then,' he says. 'You work from five in the morning until midnight for six days a week. Sabbath is, of course, your day off. You will be paid fourteen shillings and sixpence a week plus tea. There will be one break per day for use of the latrine – any others will be deducted from your wages. You may sleep on the floor of the workroom at night if you wish and if you want to purloin a bench for sleeping on you must negotiate with the other workers. I must warn you there are vermin on the floor at night though, Miss Zigofsky.'

168

I do not give him the satisfaction of watching my expression change as he gives me this news.

'Agreed?' he asks.

'Agreed,' I say, 'but I have no need of lodgings, tempting though they may sound.'

I estimate that it will take me three years to save the money for my journey to America. This is sad news, for I doubt Aaron will wait that long for me. I will need to be resourceful. On the way back to the hostel I take myself off to the Christian Society in Bethnal Green. Here I give a false name and tell the smiling woman at the entrance that I wish to convert to the Evangelical faith. The woman, a buxom grandmother who should know better, falls to her knees in front of me, raising her eyes heavenward and clasping her plump hands in prayer.

I am given a plate of kosher food for my pains, which is good enough to be sold to some of the fatter girls back at the hostel. After joining in prayers that I do not understand I am asked if I will agree to be baptised. When I inform them it is my dearest wish I am presented with a few coins, which I quickly secrete into my hankie with much relief.

As I leave the establishment I ask the woman if she works on conversions every evening. To my delight she says she does not. With any luck there will be a different grandmother there every night, and all with the same problems of deafness and short sight. My baptism could take a long time at such a rate, while my purse will become fuller.

CHAPTER SIXTEEN

ZG

THE SWEATS

In 1888 there were one thousand and fifteen tailoring workshops in Whitechapel alone. Many immigrants who could not get work in the sweatshops became costers, getting stalls and selling whatever they could. 'Greeners' found it hard to get work from the Gentiles, who often had a 'Britons first' policy to employment, while the long-settled Jews in the area could also be harsh in their criticism of the new-comers. Wages in tailoring, which had held at around two pounds a week, began to fall to one pound and lower as the steady influx increased.

Kitty,

I ache from the effort of so much work, and my only pleasure is in seeing precious Baile toiling just as hard, even though she is less suited, having had no experience of labour in Russia. I write to Aaron each night, then send all the notes once a week, for that is all the postage I can afford. As I have no address for him in America I am forced to send my packages via his mother, in the hope that she will pass them on for me. I must let Aaron know he should wait for me. If he believes me to be lost he could marry another. I have written some of my letters to him in English, to show how well I will do when I am finally in America.

I have also been in regular contact with my mother, but as yet have received no reply, either. Papa would have written. Papa would have been direct on the boat to collect me and save me from my predicament. Rintzi has neither the wit nor the money. I pray that both she and my darling brother Gregory are safe and not killed as Papa was. I force myself to cease these thoughts. Self-pity is difficult enough, but if I begin to worry for my family too I shall be mad within the month.

I tell myself all is well. Rintzi is not a natural at putting pen to paper. If anything were wrong I would know. Comforted by these and many such ideas I am left free to worry about no one save myself.

In the meantime I have fallen into a passion, though I would not admit it if my eyes were gouged out and my tongue split in two. Richard Galliard is part-owner of the business that now employs me, and the handsomest man I have seen in my entire life. Is that a wicked thing to say, when I am promised to Aaron? I think not, for I am sure Richard would be admired by any woman, whether married, betrothed or a lonely old maid.

He visits the premises once a week and the day has become the highlight of my time here. His manners are those of a gentleman and his clothes are the finest I have seen in this country. I have noticed him in three different suits so far, and each has surpassed the last in cut and finish, though all were subtle enough to imply no hint of vanity in their design.

He is tall – though not too tall – with fine auburn hair and moustache. It is his eyes, though, that I believe to be

171

his finest feature. In a country where I have seen only need, greed, or blankness in people's eyes, Richard's hold an expression of intelligence and pride.

I have seen Baile blush when he arrives in the workroom, so suppose that she, too, is fascinated by this man. When he arrives we are all to work as though our lives depended upon it, which is what we do anyway, though to keep the bosses happy we make a special show. It is difficult to watch Richard Galliard with my head bent so low over my work, so I have borrowed a small vanity mirror from one of the girls at the hostel and keep this beneath the garments on my bench, just in case. Through this I can watch him without appearing to stop work. Baile sees what I am about and seethes with jealousy at my cleverness.

I wonder he can bear to stand in this workroom at all, for the place is so fetid and airless, yet he gazes about politely, for all the world as though he were breathing the country air. There is something about him that reminds me of Gregory and I see for a moment how my brother might have looked had he kept all his wits and become a man.

I know there is no sense to be made of these emotions that I suffer, for I am to marry Aaron. However, there are moments now when I am reminded that Baile and I are little more than children ourselves, so what is in some harmless fun?

A hair fell from Richard Galliard's head as he passed my table and I have it kept in my purse. This annoys Baile so intensely that it gives me enormous pleasure to wave it in front of her nose. However much she tosses her head, I know she would kill to own that hair herself.

Through constant persistence Baile and I have forced Uncle Israel to tell us some of Richard's history. Born to a French father and German mother, both of whom began life wealthy but died half-starved and persecuted somewhere in Europe, Richard spent some time in the army before arriving in London, disembarking at the very same docks that Baile and I passed through. It was there that Richard encountered Turgis Fasukinos, the Lithuanian Jew who shares this business with him. Richard was keen to invest in a concern and saw in Turgis the skill and knowledge he himself lacked.

Richard had money, smuggled from his homeland by his father. Turgis had many years' experience in the clothing trade in Lithuania and was delighted to have bumped into the very man to back his ideas for a venture in England. In ten years they have built up a going concern, with three workshops in the East End and a high-quality salon in a better part of London.

While Turgis cracks the whip in the sweatshops Richard uses his charm and manners to woo high-class clients in the West End. While Turgis has spent his ten years in this country expanding his family along with his business, Richard is yet unmarried.

Baile and I listen to all this like children hearing a fairy story. There is meat on the bare bones now. Baile hates me for my interest in the man she considers her own infatuation, I can see this in her eyes. To enrage her further I tell little lies, informing her I met him on the steps on the way into the factory one morning and that he tipped his hat

173

and smiled. Or that the boy on the desk has told me that Richard asked him for my name. I know Baile doubts these stories, but they make her pink with rage nevertheless.

The new hostel is colder than the old but smarter too, and I am sad to know that my time here is limited, for there are many other girls in search of accommodation in much worse plights than my own. Matron knows I have employment and the offer of a place to sleep. I wonder how long it will be before I am asked to leave.

There is a great commotion one morning at the hostel. Matron comes running to me after much loud conversation in the doorway and informs me that I have a visitor. I can tell from her expression and the way she waits with folded arms that my visitor is a man.

'He says he is your cousin,' she tells me. I read doubt in her eyes and she must read doubt in my own, for I have no cousin in London.

It is Max Warkofski, the know-all young man from the boat, who waits in the porch of the building, with his hat in his hand and a look of perfect innocence on his face.

'Cousin Rosa!' he cries when I approach, and I can tell this is for the benefit of the matron who stands less than four paces behind us.

In my surprise I am rendered speechless for once.

As Max moves closer to grasp my hand he whispers, 'Tell me the address of the place where you work.' I shake his hand solemnly and mouth the address back to him, though I don't know why, for I have no great desire to see him again, as his arrogance annoys me. He has come looking for Baile, I am sure of it.

We hold a stilted conversation, during which he informs me for the matron's benefit that my aunt has been searching for me some ten weeks and will be delighted that I have now been traced.

I leave for work earlier than normal and find Max waiting, as expected, in the dark outside the factory, his hands stuffed into his pockets and looking for all the world like the rogue that he is. We walk around the corner to a crowded immigrant tea stall in Garden Street and he treats me to the best brew I have tasted since leaving home.

'So!' he says. 'Little Rosa!' His clothes are clean and smart but less expensive than those I saw on the boat. He may have lost a little weight, too, though the expression of constant amusement still burns bright in his eyes. I believe he thinks of me as sport. Perhaps he is bored in London and found himself in need of someone to tease. At any rate, I am full of suspicion that his circumstances may be no better than my own, despite his devil-may-care air. His shoes alone give hint to that, with their scuffed uppers and worn heels.

'You may have talked me out of my place at the hostel, Max,' I tell him, which only makes his smile widen.

'Excellent!' he replies. 'That flea-home is for the poor.'

'Which is exactly what I have now become!' I inform him. His smile still holds in place. Is there nothing that will remove this grin?

'And is that factory the place where you poor folk scratch a living?' he asks.

'It is certainly where we scratch for fleas!' I say, for his good humour is unfortunately infectious and I have started to laugh.

175

Perhaps there is a limit to the amount of misery a young girl can carry on her shoulders. I know I am tired of my own grief. Laughter feels good on my cheeks and in my belly. I laugh some more and Max roars with me. It feels good to be silly and girlish again.

'It's the way you view the world, young Rosa,' Max tells me, tapping me with his finger to make his point. 'Anyone can be happy if they set their mind to it. It's the way you perceive your own circumstances that counts.'

'I'd like to see you be happily employed as a pure-finder!' I tell him. These poor souls spend their time collecting dog-dirt from the London streets, for use in shoe polish. I could not imagine employment worse than that of Queer Tess's brood until I watched these unfortunates at work.

'Oh, I don't know, Rosa,' Max tells me, 'the hours aren't bad and you're in the open air. I daresay you'd like a view of the sky now and again. And maybe you could become something of an expert on the product and grow to enjoy the job . . .'

I stop him before I begin to feel ill.

When our laughter ends Max asks me the question I know he has been saving. 'Do you see anything of Baile at all?'

So that was his purpose in tracking me down. I shrug. 'I suppose I see as much as I need, as she sits at my elbow most of the day, feeding fabric into my machine.'

Max looks surprised. 'Then you'll give her my regards?' he asks.

I nod and finish my tea. 'I have to be at work,' I say. I have had enough of acting as his matchmaker.

176

Max grabs my arm to halt me. 'You haven't heard my offer yet, Rosa,' he says.

'Offer?'

'I can't bear to see you living off charity,' he says. 'I thought you were set for America. I was surprised to find your name listed at the Temporary Shelter. I went there looking for a young nephew who never arrived and saw your name as I went through the records.'

I turn away a bit at this. 'Baile's brother sold me the wrong ticket,' I say in a low voice, 'I'm reliant on charity only until I can afford my fare to America.'

Max taps me on the head with his glove. 'I have my own business now, Rosa,' he says. 'I've set up as a society photographer with prospects. My place is in Brick Lane, but not the mean end, you know. I find I have room to spare there. How would you like to rent space so that you can live within independent means again and maybe turn your luck with your employment? What about being your own boss, Rosa? You must be tired of slaving under this roof for your penny.'

I am caught by the brilliance of his eyes. Max is a great magician with his words – all sounds easy when uttered by him. He has me in his thrall and for a moment I feel my heart take a squeeze of excitement. So he is successful after all. I was wrong in my rather hasty assessment of him. I blush with guilt.

'How should I afford rent?' I ask him, with a deliberately bashful expression. 'All my money saved is for my fare.'

Max strokes his chin and I can see he is fooling with me again.

177

'Suppose we set rent so low even your little purse could accommodate the cost, and then chalk up the rest to be paid back when you're rich and famous, as I know you shall be one day?' he says.

'And why should I ever be wealthy?' I ask. I am thinking of my father's words – 'Never be poor, Rosa, and never grow old.' How quickly did I let him down!

Max looks into my eyes. 'Because you have a good brain and you have chutzpah, Rosa,' he says, 'and I've yet to meet the man or woman with both intelligence and boldness whom God did not eventually reward.'

He smiles. 'Will you think about my offer?' he asks.

In an impulse I nod before taking my leave and rushing off to my meagre employment. Thank God I am to be saved from this life at last! Max is my rescuer and in my eyes that makes him above reproach. In an instant I forget his arrogance and idiotic attempts at what he must consider a 'lady-killing' smile, and concentrate instead on his generosity and his business acumen. I write to Rintzi that night to inform her how my luck has changed, and that I am going up in the world at last.

CHAPTER SEVENTEEN

ℤG

1998

BAGHEERA
*This uncut pile velvet was once popular for evening
gowns. A fine-textured fabric, it became less fashionable in the later part of the twentieth century,
although imitation bagheera is now made from
rayon crepe.*

The wedding suit lay untouched beneath Kitty's bed, which
was where Freddy first found it.

Freddy's upbringing may have stinted a little on taste, but
could never be found wanting when it came to manners. He
neither touched the case nor asked directly about it.

'You know you have what appears to be an extremely
aged box beneath your bed and that it is shedding rust
onto the floor-tiles?' was all he said. Kitty changed from
being semi-slack and calm to defensive and emotional in
an instant. So quickly, in fact, that Freddy would have
liked to have *seen* the transition as well as *heard* it. If he
had watched Lon Chaney morph into the wolf-man on
video and then run the whole event on fast-forward it
would have had a similar effect.

179

Unfortunately he had been hanging upside-down over the rim of the mattress, searching for his glasses at the time, so he saw the case but not Kitty's expression when he raised the subject. By the time he had righted himself she was almost cross-eyed with stress.

'What? What's up?' he asked.

'Nothing.' But she could control neither her tone nor her eyes.

'Hey, hey hey!' Freddy said. He was both young and old: twenty-four going on six when there was a stupid joke around, and fifty when it came down to observing mood fluctuations, which was very unnerving.

'Hey what?' Kitty reached for the TV remote control.

'This isn't you, Kit,' he said, 'not you at all. "Nothing." That obviously means, "Yes, something." And something quite major, at that. Isn't that classed as sulking? You never sulked before. You were never evasive before.'

Kitty sighed. A pretty sigh, not a middle-aged exhalation of hopelessness. 'It's a suit,' she said. She had spots on her face for the first time in her life. Grief spots, maybe.

'Something of an heirloom, evidently,' she added. 'You're supposed –' she checked herself, suddenly.

'I'm supposed what?' Freddy asked. When she looked up he was glancing at his watch. Ordinarily that would have annoyed her – angered her, even – but today it was okay because it meant his mind was more on a meeting than her half-hidden suit.

When he was gone she pulled it from its case. She was careful because she had been taught respect for all good garments. When she laid it out across the white bedspread

180

it looked very much as though it was waiting to be worn. Or as though someone who was wearing it and lying sprawled had just de-materialized inside it.

She picked up the waistcoat and held it to the light. Then she pulled on her glasses and looked again. The stitches were so small and perfect she could barely believe a human hand had done them. She peered some more. Some were slightly different, small, but a little larger and less deft than the others. Not clumsy – certainly not clumsy. Still much tinier than most human fingers could execute. But different, all the same. So two people had stitched this.

She stopped. Looked away. There were words stitched in there, too. Kitty inhaled softly and bent her head again. It took a while to re-focus. It was small print, almost lost in the intricate design, in hebrew letters.

Why had she been so defensive and secretive when she saw Freddy find it? She started to chew her nails. He was supposed to wear it at their wedding. She stared at the garment. She hadn't even tried to see if the waistcoat would fit him. She lifted it carefully and held it to her own chest, then padded across to the mirror to have a look.

What wedding to Freddy?

Had she really thought that?

Of course they would be married – she just needed a little more time, that was all.

She touched the stitching. How much love had gone into that garment? Could what she and Freddy had ever match it?

The suit was like a reproach, reminding her of her history

and her culture but most of all setting a yardstick against which her own emotions should be measured.

She felt the dumb tears start to well again. Her father had worn the waistcoat at his own wedding, proud in the knowledge that he was carrying on the family history until he died. And now it was to stop. The business would be sold.

Kitty phoned Hester. Her mother sounded remarkably alert, almost as though she had been expecting the call. Maybe the jabs had worn off. Some of the madness had gone out of her tone.

'Is China there?' she asked. She knew already, though. She could hear kitchen noises in the background. China was as quiet as the dead in the rest of a home, but in the kitchen she became a demon, banging and crashing and whirling and washing.

'Nula says she will stay with you for a while, Kitty,' Hester told her. 'Is this a good idea?'

'I don't know, Mother,' Kitty replied. The thought of China's activity was making her feel tired. 'Look,' she said, raising her voice so Hester could hear clearly, 'about the suit, the old one you gave me . . .'

'The wedding suit,' Hester corrected her. 'You want to know what the words mean?'

Kitty paused. Was there something life had not yet told her? Was her own mother psychic?'

'It says: "Rosa, the daughter I love".' Hester hadn't waited for her reply. 'It was made by Dovid Zigofsky in Russia. He died making it, Kitty. Has Freddy seen it yet?'

'No,' Kitty told her quietly, 'he hasn't.'

*   *   *

182

The daughter I love. Had Dovid Zigofsky handed on his business to his daughter, too, along with his love and the wedding suit?

And had his daughter shuddered with fear at the prospect – the way Kitty was doing now?

CHAPTER EIGHTEEN

Z̶G

CALICO
*One of the most ancient of fabrics, calico takes its
name from Calicut, in Madras, where it was first
made. A coarse, cotton cloth, it is often used in the
trade to make up a fitting shell for a garment before
cutting the more expensive fabric.*

Kitty,

How easily am I fooled! Like Baile, Max promised a
palace and yet here I am in lodgings that make the hostel
look like a place of wondrous comfort!

Imagine the sinking of my heart as I stood outside the
Brick Lane premises of Maxwell Warkofski, Society Photographer! Count the amount of times I read the brass
wall-plate announcing this legend, all the while wondering
whether I have still possibly made a mistake in my translation! Follow me into the soot-darkened doorway, through
which even I am forced to stoop, and up the bare wooden
banisterless stairs to the attic!

Listen to the *schlemozzle* of wailing, prayers and crying
that emerges from each of the floors! It sounds as though
all the Jews in the world are packed into this one small
house! I smell *borscht* and *lockshen* and burning firewood,
and when I touch the walls the paint feels coated in grease
from all the cooking.

'Rosa!' Max has the door open before I can knock and I marvel at the fact that the shape and height of this gangling tall young man can fit into a room so small. Max *is* the room – he fills it almost entirely. I am shocked at the size of him there, suddenly, so much so that I take a step backwards before his white teeth devour me.

'Come in,' he insists, waving his arm with a flourish. It is only as he moves to one side that I see the scene in the room behind him. There is a white sheet hung from low ceiling to unclean floor and perched in the middle is a waxen-faced female clad only in a length of draped cloth.

'Miss Zigofsky,' says Max, 'meet Miss Molly d'Arboire.'

The girl rises to meet me, extending one hand while holding onto the fabric with the other.

'My name's Molly Nodd and I work as a nippy at the tearooms round the corner,' she tells me with a dimpled smile, 'but I pose for Max on me day off. He calls me d'Arboire because he says French sounds a little more classy. I don't know, though. I think he's pulling me leg. He's always pulling people's legs, did you know that, miss?'

Classy? To imagine how a man like Max would know anything about class! Richard Galliard is the one to tell you about class, breeding and business success, not Max Warkofski the conman!

Max begins to translate Molly's English, but I have understood enough to smile weakly in agreement. I look across at Max and he looks at the bags I am carrying and grins.

'So you decided to move in,' he says. I search my brains for a way out of this predicament but I have now quit the hostel and know I will be destitute if I leave this place.

185

Max doesn't wait for my answer in any event, but instead picks up my bag, though I am quicker than him and have hold of the case with the wedding suit before he can take it.

'Where is my room?' I ask, looking round. I hope it is not on the floor below because I heard barking dogs down there and wonder if there would be any sleep to be had.

'Here,' Max tells me, and Molly lets out a little spurting laugh.

Max moves to the end of the small room, which takes all of one pace, and tugs on a curtain that falls away from the wall. 'We use this to partition the place for now,' he says, 'then I will build us something more solid as soon as my last client pays me.'

I stare at him as though he is gone mad. 'I can't share this with you!' I say. 'I'm a respectable girl!'

Max smiles. 'And I'm a respectable man, Rosa,' he says, 'there's no need to fret. I use the place as a studio most of the day, which is while you'll be working, and you'll find I'm out most nights, so you'll have nothing to share. We'll barely meet to exchange greetings, let alone anything else.'

I sit on my case in the corner, thoroughly miserable at my plight, while Max finishes taking his photographs of Molly. Even in the depths of my sulk I notice how much the girl comes to life in front of the camera and how her ordinary features become almost beautiful as she changes her expression. Max, too, is a different character while he works. His long back is almost bent double over the camera and his features become serious for the first time. I feign indifference but in reality find myself totally absorbed by the strange scene in front of me. When Max straightens and announces he is finished for the night I look more disappointed than Molly.

I inform Baile of my change of address but tell her nothing of my new circumstances. The slack season in the rag trade is coming up, and we all work as hard as wasps in case we are selected for laying-off. Baile and I are already cut to a four-day week, which means I have nothing left to save. Max leaves food for me, which is all I have to exist on as I cannot afford to buy more. Sometimes he will leave a coin on the table and I will walk around to Bloomberg's on the corner of Old Montague Street to buy cheap off-cuts of delicious-tasting salami for our tea.

Max has partitioned the room more soundly and I sleep better at night behind my own little wooden-planked wall. Now that we have more than just curtain there, Max will often return home before I am asleep.

I am acutely embarrassed to be so close to a strange man. I find the smell of him in the room overpowering. He is clean enough for anyone's taste, but still I have discovered that men have a vastly different scent from women. It is an intimate smell, brashly animal and rather earthy. When I hear Max come home at night I stuff my blanket into my ears so that I will not hear him. He is a noisy sleeper. I pray I make no sound myself and take great pains to move as little as possible when I am in bed, so that my body is sore and aching in the morning from being coiled up and still all night.

Apart from the evenings, then, I find myself almost happy in the routine at Brick Lane, and the shorter week may be painful for my purse but it has greatly improved my health.

187

This is a ghetto where I live, but it is a friendly enough place nevertheless. Everyone is industrious and most people work to improve their lot and get out of the area, which is exactly what I am doing myself.

Their optimism is contagious. I am invited to visit neighbours – large families in cramped rooms where there is not one item of beauty and the beds stand with their legs in dishes of paraffin to keep bed bugs away – yet they all seem happy and proud enough and all are waiting until their business buys them places in Golders Green, where their wealthier relatives are already housed.

On the Sabbath, the Sabbath goys arrive to light up and although I have no coins for them there is one who does the job anyway, for nothing. His face was instantly recognizable to me, but it was some weeks before I identified him as one of Queer Tess's brood.

'So you have bettered yourself then?' I asked him, smiling. He looked surprised. 'You're no tosher, then?' I said. He blushed at this. 'I know your mother,' I added. 'Queer Tess works at the shelter where I first arrived. She showed me her family at work. When I saw you last you were about to go down a sewer.'

I saw by his face that I had embarrassed him. 'My name is Stanley and I am no tosher, not now,' he said, red-faced. 'My mother, who you call Queer Tess, died two weeks past of tuberculosis.'

I watched his back as he reached up to the gas mantle. I had forgotten that Tess's nickname was given by the women in the shelter.

'I'm sorry, Stanley,' I told him. He is barely a year older than myself. I asked what else he did during the week and he told me he delivered for the kosher poulterer in Wentworth Street, and that he and his friends will push a brazier around the streets on a barrow at Pesach, crying, '*Choomez, choomez*', when the Jewish folk will bring out their bread and pay the boys to take it away.

Stanley is committed to teaching me one word of proper London English a week. My first word is 'Asshole', which is a religious observance day in the English calendar, like our Sabbath. When I mentioned this day to the Evangelists they ushered me out of the building without my conversion coin.

Stanley has asked me to an evening at the Yiddish Theatre in Spitalfields. When I tell Max he looks annoyed. 'You should go if you wish, Rosa,' he says.

'I need a chaperon,' I tell him. He looks surprised.

'Why?' he asks.

'Because I am a young girl from a good family,' I say. It is the first time I have seen such an expression of seriousness on Max's face. 'My father may be dead,' I assure him, 'but there is no reason for me to become loose.'

Max is studying his large hands that are twice the size of my own. His head is dropped. Even uncombed, his hair gleams like pale seal-skin. His face, which is hidden, looks like that of an Italian nobleman, with a straight long nose and dark thick brows.

'Rosa,' he says sadly, 'all this stuff about being a well-brought up girl from a good family. You have no need to lie to me.'

I am confused.

'I am your friend, Rosa,' he says, raising his head, 'and friends are not judgmental. Whatever you have done is done. I would just ask you not to lie to me, that's all.'

'Lie?' I ask him. I feel angry at his accusation, but his tone has started me off crying.

'I know about the baby,' he says, gravely, 'I heard the talk on the ship. I'm sorry.'

I let out a wail.

'Rosa,' he says, clutching my hands, 'it doesn't matter – at least not to me. It only matters when you pretend to me to be something you're not.'

So he thinks I am a whore. I can barely draw breath for the shame that overwhelms me.

I stand up, choking.

'Rosa!' Max tries to take me in his arms and for a moment succeeds, so that I am pressed against his chest and surrounded by his smell and the soft fabric of his shirt.

'I see you now, Max!' I shout, pulling away. 'You think I am easy because of my dead child. You're wrong, you know. You understand nothing about what happened.'

I hate him for his concern and I hate him for knowing my secret. Does Baile know, too? No – she could not have kept information like that hugged to her chest for more than a moment.

As Max stands before me I see the expression in his eyes change. He is still mocking me but there is more there, too. He tries to take my hands but I am too fast for him and pull away. I dread his touch.

'Rosa,' he whispers, 'I just want to help.'

God save me from his help and his pity! My circumstances mean I am trapped like a fly in a web but I will not be grateful to Max Warkofski, photographer of half-dressed women! He might think of me as a damned and

190

lost woman, but I know the truth of my circumstances. I may be fallen lower than others of my sex, according to my religion, for what happened in the snow in my homeland, but I know I fought harder than I would for my life. Max has chosen his circumstances. Surely that must be worse?

How ugly my face must be right now, with its angry little expression!

I see the smile start to build across Max's handsome chops but I am there first with a sneer of my own.

'Rosa,' he says, 'why do you think I want to help you?'

'Oh, that is easy to answer,' I tell him. 'You wish I would tell the beautiful Baile what a gentleman you are so that she will take an interest. I am smarter than you think, Max. Did you believe I didn't know what you were about?'

Max sits down cockily on a chair and sets about lighting a cigarette. This proves to be quite a business as his matches appear to be damp.

'So why should I make a pass at you just now?' he asks once the smoke is rising.

I shrug. Who knows why men do what they do, as far as women are concerned. Menachem, Max, the man with the birthmark who raped me in the woods – can women ever understand such animal instincts?

'Could it be that it is little rabbit-faced Rosa that I love, I wonder?' Max asks. And then he laughs. He crosses his legs. His feet are big and his shoes are in need of repair. I wonder whether he knows this and I hope that it rains next time he leaves the house.

'You love Baile,' I tell him.

Max has a wonderful habit of which I am madly jealous

– namely, he can raise one eyebrow without disturbing the other. I have noticed this trick on many occasions and have always thought it the cleverest thing. It makes him appear reckless and sophisticated and I have tried to copy him for many hours while in my bed at night, but always fail. He does it now, and I feel the bile rise in the back of my throat.

'Tell me you don't, Max, and I'll call you a liar,' I say. To my shame I attempt the eyebrow stunt but only succeed in a bad imitation of Queer Tess's squint.

'Rosa,' Max says, his mouth chewing a laugh, 'at the risk of being called the greatest liar in the country I will state now that it is you I have feelings for. Maybe I should keep quiet and play the game for longer in the hope that you will come to your senses and realize this fact for yourself, but I'm not a patient man and – who knows, we could both be dead of the fever this time next week.

'I have never mentioned the child to you before because it matters not one wit to me how you came to bear it. I can only assume it was Aaron's and that this was why you were so relentless in your pursuit of him after he had fled to America.'

He pauses to inhale more of the odious smoke and I feel tears build in my eyes at the injustice of what he has just said.

'Rosa,' he is whispering now, but his voice is deep and it still fills the small room, 'it's you I have feelings for. I'm not a particularly religious man and I'm not a traditionalist. What's done is done. Did you imagine all men seek only beauty? I love your wit and your humour, though most of it is unintentional, and most of all I admire you for your spirit.

192

'We're very similar, you and I. We both want much out of life and we'll both fight to get it. You believe you want a marriage to Aaron, but I know you need more than that. Save the money for your journey if you must, but I'll stake my life you never spend it on the ticket.'

He is so smug, I could kick him.

'Once I have the money I will go,' I say.

To my intense irritation I watch his smile widen. He stands suddenly and is across the room in a leap to fetch something from a cupboard beneath the sink.

'Look,' he says, throwing a bag across at me, 'open it up.'

There is money inside the bag – enough for my trip from Liverpool and more besides.

'There it is, then,' he tells me, 'it's all yours, Rosa. You can be with your Aaron within the month. I would ask to take your wedding photographs but I'm afraid there's only enough in there for one fare.'

I stare at the notes and I look up at Max, wishing I were old enough and smart enough to play him at his own game. He has me now, though. He knows what I know. He knows America is just my dream. He knows I will never take the trip. Aaron didn't want me. I am not a fool. I know this much. If he did, he would never tolerate me after the shocking event in the snow. No good Jewish man would marry me now. I am worth less than nothing. Aaron has been my dream. He left Russia to escape me. Max has spoilt my game by calling my bluff. I hate him for this. Without our dreams and self-delusions we cease to exist. I push the money slowly back across the floor.

'Little Rosa.' He is out of the chair again and moving towards me. I see droplets of sweat on his brow and realize I have been fooled. He would never have allowed me to take it.

'Where did you get the money, Max?' I ask. He is silent for a change.

'Is it even yours?' I can't believe his cheek. He is shaking his head and smiling.

'No, Rosa, I'm looking after it for a friend.'

'So what if I had taken it?' I ask.

'I knew you wouldn't.'

'You cheat!' I cry.

'I needed to be sure,' Max tells me. 'Now I know you're staying for good.'

He believes I turned the money down for him. He thinks I have chosen him over Aaron. But it would choke me to tell him that Aaron doesn't want me.

'I am staying because I have fallen in love, Max,' I tell him, and the hope in his eyes is well worth the lie. 'I have feelings for the young man who owns the factory I work in,' I continue, 'his name is Richard Arthur Galliard and he is a gentleman with a proper business. I have written to Aaron's mother to break the news and she tells me Aaron is distraught. But who can decide whom to love? That's why I'm staying, Max. For Richard.'

I turn my back so that Max cannot see my face, which is full of the look of my own lies. He goes to move but then I hear him pause. I have ended his fun, then. He won't mock me any more, pretending to love me.

'Does this gentleman know about your child?' he asks. His voice has changed. It is so low I can barely hear it.

A baby cries from the floor below and I shudder at the coincidence.

'Of course,' I lie.

Another silence. I should feel victorious, but I don't, I feel ugly and hateful. Max just wanted to tease me. I should have laughed when he told me he loved me.

'I look forward to hearing of your betrothal, then,' Max says. He is taking the joke too far now. When I turn to face him his expression is stricken. I had no idea he was such a talented actor.

I join the game, smiling. 'Maybe you will get to take my wedding photographs after all, Max,' I tell him.

A darkness comes across his face without settling. Then it is gone and his smile is back, though there is something like anger still in his eyes. 'It would be my pleasure,' he replies.

'Rosa,' he adds, as he turns to leave the room, 'you could achieve many things if you would just be truthful to yourself.'

He is right, of course. I must forget Aaron and set myself towards other goals. Perhaps I am not so crazy in my new dreams about Richard Galliard. As Max said, not all men seek beauty in a woman, and I think he was honest enough about this, even if he lied about everything else.

Richard is wealthy and charming. Aaron did not want me and Max could not provide a good home for a goat. Would Rintzi and Gregory mind so much if I came home married to a different man, as long as he is capable of looking after us all? Perhaps I could keep my history to myself. Max has done me a good turn after all, with his teasing. I will marry Richard. I am sure of that now.

CHAPTER NINETEEN

ℤG

KIPPERS
*Girls who worked in the gentlemen's tailor shops of
Savile Row were never allowed to work on their own,
for decency's sake. So they earned the nickname
'kippers', because they always went around in pairs.*

Ever since I can remember I have been terrified of thunder-storms. Now I lie curled in my little bed one night and my stomach is sick with fear at the sight of the lightning from my window.

There is more to fear. Max is murdering Molly on the other side of the partition. I can hear her screams and am too much of a coward to move. First there was a wailing, with much shushing from Max. Then the wails rose to cries before I heard the sound suffocated, as though Max had his hand over the woman's mouth. Next he will be cutting her throat, I am sure of it.

Could our argument have prompted such murderous anger? My hands are over my mouth, stifling my own cries of fear. Could Max be the Ripper? I think back. He arrived in England the same time as us, not long after the Ripper had started his work. But was this Max's first visit? Could I have been living with a butcher for so long and not have known?

The cries are quiet now but this only makes me shake more, for I fear it means the job has been done and the woman is dead.

Somehow I fall into a sleep and when I wake it is to the smell of cigar smoke and frying eggs. I hear Max quit the room and make the long walk down to the water-closet in the yard and I creep around the partition, in mortal terror for what my eyes may find waiting.

The bed is empty and so is the room. I search everywhere but there is no body and no blood. Only eggs burning over an oil lamp.

Max returns, whistling and stamping his frozen feet.

'Rosa!' He is all smiles and his hair is uncombed. I look away quickly, for he is still in his nightshirt. 'Do you want some eggs?' he asks.

'There was a woman here,' I say, my voice trembling.

'A woman?' He is teasing me again. I wonder if he would murder me too.

'I can smell her perfume,' I tell him. He sniffs noisily and laughs.

'Are you jealous then, little rabbit?' he asks.

'Jealous?' My voice emerges as little more than a whisper. Who can be jealous of a corpse?

The following night it is much the same thing. I ask about the Ripper at work and someone gives me an old newspaper to read with much of the story inside it. My English is good enough now to make out the gist of what is written and I am sick at what I read. Could Max be this evil? I work late at the factory that night, rather than sleep in my own bed. When I do return to the house, almost fainting

197

from tiredness, I hear a woman's shrieks as I climb the final flight of stairs.

Terrified, I almost fall down the steps in my hurry to find help. I thump on the door of the downstairs room and shout until I hear the children cry and the face of old mother Grosselli, the children's grandmother, appears in the small gap between door and frame.

'There are murders upstairs!' I cry. 'I can hear Max Warkofski killing again!'

The old woman pulls a shawl off a peg behind the door and wraps it around herself before pushing past me and tramping upstairs. She is half my height but I am too nervous to walk anywhere but behind her.

Her legs are so thin and bandy I can see the bottom of our door through them as she bangs upon it with her wizened fist.

'Mr Warkofski! Mr Warkofski! What are you up to in there?' she shouts in Yiddish.

The door is pulled open and I stifle a scream. Max is there, stark naked and huge in the doorway. I look away quickly but not before I catch a glimpse of the room behind him. Molly is in his bed, smoking one of his cigars.

'You should be ashamed of yourself, Mr Warkofski!' I hear the old grandmother trill. Then there is Max's voice, amused and polite, apologizing for the noise and promising it will not happen again.

He has even charmed Mrs Grosselli, for it is me she is angry at now. 'You should learn to grow up, girl,' she says as she waddles off to her bed, 'you could have scared me to death with your shouting!'

How much of a child can I still be? How much can I

hate myself for my stupidity? The screams were a result of passion, and I thought they were cries of agony. Can this be what love is like between two people? I thought what I suffered in the snow in the forest was different from that which occurs between husband and wife, but it seems I was wrong. Do women suffer pain each and every time they are with their men?

It is at moments like this that I am at my worst, Kitty. All my courage goes and I wish to howl and be comforted. How much I miss Papa and Rintzi! To feel either of their arms about me and hear them shush me and kiss the top of my head would be worth more to me right now than my life itself.

Why does my mother not write to me? Has she heard of my current circumstances somehow? Is she shocked that her daughter has fallen so far? I think of our life in Moscow, of the days when we lived like royalty, when Papa was a master tailor and people came from miles to be fitted for his suits. The smell of the food in the house. The warm fires with the curling smoke.

Never be poor, Rosa.

'Never, Papa,' I promise out loud, 'I will never be poor again in my life.' If I am granted a way out of these circumstances I will be as wealthy as we were then, Kitty – wealthier, even.

Max appears to think this last embarrassment is all one huge joke and has not stopped laughing for over a week. He has no shame in his body, yet the neighbours still greet him warmly enough, while I am lucky for a nod.

*   *   *

199

My mood was raised a little at the workshop this week. The place is nearly empty now, as the slack season is upon us, and I had been sitting alone sewing French lace onto the collar of a frock when Richard Galliard walked into the room, accompanied by another man.

One of the machines had broken at the start of the week and it seemed Richard was about to attempt to mend it himself. From my position crouched over the work-table I watched as he removed his jacket and hung it over the back of a chair before rolling his sleeves up to reveal pale bare forearms that gleamed with downy fair hairs.

I could smell him, Kitty; not a stench of cheap soap and coal-smoke, which is how Max and I smell these days, but a scent of linen and fresh cloth and perfumed hair oil and lime cologne.

I cannot describe how this scent affected me, Kitty. It was as though part of my old life, my childhood, had walked into that grimy room to take me back to happier days. It was the smell of leisure and honour and fine values and refined pleasures. It was the smell of a man who takes time about his toilette, not a poor hungry wretch who barely splashes cold water about his person before rubbing himself with orange to mask the stench.

When Richard bent over the machine I was bold enough to raise my head. I could not have done otherwise, Kitty, even though I risked the sack. His hair fell across his brow, which was furrowed with concentration. I blushed to think that I had imagined him as my husband. What would he have ever noticed in me? And yet pride will allow its own delusions.

200

All at once he let out a cry and straightened, holding his index finger, which was covered with blood. My mouth dropped open but I was forced to double-back over my work, for fear of a reprimand.

Suddenly my name was called: 'Miss Zigofsky?' I looked up. Richard was staring at me. 'I wonder,' he asked, 'do you have any skill in first aid?' He was smiling, despite the blood. At that moment I believed I had never seen a man quite as brave.

I was off my stool and at his side in an instant, my face burning with delight at hearing my name from his lips. Not 'Rosa', or 'Rabbit', either, but 'Miss Zigofsky'.

Kitty, I cannot emphasize enough the thrill I felt at being appealed to in this way. Since leaving my homeland I had become a nobody to the outside world – my worth had diminished to the point where I could have been snuffed out like a candle and few would have noticed. The sound of status and respect made me fit to weep; that is the pitiable state I have come to, dearest. Max with his jokes and his sarcasm; the wariness of the other Jews in our ghetto, who now give me a wide berth on account of my strange circumstances; the contempt of the other bosses and employers; Kitty, it is all I can do not to agree with their assessment of me.

And yet here was the highest of them all, and he spoke to me as though I were a lady. His tone was soft and gentle. He smiled as he looked at me, but the smile was *for* me, Kitty, not caused by me. My spine straightened with pride at the sound of it.

'Miss Zigofsky.' The way Richard Galliard said those two words made me feel like the person I should have

201

been, had Papa not been forced to move us all to The Pale of Settlement.

Richard held out his wounded hand. 'I hope the sight of blood does not make you feel faint, Miss Zigofsky,' he said.

I shook my head, blushing. If only we had met in another place at another time in a different situation. If only I had been well-dressed and my cheeks had been rouged with cosmetic, rather than mortification. If my poor, pin-marked hands could have been gloved. If I had smelt of anything other than machine-grease and coal tar.

How long did I stand there, Kitty, staring at Richard's proffered hand and not daring to step forward to touch it? Can you imagine the first contact of flesh with a man from whom you had previously been banned from raising your eyes?

You are of a good family, Rosa, I told myself over and over, calm yourself or he will think you are simple in the brain.

Two drops of ruby blood fell to the floor between us, shocking me into action. I know you will think me soft, Kitty, but I feared he might bleed to death before my eyes and that it would be no one's fault but my own.

How did his flesh feel as I was bold enough to touch it? Like any other skin, but softer and warmer. It was the colour of camel-hair fabric next to my own pallid fist. Even Papa did not have hands like that, for he had always worked physically and it appeared to my eyes that Richard never had.

All I felt from this man as I examined his wound was kindness and politeness. His concern for my own well-being seemed to far outweigh any for himself. As our heights were so disparate he sat on the tailor's stool and nimbly lit a cigarette with his free hand.

We were so close, Kitty. And do you know what my thoughts were of? Of how I would crow to Baile about the whole thing. Even while my heart lay in the back of my throat, flapping like a landed fish, my main thought was of how jealous that girl would be.

My English became confused, yet I was able to tell Richard with some authority that the cut was not a deep one, but that it should be washed and bandaged.

'Well, let us do that very thing, then,' he said. I looked up into his eyes, which were directly upon me. I wanted more than anything in the whole world to return his smile and I think I did, though I cannot be sure. Perhaps I just kept the surly little rabbit face I normally wear these days. In any event, his own expression did not falter.

We walked to the sink and I turned the tap, taking care not to splash us, while he held his finger beneath it and all the while I could smell the many scents from the fabrics that he wore.

He watched me as I bandaged, not my handiwork. Looking at his wound and feeling his eyes upon me I thought all at once of Gregory and his poor fingers in the snow. I felt a rush of tender affection that was as much for my beautiful brother as for this auburn-haired man beside me, though the affection overwhelmed me, nevertheless.

'Where are you from?' he asked. I did not dare look up now, for my eyes had tears of remembrance in them, but told him in a strong enough voice that I had family in Russia but that I lived in Brick Lane.

203

'In a nice warm family house?' he asked. I paused and then nodded. What else could I say? If I told him the circumstances of my life he would have thought less of me than he already did, as a mere employee.

When I had finished tying the bandage he held the finger up for examination. 'A splendid job!' he announced, which set me off blushing again. 'If only you had not used our most expensive lace to do it,' he added. I looked up with shame. In my hurry I had pulled out the nearest cloth that had come to hand.

'Never mind, we can take it from your wages, I expect,' he said. Then he saw my expression. 'Or maybe not – look, there was a lot of blood. Have some of this, won't you? I believe we've earned it for our bravery.' He took a silver flask from his pocket and poured some liquid from it into a small cup that formed the lid, offering it to me first before downing the lot in one when I refused. Some colour returned to his face when the alcohol had taken effect.

'Thank you,' he said, smiling. I tried to hold that expression in my mind like a photograph, to cheer me through, like soup on a cold day. If only Baile had been there to see us my pleasure would have been complete.

I awake to the sound of whispering from the next room. My body is bent and my leg, which is underneath, is dead.

'Keep yourself quiet,' I hear, 'for I don't want to wake Rosa again.'

There is a woman's laugh. 'I believe there is something between you two, the way you talk of her.'

'Unfortunately not. She won't have me.'

'She?' More laughter, but suppressed. 'Max, you are joking.'

'No, but – like yourself – she is convinced that I am.'

I hear the woman's laugh turn to something else between a snort and a groan. There is silence save the movement of sheets, then I hear Max moan, low and quiet. I can stand it no more. I am shameless but I no longer have control over my actions. My room is dark but a candle flickers on the other side of the partition.

Sliding out of my low bed I tiptoe the two steps to the dividing wall. The wood feels cool as I place my face against it. I pause for a second before turning to look. The wood is old and cracked into slits. I press my whole face against the largest crack, which I can peer through into Max's half of the room.

The light is yellow and dim. There is Max's small bed, as narrow and low as my own, and on top of it the model, her face turned to the ceiling and her plump legs bent and parted. There is a blue bruise on her fat knee and another smaller one at the top of her thigh. Her eyes are closed to slits and her mouth is held open in a half-smile. It is an expression of happy reminiscence. 'Ah yes, now I remember that!' is what her face says. She gasps a small gasp and I have to turn away from the intimacy of the scene.

My body throbs in warning. I fear I will be ill from shock yet still I turn back for more. I know something of what is what – I am a child who has lived in the country and who has watched animals at work on one another in the fields. I have had the same treatment myself, though I can see nothing of my own suffering reflected on this girl's face.

205

Max is a fine beast. How could he behave in such a way? His body is huge and rippling in the candle-light. If the partner beneath him had been a horse I could understand the pleasure his heavy thrusts might cause, but she is a frail girl like myself, despite her chubby legs, and I cannot see how she can survive such an onslaught, let alone savour it. I want to cry out to stop them, for she reminds me so much of my own self, when I was taken in the snow. Max is little better than the creature with the mark on his forehead.

The whole of his body is tensed with concentration and effort, as the father's had been when he took me. He is between her legs and his torso lays where her body is most vulnerable. Without clothes to cover him his body is golden and damp.

How can they be so unashamed? There is no sheet to hide them and yet they go about their business with happy concentration. The girl begins to moan and Max bends his head to kiss her quiet. Such a kiss! His mouth is full open and devouring! Her arms fall to her sides and coins tumble out of her hand and roll onto the floor as her fingers unclasp and straighten.

She could be in a swoon now, except that her back is arched and the soft moans spill endlessly from her lips. The throbbing is worse in my body. Why do I watch when my pain almost matches the agony of my memories? Can spying be such a sin that it brings its own punishment in the form of disease? I feel my whole body burning and press it against the cold wood to cool. My breathing is so loud from fear that I am terrified they might hear me and know that I have been watching.

The veins on Max's body stand out in dark relief. His face holds an expression of such agony I am forced to wonder if the effort is worth it. His buttocks curl in and his body contorts as though a current has run through it. He pulls away from the girl suddenly and violently, throwing himself back onto the mattress with a cry of pure agony, his penis a swollen, dark wet thing that spurts fluid in an arc with each and every convulsion of his body.

I feel waves of sickness and horror coursing through my body with each and every spurt from his own. I turn away quickly, disgusted and ashamed and ill. My legs are too weak to carry my own weight and I slide to the floor, shivering.

This is no good, this is bad. I am a girl from a good Moscow family and this is the most wicked thing I have ever done or seen. What happened in the woods was not of my choosing, but this I have stood and watched like a common whore. I retch silently, trying to banish the taste of my own spit from my mouth. My stomach is in spasm from the wretchedness of it all. I must move away from this place where wickedness happens. I belong in a world like Richard's. It is my birthright. It is what Papa would have wanted for me.

When I wake in the morning I have a fever and am unable to raise my head from the pillow. Max discovers me and brings the doctor, even though I tell him I am unable to pay the fee.

'Is it the tuberculosis?' I ask when the doctor has gone. There are two sick of the same thing in our workroom and I know the disease is rife in the garment trade all over London.

'No, Rabbit,' Max tells me, smiling, 'you have a slight fever, that's all. A couple of days in bed and you should be back at your beloved machine again.'

He strokes my hair gently and I am too weak to complain. I am disgusted, repulsed and at once fascinated by him. I would never marry such an animal. A gentleman would never treat his wife in such a way. I would rather die than submit myself to such a trial.

My fever is worse than Max supposed. I drift from sleep to half-sleep and he always seems to be there.

'Tell me a story,' I ask one night, for I have become a child again in my dreams and Max is my papa, stroking my hair from my hot wet face while he waits for the fever to break.

'I won't tell you a story, little Rosa, I'll tell you a truth,' I hear Max whisper into my ear. His voice sounds kind and gentle enough. This is Max my friend again – the animal has gone.

His story is of himself when he was a small child in Russia. His parents were farmers and he was the youngest of six boys, all of whom were old enough and big enough to help their father in the field all day.

It was Max's greatest dream at the age of six to be man enough to help his papa too. There was a small stream dividing the house from the fields, though. The ditch was the symbol of manhood in the family, because only when a boy was big enough and strong enough to jump the stream could he join the others on their walk to the fields.

Each day Max would join the line of men and boys as they walked to the fields with their plough tools over their shoulders and each day he would find himself left behind as the others leapt the stream while he was left scrambling about on the bank. He would be at least twelve years before his legs were long enough, his father told him.

Max was six years and three months before he had his great idea. He disappeared from the house at night and in the morning when his father and brothers walked to the fields they found Max had toiled for hours, digging earth into the ditch to narrow it to the point where he could just about hop across on his little plump legs. He joined his brothers in the fields that day, even though his arms were too short to handle most of the adult tools.

'So you see, little Rosa,' Max whispered into my ear, 'you can achieve anything if you will only be honest about your goals and determined enough to be clever.'

At least I believe that is what he tells me, though my brain is too addled with the fever to know whether I am dreaming or not.

CHAPTER TWENTY

ZG

HAUTE COUTURE
*Exclusivity was once essential to the fashion business.
In 1868, the* Syndicale de la Couture Parisienne *was
established, becoming the* Chambre Syndicale *in 1911.
Designs lodged with the* Chambre *were protected by a
strict copyright. Today, couture is seen more as a lost
leader, with just two to three thousand clients
worldwide.*

If Kitty needed reminding about the history of her family's
business, she had only to look in the newspapers. As the
story of their tragedy rolled on, so the size and scope of
articles on the subject increased.

There were double-page spreads in the more up-market
tabloids now. Many found poetic comparisons between
Gabriel's murder and the predicted, some said, inevitable
death of the British rag trade. The *Telegraph* contained a
grisly-looking shot of the whole family arriving at the
inquest: Burgess princely and contained, his hands stuffed
into jacket pockets and eyes fixed firmly on distant hori-
zons; Hester arm-in-arm with China, both clad in understated dark sheaths and wide-brimmed hats; Chloe out
front in a navy crepe trouser suit she had purloined from
the current collection and festooned with black pearls;

Nula lagging behind away from the rest, head down and face hidden behind fly-faced shades; and then Kitty, of course. How did she look? Determined? Confused? It is difficult to read your own face. Young? Old? She looked shocked. Stricken. They all did.

And there, behind them all, strode Nicky Kofteros. Only his expression was clearly defined – one of respect, solicitude. Greed? Glee? Kitty peered more closely but the picture dispersed into impressionistic newsprint dots.

So Nicky had even wormed his way into the family group, now.

Kitty tilted back her head as a nuclear cloud of anger grew inside her. How could this happen? Gabriel would have . . . but she switched that thought off quickly. Enough people had been misquoting her father already – 'Gabriel would have wished this,' 'It's what your father would have wanted.' It didn't need one more voice interpreting his thoughts for him.

Yet she was unable to stop herself. Gabriel would have been incandescent with rage at the sight of that man walking with the family group in such a complacent manner. And at such an intimate time. He would never have allowed it. It was the type of disrespect he had died trying to prevent.

Another paper had the same photo, but with the copy reading more as a fashion spread, each outfit dissected in minute detail. What was this, funeral fashions? How much could Kitty do to avenge her father? Should more lives be ruined, for the sake of . . . what? What would she be fighting for? Her head filled with thoughts that spilt from her eyes in the shape of yet more salty tears.

She pulled off her glasses. Only they weren't *her* glasses.

211

They were her father's, the pair he wore for designing. She had picked them up in the studio and then pretended to herself she'd put them on by mistake, thinking they were her own. They were too big but not unwearable. They smelt of him. They made her look more like him. When she concentrated on the newspaper she even pulled the same face. The focus wasn't bad.

The phone rang.

'Kitty, my dear, I believe you should be informed of a certain unpleasant development.' It was the showroom manager. 'I tried to contact your brother Burgess, but he is evidently in meetings all day. At any rate, you should know too. You spent more time with us while your father was alive. Prepare yourself. Raphael has left. Walked out on us. Gone. What a bastard, eh?'

'Oh.' It was all she could say. The manager ranted for a few minutes more before Kitty placed the receiver in its cradle without further comment and stared off into space.

Her father's precious designer, Raphael, whose destiny it was to save the house single-handedly, according to Gabriel. His protégé. The first rat to leave the submerging tub. The first one to choose to avoid going down with the rest of them. Kitty wished she could be more surprised at the news. Who could blame him?

There was worse, though. Something her feigned indifference couldn't quite cope with. An unexpected low punch while her attention was momentarily diverted. Something the showroom manager had said that was taking longer to sink in than the rest.

It was Freddy's father who had poached Raphael. Of course. It was the sweetest pain, almost unbearable in its intensity which – thank God – was relatively short-lived. Kitty squeezed her eyes shut as she waited for the worst of it to pass. She heard the rational voice, the 'Kitty' voice, like soothing ointment in her mind: He had to go before we closed . . . we offered him nothing . . . he worked for our father, not us . . . why shouldn't Freddy's father take him? . . . isn't all fair in business? But the *new* voice, the voice of the anger cloud, rose up and roared louder: Raphael deserves to be trodden on, squashed, like a worm. Freddy's father warrants worse. It was disrespectful. They were taking the piss. Dancing on her father's grave.

It should never be allowed. Never.

'Fight them, Kitty. Do not allow this to happen.'

Who had said that? The woman's voice, heavily accented.

Kitty's head snapped up, her eyes wide open. Who had she heard? She looked around but the room she stood in was empty.

Fight them?

And get killed as well?

Who had said such a dangerous thing?

The phone rang again.

'Did you see the photographs I left for you, Kitty?' It was as though the receiver had become red hot in her hand. She threw it onto the floor before scrabbling to get it back onto the cradle.

Voices, so many voices. And now the murderer – phoning her to gloat. The photographs. The wedding shots. Had he been in her father's office? Did he have keys? He knew her address and her phone number. The voice had sounded sleepy and distorted. Did she know it? The phone rang again, making her jump.

213

'No!'

She let it ring. When the noise became unbearable she curled into the foetal position and closed her eyes. The clues were all there. The voices were driving her mad. She had to think. She needed time.

'Kitty, dearest?'

'Keep quiet.'

It had to be said.

CHAPTER TWENTY-ONE

ZG

LANDSLEIT

In September 1888 the Jewish Chronicle *reported the death of a four-month-old child, found '. . . suffocated in bed, probably by overlaying.' It was discovered that the child's parents lived together with their seven children in a room in Spitalfields that was only twelve foot square, and for which they were paying four shillings and sixpence per week.*

Should I tell you more about my work, Kitty? First I must say that it is something I am good at. When I watch Baile, who was first to the job before myself, I am amazed at her comparative lack of talent. While she is still classed as 'General Hand', which is the lowest grade of worker, I have been promoted to operating one of the Singer machines, which is an easier life indeed.

I arrive in the dark and I leave the same way. When my feet make their way up the narrow brick stairs – rushing, for I am usually close to being late, thanks to Max's nocturnal activities, which are difficult to sleep through – I smell hot oil from the finisher's lamps which must burn the whole day through as the old man's eyes are growing weak with age.

There is a general movement from among the piles of

old rags on the floor, which means the rest of the poor folk employed there are stirring from their sleep. The smell is none too pleasant, as you may guess, and there is a rush for the latrines as any further acts of defecation during the day will mean pay being docked in lieu of time off.

We have one worker off with tuberculosis and two stricken with the cough, which is audible above the clatter of the machines and which makes my stomach heave. During the lean season we are no more than four in the whole room, but in busier times we may number as many as twelve. There is a great amount of chattering, hawking and general groaning, but all this noise ends abruptly the minute the shift starts.

We are all made aware of this magical moment because young Mr Yanzdoff, the boy who sits at the desk by the door and who takes it upon himself to act as our overseer, will clamber onto his desk and stand to attention for a full minute, staring at his pocket watch, his arm raised in the air. When the hour strikes he will fling his arm down to his side in the most dramatic fashion, which would make us all laugh were it not for the fact that we have to commence work at that point, and quickly, too – or else!

My machine is off like a rocket, whether or not there is fabric on board.

From that moment on there is nothing but work, and the only voice heard all day is that of the new under-presser, who is ancient enough to be so close to death as makes no difference and therefore deaf as a post and unable to hear his own Yiddish mumbling.

Our main product is men's wear, and cheap and terrible

stuff it is, too. The fabric is mostly the coarsest serge, which is so thick in texture that it will buckle anything other than the largest and most cumbersome of needles, this being a fact that failed to be pointed out to me when I commenced my job, along with the rule that those needles that I did manage to bend in my labours would be replaced with money from my own pocket. The quality of this cloth is so poor and its nap so cruel that I wonder at the fate of the skin of the people who wear it, for my hands are chaffed raw as I sew it.

The colours are drab, Kitty, and the dye holds badly enough to stain our fingers. I am mainly engaged in sewing trouser-seams, and there is a gentleman tailor given the task of working on the gusset-seams, as it is considered indecorous for a young unmarried lady to be handling such areas.

On the whole I find this work hard and unfulfilling and tend to allow quality to be sacrificed to quantity. Occasionally, though, there will be garments sent in from the couture side of the business, when a rush job is needed, and then the story is different.

It was Mr Galliard who first involved me with this, careering through the factory red-faced and carrying arm-fuls of exquisite fabric.

'Where is our little miracle-worker?' he asked. My head rose slowly but my heart leapt when I discovered him looking in my direction. 'Yanzdoff tells me you can do skilled work,' he said. Yanzdoff – not master or mister! I could not resist the urge to peep at the overseer's face, which was the colour of the flesh of the ripe watermelons that are sold in the park!

'I can, sir!' I cried. And I heard Baile snort with laughter at the desperate, willing tone in my voice.

But Richard was smiling with relief. 'Can you do anything with this?' he asked, throwing the fabric down on top of my machine.

I fell silent at the first touch of the fabric. Suddenly I was back in Moscow again and my father was teaching me all about cloth and sewing. The scent of the stuff overwhelmed me and I discovered in an instant that fabric will smell as good anywhere in the world. I wished to press my face into it all and suffocate in the beauty of it. I have no memory of colour, only texture and scent. I was home again. My eyes filled with tears. It was as though Richard were bringing me my own past, piece by piece.

I pulled the garment away from my machine, for fear the oil might stain it, and shook it so that it fell the length of my lap. It was a morning-dress, partly finished, but with the bodice and sleeves unattached and much of the fine stitching and embroidery still to be done.

'We lost the tailor to TB last night,' Richard whispered, 'and the dress must be finished by tomorrow. Can you manage? There are no other workers to spare right now.' He spoke politely as always, but almost as though we were friends.

Max says the feelings I have for my boss are no more than a girlish passion, but there is more to it than that, I know it. His was the only free and untroubled soul that I had seen since Papa had died. He was there to remind me that another world existed outside my own miserable circle. He provided hope of a better life. His smile was so easy and his brow so clear. He was clean, Kitty, clean and well-mannered. I would have clung to him if I could, for he was the only hope I saw of improving my lot.

I thought for an instant of the poor wretch of a tailor who had died like my father with his work unfinished. Then I nodded. After all, none of us has a lot that is easy to bear, exactly.

'Good.' Richard looked around, relieved. 'Good!' He stopped short. I followed his gaze. To my amazement Baile had risen to her feet with an expression approaching anger on her pretty, pale-pink-pig face.

The whole room stopped work to look at her. Her hands were clenched into fists and her arms shook. The pinkness drained slowly from her face, along with the prettiness.

'I could do that work.' Her voice came out as little more than a whisper, but she could have shrieked the words for the impact they had.

Richard smiled politely enough and began to turn away.

'I said I could do that work,' Baile repeated, louder this time. I would have gasped at her daring had I had the guts in my belly to do so.

Richard turned back to face her. 'Well, the job is Miss Zigofsky's now,' he said, still with more manners in his tone than Baile deserved.

'Richard!' The word came out of Baile's mouth in a wail. I watched the boss's face redden as the smile fixed upon his mouth appeared to tighten, then he turned again and was gone.

My own jaw was hanging open like a gaping idiot's and would not close. 'Richard!' The word hung in the air as embarrassing and distasteful as a fart. I believe we all expected a combustion at that moment, the room was so

219

heavy with expectation at Baile's show of disrespect. In the end it was I who signalled the silence to stop, by spurring my machine into action, which broke the spell and sent us all back about our business.

When some sanity had returned to the room I paused in my sewing to study the dress on my lap. It was pale, silver-grey wool – the colour of the moon as seen through the grime of the small window in my bedroom. The fabric had the appearance of a *piqué* – firmly woven but soft as suede to handle, and lined with a cream sateen.

I supposed the garment to have been near completion at some stage, but then pulled apart following a fitting. At the waist hung a line of small pale yellow silk pockets, all weighted to keep the bodice in place against the corset. I ran my fingertips across the feather stitching that held the darts in position. The tailor had a good eye, but not as good as my father's. The skirt was simply cut – straight at the front but fuller at the back and hemmed in stitching that matched the tiny gold glass beads that decorated it.

I did not dare use the heavy pins I employed for the serge, so stole some finer ones from one of our tailors who was still, happily, in shock from Baile's outburst.

The skirt was so heavy it took all my efforts to stop it falling onto the floor. I needed a dummy to work on, to take the weight, yet there was only one in the building and that the size of a portly old man.

I was so excited by my task by now that thoughts of Baile and the scene she had caused merely flitted through my mind. What was she about? I caught her eyeing me more than once, but decided to pretend not to have noticed the glares that she threw me.

It was not yet dawn when Richard returned and I, to my shame, was sound asleep over my machine.

'Miss Zigofsky?' His whispered voice in my ears had me awake in an instant. His dear face was the first thing I saw as I opened my eyes. He too appeared to have slept badly. His hair was uncombed and there was a sour smell, like alcohol, on his breath.

'It's finished!' I said, watching the knot of worry in his expression unravel with relief. I held the dress up for his inspection.

'Try the thing on for me, it's no good throwing it about, and we have no stand in this place,' Richard said. I stared at him.

'Try it on?' I asked. I looked around at the live-in workers but they were mostly sound asleep and snoring. I held the garment at arm's length, thanking God I was a regular with the soap and hot water, and so would not soil the thing by putting it onto my body.

I felt this was my God-given moment come at last. In the wonderful dress Richard would see me as the well-bred girl I once was, instead of the poor, unfortunate wretch who currently graced his stinking workroom. He would be overwhelmed by the sight of Rosa Zigofsky, the master tailor's daughter from Moscow, and wonder why he had never noticed me in such a way before. I could make him love me, I was sure of that, if I could only once get him to see me in my proper position in life.

I was sent outside to the rag-room, where the air hung heavy with the stench of mildew. I had no great love of this room and avoided it when possible. Stacked high with mouldering bolts of cloth and paper awaiting collection from the rag man, it was home to many large brown rats. Clearing a space with my toe in the middle of the floor, I tore off my own shabby outer-dress and pulled the pale grey *piqué* over my head.

I should have guessed. The dress fitted me no better than a potato flour sack. It hung about my scrawny neck and my mean undergarments, which were grey with age, showed front and back of the generous bodice. Mortified, I emerged slowly from the rotting room and stood stock still as Richard struggled to prevent the pity from showing on his face.

'It is, of course, fashioned for a much larger client,' he said, kindly. I looked down at my arms and realized they were about an exact match to the colour of the fabric itself. Only my bosom appeared keen enough to be on nodding terms with the dress – the rest of my torso shunned all contact whatsoever.

I silently vowed to eat any and all food I could lay my hands upon in future so that I should never be shamed in this way again. The sight came into my mind of Max's model, Molly Nodd, laying stretched out like a cat across his bed. Her legs were as fat as little sausages and her knees had dimples. How would my legs look under such circumstances?

Suddenly, in my exhausted state, I saw myself pinned to Max's mattress like a pile of grey kindling while his entire body heaved on top of me. I heard his cries as my skinny legs rose into the air, like flagpoles, at the passion of it all . . .

'Miss Zigofsky?' Richard was looking at me. 'Are you well?' I heard him ask. 'Your face is flushed.'

My hand flew to my throat. Max Warkofski was the devil, I decided. Look what he was doing to my thoughts!

Perhaps the most galling thing of all was that, while I grew thinner, so Baile grew plumper by the day. Her uncle's family must be feeding her up for the wedding, I decided, though no mention of that event had been made for many months now and I began to suspect that it may have been consigned to the same fate as my own glorious marriage to Aaron.

I decided her delayed marriage to be the cause of her outburst in the workroom. She ignored me for days afterwards, and when she did relent and speak to me at last I was surprised at her tone, which was unexpectedly bitter for such a doll-faced girl.

'You do know how stupid you are, Bertha Zigofsky?' she asked me one morning as we passed in the street outside the sweat. 'Do you think Richard Galliard would look twice at a rabbit-faced girl like yourself? You may think you know everything, but allow me to inform you there are many things of which you are entirely ignorant – many things.'

'Ignore her, Rosa,' said the voice in my head, so I applied what I took to be a superior expression and planted it upon my face. If Baile Kluchersky was idiot enough to imagine Richard would as much as look at her twice after her show in the workroom, then she was an even greater fool than she looked.

CHAPTER TWENTY-TWO

ZG

COSTING
Costing a garment can be an elaborate business.
Besides the cost of the fabric and trimmings, the price
must include the amount of labour involved at every
stage of the outfit's evolution. A couture dress may
take as long as a month to be made up.

A fashion house showroom at season time should be a place of rabid mania. When Kitty walked into Zigo, though, the only noise to court her ears was an eerie hush. Chloe had draped the windows in acres of dramatic black tulle as a gesture of mourning. The place looked and sounded like a chapel of rest. There was more racket from the paparazzi stomping about on the pavements outside than there was from staff in the workrooms.

One or two of the finishers sat stitching in a rather aimless fashion – though more from habit than anything else – their glasses resting on the ends of their noses. Otherwise, Kitty found herself stared at in silence.

She walked to the end of the workroom, to the board where the sketches of the new range were pinned: eighty colour crayon drawings, mostly in Raphael's hand. Maybe a dozen or more were in her father's smudgy style, too. There were always eighty garments in Gabriel's off-the-peg collections – no more and no less. The first season Raphael had worked for them he had sketched eighty-two. Gabriel had lit up a cigarette and told the designer he would have to scrap two of them. They had argued for over an hour. Raphael had roared and thrown things. But at the end there had been only eighty – there always were.

'Are we finished?' asked Georgina, Gabriel's PA. Impossibly posh but grimly loyal, Georgina had once been Gabriel's house model and only moved backstage when a car accident had left her with an arthritic knee.

Kitty had always been rather in awe of Georgina. At only twenty-seven she had the air and carriage of a *grande dame* and the laugh and language of a navvy. Her face was long and pointy and her red hair cut into a sharp, earlobe-length Louise Brooks bob.

'You do know Raphael's pissed off?' she asked. Kitty nodded.

'How many of these are finished?' Her mouth pursed in concentration as she gestured towards the sketches. Georgina whistled through the characteristic gap between her front teeth. 'You know the marking system, Kitty,' she said, 'gold stars for finished, mauve dots for those done in the workroom, green for the outworkers, that's . . .' she squinted her eyes, 'fifty-five finished and costed, ten at final fitting stage, three lurking somewhere in your sister's wardrobe, two out being shot by *Vogue* for an exclusive preview deal rigged up by the PR, eight still being seamed and two at pattern stage,' she said.

Kitty frowned. 'Can they be finished in time?' she asked. Three in Chloe's wardrobe. Two being ruined on location. The anger cloud was trying to form in her head again.

225

The PA raised her eyebrows and shrugged. 'I think we all thought this season was dead in the water by now. When Raphael walked, we –'

'We have three days,' Kitty interrupted her. 'Can the range be ready for the show?'

'Oh Jesus, Kitty, without a designer?' Georgina's alarming laugh transmuted into a cough.

'Where's Alain?' Kitty asked.

A lanky, dark-haired young guy in black jeans and a baggy white shirt ambled across on cue. He said a couple of words in French to Georgina and then half-smiled at Kitty.

Alain was Mr shit-hot-graduate from St Martin's. Gabriel had snatched him from the previous year's shows at the Business Design Centre in Islington to be Raphael's workroom manager and assistant. As a manager he was crap – which was why another, more experienced man had been brought in for the job – but his talent as a designer had impressed Kitty's father immensely.

'Can you get this lot finished?' Kitty asked him. His laugh was spasmodic, like Georgina's.

There was a mania buzzing round in Kitty's head like a lazy fly, waiting to settle. Where was Burgess? Why wasn't he doing this? What about Chloe? Why was she home playing dressing dolls when she should be there kicking ass by the knicker-load?

Alain saw Kitty's expression and his laugh downgraded to a shadowy grin. 'In three days?' he asked, rubbing his chin. 'Without sleep,' he shrugged, 'maybe.' He was cropped-haired, unshaven. His eyes looked as though he had missed a few nights of slumber already. His deep voice

226

made him sound older than his twenty-three years. He smelt of French cigarettes and a surprisingly nifty lemon cologne.

Kitty led him into the machine-room. The place was noisier, friendlier. A radio was blaring pop music. Women chatted above the insistent rattle as they worked. There were boxes everywhere, all overflowing with a jumble of hats and accessories for the coming show. A girl sat beside a pile of thirty-nine pairs of shoes, taping the bottom of the soles so that the models could turn smoothly on the catwalk. In the larger studio the finished samples hung bagged and with last-minute instructions in Gabriel's hand pinned to the front of each one.

This was the first season Kitty had not been involved in since the age of ten. This was the year she was supposed to get married, not immersed in the usual chaos of missed deadlines and screaming schedules.

She fingered a couple of the outfits. There was a lull, an unseen intake of air – a pre-tempest vacuum about the place. Something vital had been sucked out of the room.

'If we go ahead with this show and it is anything less than a total financial success, we get eaten alive by the men-in-suits,' she told Georgina and Alain.

'And if it works?' Georgina asked.

'Then we probably sell to them anyway.'

'I see.'

'And are all these suit-men like the one that is sitting scratching his balls in your father's office right now?' Alain asked.

Kitty looked at him. 'Who?'

227

Georgina almost blushed. 'Nicholas Kofteros,' she said, looking down. 'He's been here for over an hour. He said he was waiting for you.'

Kofteros had his back to the door when Kitty entered – and for a frozen-in-aspic, show-stopping moment she thought it was Gabriel waiting there for her, for both men had the same broad shoulders and thick, greying hair. Therefore her anger had time to dissipate, first into hope and then into fresh-laundered grief, before he turned.

'I'm sorry,' he said politely, 'I was told I could wait for you in here. I'm afraid I became fascinated by these photographs behind your father's desk . . .'

They were the shots she had found the other evening. She stared at Kofteros's smile and a terrible suspicion started to form in her head. Could it have been his voice on the phone? Had *he* sent her the picture and left the others piled up for her to see? Was it Kofteros who had had her father killed, and who was now trying to scare her out of the business?

'I hope you know you are just exactly like a vulture, Mr Kofteros,' Kitty told him, 'circling in the skies on behalf of the Waika Group . . .'

'My actual job description is European Marketing Director for Waika,' Kofteros replied, his expression unchanging, 'and I came here to tell you some good news, not to hover.'

He paused. There *was* no good news he could tell her, Kitty thought, unless he was about to combust spontaneously and die in agony right there on the carpet.

'They have arrested your father's murderer,' Kofteros

228

said soberly, offering her her own father's chair to sit down on as the news sank in.

Kitty stood. 'How could they?' she asked. 'You're still here.'

She hated Kofteros and she loathed his arrogant manner. She wanted it to be him who had planned the execution. He was someone she could almost enjoy hating. She'd wanted to shock him – she'd hoped to wipe the expression of mock-concern off his face with her words. To her amazement she discovered she was no longer scared for herself, only determined that this man would never succeed in taking over the business.

'I wish you could understand whose side I am on, Kitty,' Kofteros said. 'I am here to help you and your family's business.' He moved towards her. His hands were even stretched out to take her by the arms. He was going to pretend he was worried for her now. Kitty stepped out of his reach. Carefully, but not nervously. Something flickered across Kofteros's face at last. Had he really looked hurt? His hands dropped to his sides.

'The man who is being questioned about killing your father was one of his outworkers. Ricky Khan,' he said quietly. 'As you undoubtedly know, Gabriel laid off his entire factory last season. Zigo was evidently their main source of regular income, and the business was due to close as a result of the lost revenue. The murder was done professionally – a revenge killing. Mr Khan must have paid a great deal of money . . .'

'Ricky Khan was one of my father's oldest friends,' Kitty interrupted him. 'He is also like an uncle to me. When Ricky first arrived in this country it was my father who

229

gave him a job and enabled him to bring the rest of his family over. He understood my father's decision was a business one, and inevitable. He would never have had my father killed.'

Kofteros shrugged. 'I understand your doubts,' he said, 'but stress can do strange things to a man's mind. Evidently Khan's business was his whole life – something I'm sure you can sympathize with. Perhaps the loss of it drove him a little crazy . . .' he looked into her eyes with an expression of apology for the news he had brought. 'I just wanted to tell you before you heard it from the press,' he said. 'I'm sorry. It must be hard to take in. I'm sure you would have preferred it to have been me.'

'You're sleeping with my sister,' Kitty said, suddenly. The idea had appeared in her head without warning, yet she knew as soon as she thought it that it had to be the truth. Where else would Chloe be getting all the New-Age jargon if not from the Waika offices? Who else would have told Kofteros all these things about Ricky Khan?

He didn't miss a beat. 'I'm sorry if you disapprove,' he said, without a trace of sarcasm.

Kitty smiled. 'You're already screwing the rest of my family,' she said, evenly, 'why shouldn't Chloe have a little fun, too?'

Kofteros stared at the floor for a second. 'Kitty, if my company does take over your business, I would like to imagine we can work together,' he said. 'It will still have the feel of a family concern and we will retain all of you in your current positions. Nobody will suffer and nobody will be out of pocket. You will be an extremely wealthy woman in your own right, without that wealth being tied up in the business, as it is now.' He moved one step closer again. 'I'm not a fool, Kitty,' he said, 'I know your passion for this business is almost as great as your father's, but believe me, you personally have nothing to lose from this take-over. If we pull out, the receivers will be at the doors within approximately two weeks.' Kitty grinned at the news as though she didn't care and Kofteros sighed.

'I believe your father left you all a stake,' he said, 'and we intend to honour his wishes once – *if* – we take controlling ownership.'

'You'll close down the couture side of the business and milk the ready-to-wear dry. You and your company haven't got the slightest interest in fashion, Mr Kofteros,' Kitty told him, 'because the product is of no importance to you at all. We could manufacture computer parts for all you care. Generations of work and pride and craftsmanship will get crushed as soon as you have what you want. You see us solely as a means to an end – just like my brother Burgess. Figures on a sheet of paper –'

Kofteros leant across the desk suddenly, cutting her off mid-sentence. His eyes were softly dark. For a moment neither spoke, they both just stared – Kitty in anger and Nicky in something that could for all the world have looked like intelligent, sincere, knowing sympathy. Kitty was the first to break the gaze. What was he trying to do now – hypnotize her? For a moment there she'd almost felt he was being kind.

'I have more interest in the fashion business than you think, Miss Zigofsky,' he said in a deep voice, 'and maybe my knowledge of your history and lineage is even greater than your own.' He paused again, looking as though he had intended to say more but then changed his mind. He smiled politely and the old, smarmy Nicky Kofteros was back again. 'I was told you were very much like your father,' he said, 'but I supposed you were a little too young to despise commercialism quite as vehemently as he did.'

'. . . and then you will get rid of us,' Kitty went on, undeterred, 'each and every member of the family, one by one. Burgess first, probably, because he understands most what you are doing and – despite the fact that he is probably wholly in your camp by now – may cause the most problems by wanting to interfere and have a voice.

'My mother will just be forgotten, along with Nula. China will go once you have paid off Stephano. Then me, because you know I won't be bought and you need to suck the last few details about the running of the business from my head.

'Chloe will last longer because her profile is the highest. The fact that you are sleeping with her will not give her the protection she hopes it will. You need a family face for the name of the business, though. She'll be eased out so gradually that she'll barely notice there are board meetings going on without her presence. You'll keep her so busy doing PR she may never realize she is nothing but a name . . .'

'If that is what you like to think,' Kofteros began, shaking his head, 'but I can assure you that you are wrong.'

'Of course she's right,' said a man's voice behind Kitty, 'it happened to most of the big fashion houses in Paris. There's no single reason to believe that it will not happen here, too.'

Kofteros's expression gelled with suppressed anger and

arrogance at this new challenge. Kitty turned to see Alain leaning behind her in the doorway, looking wonderfully sleazy and unkempt.

The two men gazed at one another for less than a second, but Kitty got the impression that a lot had been decided between them in that brief space of time. It was Kofteros who moved first, pulling his coat from the chair and extending his hand to Kitty as he murmured excuses and left.

Once he had gone, Kitty felt a desperate need to recover lost ground in the room. She spun her father's huge leather chair around and sank down into it, staring at Alain across Gabriel's desk.

'You know it rather suits you?' the designer said, throwing himself into the chair opposite.

'And you know you probably just talked your way out of a job,' Kitty told him. Alain shrugged. What were his circumstances? Kitty tried to recall her father's file on him, but she'd only glanced at it once before deciding he was an unlikely suspect. Was he from a good family? Did he need an income to survive? She didn't want him involved in her battles, especially as she knew she had every chance of losing.

There was a moment of uneasy silence. Kitty sat, lost deep in thought as Alain rocked gently backward and forward in his chair. He was a man who was comfortable in silences, she had noticed that before. It was a talent she wished she possessed. Gaps in conversations made her twitchy. Her mother had taught all her daughters that social silences were like the kiss of death. It was an inheritance Kitty still had to fight bravely to overcome.

'Do you think the new range is strong enough?' she asked at last.

'It's not bad,' Alain told her.

'Do you want to show it?' She watched his face closely.

'Why not? I didn't have much planned socially for the next few days.'

'And do you ever show more enthusiasm than you are displaying right now?'

Alain looked at her. 'No. Absolutely not. Under no circumstances. It is very un-cool.'

Kitty smiled and he responded with a grin. 'Good,' she said, 'then we'd better start work.'

It was after two o'clock by the time Kitty got back to her apartment. The bulb in the hall had blown and she searched for her keys on the stairs. As she approached her doorway something moved in the darkness. Something large, down on the floor.

'Shit!' Kitty jumped back like a scalded cat. Her brain did a quick mental inspection of the contents of her bag. Nothing, she concluded, not one solitary item that could be used as a weapon. Unless she hacked away with a credit card. Instead she raised the bag in a wild gesture of self-defence.

'Kit?' It was Nula, huddled and miserable, camped out on her doorstep.

'Oh-God-Nule-don't-speak-give-me-a-minute-fuck-fuck-fuck . . . do I need a heart attack right now? Oh Lord!' Panting with shock, Kitty leant against the wall until her heartbeat straightened. Then, when she could breathe again: 'What the hell are you doing here?'

Nula scrambled to her feet. Her hair had gone wrong and her eyes glowed with tears. 'You said I could stay,' she told Kitty. Her voice told of utter misery that was as yet unemployed.

Kitty ran a hand over her hair. 'I know, I know, I just didn't expect ... God, you gave me such a fright! I thought...' Kitty stopped herself in time. She'd thought they'd come to kill her like they killed her father. Unspeakable fear. Unutterable, unfathomable dread. How courageous had she felt in facing out Kofteros, and how stupidly, idiotically, cowardly did she look right now. Was this what bravery was like? Did it flow and ebb in waves? Somehow she'd expected it to be a more constant attribute. '... I thought you'd come over during the day, that's all,' she finished. She pulled her sister to her and hugged her. 'You shouldn't go camping on doorsteps, Nule,' she said, 'it's not safe.' Her sister smelt spicy and fresh, like a bun. She unlocked the door and pulled Nula inside. All she'd brought with her was a small rucksack.

'I thought you'd want to stay at the house,' Kitty said. With our mother, was what she meant. Nula adored Hester. Hester cherished little Nula. For the pair of them to be apart was remarkable.

'Can I stay here?' Nula asked her. 'Will Freddy mind?'

Freddy. Kitty had forgotten all about her fiancé.

'He's busy,' she told her sister, 'it's season time, remember? I'll be tied up enough myself. You can help, if you like.'

'Help?' Nula sounded weak and confused. Was she on drugs? Kitty made a mental note to check for signs. She heard Nula's face turn up towards her own and felt, rather

235

than saw, the smile that tried to spread across it in the dark.

It wasn't until Kitty turned the lights on in the hallway and caught sight of them both in the mirror that she realized they had both become nervous wrecks. Nula looked ill, but so, too, did she. She took a deep breath. She needed to be strong. She had her sister and her mother to look after. She had a murder to solve. She had a business to run.

Nula stood with her elfin face sandwiched between her hands. Her nails looked chomped. 'I couldn't stand it, Kit,' she said. Her voice had changed since their father's death. Kitty wondered whether her own had, too. 'It was that picture, the one on the piano. I couldn't live with it.' Her eyes looked wild and haunted. Her hands were shaking.

'Okay,' Kitty soothed, 'okay, okay, okay. Do you like the taste of brandy?' She led her sister into the kitchen and poured them both a shot of cognac. Nula took a sip and started to cough, but the colour came back into her cheeks and she almost managed a smile.

'We'll start at the studio tomorrow,' Kitty said, throwing her brandy back in one. The effect nearly choked her but she managed not to gasp. Start as you mean to go on, she told herself.

When she dreamt of Gabriel that night she could not be sure, but she thought that maybe his back wasn't turned quite so squarely away from her as before.

CHAPTER TWENTY-THREE

ZG

1892

VOILE

A fine, sheer fabric traditionally made from cotton, silk or wool. Simple fabrics like cotton voile and chiffon received a fashion revival amongst wealthy women at the end of the nineteenth century. Much of this was due to the growing popularity of the sewing machine, which made elaborately trimmed dresses available to the lower classes for the first time. In a move of inverted snobbery, the upper classes switched to having layers of delicate fabrics, which required massive amounts of laundering and pressing to keep them looking good. The wearing of these simple garments made a subtle statement about the numbers of staff employed by the household.

Dearest Kitty,

I have been in this country three years now and speak the language every bit as well as the others in the area. Yet for all that I still feel very much the outsider and alone. Most, if not all of the folk here, arrived in families. It is the men who come first and then send for their wives when they are settled. I, of course, have no family here and am finding it hard saving money for fares home as well as sending odd pieces of cash back to Russia when I can.

People here live very much as they did in the villages at home and a young girl alone as I am, sharing quarters as I do with a young man like Max and with no parental chaperon or guidance, is looked at very much from the corners of folks' eyes. Of course I have had offers of help and food – many from those with little enough to spare, too, I can tell you. My shame at what happened at home and the subsequent birth of my child that died has forced me to keep very much to myself though, Kitty.

Shame such as I carry will be with me all my life and I shall have to learn to bear it or collapse beneath its weight. I know now that I could never have brought such disgrace to Aaron's marriage bed. Yet I still have a dignity, Kitty, and that dignity is best left to itself. I am a young woman who was brought up well, by a good family. My father was well-respected and my mother one of the bravest women I will ever hope to know. I must carry some of this with me despite my fall. I am eighteen years old now and quite able to speak my own name with the self-esteem it deserves.

Max is so puffed up with his own conceit that he is quite unbearable. His photographic business has provided him with enough cash to expand a little and so he has placed an advertisement in the local newspaper, and the sight of his own name in print tickles him very much.

He is so full of himself now that I wonder he doesn't advertise his wonderful services in a society periodical – and tell him so to his face just to bring him down a peg or two. Imagine my expression, then, when he turns to me in all seriousness and informs me that is exactly what he has in mind, but only once he is in better premises that a lady would want to visit. I could poke his eye out for this last comment.

'So what about the lady who already lives here?' I ask him, at which he places his hand to his eyebrows and looks around the room as though hunting for the woman I refer to.

Molly Nodd, the model, is back in Max's room again tonight. I lay in silence in the darkness and my bed feels hot enough to toast me. How long can we live like this? The girl's moans slither with dull regularity from whispered pianissimo to broad fortissimo, and are full of tragic pleading, too. I wonder Max can be so cruel in ignoring her cries, but then realize she is begging for him to continue his ghastly behaviour, rather than stop.

There is a horrible contagion to the whole ritual. My own body, which I normally ignore, save to throw clothes over it in the morning and douse with soap and water after work at night, discovers demands of its own as I am forced to listen. My legs have taken on flesh around the bones at last and now my toes stretch out like a cat in the sun. My hands are balled into fists of anger that I cannot unclench. My breathing has become prominent enough to deafen me with its noise.

This is shameful! Like a ghost I am drawn from my mattress and my face is pressed again to the crack in the wall. Oh dear God, this time it is the girl who rides and Max who suffers beneath her! I stare at his face and see Richard there instead, and all at once I am so lonely there in my poor excuse of a room that I could howl out loud, were it not for the fact that Max would know I had listened and watched.

I turn into my darkened chamber. It must be possible to not listen. I force my brain to seek other stimulus. Something dull. Something perfectly mundane. Baile's wedding is very much the thing at last, and a long time it has been coming, too. Baile loses much of her prettiness by the day and if she is not soon married then I fear no one will have her.

I find the diversion I have been seeking, then. Baile the bride. I am finally able to sleep and, when I rise, I take the thought of Baile's nuptials into the factory with me. Then I have a shock. I have been trying to find a mirror to see what has become of my looks since I arrived in this country. In the end I am bold enough to climb up a step and peep into the one the tailors use when they are grooming their beards in the morning.

The face I see rise up before me like a little sun, with curiosity written all over its expression, is not my face. Instead it is Rintzi who I see there, staring into the glass. I gasp and nearly fall from my step with surprise. Have I become my mother then? I stretch up to the mirror once again, cautiously, but her face still waits there.

It is four years since I left home. Is that all it has taken for me to become my mother's doppelgänger? A fear grips me that I may inherit her madness, too. Bubba's body and Rintzi's face. I feel my features with my fingers. Is that so bad? I am a little taller than I was, that much I can tell from the way my skirts hang short to my ankles. My hair I suppose to be much the same, though I keep it plaited and pinned tight to my head all the time. I run my fingers roughly over my features, trying to recall the face I had when I left my home.

When I turn at last I find that Baile has been watching me. She never once spoke about her famous outburst over the couture garment that I stitched, though one of the girls told me she believed Richard Galliard had kissed Baile one night, after the others had gone, and that it was this shocking act that had boldened my friend into believing she could speak to him in such a disrespectful manner.

I believe this to be nothing more than a lie, of course. Baile was a victim of her own jealous temper, nothing more. She is lucky still to have employment and I will tell her this if she ever steps out of line again.

I now take regular work from the company's better garment range, which ensures my enduring unpopularity with the other workers. Sometimes I am invited to visit Baile's family at their home, but these trips are generally not pleasurable. Baile has become very quiet since her scene at the sweatshop and, if I was not so sure that her head is empty of a brain I might almost describe her as reflective in mood. When Richard arrives at the factory she stares at him hollow-eyed. Perhaps it was *she* who kissed *him*. She is vain enough to try, I know that much.

Letters from home come occasionally, but they reach me less frequently now – though they were never more than three times a year once they started. I was in great despair over the fate of my family once I understood Aaron was lost to me forever. How would they manage without my protection, or that of my husband? Would Rintzi become quite mad and relieve Gregory of the rest of his fingers?

The times when Max did not treat me to a night-time concerto I would spend tossing over these thoughts in my mind.

Then one day one of Baile's many aunts happened to mention that my mother had bettered her lot and I found myself shocked, rather than delighted at the news.

'Rintzi?' I asked her. This particular aunt of Baile's is a very old woman with little concentration for anything other than food. When she is not cooking she is to be found consuming the fruits of her labours, which has made her as fat as an ox – too large for one chair, she rests her bulk across two planks supported by chairs either end, though she complains the wood causes her sores on the backs of her legs. I wonder with some pleasure whether Baile will look like this once she is older. 'My mother is happy?'

'She's been left money from a relative and moved to a better house, according to what I hear,' the aunt said.

My letter is off to Rintzi that very night and this time her reply is quite prompt. Yes, she has come into some money and spent it all on better lodgings for Gregory and herself. Am I happy for her? Happy? How could I be anything but choked with delight! What worry I have had for her, yet all the time she was safe in a new home! Kitty, you know me well enough by now to understand that I was beside myself with rage. My whole concern has been to provide for her and my brother, and yet there she is, a well-off woman and without once thinking it worth the effort to inform me. Could some of that money not have been used to bring her daughter home?

I consider a return to Russia. Perhaps I could write begging Rintzi to fund me. My heart suffers much pain at the thought of the place, yet I know now that what I miss most is no longer there. Russia is still full of danger for Jews – greeners arrive every month with tales to make our hair stand on end. My mind finds more work for it here in London, for I realize that it is here where my dreams lie now.

This news of Rintzi's has set me thinking. I no longer need worry about returning home with a husband. I now have no responsibilities in life, save myself. This is a curious idea that will take time to come to terms with. Max, of course, has his own philosophies about my situation.

'Just think, Rosa,' he tells me, 'you are free to pursue your own destiny.'

This is the sort of talk that makes my poor brain spin and I wish he would not continue with it, but Max is like a dog with a bone when he has an idea.

'Rosa, you have great potential,' he tells me, all flushed from his latest triumphs in the local rag. 'You must make a success of your life. You're as driven as I am, if you can only see it.'

His flattery embarrasses me and I look for the ulterior motive; I know he must be mocking me, as always.

'You mean I have potential as the new flattening-iron for your bedsheets, Max,' I say. His head goes up.

'Rosa, you know how much I want you, I've told you often enough,' he says, 'but I want success for you, too. You have talent and courage. Look how you've survived. I know you only see grime and muck in this country, yet there's great wealth here too, believe me. For people like us the possibilities are endless. Don't you fancy the life of a Mayfair lady, Rosa? Look, come with me. Do you have an hour? Yes? Allow me to teach you a few truths.'

Before I can speak he has my hat upon my head, albeit back to front, and we are out in the streets and he is whistling for a cab.

Once I am bundled inside Max grabs me by the arm. 'For one time in your short life, Rosa, be quiet and listen,' he says.

I sit back with my lips pursed. I will not allow Max to get the better of me – ever – but I am curious enough to do what he says.

The cab rolls down Brick Lane, past the mean lodgings, where buxom Jewish matrons sit on doorsteps alongside young Jewish men smoking their pipes, and via the Great Synagogue with an enormous clatter upon the cobbles, pulling round Sclater Street and up Curtain Road to Old Street, where the queues for the chief rabbi's soup kitchen wait with some dignity for their salt and bread and their turn at the six huge steam-jacketed pans.

The tenements are brave new buildings looming over the older, three-storey lodgings of the sort that Max and I inhabit. These are called model dwellings and three rooms plus other conveniences can be had for four shillings and sixpence per week. Needless to say they are full to bursting with immigrants of every kind, but I would like to fancy that I may be able to save enough to move into one myself before long.

I am lost beyond Old Street. For me the world ends at City Road so I stir with undisguised interest when the cab continues its journey down Bunhill Row and on to St Paul's.

'Did you ever visit the better parts of London, Rosa?' Max asks me. There is something rather intimate about the cramped cab and we are constantly thrown together as the wheels churn on the corners. I cling to the side of the window with all my strength, which makes Max laugh.

'Am I so repellent to you?' he asks, smiling. If he showed one ounce of self-doubt I might find it easier to like him, but here is a man who is completely aware of his good looks and engaging manners. He is staring at me with those eyes that miss nothing and I watch his hand reach for mine.

'What about your young lady?' I ask. Max laughs and shakes his head.

'Oh, I should say that ours was more of a financial arrangement, Rosa,' he tells me. 'I supposed you realized that by now.'

'You pay her to do those things?' I ask.

'No, she pays me.' He is laughing out loud at me now. 'Yes, of course I pay her, what did you think, Rosa? I pay her to do what we would do, if you would only see sense and marry me. Anyway,' his eyes are back to my face, 'how did you know what we do?'

I curl up back into my seat. 'I would have to be deaf and blind not to,' I tell him in a whisper, though I am too shocked and embarrassed by this conversation to wish it to continue.

We travel in silence, punctuated only by Max's occasional head-shaking snorts of laughter. The roads are broader now and better paved, so that the cab has stopped its tooth-loosening rattle.

I will not tell Max, but I am impressed by the view – so much so that I am rendered quite dumb. We drive for many more minutes and the view improves with each street we turn into.

'This is Mayfair,' Max tells me with a flourish of his hand, 'what do you think?'

It is every bit as beautiful as Moscow. There are people everywhere on the pavements, and all dressed in the most remarkable clothes. Here are colours that I have not seen for many years: golden-sand silk crepes, Delft-blue taffeta, rose-pink linen for the women's dresses, and greenish-brown alpaca or fine midnight or slate-grey wool for the gentlemen's suits.

'Take in the buildings too, Rosa,' Max whispers at me, pleased by my expression of childish awe, but I cannot for I am too busy memorizing each stitch and tuck of the clothes.

We take tea in Regent Street and I try to ignore the waiters' faces when they spy the sad little rabbit that Max has brought with him.

'I have never known you so quiet,' Max says to me, 'and you have barely touched your cake.'

'I'm not hungry,' I tell him. In truth, I am sick with longing.

'Would you like to live like this, Rosa?' His voice is a seduction in my ear. His hand is upon my arm, but I no longer feel the urge to complain. 'One day you will walk in here again, Rosa,' Max continues, 'only you will be dressed in clothes more exquisite than any other woman in this room. You will be seated at the best table by waiters who trip over their own boots in their rush to pander to your every whim. The tip you leave for the waiter who charms you the most will exceed one week's money from the sweatshop. You will leave food on your plate – not because you are sick from the excitement of it all, but because fine food bores you and if you are confronted by one more sliver of Scotch smoked salmon or another silver spoon laden with prime caviare you will scream from *ennui*. Now, how does that sound?'

I am sitting up like a little dog, mesmerized. 'I will have all that when I marry,' I say. My mouth is dry.

'What if every woman in this room were wearing an outfit created by you?' Max asks.

'By me?' I have no notion whether he is mocking me or not. With a touch of his fingers he turns my face towards his own, so that all I see is the texture and landscape of his fine features. I have been wrong about Max, perhaps. His eyes now hold the most infinite kindness and sympathy. I stare at them. His lashes are long, dark and thick. Max's eyes are perhaps the most expressive I have ever seen, which is why I always avoid their gaze when I can. There is longing there, along with the pride and the humour. Two orbs of soft chocolate silk on a bed of dove-white satin, topped with a fringe of frayed black crepe. Hair as thick as astrakhan. There is a small crumb of teacake beside his mouth and I yearn to brush it away.

'Rosa?' his voice is soft enough to be nearly inaudible.

'Max, you are not a gentleman,' I whisper. 'You behave like an animal half the time and the rest of the time you find sport in mocking me. I may not be a beauty but I will wait for more than you can offer.' I believe this with all my heart. Max may be a good and generous enough man at times, but somehow I feel he is little better than the beasts that raped me in the snow. Perhaps it is not his fault, but it is a quality that terrifies me all the same. He is not a gentleman and never will be – no matter how well his business does. A man like Richard has been bred to treat women like ladies. He would never act as Max does in his bed at night.

Max reaches for his teacup and I notice with some surprise that his hands are shaking. Could my words have made him so angry? He looks about the room.

'I may not be a gentleman, Rosa, but I would die for you, you know. What more is there that you could want?'

This is said so quietly and evenly that I stare at him, wondering if I have misheard. Then his face changes, the neediness vanishing to be replaced by all the old arrogance.

'So, now you've seen what London has to offer, Rosa,' he says in a changed tone, 'let me tell you the bad news. The cab and this tea used up all my money. I'm afraid we're walking back. Wrap your teacake in that napkin and conceal it in a pocket – we'll need it for the journey home.'

CHAPTER TWENTY-FOUR

ZG

TROTTEUR
French for 'walking suit', the trotteur *was one of the
most popular outfits of the 1890s. It consisted of a
men's-style buttoned jacket trimmed with braid and a
skirt that was flared at the back for easy walking.*

There are curious events at the sweatshop, Kitty. First we
are informed by young Mr Yanzdoff that Richard Galliard's partner, Turgis Fasukinos, has died. At first we fear
this means the business will close, but then the rumour is
that Richard had borrowed sufficient money to buy the
place from Turgis's family. As you may imagine, Kitty, this
news alone has been enough to keep us all simmering like
kettles with speculations that we whisper around the room
when Yanzdoff's back is turned.

Then more intrigue. A fellow machinist who we all know
as Red Aggie on account of her hair, which has the colour
of the ochre dye used for hat trimmings, is seen to be
unwell, though she declines any offers of help. Baile has
been eyeing her strangely for some months now and I see
them whispering together often, which is an offence that
could relieve them of their jobs, if they are not more careful.

I have met Baile's prospective bridegroom now, Kitty,
and can only say that I hope he has a good fortune, for

his face is not the sort to win prizes and his body I can only describe as showing signs of malnourishment. I told Max about the impending nuptials as soon as I knew, watching his face carefully for signs of regret, for I still believe he carries a torch for Baile, despite all his protestations.

To his credit, though, he managed a smile of the usual gleaming variety, accompanied by a shrug and a, 'Good luck to the groom.'

Baile plans to leave the sweatshop once she is married and good luck to her too for that, though I have to admit I will miss her despite everything, as she is the nearest thing to a friend that I have in this country, for all her annoying ways.

Last night I unpacked the wedding suit from its case. This is the first time I have given it an airing since I arrived in England and the reason for that is because I fear the pain of the loss of my father will be doubled at the sight of it.

Max, needless to say, arrived in the room the minute I had the garment out of its tissue and he was full of questions that I had no desire to answer.

'Whose is the suit, Rosa?' He pushed his hands into his pockets and leant against a wall, regarding the garment with a tilt from his head. He lit a cigar, which angered me for I did not want the smoke to dirty the precious fabric.

'Mine,' I told him, sounding annoyed.

'A *gentleman's* suit, Rosa?' he asked. 'Are you tired of your own sex already and keen to change? Although you were dressed as a boy when we first met, as I recall.' He was joking again.

250

'Max, this is my husband's suit,' I told him. Already the scent of the fabric was filling me with nostalgia. I watched Max tap his foot thoughtfully.

'I wasn't aware you had a husband,' he said.

I stood up to face him. 'This is a wedding suit, Max,' I said, 'my father made it to be worn by the man that I marry on our wedding day.'

Max fingered the fabric. 'It's very fine,' he said, 'though a little small in size.'

And before I could stop him he was holding the jacket to his chest and checking the length of the sleeve.

'For you?' I asked, incredulous.

'Can it be altered, Rosa?' he says.

I snatched it away so quickly the fabric almost tore. 'Oh it will fit very well, thank you, Max,' I told him. Richard is much leaner than Max and I knew he would fit the suit perfectly.

'Oh, you still have your gentleman in mind, do you?' he asked, and there was something especially nasty about the way he pronounced the word 'gentleman'.

'Of course,' I said.

'And do you believe your prospects are any more real with this suitor than they were with Aaron?' Max asked. His tone was not unkindly, but I became angry at his words.

'You seem to think I am not good enough to make a quality marriage!' I shouted.

Max was across the room in an instant and had me by the arm. 'No, Rosa,' he told me, 'I believe you are *too* good for these men!' he said, equally annoyed. 'Aaron must have been an idiotic fool and your precious boss is no

251

better! If you think you've found a gentleman in him, perhaps you'd better speak to your friend Baile before it's too late!'

'Baile?' I asked him, but he would say no more, no matter how much I questioned him. In fact I believe he thought he had said too much, for once.

'How did *you* come to speak to Baile, Max?' I asked him after a pause.

He smiled at that because I understood he believed me to be jealous.

'I went to congratulate her on her forthcoming wedding,' he said, 'and to see if I might have the honour of taking the photographs.' He threw a card onto the table in front of me. *Max Warkofski* it said in gold leaf, *Leading Society Photographer, catering for weddings, balls and formal portraits.* 'I have new premises, Rosa,' he said, 'I'm on my way, just wait.'

I have since quizzed Baile many times about Max's comments, for I am not so stupid as to allow pride to stand in the way of curiosity. This morning she told me that Richard is, '. . . not as much of a gentleman as you would think, Rosa.' And then later informed me that he has '. . . trouble with the drink.'

Of course, Baile would have had no experience of real gentlemen in her life, growing up as she did with that prize fool Menachem presiding over the household, but I must tell you, Kitty, that I have been somewhat concerned over Richard's consumption of alcohol myself, as he frequently has the smell of it about him when he pays his visits to our poor sweatshop.

The Jewish community in the East End is on the whole

well-behaved with good moral standards, despite the poverty of its ghettos. The sense of family here is even stronger than at home, and whole areas are populated by *landsleit*, which are families that come from the same town or *shtetle* back in Russia. These people form their own communities, Kitty, with *steibels* and home-stores providing the gathering-places that ensure the rabbi's sermons on the evils of bad behaviour will be heard and discussed at length. The main vice of the men is gambling, and many have regular dealings with the local bookie, a fat man in a loud suit, who works his pitch outside the corner shop by the butcher's.

I have no idea, Kitty, how morals work in other, more affluent communities, and expect alcohol consumption to be a recognized sport among them, and so therefore not the great sin it is seen to be with us. Richard Galliard *is* a gentleman, Kitty. If you could only see him you would know at once that I am right.

CHAPTER TWENTY-FIVE

ZG

BARATHEA
*Made of wool or silk, and with a light, pebbly
pattern, barathea is mainly used for suits.*

Five months have passed, Kitty, and it is obvious – to myself at least – what the problem is with young Aggie. Her corsets are laced as tight as possible around her waist, but I notice them straining more each day and see the way her back pains her when she is bent over her machine.

I take her aside, Kitty, for I have suffered the same fate myself and remember the fear and pain that it caused me, though I suspect Aggie is not quite the innocent victim that I was when I left my home.

'Are you with child, Aggie?' I ask her. She is a pretty enough girl but her face twists with emotion at my words.

'How did you know, Rabbit?' she asks, pulling a hankie from her purse and snuffling into it.

'From your belly,' I tell her. I know I can provide her with some comfort and pity and wish I had had a similar friend myself under the same circumstances. 'Aggie,' I go on, 'you will need comradeship at this time. Will you not allow me to help you? Can I speak to the father on your behalf and tell him how alone you are?'

I look at her again and discover not tears on her face, as I had supposed, but laughter.

'You?' she starts to scream. '*You* help? What would you do, you pious little cow? Yes, you can go and tell the father what he's done, though I doubt it would do me much good if you did. But then you are Mr Galliard's favourite, and we all know you have a lust for him yourself, so maybe he will listen, after all.

'Next time he gives you some of that fine stuff to sew tell him he's to be a papa, will you? That should put a finish to your career – and mine, too, I should think!'

I look at her stomach, blushing. 'You're lying, Aggie,' I tell her politely, 'Richard Galliard is not the child's father.'

'No?' she asks, and a look at my solemn face sends her into such convulsions of laughter that I fear she might be sick.

I stare at her. 'Then you must have seduced him.'

She is clutching her sides in her mirth. 'Yes?' she asks me. 'Well, he was blind drunk at the time, I'll give you that. I doubt he'll remember his little adventure, but I believe he was a reasonably willing party to the deed.' She pushes her face into my own. 'Now why don't you fuck off, Rabbit, there's a good girl,' she says.

I leave her, as she wishes, but I will try again, Kitty, for I know she will be keen enough for my help in a few weeks' time.

Baile's wedding is a huge event, though I see no sign of the wealth that she insists is to be part of her life as a wife. In a fit of something approaching almost sisterly affection, I choose to fashion her dress, and she is well pleased with

255

the result – and surprised at the fine work too, to judge from the look on her face.

'Rosa, this is beautiful!' she tells me when I take the box to her house. I have stitched it by hand at night, for I did not dare to smuggle it into the workshop to make use of the machine. The fabric is not quality, for she had only a few shillings to spend on it, but I used broken or spent beads from some of my couture samples and worked enough of them into the design to have it looking like a dress worth ten times the price.

I am happy to see the pleasure in Baile's face, for she has softened a great deal in the final days before her marriage, and it is almost possible to like her when this less abrasive mood is upon her.

I ask her if she is to give up her job at the workroom and she says she will with time – which also makes me wonder about her new husband's finances.

Needless to say, Max is there at the wedding too, looking smart, though a little too dapper, in the new suit he has acquired for the occasion. He is now renting a shop off the Mile End Road and the idea is this: he attends the wedding to take shots of the bride and her family, then he is off in a cab back to the shop so that he can greet the new husband and wife and take their portraits in the studio there. There is usually much kerfuffle outside the shop when word gets around that a bride is about to arrive, and the pavements are often full of onlookers, which pleases Max no end, as he says crowds are good for business.

I must admit, Kitty, that at Baile's wedding I am hoping to hear some stray compliments about her dress as she walks smiling into the shop. Imagine my annoyance, then, when I discovered that she has thrown a coat about her shoulders, 'in case of draughts'. I make sure her coat is missing when she steps outside to leave again, and my face glows to see the smiles of admiration that the dress evokes among the still-waiting crowd.

Max – who as you know by now misses nothing – catches the look of pride in my eyes and returns it with a wink and a grin. Once the photographs are printed he hands one to me, too. 'A memento of your dearest friend,' he says. When I open the folder I see Baile's head has all but been cut off at the top of the shot and my handiwork on the dress is lit to full glory. I shall not, however, give Max the satisfaction of seeing that I am pleased.

All seemed quiet after Baile's wedding. Like dust tossed into the air, the atmosphere in the workroom soon settled and all was much the same as before, except that Baile returned much sobered and not, I thought, as happy as you might expect a new bride to be. But then perhaps this is the reality of marriage, Kitty. Pick your own husband with care, dear. Avoid being a bride with the same look in your eyes as that I perceive in Baile's.

A month later and it was a day like any other in the workroom, Kitty – only this day was to change my life forever.

Red Aggie, I noticed, had been pale all morning, rubbing her back and groaning when she moved. No one else seemed perturbed by this. Her story is that she is grown fatter because her uncle has taken a job in a bakery, and that the free bread he brings home at night has been enough to account for the widening of her waist. She wears a coat all through the day now, too, despite the heat of the room. This makes it hard to see exactly where the new pounds have been added.

By midday Aggie was white enough to use for notepaper and I saw her rise from her stool and walk unsteadily off towards the outside latrines.

Her return was so tardy I noticed Yanzdoff studying his pocket watch on at least three occasions. When she was finally back his voice broke the silence: 'One and a half hours docked for latrine time, Miss North.' I glanced up at her but she was back at work and the cheeks that had been paper-white now sported two bright and feverish spots of pink.

'Aggie?' I said as we were leaving at the end of the day, but she pushed right past me and I wondered if she were drunk. 'Sod off,' I believe she said, but her voice was so slurred I could not be sure.

When everyone was gone from the place, apart from the workers who slept on the floor, I walked through the rag-room and out towards the privy. The place was deserted. I lifted the lid and peered down into the pan and hunted behind the seat and down around the darkest corners of the floor. There was a stain that I believed could have been blood, but apart from that, nothing.

I went back through the rag-room and then I stopped. There were more spots of blood on the stones of the floor – a tiny, splattering trail that led off to one side. I looked in that direction. Before me lay the largest and most stinking pile of rags in the room. There was little light there, save that reflected from the workroom, and I dared not open the door wider for fear someone might come and ask what I was doing.

Taking my courage into both hands I slipped into the workroom and stole one of the passer's small paraffin lamps from the shelf. My hands shook too hard to light the matches and I must have wasted over a dozen before I could get the thing alight.

There was an acrid smell from the burning wick and suddenly the dark mouldering corner was suffused with an eerie, ochre light. I believe I preferred the dark, for the sight of the rotting stuff was a horror to me and I fell to imagining sightings of all the vermin that must have considered the heap as their home address.

To my terrified eyes, the ghastly pile appeared to writhe in the dull, flickering light. My task was a grim one, yet I was determined to complete it. Have you guessed what I sought, Kitty? I was looking for Red Aggie's child, for I was sure she had given birth out there that very afternoon. As you know the fate of my own poor child you may understand my obsession for ensuring this one at least had a decent burial.

Climbing a couple of feet up the pile, I began to pull away with my bare hands, at first with my eyes closed for fear I might see a rat, but then with them open – for it occurred to me that my fate might be better if I spotted the rat before it saw me.

I started to cry softly then, for the memory of my own awful plight on the ship brought me to tears of self-pity. I had tried to imagine that the whole episode was a dream, but the mind will always know the truth and will make you believe your own history eventually, no matter how hard you attempt to push it away.

Some of the rags were wedged into sodden blocks, but one pile came out easily when I touched it and I stood on tiptoe to peer into the gap that was left. It was as dark as pitch. I lifted the lamp to my face, fearing all the while that I could be in danger of starting a fire like the one in Koenigsberger's the furriers in Commercial Street – when five floors went up while all one hundred hands were working. This was before I arrived in London, but the story is still told as a warning to all of us in employment. The light did little to penetrate the gloom and I knew there was nothing for it but to push my bare arm into the space.

How great was the yell I had to smother when my hand encountered dampness! I fell backwards, biting my lip in my attempt to keep silent, and the lamp fell from my grasp as I hit the floor, which sent me scuttling to retrieve it even though my head had been banged on the stones and all I could see was a whirling roundabout of stars and flashing lights.

For a moment I believed my leg was broken, too, for I had fallen with it beneath me and heard a crack, which I thought must be the bone. Holding the newly retrieved lamp above my skirts I felt the length of the limb, discovering to my relief that it was whole and hearty and that the only breakage was the lamp-chimney – which would take some explaining when I finally returned it.

Sore and sick with shock I looked again at the hole in the rag-pile, knowing in my heart that I must return to it, even though my urge was to run to my home and shelter in the safety of my small bed.

Rolling my sleeve back further I regained my foothold in the rag-mountain and plunged my shaking arm back into the gap. What if it was a rat I had discovered, bleeding and trapped in its own lair? It would have my fingers off in an instant, I was sure of that. Yet the damp thing did not move when my hand encountered it this time.

Clutching at some fabric that appeared to cover it, I began to pull it forward and received no resistance. A knot of crumpled cloth slowly appeared, followed by a large bundle wrapped tightly in the same stuff. The wetness was blood and some other stain and it was then that a sadness overcame me and I started to weep silently.

This was a dead child, I was sure of it. Aggie had given birth in the privy and abandoned her infant in the rag-pile, to let it rot or be consumed by the rats. I pulled back the cloth that swaddled it carefully, whispering to it all the while, though I knew it could hear nothing on this earth, for it was so still I was certain it had to be dead. By now I had it in my muddled crazy head that this was my own child come back to me, to give its poor ignorant mother a second chance.

A small foot fell out of the bundle, no larger than that of a doll; it was blue, which made me sob more tears. The creature was tiny but perfect, and cold as the grave to touch. It was a boy. In my madness and grief I studied its forehead. There was no mark there, Kitty. Yet still I persevered in the idea that the small pathetic thing I held belonged to me.

Removing the soiled cloth that enveloped it, I wrapped it in some clean white woollen stuff that had been thrown out just that morning, with its dear face left bare, just as though it were alive. Then I clutched it to my chest and sang quietly to it, Kitty, rocking it in my arms and reciting an old Yiddish song that Rintzi had sung to me many years before.

It was at that moment that all the unfairness of life suddenly occurred to me at last, Kitty. When poverty is your lot you can be so busy working at your own survival that the great injustice of your situation passes you by. As I held that child I saw the whole perspective of our situation, and a sorry sight it was, too.

If that infant had been born to wealth it would have lived and prospered as you do, Kitty. Instead it was spawned in the immigrant ghetto and so was destined to draw less than a few breaths of rancid air before it died. Why should we be forced to live like that? My father was a good man and a skilled worker, yet he is dead and his daughter no more than a skivvy in a foreign land, along with many thousands of others consigned to the same fate. Why? Kitty, I am too stupid to provide an answer to that question.

'Never be poor and never grow old, Rosa.' That was my papa's liturgy to me and it is the message I pass on to you now, Kitty. Remember the fate of all who went before you. Seize the chance when you can and never allow the blood and sweat that was spilt to have been given in vain.

Ƶ_G

TAFFETA
*One of the finest fabrics made, taffeta must be
handled as little as possible and stitched only once, as
holes will remain after the stitches are removed.*

I took the child home, Kitty, carrying it beneath my coat. I had no plans for it but knew the pathetic thing deserved more dignity in death than my own child was afforded. Tears coursed down my face and for once I was glad of the cover of darkness.

Once in my room I washed the small scrap as carefully as if it had drawn breath, cooing to it all the while, and dried it and bound it in clean fabric. Its face was beautiful, Kitty, not ill-looking or scrawny, but as round and clear-expressioned as a cherub's, its eyes closed as if in sleep and its small round mouth curved into what I fancied to be the hint of a blissful smile.

To my relief Max was out at the theatre and not due to return for several hours. Exhausted and still sore and aching from the bruises of my tumble, I fell back onto my bed and slept for several hours.

It was dark when I woke, but I knew it was morning for I heard movements in the house below me and smelt the first scents of cooking from the stoves as the women prepared breakfasts for their husbands.

The bundle still lay crooked in my arm. A feeling of dread overwhelmed me. What had I done? Was this a sin? I had become sadly out of touch with my own religion since my arrival in London, and even though I racked my brains I could remember nothing in the rabbi's sermons that dealt with the removal of dead children.

My head ached from the battering it had received against the floor the day before, and when I opened my heavy lids I found I could barely focus my eyes. When I stared at the baby beside me I saw two pink faces peering from the blanket. There was a sound somewhere, a thin wail that I took to be issuing from my own mouth or from the kettle that Max used to heat his water for washing.

'Rosa?' I heard Max's voice, but my head still would not clear. My name bounced and echoed loudly inside my skull and the wailing danced with it. 'Rosa? Rosa!' Max's voice could have been next to my ear. Then I felt him shaking me and the fog lifted a little.

'Rosa?' Max sounded concerned and also angry. 'What have you done?'

I closed my eyes and opened them again. The room had stopped moving. 'Are you drunk?' Max's voice sounded normal. 'Rosa? What's this you have?' The wail had suddenly ceased.

I looked down at the small open mouth by my side. Instead of the blueness and white stillness I expected I saw pinks, creams and the mallow tones of warm, breathing flesh, plus wild, pearl-grey and moonstone eyes that took

264

in too much at once. The child was alive. A miracle had occurred.

'It's a baby,' I told Max. 'My baby.'

I would go down to the synagogue within the hour and pray thanks for this until my body dropped from exhaustion. I peered at the child. Its face looked angry at its fate, but it appeared well enough and its skin felt warm when I touched it.

'Max, it's a miracle,' I said, 'this child was dead last night.'

For once Max was lost for words. He sat down on the bed beside me, which caused the springs to squeal mercy, and he stared at me with what I can only describe as tempered fear in his eyes.

'You think I am mad,' I told him. I was too happy to be concerned about his opinion, but I told him my story anyway, for I needed to share it with someone and knew I could hide little from Max, owing to our living circumstances.

'You cannot keep the child,' he said when I was finished.

'Why?' I asked. 'What else should I do? Return it to its mother? Take it to the poor home? Red Aggie abandoned this child – she could have tried to kill it, for all I know. It has fallen on me to protect it, Max. Would you want to see it left to the mercy of the paupers' house?'

Max shook his head and sighed. 'What makes you think you can provide better for it, Rosa?' he asked. 'You are impoverished enough yourself.'

I smiled at Max. 'You said I could become wealthy if I wanted,' I told him, 'you always thought I had talent and prospects.'

He shook his head again. 'Rosa, this is madness,' he said.

'No, Max,' I told him, 'this is right. I *know* it is right. This child has been given a chance. I have to respect that. I can care for it and I can find it a future. In the poor house its only fate would be to live all its life in the ghetto at the mercy of others. I will find something better for it.'

I didn't tell him the absolute truth though, Kitty, that while I feigned sanity, in my thoughts this was still the soul of my own child – come back to me. I hid my euphoria beneath a cloak of rationale for Max's benefit.

Max leant across and stuck his finger in the baby's hand. 'How can you build empires now, Rosa?' he asked, but I heard in his voice a respect that was new to my ears. Although he thought my decision was wrong, I believe he was impressed by it, nevertheless.

'I'll do it, Max,' I told him. There was, of course, another piece of the story that I had not told him, and that was that the child might be Richard's.

The next day the factory was closed for the Lean Season. We had no idea until we arrived. Baile was there weeping on the pavement outside, along with the other workers, who had also lost their homes. They all looked stunned at their loss. There was a letter pinned to the door telling us to turn up again in a month's time. Aggie was there too, Kitty, though looking as close to death as her child had the previous night. I could have felt pity for her but when I smiled she simply swore at me and hurried on her way. We never saw her again.

Someone said later that she had returned to her parents

and died of tuberculosis the following spring. There was another, more awful rumour that she had either jumped from a bridge or drunk herself to death. The tales sent shivers through my entire body.

I walked back to the house quickly, as I had promised the old woman downstairs a few pennies for looking after the baby while I was at work and I wanted to get the child back before enough time had expired for her to demand payment.

I had told her the child was my sister's, Kitty, and that she had died in childbirth, leaving me to care for the infant. The old woman had looked at me oddly, for she knew most of the comings and goings of the house, and I had never had a sister visit me there. I believe she suspected the child was my own, and a result of some illicit goings-on between myself and Max. Who knows who was carrying a child with the shawls we women wore wrapped about us throughout the year, on account of the damp and the cold that persists here – even in summer, it seems. I stuck to my tale, though. This was the story I had planned to tell everyone. So here I am, dear, without a job or friend in the world and with this small baby to whom I have promised so much.

Is this Richard's child? I look at its face to see how the features resemble him. I must name the child, too. I call him David, Kitty, after my father Dovid. I heat milk for him on Max's small stove, but the old woman downstairs says I should find a wet-nurse – though that will cost money that I do not have at present.

Max tells me he has a surprise. When I get back to the

267

rooms from taking David for a walk in the park, there is a sewing machine and a tailor's dummy beside it.

'What's this?' I ask.

'It's your own business, Rosa,' Max tells me. 'It's what you will need to start building your empire.'

I turn to look at him. 'Why should you do this for me?' I ask.

'Friendship,' Max says.

I look back at the machine. 'This must have cost good money, Max,' I tell him, 'what will you expect from me in return?'

He roars with laughter at this, which sets the baby off crying and angers me very much.

'Very well, Rosa,' he says, sitting down, 'you want a good business footing for this thing. Then I will tell you my plan, shall I? I sell your wedding dresses to the brides as they book my services. In return for that you pay me a commission on every dress you make. Now how does that sound?'

I stroke my chin thoughtfully. 'How much?' I ask.

Max whistles through his teeth. 'Ten per cent of the retail price?' he asks.

'Seven,' I reply, 'and I will pay off the money for this machine in regular payments as soon as I am in profit. Agreed?'

Max sucks his teeth. 'You drive a hard bargain, Rosa,' he says. Then he puts out his hand and we shake. I smile up at him.

'Do you know, I believe that's the first time you've smiled at me?' Max says.

'One more thing, Max?' I say, still smiling.

'Anything,' he tells me.

'I need a pressing block and a steam iron,' I say.

Now we are both laughing, and it may be my imagination but I believe even baby David looks amused.

Sometimes when I look at Max, when his smile is open and genuine and without the mockery or sarcasm that so often accompanies it, I could wish that he were less of an immoral rogue so that I could perhaps be open with him and trust him and maybe even love him. But only as a brother, of course, Kitty, for my true heart is given to Richard and that will never change.

Kitty, it is now some months since I discovered David. Already he seems to have doubled in size and, despite my reduced circumstances, he seems healthy enough. Each night I lay awake in terror that he may be taken from me again, and every morning my relief at seeing his gummy smile is almost equal to how I felt when I first discovered he was alive. Sometimes in the silent darkness I will press my ear to his tiny chest, just to hear that he breathes. The responsibility fills me with dread and yet there is a growing confidence there, too. David is my gift, and a sign that I will succeed. I know that he would never have been given to me if I was destined for failure. We will not starve, I am sure of that. The apathy I felt when I was alone has gone now. Survival is crucial, for there is more than myself dependent upon it. My mind is freed for the first time in my life, and it is now that I have my other great idea.

I call on Max at his studio. He has two women there – both properly dressed, I may add, and high-class, to judge by their clothes. I have had six commissions for wedding

269

gowns since Max made the suggestion and he says there will be more once spring begins to show.

I wait until the women are photographed and gone in a cloud of expensive scents and raucous chatter. The studio is small, but Max has done much to make it look good, hanging drapes from the ceiling and adding a vast plaster urn on a pillar and filling it with lilies, which he says gives a bright feel to the place. Hung around the walls are portraits of women, mostly flattered to such a degree as to make them unrecognizable by anyone but their closest relatives.

There are at least three faces here that I see in passing every day, yet I would not have known them had it not been for their names inscribed in gold leaf along the corner of each shot.

I begin to laugh. 'Max, you are a magician, not a photographer!' I say when he emerges from his room. 'How did you make the old French polisher's wife look twenty years younger? And what about this bride over here?' I asked, pointing. 'I could swear she has a squint in real life, yet here her eyes are as straight as my own! And where are the warts in this picture?' I peer more closely as though expecting the woman's imperfections to reappear. 'Max, I swear you could even make me look beautiful!' I chuckle.

When I turn around he is watching me from the doorway with an impenetrable look upon his face. 'Do you know, Rosa,' he says, 'for a moment there I found myself imagining how it would feel if you were my wife come to visit me at work with our own child bundled in her arms.'

I wish he would not talk in this way, Kitty. I know he

270

is laughing at me but it makes me uncomfortable nevertheless.

'What are you here for?' he asks when I am silent.

'I've come for a picture, Max,' I tell him. I am all seriousness now.

'A baby portrait?' he asks, plucking David from my arms
and bouncing him about in a way that he has.

'Mother and baby, Max,' I whisper. 'I want you to do
a photograph that will look like a naming portrait.'

'But you're not his mother, Rosa,' Max tells me, his face
gone cold.

'I am as good as,' I tell him. 'Maybe I will want to pass
him off as my own child at some time.' I am careful in
what I say. To me David *is* my child already, but if I tell
Max I believe him to be the baby returned to me from its
grave in the sea I know I will never hear the end of it.

Max pulls me back roughly onto the small *chaise-longue*
and places David back into my arms.

'Tell me,' he says with anger in his voice, 'why might
you want to pass him off as your own? Who is the child's
father?' His face comes close to my own. 'Who, Rosa?' he
asks.

I look into those eyes that I sometimes feel know me
better than myself. It is Max who knows the worst side of
me, Kitty. It is Max who I fear has always understood the
truth.

'David is Richard Galliard's son,' I tell him quietly, 'sired
when my boss was too drunk to know what he was doing.
Aggie seduced him, she told me as much. If I tell him that
David is my own son instead, then I may get Richard to
marry me.'

271

I look down at the baby. 'I am not a fool, Max,' I say, 'I know a man like Richard will never want a girl like me. I am plain enough to be close to ugly and I have no money of my own. I could never charm him with my looks. But I love him and am determined to make him love me as much, and I know he will, if he will only see me in a more serious light.'

I have daring, Kitty, and I have had to learn cunning to survive. Richard may not know for sure who seduced him on that night, but he is an honourable man and I believe in my dreams that he will do the right thing by me. This plan of mine may sound insane, Kitty, but there is little deception in it. I love Richard and I love David. Does it matter so much who the real mother is?

Kitty, I could never describe the look on Max's face at these words. I had not expected him to encourage me, of course, but the violence in his eyes makes me blanche.

'You are mad, Rosa,' he tells me. He looks as though he loathes me.

'Why?' I ask, as David begins to emit a thin wail. 'Why is my plan so insane? It is founded on true feelings. Without me David would have had no future, yet through him I may be able to bargain the best prospects for all of us! Is that so lunatic, Max? Is it any worse than your dreams of a wealthy life as a society photographer?'

Max stares at me. 'You are using this child as your bait,' he says, quietly.

'No!' I cry. 'I love this child as my own and I would love him whoever his father. He *is* my child, Max! He was given to me!'

'If you want what is best for the boy, why not give him

272

straight to his father?' Max asks. 'Why allow him to grow up in poverty when he could have a good life?'

I cannot answer that question, Kitty. How could I? The impact of the guilt that accompanies it is enough to buckle my legs. Said in that manner, I must appear very evil indeed to keep David from his birthright. How can I explain my feelings? All I can say is that I feel him to be mine, and could no more give him away now than cut off my own right hand. Is this selfish, Kitty? Perhaps I am mad. Perhaps I am become like Rintzi.

'I could never part with him, Max,' I say, hugging the small babe to my chest and weeping with confusion.

And that is how we spend the night back in the house, I with my child clutched to my chest for fear he will be taken from me, while Max sets about exorcizing his own demons in the only way he knows how – by long and noisy shenanigans with his dimple-kneed model.

CHAPTER TWENTY-SEVEN

Z̶G

BLOCKS
Every fashion house has its own blocks, and it is
these blocks that create the house style. A block con-
sists of the pieces of brown paper pattern that act as a
blueprint for every outfit made by that house. The fit
of the shoulder, width of sleeve and shoulder-line are
all saved on the blocks, along with the other descrip-
tions of cut and fit that form the shape and look a
designer becomes known for.

Alain sat astride a wheel-bottomed stool, frowning at the
sample worn by the house model who stood swaying
slightly in front of him.

'It's okay,' Kitty said. Georgina nodded.

'No,' Alain told them, 'the hem is wrong. I swear I saw
puckering.'

'It's the lights in here.'

'The lights are good. The hem is wrong. Turn. Turn
again. Turn slowly. Wait. Who the fuck did this stitching?'

Four other models stood banked up behind the first:
tangerine cellophane velvet with the transparent pile; Ulster
calandered linen in over-cast grey; cinnabar nubuck leather
with sherbet faux-fur trim; laminated tweed in flame
orange and tonal grey; lichen tencel with almond-green

jersey. Kitty knew them all by description now. Each new design had been costed for wholesale and sketched for the press. Now Alain was about to unpick them, and yet they looked okay to her and to everyone else.

There had been a moment soon after midnight when someone should have cried out or wailed or sobbed, and maybe they would have stopped after all – just ground to a senseless halt. But the moment had passed unrecorded, and so Alain merely picked up his huge tailor's scissors and set about defiling the dress.

There was a vapour-cloud smell of tea and pizza in the air overhead. The workforce of twenty – ten machinists, five juniors, four pattern cutters and one presser – had been almost doubled by the arrival of agency workers, called in when things got desperate. This meant the normal hum of friendly chatter had ceased, to be replaced by an uneasy and rueful stinking silence between regular and agency staff.

The PR plunged about regardless in a puddle of undiluted optimism, splashing the air with Calvin Klein One to mask the brewing sweat-cloud, auditioning replacement models for the show, cooing to the models' agents over the mobile, booking cabs, phoning the press to assure them that, yes, the collection was still happening, despite rumours that it would be cancelled, and running off to the toilet in terror every time she got trodden underfoot when Alain went on the prowl.

Chloe arrived at dawn. 'We need to talk, Kitten,' she whispered into her sister's ear.

'I'm too fucking busy,' Kitty told her, her mouth full of pins and her brain full of crushed and smouldering resentment.

275

'He's okay, you know,' Chloe continued. That was the way she always spoke. As though Kitty had said nothing. 'Too fucking busy,' and yet she still chattered on.

Nicky Kofteros was okay. Good. Hoo-fucking-ray.

'He really is on our side, Kitten. He knows you don't like him and he respects that. He understands it. All he wants to do is see that the whole thing goes through smoothly and fairly. Nobody will get ripped off. The company is honourable. Talk to him, Kitten. Hear what he has to say.'

Kitty ignored her sister. Alain frowned across at her before glancing quickly back at his work. Then his focus settled upon the scent-filled gap where Chloe had just been standing. He stared so long Kitty had to turn around, too.

There was a young woman standing there. Chloe was looking shocked beside her. Kitty stood up. Pins tumbled from her mouth onto her chest, where they stuck, Gulliver-like, into her shirt. The visitor was about twenty years old, attractive in an unfashionable type of way: long black hair that had been badly permed and then grown out again, a pink suit that was a little too tight, a confident, chin-up posture but hands that worked nervously at the handle of her bag.

It was Ricky Khan's daughter.

'What the hell . . . ?' Chloe began. The girl ignored her. Kitty inwardly admired her chutzpah.

'I was hoping you might find time for us to speak,' she said to Kitty. Her voice sounded polite and cultured. 'I need to tell you a few things about your father's death. It's time you were told the truth.'

276

ZG

BUCKRAM
A light cloth, rather like cheesecloth in quality,
buckram is usually used with a glued finish for
hat-shaping, belt-stiffening and interfacing.

There is much knocking on the door of our old house the following day, Kitty, which is a strange thing to hear, for everyone in the ghetto knows that doors are rarely locked in this area and ours is bound to be open.

I hear voices calling out to the visitor, but the knocking does not cease. In the end I hear a man from two floors below make the slow path across his bare wood floor and out into the narrow hallway. Then it is my name I hear called: 'Miss Zigofsky! There is a gentleman here at the door for you!', in Yiddish.

It is Richard Galliard, and I am barely got together for it is still early. I smooth my hair behind my ears and then pull it out again, for I do not want to make too much of my ugliest feature.

'Miss Zigofsky?' His manners are impeccable, even in this terrible place. Then I know at once why he is there. Max has written to him about the child and he is come to reclaim it. I hold the door half-closed in readiness.

'I'm sorry,' Richard says, 'I must have startled you, but this is an urgent matter. Could you bear to take on some work for us, Miss Zigofsky? We have laid off most of our workers as you know, and need seamstresses of your calibre rather suddenly.'

'At the sweatshop?' I ask, confused. I am both terrified witless, embarrassed and also excited by the sight of him in my doorway.

Richard smiles. 'No, not there. In the couture house, Miss Zigofsky. Do you think you could manage it?'

'When?' I ask, reddening.

'Now,' is his reply.

Kitty, I am dressed in my shabbiest gear and my hair is doused in soot from the fireplace, and badly in need of a brush. While my face and hands are clean I was still awaiting Max's departure for the studio before I could see about the toilet of both David and myself! I believe Richard spots my plight, though.

'Er, I have a little business to attend to nearby,' he says, smiling. 'Perhaps half an hour?' I simper with relief.

In a flurry of excitement I have David placed with the woman downstairs, who says she will be hard-pressed to notice one squalling head more among her own vast brood, and have changed so quickly that Richard discovers me waiting in the hall on his return. I watch his smile fade as he approaches. In an effort to smell clean I have poured some of Max's cologne inside my corsets. To my shame the stench is overwhelming. I must reek like a streetwalker.

We take the carriage to the West End and I feel my poor dress turn shabbier with each rotation of the cab's wheels.

278

Richard is polite but the smell of the scent is so overpowering he has a handkerchief held to his nose before we are out of the East End.

The salon is in Berkeley Square and an extremely grand place it is too, with black-and-white marble on the floors and crystal lights all the way up the curving staircase. I step along the wood on the treads in case my boots soil the fine carpets.

The name above the door is perhaps the most impressive sight of all: 'Galliard Couture and Co. Court Dressmaker and Ladies' Tailor'.

I wonder that I am not shoved into the tradesman's entrance, and the expressions on the faces of some of the other staff when they see me make me wish that I had been. But Richard is all beams and smiles and introduces me as though we were guests at a society ball.

The salon is like a palace, Kitty. Everywhere are lights, and each light is reflected a thousand times in crystals or mirrors. The daylight throws rainbows around like confetti, dotting the floor and dancing on the walls. This is the prettiest place I have ever seen, Kitty.

They leave me in the salon and for one glorious moment I am alone there to take it all in. I am careful, though, checking my boots for mud before walking on tiptoe across the floor to stand directly beneath the central chandelier and looking up at it. Then I begin to rotate myself slowly so that I see the sparkle from each crystal in turn. In my excitement I start to spin and Bubba's coat flaps out like the wings of a rook.

Suddenly I stop and look straight ahead in the grand, gilded mirrors. Do you know what I see, Kitty? I see a small, pitch-haired girl with a face so white and so comically melancholy she could do the music halls without so much as a lick of greasepaint. She has thick, beetle-black brows that curve in permanent surprise, eyes like two chips of coal and a mean little mouth that looks as though it is spoiling for a fight.

Did you ever see those tiny dogs, Kitty? I forget their name but you will know them from my description: thin bent legs constantly splayed, barrel-bodied and round of head, they are the size of a cat yet feel themselves to be as good a fighter as the nearest mastiff. Their eyes see everything and they would challenge anything, so strong is their conviction that they would be the victor.

This is the look of the girl I see, Kitty; arrogant and cocky despite her size. Her chin juts and her head is high. I laugh at her and she laughs back and her smile splits her face and her teeth are white and her tongue pink. Her feet beneath the great coat are clown's feet – flat and long, and the ankles are thin as sticks.

I am reminded, Kitty, of the droll comedian at the variety halls, and quite tickled by all this until I realize that the woman I am looking at is myself. I try to make amends then, reaching up to smooth my hair or make good my outfit – but what is to be done? The face I see may not be much but it is my face, Kitty, so I cannot hate it. It is neither ugly nor handsome but lies somewhere between the two, which is to say it is neither as repulsive as Queer Tess's, nor as vacuous as Baile's. I like the spirit of its expression, and also its eyes, which show defiance and intelligence when they stop looking startled. Rintzi is there, but then so is Papa.

280

People think buildings are haunted, Kitty, but I believe it applies to faces, too, for it is there that one can see the ghosts of those who have died. When I hold my head so, I can see Bubba. When I smile Papa re-appears. Look in the mirror, dearest. Do you find my own face there anywhere? Search among your own handsome features some time – is there not a hint of arrogance in the tilt of the jaw? Or a trace of the same daring in your eyes? Those looks were mine, Kitty, and my mama's, papa's and Bubba's before me.

It is not Richard, thank God, who finds me in this day-dream, but another pinch-faced machinist come to collect me and take me off to the workrooms. I am full of questions as we walk. I know that I should be silent but cannot help myself, Kitty.

'Does this whole place belong to Richard Galliard?'

'*Mr* Galliard, yes.'

I am enchanted.

'To do with as he wants?'

The girl looks at me queerly. 'I suppose so, yes.'

I know I sound stupid, Kitty, but I must discover answers to the questions that are buzzing about my head.

'If Mr Galliard were to have a wife and child I suppose the place would be theirs as well, then?' I ask.

The girl stops and stares at me with her head on the tilt. 'Are you simple, or something?' she asks.

'No.'

'Then what of interest is it to the likes of you?'

I raise my nose as high as her own, proving I am just as able to put on airs when required. 'I'm just asking,' I tell her, 'would she or wouldn't she?'

'Maybe,' is all the girl will allow, but that is enough for me.

We pass through a design-room first, Kitty, a long space lined with rolls of the finest fabrics I have seen and hanging with toile, calico and paper patterns that I would give several years of my life to be allowed to look through.

There is a horsehair dummy in the midst of all this, and on it is pinned a half-made dress of peacock blue shantung. A woman as young as myself is on her knees killing the hem with stabs from a mouthful of pins, and another tacks the back with mother-of-pearl buttons so small they will need a hook to fasten them.

I am led carefully around this area by the gentleman machinist, a man large enough to make two of me, but who nevertheless proves light on his feet when we tiptoe around cloth and papers on the design-room floor. I am close enough to touch the dress and would do so too, as my fingers itch for the feel of good fabrics again, but one look from the seamstress is enough to inform me I am not good enough to be sharing the same air as the garment, let alone herself.

We dart up some narrow backstairs, which are bare of carpet, and arrive in a small room that is every bit as cramped as the sweatshop in the East End. There is natural light in this room, though, from a large skylight in the slanting roof, the effect of which is to lend an eerie, greenish glow to everything as the glass is thick enough to take on a tint.

Around the four walls are tables laden with cloths of all types and in the middle sit the rows of tables that hold the machines. At one end is a small paraffin stove and three well-dressed, long-stemmed women sit around it dipping finger biscuits into bone china cups filled with pale, aromatic tea. One of them is smoking and I am full of admiration for the way she points her rouge-painted mouth to the ceiling to emit perfect rings of billowing white smoke.

The machinist has returned to his seat. Everyone ignores me, which is of little matter, for it means I am free to stare where I will.

There must be as few as five garments being produced in here. At the sweatshop in the high season we would have more than that many on the go a-piece. The floor around the machines is covered with sheets of muslin to keep the garments free of dirt and I notice the workers wear slippers made of the same stuff over their boots.

The smell in this room is of camomile and lavender – one from the blend of tea and the other to repel the moths. To my left are wooden boxes filled with all sorts of delights – beads of every colour and size, small swatches of braid and embroidery silks and a tray of silver needles so fine and small you would need an eye like a bird even to thread them.

'Have you come as a replacement?' one of the biscuit women asks me. Her hair is pinned so tight upon her head that the skin of her face is as taut as that on a drum. I nod at her, the sudden movement of which sets Max's cologne off again, so that I am sadly aware of the stench myself.

'What grade are you?' she asks.

'Skilled,' I tell her – which is a lie in name but not deed. 'My father was a master tailor.'

She musters what might pass for a smile. 'So your father will be here to do your work for you, will he?' she says.

'No, my father is dead,' I say. She is all in black herself,

283

which makes me suspect that someone from her family must be recently deceased.

'Then we shall keep you to sewing on buttons for the time being, shall we?' she asks, re-aligning her padded buttocks on the small gilt chair.

And so this is where you discover me now, Kitty, perched on a stool so high my feet barely touch the ground when I point my toes, still in Bubba's coat for I am so ashamed of the dress I wear beneath it, sweating in the heat from the paraffin fire, holding threads between my teeth so tight my jaw aches, and furiously sewing on buttons so tiny they could be strung and used for pearls. There is a young girl beside me and, as chit-chat appears to be allowed here I attempt to strike up a conversation.

'Is her bereavement recent?' I enquire, nodding towards the woman in black. In reply I hear a muffled snorting noise and the girl presses her round, flat-featured face into some calico she is sewing.

'*Madame* Corby is attired in *noir* because she is a *vendeuse*,' she tells me, claret-faced with her mirth. 'All the *vendeuses* wear *noir*. So does the salon *première*. A *vendeuse* has a small white apron that she wears in the salon, but the *première* is all *noir*. Like a crow. I will be a *vendeuse* when I am old enough.'

I study the woman in black. 'I should imagine you will need to wait until you are at least ninety years if that woman is anything to go by,' I say, 'she looks as ancient as a tortoise.'

'She is my mother,' the girl says, and that is all the conversation I have from her for the rest of the afternoon.

*   *   *

284

Kitty, we are so busy in the salon, yet the work never exhausts me for I have such a passion for the garments that I am employed upon. Each seam and dart hold an eternal fascination for me and there is so much to learn here that I fear my head will not hold it all.

Each day I am endless with my questions until someone tires of me and I am told to keep my silence. And because we have daylight, I can see the sky. When the heat becomes unbearable a *vendeuse* will pull a green-dyed rope that hangs from the skylight and, *voilà*! From my little stool I have an adequate view of the clouds, as well as the occasional draught of fresh air, so my surroundings have improved immensely. I am also able to learn a few words of the language of fashion, which is *Français*.

There are some twenty staff employed here in all, which means it was more than three weeks before I had caught sight of them all. There is a strict order of superiority though, Kitty, and this is how it works: the salon is run by the manager, a silver-haired gentleman with a face like a cheese, named just 'Monsieur M'. Flapping at his flanks in adoration are the five *vendeuses*, all known as 'Madame', and all clad in dyed, bat-black challis from top to toe. Their hair, Kitty, is a marvel of construction and under-pinning. Each has a centre parting as straight as a rule from which the hair is combed back so severely that their scalps resemble little less than arrows. At the back are plaits so long they wrap three times around and all this is greased with pomander until it appears lacquered.

During the season there will be a dozen more *vendeuses* arriving, so I am told, and I wait to see if they all look alike.

285

Do you know, Kitty, there are no less than four women employed to clean the salon? Two work at night, polishing brass and crystal until the place gleams, and two arrive by day to ensure crumbs are swept away the minute they drop from the clients' plates.

Upstairs are the two designers, a pretty-looking couple of mice who spend their days pinning and snipping, and with them work a cutter and sewer who are both in suits as they work in full view of the clients when they arrive for their fittings.

Then there is the attic where we work, Kitty. We are governed by the *première* who is well above God in rank. When this woman arrives in the morning it is the job of the *petites mains* to take her hat and coat, polish any street mud from her boots and furnish her with a *demie-tasse* of sugared French *café*.

I am now a *seconde main*, Kitty, which means I am officially allowed to operate a machine. No fewer than two other *seconde mains* were set to watch over me when I was first set to work in such a way, no matter that I have worked machines in the sweatshop for more than a couple of years. My hands were inspected for grime before I was allowed to touch the fine fabrics and they are inspected in the same way each morning, before I start work.

Directly below our attic room I have discovered the most wonderful place, Kitty. In a long chamber without windows stand line upon line of horsehair dummies, all made to the size of the most regular and important clients.

Hannah, Madame Corby's daughter, has been involved with the making of these dummies and a fascinating story she tells, too. She was given the task of holding the pins when a certain English aristocrat came for her fitting. The woman was dressed in the *toile de corps*, which is a tight-fitting vest that moulds to the figure. The *toile* was then stuffed with horsehair to match the woman's shape exactly from neck to thigh.

Do you know, Kitty, these dummies are never seen by the women they were made for? Can you imagine why? Because most are too vain to view their true shape in the flesh! If a client is thin and straight then a more shapely dummy is shown but, if the woman is too well-rounded for her own tastes then a narrower one will be produced. All is done to keep the client happy, according to Hannah, and a more difficult job I could barely imagine, if their vanity is so great!

CHAPTER TWENTY-NINE

ZG

CHALLIS
*A light, plain weave of wool that is used mainly for
summer-weight dresses.*

The season has begun, Kitty, and a kind of madness settles over all. From my stool in the attic I can just see the street and so watch the fine carriages as they pull up around the square. The women that arrive at our door are all kinds of ages and sizes, but each one, without doubt, is very wealthy.

Each client has her own *vendeuse*, who is at *madame*'s beck and call, and who will show her all the latest styles that she knows will be suitable to her customer. Each *vendeuse* has her own list of clients that she alone will serve, and there is much hissing and spitting over any new customers that are introduced. All the saleswomen have their lists etched into small black leather-bound ledgers which are attached to their aprons by small silver chains. These clients are their life, Kitty, and anyone attempting to peep into those pages could well find themselves hacked to death by a set of well-honed talons.

I spoke of vanity before, Kitty. Let me tell you now that I have spent the past month attempting to part my own hair straight in the middle, though without much success, for my own mane is as thick and springy as the horsehair used to stuff the dummies.

Max, of course, has caught me at these endeavours and much sport he found from it, too.

'What are you about, Rosa?' he asked. I tried shushing him, Kitty, for my darling David was sound asleep in a basket at my feet, but this only drove him to come nearer and investigate more closely.

'You are trying to slice your head in two like an apple?' he asked, watching me raking my scalp with my comb.

'I am changing the style of my hair,' I told him. To my intense aggravation he squatted down on my bed to watch. I cannot bear people watching me at careful work, Kitty. My patience was all but worn out as it was, and now I found myself more than usually clumsy, thanks to Max's curiosity.

'Why?' he asked, bending over the basket to offer David a Havana cigar before lighting up himself – a joke that appears to have endless potential as far as Max is concerned, though I miss the humour of it myself.

'Because the new style is *très à la mode*,' I explained. This, of course, proceeded to tickle Max more than the cigar routine.

'And on whose authority do we receive this missive?' he asked.

'It is the style sported by the *vendeuses* at the salon,' I told him. He nodded sagely.

'Then perhaps I should be adopting it myself if it is so *à la mode*,' he said, fingering his own hair. I turned to him at that.

'I wish for once you would take me seriously, Max,' I said, 'you are nothing but jokes and satires. If I had fewer wits about me I would be all in knots and possibly in tears, too. Is there nothing you can say that does not have some other meaning? Why must your comments be so full of sarcasm?'

Max stood up slowly, shaking his head. He is so huge in my small partitioned room, Kitty. When he stands there he makes David and me look like dolls in a dolls' house.

'When I am serious you never believe me, Rosa,' he said, 'so why should I bother? Eh?'

I turned back to my mirror. My face looked pale with the hair pulled back so hard and my eyes appeared huge, like a child's. 'I cannot remember ever hearing you try,' I whispered.

At this he had his hands on my shoulders and had turned me about so quickly that my heel caught in my skirts and David started to awaken.

Max's face was so close to my own that I stared deep into his eyes and beyond. Did you ever stand in a high place, Kitty, and look far down to the ground? Then you will know of the pull I felt as I stared. What a horrible thing! For a moment I felt a magnetism that could have had me falling into his arms! Is this the trick that men use to charm women into submission?

There was much talk in London last year of a hypnotist who was working the music halls, mesmerizing members of the audience into doing acts of great stupidity against their will. While others, including Max himself, appeared to find these antics roaringly amusing, I always thought them a little sinister.

It has now occurred to me, Kitty, that Max may have been doing more than laughing at the act. What if he was also studying the techniques used? I believe the stage hypnotist employed a large pocket watch to put his patients under, while I have no memory of Max retrieving his from his pocket before I felt the magnetic pull. This is of no use as a guide, though, Kitty, for if he is so adept at the art he may also have been able to make me forget the sight of the watch altogether!

I *wanted* Max to hold me at that moment, Kitty. I would almost say I *yearned* for him to touch me more. The breath became short in my lungs and my thin legs lost their strength. Now what else could have caused that to happen if it were not some wicked skill or trick on Max's behalf?

Next time I see him reach for his watch, Kitty, I will remove myself from his presence with great speed, you may be sure of that!

My new hairstyle is not a great success in the salon as it appears many of the *vendeuses* believe a mere *seconde main* like myself should know her place and not attempt to ape her superiors. Nevertheless I shall continue with it, for I feel it gives me some style which my poor clothing, alas, sorely lacks.

Kitty, I have omitted to make much mention of David, but not because he is forgotten – rather that all those I work with inform me that I speak of very little else. He is the most marvellous child and very beautiful, too.

I stare at him for hours when he is asleep and when he wakes I feel a new joy that I cannot describe. When I hold him and feel his little skull cupped into the palm of my hand and watch his tiny fingers clenching around my own pin-scratched mitt I know that I have done the right thing in caring for him.

In the morning I carry him in my arms to the woman downstairs and I know he is happy there until I return to collect him at night. He is growing plump and healthy as I did as a babe, Kitty. When I sing to him he smiles and I still feel him to be my own infant, returned to me whole from the depths of the ocean. I am not mad, Kitty. My mind knows full well that he is not some wraith come back to haunt me, and yet my heart tells me another story at the same time. I know the child is not mine in body, but there is nevertheless an instinct in me telling me strongly that discovering him was more fate than coincidence. I believe he was intended for me, dearest. Perhaps there is some of the soul in him of the child that I lost.

Spiritualism is very much the vogue in London right now and seances take place in all the best parlours on a regular basis. The other day there was thick fog upon us and Max remarked drolly from the window that it was maybe all the left-over ectoplasm that the mediums had left leaking about the atmosphere. If so many educated people may believe in such things, though, then it is my belief that I should be allowed to as well. Bubba always told us folk tales of lost spirits and ghosts, and although they terrified poor Gregory witless I was always fascinated by them, no matter how many times they were repeated.

I have persuaded Max to take the photograph that I wanted, even though I had to trick him a little and pretend it was merely a portrait. I made David a little white robe from some lace off-cuts I saved from one of the bridal

292

gowns, and I put on my best frock and borrowed a decent hat from Baile.

Max posed us against his best backdrop, which is a rather fanciful arrangement of draped fabric and waxed fruit in front of a painting of cobalt sky and overblown clouds.

Max is very much the professional in his studio, Kitty, and it would make you laugh to watch him about his business. There is a jacket he wears for the job that I feel makes him look ridiculously pompous, though he informs me that all photographers of note wear them. The thing is made of dark crimson velvet with lapels of blood-red satin. Do you know, he even has a small matching pill-box hat with a gold braid tassel that he would place upon his head? I was forced to beg him to forget this particular item of photographer's costume, for I would have barely been able to hold my pose for laughing.

Max appeared deeply offended at this, flinging the offending item across the studio and working in studied silence for a full hour following – though I caught him putting the hat onto David's head and laughing later, when he thought I was not looking, so the thing cannot be quite so serious after all, now, can it?

The photograph is wonderful, Kitty. Max has quite captured David's expression when he is at his most cherubic and I do not look so bad, either, despite the fact that Baile's hat is a size too large and had to be stuffed with tissue to prevent it slipping around my ears. I believe Max to be quite proud of his work, too, for he has made a copy for himself that he has stuck in a little frame and placed beside his bed.

'I wonder my face does not keep you awake with the nightmares,' I said once, attempting a little joke of my own.

'It does keep me from sleeping, Rosa, but not in the way you think,' he told me, which made me blush. Sometimes I find his manner of turning an innocent comment around quite exhausting.

The season has passed now at the salon and we are a little quieter, even though there are still the fittings and makings to be done. I am worried now about my future, for I fear the same laying-off of hands that we had at the factory. I have two to feed now and worry that David may suffer if my work falls off.

In preparation for this I am hard at work getting commissions for more wedding gowns. Max has offered to keep a portfolio of photographs of the few I have already made in the studio so that the new brides can see them and judge the quality of my work. I tell him this idea has its limits, for how many brides will want to order a design that another has already worn?

Max informs me that since my designs are all copies anyway he fails to see the problem. This is of course true, but I do not like him any the more for saying it. My wedding dresses to date have all been taken from photographs Max has shown me of other brides' gowns, even though I will alter a neckline here or add some little frill or other there.

'I'm a sewer, Max,' I tell him, 'how can I be expected to design something new as well?'

Max shrugs. 'You see enough clothes, Rosa,' he tells me, 'surely you will have learnt a few tricks by now?'

294

'And you spend most of your evenings at the music halls watching the comics, Max,' I tell him indignantly, 'so I suppose by the same token you will be able to form your own routine by now.'

This is, of course, a mistake, as Max sees it as his cue to leap to his feet and begin rattling off jokes with Baile's hat pulled onto his head and a stupid expression on his face.

I would rather chew off my own nose than let Max see that any of this amuses me, and so cover my face with my hands, though David begins to crow with delight at all the racket, until I am forced to lift him from his basket and show him the whole wretched performance.

As Max comes to the end, I begin to feel a little dizzy and suddenly I am on the floor and David is crying while Max is calling my name and unbuttoning my bodice at the neck. I am about to reprimand him for this but find myself too weary to raise my head. Max is all concern now. I feel him lift me into his arms just as though I weighed as little as a rag doll, and I am placed gently upon his bed.

'When did you last eat?' he asks me.

I try to think, but I cannot remember clearly.

'Rosa!' Max is sounding serious now. I open my eyes and stare up into his face. If he pulls the pocket watch from his waistcoat I shall be crawling back into my own room despite my fatigue.

'David?' I ask. I can still hear him crying somewhere.

'The baby is fine,' Max tells me. 'I have given him your hat to play with.'

'The hat is Baile's!' I struggle to get up but Max holds me pinned to the bed.

'Rosa,' he repeats, though more gently this time, 'you are feeding the baby at the expense of yourself. Now you faint from lack of nutrition. Am I supposed to watch you starve yourself, Rosa?'

I turn my head to the pillow. Max watches me a while and then I hear him go out. His bed is softer than my own and I can do nothing but fall into a deep sleep. When I wake up Max has returned and has made tea for me to drink.

'Strudels and honeycakes,' he says. There is a platter of treats in front of me and, after breaking some off for David I am ashamed to say I eat the lot. Max sits watching me and sipping at his own cup of tea.

'Rosa,' he says quietly after a while, 'am I right in assuming you will not marry me?'

I am feeling stronger now after my feast and I snort a little and laugh, for I know he is back to his jokes again.

'Then you must make some plans,' he says, 'or you will either have to take charity or starve. The salon must fall quiet soon. Do you have work at the factory if it does?'

I shake my head. All fashion work is seasonal and all seasons are the same.

'Then what are your alternatives?' he asks.

'To make up models for some more brides,' I tell him, 'perhaps take in some private alterations and repairs.'

'Weddings are very much seasonal too, Rosa,' Max tells me. 'Didn't you know most brides like to be married in the spring? And repairs will hardly keep you in bread for a week.'

I lay back onto the pillows. 'Is all this said just to depress me, Max?' I ask. 'I know my plight. I'm not a fool.'

Max stares at me. 'You should tell your boss that you have his child here,' he says.

I have a sudden vision of Richard in my mind. I have seen him less at the salon than I did at the workshop as we are mainly segregated there and Richard does not appear much above the first floor.

'No,' I say, 'not yet.'

Max still stares. 'Then come and work for me,' he says, 'I am in need of a lady receptionist.'

I smile because of his cakes and because of his offer, which is, I believe, genuine. 'My skill is in the garment trade, Max,' I tell him. 'If I am to make my fortune then I believe it will be in that business.' I also have no wish to leave Richard's employ.

Max sighs. 'Then you will take a cut in your rent,' he tells me.

'No, Max.' I need to thank him for enough already. If he takes less rent he might be asking for favours in kind.

Did he read this in my eyes? I see a change in his own, a look of disbelief. 'You wouldn't take help from a friend?' he asks. 'Not even on behalf of the child?'

'David will never go hungry,' I tell him.

'No – not as long as you are prepared to starve on his behalf,' is Max's reply.

I sit in the design-room holding pins for the seamstress who is doing a fitting on a large matron with corsets like the sails of a ship. I am neither to stare nor to move any more than is necessary. This is difficult because the fabric of the suit we are altering has a nap that flies up like fur when it is cut and my nose itches and my eyes sting.

When the client is gone I am either allowed tea with the *vendeuses*, or they do not notice me there with them, which is the more likely option.

There are wafer biscuits on a dish that they share and my stomach groans, but I would not dare to lean and take one. I am squeezed between two of the part-time *vendeuses*, both remarkably elderly ladies with a strong scent about them of eau de cologne and mothballs. Part of their conversation is spoken in a very strangely accented French, and part of it in Yiddish, but the story I hear from them is that the older lady is about to retire.

Unfortunately both are deaf, so the conversation is of limited pleasure, but it seems that the retiring lady, known as Madame Gisele, is becoming too hard of hearing to serve the clients, and even her oldest and most loyal customers – though how many can be left alive by now I am led to ponder – have become agitated at the way orders will go astray or be completely misheard.

I gather that one elderly duchess, in particular, has been vociferous in her complaints after a brown satin tea-dress she ordered became somehow translated into a broadsilk tweed vest on the garment list. There is much rustling and twittering among the other *vendeuses* at the news of this woman's retirement, for whoever bids the most will be able to buy her client list from her when she goes.

This evening I am told I will not be needed at the salon again, though I may be called back when the next season starts. Kitty, I am sickened by this news, even though it was expected. What am I to do? I see myself a pathetic figure now – eighteen years old and soon to be queuing at the Jewish poor house for bread and hot tea. All the way home I tell myself that I have a brain in my head and that I can live on my wits, though my stomach rumbles hard enough to assure me I need bread as well.

The woman downstairs gives me a look as she returns David to me. 'There is a letter come for you,' she says. I can see she is all ears as to the contents so I deny myself the urge to rip it open there and then, stuffing it instead into the pocket of my apron as though receiving letters were an everyday occurrence.

Once in my room I place David on the floor to play while I rip open the envelope and read the letter inside.

It is from the Temporary Shelter. They have been trying to trace me for many weeks to tell me an immigrant has arrived in the country naming me as a relative they might find shelter with. I am to call at Leman Street within a day of the letter's arrival to take part in the longed-for reunion. The name that has been given is in print: ZIGOFSKY – nothing more. I wonder if one of my uncles has come from America having fallen on hard times. How pleased he will be then to see the succour that his clever little niece can provide for him!

I tell Max of this news and he is all finger-wagging and dire warnings. 'Don't take in any more strays off the street, Rosa!' he says.

I look at David and then across at Max, my eyes wide with anger. 'Strays?' I ask.

'Of course,' Max replies, walking over to the baby and lifting him shoulder high. 'You have no objection to being called a stray, do you, young man?' he asks David. He then throws his voice into the baby's mouth, saying, 'No!' in a child's tone, which is his latest trick stolen from some stage ventriloquist he has seen at the halls. He would take this joke further, but I pull David from his hands while he is still laughing at the cleverness of it all.

The fog is thick and I have no pennies for a cab and so must walk to Leman Street to meet my lost relative. I leave the house dressed in good order, for I would not want an uncle to see my true situation, but by the time I am two streets away the fog has made a huge damp halo of my hair and the mud from the carts is splashed all over the hem of my skirts.

I never relish walking about the East End after dark. I remember the tales of the Ripper that haunted me when I was a greener. The murders may have stopped but the monster was never discovered, and in my imagination he is waiting around each and every dark corner to claim me as his next victim.

A greater dread comes upon me as I approach the shelter, though. This is the place I first stayed when I arrived full of hope for my marriage to Aaron. What a child I was then! The smells here are still familiar to me. In those days I supposed I would be rid of this East End grime by now and married and living far away in Russia again, with my husband, taking care of my family. To think I came here as a saviour of them all and instead my mother is well and I am the one in need of help.

For the first time the idea occurs to me that I should save up for a ticket back to my homeland and search for my mother. But I know I can never do that now. My duty is to my own child and my dream is to marry his papa. Russia is still a cruel land for Jews and David could be slaughtered as the son of one just as easily as my own papa.

300

I am cold. The light is there in the doorway of the shelter and, although I am repulsed by the too-familiar smells of the place, I force myself to walk inside.

The warden, who greets me, is a decent sort who appears genuinely pleased that I have come to search for my relative. I had almost been expecting to see Queer Tess squatting there, before reminding myself of her death. I sign my name to some paper and am kept waiting some fifteen minutes while the warden goes off on a search. I hear two sets of footsteps returning but only the warden's voice, chatting encouragement.

'Come along, son, she's here to fetch you. Did you eat your supper? Good. Bring your coat from the peg for it's a cold enough night and you don't want a chill.'

Is this a child he has fetched for me, Kitty? I peer around the door but the corridor curves too acutely for me to see. Then I have them in my view, the warden, small and bearded, clutching a light in one hand and a coat in the other. And beside him – Gregory! Grown so much I would barely know him in the street, but my Gregory, nevertheless.

He is taller than I remembered and his face is bigger, though still quite beautiful. Like myself when I arrived he has an expression of bewilderment in his eyes. There is a sad, hand-knitted cap upon his head and his hair beneath it appears in need of a cut.

'Gregory?' I take a step further towards him. Then he raises a hand in welcome and I know it could be no one but my brother, for there are no fingers on that hand, they are buried in the woods in Russia.

'Gregory!' I am more fearful than pleased to see him.

301

How has he got here? Why has he come? He is smiling openly now at the sight of me. He breaks into a shambling run and then he has his arms about me and I feel my own tears pressed into the shoulder of his jacket, though I had no idea before then that I was crying.

Gregory rocks back and forth as he clings to me. 'Rintzi, Rintzi,' he cries. He is cold, very cold – shivering beneath his clothes. I take his coat from the warden and place it about his shoulders. I begin to speak to him in English, which is now my tongue, but realizing the confusion in his eyes switch quickly to the language of my childhood.

'How did you come here? Are you alone? What has happened? How did you arrive?'

But all he does is smile at me as fat tears snake down his face.

The warden is back with a small sack in his hands. 'Here,' he says, giving it to me. Inside are all Gregory's possessions – a comb, some soap wrapped in paper, a handful of bone collar-stiffeners and the equivalent to approximately three pounds in roubles. 'Good luck to you, son,' the warden says, raising a hand.

'What do you mean?' I ask. 'Where is he going?'

The old man smiles. 'To live with his sister,' he says.

'I have no room.' I can barely hear my own voice. 'I thought he could stay here a little while longer. I have nowhere for him to go. What shall I do?'

'The boy is fed and has enough money for lodgings,' the warden tells me. 'When the money runs out you can take him to the poor house. You know his time here is limited.'

I lead Gregory out into the street. The cold is now acute and the fog has thickened. As I take his hand I feel his

shivers have increased until his entire body seems almost
to be held in a fit. For want of anything other to do we
begin to walk in the direction of Brick Lane. Gregory holds
my hand so tight he almost breaks the bones, though I
dare not prise him off for fear I might lose him in the fog.
Carriages roll close to us, making us both jump. All noises
seem magnified in the gloom, even the sound of our own
feet.

'Are you well, Gregory?' I ask as we rush on our way,
and he nods once. 'Are you hungry?' He shakes his head,
'No.' I suspect that he is lying – Rintzi always taught us
to ask for nothing when we visit another's home – but I
am relieved, as there is little food in the house.

When we reach my place I usher Gregory up the stairs
like a reluctant dog, and into my room. I can see from his
face and the way that he pauses in the doorway that he
was expecting more. I see the room with new eyes at that
moment. It is a pauper's place, clean but impoverished.
There are not even chairs enough for us both to sit down.

'Were you expecting a palace, dear?' I ask my brother.
He shakes his head silently, rubbing his hands back and
forth on his cheeks to thaw them. Suddenly he looks at me
and smiles and it is as if my heart has opened up and been
torn from my chest.

He is the same boy that I knew and loved. Gregory,
my dear brother, here in my room in London. The same
pale-skinned face. The same calm beauty – though now
tempered with age. How old must he be? Twenty-three?
A man. Yet he smiles like a boy and his crooked teeth are
the same. His brown hair has been combed flat to his head
and ironed there by the cap. I watch as he suddenly throws

303

himself down onto the bed, exhausted. When I return from downstairs with David in my arms I find Gregory sound asleep already and bend quietly to prise the boots off his feet.

Soon he is snoring loudly. I crouch down on the floor by his feet and sit there in silence, rocking David in my arms in the dark room.

'Two children now, David,' I whisper, 'two helpless and trusting babies to care for and nourish. What is to become of us, eh? What are we to do?'

CHAPTER THIRTY

ZG

LONDON 1997

BRICK LANE
*Of all the buildings in the East End, the Great
Synagogue in Brick Lane must most represent the changing
face of the immigrants in that area. Starting life as a
French chapel, while the Huguenots wove their silk in
the neighbouring attic rooms, it was a Wesleyan
chapel before becoming a synagogue. Following that it
became a mosque.*

It was raining as they left the studio. Alain came after her. 'Take this,' he said. He eyed Khan's daughter as he handed Kitty her mobile.

'What, do you think I will try to murder her?' the girl asked him. The word 'murder' hung in the air menacingly.

'We have garments to price,' Alain said to Kitty, ignoring everything else. 'Thirty minutes max, okay?'

The two women climbed into a cab. Sitting together provided a kind of intimacy that made both uncomfortable. Riva smelt of scent and lunch. For want of something to do Kitty rolled her sleeves as though she were hot. The silence between them was unbearable. In another minute she knew she would have cracked and made some facile comment about the weather or the cost of muslin that season.

In the event it was Riva who tossed a fistful of words into the vacuum. 'Thirty minutes to prove my father did not kill yours.' She pulled the scarf off her head and shook it.

Kitty had grown up knowing the girl, but they had never been friends. Riva had always seemed fascinatingly remote. She was older, too; nearer Chloe's age. The cab smelt stale, like a damp dog. They sat side by side but both staring ahead.

Kitty was cross-eyed tired. The cab was warm and dank. Riva pulled a small perfume spray out of her purse and puffed it about fussily.

'You believe Ricky Khan killed Gabriel Zigofsky?' she asked quietly. It was as though she spoke about two strangers, just commenting on something she'd read in the press. So what is your opinion? As though it barely mattered.

'I only just heard,' Kitty said. 'I didn't believe he'd been arrested. Has he been charged?'

When Riva turned to face her she could see the calmness was all an act. Her features looked smeared in the street-lights. Kitty knew the look and she knew the feeling. Nothing worked properly any more. Eyes, nose, mouth – they all took on new functions with the shock and the grief, most of them to do with snot and tears. There was liquid bubbling up and down the back of her own nose. Ears, nose, throat – who realized their similar liquid functions until grief placed that knowledge in your path?

306

'He didn't do it,' Riva whispered. 'How could you think he did?'

Kitty stared out at the snakes of rain dripping down the glass. 'I think everyone did it right now, Riva,' she said. 'I'm so crazy with it all there's not one person I don't suspect – Kofteros, Burgess, Hester, even you, Riva, and even me. Especially me, as a matter of fact. Perhaps he was protecting the business for my sake. Christ knows the number of well-meaning people who have bothered to tell me my father intended passing everything on to me after he died. That it was me he saw as his true heir apparent. What if he got in the way of progress for *my* sake? Those are the sorts of thoughts that are currently keeping me awake at night, Riva.' She sighed. 'Did you ever have a head so full of sadness and garbage that you'd like to empty it of everything? And none of those thoughts are going anywhere, either. They just roll round and round; suspicions, technicoloured guilt-trips, giant snow-storms of grief, loneliness . . .' she turned suddenly. 'Sorry, sorry,' she mumbled. 'I'm tired. You don't want to hear all this crap.' She pushed her hair back off her face and breathed deep lungfulls of stale, nicotine-scented air.

'The cigarettes are winning again.' She laughed, nervously. Riva's hand plunged into her bag and for a moment Kitty thought the perfume spray was coming out again. Instead it was a tissue – white, with a floral border, like kitchen-towel – which Riva handed across with a small sniff of her own to accompany the gesture.

They drove to a street in East London that Kitty had never seen before – and why should she have? There was nothing there to visit; it was a middle-of-nowhere place.

The sort of street you only go down to get to somewhere else, and then probably only if you're lost. The only noise in the road was of things happening elsewhere. There were two derelict buildings; a flat-fronted cement block that looked as though it had been concocted in the fifties; some hoardings bearing layers of fucked-up posters, ragweed growing out between them.

'There,' Riva pointed, 'that was where he was found.'

A great gust of horror blew over Kitty. She stared at Riva as though she were a magician. Empty street one minute, graveyard the next. 'This is where your father died.' As easy as that. And Kitty had had no sensory warning of what was about to occur. Her own father. Her nerves should have been alive with foreboding. Some unknown perceptions should have signalled an alert. Nothing.

There was still tape. Kitty stared at the ground. Of course she had been told. But she had had no curiosity. This was not on her list of places to visit. She hadn't even looked it up on the map.

There was wet pavement and there was rubbish. She thought maybe someone should have swept it tidy, shown some respect. Golden Wonder packets and Kit-Kat wrappers hung around the spot like rubber-neckers. Someone several streets away was singing: 'I plucked a violet from my mother's grave . . .'

Kitty stared.

'Kiss me, honey, honey, kiss me . . . Thrill me honey, honey, thrill me . . .'

Her eyes were soldered to the pavement now; welded to the seal-like wetness. Every crack, bump and sweet-wrapper was being methodically consigned to that part of the brain that will never forget, no matter how hard you try. The bit that hangs on to insults like they were precious jewels. The section that has total recall over every argument you have ever had in your life. The one that can summon up all the ugly, sickening visuals of your life like an over-zealous picture library. And now a new scene had been filed away: the place where my father was killed, as seen at night, in the rain. It was an image Kitty would have preferred to forget, but now it would be with her always.

'Don't care even if I blow my top, but honey, honey . . . don't stop!' A drunk sang on, *sotto voce*.

'Kitty?'

There were objects there that she couldn't identify in the dark. Rusted bits. Lumps of dirt. Rubble. A bus ticket? Cellophane.

'Kitty?'

'Why did you bring me here?' she heard herself ask.

'Kitty, it's that guy from your showroom. He wants you to tell him you're still alive.' Riva pressed the mobile against her ear. She could just about hear Alain above the roar of the sewing machines. She badly wanted to be there, warm and normal in the workroom, not here.

'I'm just in the street,' she told him, 'I'll be back soon.'

Her eyes had still not left the spot.

'You were always your daddy's little girl, Kitty,' Riva said with a sigh. 'I hated you. He spoilt you, remember? You used to sit up on the piles of cloth where he had lifted you like a little Buddha. A pretty little doll. I was working.'

'Ricky is like an uncle to me,' Kitty whispered, 'my father loved him . . . they were friends, old friends.'

'My father hated Gabriel when he took his business

309

away,' Riva said. 'It destroyed him. But he didn't kill anyone. He died inside. He didn't ask for revenge.'

'I have to get back,' Kitty said. There was no real world
available to her now, but the salon was as close as she
could get.

'First come with me,' Riva told her. They walked further
along the street, past The Spot. Then round a corner, to a
pub – or what used to be a pub. It was boarded and black.
But there was noise, all the same.

'It's a club,' Riva told Kitty, 'a private club. Dangerous.
A sex club.'

Kitty looked at Riva.

'Tell me one other reason why your father would be in
an area like this,' the girl said, evenly. There was a white
fleck of dried toothpaste in the corner of her mouth. Kitty
heard the words in her ears, but it was minutes before they
burrowed through to her conscious mind.

'He was visiting the club, Kitty,' Riva said. 'He must
have had another life, you know – one you were not aware
of. We all have hidden sides of ourselves, Kitty,' she added,
'no one is perfect, you see – not even your father.'

CHAPTER THIRTY-ONE

ZG

PRESSERS
*Garment pressing was often done by men. They had
to be strong, because an iron for top pressing could
weigh as much as fourteen pounds.*

Kitty, I am of the belief that life consists of many levels
and we have settled at a lower one than before, and that
is the truth of our situation. Gregory has grown very feeble-
minded so that however much I love him the notion is
forced upon my poor brain that he is a burden to us all.

How can I describe my brother? His face is grown less
pretty but I feel this is more down to an habitual
expression, which is one of bewilderment and lazy depen-
dency, than a change in its features. He is big now – bigger
than me – and will sit and watch me for many hours on
end unless I find him some task to do.

I try constantly to lure tales of the *shtetle* from his mouth,
but he is not eager to communicate and often the only
reply I will receive to my endless questioning is a nod and
a smile.

I have become crafty out of desperation, Kitty. Gregory's
appetite for food is voracious, yet his manners are good.
When we sit down to eat I will place the steaming dinner

out of his reach and lean across to hold his hand and get him talking about home. His eyes fix onto the food like a dog's yet he dare not reach for it. While he is thus distracted it is easier to talk.

'How did you get here, Gregory?'

'By boat.'

'Did the family see you off?'

A shrug.

'Was it your idea to come to England?'

'Of course.'

'You were not sent, then?'

'No, Rosa. I am a man now, I think for myself.'

'Then you must have earned wages to pay for the trip?'

'No.'

The questions go in circles, Kitty, without sense or answer. It is important I employ all my patience, though. I believe in time I will discover the whole story. At the moment I keep pieces of it in my head, like a jigsaw, waiting for other bits to fit so that I can have the whole picture at last.

'How is Rintzi, Gregory?' This always evokes some strange look in his eyes before his head goes down.

'Did she receive my letters?'

'Yes.'

'Why didn't she reply? I wrote my address at the top. Did she tell you, Gregory? Did she say she would write to me or was she so terribly angry that I did not marry Aaron? Does she speak of me much, Gregory? Did you fight? Is that why you came here?'

Kitty, I received the most terrible answer to my questions last night.

312

'She is dead,' Gregory said, and his whole face seemed to burst from the effort of the words, so that mucus and tears spilled out in a torrent.

'Rintzi?'

Not happy, then. Dead.

Gregory was lost to me, though. His crying became heavier until David could stand the noise no longer and was forced to join the chorus.

'Rintzi is dead?'

'Killed,' was what I heard.

Kitty, I have more pieces for my puzzle now and spend much time sitting on my bed in the attic moving them all around in my mind in an attempt to make them fit.

Rintzi is dead, I believe this much to be true, and it seems fire was the cause – though brought about by whom I have yet to discover. At first Gregory told me she had killed herself, and this I could have believed, for my mother's mind was always unsettled, as I have mentioned before.

There were many more tears and sighs, Kitty, before I could get the idea from my brother that she had been burnt to death in a pogrom, along with many others.

This image haunted my mind for several nights and in my imagination it was the same youths who had seen my father off in the barrel. Max is away at present, sleeping at the studio so that Gregory has a bed to use. I must admit I have missed Max's common sense right now and his way of making light of things, though even he would be hard pressed to find humour in my current problems.

Much of the time I am at the machine, doing repairs that I have taken in to keep us in food while the slack season is upon us. My work is good but if I sewed day and night without stopping I would not earn enough to feed us well. Max has not asked for rent for many weeks and I am in no position to remind him. I should tell my poor brother to find employment somewhere, but I have not got the heart to ask him and am too busy discovering the truth from him to want to insist.

When Max returns I inform him there are only a few more weeks of this and then I will be back in the salon, which is true. His photographic business flourishes, thank God, and he has recently employed a sensible young girl called Isabelle to work as receptionist. She is quite smart, with an accent that implies her background must be wealthy. Max is delighted with her and says her voice alone will double trade.

This has made me think of my own voice. How do I sound to Richard? If I spoke like Isabelle perhaps he would love me. My passion for him is not subdued, Kitty. I miss him badly and each time there is a hammering on the front door of the house I imagine it is him come to fetch me back to the salon again.

If it were not for David I believe I would never leave my little attic at all, but children need fresh air and so I am methodical in our daily trips to the park.

David is not a strong child, Kitty, but I refuse to believe that he could receive better care and treatment than that which I lavish upon him. His chest is rather weak, which is a common complaint of children around here, though I cannot do more than my best when it comes to the freshest air I can find for him. When the sun comes out again to warm us he will be better, Kitty, I am sure of it.

Do you know, dearest, I am so set in my own current plight that it was many weeks before I realized that the whole ghetto suffers in a similar way? For we are all in the main tailors, pressers and sewers here, save the cabinet-makers and cobblers. Either that or our trade depends upon those who are. So we all eat together and we all starve together, depending upon the season.

Despite the poverty, though, what dignity there is here! To watch these stricken people go about their business you would think they had all the riches on earth! There is a constancy to their lives, Kitty, that leaves me feeling humbled. They talk, gather, observe the rituals and attend the synagogue through lean seasons and busy periods and if anyone mentions the harshness of it all they will raise their hands into the air as if to say, 'So?' They are the chorus of idealists, Kitty, the congregation of their suffering voices becomes a soundless echo as it travels across time.

Help is offered to me from many sources, and all from people who have little more than myself. I am proud, though, Kitty, too proud for my own good. I see myself as the provider for both David and Gregory. I am young and able-bodied and will die before either of these two goes hungry for as much as a minute.

I feel the sins of my life preclude me from joining this generally honourable society too, Kitty. Who am I to sit in their rooms and pray in their synagogues? I have had a child outside marriage and currently care for one that is, by law, not my own. If I befriended others of my community then I would fear every day that the truth of my situation would emerge and David would be taken from me and placed in the poor house. Save Gregory and Max

I am a loner, Kitty. Even Baile is something of a stranger to me since her marriage. This is how it must be, though. I have no wish for it to be otherwise, for who else can you trust in life other than yourself, Kitty?

And still I question my brother. Gregory and I are become like two old boxers, punch-drunk and weary from our nightly battle of wits yet neither able to give in.

'Who killed Rintzi, Gregory?' The food before him is not much but I can hear his stomach growl at the sight of it.

'Men,' he says. I have heard this reply for five nights running.

'What men?'

He shrugs. His face is pale but the tears have not come yet, which gives me hope.

'Were you there, Gregory?' I ask, stroking his good hand.

'No!' His tone is angry and defensive. He pushes his chair back and begins to rise. 'No!' He is shaking his head so violently his hair whips about. I pull him back down into his seat.

'Max says you should have a job, Gregory. Would you like that?' His anguish has forced me to change the subject.

'I wasn't there, Rosa.'

'Leave him, Rosa – can't you see how affected he is?' I am surprised to hear Max's voice. He is standing in the open doorway, watching in silence, smoking a cigarette.

I turn to him in exasperation. 'I *have* to find out what happened to my mother, Max, don't you see?'

Max is serious for once. He walks across to Gregory and places a hand on his shoulder. 'He's frightened,' he tells me.

316

I look at my brother. I love him but I must know. I push the bowl of food across towards him and he starts to eat noisily.

'You shouldn't force him,' Max tells me. Gregory has learnt no English so we are free to talk.

'I have to know if my mother is dead,' I say. I sound stubborn and girlish, which is not my intention.

Max takes another mouthful of smoke. 'She is,' he tells me. He pulls a small metal flask from his pocket and pours alcohol from it before handing it to me. I sniff at the drink. It is brandy – I know the smell. It reminds me of Richard.

'How do you know?' I ask.

'Your brother told me,' Max nods at Gregory.

I purse my lips to look shrewish because what I want to do is cry. Of course Gregory has told Max. Why would he not? I have used time and patience and many bowls of food to discover what Max has found out during a brief chat.

'He talks to me a lot while you are out in the park with the baby.' Of course. 'He is frightened of you, Rosa. He loves you but you scare him.'

'He told you that?' Max nods. Gregory still eats.

'Why should I scare him? I am just his little sister.' And for the first time since I have met him, Max looks uncomfortable.

'Rosa, perhaps it would be better if you left him alone,' he says. 'He is confused. Let me get him a job. If he has a salary of sorts he can rent his own room nearby. There are a lot of things he needs to forget, but that is impossible with you quizzing him each night. Pay your attentions to David instead, Rosa. His cough is getting worse, I believe.'

Max says all this in a kindly voice but I am tired and becoming angry.

'David has nothing more than a little cold,' I tell him, 'how can you imply I ignore him to deal with my brother? No one could care for a child more, Max!'

He knows this to be true enough, I can see from the way his eyes fall to the floor and the apology he is immediately forced to make.

We move around in upset silence for a bit, but in the end I have to ask, 'Why is my brother frightened of me, Max?'

Max stubs out his cigarette, unable to look me in the eye. 'He says he killed your mother,' he says in a low voice, 'he says when the men came and burnt her house he locked the door and watched her die.' He rubs his hands across his face wearily. 'He says other things at other times, Rosa. Sometimes the house burnt while he was away and he came back to find her dead. Another time he told me he started the fire himself.' Max sighs. 'He believes many things, Rosa, and all of them contradictory. Leave him. He doesn't know what he is saying. He came here for sanctuary and you must give him some peace.'

This is a very wordy speech from Max. I pick David up and clutch him to my bosom despite the fact that he, like his uncle, is happily at his food. I find it hard to sketch my emotions as I stare at the back of Gregory's head. Three images run through my mind: Rintzi dead and Gregory returning to discover the tragedy, just as I did with Papa; Rintzi leaning screaming from the window while Gregory weeps and holds the door firmly shut; Gregory throwing straw about and lighting it while Rintzi sleeps. Which one

318

do I believe? All of them, Kitty. Could my brother have murdered my mother? What a thing to have to decide! What a choice Gregory has presented me with.

But at the same time I feel that Gregory is still my darling brother and know he would never bring harm to any living thing.

'Are you all right?' Max asks. I kiss David's head. He has downy hair now. His flesh smells sweet. He is innocent and beautiful, as Gregory must have been as a baby.

'Be careful,' says Max, enigmatically.

I don't question Gregory much after that. Sometimes the truth can be unbearable. Sometimes it is better swept beneath the corner of the rug, along with the dust.

CHAPTER THIRTY-TWO

ZG

SIZING

*Until the 1930s women's clothes were sized as
'maid's' or 'matron's', then later as SW, W and WX.
It was the influx of Berlin and Viennese tailors that
led to the sizing revolution, creating a size ten to sixteen standard, and allowing women to buy a good fit
off-the-peg.*

We live in mists and fogs here, Kitty, locked safe inside
our own little dramas by the shroud the elements throw
about us. I have a candle in the window and it burns deep
yellow, like the yolk of an egg. Our house is like a doll's
house as there is no outside to be seen. I feel as though
there is no time and sometimes I feel as though I have seen
too much time and am old.

David is four years. Gregory has employment, found for
him by Max. By day he stacks fruit and by night he eats.
Max has taught him to smoke, which is something I regret.
My work at the salon has kept us going but only just. This
year the weather has been bad enough to affect trade. In
Russia we worked through as much snow as nature could
provide, but here the ladies will not come out from their
homes if there is as much as a spit of rain or – as now –
fog.

There is a smell of sulphur about the place. The fog is jonquil yellow and impenetrable. It induces a dream-like state about the place and we all move more slowly about our business, as though nothing mattered without the visual stimulus of other buildings and other people. At night I become frightened and once I woke believing the rest of the world had truly disappeared.

And who do I feel the most need of at these times? Max, that is who, for in our doll's house it is Max who is reality and Richard who barely exists. Max is solid against the mist. He is large and full of laughter and it is he who we must depend upon for our very livelihood and sanity.

Let me tell you what our day is like. I wake to the sound of Gregory banging about on the other side of the partition. He lights a candle and then he is dressing. His next thought will be of breakfast and so will David's, for already Gregory's racket has woken him and he is calling out my name.

His hair is grown longer and has started to curl a little. He wears clothes I sew for him and Papa would be proud for he is so well-dressed that people in the street must wonder how his mama comes to be so out of fashion with her own clothes.

He is a happy child when his health is good, and much in love with Max, who spoils him. I am forced to keep an eye on the pair of them constantly, for I swear Max would have him smoking and drinking already if I were not so vigilant, even though Max would tell me it is all a joke.

Gregory is strangely anxious and agitated most of the time, though I never know what about. He takes his job seriously and presents me with the money he earns at the end of every week. He watches David a lot but appears incapable of playing with the boy, even though I feel he loves him. He has never asked about David's father but calls me the child's mama nevertheless. Is it a sin for me to be grateful for his simple mind at times like these? For how would an older brother act otherwise if he arrived from the old country to discover his unmarried sister with a child?

Isabelle, Max's receptionist, adores David and Max allows her to care for him while I am at my work. We walk to the studio together and the girl will be there waiting for us with a hot barley drink ready for David, which he loves.

She is a friendly, open creature, just five years older than myself. I envy her roundness and her hair, which is ginger and curled into ringlets that hang down from the pins. I know they would laugh at her lack of fashion in the salon but her clean round face is like a breath of pure air in the midst of the choking fog.

She demands no payment for minding David as she works, but I pay her in dresses, which Max says is a fair enough bargain.

If I have work at the salon I arrive early in my best outfit. My hair is now smart enough to keep in the same style as the *vendeuses* and I have made myself a grey crepe day-dress that is passable enough.

Heavier fabrics are less popular for women's fashions now Kitty, despite the weather, and we have less stiff satin and plush at the salon than before, the newer look being for chiffons and lace, which is all very pretty.

The designer is very set on producing a new look for

spring and has settled upon something we all rate as rather daring, which consists of a high-waisted bolero bodice attached to a corselet skirt which falls almost untrimmed to the feet.

Max has a magazine called *The Lady* on a small gilt-painted table in his reception, for the women to thumb through while they wait for their portraits to be taken. I notice a lot of second-hand mantle sales in here and the prices are interesting, being as much as fifty shillings for a good quality walking-dress that sounded way past the latest mode, or seven shillings for a plain cloth skirt. I told Isabelle I could make my fortune if I only had the fabric, which I could see set her to thinking, for she is a very clever girl, I believe.

If there is no salon work I will walk Gregory to his job and then spend the morning on repairs or alterations, with maybe the odd bridal gown thrown in for good measure. I have to charge in advance for these gowns or I would not have the money for the lace, let alone the yards of satin needed. Isabelle says I could do the same with other orders but I would find it hard to take money without any proof that I could do the job.

In the afternoon I will collect David and walk him around the park. Do you know there are live cows there with women selling their milk? I buy some for David as often as I am able, for I have watched many other mothers doing the same in the hope that it will make their babies grow healthily.

David will sit and play happily in the afternoon while I work at my machine again and then I will read to him from books Max brings until Gregory is home for his supper.

Does all this sound idyllic, Kitty? With money it might be, but I am so wretchedly poor that I barely see the good moments in my life for all the worry that must accompany them. At night I am so tired I have often slept in my clothes, being too exhausted to remove them.

This night I am awoken from my sleep, though, with the fog inside the room and choking me in my throat. I cough and rub my eyes in an attempt to see clearly. Gregory must have opened a window, which is fatal in this weather, as the mists thicken inside the house so readily that you would be unable to see your own walls before five minutes have passed.

'Gregory?' I am angry with my brother for causing this inconvenience. Blinded, I stagger to the small window that we share and attempt to pull it shut, only to find it is not, as I had supposed, open.

'Gregory?' I am further awake now, though my brain is still reluctant to form proper thought. I turn but there is little to be seen around me.

'David?' In my confusion my only thought is for my child. I am still in my work clothes, which I discover as I attempt to walk quickly across the room and trip over my hem. Landing on the floor I discover the fog is less dense there and that I am able to see. Eyes still streaming, I crawl around on my knees like an animal.

'David!' I am full of dread now. There are loud cracking sounds from Gregory's room and I find I am unable to breathe. I try to stand but my legs are not strong enough and at least on the ground I can see.

I crawl along the walls until my hand touches air and I

know I am at the doorway. It is then that I realize this is no fog in my room but a fire.

'Daaaavid!'

A hand has my own hand held so firmly I jump with fear.

'Max?' I would cling to him like a limpet but my child is in the room behind me somewhere and also my brother, as far as I know.

Max lifts me into the arms of another man just as easily as if I were a child myself, and the man begins to carry me down the narrow stairs. This is not an easy task for him because I fight like a vixen to get free.

'My baby!' I scream. 'My child is inside!'

I look back and Max is staring at me. A fearfully long time seems to transpire as our eyes lock – mine round with horror and his near-concealed beneath a frown of concern. His face is white and smeared with soot. Behind him I can see the first dull red shadow of the flames that threaten to take my boy. There is much said between Max and me during that last stare, though all of it in silence.

'No jokes this time, Max,' I tell him, 'this time it is serious. If my son dies I will want to die too, it is as simple as that.' I am blindly selfish in my terror. David and Gregory. Max must save them, for without them I will perish too.

Does Max look for his own status in this equation? Do you die also if *I* die, Rosa? Would life be worth nothing for you too if I perish in these flames behind me? But his answer is obvious. Without expression he turns and is gone into the black smoke, a tall figure as dark as Beelzebub.

Kitty, I cannot tell you how long and unendurable the wait is as I stand shivering on the pavement outside my home, watching the smoke pour from my little window above. How many times am I caught as I try to run into the building and how many arms and faces do I punch as they try to prevent me?

I see the small body being tipped into the waves and hear the quiet splash that is gone so quick with the cries of the gulls.

'David.' Was he ever there to be mine at all? Or did I dream his life in some bout of madness that followed the death of my own child? Was that just a corpse I plucked from the mountain of mouldering rags in the factory? How could life have been breathed into it as it lay in my bed the long night? I howl out like a hound, Kitty, frightening all about me until I am left to stand alone as they back away in terror.

Then at last Max appears in the charred doorway, black and exhausted with smoke rising from his hair and his coat. I am upon him at once, pulling at his sleeves in desperation as neighbours do the right thing, which is banging him with their hands and swatting him with cloths and rugs before he combusts in front of us.

We are pushed from the hallway as other friends run up the stairs carrying buckets of water to deal with the flames. But the whole street could burn down for all I care. I have my hands upon Max's cheeks, pulling at his ears, his hair, screaming at him.

'David? My baby? My child, Max – is he dead? Did you leave him to perish?' I am about to unleash a stream of abuse and curses but suddenly I stop just as though struck by lightning. A scream? Was it mine?

Then I hear another scream. David. Coughing and wheezing for air Max pulls his coat open and there is my precious child, wrapped inside. He is pure pink to Max's blackness and grime. So the fire never reached him. I laugh with hysterical delight and he laughs too, terrified though he is, and Max lifts him and he is upon me, clinging ferociously and being crushed by my hugs.

Forgive my hysterics, Kitty. It seems this was not a big fire, just some smouldering cloths. Nevertheless there was a vast quantity of smoke, on account of the fact that our linen and clothing is quite damp at present as we have no warm air in which to dry it, on account of the fog – and so to me the whole terrace of hovels that we live in was in danger of being consumed in the inferno, and my beloved child along with it.

Gregory was discovered cowering in an ancient cupboard in the hall and, again, there was much relief at the sight of his tragic face. We clung together for many minutes, Kitty, all counting our blessings and saying prayers of thanks while countless alternative and thoroughly shocking endings to the tale flashed through our minds.

David is now excited by the whole adventure and Max is firmly established as his hero, as if he was not before. The blackness of our rooms enchants him, which it does not me, for all I see is raw hands and sore knees from all the scrubbing I will have to do to restore it to its more usual state of squalor again.

Thank God my sewing machine was undamaged, and

327

that I had just delivered a stack of repairs to their owners, so nothing of value is in need of replacement.

Max is, of course, beside himself at his own bravery, especially since he is to be featured in the *Whitechapel Times* in his role as blaze hero, and sketched by their artist for an accompanying print this very evening. If he has studied his own reflection in my grimy mirror once, he has studied it a thousand times, Kitty. Not one angle or tilt of the head has gone untested and his best hats have been on and off his head so much they have caused a draught.

I would laugh along with the others at his antics, Kitty, for both David and Gregory find Max uncommonly amusing, but there is a terrible secret notion inside my head and the more it brews and stews the quieter I am forced to become.

When Gregory was led out from the cupboard he hid in during the fire I held him in my arms and he held me too – though I noticed only with his poor hand, the one without the fingers. Out of curiosity I looked down at his good hand and saw it was clutched so tight around an object that the knuckles were white.

When I gently prised his fingers apart, Kitty, what do you think I discovered? A packet of matches. When I looked up at his face I saw fear in my brother's eyes and it was then I saw Rintzi again, screaming from the little window of the house in the *shtetle*, while Gregory watched in silence from below.

What am I to do? My brother is unwell, I know that – his mind was damaged the day Rintzi took him into the woods. Only I have a child of my own to think about. With Gregory in the house I now know that David is in danger, yet my brother needs me every bit as much as David since he is incapable of caring for himself if I throw him out.

The neighbours claim the fire was the act of vandals and point to the word 'Jews' that someone has scrawled on the main door to the building. I pray this to be true, Kitty.

Max remarks constantly that David is in need of schooling. A child of Richard's should attend a good school where he will learn the correct way to talk and read the best books. I am afraid the boy speaks as I do, when he should speak English the way his father does. Should he be poor all his life? I fear for his future as well as his education. Yet I could never give him up, I am too selfish to do so. He is my everything, I love him and he loves me. He calls me Mother and cries when we are apart for too long. When I work in the room he will play happily at my feet for hours, content in the knowledge that I am near.

We are in the midst of a lean period of work. I am awake all night, listening to Gregory's snores, terrified that he will wake and repeat his dreadful act. Max tells me I look unwell. When he offers me money for food, as he does more times than I care to remember, I am forced to take it, for we are hungry.

Kitty, I am beside myself with anxiety. For several weeks now David has had a return of the cough that used to plague him as a baby. At first I put it down to the effects of the smoke, which hung around our room for many days after the fire. It was Max who pointed out what I had dreaded admitting – that the cough was getting no better, even after the smoke had gone.

So many children are ill in this area. It is the poverty that causes it. We live in houses that are damp, shivering in draughts that no fires will drive away. I chew my nails with worry, Kitty. Sometimes David is well enough for me to be cheered, but then we will have another night of coughs, followed by a pale face in the morning.

'The boy is sick, Rosa,' Max told me, as gently as possible – but there was no way to say those words without invoking my hysteria.

'He will be better,' I said, 'when summer comes he will be well again.'

Max paid for a doctor, but the medicine he brought did little save make the boy sick. One morning he was so pink-faced I began to be excited, thinking he was well at last, but when I felt his cheek with the back of my hand I discovered he was feverish and wrapped him in blankets and had him on my lap for two days.

Kitty, after much sad deliberation I have written a letter to Richard. I spent badly-needed pennies on the writing paper and yet how many sheets was I forced to tear up when the right words would not come?

I have told him I am the mother of a child – his child. I have explained that I kept the knowledge from him because I did not want to burden him, yet now we are nearly penniless I have no choice. I enclosed the photograph of David and me that Max took four years ago.

I am tired of being poor, Kitty. There is no end to this and I know Richard will want to care for us both now. Perhaps I am wicked to delude him and yet there is no delusion, for to me David is my son just as much as he is

Richard's. Yet I fear for our lives if I do not do this thing. David is ill and my own health has become frail. If I do not work we will all starve.

Last night I took the wedding suit from its case and pressed it carefully before hanging it behind the door. The case lid is so snug it does not even smell of the smoke from the fire. Touching it is a bitter pleasure, Kitty. The silks are as vivid in colour as the day Papa sewed it and the fabric is as soft as the moment it came off the roll.

'Will it fit?' Max asked, seeing it hanging there that night.

I stared at him. 'I have written to David's father,' I said. 'Now all we must do is wait.'

Max looked across at Gregory but my brother was happy watching David at play. 'You believe he will marry you then?' he asked. His jaw looked set with anger though I could hear him controlling his voice carefully.

'He is a gentleman,' I replied. 'What else would he do?'

Max paced the room a bit before throwing himself down into a kneeling position in front of me.

'Don't you think this trick is a little wicked, Rosa?' he asked. 'Can't you see your idea is terribly wrong?'

I stared at the floor. 'You'll knee your trousers if you're not more careful, Max,' I said.

'Don't you mind that he'll never love you?' Max asked.

I looked him in the eye at that. 'I can make him care for me,' I said, 'I only need a chance to show what I am like. I know I'm not pretty but I share his love for the business and I'm lively enough to keep him on his toes, which is more than just a beautiful wife might do.'

'And the lie?' Max asked. 'What about the fact that you are not the boy's mother?'

331

I looked across at David. 'I feel that I am, Max,' I whispered. 'I don't know how anyone could be more of a mother to the child. There's no lie there, that I see. If Richard was too drunk to know who took advantage of his situation he won't know if it was me or not. The real mother gave birth without anyone knowing for sure, apart from me, and now she is dead.

'Most of the time we're only seen behind the machines by the other workers, so who can tell if we're a bit fatter than usual sometimes? Even proper ladies often corset themselves so tight you'd never guess – I've seen them at the salon, going all white and blue in the face as they struggle to keep the laces done up.

'Max, there's nothing evil here,' I added, 'I was given David and now I'm to find him a father and myself a husband. You know our situation. What else should I do?'

Many other things, to judge by Max's expression, but he said nothing. After a while he rose and stood by the door, staring at the suit.

'Will you walk with me, Rosa?' he asked quietly.

'It's dark,' I said.

He looked out of the window. 'But it's a beautiful night,' he told me, 'the fog has cleared and the air smells of spring at last. You can leave David downstairs for an hour. Come and allow the breeze to put the roses back into your cheeks.'

I did as he said. We walked down along Brick Lane and through Fournier Street to the market in Spitalfields, which had the smell of rotting vegetables about it at that time of the evening.

Max is, of course, a well-known figure locally now, what

with the photographic business and the article in the *Whitechapel Times*, and I lost count of the amount of people who hailed him as we walked along in the moonshine.

'Would you like to take my arm?' he asked, but I was having no part of that.

'What would decent people think, seeing me clinging to you?' I asked.

'They would think I was lucky,' he told me, and I blushed, for I had intended to match his trick of sarcasm, not to go fishing for compliments.

We found a small bench in the grounds of Christ Church and settled there for a while among the ancient tombstones that lie in stacks against the walls.

'Rosa, why do you laugh when I tell you I would marry you?' Max began.

'Because I know you are making a joke, Max,' I told him. As though the graves were not making me feel uncomfortable enough Max had to add to my squirming.

'So you would rather marry a man you barely know?' he asked after a minute or two's thought. 'First you love Aaron, who you had met once or twice, and now you love Richard, who you have barely spoken to. Why don't you love me more, then? We have had so many conversations, you should be besotted.'

What was I to tell him? A thousand retorts flew through my brain. 'Max, you are a rogue,' I informed him as lightly as I could, 'and I intend to marry a gentleman.'

He could have no idea of the size of Richard's empire. Max's little business could be gone in an instant, but Richard's had true value and history.

Max tapped his finger against his lips. 'And what yard-stick do you use to judge a rogue?' he asked quietly.

'Someone who photographs barely-clothed ladies,' I said. 'Someone who has ... relations with them after-wards.'

Max nodded, and I could not see whether he was smiling. 'Someone you could not trust,' he said.

I looked at him by way of reply.

'Yet David's father must have had ... relations ... with at least one other woman,' he said.

I sat up straight at that. 'You don't know the woman involved,' I told him. 'Some of the girls at that factory are shameless. Aggie more or less admitted she seduced him while he was in no state to know better.'

'I see,' Max said. After a while he turned to me. 'And what if I were the victim of a shameless seductress, Rosa?' he asked. 'Would you forgive me and love me in the way you love your boss?'

'Don't confuse me, Max,' I said.

'You say you don't trust me,' he continued, 'yet you trusted me with the life of your child the other night.'

I felt his hand upon my face. 'Look at me, Rosa,' he said.

Next minute his lips were pressed against my own, only the night had become so dark and the flesh of his mouth was so soft I hardly knew they were there until I felt my own begin to part in a sigh.

What else could I do but kiss him then? He had reminded me how he had saved my beloved child's life. How could I argue that that was not worth a mere kiss?

'One day you will know that I love you,' Max said in a whisper.

Can words touch your body like fingers? It would be so easy to get lost in fine thoughts, Kitty, and forget your true destiny. I could have lost myself in Max and his words if I had had a mind to believe them, which I didn't. This is how more stupid girls are fooled by men, and there is a lesson for us all there. Max is a good man but not, I believe, constant in his affections. If this joke of his about loving me were to become reality, I fear he would be back to laughing and sarcasm the following day and that I could not bear.

Richard is a fine man and will make a good husband and father. He is serious and well-mannered and Max can be accused of neither quality. Max is erratic and mocking. Yet I returned his kiss for a full half-minute and of this I am much ashamed, for I will be married to Richard before long.

CHAPTER THIRTY-THREE

ZG

RAYON
*Launched as artificial silk at the Artificial Silk
Exhibition at Olympia in 1929, manufacturers used rayon
to keep up with the demand for the new mass market
in women's wear following the Great War.*

They were exhausted now, completely washed out. Totally void. Alain still sat on his stool, but he hadn't touched the garment in front of him for over ten minutes and was staring, trance-like, at a photograph of Andy Warhol he had pinned up over his desk. He was no longer capable of judging whether the dress was finished or not. He couldn't even tell if the hem was straight.

The outfit was on a stand – they'd had to let the house model go four hours previously, after the third faint. Somewhere there were still machinists working and it was that noise that prickled their guilt and kept them sitting securely in their chairs.

Kitty had cleared weeping and hopelessness in a couple of strides, sidestepped hysteria as it was too much of a cliché, and fallen straight into the arms of empty, bottomless desolation. 'Why?' was the buzz word of the moment, 'Why? Why-in-God's-name? What-the-hell-is-this-all-for?'

People drifted in and out of the workroom, like Victorian

gentry visiting a madhouse. Chloe, China, the PR, a couple of models for the show, two very minor celebrities come to swig Chablis, and one huge star come to snort coke. Nula had arrived quietly, her little face pleading, can I help? A timid enquiry prior to settling in a pale and distant corner, gnawing at her nails and pulling at her hair in a demented manner.

Freddy had phoned but his dilemma was largely the same. What could you say? I'm exhausted? The whole of the rag trade was running on back-up batteries right then. Who had sympathy?

Years ago, Kitty had once asked her father whether the range could not be started a week earlier, so that it could be finished comfortably on time. They had all laughed at that, all the staff of the salon, everyone within earshot. Starting earlier was just not feasible. There were the fabric fairs to visit, the orders to chivvy, that was how the whole ball was set rolling. There was no scope for better planning – the whole thing was in the hands of the fabric manufacturers.

The garment in front of Alain was simple: a mud-brown coat-dress with a web of silver lamé hanging like a cloak about its shoulders.

'Shit!' he shook his head. 'It doesn't work and I don't know why.' He ripped it off the stand and threw it across at Kitty. 'Put it on,' he told her, 'I need to see if the fabric has stretched after being pressed.'

Kitty dragged the garment over her jeans and rose wearily to her feet to stand in front of the designer.

'Stop swaying,' he said, angrily, and then more politely, 'please.'

337

Kitty closed her eyes. The empty wet pavement her father had died on rolled instantly into view.

Alain smelt of smoke and soap. She listened to the noises he made as he worked, absorbing the sounds, like a child. His touch was light as he pinned and cut. Even when he ripped a seam from top to end she felt nothing.

Her father. Had he been at that club? Was Khan's daughter right? How many other dreadful things had she planted into Kitty's head?

Nula pressed an ice-cold can of diet cola into her hand and she held it first to her temples.

Gabriel was an honourable man. Faithful to his wife. Faithful to his business. Faithful to them all. He would never have been seen in such a seedy place as that boarded-up sex club.

Alarmed by her own thoughts, Kitty opened her eyes and Alain's face was her first focus – pale, tired, bristly and smudged from lack of sleep. In fact, looking very much as he usually did.

'You want this to work, don't you?' he asked her in a quiet, deep voice.

'Oh, very much,' Kitty told him, more into sleep than out of it.

'And your wedding?' Alain asked her. 'Your father spoke about it a lot. We used to say it was going to be bigger than a royal wedding. In fact, we were all pretty sick of it here, and it hadn't even started.' He laughed to show he was joking, then his face became serious again.

'Your father had begun designs for your dress, did you know that? He was compiling a portfolio of sketches to show you. It was a surprise. Raphael had worked on some of them, and so had I. Your father did the most designing, though. Sometimes he spent the whole night here, sketching. He said your dress was going to have to be the most magnificent creation ever. This did not endear us to you, as you can imagine. His little princess, eh?'

Kitty smiled. 'Where is the folio?' she asked. 'Is it in his office?'

She pulled the coat-dress off and hung it back onto the stand. Alain took a swig of her cola and led her into her father's office, where he sat her down in the huge, padded chair before laying a large folio out in front of her.

'Oh.' It was all Kitty could say. The folder smelt of Gabriel. It didn't smell of the street, of dead crisp packets. It smelt of his cologne and his clean flesh.

'Do you want to be left alone?' Alain asked, watching her face with concern. Kitty shook her head. 'No. Stay. Keep the little princess company. Please.'

Alain grinned. 'Have some wine, then,' he said. 'A bride should always have some chilled wine when she picks her dress. Have a break. Get a little pissed.'

There was champagne in the fridge in the corner. He poured two glasses and sat down beside her, so close that their legs touched.

'Alain,' Kitty asked quietly, 'tell me, do you know what a "dark room" is?'

She watched his eyes disappear behind lashes and lids the colour of marble. She knew then that his first comment would be a lie.

'It's the place where photographers do their printing,' he said. Subject closed.

She leant forward. 'You missed my inflection,' she told

him carefully, 'I asked you what a *dark room* is – two words, not one.'

He looked up. Maple syrup eyes. 'It's what they call a room in a club,' he told her, 'a room where people go to have sex. Men, usually. Men with men. A private place where it's too dark to see who they're fucking. Why?'

Kitty looked back at the sketch in front of her. 'It's a term I heard,' she said. 'I just wondered, is all.' It was where Riva Khan had said her father went. 'The dark room,' she'd told Kitty, 'I know about this. My uncle told me.'

In her mind Kitty's eyes scanned every inch of Riva's face. She had held her head high as she spoke to Kitty, as though two generations of prejudice and oppression had endowed her with an expression of one who hears nails scratching a chalkboard. Her contempt had been obvious.

'The dark room.' How romantic it sounded. A place for forbidden sex. Anonymous. Her father would never have contemplated such a place. He could have given Riva herself lessons in pride and fastidiousness. Gabriel was a strong, honourable man.

Kitty forced herself to refocus her attention on his drawings. He had been designing his daughter's wedding dress when he died. A tear splashed onto the page and Kitty blotted it up quickly with her sleeve. Alain said nothing. She thought he would be embarrassed. It was awkward now, the silence between them.

Gabriel's writing was spidery on the page. His drawings were substantial but his words and instructions surrounded them like fine, faded gauze. *Extended shoulder with pleats sitting in pads*, she read . . . *cinched waist with full taffeta*

340

bow, . . . white silk embroidered crepe lisse flouncing and white India silk . . .

Rosa, the daughter I love. It was as though the words of two fathers' voices echoed in her head.

CHAPTER THIRTY-FOUR

ZG

NUN'S VEILING
*A lightweight wool fabric made with a very plain
weave in plain colours, similar in appearance to a
wool batiste.*

There is no reply to my letter to Richard, Kitty, and I am distraught. I felt patience to be one of my virtues, yet I am pacing the room like a tethered beast.

ZG

STAYS
*For much of the nineteenth century tight-lacing was
the fashion, with women striving to have a waist no
wider than twenty inches. Many of these stays were
made of silk* coutil *and trimmed with lace and came
with 'bust-improvers'.*

A response from Richard at last. A note arrived this morning and, though not exactly wordy, it is polite enough and – once I had read it for a fifth time – I considered it to sound almost friendly and warm in tone. It read:

Dear Miss Zigofsky,
    I have studied your letter with interest. If suitable to yourself I shall send my carriage to collect you and the child on Sunday at two.
        Yours faithfully,
        R Galliard Esq.

My hands shake as I hold it. Max says I am being quixotic and this makes me angry despite the fact that I have no idea on earth what the word means.

ZG

CENDRE DE ROSE
Grey with a pink tone, cendre de rose *was one of
many colour names that became obsolete after the
nineteenth century. Others include:* esterhazy – *a
silver-grey,* fly's wing – *graphite,* terre d'Egypt – *a rust,*
dust of Paris – *ecru, and* bouffon – *a shade darker
than* eau de nil.

Kitty, Richard has taken my child. How stupid I have been,
how naïve. It has been five weeks since I took David to his
father's house and he is still there.

What hopes I had as we climbed into Richard's carriage
to make the arranged appointment. We were dressed and
ready before dawn, so acute was my excitement. David's
hair was combed flat and wetted to make it lie straight and
his little face polished by my hankie until his cheeks
gleamed like a new, shining apple. He appeared healthy
enough, Kitty, his cough had all but cleared. I had no idea
of the horrors that were to come.

The house was less grand than I had expected, but smart
enough for all that. David had caught my excitement by
the time we arrived, even though he was unaware why we
paid the visit, and his legs had him up to the door before
it was opened.

I'd expected to see Richard there waiting to greet us, but then I know nothing of these matters and it was some servant who peered out with a face like old boiled mutton.

We were shown inside the hall, with me grabbing David by the hand before he got up to some mischief with all the porcelain that was displayed in there – for although he is a good child for the most part he was rather over-excited, as I have said.

The servant showed me to a chair and, while I was being asked if I would care for refreshment, David was taken from me and led into another room without so much as a backward glance. I saw only a glimpse of the room he was taken to. There was a log fire burning well in the grate, and a tall, elderly man in a suit standing alongside a woman dressed in an outfit that I took to be a nanny's.

I waited a full two hours in that hallway and neither tea nor David were brought to me. I became frightened then, and believe I made a fool of myself, for I banged on the door that David had been led through and called out for my son.

It was Richard himself who emerged, taking my hand and leading me back to my seat with many polite apologies, which made me quiet again. His face looked concerned and rather pale, but beside that he appeared well enough.

'Well, Miss Zigofsky,' he said, 'you have given me something to think about here.'

I stared at his face.

'When was the boy born?' he asked, and I told him.

He nodded. 'Forgive me if I am rather crude at this point, Miss Zigofsky,' he said, 'but I have no memory of your

345

being . . . unwell . . . around that time. I know a few years have passed but surely . . .'

I had my answer ready for this. 'Nobody noticed,' I said. 'I was rather thin at the time and – if you remember – there was a fashion that season for the empire line so I, like a lot of the girls, had my waists hitched and tied with ribbon. You may have forgotten another important occasion because I'm afraid you were drunk when the child was conceived.'

I said this deliberately to embarrass him, for I knew it would make him uncomfortable about questioning me further. I was right. He was gentleman enough to look away.

'May I ask why you have taken until now to show the child to me?' he said.

'I explained in my letter, I had no intention of being a burden,' I replied, simply.

He turned to look at me again. There was no denying he was the boy's father, their faces were as alike as peas in a pod. When I looked at David I looked at Richard, and vice versa. His son's face must have been a shock to him.

'Miss Zigofsky . . .' he began.

'Under the circumstances I believe it would be appropriate for you to call me Rosa,' I said.

'Rosa.' The word seemed alien to him. 'We are in a very difficult situation,' he said. 'You are an honest woman, I know that much from employing you. I feel a great amount of pity for your plight. Your life with David must have been . . . difficult . . . and you have behaved well in bringing him up in these circumstances.' His eyes looked friendly and polite. 'I hope you can see the difficulty of my situation

346

too, though, Rosa,' he went on. 'I find I have a son about whom I knew nothing, and here he is and here you are . . . look, I must be blunt with you. You cannot expect decisions at once but at the same time you must understand I am keen to spend some time with the boy and get to know him a little. He seems to be a splendid chap and quite comfortable with me already. What say he stays here for a few days while we both have time to think?'

I rose from my seat at that, for the thought of leaving David was too much to contemplate.

'Take me to him,' I said. 'We must leave now, thank you.' But Richard held me by the arm in a gentlemanly fashion and for a moment we were close enough for me to feel his breath upon my cheek.

'You can't take him, Rosa,' he said in a gentle voice. 'If he is my son – and I have no reason to doubt your honesty – I must insist he stays here with me, for the time being at least. You have had him for four years now. I am probably asking for as many days. You know he will be safe and I will send him home to you directly there is any sign that he is unhappy.'

'No!' This time the hysteria must have been apparent in my voice, for Richard released my arm in shock. I ran towards the door that I had seen David led through, calling out his name as I ran.

'David! Come to me, darling!' I pulled the door wide open, no longer aware of my manners, but the room was empty, apart from the tall suited man, who stood warming his hands by the fire.

He turned in surprise as he saw me enter. 'My dear, calm yourself,' he said in a kind voice.

'Rosa,' I heard Richard say behind me, 'this is Dr McDermot, one of the noted paediatricians in London. I invited him here to examine David when he arrived.'

The doctor took my hands in his own and held them cupped there. 'I'm afraid the child is unwell, madam,' he told me.

I felt my legs begin to crumple beneath me and both he and Richard had to help me into a chair.

The doctor looked concerned. 'He may have tuberculosis, I am afraid,' he told me.

Kitty, can you imagine my distress? At this moment David came out of the room behind him, led by the servant and with as happy an expression as I had ever seen on his little face. In his hand was some toy; I do not remember what, exactly, but it was large and expensive and much more than he had ever been given in his life before.

I was out of my seat in an instant and clutching him so hard in my arms I heard him cry out.

'He is well!' I said, releasing him and looking at his face. 'Look – he is smiling, aren't you, David? He had a little cough, didn't you, dearest? But that is gone now. I will take him home right now and tuck him into his bed. He has had nothing worse than a cold. When the summer is here we will be out in the park again – I take him every day, don't I, dearest?' My tears began to fall onto the child's poor head.

When I looked up I saw that the woman, whose uniform I now recognized as that of a nurse, was standing with her hand on David's shoulder. My child was prised gently but firmly from my arms and it was all I could do to stop myself from screaming.

The doctor led me aside, away from David's earshot. 'If the boy does not receive the best of care I fear he will not see another summer, madam,' he said, gravely. 'Mr Galliard has told me your circumstances are . . . reduced. The boy will require more than you can provide for him, I'm afraid. The houses in the ghettos are damp enough to kill a healthy adult. The air is unclean. Allow the boy to be removed to better conditions, I beg you.'

My face was distorted with anguish and indecision. 'Please, Rosa,' Richard begged behind me.

What was I to do, Kitty? Tear my child from that house and take him home with me to die? Yet how could I bear to be parted from him? My dilemma was unimaginable. I had thought we would be well provided for and that Richard would take us both under his wing.

'I must be allowed to see him every day for as long as I like,' I begged, the tears a veritable downpour now.

The doctor stroked his chin. 'Perhaps after a while,' he said. 'At the moment there is a risk of extra infection. You look unwell yourself, madam. If you were to bring extra germs into his surroundings . . .' He patted my arm. 'Might I suggest you make an appointment with your own doctor?' he asked. 'He can tell if you have any contagion, and also may reassure you about your child's best interests.'

Richard's eyes were full of silent begging. I could tell he loved David already, and that I had no choice but to leave the boy as the doctor had requested.

'May I hold him one last time?' I pleaded. Kitty, his little head smelt so sweet beneath my nose. 'I will see you very soon, darling,' I whispered, without knowing for one moment whether or not that promise was true.

Max was there when I got home, but I would not tell him what had happened. Gregory was silent and would not eat his food. I wept all night, and then again in the morning when I woke and discovered David's little cot was empty beside me.

I have been summoned to a meeting with Richard, this time at the sweatshop. I tell Max I believe he is about to do the honourable thing, but Max replies that, if he were about to propose, it would not be in that Godforsaken den but somewhere with a sweeter perfume. He also adds his many-times repeated theory that I am being dishonourable in passing myself off as the boy's mother and am therefore no straighter than the bookie in the checked suit outside the greengrocer of a Sabbath.

I am about to tell him again that I am David's mama in the eyes of anyone with an ounce of decent sympathy in their veins, but discover I do not have sufficient energy, even to rise to Max's bait.

His behaviour is almost hostile these days, just when I am most in need of commiseration. Kitty, I am the loneliest soul in the world right now. Is Max right? Am I a cheat? Is it so wicked to dream of life in the room that I glimpsed in Richard's house, playing with my son in front of a warm hearth?

'That is not the way for you, Rosa,' Max says. 'You have too much going for you to want to be housemaid to a cold fish like that.'

'I plan to be Richard's wife, not his flunkey!' I shout.

Max shrugs. 'In their world it amounts to the same thing,' he says. 'Why not make your own money, Rosa?

350

Then you will be able to live as you choose, without saying thank you to anyone.'

There is a silence. I am panting with anger. 'Love is more to me than money,' I say.

Max smiles. 'Tell me that again when Richard has paid you off,' he says.

Kitty, I hit out at that, striking Max across his face with the back of my hand. He neither flinches nor ducks and his eyes never leave my face. I fully expect him to slap me back and hold myself full height to prove that I am every inch as brave as himself.

'Is that how you think you will carry on when you live in Mayfair?' he asks quietly.

'I will be without these aggravations then,' I tell him. I am so sorry for having hit him that I am almost in tears.

Max is so very good to me in many ways and I know I could well be starved in some alley without his help, Kitty. Perhaps it is this very dependence that makes me spit like a cat when I am around him. If only he could stop mocking me for one moment I could be as fond of him as I am of my own brother, but he just will not allow it, he is always baiting my bad humour with his jokes and so I suppose we will always fight.

My desperation is so acute I am early for my meeting with Richard and the sweatshop is locked when I arrive. There is snow beginning to fall and I am quite white with it by the time his carriage pulls up.

I have never seen the place empty before. Richard keeps the shutters closed and lights a candle instead, which fills the place with wisps of black smoke as it burns.

'How is my son?' I ask straightaway, wringing my hands

like one possessed. 'Is he well? Is he happy?' I cannot survive without him and feel he must be the same without me.

Richard smiles and pats my hands. 'Don't worry,' he says, 'you know he is safe. His health is quite improved already. The doctor is happy with his progress.'

I watch him light a cigarette from the match he has used for the lamp. The flame burns down so low he drops it quickly and laughs.

'I'm very proud of you, Rosa,' he says. 'You've done well with the boy. The illness was not your fault.'

'Thank you.' I smile back at him, hoping my hair still covers my ears, which must be blue with cold as well as rabbit-like in appearance.

'I would like to pay you for the cost of all your care,' he says.

I remember Max's words and my face falls. 'Then pay your son for the pleasure he has given me,' I tell him. He is at my side in a minute.

'Rosa, I have offended you!' he says. 'Please excuse me, I am nervous and clumsy. You must think I am a fool. Would you forgive me? The last thing I want to do is upset you.'

He runs his hands through his hair and lets out a nervous laugh, suddenly looking very young and very much like my child. 'Do you believe it? I already love the boy,' he tells me, and his eyes are suddenly sad and serious.

'You're asking his mother,' I say, proudly. 'I could not imagine anyone not loving him.'

The nervous laugh again. He begins to pace the small space on the floor. 'No, I mean I love him like a father,

352

Rosa,' he says. 'Isn't that incredible? Do you know for years I have been under incredible pressure from my family to marry and have children, but – to be honest with you – the idea never really appealed to me. I had no time for children or for home life. Then suddenly I am presented with a son and immediately I find he has become the focus of my universe.

'He's changed my life already, Rosa – can you believe that?' I watch the excitement on Richard's face as he speaks. This is, of course, what I wanted and yet I find myself filled with inexplicable dread at his words. 'Of course,' he goes on, 'there will be difficulties explaining his appearance, but I'm not really worried by that, to tell the truth. Scandals are quite the thing these days, especially in the fashion world.'

His enthusiasm is contagious, despite my fears, and I find myself smiling with him. This is *more* than I had hoped for, Kitty. I thought there would be many difficulties before Richard accepted David as his own. My relief at hearing David is well has made me giddy. I feel myself falling and Richard is there to catch me, leading me to a stool and watching my face with concern.

Suddenly he places his hands on mine and kisses me on both cheeks. 'You must be so proud of him,' he whispers. His face is in front of mine, close to mine. He smiles. 'Do you remember that time you bandaged my finger?' he asks. 'I never forgot that moment, Rosa. I believe I knew you were something special right then. What did you think of me? Did you imagine I was like some foolish small boy who has injured himself? Was I important to you then? Do you remember?'

How can I describe my feelings on that day? All I do is nod feebly.

He kisses me then, Kitty – so suddenly that I jump. His lips are warm upon my own cold pair. I would close my eyes, but I want to see everything and remember all.

'Rosa,' he whispers, and the pleasure I feel at hearing him say my name like that is beyond all measure.

I relax a little now, knowing that much of my struggle is over. My shivering has stopped and the warmth of Richard's body has heated my own. My eyes close. His lips are upon me again. This will stop, it has to stop, but for the moment I will allow it because my happiness is in sight at last.

'What's wrong?' Richard asks, seeing my expression. 'Did you mind the kiss?' He looks surprised, as well he might – for he has been told by me that we have been as intimate as possible on one other occasion.

I put my fingers to my lips, trying to hold Richard's kiss there, watching him walk away and light another cigarette.

'I should go,' he says, smiling. 'I need to organize the books at the salon or you'll have no job to go back to.' Another small laugh.

'Will you take me to collect David?' I ask.

'Rosa,' he begins.

'What is it?' I ask, quickly. 'You said he was well. Were you lying? Is he close to death?'

He pulls my arms back reassuringly. 'Look, Rosa, this is very difficult for me. David is not seriously ill but the doctor has told me that, apart from the illness he is a little underweight for his age and there are signs that his lungs may be permanently damaged, even once he is recovered.'

I clutch my hands to my chest. Richard pulls them away.

'Please, Rosa, you have become so pale. David is well. He is just a little malnourished, that's all. But there is so much lung disease around we will need to be careful. A few weeks on good food have made a remarkable difference in him already.'

'I feed him well and keep him out of the cold at all times . . .' I begin.

'I know you do.' The nervous laugh again. 'It's just that – as the doctor told you – there is a lot of damp in the old ghetto houses. It's not your fault, you have done your best for the boy, anyone can see that. I'm just glad you brought him to me when you did.'

'You mean to keep him,' I say in a whisper. My ears are buzzing and there are voices in my head. Why can I not understand what Richard is saying?

'Rosa, he needs the best and I can afford to give it to him,' Richard says. This is true and it is why I took my son to him. I believed he would want his child's mother too, though.

'Can he stay a little longer?' Richard asks. 'Just until he is back to strength?'

What am I to do?

'I must see him,' I say.

We drive to Richard's house and I am shaking with anguish the entire journey. When I see myself through Richard's eyes I realize how ridiculous I have been with my dreams. I am shabby and plain. Yet I thought him decent enough to marry me in spite of that. I am a poor woman he has employed and who, he believes, he was drunk enough to be seduced by several years before. I have

355

taken his child and nearly killed it for him. I must be a nightmare to him.

I am taken to an upstairs room where a warm fire burns, and discover David there, tucked sleeping in a cosy little bed with blankets up to his chin, while the kindly-faced nurse watches. David's night-clothes are so pretty; I see a little lace-trimmed silk sleeve where his arm has emerged from the side of the quilts. Does he think of his poor mother when he dreams, I wonder?

All around the bed are the most beautiful toys, Kitty.

I look at Richard. There are tears in his eyes, too.

'Can he stay?' he asks.

I nod. I have no voice to speak. I know by his tone and his expression that he means longer than a few days – that he is talking of keeping David for the rest of his life.

'Until he is properly well,' I tell him. He nods, relieved. He has already told me David's lungs may never be strong. How can I ever take him back with me to the cold grimy house I live in at present? I would be murdering my own child. I could never do that, and Richard knows this as well as I do.

We stand together in the hallway.

'I would still like to reimburse you for all the care you have given him,' Richard says.

I look him straight in the eye. 'One hundred pounds,' I say. There is a flicker of surprise across his face. He thought I would leave empty-handed. He thought I would go away and never come back. I repeat my offer.

'One hundred pounds.' My voice holds strong. He has lost the look of pity now. I have shocked him. He thinks he has judged me wrongly.

'That's rather a large amount,' he says. Even the nervous laugh has abandoned him now. So his child's mother is a hard-faced rogue, after all. I no longer care. I hold my gaze and say nothing.

'Very well. Of course. It . . . it must have been difficult for you . . .'

He is gone for several minutes but returns with a package in his hand.

'Thank you, sir,' I say. Then I walk out of his house with my back and head as straight as I can hold them.

CHAPTER THIRTY-SEVEN

ZG

ARMURE
*A rich blend of wool and silk with a barely-visible
triangle, chain or twill design on the surface.*

Do you think me very hard and terrible, Kitty? Do you believe I have sold my child? Well, allow me to tell you, dearest, that in that moment standing in Richard's hall I realized a truth that I had missed so far in my short life: I understood that Max has been right all along, and that it is everyone for themselves, and that anyone who thinks otherwise is a fool. It is a lesson I would wish you to learn too, Kitty, before you find out too late, at terrible cost, as I almost did.

If I want my son back and a gentleman for a husband I shall have to earn them, and not through mere wanting, either. Richard has bought my boy from me and I shall buy him back again. We will have all we need, David and I, and without another to provide it for us. Max has been too kind already and Richard too tolerant. I have no further need of their pity but a craving bordering on mania to see respect in their eyes instead.

I walk for many hours, but without becoming tired. My energy is ceaseless and my feet fairly fly along the cobbles. How clear things seem to me now, suddenly. I feel like a fish that has been swimming round and round in a grime-filled pond and is suddenly placed in a sparkling clear lake. I knock on doors until I discover what I need to know. Then I am off running down street after street until I reach a road called Eagle Street, in Holborn. It is a distance of some miles yet I have energy to spare and feel that I could run forever. Time is something I have little to spare now, Kitty; the longer my plan takes, the longer David will be apart from me.

A small and very smart French woman answers the door to number eighty-three – a tiny red-bricked dwelling which leans onto the side of The Eagle public house for support.

I introduce myself, trying to look pleasant enough, though my head is bursting with all that has happened and more, and she takes me through into the tiny parlour to meet her mother. The old lady does not recognize me at first and, even in my current state, I cannot help but be tickled by the fact that she does not have her teeth in at present.

'Rosa,' I say, 'Rosa Zigofsky. I work upstairs at the salon in Mayfair. I am one of the casuals – a sewer. Sometimes I come down to help with the fittings.'

When she recognizes me at last I see her back stiffen. A sewer! In her house! And she a *vendeuse*! She looks across at her daughter.

'What do you want?' she asks.

'I heard you say you are retiring,' I tell her. This is not time for polite chatter. 'I wish to purchase your client list.'

There is a sound from her mouth that could be laughter or scorn.

'How much do you want?' I ask. She tilts her small

359

scrawny head and looks up at me from the side of her eyes, like a bird.

I pull the envelope out of my vest. 'I won't argue with you,' I say, 'fifty pounds should be enough. Most of your clients are as near to death as makes no matter. This is no investment and you know it.'

She looks at me with the same scorn in her eye but then she looks at the money I hold. 'They would never allow you near the clients,' she says in French.

'They will,' I say.

There is a pause. I glance across at the daughter and catch the look of longing in her eyes as she, too, looks at the pound notes I have laid on the table. Then I look about the room. There are one or two good shawls and cloths draped about, but the furniture they cover is as rotten as my own few sticks.

'Very well,' says the mother, and I hear a sigh of relief from her daughter. I hold my hand out and she places her own claw in it reluctantly.

'*Salut.*'

'*Salut.*'

I am a *vendeuse*.

ZG

CHICOREE
Material cut with its edge left unhemmed.

Well, Kitty, as I look back I can find many things that have amused me in my new life in the salon, despite my constant distress and grief at being parted from my child. I have found it possible to laugh again, but my laughter sounds bitter and there is a new look of hard hostility in my eyes.

Imagining me as you heard me before, can you picture me now, one of the most sought-after *vendeuses* in the salon? Two years have passed since that terrible day when I gave my child to the care of his father. I am now very much the smart Frenchwoman, with long dark hair which is plaited so tight it looks varnished, and dressed in a chic black dress that flatters my pale skin.

I have tried hard to lose my accent as well as to learn the French that all the other *vendeuses* talk in. I wave my arms about less as I speak, and my walk has been copied from the deportment of all the *grandes dames* who grace our establishment in Berkeley Square.

I visit David once a week, and I cannot tell you, Kitty, how precious and yet sweetly painful these visits are. I take him to the park or the shops and I flatter myself that I am no shame to him now as we walk along together, for even though I am still living within modest means I no longer have to wear Bubba's coat or shabby, paper-lined boots.

David loves me, that much is obvious to all, but he is happy with his father. He is a beautiful boy and very bright, too – but then I am his mother and so maybe not totally impartial.

There was so much fuss the day I walked into the salon and announced I had bought the old *vendeuse*'s list you would think war had broken out. First they tried to shoo me upstairs, but I would not budge. Then they called the chief and then I was laughed at and finally they screamed at me. Then Richard arrived and the shock on his face when he saw me standing there beneath the chandelier was a picture I will never forget.

'Miss Zigofsky!' he said smiling. 'What is the problem?' The other staff agitated around behind him, flapping their skirts and pulling faces as though I were a flea-raddled cat that had somehow wandered into the room by mistake.

'There is no problem,' I said, clearly, 'I am here to start work. I have bought *Madame*'s list of clients and I will need training if I am to serve them in the correct manner.'

Richard stared at me in silence, and I could see the confusion in his eyes. I had shocked him and I was proud of that.

His laugh surprised the other staff. 'Good,' he replied after a while. He ran a hand through his hair. 'Good.' His voice had no enthusiasm, only a rasher of politeness above the more solid flesh of embarrassment.

I walked towards the back of the room, cutting a swathe through the open-mouthed staff as I went. You see, Kitty,

Richard was in a situation very like my own at last; he had no choice really, and he knew it.

He caught up with me as I was lighting the kettle for tea. 'This is a surprise, Miss Zigofsky,' he said, still smiling. 'I had no idea you had such plans for yourself.'

A decent man, fallen from grace. What fools men are, to allow alcohol to stigmatize their lives in this way. My own shame stemmed from violence beyond my control. It would never have happened any other way. Yet men like Max and Richard chart their own downfall through unnecessary and voluntary weaknesses. This was never my father's way, Kitty. We were both brought up to warm ourselves in the rays of correct behaviour, and I thank God for that, too.

And yet I still love Richard, Kitty, and perhaps it is a love that has matured with age from a childish passion to a more enduring affection.

'And neither did I, until yesterday,' I told him in reply. He coughed and looked about the room. We were alone.

'I had no intention of hurting you, you know,' he said, in a whisper. 'I only want what is the best for the boy.'

I said nothing.

'Do you intend telling anyone . . .' his voice trailed.

'That your new son is my child?' I asked. 'No.'

His shoulders slumped a little from relief and he closed his eyes. 'Perhaps it might ease your difficult situation if I found you a better job in another salon,' he said.

'Please don't bother,' I told him, 'I prefer working for you.'

He stood for a while, taking it all in, then started to

walk out, turning once he reached the drapes which were used instead of a door.

He appeared agitated and bemused. 'Did you buy that dress for the job?' he asked.

I nodded. I had bought it from a small private seamstress I knew, whose door I had nearly broken open with my knocking the night before, on the way back from Holborn. It was plain jet-black crepe with a large collar that tied into a bow and simple frills down either sleeve. The seamstress had insisted it was all the mode, and that it had been made for a fashion lady for the funeral of her sick husband, who had since recovered.

'Perhaps you would allow me to have one made here for you,' Richard said, and in that one moment I saw the dress for what it was – showy and dreadful and totally lacking in style.

I turned slowly to look in the mirror. What had looked smart and elegant last night now appeared comical in situ. My hair, as well. I had taken the whole night preparing it while Gregory watched. It was piled as tall as I could manage, to give me more height. I looked like Bubba with a hat on.

Richard watched my face but he did not smile. 'I'll send Constance down,' he said.

The girl was a helper in the salon whom I had seen many times before but never spoken to, on account of my lowly position. To my blessed relief she had a new dress ordered for me within the hour and was snipping about the one I wore with the dressmaker's shears until it took on a semblance of style that I could not have imagined myself.

She also retied my hair in a simpler fashion that had me

looking almost as smart as the other women in the salon. All this was done in solemn silence, but once it was finished she made tea and chatted in a friendly enough way about the job I would be taking on. She was to train me and watch me, she said. When that was finished I would be placed with one of the older women. I could see she was as curious about my sudden elevation as the other women, but she kept her questioning in check. She was nice, Kitty. I felt a little better that night.

CHAPTER THIRTY-NINE

ℤG

VELOURS DU NORD
*A luxurious fabric; black satin background shot with
a colour and covered with velvet flowers stamped in
relief.*

My work in the salon suits me very well, Kitty, and I am become a much better person because of it. There is not a friend in the place here, save Constance, but this does not trouble me much. Upstairs they think I have become above myself, while downstairs they treat me as if I were not worthy to spit on their boots.

The clients seem to like me, though, and this is what counts. They are all old enough to be counting their days and most are deaf, too. Their delight at being served by a younger voice and ears is obvious and prevents them minding the fact that I am new to the role.

I am treated as something of a pet, Kitty, on account of my age, and am often given sweets or little gifts as rewards for being polite and discreet. You would not believe how judicious I can be when I try, dearest! When the ladies arrive I am a model of politeness, so quiet and so quick to spot their needs before they have arisen that I could be a ghost. I have their names and titles off pat and only lift my eyes from the ground if I am spoken to directly. Never-

366

theless, I must have been noticed by many of them, for I have been given the name *Petite*, which they find easier, evidently, than learning my proper name.

Kitty, there is something else I must tell you, though I have been slow to notice it. My new hair and style of dress appears to have made me somehow more visible to men. I have been taking careful note of the younger clients who grace our salon and have fallen to copying many of their better ways. My carriage is straighter and my walk is much improved, after many nights of practice in my tiny room. I have spent precious money on a full-length mirror and, through watching my image, I have learnt how to place my hands, instead of allowing them to dangle by my sides or wave about as I speak. I have also discovered a knack of keeping my chin down but eyes up that I feel makes less of my rabbity ears and gives me a bit of a 'look'.

And now I notice the husbands of some of my clients are paying me attention. They are mostly more than nine-tenths of their way to their graves, Kitty, but it is amazing how much they pick up when I give them one of my newly-acquired 'looks'.

I even tried this glance out on Max to judge the effect, but he merely asked if I had been sitting in a draught and acquired a crick in my neck, which I suppose is one of his little jokes.

Even Richard seems rather taken with me now, when we are in the salon together. His stares are very hard to fathom but I feel he knows he has more to reckon with in me than before. He has tried to engage me in conversation several times now, even asking me what scent I wear one day when I have been bold enough to sample some *Muguet de Bois* that Constance's young man gave her as a gift. I am thrilled at this new development, but determined to keep my distance. I am pleasant enough, Kitty, but never anything more than polite. When I visit David, Richard is always absent from the house and this suits me.

I have plans now, Kitty – great plans. Learn from one who has been forced to become much wiser than you, dearest. Fight your own way in life and learn to depend on no one. How badly have I craved a family and friends about me! For these are the very bones of the society I live in – support from those dear ones during hardship and poverty. *My* only support has been from Max, and I know I will pay him back many times over once I have made my way. I mean to be rich, Kitty, for it is the only way to earn my place in the life that I want.

My work in the salon means I have access to some of the newest designs and styles. I study these fashions at great length when no one is looking, peering at stitching and seams until I have them memorized. Then I am able to sew cheaper copies at home, adapting the styles to suit more general tastes, and these I sell to any local women with more than a few pounds in their purses.

This home business of mine is proving surprisingly popular and far more lucrative than taking in repairs. I had no idea what great a part of a paltry income women will pay to be *à la mode.*

What happens is this: I have the newest style standing on a dummy but half-covered with a sheet in the corner of my little room when a customer calls to collect her repairs. While I am quietly busy making tea – taking more time than I need, I assure you – she will, of course, spot the garment and ask straightaway who it is for. I feign surprise, Kitty, rushing to cover the outfit properly with the cloth. I am shocked, I say. It should never have been seen.

After much persuading and begging from the customer I then tell her the name of a mutual acquaintance and settle to watch the many envious glances she pays to the frock as the tea is drunk. Eventually she will ask if a deposit has already been taken. I frown as though unwilling to be drawn on the matter but eventually tell her with even more reluctance that no money has changed hands so far.

'Has she seen the model?' I will be asked. When I say that she hasn't, the dress will be off the stand and over the client's head before the last sip of tea has been drained. Do you know they will often be pulling the bodice over their heads before their hats are off? I had one woman wedged tight in the neck-hole just the other evening!

Whereas Richard's dresses are modelled in places like Bond Street and the top Mayfair salons, mine receive their best airings on the hard benches of the Princes Street synagogue in Brick Lane.

My wedding frocks have received notice now, too. Just the other day the local rabbi was heard to complain about poor Jewish brides marrying on reduced fees who nevertheless managed to be conspicuous for the extravagance of their dresses, and this is, I feel, somewhat down to me.

The money I am taking has enabled me to pay a little investment into my own business. Just yesterday I took delivery of a new tailor's ham and a seam roll, for pressing, and I treated myself to a length of better quality Petersham for the waistbands, as some of the customers had

369

complained that the cheaper version scratched at their skin.

If the orders become greater I will be forced to take on my first employee. I have already made enquiries at the People's Palace, where they train poor young Jewish girls in dressmaking. When I was shown their work I discovered more than one to be of a suitably high standard and was told the girls are keen to work for a very low wage. This would be suitable for me, or else I will take on a factory worker while they are laid off during the slack period.

CHAPTER FORTY

ZG

DRESSMAKERS
*Until 1854 high-class dressmakers supplied clothes for
the upper classes by sending sketches and fabric
swatches to individual clients. In this year, though,
Yorkshireman Charles Worth set up his design establishment in Paris, producing a collection of made
samples and holding the first known fashion shows to
display them.*

The staging of the Zigo fashion show was largely down to
Chloe, who in turn enlisted an army of producers, chor-
eographers, stylists and dressers to do the real work for
her, while she contented herself with handling the lion's
share of the appropriate ranting, wailing, hair-renting,
cursing and press calls.

It was a job Kitty neither coveted nor felt herself vaguely
equal to. In previous years Gabriel would have been a
calming influence; without him, Chloe was like a hyped-up
banshee. Yet the role was somehow made for her – or she
for the role. It was one she had been rehearsing every day
of her life since the age of five.

Not an ounce of her energy, not a grimace, smile or tear
was unsuitable or surplus to requirements. The thudding
of her feet as she tore down corridors and catwalks formed

a solid, constant, pulsating beat that gave rhythm and urgency to the others' meanderings. When she shrieked she was the factory siren that galvanized the softly dazed and unproductive into meaningful activity. It was a terrible noise but comforting, at the same time. It was almost like the old days. Like before Gabriel had been killed.

As Chloe ranted, so could she simper. The focus of her charm and adoration was Alain. While he largely ignored her, both backstage and in the workroom, she pulsated around him, issuing murmurs of affectionate encouragement.

Chloe was the devil incarnate because she blamed Kitty for the last-minute decision to show. They had their press already. The range was incomplete. Alain was a complete sweetie but he was hardly Raphael and he could *never* imitate Gabriel's brilliance. It was Kitty's fault that the model team was half-rehearsed and riddled rotten with last-minute substitutions. The whole event had been *cobbled*, she told Kitty repeatedly, pronouncing the word as though speaking to a foreigner.

'*Everyone* shows at the barracks, Kitty, which is total number one reason why *we* should not be showing here. Number two? Because the place cannot – repeat, *cannot* – handle the current levels of press attention we are having to cope with since the inquest. As you are aware, the whole sodding pack are due, including not just fashion but every sodding rag that is keen to drain more juice out of the murder. The foreign press is especially prolific and suddenly we are inundated with requests for tickets from every damn celebrity who wants to get an airing.

'Gabriel would have cancelled this, Kitty – you *know*

that, don't you? And sweet Jesus,' she suddenly honed in upon a new point of controversy, 'why are you dressed like that? What in God's name possessed you?'

Kitty stared at her sister. Chloe had never looked more stunning. She had always adored slagging Kitty off more than anything else on the face of the earth and looked her best when she was doing it. Her eyes shone and her hair glowed. She was painted and swathed in sepia from top to toe. In the midst of all the colour and gleam she stood out like a cut-out from an old photo. Her hair had been cropped and dyed, her face had a luminescent glow from hours of honest toil spent peeling and exfoliating, and her lips were frosted ochre. The fabric of her trouser-suit cost two hundred and twenty pounds a metre. Kitty remembered Gabriel laughing about it when he brought the swatch back from Interstoff. Yet it was wonderfully understated. A design that looked tattooed by pinpricks and a sheen only visible under certain lights.

Kitty was wearing a boy's white singlet a size too small and jeans two sizes too large. Someone had forgotten to do her laundry. What she wore was all she had clean. Chloe battled to pull her into a quilted jacket. Kitty tried just as hard to resist.

There was a sumptuous smell in the air – the scent of fabrics that had been heated and then cooled and thrown into the air as each of the waiting models had their first outfits pulled over their heads as the last-minute fittings began. There were fatty smells of make-up and the hard-to-inhale aromas of lit matches, foreign cigarettes, burnished hair and lacquer. Then the roasting smell of gels as the lighting men went through final trials, and too-loud bursts of music that the crowds would soak up with their bodies when the auditorium was full.

Kofteros sat alone in the third row of gilt chairs, staring thoughtfully at the empty stage. He was totally rapt, with a study of locked concentration, his fingers knitted and pinned to his top lip, his legs stretched beneath the seat in front, but not in a way that looked loutish or disrespectful of the pre-show, church-like atmosphere. He was irrelevant, in his four-button suit and satin tie. A buzzard again, waiting for them to fail. Waiting to pick their bones. He smiled at Kitty when he saw her. She looked away quickly, hoping he hadn't thought she was watching.

'He's an attractive man,' Chloe said. Kitty's mouth tightened. 'He's not as wicked as you think, Kit,' her sister told her, her tone suddenly mellowed. They both stared at him out of sight now, from behind a pvc-covered screen. 'You seem to have Nicky pegged as the villain of the piece. A rotter and a scoundrel, eh?' Chloe warmed to her theme. 'And just what exactly is your role in all this buy-out foreplay? Do you see yourself as some coy Victorian heroine? I really think you should talk to him properly, Kit, instead of all this snarling. Who knows, you might even like him.'

Kitty shook her head. 'He wants this to go down the tubes, Chloe,' she told her sister. 'If the season works out the banks might view us with more sympathy. If not, we fail and we fall into Kofteros's lap. You know it and I know it. And *he* knows it, of course. Look at him, Chloe. He can't wait for the whole thing to start so that he can be there at the downfall. He'll be drooling on the runway soon.'

An aria from *Don Giovanni* flooded the hall. Two car-

374

penters scuttled across the catwalk on hands and knees, like beetles, hammering as they went. Kofteros closed his eyes, but whether to cut out the hammering or appreciate the opera, Kitty could not guess.

'We're shooting ourselves in the fucking foot, thanks to you,' Chloe said. 'If we'd cancelled the show there'd have been nothing for him to gloat over. You're the one that insisted we go down kicking and screaming for all the world to see. Where's the dignity in all this, Kitty? Do you think it's what Gabriel would have wanted? Then damn you for your fucking misplaced loyalty and schmaltz.'

Kitty looked at her sister. She was so close she could see the flecks of hazel in her irises. 'Did you really want to go down without a fight, Chloe?' she whispered. 'Is that really how you saw us? Does the money really mean that much to you? Burgess I anticipated, but I thought you might see the point in all this.' Her sister's face flushed suddenly and she looked away from Kitty's gaze. 'One last try, Chloe,' Kitty insisted, 'that's all.'

She moved even closer to say the unspeakable. 'What if it *was* them, Chloe?' Her sister's eyes came up again quickly, the pupils widened. She knew what Kitty was about to ask, it was obvious from her expression. 'What if they *did* kill our father? You must have thought about it, don't pretend you haven't. Perhaps it occurs to you now and again that you may be screwing the man who financed the assassination.'

Chloe went to walk away but Kitty pulled her back. It was the first time in their lives that she had had the courage to act in such a way with her bullying sister.

'What if it was, Chloe?' she insisted. 'What then? Roll

375

over and let them take the business as well? All those smiling faces on the screens? Grinning their little socks off at how easy it's all been? Is *that* what Gabriel would have wanted? You seem to be so tuned into his thoughts.'

Chloe pulled away. 'You're a fucking madwoman, Kit,' she said. 'You, Nula and Mother – all barking. Just excuse me if I sit this one out, will you? This is business, Kit – ask Nicky, ask Burgess. Ricky Khan murdered Gabriel. Ask the police.'

'His daughter says he didn't,' Kitty told her, receiving a look of such withering contempt in return that she wished she'd kept the last comment to herself. To change the subject she looked back at Kofteros. 'He even looks the part,' she said.

She meant that he looked like a killer. But then everyone she saw had murdered her father in her suspicious mind – even the ones who looked as though they hadn't. Kofteros looked very much as though he had.

'I don't know how you can, Chloe,' she murmured. She looked at her sister's face. Chloe was staring at Nicky and her expression looked unusually anxious.

A loud crackle of static rent the air like lightning, making both women jump and breaking the spell between them. Chloe straightened and snorted a laugh out through her nostrils, her old bravado restored. 'He is the *best* in bed, Kit,' she said, grinning. 'He does things with jelly cubes you could only guess at. If you promise to be polite to him he may even give little Freddy a few tips for free.'

Kitty looked at her sister. Was she joking? But she never knew. One thing Chloe was good at was giving nothing away. She felt a sudden rush of envy for her sister, for her shallowness, for her ability not to dwell and fester, like an open wound. Chloe was of the minute. Nothing existed for her beyond the present. Did it ever occur to her seriously for more than a fleeting millisecond that Kofteros could have arranged their father's murder?

The dark room. Kitty closed her eyes as the hammering grew nearer. Riva Khan's face hove into view. 'Your father must have been there before he died. Maybe someone he picked up in that room would have followed and killed him, think about that. Not my father, Kitty. Some pervert. A madman.'

Riva could have killed her father easily, the look on her face alone told Kitty that. If murdering Kitty would have saved her own father from prison she would have pulled a knife from her bag and gutted her on the spot, she could tell that. A proud woman. And vindictive.

Kitty shuddered, even in the heat of the spots. There was a small noise nearby. When she opened her eyes she saw Nula sitting heaped behind a rail of samples. Her hair looked wild and her large tragic eyes gleamed cyclamen as the gels were tested yet again.

'Okay?' Kitty asked her, tapping her knee with her toe. Nula nodded. The lustre in her eyes turned liquid.

'It's difficult,' Kitty said. Difficult without Gabriel. His size, his sweeping authority backstage. Difficult to forget he wouldn't appear on the catwalk at the end of the show. Chloe was happy snogging the press for now. A jittery Burgess had appeared to sit alongside Kofteros. China was home being pregnant and Hester was too sick to appear. She was holding together like Blu-tack but could become unstuck in the heat of the lights. Stephano stood at the back of the hall like a bouncer. The proud father-to-be. Kitty smiled.

And how was the chit-chat between the two suits? Burgess and Kofteros. Her uneasy-looking brother had sidled damply into the next seat and was whispering into Nicky's manicured ear. An odd couple, but at the same time well-matched; plucked from their nether world of virtual emotion to study the grubby fruits of their corporate existence.

Burgess wanted the take-over badly, Kitty knew that. She could almost smell his need from where she stood. It was Business he loved, not The Business. Like Kofteros, he could have been just as happy if they were manufacturing fitted kitchens.

The buy-out made logical, financial sense and Burgess was – above everything else – a logical man. But, like Chloe, maybe a slight malfunction in his programming had left a brain cell or two still pining for the glories of the Pyrrhic victory Kitty was attempting to pull off.

Burgess had never had a close relationship with Gabriel, who had seemed surprised and disturbed that such an odd, practical and unemotional character had apparently sprung from his loins. There had been no displays of affection between father and son. But Kitty had noticed Burgess studying them when she and Chloe had received praise and embraces as children, and felt both a dull sadness and hot-faced embarrassment that her brother had been side-lined.

There were figures on a screen and then there was real, messy life, Kitty thought. Nula unwound like a boa constrictor and rose up beside her.

'Do you want to help or watch, Nule?' Kitty asked her.

Nula thought for a minute. 'I'll help,' she said in a voice cracked with grief.

Kitty kissed her on the cheek. 'Stay together, Nules,' she whispered, 'don't fall apart on us now. We need you to be with us. Be strong. We need all the help we can get.'

ZG

CARTES-DE-VISITE
*First introduced to Britain in 1857, the trend for
these small, visiting card-size photographic portraits
was slow to catch on, but by 1861 there were one
hundred and sixty-eight portrait studios in London,
most of them specializing in the* cartes-de-visite.
*Competition became rife, with backstreet photographers
offering a 'likeness and a cigar for sixpence.' The bad
quality of these shots meant they often faded in a few
days, but the better* cartes-de-visite *form a fascinating
record of the actual fashions of the last quarter of the
nineteenth century.*

Kitty, I am now set up with a new girl to take care of extra orders, and still I find myself sewing through much of the night as well. The girl is called Ruth Levi and she has a mother involved in Slop Trade who will take on further work for a few shillings, if I wish.

Gregory is much taken with young Ruth and the improvement in his behaviour is remarkable. Knowing she is to arrive each day he is up earlier than necessary and about his toilet. When she is in the room he is far more alert and charming and I feel relieved that there has been good all round from her employment.

Ruth was born in this country of Lithuanian parents and

I believe she is almost as sharp as myself when it comes to spotting an opportunity for improvement. Just the other day I overheard her tell a customer that two of her relatives had already ordered for an up-coming *simcha* and within a week we had fittings under way for the entire party.

The family were so pleased with the result that Ruth and I were invited to the gathering and we laughed a lot to imagine how Richard would look if he could see some of his precious exclusive designs modelled by some of the fat old matrons we saw dancing to the twopenny fiddler's tunes.

It amazes me how rapidly news can spread throughout our *landsleight*, from *stieblech* to *schul*, via each Bar mitzvah, wedding and *simcha*. The women know I work in a top salon in Mayfair and each one who comes to me as a customer arrives in full possession of the knowledge that she has a right to the best looks a lady can wear, no matter how poor her circumstances.

There is a great pretence here, Kitty, and I am proud of it. The people are all poor but will not admit to such. Their poverty is something they hide inside their hovels. Courtesy makes them avert their gaze when they are forced to face the lowly circumstances of a neighbour. They live in rooms that are too small, they share their quarters with insects and vermin. Their beds stand in bowls of paraffin to rid them of bugs. And yet each day they live as though they were still in their fine homelands and dream of the time when they will be out of the ghetto and onwards to better things.

Did I tell you this place is like one huge collection area for immigrants? How we live in waiting? How the movement is upwards, no matter how remote the chance? Did I say that not once have I seen a face full of resignation? That even the old people plan for the day when their circumstances are improved?

So this is my life too now, Kitty. It is my lot to dress the optimism and pride of the oppressed and give it a face. With my twelve-shilling frocks they may sit in their badly-ventilated synagogues on the Sabbath, where the great wax candles eat up all of the air, chorusing their prayers until the windowpanes shake, and all in the knowledge that they are dressed every bit as well as the grand ladies in the tearooms up west. The fabrics may be of lowlier quality and the styles pinched and scrimped a little here and there to use up less *schmutter*, but the effect is the same – and good luck to them for that.

Schwer und bitter ist das Leben: hard and bitter is life, indeed, but at least we face it now clad in designs that could put Paris to shame!

CHAPTER FORTY-TWO

ZG

ZIBERLINE
*A thick, soft fabric of wool and mohair, with a
silky, lustrous nap.
By the 1850s, a desire to wear fashionable clothes
had affected every class in the social scale. This led to
a blurring of visual distinctions, especially as the
upper class habit of passing clothes down as soon as
they went out of fashion meant that even the quality
of fabrics worn could no longer be held as a reliable
clue to income.*

Ruth has been coaxing me to raise my prices a little. She
says our clientèle will feel more important if their purses
are squeezed. I tell her their purses are singing out with
the pain of the mashing they already suffer, but she claims
to know more – and so the prices are put up by a few
shillings, and I find that – as usual – she is right.

The Communists have already been round to enlist her,
but she is a good girl and says that they and the unions
will only have her asking for more wages and she knows
I pay her fairly already. She is a pretty girl and extremely
clever, taller than myself and with wild black hair that she
keeps tied beneath a scarf.

We are in the slack at the salon right now, so I take

Ruth down to Max's studio to see about the latest orders for brides. Max is more affluent these days and his shop is freshly painted. He wants two new outfits for his staff and he wants them identical, like uniforms. As I am taking measurements Ruth sits and sketches the designs I describe. She is only limited in her talents as an artist, though, and we all laugh when the sketches are finished.

'I'll make up a sample,' I tell Max. 'Ruth is much the same shape as your girls so I can pin it up on her and bring her round to show it.'

This causes much fuss, for the girls believe they are to have the style modelled as though they were in the salon with a mannequin parading for their benefit. Ruth's talents as a model, though, are as lacking as those of a sketcher.

'I could photograph her better,' Max says. And, Kitty, it is here that an idea occurs to me and I believe it to be such a good one that I start to sweat at my own cleverness.

'Could you photograph her in *all* my designs, Max?' I ask.

Max pulls a face, but I know he will agree. He is also rather charmed by Ruth and has been looking for an excuse to get her in front of his camera.

'How many?' he asks, rubbing his chin.

'Six, at present,' I tell him. 'And maybe the one wedding dress I have on the go.'

Before he can turn me down I am off along the street and back with armfuls of my best mantles. Ruth is pulled into each in turn and pinned to fit, while one of Max's girls has her hair combed and plaited into something half decent.

Poor Ruth! We have her holding boas and fruit, staring mournfully and smiling graciously, bending so that the more petite robes might appear long enough, and trussed into corsets two sizes too small so that she will appear slim enough for the more slender-sized orders.

Max is much impressed by the fun of all this and starts barking out orders like an army commander, which tickles all the girls but makes me blush.

Ruth begins the sitting posing shyly and nearly quivering with embarrassment, but after a few hours have passed she is posing like a dowager duchess and speaking in a voice to match, which has Max's girls in fits of hysterics.

I alone remain quiet and serious, plagued by doubts and excitements. I listen to Max playing to the girls and pray he is working professionally enough meantime. When the last one is finished he turns to me with a flourish.

'Madam,' he says. This is his new pet name for me, since my home business has shown signs of small successes. To him I am now a leading couturier, or at least that is his current tease.

Ruth comes up behind him, laughing. He turns, smiles, and places a kiss on her cheek. Kitty, there is a pang of jealousy which runs through me like a knife. What a good couple they make – she with her shining hair and quick, intelligent eyes, currently full of the admiration and longing I had been too blind to notice before, and Max with his handsome grin and huge body that dwarfs even tall Ruth. There is a moment, Kitty, more than a second but much much less than a minute, when we all wake to our own realizations. Ruth sees what appears to be prudish dis-approval written on my face while Max, who knows me best, spots it for the jealousy that it is and all at once sees his advantage.

'Rosa, you need some fun,' he says. He is still smiling. Ruth's eyes are full of what she feels to be shared sympathy.

'She works too hard,' she says, nodding.

'I need to,' I say, tersely. Max's arm is still about Ruth's waist.

'And you also need some wine,' Max says. 'I share a glass with most of my best clients so you should be no exception.' He looks at Ruth before releasing her. I know a man like Max could not fail to miss the girlish adoration in her eyes.

There is an awkward silence between Ruth and me as Max goes off to his tiny kitchen.

'Do you drink wine?' I ask Ruth while he is gone.

She stares at me. She is not stupid, she knows now how I feel. 'I have never tried it before,' she says. 'I have wanted to for a long time, though. Have you?' she asks.

'Only once,' I tell her, 'many years ago. I hated it.'

Max returns with three glasses and a bottle. 'This is burgundy,' he announces. It looks like blood. Ruth sips hers delicately and laughs. 'It's good,' she says, 'I think.'

I take my glass and drink it back in one, staring at Max as I do so. He is somewhat shocked and amused, yet rather pleased too, I think. Kitty, it is not only he who has learnt to read people's eyes over the years. I now have nearly as clear a view of Max Warkofski's thoughts as he has of my own.

He offers me a chair and then pulls one over for Ruth. 'So, what do you plan to do with your pictures, Rosa?' he asks. 'Will you have them framed and hanging on the wall of your salon?'

I ignore his sarcasm. I am holding on to my seat like grim death, for the floor is heaving and pitching like the sea. 'I plan to use them instead of samples,' I tell him. 'What Richard shows on models I can show in photographs. I can take them to my customers in a folder. They can make their selections in the privacy of their own homes.'

Max thinks a while before nodding. Ruth is clutching her glass with her eyes fired up and staring at me.

Do you know how I feel as I look at her, Kitty? I feel ugly and dull and I am so eaten with envy that I am incapable of hating her, for I am so busy hating myself. She is a nice girl. She is what I would want to be if I had the choice. That look in her eyes is the look I had when I bandaged Richard's cut hand in the sweatshop. The openness I see is the look I lost from my own eyes when I was raped in the snow in my *shtetle*. Ruth loves her mother and her father and is loved by them, while my parents are both dead. When she has a child it will be her own baby and no one will rob her of it. And she is a nice girl. And she loves Max.

'You're working outside your hours,' I tell her. And then hate myself for the blush I have put upon her face. She thought she was here as a friend and I have just reminded her she is an employee. She places her half-full glass on the table, stands to leave, lurches slightly, giggles.

Max is on his feet at once. 'I'll walk you back. Where do you live? You can't go like this. I should have mixed the wine with a little water. Excuse me, Ruth, that was my fault.'

387

There is none of the usual sarcasm or wit in his voice, only concern. Did he ever use such a tone with me? I try to remember but my head is too full of the burgundy. I am in a worse state than Ruth, but would never admit it.

It becomes dark while Max is gone, yet I do not rise to find matches for the lights. My seat is facing the empty sitter's chair. The only noise in the room is my own; heartbeat, breath, voices echoing in my empty skull.

There is a small Yiddish theatre just down the street. I hear a violin and then singing, some laughter, then a wave of hilarity. A comic song? I have no taste for such things. To my ears the song is sad. Too many melancholy notes, yet still the audience laughs.

I remember an act I caught some years before, a clown dressed as a comic bookmaker. He played the fiddle too, but the strings were joke strings that kept snapping and as they snapped he cried; great comic tears that rolled down his cheeks or squirted out into the front row. Everyone laughed, yet I cried with the clown, for I believed he truly wanted to finish the tune, and that the broken strings were preventing him.

I rise in the indigo darkness and walk silently across bare boards to the window. I can see the theatre from here. It is not much of a place, yet it appears quite grand when the lights are on.

'The Gypsy Princess.' The words are painted across boards at the front. I pull the window open to listen some more. Then I hear a cry, though I cannot hear the actual words that are screamed. There is no laughter now, just a roar, followed by more screams.

I watch the empty street curiously. A man in a dress-suit

emerges from the foyer backwards, his hands held to his face. A few people follow. Perhaps the performance is over. Or perhaps the performer has been injured on stage. People are spilling out everywhere now. The building looks like a colander with sand pouring through the holes.

I see Max cutting his way through the crowds that have now formed on the pavement. He has his hands in his pockets and his eyes fixed straight ahead. All around him is a crush of hysterical theatre-goers, yet he walks straight on like a blind man.

I return to my chair and it is there that Max finds me. Even in the darkness I can see the surprise register on his face.

'Rosa?' he says quietly. 'I thought you had gone.'

I sit very still, with my hands clasped in my lap. There is still noise from the street below; cries of anguish and laughter of relief.

Max pours himself more wine. He throws off his coat and unbuttons the neck of his shirt. 'So you mean to go into business proper?' he asks. He is massive in the room. I watch the swallow he takes go down his gullet to his chest. Has he kissed Ruth again? Yet why should he not? I am sulphurous in my bitterness. There is not a generous, well-meaning bone in my body.

I stand and the room is all whirling giddiness about me. Max is sprawled in his chair as though exhausted. Can photography be so tiring or has he become drained by his passion for Ruth?

I walk across towards him. He watches me approach and becomes eerily still. Even his breathing seems to have stopped as he watches and waits. There is no noise from either of us, save the leaf-like rustle of my skirts as I move. For a moment I stand watching him. And then I move closer still. There is a strange, dream-like weariness about me. As though I am standing on the banks of a river, contemplating throwing myself into the current and floating away until I drown.

There is nothing that matters any more, apart from this moment. I stare into the vibrant liquid blackness before me that is Max's two eyes and already I am engulfed by a carelessness I have never known before.

I stand between Max's flung-out legs – a tiny, neat and well-groomed figure before him, her hands clenched tidily and politely, small and dwarfed by the figure in the chair.

Max looks terribly puzzled. 'Rosa?'

I stretch out my arms like a somnambulist and place my hands calmly upon his shoulders. How do I look? Like an earnest child? He stays perfectly still. I am impressed by his patience.

There is laughter from the street, as high and as spiralled as the notes from the violin. Is that for me? Do I appear ridiculous, like the clown with the broken fiddle?

I bend then, to kiss Max on his broad forehead. My lips must barely touch him. I place them onto each brow, one at a time, and then the bridge of his nose. What do I want? I crave comfort, a secure shell that I can slither inside, slimy and snail-like.

I feel Max's hands about my waist. There is a cheer from the street. Do we have our own audience for this little tragedy? Yet we are in darkness and invisible to those outside.

'What is it you want, Rosa?' Max whispers into my ear.

Yet how can I tell him what I do not know for sure? How can a need so great it subjugates all sense of decency and virtue be described by someone with no experience?

I stroke his face silently. His eyes close.

'Rosa . . .'

A kiss could do no harm. I have survived a kiss from Max before, and to no ill-effect. I have hardly to bend as he is so tall, but I push my mouth against his.

Somehow this is not so easy when he is not taking the lead. I fumble on for a few seconds before raising my head.

'No, Rosa,' Max says. His voice sounds weak and I feel a sudden tremble of power. He clutches harder at my waist. 'No.'

'Max . . .' I will try again. It cannot be so hard.

Max pushes me away. 'Rosa,' he whispers, 'men are not built the same as women. There is a stage when we lose our senses and some of the power to control our own bodies. Especially when the present put before us is such a precious one. Don't offer what you mean to take away. Please.'

I have never heard him so indecisive. His words thrill me and I begin to kiss him again – only better, I feel, this time.

Our little battle of wills is over in an instant. Max pulls me in towards him, towards his body, pressing me there, holding me tight with his arms, his mouth and his legs. I throw my arms about his neck in response and we are lost, I know it.

I am laid upon a bed of lavender-sweet linen and my clothes are unpeeled, layer upon layer, until I am naked. Did you know snow can smell? It has a scent of its own

391

and it is this perfume I inhale from the cool breath of Max's mouth. I have no fear and no sense of what is to happen, only a dull and frozen certainty.

Max can bring me to pleasure or pain if he wishes, I am as unprotected as a babe.

I see no other face while Max begins his work. He is neither Richard nor my rapist. When he touches me he is Max and what I desire to touch in its nakedness is Max as well. He uses my name many times in his whispers, so I am reminded of myself enough, too. Rosa and Max.

He shows me himself without inhibition. He knows me and I know him for this honesty. Only the darkness panders to my sense of modesty, yet I know Max would too, if I wanted.

I close my eyes and Max introduces my soul to a thousand blunt emotions. There are fingers in among my hair. My ears receive whispers and my throat is laid bare with the tip of a tongue.

I am lost now, completely. My mind drifts away. There is a gasp from the crowds in the street. And then another cry echoes in the night. What has happened down there? Is the theatre spilled out onto the pavements, with all its dramas and tragedies? Or do I imagine all the noise?

I float above the sounds. The snow is so deep that first my arms are lost and now my legs in its drifts. The cold is like fire, burning my fingers. I clutch out into the air, touching another waiting hand; with a cry I try to grasp it, but it falls apart at my touch. They are Gregory's dappled little fingers, lined up like sticks in the whiteness. There is a kiss flat upon my belly. The horse will be restless with the wait. What if he goes off and takes the cart along with him?

The wedding suit! I let out a gasp as my spine arches in spasm. I have it in my hand – I feel the soft leather of the strap that Rintzi has put around it so that I can take it on the train. I am spreadeagled now, breathing the flannel of my skirt, which they have pulled up around my head to smother my screams. And because I am so ugly.

I am in water now – great waves of spume-filled greyness. Fishes nibble at my face and ears and plant kisses upon my legs and chest. I am thrown from the ship into the waves. My small face is wrapped in cotton but I feel the icy grasp of the sea the minute my body is submerged. My arms are bound – I cannot swim. I would cry out, but there is no life in my body. When my small corpse floats to the surface the gulls will peck me for their lunch and I will be happy enough to serve them, in my own way.

Max is watching in the darkness, his gleaming face above mine, waiting his turn. I can hear the sharp rasp of his breath and see the thumb-print mark upon his head.

Another roar from the street and a cry for help. Max is upon me gently but urgently and spilling inside too. His carefulness is a torture I no longer want to endure. I wish to be driven so far into the snow that I will never claw my way out again. I pull and his weight is upon me. I hear his concern but how can he crush me when the snow provides such a mattress beneath us? I hear his soft whispers turn to cries of anguish and delight and wrap him into my body at the moment of mutual ecstasy.

Even now he will not release me. I am become a part

of his own soul. He clutches at me like a lost child. I stroke his thick hair and plant kisses upon his chilling forehead.

I fall from dreaming into sleeping and the strangest sleep it is too – the sort of drowse that children take, profound and ingenuous.

When I rouse myself at last it is not quite morning and there is a purple light in the room. Max still sleeps. I pull his arms from me and leave without waking him.

The air is as sweet as London air can be – which is to say it has the scent of coal-fires and cats and the musk of rotten fruits, but I drink it down keenly as I walk. I pass the small theatre and stop for a second. There is glass and debris on the pavement, which two young coster lads are busy sweeping up into sacks. I ask them what has occurred but receive nothing but abuse for my pains. There is a policeman present, but I have been humiliated enough and so continue with my walk.

I have no desire to return home, Kitty. Gregory may be there and I fear I will find it hard to face my own brother after what has happened this night. I take myself off to Petticoat Lane instead, to the Old Clothes Exchange, to watch the poor folk there with their sorry rails of mouldering garments.

From the moment I step into Rosemary Lane there is a stench of fried fish and frizzling cut meat and onions. Even at this hour the place is full of bustle and my mood is soon lifted by the noise and various stinks, which would only appeal to one who, like me, has dwelled in London for more than a couple of years.

This whole area, from the junction of Leman and Dock

Streets to Sparrow Corner, is concerned with the selling of second-hand clothing to the very poorest creatures in London. One side of the lane is formed by a mountain of old boots and shoes, while the other is mainly hats, edgings and cheap cotton prints.

I stop in front of a vast array of some of the cheapest garments imaginable: a sea of old flannel, moleskin, fustian and corduroy. Kitty, when I compare these things with the finery I am employed in making in Mayfair! And yet there is justice here, too. Many of these items will be sent to Ireland, I am told, and the unfortunates there will be pleased for them.

I am intrigued by the sight before me, as fascinated as a healthy person walking around a graveyard. Will any of my garments finish up here? The thought tickles me and I laugh out loud. The walk has done me good – it has pushed other thoughts out of my head. It is not until I reach Commercial Street that the worries of my life return inside my head.

Will Max be waiting in my room? I tiptoe up the stairs and am relieved to find the place empty. Gregory has left it in the usual disarray and I spend some time picking up pots and plates before placing them back in their original spots.

I know Max's feet on the stairs. My hands begin to shake and I smooth my hair along my temples.

'Rosa.' He is both smiling and looking concerned. In his hand there are flowers. Roses. Their scent fills the room already.

I have never seen Max look so awkward before. He paces the room with his hat in his hands. He wears the same shirt as he wore the day before. His hair is plastered flat to his head. He looks for a vase and, when he can find none, pushes the roses into Gregory's tea-mug instead.

'That will upset my brother for certain, Max.' I laugh.

He clears his throat many times but does not speak. When he turns again I see how young he still is. 'You . . . took off without waking me,' he says at last.

I nod.

He makes a move towards me. 'Rosa, darling . . .'

'Max . . .'

His hands are at my waist again. He would kiss me, but I turn my face away.

'Don't be ashamed, dearest,' he whispers.

I allow him to hold me.

'I love you.' He repeats this many times over, until there are tears in my eyes.

I wait for what seems to be many minutes and then, at last, I hear Max ask what I know he will ask. 'Rosa, we must be married now.'

Then I have to tell him what I know has to be my reply. 'No, Max.'

I feel these words run like a sudden current through his body and I pull away politely.

'Rosa?'

'Max,' I say, 'you have always known I will marry Richard.'

He stares at me as though I am gone mad.

'Still?' he asks. His eyes are changing. The youth is going. A hard, angry man is taking his place.

'That has always been my intention,' I say.

'You came to me last night,' Max says. 'It was you,

Rosa. I have waited. I have waited so long I thought I might die.'

'Richard is to be my husband, Max,' I tell him. 'No one else. He has my child.' Did he really think I would ever be stopped in my plan to get David back? My son is still my life. All I do and work at is for him. Even if I did not love Richard I would marry him just to have my boy returned to my arms.

Max stands full height and stares down at me. 'And you may carry *my* child, now,' he says, bitterly. 'Or did that not occur to you? *Your* baby, Rosa, not someone else's. Your own flesh – and mine. It could be forming right now, as we argue. What then? Will that make you love me as much?'

I have a moment of uneasiness for, to tell the truth, this idea has not occurred to me. I clutch at my belly in shock. What if it were possible? Richard would never look at me again if I carried a child. I let out a pitiful wail at the thought and take a seat before my legs crumple beneath me.

Max sees the change in my eyes and smiles horribly. 'Think, Rosa,' he says quietly. 'Think of that idea. Imagine a child of your own, fathered by a husband who loves you more than life itself. Then think of that cold fish you desire so much. Think of the lies and deceits your relationship is based upon, and the honesty of ours.

'I know you, Rosa – better than you know yourself. Richard would have to see your name written down before he even remembered it. He will not marry you, not in a million decades! Think!'

But I will not think, Kitty, I cannot, I refuse to. All I

know is that I will marry David's father and we will be a family. It is the only way I will have David back with me again. I can imagine nothing else.

Max taps my belly. '*My* child, Rosa – what about that? Was last night your attempt to get the thought of me out of your mind? Did you hope that by giving your body what it wanted you could push me away altogether?' He stares into my eyes. 'We'll see, shall we? We'll wait.'

I have never seen Max this way before. Am I the first woman to turn him down? Well, he has plenty more to choose from, so he shouldn't let himself worry. My hands still shake with shock and I push them under my skirts and out of his sight.

'By the way,' he says as he rises to leave, 'the theatre last night – the policeman told me the whole story as I passed him just now. Someone in the balcony seats called "fire" and there was a rush to escape. What we heard as we made love was the sound of seventeen poor souls being crushed to death in the panic. What a fitting tragedy, eh? How better could our timing have been?'

I shudder as he slams his way out of the door.

For three weeks the tension has been unbearable. Max is often here but he is always silent, just watching me and waiting. God knows why, but he seems so sure that what we have done will result in a child. His presence in our rooms is terrible and even Gregory has become distressed at the sight of his friend now.

My monthly bleeding has started, Kitty. Can you imagine how great my relief is? I send a note to Max, at his studio, for I cannot bear the look on his face when he is told.

When I return from work Max is sitting in the dark and there is a terrible enough tale in his posture alone. His back is to the door and he does not move when I walk in, even though he must have heard me arrive.

I see the case opened out on the bed and the torn tissue lying over the floor.

'Max?' My terror is complete now. There is a knife in his hand. I see its glint in the moonlight. 'Max!'

I struggle with the matches and three fall from shaking hands before I have the mantle lit. I am sobbing. 'The suit!'

He has the garment across his lap. From the smell of his breath I can tell he is drunk.

I throw myself onto my knees and take the suit from him, checking it over and over again for the cuts I am sure he has made in it. When I discover it is whole my relief emerges in hysterical tears. I press the waistcoat to my face and rock to and fro on my heels.

'Don't worry, Rosa,' Max says in a hoarse tone, allowing the knife to fall from his hand to the floor, 'even I couldn't commit such a crime. Your wedding suit is whole. It should fit Richard very well. As you know, it was always several sizes too small for me.' He laughs at that, Kitty.

Was this always a joke, then? I fold the suit more carefully than ever before, stuffing each piece of shredded tissue carefully back between each fold and layer.

'You should go now, Max,' I say. He rises unsteadily to his feet and grasps me by the arm.

'I wish you well, Rosa,' he says, smiling, 'you deserve all that you are working so hard to get. David is your whole life, I realized that as I sat here waiting for you.

I just hope Richard is clever enough to see what he is missing.'

He kisses me on the forehead as he always used to do. Perhaps we are friends again. As he leaves I am sitting on the bed, clutching the re-packed case to my chest.

CHAPTER FORTY-THREE

ℤG

THE ALBUM

The celebrity cartes-de-visit *became popular in Victorian London and crowds would often form to view the latest photographs of political, sporting or theatrical figures in a studio window. Shots like these could be bought for one shilling and would often be given pride of place next to portraits in the family album, leading to confusion for later generations who were often left wondering whether they were in fact related to these famous or beautiful faces.*

Kitty, the idea of photographs is proving extremely useful. Each new design I produce is taken down to Max's studio, where he is good enough to make a picture of it for me and then either Ruth or I will take a folder of the best pieces around the neighbourhood door-to-door.

The concept is so novel that Ruth has been approaching women in rather more affluent areas and, to our delight, the reactions have been encouraging. There is no waiting for money now, either. Once a client has decided upon a model we can be bold enough to ask for a deposit up front, and this pays for the fabric, which means I have less risk to carry.

Tomorrow I will be interviewing girls to take on home

machine work, which means I can expand the business as I wish.

I have six ladies coming to see me at Max's studio today. Max has said he will be able to make extra folders of photographs and I have had the idea of sending well-spoken ladies out into places like Mayfair. It is remarkable how Max and I are able to continue with our business arrangement almost as though nothing has happened, but that is how it is. He has not mentioned the note I sent to him and, apart from a little polite coldness between us, which I believe Ruth would remark upon if she were not so tactful, things are much the same as before, apart from one terrible thing that I must live with. Since the night with Max I now see him linked in my mind with the man with the thumbnail scar between his eyebrows, and I am unable to separate what happened in his studio with what happened in the snow in Russia. I tell myself that Max is a good man at heart and remind myself of his gentleness, but the thought will not go, all the same. I concentrate my mind on business, for it is a terrible memory and one I would rather push away before I begin to doubt my sanity.

I know society women would only have their designs made couture, Kitty, at salons like Richard's, but I have noticed how each season we seem to lose a handful of clients there, and so feel that there must be many women no longer able to afford couture prices.

It is women like this I feel we must approach, who have expensive tastes but reduced incomes. If they can order my garments in the privacy of their own homes, who will know that they are not couture? There is a risk, of course, that they may turn up to Ascot or the opera and discover themselves sharing a box with a similar design, but I go to some trouble to ensure each outfit is different enough in the ways of trimming and cut to cause the minimum amount of embarrassment.

Kitty, I told you that Richard has taken to staring at me when I work in the salon. Well, now he has become quite talkative too, and just the other evening I made him laugh quite openly with a comment that I made about an elderly client of mine.

The seasons are becoming shorter at the salon and I have finished completely at the sweat, which leaves me more time to take care of my own business – though I have noticed the concern it is causing to Richard, so to hear him laugh so heartily was rewarding. He has laid off several members of staff recently, even outside the slack period – which was a surprise to us all.

Tonight, when the salon was closing, Richard asked if he might take me to supper. I have had barely enough time to run home and change, and what a decision that has been, too! I have a room full of suitable gowns to wear, but all are copies of the salon's top styles!

In the end Ruth has stayed back to help me take the bodice from one and fix it onto the skirt of another. With a silk shawl of Ruth's about my shoulders I believe Richard will never notice the similarities.

We dine at a restaurant in The Haymarket and I watch Richard relax until we are talking almost like friends.

403

'Do you know how much I have learnt to admire you this past year, Rosa?' he asks.

I look away, smiling modestly.

'When you took the job as *vendeuse* I must admit I believed you had bitten off more than you could chew. But you're popular with the clientele and that's not easy, for they're a difficult group of old baggages, as I'm sure you've discovered.'

He laughs at this and I am amazed, for I have never heard anyone at the salon speak of the clients with disrespect.

'Rosa,' he says, after a long pause, 'David is a fine boy. He is my life now, you know. The business is going through a bad patch as I'm sure you are aware. The economic climate is in decline and women are less able to afford our prices. Do you know I was advised by my bank manager to drop the costs of each garment a little to make them more affordable? Could you imagine anything worse? How can you explain to someone who is used to little more than figures on a page the value of the exclusive price tag?

'Do you think a man who has lived his life behind a desk wearing nothing better than second-rate worsted could ever grasp the concept of the heady excitement a middle-aged woman feels when she orders a model with a price-tag so high as to be well out of her husband's financial range?

'Would he know that trance-like state when a woman is presented with a bill that makes her suffer delicious waves of sickness as it is at least twice the amount she had hoped it would be? And then share the pride of modelling the dress that has been the cause of such suffering?

'If I drop my prices each frock will be less of a purchase. It is the price they are buying, Rosa, not the design.' He

404

pauses to smile and sip his wine. 'You do understand?' he asks.

'I'm sure you're right,' I tell him. His passion for the business entrances me.

His hand is upon my own. 'Would you care to see David?' he asks. 'Right now?'

We take a carriage to his house and I am ushered quietly though excitedly into my son's bedroom. The smell and the sense of him overpowers me and I have to check myself not to fall sobbing at the foot of his bed.

David lies in the midst of a deep and simple sleep. His arm is thrown above his head and his face is turned upward. I hear him breathing. *This* is what I want and what I will fight for, I tell myself. With Max, there would be no David. How could he imagine I would ever have decided otherwise?

Richard taps me on the arm and I am led reluctantly into the front lounge.

'How well he looks now!' Richard says. He is nervous. Perhaps he feels guilty, after all.

'He has a good father,' I say, and Richard's smile is full of pride and relief.

'Do you know, Rosa, the change in you is remarkable too,' he begins. 'You look more . . .'

'I look more like a lady now, Richard,' I whisper, 'is that what you mean? Well I see enough now to model myself upon. When we first met I was a poor little greener. Now I know better. I'm pleased you noticed.'

I look up quickly and, do you know, Kitty, Richard is leaning to kiss me. I stand up suddenly. 'I must go,' I tell him, watching the surprise on his face. Did he really assume

I would be so easy to catch? I know he believes we have been intimate before, when he was too drunk to remember, but surely even he must have noticed the change in my confidence and stature since then?

I shake him by the hand, as a society lady would. 'Thank you for allowing me to see my son,' I say.

He blushes. 'A pleasure,' he tells me, backing off, 'any time. Of course.'

CHAPTER FORTY-FOUR

ZG

THE BUYERS

*Retail organizations have different types of buying.
Multiples will tend to order centrally while many of
the stores can often operate on local systems. Local
buying will often guarantee more focus on the specific
customer base, while central buying has the advantage
of discounted bulk orders.*

Kitty sat in her mother's lounge, a bone china cup of brandied coffee cooling in her hand. There was a smell of pot pourri, as though she were in the back of a minicab or the ladies' rest-room of a posh department store. Hester had taken to scenting all the rooms now.

Kitty was so barely out of childhood, and yet untold nostalgias pained her savagely, like nettle rash. Her whole life was in flashback: boarding school, synagogue, births, marriages, deaths, they all blurred into dream-like lagoons where little meringue islands, whipped up by anxiety and tension, floated by with a lazy regularity.

Hester sighed and patted her uncombed hair. She would never have worn capped sleeves while Gabriel was alive. Hester's upper arms were not her best feature. There was a hammock of spare flesh swinging beneath them, and the skin there was mottled mauve.

Maybe *she* did it, Kitty thought, maybe she killed him so that she could wear short sleeves.

'Never mind,' Hester sighed. 'You did your best. Your father would have been proud of you. He always said you were the only one with his eye for the business. 'Burgess is Mr Cashflow. Chloe is Miss Gossip Column. China is Stephano's wife, nothing more. You understood what was in the blood. You inherited a talent, Kitty. Never forget that. Don't lose sight of your father's dream – it was important to him.'

It was Kitty's turn to sigh and rub her hands across her face. She still hated all this 'in the blood' talk, how they owed it to the suffering and deprivation of their forebears to make a success of what they did today, take nothing for granted, work for their sake, if not for your own.

The fashion show had been a success – though not in the way she had wanted. With too many press packed into too small a space, the atmosphere had become claustrophobic and unbearable. The audience had not come to judge the clothes, they had come to judge the family: ghouls come to visit the madhouse and study the insane. An excuse, if any were needed, to re-run every detail of Gabriel's murder across the front and inside pages of all the daily rags.

The garments themselves had barely received mention. A couple of shots on the fashion pages – some half-hearted critique as an aperitif, and then back onto the main course of murder. Many had made mention of how obviously Gabriel's touch was missing. There were a couple of lukewarm plaudits for Alain – the sort of stuff you would hear for a last-minute understudy who has had to go on stage when the star of the show is sick. Kind enough, encouraging – patronizing, even. Lipservice, nothing more, nothing less.

They were finished, then. No contrived happy endings. Kitty wasn't surprised. She had known the range was nothing great. Good, maybe. Miraculous in its conception, given the odds, but still just good. It required Gabriel's presence for it to become a lifesaver of a range. Without his touch it could never have achieved as much as she had been hoping.

She had sat in an all-nighter somewhere, drinking lemon tea and fiddling with a toasted egg sandwich. The place had been totally apt for her mood – the sort of location a movie director would have chosen in a flash. Obscenely-bright strip lighting that bathed everything in a shadowless pistachio glow. Plastic ketchup bottles with shrimp-coloured dried drips running down the sides. Pyrex plates. Comfortless but comforting – the sort of place anyone would want to sit in while they waited for the next day's papers to arrive.

Freddy had been there too, looking healthy and clean-shaven, despite the ghastly lighting. He had been good-humoured and tolerant about the café, joining in the spirit of the place, nodding to cabbies and winking at the waitress and sifting streams of white sugar into his tea.

Kitty had wanted to view Freddy with affection, only she'd found that difficult since the Raphael thing. If the collection failed it would be easy to blame his father. Blame the father, blame the son. You couldn't segregate in the rag trade. The whole family in one blinding, molten lump.

It was the Jacobs's fault. It was the Jacobs family who stitched up the Zigofskys by stealing their designer a week before the collections. No house could survive that, especially not one that had just been decapitated.

Maybe the Jacobs killed her father. So what about when she married Freddy, the much-adored and much-prized son of the clan? Would she create a new strain – the Zigofsky-Jacobs? Ripper-off and ripped-off in one? Killer and victim united?

She listed their possible reasons in her head:

1. Any Zigo success took business and money out of the Jaycee corporation. Not likely.

2. Murdering Gabriel gave them their best if not only method of headhunting Raphael. Again, not likely.

3. They wanted to stop the wedding. Inconceivable. It had been Frederick Jacobs Senior's idea in the first place, with a few encouraging hints in her direction from Gabriel.

So far the Jacobs were looking positively blemish-free compared to the Khans, Kofteros and the Zigofskys. Especially the Zigofskys. Her mind ran over familiar ground:

Motives:

Hester – so she could wear odd stockings and short
    sleeves for the first time in her life.
China and Stephano – shortage of cash-flow, owing
    to the inpending birth.
Burgess – a clinical removal of impediments to sale
    of business.

Chloe – a desire to step into the direct limelight and make herself fabulously wealthy into the bargain.
Kitty – a desire to take over the running of the business.
Nula – teenage angst.

Was it at that point that Freddy had pulled the egg sandwich away from in front of her and replaced it with the early editions? Kitty tried to remember, but the pot pourri had infused her brain, robbing it of every coherent memory, save one – The Show Was Not A Success. They should batten down the hatches and prepare for alien invasion.

ZG

BARÈGE DE PYRÉNÉES

Barège *is a fine, semi-transparent fabric made of silk
and wool. The silk is thrown up on the open mesh. A
cotton and jute blend was known as* barège grenadine,
*and one printed with foliage and brilliantly-coloured
flowers was named* barège de Pyrénées.

I have moved into better rooms in a house overlooking
Victoria Park in Hackney. Gregory was upset at leaving
Brick Lane, but now he has seen the place he is delighted.
We each have our own bedroom, with proper walls in
between instead of partitions, and there is a kitchen of our
own for the food and another room where I can work.

Even Max was impressed, although he said very little,
and I know Ruth is delighted as she says she can now
regard me as a proper boss, which made Gregory laugh.

My brother is much improved these past few months.
Max is now his friend again and it is good to see how
much Gregory learns from him that is good. He has more
friends in his job and, despite his shyness, is quite popular
with the elderly ladies around the park, who use him for
errands and spoil him like a child with cakes and sweets.

I have never mentioned the fire in Max's rooms, but
ensure all matches are kept locked away. Max's theory

was that it was the work of local boys, who are known to stick smouldering rags through Jewish letterboxes or beneath our doors. He thinks my brother was merely confused about Rintzi's death and I must say I now believe he is right about this, for Gregory is a gentle man, for all his simpleness.

I now employ fifteen women to act as agents for my models and very busy they are, too, as they work purely on a percentage of sales, which was an idea that Ruth suggested. It was not difficult to recruit locally – I have women calling all the time in the hope that I will take them on for selling, but will only employ those with a clean, smart image. Word of mouth was advertisement enough for the posts, though I also placed a carefully-worded, two-line advertisement in the newspaper, which has brought in some of the more genteel women.

The only exception to this plan of employing well-spoken women is old Mrs Ezra from Fournier Street. She is sixteen stone and hardly a model of elegance, but she is so ferocious she earns more than three of my better turned-out ladies put together, and mainly through what I can only describe as intimidation! There are women living around the Whitechapel area who would never have bought my gowns had it not been for Mrs Ezra's arriving unheralded in their parlours and drinking them out of tea and eating them out of honeycakes until they were forced to make a purchase to be rid of her.

Max has met the woman once when she called to collect her commission, and he said her stare was so fearsome he almost bought one of my mantles himself!

So this is my life now, Kitty – a flurry of manufacture

mixed with a few vital days at the salon to serve the paltry handful of clients I have left on my books, and to keep an eagle eye on designs I can copy.

Richard is always present now when I visit David and I am allowed into the house itself more as a guest than an employee. I see this as a great step forward and can tell he is more relaxed in my company.

And still there is Max. I feel we are friends again now, Kitty, for he acts as though nothing has happened, except there is a degree of coolness about him that was not there before. His time is as much taken with his business as my own. I have paid back much of what I owe him and feel proud of this fact. At night I think of him sometimes, and of what happened between us. But I know it will never happen again.

ZG

EPANGELINE
*In the 1860s epangeline was the name given to a
rep-like material, made of wool. In the latter part of the
century it was used for a slightly corded, woollen
sateen.*

There has been much fuss in the salon. A client was contacted for the coming season and replied that she would
never pay such great prices for frocks her staff might wear
on their day off. Richard took a trip to see the woman
himself and came back looking pallid with shock. We all
sat in the salon in silence while he disappeared into a meeting with his director and designers. Over the next few days
the whisper went round: the client had seen a copy of one
of her mantles being worn by next-door's cook on her
Sunday promenade. The woman had promptly fainted
clean away, which meant a doctor was alerted and the
story somehow reached the ears of the press.

Max is very delighted at this, for he found the story
himself in his local rag. 'What now then?' he asked.

'What do you mean?' I answered him.

'Well,' he said, sitting down comfortably and folding his
arms, 'how long do you think it will be before your fiancé
discovers who is copying his designs?'

I ignored the sarcasm of his tone and carried on with my sewing. 'I'm only surprised he has not guessed before,' I told him.

He looked at me carefully. 'You don't mind?'

'No.'

I stitched while he considered this. 'You know you could bankrupt him,' he said at last. 'Either that, or find yourself standing in court.'

Now it was my turn to laugh.

'What about the boy?' Max went on. 'Surely it is his inheritance you are playing with? I thought you wanted a rich marriage.'

'And so I do,' I said, cutting a length of silk thread. Max is not the only one who can play games. I rose to make tea, leaving him sitting thoughtfully.

Z̶G̶

THE EAST END
*The West End may be tourist-raddled and full of
history, but it is in London's East End that the real
ghosts play. Permeated and blackened by ancient dust,
it owes its existence to endless echoes of the past.
There are no limits to history here; what began
centuries ago has never been finished. The scars of
poverty never healed; tenements are still tenements,
immigrants still arrive and work night and day to
better their lot. There are arranged marriages and
places of prayer, and only the religions have changed,
though the industries stay roughly the same.*

Kitty took a cab to the East End. In her lap lay a Tupperware container full of home-baked cake that Hester had
given her. Since when had her mother baked? She prised
off the lid and a hot sweet smell leaked out, so she closed
it again quickly before the whole cab stank. There was
something in there covered in salmon-pink icing with
sponge butterfly wings implanted in the buttercream. Was
this how her mother filled her days now, she wondered?
Was it some kind of therapy? Would *she* find herself turning to the oven when Freddy succumbed to the near-
inevitable heart attack in old age?

She stopped off en route to check in at the wholesale showroom. The staff there tried to congratulate her on the show, but their eyes all said the same thing as her mother's mouth: 'Never mind.'

Harvey Nichols had cancelled an order because the buyer had decided on an American theme for the coming season: 'Never mind.'

She wandered out through the machine-rooms. Women were sitting drinking tea from plastic thermos cups. She realized she still held the Tupperware box so opened it and offered the contents around. They looked at her and smiled. Most of them took a cake but she guessed they were being polite and wouldn't eat it. They were older women, all about Hester's age, but unlike her mother they still had control of their figures.

Only Tilda, the house model, ate with any enthusiasm, sitting perched on a tailor's stool wearing only tights and a vest. A walking testament to the perils of anaemia, she rocked and smoked as she ate. When buttercream fell onto her front she tutted to herself before licking it off, like a cat.

They were taking short-order work to make up the figures. Gabriel would never contemplate the idea but Burgess had been insistent and so it came to pass. Betty, the sample machinist, sat lost behind a mountain of interlining, wadding, fusibles and pads. The others heard the zip of her machine and flicked their mugs in the sink before setting down to their own work. With their heads bent as though in prayer the message was the same; it rose from the tops of their scalps and permeated the air, along with the fabric fluff, steam and heat: 'Never mind.'

'Is my father's office unlocked?' Kitty asked the show-room manager.

The small room smelt stuffy. She walked around it, sniffing the air like a foxhound, opening drawers, picking things up. The manager watched from the doorway, his arms folded across his chest. He looked embarrassed. Had Burgess told him to watch out for her? That she might steal something?

She found two photographs; one was of Gabriel with his arm around another man, both smiling broadly. It was Riva's father. The shot was an old one, taken when both men had dark hair. The other photograph had been folded. Kitty straightened it out. Folding a photograph was like bending back the spine of a book – sacrilege. The boy in the shot had his back to the camera, but his turning pose meant that his face was visible. He looked like a professional model. Kitty looked closer. Raphael. Gabriel's designer. Frederick Jacobs Senior's designer now.

She flipped the shot over. There were four rings of dried yellow glue, one in each corner. Perhaps the shot had been stuck to a CV. Maybe it was sent when he applied for the job. Kitty put both pictures back in the drawer and closed it.

Think.

Why did photographs of the dead always appear to carry a message?

Think hard.

The dark room.

Kitty would have described her upbringing as open-minded but strangely moral. She had been having sex with

Freddy for two years, and yet knew very little about the darker side of the act. Nicky Kofteros could do things with jelly cubes. Kitty had no idea on earth what. Since her sister's boast she had imagined the little lumps of flavoured gelatine pushed into virtually every possible orifice, and yet none of the options seemed remotely erotic.

Was Freddy a stud? She thought not. Freddy was careful, patient, methodical. Or funny. He smelt clean and his skin tasted of the sun or of nice soap. It was Chloe who had told her Freddy was well-hung. She knew because she had once dated Freddy's brother and *he* had told her it was Freddy who had inherited all the size while he had inherited most of the intellect. Chloe had asked Kitty if she wanted to swap and Kitty had been embarrassed. Her sister always joked that that was why she was marrying Freddy. Their friends found this funny – even Freddy laughed – but Kitty couldn't share the joke, even though she knew this made Chloe worse.

'Why don't you laugh when she teases you?' China used to say when they were kids. 'She'll soon get bored. It's your little poker face that makes Chloe so wicked. Look at you.' She would hold the mirror of her powder compact up for Kitty to see.

China was always right. The face that stared back at Kitty was inevitably doleful and hapless. Yet she was an honest girl and couldn't bear to laugh when she didn't feel like it. Chloe could. Chloe could fake anything.

The dark room. Did Chloe know it? Did everyone go there?

Sex in the dark. Sex with a total stranger. Kitty became

420

absorbed by the notion. It stuck to her brain like stale gum to the bottom of a shoe. Smell and touch alone – did they ever speak to the people they fucked?

'Thank you – that was quite nice.'

'I hope my screaming didn't put you off.'

'Don't I know you? Don't I know that smell? Have we met before? Your hair and skin feel familiar. Isn't that the famous Jacobs schlong? I would have known it anywhere – you must be Freddy. It was your brother who inherited all the intellect in the family. Brain or brawn, eh?'

She had made love in the darkness but it had always been Freddy, no matter what. Freddy's chest. Freddy's stomach hairs, that rode in a thin and delicate line to his crotch. When she fingered those hairs gently his penis would rise like a drawbridge. When she touched the soft inside of his thighs his legs would part helplessly and he would give himself to her like a toy.

She could play with him for hours. Press this and this would happen. Touch that and that would occur. She liked it. She didn't want strangeness and jelly cubes. She liked the noise Freddy made when he came. Sometimes it would even make her come, too.

Kitty's taxi passed char-grilled-looking churches made of stones, speckled like acne from bomb-damage and pollution. There were brand new mosques surrounded by rows of housing so old and leaning they appeared to be tacked together by the flyposters' gum. Giant spray-blown swastikas and NF initials lay so faded on the brickwork that they appeared almost benign – as natural a part of the rotting landscape as the duckweed and billowing wisps of discarded wrappings.

There were structures tiled to waist-level in gleaming oak-brown and above in dingy cream, like decayed teeth. Cardboard boxes lay stacked and abandoned everywhere. Centuries-old signs bedecked buildings rendered unrecognizable by grime and bricked-up windows: BOYS' BATHS, RUBBER STAMP MERCHANTS, COFFEE AND CHOP HOUSE, THE EASTERN STAR, CHEVRAM SHASS SYNAGOGUE, SOUP KITCHEN FOR THE JEWISH POOR. The smell of ale and cigarettes welled out of the Jack the Ripper pub as a lunchtime drinker aired himself in the dim sunlight outside the main doors.

In the sidestreets of Brick Lane – Fournier Street, Wilkes Street, Princelet Street and Hanbury Street – the cab passed the traditional concentration of sweatshops, most of them Asian-owned. In the wider streets there were shopfronts with lengths of broad, spangled sari fabrics, swimwear and cheap children's wear on display. Outside one shop stood two life-size dummies, each dressed in sixties clothing and leering at all the passing traffic.

Riva Khan sat bent with concentration at her father's old desk. She wore a blend of traditional and modern – a khaki-green silk sari with a Conran jacket slung around her shoulders. Her feet tapped as she worked. One hand rubbed at her forehead as though trying to massage some sense out of what she was reading.

She looked up at the sound of Kitty's feet but her eyes remained dimly unfocused for a few seconds. A short guy in a raspberry pink suit came between them, pulling a rail full of polythene-clad dresses, and Kitty had to climb up the wall to get out of his way. She heard Riva start to speak but missed the first few words above the squeak of the metal castors and rustle of plastic.

'...is out of prison now?' Riva's eyes looked rattlesnake-lidded.

Kitty cupped her ear with her hand.

'I said, did you know my father has been released without charge?' she asked.

Kitty shook her head. 'No.'

Riva stared at her pencil. 'I'm trying to clear a few things up for him,' she said, 'he worries about the business. It was the only thing he asked about when they held him at the police station.

'We are all but closed down here now. He's too broken to come in. I told him I would help. Did you know I got my degree, Kitty? Did you know I passed all my accountancy exams? And yet he still wants to arrange my marriage for me. Much like your situation, eh? I heard you were engaged to Freddy Jacobs. Gabriel must have had a hard time pulling that one off. Keeping it in the family, eh? A business and political arrangement, just like my own wedding.'

Kitty cleared her throat. The walls to the workroom were bare tile, which gave her cough an echo. 'My father had no hand in my engagement,' she told Riva.

'Oh,' the girl said carefully, 'I see.' She smiled in the direction of the desk. 'So old Mr Jacobs won't be propping up the business for you, then?' she asked. 'That's very sad, Kitty, I heard your father had spent a lot of time over those negotiations. Your betrothal to Freddy was just the bait he needed.'

Kitty felt her face redden. Riva was fascinating to watch.

Her head barely moved, just her eyes. Her voice had a flat, nasal tone that was hypnotic.

'They could not find any evidence, you see,' she said, and Kitty's brain had to jump a step to keep up with the change of subject.

'Your father?' she asked.

Riva nodded. Suddenly she looked up and her expression changed. 'I'm sorry,' she said, smiling, 'I didn't even offer you tea. All that way from the glamorous side of London and I have not as much as offered you a tour of the place or refreshments. It's the grief that makes one forgetful, don't you find?'

She called for tea from a young boy who was passing. He looked surprised. Kitty caught Riva's quick frown of admonition before the polite smile returned. 'Do you think the place has changed much?' she asked, standing up and leading Kitty to the adjoining doorway. Kitty stepped through the doorless gap and looked around the workroom.

Khan had once owned two establishments, one of them a vast warehouse of a place in Old Street, with computer-programmed laser cutters and steam-injectors aiding the CMT process. When Gabriel had stopped employing him, though, he'd had to cut back to this, his older place – a ragged sweatshop with only six machines and an ancient Hoffman presser.

All the machinists were elderly women and all wore saris and tight grey buns. Soon even they would be out of a job if new orders didn't start coming in. Kitty glanced at a couple of the production panels.

'I've got them making up what you would call

schmutter,' Riva told her. 'Cheap crap for cheap prices. A far cry from the sort of stuff your father used to send us, but then who can afford to be picky when there are families to feed, eh?'

She walked around the workroom, stopping behind the chair of each machinist and telling Kitty exactly how many children and grandchildren each woman had. When her lecture was finished she stopped and smiled. 'But then I suppose a sophisticated westerner like yourself would wonder why they just didn't use a more effective birth control.' She laughed as though sharing the joke.

Kitty smiled to be polite. 'I need to ask you something,' she said when Riva was closer. The girl's eyebrows raised.

'The dark room,' Kitty whispered, 'what exactly did you mean when you told me my father must have been there?'

Riva put her head back and laughed again. 'I thought you said you didn't believe me,' she replied.

'I just need to know, Riva,' Kitty said.

The girl stared at her. 'I am a well brought-up woman, Kitty,' she said, 'exactly how much do you think I could know about a place such as that?'

'Please.' It took a lot for Kitty to say the word.

Riva's eyes gleamed like dark pebbles. 'Why don't you go and ask Raphael, Gabriel's ex-designer?' she said quietly. 'My father used to say it was one of *his* favourite haunts.' She paused. 'My father is a very moral man, Kitty. When he spoke of Raphael it was always with a tone of slight disgust. He could never work out what your father saw in the man. He adored Gabriel, but he always called Raphael his "blind spot".'

Kitty found herself politely manoeuvred to the main

425

door. 'I'm sorry,' Riva said, smiling, 'I have so much to catch up with. We may find the receivers knocking on our doors any day and I want to fend them off for as long as I can. You know how it is.'

She held out her hand. Kitty stared at it. 'What do you mean, "*see* in him"?' she asked.

Riva looked puzzled.

'You said your father could never work out what it was Gabriel *saw* in Raphael,' Kitty repeated.

Riva laughed a small, polite laugh. 'Oh,' she said, 'well, you must have known, Kitty. Raphael was your father's lover. His little toy. That was why he left after your father's death. He couldn't bear to work there anymore. He was as much in mourning as you are now.'

CHAPTER FORTY-EIGHT

ZG

LOVE
*A thin silk, striped with satin, that is used in the
making of ribbons.*

Dearest Kitty,

I am now well known in Mayfair as a copier of the
latest fashion for society ladies whose circumstances have
become reduced, but who still wish to retain an impression
of their original status and wealth.

My saleswomen pay a discreet visit to their houses with
their folios of photographs beneath their arms and, Kitty,
you would be shocked to hear some of the names of clients,
for it seems even the highest in the land have a nose for a
bargain, when it is presented in such a way.

As well as the outworkers I employ, I also make use of
a couple of sweats and at a very good rate too, for I give
them work during the slack period, so can negotiate the
lowest rates possible.

Of course there is some scrimping on designs, but on
the whole the fabrics I use look as good as the ones Richard
sells and, by using the workers during the slack and by
keeping the majority of the scrimping on the lower layers
and inner seams and tucks, I can turn out mantles that

look every bit as good as couture at less than a third of the price.

As I said, the exclusivity of each model is not assured, but we have taken to checking each client's social circle before they order and so can more or less assure none of the ladies will come face-to-face with a copy of their own style within the current season.

My only problem has been that of payment, for I find the higher the class of the client, the slower they will be at settling debts. Max tells me that this is only to be expected; that I should allow credit and not press for payment or I will lose customers. I have told him this is ridiculous. A debt is a debt, Kitty, and if my poorer souls can be prepared to scrimp their hard-earned money to ensure I am paid on time, then some of my wealthier clients can do the same with their shillings and pounds. They can pawn their jewels for all I care, Kitty. Allow one debt to go by and a hundred others will follow it.

As I said, the local souls are usually timely with their payments, for they have pride and honour and no wish to flaunt or even admit their poverty. Even so, I have been prompted to employ a group of local lads to pay visits – just as reminders. Two of these are Sabbath goys – boys who once earned their pennies lighting up on a Sabbath, and who find themselves in short demand now that the observance of kosher practices are rather in decline in the area. I have contacted Queer Tess's sons and they are more than delighted with the deal we have made. There is no menace in them at all, though I find women are pleased enough to pay up to get the scent they bring with them away from their doorsteps.

428

The same is true in Mayfair. I have taught the boys to be polite and respectful, but the sight of them alone is enough to get all bills paid promptly and I can reward the boys generously for their productive work.

Kitty, I feel at peace with myself for the first time since I left Russia. At last I am keeping Papa's warning: 'Never be poor and never grow old.' My income is flourishing and I am still young.

Gregory has shown some interest in the business and so I now employ him to manage the goys, which he thinks is splendid. Ruth is still with me, and in charge of the local outworkers, helped by her mother. I believe they rule with a rod of iron but this is all to the good, as our deliveries are known for their punctuality.

Max and I now meet as equals, as I have paid back all I owe. We talk business long into the night and I have even taken to smoking the odd cigar with him, which causes Gregory much amusement.

It is good to see respect in Max's eyes and he is much less amused by me now. I am surprised he has not wed Ruth, now that he knows there will never be anything between us. She is a very handsome girl and still much taken with him.

Gregory still moons around after her, but she treats him as a younger brother, to be indulged and made fun of.

Richard has discovered who has been cheating him at last. He came into the salon while I was serving a client and I saw him watching me with an expression of concern on his face.

'I will see you when you are finished,' he whispered

as I passed. I guessed immediately what the issue was.

'You want to speak to me?' I asked, smiling.

A muscle worked in his cheek. He stared at me for a second before nodding.

'Then you will make an appointment to come to my premises,' I said.

Kitty, you can have no idea how much this shocked him. His whole body appeared to absorb my words and his eyes widened in astonishment.

'*Your* premises?' he asked. In fact he almost spat the words out, Kitty. This was great sport – I wish you could have been there!

I had a printed card ready in my purse. 'Here,' I said, and went back to tend to my client.

Richard arrived the following day. I had the place ready for him. These are premises I have rented off Fournier Street, to house the dozen or so machines I have been forced to buy to accommodate the level of business. We are not yet to full capacity, although I intend to house some of my outworkers there, but I had Ruth's mother present sewing furiously at some good quality material, along with eleven of her colleagues.

Ruth herself was on a high stool, scratching away at an imposing-looking ledger, and I had several of my saleswomen taking tea in the corner, as well-dressed as any of Richard's *vendeuses*, and poring over their appointment books.

I led Richard to a room in the loft which I had furnished as an office, and offered him a seat on the other side of my desk.

He said nothing for a while.

'Would you have preferred coffee?' I asked.

'What?'

'Instead of the tea?'

He shook his head as though trying to clear it. 'What is all this?' he asked.

'I told you, Richard,' I said politely, 'this is my business, and very lucrative it is proving, too. I hope you'll be proud of me – most of it was founded on the money with which you bought my beloved son.'

He was watching my face now, and I saw him blush. 'Rosa . . .' he began, 'you must forgive me. I had no idea quite how much the child meant to you . . .'

I smiled. 'No, Richard,' I told him, 'you thought it was only the upper classes that have true feelings for their off-spring. To the poor like myself they are nothing short of a nuisance. We're just like wretched animals, really – incapable of feeling anything more than the basest emotions.

'Did you really believe I would allow my only child to be bought from me in such a way? Did you think me some sort of a whore from whom everything can be bought for cash? I've used your money, Richard, and I've used it cleverly. Did you ever imagine how happily two people could feed off one business? *You* make exclusive designs for leading society figures and *I* copy them more cheaply for women with less money in their purses to spare. Doesn't that sound terribly fair and decent?'

His face had gone from raspberry to puce. 'You are bankrupting me, Rosa,' he said, quietly. 'Is that what you want for your son? For him to inherit nothing but a debt when I die? For him to lead a life of poverty when my business is closed?'

I smile at this. 'There is little need to worry,' I told him. 'I am his mother and *my* business is thriving. There will be plenty to go around when I am gone.'

'Rosa!' Richard was out of his chair.

'Don't worry, Richard,' I said, my expression serious now, 'I won't let your business fail.'

He was bordering on anger now. 'I could sue you,' he said.

'And I could tell everyone that David is my son,' I replied.

He fell back and sat staring at the floor for many moments. 'What do you want?' he asked, eventually.

I stood before him, my arms down by my sides. 'I want us to be married,' I said. 'I want David to have two parents.'

There was not a sound from him, Kitty. He could have been crafted from stone for all the movement he made.

'Think about it,' I told him finally, when the silence became too much for me to bear. 'You have five days, Richard. After that I believe the banks will be in touch with you again.'

CHAPTER FORTY-NINE

ZG

POLYESTER
*First produced by J. F. Winfield and J. T. Dickson
in 1941, and made mainly of ethylene glycol and
terephthalic acid, polyester fibres are now used in
the manufacture of many fashion garments. It is
crease-resistant, keeps its shape and dries quickly
when washed.*

Nicky Kofteros's car was waiting outside Khan's sweat-shop. Kitty tried to ignore it, to make out she hadn't seen it at all, and walked on by as though it was the sort of car you'd expect to see cruising a street like that.

He didn't slam his hand on the horn and he didn't wind down the window to call her, which was just as well – at least as far as his car was concerned, as she was ripe for a little violence and Kofteros's windscreen could have been a very tempting target.

What she really wanted to do, more than anything, was to run back into the office and slap Riva's face until the terrible words stopped coming out of it. She wanted to hit the girl until she confessed that she was lying. Kitty's father was an honest man and a loyal one. Every magazine article she had ever read about him quoted him as insisting that family came first at all times.

Instead of smashing and punching, though, she watched as Kofteros climbed out of the car and called her softly by name.

She turned. He wore a dazzling white shirt, which was open at the neck, and some casual but smartly pressed trousers. She was so mad with the girl that, for a split second, she was pleased to see him there. Then she remembered who he was and scowled.

'Your brother asked me to find you,' Kofteros said. 'There is a meeting at your offices. I believe it is urgent. May I take you?'

'Do I have any choice?' Kitty asked. To his credit he did not look exasperated or feign hurt pride. Instead he just waited.

Okay, Mr jelly-cube, Kitty thought. Then there was a noise to her left and as she watched him she saw his expression change. Suddenly, as she stared at Nicky's face with something like puzzlement, she collided with someone. Her focus shortened. There was a head in front of hers. In her peripheral vision she saw Nicky vault – not run around or crawl across, but *vault* – the bonnet of his car in his haste to get to her.

'Kitty! Are you here to see me? What a nightmare, eh? Did you speak with my daughter?' Ricky Khan's face was in front of her own, so puffed with grief it was almost unrecognizable.

He was a big man – taller than Gabriel and some two feet wider. So big he had to have his suits hand-made. He had always been smart, though – dapper, even. He favoured the old colonial look – pinstripe suits, overflowing silk handkerchief in the pocket, shoes you could see your

434

face in. Now, he could have passed for any of a hundred guys pulling dress-rails around in the street. His too-tight trousers were crumpled, he wore a white vest and the short-sleeved beige shirt he had on over it was minus a button.

'What a tragedy!' he was erupting with grief, it spilled out of every gap: tears, snot, shards of spittle, spreading sweat. His eyelashes were gummed up with crying. His hands fluttered about his head as though trying to pluck some rational thought out of the air.

It was Ricky's anguish that triggered Kitty's own out-pouring. How often had she seen this huge man socializing with her father? What a pair they had made, too – noisy, rumbustious, argumentative, proud and stubborn, but always good friends. Not friends, Kitty thought – allies. They were aware that they shared the same fate, those two. The circumstances of their heritage gave them a bond. When Gabriel watched Ricky set up his business he knew he was watching his own parents and grandparents at work.

Before she could speak, though, before she could hug the man or utter a cry of empathy she was grabbed by the arm and pulled backwards. Ricky's eyes changed from slits of undiluted misery to round 'o's of shock and alarm. His hands flew out towards her but as they moved she found herself going in the same direction, further away. Then there was an eclipse of the light and she found herself staring at Kofteros's wide back.

'Kitty!' Ricky was still trying to find her. Nicky was not unnecessarily violent or threatening, he just stayed where he was.

'You have to understand this is not a good idea,' he

435

told Ricky. 'Keeping a distance between Miss Zigofsky and yourself would be in both of your interests.'

Khan was still the taller man. 'A bodyguard, Kitty?' he asked, wringing his hands. 'Do you think that I did it, then? Do you think I would ever hurt you or your father? I loved him, Kitty, you know that!'

Kofteros pulled Kitty out of the way and pushed her through the open door of his car.

'What the hell are you playing at?' she asked when he was in the driver's seat. He looked at her. He was calm and not a hair had fallen out of place. He had not even worked up a sheen of sweat.

'That was the man they arrested for killing your father,' he said. It was just a statement – with no particular emphasis or implication. 'If he *did* kill Gabriel then he might want to harm you too. I know he is like an uncle to you, Kitty, but anyone can change. Besides, if he is innocent he should not be seen talking to you, it could harm his case. The lawyers could say he threatened you.' When he spoke a trace of an accent appeared, showing his concern.

He paused as the car turned into Commercial Road. 'I'm sorry if I startled you. You will want to yell at me now. Go ahead, I'm listening.'

'That poor man,' Kitty whispered, 'he's lost everything.'

Kofteros looked at her. 'And so will you,' he said. 'Is that what you want? Surely you have done the right thing by Gabriel now, Kitty. You pulled his final collection together and staged his show. You have been the daughter he wanted. Any man would have been proud to see what you did. You must have known it was just a gesture, though. Just as you are aware you must back down now.

436

'I'm afraid the bank will not support you on the strength of that collection. Your publicity was overshadowed by the circumstances of your father's death. Women don't like to buy clothes like that. They like to read about the murder, but it doesn't make them want to wear the clothes – not for a season or so, anyway. It would make them feel ghoulish. Next year we re-launch with a new designer and you and Chloe can afford to be seen smiling again.'

'You have it all planned out, don't you?' Kitty asked him.

He shrugged. 'It's my job to plan things,' he said. 'I can't help it. It's what I'm good at – working behind the scenes. Finding things out. Making sure things go as planned.'

'Ricky Khan is a good man,' Kitty told him. 'I believe you should understand that. Maybe there are no absolutes in your life, but there are certainly some in mine and that is one of them. He could not have murdered my father.'

As she spoke the hollowness of her own words made her feel hypocritical. What was still an absolute in her life? What did she now believe? The whole landscape shifted every day.

'So you still believe that I killed him, then?' Kofteros asked. 'Of course, I must fit the bill perfectly. A slithery foreigner trying to masquerade as a pukka English businessman. Smart enough, but a little too flash. Seducing your sister and taking over the whole show. Turning up where he is least wanted like the worst kind of animal. What else do you have me pegged as, Kitty?'

She looked out of the window. 'I have no interest in you,' she said.

Kofteros laughed. 'Oh, but you have,' he said. 'You find

437

me fascinating. I'm everything you have been told to keep away from. I'm the stranger you don't accept sweets or lifts from. I'm the one who will poison your entire family if you will only allow it.

'When you lay in bed at night next to your pretty little fiancé it's the thought of men like me that makes you hide away further under the duvet and thank God the windows are securely sealed and the garlic hanging above the bed, next to the crucifix, or whatever other symbol it is beautiful Jewish princesses like yourself use to ward off the evil ones.

'Look at yourself, Kitty,' he went on, 'you say you believe I am responsible for your father's murder, and yet here you are sitting beside me in my car. What does that tell us? That you enjoy taking risks? I don't think so. You are a careful and intelligent woman. Brave to a certain extent – the way you went ahead with the fashion show tells me that – but reckless and lacking in caution?'

He smiled. 'I think it tells us you don't really believe I am capable of murder, Kitty. I believe you suspect many people, but none of them seriously. I know you are frightened, deep down in your heart. You would rather I did it than someone closer to you. You want it to be me, Kitty. How much better me than a member of your own family.'

Kitty suddenly sat upright in her seat. 'I need to stop off in the West End,' she said.

To his credit yet again Kofteros didn't argue, even though she knew they were in a hurry. Instead he drove her straight to Freddy's London showroom without question, parking the car directly outside the door and slumping down in his seat, just like a professional chauffeur.

Freddy's father was inside, drinking tea with the Selfridges

438

buyer. He half-rose from his seat as Kitty walked in, but she nodded and waved, 'okay'. Business was business, after all. She walked into the back and climbed the narrow flight of stairs to the design-room.

Freddy was there, working on some orders. He looked up, surprised and then pleased to see her. When he kissed her on the cheek she was drawn by his warmth and his familiar smell and his normality.

'Hey, Kitten,' he whispered, 'you should have phoned. We could have had lunch. Are you okay?'

'I'm fine,' Kitty lied. They both knew she didn't make impromptu visits to the showroom. The etiquette wasn't right, she was still competition, after all. Nothing would have been said, she would have been greeted warmly as a future member of the family, but it just wasn't done, especially during the Season.

Freddy put his hands on his hips. He was wearing a suit, which meant he was also selling. Kitty looked across and saw his German agent sitting by the pattern books, waiting.

'Don't let me interrupt, Fred,' she said quietly, smiling, mouthing, 'I'll see you later.' Bring jelly-cubes, she thought, only she didn't mouth that.

Raphael was at the far end of the room, staring at her obliquely. The window was behind him and she shielded her eyes from the glare.

'Hi,' she greeted him. He nodded in return. Freddy went back to the agent but Kitty guessed he was listening, along with all the other machine-room staff.

'I'm glad to see you got a new job,' Kitty told him.

Raphael straightened, wiping his hands on his jeans. He

439

pulled a couple of pins from his mouth. 'Kitty,' he said, softly, 'it's good to see you.' His tone didn't sound false, just as hers had no tone of vindictiveness.

Raphael looked just like his name sounded. He was strangely good-looking, although not instantly noticeable. His hair was a shade of brown that turned into black and his eyes were amazingly blue. His features were surprisingly irregular, though on the second glance they all worked. His appeal was subtle and serious.

Kitty had worked with him for years without really knowing him. He always seemed young, but remotely elegant and proudly sophisticated at the same time. But that was the way he was. That was Raphael.

'What did you want?' he asked. She was used to his directness. He had a busy job.

'I just wanted to see you . . .' Kitty said. So what? So now what? Did you sleep with my father? She could never have said the words. And so they just looked and whatever needed saying was said in silence. She wanted to touch him, to feel what her father had felt. She wanted to know if they had loved one another. But then she also wanted to know that her father could never have been unfaithful to Hester, too. That it was not in his nature. That Riva was a bitter, jealous liar.

'Did you find the wedding dress designs?' Raphael asked quietly.

Kitty nodded.

'Did you work on them together?' she asked. She looked at him then, and saw what she needed to see. Raphael's face was immobile but his eyes were milky with unshed tears.

'Your father did most of the work,' he said, his voice breaking, 'I only helped hunt for fabrics.'

There was something growing in Kitty's throat that threatened to choke her. 'Thank you,' she said, while the words would still come out. She held out her hand but Raphael didn't take it. The glance they exchanged was enough, though. Peace. They both loved Gabriel. What point in hatred when they both suffered from the same painful loss?

Freddy came across, curious to see what was going on. He kissed Kitty on the top of the head and his hands on her shoulders were steering her towards the door. He looked awkward. After all, his father had poached her designer.

'I think everyone imagines there might be a row brewing,' he said.

Kitty smiled. 'No, Freddy, no row.' She smiled her sweetest smile.

'Thank you,' he said. 'You would have been well within your rights.'

Kitty looked across at Freddy's father as she left. 'Never fight with pigs,' she said to herself, 'you get all dirty and they just enjoy it.' It was Frederick Jacobs Senior that she had her gripe with, not Raphael, and besides, she had worse villains than him to come to grips with.

CHAPTER FIFTY

ZG

PLISSE
A plain-weave fabric, like crepe, which has been
specially treated to keep a wrinkled appearance.

She dreamt of the club. Sometimes she would enter the dark room. She was searching for her father. The blackness was so profound she could see nothing – even her own body was invisible to her.

The silence was equally impenetrable, although – despite the quiet – she knew there would be others in there, waiting. The human body is never silent, it is a constant source of insect-like ambience. There is the hiss of breath, the whisper and bellows-sigh of the lungs, all the ferrying of mucus, the seeping of blood in the veins, the minute cracks and groans of movement – and yet she heard nothing.

But someone was waiting in there.

Who?

Raphael?

Freddy?

She took a step forward, reaching out blindly with her hands. It was like a children's party game – Blind Man's Buff. Laughing from fear. Playing, but hating it.

What if it was someone she did not know? But wasn't that the point? Anonymity. Sex with a stranger.

She lurched another step. Her blood picked up a faster rhythm. Her mouth had dried. Her tongue was like a piece of cured fruit. The darkness was threatening, but it was also like a blanket around her. The place smelt musky with the richly jewelled scent of sex.

She feared violence, but the hands that came out of the blackness to take her own were gentle enough. Dry, like a snake skin. Different flesh. Needy. Conclusive. Guiding her fingers to a face – broad features, clean-shaven, baked hot from the sun.

'It's okay, darling, you're safe.' The lips sighed the words when she touched them with her fingertips. It was a deep voice, marinating in the lower octaves. Full of the mulch created by tobacco and wine.

Gently he moved her hands further down, showing her himself by touch. Her fingers were greedy, though she feared recognition. The tips told the most – light feather-touch, to reveal texture, not shape.

Colour too, she discovered. Warm, skin-baked tan. A neck, weathered with age but not too old, supple enough, and then a bare chest, full of fine, well-sprung hairs. Older hairs – damp and springy, white or grey – she could feel the colour in their coarseness. Hairs that led a tangled route towards the groin.

'Kitty.' A younger, less crushed voice, but still tender. Another pair of hands pulled down the zipper of her dress. Her body shuddered at the cool on her back. Two more touches and she was naked. Invisible, though, safely invisible in the darkness. She felt lips pressed soft behind the soft indent of the backs of her knees, sending tingling sparks through her body like a spray of hot ash.

Then the lightest tip of a goldfish tongue, travelling slowly up the delicate belly-flesh of her inner thighs.

'Kitty.' It was the first man, the older man, who spoke this time, his voice full of urging. He directed her hands downward to his stomach and her palms touched against the rubbery tip of his penis. She felt the warm bulb of the end, wet with seeping juices.

'Kitty.' The word was lost in the warm rise of his voice, which became a whisper before evaporating, like steam, in the air above their heads.

There was a coldness, like an ice cube, upon her back. The tongue ran crazy crop circles between her thighs, making her legs uncontrollably bendy, like India rubber. Her stomach contracted in spasms of need and the flesh that was licked so greedily became the entire focus of her body. She was emptying of moisture, wet and damp in turns.

As her resistance oozed and leaked along with her bones and skin she fell into a childlike compliance: you have no choice. There is nothing you can do. Her will had been robbed by her flesh.

He turned her around easily, bending her forward like a rag doll, and she felt his penis pause politely before entering her. Her mouth was kissed by the mouth near the floor and so, too, were the insteps of her feet. So there were three of them, then. And yet all worked together like one.

They simmered and boiled together. When the delicious ache in her groin swelled and grew through her entire body so that she began to cry out it was the tender floor-mouth that kissed her throughout. He held her as she climaxed and, when the shudders had quit her body he pushed her hair from her face and blew against her forehead to cool her.

His tenderness made her weep. It was what she wished to keep above all else – to plunder from her dream and take like a trophy into wakefulness.

A door somewhere opened. A thin streak of yellow light diluted the darkness. It was the face in front of her own, full of care and concern and, now, anger at being revealed.

Kofteros.

She tried to snap shut like a flower.

'Kitty.' His expression was anguished.

She struggled to get free, but he held her pinned by her arms.

'Kitty,' he was saying, 'don't look back. Keep looking at me, Kitty, whatever you do.'

She looked back, of course she looked back.

Gabriel stood behind her, his face whey-pale in death and coated with dew. She pulled away in horror, her arms circling in an attempt to escape more quickly than her legs could manage.

Her father. Naked. The dampness on his chest and groin not sweat and semen, as she had thought in the darkness, but wet, black blood.

There was a hole where his stomach should have been. What she had taken to be cries of passion had been his agonized death throes.

Gabriel. Her father.

She woke up screaming, still feeling for her own father's blood on her bare back.

445

ZG

ALBATROSS
*The name of a lightweight woollen fabric that is soft,
with a crepe-effect weave.*

'Why not give up and retire from business altogether?'
Chloe asked. Her crossed leg ticked away impatiently.
Wherever Chloe was she wanted to be somewhere else.
She wore a rice-white pyjama suit with flat almond-green
brogues. Her hair colour had been changed to parchment
blonde, which made her skin look like toffee.

Kofteros sat beside her, reading. Next to him was Burgess, as immobile as garden statuary, apart from his right
hand, which was doing some little tense picking thing with
the arm of the chair.

'Retire?' Kitty asked. 'At nineteen? Jesus, Chloe!'

She yawned, just to annoy her sister further.

'You will have enough to live on from the deal that
Burgess is setting up,' Chloe continued, her leg thrashing,
'and you are getting married, Kit. I'm sure Freddy will
want to see you put out to pasture on the charity circuit
– you know, organizing balls and suchlike.'

There were shards of glittering hatred exchanged
between the two women.

446

'Is that what you plan to do, Chloe?' Kitty asked. 'Put yourself out to graze?'

Kofteros cleared his throat. 'I believe Kitty will be as much an integral part of Waika's future plans as you are, Chloe,' he said. Kitty tried not to look at him. The dream was still thick in her head.

Chloe sighed. 'I thought Nula was coming to this meeting,' she said, changing the subject.

Burgess studied the shine on his shoes. 'Nula doesn't have voting options any more,' he said.

They all looked at him now. Like a fly in aspic, he remained immobile beneath their stares. 'I bought her out,' he said, 'she had no interest in the business and she said she was in debt and needed the money urgently.'

'In debt?' Kitty echoed. 'For God's sake, Burgess, she's only fifteen! What could she need so much money for? Did you even ask?'

He shook his head and waved his hands. 'Maybe drugs?' he suggested.

'You gave her money for drugs?' This was Chloe.

'I was joking,' Burgess replied.

Kofteros rose to his feet. 'You selfish little bastard,' he told Burgess. Somehow he made the comment sound factual rather than spiteful. It was followed by a respectful silence. Burgess's face turned the colour of ecru. Kitty thought he looked scared.

'This is a family thing, Nicky,' he began. 'I would no more compromise my sister's safety than chew off my own arm. Of course she did not want the money for drugs. She explained her reasons for needing cash to me in some detail and there was nothing sinister there, I can assure you.

Perhaps you missed the note of irony in my voice. Perhaps you all did. I just don't feel it is appropriate to discuss family matters in public, that's all.'

Kofteros continued to stare. Kitty looked at him and was surprised by the level of anger he appeared to be concealing. 'And you could not possibly just loan her the money?' he asked.

Burgess's cheeks flushed blotting-paper pink. 'I told you,' he said, 'she has no real interest in the business.'

Kitty got up to walk out in disgust. To her surprise she saw Kofteros make a quick move to join her. Chloe noticed, too, and grabbed quickly at Kitty's arm.

'Kit, we need to come to some agreement,' she said, quietly. 'I know you want us to stay family-owned, but Dad is dead and things can never be as they were before.' Both Kitty and Kofteros gawped at Chloe in amazement, but she was shameless enough to continue.

'He would have been proud of you, Kitty,' she said. 'You pulled that show together and even I was surprised at your determination.' Kitty heard the 'but' coming from about ten miles off.

'But,' Chloe said, placing extra emphasis on the word for effect, 'it's over, Kitty, you have to see that. We owe too much. The banks won't bail us out. If we sign over to Waika at least we'll all have a job and enough money to play with. You did enough, Kit. Know when to stop.'

Kofteros still stood beside her. 'Perhaps you need more time,' he said. They all looked up in surprise at this.

'Waika need a decision now,' Burgess said in the background. 'Kitty, we all inherited equally but I could out-vote you now if I wanted. China's all for selling. Mother doesn't know what day of the week it is. But I want you to agree, Kit, don't you see?'

Kofteros was watching Kitty's face closely. 'Why don't we go for a drive?' he asked, quietly.

'Isn't that some sort of Mafia cliché?' Kitty asked him.

He grinned. 'You have my word in front of witnesses that I will bring you back in one piece,' he said.

They drove from Docklands to the West End. He bought her lunch at a deli in Soho and they ate it in his car. She was surprisingly hungry and ate quickly.

'Just mind the leather upholstery with the relish,' he told her. When she had finished she swabbed up with the paper napkins he passed to her one at a time.

'So now where?' she asked when she was finally ready.

Kofteros smiled. 'More clues, eh?' he said, almost to himself. 'Okay, Kitty, I think you need your photograph taking.'

He drove back out to the east, to an insignificant street near Khan's factory. When the car pulled up Kitty looked about. She had been to most of the area on business with her father but could see no sign of the rag trade in this particular part.

Kofteros stepped outside the car and opened her door, like a chauffeur. They were in front of a shop selling cameras and offering studio portraits. In the window were a dozen large colour shots of kids, dogs and graduating youngsters.

'Have you never been here before?' Kofteros asked.

Kitty shook her head. 'I believe most of our formal shots were done by Norman Parkinson,' she said in a snottier tone than she meant.

449

Nicky laughed. 'Then it's about time you gave someone a little more humble the chance to shoot your illustrious features,' he told her.

Kitty turned. 'Look, I don't really understand . . .' she began.

He was smiling. 'Do you trust me at all, Kitty?' he asked. 'One little bit?'

She thought about the question. 'No,' she told him.

His smile did not shrink. 'Okay,' he said, 'then I shall tell you nothing. Find things out for yourself. Just humour me, and get your portrait done. Okay?'

Kitty stared at him. 'My hair needs combing,' she said.

Grinning, he pulled a clean comb from his pocket and ran it carefully through her fringe. 'Perfect,' he told her. He chivvied her into the doorway of the place. Kitty looked inside. It was dark and old-fashioned. A joke. She turned around but Kofteros was driving off. Curiosity got the better of her. She walked inside.

There was an elderly woman sitting at a reception table, her grey hair dyed apricot and whipped into a meringue-shape upon her head. She stood up as Kitty walked in. Her sleeveless dress was made of lemon Crimplene and there were creases of white talcum powder around her bare armpits.

'May I help you, miss?' she asked, smiling.

Kitty felt awkward. 'I need a passport shot,' she said. The width of the woman's smile decreased by one centimetre.

'Passport?' She sat back down on her chair. 'Will you wait over there? The photographer has a sitting.'

Kitty lowered herself onto a padded bench which was covered with pleated turquoise satin. There were some elderly magazines on the table beside her. She felt herself being scrutinized by the receptionist and so faced it out by pretending to inspect the framed photographs on the wall beside her.

Many were old – some were ancient. There were a few vaguely recognizable faces from the sixties and seventies – minor stars who had signed their names across their shots to register their thanks and eternal appreciation of the career boost the pictures had afforded them.

The photographer appeared in the doorway, making Kitty jump in her seat.

'Passport?' he asked. He was an old man, maybe the receptionist's husband, his suit well-worn but immaculately pressed, and the wine-stain-coloured knitted waistcoat he wore beneath it matched his bow-tie perfectly.

Kitty was shown upstairs, into a small studio where an Ikea pine stool sat in the middle of a paper backdrop that had been painted to look like the sky.

'There's a mirror over there,' the photographer told her. 'Take your time, miss, I will need to set up.'

Kitty pulled a curtain back and found a small chair in front of a wall-mirror. She studied her reflection. Her fringe had been flattened by Kofteros's comb. She looked ghastly. At least that made her smile.

There were more framed shots on the wall around the mirror. Some from the fifties, this time, and one or two many years older. Directly above the mirror, in what appeared to be the place of honour, hung an ancient wedding shot in an ornate Victorian frame. The glass was dusty – too dusty to see detail. Bored with the wait, Kitty wandered out into the studio. There were plenty more shots on the walls here – the place was like a gallery in a museum. Most were Victorian wedding photos, like the one in the changing area. Kitty browsed for a bit, barely interested.

The photographer popped his head round the curtain.

'Take your time,' he said, 'take a look. You don't see many of those around these days. Enjoy.'

'Thanks.' Kitty smiled politely.

'Great,' she whispered beneath her breath. What the hell was this? Had Kofteros dumped her here to keep her out of the way while they voted to sell or something? She looked around for the exit. As she picked up her bag, though, another shot caught her eye. It was a picture of a woman holding a baby, sepia-toned and faded with age as though it had been placed in the window at some time.

'Kitty.'

It was the only shot on the wall that hadn't been taken at a wedding. Yet the woman's face looked familiar – she'd seen it staring out from one of the other frames.

'Kitty!'

She backtracked slowly. Where was it again? And why was she even looking, when she ought to be gunning back to the city? Surely she hadn't started to trust Kofteros?

There it was – the same woman in her wedding shot. Kitty peered a little closer, smiling. The couple in the photograph looked rigid with fear – at least the man did. His bride was attempting a smile. There was a small boy in the shot, too. His face was beautiful but expressionless. Hadn't they placed children's heads in clamps, to keep them still for the long exposure?

'Hey, now, what's all this?' Kitty whispered. She looked back at the baby shot. The woman looked younger than

452

she did at her wedding. The child in the wedding shot would have been about the right age to be the baby in the first one. Naughty, naughty! Kitty thought, that must have got them swallowing their teeth, eh? Child first and marry later?

'*Kitty*!'

'Ready yet, miss?' the photographer called.

'No . . . I . . .' The glass of the frame was stained with nicotine. 'Wait,' she said, sounding rude but not caring, 'wait a moment.'

With shaking hands she grabbed her glasses from her bag and pulled them on.

The wedding suit. The guy was wearing *her* wedding suit.

Kitty wiped the glass with her sleeve to clean it. She saw the old photographer standing behind her in the reflection.

'Who is this?' she asked, pointing to the picture.

The old man shrugged. 'A wedding portrait,' he said. 'If you are really interested you could turn the frame around. The names will be written on the back. Most likely they didn't pay for their sitting and so the photographer kept it and hung it himself. It's not an especially good shot – the focus is a little questionable. I keep it for historical purposes more than anything. There are better ones in stock but that was there already and the frame is rather good.'

Kitty lifted the frame down carefully. She *was* right – the groom in the photograph was wearing the suit her mother had given her, the wedding suit. She might have mistaken the jacket and trousers, but the waistcoat was too unique to confuse. She turned the picture around. *Mr and Mrs Richard and Rosa Galliard*, she read. Galliard. The name meant nothing to her. She looked at the shot once more. Rosa. She stared at the woman's face. *To Rosa – the daughter I love* – the message on the waistcoat. So this was the woman for whom the suit had been made.

'So you found a man to fit it,' Kitty whispered, smiling.

How did this Rosa look? A small woman, dark, round, but with a small waist. Large ears. Big, expressive eyes. An elegant expression, her head held high with pride.

The old man reached across and took the picture from her carefully, protectively. 'I'd rather hang it back myself,' he said earnestly. 'If you must know it is something of a keepsake. It was taken by the founder of the business, Max Warkofski, a first-generation immigrant to this country. His wedding portraiture was legendary at one time, but he lived the life of Jack the Lad. A ladies' man was what my mother used to call him – handsome as the devil, too. Successful in business and successful in the boudoir, if you know what I mean.' He shook his head sorrowfully. 'This was said to be his last portrait, though. He killed himself the day after it was taken.'

He hung the portrait with a lot of puffing. 'So you see, the life of Riley couldn't have suited him as well as everyone thought now, could it?' he said. 'My wife has always considered there was a moral there somewhere – or so she keeps saying. "Mind you don't end up like Max," has been her line for the thirty years we've been married. He was her relative though, not mine. I always said the roving eye was more likely to be in *her* blood, you see.' He laughed without humour and Kitty smiled.

454

'Look,' she said, 'does it matter if I change my mind about the passport shot?'

The man looked at her.

'I'll still pay, of course,' she added, 'only . . .' she looked around for an excuse, 'only I think I have a cold sore coming and I'd rather look my best, you know?'

She was about to leave when an idea hit her. 'Did you see the guy who brought me here, by any chance?' she asked.

'Mr Kofteros?' the photographer asked.

'You know him?' Kitty sounded surprised.

'Of course,' the photographer said, 'his family come from around here. I watched him grow up, you know. I have shots of him as a baby, if you're interested?'

The idea was tempting but Kitty was in a hurry.

'He was always fascinated by the old photos,' the man said, 'even as a child. He would try to match face to face and then trace the families through each generation. Most of our sitters come back as regular clients, you know. Christenings, weddings, silver weddings, and then more births. There's a whole social document in these albums somewhere, you know.'

He looked at the shot he had just hung back on the wall. 'Many of these people did very well for themselves, I believe,' he said, screwing up his eyes to see better. 'Nicky said he'd probably end up working for one of these families one day. I used to tell him the only way he'd meet proper society figures would be if they fiddled their tax and ended up in the same cell as him in prison.' He laughed. 'He was always a little fanciful, though. You wouldn't believe it to look at him now, would you?'

455

Kitty took one last look at the wedding photo. 'Thank you,' she said.

The man smiled. 'It doesn't look all that bad to me,' he said.

'Bad?' Kitty asked.

He tapped his mouth. 'The cold sore,' he said.

Kitty was still blushing at her lie as she left the studio. She phoned Hester as soon as she got back to her apartment. 'Can I call round for tea?' she asked.

'I'll send out for cake,' her mother said. She sounded relieved – as though she'd been waiting for Kitty's call.

CHAPTER FIFTY-TWO

ZG

TIFFANY
A semi-transparent, silk-like gauze.

'You never told us much about the family,' Kitty said.

'Darling, you never asked,' Hester told her. 'You always hated it when we went on about the old days, remember? You used to laugh. "Roots", you called it, like the Arthur Hailey book. Passing the same dull old stories down along the line.'

Hester was dressed formally, as though expecting a visit from the queen. She wore an aubergine wool dress with matching tights and shoes. And a brooch. Kitty had never seen her mother wear a brooch before.

'Rosa,' Kitty prompted, 'who was the Rosa that the suit was made for? The suit you gave me for the wedding.'

Hester sighed. 'Rosa Zigofsky,' she said. 'You have been told about her many times, Kitty. How easily one's children can become deaf when they are bored by what they hear! She was a relative on your father's side. Nothing special, Kitty, why even ask? Eh? Only that it was she who founded the business. Only that it was to that woman that we owe all this.'

'Maybe you told Chloe, Mother,' Kitty said.

457

'No, Kitty, we told you all,' Hester insisted. 'Only your ears weren't open, as usual. Since when did children listen to their parents? One day you will know this for yourself.' She smiled. 'She was a clever woman, Kitty – just like yourself. Only maybe, unlike you, she must have listened to her parents' advice now and again.'

Hester took some cake from the tray in front of them and handed it to Kitty. Then she sat watching and waiting, her mouth firmly shut and her hands clasped tightly in her lap. There would be no more talk until it was done. These were Hester's terms and her daughter understood that.

Kitty took a bite of cake. Bribery. With a small smile of victory, Hester continued with the story.

'Rosa Zigofsky started up the first mail-order house in Britain. She had the idea of getting garments photographed and selling them to order in that way. And this was in the days before the credit card!'

'So she sold out when?' Kitty asked.

Hester shrugged. 'Your father would have known – it was *his* family, after all. I can only pass on what he has told me. Rosa sold the mail-order idea because her heart was in couture. She made her money selling to the masses so that she could move upmarket. Her husband had his own business and that was the one she had her eye on all along. It is what became the Z̶G label.'

'So she died wealthy?' Kitty asked.

'She died alone,' Hester told her. 'Your father remembered her funeral in the East End. Despite all her social climbing it was where she wanted to be buried.' Hester brushed a crumb from the side of her mouth. 'She became a real demon as she got older, Kitty. People were scared of her. You wouldn't want to be in her debt. As a consequence there was no one around to see her get ill. She had been dead several days before they found her body. I believe your father had many nightmares about this as a child.'

'So was she my great-grandmother?' Kitty asked.

Hester laughed. 'Rosa Zigofsky was nobody's mother,' she said. 'Her husband Richard had a boy – David Reuben, I believe – and they both doted on him. The child died, though, a year after they married. It was said to be a terrible tragedy for them both. The boy was what they used to call "sickly" in those days.

'Rosa never got over the loss, even though he was only her stepson. The rumour was that her husband was a cold man and that the marriage was never a happy one. Your father used to say his father told him it was never even consummated. The child's death must have affected them both very hard.' Hester looked up at the ceiling as though trying to prod a memory. 'I'm sure Gabriel said she was in love with someone else. I don't know who it was, though.'

She drifted off a little, obviously lost in thought.

'So how did Dad inherit?' Kitty prompted.

Her mother smiled. 'The business passed to Rosa's brother's children when she died,' she said. 'That's where your blood comes from, Kitty – Gregory Zigofsky. He was a handsome man, just look at his photograph! Look at that strong, intelligent face!'

Hester went off out of the room and returned clutching a framed picture. Kitty had seen the shot before, she realized, but she looked at it carefully now for the first time.

459

Gregory stood, tall and handsome, behind a beautiful woman who was seated.

'That was Ruth Levi – later to become Gregory's wife,' Hester told her, pointing. 'She used to work with Rosa Zigofsky and ran some of her businesses for her. She and Gregory had three children, and they all went into the business. That must have been a true love match – look what a handsome couple they made.'

The picture was the same as the one that Kitty had found in the stack in her father's office. She knew who had left it there for her now. The same person who had sent her her parents' wedding shot. The one who had phoned. Nicky Kofteros, local historian. The little boy who had spent so much time in the old photographer's studio, studying the shots and tracing the families. She wondered exactly how far he had traced her family down its tree.

'Maybe I know more about your history than yourself, Kitty.' He had said that. And he had been right. He'd known about Rosa and Ruth. He'd left clues all the time, like crumbs of bread for a bird. But she still didn't understand why. What was he trying to achieve? Did the crumbs lead into a trap? Was she acting like a mug? She rubbed at her temples. Think, Kitty, think. Why?

Why was she being so fucking thick? She looked across at her mother. 'So Rosa died alone,' Kitty said.

'She came over from Russia during the pogroms,' Hester told her, 'but I suppose you find that story boring, too.' She was smiling, though.

'Sorry,' Kitty said.

Her mother's smile widened. She pressed more cake onto Kitty's plate.

Kitty turned the shot around and studied the back. 'Max Warkofski, portrait photographer,' she read aloud. The date was exactly the same as Rosa's photograph in the studio. The shot must have been taken shortly after Rosa and Richard's wedding. Poor Max. Making clients smile for his pictures while planning his own death.

'Would you like to keep that one?' Hester asked her.

Kitty looked at it. Gregory and Ruth. With a slight shake of her head she placed the precious photograph back into her mother's waiting hands.

CHAPTER FIFTY-THREE

ZG

GENOA PLUSH
A plush with a short, velvet-like pile.

She was sailing through the darkness, clad in a gown of black Albert crape, beneath which she wore a plain nain-sook camisole and long flannel drawers.

'Kitty.' He was there again, waiting for her. She could see nothing and when her hands reached out they touched only air.

'Kitty, my darling.'

But Gabriel was dead. She placed her hands over her face to hide her eyes. When she held her arms outstretched again it was younger flesh that they touched.

'Kitty.' His voice was hoarse with longing and the sound of it alone was enough to liquidize her flesh.

She touched his lips and then kissed them. His skin smelt of Oxo cubes. She waited for the touch of others, but this time they were alone.

Her man was already naked. He pressed against her long skirts and she folded him inside with her. They kissed full on the mouth and she felt she knew his body better than she knew her own. Her legs wound around his waist. He was tall and strong. He held her tight as they kissed, then lowered her softly to the ground without so much as a groan of effort.

His fingers worked quickly at her complicated clothes. Naked at last, apart from her stockings, she felt him lean over her and spread herself out to receive him.

He paused. 'Marry me, Kitty,' he said, 'marry me, or I shall have to die. I could never live without you, you know that.'

Kitty reached a hand up towards him, clasping his erect penis, guiding it gently down towards her, feeling it touch her body, her legs, then finally pushing softly inside her.

'I'm marrying Freddy,' she whispered as she felt his body eclipsing her own, 'I can't marry you, Nicky,' she whispered, 'you know how much I hate you.'

His lovemaking was impatient. She clung to him like a koala as he pushed inside her and cried out when he did – though he called her name with passion, while she just yelled. There was one more moment of closeness before they parted.

'That was your only time, Rosa,' he whispered into her ear, 'I wanted it to be good for you. Never forget me.'

His face pulled away. He was handsome, dark and young. He smiled at her but his eyes looked unimaginably sad. 'Max,' he said, introducing himself, touching his forehead. 'Max Warkofski.' His eyes were kind but mocking.

This time when she woke Freddy was not there beside her to comfort her as she cried. She had never felt so alone in her life. Nothing made sense. She was being told things but could understand none of it. Perhaps she was going mad.

'*Kitty.*'

463

'*Kitty, please!*'

She knew she couldn't stand much more of these voices – not now that she knew who it was that spoke to her.

CHAPTER FIFTY-FOUR

ZG

LYCRA
*Known for its stretch and recovery qualities and
introduced by Du Pont in 1958, Lycra has recently
revolutionized the textile industry. Originally used in the
manufacture of girdles and roll-ons, in the seventies
it found use in tights and exercise wear and has
currently been incorporated into many more fabrics.*

She had never used the Underground before, she didn't
even know how to buy a ticket; another commuter had
had to show her how – a young black girl with a small
child in tow. The girl's patience was saint-like. She had
taken the coins and even added a few from her own bag
when the amount had not been enough. How would she
feel the next day, when she read what she'd done?

There had been a crush at the top of the escalator, which
was puzzling because she'd chosen a time she thought
would be quiet. The bottleneck cleared once they were on
the steps, though. She liked the posters on the way down.
Glossy and *Vogue*-style. A pin-thin model in calf-skin
boots. Two youths, intertwined in matching jeans. Boys or
girls? The ad was repeated a few yards down. A boy; and
a girl. Clever. Grainy. Her reflection stared back from
between their heads. She had the same vacant, bug-eyed

stare. A pretty face, really. Just unexpressive. Like most of the other travellers, she noticed.

The escalator journey seemed eternal, but that was fine, because she liked it; into the bowels of hell. There were articles of discarded rubbish along the gap between the banister and the wall where the adverts hung: crisp packets, cigarette cartons, orange peel. She thought she heard music. Perhaps you could live on these escalators – eat, sleep, listen to music, read adverts and fuck. She took the wet gum from her mouth and pressed it against the wall. A small piece of eternity, bought for the price of a tube ticket. The gum would dry like glue. Perhaps nobody would be able to get it off. When the stairs levelled out and chucked her off she rode up and then down again in the same spot. This time she pressed her little finger against the soft gum. A fingerprint – a source of individual identity. Hers and hers alone. Had they fingerprinted her father when they found his body? Was that how they'd known who he was? Would they have had his prints on record? A match, sergeant – it's that fucking designer chappie. Shall you tell his wife, or shall I? He had parking offences. Would they have had his prints from that? Computer matched – Burgess would have approved.

She tired of the escalator ride. After the fifth trip she imagined people had begun to watch. Or that there were security cameras trained upon her. She hobbled along down the lime-green-lit tunnels instead. There was a busker with a dog. The busker looked at her with indifference but she thought she caught a speck of pity in the dog's brown eyes.

There was a whip of wind and the tunnel seemed to

466

explode with noise, while the air in it imploded. Her clothes sucked this way and that. Terrified, she pushed her hands over her ears and squeezed her eyes shut.

Two foreigners pushed past her, laughing. A train. A train had arrived at the platform. She followed the tourists. The platform was a dazzle of raw light and noise. The train invited her on board, its doors wide open. The seats looked comfortable – she could have stretched out and slept on them. But she chose the platform instead. She had to wait.

When the train had gone she looked around the place. There were two platforms, joined by a tunnel: northbound and southbound. She didn't care which. The gap at the end of both was nice and black. She stood in the adjoining tunnel, right in the middle, just in case.

Right or left? She could have bet on which would arrive first. North. Or South? She placed her hands over her mouth and laughed now that the fear of the train noise had subsided. She thought of her mother and her sister. For some reason she thought of school when she was small, which was odd, because she'd never had a moment of happiness there.

Then the wind hit her once again and she knew her time had come. It tugged at her knees and tried to ruffle her hair. It lifted her like the hurricane lifted Dorothy in *The Wizard of Oz*, so that when she went to walk she was like a model in a pair of Vivienne Westwood platforms – plink, tip, tiptoe along. But the wind helped her keep her balance; in fact, it *assisted* her death, for by the time she had reached the platform she was no longer tripping and sashaying but stomping full-pelt in a troubled nothing-can-stop-me way,

467

so that the only other person on the platform, an elderly man who had been through the war and so could have saved her had she been running in any other, less determined manner, stood back out of the way.

For this she smiled her thanks, for she had always been brought up to be polite, and then she was finished with the platform and onto air and space before falling into the darkness where the rats sleep and being pushed side-on by the force-field around the train, with the driver's face frozen: 'Oh!' and going down instead of up, because tube trains pull you under while cars will flick you over their shoulder like an enraged bull, and then – nothing.

CHAPTER FIFTY-FIVE

ZG

TULLE ARACHNE
A clear tulle embroidered in gold and silk.

It was the phone that had woken her from the dream. She sat up still for a moment, disoriented, before lifting the receiver and saying her name.

It was Burgess on the other end. His voice sounded so strange it was a moment or two before she could recognize it. Then she realized he was crying. 'It's Nula,' he said.

'Nula?' Kitty asked, rubbing her temples. 'She's here, Burgess, she's with me.'

'She's tried to kill herself, Kitty,' Burgess said.

'No,' Kitty told him, 'I told you, Burgess, she's been staying here since the collection. She's in bed, Burgess – she went off at about nine because she had homework and . . . and I took her a drink in myself around eleven and she was sound asleep. What is it? What's happened?'

'She tried to commit suicide, Kitty. Is Freddy with you? Jesus, I'm sorry. She threw herself under a tube train . . .' his voice broke up like a faulty mobile line. '. . . God, can you imagine? Why? We were all depressed by Dad's murder but nobody thought Nula was any worse than the rest . . .'

Kitty dropped the phone down and ran along the corridor to the guest bedroom. Her legs felt like lead. With every dull step she said to herself: she's in there asleep. I will open the door and wake her up and she'll get ratty with me and I'll hug her for the fright and we'll have hot milk together like Mother used to make even though we hated it as children but it's all right, I know it's all right, there's just been some creepy mistake, that's all . . .

But there was no mistake. Nula's bed had been made immaculately; the sheets folded tight and the quilt smoothed flat, like for an advert or photo shoot. On the pillow was an envelope with Kitty's name on it, only it just said, 'Kit', which was what Nula called her.

As Kitty's legs buckled beneath the leaden weight of her own body she lowered herself onto the floor rather than the bed, which Nula had obviously spent so long making perfect. As she read the note – which was really a letter, for it was four pages long – her skin seemed to cool and freeze and shrink and peel off her body like grape-skin.

A great gulf of emptiness opened up inside her and she started to vomit, though nothing came out of her mouth.

'Nula!' She read the words on the letter and suddenly the noise and the retching stopped and she was totally, utterly absorbed and lost in a new horror.

Two of the pages were handwritten, and two of them were typed. It was impossible to read them at first, she was looking too quickly for any of it to make sense. She stared at the typed sheets. They were formal, almost legal-looking. Nula had signed them at the bottom – a crazy, kid's sort of a signature that veered dangerously about the page.

Frustrated at her own lack of concentration, Kitty threw the typed pages down beside her and tried to focus on the handwritten ones.

Dear Kitty,

Sorry. Sorry for everything. no tears though because i can make you hate me more than you have ever hated anyone. I have killed myself because i can't live with any of it not what he did nor what i did either. This letter is a mess because so is my brain it was all going Kit, i wanted it as it was before we <u>were</u> happy weren't we? Remember with Burg when he and Chloe used to fight and we'd all laugh because the dog joined in too? Remember when mum and dad were so happy to and we used to have trust in the fact that that was the way it would be <u>forever</u>?

He cheated on her Kit he cheated us all he wasn't the man he told us he was the fine father the hero we had to admire and <u>trust</u>. He stole all our happiness Kit he knew i'd seen one day in the salon but god he didn't even care because i know he didn't stop because i had him followed. It didn't matter who he was with it just mattered that he wasn't with <u>us</u>.

This is what money does to you as a child Kit you were never spoilt but i grew up with everything and its amazing what you can fix if you go around with the right crowd. Raphael hated me i think. I saw the look on his face no guilt or remorse even though he knew i'd seen he must have told dad he must have mustn't he? What would mum have done if she knew? It would have killed her Kit how could he do that to us?

He was all i admired and to find out so much was wrong and so many lies means i can trust nothing and

471

never will. My head burst with it all Kit i couldn't
stand it it wouldn't go away some days it actually
<u>hurt</u>.

I'm sorry, Kit, I'm sorry, I'm sorry. I didn't want what
happened. It was easier than you'd imagine – too easy. I
just said to someone I know that he should die for what
he'd done, for being unfaithful to Mother, and next they'd
found a number for a detective agency in the *Yellow Pages*
and then there were phone numbers given to me from then
one minute it was a joke, like a movie and then the next
this man phoned because the friend had given my number
and he knew who I was and suddenly I got a call saying
it had been done.

I was so crazy upset, Kit, but he didnt care about that
or my age because he knew me and he knew I had the
money because of my name. It was so funny but then
suddenly it wasn't, and look what he did. I said I wanted
dad dead but not really, I wanted him to love us and stay
the father I thought he was, not leave us for Raphael . . .
I didn't think it was real, Kit. It was all too much like the
movies.

He kept phoning for the money, Kit. He said he'd kill
me too if I didn't pay up and keep quiet. I just gave him
the money. I didn't think it was real. How could it be? I'm
just a kid, Kit. How could that sort of thing happen?

Sorry, Kitty, sorry sorry sorry sorry sorry sorry . . .

She barely heard the doorbell. It rang so many times she
thought it was inside her head. Nula. Little Nules. Her own
sister had murdered their father. The phrase ran around her

472

head like a trapped mouse and yet it made absolutely no sense to her.

All the people she had suspected. All the photos she'd laid out on her floor. All with grudges. Each one somehow capable of such a violent act. Of course it had been a contract killing. But her own baby sister? How could it have happened? This wasn't New York! How many kids *say* they want to kill their parents at some time in their lives? Yet how many are overheard by the sort of kids that had somehow helped Nula to commit such an act?

Kitty heard the answer loud in her own head. Rich kids, that's who. The only sort of kids people will arrange this sort of thing for. Celebrity children. The type who somehow get what they want. Kids who live in unreal worlds because their parents are famous.

There was a loud crack that made Kitty look up. Where the door had once been was now a hole. Kofteros stood framed inside that hole, bent double with pain and rubbing his right arm with his left hand. Kitty almost wanted to laugh at the sight. Nothing seemed real anymore.

'Kitty?' He was able to straighten up now.

'My door . . .' It was all she could think of. It was like being high on drugs. The door. Nicky's arm. Nula's suicide.

'I was worried,' he said, 'I heard about your sister.'

Kitty stared like an idiot, trying to make sense of it all. 'I thought it was you . . .' she began. She'd thought Kofteros had arranged the killing. Not all the time, sometimes. When she wasn't blaming Stephano or Burgess. Anyone but Nula, in fact. And yet all that time . . . in the end she held Nula's letter of confession out towards Kofteros. It was a family thing, she knew that. Perhaps he should never

473

have read it. But Kitty had carried enough by herself.

He took it and glanced at it. 'She's not dead, Kitty,' he said, grabbing her arm. 'Your sister's still alive. I've come to take you to the hospital.'

There are many ways to make your mark in life, and killing your wealthy father is one of them. Kofteros was right – Nula didn't die in the Underground, the wind from the train sucked her down onto the track and she fell between the wheels, rather than under them.

The press arrived at the hospital before Kitty got there. Kofteros was like a bodyguard, pushing her through the crush with one arm around her shoulders. She couldn't have been sure but she thought she felt him mash a few faces along the way, too.

When she walked into Nula's private room there was a celebrity PR already sitting at her bedside, planning her future.

Nula's injuries were ridiculously light but the PR had arranged for a few strategically-placed plasters to be stuck to her face for the photocall. The stricken expression came free of charge. Nula's poor mind had flown elsewhere, many miles away from any of them.

Kitty had to push past a posse of lawyers and PR assistants to get to her sister's bedside.

When she sat there softly crying nobody moved to allow her room or quiet. Nula's eyes only focused on Kitty's face once.

'I did it,' she whispered, 'I don't know how but I killed him. I'm sorry, Kit, I didn't mean it to happen. It was so terrible, too. I didn't know. I never thought.'

474

'God, Nules,' Kitty replied, 'how did this nightmare ever begin to happen?'

Once Nula was transferred to a nursing home of the sort used by royals and A-list celebs, Kitty felt a yearning to return to anything that resembled real life. She craved normality. The tragedy had been great enough to bring on a stifling numbness. She hadn't cried again since her hospital visit. Her shock had been too intense.

Nula had killed their father – almost by accident. Even after she'd read the note she hadn't believed it. Her sister had had a breakdown. Sweet little Nula would never have been capable of anything so unthinkable.

But it was Burgess who had suffered most at the news. It was Burgess who went to the courts every day and patiently and deliberately reported back to Kitty everything that happened or was going to happen.

It was Burgess who suddenly became human again, and supplied the strength Kitty and Hester needed to get through it all.

Hester had known it, all the time. She had been aware of Gabriel's affairs. What Nula and Kitty had failed to realize was that their parents were a product of the sixties, when behaviour like that was the norm. Hester knew, but she didn't mind. She loved her husband. She just shielded her children from it all. Maybe that had been her mistake.

It was when Kitty saw Nula's face on her television screen that she finally knew the time had come to repair her life. Her sister was speaking on something that looked suspiciously like Oprah Winfrey. She looked beautiful and she spoke well. Her cause had been taken up in the US, where a poor little rich child who has a hitman kill her father can receive sympathy and celebrity status.

Her mind had been unbalanced, that was the verdict in the UK. Now she had been asked to participate on a book and there was talk about film rights being sold, with Winona Ryder and Gwyneth Paltrow both up for the lead role.

And all this had happened so quickly. While Kitty's own life appeared to move in slow motion.

It was time to carry on planning the wedding. Gabriel was dead. Her sister had arranged his murder, more by accident than design, but what she had done had led to a terrible, violent death. Nothing would change those facts. They had all lived with the shock. Hester had survived better than most of them because her heart had flown out to her child.

'Do something good for the family, Kitty,' she'd said recently.

Would the wedding heal anything? Kitty doubted it but knew it gave them something else to focus on than grief. She went into the salon one night to try on the dress that Alain said was ready. They had the place to themselves. Nicky had given them free use of all the facilities. She'd lost weight. Alain tutted at the way her ribs poked through her flesh, ruining the even surface of the silk.

The dress looked wildly regal. Kitty turned in front of the mirror. Then she remembered the suit.

'Look at this,' she told Alain, placing the case she had brought with her onto the cutting-table. She pulled the wedding suit from its tissue and laid it out flat, smoothing the creases with her fingers.

476

'It's old,' Alain said, feigning indifference.

'Look at it closely,' Kitty told him.

Once he had walked over and touched the fabric she could tell he was hooked. She watched his back bend over the table as he inspected every detail, squinting at the fine embroidery and sniffing the pile of the fabric.

'It's my wedding suit, Alain,' Kitty told him, 'it's been passed down the family. My father wore the waistcoat, I think. It's for Freddy to wear at our wedding.'

Alain laughed. 'Is he going to diet?' he asked.

'Can it be altered?' Kitty asked him.

Alain shrugged. 'A pity,' he said. 'It would be easier to find a new groom. The fabric is delicate. This is a beautiful garment, Kitty, it belongs in a museum. Do you really want me to start ripping its seams so that your fiancé can cram himself into it?'

Kitty looked at him. 'Try it on,' she said. He looked doubtful, but she picked up the waistcoat and held it out towards him.

Alain slipped his own thick shirt off over his head and pulled the waistcoat around his body.

'It feels strange,' he said, 'dead man's clothes. Perhaps it is unlucky to wear it.'

She put her hand over his. 'Keep it on, Alain,' she told him, 'it has brought a lot of happiness since then. It has already been altered a couple of times – look.'

They stared at themselves in the mirror.

'It looks odd with jeans,' Alain said. She could tell he was bemused by what he saw.

'You could never wear this suit together with the dress I am making for you, Kitty,' he said quietly.

477

'No?' she asked.

'No. Absolutely not. The colours would be all wrong together. You need to complement the tones of the silks – look, here.' He went to the thread bin and pulled out a handful of delicate, faded-looking colours. 'You see what these would do with this?' he asked, holding them to his chest. 'You know Gabriel had one design already in these tones. Maybe he intended it to go with the suit . . .'

They pulled Gabriel's sketchbook out again and spread it on the table. Alain flicked through a few of the pages. 'Here,' he said, folding back the paper.

It was a subtle, clever dress, simple in shape but cut on the cross to come alive on the body. Attached to the paper were swatches of fabrics and pieces of thread that exactly complemented the colours in the suit.

'You didn't choose this?' Alain asked Kitty.

She shook her head. 'I liked it, but . . .'

'But what?' Alain asked.

'I don't know, Alain, maybe it's not right for the sort of wedding the Jacobs's are looking forward to. I kind of thought they'd want a few frills and frou-frou, you know? I think it sort of goes with the territory. You'd need to really know a thing or two about design and cut to appreciate this one properly. It's not exactly knock-their-eyes-out for the back rows of a crowded synagogue, is it?'

'I like it,' Alain said. 'It was your father's favourite, too.'

Kitty picked up the sketch. 'You mean you've had me here spending hours fitting this full-blown, belle-of-the-ball number, and now you start the emotional blackmail, telling me this was what my father would have wanted all along?' Kitty asked him. 'What are you, some kind of a workaholic nut or something?'

Alain lit a cigarette and shrugged. 'Telling a bride you don't like the dress she's chosen is like telling her you don't like her choice of husband,' he said. He turned his back and started sketching something on a pad.

'So?' Kitty asked him.

'So what?'

'So, does that mean you think Freddy's wrong for me too? Is that what you're saying?'

Alain kept his back turned towards her. 'I know this suit won't fit him,' he said.

'And for that I should call the wedding off?' Kitty asked.

'Don't you believe in omens?' Alain said.

'No.'

'Then marry your Freddy.'

'He's good-looking and kind.'

'So is the guy who sweeps the floor in the salon. I don't see you marrying him.'

'Freddy comes from a good family.'

'Good God, Kitty! I never knew you were such a snob. Is he good in bed?'

'What?'

'You heard.'

Alain stood and walked towards her. He was taller. He smelt good. It was his eyes that did it, though. They looked so weary, as though they had seen everything in the world. They were large and dark now.

He took her hand and placed it on his chest, on the waistcoat that Rosa's father had stitched for her, so many

479

years before. His free hand found her chin and touched it carefully.

'Kiss me,' he whispered.

'No.'

'Kiss me,' he said.

Her chin tilted upward. His lips fell slowly towards her own. Then his eyes closed and the spell was broken.

'No,' she repeated, though even then there was very little conviction in her tone.

'Kitty?' Freddy stood in the doorway.

She looked at Alain. He was smiling.

'You knew he was coming,' she said to him.

'Of course,' he whispered, 'I took the call.'

He pressed his face against her hair. 'I owed it to your father, Kitty,' he said softly. 'Gabriel knew the marriage was wrong for you. He told me while we worked on the designs. You chose the wrong man and the wrong dress. Don't worry, you'll make the right choice ... eventually.'

CHAPTER FIFTY-SIX

ZG

JACCONET
*Currently called nainsook, jacconet was a thin
cotton fabric, something between cambric and muslin in
texture and weave.*

Freddy waited for excuses but Kitty could find none to give him. It wasn't even a proper kiss that he had seen, but she knew, above all the anger she felt towards Alain, that he was right – she could never marry Freddy. He was wrong for her. So what could she tell him?

'I'm sorry,' she said, and she was. Sorry for the coldness and disappointment that came into his eyes. Sorry for cheating him but not cheating on him. Sorry that she couldn't be the person she had planned on being. If Gabriel hadn't died then she would have married Freddy and been happy. But now she was different. Someone else had been released inside her. There were things driving her now that she had no control over.

Freddy looked across at Alain, and Kitty knew he was considering punching him hard. She knew Freddy well enough to be aware of what was going on in his mind; how he was chewing the process over, where the punch would land, how much Alain would hurt. How he himself would feel once the deed was done. In the end he settled for a quiet exit. No words, no punching, just a look and he was gone.

Kitty took a step to follow him but Alain held her by the arm.

'Are you going after him?' he asked.

She stared at him.

'To say what?' he said. 'To tell him you are sorry and that you love him and will marry him after all?' He smiled. 'Do you know what you are like when you are working, Kitty? You are happy and anxious and totally involved in the job that you are doing. Do you know how beautiful you look when that is happening? I saw this when we worked on the collection. Yet you would give it all up for a marriage you don't really want. The business is a passion for you, Kitty. Why do you let it all go so easily?'

The room was silent, lit only by the low ochre light from the desk-lamp. She watched Alain walk across to the cutting-table and she saw him lift up the giant metal shears that lay in one of the open drawers. The steel caught the light. They cut fabric like butter. Like an animal she stood stock-still, caught in a web of fear and indecision.

He came so close that his breath was upon her face. Still she was immobile, transfixed by the sight of the huge scissors.

He lifted the hem of her wedding dress with one hand. With the other he placed the open shears against the fabric, lifting them slowly but evenly so that the garment was swiftly sliced apart from the skirt to the waist. She closed her eyes. She could feel the cold metal on her bare stomach. Alain paused, staring all the while at her face, and then carried on cutting, up her ribs to her breasts and then to her throat.

Her flesh shrank in fear, but she was neither cut nor hurt. When the shears had stopped she opened her eyes and he was there in front of her, waiting for her move.

'Kitty, you know how much I want you,' he told her. His arms dropped to his sides and the shears fell to the floor with a deafening clatter.

She pulled the dress open and let it sink to the ground with a whisper. Then she began on the buttons of the waistcoat. They were small and difficult to open, but she worked on them carefully for she did not want to break the threads. All the time Alain watched her face and she could hear his breathing and smell the scent of his skin.

How many young wives had worked on these buttons? She saw Rosa on her wedding night, pulling each small fastening from its buttonhole, one by one, as careful as she was now. Did Richard wait as patiently as Alain, or would he have tried to rip at them in his haste to be with his bride? But then her mother had said the marriage was never consummated . . . Hester, too, would have folded the waistcoat for Gabriel. Did she love him on that day?

The last button fell open and Kitty looked up at Alain's face. His features were beautiful in the low light. The skin was pale nutmeg, with small violet smudges beneath each prune-dark eye. The shadows of his lashes formed a frieze along either cheek. His hair was like Nula's, cropped, dark and soft, like an animal pelt. On his chest was a down of similar hairs, though coarser and more curly. His flesh shone and pulsed with reflected colours in the half-light:

483

fly's wing, graphite, dioptase, moonstone and malachite.

She knew he ached to have her, yet she made him wait while she looked. She placed a finger to his lips and watched them form a kiss around it.

'Do you want me too, Kitty?' he asked.

She waited a while longer. 'Yes,' she told him.

He lifted her then, kissing her full on the mouth as she felt herself rise in his arms. He tasted fresh and sun-bleached like a pebble washed in the sea. Then he placed her gently and lovingly upon the high cutting-table, so that the bare wood was shock-cold against her back and buttocks.

The fat bolts of shantung and embroidered silks that lay beside her head emitted a warm and rich perfume that reminded her kindly of her childhood. Crushed beneath her skinny neck lay a pillow of dove-white velvet that should have formed the collar of her wedding gown.

Breathing carefully through her mouth like a child who senses Christmas, she watched Alain remove first the open waistcoat and then his jeans until they were naked together, moulded shroud-like in a parachute-sheet of fine pearl marocain.

He called her name inside her mouth many times as he kissed her and she pulled him close until their bodies merged into one like sodden clay. In the room there was silence, yet inside Kitty's head the ghosts of a thousand sounds kept her busily absorbed.

There was a woman's voice that sang a song she barely knew: 'I took a violet from my mother's grave . . .' the voice echoed high into the air until it faded and other voices took over. A chorus from a musical, sung in foreign voices, then fire-bells and shouting, followed by the sounds of children crying.

'Rosa?' It was her father's voice, and yet not her name. *For Rosa, the daughter I love.* There was the sound of stamping feet upon impacted snow and the smell of snow, too, and ivy and mistletoe, icy in her steaming nostrils.

'Kitty?' As Alain bored gently inside her she heard the name 'Max' called faintly in her head. Then she was lost in a tide of ancient longing that all but drowned her in its intensity. It was as though she had made love only once in her life. She felt herself open and empty, clinging to Alain like a straw in the wind, as much for safety as for lust.

As his face contorted and his back arched and became rigid in the eye of his orgasm she heard her own name roared at last like sea in a cave, and then she was gone – swept up in it totally, too lost in the stampede towards ecstasy, winced and wrinkled into her own everlasting pleasure, curling and squirming like a salt-coated slug until the pain of it had gone and she could straighten and hear normal noises again, like the tick of a wristwatch and the steady drip of her own droplets of sweat.

Wet and slippery as a pair of conger eels, Kitty and Alain lay entwined until they had cooled, then he slid back until he was spreadeagled alongside her and their mixed sweat evaporated to the point where she started to shiver. He covered her again with the fabric then, and held her until she was warm.

They left the building together and only parted once they had cabs. When Kitty got back to her apartment there was a message from Freddy on her answerphone, full of spite and slurred anger. She deleted it before the end. He was drunk. That wasn't Freddy. That was Vodka Absolut talking.

ZG

CHIFFON
Made from silk, wool or synthetics, chiffon is a gossamer-sheer fabric made from tightly twisted yarns.

When she woke it was late and her body felt flattened, like well-rolled filo pastry. She had to look in the mirror to make sure she wasn't pressed to an inch thick, like a cartoon character run over by a steamroller.

She walked about the place until body bits fell into place and she seemed less two-dimensional. Her spine felt bruised and her lips were sore. There was the trace of a rash on her cheeks and chin where his unshaven flesh had chaffed and burnt. She took some ice cubes from a tray in the freezer and pressed them to her temples and face.

When she emerged in her pyjamas to collect the post Kofteros was standing outside her door, immaculately dressed in a ghastly but expensive greige suit and cloud-white shirt.

'It's not your shade,' she told him.

'Good morning,' he said, handing her a styrofoam cup of very fresh and very bitter espresso.

'Sugar?' he asked, digging into his trouser pockets.

She allowed, rather than let him into her flat. When

she walked through a shard of gleaming daylight Kofteros raised an eyebrow at the sight of her face.

'I take it the wedding's off,' he said.

'You spoke to Freddy already?' she asked, sounding annoyed.

'No,' he told her, sipping his own coffee and wincing at the heat of it, 'only if you don't mind me saying so, he never made you look like you do right now.'

She slammed into the bathroom and poured water over her face.

'One last clue?' he shouted through the door.

Kitty sighed. 'I'm tired, Nicky.'

'But you are also curious,' Kofteros said.

'Why the hell are you doing this?' she asked when she came out. She had pulled on a sweater and a pair of faded jeans.

'Don't you have anything a bit more formal?' Kofteros asked her.

'Why, are you and Chloe getting married, or something?' Kitty asked. When he looked straight at her she remembered the dream and shuddered.

'Something more business-like would be appropriate,' he said quietly.

She changed into a trouser suit, kicking herself all the time that it was only her inquisitiveness stopping her from throwing him out on his ear.

'The last tiny piece of the puzzle,' he announced once she was beside him in the car.

'I take it there's no point asking where we're going?' Kitty said.

'You can know if you want,' he told her. She was

disappointed. Something inside her preferred the mystery of it all, like before. As much as she disliked Kofteros he had become something of a magician in her life, summoning up surprises: the photographer's studio, the insults hurled at Burgess. 'I'll wait,' she told him, sulking.

They pulled up outside a small building in a surprisingly seedy-looking street in Mayfair.

'More pictures?' Kitty asked.

'No,' Kofteros told her. He opened her door from the inside, leaning across so that his arm brushed her legs.

'I'm sorry,' he said, looking at her.

'What is this place?' she asked.

He sighed. 'If I do all the work for you, Kitty, you won't feel as though you've achieved anything. Just go inside and find out for yourself.'

She looked up at the building. 'Why are you doing these things?' she asked.

He smiled. 'Maybe I have plans to become your doting brother-in-law,' he said.

'No,' she told him evenly, 'we both know that's not it.'

His face became serious. 'One thing we share, Kitty, is a genuine interest in the business of fashion. My parents were immigrants and I was taught the importance of the continuity of history. Believe it or not, I don't enjoy breaking up your little family dynasty. I have a lot of respect for the traditional as well as the new and innovative.

'We both know that Zigo would never survive as it was, yet despite any pleasure I derive from my business manipulations – and, to be honest with you, Kitty, there have been many – I also suffer many pangs of regret that I should be the one to do the obligatory deed.'

489

'So you are helping me out of a sense of guilt?' Kitty asked.

'Maybe.' He shrugged. 'Although you should know that guilt has never been one of my prime emotions. I am a businessman, Kitty. And that's what I do – business. Who it affects and how it affects them is not my problem. I like to see things tidy, though, and the story of your family is beginning to fray around the edges.

'Burgess will stay in Zigo as long as the lawyers allow it, then he will reap his financial harvest from investing in virtual pornography. Chloe will continue as the masthead until her first bad facelift, but as she still has many years to go before the wrinkles start to appear I think we could consider her career a long and almost happy one. China is too obsessed with motherhood to be a worry and Nula . . .'

'Which just leaves me,' said Kitty. 'I'm not a charity case, Nicky. I can manage by myself.'

'And yet you have never visited this building before,' he told her. 'Why, Kitty? Do you have no curiosity or sense of history? Like I said, you are the only one of your siblings with a true taste for the business and yet you shuck the responsibility off like a snake sheds its skin. I would have thought the trail I've led you would have been enough to whet your appetite. It's *you* who has to carry on the family name, Kitty – don't you realize that?'

'How do you know so much?' Kitty asked him.

He smiled. 'Everything is there, Kitty – if you just know where to look for it.'

'Aren't you biting the hand that feeds you?' she asked.

He shrugged. 'There were many honourable men in my

490

own family's history – and many more crooks and scoundrels, too. It doesn't pay to be too straight, Kitty. Only losers reveal their entire hand of cards.'

She got out of the car. The building was an old one, in need of renovation. On the ground floor was a shop that was being re-fitted into some sort of a restaurant. She looked at the plaques on the wall near the stairway. None of the businesses sounded familiar, but one was a fashion firm, so she climbed to the first floor, where the company was sited.

There were heavy wooden doors with frosted glass inserts and a plastic sign above them: Seigfried and Sons, Fashion Importers. Kitty pressed a button on the intercom and the doors buzzed open.

Inside was a small showroom, unremarkable save for two massive and ornate windows that stretched the length of one end of the room. The place looked untidy. There were half-open packing boxes strewn about and half-empty rails with the odd hanging garment.

'Can I help you?' The elderly man who approached her looked polite but suspicious.

'Are you closing down?' Kitty asked.

'Selling up,' he told her. 'The overheads here are too great. We ran until the end of our lease and then – well, you can imagine property prices around here! Are you a buyer?'

'No,' Kitty said, 'I'm a manufacturer – well, I used to be. My father was Gabriel Zigofsky.'

The old man peered at her, his face a sudden mask of condolence. 'I knew I recognized your face!' he said. 'Please, sit down – look, I can clear a few of these boxes

491

away. Let me get tea – I'm sorry, we have had so many people come to look around . . .'

She touched his arm. 'Don't worry about the chair,' she said. 'I wonder – could I be another one of your visitors that comes to look around? Would you mind very much? A friend recommended I visit you.'

The man smiled. 'Of course, of course!' he said. 'I'm a little surprised you never came before. Look where you like – I'll carry on in my office, if you don't mind. Most of the stuff is packed away, I'm afraid. But the workrooms are still stuff-full. I collect too much, you see, I never could throw anything away. If there's anything you want to keep, just let me know, though I doubt it will interest a young lady like yourself very much. Still, enjoy!'

Kitty stared at him as he walked off. Help herself? She wandered across to the windows. They were so dusty the sunlight was diffused. The carpet she walked on was threadbare in places and the boards creaked painfully as she moved across the room.

He had given her the run of the place. She had no idea why, but curiosity drove her on. Did he think she might be buying the property? Maybe he was a little eccentric. Or perhaps her father's name opened more doors than she'd thought.

The workroom was long and narrow with a skylight in the ceiling. There was a handful of ancient machines and a cutting-table so gnarled and bent with age it would have defied even Alain's expert hand.

A woman eating lunch at the desk smiled as she approached. 'More like a museum, eh?' she asked Kitty. 'It's a shame these places have to close. They're all going now, though. Nobody wants couture these days, do they?'

Kitty returned the smile. 'I thought you were importers,' she said.

'Nooo . . .' the woman told her, 'agents for a German coat range, yes – but then there's this other side of the business, too. When the place was bought originally it was just couture. There's still a dressmaking service for the elderly ladies of Mayfair. Not a lucrative business, I must confess, but it's been running for donkey's years and the old man was rather loathe to knock it on the head. I think he rather likes the idea of the individually-made garment. He's always been proud of his little sideline and the ladies love it. I don't know what they'll do now it's closing – though most of them have kicked the bucket by now.'

She folded the wrapping from her lunch and threw it into a bin. 'Are you interested in fashion?' she asked. 'Would you like to see some of the old stuff that he's kept over the years?'

Kitty nodded. The woman led her into a large walk-in cupboard.

'All the old order books and sketchpads are here,' she said, pulling a lightswitch. 'Some of them date back to the last century. You can have a poke around if you like – I sometimes thumb through them while I'm taking a break, though the dust tends to set my asthma off if I'm not careful. There's a washroom over there if you need to scrub up when you're finished. Mind that nice suit – it's a Zigo, isn't it?'

Kitty barely heard the question. She had entered the cupboard and was staring at the workbooks. She didn't even hear the woman walk off. The sense of the place was overpowering enough to make her giddy.

The design books were coated with grey dust but still stacked in numerical order. The most recent was '96. Kitty pulled it off the pile and flicked through it. The dresses were mainly Hartnell rip-offs, designed for what Gabriel would have called 'the more mature client'.

Each drawing had been carefully executed in pen and a swatch of the fabric stapled to the side of the page. There was nothing exciting about either the styles or the colours. But then the sort of clients that these had been made for wouldn't have wanted anything more innovative.

Kitty put the book back with a sigh. She'd started at the end so she may as well finish at the beginning. She couldn't read the exact year on the spine of the first book on the shelves, as the numbers had faded, but it was compiled in the 1800s.

After an amount of tugging it fell out, bringing its own dust-cloud with it. Kitty coughed at the fumes and waved her hand about until the air cleared a little. There was a small table and a stool in the cupboard. She placed the book on the table and squatted down on the stool. There was a wad of tissues in her pocket and she used a couple as a duster to wipe the front of the book before opening it.

Maison Rosa, she read, in thin gold lettering. A thrill ran through her body like an electric current. She pulled the first page open. There was some spidery writing on the left and then an amateurish drawing of a woman's shape, with a floor-length garment sketched roughly on it. She barely made out the words that were scrawled beneath

494

it: *Princess dress of rose-pink foulard with striped pekin overskirt.*

A few pages on and the sketches were getting more assured, even though the proportions of the figures made Kitty smile. It was as though a child had done them. As she flicked the pages over, though, she realized that the artist was precocious – a very quick learner indeed. The lines became bolder and expressions even appeared on the models' faces.

An Empire dress of plain bengaline, she read from one page, *the panels of the skirt in jet crepe de Chine and the bodice stitched in embroidered flowers. Full sleeves of beaded lisse.*

The fabric swatches that accompanied each sketch were a deal less grand than the words, though. When 'fine woollen fabric' was described there was often a torn patch of dyed serge, or other cheap material.

'She was knocking off!' Kitty whispered, smiling. 'Rosa, you bad girl!'

She was in the cupboard for two hours without realizing. A mug of tea was placed at her elbow and she drank it without even wondering where it had come from.

Rosa Zigofsky. The books were her own personal diary – a complete record of her business as it was built up, and all in sketches and scrawled writing and little scraps of faded fabric and column upon column of figures.

There was a heart-stopping moment when she saw the first photograph. It was an old studio portrait of an awkward-looking young woman in a simple bridal gown. Kitty's fingers flew to her mouth with the shock of the change from sketches to photographs. So this was the

495

beginning of the mail-order business that had built up and morphed into Zigo fashions.

There was a polite tap on the open door behind her. Kitty turned slowly, rubbing at her stiff and aching neck.

'Alain?'

He stood in the doorway, his expression as curious as Kitty's had been when she first arrived.

'I phoned you all morning,' he said, 'in the end I had to get the thumbscrews out on Mr Smoothie to find out where you were. I thought you'd vanished off the face of the earth, Kitty. Even your mobile's turned off. What the hell is all this?' He looked at the design books with mounting fascination.

She pulled him towards the small table. 'Look, Alain,' she said, 'this is like watching conception for me. This is a record of the founding of our fashion business.'

'*Your* business, Kitty,' Alain said, poring over the sketches and photographs. 'I was a little rude when Mr Smoothie refused to tell me where you were. He fired me.'

'I'm sorry,' Kitty said.

'Don't be,' he told her, sniffing at a small square of ancient brocade. 'How many of these are there?' he asked.

'One per year since the late 1800s,' she told him. 'This must have been Rosa's premises at some time, Alain. I had no idea. The only business I ever knew about was the one in Berkeley Square.' She stopped as a loose photograph fell out of the book and onto the floor.

'Look,' she said, 'it's her wedding shot again.' It was a larger version of the picture in the photographer's studio. Behind it, and slightly stuck to it, was another portrait, of a man standing by himself.

496

'Max Warkofski,' Kitty read from the back. 'It's the photographer, Alain, the one who did the wedding shot. She must have kept them both together.'

Alain stepped back. 'This place is too small for both of us, Kitty,' he said. 'You carry on looking. I'll wait outside.'

He was gone less than five minutes before Kitty heard him calling her. She walked out into the workroom, rubbing her eyes at the sudden light.

'Did you see these?' Alain asked her. He held out a couple of plain cotton blouses with the necklines turned inside-out. 'Look, Kitty,' he said, 'look at the label.'

Kitty read the heavily embroidered italics: 'Rosa Zigofsky Couture,' she said. She looked at the woman, who was now back at her desk. 'But these are new,' she said.

The woman nodded. 'It's a label that's been running since the old days. The couture house closed down but the old man kept the name going for his ladies, who liked to think they were getting something a bit special.'

'Didn't anyone question the copyright?' Kitty asked.

The woman shook her head. 'Search me,' she said.

Kitty took the blouses to the old man who ran the place.

'So you found your name!' he said, smiling.

'How did you manage to keep hold of it?' Kitty asked him. 'Surely someone at Zigo would have put a stop to this years ago!'

The old man nodded. 'It was a gentleman's agreement,' he said. 'Your father knew the name was being used, as did his father before him, but the place was started by Rosa Zigofsky and I think they allowed the name to stay as a little memorial to the woman. The business was her whole life, I believe. Who would have dared to make it otherwise?'

'So this is legal?' Kitty asked.

'Talk to my legal eagles if you think it isn't!' the old man smiled.

Kitty's expression froze. Suddenly she turned and ran out of the building. Alain followed her down the stairs.

'Kitty!' he shouted. 'Where are you going?'

'To speak to my solicitors,' she replied.

ZG

SILISTRIENNE
A firm-textured wool and silk textile.

Dearest Kitty,

So now you know my story. And now that the world has turned full circle again, I shall watch with great pride as you work your way in the business that I founded.

Kitty, there were so many mistakes in my life that I should hate to see you make, yet your youth is all to advantage, whilst my own was a handicap, I believe.

While I arrived penniless in what is now your country my hardships and mean circumstances were as much an impediment to me as I believe your ease of life has been to you. My hurdle was starvation while yours has been apathy and an inability to survive alone.

I have done terrible things, Kitty, and I would not wish the same mistakes upon you. I have killed, dearest – for what would you call my treatment of Max, other than outright murder? How can I blame my own insecurities and lack of experience for such an outrage?

He loved me, Kitty, and I did not see it. Instead I sought to be as much the cynic as I thought him to be, even asking him to take my wedding photograph, for which final act of humiliation he took his own life. Look around you, Kitty. Never allow pride to blur your judgment. A gentleman is not always marked out by his manners and the cut of his suit. If such a man loves you, dearest, work hard to forgive his imperfections before dismissing him altogether.

And then, dear, as a punishment for all my sins my darling son David was taken from me, too. Even now the grief makes me ache with pain.

So what was I left with? A sham marriage, to be sure, for Richard hated me every bit as much as Max loved me. He treated me well enough, but his mind was elsewhere once David died. It was for that child's sake we had been joined and without him we had nothing. My marriage was never consummated, Kitty. Max was the only man I ever knew, save the monster in my homeland.

So the business became my life once again. With Richard's interest in the place all but gone, I worked day and night to make the money come in. And it worked, dearest. With Ruth's help I became famous in my own time. I was the one who persuaded her to marry my brother Gregory. When Max died, all her girlish hopes went with him and so a business-like union suited her very well. They were happy enough, Kitty. Their blood is in your veins along with my own.

Your wealth from the sale of the business enabled you to buy again the place that I sadly neglected, Kitty, and sold on the day of my marriage. My concern was to re-build my husband's business, for it was all I had aimed for, along with his love. Yet so much of me went into the small place you now have, Kitty. Your life is there, child, just as mine was at one time.

Now the name will not die and the family will own what I owned. Let other people do what they will with the main business – keep yourself small and exclusive, it is the only way to be true to the passion I know is inside you. You will find new clients, Kitty. Good quality is always in demand and as the old company begins to sell out to profit so yours can keep the name of which I was so proud.

Never lose the wedding suit, Kitty. It was my most cherished possession and should be yours, too. My marriage to Richard was the most splendid day of my life, for I had no way of knowing what lay ahead. How huge were my dreams then, Kitty! Yet you should make your own happiness and look to no others to achieve it, which is something I learnt at my cost.

Kitty, make no similar mistakes, I beg you. The business was my life, but love of cloth and cut is not all you will need. I died wealthy but I died alone, with only my pride to keep me company. You are young, Kitty, as I once was. Be generous with your love, child, and forgive those who appear to stray, for their love is no less strong. I discovered that only when it was too late. Max took his own life on account of me, Kitty. The memory of what he did has haunted me forever.

The new couture salon opened six months later, amid a welter of publicity that for once focused on the business, rather than Gabriel's murder.

Waika did all they could to prevent the launch, yet the pay-off they had given Kitty enabled her to afford the better legal team. They under-estimated her determination. In the end there was nothing they could do. When Zigofsky opened, it took with it all the traditions of quality and prestige that Waika had milked out of the Zigo name.

Kitty was proud, but Hester was prouder. She arrived at the opening in her odd stockings – a look which now had a cult following among women of a certain age who still wanted to appear innovative – with China's daughter clutched in her arms. Both were dressed in specially-made outfits from the Zigofsky 'Diffusion' range.

Alain's first collection was a masterpiece of exquisite understatement, making the garments at Zigo and Jacobs appear tacky and gaudy by contrast. Kitty had bought in an older Parisian couturier to add heavyweight experience to the designs and to give them the quality touches that would bring society names to their door.

Kofteros was not, of course, at the opening, though he phoned Kitty from his car once the main party was over.

'Are you coming over?' Kitty asked him.

'Me?' he laughed. 'Do you want to see me end up wearing a pair of cement boots in the Thames? No, Kitty, I don't think so. Waika are still going apeshit about all this as it is. Maybe later, under the cover of darkness, like a vampire.'

'You risked your job,' Kitty told him.

'No,' he said, 'nothing remotely as dramatic. All I did was give you a lift in the car. Nobody could ever blame a lowly chauffeur for what's happened. Anyway, there's no real damage done – only a dent to Waika's fragile ego. They can afford to ignore the problem. Just sit tight for a couple of years, Kitty, and they'll be buying you out ten times over.'

'But they must have blamed you for not checking out the legal implications?' Kitty asked.

'No,' Kofteros said, 'they blamed another guy in another suit. The man who was about to be given my job, in fact. I was going to be made redundant about the same time as you and your brother. It just happened that I noticed a small glitch in the paperwork which their newest blue-eyed boy failed to spot.'

'So you helped me in order to save your own skin?' Kitty asked.

'I never said you should say thank you,' Kofteros told her.

'Thanks anyway,' Kitty said.

There was an awkward pause.

'So I suppose you go off and marry your little swarthy Frenchman now?' he asked.

'Maybe,' Kitty told him, 'maybe not. Business comes first.'

'Well,' Kofteros began, 'if you ever need anything, you know . . .'

'There is one thing I still need to know,' Kitty said.

'Ask,' he told her.

'What exactly is it you do with jelly-cubes?'

'Chloe told you about that?' he asked.

'She did.'

There was a crackle of static before Kitty could hear him laughing.

'She was joking, Kitty, winding you up,' he said at last. 'Do you know, you are almost perfect – beautiful, talented, quite kind to people you like. There's only one thing that never got passed down in your genes, Kitty – a sense of humour.'

'I don't believe you,' Kitty said, smiling.

'You don't *want* to believe me,' Nicky replied. He sighed. 'Okay, if you really have to know. What I do with the jelly-cubes is I place them very carefully up . . .'

But Kitty had rung off.

'*Kitty*!'

The voice in her head again.

'*Kitty*!'

Sighing, she got his number on redial. He picked up after one ring.

'So will it be two years before I see you again? After the dust has settled?' she asked.

'Marry your Frenchman.' Nicky laughed. 'The suit fits him better.'

Kitty smiled. 'How about under the cover of darkness?' she asked.

'Maybe.'

This time it was he who hung up on her.

She waited until the phone rang again.

'Do you know a good tailor who can do alterations?' he said.

GLOSSARY

Pesach	Passover
Shiva	wake, the first week after the funeral
Chevra Kadisha	burial society
Talmud	fundamental code of Jewish law
Kichels	biscuits
Minyan	the required number – ten males over the age of thirteen – for parts of services or readings
Shtetle	Jewish village communities of Eastern Europe
Shema	a Jewish prayer declaring the oneness of God
Yamulkh	a man's skullcap
Simcha	celebration
Challah	bread
Schlemozzle	uproar

DEATH

VINTA

ARTISTS IN CRIME

Dame Ngaio Marsh was born in New Zealand in 1895 and died in February 1982. She wrote over 30 detective novels and many of her stories have theatrical settings, for Ngaio Marsh's real passion was the theatre. Both actress and producer, she almost single-handedly revived the New Zealand public's interest in the theatre. It was for this work that she received what she called her 'damery' in 1966.

'The finest writer in the English language of the pure, classical puzzle whodunit. Among the crime queens, Ngaio Marsh stands out as an Empress.'   *The Sun*

'Ngaio Marsh transforms the detective story from a mere puzzle into a novel.'   *Daily Express*

'Her work is as nearly flawless as makes no odds. Character, plot, wit, good writing, and sound technique.'   *Sunday Times*

'She writes better than Christie!'   *New York Times*

'Brilliantly readable . . . first class detection.'   *Observer*

'Still, quite simply, the greatest exponent of the classical English detective story.'   *Daily Telegraph*

'Read just one of Ngaio Marsh's novels and you've got to read them all . . . '   *Daily Mail*

BY THE SAME AUTHOR

NGAIO MARSH

Death in Ecstasy

Vintage Murder

Artists in Crime

AND

Death on the Air

HARPER

HARPER

an imprint of HarperCollins*Publishers*
1 London Bridge Street
London SE1 9GF
www.harpercollins.co.uk

This omnibus edition 2009

Death in Ecstasy first published in Great Britain by Geoffrey Bles 1936
Vintage Murder first published in Great Britain by Geoffrey Bles 1937
Artists in Crime first published in Great Britain by Geoffrey Bles 1938
Portrait of Troy and Death on the Air first published in Great Britain in
Death on the Air and Other Stories by HarperCollins*Publishers* 1995

Ngaio Marsh asserts the moral right to
be identified as the author of these works

Copyright © Ngaio Marsh Ltd 1936, 1937, 1938
Portrait of Troy and Death on the Air copyright © Ngaio Marsh
(Jersey) Ltd 1989

ISBN 978 0 00 732870 3

Printed by CPI Group (UK) Ltd, Croydon CR0 4YY

MIX
Paper from
responsible sources
FSC® C007454

FSC is a non-profit international organisation established to promote the
responsible management of the world's forests. Products carrying the FSC
label are independently certified to assure consumers that they come
from forests that are managed to meet the social, economic and
ecological needs of present and future generations.

Find out more about HarperCollins and the environment at
www.harpercollins.co.uk/green

CONTENTS

Portrait of Troy

Troy made her entrance with the sixth of the books about Alleyn. In those days, I still painted quite a lot and quite seriously, and was inclined to look upon everything I saw in terms of possible subject matter.

On a voyage out to New Zealand from England, we called at Suva. The day was overcast, still and sultry. The kind of day when sounds have an uncanny clarity, and colour an added sharpness and intensity. The wharf at Suva, as seen from the boat-deck of the *Niagara*, was remarkable in these respects: the acid green of a bale of bananas packed in their own leaves; the tall Fijian with a mop of hair dyed screaming magenta, this colour repeated in the sari of an Indian woman; the slap of bare feet on wet boards and the deep voices that sounded as if they were projected through pipes. All these elements made their impressions, and I felt a great itch for a paint brush between my fingers.

The ship drew away, the wharf receded, and I was left with an unattempted, non-existent picture that is as vivid today as it was then.

I don't think it is overdoing it to say that when I began *Artists in Crime*, it was this feeling of unfulfilment that led me to put another painter on another boat deck making a sketch of the wharf at Suva and that she made a much better job of it than I ever would have done.

This was Troy. It was in this setting that she and Alleyn first met.

I have always tried to keep the settings of my books as far as possible within the confines of my own experience. Having found Troy and decided that Alleyn was to find her, too, the rest of the book developed in the milieu of a painters' community. It was written before capital punishment was abolished in Great Britain, and Troy shared my own repugnance for that terrible practice: I had talked with a detective-inspector and learnt that there were more men in the force who were for abolition than was commonly supposed. I knew Alleyn would be one of them. He would sense that the shadow of the death penalty lay between himself and Troy. It was not until the end of the next book, *Death in a White Tie*, that they came finally together. In *Death and the Dancing Footman*, they are already married.

My London agent, I remember, was a bit dubious about marrying Alleyn off. There is a school of thought that considers love interest, where the investigating character is involved, should be kept off stage in detective fiction or at least handled in a rather gingerly fashion and got rid of with alacrity. Conan Doyle seems to have taken this view.

'To Sherlock Holmes she is always *the* woman', he begins, writing of Irene Adler. But after a couple of sentences expressive of romantic attachment, he knocks that idea sideways by stating that, as far as Holmes was concerned, all emotions (sexual attraction in particular) were 'abhorrent to his cold, precise, but admirably balanced mind'.

So much for Miss Adler.

An exception to the negative attitude appears in Bentley's classic *Trent's Last Case*, where the devotion of Trent for one of the suspects is a basic ingredient of the investigation. Dorothy L Sayers, however, turns the whole thing inside out by herself regrettably falling in love with her own creation and making rather an ass of both of them in the process.

Troy came along at a time when thoroughly nice girls were often called Dulcie, Edith, Cecily, Mona, Madeleine. Even, alas,

Gladys. I wanted her to have a plain, rather down-to-earth first name and thought of Agatha – not because of Christie – and a rather odd surname that went well with it, so she became Agatha Troy and always signed her pictures 'Troy' and was so addressed by everyone. *Death in a White Tie* might have been called *Siege of Troy*.

Her painting is far from academic but not always non-figurative. One of its most distinguished characteristics is a very subtle sense of movement brought about by the interrelationships of form and line. Her greatest regret is that she never painted the portrait of Isabella Sommita, which was commissioned in the book I am at present writing.* The diva was to have been portrayed with her mouth wide open, letting fly with her celebrated A above high C. It is questionable whether she would have been pleased with the result. It would have been called *Top Note*.

Troy and Alleyn suit each other. Neither impinges upon the other's work without being asked, with the result that in Troy's case she does ask pretty often, sometimes gets argumentative and uptight over the answer and almost always ends up by following the suggestion. She misses Alleyn very much when they are separated. This is often the case, given the nature of their work, and on such occasions each feels incomplete and they write to each other like lovers.

Perhaps it is advisable, on grounds of credibility, not to make too much of the number of times coincidence mixes Troy up in her husband's cases: a situation that he embraces with mixed feelings. She is a reticent character and as sensitive as a sea urchin, but she learns to assume and even feel a certain detachment.

'After all,' she has said to herself, 'I married him and I would be a very boring wife if I spent half my time wincing and showing sensitive.'

I like Troy. When I am writing about her, I can see her with her shortish dark hair, thin face and hands. She's absent-minded, shy and funny, and she can paint like nobody's business. I'm always glad when other people like her, too.

NGAIO MARSH
1979

* Photo-Finish

Death in Ecstasy

For the family in Kent

Contents

Foreword

In case the House of the Sacred Flame might be thought to bear a superficial resemblance to any existing church or institution, I hasten to say that if any similarity exists it is purely fortuitous. The House of the Sacred Flame, its officials, and its congregation are all imaginative and exist only in Knocklatchers Row. None, as far as I am aware, has any prototype in any part of the world.

My grateful thanks are due to Robin Page for his advice in the matter of sodium cyanide; to Guy Cotterill for the plan of the House of the Sacred Flame, and to Robin Adamson for his fiendish ingenuity in the matter of home-brewed poisons.

NGAIO MARSH
Christchurch, New Zealand

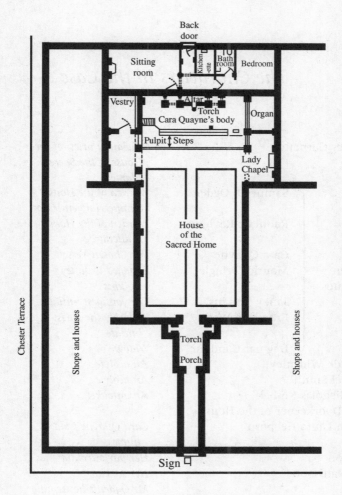

Back
door

Sitting
room

Kitchenette

Bathroom

Bedroom

Vestry

Altar

Torch

Cara Quayne's body

Organ

Pulpit ↕ Steps

Lady
Chapel

House
of the
Sacred Home

Chester Terrace

Shops and houses

Shops and houses

Torch

Porch

Sign ⌷

Knocklatchers Row

The Characters in the Case

Jasper Garnette		Officiating priest of the House of the Sacred Flame
	Samuel J. Ogden	Warden of the House. A commercial gentleman
	Raoul de Ravigne	Warden of the House. A dilettante
The Seven Initiates	Cara Quayne	The Chosen Vessel
	Maurice Pringle	Engaged to Janey Jenkins
	Janey Jenkins	The youngest initiate
	Ernestine Wade	Probably the oldest initiate
	Dagmar Candour	Widow
Claude Wheatley		An acolyte
Lionel Smith		An acolyte
Dr Nicholas Kasbek		An onlooker
The Doorkeeper of the House		
Edith Laura Hebborn		Cara Quayne's old nurse
Wilson		Her parlourmaid
Mr Rattisbon		Her solicitor
Elsie		Mr Ogden's housemaid
Chief Detective-Inspector Alleyn		Criminal Investigation Department, Scotland Yard
Detective-Inspector Fox		His assistant
Detective-Sergeant Bailey		His fingerprint expert
Dr Curtis		His Divisional Surgeon
Nigel Bathgate		His Watson

Part One

CHAPTER 1

Entrance to a Cul-de-sac

On a pouring wet Sunday night in December of last year a special meeting was held at the House of the Sacred Flame in Knocklatchers Row.

There are many strange places of worship in London, and many remarkable sects. The blank face of a Cockney Sunday masks a kind of activity, intermittent but intense. All sorts of queer little religions squeak, like mice in the wainscoting, behind its tedious façade.

Perhaps these devotional side-shows satisfy in some measure the need for colour, self-expression and excitement in the otherwise drab lives of their devotees. They may supply a mild substitute for the orgies of a more robust age. No other explanation quite accounts for the extraordinary assortment of persons that may be found in their congregations.

Why, for instance, should old Miss Wade beat her way down the King's Road against a vicious lash of rain and in the teeth of a gale that set the shop signs creaking and threatened to drive her umbrella back into her face? She would have been better off in her bed-sitting-room with a gas-fire and her library book.

Why had Mr Samuel J. Ogden dressed himself in uncomfortable clothes and left his apartment in York Square for the smelly discomfort of a taxi and the prospect of two hours without a cigar?

What induced Cara Quayne to exchange the amenities of her little house in Shepherd Market for a dismal perspective of wet pavements and a deserted Piccadilly?

What more insistent pleasure drew M. de Ravigne away from his Van Goghs, and the satisfying austerity of his flat in Lowndes Square?

If this question had been put to these persons, each of them, in his or her fashion, would have answered untruthfully. All of them would have suggested that they went to the House of the Sacred Flame because it was the right thing to do. M. de Ravigne would not have replied that he went because he was madly in love with Cara Quayne; Cara Quayne would not have admitted that she found in the services an outlet for an intolerable urge towards exhibitionism. Miss Wade would have died rather than confess that she worshipped, not God, but the Reverend Jasper Garnette. As for Mr Ogden, he would have broken out immediately into a long discourse in which the words 'uplift,' 'renooal,' and 'spiritual regeneration' would have sounded again and again, for Mr Ogden was so like an American as to be quite fabulous.

Cara Quayne's car, Mr Ogden's taxi, and Miss Wade's goloshes all turned into Knocklatchers Row at about the same time.

Knocklatchers Row is a cul-de-sac leading off Chester Terrace and not far from Graham Street. Like Graham Street it is distinguished by its church. In December of last year the House of the Sacred Flame was obscure. Only members of the congregation and a few of their friends knew of its existence. Chief Detective-Inspector Alleyn had never heard of it. Nigel Bathgate, looking disconsolately out of his window in Chester Terrace, noticed its sign for the first time. It was a small hanging sign made of red glass and shaped to represent a flame rising from a cup. Its facets caught the light as a gust of wind blew the sign back. Nigel saw the red gleam and at the same time noticed Miss Wade hurry into the doorway. Then Miss Quayne's car and Mr Ogden's taxi drew up and the occupants got out. Three more figures with bent heads and shining mackintoshes turned into Knocklatchers Row. Nigel was bored. He had the exasperated curiosity of a journalist. On a sudden impulse he seized his hat and umbrella, ran downstairs and out into the rain. At that moment Detective-Inspector Alleyn in his flat in St James's looked up from his book and remarked to his servant: 'It's blowing a gale out there. I shall be staying in tonight.'

CHAPTER 2

The House of the Sacred Flame

In Chester Terrace the wind caught Nigel broadside-on, causing him to prance and curvet like a charger. The rain pelted down on his umbrella and the street lamps shone on the wet pavement. He felt adventurous and pleased that he had followed his impulse to go abroad on such a night. Knocklatchers Row seemed an exciting street. Its name sounded like a password to romance. Who knows, he thought hopefully, into what strange meeting-place I may venture? It should be exotic and warm and there should be incense and curious rites. With these pleasant anticipations he crossed Chester Street and, lowering his umbrella to meet the veering wind, made for the House of the Sacred Flame.

Two or three other figures preceded him, but by the time he reached the swinging sign they had all disappeared into a side entry. As he drew nearer Nigel was aware of a bell ringing, not clearly, insistently, like the bell of St Mary's, Graham Street, but with a smothered and inward sound as though it was deep inside a building. He turned left under the sign into shelter, and at that moment the bell stopped ringing. He found himself in a long covered passage, lit at the far end by a single lamp, or rather by a single light, for as he approached he saw that a naked flame rose from a bronze torch held in an iron sconce. Doubtless in deference to some by-law this unusual contrivance was encased in a sort of cage. Beyond the torch he saw double doors. A man came through, closed the doors, locked them, and seated himself on a stool under the torch. Nigel furled his umbrella and approached this doorkeeper. He was a thinnish young man, pale and spectacled, with an air of gentility.

'I'm afraid you are too late,' he said.

'Too late?' Nigel felt ridiculously exasperated and disappointed.

'Yes. The bell has stopped. I have just locked the doors.'

'But only this second. I saw you do it as I lowered my umbrella. Couldn't you open them again?'

'The bell has stopped.'

'I can hear that very well. That, too, has only just occurred. Could not you let me in?'

'I see you do not know our rules,' said the young man, and pointed to a framed notice which hung beside the doors. Nigel turned peevishly and read the sentence indicated by the young man: 'The bell ceases ringing as the Priest enters the temple. The doors are then locked and will not be reopened until the ceremony is ended.'

'There, you see,' said the young man complacently.

'Yes, I see. But if you will allow me to say so, I consider that you make a mistake in so stringently enforcing this rule. As you have noticed I am a new-comer. Something prompted me to come – an impulse. Who knows but what I might have proved an enthusiastic convert to whatever doctrine is taught behind your locked doors?'

'There is a Neophytes' Class at six-fifteen on Wednesdays.'

'I shall not attend it,' cried Nigel in a rage.

'That is as you please.'

Nigel perceived very clearly that he had made a fool of himself. He could not understand why he felt so disproportionately put out at being refused entrance to a ceremony of which he knew nothing and, he told himself, cared less. However he was already a little ashamed of his churlish behaviour and with the idea of appeasing the doorkeeper he turned once again to the notice.

At the top was a neat red torch set in a circle of other symbols, with most of which he was unfamiliar. Outside these again were the signs of the Zodiac. With a returning sense of chagrin he reflected that this was precisely the sort of thing his mood had demanded. Undoubtedly the service would be strange and full of an exotic mumbo-jumbo. He might even have got a story from it. A muffled sound of chanting beyond the doors increased his vexation. However he read on:

In the Light of the Sacred Flame all mysteries are but different facets of the One Mystery, all Gods but different aspects of one Godhead. Time is but an aspect of Eternity, and the doorway to Eternity is Spiritual Ecstasy.

JASPER GARNETTE

'Tell me,' said Nigel, turning to the doorkeeper, 'who is Jasper Garnette?'

'Our Founder,' answered the young man stiffly, 'and our Priest.'

'You mean that not only does he write about eternity but he actually provides the doorway which he mentions in this notice?'

'You may say,' said the young man with a glint of genuine fervour in his eye, 'that this *is* The Doorway.'

'And are you fated to stay for ever on the threshold, shutting out yourself and all later arrivals?' inquired Nigel, who was beginning to enjoy himself.

'We take it in turns.'

'I see. I can hear a voice raised in something that sounds like a lament. Is that the voice of Mr Jasper Garnette?'

'Yes. It is not a lament. It is an Invocation.'

'What is he invoking?'

'You really should attend the Neophytes' Class at six-fifteen on Wednesdays. It is against our Rule for me to gossip while I am On Guard,' pronounced the doorkeeper, who seemed to speak in capitals.

'I should hardly call this gossip,' Nigel objected. Suddenly he jumped violently. A loud knock had sounded on the inside of the door. It was twice repeated.

'Please get out of the way,' cried the young man. He removed the wire guard in front of the torch. Then he took a key from his pocket and with this he opened the double doors.

Nigel drew to one side hurriedly. There was a small recess by the doors. He backed into it.

Over the threshold came two youths dressed in long vermilion robes and short overgarments of embroidered purple. They had long fuzzy hair brushed straight back. One of them was red-headed with a pointed nose and prominent teeth. The other was dark with languorous eyes and full lips. They carried censers and advanced one to each side of the torch making obeisances. They were followed by an extremely tall man clad in embroidered white robes of a Druidical cut and flavour. He was of a remarkable appearance, having a great mane of silver hair, large sunken eyes and black brows. The bone of his face was much emphasized, the flesh heavily grooved. His mouth was abnormally wide with a heavy underlip. It might have been the head of an actor, a saint, or a Middle-West American purveyor of patent medicines. Nigel had ample opportunity to observe him, for he stood in front of the torch with his short hands folded over an unlighted taper. He whispered and muttered for some time, genuflected thrice, and then advanced his taper to the flame. When it was lit he held it aloft. The doorkeeper and the two acolytes went down on their knees, the priest closed his eyes, and Nigel walked into the hall.

He found himself in a darkness that at first seemed to be absolute. In a few seconds, however, he could make out certain large shapes and masses. In the distance, perhaps on an altar, a tiny red light shone. His feet sank into a thick carpet and made no sound. He smelt incense. He felt the presence of a large number of people all close to him, all quite silent. A little reflected light came in through the doors. Nigel moved cautiously away from it towards his right and, since he met with no obstruction, thought that he must be in a cross-aisle. His eyes became accustomed to the darkness, he saw veils of moving smoke, lighter shapes that suggested vast nudities, then rows of bent heads with blurred outlines. He discovered that he was moving across the back of the church behind the last row of pews. There seemed to be an empty seat in the far corner. He made for this and had slid into it when a flicker of light, the merest paling of gloom, announced the return of the priest – surely Jasper Garnette himself – with his taper. He appeared in the centre aisle, his face and the rich embroidery of his robe lit from beneath by the taper. The face seemed to float slowly up the church until it changed into the back of a head with a yellow nimbus. The taper was held aloft. Then, with a formidable plop, an enormous flame sprang up out of the dark. The congregation burst into an alarming uproar. An organ uttered two or three of those nerve-racking groans that are characteristic of this instrument and red lamps came to life at intervals along the walls.

For several minutes the noise was intolerable, but gradually it revealed itself as a sort of a chant. Next to Nigel was a large lady with a shrill voice. He listened attentively but could make nothing of her utterances, which seemed to be in no known language.

'Ee-ai-ee-yah-ee,' chanted this lady.

Presently the organ and the congregation together unexpectedly roared out a recognisable Amen. Everyone slid back from their knees into their seats and there was silence.

Nigel looked about him.

The House of the Sacred Flame resembled, in plan, any Anglican or Roman church. Nave, transept, sanctuary and altar – all were there. On the left was a rostrum, on the right a reading-desk. With these few specious gestures, however, any appearance of orthodoxy ended. Indeed the hall looked like nothing so much as an ultra-modern art exhibition gone completely demented. From above the altar projected a long sconce holding the bronze torch from which the sanctuary flame rose in all its naptha-like theatricality. On the altar itself was a feathered serpent, a figure carved in wood with protruding tongue and eyes made of pawa shell, a Wagnerian sort of god, a miniature totem-pole and various other bits of heathen bric-a-brac, as ill-assorted as a bunch of plenipotentiaries at Geneva. The signs of the Zodiac decorated the walls, and along the aisles were stationed at intervals some remarkable examples of modern sculpture. The treatment was abstract, but from the slithering curves and tortured angles emerged the forms of animals and birds – a lion, a bull, a serpent, a cat and a phoenix. Cheek by jowl with these, in gloomy astonishment, were ranged a number of figures whom Nigel supposed must represent the more robust gods and goddesses of Nordic legend. The gods wore helmets and beards, the goddesses helmets and boots. They all looked as though they had been begun by Epstein and finished by a frantic bricklayer. In the nearest of these figures Nigel fancied he recognized Odin. The god was draped in an angular cloak from the folds of which glared two disconsolate quadrupeds who might conceivably represent Geri and Freki, while from behind a pair of legs suggestive of an advanced condition of elephantiasis peered a brace of disconsolate fowls, possibly Huginn and Muninn. Incense burned all over the place. Everything was very expensive and lavish.

Having seen this much, Nigel's attention was arrested by a solitary voice of great beauty. The Rev. Jasper Garnette had mounted the pulpit.

Afterwards, when he tried to describe this part of the service to Chief Detective-Inspector Alleyn, Nigel found himself quite unable to give even the most general resumé of the sermon. Yet at the time he was much impressed. It seemed to him that these were the utterances of an intellectual. He had an extraordinary sense of rightness as though, in a series of intoxicating flashes, all mental and spiritual problems were reduced to a lovely simplicity. Everything seemed to fit with exquisite precision. He had a vivid impression of being personally put right. At first it appeared that the eyes of the preacher were on him alone. They looked into each other's eyes, he thought, and he was conscious of making a complete surrender. Later the preacher told him to look at the torch and he did so. It wavered and swelled with the voice. He no longer felt the weight of his body on the seat. Nigel, in short, had his first experience of partial hypnotism and was well under way when the large lady gave utterance to a stentorian sneeze and an apologetic gasp: 'Oh, dear me!'

That, he told Alleyn, tore it. Back to earth he came just as Father Garnette spoke his final period, and that was the one utterance Nigel did retain:

'Now the door is open, now burns the flame of ecstasy. Come with me into the Oneness of the Spirit. You are floating away from your bodies. You are entering into a new life. There is no evil. Let go your hold on the earth. Ecstasy – it is yours. Come, drink of the flaming cup!'

From all round the hall came a murmur. It swelled and was broken by isolated cries. The large lady was whimpering, further along a man's voice cried out incoherently. The priest had gone to the altar and from a monstrance he drew out a silver flagon and a jewelled cup. He handed the flagon to the dark acolyte and passed his hand across the cup. A flame shot up from within, burned blue and went out. In the front rank a woman leapt to her feet. The rest of the congregation knelt. The woman ran up the chancel steps and with a shrill 'Heil!' fell prostrate under the torch. The priest stood over her, the cup held above his head. She was followed by some half-a-dozen others who ranged themselves in a circle about her, knelt and raised their hands towards the cup. They, too, cried out incoherently. There was something indecent about these performances and Nigel, suddenly sane, felt ashamed and most uncomfortable. Now the priest gave the cup to one of the kneeling circle, a large florid woman. She, with the exclamation of 'Y'mir,' pronounced with shrill emphasis, took the silver flagon from the attendant acolyte, poured something into the cup and passed it to her neighbour. He was a dark and well-groomed man who repeated the ritual uttering a different word. So the cup went round the circle. Each Initiate took it from his neighbour, was handed the flagon by the acolyte, poured wine from the flagon into the cup, passed the cup to the next Initiate, and returned the flagon to the acolyte. Each uttered a single word. Nigel thought he detected the names of 'Thor,' of 'Ar'riman' and 'Vidur' among others so outlandish as to be incomprehensible. The circle completed, the priest again received the cup. The prostrate woman sprang to her feet. Her arms twitched and she mouthed and gibbered like an idiot, turning her head from side to side. It was a nauseating, a detestable performance, doubly so since she was a beautiful creature; tall, not old, but white-haired. She was well and fashionably dressed, but her clothes were disarranged by her antics, her hat had slipped grotesquely sideways and one of her sleeves was twisted and dragged upwards. She began to speak, a long stream of incoherences in which were jumbled the names of antique gods with those of present-day beliefs. 'I am one and I am all.' The kneeling circle kept up an obbligato of 'Heils' in which, at the last, she joined, clapping her hands together and rocking to and fro.

Suddenly, perhaps at some signal from the priest, they were all silent. The woman stretched both her hands out and the priest gave her the cup.

'The wine of ecstasy give you joy in your body and soul!'

'Tur-aie!'

'The holy madness of the flame possess you!'

'Heil! Tur-aie! Tur-aie!'

She raised the cup to her lips. Her head tipped back and back until the last drop must have been drained. Suddenly she gasped violently. She slewed half round as if to question the priest. Her hands shot outwards as though she offered him the cup. Then they parted inconsequently. The cup flashed as it dropped to the floor. Her face twisted into an appalling grimace. Her body twitched violently. She pitched forward like an enormous doll, jerked twice and then was still.

CHAPTER 3

Death of an Ecstatic Spinster

At first Nigel, though greatly startled, imagined that this performance was merely the climax of the ceremony. He found the whole
business extremely unpleasant but was nevertheless interested.
Perhaps a minute passed before he realized that the woman's collapse
was not anticipated by the congregation or by Father Garnette himself. A young man in the group of Initiates gave the first indication.
He rose from his knees and stood looking from the woman to the
priest. He spoke, but so quietly that Nigel could not hear what he
said. The rest of the circle remained kneeling, but rather as though
they had forgotten to rise or were stricken into immobility. The
ecstatic fervour of the ceremony had quite vanished and something
infinitely more disquieting had taken its place. The priest spoke.
Perhaps because he had heard the words so often that evening, Nigel
heard them then.

'Spiritual ecstasy . . .' He pronounced this word 'ecstasah.'
'Manifestation . . .'

The Initiate hesitated and looked fixedly at the prostrate figure.

'My friends,' said the priest loudly, with an air of decision. 'My
friends, our beloved sister has been vouchsafed the greatest boon of
all. She is in ecstasy. Let us leave her to her tremendous experience.
Let us sing our hymn to Pan, the God-in-all.'

He stopped. The organ uttered a tentative growl. The congregation, murmuring and uneasy, got to its feet.

'Let us sing,' repeated Jasper Garnette with determination, 'the
hymn – '

16

A scream rang out. The dowdy woman had broken away from the circle and stood with her head thrust forward and her mouth wide open.

'It's not. It's not. She's dead. I touched her. She's dead!'

'Miss Wade, quiet!'

'I won't be quiet! She's dead.'

'Wait a moment,' said a placid voice near Nigel. An elderly solid-looking man was working his way out of the row of pews. He pushed himself carefully past the large lady. Nigel moved out to make way for him and then, on a journalistic impulse, followed him up the aisle.

'I think I had better have a look at this lady,' said the man placidly.

'But, Dr Kasbek – '

'I think I had better have a look at her, Father Garnette.'

Nigel unobserved, came up with the group under the torch. He had the sensation of walking on to a stage and joining in the action of a play. They appeared a strange enough crew, white-faced and cadaverous looking in the uneven glare of the single flame. This made a kind of labial bubbling. It was the only sound. The doctor knelt by the prostrate figure.

She had fallen half on her face, and head downwards across the chancel steps. The doctor touched her wrist and then, with a brusque movement, pulled away the cap that hid her face. The eyes, wide open and protuberant, stared straight up at him. At the corners of the mouth were traces of a rimy spume. The mouth itself was set, with the teeth clenched and the lips drawn back, in a rigid circle. The cheeks were cherry-red, but the rest of the face was livid. She may have been in a state of ecstasy but she was undoubtedly dead.

On seeing this dreadful face, the Initiates who had gathered round drew back quickly, some with exclamations, some silently. The elderly drab lady, Miss Wade, uttered a stifled yelp in which there was both terror and, oddly enough, a kind of triumph.

'Dead! I told you she was dead! Oh! Father Garnette!'

'Cover it up for God's sake,' said the tall young man.

The doctor knelt down. He sniffed twice at the rigid lips and then opened the front of the dress. Nigel could see his hand pressed firm-ly against the white skin. He held it there for some time, seconds that seemed like minutes. Still bent down, he seemed to be scrutinising the woman's face. He pulled the hat forward again.

'This is turrible, turrible. This certainly is turrible,' murmured the commercial-looking gentleman, and revealed himself an American.

'You'd better get rid of your congregation,' said the doctor abruptly. He spoke directly to the priest.

Father Garnette had said nothing. He had not moved. He still looked a striking enough figure, but the virtue had gone out of him. He did not answer.

'Will you tell them to go?' asked Dr Kasbek.

'Wait a moment.'

Nigel heard his own voice with a sensation of panic. They all turned to him, not in surprise, but with an air of bewilderment. He was conscious of a background of suppressed murmurs in the hall. He felt as though his vocal apparatus had decided to function independently.

'Has this lady died naturally?' he asked the doctor.

'As you see, I have only glanced at her.'

'Is there any doubt?'

'What do you mean?' demanded the priest suddenly, and then: 'Who are you?'

'I was in the congregation. I am sorry to interfere, but if there is any suspicion of unnatural death I believe no one should – '

'Unnatural death? Say, where d'you get that idea?' said the American.

'It's the mouth and eyes, and – and the smell. I may be wrong.' Nigel still looked at the doctor. 'But if there's a doubt I don't think anybody should leave.'

The doctor returned his look calmly.

'I think you are right,' he said at last.

They had none of them raised their voices, but something of what they said must have communicated itself to the congregation. A number of people had moved out into the centre aisle. The murmur had swelled. Several voices rang out loudly and suddenly a woman screamed. There was a movement, confused and indeterminate, towards the chancel.

'Tell them to sit down,' said the Doctor.

The priest seemed to pull himself together. He turned and walked quickly up the steps into the pulpit. Nigel felt that he was making a deliberate effort to collect and control the congregation and to bend the full weight of his personality upon it.

'My friends' – the magnificent voice rang out firmly – 'Will you all return to your seats and remain quiet? I believe, I firmly believe that the great rushing powers of endless space have chosen this moment to manifest themselves. Their choice has fallen upon our beloved sister in ecstasy, Cara Quayne.' The voice wavered a little, then dropped a tone. 'We must strengthen our souls with the power of the Word. I call upon you to meditate upon the word "Unity." Let there be silence among you.'

He was at once obeyed. A stillness fell upon the hall. The rustle of his vestments sounded loudly as he came down the steps from the pulpit. To Nigel he seemed a fabulous, a monstrous creature.

He turned to the two acolytes, who stood, the one mechanically swinging his censer, the other holding the jug of wine.

'Draw the chancel curtains,' whispered Father Garnette.

'Yes, Father,' lisped the red-headed acolyte.

'Yes, Father,' minced the dark acolyte.

A rattle of brass, the sweep of heavy fabric, and they were swiftly shut away from the congregation by a wall of thick brocade. The chancel became a room, torch-lit and rather horribly cosy.

'If we speak low,' said Father Garnette, 'they cannot hear. The curtains are interlined and very thick.'

'For Gard's sake!' said the American. 'This is surely a turrible affair. Doctor, are you quite certain she's gone?'

'Quite,' answered the doctor, who had again knelt down by the body.

'Yes, but there's more in it than that,' began the young man. 'What's this about no one leaving? What does it mean?' He swung round to Nigel. 'Why do you talk about unnatural death, and who the hell are you?'

'Maurice,' said Father Garnette. 'Maurice, my dear fellow!'

'This woman,' the boy went on doggedly, 'has no business here. She had no right to the Cup. She was evil. I know you – Father Garnette, I *know*.'

'Maurice, be quiet.'

'Can it, Pringle,' said the American.

'I tell you I *know* – ' The boy broke off and stared at the priest with a sort of frantic devotion. Father Garnette looked fixedly at him. If there was some sort of conflict between them the priest won, for the boy suddenly turned aside and walked away from them.

'What is it?' Nigel asked the doctor. 'Is it poison?'

'It looks like it, certainly. Death was instantaneous. We must inform the police.'

'Is there a telephone anywhere near?'

'I believe there's one in Father Garnette's rooms.'

'His rooms?'

'Behind the altar,' said the doctor.

'Then – may I use it?'

'Is that absolutely necessary?' asked the priest.

'Absolutely,' said Dr Kasbek. He looked at Nigel. 'Will you do it?'

'I will if you like. I know a man at the Yard.'

'Do. What about the nearest relative? Anybody know who it is?'

'She lives alone,' said a girl who had not spoken before. 'She told me once that she had no relations in England.'

'I see,' said Dr Kasbek. 'Well, then, perhaps you' – he looked at Nigel – 'will get straight through to the police. Father Garnette, will you show this young man the way?'

'I had better return to my people, I think,' replied Father Garnette. 'They will need me. Claude, show the way to the telephone.'

'Yes, Father.'

In a kind of trance Nigel followed the dark acolyte up the sanctuary steps to the altar. The willowy Claude drew aside a brocaded curtain to the left of the altar and revealed a door which he opened and went through, casting a melting glance upon Nigel as he did so.

'Nasty little bit of work,' thought Nigel, and followed him.

Evidently Father Garnette lived behind the altar. They had entered a small flat. The room directly behind was furnished as a sort of mythological study. This much he took in as Claude glided across the room and snatched up something that looked like a sacramental tea-cosy. A telephone stood revealed.

'Thank you,' said Nigel, and hoped Claude would go away. He remained, gazing trustfully at Nigel.

Sunday evening. Unless he had an important case on hand, Alleyn ought to be at home. Nigel dialled the number and waited, conscious of his own heart-beat and of his dry mouth.

'Hullo!'

'Hullo – May I speak to Chief Detective-Inspector Alleyn? Oh, it's you. You are in, then. It's Nigel Bathgate here.'

'Good evening, Bathgate. What's the matter?'

'I'm ringing from a hall, the – the House of the Sacred Flame in Knocklatchers Row off Chester Terrace, just opposite my flat.'

'I know Knocklatchers Row. It's in my division.'

'A woman died here ten minutes ago. I think you'd better come.'

'Are you alone?'

'No.'

'You wretched young man, what's the matter with you? Is the lady murdered?'

'How should I know?'

'Why the devil didn't you ring the Yard? I suppose I'd better do it.'

'I think you ought to come. I'm holding the congregation. At least,' added Nigel confusedly, 'they are.'

'You are quite unintelligible. I'll be there in ten minutes.'

'Thank you.'

Nigel hung up the receiver.

'Fancy you knowing Alleyn of Scotland Yard,' fluted Claude. 'How perfectly marvellous! You are lucky.'

'I think we had better go back,' said Nigel.

'I'd much rather stay here. I'm afraid. Did you ever see anything so perfectly dreadful as Miss Quayne's face? Please do tell me – do you think it's suicide?'

'I don't know. Are you coming?'

'Very well. You seem to be a terrifically resolute sort of person. I'll turn the light out. Isn't Father Garnette marvellous? You're new, aren't you?'

Nigel dived out of the door.

He found the Initiates grouped round the American gentleman, who seemed to be addressing them in a whisper. He was a type that is featured heavily in transatlantic publicity, tall, rather fat and inclined to be flabby, but almost incredibly clean, as though he used all the deodorants, mouth washes, soaps and lotions recommended by his prototype who beams pep from the colour pages of American periodicals. The only irregularities in Mr Ogden were his eyes, which were skewbald – one light blue and one brown. This gave him a comic look and made one suspect him of clowning when he was most serious.

To Nigel's astonishment the organ was playing and from beyond the curtains came a muffled sound of singing. Father Garnette's voice was clearly distinguishable. Someone, the doctor perhaps, had covered the body with a piece of gorgeously embroidered satin.

When he saw Nigel the American gentleman stepped forward.

'It appears to me we ought to get acquainted,' he said pleasantly. 'You kind of sprang up out of no place and took over the works. That's OK by me, and I'll hand it to you. I certainly appreciate prompt action. My name's Samuel J. Ogden. I guess I've got a card somewhere.' The amazing Mr Ogden actually thrust his hand into his breast pocket.

'Please don't bother,' said Nigel. 'My name is Bathgate.'

'Pleased to meet you, Mr Bathgate,' said Mr Ogden, instantly shaking hands. 'Allow me to introduce these ladies and gentlemen. Mrs Candour, meet Mr Bathgate. Miss Wade, meet Mr Bathgate. Mr Bathgate, Miss Janey Jenkins. Monsieur de Ravigne, Mr Bathgate. Dr Kasbek, Mr Bathgate. Mr Maurice Pringle, Mr Bathgate. And these two young gentlemen are our acolytes. Mr Claude Wheatley and Mr Lionel Smith, meet Mr Bathgate.'

The seven inarticulate Britishers exchanged helpless glances with Nigel. M de Ravigne, a sleek Frenchman, gave him a scornful bow.

'Well now – ' began Mr Ogden with a comfortable smile.

'I think, if you don't mind,' said Nigel hurriedly, 'that someone should go down to the front door. Inspector Alleyn is on his way here, and as things are at the moment he won't be able to get in.'

'That's so,' agreed Mr Ogden. 'Maybe one of these boys – '

'Oh, do let me go,' begged Claude.

'Fine,' said Mr Ogden.

'I'll come with you, Claude,' said the red-headed acolyte.

'There's no need for two, honestly, is there Mr Ogden?'

'Oh, get to it, Fauntleroy, and take little Eric along!' said Mr Ogden brutally. Nigel suddenly felt that he liked Mr Ogden.

The acolytes, flouncing, disappeared through the curtain. The sound of organ and voices was momentarily louder.

'Do acolytes have to be that way?' inquired Mr Ogden of nobody in particular.

Somebody laughed attractively. It was Miss Janey Jenkins. She was young and short and looked intelligent.

'I'm sorry,' she said immediately. 'I didn't mean to laugh, only Claude and Lionel are rather awful, aren't they?'

'I agree,' said Nigel quickly.

She turned, not to him, but to Maurice Pringle, the young man who had spoken so strangely to the priest. He now stood apart from the others and looked acutely miserable. Miss Jenkins went and spoke to him, but in so low a voice that Nigel could not hear what she said.

'Dr Kasbek,' said the little spinster whom Mr Ogden had called Miss Wade, 'Dr Kasbek, I am afraid I am very foolish, but I do not understand. Has Cara Quayne been murdered?'

This suggestion, voiced for the first time, was received as though it was a gross indecency. Mrs Candour a peony of a woman, with ugly hands, uttered a scandalized yelp; M de Ravigne hissed like a steam-boiler; Mr Ogden said: 'Wait a minute, *wait* a minute'; Pringle seemed to shrink into himself, and Janey Jenkins took his hand.

'Surely not, Miss Wade,' said Dr Kasbek. 'Let us not anticipate such a thing.'

'I only inquired,' said Miss Wade. 'She wasn't very happy, poor thing, and she wasn't very popular.'

'Miss Wade – please!' M de Ravigne looked angrily at the little figure. 'I must protest – this is a – a preposterous suggestion. It is ridiculous.' He gesticulated eloquently. 'Is it not enough that this tragedy should have arrived? My poor Cara, is it not enough!'

The voice of Father Garnette could be heard, muffled but sonorous, beyond the curtains.

'Listen to him!' said Pringle. 'Listen! He's keeping them quiet. He's kept us all quiet. What are we to believe of him?'

'What are you talking about?' whispered Mrs Candour savagely.

'You know well enough. You'd have taken her place if you could. It's not his fault – it's yours. It's all so – so beastly – '

'Maurice,' said Miss Jenkins softly.

'Be quiet, Janey. I will say it. Whatever it is, it's retribution. The whole thing's a farce. I can't stand it any longer. I'm going to tell them – '

He broke away from her and ran towards the curtains. Before he reached them they parted and a tall man came through.

'Oh, there you are, Bathgate,' said Chief Detective-Inspector Alleyn. 'What's the trouble?'

CHAPTER 4

The Yard

The entrance of Chief Detective-Inspector Alleyn had a curious effect upon the scene and upon the actors. It was an effect which might be likened to that achieved by the cinema when the camera is shifted and the whole scene presented from a different viewpoint. Nigel had felt himself to be involved in a nightmare, but it now seemed to be someone else's nightmare of which he was merely the narrator. He wondered wildly whether he should follow Mr Ogden's example and embark on an elaborate series of introductions. However, he avoided this complication and in as few words as possible told Alleyn what had happened. The others remained silent, eyeing the inspector. Janey Jenkins held Pringle's hand between her two hands; Miss Wade kept a handkerchief pressed against her lips; M.de Ravigne stood scornfully apart; Mrs Candour had collapsed into a grand-opera throne on the left of the altar; Mr Ogden looked capable and perturbed and the two acolytes gazed rapturously at the inspector. Alleyn listened with his curious air of detachment that always reminded Nigel of a polite faun. When Nigel came to the ecstatic frenzy, Alleyn made a slantwise grimace. Speaking so quietly that the others could not overhear him, Nigel repeated as closely as he could remember them the exclamations made by Pringle, Miss Wade and de Ravigne. Alleyn asked for the names of persons who should be informed. Beyond Miss Quayne's servants there seemed to be nobody. Miss Jenkins, appealed to, said she had overheard Miss Quayne saying that her staff were all out on Sunday evening. She volunteered to ring up and find out and retired to Father Garnette's room to do so. She returned to say there was no answer. Alleyn took the number and said he would see the house was informed later. As soon as he had learnt the facts of the case, Alleyn lifted the satin drapery and looked at the distorted face beneath it, spoke a few words aside to Dr Kasbek, and then addressed them all quietly. At this moment Father Garnette, having set his congregation going on another hymn, returned to the group. Nigel alone noticed him. He stood just inside the curtains and never took his eyes off the inspector.

Alleyn said: 'There is, I think, no reason why you should not know what has happened here. This woman has probably died of poisoning. Until we know more of the circumstances and the nature of her death I shall have to take over the case on behalf of the police. From what I have heard I believe that there is nothing to be gained in keeping the rest of the congregation here.' He turned slightly and saw the priest.

'You are Mr Garnette? Will you be good enough to ask your congregation to go home – when they have quite finished singing, of course. I have stationed a constable inside the door. He will take their names. Just tell them that, will you?'

'Certainly,' said Father Garnette and disappeared through the curtains.

They heard him pronounce a benediction of sorts. Beyond the curtains there was a sort of stirring and movement. One or two people coughed. It all died away at last. A door slammed with a desolate air of finality and there was complete silence in the building, save for the slobbering of the torch. Father Garnette returned.

'Phew!' said Alleyn. 'Let's have the curtains drawn back, may we?'

Father Garnette inclined his head. Claude and Lionel flew to the sides of the chancel and in a moment the curtains rattled apart, revealing the solitary figure of the doorkeeper, agape on the lowest step.

'Is there anything I can do, Father?' asked the doorkeeper.

'Lock the front door and go home,' said Father Garnette.

'Yes, Father,' whispered the doorkeeper. He departed hurriedly pulling the double doors to with an apologetic slam. For a moment there was silence. Then Alleyn turned to Nigel.

'Is there a telephone handy?'

'Yes.'

'Get through to the Yard, will you, Bathgate, and tell them what has happened. Fox is on duty. Ask them to send him along with the usual support. We'll want the divisional surgeon and a wardress.'

Nigel went into the room behind the altar and delivered this message. When he returned he found Alleyn, with his notebook in his hand, taking down the names and addresses of the Initiates.

'It's got to be done, you see,' he explained. 'There will, of course, be an inquest and I'm afraid you will all be called as witnesses.'

'Oh, God,' said Pringle with a snort of disgust.

'I'd better start with the deceased,' Alleyn suggested. 'What is her name, please?'

'She was a Miss Cara Quayne, Inspector,' said Mr Ogden. 'She owned a very, very distinctive residence in Shepherd Market, No.101. I have had the honour of dining at the Quayne home, and believe me it surely was an aesthetic experience. She was a very lovely-natured woman with a great appreciation of the beautiful – '

'No. 101 Shepherd Market,' said Alleyn. 'Thank you.' He wrote it down and then glanced round his audience.

'I will take yours first if I may, Doctor Kasbek.'

'Certainly. Nicholas Kasbek, 189a Wigmore Street.'

'Right.' He turned to Miss Wade.

'My name is Ernestine Wade,' she said very clearly and in a high voice, as though Alleyn was deaf. 'I live at Primrose Court, King's Road, Chelsea. Spinster.'

'Thank you.'

Miss Jenkins came forward.

'I'm Janey Jenkins. I live in a studio flat in Yeomans Row, No.99d. I'm a spinster too, if you want to know.'

'Well,' said Alleyn, 'just for "Miss" or "Mrs," you know.'

'Now you, Maurice,' said Miss Jenkins.

'Pringle,' said that gentleman as though the name was an offence. 'Maurice. I'm staying at 11 Harrow Mansions, Sloane Square.'

'Is that your permanent address?'

'No. Haven't got one unless you count my people's place. I never go there if I can help it.'

'The Phoenix Club will always find you, won't it?' murmured Miss Jenkins.

'Oh, God, yes,' replied Mr Pringle distastefully.

'Next please,' said Alleyn cheerfully. Mrs Candour spoke suddenly from the ecclesiastical throne. She had the air of uttering an appalling indecency.

'My name is Dagmar Candour. Mrs. Queen Charlotte Flats, Kensington Square. No.12.'

'C.a.n. – ?' queried Alleyn.

'd.o.u.r.'

'Thank you.'

Mr Ogden, who had several times taken a step forward and as often politely retreated, now spoke up firmly.

'Samuel J. Ogden, Chief. I guess you're not interested in my home address. I come from the States – New York. In London I have a permanent apartment in York Square. No.93, Achurch Court. I just can't locate my card-case, but – well, those are the works.'

'Thank you so much, Mr Ogden. And now you, if you please, sir.'

Father Garnette hesitated a moment, oddly. Then he cleared his throat and answered in his usual richly inflected voice:

'Father Jasper Garnette.' He spelt it. 'I am officiating priest of this temple. I live here.'

'Here?'

'I have a little dwelling beyond the altar.'

'Extremely convenient,' murmured Alleyn. 'And now, these two' – he looked a little doubtfully at Claude and Lionel – 'these two young men.'

Claude and Lionel answered together in a rapturous gush.

'What?' asked Alleyn.

'Do be quiet, Lionel,' said Claude. 'We share a flat in Ebury Street; "Ebury Mews." Well, it isn't actually a flat, is it, Lionel? Oh dear, I always forget the number – it's too stupid of me.'

'You *are* hopeless, Claude,' said Lionel. 'It's 17 Ebury Mews, Ebury Street, Inspector Alleyn, only we aren't very often there because I'm in the show at the Palladium and Claude is at Madame Karen's in Sloane Street and – '

'I do not yet know your names.'

'Lionel, you are perfectly maddening,' said Claude. 'I'm Claude Wheatley, Inspector Alleyn, and this is Lionel Smith.'

Alleyn wrote these names down with the address, and added in brackets: 'Gemini, possibly heavenly.'

M. de Ravigne came forward and bowed.

'Raoul Honoré Christophe Jérôme de Ravigne, monsieur. I live at Branscombe Chambers, Lowndes Square. My card.'

'Thank you. M. de Ravigne. And now will you all please show me exactly how you were placed while the cup was passed round the circle. I understand the ceremony took place in the centre of this area.'

After a moment's silence the priest came forward.

'I stood here,' he said, 'with the chalice in my hands. Mr Ogden knelt on my right, and Mrs Candour on my left.'

'That is correct, sir,' agreed Ogden and moved into place. 'Miss Jenkins was on my right, I guess.'

'Yes,' said that lady, 'and Maurice on mine.'

Mrs Candour came forward reluctantly and stood on Garnette's left.

'M. de Ravigne was beside me,' she whispered.

'Certainly.' M. de Ravigne took up his position and Miss Wade slipped in beside him.

'I was here,' she said, 'between Mr de Ravigne and Mr Pringle.'

'That completes the circle,' said Alleyn. 'What were the movements of the acolytes.'

'Well you see,' began Claude eagerly, 'I came here – just here on Father Garnette's right hand. I was the Ganymede you see, so I had the jug of wine. As soon as Father Garnette gave Mrs Candour the cup, I gave her the wine. She holds the cup in her left hand and the wine in her right hand. She pours in a little wine and speaks the first god-name. You are Hagring, aren't you Mrs Candour?'

'I *was*,' sobbed Mrs Candour.

'Yes. And then I take the jug and hand it to the next person and – '

'And so on,' said Alleyn. Thank you.'

'And I was censing over here,' struck in Lionel with passionate determination. 'I was censing all the time.'

'Yes,' said Alleyn; 'and now, I'm afraid I'll have to keep you all a little longer. Perhaps, Mr Garnette, you will allow them to wait in your rooms. I am sure you would all like to get away from the scene of this tragedy. I think I hear my colleagues outside.'

There was a resounding knock on the front door.

'Oh, may I let them in?' asked Claude.

'Please do,' said Alleyn.

Claude hurried away down the aisle and opened the double doors. Seven men, three of them constables, came in, in single file, headed by a tall thick-set individual in plain clothes who removed his hat, glanced in mild surprise at the nude statues, and walked stolidly up the aisle.

'Hullo, Fox,' said Alleyn.

'Evening, sir,' said Inspector Fox.

'There's been some trouble here. One of you men go with these ladies and gentlemen into the room at the back there. Mr Garnette will show you the way. Will you, Mr Garnette? I'll keep you no longer than I can possibly help. Dr Kasbek, if you wouldn't mind waiting here – '

'Look here,' said Maurice Pringle suddenly, 'I'm damned if I can see why we should be herded about like a mob of sheep. What has happened? Is she murdered?'

'Very probably,' said Alleyn coolly. 'Nobody is going to herd you, Pringle. You are going to wait quietly and reasonably while we make the necessary investigations. Off you go.'

'But – '

'I knew,' cried Mrs Candour suddenly. 'I knew something dreadful would happen. M. de Ravigne, didn't I tell you?'

'If you please, madame!' said de Ravigne with great firmness.

'All that sort of thing should have been kept out,' said little Miss Wade. 'It should never – '

'I think we had better follow instructions,' interrupted Father Garnette loudly. 'Will you all follow me?'

They trooped away, escorted by the largest of the constables.

'Lumme!' ejaculated Alleyn when the altar door had shut. 'As you yourself would say, Fox, *"quelle galère."'*

'A rum crowd,' agreed Fox, 'and a very rum place too, seemingly. What's happened, sir?'

'A lady has just died of a dose of cyanide. There's the body. Your old friend Mr Bathgate will tell you about it.'

'Good evening, Mr Bathgate,' said Fox mildly. 'You've found something else in our line, have you?'

'It was at the climax of the ceremony,' began Nigel. 'A cup was passed round a circle of people, these people whom you have just seen. This woman stood in the middle. The others knelt. A silver jug holding the wine was handed in turn to each of them and each poured a little into the cup. Then the priest, Father Garnette, gave her the cup. She drank it and – and fell down. I think she died at once, didn't she?'

He turned to Dr Kasbek.

'Within twenty seconds I should say.' The doctor looked at the divisional surgeon.

'I would have tried artificial respiration, sent for ferrous sulphate and a stomach tube and all the rest of it but' – he grimaced – 'there wasn't a dog's chance. She was dead before I got to her.'

'I know,' said the divisional surgeon. He lifted the drapery and bent over the body.

'I noticed the characteristic odour at once,' added Kasbek, 'and so I think did Mr Bathgate.'

'Yes,' agreed Nigel, 'that's why I butted in.'

Alleyn knelt by the fallen cup and sniffed.

'Stinks of it,' he said. 'Bailey, you'll have to look at this for prints. Not much help if they all handled it. We'll have photographs first.'

The man with the camera had already begun to set up his paraphernalia. He took three flashlight shots, from different viewpoints, of the body and surrounding area. Alleyn opened the black bag, put on a pair of rubber gloves and took out a small bottle and a tiny funnel. He drained off one or two drops of wine from the cup. While he did this Nigel took the opportunity to relate as much of the conversation of the Initiates as he could remember. Alleyn listened, grunted, and muttered to himself as he restored the little bottle to his bag. Detective-Sergeant Bailey got to work with an insufflator and white chalk.

'Where's the original vessel that was handed round by one of these two hothouse flowers?' asked Alleyn. 'Is this it?' He pointed to a silver jug standing in a sort of velvet-lined niche on the right side of the chancel.

'That's it,' said Nigel. 'Claude must have kept his head and put it there when – after it happened.'

'Is Claude the black orchid or the red lily?'

'The black orchid.'

Alleyn sniffed at the silver jug and filled another bottle from it.

'Nothing there though, I fancy,' he murmured. 'Let me get a picture of the routine. Miss Quayne stood in the centre here and the others knelt round her. Mr Garnette – I really cannot bring myself to allude to the gentleman as "Father" – Mr Garnette produced the cup and the – what does one call it? Decanter is scarcely the word. The flagon, perhaps. He gave the flagon to Master Ganymede Claude, passed his hand over the cup and up jumped a flame. A drop of methylated spirits perhaps.'

'I suppose so,' said Kasbek, looking amused.

'Well. And then the cup was passed from hand to hand by the kneeling circle and each took the flagon from Claude and poured in a libation.'

'Each of them uttered a single word,' interrupted Nigel. 'I really have no idea what some of them were.'

'The name of a diety, I understand,' volunteered Kasbek. 'I am not a member of the cult, but I've been here before. They pronounce the names of six deities. "Hagring," "Haco," "Frigga," and so on. Garnette is Odin and the Chosen Vessel is always Frigga. The idea is that all the godheads are embodied in one godhead and that the essence of each is mingled in the cup. It's a kind of popular pantheism.'

'Oh, Lord!' said Alleyn. 'Now then. The cup went round the circle. When it got to the last man, what happened?'

'He handed it to the acolyte, who passed it on to the priest, who gave it to Miss Quayne.'

'Who drank it,'

'Yes,' said Dr Kasbek, 'who drank it, poor thing.'

They were silent for a moment.

'I said "when it got to the last man" – it *was* a man you said? Yes, I know we've been over this before, but I want to be positive.'

'I'm sure it was,' said Nigel. 'I remember that Mr Ogden knelt at the top of the circle, as it were, and I seem to remember him giving the cup to the acolyte.'

'I believe you're right,' agreed the doctor.

'That agrees with the positions they took up just now.'

'Was there any chance of Miss Quayne herself dropping anything into the cup?'

'I don't think so,' Nigel said slowly. 'It so happens that I remember distinctly she took it in both hands, holding it by the stem. I've got a very clear mental picture of her, standing there, lit by the torch. She had rings on both hands and I remember I noticed that they reflected the light in the same way as the jewels on the cup. I feel quite certain she held it like that until she drank.'

'I have no such recollection,' declared the doctor.

'Quite sure, Bathgate?'

'Yes, quite sure. I – I'd swear to it.'

'You may have to,' said Alleyn. 'Dr Kasbek, you say you are not one of the elect. Perhaps, in that case, you would not object to telling me a little more about this place. It is an extremely unusual sort of church.' He glanced round apologetically. 'All this intellectual sculpture. Who is the lowering gentleman with the battle-axe? He makes one feel quite shy.'

'I fancy he is Wotan, which is the same as Odin. Perhaps Thor. I really don't know. I imagine the general idea owes something to some cult in Germany, and is based partly on Scandinavian mythology, though as you see it does not limit itself to one, or even a dozen, doctrines. It's a veritable *olla podrida* with Garnette to stir the pot. The statues were commissioned by a very rich old lady in the congregation.'

'An old lady!' murmured Alleyn. 'Fancy!'

'It is rather overwhelming,' agreed Kasbek. 'Shall we move into the hall? I should like to sit down.'

'Certainly,' said Alleyn. 'Fox, will you make a sketch-plan of the chancel? I won't be more than two minutes and then we'll start on the others. Run a line of chalk round the body and get the bluebottle in there to ring for the mortuary-van. Come along with us, won't you, Bathgate?'

Nigel and Dr Kasbek followed the inspector down to the front row of chairs. These were sumptuously upholstered in red embossed velvet.

'Front stalls,' said Alleyn, sitting down.

'There are seven of them, as you see. They are for the six Initiates and the Chosen Vessel. These are selected from a sort of inner circle among the congregation, or so I understand.'

Dr Kasbek settled himself comfortably in his velvet pew. He was a solid shortish man of about fifty-five with dark hair worn *en brosse*, a rather fleshy and pale face, and small, intelligent eyes.

'It was founded by Garnette two years ago. I first heard of it from an old patient of mine who lives nearby. She was always raving about the ceremonies and begging me to go. I was called in to see her one Sunday evening just before the service began and she made me promise I'd attend it. I've been several times since. I am attracted by curious places and interested in – how shall I put it? – in the incalculable vagaries of human faith. Garnette's doctrine of drama-tized pantheism, if that's what it is, amused and intrigued me. So did the man himself. Where he got the money to buy the place – it was originally a nonconformist club-room, I think – and furnish it and keep it going, I've no idea. Probably it was done by subscription. Ogden is Grand Warden or something. He'll be able to tell you. It's all very expensive, as you see. Garnette is the only priest and literally the "onlie begetter," the whole show in fact. He undoubtedly practises hypnotism and that, too, interests me. The service you saw tonight, Mr Bathgate, is only held once a month and is their star turn. The Chosen Vessel – Miss Quayne on this occasion – has to do a month's preparation, which means, I think, intensive instruction and private meditation with Garnette.'

'Odin and Frigga,' said Alleyn. 'I begin to understand. Are you personally acquainted with any of the Initiates?'

'Ogden introduced himself to me some weeks ago and Garnette came and spoke to me the first evening I was here. On the look-out for new material, I suppose.'

'None of the others?'

'No. Ogden suggested I should "get acquainted," but' – he smiled – 'I enjoy being an onlooker and I evaded it. I'm afraid that's all I can tell you.'

'It's all extremely suggestive and most useful. Thank you very much, Dr Kasbek. I won't keep you any longer. Dr Curtis may want a word with you before you go. I'll send him down here. You'll be subpoenaed for the inquest of course.'

'Of course. Are you Chief Detective-Inspector Alleyn?'

'Yes.'

'I remembered your face. I saw you at the Theodore Roberts trial.'

'Oh, yes.'

'The case interested me. You see I'm an alienist.'

'Oh, yes,' said Alleyn again with his air of polite detachment.

'I was glad they brought in a verdict of insanity. Poor Roberts. I suppose in a case of that sort the police do not push for the – the other thing.'

'The police force is merely a machine. I must fly I'm afraid. Goodnight. Bathgate, will you let Dr Kasbek out when he has spoken to Curtis?'

Alleyn returned to the top of the hall. The divisional surgeon joined Kasbek and the two doctors walked down the aisle with that consultation manner, heads together, faces very solemn, like small boys in conference. Nigel followed sheepishly at a tactful distance. The word cyanide floated at intervals down the aisle. At last Dr Curtis said: 'Yes. All right. Goodnight.' They shook hands. Nigel hurried up to wrestle with the elaborate bolts and lock that secured the double doors.

'Oh, thank you very much,' said Kasbek. 'You've made yourself quite invaluable this evening, Mr Bathgate.'

'To tell you the truth, sir,' said Nigel, 'I am surprised at my own initiative. It was the smell that did it.'

'Oh, quite. I was just going to say no one must leave when you spoke up. Very glad of your support. Can you manage? Ah – that's done it. I see there's a constable outside. I hope he lets me out! Goodnight, Mr Bathgate.'

CHAPTER 5

A Priest and Two Acolytes

The constable had arrived with the mortuary-van. A stretcher was brought in. Nigel, not wishing to see again that terrible figure, hung back at the entrance, but after all, try as he would, he could not help watching. The group up in the chancel looked curiously theatrical. Alleyn had turned on all the side lamps but they were dull red and insignificant. The torch flickered confusedly. At one moment it threw down a strong glare, and at the next almost failed, so that the figures of the men continually started to life and seemed to move when actually they were still. Alleyn drew the brocaded satin away from the body and stood contemplating it. The body, still in its same contracted, headlong posture, looked as though some force had thrown it down with a sudden violence. Dr Curtis said something. His voice sounded small and melancholy in the empty building. Nigel caught the words 'rigor mortis – rapid.' Alleyn nodded and his shadow, starting up on the wall as the torch flared again, made a monstrous exaggeration of the gesture. They bent down and lifted the body on to the whitish strip of the stretcher. One of the men pulled a sheet up. Curtis spoke to them. They lifted the stretcher and came slowly down the aisle, black silhouettes now against the lighted chancel. They passed Nigel heavily and went out of the open door. The constable stayed in the entrance, so Nigel did not relock the doors. He returned to the chancel.

'I'm glad that part is over,' he said to Alleyn.

'What? Oh, the body.'

'You appear to be lost in the folds of your professional abstraction,' remarked Nigel tartly. 'Pray, what are you going to do next?'

'Your style is an unconvincing mixture of George Moore and
Lewis Carroll, my dear Bathgate. I am about to interview the ladies
and gentlemen. I dislike this affair. I dislike it very much. This is a
beastly place. Why did you come to it?'

'I really can't tell you. I was bored and I saw the sign swinging in
the rain. I came in search of adventure.'

'And I suppose, with your habitual naîveté, you consider that you
have found it. Fox, have you made your plan?'

'Not quite finished, sir, but I'll carry on quietly.'

'Well, give an ear to the conversation. When we get to M. de
Ravigne, you may like to conduct the examination in French.'

Fox smiled blandly. He had taken a course of gramophone lessons
in French and now followed closely an intermediate course on the
radio.

'I'm not quite up to it as yet, sir,' he said, 'but I'd be glad to listen
if you feel like doing it yourself.'

'Bless you, Fox, I should make a complete ass of myself. Got your
prints, Bailey?'

'I've been over the ground,' said Detective-Sergeant Bailey
guardedly.

'Then call in the first witness. Find out if any of them are particularly anxious to get away, and I'll take them in order of urgency.'

'Very good, sir.'

Bailey, with an air of mulish indifference, disappeared through
the altar door. In a moment he came back.

'Gentleman just fainted,' he grumbled.

'Oh, Lord!' apostrophized Alleyn. 'Have a look, will you, Curtis?
Which is it, Bailey?'

'One of those affairs in purple shirts, the dark one.'

'My oath,' said Alleyn.

Dr Curtis uttered a brief 'Tsss!' and disappeared. Bailey emerged
with Father Garnette.

'I'm extremely sorry to have kept you waiting, sir,' said Alleyn,
'but you will understand that there were several matters to deal
with. Shall we go down into the chairs there?'

Garnette inclined his head and led the way. He seated himself
unhurriedly and hid his hands in his wide sleeves. Fox, all bland
detachment, strolled to a nearby pew and seemed to be absorbed in

his sketch-plan of the chancel and sanctuary. Nigel, at a glance from Alleyn, joined Inspector Fox and took out his notebook. A short-hand report of the interviews would do no harm. Father Garnette did not so much as glance at Nigel and Fox. Alleyn pulled forward a large fald-stool and sat on it with his back to the flickering torch. The priest and the policeman regarded each other steadily.

'I am appalled,' said Father Garnette loudly. His voice was mellifluous and impossibly sorrowful. 'Ap-PALL-ed.'

'Unpleasant business, isn't it?' remarked Alleyn.

'I am bewildered. I do not understand, as yet, what has happened. What unseen power has struck down this dear soul in the very moment of spiritual ecstasah?'

'Cyanide of potassium I *think*,' said Alleyn coolly, 'but of course that's not official.'

The embroidery on the white sleeves quivered slightly.

'But that is a poison,' said Father Garnette.

'One of the deadliest,' said Alleyn.

'I am appalled,' said Father Garnette.

'The possibility of suicide will have to be explored, of course.'

'Suicide!'

'It does not seem likely, certainly. Accident is even more improbable, I should say.'

'You mean, then, that she – that she – that murder has been done!'

'That will be for a jury to decide. There will be an inquest, of course. In the meantime there are one or two questions I should like to ask you, Mr Garnette. I need not remind you that you are not obliged to answer them.'

'I know nothing of such matters. I simply wish to do my duty.'

'That's excellent, sir,' said Alleyn politely. 'Now as regards the deceased. I've got her name and address, but I should like to learn a little more about her. You knew her personally as well as officially, I expect?'

'All my children are my friends. Cara Quayne was a very dear friend. Hers was a rare soul, Inspector – ah?'

'Alleyn, sir.'

'Inspector Alleyn. Hers was a rare soul, singularly fitted for the tremendous spiritual discoverahs to which it was granted I should point the way.'

'Oh, yes. For how long has she been a member of your congregation?'

'Let me think. I can well remember the first evening I was aware of her. I felt the presence of something vital, a kind of intensitah, a – how can I put it? – an increased receptivitah. We have our own words for expressing these experiences.'

'I hardly think I should understand them,' remarked Alleyn dryly. 'Can you give me the date of her first visit?'

'I believe I can. It was on the festival of Aeger. December the fifteenth of last year.'

'Since then she has been a regular attendant?'

'Yes. She had attained to the highest rank.'

'By that you mean she was a Chosen Vessel?'

Father Garnette bent his extraordinary eyes on the inspector.

'Then you know something of our ritual, Inspector Alleyn?'

'Very little, I am afraid.'

'Do you know that you yourself are exceedingly receptive?'

'I receive facts,' said Alleyn, 'as a spider does flies.'

'Ah.' Father Garnette nodded his head slowly. 'This is not the time. But I think it will come. Well, ask what you will, Inspector.'

'I gather that you knew Miss Quayne intimately – that in the course of her preparation for tonight's ceremony you saw a great deal of her.'

'A great deal.'

'I understand she took the name of Frigga in your ceremony?'

'That is so,' said Father Garnette uneasily.

'The wife of Odin, I seem to remember.'

'In our ritual the relationship is one of the spirit.'

'Ah, yes,' said Alleyn. 'Had you any reason to believe she suffered from depression or was troubled about anything?'

'I am certain of the contrarah. She was in a state of tranquilitah and joy.'

'I see. No worries over money?'

'Money? No. She was what the world calls rich.'

'What do you call it, sir?'

Father Garnette gave a frank and dreadfully boyish laugh.

'Why, I should call her rich too, Inspector,' he cried gaily.

'Any unhappy love affair, do you know?' pursued Alleyn.

Father Garnette did not answer for a moment. Then he said sadly:

'Ah, Inspector Alleyn, we speak in different languages.'

'I didn't realize that,' said Alleyn. 'Can you translate my question into your own language, or would you rather not answer it?'

'You misunderstand me. Cara Quayne was not concerned with earthly love; she was on the threshold of a new spiritual life.'

'And apparently she has crossed it.'

'You speak more faithfully than you realize. I earnestly believe she has crossed it.'

'No love affair,' said Alleyn, and wrote it down in his notebook. 'Was she on friendly terms with the other Initiates?'

'There is perfect loving kindness among them. Nay, that does not express my meaning. The Initiates have attained to the third plane where all human relationships merge in an ecstatic indifference. They cannot hate for there is no hatred. They realize that hatred is *maya* – illusion.'

'And love?'

'If you mean earthlah love, that too is illusion.'

'Then,' said Alleyn, 'if you follow the idea to a logical conclusion, what one does cannot matter as long as one's actions spring from one's emotions for if these are illusion – or am I wrong?'

'Ah,' exclaimed Father Garnette, 'I knew I was right. We must have a long talk some day, my dear fellow.'

'You are very kind,' said Alleyn. 'What did Miss Wade mean when she said: "All that sort of thing should have been kept out"?'

'Did Miss Wade say that?'

'Yes.'

'I cannot imagine what she meant. The poor soul was very distressed no doubt.'

'What do you think Mrs Candour meant when she said she knew something dreadful would happen and that she had said so to M. de Ravigne?'

'I did not hear her,' answered Father Garnette. His manner suggested that Alleyn as well as Mrs Candour had committed a gross error in taste.

'Another question, Mr Garnette. In the course of your interviews with Miss Quayne can you remember any incident or remark that would throw any light on this matter?'

'None.'

'This is a very well-appointed hall.'

'We think it beautiful,' said Father Garnette complacently.

'Please do not think me impertinent. I am obliged to ask these questions. Is it supported and kept up by subscription?'

'My people welcome as a privilege the right to share in the hospitalitah of the Sacred Flame.'

'You mean they pay the running expenses?'

'Yes.'

'Was Miss Quayne a generous supporter?'

'Dear soul, yes, indeed she was.'

'Do you purchase the wine for the ceremony?'

'I do.'

'Would you mind giving me the name of this wine and the address of the shop?'

'It comes from Harrods. I think the name is – let me see – "Le Comte's Invalid Port".'

Alleyn repressed a shudder and wrote it down.

'You decant it yourself? I mean you pour it into the silver flagon?'

'On this occasion, no. I believe Claude Wheatley made all the preparations this evening.'

'Would you mind telling me exactly what he would have done?'

'Certainly. He would take an unopened bottle of wine from a cupboard in my room, draw the cork and pour the contents into the vessel. He would then make ready the goblet.'

'Make ready – ?'

Father Garnette's expression changed a little. He looked at once mulish and haughty. 'A certain preparation is necessarah,' he said grandly.

'Oh, yes, of course. You mean the flame that appeared. How was that done? Methylated spirit?'

'In tabloid form,' confessed Father Garnette.

'I know,' cried Alleyn cheerfully. 'The things women use for heating curling-tongs.'

'Possiblah,' said Father Garnette stiffly. 'In our ritual, Inspector Alleyn, the goblet itself is holy and blessed. By the very act of pouring in the wine, this too becomes sacred – sacred by contact with the Cup. Our ceremony of the Cup, though it embraces the virtues of various communions in Christian churches, is actually entirely different in essentials and in intention.'

'I was not,' said Alleyn, coldly, 'so mistaken as to suspect any affinity. Having filled the flagon Mr Wheatley would then put it – where?'

'In that niche over there on our right of the sanctuarah.'

'And what is the procedure with the methylated tablet?'

'Prior to the service Claude comes before the altar and after prostrating himself three times, draws the Sacred Cup from its Monstrance. As he does this he repeats a little prayer in Norse. He genuflects thrice and then rising to his feet he – ah – he – '

'Drops in the tablet and puts the cup away again?'

'Yes.'

'I see. Mr Bathgate tells me the flame appeared after you laid your hands over the cup. How is this done?'

'I – ah – I employ a little capsule,' said Father Garnette.

'Really? What does it contain?'

'I believe the substance is known as zinc – ah – ethyl.'

'Oh, yes. Very ingenious. You turn away for a moment as you use it perhaps?'

'That is so.'

'It all seems quite clear now. One more question. Has there, to your knowledge, ever been any form of poison kept on the premises of this building?'

Father Garnette turned as white as his robes and said no, definitely not.

'Thank you very much. I greatly appreciate your courtesy in answering so readily. I hope you will not mind very much if I ask you to wait in the – is that a vestry over there? It is! – in the vestry, while I see these other people. No doubt you will be glad to change into less ceremonial dress.'

'I shall avail myself of the opportunitah to regain in meditation my tranquilitah and spiritual at-oneness.'

'Do,' said Alleyn cordially.

'My subconscious mind, impregnated with the word, will flow to you-wards. In all humilitah I believe I may help you in your task. There are more things in Heaven and earth, Inspector Alleyn – '

'There are indeed, sir,' agreed the inspector dryly. 'Have you any objection to being searched before you go?'

'Searched? No – er – no, certainly not. Certainly not.'

'That's very sensible. Pure routine you know. I'll send a man in.'

Father Garnette withdrew to the vestry accompanied by a plain-clothes man.

'Damn', sickly, pseudo, bogus, mumbo-jumbo,' said Alleyn with great violence. 'What do you think of him, Fox?'

'Well, sir,' said Fox placidly, 'I must say I wondered if the gentleman knew much more about what he seemed to be talking about than I did.'

'And well you might, my Foxkin, well you might. Hullo, Bathgate.'

'Hullo,' said Nigel guardedly.

'Enjoying yourself?'

'I'm taking shorthand notes. I seem to remember that you have a passion for shorthand notes.'

'Ain't dat de truff, Lawd! Have you read "Ole Man Adam"?'

'Yes.'

'I wish Garnette had. Fox!'

'Yes, sir?'

'Send someone else into the vestry with Mr Garnette, will you, and get them to look him over. And any of the others I send in. Where's the wardress?'

'In the porch out there.'

'She can deal with the ladies. Tell them to look for a small piece of crumpled paper or anything that could have held powder. I don't think they'll find it. Bailey!'

Detective-Sergeant Bailey moved down from the sanctuary.

'Yes, sir?'

'The next, if you please.'

Bailey went through the little door and reappeared with Claude Wheatley and a general air of having taken an unlucky dip in a bran-tub. Fox returned with another plain-clothes man who went into the vestry.

'This gentleman isn't feeling too good, sir. He wants to go home,' said Bailey.

'Oh, yes,' said Claude. 'Oh, yes, please. Oh, yes.'

'Sorry you're upset, Mr Wheatley,' said Alleyn.

'Upset! I'm fearfully ill, Inspector. You can't think. Oh, please may I sit down.'

'Do.'

Claude sank into one of the Initiates' chairs and gazed wide-eyed at the inspector.

'I feel too ghastly,' he moaned.

'What upset you?'

'That appalling old woman. She said such frightful things. I do think old women are awful.'

'Whom do you mean?'

'The Candour female.'

'What did she say to upset you?'

'Oh, I don't know. I do feel shocking.'

Dr Curtis came out of Garnette's room and strolled down.

'Mr Wheatley felt a bit squeamish,' he said cheerfully, 'but he'll be all right. He's had a peg of some really excellent brandy. Father Garnette's a lucky man.'

'Splendid,' rejoined Alleyn. 'Would you be a good fellow and go back to them, Curtis? Some of the others may need attention.'

'Certainly.' Curtis and Alleyn exchanged a glance and the doctor returned.

'Now, Mr Wheatley,' Alleyn began. 'I think you look much better. I've a few questions I'd like to put to you. You can refuse to answer if you think it advisable.'

'Yes, but that's all very well. Suppose I do refuse, then you'll start thinking things.'

'I might, certainly.'

'Yes – well – there!'

'Difficult for you,' remarked Alleyn.

'Well, anyway,' said Claude very peevishly, 'you can ask them. I may as well know what they are.'

'I have already asked the first. What did Mrs Candour say to upset you?'

Claude wriggled.

'Jealous old cat. The whole thing is she loathes Father Garnette taking the slightest notice of anybody else. She's always too loathsomely spiteful for words – especially to Lionel and me. How she dared! And anyway everybody knows all about it. I'd hardly be stupid enough to – ' Here Claude stopped short.

'To do what, Mr Wheatley?'

'To do anything like that, even if I wanted to, and anyway I always thought Cara Quayne was a marvellous person – so piercingly decorative.'

'What would you hardly be stupid enough to do?' asked Alleyn patiently.

'To – well – well – to do anything to the wine. Everybody knows it was my week to make preparation.'

'You mean you poured the wine into the silver flagon and put the methylated tablet into the cup. What did Mrs Candour suggest?'

'She didn't actually suggest anything. She simply said I did it. She kept on saying so. Old cat.'

'I shouldn't let it worry you. Now, Mr Wheatley, will you think carefully. Did you notice any peculiar, any unusual smell when you poured out the wine?'

'Any smell!' ejaculated Claude opening his eyes very wide. 'Any *smell!*'

'Any smell.'

'Well, of course I'd just lit all the censers you know. Don't you think our incense is rather divine, Inspector? Father Garnette gets it from India. It's sweet-almond blossom. There's the oil too. We burn a dish of the oil in front of the altar. I lit it just before I got the wine. It's a gorgeous perfume.'

'Evidently. You got the bottle of wine from Mr Garnette's room. Was it unopened?'

'Yes. I drew the cork.'

'You put nothing else in the flagon?'

Claude looked profoundly uncomfortable.

'Well – well, anyway I didn't put any poison in, if that's what you're hinting.'

'What else did you put?'

'If you must know it's something from a little bottle that Father Garnette keeps. It has a ceremonial significance. It's always done.'

'Have you any idea what it is?'

'I don't know.'

'Where is this bottle kept?'

'In the little cupboard in Father Garnette's room.'

'I see. Now as I understand it you took the wine to each of the Initiates in turn. Did you at any time notice an unusual smell from the cup?'

'I never touched the cup, Inspector. I never touched it. They all handed it round from one to the other. I didn't notice any smell except the incense. Not ever.'

'Right. Did you notice Miss Quayne at all when she took the cup?'

'Did I notice her? My God, yes.'

'What happened exactly?'

'It was simply appalling. You see I thought she was in Blessed Ecstasy. Well, I mean she was, up to the time she took the cup. She had spoken in ecstasy and everything. And then she drank. And then oh, it was frightful! She gave a sort of gasp. A fearfully deep gasp and sort of sharp. She made a face. And then she kind of slewed round and she dropped the cup. Her eyes looked like a doll's eyes. Glistening. And then she twitched all over – jerked – ugh! She fell down in a sort of jerk. Oh, I'm going to be sick, I think.'

'No, you're not,' said the inspector very firmly. 'You are going home. Go into the vestry and change your clothes.'

'Where's Lionel?'

'He'll join you in a moment. Goodnight.'

'Oh,' said Claude rolling a languishing eye at Alleyn, 'you are marvellous, Inspector. Oh, I would so very much rather not be sick. Goodbye.'

'Goodnight.'

Claude, under escort, walked with small steps into the vestry where they could hear him talking in a sort of feeble scream to the officer who searched him.

'Oh,' cried Inspector Fox suddenly in a falsetto voice, 'oh, Inspector, I think I'm going to be sick.'

'And well you might be,' said Nigel, grinning. 'What a loathly, what a nauseating, what an unspeakable little dollop.'

'Horrid, wasn't it?' agreed Alleyn absently. 'Damn that incense,' he added crossly. 'Sweet almond too, just the very thing – ' he paused and stared thoughtfully at Fox. 'Let's have Lionel,' he said.

Lionel was produced. His manner was a faithful reproduction of Claude's and he added nothing that was material to the evidence. He was sent into the vestry, whence he and Claude presently emerged wearing, the one, a saxe-blue and the other, a pinkish-brown suit. They fussed off down the aisle and disappeared. Alleyn sent for Mrs Candour.

CHAPTER 6

Mrs Candour and Mr Ogden

Mrs Candour had wept and her tears had blotted her make-up. She had dried them and in doing so had blotted her make-up again. Her face was an unlovely mess of mascara, powder and rouge. It hung in flabby pockets from the bone of her skull. She looked bewildered, frightened and vindictive. Her hands were tremulous. She was a large woman born to be embarrassingly ineffectual. In answer to Alleyn's suggestion that she should sit on one of the chairs, she twitched her loose lips, whispered something and walked towards them with that precarious gait induced by excessive flesh mounted on French heels. She moved in a thick aura of essence of violet. Alleyn waited until she was seated before he gave her the customary information that she was under no obligation to answer any questions. He paused, but she made no comment. She simply stared in front of her with lacklustre eyes.

'I take it,' said Alleyn, 'that you have no objection. Was Miss Cara Quayne a personal friend of yours?'

'Not a great friend.'

'An acquaintance?'

'Yes. We – we – only met here.' Her voice was thin and faintly common. 'At least, well, I did go to see her once or twice.'

'Have you got any ideas on the subject of this business?'

'Oh my God!' moaned Mrs Candour. 'I believe it was a judgment.'

'A judgment?'

Mrs Candour drew a lace handkerchief from her bosom.

'What had Miss Quayne done,' asked Alleyn, 'to merit so terrible a punishment?'

'She coveted the vow of Odin.'

'I'm afraid I do not know what that implies.'

'That is how I feel about it,' said Mrs Candour, exactly as if she had just finished a lucid and explicit statement. 'Father Garnette is above all that sort of thing. He is not of this world. He had told us so, often and often. But Cara was a very passionate sort of woman.' She dropped her voice and added with an air of illicit relish: 'Cara was dreadfully over-sexed. Pardon me.'

'Oh,' said Alleyn.

'Yes. Of course I know that ecstatic union is blessed, but ecstatic union is one thing and – ' Here Mrs Candour stopped short and looked frightened.

'Do you mean,' said Alleyn, 'that – ?'

'I don't mean anything definite,' interrupted Mrs Candour in a hurry. 'Please, please don't attach any importance to what I've just said. It was only my idea. I'm so dreadully upset. Poor Cara. Poor, poor Cara.'

'Mr Claude Wheatley tells me – '

'Don't you believe anything that little beast says, Mr – er – Inspector – er – '

'Inspector Alleyn, madam.'

'Oh – Inspector Alleyn. Claude's a little pig. Always prying into other people's affairs. I've told Father, but he's so *good* he doesn't *see.*'

'I gather you rather upset Mr Wheatley by referring to his preparations for the service.'

'Serves him right if I did. He kept on saying it was murder, he knew it was murder, and that Cara was such a lovely woman and everyone was jealous of her. I just said: "Well," I said, "if she was murdered," I said, "who prepared the goblet and the flagon?" And then he fainted. I thought it looked very queer.'

'Miss Quayne *was* a very beautiful woman, I believe?' said Alleyn casually.

'I never could see it. Of course, if you admire that type. But just because that M. de Ravigne went silly over her – I mean everyone knows what foreigners are like. If you give them any encouragement, that is. Well, I myself – I suppose Claude told you that – about her looks, I mean. Or was it Father Garnette? *Was* it?'

'I'm afraid I don't remember,' said Alleyn.

Mrs Candour jerked her chin up. For a second her face was horrible. 'Cara doesn't look very pretty now,' she said softly.

Alleyn turned away.

'I mustn't keep you any longer,' he said. 'There's only one other point. You were the first, after Mr Garnette, to take the cup. Did you notice any peculiar smell?'

'I don't know. I don't remember. No, I don't think so.'

'I see. Thank you. That is all, I think.'

'I may go home?'

'Certainly. There is a wardress in the lobby. Would you object to being examined?'

'Searched!'

'Just looked over, you know. It's the usual thing.'

'Oh, yes, please – I'd rather – much rather.'

'Thank you. You will be given notice of the inquest.'

'The inquest! Oh, how dreadful. I don't know how I'm to get over this – I'm so shockingly sensitive. Inspector Alleyn, you've been marvellously kind. I always thought that police methods were brutal.' She looked up at him with a general air of feminine helplessness somewhat negatived by a glint of appraisal in her eye. It was a ghastly combination. She held out her hand.

'Goodbye, Inspector Alleyn.'

'Good evening, madam,' said Alleyn.

She wobbled away on her French heels.

'This is a very unsavoury case,' said Nigel.

'It's murder,' said Inspector Fox mildly.

'Most foul,' added Alleyn, 'as at the best it is. But this *most* foul – Yes, I agree with you, Bathgate. Bailey!'

'Here,' said that worthy, rising up from behind the lectern.

'Next please.'

'Right, sir.'

'What did you make of Mrs Candour?' asked Alleyn.

'A perfectly appalling old girl,' said Nigel fervently.

'Oh, yes. All that. Almost a pathological case, one might imagine. Still, the exhibition of jealousy was interesting, didn't you think, Fox?'

'Yes, I did,' agreed Fox. 'This Father Garnette seems to be a peculiar sort of man for the ministry.'

'Exactly.'

'When she made that appalling remark about Cara not looking very pretty now,' said Nigel, 'she was positively evil. Without a shadow of doubt she loathed the poor woman. I am surprised at your allowing her to escape. She should have been handcuffed immediately, I consider.'

'Don't show off,' said Alleyn abstractedly.

'I'll be right there, Ahfficer. Where's the Chief?' cried Mr Ogden from afar. He appeared with Bailey by the altar, saw Alleyn, and made straight for him.

'Well, well, well. Look what's here!' exclaimed Mr Ogden.

'Yes, look,' said Alleyn. 'It's a pathetic sight, Mr Ogden. Here we go grubbing along – however.'

'Say, Inspector, what's the big idea? You look kind of world-weary.'

'Do I, Mr Ogden, do I?'

'And just when I was congratulating myself on sitting right next the works for an inside survey of British criminal investigation.'

'And now you'll never talk again about our wonderful police.'

'Is that so? Well, I'm not saying anything.'

'You won't mind if I ask you a few dreary questions, perhaps? We have to do our stuff, you know.'

'Go right ahead. My, my!' said Mr Ogden contemplating Alleyn with an air of the liveliest satisfaction. 'You certainly are the goods. I guess you've got British Manufacture stamped some place where it won't wear off. All this quiet deprecation – it's direct from a sure-fire British best-seller. I can't hardly believe it's true.'

Nigel, from his unobtrusive seat by Fox, allowed himself an irritating grin. Alleyn saw it and looked furious.

'That sounds a very damning description, Mr Ogden,' he said, and hurried on. He asked Ogden if he had noticed a peculiar smell and got the now customary reply that the reek of incense was so strong that it would drown any other smell.

'Though, now I get to thinking about it,' added Mr Ogden, 'I do seem to remember it was uncommon powerful tonight. Yes, sir, I believe I thought those two he-he boys were certainly hitting up the atmosphere.'

'Can you remember at what precise moment you thought this?'

Mr Ogden's face became very pink. For the first time since Alleyn met him he hesitated.

'Well, Mr Ogden?'

'Well now, Inspector, I can't remember. Isn't that just too bad?'

'Miss Jenkins was next to you in the circle, wasn't she?'

'That is correct,' said Mr Ogden tonelessly.

'Yes. Now look here, sir. You're a business man I take it?'

'Surely.'

'Thank God for that. I don't know how much this organisation means to you, and I don't want to say anything that will be offensive, but I'm longing for a sensible man's view of the whole situation. An intelligent and knowledgeable view.'

'Inside dope,' said Mr Ogden.

'Exactly.'

'Go right ahead. Maybe I'll talk and maybe not. Maybe I don't know anything.'

'I gather you are an officer of the executive?'

'That's so. A Warden.'

'You know all these people quite well, I suppose?'

'Why, yes. We are all enthusiastic about uplift. The spirit of comradeship pervades our relationship. You Britishers are weaned on starch, I guess, but I hand myself out a whole lot of roses for the way I've got this bunch started. Right at the commencement of the movement they used to sit round looking at each other like they all suffered from frostbite. Now they've got together like regular fellows. They're a great little crowd.'

'You've been interested in the organisation since its foundation?'

'That's so. That was way back in – why, it must be two years ago. I met up with Father Garnette coming across to England. I move about some, Inspector. That's my job. That trip it was the Brightwater Creek Gold Mining Company. Yes, that's what it would be. I recollect I had Father Garnette accept a small nugget as a souvenir. That would be May two years ago. I was very, very much impressed with Father Garnette's personality.'

'Really,' said Alleyn.

'Yes, sir. I'm a self-made man, Chief. I was raised in a ten-cent fish joint, and my education simply forgot to occur, but when I meet culture I respect it. I like it handed out good and peppy, and that's the way Father Garnette let me have it. By the time we hit Southampton we'd doped out a scheme for this church, and before six months had passed we were drawing congregations of three hundred.'

'Remarkable,' said Alleyn.

'It was swell.'

'Where did the money come from?'

'Why, from the flock. Father Garnette had a small hall 'way down Great Holland Road. Compared with this it was a bum show, but say, did we work it? The Father had a service every night for a month. He got right down to it. A small bunch of very influential people came along. Just one or two, but they roped in more. When he'd got them all enthusiastic he had an appeal week and loosed a line of high-voltage oratory. Sob-stuff. I gave five grand and I'm proud to spill the beans.'

'Who were the other subscribers?'

'Why, Dagmar Candour was in on the plush seats with a thousand pounds and poor Cara checked in at the same level. Each of those ladies seemed ambitious to carry off the generosity stakes. Then there was M. de Ravigne and – and all the bunch of Initiates. I guess I'd hold up operations some if I recited all the subscribers.'

'Miss Quayne must have been a very wealthy woman?'

'She was very, very wealthy, and she had a lovely nature. Why, only last month she deposited five thousand in bearer bonds in the safe back there beyond the altar. They are waiting there until another five is raised among the rest of us and then it's to form a building fund for a new church. That's how generous she was.'

Nigel had paused, pen in air, to gape at Mr Ogden's enthusiastic countenance, and to reflect a little childishly on the gullibility of average men and women. None of these people was particularly stupid, he would say, except perhaps Mrs Candour. Miss Quayne had looked interesting. Mr Ogden was obviously an intelligent business man. Janey Jenkins, Maurice Pringle, M. de Ravigne were none of them idiots. He forgot all about Miss Wade. Yet all these apparently sensible individuals had been duped by Garnette into parting with sums of money. Extraordinary! At this moment he remembered his own reaction to Father Garnett's oratory and felt less superior.

'That's how generous she was,' repeated Mr Ogden.

'What was the relationship between M. de Ravigne and the deceased?'

'Crazy about her,' answered Mr Ogden succinctly.

'Yet I rather gathered that the Initiates were a cut above earthly love,' ventured Alleyn.

'I guess M. de Ravigne has not altogether cast off the shackles of the body,' said Mr Ogden dryly. 'But get this: Cara was not interested. No, sir. Her soul was yearning after the inner mysteries of the spirit.'

'Did you hear what Mr Pringle and Mrs Candour said immediately after the tragedy?'

Mr Ogden looked uncomfortable.

'Well, I can't say – '

Alleyn consulted his notebook and read aloud the conversation as Nigel had reported it to him.

'Mr Pringle said: "The whole thing is a farce." He talked about retribution. He said to Mrs Candour: "You would have taken her place if you could." What do you think he meant, Mr Ogden?'

'I don't know, Chief, honest I don't,' said Mr Ogden, looking very worried. 'Maybe there was a little competition between the ladies for spiritool honours. Maybe Pringle kind of thought Mrs Candour would have enjoyed a spell as Chosen Vessel.'

'I see.'

'You don't want to make too much of it. They were all het up. That boy's three hundred per cent nerves. Garsh!' Mr Ogden went on fervently, 'I wish to hell we could smoke.'

'Same here,' agreed Alleyn. 'I'd give my soul for a pipe. No hope for me, I'm afraid, but I don't think I need keep you much longer, Mr Ogden.'

Mr Ogden looked astounded.

'Well, say!' he remarked, 'that's certainly a surprise to me. I don't get the works this trip?'

'Nor the next, I hope. Unless you can think of anything you feel we ought to know I shan't worry you any more until after the inquest. Of course, if you have any theory I should be extremely glad – '

'For Gard's sake!' ejaculated Mr Ogden. 'Listen. Are they all this way around the Yard?' He looked at Fox and lowered his voice to a penetrating whisper. 'He looks more like a regular dick. An' yet if I worded him maybe he'd talk back like a bud's guide to society stuff. Is that so?'

'You must meet Inspector Fox and find out,' said Alleyn. 'Fox!'

'Hullo, sir?' Fox hoisted himself up and walked solemnly round the pews towards them.

'Mr Ogden finds our methods a little lacking in colour.'

'Indeed, sir?'

'Yes. Can you suggest any improvements? Have you any questions you would like to put to Mr Ogden, Fox? Something really startling, you know.'

'Well, sir, I can't say I have. Unless' – Fox paused a moment and stared at Alleyn – 'unless Mr Ogden can tell us anything about the – er – the ingredients of the cup.'

'Can you, Mr Ogden.'

'Surely. It's some sissy dope from a departmental store. I've seen the bottles. Invalid Port. One half per cent alcohol. But – '

'Yes?'

'Well, since you're asking, Chief, I reckon Father Garnette has it pepped up some. A drop of brandy I'd say. Mind, I don't know.'

'There you are, Fox. Anything else?'

'I don't think so, sir,' said Fox with a smile, 'unless the gentleman would like to be searched.'

'Would you care to be searched, Mr Ogden? We do that sort of thing rather neatly.'

'Well, for crying out loud!' exclaimed Mr Ogden. He looked from Alleyn to Fox, cast up his eyes, passed a plump hand over his head and burst out laughing.

'Get to it,' he begged,' get to it. For the Lord's sake get to it. Would I care to be searched!'

'Carry on, Fox,' said Alleyn.

Fox took out a notebook and Alleyn, with the swift precision of a pick-pocket, explored the inner fastnesses of Mr Ogden's suit.

'Note-case. One fiver and three singles. Pocket-book. Letter. Typewritten, stamped and sealed. Address "Hector K. Manville, Ogden-Schultz Gold-refining and Extracting Co., 81 East forty-fifth Street, Boston, Massachusetts." Letter refers to a new gold refining process. It's rather technical.'

Fox read it with difficulty.

'Bill from Harrods. £9 10s. 8d. To account rendered. Date: November 2nd of this year. Letter beginning "Dear Sam," signed Heck. Date – '

Alleyn murmured on. It was all over before Mr Ogden had left off chuckling.

'No phials of poison,' said Alleyn lightly. 'That's all, sir.'

'It was real smart,' declared Mr Ogden handsomely. 'They don't fan a man neater than that in the States. That's saying some. Well, Inspector, if that's all I guess I'll move off. Say, it seems real callous for me to be standing here talking facetious when Cara Quayne is lying – See here, Chief, have I got to say murdered?'

'We must wait for the inquest, Mr Ogden.'

The American's genial face had suddenly become preternaturally solemn like that of a clown, or a child who has been reproved for laughing.

'If it is murder,' he said quietly, 'and the trail's not just all that easy and – aw hell, Chief, I've got the dollars and I ain't paralysed yet.'

With which cryptic remark Mr Ogden took himself off.

'Is he real?' asked Nigel, 'or is he a murderer with unbridled histrionic ambitions? Surely no American was ever so American. Surely – '

'Do stop making these exclamatory interjections. You behave for all the world like a journalistic Greek chorus. Fox, what *did* the gentleman mean by his last remark. The one about not suffering from paralysis?'

'I understood him to be offering unlimited sums of money to the police and the prosecution, sir.'

'Bribery, thinly disguised, depend upon it,' said Nigel. 'I tell you no American was ever – '

'I don't know. His eyes, at all events, are original. People do run true to type. It's an axiom of police investigation. Next please, Bailey.'

Janey Jenkins was next.

CHAPTER 7

Janey and Maurice

Miss Jenkins was one of those women who are instinctively thought of by their Christian names. She looked like a Janey. She was short-ish, compact, with straight hair, well brushed, snapping black eyes, snub nose, and an amusing mouth. Without being pretty she was attractive. Her age was about twenty-two. She walked briskly towards Alleyn, sat down composedly and said: 'Well, Inspector Alleyn, let's get it over. I'll answer any questions you like, compro-mising or uncompromising, as long as it's over quickly.'

'I thank whatever gods may be,' rejoined Alleyn, 'and there are enough to begin with on the premises, if you'll excuse my saying so.'

'We *are* rather generously endowed, aren't we?' said Janey.

'You must forgive me. I didn't mean to be offensive.'

'You weren't. I'm not altogether an ass. This is rather a rum show, I dare say.'

'You don't talk like my idea of an Initiate.'

'Don't I? Well perhaps I'm not a very good one. I'm thinking of back-sliding, Inspector Alleyn. Oh, not because of this awful busi-ness. At least – I don't know. Perhaps it has shown us up in rather an unattractive light.' She paused and wrinkled her forehead. 'It all seems very bogus to you I expect, but – but – there's something in it or I thought so.'

'When I was an undergraduate I became a Plymouth Brother for two months. It seemed frightfully important at the time. I believe nowadays they go in for Black Magic.'

'Yes, Maurice tried that when he was up. Then he switched over to this.'

'You speak of Mr Pringle?'

'Yes.'

'Did he introduce you to this church?'

'Clever of you,' said Janey. 'Yes, he did.'

'When was this?'

'Oh, about six months ago.'

'You have advanced rather quickly, surely.'

'This was my first evening as an Initiate. Maurice has been one for some time. I was to have begun special instruction next week.'

'You don't mean to go on with it?'

'I don't,' said Janey.

'Would you mind telling me why?'

'I think perhaps I would.' She looked thoughtfully at Alleyn. 'No, I'll tell you. I've got my doubts about it. I've had my doubts about it for some time, to be quite honest.'

'Then why – '

'Maurice was so terribly keen. You see we're engaged. He could talk of nothing else. He's awfully highly strung – terribly sensitive – and – sort of vulnerable, and I thought – '

'You thought you would keep an eye on him – that it?'

'Yes. I don't know why I'm telling you this.'

'I am sure you will not regret doing so. Miss Jenkins, do you know what Mr Pringle was driving at when he said that Mr Garnette was keeping them all quiet, that Mrs Candour would have taken Miss Quayne's place if she could, and that he was going to tell everybody something?'

'How do you know Maurice said that?'

'You may remember he was in the middle of it when I arrived. He stopped short when he saw me. I heard some of it. Mr Bathgate has told me the rest. What is the explanation?'

'I don't think I can answer that.'

'Can't you? Why not?'

'I don't want to stir it all up. It has got nothing to do with this dreadful thing. I'm sure of that.'

'You cannot possibly be sure of that. Listen to me. Mr Bathgate is prepared to swear that Miss Quayne put nothing into the cup after it was handed to her. She took it by the stem in both hands and drank from it without changing their position. She died two minutes after she drank from the cup. It had gone round the circle of Initiates. No one else, except the acolyte and Mr Garnette, had handled it. Can you not see that the inter-relationships of those six people are of importance? Can you not see that I must learn all I may of them. I must not try to persuade you to speak against your judgment – if I did this I should grossly exceed my duty. But please, Miss Jenkins, *don't* say: "It's got nothing to do with the case." We don't know what may or may not bear on the case. There is only one person who could tell us that.'

'Only one person? You mean – a guilty person?'

'I do. If such a one exists.'

There was a long silence.

'I'll tell you this much,' said Janey at last. 'Maurice hero-worshipped Father Garnette. He went, as Mr Ogden would say, crazy about him. I think Father Garnette took hold of his imagination. Maurice is very responsive to personal magnetism.'

'Yes.'

'I fell for it myself. When he preaches – it's rather extraordinary – one feels as though the most terrific revelation is being made. No, that's not quite it. Everything seems to be beautifully dovetailed and balanced.'

'A sense of exquisite precision,' murmured Alleyn. 'I believe opium smokers experience it.'

Janey flushed.

'You mean we were drugged with words. I don't think I quite admit that. But where was I? Oh. Well, a little while ago Maurice began to suspect that things were happening all the time in the background. He had put Father Garnette on a pedestal, you see, and the least suggestion of – of wordly interest seemed wrong to Maurice. Some of the women in the congregation, Mrs Candour and poor Cara too, I'm afraid, were rather blatantly doting. Maurice got all worked up about it. He minded most dreadfully. That's what he meant when he talked like that about Mrs Candour.'

'He meant that Mrs Candour was jealous of Miss Quayne and that Mr Garnette had kept it quiet?'

'Yes.'

'I see.'

'But not that Mrs Candour was so jealous that – he didn't mean that. Please, please don't think that. It was nothing. Maurice was hysterical. He sees everything in an exaggerated light. You do believe me, don't you? Don't you?'

'I'm not sure,' said Alleyn, 'I think you are understating things, you know.'

'I'm not. Oh, why did I say anything! I won't answer any more questions. Let me go.' Janey's voice shook. She stood up, her hands clenched, her pupils dilated.

'Of course you may go, Miss Jenkins,' said Alleyn very quietly. 'You have had a wretched experience and it's unnerved you. Believe me, you need not reproach yourself for anything you have told me. Really. If only people would understand that in these cases they are under a moral obligation to help the police, that by keeping things back they may actually place an innocent man or woman in the gravest danger! However, I grow pompous and in a minute I might become facetious. Save yourself, Miss Jenkins, and go home.'

Janey managed a smile and brushed her hand across her face.

'Oh dear,' she whispered.

'You're done up,' said Alleyn quickly. 'Bathgate, dodge out and get a taxi for Miss Jenkins, will you?'

'I think I'd better wait for Maurice, please.'

'Do you? Would you like some of Mr Garnette's brandy?'

'No thank you. I'll just wait in the back pews if I may.'

'Of course you may. If it wouldn't bother you too much the wardress will run over you. Have you ever been searched?'

'Never. It sounds beastly, but I suppose I must.'

'That's very sensible. Inspector Fox will take you to the wardress. I'll see your young man now.'

Janey walked firmly down the aisle with Fox and disappeared into the shadows. Fox returned and Bailey produced Maurice Pringle.

Maurice looked quickly about him, and stopped like a pointer when he saw Alleyn. At the inspector's suggestion he came into the hall but refused to sit down. He thrust his hands into his pockets and seemed unable to stand still.

'Now then, Mr Pringle,' began Alleyn cheerfully.

'Where's Janey? Miss Jenkins?' demanded Maurice.

'Waiting for you.'

'What do you want to know?'

'Anything you can tell me that's to the purpose.'

Maurice was silent. Alleyn asked about the smell and heard about the incense. He read Maurice's previous statements from his notebook.

'What were you going to say when I came in?'

'Nothing.'

'Do you usually speak in half-phrases, Mr Pringle?'

'What d'you mean?'

'You said: "I'm going to tell them that – "and then you know I walked in and you stopped.'

Maurice snatched his left hand out of his pocket and bit at one of his fingers.

'Come. What did you mean by retribution? What would Mrs Candour have had so willingly from Miss Quayne? What had Mr Garnette kept quiet? What were you going to tell them?'

'I refuse to answer. It's my affair.'

'Very good. Fox!'

'Sir?'

'Will you tell Miss Jenkins that Mr Pringle does not wish to make any statements at present and that I think she need not wait? See that she gets a taxi, will you? She's a bit done up.'

'Very good, sir.'

'What do you mean?' said Maurice angrily. 'I'm taking her home.' Fox paused.

'I'm afraid I'll have to ask you to stay a little longer,' said Alleyn.

'My God, how I hate officials! Sadism at its worst.'

'Off you go, Fox.'

'Stay where you are,' said Maurice. 'I'll – what's the damn' phrase – I'll talk.'

Alleyn smiled and Fox blandly returned to his pew.

'You are interested in psycho-analysis, Mr Pringle?' asked Alleyn politely.

'What's that got to do with it?' rejoined Maurice, who seemed to have set himself some impossible standard of discourtesy. 'I should have thought the British Police Force scarcely knew how to pronounce the word – judging by results.'

'Someone must have told me about it,' said Alleyn vaguely.

Maurice looked sharply at him and then turned red.

'I'm sorry,' he muttered. 'This filthy show's got me all jumpy.'

'Well it might. I only asked you if you were interested in psycho-analysis because you used that password to the intelligentsia – "sadism." I don't suppose you know what it means. What are your views on crowd psychology?'

'Look here, what the hell are you driving at?'

'On the psychology of oratory, for instance? What do you think happens to people when they come under the sway of, shall we say, a magnetic preacher?'

'What happens to them! My God, they are his slaves.'

'Strong,' said Alleyn. 'Would you describe this congregation as Mr Garnette's slaves?'

'If you must know – yes. Yes. Yes. Yes!'

'Yourself included?'

The boy looked strangely at Alleyn as though he was bringing the inspector into focus. His lips trembled.

'Look,' he said.

Alleyn walked up to him, looked steadily in his face, and then murmured, so quietly that Nigel did not hear, a single word. Maurice nodded.

'How did you guess?'

'You told me to look. It's your eyes, you know. Contracted pupils. Also, if you'll forgive me, your bad manners.'

'I can't help it.'

'I suppose not. Is this Mr Garnette's doing?'

'No. I mean somebody gets them for him. He – he gave me special cigarettes. Quite mild really. He said it helped one to become receptive.'

'No doubt.'

'And it does! It's marvellous. Everything seems so clear. Only – only – '

'It's more than mild cigarettes now, I think.'

'Don't be so bloody superior. Oh, God, I'm sorry!'

'Do the other Initiates employ this short cut to spiritual ecstasy?'

'Janey doesn't. Janey doesn't know. Nor does Ogden. Don't tell Janey.'

'I won't if I can help it. All the others?'

'No. Cara Quayne had begun. The Candour does. She did before Father Garnette found her. Ogden and de Ravigne don't. At least I'm not sure about de Ravigne. I want him to try. Everyone ought to try and you can always leave off.'

'Can you?' said Alleyn.

'Of course. I don't mean to go on with it.'

'Did you all meet here in Mr Garnette's rooms and – smoke his cigarettes.'

'At first. But lately those two – Mrs Candour and Cara – came at separate times.' Maurice put his hand to his mouth and pulled shakily at his under lip. 'And then – then Cara began to make her preparations for Chosen Vessel and she came alone.'

'I see.'

'No, you don't. You don't see. You don't know. Only I know.' He now spoke rapidly and with great vehemence as though driven by an intolerable urge. 'It was one afternoon about three weeks ago when I came in to see him. No one in the church. So I went straight up here – past here – up to the door, his door. I spoke: "Are you there, Father?" They couldn't have heard. I went in – half in – they didn't see me. Oh, God! Oh, God! Frigga and Odin. The Chosen Vessel!' He gave a screech of laughter and flung himself into one of the chairs. He buried his face in his arm and sobbed quite loudly with an utter lack of restraint.

Inspector Fox strolled across the nave and stared with an air of calm appreciation at a small effigy of a most unprepossessing Nordic god. Nigel, acutely embarrassed, bent over his notebook. Detective-Sergeant Bailey emerged from his retreat, cast a glance of weary disparagement at Maurice, and went back again.

'So that is what you meant by retribution,' said Alleyn. Pringle made a sort of shuddering movement, an eloquent assent.

A little figure appeared out of the shadows at the end of the hall.

'Have you quite finished, Inspector Alleyn?' said Janey.

She spoke so quietly that it took Nigel a second or two to realize how furiously angry she was.

'I've quite finished,' said Alleyn gravely. 'You may both go home.'

She bent over Pringle.

'Maurice. Maurice darling, let's go.'

'Let me alone, Janey.'

'Of course I won't. I want you to take me home.'

She spoke softly to him for a minute and then he got up. She took his arm. Alleyn stood aside.

'I could murder you for this,' said Janey.

Oh, my child, don't talk like that!' exclaimed Alleyn with so much feeling that Nigel stared.

Janey looked again at the inspector. Perhaps she saw something in his dark face that made her change her mind.

'All right, I won't,' said Janey.

CHAPTER 8

The Temperament of M. de Ravigne

After Maurice had been searched and sent home Nigel approached Alleyn with a certain air of imbecile fractiousness that he assumed whenever he wished to annoy the inspector.

'Will somebody,' asked Nigel plaintively, 'be good enough to explain that young man's behaviour to me?'

'What?' asked Alleyn absently.

'I want to know your explanation for Pringalism. Why did Pringle ask you to look at him? Why *did* you look at him? What did you say to Pringle? And why did Pringle cry?'

'Fox,' said Alleyn, 'will you take Form One for this evening?'

'Very good,' said Fox, returning from his god. 'What is it you were inquiring about, Mr Bathgate?'

'Pringalism.'

'Meaning the young gentleman's behaviour, sir? Well, it was rather unusual I must say. My idea is he takes something that isn't good for him.'

'What do you mean, Inspector Fox? Something dietetically antagonistic? Oysters and whisky?'

'Heroin and hot air,' snapped Alleyn. 'Oh, Mr Garnette, Mr Garnette, it shall go hard if I do not catch you bending.'

'I say!' said Nigel. 'Do you think *Garnette* – '

'Let us have the French gentleman, please, Bailey,' interrupted Alleyn.

Monsieur de Ravigne emerged with an air of sardonic aloofness. He was a good-looking man, tall for a Frenchman and extremely well groomed. He saw Alleyn and walked quickly down towards him.

'You wish to speak to me, Inspector Alleyn?'

'If you please, M. de Ravigne. Will you sit down?'

'After you, monsieur.'

'No, no, monsieur, please.'

They murmured and skirmished while Fox gazed at them in mild enchantment. At last they both sat down. M. de Ravigne crossed his legs and displayed an elegant foot.

'And now, sir?' he inquired.

'You are very obliging, monsieur. It is the merest formality. A few questions that we are obliged to ask in our official capacity. I am sure you understand.'

'Perfectly. Let us discharge this business.'

'Immediately. First, were you aware of any unusual or peculiar odour during the ceremony of the cup?'

'You allude, of course, to the odour of prussic acid,' said M. de Ravigne.

'Certainly. May I ask how you realize the poison used was a cyanide?'

'I believe you yourself mentioned it, monsieur. If you did not it is no matter. I understood immediately that Cara was poisoned by cyanide. No other poison is so swift, and after she fell – ' he broke off, became a little paler and then went on composedly '– after she fell, I bent over her and then – and then – I smelt it.'

'I see. But not until then?'

'Not until then – no. The odour of the incense – sweet almond the acolyte tells me – was overpowering and, strangely enough, similar.'

De Ravigne turned stiffly towards Alleyn.

'My Cara was murdered. That I know well. Is it possible, Mr Inspector, that this similarity is a little too strange?'

'It is a point I shall remember, monsieur. You have used the expression "My Cara." Am I to understand that between you and Miss Quayne – '

'But yes. I adored her. I asked her many times to do me the honour of becoming my wife. She was, unhappily, indifferent to me. She was devout, you understand, altogether dedicated to the religious life. I see you look fixedly at me, monsieur. You are thinking perhaps that I am too calm. You have the idea of the excitable Frenchman. I should wave my hands and weep and roll about my eyes and even have a hysteric, like that little animal of a Claude.'

'No, Monsieur de Ravigne. Those were not my thoughts.'

'*N'importe,*' murmured de Ravigne.

'*On n'est pas dupe de son coeur –* ' began Alleyn.

'I see I misjudged you, M. l'Inspecteur. You have not the conventional idea of my countrymen. Also you speak with a charming and correct accent.'

'You are too kind, monsieur. Has the possibility of suicide occurred to you?'

'Why should she wish to die? She was beautiful and – loved.'

'And not poor?'

'I believe, not poor.'

'Did you notice her movements when she held the cup?'

'No. I did not watch,' said de Ravigne.

'You are religious yourself, of course, or you would not be here?' remarked Alleyn after a pause.

M. de Ravigne delicately moved his shoulders: 'I am intrigued with this church and its ceremonial. Also the idea of one godhead embracing all gods appeals to my temperament. One must have a faith, I find. It is not in my temperament to be an atheist.'

'When did you first attend the services?'

'It must be – yes, I think about two years ago.'

'And you became an Initiate – when?'

'Three months ago, perhaps.'

'Are you a subscriber to the organisation? We must ask these questions, as I am sure you understand.'

'Certainly, monsieur, one must do one's job. I subscribe a little, yes. Five shillings in the offertory always and at special times a pound. Fifty pounds when I first came. This temple was then recently established. I presented the goblet – an old one in my own family.'

'A beautiful piece. Baroque at its best,' said Alleyn.

'Yes. It has its history, that cup. Also I gave a statuette. In the shrine on your right, monsieur.'

Alleyn looked at the wall and found M. de Ravigne's statuette. It was cast in bronze with a curious plucked technique and represented a nebulous nude figure wearing a winged helmet from which there emerged other and still more nebulous forms.

'Ah yes,' said Alleyn, 'most interesting. Who is the artist?'

'Myself in ecstasy, monsieur,' replied M. de Ravigne coolly.

Alleyn glanced at his shrewd, dark face and murmured politely.

'My temperament,' continued M. de Ravigne, 'is artistic. I am, I fear, a dilettante. I model a little, *comme çi, comme ça.* I write a little, trifles of elegance. I collect. I am not rich, M. l'Inspecteur, but I amuse myself.'

'A delightful existence. I envy you, monsieur. But we must get back to business.'

A dim bass rumble from the rear seemed to suggest that Inspector Fox had essayed: *"Revenons à nos moutons,"* and had got lost on the way.

'I understand,' said Alleyn, 'that Miss Quayne has no relations in England. There must be *someone* surely?'

'On the contrary. She has told me that there are none. Cara was an only child and an orphan. She was educated abroad at a convent. Her guardians are both dead.'

'You met her abroad perhaps?'

'Yes. In France years ago at the house of a friend.'

'Did Miss Quayne introduce you to this hall?'

'No, monsieur. Alas, it was I who introduced her to the ceremonies.'

'Returning to her connections, monsieur. Is there no one with whom we should get in touch?'

'Her notary – her solicitor.'

'Of course. Do you know who that is?'

'I have heard. One moment. It is – *tiens!* – a name like Rats. No. Rattingtown. No.'

'Not Rattisbon by any chance?'

'That is it. You know him?'

'Slightly. Where will the money go, Monsieur de Ravigne?' M. de Ravigne hitched up his shoulders, elevated his brows, protruded his eyes and pursed his lips.

'I see,' said Alleyn.

'This I do know,' conceded M. de Ravigne. 'Much will go to this church. Five thousand pounds are reposed in the safe here in bearer bonds to await a further subscription. But there will be more for this church. Once Cara told me she had altered her Will for the purpose. It was then I heard the name of this Mr Rats.'

'Oh, yes,' said Alleyn politely. 'To go to another aspect of the case, do you know anything of the procedure for preparing the cup?'

'Nothing, monsieur. I am not interested in such affairs. To know the machinery of the service would damage my spiritual poise. Such is my temperament.'

'You do not choose to look behind the scenes?'

'Precisely. There must be certain arrangements. A flame does not make itself from nothing, one realizes, but I do not wish to inquire into these matters. I enjoy the results.'

'Quite so,' said Alleyn. 'I think that will be all, monsieur. Thank you a thousand times for your courtesy.'

'Not at all, monsieur! It is you who have displayed courtesy. If I can be of further use – It is perhaps a matter of some delicacy, but I assure you that anything I can do to help you – I shall not rest content until this animal is trapped. If there should be a question of expense – you understand?'

'You are very good.'

'Tout au contraire, monsieur.'

'– but it is for information we ask. Do you object to our searching you, monsieur?'

'I object very much, monsieur, but I submit.' Fox searched him and found nothing but money, a chequebook and a photograph.

'Mon Dieu!' said de Ravigne. 'Must you paw it over in your large hands? Give it to me.'

'Pardon, monsoor,' said Fox hastily, and gave it to him.

'It is Cara Quayne,' said de Ravigne to Alleyn. 'I am sorry if I was too hasty.'

'I am sure Inspector Fox understands. Goodnight, M. de Ravigne.'

'Goodnight, M. l'Inspecteur.'

'Well,' said Fox when the Frenchman had gone. 'Well, that was a fair treat, sir. As soon as you spoke to the gentleman in his own tongue he came along like a lamb. There's the advantage of languages. It puts you on an equal footing, so to speak. I wonder you didn't carry on the rest of the interview in French.'

'Fox!' said Alleyn with the oddest look at him. 'You make me feel a bloody fool sometimes.'

'Me?' exclaimed Fox, looking blandly astonished.

'Yes, you. Tell me, have you any comments to make on the Frenchman?'

Fox wiped his enormous paw slowly down his face.

'Well, no,' he said slowly, 'except he seemed – well, sir, it's a rum thing two of the gentlemen should offer money for the police investigations. An unheard of idea. But of course they were both foreigners. As far as Mr Ogden is concerned, well, we have heard of the word "racket," haven't we?'

'Exactly,' agreed Alleyn dryly. 'I imagine his proposal is not unusual in the States.'

'Ogden's too good to be true,' interrupted Nigel. 'You mark my words,' he added darkly, 'he was trying to bribe you.'

'Bribe us to do what, my dear Bathgate? To catch a murderer?'

'Don't be ridiculous,' said Nigel loftily.

'And was M. de Ravigne also attempting to undermine the honour of the force?'

Oh,' said Nigel, 'de Ravigne's a Frenchman. He is no doubt over-emotionalized and – and – oh, go to the devil.'

'It seems to me,' rumbled Fox, 'that we ought to have a look at that little bottle in the cupboard – the one Mr Wheatley talked about.'

'I agree. We'll move into Mr Garnette's "little dwelling." By the way, where is Mr Garnette? Is he still in the vestry being searched?'

As if in answer to Alleyn's inquiry, the vestry door opened and the priest came out. He was now dressed in a long garment made of some heavy, dark-green material. The plain-clothes man who had escorted him into the vestry came to the door and stared after the priest with an air of disgusted bewilderment.

'Ah, Inspector!' cried Father Garnette with holy cheeriness. 'Still hard at work! Still hard at work!'

'I'm most frightfully sorry,' said Alleyn. 'There was no need for you to wait in there. You could have returned to your rooms.'

'Have I been long? I was engaged in an ecstatic meditation and had passed into the third portal where there is no time.'

'You were fortunate.'

Bailey came out of Father Garnette's room and approached the inspector.

'That Miss Wade, sir,' he said, 'is getting kind of resigned. I think she's dropped off to sleep.'

Alleyn gazed at Fox and Fox at Alleyn.

'Cripes!' said Inspector Fox.

'Lummie!' said Inspector Alleyn, 'I must be in ecstasy myself. I'd quite forgotten her. Lord, I am sorry! Show the lady down, Bailey.'

'Right oh, sir.'

CHAPTER 9

Miss Wade

Father Garnette showed an inclination to hover, but was most firmly removed to his own rooms. He and Miss Wade met on the chancel steps.

'Ah, you poor soul!' intoned Father Garnette. 'Very weary? Very sad?'

Miss Wade looked from Bailey to the priest.

'Father!' she whispered. 'They are not – they don't suspect – '

'Courage, dear lady!' interposed Father Garnette very quickly and loudly. 'Courage! We are all in good hands. I shall pray for you.'

He hurried past and made for his door, followed by Bailey. Miss Wade looked after him for a moment and then turned towards the steps. She peered shortsightedly into the hall. Alleyn went up to her.

'I cannot apologize enough for keeping you so long.'

Miss Wade examined him doubtfully, 'I am sure you were doing your duty, officer,' she said.

'You are very kind, madam. Won't you sit down?'

'Thank you.' She sat, very erect, on the edge of one of the chairs.

'There are certain questions that I must ask,' began Alleyn, 'as a matter of official routine.'

'Yes?'

'Yes. I'll be as quick as I can.'

'Thank you. It will be nice to get home,' said Miss Wade plaintively. 'I am distressed by the thought that I have perhaps left my electric heater turned on. I can remember *perfectly* that I *said* to myself: "Now I must not forget to turn it off," but – '

71

Here Miss Wade stopped short and gazed pensively into space for at least seven seconds.

'I recollect,' she said at last, 'I *did* turn it off. Shall we commence? You were saying?'

'That I should like, if I may, to ask you one or two questions.'

'Certainly. I shall be glad to be of any assistance. I am not at all familiar with the methods of the police, although I have a very dear brother who was an officer in the Cape Mounted Police during the Boer War. He suffered great privations and discomforts and his digestion has never quite recovered.'

Alleyn stooped abruptly and fastened his shoe.

'The questions, Miss Wade, are these,' he began when he had straightened up again. 'First: did you notice any unusual smell when you received the cup from M. de Ravigne?'

'Let me think. Any odour? Yes,' said Miss Wade triumphantly, 'I did. Decidedly. Yes.'

'Can you describe it?'

'Indeed I can. Peppermint.'

'Peppermint!' ejaculated Alleyn.

'Yes. And onion. You see Claude, the lad who acted as cup-bearer, was bending over me and – and it was rather overwhelming. I have noticed it before and wondered if I should speak to Father about it. Evidently, the lad is passionately fond of these things, and I don't, I really *don't* think it is quite reverent.'

'I agree,' said Alleyn hurriedly. 'Miss Wade, you have said once before this evening that Miss Quayne was not very happy and not very popular. Can you tell me a little more about her? Why was she unpopular?'

'But you were not here when I said that, officer. I am positive of that because when we were in there waiting – no. I'm not telling the truth – that's a fib. It was *before* you came, and it was before that young man went to the telephone and' – Miss Wade again stared fixedly at the inspector for some seconds – 'and Father Garnette said to me: "I implore you not to speak like that to the police," so you see I know you were not here, so how did you know?'

'Mr Bathgate remembered and told me. Why was Miss Quayne unhappy?'

'*Because* she was unpopular,' said Miss Wade triumphantly.

'And why was she unpopular, do you think?'

'Poor thing! I think there was a certain amount of jealousy. I'm afraid that there was, although perhaps I should not say so. Father Garnette seemed to think I should not say so.'

'I am sure you want to help us.'

'Oh, yes, of *course* I do. At least – Would you be good enough to tell me if poor Cara was murdered?'

'I believe so. It looks like it.'

'Then if I say that *somebody* was jealous of her you may grow suspicious and begin to think all sorts of things, and I don't believe in capital punishment.'

'Jealousy is not invariably followed by homicide.'

'Isn't that *precisely* what I was saying! So you see!'

'Mrs Candour,' said Alleyn thoughtfully, 'tells me that Miss Quayne was not a particularly striking personality.'

'Now that's really naughty of Dagmar. She should try to conquer her feelings. It is not as though Father gave them any encouragement. I am afraid she wilfully misunderstood. He is too noble and too pure even to guess – '

'Guess what, Miss Wade?'

Miss Wade compressed her faded lips and looked acutely uncomfortable.

'Come!' said Alleyn. 'I shall jump to some terrible conclusion if you are so mysterious.'

'I don't believe what they say,' cried Miss Wade. Her voice shook and her thin hands trembled in her lap. 'It is wicked – wicked. His thoughts are as pure as a saint's. Cara was a child to him. Dagmar is a wicked woman to speak as she does. Cara was excitable and impulsive, we know that, and generous – generous. Rich people are not always to be envied.' Alleyn was silent for a moment.

'Tell me,' he began at last,' were your eyes closed during the ceremony of the cup?'

'Oh, yes. We all must keep our eyes closed, except, of course, when we pour out the wine. One has to open them then.'

'You did not notice any of the other Initiates when they poured out the wine?'

'Of course not,' said Miss Wade uncomfortably. She became very pink and pursed up her lips.

'I should have thought,' pursued Alleyn gently, 'that when you took the cup from M. de Ravigne – '

'Oh, *then* of course I had to peep,' admitted Miss Wade.

'And when you passed it on to Mr Pringle?'

'Well, of course. Especially with Mr Pringle, he has such very tremulous hands. Exceedingly tremulous. It's smoking too many cigarettes. I told him so. I said frankly to him: "Mr Pringle, you will undermine your health with this excessive indulgence in nicotine." My dear brother is also a very prolific smoker, so I *know.*'

'Mr Pringle did not spill any wine, I suppose?'

'No. No, he didn't. But more by good fortune than good management. He took the cup by the stem in one hand and it quivered and, if I may say so reverently, jigged about so much that he was obliged to grasp it by the rim with the other. Then, of course, he had great difficulty in taking the wine-vessel – the silver jug, you know – from Claude, and in pouring out the wine. It wasn't at all nice. Not reverent.'

'No. M. de Ravigne?'

'Ah. There, *quite* a different story. Everything very nice and respectful,' said Miss Wade. 'Dagmar had left a little trickle on the rim and he drew out a *spotless* handkerchief and wiped it. Nothing could be nicer. He might almost be an Englishman.'

'In your anxiety – your very natural anxiety about Mr Pringle – perhaps you just looked to see – '

'When he passed it to dear Janey? Yes, Inspector, I did. Janey must have felt as nervous as I did for she reached out her hands and *took* it as soon as Mr Pringle had poured in the wine. Well, I say "poured," but it is my impression that although he made an attempt he did not actually succeed in doing so. Mr Ogden is always quite the gentleman, of course,' added Miss Wade with one of her magnificent *non sequiturs.* 'He receives the cup in *both* hands by the bowl and grasps the vessel firmly by the neck. That sounds a little as though he had three hands, but of course the mere idea is ludicrous.'

'And then gives the cup to Mr Garnette.'

'To Father Garnette. Yes. Of course when Father Garnette took it, I did raise my eyes. He does it so beautifully, it is quite uplifting. *One* hand on the stem,' described Miss Wade holding up genteel little claws, 'and the *other* laid over the cup. Like a benison.'

'I suppose you all watch the Chosen Vessel?'

'Oh, yes. As soon as poor Cara took it we all raised our eyes. You see she was speaking in ecstasy. It was a wonderful experience. I thought she was going to dance.'

'To dance!' ejaculated the inspector.

'Even,' chanted Miss Wade in a pious falsetto, 'even as the priests danced before the Stone of Odin. It has happened before. A lady who has since passed through the last portal.'

'You mean she has died?'

'Yes.'

'What did this lady die of?' asked Alleyn.

'They *called* it epilepsy,' replied Miss Wade doubtfully.

'Well, Miss Wade,' said Alleyn after a pause, 'it has been perfectly charming of you to be so patient with me. I am most grateful. There's only one other thing.'

'And that is?' asked Miss Wade with a perky air of being exceedingly businesslike.

'Will you allow the wardress to search you?'

'To *search* me! Oh dear. I – I – must confess. It is such a very cold evening and I did not anticipate – '

'You would not have to – remove anything,' said Alleyn hurriedly. 'Or rather' – he looked helplessly at Miss Wade's dejected little fur tippet and drab raincoat and, since the raincoat was unbuttoned, at layers of purple and black cardigans – 'or rather only your outer things.'

'I have no desire,' said Miss Wade, 'to obstruct the police in the execution of their duty. Where is this woman?'

'In the porch outside.'

'But that is very public.'

'If you would prefer the vestry.'

'I don't think the robing-chamber would be quite nice. Let it be the porch, officer.'

'Thank you, madam.'

Detective-Sergeant Bailey came down from the chancel and whispered to Inspector Fox. Inspector Fox moved to a strategic position behind Miss Wade and proceeded to raise his eyebrows, wink with extreme deliberation, contort his features into an expression of cunning profundity and finally to hold up a small fragment of paper.

'Eh?' said Alleyn. 'Oh! Do you know, Miss Wade, I don't think I need bother you with this business. Just let the wardress see your bag and pockets if you have any. And your gloves. That will be quite enough.'

'More than sufficient,' said Miss Wade. 'Thank you. Good evening, officer.'

'Good evening, madam.'

'Have you been through the Police College?'

'Not precisely, madam.'

'Indeed?' said Miss Wade, squinting curiously at him. 'But you speak nicely.'

'You are very kind.'

'A superior school perhaps? The advantages – '

'My parents gave me all the advantages they could afford,' agreed Alleyn solemnly.

'Chief Detective-Inspector Alleyn, ma'am,' began Fox with surprising emphasis, 'was – '

'Fox,' interrupted Alleyn, 'don't be a snob. Get Miss Wade a taxi.'

'Oh, thank you, I have my overshoes on.'

'My superiors would wish it, madam.'

'Then in that case – my grandfather kept his carriage at Dulwich – thank you, I will take a taxi.'

CHAPTER 10

A Piece of Paper and a Bottle

'Well, Brer Fox,' said Alleyn when that gentleman returned, 'has the lady been looked at?'

'Mrs Bekin went through her bag and pockets,' replied Fox.

'And what was the trophy you waved at me just now?'

'Bailey found something up in the chancel. It was simply lying on the floor. It had been ground into the carpet by somebody's heel. We thought it was the article you wanted.'

'I hope it is. Let's see it.'

'It wasn't the same bit I showed you,' explained Fox. 'That was just, as you say, a hint. There's the original.'

He produced a small box. Nigel drew near. Alleyn opened the box and discovered a tiny piece of very grubby reddish paper. It had been pressed flat and was creased by a heavy indentation.

'M'm,' grunted Alleyn, 'Wait a bit.'

He went to his bag and got a pair of tweezers. Then he carried the paper in the box to one of the side lights and looked closely at it. He lifted it a little with the tweezers, holding it over the box. He smelt it.

'That's it, sure enough,' he said. 'Look – it's an envelope. A cigarette-paper gummed double. By Jove, Fox, he took a risk. It'd need a bit of sleight-of-hand.' He touched it very delicately with the tip of his fingers.

'Wet!' said Alleyn. 'So that's how it was done.'

'What do you mean?' asked Nigel, 'It's red. Is it drenched in somebody's life-blood? Why must you be so tiresomely enigmatic?'

'Nobody's being enigmatic. I'm telling you, as Mr Ogden would say. Here's a bit of cigarette-paper. It's been doubled over and gummed into a tiny tube. One end has been folded over several times making the tube into an envelope. It has been dyed – I *think* with red ink. It's wet. It smells. It's a clue, damn your eyes, it's a clue.'

'It will have to be analysed, won't it, sir?' asked Fox.

'Oh rather, yes. This is the real stuff. "The Case of the Folded Paper." "Inspector Fox sees red."'

'But, Alleyn,' complained Nigel, 'if it's wet do you mean it's only recently been dipped in red ink? Oh – wait a bit. Wait a bit.'

'Watch our little bud unfolding,' said Alleyn.

'It's wet with wine,' cried Nigel triumphantly.

'Mr Bathgate, I do believe you must be right.'

'Facetious ass!'

'Sorry. Yes, it floated upon the wine when it was red. Bailey!'

'Hullo, sir?'

'Show us just where you found this. You've done very well.' A faint trace of mulish satisfaction appeared on Detective-Sergeant Bailey's face. He crossed over to the chancel steps, stooped, and pointed to a sixpenny piece.

'I left that to mark the place,' he said.

'And it is precisely over the spot where the cup lay. There's my chalk mark. That settles it.'

'Do you mean,' asked Nigel, 'that the murderer dropped the paper into the cup?'

'Just that.'

'Purposely?'

'I think so. See here, Bathgate. Suppose one of the Initiates had a pinch of cyanide in this little envelope. He – or she has it concealed about his or her person. In a cigarette-case, perhaps, or an empty lipstick holder. Just before he goes up with the others he takes it out and holds it right end up – wait a moment – like this perhaps.'

'No,' said Nigel, 'like this.' He folded his hands like those of a saint in a mediaeval drawing, 'I noticed they all did that.'

'Excellent. The flat open end would be slipped between two fingers, and the thing would be held snug. When he – call it he for the moment – takes the cup, he manages to let the little envelope fall in. Not so difficult as it sounds. We'll experiment later. The paper floats. The folded end uppermost, the open end down. The powder falls out.'

'But,' objected Fox, 'he's running a big risk, sir. Suppose somebody notices the paper floating about on the top of the wine. Suppose, for the sake of argument, Miss Jenkins or Mr Ogden say they saw it, and Mr Pringle and the rest don't mention it – well, that won't look too good for Mr Pringle. If he's the murderer he'll think of that. I mean – '

'I know what you're driving at, Inspector,' said Nigel excitedly. 'But the gentleman says to himself that if anyone notices the paper he'll notice it too. That will switch it back a place to the one before him.'

'Um,' rumbled Fox doubtfully.

'I don't think they would see it,' Alleyn murmured. 'You say, Bathgate, that during the ceremony of the cup the torch was the only light?'

'Yes.'

'Quite so. It's nearly burnt out now, but I think you will find that when it's going full blast there will be a shadow immediately beneath it where they knelt, a shadow cast by its own sconce.'

'I think there was,' agreed Nigel. 'I remember that they seemed to be in a sort of pool of gloom.'

'Exactly. And in addition, their own heads, bent over the cup, would cast a further shadow. All the same, you're right, Fox. He *is* taking a big risk. Unless – ' Alleyn stopped short, stared at his colleague, and then for no apparent reason made a hideous grimace at Nigel.

'What's that for?' demanded Nigel suspiciously.

'This is all pure conjecture,' said Alleyn abruptly. 'When the analyst finds traces of cyanide we can start talking.'

'I can't see why he'd drop the paper in,' complained Nigel. 'It must have been accidental.'

'I don't know, Mr Bathgate,' said Fox in his slow way. 'There are points about it. No fingerprints. Nothing to show if he's searched.'

'That's right,' said Bailey suddenly. 'And he'd reckon the lady'd be sure to drop the cup. He'd reckon on it falling out and getting tramped into the carpet like it was.'

'Say it stuck to the side?' objected Fox.

'Well, say it did,' said Bailey combatively. 'What's to stop him getting it out when they're all looking at the lady throwing fancy fits and passing in her checks?'

'Say it slid out on to her lips,' continued Fox monotonously.

'Say she drank it? You make me tired, Mr Fox. It wouldn't slide out, it'd slide back on the top of the wine. Isn't that right?'

'Um,' said Fox again.

'What d'yer mean "Um"! That's fair enough, isn't it, sir?' He appealed to Alleyn.

'Conjecture,' said Alleyn. 'Surmise and conjecture.'

'You started it,' remarked Nigel perkily.

'So I did. That's all the thanks I get for thinking aloud. Come on, Fox. It grows beastly late. Shut up your find. We'll know more about it when the analyst has spoken his piece.'

Fox took the little box from him, shut it, and put it into the bag.

'What's next, sir?' he asked.

'Why, Mr Garnett's little bottle. Where is Mr Garnette?'

'In his rooms. Dr Curtis is there and one of our men.'

'I wonder if he has converted them. Let us join the cosy circle. You can tackle the vestry now, Bailey.'

Fox, Alleyn and Nigel went up to Father Garnette's room, leaving Bailey and his satellites to continue their prowling.

Father Garnette sat at his desk which, with its collection of *objects de piété*, so closely resembled an altar. Dr Curtis sat at the table. A uniformed constable with a perfectly expressionless face stood by Father Garnette's prie-dieu, furnishing a most fantastic juxtaposition of opposites. They all had the look of persons who have not spoken for a considerable time. Father Garnette was pallid and a little too dignified; Dr Curtis was wan and puffed with suppressed yawning; the constable was merely pale by nature.

'Ah, Mr Garnette,' said Alleyn cheerfully, 'here we are at last. You must long for your bed.'

'No, no,' said Father Garnette. 'No, no.'

'We shan't keep you very much longer. I wonder if you will allow me to make an inspection of these rooms? I'm afraid it ought to be done.'

'An inspection! But really, Inspector, is that necessarah? I must confess I – ' Father Garnette stopped and then added a throaty sound suggestive of sweet reasonableness coupled with distress.

'You object?' said Alleyn briskly. 'Then I shall have to leave my men here for the time being. I'm so sorry.'

'But – I cannot understand – '

'You see I'm afraid there is little doubt that this is a case of homicide. That means there is a certain routine that we are obliged to follow. A search of the premises is part of this routine. Of course, if you object – '

'I – no – I – '

'You don't?'

'Not if – no. It is merely that this little dwelling is very precious to me. It is filled with the thoughts – the meditations of a specially dedicated life. One shrinks a little from the thought of – ah – '

'Of fools stepping in where – but no, of course this is one of the places where angels tread all over the place. We'll be as quick as we can. You can help us if you will. The bedroom is through there, I suppose.'

'Yes.'

'Any other rooms?'

'The usual offices,' said Father Garnette grandly: 'bathroom, etceterah, etceterah.'

'Any back door?'

'Ah – yes.'

'Is it locked?'

'Invariablah.'

'Have a look, will you, Fox? I'll take this room'

Fox dived past a black velvet portière. The constable, at a nod from Alleyn, followed him.

'Would you rather stay here?' asked Alleyn of Father Garnette. Father Garnette cast a somewhat distracted glance round the room and said he thought he would.

'Finished with me, Alleyn?' asked Dr Curtis.

'Yes, thanks, Curtis. Inquest on Tuesday, I suppose. They'll want a post-mortem, of course.'

'Of course. I'll be off.'

'Lucky creature. Goodnight.'

'Goodnight. Goodnight, Father Garnette.'

'Goodnight, my dear doctor,' ejaculated Father Garnette on a sudden gush of geniality.

The little divisional surgeon hurried away. Nigel attempted to make himself inconspicuous by standing in a corner and was at once told to come out of it and give a hand.

'Make a note of anything I tell you about. Now, Mr Garnette, I understand that in preparing the wine for tonight's ceremony Mr Wheatley used two ingredients. Where did he find the bottles?'

Father Garnette pointed to a very nice Jacobean cupboard. It was unlocked. Alleyn opened the doors and revealed an extremely representative cellar. All the ingredients for the more elaborate cocktails, some self-respecting port, the brandy that had been recommended by Dr Curtis, and a dozen bottles of an aristocrat in hocks. On a shelf by themselves stood four bottles of dubious appearance – 'Le Comte's Invalid Port.' One was empty.

'That will be the one broached tonight?' asked Alleyn.

'Ah – yes,' said Father Garnette.

Alleyn moved the others to one side and discovered a smaller label-less bottle, half full. He took it out carefully, holding it by the extreme end of the neck. The cork came out easily. Alleyn sniffed at the orifice and raised an eyebrow.

'Big magic, Mr Garnette,' he remarked.

'I beg your pardon?'

'Did this provide the second ingredient in the potion mixed by Mr Wheatley?'

'A – broomp,' said Father Garnette, clearing his vocal passage, 'yes. That is so.'

Alleyn drew a pencil from his pocket, dipped it into the bottle and then sucked it pensively.

'How much of this was used?' he asked.

Father Garnette inclined his head.

'The merest *soupçon*,' he said. 'It is perfectly pure.'

'The best butter,' murmured Alleyn. He put the bottle in his bag, which Fox had left on the table.

'You have a complete cellar without it, I see,' he said coolly.

Ah yes. Will you take something, Inspector? This has been a trying evening – for all of us.'

'No, thank you so much.'

'Mr – ah – Bathgate?'

Nigel's tongue arched longingly but he too refused a drink.

'I am very much shaken,' said Father Garnette. 'I feel wretchard. Quite wretchard.'

'You had better have a peg yourself, perhaps,' suggested Alleyn. Father Garnette passed his hand wearily across his forehead and then let his arm flop on the desk.

'Perhaps I had, perhaps I had,' he said with a sort of brave smile. He poured himself out a pretty stiff nip, took a pull at it, and sat down at the table.

Alleyn went on with his investigation of the room. He moved to the desk. Father Garnette watched him.

'I wonder if you would mind moving into the next room, Mr Garnette,' said Alleyn placidly.

'I – but – I – Surely, Inspector, I may at least watch this distasteful proceeding.'

'I think you should spare yourself the pain. I want Inspector Fox to search you.'

'I have already been searched.'

'That was before you changed, I think. I expect Fox will have almost finished there. I suggest you go to bed.'

'I do not want to go to bed,' complained Father Garnette. He took another resolute pull at his drink.

'Don't you? It would be simpler. However, I'll get Fox to look you over now. You will have to strip, I'm afraid. Fox.'

'Sir?' Inspector Fox thrust a large bland face round the curtain. Father Garnette suddenly leapt to his feet.

'I refuse,' he said very loudly. 'This is too much. You exceed your duty. I refuse.'

'What's up, sir?' asked Fox.

'Mr Garnette doesn't want to be searched again, Fox. Did he object the first time?'

'He did not.'

'Curious. Ah well!'

'I just thought I'd mention it, sir. The back door is not locked.'

'Oh,' said Alleyn. 'I thought, Mr Garnette, that you said it was invariably locked.'

'So it is, Inspectah. I cannot understand – I locked it myself, this afternoon.'

Alleyn took out his notebook and wrote in it. Then he handed it to Fox, who came through the curtain, put on a pair of spectacles, and read solemnly. Father Garnette's eyes were glued on the note-book.

'That's very peculiar, sir,' said Fox. 'Look here.' He swung round with his back to Alleyn and held up a tightly clenched paw. Father Garnette stared at Fox wildly.

'Very peculiar,' repeated Fox.

Nigel could have echoed his words, for Alleyn with amazing swiftness whipped the bottle from his bag and, holding it delicately, tipped a handsome proportion of its contents into Father Garnette's glass. He returned the bottle to the bag and strolled over to Fox.

'Ah yes,' he said. 'Remarkable.'

'What d'you mean?' asked Garnette loudly. 'What are you talk-ing about?'

'It's of no consequence,' murmured Alleyn. 'of no consequence whatever.'

'I demand – ' began Garnette. He glared unhappily at the two detectives, suddenly flopped down into his chair, and drank off the contents of the glass.

'Carry on, Fox,' said Alleyn.

CHAPTER 11

Contents of a Desk, a Safe, and a Bookcase

The behaviour of Father Garnette underwent a rapid and most perceptible change. This difference was first apparent in his face. It was rather as though a facile modeller in clay had touched the face in several places, leaving subtle but important alterations in its general expression. It became at once bolder and more sly. The resemblance to a purveyor of patent medicines triumphed over the more saintly aspect. Indeed, Father Garnette no longer looked in the least like a saint. He looked both shady and blowsy.

Nigel, fascinated, watched this change into something rich and strange. Alleyn, busy at the desk, had his back to the priest. Inspector Fox had returned to the bedroom where he could be heard humming like a Gargantuan bumble-bee. Presently he burst into song:

'Frerer Jacker, Frerer Jacker,
Dormy-vous, dormy-vous.'

It was an earnest attempt to reproduce the intermediate radio French lesson.

The clock on the mantelpiece ticked loudly, cleared its throat, and struck twelve.

'Say, bo!' said Father Garnette suddenly and astonishingly: 'Say, bo, why can't we get together?'

Alleyn turned slowly and regarded him.

'That's the way Ogden talks when he talks when he talks,' added Father Garnette with an air of great lucidity.

'Oh, yes?' said Alleyn.

'Get together,' repeated Father Garnette, 'let's get together at the river. The beautiful the beautiful the river. Why can't we gather at the river? I ran a revivalist joint way down in Michitchigan back in '14. It was swell. Boy, it was swell.'

'Was Mr Ogden with you in Michigan?' asked Alleyn.

'That big sap!' said Father Garnette with bitter scorn. 'Why, he thinks I'm the sand-fly's garters.' He appeared to regret his last observation and added, with something of his former manner: 'Mr Ogden is sassherated in holy simplicity.'

'Oh,' said Alleyn. 'When *did* you meet Mr Ogden?'

'Crossing th' 'Tlantic. He gave me a piece of gold. Ogden's all right. Sassherated in simplicity.'

'So it would appear.'

'Listen,' said Father Garnette. 'You got me all wrong. I never did a thing to that dame. Is it likely? Little Cara! No, sir.'

He looked so obscene as he made this statement that Nigel gave an involuntary exclamation.

'Be quiet, Bathgate,' ordered Alleyn very quietly.

'Why can't we get together?' resumed Father Garnette. 'I'll talk.'

'What with?' asked Alleyn.

'With the right stuff. You lay off this joint and you won't need to ask for the say-so. What's it worth?'

'What's it worth to you?'

'It's your squeak,' said Father Garnette obscurely.

'You're bluffing,' said Alleyn, 'you haven't got tuppence.'

Father Garnette was instantly thrown into a violent rage.

'Is that so!' he said, so loudly that Fox came back to listen. 'Is that so! Listen, you poor simp. In my own line there's no one to touch me. Why? Because I got brains sanimaginasshon and mor'n that – because I got one hundred per cent essay.'

'What's that?' asked Alleyn.

'Essay! Ess-shay. "It."'

'So you say,' grunted Alleyn most offensively.

'So I say and what I say's so I say,' said Father Garnette with astounding rapidity, 'If you don't believe me – look f'yourself.'

He made an effort to rise, fell back in his chair, fumbled in his pocket and produced a ring of keys.

'Little leather box in desk,' he said. 'And not only that. Safe.'

'Thank you,' said Alleyn. Father Garnette instantly fell asleep.

Alleyn, without another glance at him, returned to the desk and pulled out the bottom drawer.

'Lor, sir,' said Fox, 'you've doped the gentleman.'

'Not I,' Alleyn grunted. 'He's merely tight.'

'Tight!' ejaculated Nigel. 'What was in the bottle?'

'Proof spirit. Over-proof as like as not.'

'Pure alcohol?'

'Something of the sort. That or rectified spirit, I imagine. Have to be analysed. This is a very exotic case. Thorndyke stuff. Not my cup of tea at all.'

'What,' asked Nigel, 'did you write on that paper you gave Fox?'

'A suggestion that he should attract Mr Garnette's attention.'

'You bad old Borgia!'

'Stop talking. Can't you see I'm detecting. What's the back door like, Fox?'

'Ordinary key and bolts. Funny it was open.'

'Very funny. Go through that waste-paper basket, will you? And the grate.'

Fox knelt on the hearth-rug. The fire had almost burnt out. For some time the detectives worked in silence. Suddenly Fox grunted.

'How now, brown cow?' asked Alleyn.

'If you mean me, sir, here's a bit of something.'

'What?'

Fox, using tweezers, drew two scraps of burnt paper from the ashtray and laid them before Alleyn. Nigel got up to look. They were the merest fragments of paper, but there were one or two words printed on them in green pencil:

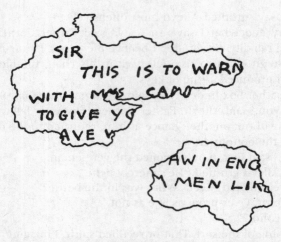

'Oh, Lord!' said Alleyn, 'what now! Let's see. Same paper as this stuff on his desk? No. I can't see a green pencil anywhere. We'll have to find out when that thing was last cleaned out. Any more bits?'

'That's the lot,' said Fox.

'Put it away tenderly. We'll have to brood over it. I want to get this desk cleaned up. Ah, here we are.' He drew out a purple suède case and examined the keys. Father Garnette uttered a stertorous snore. Fox, still looking scandalized, walked over to him.

'He'd be better in bed,' said Fox.

'So he would. Make it so, will you, Fox? Mr Bathgate will help you. And from his fair and unpolluted breath may violets spring. Ugh, you horrid old man!' added Alleyn with sudden violence. He had taken a bundle of letters from the box and was reading one of them.

Fox assisted by Nigel, heaved and hauled Father Garnette into the bedroom, which was draped in rose-coloured plush and satin. Here were more idols, more Nordic bijouterie, more cushions.

'Very classy, isn't it, sir?' remarked Fox as he lowered Father Garnette on to the divan bed.

'It's villainous, Fox,' said Nigel. He contemplated Father Garnette with distaste.

'Must we undress this unpleasant old blot?' he asked.

'I'm afraid so, sir. Can you find his pyjamas?'

From under a violently embroidered coverlet Nigel drew out a confection in purple silk.

'Look, Inspector, look! Really, it's too disgusting.'

'Not quite my fancy, I will say, sir,' conceded Fox who had attacked Father Garnette's right boot. 'I believe in wool next the skin, summer and winter. I'd feel kind of slippery in that issue.'

Nigel tried to picture Inspector Fox in purple satin pyjamas, failed to do so and laughed himself into a good humour. They put Father Garnette to bed. He muttered a little, opened his eyes once, said: 'Thank you, my son' in faultless English, showed signs of feeling very ill, but appeared to get over it, and finally sank again into the deepest slumber.

They rejoined Alleyn and found him poring over an array of letters.

'Something doing, sir?' asked Fox.

'Much. Most of it odious. These are all letters from women.'

'Any from the deceased?'

'Yes.' Alleyn grimaced. 'There it is. Read it. A mixture of pseudo-mystic gibberish and hysterical adulation. Garnette seems actually to have persuaded her that the – the union – was blessed, had a spiritual significance – puh!' He made a violent gesture. 'Read it. It's important.'

Nigel read over Fox's shoulder. The letter was written on mauve paper printed with Cara Quayne's address in Shepherd Market. It was undated. It began:

> *Beloved Father and Spouse in Ecstasy,*
> I know you will be out this afternoon, but I feel I must make oblation for the divine, glorious, ecstatic bliss that has been mine ever since last night. I am half frightened, tremulous. Am I worthy? I – the Chosen Vessel? How can I make oblation? With this you will find a parcel. It contains the bonds I told you of. £5,000. Oh, how hateful to speak of money, but – I know you will understand – it is a thank-offering. Tell them about it, and let them give too until we have enough for a new temple. I want you to find it when you come in – after I have gone. Oh, beloved holy –

The letter ran on to eight pages.

'Very peculiar indeed, sir,' said Fox who read the whole thing through with a perfectly impassive demeanour. 'That will be the money Mr Ogden and monsieur talked about. In the safe here, they said.'

'They did. I'm about to tackle the safe.'

Alleyn moved across the room, pulled aside a strip of Javanese tapestry, and disclosed a small built-in safe. He found the key on the ring Father Garnette had given him, opened the safe and began, with great method, to remove the contents and array them neatly on the table.

'Bank-book. Let's see. He paid in fifty pounds last Monday. I suppose we shan't find much cash. Any offertory tonight, Bathgate?'

'No. I imagine we didn't get so far.'

'I suppose not. There's a bag of something. Petty cash, perhaps. What's this? Cheque from Mr Ogden. Twenty pounds. Dated last Wednesday.'

'How he gets it out of the *gentlemen* fairly beats me,' said Fox.

'Extraordinary, isn't it? But you know, Fox, there is a kind of simple, shrewd business brain that'll believe any tarradiddle outside its own province.'

'Would you say Mr Ogden's was that sort, sir?' Alleyn flipped the cheque at him.

'Looks like it,' he said, and turned again to the safe. 'Hullo! This is more the sort of thing.'

He pulled out a package and laid it on the table. It was a largish brown-paper parcel tied up with red ribbon. It was addressed to 'The Reverend Father Jasper Garnette,' and the writing was undoubtedly Cara Quayne's. Alleyn stared fixedly at the ribbon. He turned the parcel over once or twice.

'Aren't you going to open it?' asked Nigel.

'Oh, yes. Yes.' But he hesitated a little while longer and at last, laying the parcel on the table, slipped the ribbon very gingerly over one end, cautiously pulled out the folds of paper, and peered into the open end. He held the parcel under a lamp, and examined it even more closely. Then he dropped it back on to the table.

'Well?' asked Nigel.

'Well, Bathgate, I wish Mr Garnette was not so sound asleep.'

'Why on earth?'

'I should like him to have a look at this.' Fox lifted the parcel by the open end and looked in.

'Cripes!' he said.

'Here!' Nigel ejaculated. 'Let me look.'

'Don't pick it up. Look inside.'

Nigel did so. Fox flashed his torch into the parcel. Nigel glanced up at the two policemen, peered again into the parcel, grinned, looked doubtful, and at last said:

'But is that all?'

'I think so, oh yes,' answered Alleyn.

'But,' said Nigel, 'it's – it's all newspaper.' He thrust a finger in and ferreted round.

'So it is,' agreed Alleyn.

'By gum!' ejaculated Nigel. 'The motive!'

'Very like, very like.'

'Garnette has pinched the bonds.'

'Somebody's pinched them. Ask Bailey to come in and get the prints, if any, will you, Bathgate?'

Bailey was grubbing about in the vestry. He returned with Nigel, produced his insufflator and got to work on the parcel. Alleyn had sat down at the table and was tackling the rest of the material from the safe. Fox embarked on a meticulous search of the sideboard drawers. Nigel, with a sidelong glance at the Chief Detective-Inspector, pulled out his pad, sank into Father Garnette's most spacious armchair, lit a cigarette, and began to write.

'Copy?' inquired Alleyn mildly.

'And why not?' said Nigel defiantly.

'No reason at all. Let me see it before you send it in.'

'That's a pretty piece of effrontery, that is,' said Nigel hotly. 'Who was here from the start? Who called you in? I consider I displayed remarkable presence of mind. You've come in on a hot scent. This is a big story and I'm going to make it so. Eyewitness of a murder. That's what I was, and they're going to know it.'

'All right. All right. I merely ask to see your story.'

'Yes, and you'll blue pencil it out of existence.'

'No, I won't. Don't mention the bearer bonds.'

'There you go, you see!'

'And pray, Bathgate, don't refer to me as "The indefatigable Chief Detective-Inspector Alleyn."'

'But, Alleyn,' Nigel protested, 'That is altogether unfair. I have never made use of such a phrase. You merely speak for your own amusement.'

'What style are you adopting? You have been reading George Moore again, I notice.'

'What makes you suppose that?' asked Nigel, turning pink.

'His style has touched your conversation and left it self-conscious.'

'Nonsense.'

'Nevertheless it is an admirable style, though I shall be interested to see how you apply it to journalism and the mechanics of police investigation.'

'That is merely ridiculous,' said Nigel. He returned pointedly to his work and after a moment's consideration erased a word or two.

'Any prints on the parcel, Bailey?' asked Alleyn.

'Yes, sir. All one brand. The Reverend, I'll bet. I've got a sample of him off that glass.'

'Ah,' said Alleyn.

'Ah-ha,' said Nigel.

'No, not quite "Ah-ha" I fancy,' murmured the inspector.

'Hullo!' exclaimed Fox suddenly.

'What's up?' asked Alleyn.

'Look here, sir.' Fox came to the table and put down a small slip of paper.

'I found it in the cigarette-box,' he said. 'It's the lady again.'

'Yes,' agreed Alleyn, 'it's the lady. Bless my soul,' he added, 'the damn' place is choc-a-bloc full of dubious correspondence.'

Nigel came across to look. Fox's new find was a very small page of shiny paper. Monday's date was printed in one corner and underneath was scribbled the word: 'Sunday.' Three edges were gilt, the fourth was torn across at an angle as though it had been wrenched from a book. Cara Quayne had written in pencil: 'Must see you. Terrible discovery. After service tonight.'

'Where exactly was it?' asked Alleyn.

'In this.' Fox displayed an elaborate Benares box almost full of Turkish cigarettes. 'It was on the sideboard and the paper lay on top of the cigarettes. Like this.' He picked up the paper and put it in the box.

'This is very curious,' said Alleyn. He raised an eyebrow and stared fixedly at the little message. Get the deceased's handbag,' he said after a minute. 'It's out there.'

Fox went out and returned with a morocco handbag. Alleyn opened it and turned out the contents, and arranged them on the table. They were: A small case containing powder, a lipstick, a hand-kerchief, a purse, a pair of gloves, and a small pocket-book bound in red leather with a pencil attached.

'That's it,' said Alleyn.

He opened the book and laid the note beside it. The paper corre-sponded exactly. He scribbled a word or two with the pencil.

'That's it,' he repeated. 'The lead is broken. There's the same dou-ble line in each case.' He turned the leaves of the book. Cara Quayne had written extensively in it – shopping lists, appointments, memo-randa. The notes came to an end about half-way through. Alleyn read the last one and looked up quickly.

'Got an evening paper, either of you?'

'I have,' said Fox, producing one, neatly folded, from his pocket.

'Does the new show at the Criterion open tomorrow?'

'You needn't bother to look,' interrupted Nigel. 'It does.'

'You have your uses,' grunted the inspector. 'That fixes it then. She wrote that note today.'

'How do you know?' demanded Nigel.

'There is a note on today's page: "Dine and go 'Hail Fellow' Criterion, Raoul, tomorrow." I wanted to be sure she stuck to the printed date. The next page, tomorrow's, is the one she tore out. There's the date. She must have torn it out today.'

'Things are looking up a bit, aren't they, sir?' ventured Fox.

'Are they, Fox? Perhaps they are. And yet – it's a sticky business, this. Light your pipe, my Foxkin, and do a bit of 'teckery. What's in your mind, you sly old box of tricks?'

Fox lit his pipe, sat down, and gazed solemnly at his superior.

'Come on, now,' said Alleyn.

'Well, sir, it's a bit early to speak anything like for sure, but say the lady knew what we know about that parcel there. Say she found it out today, when the parson was out – called in to see him perhaps.'

'And found the safe open?'

'Might be. Sounds kind of careless, but might be. Anyway, say she found out somehow and wanted to tell him. Say he came in, read the note, and – well, sir, say he thought something would have to be done about it.'

'I don't think he has read the note, Fox.'

'Don't you, sir?'

'No. We can see if his prints are on it. If he has read it I don't think he's a murderer.'

'Why not?' asked Nigel.

'He'd have destroyed it.'

'That's so,' admitted Fox.

'But,' Alleyn went on, 'as I say, I don't think he's read it. There are no cigarette-ends of that brand about, are there?'

They hunted round the room. Alleyn went into the bedroom and came back in a few moments.

'None there,' he said, 'and dear Mr Garnette looks very unattractive with his mouth open. But I think we'd better look for prints in there, Bailey. There's that open door. Did you run anything to earth in the bedroom, Fox?'

'A very small trace of a powder in the wash-stand cupboard, sir. That's all.'

'Well, what about cigarette-butts?'

'None here,' announced Fox, who had examined the grate as well as all the ashtrays in the room. 'There are several Virginians – Mr Bathgate's and Dr Curtis's I think they are – no Turkish anywhere.'

'Then he hasn't opened the box.'

'I must say I can't help thinking that note's got a bearing on the case,' said Fox.

'I think you're right, Fox. Put it in my bag, box and all. Let's finish off and go home.'

'And tomorrow?' asked Nigel.

'Tomorrow we'll get Mr Garnette to open the surprise packet.'

'What about the gentleman in question, sir?'

'What about him?'

'Will he be all right? All alone?'

'Good heavens, Fox, what extraordinary solicitude! He'll wake up with a hirsute tongue and a brazen belly. And he will be very, very troubled in his mind. There's that back door.'

'Yes, sir.'

'We'll have to leave a couple of men here. Let's tidy up. Put all that stuff back in the safe, Fox, will you? I'll tackle the desk.'

The two detectives replaced everything with extreme accuracy. Alleyn locked the safe and the desk and pocketed the keys. He strolled over to the bookcase, and as Fox packed up the police bag he murmured titles to himself: *The Koran, Spiritual Experiences of a Fakir, From Wotan to Hitler, The Soul of the Lotus Bud, The Meaning and the Message, Jnana Yoga* . . . 'Hullo, here's something of his own invent. As I live, a little book of poems. Purple suède, Heaven help us, purple suède! *Eros on Calvary and Other Poems,* by Jasper Garnette. Old pig!'

He opened the book and read.

> *The grape and thorn together bind my brows;*
> *Delight and torment is my double mead.*

'Oh, Lord, oh, Lord, how inexpressibly beastly!'

He shoved the poems back and then, with a grimace at Nigel, thrust his hand behind the books and, after a little groping, pulled out several dusty volumes, all covered in brown paper.

'Petronius,' he said, 'and so on. This is his nasty little secret hoard. Notice the disguise, will you! Hullo, what's this?'

He turned to the table and held a very battered old book under the lamp.

'Abberley's *Curiosities of Chemistry.* What a remarkably rum old book! Published by Gasock and Hauptmann, New York, 1865. I've met it before somewhere. Where was it?'

He screwed up his face with an effort to remember and, holding the book lightly in his long, fastidious hands, let it fall open.

'I've got it,' said Alleyn. 'It was in the Bodleian, twenty years ago.'

He opened his eyes and turned to Nigel. That young man was standing with his mouth agape and his eyes bulging.

'What's the matter with you?' asked Alleyn.

Nigel pointed to the book in the inspector's hands. Fox and Alleyn both looked down.

'The book had fallen open at a page headed: 'A simple but little-known method of making sodium cyanide.' chapter 12

CHAPTER 12

Alleyn Takes Stock

'Dear me!' said Alleyn as he laid the book on the table. 'This is a quaint coincidence.' He paused a moment and then murmured: 'I wonder if coincidence is quite the right word.'

'H'm' said Fox, deeply.

'I'd call it the Hand of – of Fate, or Providence, or Nemeses or something,' said Nigel.

'I dare say you would – on the front page. Not this time, however.' But Nigel was reading excitedly.

'Do listen, Alleyn. It says you can make sodium cyanide from wool and washing soda.'

'Really? It sounds a most unpalatable mixture.'

'You have to heat them terrifically in a retort or something. It says: "it is, perhaps, a fortunate circumstance that this simple recipe is not generally known. The tyro is advised to avoid the experiment as it is attended by a certain amount of danger, so deadly is the poison thus produced."'

'Yes. Don't blow down my neck and don't touch the book, there's a good chap. Bailey will have to get to work on it. Not nearly so much dust on this as on the other hidden books, you notice, Fox, and the brown paper cover is newer. The others are stained. Blast! I don't like it at all.'

Bailey reappeared and was given the book.

'I don't think the results will be very illuminating,' said Alleyn. 'Try the open page as well as the cover. What *is* it these books smell of?'

He sniffed at them.

'It's those stains, I seem to imagine. It's very faint. Perhaps I *do* imagine. What about you, Bailey?'

Alleyn examined the *Curiosities* closely. 'It smells faintly. There's no stain on the cover.' He slipped the blade of his pocket-knife beneath the brown paper and peered under it: 'And there is no stain on the red cover of the book. There you are, Bailey.'

'But, Alleyn,' interrupted Nigel, 'surely it's of the first importance. If the pathologist finds cyanide – sodium cyanide – and Garnette has this book and – '

'I know, I know. Extraordinarily careless of him to leave it there, don't you think? Stupid, what?'

'Do you think it is coincidence?'

'Bless my soul, Bathgate, how on earth am I to know? Your simple faith is most soothing, but I can assure you it's misplaced.'

'Well, but what do you *think?* Tell me what you *think.*'

'I "think naught a trifle, though it small appear."'

'That has the advantage of sounding well and meaning nothing.'

'Not altogether. Look here. We know Miss Quayne was probably murdered by cyanide poisoning. We believe that it must have been done by one of eight persons.'

Nigel counted beneath his breath.

'Only seven, six Initiates and Garnette.'

'Mr Wheatley, sir,' Fox reminded him. 'The young fellow that handed round, you know.'

'Oh – true. Well?'

'Well,' Alleyn went on composedly, 'we have reason to suppose the stuff was dropped into the cup in a cigarette-paper. The paper was later found on the place where the cup fell. So much for the actual event. We have learned that Miss Quayne had deposited bearer-bonds, to the tune of five thousand, in the safe. We have found a parcel that appeared to be the original wrapping of these bonds. If so the bonds have been taken and newspaper substituted. We have found a message in Cara Quayne's writing, addressed yesterday, presumably to Garnette. This message says she must see him at once as she had made a terrible discovery. I think the odds are he has not read the message. Whether it referred to the bonds or not we have no idea. We have found an antique work on chemistry hidden among Garnette's books. It falls open at a recipe for home-made cyanide. So much for our tangible data.'

'What about motive?' suggested Nigel.

'Motive. You mean Garnette's motive, don't you? I gather you are no longer wedded to Mr Ogden as the villain of the piece?'

'I wasn't really serious about Ogden, but I wouldn't be surprised if he and Garnette were rogues together in the States.'

'What's your view, Fox?' asked Alleyn.

'Well, sir, I must say I don't think so. Father Garnette was very frank under the influence and he said he met Mr Ogden crossing the Atlantic. That tallies with Mr Ogden's statement.'

'Exactly, Fox.'

'And I must say, sir, Mr Ogden isn't my notion of a Chicago racketeer.'

'Not mine either. Perhaps we are too conservative, Brer Fox. But because two men come from the United States of America and one's a rogue, it doesn't mean they are old associates.'

'If you put it like that,' said Nigel, 'it does sound a bit far-fetched.'

'Of course they *are* associates now,' ruminated Fox, 'but Mr Ogden seems more like a victim than a crook.'

'Well, then – Garnette,' urged Nigel.

'If,' said Alleyn, 'Mr Garnette stole the bonds and killed Miss Quayne with a jorum of sodium cyanide, he set about it in a most peculiar manner. He chose a moment when he and seven other persons would be equally suspected. He must have known that a search would be made of these rooms, yet he left his recipe book in a place where it was sufficiently concealed to look furtive, and not well enough hidden to escape discovery. He destroyed, so far as we know, none of her letters. He left, inside a cigarette-box, her note, suggesting that she had discovered something very upsetting.'

'But you said he never found it,' objected Nigel.

'If that's so why did he think it necessary to kill her?'

'She may have rung up or something.'

'She may, certainly, but wouldn't she have mentioned the note?'

'Perhaps,' said Nigel doubtfully.

'I quite agree it's not cast-iron,' Alleyn continued, 'I am breaking my own rule and going in heavily for conjecture. So far, I am convinced, we have only scratched the surface of an extremely unsavoury case.'

'What about the others?' said Fox. 'They are a very strange lot – very strange indeed. There may be motives among them, Chief.'

'Oh, yes.'

'Such as jealousy,' began Nigel eagerly. 'Jealousy, you know, and passion, and religious mania.'

'*Now* you're talking exactly like the Dormouse. Really, Bathgate, you are a perfect piece of pastiche this evening.'

'Don't be ridiculous. Let us take the others in turn.'

'Very well,' said Alleyn resignedly, 'It's hideously late but let us. A. Mrs Candour.'

'There you are!' cried Nigel. 'A warped nature if ever there was one. Did you notice how she behaved when you said you supposed Miss Quayne was very beautiful? She fairly writhed. She's even jealous of that little squirt Wheatley. There are those two bits of paper Fox got from the grate. Obviously a letter beginning: "This is to warn you – " and then later on M – S and CA and what might be the top of an N. Mrs Candour again. And did you notice her face when she said: "Cara doesn't look so pretty now?" It was absolutely obscene.'

'It was,' said Alleyn quietly. 'You do see things, Bathgate.'

'I suppose you are making mock of me as usual.'

'My dear fellow,' said Alleyn quickly, 'indeed I am not. Please forgive me if I am odiously facetious sometimes. It's a bad habit I've got. I assure you that if I really thought you slow in the uptake I should never dream of ragging you. You're kind enough to let me show off and I take advantage of it. Do forgive me.'

He looked so distressed and spoke with such charming formality that Nigel was both embarrassed and delighted.

'Chief Detective-Inspector,' he said, 'I am your Watson, and your worm. You may both sit and trample on me. I shall continue to offer you the fruits of my inexperience.'

'Very nicely put, Mr Bathgate,' said Fox.

Alleyn and Nigel stared at him, but he was perfectly serious.

'Well,' said Alleyn hurriedly,' to return to the Candour. She gave, as you say, a very nasty little exhibition. Would she have done so if she'd killed Miss Quayne? It's possible. She certainly tried to ladle out sympathy later on. She was the first to take the cup. That's a naught that may be a trifle. So much for her. B. M. de Ravigne.'

'Ah, now, the French gentleman,' said Fox. 'He was in love with the deceased and owned up quite frank to it. Well now, it would have come out anyway, so there's not a great deal in his frankness, I must say. There seem to have been some nice goings-on between deceased and the minister. Mr Pringle evidently was an eyewitness. Now monsieur never hinted at anything of the sort.'

'And therefore thought the more,' murmured Alleyn. 'Yes, Fox, he was very cool, wasn't he?'

'Remarkable,' said Fox, 'until I handled deceased's photograph and then he blazed up like a rocket. What about this *crime passionel* the French jokers are always dragging in? They let 'em off for that sort of thing over there. Did you notice what Miss Wade said about the handkerchief?'

'I did.'

'He's a very cool hand is monsieur,' repeated Fox.

'We'll have to trace their friendship back to Paris, I dare say,' said Alleyn wearily. 'Oh, Lord! C. Miss Wade. I'm taking them in the order in which they knelt. She comes next.'

'Nothing there,' said Nigel. 'She's just a little pagan church-hen with a difference. Rather a nice old girl, I thought.'

'She spoke very silly to the chief,' pronounced Fox with unex- pected heat. ''Have you been through the Police College, officer?'' These old ladies! You could write a book on them. She's the sort that makes point-duty what it is.'

'I adored the way she said she had her eyes shut all through the cup ceremony, and then told you what each of them did,' said Nigel. 'Didn't you, Alleyn?'

'Yes,' said Alleyn. 'It was extremely helpful and rather interesting.'

'D. will be Mr Pringle,' observed Fox. 'And here we go again. To my way of thinking he's the most likely type. Neurotic, excitable young gentleman and dopes, as you found out, sir.'

'I agree,' said Alleyn. 'He is a likely type. He's in a bad way. He's had a violent emotional jolt and he's suffering from the after-effects of unbridled hero-worship. Silly young dolt. I hope it's not Pringle.'

'Obviously,' ventured Nigel, 'he would look on Miss Quayne as Garnette's evil genius.'

'Yes,' murmured Alleyn. 'I don't pretend to speak with any sort of authority, but I should expect a person in Pringle's condition to turn against the object of his worship rather than against the – what shall I call her? – the temptress. I should expect him in the shock of his discovery to direct his violence against Garnette there and then, not against Miss Quayne some three weeks later. I may be quite wrong about that,' he added after a minute or two. 'However – there is Pringle. He's neurotic, he's dopey, and he's had a severe emotional shock. He hero-worshipped Garnette and made a hideous discovery. He's probably been living in an ugly little hell of his own for the last three weeks. By the way, we haven't sampled Mr Garnette's cigarettes, have we? Another little job for the analyst.'

'Now Miss Jenkins,' said Fox. 'She's E.'

'She struck me as being a pleasant creature,' said Nigel. 'Rather amusing I should think. Not a "lovely" of course, but moderately easy to look at. Intelligent.'

'Very intelligent,' agreed Alleyn.

'How she got herself mixed up in this show beats me,' confessed Fox. 'A nice young lady like that.'

'She practically said herself,' Nigel interrupted. 'She's attached to that ass Pringle. Women are – '

'Yes, yes,' interrupted Alleyn hastily. 'We needn't go into all that, I think, As far as we've got there's no motive apparent in Miss Jenkins's case. We are back at Ogden.'

'F. Mr Ogden,' said Fox solemnly. 'It seems to me, sir, the only call we've got for suspecting Mr Ogden more than anybody else is that he's an American, and it seems as if Father Garnette's another. It don't amount to much.'

'It don't,' said Alleyn. 'Personally I fancy the Atlantic meeting was their first one. I agree with you, Fox.'

'As regards Father Garnette's later utterances,' said Nigel, 'we had a clear case of *in vino veritas*.'

'Someone was bound to say *in vino veritas* sooner or later,' said Alleyn, 'but you are quite right, Bathgate.'

'That's the lot, then,' said Nigel.

'No. Again you've forgotten Opifex.'

'Opifex? What do you mean?'

'Another classical touch. Don't you remember the rhyme in the Latin text-books:

> Common are to either sex
> Artifex and Opifex.

'Quite good names for Lionel and Claude.'

'Really, Inspector!' protested Nigel, grinning broadly.

'Artifex was busy with the censer and seems unlikely. Opifex had, of course, less opportunity than the others. I understand he did not handle the cup?'

'I don't *think* he did,' said Nigel. 'Of course he was bending over the Initiates while they passed it round.'

'Meaning Mr Wheatley?' asked Fox.

'Yes. Mr Claude Wheatley.'

'Hardly got the guts to kill anybody, would you think, sir?'

'I'd say not,' agreed Nigel heartily.

'They call poison a woman's weapon, don't they?' asked Alleyn vaguely. 'A dangerous generalisation. Well, let's go home. There's one more point I want to clear up. Any prints of interest, Bailey?'

Detective-Sergeant Bailey had returned from the bedroom and had been at work on the parcel and the book. He had not uttered a word for some time. He now said with an air of disgruntled boredom: 'Nothing on the book. Reverend Garnette on the parcel, I think, but I'll take a photograph. There's some prints in the bedroom besides the Reverend's. I think they are Mr Pringle's. I got a good one of his from that rail out there. Noticed him leaning on it.'

'Did you find out how the torch is worked?'

'Yes. Naphtha. Bottle in the vestry.'

'Can you ginger it up for a moment, Bailey?'

'Very good, sir.'

'Have you got any cigarette-papers on you?'

Bailey, looking completely disinterested, produced a packet and went out. Alleyn got a silver cup from the sideboard, half filled it with some of Father Garnette's Invalid Port, emptied some salt into a cigarette-paper, stuck the margins together, and screwed up the end. Meanwhile, Fox locked the safe and sealed it with tape and wax. Alleyn pocketed the keys.

'Come on out,' he said.

'They all returned to the sanctuary. Bailey had got the torch flaring again. The hall had taken on a new but rather ghastly lease of life. It looked like a setting for a film in extremely bad taste. The nude gods, the cubistic animals, the velvets and the elaborate ornaments flickered in the torchlight with meretricious theatricality. It was, Nigel told himself, altogether too much of a good thing. And yet, over-emphasized as it was, it did make its gesture. It was not, as it might well have been, merely silly. As the light flared up, the faces of the plaster figures flushed and seemed to move a little. The shadows under the eyes and nostrils of the Wotan wavered and the empty scowl deepened. One god seemed to puff out his cheeks, another to open and close his blank eyes. It was very still; there was no sound at all but for the roar of the naphtha. The men's voices sounded forlorn and small. It had grown very cold.

Alleyn walked down to the chancel steps and peered out into the body of the hall.

'I want you all up here for a moment,' he said.

His voice seemed to echo a little. A plain-clothes man came out of the vestry and another appeared in the aisle. A constable came out of the porch.

When they were all assembled under the torch Alleyn asked them to kneel in a circle. They did this, the constable and Fox very stolidly, Bailey with morose detachment, and two plain-clothes men with an air of mild interest. Nigel was unpleasantly moved by this performance. His imagination fashioned out of shadows the figure of Cara Quayne.

Alleyn knelt with them. All their hands were shadowed by the sconce. They held them folded as Nigel showed them. They passed the cup from hand to hand, beginning with Fox who knelt in Mrs Candour's place. Alleyn made them send it twice round the circle. Then they all stood up.

'Notice anything?' asked Alleyn.

Nobody spoke.

Alleyn suddenly flung the cup from him. It fell with a dull thud and the wine seeped into the carpet. Alleyn bent down and invited them all to look. In the bottom of the cup were the dregs of the wine and a tiny piece of paper.

'You see it's stuck to the side,' said Alleyn.

'When did you put it in, sir?' asked Fox.

'The first time round. You see, none of you noticed it. It's much too dark. The little tube tipped up, the salt slipped out of the open end, the paper went transparent. I hadn't coloured mine red, but still you didn't see it.'

'By Gum,' said Fox.

Bailey said: 'Cuh!' and bent down again to examine the paper.

'Yes,' added Fox suddenly, 'but how did the murderer know it would be so safe?'

'That,' said Alleyn, 'is another matter altogether. I rather think it's the crux of the whole case.'

Part Two

CHAPTER 13

Nannie

When Nigel woke on the morning after his visit to the House of the Sacred Flame, it was with a vague sense of disquietude as though he had been visited by nightmare. As the memory of the night's adventure came back to him it still seemed unreal. He could scarcely believe that, only a few hours ago, he had knelt under a torch among images of Nordic gods, that he had seen a woman, who seemed to be possessed of an evil spirit, drink and die horribly. He closed his eyes and the faces of the Initiates appeared again. There was Miss Wade with prim lips, Pringle talking, talking, Ogden perspiring gently, M. de Ravigne who seemed to bow his head with grotesque courtesy, Janey Jenkins, and Mrs Candour who opened her mouth wider and wider –

He jerked himself back from sleep, got out of bed, and went to his window. The rain still poured down on the roofs. Wet umbrellas bobbed up and down Chester Terrace. A milkman's cart with a dejected and irritated pony was drawn up at the corner of Knocklatchers Row. Nigel looked down Knocklatchers Row. Perhaps he would not have been very surprised if there had been no Sign of the Sacred Flame, but there it was, swinging backwards and forwards in the wind, and underneath it he could just see the narrow entry.

He bathed, breakfasted, opened his paper and found no reference to the tragedy. So much the better. He rang up his office, got out his notes, sat down to the typewriter and worked solidly for an hour. Then he rang up Scotland Yard. Chief Detective-Inspector Alleyn was in his room and would speak to Mr Bathgate.

'Hullo!' said Nigel with extreme cordiality.

'What do *you* want?' asked Alleyn guardedly.

'How are you?'

'In excellent health, thank you. What do you want?'

'It's just a matter of my copy – '

'I knew it.'

'I want to put it in as soon as possible.'

'I'm seeing the A.C. in half an hour, and then I'm going out.'

'I'll be with you in ten minutes.'

'Come, birdie, come,' said Alleyn.

Nigel gathered up his copy and hurried out.

He found Alleyn in his office, writing busily. The inspector grinned at Nigel.

'You persistent devil,' he said, 'sit down. I won't be five minutes.'

Nigel coyly laid the copy before him and subsided into a corner. Alleyn presently turned to the copy, read it, blue-pencilled a word or two, and then handed it back.

'You are learning to behave quite prettily,' he said, 'I suppose you'll take that straight along to Fleet Street.'

'I'd better,' agreed Nigel, 'It's front-page stuff. They'll pull the old rag to bits for me this time. What are you up to this morning, Inspector?'

'I'm going to Shepherd Market when I've seen the boss-man.'

'Cara Quayne's house? I'll meet you there.'

'Will you indeed?'

'Don't you want me?'

'I'll be very glad to see you. Don't let any of your brother blood-suckers in.'

'I can assure you there is no danger of that. I'll sweep past like a May Queen.'

'You'd better have my card. Give it back to me – I remember your previous performances, you see.' He flipped a card across to Nigel, 'I feel like a form master who goes in for favourites.'

'Oh, sir, thanks most horribly, sir. It's frightfully decent of you, sir,' bleated Nigel.

'For the honour of the Big Dorm., Bathgate.'

'You bet, sir.'

'Personally,' said Alleyn, 'I consider schoolboys were less objectionable when they *did* talk like that.'

'When cads were cads and a' that?'

'Yes. They talk like little men nowadays. They actually take refuge in irony, a commodity that should be reserved for the middle-aged. However, I maunder. Meet me at the Château Quayne in half an hour.'

'In half an hour.'

Nigel hurried to his office where he made an impressive entry with his copy and had the intense satisfaction of seeing sub-editors tear their hair while the front page was wrecked and rewritten. A photographer was shot off to Knocklatchers Row and another to Shepherd Market. Nigel accompanied the latter expert, and in a few minutes rang the bell at Cara Quayne's front door.

It was opened by a gigantic constable whom he had met before, PC Allison.

'I'm afraid you can't come in, sir,' began this official very firmly.

'Do you know, you are entirely mistaken?' said Nigel, 'I have the entrée. Look.'

He produced Alleyn's card.

'Quite correct, Mr Bathgate,' said PC Allison. 'Now you move off there, sir,' he added to a frantic young man who had darted up the steps after Nigel and now endeavoured to follow him in.

'I'm representing – ' began the young man.

'Abandon hope,' said Nigel over his shoulder. The constable shut the door.

Nigel found Alleyn in Cara Quayne's drawing-room. It was a charming room, temperately, not violently, modern. The walls were a stippled green, the curtains striped in green and cerise, the chairs deep and comfortable and covered in dyed kid. An original Van Gogh hung over the fireplace, vividly and almost disconcertingly alive. A fire crackled in the grate. Alleyn sat at a pleasantly shaped writing-desk. His back was turned towards Nigel, but his face was reflected in a mirror that hung above the desk. He was absorbed in his work and apparently had not heard Nigel come in. Nigel stood in the doorway and looked at him.

'He isn't in the least like a detective,' thought Nigel. 'He looks like an athletic don with a hint of the army somewhere. No, that's not right: it's too commonplace. He's faunish. And yet he's got all the right things for 'teckery. Dark, thin, long. Deep-set eyes – '

'Are you lost in the pangs of composition, Bathgate?' asked Alleyn suddenly.

'Er – oh – well, as a matter of fact I was,' said Nigel. 'How are you getting on?'

'Slowly, slowly. Unfortunately Miss Quayne has very efficient servants. I'm just going to see them. Care to do your shorthand stuff? Save calling in the sergeant?'

'Certainly,' said Nigel.

'If you sit in that armchair they won't notice you are writing.'

'Right you are,'

He sat down and took out his pad.

'I'll see the staff now, Allison,' Alleyn called out.

'Very good, sir.'

The first of the staff to appear was an elderly woman dressed in a black material that Nigel thought of as bombazine, but was probably nothing of the kind. She had iron-grey hair, a pale face, heavy eyebrows, and a prim mouth. She had evidently been weeping but was now quite composed. Alleyn stood up and pushed forward a chair.

'You are Miss Edith Hebborn?' he said.

'Yes, sir.'

'I am Inspector Alleyn. We are obliged, as you know, to inquire into Miss Quayne's death. Won't you sit down?'

She seemed to hesitate and then sat rigidly on the edge of the chair.

'I am afraid this has been a great shock to you,' said Alleyn.

'It has.'

'I hope you will understand that I have to ask you certain questions about Miss Quayne.'

He paused for a moment but she did not answer.

'How long have you been with Miss Quayne?' asked Alleyn.

'Thirty-five years.'

'Thirty-five years! That must be nearly all her life.'

'She was three months old when I took her. I was her Nannie.'

She had a curious harsh voice. That comfortable word "Nannie" sounded most incongruous.

'I see,' said Alleyn. 'Then it is a sorrow as well as a shock. You became her maid after she grew up?'

'Yes, sir.'

'Will you tell me a little about her – her childhood and where she lived? Her people?'

She waited for a moment. Nigel wondered if she would refuse to give anything but flat responses to questions, but at last she spoke:

'She was an only child, born after her father died.'

'He was Colonel Quayne of Elderbourne Manor, Sevenoaks?'

'Yes. He was in India with the mistress. Killed playing polo. Mrs Quayne came to England when Miss Cara was a month old. They had a black woman for nurse, an Eh-yah or some such thing. She felt the cold and went back to her own country. I never fancied her. The mistress only lived a year after they came home.'

'A tragic entrance into the world,' said Alleyn.

'Yes, sir.'

'Where did you and the baby go?'

'To France,' said Nannie and implied 'of all places.'

'Why was that?'

'There were no relations in England. They had all gone abroad. There were no near relatives at all. A second cousin of the Colonel's in New Zealand or some such place. They had never met. The nearest was an aunt of the mistress. A French lady. The mistress was half French, sir, though you'd never have known it.'

Something in Alleyn's manner seemed to have thawed her a little. She went on:

'We settled in a little house near this aunt – Madame Verné, was the name – who had a Shatter, one of those big places, near Antibes. The Shatter Verné it was. We were there for eight years. Then Miss Cara went to a convent school, a Papist place. Madame Verné wished it and so did the other guardian, a gentleman who has since died. I moved to the Shatter, and Miss Cara came home for the holidays.'

'That went on for how long?'

'Till she was seventeen. Then Madame died. The Shatter was sold.'

'There was always – There was no difficulty about ways and means?'

'Miss Cara was an heiress, sir. The Colonel, Mrs Quayne, and then Madame; they all left something considerable. We were very comfortable as far as that went.'

'You stayed on in France?'

'In Paris. Miss Cara liked it. She had formed friendships there.'

'Was M. de Ravigne one of these friends?'

'He was,' said Miss Hebborn shortly.

'Did you not think this a suitable friendship?'

'I *did*. Until recently.'

'Why did you change your opinion?'

'At first I had no fault to find with Mr Ravigne. He was an old friend of Madame's and often stayed at the Shatter. He seemed a very pleasant gentleman, steady, quiet in his ways, not a lot of high-falutin' nonsense like so many of that nation. A foreigner, of course, but at times you would scarcely have noticed it.'

'Miss Wade's very words,' murmured Alleyn.

'Her!' said Miss Hebborn. 'H'm! Well, sir, it was after we came to London that Mr Ravigne changed. For the worse. He called soon after we were settled in and said London appealed to his – some expression – '

'His temperament?'

'Yes, sir. Of course it was Miss Cara that did the appealing. He was always very devoted, but she never fancied him. Never. Then he commenced to talk a lot of stuff and nonsense about this new-fangled religion he'd got hold of. A lot of wicked clap-trap.'

The pale face flushed angrily. She made a curious gesture with her roughened hand, passing it across her mouth and nose as if to wipe away a cobweb.

'You mean the House of the Sacred Flame and its services?'

'Sacred Flame indeed! Bad, wicked, heathen humbug. And that Mr Garnette with his smooth ways and silly dangerous talk. I've never forgiven Mr Ravigne and he knows it. It changed Miss Cara. Changed her whole nature. She was always one of the high-strung, nervous sort. Over-excitable as a child and over-excitable as a woman. I recollect the time we went through when she was four-teen. Wanted to turn Papist. I showed her the rights of that. I'd always brought her up strict Anglican. I'm Chapel myself. Primitive Methodist. But it was the parents' wish and I saw it carried out.'

'That was very honourable of you, Nannie. I'm sorry, the "Nannie" slipped out.'

'You're very welcome, sir. I've always been Nannie, ever since – she could talk.'

She bit her lip and then went on:

'From the time she went into that wicked place everything went badly. And I couldn't do anything to stop it. I couldn't do anything. I had to stand by and watch my – my – Miss Cara turn her back on the Lord and go down the way of damnation. She took me with her once,' added Nannie, ambiguously. 'The sight of the place, full of naked heathen idols and all the baubles of Satan – it was worse than Rome. There! And when I found out she was going to be the leader in that lewd mockery of her own Church I wished she had died when she was an innocent baby. I wished – '

She broke off abruptly. She was shaking from head to foot. The whole of her last speech had been reeled off in a high key as though she was giving an oration. Nigel was reminded of a woman he had heard preaching at the Marble Arch. Here was real revivalist fervour, pig-headed, stupid, arrogant. After last night it seemed blessedly straightforward and clean.

'Steady, Nannie,' said Alleyn.

'Yes, sir. Thank you. But I don't feel steady when I think of my poor lamb cut off in the midst of her silly wickedness, like as not with heathenish words on her lips. As the Lord's my judge, sir, I'd have rather she'd gone over to Rome that time when she was still an innocent baby, that I would.'

'Was it entirely through M. de Ravigne that she became interested in this Church?'

'He started it. He took her off there one evening. Said he thought it would "amuse" her. Amuse! Not much amusement in any respectable sense of the word. And that Mr Garnette – Reverend I will not call him – he made what was bad enough, goodness knows, ten thousand times worse. If it had been Satan himself speaking straight out of hell, he couldn't have spoke wickeder. And the goings on! She thought I didn't know. I knew.'

'How did you know?'

Nannie looked slightly taken aback at this question.

'I heard remarks passed when that lot came here to see her. That Mrs Candour. You could tell at a glance. Not a *nice* woman, and not a lady either. And Miss Wade, who ought to know better at her age, always talking, talking, talking about "Dear Father Garnette." Father! Father of lies! And I had to stand aside and watch my baby drawing nearer and nearer to hell fire – '

She broke off again. Her lips trembled. She passed her hand over them and fell silent.

'What were Miss Quayne's movements yesterday?' asked Alleyn.

She had spent the morning in her room, it appeared, engaged in meditation. She had not lunched. At about two o'clock she had sent for her car and the chauffeur had told Nannie that he had driven her to the church. He remembered glancing at his watch a second or two before she came out. It was then ten to three. He had said to the other servants that Miss Quayne seemed very upset when she came out. He drove her straight home.

'One more question,' said Alleyn. 'Where were you last night when we tried to get you on the telephone?'

'I was out for a walk.'

'Out for a walk! In that weather?'

'Yes, sir. She'd told me it was her first evening as Chosen Whatever-it-was, and I was that upset and wretched! I tried to talk her out of it but she hardly listened. She just went away as if she didn't hear me. When the door shut and I was left to myself I couldn't endure it. I'd meant to go to chapel but I couldn't. I put on my hat and jacket and I followed her.'

'To the hall?'

'Yes, sir. Miss Cara had taken the car, of course, so I knew I wouldn't catch her up, but somehow I felt I'd walk. I was desperate, sir.'

'I think I understand. What did you mean to do when you got there?'

'I hardly know. I think I'd have gone in and – and stood up for the Lord in the midst of His enemies. I think I meant to do that, but when I got there the doors were shut and a pimply-faced fellow said I couldn't get in. He said he'd been had once already that evening. I don't know what he meant. So I went away and as I went I heard them caterwauling inside, and it drove me nearly demented. I walked in the rain a long way and it was late when I got in. The others were back and in bed. I waited for her. I was still waiting when the police rang up. Morning it was then.'

'Oh, yes. By the way, when did you write to Mr Garnette to warn him off Miss Cara?'

It would be difficult to say which looked the more astounded at this, Nigel or Nannie. Nannie stared into the mirror over Alleyn's head for some seconds, and then said with a snap:

'Friday night.'

'He got it on Saturday?'

'Yes.'

'And you went to the hall to see if he had taken heed?'

'Yes.'

'I see. Thank you, Nannie.'

The old woman hesitated and when she spoke again it was more haltingly.

'There's more to it than that. When I got there and the door was shut in my face, I couldn't rest till I knew – knew if she was doing it. I walked round the block to the back of the building. I came to a sort of a yard, I could still hear the noise inside. There was a door. I stood by it listening. There was one voice, louder than the others. Then I saw the door was not quite shut – and – and – '

'You walked in.'

'Yes, sir, I did. I felt I had to. I had to *know*. It was that man's rooms I'd got into. There was a light in the sitting-room. The voice got louder all the time. I – I went in. Miss Cara had told me about him living on the premises in that hole-and-corner fashion, so I knew about the other door – the one into the hall. I opened it a little way. There's a curtain, but I pulled it aside.'

A dark flush crept into the pale face. She looked defiantly at Alleyn.

'I tell you I could not help myself.'

'I know. What did you see?'

'They were moving. I could see the front row. I saw her – Miss Cara. She came running up the steps towards me. That man was quite close. His back was turned to me. Her face. Her pretty face – it looked dreadful. Then she turned and faced them. She was calling out. Screaming. I tried to go in and stop it. I couldn't. I couldn't move. Only watch. I might have saved her. No, don't say anything – I might. Then I saw that lot coming up after her. Skirmishing round.'

'Yes. Go on,' said Alleyn quickly. 'Tell me exactly – '

'I'll remember to my dying day. First that American gentleman, Ogden. Then one or two of them together, then the young man and Miss Jenkins. The only one of the lot I'd care to have anything to do with. Led astray like my poor child. Mrs Candour and old Mrs Wade were trying to get one on each side of that man. I saw Mrs Candour push in by him. Miss Wade tried to get in on the other side. She was in a great taking-on. In the end she didn't get there. Collided with the American gentleman and nearly fell over. It's my belief he stopped her on purpose, having some sense of decency.'

'Oh. What did she do then?'

'He put her next Mr Ravigne and went next that man himself. Then my poor child began again. Don't ask me. I can't – I couldn't watch. Something seemed to break in me. I turned and – and somehow I got out into the street.'

She turned her head aside, gave a harsh sob and then blew her nose defiantly.

Alleyn stood up.

'You must try to get some sleep now.'

Nannie was silent.

'At least your Miss Cara is out of it all.'

'I thank God for that,' said Nannie.

'I won't keep you a moment longer. Do you know if Miss Quayne has left a Will?'

'She made one years ago, sir, when she came of age, but I think she's changed it. She told me she was going to Mr Rattisbon – that's her lawyer – about it. That lot have been getting money out of her as well I know.'

'Much?'

'I don't know, sir, but I have ideas. A great deal, if you ask me. And I dare say she'll have left them the rest.' She hesitated and then raised her voice. 'And if she's been murdered, sir, it's for her money. Mark my words, it's for her money.'

'It often is,' said Alleyn. 'Thank you. Go and rest somewhere. You need it, you know.'

Nannie glared down her nose, muttered: 'Very considerate, I'm sure,' and tramped to the door. Here she paused and turned.

'May I ask a favour, sir?'

'Certainly.'

'Can I – will they let me have her home again before she's put away?'

'Not just yet, Nannie,' said Alleyn gently. 'Tomorrow perhaps – but – I think it would be better not.'

She looked fixedly at him and then, without another word, went out of the room.

CHAPTER 14

Nigel Takes Stock

'Grand old girl, that,' agreed Nigel from his armchair.

'Wasn't she?' agreed Alleyn. 'That doorkeeper in the house of the ungodly will have to be seen.'

'To check up on her visit?'

'Just that.'

'Look here,' said Nigel, 'how did you know?'

'Never you mind. Keep quiet. Now I'll have to see the rest of the staff.'

The rest of the staff proved to be unproductive of much intelligence. Two housemaids, a parlourmaid, a chauffeur and a cook, who all seemed excited and perturbed as if they had one eye on the tragedy and the other on losing their jobs. The parlourmaid, outwardly a frigid woman, obviously regarded the affair as a personal affront and seemed at the same time to be in a semi-explosive condition. The upper-housemaid was excited, the under-housemaid was incoherent. The cook wept, but absent-mindedly and rather as though she felt it incumbent on her as a fat, comfortable woman to do so. They bore out Nannie's statements as regard their movements on the preceding day. The chauffeur repeated his previous statement that he had driven Miss Quayne to the church at two-thirty and had brought her home at five to three. He had certainly thought she seemed most upset when she came out of the church. 'Kind of flabbergasted,' was the way he'd describe it. She was very pale and, he thought, out of breath. He had got tired of sitting in the car and had walked up the side entry to the double doors. Miss Quayne had left one door open and he looked into the hall. He saw her come out of the door by the altar. He thought she said something and supposed she was speaking to Father Garnette. One or two people had gone into the church while he waited. Alleyn asked the parlourmaid, who had been with Miss Quayne since she took the house, how many of the Initiates were regular visitors. He gave her a list of their names which she held in genteel fashion with her little finger crooked.

'Most of these neemes are familiar,' she said.

'Have all of them visited Miss Quayne?'

'Yes.'

'Some more frequently than others?'

'Quayte,' said the parlourmaid, whose name was Wilson.

'Which were the most regular visitors?'

'Mr Ravinje,' it appeared, Mr Ogden and Mrs Candour.

'Mrs Candour? When was she last here?'

'I could ascertain,' said Wilson, 'from the appointment book.'

'Please let me see it.'

Wilson produced the appointment book. It was a diary, and Alleyn spent some minutes over it.

'I notice,' he said at last, 'that Mrs Candour was quite a regular visitor until some three weeks ago. She seems to have lunched or dined pretty well every week. Then her name does not appear again. He raised an eyebrow at Wilson. 'Any reason for that, do you know?'

'There was words,' said Wilson.

'What about?'

'A certain party.'

'Oh. What party? Or don't you know?'

Wilson drew down the corners of her mouth.

'Come on, Wilson,' said Alleyn, 'Let's know the worst.'

'Well, reely, I never am in the habit of repeating the drawing-room in the kitchen,' said Wilson.

'This isn't the kitchen and it may be important. Did Mrs Candour and Miss Quayne have words about Mr Garnette?'

'Yes, sir,' said Wilson who seemed to have weighed Alleyn in the balance and found him quality.

'Tell me about it, Wilson. You'll be speaking in the cause of justice, you know. Think of that and expand. Did this row take place at lunch on Wednesday, November 14th, the last time Mrs Candour was here?'

'Yes, sir. Or rather it was after lunch. Over the coffee in here.'

'You brought the coffee in?'

'Yes. Voices was raised and I heard words as the ladies came out of the dining-room. I was coming into the hall with the tray and I didn't actually know what to do.'

'Very awkward for you. What where they saying?'

Wilson suddenly cast off all parlourmaidenly restraint and launched herself into a verbatim account.

'Mrs Candour said to Miss Quayne: "You know what I mean, quite well," sh' said, "I've been watching you," sh' said, "and I was disgusted," sh' said. That was when they came out of the dining-room and they never noticed me standing there they was so carried away. And Miss Quayne looked at her and said: "I hope I don't understand you, Dagmar," sh' said. And the way she said it! "I hope I don't understand you, Dagmar," sh' said, "because I can't believe you would let your soul come down to such an earth-plane," sh' said, "as to think of Father Garnette and me in such a way," sh' said. And Mrs Candour laughed and she said: "Earth-plane!" sh' said. "If you're not revelling on the earth-plane at this very moment I'd like to know who is? Don't pretend, Cara," sh' said. Then they went into the drawing-room and I waited and I didn't like to go in and they never shut the door and Miss Quayne said very loud: "It's pathetically clear," sh' said, "what's the matter with you. You're devoured by jealousy." Mrs Candour gave a kind of – well, a kind of screech, sir, but Miss Quayne said, sh' said: "Because Father Garnette has chosen me to discover the hidden mysteries of the spirit and the body," sh' said – or something like that it was, and then Mrs Candour laughed. And the way she laughed! Well! And she said: "Cara," sh' said, "don't think you can take me in," sh' said, "because I know." And she said: "I promise you, I'm not going to stand aside and see it," sh' said. And then I was that upset I kind of quivered if you understand me, and the cups rattled and Miss Quayne said: "S'ssh!" sh' said, "Wilson," sh' said. So I walked in.'

'Extraordinarily dramatic!' exclaimed Alleyn. 'A princely entrance. And did they drink their coffee?'

'Their hands shook that much they could hardly pour it out, sir.'

'And you withdrew?'

'Yes, sir, and closed the door,' said Wilson, righteous but regretful. A moment later she followed her own example and Alleyn and Nigel were left alone.

'Could you possibly keep up with all that?' asked Alleyn.

'I may have left out an occasional "sh' said." Otherwise it's all here. Do you think Mrs Candour really talked like that?'

'Wouldn't be surprised. She's a very common woman. She's a liar, what's more. She said she'd only been twice to this house.'

'I wonder if she's a murderess,' said Nigel.

'Too stupid, I'd have thought,' said Alleyn, 'but you never know. There's a certain kind of low cunning that comes out very strong on occasion. I wish I had it. I'm scared to death I'll make a fool of myself over this case. The boss-man is very excited about it. It *ought* to be easy – it's so startling. Startling cases are generally easy. The difficult cases are the ones when one drunk heaves a brick at another drunk and leaves him lying in the road. Once they go in for fancy touches it's usually kindergarten stuff. And this is so very fancy, so very extra, so specially Susie. Like to make one of your analyses, Bathgate?'

'What do you mean? My analyses?'

'On paper. All the people and their motives and opportunities with neat little sub-headings. Like a balance-sheet.'

'Do you really want me to?'

'Yes, if you will. I shall be able to cast a superior eye over it and then shatter it with a few facetiae. It will restore my self-respect. No, do make it. You will look at the show from a different point of view. It may easily suggest something. It will be a help. Really.'

'I shall be delighted,' said Nigel and set to work.

Alleyn returned to Cara Quayne's desk and carried on with the job of sorting her papers. There was a long silence broken only by the rustle of paper, the snap and crackle of the fire, and the sound of Nigel's pen. Presently he looked up and said:

'There. Finished.'

'Let me see,' said Alleyn.

With a smug but slightly anxious air, Nigel laid his paper before the inspector. This is what he had written:

MURDER OF CARA QUAYNE

Suspects

The Initiates, the priest, and the acolyte.

All of these had the opportunity to slip the cigarette-paper possibly containing cyanide into the cup.

Circumstances

Cara Quayne drank the wine while in a state of great nervous excitement. She seemed to me to be self-hypnotized and scarcely conscious of her actions. I was reminded of a dervish or a negro priestess.

'Have you ever seen one?' asked Alleyn.
'No. That didn't prevent me from being reminded of one.'
Alleyn read on:

The other Initiates were also in a highly emotional condition, and it is unlikely that they would notice any hanky-panky with the cup.

Garnette. Probably the only normal person there. He handled the cup twice. He started it off, took it back from Ogden and gave it to Cara Quayne. He had the greatest opportunity. Miss Wade said he covered the cup with one hand so he could have easily dropped the paper into the wine. *Motive.* Deceased had left £5,000 in bearer bonds in his safe. These have been pinched. She had made a 'terrible discovery' and may have told him of it. If he stole the bonds this might induce him to kill her. She may have left him a large sum in her Will. *Note. A* work on poisons was hidden behind his books. It fell open at a recipe for home-made cyanide. Garnette spoke like an American when tight.

Mrs Candour. First Initiate to take cup. Jealous of Miss Quayne. *Motive.* Quarrelled with her over Garnette. Over-sexed, unattractive, stupid, vindictive. The scrap of paper found in the grate seems to refer to her: – 'Sir, this is to warn – with M–S CA,' etc. Could this have been a warning against Mrs Candour? If so, from whom?

M. de Ravigne. Second Inititate to handle cup. Miss Wade says he used handkerchief to wipe rim. Might have palmed poison with this. *Motive.* In love with Miss Quayne, who was evidently Garnette's mistress. A very cool customer. Has known deceased longer than any of the others.

Miss Wade. Third Initiate to handle cup. Unlikely. *Motive.* None apparent. She seems unaware of the Quayne-Garnette situation.

Pringle. Fourth to handle cup. Neurotic. Takes drugs. Worships Garnette. *Motive.* He surprised Garnette and Miss Quayne. Possibly shock unhinged him and he was determined to save G. Miss W. says he made a botch of handling cup.

Janey Jenkins. Fifth to handle cup. Engaged to Pringle. Very unlikely. *Motive.* None.

Ogden. Last. American. Met Garnette coming over to England. Very keen on the church. *Seems* straightforward, but you never know. Has given largely to church funds. *Motive.* Possibly he and Garnette were rogues together in the States and are in this together. If so Ogden may have offered to do the killing. Garnette bore out Ogden's statement when he (G.) was tight.

Claude Wheatley. Carried round flagon with wine. Could have dropped cyanide into cup. Horrible youth. Dotes on Garnette. Perhaps the Greeks have a word for him. *Motive.* Jealousy. Unlikely. Wouldn't have the guts. *Note.* If sodium cyanide is found at autopsy it seems certain the book on chemistry is a definite clue. That points to Garnette. Garnette is the obvious man, I think. The chauffeur's statement about Miss Quayne's afternoon visit to the church seems to suggest that she found something there that upset her and caused her to write the note to Garnette which Fox found in the cigarette-box.

Here Nigel's summary stopped abruptly. He had added a few words and scored them out.

'Excellent,' said Alleyn.

'It says nothing new, I'm afraid.'

'No, but it raises several disputable points, which is always helpful. By the way, the analyst rang up just before you came. He has found sodium cyanide in the cigarette-paper, but of course the autopsy will take some time yet.'

'Then the *Curiosities of Chemistry* is an important clue.'

'I don't know,' said Alleyn slowly, 'but I rather fancy it's not important in quite the way you fancy.'

'Whatever does that mean?'

'There were no prints on that book. Bailey has tried all the stock dodges of dactylography.'

'What may that be? Oh, wait a bit. Dactyl. Why not say "finger-printery"?'

'As you please. He's dabbed nitrate of silver solution on it and developed the pages. Nothing there. It's a glossy paper, so someone must have dealt with the book. If Garnette got his big idea from it he must have wiped his fingerprints off and put it where he knew we would find it. A curious combination of forethought and stupidity, don't you think?'

'Yes, but still – Oh, I don't know. Go on with Garnette.'

'You note that Garnette was probably the only completely self-possessed person present. A very good point to make. Should you say this crime looks more like the work of a calculating, shrewd, unscrupulous individual, or a hysterical monomaniac with a streak of cunning?'

'The latter, I suppose,' said Nigel slowly, 'which Garnette is not. All the same, he might have meant us to think that.'

'Ah,' said Alleyn, 'that's very subtle, Bathgate.'

'Garnette strikes me as being subtlish,' said Nigel. 'What do you think about Garnette and Ogden being old partners in infamy?'

'Not a great deal. As I said last night, I think Garnette told the truth when he was tight. If you remember he advanced the colourful suggestion that Ogden looks upon him as the sand-fly's garters. I'm not well up in Americanese, but I had the distinct impression that Mr Garnette regards Mr Ogden as fair and easy game.'

'Look here,' said Nigel suddenly, 'let's pretend it's a detective novel. Where would we be by this time? About half-way through, I should think. Well, who's your pick.'

'I am invariably gulled by detective novels. No herring so red but I raise my voice and give chase.'

'Don't be ridiculous,' said Nigel.

'Fact. You see in real detection herrings are so often out of season.'

'Well, never mind, who's your pick?'

'It depends on the author. If it's Agatha Christie, Miss Wade's occulted guilt drips from every page. Dorothy Sayers's Lord Peter would plump for Pringle, I fancy. Inspector French would go for Ogden. Of course Ogden, on the face of it, is the first suspect.'

'What are you saying! Ogden! Then you *do* think he's a bad hat.'

'No. *No!* He seems a perfectly good hat. I merely say that the immediate circumstances – the actual situation at the time of the murder – point to Ogden.'

'Why?'

'My dear Bathgate, this is a sad falling-off. Think of his position.'

'I'm damned if I know what you are driving at. His position seems to be very comfortable. He's a rich business man.'

Alleyn cast his eyes up but said nothing.

'Don't make that maddening grimace, Alleyn. What are you getting at? Do you or do you not suspect Mr Ogden?'

'I suspect the whole lot of them. Apart from the one point I have noted I don't think he's any likelier than the others.'

'Surely he's likelier than Janey Jenkins and Miss Wade.'

There was a tap at the door and Inspector Fox came in.

'Another report from Bailey, sir,' he said. 'Good morning, Mr Bathgate.'

'What's Bailey say?' asked Alleyn.

'Nothing new. He's got to work properly on the prints. Very smart chap, Bailey. He's found Father Garnette's prints on the parcel of newspaper, and he thinks there's a trace of them on the top of the poison book. Nothing on the cyanide page, as you know. Miss Quayne's on the page torn out of the notebook.'

'When did he get a pattern to compare them with?'

'That would be from the body, sir.'

'Oh, of course.'

'There's another print come out on the book,' Fox continued, 'and he hasn't been able to trace it. He'd like to get impressions from the rest of them.'

'He shall have them,' said Alleyn, 'this afternoon. When's the inquest? Tomorrow at eleven?'

'That's right, sir.'

'Well, we'd better call it a day here.'

'Have you found anything?' Nigel asked. 'Any clues?'

'Nothing spectacular. De Ravigne's love letters. A smug and guarded epistle from the Garnette.'

'May I see M. de Ravigne's letters, sir?' asked Fox.

'There you are. The one on the top's the most interesting.'

Fox seated himself at the table, adjusted a large pair of spectacles and spread out the first of the letters. Nigel strolled up behind him.

'What are *you* up to?' inquired Alleyn.

'Nothing,' said Nigel, reading frantically at long range.

M. de Ravigne wrote a large flowing hand. It was dated Friday of last week.

My Adored Cara [the letter began], I distress myself intolerably on your behalf. It is not that you reject me, for that is the fortunes of love which are ever as hazardous as those of war. To accept defeat I can compose myself with dignity and remain, however wounded, your devoted friend. So far have I adopted, at all events outwardly, your English phlegm. It is as your friend I implore you to continue no longer in your design for the role of Chosen Vessel. It is a project fraught with danger to yourself. You are blinded with a false glamour. One may amuse oneself and interest oneself in a religion, but there should be a careful moderation in this as in all things. In becoming the Chosen Vessel you would cast away your moderation and abandon yourself to detestable extremities. I beg, I implore you to refuse this role, so injurious to your *amour propre*. You do not comprehend what you undertake. I repeat you are in a danger to lose that which one most prizes. You are in a grave peril. I kiss your hand and entreat again that you take the advice of

Your devoted,

Raoul

I beg that you destroy this as all other of my letters.

'And she didn't,' said Nigel.

CHAPTER 15

Father Garnette Explores the
Contents of a Mare's Nest

'No,' said Alleyn, 'she kept his letters. Women keep love letters for much the same reason as a servant keeps references. They help to preserve, as M. de Ravigne might say, the *amour propre*, and can always be produced upon occasion.'

'Angela never shows my letters to anyone,' said Nigel hotly. 'Never.'

'Not to her bosomest friend? No? You are fortunate. Perhaps she hopes they may be found, smelling faintly of orris-root, if she pre-deceases you.'

'That is a remark in bad taste, I consider.'

'I agree and apologize. You don't question the taste of reading Miss Quayne's love letters over Fox's shoulder, I notice,' said Alleyn mildly.

'That's entirely different,' blustered Nigel. 'Miss Quayne was murdered.'

'Which makes her fair game. I know, I know. Well, what do you think of M. de Ravigne's effusion?'

'It looks monstrous fishy to me,' said Nigel. 'What does he mean about her putting herself in a position that is fraught with danger? It looks remarkably like a threat. "Take on the Chosen Vessel job and your life will be in danger."'

'He doesn't actually say her life, Mr Bathgate,' said Fox, glancing up from another of the letters.

'No,' agreed Alleyn. 'He may be old-fashioned enough to think there is something a woman values more than her life.'

'Well,' said Nigel, 'what do you think inspired the letter?'

'An interesting point, Bathgate. I don't know. Jealousy perhaps or – yes – it might be fear. He was very agitated when he wrote it.'

'How do you make that out?'

'The phraseology betrays him. The English is much less certain than in the other letters. There are several little mistakes.'

'I think the postscript looks very shady.'

'It does, doesn't it? What do you say, Fox?'

'Well, sir, I'd say the gentleman knew something that he didn't exactly like to mention in black and white. It might be he knew there'd be goings-on with the Reverend, and it might be something he was afraid she'd find out. That postscript to me looks as though he was scared.'

'You wise old bird. Well, I've finished here. We'll leave your mates to do the toothcombing, Fox. They are upstairs at the moment. I've a date with Mr Rattisbon.'

'He was the solicitor in the O'Callighan case, wasn't he?' asked Nigel.

'He was. He's everything that a lawyer ought to be. Desiccated, tittuppy, nice old fuss-pot. Gives one the idea that he is a good actor slightly overdoing his part. I must away, Fox. Meet you at the Garnette apartment, as Mr Ogden would say.'

'Right-oh, sir.'

'Anyone else going?' Nigel inquired.

'No doubt you will appear. I expect the Initiates to turn up in full force. Two o'clock.'

'Certainly, I shall come,' said Nigel. *'Au revoir.'*

Nigel returned to his office and Alleyn went down the Strand to the little street where Mr Rattisbon kept office.

It was one of those offices that look as if they were kept going as a memorial to Charles Dickens. A dingy entry smelt of cobwebs and old varnish. A dark staircase led to a landing, where a frosted-glass skylight let in enough light to show Mr Rattisbon's name on the door. Beyond the door Alleyn found Mr Rattisbon himself in an atmosphere of dust, leather, varnish, dry sherry, and age. The room was not dusty, but it made one think of discreet dust. Mr Rattisbon was not dressed in Victorian garments, but he conveyed an impression of being so dressed. He was a thin, eager old man with bluish hands and sharp eyes. He spoke rapidly with a sort of stuttering volubility, and had a trick of vibrating the tip of his long tongue between his lips. He dealt, as his father and grandfather had done before him, with the estates of the upper-middle class. He was a very shrewd old gentleman.

'I hope I'm not late, sir,' said Alleyn.

'No, no, Chief Inspector, not at all. Quite punctual, quite punctual. Pray sit down. Yes. Let me see. I don't think we have met since that unfortunate affair – um?'

'No. I am sorry to bother you. I expect you have guessed what brought me?'

'Brought you. Yes. Yes. This miserable business of Miss Cara Valerie Quayne. I have received word of it this morning. A most distressing affair, most.'

'How did you hear of it, sir?'

'Through the maid, the confidential maid. A Miss – ah – Miss Edith Laura Hebborn. Miss Hebborn felt I should be advised immediately and very properly rang me up. One of the old type of domestic servants. The old type. I suppose there's no doubt about it being a case of homicide. Um? No.'

'None, I'm afraid. It's a bizarre case.'

'Bizarre!' ejaculated Mr Rattisbon with distaste. 'Tch! Well, Chief Inspector, how can I assist you?'

'By giving me any information you can about Miss Quayne and by letting me see the Will. The inquest is tomorrow. Perhaps it would save time if I told you what I have learned up to date.'

Alleyn gave Mr Rattisbon the gist of the information he had received from Nannie and from the Initiates. The little lawyer listened attentively.

'Precisely,' he said when Alleyn had finished. 'An excellent account and substantially correct. Accurate.'

'Miss Quayne's affairs have always been in your hands, sir?'

'Oh, yes. Yes. Colonel Quayne – her father – old family clients. Charming fellow.'

'You have seen Miss Quayne recently?'

'Five weeks ago tomorrow.'

'On that occasion did she wish to alter her Will?'

'Um? You heard of that?'

'From M. de Ravigne. I hope you will tell me anything that strikes you as being relevant.'

'It is exceedingly distasteful to me to discuss my clients' affairs, Chief Inspector. Of course, I quite appreciate the extraordinary nature of the matter. Since you rang up I have considered the advisability of – of – speaking with complete frankness, and – I – in short I have decided to lay the whole matter before you.'

Mr Rattisbon suddenly snatched his pince-nez from his nose and waved them at Alleyn.

'As follows,' he said. 'Five weeks ago I received a visit from Miss Cara Valerie Quayne. She had advised me first that she wished to make an extensive alteration in her Will, and then that she desired me to draw up a new Will. I therefore had the existing document in readiness for her visit. She arrived.' He rubbed his nose violently. 'And I may say she astounded me.'

Alleyn was silent. After contemplating him with severity for some seconds Mr Rattisbon leant across the desk and continued:

'She astounded me. The previous Will had been a very proper and sensible disposition of her considerable fortune. Several large sums to various worthy charities. Annuities to her servants. Various legacies. The residuary legatee was a third cousin in New Zealand. A boy whom she has never seen, but he bears her father's name. And so on and so on and so on. Perfectly proper. She now informed me that she wished me completely to revise these terms and – in short to draw up a new document. On these lines: She wished the annuity of two hundred pounds per annum to Miss Edith Laura Hebborn to be increased to three hundred pounds per annum. The lease of her house, its contents, her pictures, jewels and so on to M. Raoul Honoré Christophe de Ravigne. A – a handsome legacy to Father Jasper Garnette. The rest of her very considerable fortune – every penny piece of it – she would leave to the House of the Sacred Flame, 89 Knocklatchers Row, Eaton Place, making Father Garnette the sole trustee.'

'Gosh!' said Alleyn.

'You may well say so. I – frankly, Chief Inspector – I was horrified. I had known Miss Quayne from her childhood. Her father was a personal friend as well as a client. In a sense I may say I had considered myself *in loco parentis*, since both guardians were deceased. When

I first became aware of Miss Quayne's increasing interest in Mr Garnette's sect I went so far as to make inquiries about him. What I discovered did not reassure me. On the contrary I became gravely suspicious. Then, to crown everything, she came to me with the request that I should draw up a Will on the lines I have indicated.'

'Extraordinary.'

'Most extraordinary. As a solicitor I have become accustomed to testamentary – ah – vagaries. I have become accustomed to them. But this caused me the greatest concern. I exceeded the strict limits of propriety by urging her again and again to reconsider. I represented to her that this Father Garnette might not be all she thought him. I strongly urged her to allow me to make further inquiries. When all else failed I begged that she at least left this very considerable sum to be administered by other trustees on behalf of the – the – religious body in which she had become so interested. Not a bit of it!'

'She insisted on leaving Mr Garnette as sole trustee?'

'Precisely. She was in a most excitable frame of mind and was impatient, I may say intolerant, of any suggestions. I put it to her that her father would have regarded the terms of the new Will with abhorrence. She would not listen. She – in short, she said that if I made any further difficulties she would get a Will form from – from a Smith's bookstall and fill it in herself.'

Mr Rattisbon dropped his pince-nez delicately on his blotting-paper and by this moderate gesture conveyed a sense of overwhelming defeat.

'I drew up the Will,' he said. 'Three days afterwards, she came here and signed it.'

'So that's that,' grunted Alleyn. 'By how much does the sect benefit?'

'In round figures, twenty-one thousand pounds.'

'And may I ask, sir, by how much Mr Jasper Garnette is to be a richer man?'

'Ten thousand pounds.'

'Damn!' said Alleyn.

Mr Rattisbon shot a shrewd glance at him.

'May I take it as your personal opinion that he will live to – to enjoy it?' he asked.

'He'll need it before I'm done with him.'

'That is a cryptic answer, Chief Inspector.'

'Yours was a leading question, sir.'

Mr Rattisbon suddenly sucked in his breath three or four times very rapidly and uttered a little whooping noise. He had laughed.

'In any case,' Alleyn went on, 'couldn't the Will be contested? What about the young Quayne, down under? What about coercion? Or her mental condition? I'm entirely ignorant of the law, sir, but suppose – well, suppose he'd been giving her drugs?'

Mr Rattisbon stared at the inspector for some seconds.

'If you find evidence of that,' he said at last, 'I would be greatly obliged if you would call on me again.'

'Certainly.' Alleyn stood up. 'By the way, have you any idea why she increased the bequest to Miss Hebborn?'

'I received an impression that – that it was in the nature of a – how shall I put it? – of a peace-offering. Miss Hebborn had, I believe, expressed herself somewhat warmly on the subject of the sect, which she regarded in a most unfavourable light. There had been a heated argument, hasty words amounting to a quarrel. Miss Quayne was greatly attached to her old nurse, who had given her devoted service. From certain remarks she let fall I gathered that she wished to – in a sense to make reparation.'

'And the bequest to M. de Ravigne? It will amount to something pretty considerable, I imagine. The pictures alone are worth a great deal. There's a very fine Van Gogh and I noticed a Famille Verte "ginger" jar that wouldn't be had for the asking.'

'Precisely. M. de Ravigne is an old friend of the family and, I understand, a collector. I have not the pleasure of his acquaintance.'

'He has an intriguing temperament. I must go. Goodbye, sir, and thank you a thousand times.'

'Goodbye. Yes. Thank-yer. Thank-yer. Don't mention it. Yes,' gabbled Mr Rattisbon with extreme rapidity. He walked out first on to the landing and there leant forward and peered up into Alleyn's face. 'And I hope you're going to – eh? By the heels? Eh? Always interested in your work. This time – natural anxiety. Well. Mind the steps.'

'I hope so. Of course. Thank you,' said Alleyn.

He had a short interview with his Assistant Commissioner, lunched in the Strand and went straight to Knocklatchers Row. Here he found Claude and Lionel and all the Initiates who had been rung up from the Yard grouped in a solid phalanx round Father Garnette's sitting-room under the eye of Detective-Sergeant Bailey. The priest, looking extremely cadaverous and yellow, was seated at the centre table. Nigel, who had hung about the entrance with Inspector Fox, followed the detectives into the room.

'Good afternoon, ladies and gentlemen,' said Alleyn cheerfully. 'Forgive me if I've kept you waiting.'

Janey Jenkins said: 'You're punctual. It's just struck two.'

Mr Ogden stood up and said: 'Well, well, well, look who's here.'

The rest of the ladies and gentlemen uttered self-conscious noises.

'I shan't keep you long,' Alleyn went on. 'First of all, if you don't mind, we would like to take your fingerprints. It's the usual thing. I could get them on the sly by offering you shiny photos to identify as your third cousins, but there really isn't time. Detective-Sergeant Bailey will fix you up.'

Janey looked interested, Maurice disgusted, Ogden solemn and de Ravigne faintly amused, while Mrs Candour and Miss Wade were obviously terrified. The acolytes turned pale and Father Garnette remained ghastly and rather remote. Bailey took their prints by getting them to roll the cushion of each finger on a little printer's ink and then on a sheet of white paper. He thoughtfully offered them an oiled rag to clean up with. This ceremony ended, Alleyn invited them all to sit round the table.

'First of all,' he began, 'I should like you all to tell me as far as you can remember what are the contents of the safe. I understand that several of you had access to it.'

There was a moment's silence and then Mr Ogden said bluntly:

'We all know where the key was kept, Chief, but I guess none of us worried.'

'Where was the key kept.'

'On my desk,' said Father Garnette, 'sometimes.'

'In your pocket,' said Mr Ogden. 'It wasn't just laying around all the time, Chief. Sometimes there's quite a little bit of coin in that safe.'

'How much is there at the moment?' asked Alleyn.

'I – ah – I really forget,' said Father Garnette. 'Let me see. There should be last Wednesday's offertory. I really don't remembah – '

'It was £61 8s. 6d.' announced M. de Ravigne.

'You've got it pat!' said Maurice Pringle unpleasantly.

'I am a warden,' replied de Ravigne very placidly, 'I counted it. Father Garnette and Mr Ogden were here. It was, I repeat, £61 *8s. 6d.*'

'*And* a cheque for twenty pounds,' said Mr Ogden dryly. 'You might remember that.'

'Your own offering, Monsieur Ogden. I remember.'

'What else?' asked Alleyn.

'There is more importantly, M. l'Inspecteur, a parcel of bearer bonds of which I have told you. They are issued by the Kasternek Oil Company. These were given by Miss Quayne to this church to await the raising of the same amount for a building fund. They are in value five thousand pounds. Since they were here you have always kept the key on your person, is it not so, Father?'

'Quite right, my dear Raoul. You advised me to take this precaution, if you remember.'

'Certainly.'

'Quite correct,' said Mr Ogden emphatically. 'We may all be OK but that doesn't say we've got to act crazy.' He stopped short, turned bright red, and glanced uneasily at Father Garnette.

'Anything else in the safe? ' asked Alleyn.

'The banking-book is there. That, I believe, is all,' murmured M. de Ravigne.

'Right. Well, we'll just check it over. I'll ask Mr Garnette to do that. It's purely a matter of form. You will notice we sealed it last night. The usual procedure under the circumstances. Now, Mr Garnette, if you please.'

He produced the bunch of keys, gave them to Father Garnette and himself broke the police seal. Father Garnette rose, opened the safe and took out the contents one by one, laying them on the table. Nigel noticed that the parcel had been replaced. Bailey must have done that and put a fresh seal on the safe. The cash was counted by Fox who found it correct.

'Have you looked at the parcel of bearer bonds?' asked Alleyn.

Father Garnette glanced at him.

'No,' he said. He sounded anxious and surprised. 'No, I have not.'

'Just open it,' suggested Alleyn, 'and make sure there has been no theft. We've got to explore every possibility.'

Father Garnette undid the red ribbon and pulled open the brown paper.

A neat wad of newspaper lay revealed.

One would have thought it impossible for Father Garnette's face to look more unhealthy than it already was that morning, but it undoubtedly became a shade more livid when the contents of the parcel were displayed. It also became absolutely expressionless. For about three seconds he stood still. Then he raised his eyes and stared inimically at Alleyn. Nigel wondered if, for a moment, the priest had a mad idea that the police had played a practical joke on him. Alleyn returned his glance gravely. Suddenly Father Garnette seized the newspaper and with an ugly fumbling movement clawed it apart, shook the leaves open, and then as abruptly, let them fall again. When he spoke it was in a curiously dead voice, as though his throat had closed.

'Robbed!' he said, 'I've been robbed – robbed.'

They had watched Father Garnette and Father Garnette only, so that when Mr Ogden produced his national classic expression of incredulity it made them all jump.

Mr Ogden placed both hands on the table and leant towards his spiritual leader.

'Oh, yeah?' said Mr Ogden.

CHAPTER 16

Mr Ogden Puts his Trust
in Policemen

'Is that so?' continued Mr Ogden; and then, for all the world as though he was an anthology of Quaint American Sayings, he completed the trilogy by adding in a soft undertone:

'Sez you?'

They all turned to watch Mr Ogden. His good-natured face had settled down into a definitely hard-boiled expression. His lower lip stuck out, his eyes were half-closed. He spoke out of one corner of his mouth. He leant easily on the table, but the very seams of his coat looked tense. He did not remove his gaze from Father Garnette, but he addressed the table at large.

'Folks,' he said, 'I guess we're the Simps from Simpleton. Cable address Giggle-Giggle. No flowers by request.'

'What the hell do you mean?' asked Maurice Pringle.

De Ravigne swore very softly in French.

'What do you mean?' replied Mr Ogden, never taking his eyes off Garnette. 'What do I mean? Aren't you conscious yet? Who's taken care of the keys ever since Cara parked those bonds in the safe? Didn't we say, right now, Father Garnette had been wearing his keys for safety's sake? Safety is right. 'I reckon those bonds are so darned safe we'll never see them any more.'

'What do you mean, Mr Ogden?' asked Miss Wade. 'I'm afraid 'I don't quite follow. Has this money been stolen?'

'Nope,' answered Mr Ogden. 'It's just kind of disguised itself as the Daily Mail.'

'But I don't understand – '

'Cara's bonds have been stolen, Miss Wade,' said Janey impatiently, 'and newspaper substituted. You can see for yourself.'

'Who has done this?' demanded Father Garnette suddenly. He had drawn himself up to his full height. The resonance had come back to his voice, and something of the old dominance to his manner. He was wearing that dark-green garment – a sort of cassock that covered his neck and hung heavily about his feet. In a raffish, theatrical kind of fashion he looked extremely impressive. He puzzled Nigel, who had expected him to crumble up when the theft of the bonds was revealed. He had watched Garnette, and the priest was either dumbfounded or the best actor off the stage that Nigel had ever seen.

'Who has done this?' repeated Garnette. He turned his head and stared round the circle of Initiates.

'I swear I never touched the safe,' bleated Claude Wheatley in a hurry.

'I suggest, Father, that you yourself are best situated to answer this question,' said de Ravigne softly. 'It makes itself apparent. As we have said and you have also agreed – you have kept these keys about your person since our poor Cara made her gift.'

'How dare you!' cried Mrs Candour shrilly. 'How dare you suggest such a thing, M. de Ravigne? Father!'

'Quiet, my child,' said Father Garnette.

Maurice Pringle burst out laughing. The others stared at him scandalized.

'Look at him,' coughed Maurice, 'look! To the pure all things are pure.'

'Maurice!' cried Janey.

'Just a minute, please,' said Alleyn.

They had forgotten all about Alleyn, but now they listened to him.

'Mr Pringle,' he said, 'will you be good enough to pull yourself together? You are behaving like a hysterical adolescent. That's better. I gather from what you have all said that no one is prepared to volunteer information about the missing bonds.' Father Garnette began to speak, but Alleyn raised a finger. 'Very well. I now wish to bring another exhibit to your notice. The book, if you please, Fox.'

Inspector Fox loomed forward and put a book into Alleyn's hand. Alleyn held it up. It was a copy of Abberley's *Curiosities of Chemistry*.

'Quis?' said Alleyn lightly.

Garnette turned and looked calmly at it. Mrs Candour gaped at it with her mouth open. Maurice stared at it as if it were an offensive relic, Janey looked blank, M. de Ravigne curious. Mr Ogden still glared at Father Garnette. Miss Wade balanced her pince-nez across her nose and leant forward to peer at the book. Claude Wheatley said: 'What's that? I can't see.'

'It is Abberley's *Curiosities of Chemistry,*' said Alleyn.

'Hey?' exclaimed Mr Ogden suddenly and wheeled round in his chair. He saw the book and his jaw dropped.

'Why – ' he said. 'Why – '

'Yes, Mr Ogden?'

Mr Ogden looked exceedingly uncomfortable. A dead silence followed.

'What is it?' continued Alleyn patiently.

'Why nothing, Chief. Except that I'm quite curious to know where you located that book.'

'Anybody else know anything about it?' asked Alleyn.

'Yes,' said Father Garnette, 'I do.'

He was still on his feet. He stretched out his hand and Alleyn gave him the book.

'This volume,' said Father Garnette, 'appeared in my shelves some weeks ago. It is not mine and I do not know where it came from. I did not even open it. I simply found it there.'

'Next an unexpurgated translation of Petronius?'

'Ah – preciselah!' said Father Garnette.

He still held the book in his hands. Perhaps the habit of the pulpit caused him to let it fall open.

'Who left this book in my room?' he demanded.

'Look at it,' said Alleyn.

Garnette hesitated as though he wondered what Alleyn meant. Then he looked at the book. It had again fallen open at the page which gave the formula for sodium cyanide. For a moment Garnette scarcely seemed to take it in. Then with sudden violence he shut the book and dropped it on the table.

'I am the victim of an infamous conspiracy,' he said. The baa-ing vowel-sounds had disappeared, and the hint of a nasal inflection had taken their place.

'You tell us,' said Alleyn, 'that this book was left in your shelves. When did you first discover it?'

'I do not remembah,' declared Garnette, rallying slightly.

'Try to remember.'

'It was there three Sundays ago, anyway,' volunteered Claude.

'Oh?' said Alleyn. 'How do you know that, Mr Wheatley?'

'Because, I mean, I saw it. And I know it was three Sundays ago because you see I do temple service – cleaning the silver, you know – and all that, every fortnight. And it was while I was doing that, I found it, and it wasn't last Sunday, so it must have been three Sundays ago.'

'How did you come to find it?'

'Well, I – well, you see – well, I'd finished and Father was out and I thought I'd wait till he came in and so I went into his room to put some things away.'

'Where was the book?'

'Well, it was in the shelves.'

'Where you could see it?'

'Not quite.'

'It was behind the other books?'

'Yes, if you must know, it was,' said Claude turning an unattractive crimson. 'As a matter of fact I had put all the books there myself – he stopped and looked nervously from Ogden to Garnette – 'about a week before that. I was – I was tidying up in here. I didn't look at them, then. The book on Chemistry wasn't there that day. But it was there on the Sunday – a week later. You see I'd read most of the other books and I thought I'd try and find something else, and so – '

'Did you handle it?'

'I – I – just glanced at it.'

'You touched it. You're sure of that?'

'Yes, I am. Because I remember I had my gloves on. The ones I do the polishing in. I like to keep my hands nice. I wondered if they'd marked it. Then I put it away and – and I read something else, you see.'

'Petronius, perhaps.'

'Yes, it was. I thought it marvellous.'

'Thank you.'

'I don't understand,' began Miss Wade.

'Nor do I,' interrupted Mrs Candour. 'Why is such a fuss being made about this book?'

'It's a treatise on poisons,' said Maurice. 'Cara was poisoned. Find the owner of the book and there's your murderer. Q.E.D. Our wonderful police!'

'I've got an idea,' said Mr Ogden with a curious inflection in his voice, 'that it's not just as simple as all that.'

'Really?' jeered Maurice. 'You seem to know a damn' sight too much to be healthy.'

'Maurice, please!' said Janey.

'Oh, God, I'm sorry, Jane.'

'The interesting thing about the book,' said Alleyn in his quietest voice, 'is that if you handle it as Mr Garnette did, it falls open at a discourse on cyanide.' He took the book and handed it to de Ravigne. 'Like to try?' he asked.

De Ravigne took the book, but he must have handled it differently. It fell open at another place. He examined it closely, a curiously puzzled expression in his eyes.

'Let me see,' said Lionel. 'Do, please.' With him the experiment worked successfully.

'How too marvellous!' said Claude.

'Here,' shouted Mr Ogden suddenly, 'lemme see.'

Lionel handed him the book and he experimented with it while they all watched him. The book fell open repeatedly and each time at the same page

'Well, for crying out loud!' said Mr Ogden, and slammed it down on the table.

'Now,' Alleyn went on, 'there's one more exhibit. This box of cigarettes. Yours, isn't it, Mr Garnette?' He laid the Benares Box on the table.

'Ah, yes.'

'Will you open it?'

'Is this a sleight of hand act?' asked Maurice Pringle. 'no deception practised.'

'None, on my part,' replied Alleyn good-humouredly, 'as I think you will agree, Mr Garnette.'

Garnette had opened the box. Cara Quayne's note lay on the top of the cigarettes.

'What is this?' asked Garnette. And then: 'My God, it's her writing.'

'Will you read it aloud?'

Garnette read slowly. The habit of the pulpit was so strong in him that he pitched his voice and read deliberately with round vowels and stressed final consonants.

'Must see you. Terrible discovery. After service tonight.'

He put the paper down on the table and again looked at Alleyn. His lips twitched, but he did not speak. He moved his hands uncertainly. He looked neither guilty nor innocent but simply puzzled.

'Where did this come from?' he said at last.

'It was found last night in that box,' Alleyn said.

'But – I did not know. I did not see it there.'

'Does anyone,' asked Alleyn, 'know anything of this note?' Nobody spoke.

'Had Miss Quayne spoken to any of you of this terrible discovery she had made?'

'When was it written?' asked Maurice suddenly.

'Yesterday.'

'How do you know?'

'Because it is dated,' answered Alleyn politely.

'Oh, Maurice, my poor pet!' said Janey, and for the first time that morning somebody laughed.

'Shut up!' exclaimed Maurice.

'You did not open this box yesterday, Mr Garnette?' Alleyn went on.

'No.'

'When did Miss Quayne call?'

'I do not know. I did not see her. I was out from midday until about three o'clock.'

'Where were you?'

'Father Garnette was my guest at luncheon,' said de Ravigne. 'I had invited Cara also, but she desired, she said, to spend the day in meditation in her own house.'

'She changed her mind, it seems. How would she get in here?'

'The key to the front door of the church is always left in the porch, monsieur. It is concealed behind the torch there. We all use it.'

'Did any of you come here yesterday between two-thirty and three o'clock while Miss Quayne was in the hall?'

No one had come, it seemed. Alleyn asked them all in turn where they had been. Maurice had lunched with Janey in her flat and had stayed there till four. Mrs Candour had been at home for lunch, and so had Miss Wade. Miss Wade to everybody's surprise said she had been in the hall when Cara went through and into Garnette's flat. Miss Wade had been engaged in a little meditation, it appeared. She had seen Cara come out again and had thought she seemed 'rather put out.'

'Why did you say nothing of this before?' asked Alleyn.

'Because you did not ask me, officer,' said Miss Wade.

'*Touché,*' said Alleyn, and turned to the others.

Mr Ogden had lunched at his club and afterwards taken a 'carn-stitootional' in the park, arriving home at tea-time. Garnette and de Ravigne had remained in the latter's house until two-forty, when de Ravigne had asked Garnette the time in order to set his clock right. About ten minutes later, Garnette left. He had a Neophytes' class at three-thirty, and it seemed that two selected advanced Neophytes always stayed on for what Father Garnette called a little repast in his flat, and then went to the evening instruction. This was a regular routine. That would account, Nigel reflected, for Cara Quayne leaving the note in the cigarette-box. Whatever her terrible discovery was, she would know she had no chance of a private conversation before the evening ceremony. After he left de Ravigne's house Father Garnette had gone straight to the hall. There he found one or two people who had come in early for the ceremony. He had not looked at the safe, but he felt sure he would have noticed if it had been open. De Ravigne lived in Lowndes Square, so it would not have taken many minutes for the priest to walk back to Knocklatchers Row. He probably arrived at about three o'clock. De Ravigne said he had remained at home until it was time to go to the evening ceremony. Claude and Lionel it transpired, had not got up until half-past three in the afternoon.

'Ah, well,' said Alleyn, with the ghost of a sigh, 'I shall not keep you here any longer, ladies and gentlemen. The meeting is adjourned.'

One by one the Initiates got to their feet. Garnette remained seated at the table, his face buried in his hands. Evidently most of them felt desperately uncomfortable at the thought of Father Garnette. They eyed him surreptitiously and made uneasy noises in their throats.

Ogden still glared at him and, alone of the Initiates, seemed disinclined to leave. M. de Ravigne clicked his heels, made a formal bow which included Alleyn and Garnette, said 'Gentlemen'; made a rather more willowy bow, said 'Ladies,' and walked out with an air of knowing how to deal with the stiffest social contretemps.

Miss Wade, after some hesitation, made a sudden dart at Garnette, extended a black kid claw and said:

'Father! Faithful! Last ditch! Trust!'

Whereupon Mrs Candour, who had been waiting for a cue from somebody, uttered a lamentable bellow and surged forward, saying: 'Yes – yes – yes.'

Garnette pulled himself together and cast upon both ladies a sort of languishing glare.

He said: 'Faithful! Faithful unto – ' and then, disliking the sound of the phrase, hurriedly abandoned it.

Ogden let them all go and then walked up to Alleyn.

'Can I have a word with you, Chief?' he asked.

'Certainly, Mr Ogden.'

'What are you going to say?' demanded Garnette.

'That's nobody's business, Garnette,' said Ogden. 'C'm on, Chief!'

He led the way out into the hall, followed by Alleyn, Nigel and Fox. When they were down in the aisle, he jerked his thumb at Nigel.

'I ain't giving interviews this trip, Mr Bathgate,' he said, 'and something seems to tell me you're a Pressman.'

'Mr Bathgate is not here in his official capacity,' said Alleyn. 'I think we can trust him.'

'Seems like I'm doing a helluva lot of trusting. Well – if you say so, Chief, that's OK by me.'

Nigel returned to his old perch in the front pews, and Mr Ogden paid no further attention to him. He addressed himself to Alleyn.

'Listen, Chief. I've spent quite a lot of my time in this little old island, but right now is the first occasion I've come into contact with the Law. Back home in God's Own Country I'd say a guy was crazy to do what I'm doing. But listen, Chief. I guess you're on the level, and I guess you ain't so darned polite you can't do your stuff.'

Here Mr Ogden paused, drew out a large silk handkerchief and wiped his neck with it.

'Hell,' he said. 'This has got me all shot to bits.'

'What's on your mind, Mr Ogden?' asked Alleyn.

'Hell,' repeated Mr Ogden. 'Well, listen. They opine that in this country you don't get the hot squat, not without you earn it good and plenty.'

'I beg your pardon?' said Alleyn, gazing at him. 'Oh! I see. I think you're quite right. There are no miscarriages of justice in capital charges on the conviction side. Only, we hang them over here, you know.'

'That's so,' agreed Mr Ogden, 'but the principle's the same.'

'True,' said Alleyn.

Mr Ogden seemed to find extreme difficulty in coming to the point. He rolled his eyes and goggled solemnly at Alleyn.

'Listen, Chief,' he said again. 'I guess that you've got it figured out that whoever owns the book of the words and songs did the murder.'

'You mean the book on chemistry?'

'Yup.'

'It certainly looks rather like that.'

'Then it looks all cock-eyed,' said Mr Ogden violently. 'It looks all to – Hell! Do you know why?'

'I think I can guess,' said Alleyn smiling.

'You can! Well I'd be – '

'I rather fancied the book belonged to you.'

'Chief, you said it,' said Mr Ogden.

CHAPTER 17

Mr Ogden Grows Less Trustful

You said it,' repeated Mr Ogden and collapsed into a pew.

'Cheer up, Mr Ogden,' said Alleyn.

Mr Ogden passed his handkerchief across his brow and contemplated the inspector with a certain expression of low cunning that reminded Nigel of a precocious baby.

'Maybe I seemed a mite too eager about that book,' he said. 'Maybe I kinda gave you the works.'

'My inspiration dates a little further back than that,' said Alleyn. 'You told us last night that you were interested in gold-refining. A letter which we found in your pockets referred rather fully to a new process. It assumed a certain knowledge of chemistry on your part. The book is an American publication. It was a little suggestive, you see.'

'Yup,' said Mr Ogden, 'I see. Now listen. I bought that book years ago, way back in the pre-war period when I first began to sit up and take notice. I was a junior clurk at the time in the offices of a gold-refining company. Junior clurk is a swell name for office-boy. I lit on that book laying out in the rain on a five-cent stall, and I was ambitious to educate myself. It's kinda stayed around ever since. The book, I mean. When I came over here it was laying in one of my grips, and I let it lay. I know a bit more than I useter, and some of them antique recipes tickled me. Well, anyhow, it stuck and, and when I got fixed where I am now I packed it in the bookshelves along with the Van Dines and National Geographics and the *Saturday Evening Posts.* I never opened it. And get this, chief, I never missed it till last night.'

'Last night? At what time?'

'After I got home. I got to thinking about Cara, and I figured it out that she passed in her checks very, very sudden, and that the suddenest poison I knew was prussic acid. Hydrocyanic acid if you want to talk Ritzy. I thought maybe I'd refresh my memory and I looked for the old book. Nothing doing. It was gone. What do you know about that?'

'What do *you* know about it?' rejoined Alleyn.

'Listen,' said Mr Ogden for about the twentieth time that afternoon. 'I know this far. It was there four weeks back. Four weeks back from tonight I threw a party. All the Sacred Flame crowd was there. Garnette was there. And Raveenje. And Cara Quayne. All the gang, even Miss Wade, who has a habit of getting mislaid or over-looked: she was there and cracking hardy. Well, Raveenje, he's enthusiastic about literature. First editions are all published by Pep and Kick as he sees it. I saw him looking along the shelves and yanked down the old *Curiosities* for him to have a slant at. Well, maybe it hadn't enough whiskers on it, but it seemed to excite him about as much as a raspberry drink at a departmental store. He gave a polite once-over and lost interest. But that's how I remember it was there. From that night till last evening I never gave it a thought.'

'Did anyone take it away that night?'

'How should I know? I never missed the blamed thing.'

'You can't remember anything that would help? The next time you looked at your bookshelves?'

'Nope. Wait a while. Wait a while.'

Mr Ogden clapped a plump hand on top of his head as if to prevent an elusive thought from escaping him.

'The next day or maybe the day after – it was around that time – Claude stopped in and he took Garnette's books away with him. I was out at the time.'

'Mr Garnette's books? What books?'

Mr Ogden looked remarkably sheepish.

'Aw Gee!' he said. 'Just something for a rainy day. He loaned 'em to me. He said they were classics. Classics. And how? Boy, they were central-heated.'

'Are they among the lot in brown paper covers, behind the others?'

'You said it.'

'And Claude Wheatley took them away?'

'Sure. He told the maid Garnette had sent him for them. He wanted to keep hold of them because they were rare. I'll say they were rare! Anyhow, that's when I last remember anything about books. I suppose Garnette told Claude where they were.'

'Was the *Curiosities* in your shelves then?'

'Isn't that what I'm aiming to remember!' exclaimed Mr Ogden desperately. 'Lemme think! Next day Claude told me he'd called for Garnette's books and I said: "Those were the ones in brown-paper overalls," and he said he'd recognized them by that.'

'The *Curiosities* was not in a brown paper, then?'

'No, sir. I'd no call to camouflage it. It was respectable.'

Alleyn laughed.

'Can you remember noticing it that day?'

'Nope.'

'Would you have noticed if it had already gone?'

'Lordy, no!' said Mr Ogden.

He stared wildly into space for an appreciable time and then said slowly:

'Not in that way. I wouldn't have definitely missed it. But in another way I seem to remember *not* seeing it if you get me. It's a red book. Seems like I remember *not* seeing a red book. That sounds crazy, I guess.'

'On the contrary, this is all extremely interesting,' said Alleyn.

'Yeah? Well, here's hoping it doesn't interest you in Sam J. Ogden. Maybe Raveenje will recall me showing him the book. Or maybe one of the rest will. That,' added Mr Ogden with a naïve smile, 'is just why I thought I'd better come clean.'

'Do you incline to think somebody took the book that evening, Mr Ogden?'

'What the hell? I haven't a notion when it was lifted.'

'Have any of the Initiates been to see you since then?'

'Sure, they have. I gave a little lunch last Wednesday for Cara and Raveenje and Garnette and Dagmar. Lemme see. Maurice and Janey were around last Sunday. That was the night Dr Kasbek came in. I haven't had Claude and Lionel come in again. Those two queens give me a pain.'

'Now look here, Mr Ogden, you've got your own ideas on the subject, haven't you? You practically stated, just now, that you believed Mr Garnette had taken these bonds.'

Mr Ogden looked extremely uncomfortable.

'Didn't you?' pressed Alleyn.

'I'm not saying a thing.'

'Very well,' said Alleyn shortly, 'I can't do anything against that,'
Ogden gave him a sidelong but not unattractive grin.

'Seems like the British police is kinda helpless,' he said.

'Seems like it,' agreed Alleyn dryly. 'How many of you are in this
thing with Garnette?'

'What the hell? In what thing?'

He broke off, got to his feet, and stood glaring down at Alleyn, his
face white and his eyes very angry.

'See here,' he said. 'Just what do you mean? I'm not muscling in
on any homicide rackets. I've told you a straight story about that
book and I'm sticking to it. If you don't believe me – find out.'

'Mr Ogden, I fully believe your story. But there are more rackets
than one, you know.'

'Yeah? Just what are you aiming to insinuate?'

'Merely that I have far too high an opinion of your intelligence to
suppose that you would allow yourself to become as enamoured of
transcendental mumbo-jumbo as you would have me believe.'

'Are you telling me the spiritual dope we hand out here is phoney?'

'I'm saying that you aren't so hypnotized by it that you've lost
your business man's acumen.'

Mr Ogden looked very hard at the inspector and a slow grin
began to dawn on his face.

'And I'm saying,' Alleyn continued, 'that you don't float anything
with big fat cheques unless you're going to get a more tangible
return for your money than a dose of over-proof spiritual uplift.'

'Maybe,' said Mr Ogden with a fat chuckle.

'In short, Mr Ogden, I want to know how you stand as regards the
finance of this affair. I've got to find out how everybody stands. It's
no good mincing matters. All of the Initiates come under suspicion
of this crime; yourself as much as anyone. Believe me, you cannot
afford to keep back any information when there's a capital charge in
the offing.'

'Just when did you get your big idea that I'm interested financially?'

'I got it the first time I saw you. I know that there are, if you will
forgive me for saying so, many hard-headed Americans who can be

taken in by highly-coloured religious sects. I told myself you might be one of them, but somehow I didn't think you were. You seemed to me to be too shrewd. Your attitude towards Mr Garnette, when the theft of the bonds was discovered, confirmed my opinion. Of course, if you prefer not to tell me how matters stand, we can ferret round and find out. Mr Garnette is now so alarmed he will no doubt be ready to give me his version.'

'Like hell he will, the dirty what's it,' said Mr Ogden indignantly. 'See here, Chief, you win this deal, hands down. Bar one point. Until today I was putting my OK stamp on the doctrine of the Sacred Flame. I've never backed a phoney deal in my life and I'm not starting in now. No, sir. The Sacred Flame and Jasper Garnette looked like clean peppy uplift to me. When Garnette and me met up on that trip, he outlined his scheme and he slipped me the line of talk. He told me it'd need capital. Well, I heard him address the passengers and the way he had those society dames asking if he'd accept ten dollars as a favour for the Seamen's Fund got me thinking. Before we landed I'd figured it out. I floated the concern on a percentage basis and Garnette couldn't have done it without me. We were in cahoots, and now, the dirty so-and-so, he's pulled out those bonds on me.'

'Are there any other shareholders?'

'M. de Raveenje put five hundred pounds into it. All he could find. The slump hit him up some. Say, I reckon he'll want to know the how-so about those bonds. He's white all through, and he saw Cara way up among the gods.'

'Did you,' asked Alleyn, 'have a written agreement?'

'Certainly we did. Drawn up by a lawyer. Each of us got a copy. Want to see it, Chief?'

'Yes, we'd better have a look at it. I wonder where Mr Garnette keeps his.'

'Most likely at his bank. He's a wise coon!'

'You are convinced Garnette took the bonds?'

'I wish to God I wasn't,' said Mr Ogden unexpectedly. 'I – I kind of reverenced that guy. Me! Maybe I'll learn sense – next year.'

'Did you keep books?'

'Yes, sir. I did the books and Raveenje and Garnette could see them at any time. Raveenje has got them home right now.'

'How did it work?'

'Like any regular company. I'm the biggest shareholder – I put up the most dollars. Garnette is paid a salary and he draws twenty per cent of the profits. That was square enough.'

'Do you know Mr Garnette is a fellow-countryman of yours?'

'Mr Ogden looked as if he might be a sign for an inn called *The Incredulous Man*. 'Forget it,' he said briefly. 'Him! No, sir! We certainly breed one brand of polecat, but it ain't called Garnette. Look at his line of talk! Where do you get that stuff anyway?'

'You might say,' said Alleyn with a glance at Fox, 'that the gentleman told me himself.'

'Then he piled up one more lie on to his total.'

'Ah, well,' sighed Alleyn, 'I think that's all for the moment, Mr Ogden.'

'Good! But listen, Chief, I don't want to get in wrong over the financial side of his joint. Get this. I put up the dollars. I saw it as a commercial proposition and I backed it. I've run my department straight and I've had no more'n my fair share. Same goes for Raveenje. He's on the level all right. I look at it this way. This temple has brought colour and interest into folk's lives. I'd thought it was something more than that, day-before-yesterday, when Garnette looked like a regular guy. But even if Garnette's synthetic, and he certainly is, it's been a great little party.' He paused and then repeated as though it was a manufacturer's slogan: 'It has brought colour and interest into otherwise drab and grey lives.'

'Together with hysteria and heroin, Mr Ogden.'

Nigel, who had managed to make unostentatious shorthand notes throughout this interview, now watched Ogden eagerly. Would this shot go home? He decided that the American's astonishment bore the unmistakable stamp of sincerity.

'What the sweltering hell d'you mean?' asked Ogden. 'Heroin? Snow? Who's doping in this crowd? By heck!' he added after a moment's pause, 'is that what's wrong with young Pringle? Who's started it?'

'To the best of my belief, Mr Garnette.'

The American swore, heartily, solidly, and with lurid emphasis. Alleyn listened politely, Fox with a dispassionate air of expert criticism.

'By God,' ended Mr Ogden, 'I wish to – I'd never touched this – concern. Never no more! It's taken a murder to put me wise, but never no more. Say, listen. Chief, as God's my witness I never – Aw, what's the use?'

'It's all right,' said Alleyn quietly. 'We have been told you were not mixed up in it.'

'How's that?'

'Pringle told me. Don't worry about it too much, Mr Ogden. We're not going to pull you in for drug-running.'

Ogden looked nervously from Fox to Alleyn.

'Not for *drug-running*,' he said. 'I'm not raving about the way you said it.'

'Now look here,' said Alleyn, 'don't you go making things more difficult by getting the wind up. I can't go round like a child in a nursery game saying: "It isn't you! It isn't you!" until I get to the "he." I can only repeat my well-worn slogan that the innocent are safe as long as they stick to the truth.'

'I hope to hell you're right.'

'Of course I'm right. It'll come out what the Australians call "jakealoo." Have any of the Initiates ever been to Australia, do you know?'

'I don't know, Chief. I haven't.'

'They have a strong way of putting things there. But I wander. Don't worry, Mr Ogden.'

'That blamed book! If only I knew when it went.'

'Never mind about the book. I think I can guess when it went and who took it.'

'Well, ain't you the clam's cuticle!' said Mr Ogden.

CHAPTER 18

Contribution from Miss Wade

After Miss Ogden had gone Alleyn thrust his hands into his trouser pockets and stood staring at Fox.

'What are we to make of all this, Fox?' he asked. 'What do *you* make of it? You're looking very blank and innocent, and that means you've got hold of an idea.'

'Not to say an idea, sir. I wouldn't go so far as that. I've been trying to string up a sequence as you might say.'

'May we hear it? I've got to such a state I hardly know which of these creatures is which.'

'Now, then, sir,' said Fox good-humouredly, 'you know we won't believe that. Well, this is as far as I've got. We know Miss Quayne went out yesterday afternoon. We know she came here between two-thirty and three. We know she got some sort of a shock while she was here. We know the bonds were stolen, but we don't know when. We know she was murdered last night.'

'True, every word of it.'

'Starting from there,' continued Fox in his slow way, 'I've wondered. I've wondered whether she discovered the theft yesterday afternoon and whether the thief knew she discovered it. She used the word "discovery" in her note. Now if Garnette pinched the bonds she didn't know it was him or she wouldn't have left that note for him. That's if the note *was* meant for him, and I don't see how it could be otherwise. Well, say the safe was open when she got here and for some reason she wanted to see the bonds and found they were gone. She perhaps hung round waiting for him until the people began to come in for the afternoon show – the chauffeur chap said they did – and then came away leaving the note. I don't quite like this,' continued Fox. 'It's got some awkward patches in it. Why did she put the bonds away all tidily? Would the safe be unlocked?'

'She might,' said Alleyn, 'have met somebody who said something to upset her. Something about – '

'I say,' interrupted Nigel. 'Suppose she met somebody who said they suspected Garnette of foul play and she wanted to warn Garnette against them? How's that?'

'Not a bad idea, sir. Not a bad idea at all. Garnette got wind of it and thought he'd polish the lady off before she had time to alter the Will.'

'But how did she get wind of it?' objected Alleyn. 'Not through the note. He never read it. And if she wanted to warn him, why should she alter her Will?'

'That's so,' sighed Fox. 'By the way, sir, what *are* the terms of the Will? Has she left him a fair sum?'

Alleyn told him and Fox looked intensely gratified.

'Ten thousand. And twenty-one thousand for the Church. That's motive enough if you like.'

'How much further did you get with your wondering, Brer Fox? Had you fitted in the two scraps of paper we found in the fireplace?'

'Can't say I did, sir. Somebody warning the Reverend about something, and it seems to refer to Mrs Candour, as Mr Bathgate pointed out. Judging from their position in the grate they were part of a letter thrown there some time during the evening, or at any rate some time yesterday.'

'Certainly, but I don't agree about Mrs Candour. I've got the thing here. Take another look at it.'

Alleyn produced the two scraps of paper.

'I thought at the time,' he said slowly, 'that they were written by Miss Quayne's old nurse.'

'Good Lord!' ejaculated Fox. 'How d'you get that out of it?'

'Yes,' said Nigel, 'how the devil did you? He wouldn't tell me, Inspector Fox.'

'Pretty good, isn't it?' said Alleyn complacently. 'Not so good, however, when the first glory wears off. It's written in green pencil and there was a green pencil on Miss Quayne's desk. The M-S is the remains of "Miss" and the CA the beginnings of "Cara." That's the top of an R, not an N. The old girl wrote to Garnette warning him off. I fancy it read something like this: "Sir: this is to warn you that if you [something or other] with Miss Cara, I am determined to give you in charge. There's a law in England to save women from men like you." Something like that.'

'Yes,' said Fox, 'that fits.'

'She made that trip here last night to see if the letter had borne any fruit and watched the show from Garnette's room. Don't be cross, Fox! I haven't had time to tell you before. I'll let you see the notes of my interview with Nannie Hebborn. The old lady came clean and was very helpful. But that disposes of the note. Garnette must have chucked it in the grate some time yesterday. Now, Fox, what about the book?'

'I reckon Garnette heard Ogden showing it to M. de Ravigne at the party and pinched it,' said Fox. 'After all, sir, his prints are on the top of the book and on the wrappings of the parcel. He might have missed wiping them off that part of the book.'

'What about that little drip Claude?' demanded Nigel. 'You heard Ogden say he was out when he came for the books. And you remember Claude said that a week before he saw the *Curiosities* here he had put the other books at the back of the shelf. He looked mighty uncomfortable over that. Of course that was when he brought them back from Ogden's. Suppose *he* pinched it and didn't want to say so?'

'That's got to be considered too,' said Alleyn. 'I think the stray prints on the top of the leaves are possibly Claude's, and not Garnette's. Bailey hasn't had much success with them.'

'You think *Mr Wheatley* took the book?' said Fox.

'But,' said Nigel, flushed with triumph, 'it hadn't got a brown-paper cover on, so if Claude took it he did so deliberately.'

'Don't overdo it, Bathgate,' said Alleyn kindly. 'This is the pace that kills.'

'Garnette told him to take it,' continued Nigel. 'Depend upon it, Garnette told him to take it.'

'He'd never do that, Mr Bathgate,' objected Fox. 'Not if he meant to make use of it. No, I still think Garnette pinched the book himself.'

'Here we go round the mulberry bush for about the millionth time,' said Alleyn wearily, 'and why the devil we're hanging about this beastly place is more than I can tell. Let's get back to the Yard, Fox. There's an unconscionable lot of drudgery ahead. Have they tackled the fingerprint game?'

'They're at it now,' said Fox, as they all walked down the aisle. 'And by the way, sir, we've checked Dr Kasbek's story. He seems to be all right.'

'Good. I rang New York early this morning. They were very polite and will try to find us something about Garnette and Ogden. They can check up Ogden through the address on that letter we found on him. Come on.'

But they were not quite finished with the House of the Sacred Flame. In the closed entry, watched over by an enormous constable, was Miss Wade.

'Oh, officer,' said Miss Wade. She peered up at Alleyn and pitched her voice in a genteel falsetto. 'I would like to speak to you for a moment.'

'Certainly,' said Alleyn politely. 'I'll see you in the car, Fox.'

Nigel and Fox walked on, and the constable, with massive tact, withdrew to the outer end of the alley.

'What can I do for you, Miss Wade?' asked Alleyn.

'It is a little matter that has rather troubled me. I am afraid I cannot keep pace with all the dreadful things that have happened since yesterday afternoon. Dear Janey says someone has stolen the money that dear Cara so generously gave to the temple. When did they do this?'

'We don't know, unfortunately. The bonds were deposited in the safe last month. They had disappeared last night.'

'Were they stolen yesterday afternoon?'

'Why do you ask that, Miss Wade?' said Alleyn quickly.

'I only thought that perhaps that was what poor Cara meant when she said she would tell Father Garnette about it.'

Alleyn gazed at Miss Wade rather as though she had suddenly produced a rabbit from somewhere behind her back teeth.

'Would you mind saying that again?' he asked.

Miss Wade repeated her last remark in a somewhat louder voice but with perfect equanimity.

'When,' said Alleyn, 'did Miss Quayne say this, and to whom?'

'Yesterday afternoon, to be sure. When else?'

'When else, of course,' repeated Alleyn with some difficulty. 'How do you know she said it, if I may ask?'

'Really, officer! Because I overheard her. Naturally.'

'Naturally. In the – the temple?'

'In the temple. Naturally, in the temple.'

'Naturally.'

'It quite upset my meditation. I had come down early before the Neophytes' instruction to make my preparation for the evening ceremony. I had chosen the word "bliss" and had just reached the Outer Portal of the Soul when this interruption occurred. It was provoking. I wished, afterwards, that I had chosen a back pew instead of my Initiate's throne.'

'I am extremely glad you didn't,' Alleyn managed to say.

'Shall I continue?'

'Please do.'

'I had held my breath up to forty-five and exhaled slowly while inwardly repeating the word and, as I say, was about to enter the Outer Portal when she opened the door.'

'Miss Quayne did?'

'Who else? Before that I had not been aware of her presence in Father Garnette's rooms. She had arrived before I did and had gone through the hall, no doubt. I left my overshoes outside,' added Miss Wade with magnificent irrelevancy.

'She opened the door into Mr Garnette's rooms, and then you heard her?'

'Yes. The curtain was hiding her, of course, but she raised her voice and, being in the front, I heard her. Indeed, I felt a little annoyed with dear Cara. The altar door should never be used in meditation hours. Except, of course, by Father himself. And it was well after meditation began. I glanced at my watch. Quarter to three it was.'

'Miss Wade, can you repeat exactly what you overheard Miss Quayne say?'

'Her very words. "I don't believe you are speaking the truth" was what dear Cara said, "and I shall tell Father Garnette what you have done."'

Here Miss Wade paused and drew herself up with a little quiver.

'To whom did she speak?'

'I haven't a notion,' said Miss Wade cosily.

Alleyn stifled a groan.

'No,' she went on, '*that* I do *not* know. Not Father, naturally.'

'Naturally,' repeated poor Alleyn.

'Whoever it was, was *quite* inaudible. And then she came hurrying down in to the temple with a great lack of reverence, poor thing. She rushed past me without seeing me, though I remained kneeling and gave her a reproachful glance. There were some neophytes in the back pews. It really *was* naughty of Cara. Such a bad example.'

'Did she seem much upset?'

'Distracted,' said Miss Wade.

'Did anybody come out after her?'

'On the contrary. Father Garnette came *in* at this door about five minutes later. He had been to lunch with M. de Ravigne. He spoke a few words to me. I had quite given up my meditation.'

'Did you mention the incident to him?'

'Now did I?' mused Miss Wade with her head on one side. 'No! Definitely not. I would have done so, but he spoke of Higher Things.'

'Have you told anybody else?'

'No, I think not.'

'Then let me implore you not to do so, Miss Wade. What you have just told me is of the very greatest importance. Please promise me you will not repeat it.'

Miss Wade bridled.

'Really, officer,' she said, 'I am not accustomed – '

'No, no. Never mind all that. Please don't think me overbearing, but unless you will give me your word that you will keep this incident to yourself I – I shall be obliged to take very drastic measures. Miss Wade, it is for your own sake I insist on this silence. Do you understand?'

'That I don't,' said Miss Wade with spirit.

Alleyn took one of the little black kid claws in his hand, and he bent his head and smiled at Miss Wade.

'Please,' he said, 'to oblige a poor policeman. Do promise.'

She blinked up at him. Something rather youthful came back into her faded eyes. Her cheeks were pink.

'It is a pity you have come down to this sort of work,' said Miss Wade. 'You have what my dear Mama used to call quite an air. Very well, I promise.'

Alleyn made her a bow. She tossed her head and went off down the alleyway at a brisk trot.

He stood there and looked thoughtfully after her, his hat in his hand. At last, with a shrug, he went out to where Inspector Fox waited for him in a police car.

'What's wrong with the old lady?' asked Fox.

'Nothing much. She just felt chatty.'

'Anything of interest?'

'Merely that she overheard Cara Quayne telling her murderer she'd speak to Garnette about him or her as the case may be.'

'Lor'!' said Fox. 'When, for Gawd's sake?'

'At about a quarter to three yesterday afternoon.'

'In the hall?'

'Naturally,' said Alleyn promptly. 'Listen.'

He repeated Miss Wade's statement. Fox stared solemnly out of the window.

'Well, that's very interesting, sir,' he said when Alleyn had finished. 'That's very interesting indeed. Do you think she caught him red-handed with the bonds?'

'I wouldn't be surprised. Or else he (or she, you know, Fox) refused to let her see them. There's been some talk of her adding to those bonds. She may have wanted to do so on the eve of her first innings as Chosen Vessel.'

'That's right, sir. D'you think she was poisoned to keep her quiet?'

'I think she was killed, in the end, to keep her quiet. But he meant to do it anyway.'

'How do you make that out?'

'If it's sodium cyanide he couldn't make it between three and eight o'clock. He must have had it ready.'

'Then what was the motive?'

'Same as before, Fox. Why are we sitting in this car?'

'I dunno, sir.'

'Tell him to drive – yes, tell him to drive to M. de Ravigne's house.'

Fox gave the order.

'What happened to Mr Bathgate?' asked Alleyn.

'He went up to his flat, sir. I think he took Miss Jenkins and Mr Pringle with him.'

'He's a great hand at cultivating suspects,' said Alleyn.

'It's been useful before now.'

'So it has.'

They lapsed into silence. At a telephone-box Alleyn stopped for a moment to ring the Yard. A message had come through from Bailey who was at Cara Quayne's house. The blotting-paper in her bedroom desk had proved to be interesting. Lots of writing but in some foreign lingo. Alleyn could hear Bailey's disparagement in this phrase. They had made out yesterday's date and an address: 'Madame la Comtesse de Barsac, Château Barsac, La Loupe, E. et L., France.' This had been checked up from an address book. They had also found evidence on the blotting-paper and on a crumpled sheet in the waste-paper basket of something that looked very much like a Will. Mr Rattisbon had rung up and would ring again.

'So put that on your needles and knit it,' said Alleyn when he had told Fox.

The car turned into Lowndes Square and drew up by M. de Ravigne's flat.

Branscome Chambers proved to be a set of small bachelor flats, and M. de Ravigne appeared to live in the best of them. This was on the fourth floor. They went up in the lift.

'Any flats vacant here?' asked Alleyn of the liftman.

'Yes, sir. One. Top floor.'

'How many rooms.'

'Three recep., one bed, one servant's bed, bath and the usual, sir,' said the liftman. 'These are service flats you know. Food all sent up.'

'Ah, yes. Central heating throughout the building, isn't it?'

'Yes, sir.'

'I can't do without an open fire,' said Alleyn.

'No, sir? These electric grates are very convincing though. There's a blazing log effect in No. 5.'

'Really? That's not M. de Ravigne's, is it?'

'No, sir. He's just got the usual heaters. Here you are, sir.'

'Oh, yes. Sorry. Thank you.'

'Thank you very much, sir.'

A discreet dark man with a bluish chin opened the door to them. The voice of a piano came softly from within the flat. Monsieur was at home? He would inquire. He took Alleyn's card and returned in a moment. Monsieur was at home and would they come in? The flat proved to be, if anything, overheated. The little hall where they left their hats was as warm as a conservatory and smelt like one. An enormous bowl of freesias stood on a very beautiful Louis Seize table. From here the servant showed them into a long low drawing-room panelled in cream and very heavily carpeted. It was not over-furnished, indeed, the general effect was one of luxurious restraint. The few pieces were 'period' and beautiful. Three T'ang ceramics stood alone in a magnificent lacquer cabinet. The only modern note was struck by the pictures – a Van Gogh, a Paul Nash and a Gerald Brockhurst. Seated at a baby grand piano was M. Raoul de Ravigne.

CHAPTER 19

Alleyn Looks for a Flat

M. de Ravigne greeted them with a suavity so nicely tempered that it could not be called condescension. He looked very *grand seigneur*, standing with one long white hand on the piano, grave, polite, completely at his ease.

'Will you be seated, messieurs? You come to pursue your inquiries about this tragedy?'

'Yes,' said Alleyn in his most official voice, 'we followed you here in the hopes that we might have a word or two in private. It is an unfortunate necessity in these affairs that the police must constantly make nuisances of themselves and must continually bring the realisation of an unhappy occurrence before those who would prefer to forget it.'

'One understands that very readily. For myself I am only too anxious to be of any assistance, however slight, in bringing this animal to justice. What can I do for you, messieurs?'

'You are extremely courteous, M. de Ravigne. First I would like to bring this letter to your notice.'

De Ravigne held out his hand. Alleyn gave him his own letter, written to Cara Quayne the preceding Friday. De Ravigne glanced at it, read a word or two and then laid it on the arm of his chair. Fox took out his notebook.

'You are correct,' said de Ravigne, 'when you say that much unpleasantness attends the activities of the police. I have a profound distaste for having my correspondence handled by those whom it does not concern.'

'Unhappily, the police are concerned in every scrap of evidence, relevant or irrelevant, which comes into their hands. Perhaps you can assure us of the irrelevance of this letter.'

'I do so most emphatically. It has no bearing on the case.'

Alleyn picked it up and looked through it.

'Against what danger did you warn her so earnestly?' he asked quietly.

'It was a personal matter, M. l'Inspecteur.'

'Make that quite clear to us, monsieur, and it will be treated as such. You will see, I am sure, that a letter warning Miss Quayne against some unknown peril cannot be passed over without inquiry.'

De Ravigne inclined his head slightly.

'I see your argument, of course. The danger to which I refer had nothing to do with physical injury.'

'You did not anticipate this tragedy?'

'A thousand times, no. I? How should I?'

'Then what was threatened?'

'Her virtue, M. l'Inspecteur.'

'I see,' said Alleyn.

De Ravigne eyed him for a moment and then got up. He moved restlessly about the room, as though he was trying to come to some decision. At last he fetched up in front of Alleyn and began to speak in French rapidly and with a certain suppressed vehemence. Inspector Fox breathed heavily and leant forward slightly in his chair.

'Judge of my position, monsieur. I loved her very much. I have loved her very much for so many years. Ever since she was a dark *jeune fille* at a convent with my sister. At one time I thought that she would consent to a betrothal. It was in France when she had first made her *début*. Her guardian, Madame de Verné, approved. It was in every way suitable. My own family, too. Then – I do not know how it came about, but perhaps it was her temperament to change as it was mine to remain constant – but she grew colder and – but this is of no importance. She came to London where we met again after a year. I found myself still her slave. She allowed me to see her. We became, after your English fashion, "friends." It was to amuse her, to interest her, that I myself introduced her to this accursed temple. I did not know then what I know now of the character of Father Garnette.'

'How long did it take you to find him out?' asked Alleyn.

De Ravigne lifted his shoulders very slightly and returned to English.

'I do not know. I was not interested in his morals. It was the ceremonies, the ritual, the bizarre but intriguing form of paganism, that appealed to me. If I became aware that he amused himself, that he had his mistresses, it did not at all disconcert me. It was not inconsistent with the pagan doctrine. One lives one's own life. I cannot say when I first realized that the rôle of Chosen Vessel held a certain significance for this priest. But I am not blind. Dagmar was elected, and – in short, monsieur, I am a man of the world and I saw, accepted, and disregarded *l'affaire Candour*. It was none of my business.'

'Precisely,' said Alleyn, 'but when Miss Quayne became a candidate – '

'Ah, then, monsieur, I was in agony. Again, judge of my position. I had introduced her to this place, forgetting her temperament, her enthusiasms, her – what is your word? – her whole-heartedness. I myself was responsible. I was revolted, remorseful, distracted. I wrote the letter you hold in your hand.'

'And continued,' said Alleyn, 'to draw your dividends?'

'*Sacré nom!*' said de Ravigne. 'So you know of that also?'

'Oh, yes.'

'Then it will be difficult to persuade you that it was my intention yesterday and is doubly so today, to withdraw my capital from this affair.'

'Five hundred, isn't it? asked Alleyn.

'Yes. If I did not make this gesture before, M. l'Inspecteur, it was because I was unwilling to bring about a fracas which would have involved more persons than Father Garnette himself. When I first attended the little temple in Great Holland Road I found it in need of funds. I could not afford to give this sum, but I could afford to lend it. Mr Ogden was also willing, and on a larger scale, to invest money. I left the business arrangements to Father Garnette and Mr Ogden, who is a man of commerce. Myself, I have not the business temperament. But rest assured I shall withdraw. One cannot suffer oneself to become financially associated with such *canaille*.'

'Do you call Mr Ogden *canaille*, monsieur?'

'Monsieur, I refer rather to the priest. But Ogden, he is very much of the people. His perceptions are not acute. He is not fastidious. No doubt he will not feel any delicacy in accepting his interest from this investment. As for the priest – but I prefer not to discuss the priest.'

'Do you know that Mr Garnette has been giving drugs to Pringle, Mrs Candour and Miss Quayne?'

De Ravigne did not answer at once. He lit a cigarette and then with an apology offered the box.

'No?' he said. 'Then perhaps your pipe?'

'Not just at the moment, thank you very much. About this drug business?'

'Ah, yes. Your information does not surprise me.'

'You knew, then?'

'Monsieur, I must repeat that the private affairs of the Initiates does not interest me.'

'But – Miss Quayne?'

'I cannot believe that she indulged in the vice.'

'Nevertheless – '

'I cannot believe it,' said de Ravigne violently, 'and I will not discuss it.'

'Ah, well,' said Alleyn. 'let us leave it then. Apropos of the letter, monsieur. Why did you emphasize your desire that she should destroy it?'

'I have already told you of my distaste for having my letters read. That old Hebborn! She has her nose in everything and she is antagonistic to me. I could not endure that she should intrude her nose into it.'

'Then why not write in French?'

'But I wished to impress her of my calmness and deliberation,' said M. de Ravigne smoothly. 'If I wrote in French, allowing my emotion full scope, what would she think? She would think: "Ah, he has shot himself off at the deep ending. This Gallic temperament! Tomorrow he will be calm again." So I write coolly in English and request that she destroys this letter.'

'Ah, yes, that explains the postscript.' Alleyn got to his feet and then, as if it were an afterthought, he said:

'The book on chemistry. I understand you have seen it before?'

De Ravigne hesitated for the fraction of a moment before he replied: 'It is strange you should say that. I myself received the impression that I had encountered the book, but where? I cannot recollect.'

'Was it in Mr Ogden's house?'

'But of course! In his house. He showed it to me. How could I have forgotten? The priest was there and looked at it too. And the others. It was too stupid of me to forget. I remember I upset a glass of whisky and soda near it. Ogden fancied the book might be of value, I think, but it was of no interest to me. That is why I did not remember it. So the book is the good Ogden's book? That is interesting, monsieur, is it not?'

'Any information about the book is interesting. And speaking of books, M. de Ravigne, may I have the books of the Sacred Flame Company? I understand you've got them here.'

'The books? Ah, yes. The good Ogden insisted that I glance at them. They seem to be in order. Naturally the theft of the bonds would not appear. Perhaps the good Ogden himself has seen to that. Perhaps he and the priest together have arranged these little matters. You see I am bitter, monsieur. I am not easily made suspicious, but when my suspicions are aroused – But the books! You shall have them, certainly.'

He rang for his servant, who produced the books and gave them to Alleyn.

'There's one other question, M. de Ravigne, and then I shall trouble you no further. Do you know anything of a Madame la Comtesse de Barsac?'

'My sister, monsieur,' said de Ravigne very frigidly.

'Forgive me. I really didn't know. She was the confidante of Miss Quayne, I think ? A very great friend?'

'That is so.'

Alleyn got up.

'A thousand thanks,' he said. 'Is there anything else, Fox? Perhaps you –'

'No thank you, sir,' said Fox cheerfully. 'I think you've covered the ground.'

'Then we will make our adieux, monsieur. You will have received notice of the inquest tomorrow?'

'At eleven o'clock, yes. It will, I imagine, be purely formal.'

'One never knows with inquests, but I expect so. The terms of the Will may come out. You know them, I expect?'

'No, monsieur.'

'No? Come along, Fox. Where are those books?'

'You've got them under your arm, sir.'

'Have I? So I have. *Au 'voir*, Monsieur de Ravigne. I am afraid we have been a great nuisance.'

'Not at all, Monsieur l'Inspecteur. I am only too glad – though I am afraid I have been of little assistance – '

'*Tout au contraire, monsieur.*'

'*Vraiment? Au 'voir*, monsieur. Good afternoon, monsieur.'

'Oh reevor, monsieur,' said Fox very firmly.

On their way down the liftman extolled the virtues of the flats, and Alleyn warmly agreed with him, but still insisted that he preferred the solace of an open fire. Inspector Fox listened gravely to his conversation, occasionally uttering a profound noise in his throat. As they got into the car his good-natured face wore the nearest approach to a sardonic smile of which it was capable.

'The Yard,' said Alleyn to the driver. 'You'll be able to improve your French if we see much more of that gentleman,' he added with a smile at Fox.

'It's a rum thing,' said Inspector Fox, 'that I can follow that radio bloke a fair treat, and yet when the monsieur gets under way it sounds like a collection of apostrophes.

What do we do when we get back to the office?'

'We send a cable to Australia.'

'To Australia?'

'Yes, Brer Fox.'

'What's that in aid of?'

'You've never been to Australia?'

'I have not.'

'I have. Let me tell you about it.'

Alleyn discoursed at some length about Australia. They got back to the Yard at five o'clock. The fingerprint people reported that they had been unable to find any of the Sacred Flame prints in the records. Mr Rattisbon had sent a letter round for Alleyn. The report from Cara Quayne's house together with the blotting-paper and crumpled sheet from the waste-paper basket awaited him in his room. He went there, accompanied by Fox, and tackled Mr Rattisbon's letter first.

'Let's smoke a pipe apiece,' he said. 'I'm longing for one.'

They lit up, and Fox watched him gravely while he opened the long envelope. Alleyn's eyebrows rose as he read the enclosures. Without a word he handed them across to his subordinate. Mr Rattisbon wrote to say that the morning mail had brought a new Will from Miss Quayne. She had evidently written it some time yesterday afternoon. It was witnessed by Ethel Parker and May Simes. As regards the bequests to de Ravigne and Laura Hebborn it was a repetition of the old Will. For the rest it was startlingly changed. The entire residue was left to Mr Jasper Garnette of Knocklatchers Row, Eaton Place. Miss Quayne had written to say she hoped that the new Will was in order, and that if it was not, would Mr Rattisbon please draw up a fresh document to the same effect. The alteration was so straightforward that she believed this to be unnecessary. She had urgent reasons for making the alteration, reasons connected with a 'terrible discovery.' She would call and explain. Her dear Father Garnette, she said, was the victim of an unholy plot. In his covering letter Mr Rattisbon explained that at the time Alleyn called he had not looked at his morning post. He added that he found the whole affair extremely distressing; an unexpectedly human touch.

'By gum!' said Fox, putting the papers down, 'it looks as if you're right, sir.'

'Gratifying, isn't it? But how the devil are we going to ram it home? And what about our Jasper? Oh, Garnette, my jewel, my gem above price, you will need your lovely legacy before we've done with you. Where's the report on those cigarettes, Fox? Has it come in? Where's my pad? Here we are. Yes. Oh excellent priest! Perdition catch my soul, but I do love thee. All the top cigarettes as innocent as the wild woodbine, but underneath, in a vicious little mob, ten doped smokes. A fairly high percentage of heroin was found, from one-tenth to as much as one-seventh of a grain per cigarette. It is possible that the cigarette tobacco has been treated with a solution of diamorphine? Oh, Jasper, my dear, my better half, have I caught my heavenly jewel?'

'Come off it, sir,' said Fox with a grin.

'How right you are, my Foxkin. Is there any reason why we should not prise the jewel from its setting?'

'Do you mean you'd like to arrest Garnette?'

'Would I like to? And how! as Mr Ogden would say. And how, my old foxglove, my noxious weed. Has anyone ever written a poem to you, Fox?'

'Never, sir.'

'I wish I had the art:

> "Hercules or Hector? Ah, no!
>   This is our Inspector Fox,
> Mens sana in corpore sano,
>   Standing in the witness-box.

'Very feeble, I'm afraid. What about the analyst? Autopsy on body of Miss Cara Quayne. Here we are. He's been very quick about it. "External appearances: blue nails, fingers clenched, toes contracted, jaws firmly closed." We know all that. "Internally" – This is it. "On opening the stomach the odour of hydrocyanic acid was clearly distinguishable." How beastly for him. He found the venous system gorged with liquid blood, bright red and arterial in character. The stomach and intestines appeared to be in their natural state. The mucous membrane of the stomach – How he does run on, to be sure. Let's see. The silver test was carried out. The precipitate gave the characteristic reactions – '

Alleyn read on in silence. Then he dropped the report on his desk and leant back.

'Yes,' he said flatly, 'it's sodium cyanide. I do well, don't I, to sit here being funny-man, and not so damn' funny either, while a beautiful woman turns into a cadaver, an analyst's exercise, and her murderer – ? Fox, in many ways ours is a degrading job of work. Custom makes monsters of us all. Do you ever feel like that about it, Fox? No, I don't think you do. You are too nice-minded. You are always quite sane. And such a wise old bird, too. Damn you, Fox, do you think we're on the right lay?'

'I think so, sir. And I know how you feel about homicide cases. I'd put it down to your imagination. You're a very imaginative man, I'd say. I'm not at all fanciful myself, but it does seem queer to me sometimes, how calm-like we get to work, grousing about the routine, put out because our meals don't come regular, and all the time there's a trap and a rope and a broken neck at the end if we do our job properly. Well, there it is. It's got to be done.'

'With which comfortable reflection,' said Alleyn, 'let us consult Mr Abberley on the subject of sodium cyanide.'

He picked the book out of his bag which had been brought back from the church, and once again it opened at the discourse on sodium cyanide.

'You see, Fox, it's quite an elaborate business. List, list, oh list. You take equal weights of wool and dried washing-soda and iron filings. Sounds like Mrs Beaton gone homicidal. Cook at red heat for three or four hours. Allow to cool. Add water and boil for several more hours. Tedious! Pour off clear solution and evaporate same to small volume. When cool, yellow crystals separate out. And are these sodium cyanide? They are not. To the crystals add a third of their weight of dried washing-soda. Heat as before for an hour or two. While still hot, pour off molten substance from black residue. It will solidify, on cooling, to a white cake. *Alley Houp!* Sodium cyanide as ordered. Serve *à la Garnette* with Invalid Port to taste. *Loud* cheers and *much* laughter. This man is clever.'

He re-read the passage and then shut the book.

'As far as one can see this could all be done without the aid of laboratory apparatus. That makes it more difficult, of course. A house-to-house campaign is indicated, and then we may not get much further. Still it will have to be done. I think this is an occasion for Mr Bathgate, Fox. You tell me he went off with Pringle and Miss Jenkins.'

'That's right. I saw them walk down Knocklatchers Row and go into his flat in Chester Terrace.'

'I wonder if I'd be justified – He can't get into trouble over this. It's so much better than going ourselves. He's an observant youth, and if they've got all matey – What d'you think, Fox?'

'What are you driving at, sir?'

'Wait and see.'

He thought for a moment and then reached for his telephone. He dialled a number and waited, staring abstractedly at Fox. A small tinny quack came from the telephone. Alleyn spoke quietly.

'Is that you, Bathgate? Don't say my name. Say "Hullo, darling."
That's right. Now just answer yes and no in a loving voice if your
guests are still with you. Are they? Good. It's Angela speaking.'

'Hullo, darling,' quacked the little voice.

'Is your telephone the sort that shouts or whispers? Does it
shout?'

'No, my sweet. It's too marvellous to hear your voice,' said Nigel
in Chester Terrace. Without covering the receiver he addressed
somebody in the room: 'It's Angela – my – I'm engaged to her.
Excuse the raptures.'

'Are you sure it's all right for me to talk?' continued Alleyn.

'Angela, darling, I can hardly hear you. This telephone is almost
dumb.'

'That's all right then. Now attend to me. Have you got very
friendly?'

'Of *course* I have,' said Nigel rapturously.

'Well. Get yourself invited to either or both of their flats. Can you
do that?'

'But Angel, I did all that ages ago. When am I going to see you?'

'Do you mean you have already been to their flats?'

'No, no. Of course not. How are you?'

'Getting bloody irritable. What *do* you mean?'

'Well, at the moment I am sitting looking at your photograph. As
a matter of fact I've been showing it to somebody else.'

'Blast your eyes.'

'No, my sweet, nobody you know. I hope you will soon. They're
engaged like us. We're all going to a show. Angela, where are you?'

'At the Yard.'

'Darling, how expensive! Yarborough! A toll call. Never mind.
When are you coming to London? Is there anything I can do for
you?'

'Yes, there is. If you're going to a show, can you engineer a round
trip to their flats afterwards?'

'Rather! As a matter of fact I'd rather thought of doing that.
Darling – '

'Shut up. Listen carefully now.'

'At Harrods? Must it be pink, my sweet?'

'Now don't you be too clever. Miss Angela would cast you off for ever if you mooed at her like that. Pay attention. When you are there I want you to observe certain things.'

'All right, darling, I was only being facetious. Let me know the worst.'

'I will. This is what I want you to look for – ' Alleyn talked on. Fox listened solemnly. Nigel, over in Chester Terrace, blew kisses into the receiver and smiled apologetically at Janey Jenkins and Maurice Pringle.

CHAPTER 20

Fools Step In

'It annoys Angela beyond endurance if I hold modern conversations with her on the telephone,' said Nigel hanging up the receiver on a final oath from Alleyn.

'If that was a sample, I'm not surprised,' said Janey Jenkins. 'I absolutely forbid Maurice to call me his sweet. Don't I, Blot?'

'Yes,' said Maurice unresponsively. He got up and moved restlessly about the room, fetching up at the window where he stood and stared out into the street, biting his fingers.

'What is your Angela's other name?' asked Janey.

'North. She's darkish with a big mouth and thin.'

'When are you going to be married?'

'In April. When are you?'

Janey looked at Maurice's back. 'It's not settled yet.'

'I'd better do something about getting seats for a show,' said Nigel. 'Where shall we go? It's such fun your coming here like this. We must make it a proper party. Have you seen "Fools Step In" at the Palace?'

'No. We'd love to, but look here, we're not dressed for a party.'

'Oh. No, you're not, are you? Wait a moment. Let's make it a real gala. I'll change now and then we'll take a taxi and go to your flat and then to Pringle's. We'll have a drink here first. Pringle, would you make the drinks while I change? The things are all in that cupboard there. It's only half-past five. I'll have a quick bath – won't be ten minutes. Do you mind? Will it amuse you? Not my bath, but everything else?'

'Of course it will,' said Janey.

Maurice swung round from the window and faced Nigel. 'Look here,' he said, 'aren't you rather rash to rush into parties with people that are suspected of murder?'

'Don't Maurice!' whispered Janey.

'My good ass,' said Nigel, 'you embarrass me. You may of course be a homicidal maniac, but personally I imagine Alleyn has definitely ruled you out.'

'I suppose he's told you to say that. You seem to be very thick with him.'

'Maurice, please!'

'My dear Jane, it's not impossible.'

'No,' said Nigel calmly, 'of course it's not. Alleyn is by way of being a friend. I think you're suspicions are perfectly reasonable, Pringle.'

'Oh, God, you are a little gentleman. I suppose you think I'm bloody unpleasant.'

'As a matter of fact I do, at the moment, but you'll be better when you've had a cocktail. Get to work, there's a good chap. And you might ring up the Palace for seats.'

'Look here, I'm damned sorry. I'm not myself. My nerves are all to hell. Janey, tell him I'm not entirely bogus. I can't be if you say so.'

Janey went to him and held him firmly by one ear.

'Not entirely bogus,' she told Nigel.

'That's all right then,' said Nigel hurriedly. 'Look after yourselves.'

'As he bathed he thought carefully about his instructions. In effect Alleyn had told him to cultivate these two with a view to spying on them. Nigel winced. Stated baldly it sounded unpleasant. He had had this sort of thing out with Alleyn on former occasions. The Chief Inspector had told him roundly that his scruples had merely pointed to a wish to have the ha'pence without the kicks, to follow round with the police, write special articles from first-hand experience, and turn squeamish when it came to taking a hand. Alleyn was right of course. If Maurice and Janey were innocent he would help to prove it. If they were guilty – But Nigel was quite sure neither Janey nor Maurice, for all his peculiar behaviour, was guilty of Cara Quayne's death. He dressed hurriedly and went out into the little hall to get his overcoat. He dived into the cupboard. It was built into the drawing-room wall and the partition was thin. He heard Janey Jenkin's voice, muffled and flat but distinct:

'But *why* can't you tell me? I know quite well there's something. Maurice, this *can't* go on.'

'What do you mean? Are you going to turn me down? I don't blame you.'

'You know I won't turn you down. But why can't you trust me?'

'I do trust you. I trust you to stick to what we've said.'

'About yesterday afternoon – ?'

'Sst!'

'Maurice, is it anything to do with – with your cigarettes? You're smoking one of them now, aren't you? Aren't you?'

'Oh, for God's sake don't start nagging.'

'But – '

'When this is over I'll give it up.'

' "When." "When." It's always "when." '

'Will you shut up, Jane! I tell you I can't stand it.'

'Ssh! He'll hear you.'

Silence. Nigel stole out and back to his bedroom. In three minutes he rejoined them in the drawing-room. Maurice had mixed their drinks, and Janey had turned on the radio. With an effort Nigel managed to sustain his rôle of cheerful host. Maurice suddenly became more friendly, mixed a second cocktail and began to talk loudly of modern novelists. It appeared that he was himself engaged on a first novel. Nigel was not surprised to learn that it was to be a satire on the upper middle classes. At six o'clock they took a taxi to Janey's studio flat in Yeoman's Row, and while she changed Maurice made more cocktails. Janey, it seemed, was at the Slade. Nigel found the studio very cold though they had put a match to the gas-heater. Shouting at them from the curtained-off recess that served as a bedroom Janey explained that she meant to seek warmer quarters. Even the kitchenette-bathroom was cold, she said. She did her cooking over a gas-ring, and you couldn't warm yourself at the bath-geyser. Some of her drawings were pinned up on the walls. She used an austere and wiry line, defined everything with uncompromising boundaries, and went in extensively for simplified form. The drawing had quality. Nigel wandered round the studio and into the kitchen. Everything was very tidy, and rather like Janey herself.

'What are you doing?' called Janey. 'You're both very silent.'

'I'm looking at your bathkitchenry,' said Nigel. 'You haven't got nearly enough saucepans.'

'I only have breakfast here. There's a restaurant down below. One of ye olde brasse potte kind – all orange curtains and nut salads. Yes,' said Janey emerging in evening dress, 'I must leave this place. The problem is, where to go.'

'Come to Chester Terrace and be neighbours. Angela and I are going to take a bigger flat in my building. It's rather nice. You could have mine.'

'Your Angela might hate me at first sight.'

'Not she. Are we ready?'

'Yes. Come on, Blot.'

'I'm finishing my drink,' said Maurice. 'You're right, Jane, this is an appalling place. I should go mad here. Come on.'

'We should have gone to you first,' said Janey. 'He is in Lower Sloane Street, Mr Bathgate. How silly! Maurice, why didn't we go to you first?'

'You can drop me there now. I don't think I'll join the party.'

'Maurice! Why ever not?'

'I'm hopelessly inadequate,' he muttered. He looked childishly obstinate, staring straight in front of him and smiling sardonically. Nigel could have kicked him.

'Your boyfriend has a talent for quick changes,' he said to Janey and hailed a taxi. Janey spoke to Maurice in an urgent undertone. Out of the corner of his eye Nigel saw him shrug his shoulders and give a gloomy assent. When they were in the taxi Janey said:

'Maurice is afraid he's too much upset by last night to be much use to anybody, but I've decided to pay no attention to him. He's coming.'

'Splendid!' cried Nigel.

'Marvellous, isn't it?' said Maurice with a short laugh.

He was very restless in the taxi, complained that the man should have gone down Pont Street instead of through Cadogan Square, thought they were going to be run over in Sloane Street, insisted on paying the fare, and had a row with the driver over the change. He lived in a small service flat at the top of Harrow Mansions in Lower Sloane Street – sitting-room, bedroom, bathroom. It was comfortable enough, but characterless.

'At least it's warm,' said Maurice, and switched on the heater. He opened a cupboard.

'We don't want more drinks, do we?' ventured Janey.

'Isn't this a party?' asked Maurice loudly, and dragged out half a dozen bottles.

He left them as soon as he had made the cocktails, carrying his own with him. The bathroom door slammed and a tap was turned on. Janey leant forward.

'There's something I must tell you,' she said urgently.

Nigel found nothing to say and she went on, speaking nervously and quickly:

'It's about Maurice. I know you must think him too impossible. He's been poisonous' – she caught herself up with a gasp – 'perfectly odious ever since you asked us up to your flat. It was nice of you to do that, and to take us out. But I want to tell you. Maurice can't help himself. I suppose you know why?'

'Yes, I think so. It's bad luck.'

'It's frightful. Not only the cigarettes, but – worse than that. He's taking it now, I know he is. You'll see. When he comes back he'll be excited and – and dreadfully friendly. He's turning into a horrible stranger. You don't know what the real Maurice is like.'

'How did he start?'

'It's Father Garnette. He's responsible. I think he must be the wickedest, foulest beast that ever lived. You can tell your friend Alleyn that if you like. But he knows. Maurice told him last night. Mr Alleyn could help Maurice if – He doesn't think Maurice did it, does he? He can't.'

'I honestly don't believe he does. Honestly.'

'I *know* Maurice is – is innocent. But there's something else. Something he knows and he won't tell Mr Alleyn. He won't tell. He's made me promise. Oh *what* am I to do?'

'Break your promise.'

'I can't, I can't. He'd never trust me again and, you see, I can help him as long as he trusts me.' Her voice trembled. 'It's a shame to bother you with it.'

'Good Heavens, what nonsense. I'd like to help you both but – look here, don't tell me anything unless you want Alleyn to know. I ought not to say that. I'm on his side, you see. But if you are hiding anything for Pringle's sake – don't, don't, don't. And if he's hiding something for anybody else's sake you must *make* him tell Alleyn. Do you remember the Unicorn Theatre case?'

'Yes, vaguely. It's queer how one reads every word of murder trials and then forgets them. I'll never forget this one, will I? We must speak softly. He'll be back in a minute.'

'In the Unicorn case a man who knew and didn't tell was – killed.'

'I remember now.'

'Is it something to do with this drug he's taking?'

'How did you guess?'

'Then it *is* Garnette!' said Nigel.

'Ssh! No, for pity's sake! Oh, what have I done!'

'What are you two burbling about?' called Maurice.

He sounded very much more cheerful. Janey looked up sharply and then made a despairing little gesture.

'About you, good-looking,' she called out.

Maurice laughed. 'I must come out and stop that,' he said.

'Oh, God,' whispered Janey. She suddenly gripped Nigel's arm. 'It's not Garnette, it's not, it's not,' she said fiercely. 'I must see you again.'

'After the show,' murmured Nigel hurriedly. 'I'll come to the flat.'

'But – no – it's impossible.'

'Tomorrow, then. Tomorrow morning. About eleven.'

'The inquest is at eleven.'

'Earlier, then.'

'What can you do, after all?'

'Don't worry. I'll fix it.'

Janey got up and went to the gramophone. The theme song from 'Fools Step In' blared out.

> *You're no angel, I'm no saint,*
> *You've a modern body with a super coat of paint.*
> *My acceleration's speedy,*
> *You've broken every rule,*
> *You may say that I am greedy,*
> *You may call me just a fool.*
> *You're no angel and I sometimes lost my head,*
> *But fools step in where angels fear to tread.*

'The tune's all right,' said Maurice, emerging from the bedroom, 'but the words are fatuous, as usual.'

Nigel gazed at him in astonishment. His eyes were very bright. He had an air of spurious gaiety. He was like a mechanical figure that had been overwound and might break. He talked loudly and incessantly, and laughed at everything he said. He kept repeating that they had plenty of time.

'Loads of time. Fifty gallons of time. Time, the unknown quantity in the celestial cocktail. Time, like an ever-rolling drunk. Jane, you're looking very seductive, my angel. "You're no angel and I'm no saint".'

He sat on the arm of her chair and began to stroke her neck. Suddenly he stooped and kissed her shoulder.

' "And I sometimes lose my head." Don't move.'

She sat quite still, staring miserably at Nigel.

'I think we'd better dine,' said Nigel. 'It's after seven.'

Maurice had slid down behind Janey and now pulled her to him. He slipped his arms round her and pressed his face against her bare shoulder.

'Shall we go with him, Janey? Or shall we stay here and step in where angels fear to tread?'

'Don't do that, Blot. And don't be rude about Mr Bathgate's party. No, get up, do.'

He laughed uproariously and pushed her away from him.

'Come on, then,' he said, 'come on. I'm all for a party.'

They dined at the Hungaria. Maurice was very gay and rather noisy. He drank a good deal of champagne and ate next to nothing. Nigel was thankful when they got away. At the theatre Maurice seemed to quieten down. Towards the end of the second act he suddenly whispered that he had a splitting headache and leant forward in his stall with his head between his hands. The people round about them obviously thought he was drunk. Nigel felt acutely uncomfortable. When the lights went up for the final curtain Maurice was leaning back, his eyes half closed and his face lividly white.

'Are you all right?' asked Nigel.

'Perfectly, thank you,' he said very clearly. 'Is it all over?'

'Yes,' said Janey quickly, 'stand up, Maurice. They're playing The King.'

He got up as though he was exhausted, but he was quiet enough as he followed them out into the street. In the taxi he sat absolutely still, his hands lying palm upwards on the seat. In the reflected light for the streets Nigel saw that his eyes were open. The pupils were the size of pin-points. Nigel looked questioningly at Janey. She nodded slightly.

'I'll see you in, Pringle,' said Nigel.

'No, thank you,' he said loudly.

'But Maurice – '

'No, thank you; no, thank you; *no, thank you*. Damn you, for—'s sake leave me alone, will you.'

He had got out and now slammed the door shut, and without another look at them went quckly up the steps to the flats.

'Let him go,' said Janey.

Nigel said '99, Yeoman's Row' to the man, and they drove away.

Janey began to laugh.

'Charming guest you've had for your party. Has anyone ever been quite so rude to you before? You must have enjoyed it.'

'Don't!' said Nigel. 'I didn't mind. I'm only so sorry for you both.'

'You are nice about it. I won't have hysterics; don't look so nervous. Your Angela's a lucky wench. Tell her I said so. No, don't. Don't talk to me, please.'

They finished the short journey in silence. As he saw her into her door Nigel said:

'I'm coming in the morning. Not early, so don't get up too soon. And please remember you'd much better tell Alleyn.'

'Ah, but you don't know,' said Janey.

CHAPTER 21

Janey Breaks a Promise

When Nigel got home it was half-past eleven. He rang Alleyn up.

'Were you in bed?' asked Nigel.

'In bed! I've just got back from the Yard.'

'What have you been doing?'

'Routine work.'

'That is merely the name you give to the activities you keep a secret from me.'

'Think so? What have you been up to yourself?'

'Cultivating a pair of fools.'

'That's your opinion of them, is it?'

'It'll be yours when I reveal all. She's a nice fool and he's inexpressibly unpleasant. Look here, Alleyn, Pringle's keeping something up his sleeve. Yesterday afternoon – '

'Hi! No names over the telephone. Your landlady may be lying on her stomach outside the door.'

'Shall I come round to your flat?'

'Certainly not. Go to bed and come to the Yard in the morning.'

'You might be grateful. I've endured a frightful party and paid for a lot of champagne, all in the cause of justice. Really, Alleyn, it's been a ghastly evening. Pringle's soaked to the back teeth in drugs and – '

'*No names over the telephone.* I am grateful. What would we do without our Mr Bathgate? Can you get to my office by nine?'

'I suppose so. But I want you to come with me to Janey Jenkins's flat. 'I think if you tackle her she may tell you about Mau – '

177

'*Not over the telephone.*'

'But why not? Who do you think is listening? What about your own conversations? Has Miss Wade swarmed up a telegraph pole and tapped the wires?'

'Good night,' said Alleyn.

Nigel wrote an article on the beauty and charm of Cara Quayne. The article was to be illustrated with two photographs he had picked up in her flat. Then he cursed Alleyn and went to bed.

The next morning he went down to the Yard at nine and found Alleyn in his room.

'Hullo,' said Alleyn. 'Sit down and smoke. I won't be a minute. I've just been talking to New York. Mr Ogden seems to be as pure as a lily as far as they can tell. We rang them up yesterday and they've been pretty nippy. The Ogden-Shultz Gold Refining Company seems to be a smallish but respectable concern. It did well during the gold fever in '31, but not so well since then. Of Mr Garnette they know nothing. They are going to have a stab at tracing the revivalist joint that was such a success way down in Michigan in '14. The wretched creature has probably changed his name half a dozen times since then.'

He pressed his desk-bell and to the constable who answered he gave an envelope and a telegram form.

'Deferred cable for Australia,' he said, 'and urgent to France. Read out the telegram, will you?'

The constable, with many strange sounds, spelt out a long message in French to the Comtesse de Barsac. As far as Nigel could make out, it broke the news of Miss Quayne's death, and said that a letter would follow, and gave an earnest assurance that the entire police force of Great Britain would be infinitely grateful if Madame la Comtesse would refrain from destroying any letters she received from Miss Cara Quayne. The constable went out looking baffled but impressed.

'What's all that for?'

Alleyn told him about the letter to Madame de Barsac and also about the new Will.

'I've got it here,' said Alleyn. 'With the exception of the three hundred pounds a year to Nannie and the house to de Ravigne – everything to the glowing Garnette.'

'And it was done on Sunday?'

'Yes. At three-thirty. She actually has put the time.'

'That's *very* significant,' pronounced Nigel.

'Very,' agreed Alleyn dryly.

'She had been back from the mysterious visit to the temple about half an hour,' continued Nigel with the utmost importance, 'and had evidently made up her mind to alter the Will as a result of whatever had taken place in Garnette's room.'

'True for you.'

'Had she learned about the commercial basis on which the House of the Sacred Flame was established? Or had she heard something derogatory about Garnette himself and wished to make a gesture that would illustrate her faith in Garnette? Doesn't the note in the cigarette-box seem to point to that?'

'Am I supposed to answer these questions or are they merely rhetorical?'

'What do you think yourself? About the new Will?'

'*If* we are right in supposing the interview with the unknown at two-forty-five on Sunday afternoon has got a definite bearing on the case and *if* the unknown was the murderer then I think the alteration in the Will is the direct outcome of the interview. *If* this is so, then I believe the case narrows down to one individual. But all this is still in the air. Miss Quayne may have found Cyril swigging invalid port and written the note to let Garnette know about it. She may have altered the will simply because she wished to shower everything on Garnette. The whole of Sunday afternoon may be irrelevant. 'Morning, Fox.'

'Good morning, sir,' said Inspector Fox, who had come in during his speech. 'What's this about Sunday afternoon being irrelevant? Good morning, Mr Bathgate.'

'Well, Fox, it's possible, you know. We are still in the detestable realms of conjecture. I hope to Heaven Mme de Barsac has not burned that letter. I wired to her last night and got no answer. I've just sent off another telegram. I could get on to the Sûreté, but I don't want to do it that way. We badly need that letter.'

'You've got a certain amount from the blotting-paper, haven't you?' asked Fox.

'Bits and pieces. Luckily for us Miss Quayne used medium-sized sheets of notepaper and a thick nib. The result is lots of wet ink and

good impressions on the blotting-paper. Here they are. No translation necessary for you, you old tower of Babel.'

'May I see?' said Nigel.

'Yes. But they're not for publication.'

Fox took out his spectacles and he and Nigel read the sentences
from the blotting-paper,

> *Raoul est tout-à-fait impitoyable –*
> *Une secousse electrique me bouleversa –*
> *Cette supposition me révoltait, mais que voul –*
> *Alarmé en me voyant –*
> *il pay - a - sès crimes.*
> *– le placèrent en qualité d'administrateur d – '*

'What's "secousse"?' asked Fox.

'A shock, a surprise.'

'Does she mean she's had an electric shock, sir?'

'It's a figure of speech, Fox. She means she was much put out.
The phraseology suggests a rather exuberant hysterical style. I do not
advise you to adopt it.'

'What do you make of it, Mr Bathgate?' asked Fox.

'It's very exciting.' said Nigel. 'The first bit is clear enough. Raoul –
that's de Ravigne – is completely indifferent – pitiless. She had a shock.
Then she was horrified at her own – what's the word?'

'This hypothesis revolted me,' suggested Alleyn.

'Yes. Then somebody took fright when he saw her. And somebody
will – I suppose this was "payera" – will answer for his crimes. And
somebody was made a trustee. That's the last bit. That's Garnette,'
continued Nigel in high feather. 'He's a trustee in the first Will. By
gum, it looks as if she was talking about Garnette all along.'

'Except when she wrote of de Ravigne?' said Alleyn mildly.

'Oh, of course,' said Nigel. 'Good Lord! Do you suppose she confided in de Ravigne?'

'I refuse to speculate. But I don't like your very free rendering of
the last sentence. And now what's all this about Miss Janey
Jenkins?'

Nigel launched into an account of his evening's experiences. The
two detectives listened in silence.

'You did very well,' said Alleyn when Nigel came to a stop. 'Thank you, Bathgate. Now let me be quite sure of what you overheard from the perfumed depths of your clothes cupboard. Pringle asked Miss Jenkins to stick to their story about Sunday afternoon?'

'Yes.'

'And she asked if it had anything to do with his cigarettes?'

'Yes. That's it.'

'Right! You arranged to visit her this morning?'

'Yes. Before the inquest.'

'Would you mind if I took your place?'

'Not if you swear you'll tell me what happens.'

'What's the time?'

'Half-past nine,' said Fox.

'I'll be off. See you at the inquest.'

Alleyn took a taxi to Yeoman's Row. Janey's studio was at the far end. It was a sort of liaison office between Bohemia and slumland. Five very grubby little boys and a baby were seated on the steps.

'Hullo,' said Alleyn. 'What's the game?'

'Ain't no game. Just talkun,' said the grubbiest and smallest of the little boys.

'I know,' said Alleyn. 'Who's going to ring this bell for me?'

There was a violent assault upon the bell.

'I done it, Mister,' said the largest of the little boys.

The baby rolled off the second step and set up an appalling yell.

'Stan-lee!' screamed a voice from an upper window, 'what are you doing to your little bruwer?'

' 'Snot me; it's 'im,' said Stanley, pointing to Alleyn.

'I'm frightfully sorry,' said Alleyn. 'Here. Wait a moment. Is he hurt?'

' 'E won't leave 'is 'oller not without you picks 'im up,' said Stanley.

Alleyn picked the baby up. The baby instantly seized his nose, screamed with ecstasy, and beat with the other hand upon Alleyn's face.

It was on this tableau that Janey opened her door.

The Chief Inspector hurriedly deposited the child on the pavement, gave Stanley a shilling for the party, took off his hat, and said:

'May I come in, Miss Jenkins?'

'Inspector Alleyn?' said Janey. 'Yes. Of course.'

As she shut the door Stanley was heard to say 'Coo! It's a cop,' and the baby instantly began to roar again.

Without speaking Janey led the way upstairs to the studio. A solitary chair was drawn up to the gas-fire. The room was scrupulously tidy and rather desolate.

'Won't you sit down?' said Janey without enthusiasm.

'I'll get another chair,' offered Alleyn and did so.

'I suppose Mr Bathgate sent you here?' asked Janey.

'Yes. In effect he did.'

'I was a fool.'

'Why?'

'To make friends with – your friend.'

'On the contrary,' said Alleyn, 'you were very wise. If I may say so without impertinence you would do well to make friends with me.'

Janey laughed unpleasantly.

'Dilly, dilly, dilly,' she said.

'No. Not "dilly, dilly, dilly." You didn't murder Miss Quayne, did you?'

'You can hardly expect me to answer "yes."'

'I expect an answer, however.'

'Then,' said Janey, 'I did not murder Cara Quayne.'

'Did Mr Pringle murder Miss Quayne?'

'No.'

'You see,' said Alleyn with a smile, 'we get on like a house on fire. Where was Mr Pringle at three o'clock on Sunday afternoon?'

She drew in her breath with a little gasp.

'I've told you.'

'But I'm asking you again. Where was he?'

'Here.'

'That,' said Alleyn harshly, 'is your story and you are sticking to it? I wish you wouldn't'

'What do you mean!'

'It's not true you know. He may have lunched with you but he did not stay here all the afternoon. He went to the temple.'

'You knew – '

'Now you give me an opportunity for the detective's favourite cliché. "I didn't know, but you have just told me."'

'You're hateful!' she burst out suddenly. 'Hateful! Hateful!'

'Don't cry!' said Alleyn more gently. 'It's only a cliché and I would have found out anyway.'

'To come prying into my house! To find the weak place and go for it! To pretend to make friends and then trap me into breaking faith with – with someone who can't take care of himself.'

'Yes,' he said, 'it's my job to do those sorts of things.'

'You call it a smart bit of work, I suppose.'

'The other word for it is "routine."'

'I've broken faith,' said Janey. 'I'll never be able to help him again. We're done for now.'

'Nonsense!' said Alleyn crisply. 'Don't dramatize yourself.'

Something in his manner brought her up sharply. For a second or two she looked at him and then she said very earnestly:

'Do you suspect Maurice?'

'I shall be forced to if you both insist on lying lavishly and badly. Come now. Do you know why he went to the temple on Sunday afternoon?'

'Yes,' said Janey, 'I think I know. He hasn't told me.'

'Is it something to do with the habit he has contracted?'

'He told you himself about that, didn't he?'

'He did. We have analysed Mr Garnette's cigarettes and found heroin. I believe, however, that Mr Pringle has gone further than an indulgence in drugged cigarettes. Am I right?'

'Yes,' whispered Janey.

'Mr Garnette is responsible for all this, I suppose.'

'Yes.' She hesitated, oddly, and then with a lift of her chin repeated: 'Yes.'

'Now,' Alleyn continued, 'please will you tell me when Mr Pringle left here on Sunday afternoon?'

She still looked very earnestly at him. Suddenly she knelt on the rug and held her hands to the heater, her head turned towards him. The movement was singularly expressive. It was as though she had come to a definite decision and had relaxed.

'I will tell you,' she said. 'He went away from here at about half-past two. I'm not sure of the exact time. He was very restless and – and difficult. He had smoked three of those cigarettes and had got no more with him. We had a scene.'

'May I know what it was about?'

'I'll tell you. Mr Alleyn, I'm sorry I was so rude just now. I must have caught my poor Maurice's manners, I think. I do trust you. Perhaps that's not the right word because you haven't said you think him innocent. But I know he's innocent and I trust you to find out.'

'You are very brave,' said Alleyn.

'The scene was about – me. When he's had much of that stuff he wants to make love. Not as if it's me, but simply because I'm there. I'm not posing as an ingenue of eighteen – and they're not so "ingenue" nowadays either. I'm not frightened of passion and I can look after myself, but there's something about him then that horrifies me. It's like a nightmare. Sometimes he seems to focus his – his senses on one tiny little thing – my wrist or just one spot on my arm. It's morbid and rather terrifying.'

She spoke rapidly now as though it was a relief to speak and without any embarrassment or hesitation.

'It was like that on Sunday. He held my arm tight and kissed the inside. Just one place over and over again. When I told him to stop he wouldn't. It was horrible. I can give you no idea. I struggled and when he still went on, I hit his face. Then there was the real scene. I told him he was ruining himself and degrading me and all because of the drugs. Then we quarrelled about Father Garnette, desperately. I said he was to blame and that he was rotten all through. I spoke about Cara.' She stopped short.

'That made him very angry?'

'Terribly angry. Hatefully angry. For a moment I was frightened. He said if that was what *they* did – You understand?'

'Yes,' said Alleyn

'Then he suddenly let me go. He had been almost screaming, but now he began to speak very quietly. He simply told me he would go to the church flat and get more of – more heroin. "A damn' big shot of it," he said. He told me quite slowly and distinctly that Father Garnette had some in the bedroom and that he would take it. Then he laughed, gently, and went away. And then, in the evening, when he'd had more of that stuff, I suppose, he met me as though nothing had happened. That's a pretty good sample of the happy wooing we enjoy together.'

She still knelt on the rug at Alleyn's feet. She had gone very white and now she began to tremble violently.

'I'm sorry,' she stammered. 'It's silly. I don't know why – I can't help it.'

'Don't mind!' said Alleyn. 'It's shock, and thinking about it again.'

She laid her hand on his knee and after a second he put his lightly over it.

'Thank you,' said Janey. 'I didn't see him again until the evening. After you had finished with us I walked back with him to his door. He told me I was to say he had been here all the afternoon. I promised. I promised: that's what is so awful. He said: "If they go for the wrong man – " and then he stopped. I came on here by myself. That's all.'

'I see,' said Alleyn. 'Have you got any brandy on the premises?'

'There's some – over there.'

He got a rug off the couch and dropped it over her shoulders. Then he found the brandy and brought her a stiff nip.

'Down with it,' he ordered.

'All right,' answered Janey shakily. 'Don't bully.' She drank the brandy and presently a little colour came back into her face.

'I have made a fool of myself. I suppose it's because I'd kept it all bottled up inside me.'

'Another argument in favour of confiding in the police,' said Alleyn.

She laughed again and put her hand on his knee.

'– who are only human,' Alleyn added and stood up.

'You're a very aloof sort of person to confide in, aren't you?' said Janey abruptly. 'Still, I suppose you must be human or I wouldn't have done it. Is it time we went to the inquest?'

'Yes. May I drive you there or do you dislike the idea of arriving in a police car?'

'No, but I think I'd better collect Maurice.'

'In that case I shall go. Are you all right?'

'I'm not looking forward to it. Mr Alleyn, shall I have to repeat all – this – to the coroner?'

'The conduct of an inquest is on the knees of the coroner. Sometimes he has housemaid's knees and then it's all rather trying. This gentleman is not of that type, however. I think we shall have a quick show and an adjournment.'

'An adjournment? For what?'

'Oh,' said Alleyn vaguely, 'for me to earn my wages, you know.'

CHAPTER 22

Sidelight on Mrs Candour

The inquest was as Alleyn had said it would be. Only the barest bones of the case were exhibited to the jury. Owing, no doubt, to Nigel's handling of a 'scoop' the public interest was terrific. Alleyn himself had by this time become a big draw. It would be a diverting pastime to discuss how far homicide cases have gone to cater for the public that used to patronize stock 'blood-and-thunder' at Drury Lane. In the days when women of breeding did not stand in queues to get a front seat at a coroner's inquest or a murder trial, melodrama provided an authentic thrill Nowadays melodrama is not good enough when with a little inconvenience one can watch a real murderer turn green round the gills, while an old gentleman in a black cap, himself rather pale, mumbles actor-proof lines about hanging by the neck until you are dead and may God have mercy on your soul. No curtain every came down on a better tag. The inquest is a sort of curtain-raiser to the murder-trial, and, in cases such as that of Cara Quayne, provides an additional kick. Which of these people did it? Which of these men or women will hang by the neck until he or she is dead? That priest, Jasper Garnette. Darling, such an incredible name, but rather compelling, don't you think? A definite thrill? Or don't you? He seems to have been . . . Can *anyone* go to the temple? . . . Chosen Vessel . . . My sweet, you *have* got a mind like a sink, haven't you! The American? . . . *too* hearty and wholesome . . . Still, one never knows. I must say . . . De Ravigne? My dear, I *know* him. Not frightfully well. His cousin . . . No, it was his sister ... Of course one never knows. That Candour female . . . God, what a mess! The

boy? Pringle? Wasn't he one of the Essterhaugh, Browne-White lot?
Of course one knows what they're like. He looks as if he might be
rather fun. Darling, *did* you ever see anything to *approach* Claude and
Lionel? Still, one never knows. One never knows until the big show
comes on. One never knows.

In all this undercurrent of conjecture Alleyn, little as he heeded
it, played a star part. His was as popular a name as that of the learned
pathologist, or the famous counsel who would be briefed if Alleyn
did his bit and produced an accused to stand trial. Chief Inspector
Alleyn himself, as he assembled the bare bones of the case before the
coroner, glanced once round the court and thought vaguely: 'All the
harpies, as usual.'

Nigel Bathgate, Dr Kasbek, Dr Curtis and the pathologist were the
first witnesses. Dr Kasbek was asked by a very small juryman why
he had not thought it worth while to send for remedies. He said
dryly that there was no remedy for death. The ceremony of the cup
was outlined and the finding of sodium cyanide described. Alleyn
then gave a brief account of his subsequent investigations in the
House of the Sacred Flame.

Father Jasper Garnette was called and gave a beautiful rendering of a saint among thieves. He was followed by the rest of the
Initiates. Mr Ogden's deportment was so elaborately respectful that
even the coroner seemed suspicious. M. de Ravigne was aloof and
looked as if he thought the court smelt insanitary. Mrs Candour
wore black and a stage make-up. Miss Wade wore three cardigans
and a cairngorm brooch. She showed a tendency to enlarge on
Father Garnette's purity of soul and caused the solicitor who
watched the proceedings on Father Garnette's behalf to become
very fidgety. Maurice Pringle was called on the strength of his
being the first to draw attention to Cara Quayne's condition. He
instantly succeeded in antagonising the coroner. Claude Wheatley,
who followed him, got very short commons indeed. The coroner
stared at him as though he was a monster, asked him precisely
what he *did* mean, and then said it seemed to be so entirely irrelevant that Mr Wheatley might stand down. Janey merely corroborated the rest of the evidence. It was all over very quickly. The
coroner, a crisp man, glanced once at Alleyn and ordered an
adjournment.

'He's a specimen piece, that one,' said Alleyn to Fox as they walked away. 'I only wish there were more like him.'

'What are the orders for this afternoon, sir?'

'Well, Fox, we must come all over fashionable and pay a round of calls. There are still two ladies and a gentleman to visit. I propose we have a bite of lunch and begin with Mrs Candour. She's expecting us.'

They had their bite of lunch and then made their way to Queen Charlotte flats, Kensington Square, where, in a setting of mauve and green cushions, long-legged dolls and tucked lampshades, Mrs Candour received them. She seemed disappointed that Alleyn had not come alone, but invited them both to sit down. She herself was arranged on a low divan and exuded synthetic violets. She explained that she suffered from shock. The inquest had been too much for her. The room was stiflingly heated by two ornate radiators and the hot water pipes gurgled like a dyspeptic mammoth.

Alleyn engulfed himself in a mauve satin tub hard by the divan. Inspector Fox chose the only small chair in the room and made it look foolish.

'My doctor is coming at four o'clock,' said Mrs Candour. 'He tells me my nerves are shattered. But shattered!'

She gesticulated clumsily. The emeralds flashed above her knuckles. Alleyn realized that she wished him to see a hot-house flower, enervated, perhaps a little degenerate, but fatal, fatal. With a mental squirm he realized he had better play up. He lowered his deep voice, bent his gaze on her and said:

'I cannot forgive myself. You should rest.'

'Perhaps I should. It doesn't matter. I must not think of myself.'

'That is wonderful of you,' said Alleyn.

She shrugged elaborately and sighed.

'It is all so ugly. I cannot bear ugliness. I have always surrounded myself with decorative things. I must have beauty or I sicken.'

'You are sensitive,' pronounced Alleyn with a strong man's scowl.

'You feel that?' She looked restively at Inspector Fox. 'That is rather clever of you, Mr Alleyn.'

'My consciousness of it brought me here this afternoon. We want your help, Mrs Candour. It is the sensitive people who see things, who receive impressions that may be invaluable.'

'Ah,' said Mrs Candour with a sad sardonic smile.

'Before I ask you for this particular kind of help I just want to confirm your statement about your own movements on Sunday. It's purely a matter of form. You were here all day, I think you said.'

'Yes, all day. How I wish it had been all the evening too!'

'I bet you do,' thought Alleyn. Aloud he said: 'Perhaps your servants would be able to confirm this. No doubt they will remember that you were indoors all day.'

'There are only two maids. I – I expect they will remember.'

'Perhaps Inspector Fox might have a word with them.'

'Of course,' said Mrs Candour very readily indeed.

'You would like to see them alone, I expect, Inspector? I'll ring.'

'Thank you, ma'am,' said Fox. 'I won't keep them long.' A musical-comedy parlourmaid who had shown them in, showed Fox out. His voice could be heard rumbling distantly in the flat.

'And now,' said Mrs Candour turning intimately to Alleyn, 'and now, Mr Alleyn.'

Alleyn leant back in his chair and looked at her until she glanced down and up again. Then he said:

'Do you remember a party at Mr Ogden's four weeks ago, yesterday?'

'Just a moment. Will you get me a cigarette? On the table over there. No, not those,' said Mrs Candour in a hurry. 'The large box. The others are Virginian. I loathe Virginian cigarettes.'

Alleyn opened the wrong box.

'Do you?' he said. 'What make is this? I don't know the look of them.' He took one out and smelt it.

'They are hateful. Someone sent them. I meant to have them thrown away. I think the servants must have upset – My cigarette, Mr Alleyn. Mayn't I have it?'

'I'm so sorry,' said Alleyn and brought the other box.

He lit hers for her, stooping over the divan. She made a great business of it.

'You?' she murmured at last.

'Thank you. I prefer Virginians,' he said. 'May I have one of these?'

'Oh, please don't. They are disgusting. Quite un-smokable.'

'Very well,' said Alleyn and took out his case. 'Do you remember the party?'

'At Sammy Ogden's? Do I? Yes, I believe I do.'

'Do you remember that M. de Ravigne looked at one of the books?'

She closed her eyes and laid the tips of her thick fingers on the lids.

'Let me think. Yes!' She opened her eyes wide. 'I remember. M. de Ravigne collects old books. He was browsing along the shelves. I can see it all now. I was talking to Father and poor Cara had joined us. Then Sammy came up. I remember that M. de Ravigne called to him: "Where did you find this?" And he looked across and said: "On a bookstall. Is it worth anything?" And Father went across and joined them. He adores books. They draw him like a magnet.'

'He has a remarkable collection,' said Alleyn. 'Was he interested in this particular one?'

'Let me think. He went across and – What was the name of the book?' She gaped stupidly. 'It wasn't – ! Oh, it was! You mean it was that book you showed us, on poisons. My God, is that what you mean?'

'Don't distress yourself. Don't be alarmed. Yes, that was it. You see we want to trace the book.'

'But if that was the one it belongs to Sammy Ogden. It's his. And he never said so. When you showed it to us he simply sat there and – ' Her eyes brightened; she was avid. 'Don't you see what that means? He didn't own up.'

'Oh, yes,' said Alleyn. Her excitement was horrible. 'Oh, yes, he told us it was his book. He hadn't missed it.'

'But – Oh.' For a moment she looked disappointed. Then he could see an anticipation of deeper pleasure come into her eyes. Her lips trembled. 'Then, of course, it was the Frenchman. Listen. I'll tell you something. Listen.'

Alleyn waited. She lowered her voice and hitched herself nearer to him.

'He – Raoul de Ravigne I mean – made a fool of himself over Cara. She encouraged him. You know what foreigners are. If I had chosen to let him – ' She laughed shrilly. 'But I wasn't having any. There was quite a scene once. I had a lot of bother with him. It was after that he turned to Cara. In pique, I always thought. And then – I hardly like to tell you. But Cara was dreadfully – you know. I've read quite a lot of psycho-analysis, and it was easy to see she was *mad* about Father Garnette. De Ravigne saw it. I watched him. I *knew*. He was furious. And when she got herself elected Chosen Vessel, he realized what *that* meant. You know what I mean?'

Alleyn really couldn't manage more than an inclination of his head.

'Well, perhaps it was too much for him. He's a very passionate sort of man. You know. The Celtic – I mean the Gallic temperament. Why didn't he say he'd seen the book before? That's what I'd like to know. I'm right. Don't you think I am right?'

'Did he take the book away with him?' asked Alleyn.

She looked furtively at him.

'I don't know but he was very interested in it. You could see. He was very interested. He asked Sammy Ogden where he got it. He fossicked about till he found it.'

'Mr Ogden said that he himself drew M. de Ravigne's attention to the book and that M. de Ravigne showed little interest in it.'

'He may have *pretended* not to be interested,' she said. 'He *would* do that. He makes a pose of being uninterested, the dirty beast.'

At this last vindictive descent into devastating vulgarity Alleyn must have shown some sort of distaste. A dull red showed through her make-up and for a moment she looked frightened.

'I expect you think I'm awful,' she said, 'But you see I know what he's like.'

'You tell me you had an unpleasant encounter with M. de Ravigne. May I hear a little more about that?'

But she would not tell him more. She was very uneasy and began to talk about self-respect. The encounter had no bearing on the case. She would rather not discuss it. She would not discuss it. He pressed a little further and asked when it had happened. She could not remember.

'Was it about the time you discontinued your visits to Miss Quayne?'

That shot went home. She now turned so white that he wondered if she would collapse. She seemed to shrivel back into the cushions as though she was scorched.

'What do you mean! Why are you talking like this? What are you thinking?'

'You mustn't distress yourself in this way,' said Alleyn.

'How can I help it when you start – I'm not well. I told you I was ill. I must ask you to go.'

'Certainly,' said Alleyn. He got up. 'I am sorry. I had no idea my question would have such an unfortunate effect.'

'It's not that. It's my nerves, I tell you. I'm a nervous wreck.'

She stammered, clenched her hands, and burst into a storm of ungracious tears. With a word of apology Alleyn turned and walked to the door.

'Stop!' cried Mrs Candour. 'Stop! Listen to me.' He turned.

'No, no,' she said wildly, 'I won't say any more. I won't. Leave me alone.'

He went out.

Fox waited for him outside.

'Bit of a rumpus in there, seemingly,' said Fox.

'Heavens, yes! There's been a loathsome scene. I'll have a bad taste in my mouth for weeks. I'll tell you about it in the car. We go to Ogden's house now.'

On the way to York Square he related the details of his interview. 'What do you make of all that?' he asked.

'Well, it sounds as if Mrs Candour had tried to do a line with the French gentleman and failed. Then I suppose she turned round and took a dislike to him like these sort of women do. She wouldn't feel too friendly towards Miss Quayne either, seeing Miss Quayne pinched the monsieur and the Reverend as well. No, she wouldn't feel very friendly in that quarter.'

'No.'

'The point is,' continued Fox with a sort of dogged argumentativeness, 'did she tell you anything that supports our theory or sets us off on another lay? That's the point.'

'She said that de Ravigne found the book and that nobody drew his attention to it until Ogden asked him what it was worth. She was very emphatic about that.'

'Was she telling the truth?'

'I wish I knew,' said Alleyn.

'And Father Garnette?'

'He saw it too. For the matter of that they may all have glanced at it afterwards. But the question is – '

'Did any of them see enough of it to put ideas of sodium cyanide into their heads?'

'Exactly, Brer Fox, exactly. How did you get on with that remarkably frisky-looking soubrette who showed us in?'

'Oh, her! Rita's her name. And the cook's a Mrs Bulsome. A very pleasant, friendly woman, the cook was. Made me quite welcome in the kitchen, and answered everything nice and straightforward. Rita took in the coffee at a quarter to two on Sunday. She went and got the cups about ten minutes later and Mrs Candour was then stretched out on the sofa, smoking and listening to the radio. She was still there when Rita took tea in at four-thirty and they heard the radio going all the afternoon.'

'Not exactly a cast-iron alibi. Did you pick up any gossip about that – that inexpressibly tedious lady?'

'Mrs Candour? Well, she's not very much liked in the hall, sir. Rita said it was her opinion the mistress was half-dopey most of her time, and Mrs Bulsome, who's a very plain-spoken woman, said the kitchen cat, a fine female tortoiseshell, had a better sense of decency. That was the way Mrs Bulsome put it.'

'You have all the fun, Fox.'

'Rita says Mrs Candour set her cap at monsieur and was always ringing him up and about three weeks ago she got him there and there was a scene. They heard her voice raised and after he'd gone Rita went in and she found Mrs C. in a great state. She never rang up after that and monsieur never came back. About that time, they said, she left off visits to Miss Quayne.'

'As we saw by Miss Quayne's appointment book. Here we are at the Château Ogden. Don't let me forget any important questions, Fox. I'll have to go carefully with Ogden He's feeling rather self-conscious about his book.'

'That's not to be wondered at,' said Fox grimly.

'There's a telephone-box. Pop in and ring up the Yard, Foxkin. I'd like to know if there's an answer from Madame la Comtesse.'

Fox was away for some minutes. He returned looking more than usually wooden.

'There's an answer. I've taken it down word for word. It's in French, but as far as I can make it out the Comtesse is in a private hospital and can't be disturbed.'

'Hell's boots!' said Alleyn. 'I'll disturb her if I have to dress up as a French gynaecologist to do it!'

CHAPTER 23

Mr Ogden at Home

Mr Ogden lived in an old-fashioned maisonette. His sitting-room was on the street level and opened off a small hall from which a break-neck stair led up to his dining-room and kitchen and then on to his bedroom and bathroom. He was served by a family who lived in the basement. He answered his own door and gave Alleyn and Fox a hearty, but slightly nervous, greeting.

'Hello! Hello! Look who's here! Come right in.'

'You must be sick of the sight of us,' said Alleyn.

'Where d'you get that stuff?' demanded Mr Ogden with some-what forced geniality. 'Say, when this darn business is through, maybe we'll be able to get together like regular fellows.'

'But until then – ?' suggested Alleyn with a smile.

Mr Ogden grinned uncomfortably.

'Well, I won't say nothing,' he admitted, 'but I'll try and act like I was a pure young thing. What's new, Chief?'

'Nothing much. We've come to look at your house, Mr Ogden.'

Mr Ogden paled slightly.

'Sure,' he said. 'What's the big idea?'

'Don't look so uncomfortable. We're not expecting to find a body in the destructor.'

'Aw gee!' protested Mr Ogden. 'You make me nervous when you pull that grim British humour stuff.'

He showed them over the maisonette, which had the peculiarly characterless look of the ready-furnished dwelling. Mr Ogden, however, appeared to like it.

'It's never recovered from the shock it got when Queen Victoria okayed gas-lighting,' he said. 'It's just kind of forgotten to disappear. Look at that grate. I reckon it would have a big appeal in the States as a museum specimen. Some swell apartment! When I first saw it I thought I'd side-slipped down time's speedway. I asked the real estate agent if it was central heated and the old guy looked so grieved I just hadn't the nerve to come at it again.'

'There are plenty of modern flats in London, sir,' said Inspector Fox rather huffily, as they went into the kitchen.

'Sure there are. Erected by Rip Van Winkle and Co. You don't want to get sore, Inspector. I'm only kidding. I took this apartment *because* it's old-world and British. I get a kick out of buying coal for this grate and feeling Florida in front and Alaska down the back.'

'It's a very cosy little kitchenette, sir,' said Fox, still on the defensive. 'All those nice modern Fyrexo dishes!'

'I've pepped it up some. There was no ice-chest and a line of genuine antiques for fixing the eats. And will you look at that hot-squat, coal-consuming range? I reckon that got George Whatsit Stevenson thinking about trains.'

Fox mumbled impotently.

They completed their tour of the maisonette and returned to the sitting-room. Mr Ogden drew armchairs up to the hearth and attacked the smouldering coals with a battered stump of a poker.

'How about a drink?' he asked.

'Thank you so much, not for me,' said Alleyn.

Mr Ogden again looked nervous.

'I forgot,' he mumbled, 'I kinda asked for that.'

'Good Heavens,' protested Alleyn, 'you mustn't jump to conclusions like this, Mr Ogden. We're on duty. We don't drink when we're on duty. That's all there is to it.'

'Maybe,' said Mr Ogden eyeing him doubtfully. 'What can I do for you, Chief?'

'We're still trying to untangle the business of the book. I think you can help us there, if you will. I take it that this is the room where you held your party?'

'Yup.'

'And where are your books,' continued Alleyn, pointing to where a dispirited collection of monthly journals and cheap editions propped each other up in an old bookcase.

'That's the library. Looks world-weary, doesn't it? I'm not crazy about literature.'

'I notice there are no red backs there, so the *Curiosities* must have showed up rather well.'

'That's so. It looked like it was surprised at being there,' said Mr Ogden with one of his imaginative flights.

'Well now, can you show me where it was on the night of your party?'

'Lemme see.'

He got up and walked over to the shelves.

'I reckon I can,' he said. 'M. de Ravigne had parked his drink in that gap along by the stack of *Posts* and spilled it over. I remember that because it marked the shelf and he was very repentant about it. He called me over and apologized and I said: "What the hell's it matter," and then I saw the old book. That's how I came to show it to him.'

'You showed it to him. You're positive of that? He did not find it for himself, and you didn't see him with it before anything was said about it?'

Mr Ogden thought that over. The significance of Alleyn's question obviously struck him. He looked worried, but he answered with every appearance of complete frankness.

'No, *sir*. Raoul de Ravigne did no snooping around those books. I showed it to him. And get this, Chief. If I hadn't showed it to him he'd never have seen it. He had turned away from the books and was telling Garnette how thoughtless he'd acted putting his glass down on the shelf.'

'But he would have seen it before, when he put his glass down.'

'Yeah? Well, that's so. But even if that is so you can bet your suspenders Ravigne is on the level. See here, Chief, I get you with this book stuff and God knows I feel weak under my vest whenever I remember the *Curiosities* belonged to me. But if you're thinking of Raoul de Ravigne for the quick hiccough, forget it. He worshipped Cara. He surely worshipped her.'

'I know, I know,' said Alleyn abstractedly.

Fox, who had examined the shelf, suddenly remarked:

'There's the mark of the stuff there still. Spirit, it's lifted the varnish.'

'So it has,' said Alleyn. 'After you had shown him the book what happened to it?'

'Why, I don't just remember. Wait a while. Yeah, I got it. He looked at it sort of polite but not interested, and handed it to Garnette.'

'And then?'

'I can't remember. I guess we walked away or something.'

'Previous to the glass incident what had you all been doing?'

'Search me. Talking.'

'Had you been talking to Mrs Candour, Miss Quayne and Mr Garnette?'

'That's so. Checking up, are you? Well, I reckon that's right. We were here by the fire, I guess.'

'And you don't remember seeing the book after that evening?'

'No. But I don't remember *not* seeing it till the day that sissy stopped in for Garnette's books. I'm dead sure it wasn't here then. Dead sure.'

'That's a most important point. It seems to show – ' Alleyn paused and then said: 'Look here, Mr Ogden, as far as I can see there's no reason why I shouldn't be perfectly frank with you. Tell me, is it your opinion the book disappeared on the night of your party?'

'Honest, Chief, I'm not sure. I don't know. I can't go any further except that I'd stake a couple of grand Ravigne doesn't come into the picture.'

'Who looks after you here and does the housemaiding?'

'The girl Prescott. The daughter of the janitor.'

'Could we speak to her, do you think?'

'Sure! She'll be down in the dungeon they call their apartment. I'll fetch her.'

He went out into the little hall and they could hear him shouting: 'Hey! Elsie! Cm' on up here, will you?'

A subterranean squeak answered him. He came back grinning.

'She'll be right up. Her old man does the valeting and butling, her ma cooks, and Elsie hands out the cap and apron dope. The bell doesn't work since they forgot to fix it way back eighteen-twenty-five.'

Elsie turned out to be a pleasant-faced young woman. She was neatly dressed, and looked intelligent.

'Listen, Elsie. These gentlemen want to ask you something.'

'It's about a book of Mr Ogden's that was stolen,' said Alleyn. 'It's a valuable book and he wants us to trace it for him.'

Elsie looked alarmed.

'Don't worry,' said Alleyn, 'we rather think it was taken by a man who tried to sell him a wireless. Do you remember the night Mr Ogden had a large party here? About three weeks ago?'

'Yes, sir. We helped.'

'Splendid. Did you do the tidying next day?'

'Yes, sir.'

'I suppose you dusted the book-shelves, didn't you?'

'Oh, yes, sir. They were in a terrible mess. A gentleman had upset a glass. Just there it was, sir.'

She pointed to the shelf.

'Were any of the books damaged?'

'The one next the place was, sir. It was stained-like.'

'What book was that?'

'I never noticed the name, sir. It had brown paper on it. You couldn't see.'

'Was there a red book there?'

'You mean the queer-looking old one. That hasn't been there for a – well, for some time.'

'That's the one we are trying to trace, Elsie. You think it was not there that morning?'

'No, sir. I'm sure it wasn't. You see that's where it always stood, and I noticed it wasn't there because I thought it was a pity because it wouldn't have mattered if that old book had been marked because I didn't know it was a valuable book, sir. I just laid the other one down by the fire to dry off and put it back again. I didn't take the cover off because I didn't like. It was put on very neat with nice shiny paper.'

Alleyn glanced at Mr Ogden, who turned bright pink.

'But it wasn't the old book, sir. The old book was bigger and it hadn't got a cover. Now I come to think of it, I remember I says to Mr Ogden, I says: "Where's the big red book?" Didn't I, sir? When you was looking through them to see the damage.'

'By heck, I believe she did,' shouted Mr Ogden.

'Splendid, Elsie. So one way and another you're absolutely certain there was no big red book?'

'Yes, sir, certain sure. There was just a row of five in brown paper covers and then the ones that are there now. I remember it all so distinct because that was the day before we went for our holidays, and I says I'd like to get things nice for a start off because Mr Ogden was going to do for himself and get his meals out, and he'd been that kind, and it seemed such a pity like, anything should be missing, so I was quite anxious to make everything nice, so I did and so that's how I remember.'

'Thank you very much indeed, Elsie.'

She went away in high feather.

'Just as well she didn't look at the book, Mr Ogden,' said Alleyn dryly. 'Which was it? *Petronius?*'

'Aw, hell!' said Mr Ogden.

'Well, Fox, we must go our ways.' Alleyn wandered over to the shelves. 'M. de Ravigne certainly left his mark,' he said. 'The stuff ran some way along. What was it?'

'A highball.'

'Ah, well,' said Alleyn, 'we'll have to find out what Mr Garnette did with the *Curiosities.*'

'By God,' began Mr Ogden violently, 'if Garnette – ' He stopped short. 'I ain't saying a thing,' he added darkly.

'Come along, Fox,' said Alleyn. 'We've kept Mr Ogden too long already. I must present Elsie with the wherewithal for a new bonnet. She skipped away before I could do it. I'll find her on the way down.'

They said goodbye. Elsie was hovering in the little hall. Alleyn winked at Fox who went on ahead. Alleyn joined him in the car five minutes later.

'Very talkative girl that,' said Fox dryly.

'She is. In addition to being swamped with thanks I've heard all about her sister's miscarriage, the mystery of the drawing-room poker (it seems Elsie suspects someone of chewing at the tip), her young man who is a terror for crime stories, how Mr Ogden broke a Fyrexo pot and why Elsie likes policemen. She remembers the day Claude came for the books. She put them in his attaché-case for him. Ogden was out, as he said. Elsie says there were six, which is rum, as she spoke of five before that. What's the time?'

'Five-thirty.'

'I made an appointment with young Pringle for six. I expect he'll be in. Look here, Fox. I'll drop you at Knocklatchers Row. If Garnette is in, ask him what he did with the book that night at Ogden's. Go easy with him. It would be lovely to hear the truth for once from those perfect lips. He'll swear he left it behind him, of course, but try and get some means of checking up on it. Then, if you've time, look up the unspeakable Claude. Ask him how many books he collected from Ogden for Garnette. He'll probably say he's forgotten, but ask him. Oh, and ask Garnette if he examined them when they came in. Will you do all that, Fox?'

'Right-oh, sir. What's your view now? Things are a bit more ship-shape, aren't they?'

'They are, Fox, they are. It's closing in. I've little doubt in my own mind now. Have you?'

'No. It looks as if you're right.'

'We haven't got enough for an arrest, of course. Still, the cable from Australia *may* bring forth fruits, and I'll *have* to get in touch with Madame de Barsac. You were quite right. She's in a nursing home. The telegram was from her housekeeper. I hope to Heaven Cara Quayne's letter has survived. I'll ring up the Sûreté tonight. Old Sapineau is by way of being a pal of mine. Perhaps he can do something tactful for me. Here we are at Knocklatchers Row. In you go, Fox. It's better I should see Pringle alone. I've got to convince him we know he came to this church on Sunday afternoon without giving away the source of information. I'll have to bluff, and I can do that better without your eye on me. It may come to taking an extreme measure. Watkins and Bailey are meeting me there. I'll be back at the Yard some time this evening. What a life, ye screeching kittens, what a life!'

Alleyn drove on to Lower Sloane Street, where he was joined by Detective-Sergeants Bailey and Watkins.

'Stay down opposite the door,' said Alleyn, 'and try not to look like sleuths, there's good fellows. If you see me come to the window, wander quietly upstairs. Hope it won't be necessary.'

He went upstairs to the flat, where he found Maurice Pringle.

Maurice looked a pretty good specimen of a wreck. His face was the colour of wet cement, there were pockets of green plasticine under his eyes, and he had the general appearance of having spent the day on an unmade bed. Alleyn dealt roundly with him.

'Good evening, Mr Pringle. You're looking ill.'

'I'm feeling bloody if it's of any interest,' said Maurice. 'Sit down, won't you?'

'Thank you.' Alleyn sat down and proceeded to look calmly and fixedly at Maurice.

'Well, what's the matter?' demanded Maurice. 'I suppose you haven't come here to memorize my face, have you?'

'Partly,' said Alleyn coolly.

'What the devil do you mean? See here, Inspector Alleyn, if that's your name, I'm about fed up with your methods. You're one of the new gentlemen-police, aren't you?'

'No,' said Alleyn.

'Well, what the hell are you?'

'Just police.'

'I'd be obliged,' said Maurice loftily, 'if you'd get your business done as quickly as possible. I'm busy.'

'So am I, rather,' said Alleyn. 'I should be delighted to get it over. May I be brief, Mr Pringle?'

'As brief as you like.'

'Right. Who supplies you with heroin?'

'None of your cursed business. You've no right to ask questions of that sort. I'll damn well report you.'

'Very good,' said Alleyn.

Maurice flung himself down in his chair, bit his nails and glowered.

'I wish to God I hadn't told you,' he said.

'Your behaviour and your looks told me long before you did,' rejoined Alleyn.

Maurice suddenly flung his hands up to his face.

'If my manner is discourteous I must apologize,' Alleyn went on, 'but this is a serious matter. You have deliberately lied to me. Please let me go on. You informed me that you spent Sunday afternoon with Miss Jenkins in Yeoman's Row. That was a lie. You were seen in Knocklatchers Row on Sunday afternoon. You went into the House of the Sacred Flame. Am I right?'

'I won't answer.'

'If you persist in this course I shall arrest you.'

'On what charge?'

'On the charge of receiving prohibited drugs.'

'You can't prove it.'

'Will you risk that?'

'Yes.'

'Do you hold to your statement that you did not go to the House of the Sacred Flame on Sunday afternoon?'

'Yes.'

'Are you protecting yourself – or someone else?'

Silence.

'Mr Pringle,' said Alleyn gently, 'if you are placed under arrest what will you do about your heroin then?'

'Damn your eyes!' said Maurice.

'I am now going to search your flat. Here is my warrant. Unless, of course, you prefer to show me how much dope you have on the premises?'

Maurice stared at him in silence. Suddenly his face twisted like a miserable child's.

'Why can't you leave me alone? I only want to be left alone! I'm not interfering with anyone else. It doesn't matter to anyone else what I do.'

'Not to Miss Jenkins?' asked Alleyn.

'Oh, God, they haven't sent you here to preach, have they?'

'Look here,' said Alleyn, 'you won't believe me, but I don't particularly want to search your flat or to arrest you. I came here hoping that you'd give me a certain amount of help. You went to Knocklatchers Row on Sunday afternoon. I think you went into Garnette's rooms. There you must either have overheard a discussion between Miss Quayne and another individual, or had a discussion with her yourself. For some reason you kept all this a secret. From our point of view that looks remarkably fishy. We must know what happened in Garnette's rooms between two-thirty and three on Sunday afternoon. If you persist in your refusal I shall arrest you on the minor charge, and I warn you that you'll be in a very unpleasant position.'

'What do you want to know?'

'To whom did Miss Quayne say: "I shall tell Father Garnette what you have done"?'

'You know she said that?'

'Yes. Was it to you?'

'No.'

'Was it to M. de Ravigne?'

'I won't tell you. It wasn't to me.'

'Had you gone there to get heroin?'

'I won't tell you.'

Alleyn walked over to the window and looked down into the street. 'Does Mr Garnette supply you with heroin?' he asked.

'I'll tell you one thing,' said Maurice suddenly. 'Garnette didn't kill Cara Quayne.'

'How do you know that, Mr Pringle?'

'Never you mind. I do know.'

'I am afraid that sort of statement would not be welcomed by learned counsel on either side.'

'It's all you'll get from me.'

'– and if you happened to be in the dock, the information would be superfluous.'

'I didn't kill her. You can't arrest me for that. I tell you before God I didn't kill her.'

'You may be an accessory before the fact. I'm not bluffing, Mr Pringle. For the last time will you tell me who supplies you with heroin?'

'No.'

'Oh, come in, you two,' said Alleyn disgustedly.

Bailey and Watkins came in, their hats in their hands. Alleyn was rather particular on points of etiquette.

'Just look round, will you,' he said.

The look-round consisted of a very painstaking search of the flat. It lasted for an hour, but in the first ten minutes they found a little white packet that Alleyn commandeered. No written matter of any importance was discovered. A hypodermic syringe was their second find. Alleyn himself took six cigarettes and added them to the collection. Throughout the search Maurice remained seated by the electric radiator. He smoked continually, and maintained a sulky silence. Alleyn looked at him occasionally with something like pity in his eyes.

When it was all over he sent the two Yard men out into the landing, walked over to where Maurice sat by the heater, and stood there looking down at him.

'I'm going to tell you what I think is at the back of your obstinacy,' he said. 'I wish I could say I thought you were doing the stupid but noble protection game. I don't believe you are. Very few people go in for that sort of heroism. I think self, self-indulgence if you like, is at the back of your stupid and very churlish behaviour. I'm going to make a guess, a reprehensible thing for any criminal investigator to do. I guess that on Sunday afternoon you went to Garnette's flat to get the packet of heroin we found in your boot-box. I think that Garnette is a receiver and disperser of such drugs, and that you knew he had this packet in his bedroom. I think you went in at the back door, through into the bedroom. While you were there someone came into the sitting-room from the hall. You were not sure who this person was, so you kept quiet, not moving for fear they should hear you and look in at the connecting door. While you stood still, listening, this unknown person came quite close to the door. You heard a faint metallic click and you knew the key had been turned in the lock of the safe. Then there was an interruption. Someone else had come into the sitting-room. It was Cara Quayne. There followed a dialogue between Cara Quayne and the other person. I shall emulate the thrilling example of learned Counsel and call this other person X. Cara Quayne began to make things very awkward for X. She wanted to know about her bonds. I think perhaps she wanted to add to them on the occasion of her initiation as Chosen Vessel. It was all very difficult because the bonds were not there. X tried a line of paci- fying reasonable talk, but she wasn't having any. She was very excited and most upset. X had a certain amount of difficulty in keeping her quiet. At last she said loudly: "I shall tell Father Garnette what you have done," and a second later you heard the rattle of curtain rings and the slam of the outer door. She had gone. Now your actions after this are not perfectly clear to me. What I think, however, is this: You behaved in rather a curious manner. You did not go in to the sitting-room, strike an attitude in the doorway, and say: "X, all is discovered," or: "X, X, can I believe my ears?" No. You tiptoed out of the bedroom and through the back door which you did not lock and which remained unlocked all through the evening. Then you scuttled back here and proceeded to make a beast of your- self with the contents of the little white packet. Now why did you do this? Either because X was a person who had a very strong hold of some sort over you, or else because X was someone to whom you were deeply attached. There is of course, a third – damn it, why can't one say a third alternative? a third explanation. You may have drugged yourself into such a pitiable condition that you haven't the nerve to tackle a white louse, much less X.'

'God!' said Maurice Pringle. 'I'll tackle you if there's much more of this.'

'There's very little more. You asked me to be brief. You had to take Miss Jenkins into your confidence over this because you wanted her to tell us you'd been in her flat all the afternoon. Now if you refuse to tell me who X is you're going to force me to do something very nasty about Miss Jenkins. She's a secondary accessory *after* the fact. With you, of course. You're going to force me to arrest you on the dope game. If you persist in your silence after your arrest you will be the direct cause of fixing the suspicion of homicide on the man who you say is innocent. There will be no more heroin. I should imagine your condition is pathological. You should go into a home and be scientifically treated. How you'll stand up to being under lock and key in a police station is best known to yourself. Well, there you are. Is it to be a wholesale sacrifice of yourself, Miss Jenkins and – possibly – an innocent person? Or are you going to clear away the sacrificial smoke at present obscuring the features of Mr or Madam X?'

Alleyn stopped abruptly, made a curious self-deprecatory grimace, and lit a cigarette. In the silence that followed, Maurice stared at him piteously. His fingers trembled on the arm of the chair. He seemed scarcely to think. Suddenly his face twisted and with the shamefaced abandon of a small boy he turned and buried his eyes in the cushions.

After a moment Alleyn stretched out a thin hand and touched him.

'It's best,' he said. 'I'm not altogether inhuman, and believe me, in every way, it's best.'

He could not hear the answer.

'Do you agree?' asked Alleyn gently.

Without raising his head Maurice spoke again. '– want to think – tomorrow – give me time.'

Alleyn thought for a moment.

'Very well,' he said at last, 'I'll give you till tomorrow. But don't commit suicide. It would be so very unprincipled, and we should have to arrest Miss Jenkins for perjury or something, and hang Mr Garnette. Perhaps I'd better leave someone here. You are a nuisance, aren't you? Good evening.'

CHAPTER 24

Maurice Speaks

On a stormy evening of December last year, five days after the murder of Cara Quayne, Nigel Bathgate stood at the window of his flat in Chester Terrace and looked across the street into Knocklatchers Row. It was blowing a gale and the rain made diagonal streamers of tinsel against the wet black of the houses. The sign of the Sacred Flame swung crazily out and back. A faint light shone from the concealed entry and ran in a gleaming streak down the margin of a policeman's cape. The policeman had just arrived, relieving a man who had been on duty there all afternoon. As Nigel looked down through the rain Miss Wade's umbrella appeared from the direction of Westbourne Street. He knew it was Miss Wade's umbrella because of its colour, a dejected sap-green, and because Miss Wade's goloshes and parts of herself were revealed as she struggled against the wind. The goloshes turned in at Knocklatchers Row just as a taxi came up from the opposite direction. It stopped at the House of the Sacred Flame. Mr Ogden got out, paid his fare, threw away his cigar and nodding to the policeman, disappeared down the entry. Then Maurice Pringle came down Chester Terrace, the collar of his mackintosh turned up and the brim of his hat pulled down over his eyes. Another taxi followed Mr Ogden's. It overtook and passed Maurice Pringle and a man who came from the same direction as Maurice. There was an interval, and then Lionel and Claude appeared under one umbrella. Then two more taxis and at last a closed car that whisked round the corner and drew up stylishly under the Sign of the Sacred Flame. Two men got out of this car. The first was large and solid, the second tall with a good figure, and a certain air of being well-dressed.

When Nigel saw this last figure he turned from the window, picked up his hat and umbrella, and went out into the rain.

In Chester Terrace the wind blew as violently as it had done on the night of the murder. The whole scene was a repetition so exact that Nigel had a curious sensation of suspended time, as though everything that had happened since Sunday evening was happening still. Even as he lowered his umbrella to meet the veering wind, Cara Quayne raised the cup to her lips, Garnette drank brandy and rectified spirit in the room behind the altar, his face veiled by the smoke of Maurice Pringle's cigarette. De Ravigne stood with the book in his hand, and Ogden stared at him with his mouth open. Mrs Candour, Miss Wade and the two acolytes nodded like mandarins in the background, and the doorkeeper repeated incessantly: 'I'm afraid you're too late. May I draw your attention to our regulations?'

'It would be fun to write it all up on those lines,' thought Nigel, 'but not precisely what the Press-lord ordered.'

This reflection brought him to the entry and the end of his fancies.

The torch in the wire frame was unlit. A large constable stood in the doorkeeper's place and beside him were Chief Detective-Inspector Alleyn and Detective-Inspector Fox.

'They're all in, sir,' said the constable.

'Ah,' answered Alleyn. 'We'll give them a minute to get comfortably settled and then we shall gate-crash.'

'Good evening,' said Nigel.

'Hullo. Here's Public Benefactor No. 1. Well, Bathgate, your information was correct and we're all much obliged. How did you find out?'

'Through Janey Jenkins. I rang up to see if she was all right after our ghastly night out with Pringle, and she told me they were meeting at Garnette's flat this afternoon. It's Ogden's idea. He thought they ought to get together like regular fellows and figure things out.'

'Americans are a gregarious race,' said Alleyn. 'Did you get the eavesdropper fixed up, Fox?'

'We did, sir. The Reverend went for a constitutional this afternoon and we fixed it all up nice and quiet while he was away. It's a small room and everything ought to come through very clear.'

'What are you talking about?' asked Nigel composedly.

'A cunning device, Bathgate, a cunning device. We shall sit among pagan gods and listen, like a Sforza in a Renaissance palace, to tales of murder. It will probably be inexpressibly tedious, but we may pick up a bit here and there.'

'You mean, I suppose, that you have installed a dictaphone.'

'Not quite that. We have installed a microphone with wires leading to a small loudspeaker. What a pity Leonardo is not alive today. I believe he is the only man of his time who would not be disconcerted by modern contraptions.'

'He wouldn't like the women,' said Nigel.

'He wouldn't recognize them as such. I think we might go in, Fox, don't you?'

They went quietly into the hall. Alleyn led the way to a recess on the right where Monsieur de Ravigne's statuette stood above a small altar. The whole recess only held six rows of chairs and was like a miniature shrine. The entrance was framed with heavy curtains which Fox drew after them. They were thus completely hidden from the main body of the hall. Fox switched on his torch and pointed it at the far corner by the altar. Nigel saw a glint of metal. They moved forward. Fox stooped down. A tiny metallic sound broke the silence. It was like a minute telephone under a heap of cushions. At a sign from Alleyn they squatted on the ground. Nigel's knees gave two stentorian cracks and Alleyn hissed at him. A Lilliputian Mr Ogden remarked:

'O.K. by me. Well folks, there's no cops listening in. The plain-clothes guy that's been sticking around the back door came unglued this morning, and the dick at the front's only there for show. I guess we'd better square up and make it a regular meeting. There's no sense in sitting around and handing out hot air. The first thing to do is to appoint a chairman.'

'Oh, God!' said Pringle's voice.

'But surely, Mr Ogden,' said Father Garnette, 'there is no neces-sitah – '

'I agree with Mr Ogden.' That was de Ravigne. 'It is better to make this affair formal. Let us appoint a chairman. I propose Mr Ogden should fill this office.'

'Aw say, I wasn't putting out feelers – '

'I second that. Hem!' Miss Wade.

'Well, thanks a lot. I certainly appreciate – '

'Good Lord,' said Alleyn, 'he's going to make a speech!' And sure enough, make a speech Mr Ogden did. He used every conceivable American business phrase, but what he said might be summed up as follows: They were all under suspicion of murder, and they all wished to clear themselves. No doubt each of them had his or her own theory. He thought it would be to their mutual benefit to share these theories. After the disaster of Sunday it was unlikely that their ceremonies should or could be continued. The House of the Sacred Flame was a business concern and therefore should be wound up in a businesslike manner. At this juncture there was a confused but energetic protest from Father Garnette, Mrs Candour and Miss Wade. The word 'spiritual' was used repeatedly.

'Sure, I'm alive to the spiritual dope,' interrupted Mr Ogden. 'I thought it was sure-fire honest-to-God uplift. Otherwise I'd never have backed it. It looked good-oh to me.'

Alleyn gave a curious little exclamation.

'But,' the voice went on, 'now I think different. And right here is where I hand out the inside stuff. Listen.'

He then gave them an account of the financial basis on which the House of the Sacred Flame was built. It agreed in every detail with the statement he had made to Alleyn. Mr Ogden backed the organization, paid for the building in which they now sat, and held the bulk of the shares. Mr de Ravigne was a much smaller shareholder, Father Garnette received twenty per cent of the profits and a salary.

When Mr Ogden finished speaking there was a silence so long that Nigel wondered if the microphone had broken down. Suddenly someone began to laugh. It was Maurice Pringle. He sounded as though he would never stop. At last he began to splutter out words.

'All this time – thank-offerings – self-denials – Oh, God! It's too screechingly funny!'

A babel of voices broke out.

'Quite appalling – '

'Business arrangement – '

'All so sordid and worldly. I never thought – '

'I don't pretend to understand business. My only care is for my flock – '

'If Father says it is – '

'Oh, shut up!'

'Lionel, do be quiet. I must say – '

'Cut it out,' shouted Mr Ogden.

Silence

'This is no way to act,' continued Mr Ogden firmly, 'I said this was to be a regular well-conducted meeting, and by heck, I'm going to have it that way. There's the copies of our agreement. Pass them round. Read them. They're the goods. They've been okayed by a lawyer and they're law. Laugh that off!'

A rustle, a clearing of throats, and then a murmur.

'Now,' said Ogden, 'get this. The profits of this outfit belong legally to me, Garnette and Monsieur de Ravigne. In that order. Any money coming in is ours. In that order. We kept up the temple and handed out the goods. Cara Quayne's donation of five thousand pounds in bearer bonds was our property – '

'No, it wasn't,' interrupted Maurice. 'Cara gave that money to a building fund, and it should have been used for nothing else.'

'It wouldn't have been used any other way, Pringle, if I'd had the say-so. But it was ours to administer. Yeah, that's so. Well, someone here present got a swell idea about that packet of stuff and lifted it. After that, it was just too bad about Cara.'

'You think,' de Ravigne spoke for the first time, 'that whoever stole this money also murdered my poor Cara. I incline to agree with you.'

'Sure. And these Ritzy cops think so too. Something happened in this room around two-thirty on Sunday. Cara came here then. Alleyn may talk queeny, but he's doped that out. Yeah, he seems like he was too refined to get busy, but he's got busy. Too right he has. Well, I guess I know what his idea is. He reckons Cara came here Sunday to add to those bonds and caught the double-crosser red-handed. I don't know just how you folks respond to this idea, but it looks good to me. Find the man or woman who was in this room at two-thirty on Sunday and you've got the killer.'

'Certainly,' said de Ravigne smoothly.

'But, I don't see – ' began Father Garnette.

'Just a moment, Garnette,' interrupted Mr Ogden. 'I'm coming to you. Who was in Cara's confidence? Who lifted my book on poisons. Oh, yeah, it was my book.'

'Why didn't you say so?' asked Janey.

'Because I thought you all knew. I reckon M. de Ravigne remembered looking at that book the night of my party and was too white to say so. It was swell, and I'm surely grateful.'

'It was nothing,' said de Ravigne.

'But I reckoned I hadn't a thing to conceal and I came clean about the book to Alleyn. But who lifted that book and put a brown-paper wrapper on it? Who put it way back behind that shelf where it wouldn't be seen? Who got the book that way it opened itself up like it was tired, at the straight dope on sodium cyanide?'

'It does not always open in this manner,' said de Ravigne.

'Practically, it does,' interrupted either Lionel or Claude. 'When I tried it – '

'Wait a moment. Wait a moment. Lemme get on with my whosits. Who had control of the keys after Cara's bonds were parked in the safe? Who lifted the bonds? Who kidded Cara into leaving him enough to re-christen himself Rockefeller?'

'What do you say?' cried Garnette suddenly. 'She left the money to the temple not to me.'

'How the blazing hell do you know?'

'She told me, poor soul, she told me.'

'That's right.' Mrs Candour's voice sounded shrilly. 'She told me herself weeks ago – well, about three weeks ago – when she first knew she was chosen. And she left her house and everything in it to Raoul de Ravigne. Ask him! he knows. Ask him! There are pictures worth hundreds. Ask him!'

'I do not wish to discuss it,' said de Ravigne. 'If she did this, and it was true she spoke of it, I am most grateful. But I will not discuss it.'

'Because you know – '

'Quit it, Dagmar. Where do you get that stuff?'

'What stuff?' cried Mrs Candour in alarm. 'What stuff? Do you mean – '

'He only means: "What are you talking about?" ' said Pringle hurriedly.

'I thought you meant *the* stuff. That detective, Alleyn; I'm sure he suspects. Sammy, can they – ?'

'Shut up,' said Maurice violently.

'Stick to the point,' begged Mr Ogden. 'I'm interested in Garnette.'

'I, too,' said de Ravigne. 'It seems to me that you make the argument very clear against this priest, Mr Ogden.'

'A murderer! Father Garnette, this is infamous.' That was Miss Wade.

'It's a fact. Listen, you, Garnette – '

'Stop!'

Maurice Pringle's voice rose above the others. Nigel could picture him on his feet, confronting them.

'Sit down, Pringle,' said Mr Ogden angrily.

'I won't. I'm going to – '

'That's my cue,' whispered Alleyn. 'Come on.'

Nigel followed him out of the little shrine and up the aisle. The voices of the Initiates sounded confusedly from behind the altar. Alleyn led the way up the hall to Father Garnette's door. He motioned to Nigel. They stood one on each side of the door. Very stealthily Alleyn turned the handle and pulled it ajar. The curtain inside was bunched a little towards the centre and by squinting slantways they were able to see into the room beyond. Nigel glued his eyes to the crevice beneath the hinge. He was reminded, ridiculously, of Brighton Pier. He found himself looking across the top of Miss Wade's purple toque straight into Maurice Pringle's eyes.

Maurice stood on the far side of the table. His face was ashen. A lock of hair had fallen across his forehead. He looked impossibly melodramatic. He seemed to have come to the end of a speech, interrupted perhaps by the hubbub that had broken out among the other Initiates. Miss Wade's hat bobbed and bobbed. A dark object momentarily hid this picture. Someone was standing just on the other side of the door. It was on this person Maurice had fixed his gaze. Whoever it was moved again and the picture reappeared in a flash. Mr Ogden's voice sounded close to Nigel's ear.

'The kid's crazy. Sit down, Pringle.'

'Go on, Maurice,' said Janey clearly from somewhere.

'Courage, my dear lad,' boomed Father Garnette with something of his old unctuousness.

Maurice jerked his head as though he had been struck.

'For God's sake don't start that stuff again or I'll let them hang you. Don't imagine I still worship at your shrine. I know what you're like now; I think I've known for a long time. A little bit of bloody

Brummagen. I've let myself be ruined aesthetically and, if you like, morally, for a plaster reproduction that wouldn't take in a house-maid. If I let them get you I'd be helping at a bit of spring-cleaning. God knows why I'm doing this. That's not true, either. I'm doing it because I can't help myself.'

'What the hell are you talking about, Pringle? You're dopey.'

'Dopey!' He turned to stare again at the hidden Ogden. 'For the first time in six months I'm not more or less doped. For Christ's sake let's speak the truth. Dope! Half of us are soaked in it. Dagmar, Cara, Me! You two bloody little pansies. You've been experimenting, haven't you? Just trying to see what it's like. Dear Father Garnette's been giving you cigarettes. And where does dear Father Garnette get his heroin? You none of you know. He doesn't know himself. He knows it comes from Paris through an agent in Seven Dials. He doesn't know who the agent is. I do.'

'He's mad,' screamed Mrs Candour.

'Sure, he's crazy,' said Mr Ogden soothingly. 'You don't want to get this way, Dagmar.'

A slight movement beside Nigel caused him to turn. Alleyn had opened the door a little wider and now slid in behind the curtain.

'I'm sane, and there's one of you who knows it. Keep still, all of you. I'm going to tell you what happened on Sunday afternoon.'

'By all means,' said de Ravigne softly, 'let us hear.'

'I came here on Sunday afternoon to pick up a packet of stuff Garnette had arranged to let me have. Cigarettes aren't good enough for me. I need more than the rest of you. This lot cost me ten pounds. Father Garnette has spiritual qualms about handing it over. Haven't you, Father? It makes him feel self-conscious, you know. So he leaves it in his little bedside cupboard and I get it for myself and plant the cash. He says heroin helps to divorce the psyche from the body. I came here some time after half-past two. Jane and I had had a row and I needed the stuff. I came in at the front door and went through into the bedroom. I just got the stuff and was going when I heard someone come out of the temple into this room. It wasn't our spiritual father. I knew his step.'

'Oh, for Heaven's sake – '

'Go on, Maurice.'

'Yes, Jane. Let me alone. I didn't quite like to reveal myself. It looked a bit queer my being there. I hesitated. Then I heard a click. Then two or three clicks. It dawned on me that someone was monkeying with the safe. The door wasn't quite shut. I looked through and saw who it was. It was – '

'I'm chairman of this meeting and I'm not standing for this. It's out of order. Sit down!'

'No.'

'*Sit down*'

'By God, if you don't shut up yourself I'll make you.'

'Yeah? You and who else?'

'Me,' said Alleyn. 'You're covered, Mr Ogden.'

CHAPTER 25

Alleyn Snuffs the Flame

Chief Detective-Inspector Alleyn once confessed to Nigel Bathgate that he enjoyed a dramatic close to a big case. 'It casts,' he explained, 'a spurious but acceptable glamour over the more squalid aspect of my profession.' In the case of Cara Quayne this preference must have been gratified. The close could scarcely have been more dramatic.

At the precise moment when Alleyn gripped his arms from behind, Ogden had reached for his gun, whether to shoot Pringle or himself, will never be known. At that same moment Detective-Sergeant Bailey came in from Garnette's bedroom, followed by two other officers. Bailey, looking liverish, carried an automatic. Ogden struggled savagely for about a minute. They had to handcuff him. Then Alleyn charged him. Mrs Candour, seconded by Claude and Lionel, screamed steadily throughout this performance and fainted, unnoticed, at the end of it. The others were silent. Ogden did not speak until they told him to come away. Then he twisted round and confronted Pringle.

'Let him finish,' he said. 'He's got nothing I can't answer. Let him finish.'

Maurice glanced at Alleyn, who nodded. Maurice turned his eyes towards Ogden, and began to speak.

'I saw you at the safe. You had just opened it. You had the bonds in your hand. Or rather you had the faked packet, I suppose. Then Cara came in quietly. She asked you what you were doing with the bonds. You told her Garnette had said you were to look at them. She just stared at you. I think you knew she didn't believe you because almost at once you began to talk about the stuff, heroin.'

He paused for a second, moistened his lips, and looked at Alleyn.

'He said he knew she was at it. He asked her if she would miss it very much if she couldn't get any more. He was very genial and friendly and said he felt like taking her into his confidence. Then he told her about the place in Seven Dials where Garnette got the stuff. He said quite calmly that he owned the racket. It would just be a little secret between himself and Cara, he said, and even Garnette himself didn't know he had anything to do with it. Then, when Cara said nothing, he added that it would be just too bad if anyone got curious about him because if he was put in an awkward position he'd have to come across with the whole story and then – He made it quite clear that if she gave him away he'd drag her name in and Garnette's as well. All of us. He told her that a word from him about her would cut her off from all chance of supply. He had only to suggest she was an agent of the police, and no one would sell it to her. While he was talking he put the packet back into the safe. He said: "So that's O.K." His back was turned while he re-locked the safe and I think it was then she wrote that note you found – it was only a few words – and put it in the cigarette-box, because I heard the lid drop and then a match was struck. She took a cigarette and lit it. All that time she said nothing. Just before she went away, he said very softly: 'And if that isn't enough – well, it'd be too bad if we had to look around for another Chosen Vessel.' There was a long silence after that. Then, Cara said loudly: 'I shall tell Father Garnette what you have done.' Ogden said: 'No you won't, Cara.' Without another word she went away. I realized he might come through into the bedroom and I got out by the back door.'

'Why did you say nothing of all this?' demanded de Ravigne.

'Because I'm a bloody skunk,' answered Maurice immediately. 'Because I hadn't got as much courage as she had, if you want to know. I was in the same boat. I've got to have the stuff. I'll go mad without it. I thought he'd put the bonds back. When I found he hadn't, it didn't make any difference. I've got to have it. God, can't you understand?'

'Then why have you done this?' asked Miss Wade. 'I'm afraid I don't quite understand.'

'Because he's *not* a bloody skunk,' said Janey loudly.

'Janey, dear!'

'It's an admirable explanation, Miss Wade,' said Alleyn. 'Let us leave it at that. Mr Garnette, I am afraid I must ask you to come to the police station with us.'

'On what charge? This is an infamous conspiracy. I am innocent. This man whom I have taken to my bosom – this viper – '

'Aw, can it, you – !' said Ogden so savagely that Garnette was suddenly silent and suffered himself to be led away without further protest.

'Ready, Mr Ogden?' asked Alleyn. 'Right, Fox!'

Inspector Fox, who had come in immediately after the arrest, approached Ogden with his customary air of placid courtesy.

'We'll just move along now, if you please, sir,' he said.

Ogden seemed to come out of a morose trance. He raised his skewbald eyes and looked from Alleyn to Fox.

'You – Britishers,' he said.

'But aren't Australians British?' asked Alleyn. For the first time Ogden looked frightened.

'I was born in Michigan,' he said.

'Australia may congratulate herself,' answered Alleyn.

'Sez you!'

'Mr Ogden,' said Alleyn, 'you are too vulnerable. What are you waiting for, Fox?'

They took Ogden out. One by one the Initiates drifted away. Mrs Candour, Claude and Lionel, who seemed to have discovered some mysterious affinity, left together. De Ravigne, who had remained completely unruffled, made ceremonious adieux.

'I imagine, M. l'Inspecteur, that there is something more than hops to the eye in this affair.'

'It will be all hop to the eye soon enough, M. de Ravigne,' said Alleyn sombrely.

'I can believe it. So long as my poor Cara is revenged I am satisfied. I must confess I myself suspected the priest. Without a doubt he is on an equality with Ogden. He introduced to Cara so many infamies. The drugs – to one of her temperament – '

'Did you never suspect the drug?'

'Certainly. I confronted her with it. Monsieur, I am myself almost as culpable. I introduced her to this accursed place. For this I can never forgive myself.'

'There is one question I should like to ask you,' said Alleyn. 'Did you remember the *Curiosities of Chemistry* when you saw it again in this room?'

'I remembered that I had held it in my hands, but I could not recollect where, or upon what occasion. It had not interested me. Later, in my flat, the whole scene returned to me. I had upset the glass. The book was stained. I cannot conceive why I had forgotten.'

'I see,' said Alleyn politely. 'You discovered the book?' Ogden did not show it to you?'

'I discovered it, monsieur. Had I not upset my glass that evening the book would not have been taken from the shelf. I myself called Ogden's attention to it. He was, as I remember, speaking to Mrs Candour at the time. I called him to me in order to ask about the book.'

'Ah,' said Alleyn, 'that tallies. Thank you very much, monsieur.'

'Not at all, monsieur. If you will excuse me – '

De Ravigne went out, unruffled. Miss Wade approached Alleyn. As usual she had a deceptive air of perspicacity.

'Good evening, officer,' she said.

'Good evening, Miss Wade,' said Alleyn gravely.

'I am most upset,' announced Miss Wade. 'Mr Ogden has always impressed me as being a very gentlemanly fellow, for a foreigner of course. And now you say he is a poisoner.'

'He is charged with murder,' murmured Alleyn.

'Exactly,' said Miss Wade. 'My dear brother was once in Michigan. The world is very small, after all.'

'Indubitably!'

'Obviously,' continued Miss Wade, 'Father Garnette has been greatly abused. By whom?'

'Miss Wade,' said Alleyn, 'if I may make a suggestion, I – I do most earnestly advise that you put this place and all its associations right out of your mind.'

'Nonsense, officer. I shall continue to attend the ceremonies.'

'There will be no ceremonies.'

Miss Wade stared at him. Gradually a look of desolation came into her faded eyes.

'No ceremonies? But what shall I do?'

'I'm so sorry,' said Alleyn gently.

She instantly quelled him with a look that seemed to remind him of his place. She tweaked her shabby gloves and turned to the door.

'Good evening,' said Miss Wade, and went out into the deserted hall.

'Oh, Mr Garnette!' swore Alleyn, 'and oh, Mr Ogden!' Maurice and Janey were the last to leave.

'Look here,' said Alleyn, 'I'm not going to be official with you two people. Miss Wade has snubbed me, poor little thing, and you can too if you think fit. Mr Pringle, I have to thank you most sincerely for the stand you took just now. It was, of course, an extremely courageous move. You spoke frankly about the habit you have contracted. I shall speak as frankly. I think you should go into a nursing home where such cases are treated. I know of an excellent place. If you will allow me to do so I can write to the doctor-in-charge. He will treat you sympathetically and wisely. It won't be pleasant, but it is, I believe, your only chance. Don't answer now. Think it over and let me know. In the meantime, I have asked Dr Curtis to have a look at you and he will help you, I am sure. This is an inexcusable bit of cheek on my part, but I hope you will forgive me.'

Maurice stood and stared at him.

'Can I come and see you?' he said suddenly.

'Yes, when I'm not too busy,' answered Alleyn coolly. 'But don't go and distort me into an object for hero-worship. I seem to see it threatened in your eye. I'm too commonplace and you're too old for these adolescent fervours.'

He turned to Janey.

'Goodbye,' he said. 'I'm afraid you'll both be called as witnesses.'

'I suppose so,' said Janey. 'Am I allowed to do a spot of hero-worship?'

'You reduce me to the status of an insufferable popinjay,' replied Alleyn. 'Goodbye and God bless you.'

'Same to you,' said Janey. 'Come on, Blot.'

'Well, Bathgate,' said Alleyn.

'Hullo,' said Nigel.

'You were right again, you see.'

'Was I? When?'

'You warned me on Sunday that Ogden was too good to be true.'

'Good Lord!' said Nigel. 'So I did. I'd forgotten. Extraordinarily clever of me. Look here. Could you bear to sit down for ten minutes and – and – confirm my first impression?'

'I knew this was coming. All right. But let it be in your flat.'

'Oh, of course.'

They locked up Father Garnette's flat and went out into the hall. Only two side lamps were alight and the building was almost full of shadows as it had been when Nigel walked in, unbidden, on Sunday night. It was so still that the sound of rain beating on the roof filled the place with desolation. The statues, grey shapes against the walls, assumed a new significance. The clumsy gesture of the Wotan seemed indeed to threaten. The phœnix rose menacingly from the sacred flame. Alleyn followed Nigel down the centre aisle. At the door he turned and looked back.

'I wonder what will happen to them,' he said. 'One of Garnette's symbols, at least, is true. The phœnix of quackery rises again and again from its own ashes. Tonight we slam the door on this bit of hocus-pocus and tomorrow someone else starts a new sideshow for the credulous. Come on.'

They went down the outside passage and out into the rain. The constable was still on duty.

'It's all over,' said Alleyn.' 'You can go home to bed.'

Up in Nigel's flat they built themselves a roaring fire and mixed drinks.

'Now then,' said Nigel.

'What do you want to know?' asked Alleyn a little wearily.

'I don't want to bore you. If you'd rather – '

'No, no. It's only the beastly anti-climax depression. Always sets in after these cases. If I don't talk about it I think about it. Go ahead.'

'When did you first suspect him?'

'As soon as I learnt the order in which they had knelt. He was the last to take the cup before it returned to Garnette. That meant that he had least to risk. Except Garnette, of course. Miss Wade told us that the priest always took the cup in one hand and laid the other over the top. That meant he would not see the little tube of paper. Do you remember I said that Ogden's position made him the first suspect?'

'Yes. I thought you meant – Never mind. Go on.'

'Ogden would know that Garnette handled the cup in that way. He would also know that Miss Qayne would spend some time over her hysterical demonstration before she drank the wine. There would be time for the cyanide to dissolve. The point you made about the uncertainty of whether the paper would be seen is a good one. It pointed strongly to Ogden. He is the only one, except Garnette and Claude, who could be sure it would not be noticed. I felt that the others would be unlikely to risk it. Claude had neither the motive nor the guts. Garnette had an overwhelming motive, but he's an astute man and I simply couldn't believe that he would be ass enough to leave the book lying about for us to find.'

'Did Ogden plant the book?'

'No. Master Claude did that.'

'Claude?'

'Yes, when he called for Garnette's books, three weeks ago, after the party.'

'On purpose?'

'No. Accidentally.'

'How do you know?'

'The books Garnette lent Ogden were in brown-paper wrappers. There were five of them. Ogden's maid said so and when we saw them in Garnette's flat there were five that were so covered. Six, counting the *Curiosities*. But Claude told Fox he knew he returned six books to Garnette. He took them in an attaché case, and they just fitted it. What happened, I believe, was something like this. For some time Ogden had thought of murdering Cara Quayne. He may even have pondered over the sodium cyanide recipe, but I think that came later. He knew she was leaving her fortune to Sacred Flame Limited, and he was the biggest shareholder. He may have meant to destroy the book and then have thought of a brighter idea, that of planting it in Garnette's flat. When de Ravigne drew everybody's attention to the book at the party, I believe Ogden made up his mind to risk this last plan. As soon as they had gone he covered the *Curiosities* in brown paper. Next morning when the maid cleaned up the mess she noticed it had gone. It hadn't gone. It was disguised as one of Garnette's bits of hot literature. When Claude called for the books he took the ones with brown-paper wrappers: the *Curiosities* among them. I suppose when Ogden found what had happened he waited for developments, but there were none. The six books had been shoved back behind the others and neither Garnette or Claude had noticed anything. This was a phenomenal stroke of luck for Ogden. No doubt if it hadn't happened he would have planted the book himself, but Claude had saved him the trouble. He must have waited his chance to find the book and wipe off any prints. He was emphatic about drawing de Ravigne's attention to the *Curiosities*, but the others, questioned independently, said that de Ravigne himself found the book. If he had already laid his plans this chance discovery by de Ravigne must have disconcerted our Samuel, as it brought the book into unwelcome prominence. He may have thought then of the pretty ruse of incriminating Garnette and pulling in his share of the bequest. But I rather fancy that chance finding by de Ravigne put the whole idea into his head. Otherwise the book would not have been on show. Yes. I think the cyanide scheme was born on the night of the party. It sounds risky, but how nearly it succeeded! There was Elsie, the maid, to swear the book had gone the morning after the party. There were the others to say Garnette and de Ravigne had both handled it the night before. Ogden made a great show of defending de Ravigne, but, of course, if I'd gone for de Ravigne it would have suited his book almost as well as if I'd gone for Garnette. Ogden played his cards very neatly. He owned up to the book with just the right amount of honest reluctance. He gave a perfectly true account of the business arrangement with de Ravigne and Garnette. He had to bring that out, of course, in order to collect when the Will was proved. He made a great point of the legality of their contract. He's a fly bird, is our Samuel.'

'I'm sure you're right about all this,' said Nigel diffidently, 'but it seems very much in the air. Without Pringle's evidence could you ever bring the thing home to him? Isn't it altogether too speculative?'

'It's nailed down with one or two tin-tacks. Ogden and Garnette were the only two who could have concocted the sodium cyanide at what house-agents call the Home Fireside.'

'Really?'

'Yes. They are the only two who have open fires. The others, if you wash out Miss Jenkins's gas-ring, all live in electrically heated, or central-heated, service flats. The cooking of sodium cyanide is not the sort of thing one would do away from the Home Fireside, and

anyway they have, none of them, been out of residence for the last
six months. Then Elsie told me that two days after the party the
servants all went on their holiday and Mr Ogden, who was so kind,
"did" for himself. A dazzling chance for him to do for Cara Quayne
at the same time. When Elsie returned from the night-life of Marine
Parade, Margate, she no doubt found everything in perfect order. A
little less washing-soda in the wooden box over the sink, perhaps,
one new Fyrexo patent heat-proof crock. Mr Ogden had unfortunately dropped the old one and it was just too bad, but he had got
her another. He didn't say anything about it, but bright little Elsie
spotted the difference. While she was away he had made his sodium
cyanide.'

'Yes, but you don't *know* – '

'Here's another tin-tack.'

Alleyn went to his overcoat and took out a thin object wrapped
in paper.

'I brought it to show you. I stole it from Ogden's flat.'

He unwrapped the paper. A very short and extremely black iron
poker was disclosed.

'Here's where he got his iron filings. I noticed the corrugations on
the tip. He had made it nice and black again, but pokers don't wear
away in minute ridges. Elsie agreed with me. It wasn't like what it
was before she went away, that it wasn't.'

'And what, may I ask, was the meaning of the cable to Australia?'

'Do you remember another very intelligent remark you made on
Sunday evening?'

'I made any number of intelligent remarks.'

'Possibly. This was to the effect that Ogden's Americanese was too
good to be true. It seemed to me no more exaggerated than the
sounds that fill the English air in August, but after a bit I began to
think you were right. I was sure of it when, under stress, he came
out with a solecism. He said "Good-oh." Now "Good-oh" is purest
dyed in the wool Australian. It is the Australian comment on every
conceivable remark. If you say to an Australian: "I'm afraid your
trousers are on fire," he replies "Good-oh." Mr Ogden, on a different
occasion, ejaculated "Too right!" Another bit of undiluted Sydney.
And yet when I ased him if he had been to Australia he denied the
soft impeachment. So we've asked headquarters, Sydney, if it knows

anything about a tall man with an American accent and skewbald eyes. It may be productive. One never knows. But the longest and sharpest tack is Madame la Comtesse de Barsac.

'From the fastness of her nursing home she has come out strong with a telegram that must have cost her a pretty sum. It is this sort of thing. "Madame la Comtesse de Barsac has just learned of the death of Mademoiselle Cara Quayne. She believes that she has evidence of the utmost importance and urges that the officials in charge of the case apprehend one Samuel Ogden. Mademoiselle Quayne's letter of December tenth follows and will explain more fully the reasons that commend this action." '

' 'Struth!' said Nigel, 'that puts the *diamanté* clasp on it.'

'I rather fancy it does.'

'I suppose it's the letter Cara Quayne wrote after she got back to the flat on Sunday afternoon.'

'That's it. With the help of the bits we got from the blotting-paper I think we can make a pretty shrewd guess at what's in it. Cara may describe her visit to the temple, her encounter with Ogden and her fears for the consequences. She has gone so far with the heroin habit that she cannot face the prospect of being done out of it. She implores her old friend to help her, perhaps asks if Madame de Barsac could put her on to an agent for the stinking stuff. I hope she'll say he threatened her, specifically. If she does – '

'Yes,' said Nigel, 'if she says that it'll look murky for Mr Ogden.'

'There's another useful bit of information. Old Nanny Hebborn, as I think you heard her tell me, lurked in Mr Garnette's parlour on Sunday night and saw the beginnings of the cup ceremony. She described the movements of the Initiates when they formed their circle. She said Ogden went up first. When Miss Wade and the Candour skirmished to get one on each side of Garnette, Ogden out-manœuvred them and himself got in on Garnette's right hand. Nanny said he deliberately stopped Miss Wade and took her place. Of course he did. It was the only safe place for him.'

'I suppose Ogden's counsel will go for Garnette?'

'Oh yes. I've no doubt Mr Garnette's trans-Atlantic origin and activities will all be brought out into the fierce light that beats upon the witness-box. I hope it will be the dock. Him and his heroin! Devil take me, but I swear he's the nastier sample of the two.'

'Will he get the money?'

'Not if Mr Rattisbon can help it.'

The telephone rang. Nigel answered it.

'It's for you,' he said. 'Fox, I think.'

Alleyn took the telephone from him. Nigel walked over to the window and stared out into the street.

'Hullo, Fox,' said Alleyn, 'you've run me to earth. What is it?'

The telephone quacked industriously.

'I see,' said Alleyn. 'That's all very neat and handy. Thank you, Foxkin. Are you at the Yard? Well, go home to bed. It's late. Good night.'

He hung up the receiver and swung round in his chair.

'Cable from Australia. "Sounds like S. J. Samuels, American sharp, convicted sale prohibited drugs. Two years. Involved Walla-Walla homicide case!"'

He paused. Nigel did not answer.

'And Mr Garnette has decided to make a statement. He says he has had some interesting confidences from Ogden. Little charmer! What are you looking at?'

'I'm looking down into Knocklatchers Row. It's very odd, but someone seems to be taking away the Sign of the Sacred Flame. Only it's raining so hard I can hardly see.'

'You're quite right. It's a man from the Yard. Crowds collect and gape at the thing. I told them to take it away.'

Vintage Murder

*For Allan Wilkie and
Frediswyde Hunter-Watts
In memory of a tour in New Zealand*

Contents

Cast of Characters

Roderick Alleyn		*Of the Criminal Investigation Department, Scotland Yard*
Susan Max		*Character Woman*
Hailey Hambledon		*Leading Man*
Courtney Broadhead		*Second Juvenile*
St John Ackroyd		*Comedian*
Carolyn Dacres		*Leading Lady*
Alfred Meyer		*Her husband: Proprietor and Managing Director of Incorporated Playhouses Ltd*
	Of the Carolyn Dacres Comedy Company	
Valerie Gaynes		*A Beginner*
George Mason		*Meyer's partner: Business Manager, Incorporated Playhouses Ltd*
Ted Gascoigne		*Stage Manager*
Francis Liversidge		*First Juvenile*
Brandon Vernon		*Character Man*
Fred	*Of the Stage Staff*	*Head Mechanist*
Bert		*Stage-hand*
Bob Parsons		*A dresser*
Gordon Palmer		*A bear-cub*
Geoffrey Weston		*His Leader*
Dr Rangi Te Pokiha		*A Maori physician*
Detective-Sergeant Wade		
Detective-Inspector Packer		*Of the New Zealand Police Force*
Detective-Sergeant Cass		
Superintendent Nixon		
Singleton		*Stage door keeper at the Royal*

Foreword

Although I agree with those critics who condemn the building of
imaginary towns in actual countries I must confess that there is no
Middleton in the North Island of New Zealand, nor is 'Middleton' a
pseudonym for any actual city. The largest town in New Zealand is
no bigger than, let us say, Southampton. If I had taken the Dacres
Comedy Company to Auckland or Wellington, Messrs Wade, Packer,
and Cass, to say nothing of Dr Rangi Te Pokiha, might have been
mistaken for portraits or caricatures of actual persons. By building
Middleton in the open country somewhere south of Ohakune, I
avoid this possibility, and, with a clear conscience, can make the
usual statement that:

*All the characters in this story are purely imaginary and bear no relation
to any actual person.*

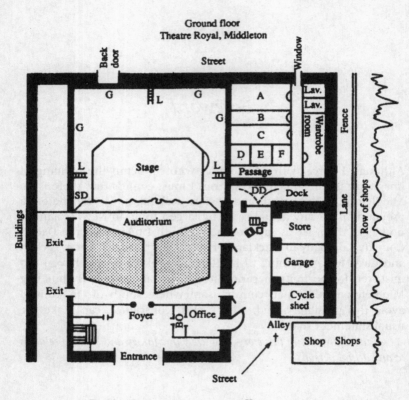

Ground floor
Theatre Royal, Middleton

Dressing rooms

A – Liversidge, Vernon, Broadhead
B – Valerie Gaynes
C – St John Ackroyd
D – Carolyn Dacres
E – Hailey Hambledon
F – Susan Max

Key

L – Ladders
DD – Double doors
SD – Stage-door
BO – Box office
Cs – Cases
G – Grid

CHAPTER 1

Prologue in a Train

The clop and roar of the train was an uneasy element somewhere at the back of the tall man's dreams. It would die away – die away and fantastic hurrying faces come up to claim his attention. He would think 'I am sure I am asleep. This is certainly a dream.' Then came a jolt as they roared, with a sudden increase of racket, over a bridge and through a cutting. The fantastic faces disappeared. He was cold and stiff. For the hundredth time he opened his eyes to see the dim carriage-lamps and the rows of faces with their murky highlights and cadaverous shadows.

'Strange company I've got into,' he thought.

Opposite him was the leading man, large, kindly, swaying slightly with the movement of the long narrow-gauge carriage, politely resigned to discomfort. The bundle of rugs in the next seat to the tall man was Miss Susan Max, the character woman. An old trouper, Susan, with years of jolting night journeys behind her, first in this country, then Australia, and then up and down the provinces in England, until finally she made a comfortable niche for herself with Incorporated Playhouses in the West End. Twenty years ago she had joined an English touring company in Wellington. Now, for the first time, she revisited New Zealand. She stared, with unblinking eyes, at the dim reflections in the window-pane. The opposite seat to Susan's was empty. In the next block George Mason, the manager, a dyspeptic, resigned-looking man, played an endless game of two-handed whist with Ted Gascoigne, the stage-manager.

And there, nodding like a mandarin beside old Brandon Vernon, was little Ackroyd, the comedian, whose ill-temper was so much at variance with his funny face. Sitting in front of Mason, a pale young man fidgeted restlessly in his chair. This was Courtney Broadhead. 'Something the matter with that youth,' thought the tall man. 'Ever since Panama–' He caught the boy's eye and looked beyond him to where Mr Francis Liversidge, so much too beautifully dressed, allowed Miss Valerie Gaynes to adore him. Beyond them again to the far end of the long carriage were dim faces and huddled figures. The Carolyn Dacres English Comedy Company on tour in New Zealand.

He felt very much an outsider. There was something about these people that gave them a united front. Their very manner in this night train, rattling and roaring through a strange country, was different from the manner of other travellers. Dozing a little, he saw them in more antiquated trains, in stage-coaches, in wagons, afoot, wearing strange garments, carrying bundles, but always together. There they were, their heads bobbing in unison, going back and back.

A violent jerk woke him. The train had slowed down. He wiped the misty window-pane, shaded his eyes, and tried to look out into this new country. The moon had risen. He saw aching hills, stumps of burnt trees, some misty white flowering scrub, and a lonely road. It was very remote and strange. Away in front, the engine whistled. Trees, hills and road slid sideways and were gone. Three lamps travelled across the window-pane. They were off again.

He turned to see old Susan dab at her eyes with her handkerchief. She gave him a deprecatory smile.

'Those white trees are manuka bushes,' she said. 'They bloom at this time of the year. I had forgotten.'

There was a long silence. He looked from one dimly-lit slumping figure to another. At last be became aware of Hambledon's gaze, fixed on himself.

'Do you find us very queer cattle?' said Hambledon, with his air of secret enjoyment.

'Why do you ask that?' said the tall man quickly.

'I noticed you looking at us and wondered what were your thoughts. *Do* you think us queer cattle?'

In order not to disturb Susan Max and to make himself heard above the racket of the train, he bent forward. So did the tall man. With their heads together under the murky lamp, they looked like conspirators.

'That would be an ungracious thought,' said the tall man, 'after your kindness.'

'Our kindness? Oh, you mean George Mason's offer of a seat in our carriage?'

'Yes. The alternative was a back-to-the-engine pew by a swinging door, among commercial travellers, and next a lavatory.'

Hambledon laughed silently.

'Ah well,' he said, 'even queer cattle may be preferable to all that.'

'But I didn't say I thought – '

'If you had it would not have been very strange. Actors are a rum lot.'

'The last man I heard say that was an actor – and a murderer,' said the tall man.

'Really?' Hambledon raised his head. 'You don't by any chance mean Felix Gardener?'

'I do. How did you guess – ?'

'*Now* I know who you are. Of course! How stupid of me! I have seen your photograph any number of times in the papers. It's been worrying me.'

His companion looked at Susan Max. Her three chins were packed snugly down into her collar and her eyes were closed. Her whole person jogged rhythmically with the motion of the train.

'She knew me,' he said, 'but I asked her not to give me away. I'm on a holiday.'

'I should have guessed from your name of course. How inadequate one's memory is. And without your – your rank – '

'Exactly. They spelt me wrongly in the passenger list.'

'Well, this is very interesting. *I* shan't give you away.'

'Thank you. And at any rate we part company in Middleton. I'm staying for a few nights to see your show and look round, and then I go on to the South Island.'

'We may meet again,' said Hambledon.

'I hope so,' said his companion cordially.

They smiled tentatively at each other, and after an uncertain pause leant back again in their seats.

The train roared through a cutting and gathered speed. 'Racketyplan, rackety-plan,' it said, faster and faster, as though out of patience with its journey. The guard came through and turned down the lamps. Now the white faces of the travellers looked more cadaverous than ever. The carriage was filled with tobacco smoke. Everything felt grimy and stale. The shrill laughter of Miss Valerie Gaynes, in ecstasy over a witticism of Mr Liversidge's, rose above the din. She stood up, a little dishevelled in her expensive fur coat, and began to walk down the carriage. She swayed, clutched the backs of seats, stumbled and fell half across George Mason's knees. He gave her a disinterested squeeze, and made a knowing grimace at Gasgoigne who said something about: 'If you *will* go native.' Miss Gaynes yelped and got up. As she passed Hambledon and the tall man she paused and said:

'I'm going to my sleeper. They call it "de luxe". My God, what a train!'

She staggered on. When she opened the door the iron clamour of their progress filled the carriage. Cold night air rushed in from outside bringing a taint of acrid smoke. She struggled with the door, trying to shut it behind her. They could see her through the glass panel, leaning against the wind. Hambledon got up and slammed the door and she disappeared.

'Have you taken a sleeper?' asked the tall man.

'No,' said Hambledon. 'I should not sleep and I should probably be sick.'

'That's how I feel about it, too.'

'Carolyn and Meyer have gone to theirs. They are the only other members of the company who have risked it. That young woman has just got to be expensive. Valerie, I mean.'

'I noticed that in the ship. Who is she? Any relation of old Pomfret Gaynes, the shipping man?'

'Daughter.' Hambledon leant forward again. 'Academy of Dramatic Art. Lord knows how big an allowance, an insatiable desire for the footlights and adores the word "actress" on her passport.'

'Is she a good actress?'

'Dire.'

'Then how – ?'

'Pomfret,' said Hambledon, 'and push.'

'It seems a little unjust in an overcrowded profession.'

'That's how it goes,' said Hambledon with a shrug. 'The whole business is riddled with preferment nowadays. It's just one of those things.'

Susan Max's head lolled to one side. Hambledon took her travelling cushion and slipped it between her cheek and the wall. She was fast asleep.

'There's your real honest-to-God actress,' he said, leaning forward again. 'Her father was an actor-manager in Australia and started life as a child performer in *his* father's stock company. Susan has trouped for forty-five years. It's in her blood. She can play anything from grande dame to trollop, and play it well.'

'What about Miss Dacres? Or should I say Mrs Meyer? I never know with married stars.'

'She's Carolyn Dacres all the time. Except in hotel registers, of course. Carolyn is a great actress. Please don't think I'm using the word "great" carelessly. She is a great actress. Her father was a country parson, but there's a streak of the stage in her mother's family, I believe. Carolyn joined a touring company when she was seventeen. She was up and down the provinces for eight years before she got her chance in London. Then she never looked back.' Hambledon paused and glanced apologetically at his companion. 'In a moment you will accuse me of talking shop.'

'Why not? I like people to talk shop. I can never understand the prejudice against it.'

'You don't do it, I notice.'

The tall man raised one eyebrow.

'I'm on a holiday. When did Miss Dacres marry Mr Alfred Meyer?'

'About ten years ago,' said Hambledon, shortly. He turned in his seat and looked down the carriage. The Carolyn Dacres Company had settled down for the night. George Mason and Gascoigne had given up their game of two-handed whist and had drawn their rugs up to their chins. The comedian had spread a sheet of newspaper over his head. Young Courtney Broadhead was awake, but Mr Liversidge's mouth was open and those rolls of flesh, so well disciplined by day, were now subtly predominant. Except for Broadhead they were all asleep. Hambledon looked at his watch.

'It's midnight,' he said.

Midnight. Outside their hurrying windows this strange country slept. Farm houses, lonely in the moonlight, sheep asleep or tearing with quick jerks at the short grass, those aching hills that ran in curves across the window-panes, and the white flowering trees that had made old Susan dab her eyes. They were all there, outside, but remote from the bucketing train with its commercial travellers, its tourists and its actors.

'The fascination of a train journey,' thought the tall man, 'lies in this remoteness of the country outside, and in the realisation that it is so close. At any station one may break the spell of the train and set foot on the earth. But as long as one stays in the train, the outside is a dream country. A dream country.' He closed his eyes again and presently was fast asleep and troubled by long dreams that were half broken by a sense of discomfort. When he woke again he felt cold and stiff. Hambledon, he saw, was still awake.

Their carriage seemed to be continually turning. His mind made a picture of a corkscrew with a gnat-sized train twisting industriously. He looked at his watch.

'Good lord,' he said. 'It's ten past two. I shall stay awake. It's a mistake to sleep in these chairs.'

'Ten past two,' said Hambledon. 'The time for indiscreet conversation. Are you sure you do not want to go to sleep?'

'Quite sure. What were we speaking of before I dozed off? Miss Dacres?'

'Yes. You asked about her marriage. It is difficult even to guess why she married Alfred Meyer. Not because he is the big noise in Incorporated Playhouses. Carolyn had no need of that sort of pull. She had arrived. Perhaps she married him because he was so essentially commonplace. As a kind of set-off to her own temperament. She has the true artistic temperament.'

The tall man winced. Hambledon had made use of a phrase that he detested.

'Don't misunderstand me,' Hambledon continued very earnestly. 'Alf is a good fellow. He's very much liked in the business. But – well, he has never been a romantic figure. He lives for the firm, you know. He and George Mason built it between them. I've played in I.P.

productions for twelve years now. Eight pieces in all and in five of them I've played opposite Carolyn.'

He had the actor's habit of giving full dramatic value to everything he said. His beautiful voice, with its practised inflexions, suggested a romantic attachment.

'She's rather a wonderful person,' he said.

'He means that,' thought his companion. 'He is in love with her.'

His mind went back to the long voyage in the ship with Carolyn Dacres very much the star turn, but not, he had to admit, aggressively the great actress. She and her pale, plump, rather common, rather uninteresting husband, had sat in deck chairs, he with a portable typewriter on his knees and she with a book. Very often Hambledon had sat on the other side of her, also with a book. They had none of them joined in the all-night poker parties with young Courtney Broadhead, Liversidge and Valerie Gaynes. Thinking of these three he turned to look up the dim carriage. There was young Broadhead, still awake, still staring at the blind window-pane with its blank reflections. As if conscious of the other's gaze he jerked his head uneasily and with an abrupt movement rose to his feet and came down the carriage. As he passed them he said:

'Fresh air. I'm going out to the platform.'

'Young ass,' said Hambledon when he had gone through the door. 'He's been losing his money. You can't indulge in those sorts of frills, on his salary.'

They both looked at the glass door. Broadhead's back was against it.

'I'm worried about that boy,' Hambledon went on. 'No business of mine, of course, but one doesn't like to see that kind of thing.'

'They were playing high, certainly.'

'A fiver to come in, last night, I believe. I looked into the smoke-room before I went to bed. Liversidge had won a packet. Courtney looked very sick. Early in the voyage I tried to tip him the wink, but he'd got in with that bear leader and his cub.'

'Weston and young Palmer, you mean?'

'Yes. They're on the train. The cub's likely to stick to our heels all through the tour, I'm afraid.'

'Stage-struck?'

'What they used to call "shook on the pros." He hangs round Carolyn, I suppose you've noticed. She tells me his father – he's a Sir Something Palmer and noisomely rich – has packed him off to New Zealand with Weston in the hope of teaching him sense. Weston's his cousin. The boy was sacked from his public school, I believe. Shipboard gossip.'

'It is strange,' said the tall man, 'how a certain type of Englishman still regards the Dominions either as a waste-paper basket or a purge.'

'You are not a colonial, surely?'

'Oh, no. I speak without prejudice. Hullo, I believe we're stopping.'

A far-away whistle was followed by the sound of banging doors and a voice that chanted something indistinguishable. These sounds grew louder. Presently the far door of their own carriage opened and the guard came down the corridor.

'Five minutes at Ohakune for refreshments,' he chanted, and went out at the near door. Broadhead moved aside for him.

'Refreshments!' said Hambledon. 'Good lord!'

'Oh, I don't know. A cup of coffee, perhaps. Anyway a gulp of fresh air.'

'Perhaps you're right. *What* did he say was the name of the station?'

'I don't know. It sounded like a rune or incantation.'

'Oh – ah – coo – nee,' said Susan Max, unexpectedly.

'Hullo, Susie, you've come up to breathe, have you?' asked Hambledon.

'I haven't been to sleep, dear,' said Susan. Not really asleep, you know.'

'I'd forgotten you were an Australian.'

'I am not an Australian. I was born in New Zealand. Australia is a four-day journey from – '

'I know, I know,' said Hambledon with a wink at the tall man.

'Well, it *is* provoking, dear,' said Miss Max huffily. 'We don't like to be called Australian. Not that I've anything against the Aussies. It's the ignorance.'

A chain of yellow lights travelled past their windows. The train stopped and uttered a long steamy sigh. All along the carriage came the sound of human beings yawning and shuffling.

'I wish my father had never met my mother,' grumbled the comedian.

'Come on,' said Hambledon to the tall man.

They went out through the door. Courtney Broadhead was standing on the narrow iron platform of their carriage. His overcoat collar was turned up and his hat jammed over his eyes. He looked lost and miserable. The other two men stepped down on to the station platform. The cold night air smelt clean after the fug of the train. There was a tang in it, salutary and exciting.

'It smells like the inside of a flower shop,' said Hambledon. 'Moss, and cold wet earth, and something else. Are we very high up in the world, I wonder?'

'I think we must be. To me it smells like mountain air.'

'What about this coffee?'

They got two steaming china baths from the refreshment counter and took them out on to the platform.

'Hailey! Hailey!'

The window of one of the sleepers had been opened and through it appeared a head.

'Carolyn!' Hambledon walked swiftly to the window. 'Haven't you settled down yet? It's after half past two, do you know that?'

The murky lights from the station shone on that face, finding out the hollows round the eyes and under the cheek bones. The tall man had never been able to make up his mind about Carolyn Dacres's face. Was it beautiful? Was it faded? Was she as intelligent as her face seemed to promise? As he watched her he realized that she was agitated about something. She spoke quickly, and in an undertone. Hambledon stared at her in surprise and then said something. They both looked for a moment at the tall man. She seemed to hesitate.

'Stand clear, please.'

A bell jangled. He mounted the platform of his carriage where Courtney Broadhead still stood hunched up in his overcoat. The train gave one of those preparatory backward clanks. Hambledon, still carrying his cup, hurriedly mounted the far platform of the sleeper. They were drawn out of the station into the night. Courtney Broadhead, after a sidelong glance at the tall man, said something inaudible and returned to the carriage. The tall man remained outside. The stern of the sleeping-carriage in front swayed and wagged, and the little iron bridge that connected the two platforms jerked backwards and forwards. Presently Hambledon came out of the sleeper and, holding to the iron rails, made towards him over the bridge. As soon as they were together he began to shout:

'... very upset ... most extraordinary ... wish you'd ...' The wind snatched his voice away.

'I can't hear you.'

'It's Meyer – I can't make it out. Come over here.'

He led the way across the little bridge and drew his companion into the entrance lobby of the next carriage.

'It's Meyer,' said Hambledon. 'He says someone tried to murder him.'

CHAPTER 2

Mr Meyer in Jeopardy

The tall man merely stared at Hambledon who came to the conclusion that his astonishing announcement had not been heard.

'Someone has tried to murder Alfred Meyer,' he bawled.

'All right,' said the tall man. He looked disgusted and faintly alarmed.

'Carolyn wants you to come along to their sleeper.'

'You haven't told her – ?'

'No, no. But I wish you'd let me – '

The inside door of the little lobby burst open, smacking Hambledon in the rear. The pale face of Mr Alfred Meyer appeared round the side.

'Hailey – do come along. What are you – oh!' He glanced at the tall man.

'We are both coming,' said Hambledon.

They all lurched along the narrow corridor off which the two sleepers opened. They passed the first door and Meyer led them in at the second. The "de luxe" sleeper was a small cabin with two narrow bunks and a wash-basin. Carolyn Dacres, wearing some sort of gorgeous dressing-robe, sat on the bottom bunk. Her arms were clasped round her knees. Her long reddish-brown hair hung in a thick twist over her shoulder.

'Hullo!' she said, looking at the tall man. 'Hailey says he thinks you'd better hear all about it.'

'I'm sure you'd rather talk over whatever has happened among yourselves. I assure you I've no desire to butt in.'

243

'Look here,' said Hambledon, *'do* let me explain – about you, I mean.'

'Very well,' said the tall man, looking politely resigned.

'We all knew him as "Mr Allen" on board,' began Hambledon. 'That's what he was in the passenger list. It was only tonight, in the train, that I realized he was Roderick Alleyn – E-Y-N – Chief Detective-Inspector, CID, and full musical honours with a salute of two sawn-off shotguns.'

'My God!' said Mr Meyer plaintively. It was his stock expression.

'Why – ' said Carolyn Dacres, 'why then you're – yes, of course. "The Handsome Inspector." Don't you remember, Pooh? The Gardener case? Our photographs were side by side in the *Tatler* that week, Mr Alleyn.'

'The only occasion,' said Chief Detective-Inspector Alleyn, 'on which I have felt there was any compensation for newspaper publicity.'

'Any *compensation,*' broke in Mr Meyer. 'My God! Well now, as you are an expert, will you listen to this? Sit down for God's sake. Move up, Carol.'

Alleyn sat on a trunk, Hambledon on the floor, and Meyer plumped down beside his wife. His large face was very white and his fat hands shook slightly.

'I'm all upset,' he said.

'I'll try to explain,' said Miss Dacres. 'You see, Hailey darling – and Mr Alleyn – Alfie-Pooh sat up late. He had a lot of correspondence to get through, and he brought his typewriter in here. Some time before we got to the last station he thought he would go out to that shocking little platform for a breath of fresh air. Didn't you, darling?'

Mr Meyer nodded gloomily.

'We were at that time travelling up or down a thing that I think they call the corkscrew. The guard, who is an exceedingly nice man, and so, so well informed, told us all about it. It appears that this corkscrew – '

'Spiral,' corrected Mr Meyer.

'Yes, darling. This spiral is quite remarkable as railway lines go. One is continually catching one's own tail and the guard's wagon is quite often in front of the engine.'

'Really, Carolyn!' expostulated Hambledon.

'Something of the sort, darling. However, that is of no real importance as far as this story goes. The only thing we must all remember
is that when it is corkscrewing the train keeps on turning round and
round.'

'What can you mean?'

'Cut out the comedy, Carolyn,' begged Mr Meyer. 'This is serious.'

'Darling, *of course* it is. You see, Mr Alleyn, Alfie went out on the
little platform and stood there, and all the time the train kept turning corners very fast and it was all rather impressive. Alfie was very
excited and thrilled with the view, although it was so dark he could
not see much, except the other parts of the train corkscrewing above
and below him. He heard a door bang, but he did not look round
because he thought it was just someone going along the train. He
was holding on very tight with both hands. Luckily. Because otherwise when this person pushed him he would have – '

'Here!' said Mr Meyer firmly. 'I'll tell them. I was on the platform
facing outwards. I noticed the iron door to the steps was opened back
and there was nothing between me and God knows all. It was blowing a gale. I kind of knew people were going past me on their way
through the train, but I didn't look round. We came to one of these
hairpin-bends and as we swung round someone kicked me on the
behind. Hard. By God, I nearly went over. As nearly as damn it. I tell
you I lurched out over the step. I grabbed at the door with my left
hand, but I must have pulled it away from the catch on the wall as if
I was going through and shutting it after me. See what I mean? I
clutched the platform rail with my right hand – just caught it close to
the iron stanchion by the steps. It seemed to last a lifetime, that hanging outwards. Then the train swung round the opposite way and I got
back. Of course when I was all right again and turned round the man
had gone. God, I'm all to pieces. Look in that case there, Hailey.
There's a bottle of brandy.' He turned pale bulging eyes on Alleyn.

'What the hell do you make of that?'

'Extremely unpleasant,' said Alleyn.

'Unpleasant! Listen to him, will you!'

'My poor Alfie,' said his wife. 'You shall have quantities of brandy.
Pour it out, Hailey. There are glasses there, too. We shall all have
brandy while Mr Alleyn tells us who tried to assassinate my poor
Pooh. Don't spill it, Hailey. There! Now, Mr Alleyn?'

She looked up with an air of encouragement at the chief inspector. 'Is she being deliberately funny?' Alleyn wondered. 'She's not
really one of those vague women who sound like fools and are as
deep as you make them. Or is she? No, no, she's making a little
"cameo-part" of herself, for us to look at. Perhaps she has done it for
so long that she can't stop.'

'What I want to know is, what do I do?' Meyer was saying.

'Stop the train and tell the guard?' suggested Carolyn, sipping her
brandy. 'You pull the communication cord and pay five pounds and
then some woman comes forward and says you attempted to – '

'Carolyn, do be quiet,' begged Hambledon, smiling at her. 'What
do you think, Alleyn?'

'You are quite sure that you were deliberately kicked?' asked
Alleyn. 'It wasn't someone staggering along the train who lost
his balance and then his head, when he thought he'd sent you
overboard?'

'I tell you I was kicked. I bet you anything you like I've got a black
and blue behind.'

'Darling! We must put you in a cage and take you on tour.'

'What ought I to do, Alleyn?'

'My dear Mr Meyer, I – really I don't quite know. I suppose I
ought to tell you to inform the guard, and telegraph the police from
the next station. There are some very tight footballers farther along
the train. I wonder – '

'Of *course*,' said Carolyn with enthusiasm. 'How brilliant of you,
Mr Alleyn. It was a drunken footballer. I mean, it all fits in so splen-
didly, doesn't it? He would know how to kick. Think of the All
Blacks.'

Mr Meyer listened solemnly to this. Hambledon suddenly began
to laugh. Alleyn hurriedly lit a cigarette.

'It's all very well for you to laugh,' said Mr Meyer. He felt his stern
carefully, staring at Alleyn. 'I don't know about the police,' he said.
That'd mean the Press, and we've never gone in for that sort of
publicity. What do you think, Hailey? "Attempted Murder of Well-
known Theatrical Manager." It's not too good. It isn't as if it had
been Carolyn.'

'I should think not indeed,' agreed Hambledon with difficulty.

'So should I think not indeed,' said Carolyn.

'Mr Meyer,' said Alleyn, 'have you any enemies in your company?'

'Good God, no. We're a happy little family. I treat my people well and they respect me. There's never been a word.'

'You say that several people went past you while you were on the platform,' said Alleyn. 'Did you notice any of them in particular?'

'No. I stood with my back to the gangway.'

'Do you remember,' asked Alleyn after a pause, 'if there was anyone standing on the opposite platform, the one at this end of our carriage that was linked to yours by the iron bridge?'

'I don't think so. Not when I went out. Someone might have come out later. You know how it is – all dark and noisy and windy. I had my hat pulled down and my scarf up to my eyes. I simply stood with my back half turned to that platform looking out at the side.'

'How long was it before we got to the last station – Okahune?'

'I should think about half an hour.'

'What time was it,' Alleyn asked Hambledon, 'when I woke up and we began to talk? I looked at my watch, do you remember?'

'It was ten past two. Why?'

'Oh, nothing. We got to Okahune at two-forty-five.'

Hambledon glanced sharply at Alleyn. Carolyn yawned extensively and began to look pathetic.

'I'm sure you are longing for your beds,' said Alleyn. 'Come on, Hambledon.'

He got up and was about to say good night when there was a bang at the door.

'Mercy!' said Carolyn. 'What now? Surely they can't want to punch more holes in our tickets. Come in!' Valerie Gaynes burst into the little sleeper. She was dressed in a shiny trousered garment, covered with a brilliant robe, and looked like an advertisement for negligées in an expensive magazine. She made a little rush at Carolyn, waving her hands.

'I heard you talking and I simply *had* to come in. Please forgive me, darling Miss Dacres, but something rather awful has happened.'

'I know,' said Carolyn promptly, 'you have been kicked by a drunken footballer.'

Miss Gaynes stared at her.

'But why – ? No. It's something rather awkward. I've – I've been robbed.'

'Robbed? Pooh darling, this is a most extraordinary train. Do you hear what she says?'

'Isn't it too frightful? You see, after I had gone to bed – '

'Valerie,' interrupted Carolyn. 'You do know Mr Alleyn, don't you? It appears he is a famous detective, so he will be able to recover your jewels when he has caught Pooh's murderer. Really, it is very lucky you decided to come to New Zealand, Mr Alleyn.'

'I am glad you think so,' said Alleyn tonelessly. 'I'd be extremely grateful,' he added, 'if you kept my occupation a secret. Life's not worth living if one's travelling companions know one is a CID man.'

'Of course we will. It will be so much easier for you to discover Valerie's jewels if you're incog., won't it?'

'It's not jewels, it's money,' began Miss Gaynes. 'It's quite a lot of money. You see, Daddy gave me some English notes to change when I got to New Zealand because of the exchange, and I kept some of them out for the ship, and gave some of them to the purser, and the night before we landed I got them from the purser and – and – they were all right, and I – I – '

'Have some brandy?' invited Carolyn suddenly.

'Thank you. Daddy will be simply livid about it. You see, I can't remember when I last noticed I still had them. It's all terribly confusing. I put them in a leather folder thing in my suitcase when I got them from the purser.'

'That was a damn' silly thing to do,' said Mr Meyer gloomily.

'I suppose it was, but I'm awful about money. *Such* a fool. And, you see, this morning, before I shut the suitcase, I felt the folder and it rustled, so I thought, well, that's all right. And then, just now, I couldn't sleep in this frightful train, so I thought I'd write a letter, and I got out the folder and it was full of paper.'

'What sort of paper?' asked Carolyn, sleepily.

'Well, that's what makes me wonder if it's just a low joke someone's played on me.'

'Why?' asked Alleyn.

'Oh!' said Miss Gaynes impatiently, 'you must be *too* pure and clean-minded at Scotland Yard.'

Hambledon murmured something to Alleyn who said: 'Oh, I see.'

'It was the brand they had in the ship. I noticed that. I call that pretty good, don't you? I mean, to notice that. Do you think I'd make a sleuthess, Mr Alleyn? No, but really, isn't it a bore? *What* ought I to do? Of course I've got a letter of credit for Middleton, but after all one doesn't like being burgled.'

'Did you look at your folder, or whatever it was, after breakfast this morning?' asked Meyer suddenly.

'Er – no. No, I'm sure I didn't. Why?'

'How much was in it?'

'I'm not sure. Let me think. I used four – no, five pounds for tips and then I paid Frankie ten that I lost at – '

She stopped short, and a kind of blankness came into her eyes.

'Oh, what's the use, anyway,' she said. 'I suppose it was about ninety pounds. It's gone. And that's that. I mustn't keep you up, darling Miss Dacres.'

She made for the door. Alleyn opened it.

'If you would like to let me see the leather case – ' he said.

'Too sweet of you, but honestly I'm afraid the money's gone for good.'

'Well, I should let him see it,' said Carolyn, vaguely. 'He may be able to trace it directly to the murderous footballer.'

'*What* murderous footballer?'

'I'll tell you in the morning, Valerie. Good night, I'm so sorry about your money, but Mr Alleyn will find it for you as soon as he has time. We've all had quite enough excitement for one night. Let us curl up in our horrid little sleepers.'

'Good night,' said Miss Gaynes and went out.

Alleyn looked at Carolyn Dacres. She had shut her eyes as soon as Valerie Gaynes had gone. She now opened one of them. It was a large, carefully made-up eye, and it was fixed on Alleyn.

'Good night, Carol,' said Hambledon. "Night, Alf. Hope you get some sleep. Not much of the night left for it. Don't worry too much about your adventure.'

'Sleep!' ejaculated Mr Meyer. 'Worry! We get to Middleton in an hour. Scarcely worth trying. I can't lie down with any hope of comfort and *you'd* worry if someone tried to kick you off a train on the top of a mountain.'

'I expect I should. Coming, Alleyn?'

'Yes. Good night, Miss Dacres.'

'Good night,' said Carolyn in her deepest voice.

'So long,' said Mr Meyer bitterly. 'Sorry you've been troubled.'

Hambledon had already gone out into the little corridor, and Alleyn was in the doorway, when Carolyn stopped him.

'Mr Alleyn!'

He turned back. There she was, still looking at him out of one eye, like some attractive, drowsy, but intelligent bird.

'Why didn't Valerie want you to see the leather writing-folder?' asked Carolyn.

'I don't know,' said Alleyn. 'Do you?'

'I can make a damn' good guess,' said Carolyn.

CHAPTER 3

Off-stage

The Dacres Company arrived at Middleton in time for breakfast. By ten o'clock the stage staff had taken possession of the Theatre Royal. To an actor on tour all theatres are very much alike. They may vary in size, in temperature, and in degree of comfort, but once the gas-jets are lit in the dressing-rooms, the grease-paints laid out in rows on the shelves, and the clothes hung up in sheets on the walls, all theatres are simply 'theatre'. The playhouse is the focus-point of the company. As soon as an actor has 'found a home', and, if possible, enjoyed a rest, he goes down to the theatre and looks to the tools of his trade. The stage-manager is there with his staff, cursing or praising the mechanical facilities behind the curtain. The familiar flats are trundled in, the working lights are on, the prompter's table stands down by the footlights and the sheeted stalls wait expectantly in the dark auditorium.

Soon the drone of the run-through-for-words begins. Mechanics peer from the flies and move, rubber-footed, about the stage. The theatre is alive, self-contained and warm with preparation.

The Royal, at Middleton, was a largish playhouse. It seated a thousand, had a full stage and a conservative but adequate system of lighting and of overhead galleries, grid, and ropes. Ted Gascoigne, who was used to the West End, sniffed a little at the old-fashioned lighting. They had brought a special switchboard and the electrician morosely instructed employees of the local power-board in its mysteries.

At ten o'clock Carolyn and her company were all asleep or breakfasting in their hotels. Carolyn, Valerie Gaynes, Liversidge, Mason

251

and Hambledon stayed at the Middleton, the most expensive of these drear establishments. For the rest of the company, the splendour of their lodgings was in exact ratio to the amount of their salaries, from Courtney Broadhead at The Commercial down to Tommy Biggs, the least of the staff, at 'Mrs Harbottle, Good Beds'.

George Mason, the manager, had not gone to bed. He had shaved, bathed, and changed his clothes, and by ten o'clock, uneasy with chronic dyspepsia, sat in the office at The Royal talking to the 'advance', a representative of the Australian firm under whose auspices the company was on tour.

'It's going to be big, Mr Mason,' said the advance. 'We're booked out downstairs, and only fifty seats left in the circle. There's a queue for early-door tickets. I'm very pleased.'

'Good enough,' said Mason. 'Now listen.'

They talked. The telephone rang incessantly. Box-office officials came in, the local manager of the theatre, three slightly self-conscious reporters, and finally Mr Alfred Meyer, carrying a cushion. This he placed on the swivel chair, and then cautiously lowered himself on to it.

'Well, Alf,' said Mason.

"Morning, George,' said Mr Meyer.

Mason introduced the Australian advance, who instantly seized Mr Meyer's hand in a grip of iron and shook it with enthusiasm.

'I'm very glad to meet you, Mr Meyer.'

'How do you do?' said Mr Meyer. 'Good news for us, I hope?'

The reporters made tentative hovering movements.

'These gentlemen are from the Press,' said Mason. 'They'd like to have a little chat with you, Alf.'

Mr Meyer rolled his eyes round and became professionally cordial.

'Oh, yes, yes,' he said, 'certainly. Come over here, gentlemen, will you?'

The advance hurriedly placed three chairs in a semi-circle close to Meyer, and joined Mason, who had withdrawn tactfully to the far end of the room.

The reporters cleared their throats and handled pads and pencils.

'Well now, what about it?' asked Mr Meyer helpfully.

'Er,' said the oldest of the reporters, 'just a few points that would interest our readers, Mr Meyer.'

He spoke in a soft gruff voice with a slight accent. He seemed a very wholesome and innocent young man.

'Certainly,' said Mr Meyer. 'By God, this is a wonderful country of yours . . . '

The reporters wrote busily the outlines for an article which would presently appear under the headline: 'Praise for New Zealand: An Enthusiastic Visitor.'

II

Two young men and a woman appeared in the office doorway. They were Australians who had travelled over to join the company for the second piece, and now reported for duty. Mason took them along to the stage-door, pointed out Gascoigne, who was in heated argument with the head mechanist, and left them to make themselves known.

The stock scene was being struck. The fluted columns and gilded walls of all stock scenes fell forward as softly as leaves, and were run off into the dock. An Adam drawing-room, painted by an artist, and in excellent condition, was shoved together like a gigantic house of cards and tightened at the corners. Rack, flack, went the toggles as the stagehands laced them over the wooden cleats.

'We don't want those borders,' said Gascoigne.

'Kill the borders, Bert,' said the head mechanist, loudly.

'Kill the borders,' repeated a voice up in the flies. The painted strips that masked the overhead jerked out of sight one by one.

'Now the ceiling cloth.'

Outside in the strange town a clock chimed and struck eleven. Members of the cast began to come in and look for their dressing-rooms. They were called for eleven-thirty. Gascoigne saw the Australians and crossed the stage to speak to them. He began talking about their parts. He manner was pleasant and friendly, and the Australians, who were on the defensive about English importations, started to thaw. Gascoigne told them where they were to dress. He checked himself to shout:

'You'll have to clear, Fred; I want the stage in ten minutes.'

'I'm not ready for you, Mr Gascoigne.'

'By – you'll have to be ready. What's the matter with you?'

He walked back to the stage. From up above came the sound of sawing.

Gascoigne glared upwards.

'What are you *doing* up there?'

An indistinguishable mumbling answered him.

Gascoigne turned to the head mechanic.

'Well, you'll have to knock off in ten minutes, Fred. I've got a show to rehearse with people who haven't worked for four weeks. And we go up tonight. Tonight! Do you think we can work in a sawmill. What is he *doing?*'

'He's fixing the mast,' said the head mechanic. 'It's got to be done, Mr Gascoigne. This bloody stage isn't – '

He went off into mechanical details. The second act was staged on board a yacht. The setting was elaborate. The lower end of a mast with 'practical' rope ladders had to be fixed. This was all done from overhead. Gascoigne and the head mechanic stared up into the flies.

'We've flied the mast,' said the mechanic, 'and it's too long for this stage, see. Bert's fixing it. Have you got the weight on, Bert?'

As if in answer, a large black menace flashed between them. There was a nerve-shattering thud, a splintering of wood, and a cloud of dust. At their feet lay a long object rather like an outsize in sash-weights.

Gascoigne and the mechanic instantly flew into the most violent of rages. Their faces were sheet-white and their knees shook. At the tops of their voices they apostrophized the hidden Bert, inviting him to come down and be half killed. Their oaths died away into a shocked silence. Mason had run round from the office, the company had hurried out of the dressing-rooms and were clustered in the entrances. The unfortunate Bert came down from the grid and stood gaping in horror at his handiwork.

'Gawdstreuth, Mr Gascoigne, I don't know how it happened. Gawdstreuth, Mr Gascoigne, I'm sorry. Gawdstreuth.'

'Shut your – face,' suggested the head mechanic, unprintably. 'Do you want to go to gaol for manslaughter?'

'Don't you know the first – rule about working in the flies? Don't you know – ?'

Mason went back to the office. One by one the company returned to their dressing-rooms.

III

'And what,' said the oldest of the three reporters, 'is your opinion of our railroads, Mr Meyer? How do they compare with those in the Old Country?'

Mr Meyer shifted uncomfortably on his cushion and his hand stole round to his rear.

'I think they're marvellous,' he said.

IV

Hailey Hambledon knocked on Carolyn's door.

'Are you ready, Carol? It's a quarter past.'

'Come in, darling.'

He went into the bedroom she shared with Meyer. It looked exactly like all their other bedrooms on tour. There was the wardrobe trunk, the brilliant drape on the bed, Carolyn's photos of Meyer, of herself, and of her father, the parson in Bucks. And there, on the dressing-table, was her complexion in its scarlet case. She was putting the final touches to her lovely face and nodded to him in the looking-glass.

'Good morning, Mrs Meyer,' said Hambledon and kissed her fingers with the same light gesture he had so often used on the stage.

'Good morning, Mr Hambledon.' They spoke with that unnatural and half-ironical gaiety that actors so often assume when greeting each other outside the theatre.

Carolyn turned back to her mirror.

'I'm getting very set-looking, Hailey. Older and older.'

'I don't think so.'

'Don't you? I expect you do, really. You think to yourself sometimes: "It won't be long before she is too old for such-and-such a part." '

'No. I love you. To me you do not change.'

'Darling! So sweet! Still, we do grow older.'

'Then why, why, why not make the most of what's left? Carol – do you really believe you love me?'

'You're going to have another attack. Don't.'

She got up and put on her hat, giving him a comically apprehensive look from under the brim. 'Come along now,' she said.

He shrugged his shoulders and opened the door for her. They went out, moving beautifully, with years of training behind their smallest gestures. It is this unconscious professionalism in the everday actions of actors that so often seems unreal to outsiders. When they are very young actors, it often is unreal, when they are older it is merely habit. They are indeed 'always acting', but not in the sense that their critics suggest.

Carolyn and Hambledon went down in the lift and through the lounge towards the street door. Here they ran into Chief Detective-Inspector Alleyn, who was also staying at the Middleton.

'Hullo!' said Carolyn. 'Have you been out already? You *are* an early one.'

'I've been for a tram ride up to the top of those hills. Do you know, the town ends quite suddenly about four miles out, and you are on grassy hills with little bits of bush and the most enchanting view.'

'It sounds delicious,' said Carolyn vaguely.

'No,' said Alleyn, 'it's more exciting than that. How is your husband this morning?'

'Still very cross, poor sweet. And black and blue, actually, just as he prophesied. It *must* have been a footballer. Are you coming to the show tonight?'

'I want to, but, do you know, I can't get a seat.'

'Oh, nonsense. Alfie-Pooh will fix you up. Remind me to ask him, Hailey darling.'

'Right,' said Hambledon. 'We ought to get along, Carol.'

'Work, work, work,' said Carolyn, suddenly looking tragic. 'Goodbye, Mr Alleyn. Come round to my dressing-room after the show.'

'And to mine,' said Hambledon. 'I want to know what you think of the piece. So long.'

'Thank you so much. Goodbye,' said Alleyn.

'*Nice* man,' said Carolyn when they had gone a little way.

'Very nice indeed. Carol, you've got to listen to me, please. I've loved you with shameless constancy for – how long? Five years?'

'Surely a little longer than that, darling. I fancy it's six. It was during the run of *Scissors to Grind* at the Criterion. Don't you remember – '

'Very well – six. You say you're fond of me – love me – '

'Oughtn't we to cross over here?' interrupted Carolyn. 'Pooh said the theatre was down that street, surely. Oh, do be careful!' She gave a little scream. Hambledon, exasperated, had grasped her by the elbow and was hurrying her across a busy intersection.

'I'm coming to your dressing-room as soon as we get there,' he said angrily, 'and I'm going to have it out with you.'

'It would certainly be a better spot than the footpath,' agreed Carolyn. 'As my poor Pooh would say, there is a right and wrong kind of publicity.'

'For God's sake,' said Hambledon, between clenched teeth, 'stop talking to me about your husband.'

V

Before going to the theatre young Courtney Broadhead called in at the Middleton and asked for Mr Gordon Palmer. He was sent up to Mr Palmer's rooms, where he found that young man still in bed and rather white about the gills. His cousin and mentor, Geoffrey West, sat in an arm-chair by the window, and Mr Francis Liversidge lolled across the end of the bed smoking a cigarette. He, too, had dropped in to see Gordon on his way to rehearsal it seemed.

The cub, as Hambledon had called Gordon Palmer, was seventeen years old, dreadfully sophisticated, and entirely ignorant of everything outside the sphere of his sophistication. He had none of the awkwardness of youth and very little of its vitality, being restless rather than energetic, acquisitive rather than ambitious. He was good-looking in a raffish, tarnished sort of fashion. It was entirely in keeping with his character that he should have attached himself to the Dacres Comedy Company and, more particularly, to Carolyn Dacres herself. That Carolyn paid not the smallest attention to him made little difference. With Liversidge and Valerie he was a great success.

'Hullo, Court, my boy,' said Gordon. 'Treat me gently. I'm a wreck this morning. Met some ghastly people on that train last night. What a night! We played poker till – when was it, Geoffrey?'

'Until far too late,' said Weston calmly. 'You were a young fool.'

'He thinks he has to talk like that to me,' explained Gordon. 'He does it rather well, really. What's your news, Court?'

'I've come to pay my poker debts,' said Courtney. He drew out his wallet and took some notes from it. 'Yours is here too, Frankie.' He laughed unhappily. 'Take it while you can.'

'That's all fine and handy,' said Gordon carelessly. 'I'd forgotten all about it.'

VI

Mr Liversidge poked his head in at the open office door. He did not come on until the second act, and had grown tired of hanging round the wings while Gascoigne thrashed out a scene between Valerie Gaynes, Ackroyd, and Hambledon. Mr Meyer was alone in the office.

'Good morning, sir,' said Liversidge.

"Morning, Mr Liversidge,' said Meyer, swinging round in his chair and staring owlishly at his first juvenile. 'Want to see me?'

'I've just heard of your experience on the train last night,' began Liversidge, 'and looked in to ask how you were. It's an outrageous business. I mean to say – !'

'Quite,' said Meyer shortly. 'Thanks very much.'

Liversidge airily advanced a little farther into the room.

'And poor Val, losing all her money. Quite a chapter of calamities.'

'It was,' said Mr Meyer.

'Quite a decent pub, the Middleton, isn't it, sir?'

'Quite,' said Mr Meyer again. There was an uncomfortable pause. 'You seem to be in funds,' remarked Mr Meyer suddenly.

Liversidge laughed melodiously. 'I've been saving a bit lately. We had a long run in Town with the show, didn't we? A windfall this morning, too.' He gave Meyer a quick sidelong glance. 'Courtney paid up his poker debts. I didn't expect to see *that* again, I must say. Last night he was all down-stage and tragic.'

'Shut that door,' said Mr Meyer. 'I want to talk to you.'

VII

Carolyn and Hambledon faced each other across the murky half-light of the star dressing-room. Already, most of the wicker baskets had been unpacked, and the grease-paints laid out on their trays. The room had a grey, cellar-like look about it and smelt of cosmetics. Hambledon switched on the light and it instantly became warm and intimate.

'Now, listen to me,' he said.

Carolyn sat on one of the wicker crates and gazed at him. He took a deep breath.

'You're as much in love with me as you ever will be with anyone. You don't love Alfred. Why you married him I don't believe even God knows, and I'm damn' certain you don't. I don't ask you to live with me on the quiet, with everyone knowing perfectly well what's happening. That sort of arrangement would be intolerable to both of us. I do ask you to come away with me at the end of this tour and let Alfred divorce you. Either that, or tell him how things are between us and give him the chance of arranging it the other way.'

'Darling, we've had this out so often before.'

'I know we have but I'm at the end of my tether. I can't go on seeing you every day, working with you, being treated as though I was – what? A cross between a tame cat and a schoolboy. I'm forty-nine, Carol, and I – I'm starved. Why won't you do this for both of us?'

'Because I'm a Catholic.'

'You're not a good Catholic. I sometimes think you don't care tuppence about your religion. How long is it since you've been to church or confession or whatever it is? Ages. Then why stick at this?'

'It's my Church sticking to me. Bits of it always stick. I'd feel I was wallowing in sin, darling, truthfully I would.'

'Well, wallow. You'd get used to it.'

'Oh, Hailey!' She broke out into soft laughter, but warm soft laughter that ran like gold through every part she played.

'Don't!' said Hambledon. 'Don't!'

'I'm so sorry, Hailey. I am a pig. I do adore you, but, darling, I can't – simply can't live in sin with you. Living in sin. Living in sin,' chanted Carolyn dreamily.

'You're hopeless,' said Hambledon. 'Hopeless!'

'Miss Dacres, please,' called a voice in the passage.

'Here!'

'We're just coming to your entrance, please, Mr Gascoigne says.'

'I'll be there,' said Carolyn. 'Thank you.' She got up at once.

'You're on in a minute, darling,' she said to Hambledon.

'I suppose,' said Hambledon with a violence that in spite of himself was half whimsically-rueful, 'I suppose I'll have to wait for Alf to die of a fatty heart. Would you marry me then, Carol?'

'What is it they all say in this country? *"Too right." Too right* I would, darling. But, poor Pooh! A fatty heart! Too unkind.' She slipped through the door.

A moment or two later he heard her voice, pitched and telling, as she spoke her opening line.

' "Darling, what do you think! He's asked me to marry him!" ' And then those peals of soft warm laughter.

CHAPTER 4

First Appearance of the Tiki

The curtain rose for the fourth time. Carolyn Dacres, standing in the centre of the players, bowed to the stalls, to the circle and, with the friendly special smile, to the gallery. One thousand pairs of hands were struck together over and over again, making a sound like hail on an iron roof. New Zealand audiences are not given to cheering. If they are pleased they sit still and clap exhaustively. They did so now, on the third and final performance of Ladies of Leisure. Carolyn bowed and bowed with an air of enchanted deprecation. She turned to Hailey Hambledon, smiling. He stepped out of the arc and came down to the footlights. He assumed the solemnly earnest expression of all leading actors who are about to make a speech. The thousand pairs of hands redoubled their activities. Hambledon smiled warningly. The clapping died away.

'Ladies and gentlemen,' began Hambledon reverently, 'Miss Dacres has asked me to try and express something of our' – he looked up to the gallery – 'our gratitude, for the wonderful reception you have given the first play of our short' – he looked into the stalls – 'our all *too* short season in your beautiful city.' He paused. Another tentative outbreak from the audience. 'This is our first visit to New Zealand, and Middleton is the first town we have played. Our season in this lovely country of yours is, of necessity, a brief one. We go on to – to – ' he paused and turned helplessly to his company. 'Wellington,' said Carolyn. 'To Wellington, on Friday. Tomorrow, Wednesday and Thursday we play *The Jack Pot*, a comedy which we had the honour of presenting at the Criterion Theatre in London.

Most of the original cast is still with us, and, in addition, three well-known Australian artists have joined us for this piece. May I also say that we have among us a New Zealand actress who returns to her native country after a distinguished career on the London stage – Miss Susan Max.' He turned to old Susan, who gave him a startled look of gratitude. The audience applauded vociferously. Old Susan, with shining eyes, bowed to the house and then, charmingly, to Hambledon.

'Miss Dacres, the company, and I, are greatly moved by the marvellous welcome you have given us. I – I may be giving away a secret, but I am going to tell you that today is her birthday.' He held up his hand. 'This is her first visit to Middleton; I feel we cannot do better than wish her many happy returns. Thank you all very much.'

Another storm of hail, a deep curtsy from Carolyn. Hambledon glanced up into the OP corner, and the curtain came down.

'And God forbid that I should ever come back,' muttered little Ackroyd disagreeably.

Susan Max, who was next to him, ruffled like an indignant hen.

'You'd rather have the provinces, I suppose, Mr Ackroyd,' she said briskly.

Old Brandon Vernon chuckled deeply. Ackroyd raised his comic eyebrows and inclined his head several times. 'Ho-ho. *Ho-ho*!' he sneered. 'We're all touchy and upstage about our native land, are we!'

Susan plodded off to her dressing-room. In the passage she ran into Hailey Hambledon.

'Thank you, dear,' said Susan. 'I didn't expect it, but it meant a lot.'

'That's all right, Susie,' said Hambledon. 'Go and make yourself lovely for the party.'

Carolyn's birthday was to be celebrated. Out on the stage the hands put up a trestle-table and covered it with a white cloth. Flowers were massed down the centre. Glasses, plates, and quantities of food were arrayed on lines that followed some impossible standard set by a Hollywood super-spectacle, tempered by the facilities offered by the Middleton Hotel, which had undertaken the catering. Mr Meyer had spent a good deal of thought and more money on this party. It was, he said, to be a party suitable to his wife's position as the foremost English comedienne, and it had been planned with one eye on the Press and half the other on the box-office. The *pièce de résistance* was to be in the nature of a surprise for Carolyn and the guests, though one by one, he had taken the members of his company into his confidence. He had brought from England a jeroboam of champagne – a fabulous, a monstrous bottle of a famous vintage. All the afternoon, Ted Gascoigne and the stage hands had laboured under Mr Meyer's guidance and with excited suggestions from George Mason. The giant bottle was suspended in the flies with a counterweight across the pulley. A crimson cord from the counterweight came down to the stage and was anchored to the table. At the climax of her party, Carolyn was to cut this cord. The counterweight would then rise and the jeroboam slowly descend into a nest of maiden-hair fern and exotic flowers, that was to be held, by Mr Meyer himself, in the centre of the table. He had made them rehearse it twelve times that day and was in a fever of excitement that the performance should go without a hitch. Now he kept darting on to the stage and gazing anxiously up into the flies, where the jeroboam hung, invisible, awaiting its big entrance. The shaded lamps used on the stage were switched on. With the heavy curtain for the fourth wall, the carpet and the hangings on the set, it was intimate and pleasant.

A little group of guests came in from the stage-door. A large vermilion-faced, pleasant-looking man, who was a station-holder twenty miles out in the country. His wife, broad, a little weather-beaten, well dressed, but not very smart. Their daughter, who was extremely smart, and their son, an early print of his father. They had called on Carolyn, who had instantly asked them to her party, forgotten she had done so, and neglected to warn anybody of their arrival. Gascoigne, who received them, looked nonplussed for a moment, and then, knowing his Carolyn, guessed what had happened. They were followed by Gordon Palmer, registering familiarity with backstage, and his cousin, Geoffrey Weston.

'Hullo, George,' said Gordon. 'Perfectly marvellous. Great fun. Carolyn was too thrilling, wasn't she? I must see her. Where is she?'

'Miss Dacres is changing,' said Ted Gascoigne, who had dealt with generations of Gordon Palmers.

'But I simply can't wait another *second*,' protested Gordon in a high-pitched voice.

'Afraid you'll have to,' said Gascoigne. 'May I introduce Mr Gordon Palmer, Mr Weston, Mrs – mumble-mumble.'

'Forrest,' said the broad lady cheerfully. With the pathetic faith of most colonial ladies in the essential niceness of all young Englishmen, she instantly made friendly advances. Her husband and son looked guarded and her daughter alert.

More guests arrived, among them a big brown man with a very beautiful voice – Dr Rangi Te Pokiha, a Maori physician, who was staying at the Middleton.

Alleyn came in with Mason and Alfred Meyer, who had given him a box, and greeted him, after a final glance at the supper-table. They made a curious contrast. The famous Mr Meyer, short, pasty, plump, exuded box-office and front-of-the-house from every pearl button in his white waistcoat. The famous policeman, six inches taller, might have been a diplomat. 'Magnificent appearance,' Meyer had said to Carolyn. 'He'd have done damn' well if he'd taken to "the business".'

One by one the members of the company came out from their dressing-rooms. Most actors have an entirely separate manner for occasions when they mix with outsiders. This separate manner is not so much an affectation as a *persona*, a mask used for this particular appearance. They wish to show how like other people they are. It is an innocent form of snobbishness. You have only to see them when the last guest has gone to realize how complete a disguise the *persona* may be.

Tonight they were all being very grown-up. Alfred Meyer introduced everybody, carefully. He introduced the New Zealanders to each other, the proprietor and proprietress of the Middleton to the station-holder and his family, who of course knew them perfectly well *de haut en bas*.

Carolyn was the last to appear.

'Where's my wife?' asked Meyer of everybody at large. 'It's ten to. Time she was making an entrance.'

'Where's Carolyn?' complained Gordon Palmer loudly.

'Where's *Madame?*' shouted George Mason jovially.

Led by Meyer, they went to find out.

Alleyn, who, with Mason, had joined Hambledon, wondered if she was instinctively or intentionally delaying her entrance. His

previous experience of leading ladies had been a solitary professional one, and he had very nearly lost his heart. He wondered if by any
chance he was going to do so again.

At last a terrific rumpus broke out in the passage that led to the
dressing-rooms. Carolyn's golden laugh. Carolyn saying 'O-o-oh!' like
a sort of musical train whistle. Carolyn sweeping along with three
men in her wake. The double doors of the stage-set were thrown open
by little Ackroyd, who announced like a serio-comic butler:

'Enter *Madame!*'

Carolyn curtsying to the floor and rising like a moth to greet guest
after guest. She had indeed made an entrance, but she had done it
so terrifically, so deliberately, with a kind of twinkle in her eye, that
Alleyn found himself uncritical and caught up in the warmth of
her famous 'personality'. When at last she saw him, and he awaited
that moment impatiently, she came towards him with both hands
outstretched and eyes like stars. Alleyn rose to the occasion, bent his
long back, and kissed each of the hands. The Forrest family goggled
at this performance, and Miss Forrest looked more alert than ever.

'A-a-ah!' said Carolyn with another of her melodious hoots.
'My distinguished friend. The famous – '

'No, no!' exclaimed Alleyn hastily.

'Why not! I insist on everybody knowing I've got a lion at my
party.'

She spoke in her most ringing stage voice. Everybody turned to
listen to her. In desperation Alleyn hurriedly lugged a small packet
out of of his pocket and, with another bow, put it into her hands.
'I'm making a walloping great fool of myself,' he thought.

'A birthday card,' he said. 'I hope you'll allow me – '

Carolyn, who had already received an enormous number of
expensive presents, instantly gazed about her with an air of flabbergasted delight that suggested the joy of a street waif receiving a
five-pound note.

'It's for *me!*' she cried. 'For *me*, for *me*, for *me.*' She looked brilliantly at Alleyn and at her guests. 'You'll all have to wait. It must be
opened now. Quick! Quick!' She wriggled her fingers and tore at the
paper with excited squeaks.

'Good lord,' thought Alleyn, 'how does she get away with it? In
any other woman it would be nauseating.'

His gift was at last freed from its wrappings. A small green object appeared. The surface was rounded and graven into the semblance of a squat figure with an enormous lolling head and curved arms and legs. The face was much formalized, but it had a certain expression of grinning malevolence. Carolyn gazed at it in delighted bewilderment.

'But what is it? It's jade. It's wonderful – but – ?'

'It's greenstone,' said Alleyn.

'It is a tiki, Miss Dacres,' said a deep voice. The Maori, Dr Rangi Te Pokiha, came forward, smiling. Carolyn turned to him. 'A tiki?'

'Yes. And a very beautiful one, if I may say so.' He glanced at Alleyn.

'Dr Te Pokiha was good enough to find it for me,' explained Alleyn.

'I want to know about – all about it,' insisted Carolyn.

Te Pokiha began to explain. He was gravely explicit, and the Forrests looked embarrassed. The tiki is a Maori symbol. It brings good fortune to its possessor. It represents a human embryo and is the symbol of fecundity. In the course of a conversation with Te Pokiha at the hotel Alleyn had learned that he had this tiki to dispose of for a *pakeha* – a white man – who was hard-up. Te Pokiha had said that if it had been his own possession he would never have parted with it, but the *pakeha was* very hard-up. The tiki was deposited at the museum where the curator would vouch for its authenticity. Alleyn, on an impulse, had gone to look at it and had bought it. On another impulse he had decided to give it to Carolyn. She was enthralled by this story, and swept about showing the tiki to everybody. Gordon Palmer, who had sent up half a florist's shop, glowered sulkily at Alleyn out of the corners of his eyes. Meyer, obviously delighted with Alleyn's gift to his wife, took the tiki to a lamp to examine it more closely.

'It's lucky, is it?' he asked eagerly.

'Well you heard what he said, governor,' said old Brandon Vernon. 'A symbol of fertility, wasn't it? If you call that luck!'

Meyer hastily put the tiki down, crossed his thumbs and began to bow to it.

'O tiki-tiki be good to little Alfie,' he chanted. 'No funny business, now, no funny business.'

Ackroyd said something in an undertone. There was a guffaw from one or two of the men. Ackroyd, with a smirk, took the tiki from Meyer. Old Vernon and Mason joined the group.

Their faces coarsened into half-smiles. The tiki went from hand to hand, and there were many loud gusts of laughter. Alleyn looked at Te Pokiha who walked across to him.

'I half regret my impulse,' said Alleyn quietly.

'Oh,' said Te Pokiha pleasantly, 'it seems amusing to them naturally.' He paused and then added: 'So may my great grandparents have laughed over the first crucifix they saw.'

Carolyn began to relate the story of Meyer's adventure on the train. Everybody turned to listen to her. The laughter changed its quality and became gay and then helpless. Meyer allowed himself to be her foil, protesting comically.

She suddenly commanded everyone to supper. There were place-cards on the table. Alleyn found himself on Carolyn's right with Mrs Forrest, for whom a place had been hurriedly made, on his other side.

Carolyn and Meyer sat opposite each other halfway down the long trestle-table. The nest of maiden-hair fern and exotic flowers was between them, and the long red cord ran down to Carolyn's right and was fastened under the ledge of the table. She instantly asked what it was there for, and little Meyer's fat white face became pink with conspiracy and excitement.

It was really a very large party. Twelve members of the company, as many more guests, and the large staff, whom Carolyn had insisted on having and who sat at a separate table, dressed in their best suits and staring self-consciously at each other. Candles had been lit all down the length of the tables and the lamps turned out. It was all very gay and festive.

When they were settled Meyer, beaming complacently, rose and looked round the table.

'Ladies and gentlemen,' said Meyer, 'I suppose this is quite the wrong place for a speech, but we can't have anything to drink till I've made it, so I don't need to apologize.'

'Certainly not' – from Mason.

'In a minute or two I shall ask you to drink the health of the loveliest woman and the greatest actress of the century – my wife.'

'Golly!' thought Alleyn. Cheers from everybody.

'But before you do this we've got to find something for you to drink it in. There doesn't appear to be anything on the table,' said Meyer, with elaborate nonchalance, 'but we are told that the gods will provide so I propose to leave it to them. Our stage-manager tells me that something may happen if this red cord here is cut. I shall therefore ask my wife to cut it. She will find a pair of shears by her plate.'

'Darling!' said Carolyn. '*What* is all this? Too exciting. I shan't cause it to rain fizz, shall I? Like Moses. Or was it Moses?'

She picked up the enormous scissors. Alfred Meyer bent his fat form over the table and stretched out his short arms to the nest of fern. A fraction of a second before Carolyn closed the blades of the scissors over the cord, her husband touched a hidden switch. Tiny red and green lights sprang up beneath the fern and flowers, into which the jeroboam was to fall and over which Meyer was bending.

Everyone had stopped talking. Alleyn, in the sudden silence, received a curious impression of eager dimly-lit faces that peered, of a beautiful woman standing with one arm raised, holding the scissors as a lovely Atropos might hold aloft her shears, of a fat white-waistcoated man like a Blampied caricature, bent over the table, and of a red cord that vanished upwards into the dark. Suddenly he felt intolerably oppressed, aware of a suspense out of all proportion to the moment. So strong was this impression that he half rose from his chair.

But at that moment Carolyn cut through the cord.

Something enormous that flashed down among them, jolting the table. Valerie Gaynes screaming. Broken glass and the smell of champagne. Champagne flowing over the white cloth. A thing like an enormous billiard ball embedded in the fern. Red in the champagne. And Valerie Gaynes, screaming, screaming. Carolyn, her arm still raised, looking down. Himself, his voice, telling them to go away, telling Hambledon to take Carolyn away.

'Take her away, take her away.'

And Hambledon: 'Come away. Carolyn, come away.'

CHAPTER 5

Intermezzo

'No, don't move him,' said Alleyn.

He laid a hand on Hambledon's arm. Dr Te Pokiha, his bronze fingers still touching the top of Meyer's head, looked fixedly at Alleyn.

'Why not?' asked Hambledon.

George Mason raised his head. Ever since they had got rid of the others Mason had sat at the end of the long table with his face buried in his arms. Ted Gascoigne stood beside Mason. He repeated over and over again:

'It was as safe as houses. Someone's monkeyed with it. We rehearsed it twelve times this morning. I tell you there's been some funny business, George. My God, there's been some funny business.'

'Why not?' repeated Hambledon. 'Why not move him?'

'Because,' said Alleyn, 'Mr Gascoigne may be right.'

George Mason spoke for the first time.

'But who'd want to hurt him? Old Alf! He hasn't an enemy in the world.' He turned a woebegone face to Te Pokiha.

'You're sure, Doctor, he's – he's – gone?'

'You can see for yourself, Mr Mason,' said Te Pokiha; 'the neck is broken.'

'I don't want to,' said Mason, looking sick.

'What ought we to do?' asked Gascoigne. They all turned to Alleyn. 'Do I exude CID?' wondered Alleyn to himself, 'or has Hambledon blown the gaff?'

'I'm afraid you must ring up the nearest police station,' he said aloud. There was an instant outcry from Gascoigne and Mason.

'Good God, the police!'

'What the hell!'

' . . . but it was an accident!'

'That'd be finish!'

'I'm afraid Mr Alleyn's right,' said Te Pokiha; 'it is a matter for the police. If you like I'll ring up. I know the superintendent in Middleton.'

'While you're about it,' said Mason with desperate irony, 'you might ring up a shipping office. As far as this tour's concerned – '

'Finish!' said Gascoigne.

'We've got to do something about it, Ted,' said Hambledon quietly.

'We built it up between us,' said Mason suddenly. 'When I first met Alf he was advancing a No. 4 company in St Helens. I was selling tickets for the worst show in England. We never looked back. We've never had a nasty word, never. And look at the business we've built up.' His lips trembled. 'By God, if someone's killed him – you're right, Hailey. I'm – I'm all anyhow – you fix it, Ted. I'm all anyhow.'

Dr Te Pokiha looked at him.

'How about joining the others, Mr Mason? Perhaps a whisky would be a good idea. Your office – ?'

Mason got to his feet and came down to the centre of the table. He looked at what was left of Alfred Meyer's head, buried among the fern and broken fairy lights, wet with champagne and with blood. The two fat white hands still grasped the edges of the nest.

'God!' said Mason. 'Do we have to leave him like that?'

'It will only be for a little while,' said Alleyn gently. 'I should let Dr Te Pokiha take you to the office.'

'Alf,' murmured Mason. 'Old Alf!' He stood there, his lips shaking, his face ugly with suppressed emotion. Alleyn, who was accustomed to scenes of this sort, was conscious of his familiar daemon which took little at face value, and observed so much. The daemon prompted him to notice how unembarrassed Gascoigne and Hambledon were by Mason's emotion, how they had assumed so easily a mood of sorrowful correctness, almost as if they had rehearsed the damn' scene, and the daemon.

They got Mason away. Te Pokiha went with him and said he would ring up the police. The unfortunate Bert, the stage-hand who had rigged the tackle under Meyer's and Gascoigne's directions, was hanging about in the wings and now came on the stage. He began to explain the mechanics of the champagne stunt to Alleyn.

'It was like this 'ere. We fixed the rope over the pulley, see, and on one end we fixed the bloody bottle and on the other end we hooked the bloody weight. The weight was one of them corner weights we used for the bloody funnels.'

'Ease up on the language, Bert,' suggested Gascoigne moodily.

'Good-oh, Mr Gascoigne. And the weight was not so heavy as the bottle, see. And we took a lead with a red cord from just above the weight, see, and fixed it to the table. So when the cord was cut she came down gradual like, seeing she was that much heavier than the weight. The weight and the bottle hung half-way between the pulley and the table, see, so when she came down, the weight went up to the pulley. It was hooked into a ring in the rope. We cut out the lights and used candles so's nothing would be noticed. We tried her out till we was sick and tired of her and she worked corker every time. She worked good-oh, didn't she, Mr Gascoigne?'

'Yes,' said Gascoigne. 'That's what I say. There's been some funny business.'

'That's right,' agreed Bert heavily. 'There bloody well must of.'

'I'm just going aloft to take a look,' said Gascoigne.

'Just a moment,' interrupted Alleyn. He took a notebook and pencil from his pocket. 'Don't you think perhaps we had better not go up just yet, Mr Gascoigne? If there has been any interference, the police ought to be the first on the spot, oughtn't they?'

'I think I'll go and see how Carolyn is,' said Hambledon suddenly.

'They're all in their dressing-rooms,' said Gascoigne.

Hambeldon went away. Alleyn completed a little sketch in his notebook and showed it to Gascoigne and Bert. 'Was it like that?'

'That's right, mister,' said Bert, 'you got it. That's how it was. And when she cut the bloody cord, see . . . ' he rambled on.

Alleyn looked at the jeroboam. It had been cased in a sort of net which closed in at the neck, and was securely wired to the rope.

'Wonder why the cork blew out,' murmured Alleyn.

'The wire was loosened a bit before it came down,' said Gascoigne. 'He – the governor himself – he went aloft after the show specially to do it. He didn't want a stage-wait after it came down. He said the wire would still hold the cork.'

'And it did till the jolt – yes. What about the counterweight, Mr Gascoigne? That would have to be detached before the champagne was poured out.'

'Bert was to go up at once and take it off.'

'I orfered to stay up there, like,' said Bert. 'But 'e says "No,", 'e says, "you can see the show and then go up. I'll watch it." Gawd, Mr Gascoigne – '

Alleyn slipped away through the wings. Off-stage it was very dark and smelt of theatre. He walked along the wall until he came to the foot of an iron ladder. He was reminded most vividly of his only other experience behind the scenes. 'Is my mere presence in the stalls,' he thought crossly, 'a cue for homicide? May I not visit the antipodes without elderly theatre magnates having their heads bashed in by jeroboams of champagne before my very eyes? And the answer being "No" to each of these questions, can I not get away quickly without nosing into the why and wherefore?'

He put on his gloves and began to climb the ladder. 'Again the answer is "No." The truth of the matter is I'm an incurable nosy parker. Detect I must, if I can.' He reached the first gallery, and peered about him, using his electric torch, and then went on up the ladder. 'I wonder how she's taking it? And Hambledon. Will they marry each other in due course, provided – After all, she may not be in love with Hambledon. Ah, here we are.'

He paused at the top gallery and switched on his torch.

Close beside him a batten, slung on ropes, ran across from his gallery to the opposite one. Across the batten hung a pulley and over the pulley was a rope. Looking down the far length of the rope, he saw it run away in sharp perspective from dark into light. He had a bird's-eye view of the lamplit set, the tops of the wings, the flat white strip of table; and there, at the end of the rope in the middle of the table, a flattened object, rather like a beetle with a white head and paws. That was Alfred Meyer. The other end of the rope, terminating in an iron hook, was against the pulley. The hook had been secured to a ring in the end of the rope, and the red cord which Carolyn had cut was also tied to the ring. The cut end of the cord dangled in mid-air. On the hook he should have found the counterweight.

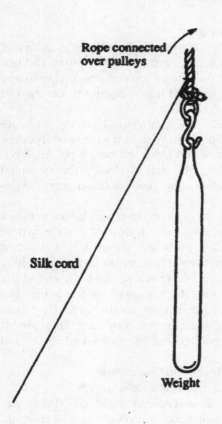

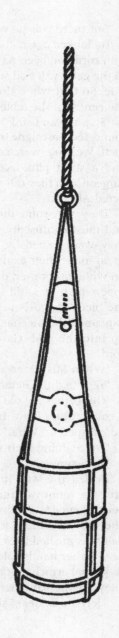

But there was no counterweight.

He looked again at the pulley. It was as he had thought. A loop of thin cord had been passed round the near end of the batten and tied to the gallery. It had served to pull the batten eighteen inches to one side. So that when the bottle dropped it was slightly to the right of the centre of the table.

'Stap me and sink me!' said Alleyn and returned to the stage. He found Ted Gascoigne by the stage-door. With him were two large dark men, wearing overcoats, scarves, and black felt hats; a police officer, and a short pink-faced person who was obviously the divisional surgeon. 'Do they call them divisional surgeons in this country?' wondered Alleyn.

They were some time at the stage-door. Gascoigne talked very fast and most confusedly. At last he took them on to the stage, where they were joined by Te Pokiha. From the wings Alleyn watched them make their examination. It gave him a curious feeling to look on while other men did his own job. They examined the end of the rope which was still knotted into the net enclosing the bottle, and the piece of red-bound wire cord that lay on the table. Gascoigne explained the mechanism of the descending jeroboam. They peered up into the grid. Gascoigne pointed out the other end of the red cord.

'When Miss Dacres cut it, it shot up,' he explained.

'Yes,' said the detective. 'Ye-ees. That's right. Ye-ees.'

'Out comes the old notebook,' said Alleyn to himself. 'Hullo,' said a voice at his elbow. It was Hambledon. 'Carolyn wants to see you,' he whispered. 'What's happening out there?'

'Police doing their stuff. Wants to see me, does she?'

'Yes, come on.'

He led the way into the usual dark wooden passage. The star dressing-room was the first on the left. Hambledon knocked on the door, opened it, and led the way in. Carolyn sat at her dressing-table. She still wore the black lace dress she had put on for the party. Her hair was pushed back from her face as though she had sat with her head in her hands. Old Susan Max was with her. Susan sat comfortably in an armchair, radiating solid sense, but her eyes were anxious. They brightened when she saw Alleyn.

'Here he is, dear,' she said.

Carolyn turned her head slowly.

'Hullo,' she said.

'Hullo,' said Alleyn. 'Hambledon says you want me.'

'Yes, I do.' Her hands were trembling violently. She pressed them together between her knees.

'I just thought I'd like you here,' said Carolyn. 'I've killed him, haven't I?'

'No!' said Hambledon violently.

'My dear!' said Susan.

'Well, I have. I cut the cord. That was what did it, wasn't it?' She still looked at Alleyn.

'Yes,' said Alleyn in a very matter-of-fact voice, 'that was what set the thing off. But you didn't rig the apparatus, did you?'

'No. I didn't know anything about it. It was a surprise.'

She caught her breath and a strange sound, something like laughter, came from her lips. Susan and Hambledon looked panicky.

'Oh!' cried Carolyn. 'Oh! Oh!'

'Don't!' said Alleyn. 'Hysterics are a bad way of letting things go. You feel awful afterwards.'

She raised one of her hands and bit on it. Alleyn picked up a bottle of smelling-salts from the dressing-table and held it under her nose.

'Sniff hard,' he said.

Carolyn sniffed and gasped. Tears poured out of her eyes.

'That's better. You're crying black tears. I thought that stuff was waterproof. Look at yourself.'

She gazed helplessly at him and then turned to the glass. Susan gently wiped away the black tears.

'You're a queer one,' sobbed Carolyn.

'I know I am,' agreed Alleyn. 'It's a pose, really. Would you drink a little brandy if Hambledon got it for you?'

'No.'

'Yes, you would.' He looked good-humouredly at Hambledon, who was standing by her chair. 'Can you?' asked Alleyn.

'Yes – yes, I'll get it.' He hurried away.

Alleyn sat on one of the wicker baskets and spoke to old Susan.

'Well, Miss Max, our meetings are to be fraught with drama, it seems.'

'Ah,' said Susan with a sort of grunt.

'What do you mean?' asked Carolyn. She turned to the mirror and, very shakily, dabbed at her face with a powder-puff.

'Mr Alleyn and I have met before, dear,' explained Susan. 'Over that dreadful business with Felix Gardener, you know.'

'Yes. We spoke about it that night on the train.' Carolyn paused, and then she began to speak rapidly, urgently and with more command over her voice.

'That's why I wanted to see you. That night on the train. You remember what – he – said. Someone had tried to kill him. Have you thought of that?'

'I have,' said Alleyn.

'Well then – I want you to tell me, please, is this anything to do with it? Has someone – the same someone – done tonight what they failed to do on the train? Mr Alleyn – has someone murdered my husband?'

Alleyn was silent.

'Please answer me.'

'That's a question for the police, you know.'

'But I want *you* to tell me what you think. I must know what you think.' She leant towards him. 'You're not on duty. You're in a strange country, like all of us, and far away from your job. Don't be official, please don't. Tell me what you think!'

'Very well,' said Alleyn after a pause. 'I think someone has interfered with the tackle that was rigged up for – for the stunt with the champagne, you know.'

'And that means murder?'

'If I am right – yes. It looks like it!'

'Shall you speak to the police? They are there now, aren't they?'

'Yes. They are out there.'

'Well?'

'I regard myself as a layman, Miss Dacres. I shall certainly not butt in.' His voice was not final. He seemed to have left something unsaid. Carolyn looked fixedly at him and then turned to old Susan.

'Susie, darling, I want to talk to Mr Alleyn. Do you mind? You've been an angel. Thank you so much. Come back soon.'

When Susan had gone Carolyn leant forward and touched Alleyn's hand.

'Listen,' she said, 'do you feel friendly towards me? You do, don't you?

'Quite friendly.'

'I want you for my friend. You don't believe I could do anything very bad, do you? Or let anything very bad be done without making some effort to stop it?'

'What is in your mind?' he asked. 'What are you trying to say?'

'If I should want your help – yes, that's it – would you give it me?'

Her hand was still on his. She had patched up the stains made by her tears and her face looked beautiful again. He had seen her lean forward like that on the stage; it was a very characteristic gesture. Her eyes seemed to cry out to him.

'If I can be of any help,' said Alleyn very formally, 'of course I shall be only too glad – '

'No, no, no. That's not a bit of good. Sticking out all your prickles like that,' said Carolyn, with something of her old vigour. 'I want a real answer.'

'But, don't you see, you say too much and too little. What sort of help do you want from me?'

'I don't know, I don't know.'

'Come,' said Alleyn, 'I'll promise to stay in Middleton a little longer. When do you go on to Wellington?'

'When? We were to open there next week, but now – I don't know.'

'Listen to me. I give you one piece of advice. Don't try and keep anything in the dark, no matter what it is. Those fellows out there will want to talk to you. They'll have to ask you all sorts of questions. Answer them truthfully, no matter what it means, no matter how painful it may be, no matter where you think their questions are leading you. Promise me that and I'll pledge you my help, for what it's worth.'

Carolyn still leant towards him, still looked straight at him. But he felt her withdrawal as certainly as though it had been physical.

'Well?' he asked. 'Is it a bargain?'

But before she could answer him Hailey Hambledon came back with the brandy.

'The detectives want us all to wait in the wardrobe-room,' he said. 'I don't know about you, Alleyn.'

'You haven't given me away to anyone, have you?' asked Alleyn.

'No, no. Only we three realize you're a detective.'

'Please let it stay like that, will you?' asked Alleyn. 'I'm most anxious that it should be so.'

'I'll promise you *that*,' said Carolyn.

Their eyes met.

'Thank you,' said Alleyn quietly. 'I'll join you later.'

CHAPTER 6

Second Appearance of the Tiki

'Who's that?' demanded the largest of the three detectives. 'Just a minute there, please.' He was on the stage and had caught sight of Alleyn through the open door of the prompt entrance.

'It's me,' said Alleyn in a mild voice and walked through. The detective, Te Pokiha, and the police doctor, were all standing by the table.

'Who's this gentleman, Mr Gascoigne?' continued the detective.

'Er – it's – er – Mr Alleyn, Inspector.'

'Member of the company?'

'No,' said Alleyn, 'just a friend.'

'I thought I said no one was to come out here. What were you doing, sir? Didn't you understand – ?'

'I just thought – ' began Alleyn with that particular air of hurt innocence that always annoyed him when he met it in his official capacity. 'I just thought – '

'I'll have your full name and address, if *you* please,' interrupted the inspector, and opened his notebook. 'Allan, you said. First name?'

'Roderick.'

'How do you spell – ?' The inspector stopped short and stared at Alleyn. 'A-l-l-e-y-n, Inspector.'

'Good God!'

'New Scotland Yard, London,' added Alleyn apologetically.

'By cripes, sir, I'm sorry. We'd heard you were – we didn't know – I mean – '

'I shall call at headquarters when I get to Wellington,' said Alleyn. 'I've got a letter somewhere from your chief. Should have answered it. Very dilatory of me.'

'I'm very, very sorry, sir. We thought you were in Auckland. We've been expecting you, of course.'

'I changed my plans,' said Alleyn. 'All my fault, Inspector – ?'

'Wade, sir,' said the inspector, scarlet in the face.

'How do you do?' said Alleyn cheerfully, and held out his hand.

'I'm very very pleased to meet you, Chief Inspector,' said Inspector Wade, shaking it relentlessly. 'Very very pleased. We had word that you were on your way, and as a matter of fact, Superintendent Nixon was going to look in at the Middleton as soon as you came down. Yes, that's right. The super was going to call. We've all been trained on your book.* 'It's – it's a great honour to meet the author.'

'That's very nice of you,' said Alleyn, easing his fingers a little. 'I should have called at your headquarters on my arrival, but you know how it is in a new place. One puts off these things.' He glanced through the wings on to the stage.

'That's right. And now we meet on the job as you might say. Ye-ees.'

'Not *my* job, thank the Lord,' said Alleyn, 'and, look here. I want to hide my job under a bushel. So – if you don't mind – just don't mention it to any of these people.'

'Certainly, sir. I hope you'll let the boys here meet you. They'd be very very pleased, I know.'

'So should I – delighted. Just tip them the wink, if you don't mind, to forget about the CID. And as I'm a layman, I suppose you want to ask me a few questions, Inspector?'

The New Zealander's large healthy face again turned red.

'Well now, sir, that makes me feel a bit foolish but – well – yes, we've got to do the usual, you know.'

'Of course you have,' said Alleyn very charmingly. 'Nasty business, isn't it? I shall be most interested to see something of your methods if you will allow me.'

---

* *Principles and Practice of Criminal Investigation*, by Roderick Alleyn, MA (Oxon), CID. (Sable & Murgatroyd, 21s.)

'It's very fine of you to put it that way, sir. To be quite frank I was wondering if you would give us an account of what took place before the accident. You were in the party, I understand.'

'A statement in my own words, Inspector?' asked Alleyn, twinkling.

'That's right,' agreed Wade with a roar of laughter, which he instantly quelled. His two subordinates, hearing this unseemly noise, strolled up and were introduced. Detective-Sergeants Cass and Packer. They shook Alleyn's hand and stared profoundly at the floor. Alleyn gave a short but extremely workmanlike account of the tragedy.

'By cripes!' said Inspector Wade with great feeling. 'It's not often we get it like that. Now, about the way this champagne business was fixed. You say you made a sketch of it, sir?'

Alleyn showed him the sketch.

'Ought to have worked OK,' said Wade. I'll go up and have a look-see.'

'You'll find it rather different, now,' said Alleyn. 'I ventured to have a glance up there myself. I do hope you don't mind, Inspector. It was damned officious, I know, but I didn't get off the ladder and I'm sure I've done no harm.'

'That's quite all right, sir,' said Wade heartily. 'No objections here. We don't have Scotland Yard alongside us every day. You say it's different from your sketch?'

'Yes. May I come up with you?'

'Too right. You boys fix up down here. Get the photographs through and the body shifted to the mortuary. You'd better ring the station for more men. Get a statement from the stage-manager and the bloke that rigged this tackle. You can take that on, Cass. And Packer, you get statements from the rest of the crowd. Are they all in the wardrobe-room?'

'I think they will be there by now,' said Alleyn. 'The guests have gone, with the exception of a Mr Gordon Palmer and his cousin Mr Weston who, I believe, are still here. Mr George Mason, the business manager, has a list of the names and addresses. The guests simply came behind the scenes for the party and are casual acquaintances of the company. Mr Palmer and his cousin came out in the same ship as the company. I – I suggested that perhaps they might be of use. They were,' said Alleyn dryly, 'delighted to remain.'

'Good-oh,' said Wade. 'Get to it, you boys. Are you ready, Mr Alleyn?'

He led the way up the iron ladder. When he reached the first gallery he paused and switched on his torch.

'Not much light up there,' he grunted.

'Wait a moment,' called Alleyn from below. 'There's a light-border. I'll see if I can find the switch.'

He climbed up to the electrician's perch and, after one or two experiments, switched on the overhead lights. A flood of golden warmth poured down through the dark strips of canvas.

'Good-oh,' said Wade.

'It is extraordinary,' thought Alleyn, 'how ubiquitous they make that remark. It expresses anything from acquiescence to approbation.'

He mounted the iron ladder.

'Well now, sir,' said Wade, 'it all looks much the same as your sketch to me. Where's the difference?'

'Look at the rope by the pulley,' suggested Alleyn, climbing steadily. 'Look at the end where the counterweight should be attached. Look – '

He had reached the second platform where Wade sat, dangling his legs. He turned on the ladder and surveyed the tackle.

'Hell's gaiters!' said Alleyn very loudly. 'They've put 'em back again.'

A long silence followed. Alleyn suddenly began to chuckle.

'One in the eye for me,' he said, 'and a very pretty one, too. All the same it's too damn' clever by half. Look here, Inspector, when I came up here twenty minutes ago the counterweight was *not* attached to the rope over there, and the pulley *had* been moved eighteen inches this way by a loop of cord.'

'Is that so?' said Wade solemnly. After another pause he glanced at Alleyn apologetically. It'd be very dark then, sir. No lights at all, I take it. I suppose – '

'I'll go into the box and swear my socks off and my soul pink,' said Alleyn. 'And I had a torch, what's more. No – it's been put right again. It must have been done while I was in the dressing-room. By George, I wonder if the fellow was up here on the platform when I came up the ladder. You had just got to the theatre when I went down.'

'D'you mean,' asked Wade, 'd'you mean to tell me that this gear was all different when we came in and someone's changed it round since? We'd have known something about that, Mr Alleyn.'

'My dear chap, but would you? Look here, kick me out. I've no business to gate-crash on your job, Inspector. It's insufferable. Just take my statement in the ordinary way and I'll push off. Lord knows, I didn't mean to buck round doing the CID official.'

Wade, whose manner up to now had been a curious mixture of deference, awkwardness, and a somewhat forced geniality, now thawed completely.

'Look, sir,' he said, 'you don't need to make any apologies. I reckon I know a gentleman when I meet one. We've read about your work out here, and if you like to interest yourself – well, we'll be only too pleased. Now! Only too pleased.'

'Extraordinary nice of you,' said Alleyn. 'Thank you so much for those few nuts and so on. All right. Didn't you stay by the stage-door for a bit, when you came in?'

Yes, that's right, we did. Mr Gascoigne met us there and started some long story. We didn't know what was up.

Simply got the message, there'd been an accident at the theatre. It took me a minute or two to get the rights of it and another minute or two to find out where the body was. You know how they are.'

'Exactly. Well now, while that was going on, I fancy our gentleman was up here and very busy. He came up under cover of all the hoo-hah on the stage some time after the event. He was just going to put things straight, when he heard me climbin' up de golden stair, as you might say. That must have given him a queasy turn. He took cover somewhere up here in the dark and as soon as I went down again he did what he had to do. Then, when you were safely on the stage and shut off by the walls of scenery, down he came pussy-foot, by the back-stage ladder, and mixed himself up with the crowd. Conjecture, perhaps – '

'I've just been reading your views on conjecture, sir,' said Wade.

'For the Lord's sake, Wade, don't bring my own burblings up against me, or I shall look the most unutterable ass. Conjecture or not, I think you'll find traces of this performance if you look round up here.'

'Come on, then, sir. Let's go to it.'

'Right you are. Tread warily, I would. Damn – it's slatted.'

The gallery turned out to be a narrow stretch of steel-slatted platform extending from the prompt corner to the back wall, round the back wall, and along the opposite side to the OP corner. It was guarded by a rail to which the ropes that raised the scenic clothes were made fast. They began to work their way round, hugging the wall and taking long steps on the tips of their toes.

'There's plenty of dust in these regions,' said Alleyn. 'I had a case that hung on just such another spot. Hung, by the way, is the right word. The homicide swung his victim from the grid.'

'You mean the Gardener case, sir? I've read about that.'

'Bless me, Inspector, if you're not better up in my cases than I am myself. Stop a moment.'

They had moved out of the area of light, and switched on their torches. Alleyn swung his towards the rail.

'Here, you see, we are opposite the pulley. Now when I came up here before, a piece of cord had been passed round the batten on which the pulley is rigged. That beam, there. The rope to the beam stopped it from slipping and it was made fast to this cleat on the rail here. The effect was to drag the pulley eighteen inches or so this way.'

'What for, though?' asked Wade.

'In order that the jeroboam of fizz should fall, not into the nest of ferns and fairy lights, but on to the naked pate of poor Alfred Meyer.'

'Geeze!'

'And here, I think, I very much suspect, is the piece of cord. Neatly rolled round the cleat. Clever fellow, this. Keeps his head. What? Shall we move on?'

'I'll collect that cord on the way back,' grunted Wade. 'On you go, sir. After you.'

'There are any number of footprints on these damn' slats. The stage hands have been all over the place, of course.'

'Not much chance of anything there,' agreed Wade, 'but we'll have to see. If you're right, sir, the suspect's prints will be on top.'

'So they will. Here's the back wall. Another ladder here you notice. I daren't look down, I'm terrified of heights. Round we go. This, no doubt, is where he crouched with blazing eyes and bared molars while I climbed the ladder. Dramatic, ain't it? Also remarkably grubby. Bang goes the old boiled shirt. Hullo! Another ladder going down to the back of the stage. That'll be the one he used, I should think. Turn the corner gently. Now we're on the last lap.'

'And there's the pulley again.'

They had worked round to the OP gallery and were close by the pulley which hung within easy reach from its batten. 'Yes,' said Alleyn, 'and there hangs the counterweight on the hook. I understand the weight is one of the sort that is used in the second act, to lead the ship's funnel down to the right spot. They've got several of them. Look. There is the funnel with the weight on it, just above our heads. And here, along the side, are several spare weights. Different sizes. You'll notice that the ring at the top of the hook would serve as a chock and prevent the rope whizzing through the pulley when the weight was removed. The weight hung exactly half-way, so there would be no slack rope on the table. '

'And you say there was no weight on this rope when you looked up here before?'

There was no weight. The rope with the cut end of red cord simply hung in the pulley.'

He flashed his light on the beam. You'll notice the whole thing is within arm's length of the gallery. The table was placed well over to the side for that reason.'

'Well, I'll test the lantern for prints,' said Wade, 'but it's a bit hopeless. Anyway he'd use gloves. Don't you reckon it's a mistake sir, the way they've advertised the fingerprint system? Any fool crook knows better than to forget his gloves, these days.'

'There are times,' said Alleyn, 'when I could wish the penny Press-lords in the nethermost hell. Yet they have their uses, they have their uses. Nay, I can gleek on occasion.' Sensing Wade's bewilderment he added hurriedly: 'You're right, Inspector, but of course they have to come out in evidence. Prints, I mean. I grow confused. It must be the smell of fizz.'

'It was certainly a high-class way of murdering anybody,' said Wade dryly. 'Dong him one with a gallon of champagne. Good-oh!'

'I doubt if I shall enjoy even the soundest vintage years for some time to come,' said Alleyn. 'The whole place reeks of it. You can even smell it up here. Great hopping fleas!'

'What's wrong, sir?'

Alleyn was staring from the counterweight on the rope to those on the platform.

'My dear Wade, we have come within an ace of making the most frightful fools of ourselves. Look at that weight.'

'I am,' said Wade.

'Well, my dear chap, what's keeping it there?'

'The weight of the – Cripey, sir, the cork blew out and half the champagne with it. That weight ought to be on the stage. It ought to be heavier than the half-empty bottle.'

'Exactly. Therefore it is *very much* lighter than the full bottle. Therefore it is not the weight they rehearsed with. And what's more, the original weight must have hung hard by the lower gallery, half-way down to the stage, within easy reach. He didn't come up here for the first visit. He did his stuff from the lower gallery.'

'You're right, sir. And if you hadn't come up the first time, it would have looked more like an accident and less like homicide.'

Alleyn pulled in the rope and grasped it above the weight.

'Nothing like heavy enough,' he said. 'It must have been one of the big ones. Well – that's that. Are we staying aloft, Inspector?'

'I think we'll go down now, sir. I'll send Cass up to collect the stuff here. It'll need careful handling, and I think had better be done by daylight. I'll leave a man here, of course. Ye-es.'

Footsteps sounded on the stage below, and voices. They looked down and had a bird's eye view of a little procession. The police constable, whom Wade had left mounting guard over Meyer's body, opened the door in the box set. Through it came Dr Tancred, Dr Te Pokiha, and two men with a stretcher. The stretcher was laid on the stage. Tancred looked up into the grid, his hand over his eyes.

'You up there, Inspector?' he called.

'Here I am, Doctor.'

'All right if we move the body?'

'Has Cass got his photos OK?'

'Yes.'

'Good-oh, then, Doctor.'

They lifted the terrible head. Tancred and Te Pokiha examined it again. It lolled back and seemed to stare up to where the two men watched from above. Pieces of fern were stuck on the face, and it was cut with glass from the broken lights. Te Pokiha brushed the fern away. They hauled the body up from the chair. It seemed to be very heavy. At last they got it on the stretcher and covered it.

'All right,' said Tancred.

They carried Meyer away, the policeman holding the door open. Te Pokiha remained behind.

'Well, we may as well go down,' said Wade.

Alleyn did not answer. Wade turned to look at him. He was in the act of stooping. His long fingers reached for something that lay between two of the steel slats at his feet. His fingers edged at this little object, coaxed it up, and grasped it. He straightened, glanced down beneath him to where Te Pokiha stood, and then made a slight gesture of warning.

'What's up?' asked Wade softly.

Alleyn stretched out his hand into the light. On the palm lay a small green object of a singular shape. Its head lolled over to one side and it seemed to be grinning.

'Are you coming down?' called Te Pokiha from the stage.

CHAPTER 7

Wardrobe-room Muster

'It's a tiki,' said Wade.

'Yes. May be of some importance. Wait a moment.'

Alleyn pulled a handkerchief from his pocket, dropped the tiki on it and folded it over carefully.

'There you are, Inspector. I'll give you the history when we get down. In the meantime, if I may make a suggestion, keep it under your hat.'

They climbed down the OP ladder to the stage. Te Pokiha waited for them.

'If you've no further use for me, Mr Wade, I think I'll clear out,' he said. 'It's one o'clock.'

'Right-oh, then, Doctor,' agreed Wade. 'We'll want you for the inquest.'

'I suppose so.' He turned to Alleyn. 'I had no idea you were the famous Roderick Alleyn,' he said in his warm voice. 'It's strange that this should be your introduction to New Zealand. I have read – '

'Have you?' said Alleyn quickly. 'I'm supposed to be on a holiday for my health. And by the way, I particularly *don't* want my identity made public. As far as this affair goes, I'm a layman, Dr Te Pokiha. Inspector Wade very kindly allowed me to have a look at the pulley up there.'

'Has it been interfered with?' asked Te Pokiha.

'We're going to make a thorough examination by daylight, Doctor,' said Wade. 'I'll just see these other people now.'

Te Pokiha's dark eyes gleamed in his dark face.

'I'll wish you good night, then. Good night, Mr Alleyn. You seemed to be interested in my people. If you would care to come and see me while you are here – '

'I should be delighted,' said Alleyn cordially.

'Dinner tomorrow? Splendid. It's not far out. Twenty miles. I'll call for you at six.'

Alleyn shook the thin brown hand that Te Pokiha extended, and watched the Maori go out.

'Very, very fine fellow, Rangi Te Pokiha,' said Wade. 'Fine athlete, and brainy, too. Best type of Maori.'

'I met him at the hotel,' said Alleyn, 'and found him very interesting. There is no colour prejudice in this country, apparently.'

'Well, not in the way there is in India, for instance. Mind, there are Maoris and Maoris. Te Pokiha's high caste. His mother was a princess and his father a fine old chief. The doctor's had an English college education – he's ninety per cent civilized. All the same, sir, there's the odd ten per cent. It's there, no matter how civilized they are. See him when he goes into one of the back-country pas and you'll find a difference. See him when he goes crook! By gee, I did once, when he gave evidence on a case of – well, it was an unsavoury case and the doctor felt strongly about it. His eyes fairly flashed. He looked as if he might go off at the deep end and dance a haka in court.'

'A haka?'

'War-dance. They pull faces and yell. Great affair, it is. Well now, what about this tiki, Mr Alleyn?'

'Ah, yes.' Alleyn lowered his voice. 'Dr Te Pokiha put me in the way of buying that tiki. I gave it to Miss Carolyn Dacres as a birthday present tonight.'

'To the Dacres woman?' asked Wade, suddenly looking very sharp. 'You did? Is that so?'

'She is not "the Dacres woman" so far, you know,' said Alleyn. 'The tiki passed from hand to hand. It may be of interest to find out where it fetched up.'

'Of interest! I should say so. I'll see these people now. Cass!'

Detective-Sergeant Cass opened the door in the set and looked in.

'I'm going to the office, Cass. Send these people along one by one. You haven't left them alone, I hope?'

'No, sir. We've got them all together in one room now. Packer's in there.'

'All right.' He turned to Alleyn. 'Are you sticking to it a while longer, Mr Alleyn?'

'I think I'll wander in and join the party for a bit, if you've no objections.'

'That's quite all right, sir, that's quite all right. You just please yourself,' said Wade in his heartiest voice. Alleyn knew that the inspector was at once relieved to think that he would be left alone for examination of the others, and slightly disappointed at losing his chance of exhibiting his ability before the representative of Scotland Yard.

'I suppose,' thought Alleyn, 'I must give him an inferiority complex. He feels I'm criticising him all the time. If I don't remember to be frightfully hearty and friendly, he'll think I'm all English and superior. I know he will. I would myself, I suppose, in his shoes. He's been damn' pleasant and generous, too, and he's a very decent fellow. Dear me, how difficult it all is.'

He found his way along the dressing-room passage and, guided by the murmur of voices, knocked at the last door. It was opened by Detective-Sergeant Packer, who came half through the door. He was a fine specimen, was Packer; tall, magnificently built, with a good head on him. When he saw Alleyn he came to attention.

'Sergeant Packer,' said Alleyn, 'your inspector tells me I may come in here if I behave nicely. That all right?'

'Certainly, Chief Inspector,' said Packer smartly.

Alleyn looked at him.

'We shan't bother about the "Chief Inspector",' he murmured. 'Can you come outside for a second?'

Packer at once stepped out and closed the door.

'Look here,' said Alleyn, 'do those people in there realize I'm from the Yard?'

'I don't think they do, sir. I heard them mention your name, but they didn't seem to know.'

'Good. Leave 'em in outer darkness. Just any old Allen. I asked Inspector Wade to warn you, but I suppose he hasn't had a chance. Miss Dacres, Miss Max, and Mr Hambledon know, but they'll keep quiet, I hope. Understand?'

'Yes, sir.'

'Splendid. Then just let me loose among 'em, Packer. I'll do no harm, I promise you.'

'Harm, sir? I should say *not*. If you'll excuse me mentioning it, sir, I've just read – '

'Have you? I'll give you a copy for yourself. Now usher me in. And chidingly, Packer. Be severe with me.'

Detective-Sergeant Packer was a young officer. He looked at the tall figure of Chief Inspector Alleyn and developed instant and acute hero-worship. 'He looks like one of those swells in the English flicks,' he afterwards confided to his girl, 'and he talks with a corker sort of voice. Not queeny, but just corker. I reckon he's all right. Gosh, I reckon he's a humdinger.'

Under a fearful oath of secrecy, long after there was any need for discretion, Packer described to his best girl the scene in the wardrobe-room.

'He said to me, kind of laughing – and he's got a corking sort of laugh – he said: "Be severe with me, Packer." So I opened the door and, as he walked through, I said: "Move along in there, if *you* please, sir. And kindly obey instructions." Very stiff. And he walked in and he said, "Frightfully sorry, officer," in a real dude voice. "Fright-fullah sorrah, officahh" – only it sounded decent the way he said it. Not unnatural. Just English. "Frightfulla sorra – " I can't seem to get it.'

'And then what?' asked Packer's best girl.

'Well, and then he walked in. And I stayed on the outside of the door. He didn't tell me to, but I reckoned if I stayed out he'd get them to talk. I left the door a crack open and I walked noisily away and then quietly back again. I dunno what old Sam Wade would 'uv said if he'd come along. He'd 'uv gone horribly crook at me for not staying inside. Well, as soon as the Chief walks in they all start in squealing. "Oh, Mr Alleyn, what's happening? Oh, Mr Alleyn, what's the matter?" The girl Gaynes – Valerie Gaynes. You know – '

'She's the one that wore that corking dress in the play. I think she's lovely.'

'She makes me tired. She started squealing about the disgraceful way she'd been treated, and how she'd write to her old man and complain, and how they'd never dream of shutting her up like this

in England, and how she reckoned the police in this country didn't
know the way to behave. Give you a pain in the neck, dinkum, she
would. Well, as I was telling you – '

Packer told his girl many times of this scene.

The fact of the matter was that Alleyn got an unpleasant shock
when he walked into the wardrobe-room. He suddenly remembered
that, during that night in the train Carolyn had told Valerie Gaynes
he was a CID official, and here was Valerie Gaynes rushing at him
with complaints about the New Zealand police, about the way she
was being treated. Any moment she might give the show away. He
glanced at Carolyn. She called Miss Gaynes, murmured something in
her ear, and drew her down beside her.

'Oh!' said Valerie Gaynes flatly. 'Well, I think – '

'Of course you do,' said Carolyn quickly, 'but if you could manage not to *talk* quite so much, darling, it would be such a good idea.'

'But, Miss Dacres – '

'Yes, darling, but do you know, I think if I were you, I should just
go all muted – like you did over your money, do you remember,
when Mr Alleyn offered to look at your notecase.'

Valerie Gaynes suddenly sat down.

'That's right, darling,' said Carolyn jerkily. 'Come and sit down, Mr
Alleyn. It seems we are all to be shut up in here while they find out
whether my poor Pooh was – whether it was all an accident or not.'

Her voice was pitched a note too high and her hands moved
restlessly in her lap.

'That's the idea, I believe,' said Alleyn.

'What are they *doing* out there?' asked little Ackroyd peevishly.

'How much longer – ?'

'Mr Alleyn, can you tell us – ?'

They all began again.

'I know no more than you do,' said Alleyn, at last. 'I believe they
propose to interview us all, singly. I've just had my dose. I got ticked
off for loitering.'

'What did they ask you?' demanded young Palmer.

'My name and address,' said Alleyn shortly. He dragged forward
a small packing-case, sat on it, and surveyed the company.

The wardrobe-room at the Royal was simply a very large dressing-
room, occupied by the chorus when musical-comedy companies

visited Middleton. The Dacres Company used it to store the wardrobes for their second and third productions. An ironing-table stood at one end, an odd length of stage-cloth carpeted the floor, and a number of chairs, covered with dustcloths, were ranged round the walls. It served the company as a sort of common-room – an improvized version of the old-fashioned green-room. Carolyn tried to create something of the long-vanished atmosphere of the actor-manager's touring company. She was old enough to have served her apprenticeship in one of the last of these schools and remembered well the homely, knit-together feeling of back-stage, the feeling that the troupe was a little world of its own, moving compactly about a larger world. With Meyer's help she had tried, so far as she was able, to keep the same players about her for all her productions. She used to beg Meyer to look for what she called useful actors and actresses, by which she meant adaptable people who could pour themselves into the mould of a part and who did not depend upon individual tricks. 'Give me actors, Pooh darling, not types.' Perhaps that was why, with the exception of Valerie Gaynes and Courtney Broadhead, none of her company was very young. Valerie she had suffered only after a struggle, and, she confided in Hambledon, because she was afraid they might all begin to think she was jealous of young and good-looking women. Courtney came of an old acting family and took his work seriously. The rest – Ackroyd, Gascoigne, Liversidge, Vernon, Hambledon and Susan Max, were all over forty. They were, as Hambledon would have said, 'old troupers', used to each other's ways, and to the sound of each other's voices. There is a kind of for-tuitous intimacy among the members of such companies. It would be difficult to say how well they really know each other, but they often speak of themselves as 'a happy family'. As he looked from one face to another Alleyn was aware of this corporate feeling in the Dacres Company. 'How are they taking it?' he wondered. He asked himself the inevitable question: 'Which? Which of these?' And one by one he watched them.

Hambledon had moved away from Carolyn and sat opposite her and beside George Mason. They were both very pale and silent. Mason's undistinguished face was blotched, as if he had been crying. He looked apprehensive and miserable and rather ill. Hambledon's magnificent head was bent forward. He held one long-fingered hand

over his eyes, as though the light bothered him. Old Brandon
Vernon sat with his arms folded and his heavy eyebrows drawn
down. He had the peculiar raffish look of a certain type of elderly
actor. His face was pale, as if it had taken on the texture of grease-
paint, his mobile mouth seemed always about to widen into a sardonic grin; his eyes, lacklustre, had an impertinent look. There were
traces of No 9 in the hair on his temples and his chin was bluish. He
played polished old men-of-the-world with great skill. When Alleyn
came in Vernon was deep in conversation with little Ackroyd, with
whom he seemed to be annoyed. Ackroyd, whose amusing face was
so untrustworthy a guide to his character, listened irritably. He grimaced and fidgeted, glanced under his eyelids at Carolyn.

Next to Ackroyd sat Liversidge, with an empty chair beside him.
Valerie Gaynes had moved out of it when Carolyn called her. Alleyn
was a little surprised to see how shaken Liversidge seemed to be. His
too full, too obviously handsome face was very white. He was
unable to sit still, and when he lit one cigarette from the butt of
another his hands shook so much that he could scarcely control
them.

Young Courtney Broadhead, on the other hand, looked solemn,
but much less unhappy than he had appeared to be that night in the
train. 'They have changed their roles,' thought Alleyn. For in the
train Broadhead had stood huddled in his overcoat on the little iron
platform, speaking to nobody; while Liversidge had shouted and
shown himself off. Alleyn's thoughts returned persistently to the
night in the train.

Ted Gascoigne had joined young Gordon Palmer and his cousin,
Geoffrey Weston. The stage-manager was describing the mechanism
of the pulley and the bottle. Gordon listened avidly, bit his nails, and
asked innumerable questions. Weston said very little.

The stage-hands stood in an awkward and silent group at the far
end of the room.

Alleyn had not been long in the room before he realized that the
members of the company felt themselves constrained and embarrassed by the presence of Carolyn, and perhaps of Hambledon.
Through their conversation ran a chain of sidelong glances, of half-
spoken phrases. This, he told himself, was natural enough, since
they must assume that they were in the presence of grief and there

is nothing more embarrassing than other people's sorrow. 'But not to these people,' thought Alleyn, 'since they have histrionic precedents for dealing with sorrow. They are embarrassed for some other reason.'

Under cover of the general conversation he turned to Carolyn and said quietly: 'I am plagued with a horrible feeling that you may think I have brought misfortune to you.'

'You?' She looked at him in bewilderment. 'How should I think that?'

'By my gift.'

'You mean – the green figurine – the tiki?'

She glanced swiftly at Hambledon and away again.

'I wish you would return it to me and let me replace it by another gift,' said Alleyn.

Carolyn looked fixedly at him. Her hand went to her breast.

'What do you mean, Mr Alleyn?' she asked hurriedly.

'Is it in your bag?'

'I – yes. No.' She opened her bag and turned it out on her lap. 'No. Of course it's not. I haven't had it since – since before supper. Somebody took it from me – they were all looking at it. I remember distinctly that I did not have it.'

'May I ask who has it now?'

'Of course – if you want to.'

Alleyn raised his voice.

'Who's got Miss Dacres's tiki, please? She would like to have it.'

Dead silenece. He looked from one figure to another. They all looked bewildered and a little scandalized, as though Carolyn, by asking for her little tiki, had stepped outside the correct rendering of her part of tragic wife.

'It must be on the stage,' said Courtney Broadhead.

'Sure none of you has it?' pursued Alleyn.

The men felt in their pockets.

'I remember handing it on to you,' said Brandon Vernon to Ackroyd.

'Somebody took it from me,' said Ackroyd. 'You did, Frankie.'

'I?' said Liversidge. 'Did I? I haven't got it now. As a matter of fact, I think I gave it to – ' He hesitated and glanced at Carolyn.

'Yes?' asked Alleyn.

'– to Mr Meyer,' said Liversidge uncomfortably.

'Oh!' Carolyn drew in her breath swiftly. Old Susan looked direct-ly at Alleyn with a curious expression that he could not read. Suddenly Valerie Gaynes cried out:

'It's unlucky – I thought at the time it looked unlucky. Something seemed to tell me. I've got a queer intuition about things – '

'I am quite sure,' said Carolyn steadily, 'that my tiki is not unlucky. And I know Alfie hadn't got it when we sat down to supper.'

'How do you know that, Miss Dacres?' asked Alleyn.

'Because he asked me for it. He wanted to look at it again. And I hadn't got it either.'

'But I say – '

Alleyn turned swiftly. Young Gordon Palmer stood with his mouth half open and a curiously startled look on his face.

'Yes, Mr Palmer?' asked Alleyn.

'Oh, nothing.' And at that moment Packer opened the door and said:

'Inspector Wade would like to speak to Mrs Meyer, please.'

'I'm coming,' said Carolyn. Her long graceful stride took her quickly to the door. Hambledon got there before her.

'May I take Miss Dacres to the office?' he asked. 'I'll come straight back.'

'Well, sir – ' said Packer uncomfortably. He looked for a fraction of a second at Alleyn, who gave him the ghost of a nod.

'I'll just inquire,' said Packer. He went outside and closed the door. They could hear him talking to Sergeant Cass. He returned in a moment.

'If you would care to go along with Sergeant Cass and Mrs Mey – beg pardon – Miss Dacres, sir, that'll be all right. Sergeant Cass will come back with you.'

Alleyn strolled over to the door.

'I really cannot understand, officer,' he said, 'why I should be kept hanging about here. I've nothing whatever to do with this miserable business.' He added swiftly, under his breath: 'Keep Mr Hambledon talking outside the door if he returns.' And to Hambledon: 'Stay out-side if you can.'

Hambledon stared, but Packer said loudly:

'Now that'll be quite enough from you, Mr Alleyn. We're only doing our duty, as you ought to realize. You go back to your chair, if you please, sir. Everything will be quite all right.'

'Oh, excellent Packer!' thought Alleyn and returned churlishly to his upturned case.

Carolyn and Hambledon went out with Packer, who shut the door.

At once the others seemed to relax. There was a slight movement from all of them. Courtney Broadhead said:

'I simply can't take it in. It's so horrible. So horrible.'

'That is how *you* feel about it, is it?' said Liversidge.

'I should think that's how everybody feels about it,' said old Susan Max. 'It's been a terrible experience. I shan't forget it in a hurry.'

'He looked so awful.' Valerie Gaynes's voice rose hysterically. 'I'll see it all my life. I'll be haunted by it. His head – all that mess!'

'My God!' choked George Mason suddenly, 'I've got to get out of this. I'm going to be sick. Here – let me out.'

He rushed to the door, his handkerchief clapped to his mouth, and his eyes rolling lamentably. 'Get me out!'

Packer opened the door, cast one glance at Mason's face, and let him through. Unpleasant noises were followed by the bang of a door.

'He's been slowly turning green ever since we came in here,' said Ackroyd. 'Damned unpleasant sight, it was. Why the devil does *he* have to turn queasy?'

'It's his stomach, dear,' said Susan. 'George suffers from dyspepsia, Mr Alleyn. Martyr to it.'

'You had to finish him off, Val,' Brandon Vernon pointed out, 'by talking about the mess. Why did you have to bring that up?'

'Don't talk about bringing things up, for God's sake,' complained Liversidge.

'You look as if you were going on for Hamlet senior yourself, Frankie,' sneered Ackroyd.

'Oh, shut up,' said Liversidge violently.

'Well, nobody could feel iller than I do. I feel terrible,' said Valerie. 'Do you know that? I feel terrible.'

Nobody paid the slightest attention.

'What'll happen to the Firm?' asked Ackroyd of no one in particular. They all stirred uneasily. Gascoigne paused in his dissertation on counterweights and swung round.

'The Firm?' he said. 'The Firm will go on.'

'Do you mean Incorporated Playhouses?' asked Gordon Palmer eagerly.

'No,' snapped Ackroyd rudely, 'he means Wirth's Circus.'

'We always call Incorporated Playhouses "the Firm",' explained Susan good-naturedly.

'The great firm of Inky-P,' rumbled old Vernon.

'It was founded and built up by Mr Meyer, wasn't it?' asked Alleyn. 'He was actually the only begetter?'

'He and George Mason,' said Gascoigne. 'They made it together. George was a damn' good actor in his day – character, you know – never played straight parts. The governor met him somewhere and they doubled up. Yes, they started forty years ago as Mason & Meyer's Dramas Limited. A lot of omies the others were then, doing umpty-shows in the smalls.'

'That leaves me gaping,' said Alleyn apologetically. 'What is an "omie", Miss Max, and how does one recognize an "umpty-show"?'

'Ted means they were bad actors doing worse shows in one-eyed towns up and down the provinces,' said Susan.

'Yes,' continued Gascoigne, 'and today it's the biggest theatre combine in Europe. Wonderful achievement.'

'It'll be "George Mason" only now,' said Liversidge suddenly.

There was an uncomfortable silence.

'Yes,' said little Ackroyd. He looked under his lashes at Gascoigne. 'George will be a very wealthy man.'

At once Alleyn sensed a feeling of panic, of protest. Susan Max, who obviously disliked Ackroyd, planted her fat little hands on her knees and squared her shoulders.

'George Mason,' she said loudly, 'would rather be back advancing "The Worst Woman in London" than have this happen.'

'*Certainly.*' Gascoigne backed her up emphatically. 'I've stage-managed for the Firm for twenty-five years and it's been a happy little family for every day of it. Every day of it. Big as they are, they've gone on taking a personal interest. They run their own shows. Of course, this is just a holiday – but look at the way they've kept with the crowd. Mr Meyer was down in the office every morning and, make no mistake, he came down to work. He was *honest*, and by God, you can't say that for many of 'em. He and George were the whitest men in management.'

'Ah!' said Susan, ruffling her plumage, and looking with approval at Gascoigne.

'Well,' rumbled old Vernon, 'I've no quarrel with Inky P, and I hope to God George keeps me with him.'

'All right, all right,' protested Ackroyd. 'I'm not saying George isn't the curly-headed boy, am I, even if he hasn't always been quite quite?'

'What d'you mean by that?' demanded Vernon.

'I seem to remember hearing something about a company left stranded in America in the good old days,' said Ackroyd. 'Just one of those stories, you know, just one of those stories.'

'Then why repeat it?' snapped Vernon.

'Hear, hear,' said Gascoigne.

'Oh, dear, dear, *how* I do get myself in wrong, don't I?' cooed Ackroyd. He turned to Gascoigne. 'You keep on yammering about this bloody champagne stunt, Ted. You say it was fool-proof, accident-proof, all the rest of it.

Well – if it was, somebody's murdered Alfred Meyer. Now!'

Valerie Gaynes screamed and rushed across the room to the empty chair by Liversidge.

'Frankie!' she sobbed. 'Frankie! Not that! It's not true what they're saying – not true.'

'There, kiddy, there there!' crooned Mr Liversidge, stroking her arm and looking unpleasantly protective.

The door opened and George Mason returned. His round face was still very white.

'I'm very sorry, everyone,' he said simply, and returned to his seat.

'Better, Mr Mason?' asked Susan.

'Yes, thanks, Susie. Ashamed of myself. Where's Carolyn and Hailey?'

'Still out there.'

'While we're all together,' said Mason quietly, 'I'd just like to say that whatever happens I think I'd better call the company for midday tomorrow. I'll try and work out what's best to be done. Everyone on the stage at twelve, please, Mr Gascoigne.'

'Certainly, Mr Mason,' said Ted Gascoigne. 'Twelve o'clock tomorrow morning, please, ladies and gentlemen.'

Packer came in.

'The chief would like to see the stage staff.'

The little group at the far end of the room came forward and filed out through the door.

'Just a moment,' said Mason suddenly. 'Where are Miss Dacres and Mr Hambledon?'

'I think they've gone, sir.'

'Gone?'

'They've arrested them!' screamed Valerie Gaynes. 'My God, they've arrested them!'

'C-st!' said Mason savagely. 'Can no one keep that girl quiet!'

'They've just gone home, miss,' said Packer.

CHAPTER 8

Money

'The sooner you get down-stage and find yourself the better, young lady,' said Mason, when the staff had gone. 'What's the idea of all this tragedy stuff?'

'Oh, I can't help it,' wailed Valerie. 'I can't help it. I can't help it.'

'Nonsense,' said old Susan very loudly. 'Carolyn and Hailey arrested! The very idea!'

'I'm sorry. It was just him saying they'd gone. And it flashed through my mind – my poor tormented mind – how fond he is of her. I mean, we all know, and it was just – '

'Never mind, now,' interrupted Liversidge. 'Think of something else.'

'That's a suggestion,' said Alleyn cheerfully. 'Think of all the money you lost, Miss Gaynes. It's never turned up, I suppose?'

This had a salutary effect. Valerie stopped sobbing and caught her breath.

'No – I – no, it hasn't. But Mr Meyer was – awfully sweet. He – he advanced it to me – the same amount. And to think – '

'Really! Very kind of him.'

'Yes. He said he felt responsible, as I was under his wing. He said the Firm wouldn't let its people be out of pocket. And to think he's d – '

'D'you mean he gave it to you?' asked Ackroyd.

'Well – yes. He made me take it. I said it didn't matter – but he made me. And now he's lying there – mur – '

'That's just like him,' said Courtney Broadhead. 'He was wonderfully generous.'

'You've experienced his generosity, have you, Court?' asked Liversidge.

'Yes.' Broadhead looked straight at him. I have indeed.'

'Tell us about it, Court,' invited Gordon Palmer.

'Shut up, Gordon,' said Mr Weston, speaking for the first time since Alleyn had been in the room. 'Don't nosy-park.'

'Well,' said Liversidge, who seemed to have recovered a good deal of his composure. 'Well. It's nice to have an extra quid or two in your pocket. Thanks to you, Court, old boy, I've got one or two. I'll take you on again at Two's Wild whenever you like.'

'You were lucky at poker, were you, Mr Liversidge?' asked Alleyn lightly.

'I was. And poor old Court couldn't hold a court card.' He laughed.

'Must you?' said little Ackroyd. 'Oh, must you?'

'I think it's awful to make jokes,' began Valerie, 'when you think – '

'We're making epitaphs,' said Gordon Palmer. 'Or Court is, at any rate.' He glanced defiantly at Weston, and then turned to Broadhead. 'I've got a particular reason for asking it.'

'What is it?' said Broadhead.

'It's this. Where did you get the money to pay your poker debts?'

In the shocked silence that followed this amazing sentence Alleyn watched Liversidge. Liversidge himself watched Courtney Broadhead.

'I haven't the smallest objection to telling you,' said Broadhead. His face was scarlet, but he faced young Palmer collectedly. 'Mr Meyer lent it to me.'

'Oh,' said Gordon. He glanced sheepishly at Liversidge.

'Gordon!' Geoffrey Weston remarked dispassionately. 'You're a bounder.'

' "Carruthers, you cad, you have disgraced the old school tie," ' jeered Gordon. 'Really, Geoff, you're too superb.'

'You're asking for a hiding,' continued Mr Weston, 'and I've a damned good mind to give it you.'

'I shall run away. I run faster than you. Don't be a ninny, Geoff. I said I had a reason for asking my question. I had. A damn' good reason. The day we left the ship Courtney asked me if I'd mind waiting for my winnings till he began to draw his money. I said no,

that was all right. He said he had been a fool and was in the soup.
That night, in the train, Val found she'd been robbed of a hundred
quid. The next day Courtney paid Frankie Liversidge and me every
penny he owed us. He said afterwards he'd had a windfall. Now he
says Mr Meyer lent him the cash. Well, that's very charming. Pity, in
a way, that Mr Meyer isn't here to – '

'You damned little tripe-hound,' bawled Courtney Broadhead,
and made for him.

'Broadhead!' Alleyn made them all jump. Courtney swung round
angrily.

'I shouldn't, really,' said Alleyn.

'By God, no one's going to talk to me like – '

'If there's an explanation,' said Gordon Palmer, who looked
frightened but obstinate, 'why don't you give it? You seem to be out
for blood this evening, don't you?'

Courtney Broadhead made a wild swipe at him. Alleyn caught his
arm, did something neat and quick with it, and held him.

'Do you want the sergeant outside to referee, you unspeakable
donkey?' inquired Alleyn. 'Go back to your seat.'

To the intense astonishment of everybody Courtney went.

'Now,' said Alleyn to Gordon Palmer, 'you will listen to me, if you
please. If you have any information that is relevant to this business,
you will give it to the police.'

'I'm at liberty to say what I choose,' said Gordon, backing away.

'Shut up,' said Weston.

'If you go about making statements that may be criminally slan-
derous, you won't be at liberty to do anything at all for some considerable time,' Alleyn told him. 'Sit down and attend to your elders
and betters, and don't be rude. You are a thoroughly tiresome and
stupid young cub, and I see small hope of your growing up into anything that remotely resembles a human being.'

'Look here, who the hell – ?'

'Shut up,' said Weston.

Gordon retired, muttering.

'I think,' said Liversidge, 'that if I were in your place, Court, old
boy, I'd just explain quietly. You owe it to yourself, you know.'

'There's nothing more to say,' began Broadhead. 'I lost at poker
and couldn't pay my debts. I went to Mr Meyer the morning we got

here and told him about it. He was extraordinarily decent and advanced me the money. I was to pay it back out of my salary.'

'Well then, old boy,' said Liversidge, 'you've no need to worry. It'll all be on the books, won't it, Mr Mason? I suppose Mr Meyer told you about it?'

'I agree with Mr Alleyn,' said Mason quietly, 'that there is nothing to be gained by discussing this matter here.'

'It won't be on the books,' said Courtney Broadhead. it was a private loan.'

There was a long, uncomfortable silence.

'I don't understand,' said Valerie Gaynes suddenly. 'Of course, Court didn't take my money. What's my money got to do with it? It was stolen in the ship. Probably a steward took it.'

Her voice flattened. She looked at Liversidge and away again.

'I'm sure a steward took it, Frankie,' she said. It was almost as though she pleaded with him.

'I'll bet it was a steward,' said Liversidge very heartily indeed. He flashed an intolerably brilliant smile at Courtney Broadhead.

'Well,' said Susan Max roundly, 'it may have been a steward or it may have been the captain of the ship, but it wasn't Courtney Broadhead, and only a fool or a rogue would suggest that it was.'

'Quite a champion of – ah – good causes tonight, aren't you, Susie?' said Liversidge winningly.

'For God's sake,' said George Mason, 'can't you cut out all this stuff about Miss Gaynes's money and Courtney's money. We're up against a terrible tragedy and, my God, you all start selling a lot of cross-talk. What's going to happen to the show? That's what I'd like to know. What's going to happen to the show?'

And as if he had indeed sounded the very bottom of their trouble they at once became silent and anxious.

'The show!' said Gordon Palmer shrilly. 'You are an extraordinary crowd. The show doesn't matter – what's going to happen to *us?*'

At this protest from outside they all seemed to draw together. They looked anxiously at each other, ignoring Gordon.

'You don't seem to realize a man's been murdered,' he went on. His voice, trying to be compelling and indignant, was boyishly lame.

'Shut up,' said Geoffrey Weston.

'I won't. There's poor Mr Meyer – ' The voice wobbled uncertainly.

'If Alfred Meyer can think at all where he's gone,' said little George Mason surprisingly, 'he's thinking about the show. The Firm came first with Alfred – always.'

There was a short silence.

'I'm very sorry it happened, ladies and gentlemen,' added Mason, 'very sorry for your sakes, I mean. We've brought you all this way. I – I can assure you you'll be – looked after. My partner wouldn't have wanted it otherwise. We're old friends, all of us. I can't just sort things out in my own mind but – if I've got anything to do with it there'll be no difference.'

He looked solemnly at his company. There was a little stir among them as they were touched by his sudden assumption of formality, and by the illusion of security that his words had given to them. And, as he watched them, it seemed to Alleyn that of all things security is most desired by actors since it is the one boon that is never granted them. Even when they are in great demand and command absurdly large salaries, he reflected, few of them contrive to save much money. It is almost as though they were under the compulsion of some ancient rule of their guild, never to know security but often to desire it. And he fell to thinking of their strange life and of the inglorious and pathetic old age to which so many of them drifted.

Packer came in interrupting his thought.

The inspector, said Packer, would now speak to Mr Mason, if the latter was feeling better. Mr Mason turned pale, said he felt much better, and followed the sergeant out.

'I hope to God he meant what he said,' rumbled old Brandon Vernon. 'I've been so long with the Firm I've forgotten what other managements are like.'

Gradually they settled down to the actor's endless gossip about 'shop'. It was obvious that they were all shocked – some of them deeply moved perhaps – by Meyer's death. But they slipped into their habitual conversation quite unconsciously and soon were talking peaceably enough. Courtney Broadhead had gone to the far end of the room and stayed there, glowering, till old Vernon strolled across and tried to talk him into a better humour. They all completely ignored Gordon Palmer who sulked in a corner with his silent bear-leader.

Presently Packer returned.

'Inspector Wade would like to speak to you now, Mr Alleyn,' said Packer.

Alleyn followed him into the dark passage.

'Mr Wade was wondering if you'd be glad of the chance to get out of there, sir,' murmured Packer.

'I see. Very thoughtful of him.'

'Goodnight, sir.'

'Goodnight, Packer. I'll see you again, I expect.'

'Good-oh, sir,' said Packer with enthusiasm.

Alleyn made his way to the office where he found Wade seated at Alfred Meyer's desk with the colossal Cass in attendance.

'I thought perhaps you were getting a bit fed up in there, sir,' said Wade.

'It wasn't dull,' said Alleyn. 'The conversation took rather an interesting turn.'

'Yes?'

Alleyn related his experiences in the wardrobe-room.

'Oh,' said Wade, 'that's a bit of news, now, all that about Mr Courtney Broadhead and the Gaynes woman. We'll just get some notes on that, if we may, sir. Cass'll take it down in shorthand. Now, how does it go?'

'Briefly,' said Alleyn, 'like this. Liversidge, Miss Gaynes, young Gordon Palmer, his cousin, Geoffrey Weston, who seems to have strange ideas on the duties of a bear-leader, and Courtney Broadhead, all played poker for high stakes on the voyage out. Gordon Palmer and Liversidge were conspicuous winners, Broadhead a conspicuous loser. Some time between the last evening on board ship and the following evening on board the train, approximately a hundred pounds in notes was stolen from Miss Valerie Gaynes. The notes were in a leather writing-folder which she kept in a suitcase. In the train I noticed that Broadhead seemed greatly worried and I said so to Mr Hambledon. I had a seat in the company's carriage. Mr Broadhead spent a good deal of time on the platform. I can give you a more detailed, though incomplete, record of his movements, if you wish.'

'If you please, sir.'

'Well, here goes. I've a shocking memory, but it has retained one or two small items. At midnight the company, with the exception of

Mr and Mrs Meyer – Miss Dacres you know – and Miss Gaynes, were in the carriage. The other three had gone to their sleepers. At about ten minutes past twelve, I went to sleep. I woke at two-ten. The company were as they had been before I dozed off. A few minutes later, Mr Broadhead went out on the platform. He was visible through the glass door. At two-forty-five we reached Ohakune. Mr Hambledon and I went out and got coffee. Miss Dacres called us into her sleeper. We were met on the way by Mr Meyer who took us there. He said someone had tried to tip him overboard from the sleeper platform, about an hour before we got to Ohakune. He was not certain of the time. It may have been forty minutes or longer. If so this attempt was made while I was asleep. While Mr Meyer was relating his experience to us, Miss Gaynes came in and reported the loss of her money. When I offered to cast the eye at her ravished suitcase she was unflatteringly tepid and melted away.'

'Er,' said Cass.

'Yes?' asked Alleyn.

'That last sentence, sir – er – "when I offered to look" – '

'I phrased it badly,' said Alleyn. 'I offered to examine Miss Gaynes's leather folder. She declined, and shortly afterwards withdrew.'

'Thanks,' said Cass.

'Returning to the wardrobe-room. While I was there Mr Gordon Palmer remarked that Mr Courtney Broadhead had paid his poker debts the morning after our train journey. Mr Palmer told us that Mr Broadhead had previously asked for time in the settlement of these debts. Mr Palmer asked Mr Broadhead where he had raised the wind.'

'Obtained the requisite sum,' murmured Cass.

'Certainly, Cass. Mr Broadhead showed signs of the liveliest indignation and offered violence.'

'Did he strike Palmer?' asked Wade.

'No. I ventured to apply a back-arm bend. Mr Broadhead informed us that he had confided in the deceased, who had advanced him the money. Mr Palmer then remarked that it was unfortunate that Mr Meyer could not substantiate this statement. It was at this stage that the attempt at violence occurred. How's that for official language?'

'Pardon?'

'No matter. Now, look here, Inspector. I had the impression that young Palmer was not doing his nasty stuff quite off his own bat. I rather fancy someone had egged him on to bait Courtney Broadhead.'

'Do you, sir? Any idea who?'

'Mr Liversidge,' said Alleyn abstractedly, 'was *so* helpful and kind. He suggested that no doubt Mr Meyer had made a note of the loan and that this would clear the whole matter up.'

'Well, so it would, sir, wouldn't it?'

'Yes. Mr Broadhead explained that the loan was a personal matter and was not recorded on the books.'

'Is that so?' said Wade. He regarded Alleyn solemnly. 'Well now, sir, that's very interesting. You might look at it this way. A young fellow who hasn't got the cash to pay his debts suddenly pays them and when people get inquisitive he says he was given the money by someone who's just been murdered.'

'Yes, that's how Master Palmer put it,' said Alleyn.

'About the tiki,' said Wade after a pause. 'I asked the Dacres wom – Mrs Meyer where it was, and she said she gave it to someone before supper. Neither she nor Hambledon could remember anything about it according to themselves. Nor could Mr Mason. Now there's this Mason. I understand he comes in for the money. I suppose it's a big estate, but you never know with theatricals. We'll have to watch Mr Mason.'

'Yes,' agreed Alleyn. 'I watched him go green in the face just now. He got out just in time – only just.'

'He said something about that. When did it happen?'

'Just after I asked my question about the tiki.'

'Get this down,' said Wade to Cass.

Alleyn described Mr Mason's dilemma.

'So he went out, did he?' grunted Wade. 'I'll have something to say to young Packer about that. Too right, I will. Letting him out just because he kidded he felt crook. These blasted youngsters. It may have been one big bluff. What if Mason was the one who had the tiki last and suddenly remembered it? Say he kidded he was crook so's he could see if he had it in his pockets? I'll talk to young Packer.'

'Er – yes. Quite so,' agreed Alleyn diffidently. 'But I assure you, Wade, the gentleman would most certainly have been ill where he stood if Packer had restrained him. Judging from the lamentable sounds that reached us, he got no farther than the passage. I don't think he escaped Packer's eye, you know.'

'You mean,' said Wade with scriptural accuracy, 'he vomited?'

'I do,' said Alleyn, 'and to some purpose.'

'Then he wasn't kidding he was crook?'

'He *may* be a crook, but why should he – '

'No, no. I mean, he wasn't making out he *felt* crook.'

'I – I beg your pardon. No. I should say definitely not.'

'Ugh!' grunted Wade.

'Of course,' said Alleyn mildly, 'he may have palmed a piece of soap and eaten it on the sly in order to make himself sick. But no – he didn't foam at the mouth.'

'I wonder what's the strength of this Firm of theirs – Incorporated Playhouses, or whatever they call it. Any idea, sir?'

'When Mason went out they all began talking about it. One of them – Ackroyd, I think – remarked that Mr Mason would be a very wealthy man.'

'Did he, though? Well – there's motive, sir.'

'Oh, rather. Money. The first motive, I always say,' agreed Alleyn.

'He's just gone – Mason, I mean. I asked him about this Incorporated Playhouses. He said, quite frank, that he'd be the whole works now Meyer was out of it. 'Course, he *would* be frank about that. We'd find out, anyway. He made no trouble about our looking at the books, either, though I must say he didn't seem too pleased when I sat down here and started going through the drawers.'

'That was Mr Meyer's desk, wasn't it?' asked Alleyn.

'Yes, that's right. I said: "This was deceased's private property, like, I suppose?" and he just nodded, and I must say he did look a bit sick. Kind of annoyed, too, as if he might go crook at me, any moment.'

'What, oh what,' wondered Alleyn, '*is* the fine shade of meaning attached to this word "crook"?' Aloud he asked:

'Have you been through the desk?'

'Not yet, sir. There's a whale of a lot of stuff. All very neat and business-like, though. He actually carted round the desk itself. Can you beat that? Couldn't do without it, Mason said. It's not much of an affair, either. Seems deceased had it for years and reckoned it brought him luck. Very superstitious gang, theatricals. It's a rickety old show too.'

Wade reached down to a lower drawer and pulled at the knob.

'A real old-timer,' he said and gave it a vigorous jerk. The drawer shot out suddenly. He looked down. 'Hul-lo!' said Wade. 'What's this? What's this!'

'It looks rather like a will,' said Alleyn.

CHAPTER 9

Courtney Broadhead's Scene

'By cripes, that's just what it is,' said Wade with the liveliest satisfaction.

He opened out his find and laid it on the desk. 'Quite short, too, it seems to be. Look here, sir.'

Alleyn read over his shoulder. Cass, with heavy nonchalance, moved a step or two nearer. A long silence followed, broken occasionally by a stertorous whispering noise made by Inspector Wade when he came upon a passage of involved legal phraseology. At last Alleyn straightened his long back and Wade brought his palm down with a slap on the open will.

'Money!' he said. 'We've got it here all right. Yee-ers. Notice the date? Two years ago. And three months. Seems Mr Mason is a principal legatee. Can you beat that? Meyer fixed the wife up with a whacking big lump sum and leaves the rest to his partner in – how does it go? – "in recognition of his lifelong devotion to the firm of Incorporated Playhouses and in memory of a friendship that only death can sever." '

'Pleasantly Victorian,' remarked Alleyn, 'and rather charming.'

'Well, they certainly hit the right note when they said Mason'd be a rich man,' said Wade. 'They did, didn't they?'

'Sixty thousand to the wife – and look at the residue. Forty thousand. Forty thousand, his share in the business, all to Mason. By gosh! Well, I'd better get on with the job, I suppose. I think we'll see this young Broadhead next. Looks to me as if there might be something in that, though it's too early to speculate. I reckon you'd say it's always too early to do that, wouldn't you, sir?'

'I say so, Mr Wade, but I do it just the same.'

Wade gave his great shout of laughter.

'It's human nature,' he said. 'Wondering! People spend half their time wondering about each other. That's what sells this detective fiction, I reckon.'

'I think you're right,' said Alleyn. 'It's what made policemen out of both of us, I wouldn't mind betting. Are you keen on your job, Wade?'

'Well now, that's a bit of a power, that is.' And Wade stared solemnly at Alleyn. 'Yes. Taking it all round, I'd say I was. Not but what it doesn't give you a pain in the neck sometimes. Making the usual inquiries. Following up information received. And the first two or three years are enough to break your heart, they're that slow. Police-constable duty, I mean. Of course, you didn't have any of that, sir.'

'Did I not?' asked Alleyn grimly.

'Why, I reckoned you'd be kind of – ' He hesitated. 'You came at it from college, didn't you, sir? I mean you were kind of – '

'I went into the force before the days of Lord Trenchard's scheme. I came down from Oxford, and after three years soldiering, and a brief sojourn in the Foreign Office, signed on in the usual way and went on night duty in Poplar.'

'Is that so? Is that so?' Wade stared at Alleyn's fastidiously ironical face and looked as if he was trying to picture it beneath a helmet.

'How about Mr Broadhead?' said Alleyn.

'That's right. Get him, Cass.'

'Hadn't I better disappear?' suggested Alleyn when Cass had gone, 'It'll look a little odd if I don't.'

'I've been thinking about that, sir. Now, you say you don't want this crowd to know you're what you are. Well now, if you feel that way it's up to us to respect your wishes. It's just for you to say. And I'm very, very glad to have had your report on what you've heard. Still, it seems to me that with four of these theatricals knowing you're a Chief Inspector from the Yard, it's not going to be a secret for long.'

'You're perfectly right,' groaned Alleyn.

'Well now, sir, what if I was to tell them who you are? Mind, if you want to keep out of it, you've only to say so and we'll respect your wishes, but if you're interested, we'd be only too pleased. I had a chat just now over the phone with the super, and I told him you were helping us anonymously, and he said he'd call on you in the morning, as maybe you'd be wanting to get home to bed shortly. He said we were to show you every courtesy, sir, and I'm sure we want to, but if you feel like sitting in official-like, well – ' And here Inspector Wade, having wound himself up into a sort of struggling verbal cocoon, gave up the unequal contest and stared rather helplessly at Alleyn.

'My dear fellow,' said Alleyn quickly, 'of course I'll sit in if you'd like me to. It's extraordinarily nice of you to ask me. Tell them I'm a busy, by all means, if you think it'll serve any useful purpose. There comes young Broadhead now.'

Courtney Broadhead was ushered in by Cass. His face looked white and drawn in the harsh light shed by the office lamp. He stopped short just inside the door, stared unhappily at Wade, and then saw Alleyn.

'Hullo, Mr Alleyn,' he said. 'You still up?'

'Yes,' said Alleyn. 'This is Inspector Wade – Mr Courtney Broadhead.'

'Good evening, Mr Broadhead,' said Wade, with a kind of official heartiness. 'I'd just like a word with you, if you don't mind. You may be able to help us with one or two points.'

'Oh,' said Broadhead, still staring at Alleyn. Wade glanced at the notes before him on Alfred Meyer's old desk.

'Now, Mr Broadhead, there are a few details I'd like to have from you about your journey down from Auckland in the Limited on Friday night.'

'Oh,' said Broadhead again. His mouth shaped itself into a curious half-smile and still he looked at Alleyn.

'I understand,' continued Wade, 'that up to a few minutes before the train reached Ohakune you were in the reserved carriage with the rest of the company. That is correct?'

'I think so. I really don't remember. You were in our carriage that night, weren't you, Mr Alleyn?'

'I was, yes,' said Alleyn.

Broadhead laughed unpleasantly.

'Perhaps you remember where I was before the train got to wherever-it-was.'

'I think I do.'

'Did you go out on the platform before the train reached Ohakune, Mr Broadhead?' asked Wade with rather unconvincing airiness.

'Believe I did. Ask Mr Alleyn.'

Wade looked blandly at Alleyn.

'I believe he did,' said Alleyn.

'At what time?' pursued Wade.

'Ask Mr Alleyn.'

'About two-thirty-five,' said Alleyn cheerfully.

'Wonderful memory you've got,' remarked Broadhead. 'Do they pay you for this?'

'Now, Mr Broadhead,' said Wade. 'Was Mr Meyer on the opposite platform to the one on which you stood? The sleeper-platform?'

'Doesn't Mr Alleyn know that too?' asked Broadhead.

'Chief Detective-Inspector Alleyn,' said Wade with a certain amount of relish, 'has been kind enough to make his own statement.'

Courtney Broadhead looked bewildered, then flabbergasted and then, strangely enough, relieved. Unexpectedly he burst out laughing.

'Oh, no!' he said. 'Not really. A genuine sleuth and in at the death! I got you wrong. I thought you were being the helpful little amateur. Sorry.' He examined Alleyn with interest. 'Good lord, you're the man with the marvellous press. The *Daily Sun* ran you in the Gardener case, didn't it?'

'Spare me,' said Alleyn.

'"The Handsome Sleuth or the Man Who Never Gives Up." I thought your name was spelt – '

'It is,' said Alleyn. 'The passenger list got it wrong.'

Broadhead was silent. He seemed to be turning over this new piece of information in his mind. Something of his former manner appeared when he spoke again.

'Are you interested professionally in this – this case?'

'We hope that the chief inspector,' said Wade, 'will very kindly give us the benefit of his advice.'

'Do you!' said Broadhead.

'Now about Mr Meyer on the sleeper-platform,' said Wade briskly. 'Was he there?'

'No. Not while I was outside.'

'You're sure about that?'

Cass glanced up from his notebook. Wade leant forward. Alleyn, who had an unlit cigarette between his lips, paused in the act of striking a match.

'Absolutely,' said Broadhead firmly.

Alleyn lit his cigarette.

'Yee-ers,' said Wade thoughtfully. He turned to Alleyn. 'I don't know if you'd care to put a question, sir?'

'Oh, thanks,' said Alleyn. 'Do you know I would, rather? Mr Broadhead, did you fall asleep in the carriage before we got to Ohakune?'

Broadhead stared.

'Yes. At least I dozed. Had a nightmare.'

'Any idea how long you were asleep?'

'No. Ten minutes perhaps. I don't know.'

'I was sound asleep myself. I remember noticing, just before I dozed off, that you and Mr Hambledon seemed to be the only other persons awake in the carriage.'

'I watched you fall asleep,' volunteered Broadhead. 'I remember that. You just shut your eyes and went still. The others all had their mouths open. I wondered if you were foxing.'

'Why?' said Alleyn sharply.

'I don't know. I thought you might be bored with the great HH.'

'With Hambledon? No. Did he go to sleep?'

'I don't think so. Wait a moment. The last thing I remember before I shut my own eyes was – was looking along the carriage towards the door. I thought they all looked half dead, swaying in their seats with their mouths open. I saw Hailey pick up a paper and hold it sideways to catch the light. His back was towards me, you know. I could see his arm and half the back of his head. That's the last thing I remember before I fell asleep.'

'And when you woke?'

'Nobody seemed to have moved. It was all rather unreal and smoky and noisy. Then you woke up and began to speak to Hambledon.'

'No one had moved,' murmured Alleyn to himself.

'At least – ' Broadhead stopped short.

'Yes?'

'I've got a sort of hazy idea someone went down the corridor, past my chair. You know how one gets the impression of things when one dozes in a train. I might have dreamt it. No – I don't think I did. Someone went past. I think it half-woke me.'

'Do you mean that this person walked back from the direction of the platform at the head of the carriage, or towards it from the rear of the carriage?'

'Back. He was facing me. Probably been to the lav. at the rear of the sleeper.'

'He?'

'Yes. I think so. He must have sat down in one of the seats behind me.'

'He may have gone right through.'

'No. I remember waiting for the door to slam. It didn't. I went to sleep again.'

'Thank you,' said Alleyn. 'I've no other questions, Inspector Wade.'

'Good-oh, sir.' Wade turned to Broadhead. 'What did you do with Mrs Meyer's tiki?' he asked.

'What? Nothing. I never had it. Look here, what *is* all this about that damned little monster? You started it in the wardrobe-room, Mr Alleyn. What's the dazzling idea?'

'We simply want to trace the tiki, Mr Broadhead,' said Wade. 'Mrs Meyer has lost it.'

'She's also lost a husband,' said Broadhead tartly, 'I thought you were looking for a murderer, not a thief.'

'That's certainly – '

'What's more, I don't believe she cares tuppence whether the tiki's lost or found. What the hell are you driving at? Am I supposed to have pinched the filthy little object? I've had about as much as I can stand. You think I stole Val Gaynes's money, don't you? You think it's all a lie about Meyer lending me the cash. You think I'm a thief and a murderer – ' His voice rose hysterically. Cass looked perturbed and moved a step or two nearer to Broadhead. Wade stood up hastily.

'Keep off,' shouted Broadhead; 'you can't arrest me – you can't – '

'My good ass,' advised Alleyn, 'don't put ideas in our heads and don't dramatize yourself. As you have suggested, this is a serious matter. Nobody's trying to arrest you. Inspector Wade has asked you a perfectly reasonable question. Why not answer it?'

'There now, Mr Broadhead,' said Wade, 'that's the way to look at it.'

'I suppose,' said Broadhead more quietly, 'you've heard all about the scene in the wardrobe-room. I suppose your distinguished colleague has told you what that little stinker Palmer said about me.'

'*And* all about your subsequent attempt upon the stinker,' murmured Alleyn. 'Yes.'

'Don't you think it was a pretty foul thing to sit there as if you were one of us, playing the spy, all agog to report to the police? Don't you? Don't you think it would have been the decent thing to say – to say – '

'To say,' suggested Alleyn helpfully: '"I'm a detective, so if one of you killed this very honest little gentleman whom you all profess to admire so much, don't do anything to give yourself away." No, Mr Broadhead.'

'My God, I was as fond of him as any of them. He was a damn' good friend to me.'

'Then,' said Alleyn, 'see if you can help Inspector Wade to trace the little greenstone tiki.'

'Oh, hell!' said Broadhead. 'All right! All right! Though what the suffering cats it's got to do with the case – All right. Go ahead.'

'Well, now,' said Wade. 'I understand you all took a look at this tiki before you sat down to supper. Did you handle it, Mr Broadhead?'

'Yes. I had it in my hand for a moment. Someone took it from me.'

'Who?'

'I think it was Frankie Liversidge. I'm not sure. It was passed round.'

'Yes. Now, Mr Broadhead, I want you to go back to the end of the performance, last night. Were you acting right up to the finish?'

'Acting!' said Broadhead distastefully. 'No, I wasn't "acting". I finished just before Miss Dacres's big scene.'

'What did you do then?'

'Stood in the wings for the company call at the curtain.'

'Then you *were* acting, as you might say,' insisted Wade crossly.

'If you call hanging about off-stage – '

'Let it go. After the play was over, what did you do?'

'Bolted to the dressing-room and took off my make-up.'

'Anyone with you?'

'Yes. Vernon and Frankie Liversidge.'

'All the time?'

'Vernon and I went back together. Frankie came in a minute or two later, I think. And Ackroyd joined us before we went along to the party.'

'All right. Now after the accident I understand that at the suggestion of Dr Te Pokiha and the chief inspector here you all went to your dressing-rooms and later to the wardrobe-room. Did you go directly to the wardrobe-room, Mr Broadhead?'

'No. I went into my dressing-room on the way.'

'What for?'

'To get my overcoat. I was shivering.'

'How long were you in the dressing-room?'

'About five minutes.'

'Five minutes to fetch a coat?'

'Well – Branny was there.'

'Who's he?'

'Brandon Vernon – the heavy. I told you we share the dressing-room. Branny had a flask there. We had a nip. Needed it. Frankie came in later and had one, too. Then we all went to the wardrobe-room.'

'To get to the dressing-room, you passed the iron ladder that goes up to the platform?'

'What platform?'

'I think it's called the grid,' said Alleyn diffidently. 'Or is it the flies?'

'Oh,' said Broadhead. 'Yes. I suppose we did. It's just by the dressing-room passage, isn't it?'

Wade shifted his position and became elaborately casual.

'You didn't happen to glance up towards the platform at all, I suppose?'

'Good lord, I don't know. Why should I?'

'You didn't get the impression anyone was up there?'

'I didn't get any impression at all.'

'Did you all leave the stage together – the whole company, I mean, and the guests?'

'Pretty well. Everyone was very quiet. The guests just petered away as soon as they could. We stood for a moment by the entrance to the passage to let Miss Dacres go first. Then we followed.'

'All together?'

'We didn't make a football scrum of it,' said Broadhead crossly. 'It's a narrow passage.'

'When you got to the wardrobe-room, was everyone there?'

'I wasn't the last.'

'Who came in after you, Mr Broadhead?'

'Oh, lord!' said Broadhead again. 'Let's see. Well, Gascoigne was after me, and Mr Mason. Susan and Hailey Hambledon came in just before that, I think, with Miss Dacres. I'm not sure. No, by George, Mr Alleyn was last.'

'Quite right,' agreed Alleyn. 'I was a bad last.'

'Well,' said Wade, 'I think that'll be all, sir. If you've no objection, I'll get you to sign these notes later on when they've been put into longhand. We've got your address. Perhaps you'd look in some time tomorrow morning at the station.'

'Where is it?'

'Hill Street, Mr Broadhead. Top of Ruru Street. Anyone will direct you.'

'I suppose so. I could ask a policeman. At least he would know that.'

'Goodnight, Mr Broadhead,' said Wade coldly.

CHAPTER 10

The Case is Wide Open

'I wish I knew,' said Alleyn when Broadhead had gone, 'whether to give myself a kick in the neck or a slap on the back.'

'How's that, sir?' asked Wade.

'After the main body had retired to the dressing-rooms, Mr Mason, Mr Gascoigne, Dr Te Pokiha, the chief mechanist and I were left on the stage with the body. Until then I had imagined the whole show was simply a ghastly accident, but almost automatically I had suggested that none of the company left the theatre. The official mind must have functioned – reaction to sudden death or something. If I *had* suspected homicide, I should have done my best to keep them all on the stage. I don't think I would have succeeded without producing the Yard. But at that stage I didn't actually suspect, although I suppose I asked myself the routine question – "Homicide or Accident?" Well, as soon as we were alone the unhappy Bert gave tongue. He protested many times and with sanguinary monotony that there had been some funny business. So did Mr Gascoigne. They were all for going up aloft to take a look at the tackle. From being almost official I now became quite officious. I said: "No, no, gentlemen; we must must leave this for our wonderful police." "Scale not the heights," the old man said, and they heeded and gave over.'

'Quite right, too.'

'But was it? Suppose they had gone aloft? They would have found the tackle as it was when the bottle fell. They would have found it as I found it a few minutes later when I snooped up the ladder. Now what would have been the effect of this discovery on the murderer?

If the murderer is not Mr Mason, or Mr Gascoigne, or Te Pokiha, or Bert, he would presumably have come out of his hole, found the stage empty, heard voices on the grid, and gone back into his hole. He would never have tidied up.'

'That's so. But we've got your evidence, anyway,' objected Wade.

'Yes, we have. We've caught him out in a bit of elaboration,' agreed Alleyn. 'If – if – ' He rubbed his nose vexedly. 'I usually welcome elaborations. "Beware of fancy-touches" should be neatly printed and hung above every would-be murderer's cot. But this time I felt that, as far as we're concerned, there's a catch in it. Well, now, if our man is Te Pokiha, or Mason, or Gascoigne, or Bert, he would still have been unable to tidy up. By preventing the inspection of the tackle I made possible the alteration.'

'Well, sir, according to your way of looking at it, that's all to the good. The alteration was a blunder, as it turned out.'

'And we should never have found the tiki.'

'That's two blunders.'

'Is it?' said Alleyn. 'I've got my doubts about that.'

'I don't get you there, sir. Surely we ought to trace the tiki?'

'Oh, yes,' agreed Alleyn, screwing up one side of his face. 'We'll have to try. What did Hambledon and Mason have to say about it?'

'Oh, same story as young Broadhead. Mr Hambledon said he took it from Mrs Meyer soon after you gave it to her. He says he had a look at it and handed it onto someone else – thinks it was old Mr Vernon, but isn't sure. Mr Mason says he can't say who gave it to him, but he handled it and remembers giving it back to Mrs Meyer just before you all sat down to supper.'

'And Mrs Meyer?'

'Thinks she remembers he gave it to her and fancies she put it down on the table somewhere. There you are!'

'Yes,' said Alleyn, 'it's wide open.'

'Mrs Meyer – ' began Wade and stopped abruptly.

'Look here, sir, what *do* I call the lady? Mrs Meyer or Miss Dacres?'

'Miss Dacres, I fancy.'

'Seems hardly nice in some ways. Well, then, Miss Dacres seemed a bit surprised when I asked her about the tiki. She gave me a look.'

'That's because I had already spoken to her about it.'

'Is that so? Did you get the same answer?'

'More or less. She looked in her bag and then said she didn't know what had become of it. All the same – '

'Well – there it is,' said Wade without noticing Alleyn's hesitation. 'Better get a move on, I suppose. Who'll we take next, sir?'

'If I might suggst, I think it would be as well to ask Gascoigne, the stage-manager, if he knows who was the last person, officially, to examine the apparatus.'

'Good enough,' said Wade, and sent for Gascoigne.

Gascoigne said that the last official inspection took place just before the end of the third act.

'Mr Meyer came round from the front of the house. He was as fussy about it as if it'd been a first night in town,' said Gascoigne. 'He asked me if everything was all right. I'd been up myself and seen it and we'd rehearsed it God knows how often. But to humour him I sent Bert up again and I'm blessed if the governor didn't climb up after Bert. It was then that he loosened the wire, I think. He was in a great flutter. By God, you'd almost think he knew something would happen. That was actually just before the last curtain. I remember they came down the ladder after we'd run down.'

'Which of them came first?'

'Bert. He came to me in the prompt-box and said it was all OK. Mr Meyer went off to the front of the house, I think.'

'And what did you do?'

'Me?' said Gascoigne, looking surprised. 'I got the staff to work setting the stage for the party. Bert and the local men did it.'

'Did you notice anyone go up the ladder after that?' asked Wade without hope.

'Of course I didn't. Wouldn't I be asking you to go after them if I had? Look here, Inspector, had that gear been interfered with? I'd like to go up and take a look at it.'

'You'd find no difference, Mr Gascoigne,' said Wade.

'But I tell you,' said Gascoigne violently, 'there must have been some funny business – there must have been.'

'Now listen, sir,' said Wade. 'When everybody left the stage at Chief Inspector Alleyn's suggestion – '

'What! Chief Inspector how much?' ejaculated Gascoigne.

Wade explained.

'Here!' said Gascoigne. 'Is there anything fishy about our company? Have you been tailing round after us, Mr Alleyn? What's the idea of all this?'

'I'm on a holiday,' explained Alleyn apologetically, 'and I've not been tailing anybody at all, Mr Gascoigne.'

'So you say,' muttered Gascoigne.

'It's true,' said Alleyn. 'S'welp me.'

'Now, Mr Gascoigne,' continued Wade doggedly, 'when they all left the stage after the accident, what did you do?'

'I stayed put. I wanted to go up and look at the gear, but Mr – Inspector – Alleyn said wait for the police. Why didn't you tell us who you were then?'

'It would have been in doubtful taste, don't you think?' asked Alleyn. 'You remained on the stage until the arrival of the police, I think?'

'Yes, I did,' said Gascoigne.

Wade glanced at Alleyn.

'Well, Mr Gascoigne, I think that's all I want to know just now. You're staying – where?'

'The Railway Hotel.'

'Good-oh, sir. Perhaps you'd look in at the station tomorrow. The inquest – ' Wade shepherded Gascoigne out and came back looking worried.

'I reckon,' he said, 'we can cross him off unless there's been any collusion. He met us at the door and you left him on the stage. He never had a chance to go up into the grid. Seems to me that the point we want to get at is what they all did when they left the stage. Isn't that right, sir?'

'I think so,' agreed Alleyn. 'Between the event and the time you and I went aloft, someone managed to climb one of the ladders and put things straight. It seems to me, Wade, that the most likely moment for this would be when they all left the stage. Off-stage it was quite dark. It would be a perfectly easy matter for one of them to slip aside behind the scenery, snoop round to the ladder at the back, and climb up. Whoever it was probably took off his or her shoes. Now, if this person went up during the time of the general exodus, he was probably hiding up there when I made my first visit. He'd want to get the job done as soon as possible and before the police arrived. It sounds more risky than it actually was. If he *had* been spotted he'd have said he was damn' well going to have a look at the gear and have made a song about its having been interfered with. We know Gascoigne could not have done this.'

'Nor Broadhead either, if Brandon Vernon agrees that they went together to the dressing-room,' said Wade.

'Right. Now let's look at the other half of the picture, shall we? The first visit, when the murderer cut the weight off the rope and moved the pulley. Again Broadhead says he and Vernon went together to the dressing-room, after the final curtain. That is, after Bert came down and reported the tackle all correct. If Vernon gives the same account, that lets both of them out. If Bert and his mates say Gascoigne was with them while they got ready for the party, that lets him out.'

'Looks as if it's a crack less wide open, sir, when you get at it like that. Now, when I talked to Mason, he said he was in the box-office during the last act. When the people began to come away, he went to his own office – this room we're in now – to have a word with the deceased. He says deceased left him here, saying he was going round to the stage. Mason says he then made a note of the night's takings and did one or two jobs here. He went out once, ran along to tell the old chap who stage-door-keeps to show all the guests straight to the stage but to be sure and check up their names in order to keep off any hangers-on who hadn't been invited. I've spoken to old Singleton, the doorkeeper, and he remembers Mason running along the alley to give him this message. He says Mason came back here. So does Mason. The old chap stood by the stage-door looking after him. And to make it a bit tighter, the old bloke says he strolled along to the office a bit later to ask about something, and Mason was there at his desk. Dr Te Pokiha says he looked in before going to the party – he'd met Mason before – and stayed there yarning for a while, leaving Mason in the office. Now, Mr Alleyn, the only way Mason could have got behind the scenes without Singleton seeing him is by going through this door into the box-office, out at the front entrance where someone might have seen him, and round the block to the back of the theatre. The door at the back is locked on the inside. Even if he had the key he couldn't have done it in the time. He couldn't have got back before Singleton walked across, which he says was about five or six minutes later. That's that. Mason said he stayed on here – looking up his papers and so on – for a while – not long – and then joined the party. Singleton remembers Mason coming back and swears he didn't go behind the scenes until the last of the guests were in.'

'I was among the last of the guests,' said Alleyn, 'and I overtook Mr Mason at the stage-door.'

'Did you, sir? Did you, now! Well, I suppose you might say that's a pretty fair alibi for Mr Mason. Would he have time to go up aloft after he went in with you, now?'

'Plenty of time,' said Alleyn sadly, 'but he didn't do it. I remember perfectly well that he was on the stage all the time. He stood near me and I talked to him and to Hambledon.'

'That's what Hambledon said,' agreed Wade gloomily. It's a blooming nark, dinkum it is. Still, there's better alibis than that have gone west before now, and I'm not going to forget this will. Mason's a whole lot better off by this murder.'

'Was he badly off before?' asked Alleyn lightly.

That's what I reckon we'll have to find out, sir. Do you think the Yard – ?'

'Oh, yes. They'll do it for you if it can be done. We call it making tactful inquiries. *Aren't* I glad I'm not there.'

'You're here, though,' said Wade, 'and I suppose they know it.'

'I don't like the way you said that, Inspector,' said Alleyn with a wry smile. 'And I know jolly well what you're thinking.'

Wade grinned sheepishly.

'Well, sir,' he said, 'it looks as if it's an English case more than a New Zillund one, now, doesn't it?'

'Wait and see,' said Alleyn. 'What about your tiki? And talking about the tiki, did you ask Mr Mason where he went with Dr Te Pokiha after the event? He was very much shaken and Te Pokiha took him off somewhere to give him a drink.'

'The doctor brought him here. There's a bottle of whisky and a couple of glasses in that cupboard there. I put 'em away to get Mason's prints. They seem to have taken it neat.'

'So Dr Te Pokiha felt a bit groggy, too,' said Alleyn. 'He seemed so very sedate and professional at the time. What happened when they'd had their neat whiskies?'

'The doctor rang us up and left Mason here with his grog, when we arrived. Mason says he was still here when we went past. I remember noticing that door was open on the alleyway and the lights in here were up. I fancy I caught sight of him. Anyway, the doorkeeper says he mooched along the yard after we'd come in, saw Mason in the office and talked to him. He says he went along as soon as he'd let us in and stayed until Mason went to the wardrobe-room. They walked along together.'

'That's right, too, sir,' said the silent Cass unexpectedly. 'I was just inside the stage-door when he came through. I sent him along. He was looking horribly crook.'

'Ill?' asked Alleyn cautiously.

'Too right, sir.'

'Crook or not,' said Wade, 'I'm not taking anything for gospel where Mr George Mason's concerned, by cripey I'm not. Now the D – Miss Dacres hasn't got even half an alibi for the first stunt – fixing the gear before the murder. She says she went to her dressing-room and was alone there till she came to the party.'

'What about her dresser?'

'Says she sent her off to doll herself up for the party. Now Miss Dacres *could* have slipped round to the ladder at the back, fixed the gear, and then gone to her room. When did she come in to the party, sir?'

'She came in last,' said Alleyn, and up through his mind welled the memory of Carolyn hooting melodiously as she came down the passage, of Ackroyd opening the door on to the stage, of Carolyn making her entrance, of himself going to meet her.

'Last!' exclaimed Wade. 'Last of the lot, and alone.'

'No. Not alone, Hailey Hambledon, Mr Mason and Mr Meyer went and fetched her.'

'That makes no odds,' said Wade.

'What about Mr Hambledon?' asked Alleyn.

'He says he left the stage with the others after the final curtain and went to his dressing-room. His dresser was there but he didn't want him and sent him away.'

'Yes. He was wearing a dinner-jacket. He'd only need to take his make-up off.'

'He could have gone up the first time, sir. As soon as the dresser had gone he could have slipped back to the stage and round to the ladder at the rear. It would have been after Mr Meyer and Bert okayed the gear.'

'How does he stand for the second visit? He stayed behind with us – and the body – and left the stage while Gascoigne, Bert and I were still there. Said he was going to Miss Dacres's room. He was there when I arrived later on. He went out, at my suggestion, to get some brandy. I don't think he was away long enough to go up to the grid and get the brandy as well. *Might* have had time, I suppose, but it would have been damn' quick work.'

'As far as Mr Hambledon is concerned we haven't got a motive, sir, have we?'

Alleyn raised an eyebrow.

'I suppose you may say we haven't,' he said slowly. 'Is there anything – ' began Wade. 'No, no. Nothing.'

A knock on the outside door heralded the entrance of Packer.

'Beg pardon, sir,' he said, 'but are you ready for another?'

'Yes – all right – all right,' said Wade impatiently. 'Send – '

'Beg pardon, sir, but Mr Ackroyd says could you see him next? He says there's something he'd like to tell you, particular.'

'Ackroyd? Which is he?'

'The comedian,' said Alleyn.

'Good-oh, then, Packer. Send him along.'

Packer went away with Cass.

'What's biting Mr Ackroyd, I wonder?' said Wade.

'I wonder,' murmured Alleyn.

'Is he one of their swell turns, sir? The funny man, is he?'

'Dreadfully funny,' said Alleyn.

'I haven't seen the show. I like a good laugh, but these stage plays seem kind of feeble-minded after the flicks, I reckon. Nothing but talk. I don't mind a bit of vordervil. Still, if it's funny – '

'Mr Ackroyd is a good comedian on the stage. I find him less entertaining when he's off it.'

'He looks a scream,' said Wade.

The scream appeared, ushered in by Cass.

Ackroyd was a dot of a man; beside the gigantic Cass he looked like a dwarf. 'And his face *is* funny,' thought Alleyn. 'That button of a nose was made to be painted red. He ought to be in pantomime rather than polite comedy. No, that's not fair – he's a really good actor. There are brains behind his work and that kind of humour that comes from inside – the Chaplin brand. But I don't think he's a very nice little man. Waspish.'

Ackroyd walked across to Inspector Wade with neat assurance. His stage mannerisms were faintly imposed on his everyday behaviour. One expected him to say something excruciatingly funny.

'I hope I don't intrude,' said Ackroyd.

'That's all right, sir,' said Wade heartily. 'Take a seat. You wanted to see me about something?'

'That's right. Mind, I don't want you to take too much notice of it. It's probably of no account. Still, I feel you ought to know about it. It's dead against the grain with me to butt in on other people's business, you know.'

'Lie,' thought Alleyn.

'We quite understand that, Mr Ackroyd,' said Wade. 'It's a confidential matter.' Ackroyd turned to Alleyn. 'No offence, you know, old boy.'

'None in the world,' said Alleyn cheerfully.

'– so if you wouldn't mind – '

'Mr Alleyn is a detective,' said Wade. 'He's in this case with us.'

'A detective?' shouted Ackroyd. 'By George, Meyer knew about it all the time, did he! Working for Meyer, were you?'

'I'm afraid I don't follow you, Mr Ackroyd. I am a policeman,' said Alleyn, 'not a private detective.'

'A Yard man?'

'Yes.'

'Then it couldn't have been him you were after.'

'Who d'you mean?' asked Wade.

'Why, Hambledon, of course,' said Ackroyd.

CHAPTER 11

St John Ackroyd and Susan Max

'Hambledon!' said Alleyn sharply. 'What the – I beg your pardon, Wade,' he added instantly. 'This is your show.'

'Go right ahead, sir.'

'Thank you so much.' Alleyn turned to Ackroyd. 'I must confess I'm curious to know why you thought I was interested in Mr Hambledon.'

'Don't mind me, old boy,' said Ackroyd easily. 'When the inspector here said you were a 'tec, I thought Alf Meyer had put you on to follow Hailey and the fair Carolyn. That's all. Quite natural, you know, under the circs.'

'I see,' said Alleyn, and was silent.

'It's like that, is it?' said Wade.

Ackroyd pulled a serio-comic face, thrusting his lower lip sideways with the tip of his tongue. 'Very much like it,' he said.

'Common little stinker,' thought Alleyn.

'D'you mean,' asked Wade, 'that she gave him cause for divorce?'

'That's my idea. No business of mine, mind.'

'Was it this you were wanting to tell me, Mr Ackroyd?'

'Oh God, no. At least, it's something to do with it. I was going to keep it under my hat, but Alf Meyer was a white man, and if he's been murdered – ' He paused.

'That's right,' encouraged Wade. Alleyn was conscious of an illogical distaste for both of them.

'Well, it's like this,' said Ackroyd. 'The morning we got here I came down to the theatre. We had a call at ten-thirty. I got here early and went to my dressing-room. It's round the corner of the passage and up a right-angled one, so that actually it backs on to the star dressing-room. Well, in these wooden buildings of yours you can hear each other thinking. The walls are only thin partitions in this show. I was getting my stuff out when I heard Hailey and the Great Actress talking in the star-room.'

'Mr Hambledon and Miss Dacres?'

'None other. Hailey was in the devil of a temper, trying to get her to say she'd levant with him at the end of this tour. Fact! And she said she wouldn't because she's a Catholic and doesn't believe in divorce. She was doing her "little devil" stuff. Seemed to be big with Hailey – he got all he-man and violent. Ttff! Then he said something like: "Would you marry me if Alf was dead?" And the Great Actress said she would. That took her off. She went out on the stage, and a minute later I heard her give her opening line.'

'Yes,' said Wade after a moment. 'Thanks, Mr Ackroyd. Doesn't sound exactly as if she was Hambledon's mistress, though, do you reckon?'

'God knows what she is. She'll be his wife before long, I don't mind betting you. Well, that's that. Probably nothing in it. I'll be off.'

'If you don't mind waiting a minute longer, sir, there are one or two formal questions.'

Wade asked Ackroyd what he did after the final curtain. He went straight to his dressing-room, it seemed. He was alone there until he came out for the party. He looked in at Liversidge's room and they then joined Vernon and Broadhead and went along to the party. After the catastrophe he left the stage with the others, went to his dressing-room, had a stiff nip and then joined the rest of the company in the wardrobe-room. On both these occasions he had repeatedly called out to the others from his own room. Asked about the train journey he said he slept solidly for at least an hour before they got to Ohakune, and had not the remotest idea who entered or left the carriage.

Cass took notes of this, as of all the former interviews. Ackroyd took it all very easily and gave some of his replies with an air of mock solemnity that the sergeant and Wade found extremely diverting. When it was all over Ackroyd turned to Alleyn.

'And what, may one ask,' he said, 'is Scotland Yard's part in the proceedings?'

'Noises off, Mr Ackroyd,' replied Alleyn good-humouredly. 'I'm here by accident and the courtesy of Inspector Wade.'

'Funny me thinking you were a private sleuth. I say, old boy, you'll keep it under your hat won't you – about Hailey and the Dacres, you know. You're rather pally with them, I've noticed. That's what made me think you were watching them. Don't give me away, now, will you?'

'To Miss Dacres and Mr Hambledon? No,' said Alleyn bleakly.

Ackroyd walked over to the door.

'Of course,' he said, 'that fascinating blah stuff of hers goes down with the nit-wits. I've worked with her for six years and I know the lady. She's as hard as nails underneath. That's only my opinion, you know, for what it's worth. It's based on observation.'

'Was your suggestion about Mr Mason's past also based on observation?' asked Alleyn pleasantly.

'What's that, old boy? Oh George! No, I wasn't in the company he stranded in the States. I don't go out with bad shows.'

'But it's a true story?'

'Don't ask me. I was told it for gospel. You never know. But I get fed up with all this kow-towing to the Firm. Alf and George are no better than anybody else in management. Now Alf s gone I suppose all the spare spotlights will be trained on George. "Our Mr Mason." *And* of course on the Great Actress. By the way what's all the fuss about the little green whatsit you gave her?'

'Merely that it is lost and we should like to recover it.'

'Well if it's lost, she did the losing. She had it last.'

'Is that so!' exclaimed Wade.

'Certainly. Branny put it down on the table and she picked it up and slipped it inside her dress. I'll swear to that in six different positions. Cheerio!'

And, like a good actor, on this effective line he made his exit.

'He's a hard case, that one,' said Wade appreciatively. 'I reckon he's a real shrewdy.'

'Yes,' agreed Alleyn, 'he's shrewd.'

'I'd like to know how much there is in that stuff about Hambledon. "Would you marry me if Alf was dead?" And she said she would. I'd like to know just how he said it. And, by gum, I'd like to know if there's a free passage from the top of Miss Dacres's dress downwards.'

'And I,' said Alleyn, 'would like to know when Miss Dacres found occasion to snub Mr Ackroyd, and why.'

'Hullo!' said Wade. 'Where d'you get that notion, sir?'

'From the funny gentleman's behaviour. He radiated a peculiar malevolence that I associate with snubs from the opposite sex.'

'Still, sir, he'd hardly want to involve her in a murder charge, now, would he? And that statement about the tiki – well.'

'It is Hambledon, I fancy, whom he would like to involve.'

Wade chewed this over, eyeing Alleyn with a sort of guarded curiosity.

'Well,' he said at last, 'We'd better get on. Let's see: there's that old lady, Miss Max, and Miss Gaynes, Mr Liversidge, Mr Weston, who's not a member of the company, his cousin, Young Palmer (ditto), and Mr Brandon Vernon. Suppose we see the old girl first, Cass.'

Cass went off.

'Miss Max is an old acquaintance of mine,' said Alleyn; 'she was in the Felix Gardener show.'

'Is that so, sir? Well, now, perhaps you would talk to her. I'd like to listen to your methods, sir. We've got our own little ideas here about interviews and it'd be very interesting to compare them.'

'Bless me, Wade, I'm afraid you won't find much to analyse in my remarks, especially to Miss Max. I'll talk to her if you like, only don't, for the Lord's sake, expect fireworks. Here she comes.'

In came old Susan Max. Her roundabout figure was neat in its velveteen evening dress. Her faded blonde hair had been carefully dressed for the party, her round honest face with its peculiar pallor, induced by years of grease-paint, had been delicately powdered but not made-up. She looked what she was, an actress of the old school. She waddled forward, her face lighting as she saw Alleyn.

'Well, Miss Max,' said Alleyn, pushing a chair up to the fire, 'I'm afraid you've had a long wait in the wardrobe-room. Sit down by the fire and cheer us up.'

'Me cheer you up,' said Susan. 'I like that.'

She gave a cackle of laughter, but when she looked up at him her faded blue eyes were anxious.

'I never thought we'd meet again – like this,' said old Susan.

'I know,' said Alleyn. 'It's strange, isn't it?'

'They'll be calling me a Jonah,' she said. The pudgy old hands moved restlessly in her lap.

'You a Jonah! Not a bit of it. You've met Inspector Wade, haven't you?'

Susan gave Wade a grand nod.

'He's asked me to have a talk with you about this beastly affair. Do the others still think I'm a harmless civilian?'

'Would you credit it, dear,' said Susan indignantly, 'that just before I came along here that girl blurted it all out!'

'Miss Valerie Gaynes?'

'Little idiot. I've no patience. Doing her emotional act all over the room. What business is it of hers?'

'None at all, I should have thought,' said Alleyn comfortably. 'Have a cigarette and tell me some scandal. How did she get her job?'

'Who? Gaynes? My dear, through influence, like everybody else nowadays. Her father's a lessor of our theatre in Town. The girl knows nothing about the business. No poise. No charm. No personality. You were in front, weren't you? Well! What a *naughty* performance.'

'I wonder Miss Dacres puts up with it.'

'My dear, she has to. Some leading women don't mind poor supports, of course. Selfish. But Carolyn Dacres is an artist. Different type altogether,' said Susan, settling her chins.

'Anything between Liversidge and Valerie Gaynes?' asked Alleyn.

'Somebody ought to tell that girl to look after herself,' said Susan darkly. 'Not that they'd get any thanks for it. I've known Frankie Liversidge a good many years and I wouldn't care for any daughter of mine to be on those terms with him.'

'Anything in particular wrong with him?' asked Alleyn.

'Well, dear, he's not – not quite straight, shall we say, especially where women are concerned. But I mustn't sit here gossiping. It's all hours of the night as it is. What can I tell you?'

Alleyn asked her about her movements before and after the catastrophe. Like everyone else, she had spent the two significant periods in her dressing-room. At the end of the play she had gone straight there, removed her make-up and changed her dress. Miss Dacres's dresser had, at old Susan's invitation, also used the room to smarten herself up for the party.

'She's a nice woman – been with Miss Dacres for years, and she helped me with my change. The dress I wear in the last act is a beast to get out of. I was only just ready when the last of the guests arrived.'

After the catastrophe Susan had gone to the door of the star-room with Carolyn Dacres and had offered to go in with her.

'She said she'd rather be by herself, so I went on to my own room, dear. Minna – the dresser, you know – came in a little later. Miss Dacres had sent her away too. After a little while Minna said she couldn't bear to think of her there alone so she went back, and in a minute or two she came for me. The poor child – I mean Miss Dacres. for to me she *seems* a child – had thought she would like my company. She was sitting there quite quietly, staring in front of her. Shock. Couldn't talk about it or weep or do anything to ease her mind. Then she suddenly said she'd like to see you. Hailey Hambleon had come in and went to fetch you.'

'How long had he been there, Miss Max?'

'Let me see. He came in soon after I did. About ten minutes, I should say.'

'Ah,' said Alleyn with a sort of satisfied grunt. After a moment he leant forward.

'What sort of a fellow was Alfred Meyer?' he asked.

'One of the very best,' said Susan energetically. 'The right type of manager, and there aren't many of them left in the business. Always the same to everybody. Devoted to her.'

Alleyn remembered the pale commonplace little man, who had been so quiet in the ship and so frightened on the train.

'And she to him?' he asked.

Old Susan glanced at Cass and Wade.

'Very,' she said dryly.

'We've got to learn the truth, you know,' said Alleyn gently. 'We'll have to pry and pry. It's one of the most revolting aspects of a murder-case, and the victim is sometimes the greatest sufferer.'

'Then it is murder?'

'I'm afraid so.'

There was a long silence.

'Well,' said old Susan at last, 'it's no good making mysteries where there are none. She *was* very fond of Meyer. Not perhaps in a romantic fashion, exactly. He wasn't a figure for romance. But she was fond of him. You might say she felt safe with him.'

'And Hambledon?' asked Alleyn quietly.

Susan squared her fat shoulders and stared straight in front of her.

'If you mean anything scandalous, my dear, there's not a word of truth in it. Not a morsel. Mind, I don't say Hailey isn't devoted to her. He is, and has been for years, and he makes no bones about it. I've been with the Firm off and on for a long time and I know. But there's been no funny business between them, and don't let anybody tell you there has.'

'They've been trying,' said Alleyn. Susan suddenly slapped her hands on her lap. 'Ackroyd!' she cried. 'It was, but don't say so.'

'I'll be bound. Little beast. He's never forgiven her – never.'

'For what?'

'It was when he rejoined us for the revival of *Our Best Intentions* – a year ago it was. He's the type that always hangs round the leading woman and tries to go big with the management. You can smell 'em a mile off. Well, he tried it on with Carolyn Dacres and believe me it took him right off,' said Susan, becoming technical. 'As soon as the funny business started she was *well* up-stage and Mr Ackroyd made a quiet exit with no rounds of applause. He's a spiteful little beast and he's never forgiven her or Hailey. Hailey actually spoke to him about it, you know. I believe George Mason did, too. He's never forgotten it. You heard how he spoke about George tonight. Dragging in that American business.'

'Nothing in it?'

'My dear,' said Susan resignedly, 'I dare say something did happen. I rather think it did, but if we knew all the circumstances I've no doubt we'd find faults on both sides. George Mason started in a small way and he's not the only one, by a long chalk, that's got an incident of that sort to live down. My advice to you is, forget all about it. Whatever happened in the early days, he's an honest man now. I've worked for him for a good many years and you can take my word for it. And what's more I wouldn't say the same for Ackroyd.'

'I see,' said Alleyn.

'Anything more?' asked Susan.

'I don't think so. Thank you so much. Perhaps Inspector Wade – '

'No thanks, sir, no thanks,' said Wade, getting up from the desk where he had sat in silence. 'Unless – the train – '

'Miss Max sat opposite me. She slept all the time, I fancy.'

'The train!' ejaculated Susan. Alleyn explained.

'Yes,' said Susan, 'I was asleep. Do you mean you think that business on the train had something to do with this?'

'Who can tell?' murmured Alleyn vaguely. 'You're longing to get home to your bed, aren't you?'

'Well, I am.'

She hitched herself off the chair and waddled to the door. Alleyn opened it. She stood, a roundabout and lonely little figure, looking up at him very earnestly.

'In that other case in London someone nearly killed you by dropping a chandelier from the grid, didn't they?'

'So they did.'

'You don't think it's – it's given anyone an idea?'

Alleyn stared at her.

'I wonder,' he said.

CHAPTER 12

Liversidge Fluffs his Lines

'What was she driving at?' asked Wade when Susan had gone.

'Oh – the Gardener case. A neurotic property-man dumped half a ton of candelabra on the stage in a childish attempt to distract my attention. Later on he became victim No. 2, poor booby. Knew too much. It all came out in the evidence. I imagine they take a lot of trouble when men are working aloft. I remember the stage-manager told me the hands always have their tools tied to their wrists, in case of accidents.'

'Well, sir, you got some nice little bits out of the old lady. Of course her being a friend made a difference.'

'Of course,' agreed Alleyn cordially.

'Do you reckon there's anything in this story of Ackroyd's about Mason stranding a company in America?'

'I am inclined to agree with Miss Max's opinion of Ackroyd as a witness, but we'd better look into Mr Mason's history, of course. I'll get them to do that at the Yard.'

'Ackroyd means Mason walked out and left his company cold?'

'Yes. Not an unusual proceeding with small companies, I fancy, in the old days. A dirty trick, of course.'

'Too right – and if he's that sort – still, it doesn't mean every manager that strands a company would do in his partner.'

'Indeed not. The routes of touring companies would have been strewn with managerial corpses, I'm afraid.'

'There's the motive, though. You can't get away from that, sir,' persisted Wade.

'Oh, rather not. There's also the perfectly good alibi.'

'Don't I know it? Oh, well, Miss Max seems OK as far as the two important times are concerned.'

'What's happened to the dresser?' asked Alleyn.

'Oh, I saw her and the two Australians in the company and most of the staff soon after we got here. We just took statements and let them go. We've got their addresses. They're out of the picture as you might say. The Australians have only just joined the company and the stagehands are local men with good characters.'

'I know,' said Alleyn.

'How about having a pop at Mr Liversidge, sir?'

'Who, me?'

'That's right. Will you, sir?'

'At your service, Inspector.'

So Cass was dispatched to the wardrobe-room and returned with Mr Frank Liversidge, who came in looking very beautiful. His black hair was varnished down to his head and resembled an American leather cap. His dinner-jacket, a thought too waisted, his boiled shirt, his rather large tie, were all in perfect order, and so was Mr Liversidge. As soon as he saw Alleyn he uttered a musical laugh and advanced with manly frankness.

'Well, well, well,' said Mr Liversidge, in a dreadfully synthetic language that was so very nearly the right thing. 'Who'd have thought it of you? I've maintained that you were an ambassador incog., and Val was all for the Secret Service.'

'Nothing so exciting, I'm afraid,' murmured Alleyn. 'This is Inspector Wade, Mr Liversidge. He has asked me to talk to you about one or two features of this business. Will you sit down?'

'Thanks,' said Liversidge gracefully. 'So the Yard is coming into the show, is it?'

'By courtesy. Now, will you please give us an account of your movements after the final curtain tonight?'

'My movements?' He raised his eyebrows and took out his cigarette-case. All his actions were a little larger than life. Alleyn found himself thinking of them in terms of stage-craft. 'Bus. – L. taps cigarette. Takes lighter from packet. Lights cigarette with deliberation.'

'My movements,' repeated Liversidge, wafting smoke-rings in Alleyn's direction. 'Let me see. Oh, I went to my dressing-room and demolished the war-paint.'

'Immediately after the final curtain?'

'I think so. Yes.'

'You found Mr Vernon and Mr Broadhead there?'

'Did I? Yes, I believe I did. It's a big room. We share it.'

'They were on at the final curtain, of course?'

'We all take the call.'

'But they reached the dressing-room before you did?'

'Marvellous deduction, Inspector! Now I think of it, I was a little late getting there. I stayed off-stage for a minute or two.'

'Why did you do this?'

'Oh, I was talking.'

'To whom?'

'My dear old boy, I don't know. Who was it now? Oh, Valerie Gaynes.'

'I'm sure,' said Alleyn formally, 'you will understand that these questions are not prompted by idle curiosity.'

'My dear old boy!' repeated Liversidge. Alleyn restrained a wince.

'Then perhaps you will not object to telling us what you and Miss Gaynes talked about.'

Liversidge looked from Wade to Cass and back again at Alleyn.

'Well, as a matter of fact, I don't remember.'

'Please try to remember. It's only a couple of hours ago. Where were you standing?'

'Oh, just off-stage somewhere.'

'On the prompt side.'

'Er – yes.'

'Then perhaps Mr Gascoigne will remember. He was there.'

'He was nowhere near us.'

'You remember that,' said Alleyn vaguely.

Liversidge lost a little of his colour.

'As a matter of fact, Alleyn,' he said after a moment, 'our conversation was about a personal matter. I'm afraid I can't repeat it. Nothing that could have the remotest interest to anyone but ourselves. You *do* understand.'

'Oh, rather. How long did it last?'

'Two or three minutes, perhaps.'

'If you were near the prompt entrance you were not far from the steel ladder that goes up into the grid. Did anyone come down that ladder while you were there?'

'Yes,' answered Liversidge readily enough. 'Just as I turned away to go down the dressing-room passage, Alfred Meyer and the head mechanist came down.'

'Did you stay on the stage after that?'

'No. I went on down the passage.'

'Thank you so much,' said Alleyn. 'That, really, was the point we wanted to get at. Now, after the tragedy, when we cleared the stage – where did you go?'

'I stood with all the others by the entrance to the passage. That was while Hailey was shepherding the guests out. Then I went to the dressing-room.'

'Anyone else there when you arrived?'

'Yes. Branny and poor old Court. He felt very shaken. Branny was giving him a nip.'

'Were you among the last to leave the stage?'

'I suppose I was. I think we were the last.'

'Who was with you?'

'Oh – Val Gaynes.'

'Did you have a second conversation?'

'Just about the tragedy,' said Liversidge. 'I left her at her dressing-room door. She went on to the wardrobe-room, I think.'

'Now, Mr Liversidge, can you tell me if anyone remained on the stage after you left it?'

'Hailey Hambledon went back to – to where you were after the guests had gone.'

'Yes, yes, I know. I don't mean the actual stage within the scenery but the area, off-stage. Did anyone stay behind, off-stage?'

'I didn't notice anyone do so,' said Liversidge.

'Right. Now about this scene in the wardrobe-room. Had Master Gordon Palmer spoken to you about his curious theories?'

Liversidge passed his rather coarse and very white hand over his gleaming head.

'He – well, he did say something about it. Sort of mentioned it, don't you know. I was astounded. I simply can't believe it of dear old Court. Simply *can not* credit it.' Mr Liversidge added that Courtney Broadhead was a white man, a phrase that Alleyn had never cared for and of which he was heartily tired.

'I wish,' he said, 'that you would repeat as much of the conversation as you can remember. How did it begin?' Liversidge hesitated for some time.

'Never mind,' said Alleyn, 'about getting it quite correct. We can get Gordon Palmer's version too, you know.'

This was far from having a reassuring effect on Mr Liversidge. He darted a glance full of the liveliest distaste at Alleyn, made several false starts, and finally bent forward with an air of taking them into his confidence.

'Now look, Inspector,' he said earnestly, 'this is damned awkward for me. You see someone had said something about Val's money to both Gordon and me, and Gordon afterwards asked me what I thought was the true story. That was just after poor old Court had paid up. Well, I said – not meaning Gordon to take it up seriously – just a joke – I mean I never dreamt he'd think for a moment – ' Mr Liversidge waved his hands.

'Yes?' said Alleyn.

'Gad, I wouldn't have had it happen for the world. I said laughing – something about – "Well – Court's suddenly flush – p'raps he's the dirty-dog." Something like that. I mean, never dreaming – '

'Did you pursue this joke?' asked Alleyn.

'Well, don't you know, chaffingly,' explained Liversidge. 'What!'

'My God,' thought Alleyn, 'it's supposed to be Oxford, that language.' Aloud he said: 'Did you also talk about the attempt on Mr Meyer in the train?'

'In point of fact – yes. It was all meant for comedy, you know. I just said, all laughingly, that perhaps Alfred Meyer had caught him at it, and so he'd tried to tip him overboard. Well, I mean to say! When I heard Gordon tonight! Well, of course! I was flabbergasted!'

'Did you have any further joking references tonight – after the fatality?' inquired Alleyn, evenly.

'My dear Mr Alleyn!' expostulated Liversidge, greatly shocked.

'No reference of any sort?'

'Actually, do you know, Gordon did say something to me in the passage. I don't remember what it was. I was too shocked and grieved to pay attention. I think he just said something about, did I remember what we had talked about.'

'I see,' said Alleyn. 'Mr Liversidge, do you know at what time during our train journey the attempt on Mr Meyer was made?'

'Eh. Let me see, let me see. Do I remember? Yes – it was sometime before we got to that place where we stopped for refreshments. Isn't that right? I remember the dear old governor telling us about it. Poor old governor! It's hard to realize – '

'Frightfully hard, isn't it! Now before we reached that station – Ohakune – the guard came through the train chanting an announcement.'

'So he did.'

'Were you awake or did he wake you?'

'He woke me.'

'Had you been asleep for long?'

'Ages. I dropped off soon after Val went along to her sleeper.'

'Do you remember that you were disturbed by anyone getting up and leaving the carriage before the guard went through?'

'Didn't Court Broadhead go out to the platform? I seem to remember – good God, old man, I don't mean – you can't mean – !'

'I don't mean anything at all, Mr Liversidge,' said Alleyn. 'Nobody else?'

'I don't think so. No.'

'Thank you. Now about the greenstone tiki. We are anxious to trace it if possible. Miss Dacres has lost it.'

'Is it valuable?'

'It is rather, I imagine.'

'Well, you ought to know,' said Liversidge.

'Quite so. Do you remember handling it?'

'Certainly,' said Liversidge with huffy dignity. 'I also remember returning it.'

'To whom?'

'To – to Branny, I think. Yes, it was to Branny. And he gave it to Carolyn and she put it on the table. I remember that quite well.'

'Whereabouts on the table?'

'At the end on the OP side. It was before we sat down. Funny me remembering.'

'Do you remember anyone picking it up from the table?'

'No. No, I don't.'

'Have you any theory,' asked Alleyn abruptly, 'about the disappearance of Miss Gaynes's money?'

'I? Lord, no! I should think very likely a steward pinched it.'

'It's happened before,' agreed Alleyn. 'She seems to have been pretty casual about her cash.'

'Casual! God, she's hopeless. Fancy leaving a packet of tenners in an open suitcase. Well, of course!'

'All in tenners, was it?' asked Alleyn absently.

'I think so. She told me so.'

Wade cleared his throat.

'I seem to remember,' continued Alleyn vaguely, 'that she said something about paying you a tenner she'd lost at poker. When did she do that?'

'On the last night we were in the ship. After we'd finished playing. Actually it was about one o'clock in the morning.'

'She still had her money then, evidently.'

'Yes.'

'She got this tenner from the hoard in the suitcase, did she?'

'I – I think so. Yes, she did.'

'You saw her, did you, Mr Liversidge?'

'Well – not exactly. I walked along to her cabin and waited outside in the corridor. She came out and gave me the tenner. I didn't know, then, where she got it from.'

'You couldn't see her?'

'No, I couldn't. Damn it all, Alleyn, what's the idea of all this?'

'No offence in the world. Goodnight, Mr Liversidge.'

'Eh?'

'Goodnight,' repeated Alleyn cheerfully.

Liversidge stared uncomfortably at him and then got to his feet. Wade made a movement and was checked by a glint in Alleyn's eye.

'Well, so long,' said Mr Liversidge and went away.

'Let him go,' said Alleyn when the door had slammed. 'Let him go. He's *so* uncomfortable and fidgety. You can get him again when he's spent a beastly night. He'll do very nicely for the time being. Let him go.'

CHAPTER 13

Miss Gaynes Goes Up-stage

'Now, Miss Gaynes,' said Alleyn patiently, 'it's a very simple question. Why not let us have the answer to it?'

Valerie Gaynes lay back in the office armchair and stared at him like a frightened kitten. At the beginning of the interview she had been in good histrionic form and, it seemed to Alleyn, thoroughly enjoying herself. She had accounted for her whereabouts during the two crucial periods, she had taken the tiki in her stride, with many exclamations as to its ill-omened significance, she had discoursed at large on the subject of her own temperament, and she had made use of every conceivable piece of theatrical jargon that she could haul into the conversation in order to show them how professional she was. Alleyn had found all this inexpressibly tedious and quite barren of useful information, but he had listened with an air of polite interest, chosen his moment, and put the question that had so greatly disconcerted her:

'What did you and Mr Liversidge talk about before you left the stage after the final curtain?'

He could have sworn that under her make-up she turned white. Her enormous brown eyes blinked twice exactly as though he had offered to hit her. Her small red mouth opened and literally her whole body shrank back into the chair. Even after he had spoken again, she made no attempt to answer him, but lay there gaping at him.

'Come along,' said Alleyn.

When she did at last muster up her voice it was almost comically changed. 'Why – nothing in particular,' said Miss Gaynes.

'May we just hear what it was?'

She moistened her lips.

'Didn't Frankie tell you? What did he say?'

That's the sort of question we particularly never ask a policeman,' said Alleyn. 'I want *you* to tell me.'

'But – it was just about poor Mr Meyer – nothing else.'

'Nothing else?'

'I tell you I don't remember. It was nothing.'

'It wasn't something very private and personal – between you and Mr Liversidge?'

'No. Of course not. We haven't anything – like that – to say.'

'Funny!' said Alleyn. 'Mr Liversidge told us you had.' Miss Gaynes burst into tears.

'Look here,' said Alleyn after a pause, 'I'm going to give you a very hackneyed bit of advice, Miss Gaynes. It's extremely good advice and you may land yourself in a very uncomfortable position if you don't take it. Here it is. Don't lie to the police when there's a murder charge brewing. Nobody else can make things quite as awkward for you as they can. *Nobody.* If you don't want to answer my question you can refuse to do so. But don't lie.'

'I – I'm frightened.'

'Would you rather refuse to give us your answer?'

'But if I do that you'll think – you'll suspect – terrible things.'

'We shall merely note that you decline – '

'No. No. What are you thinking? You're suspecting *me!* I wish I was out of it all. I wish I'd never told him. I wish I'd never met him. I don't know *what* to do.'

'What do you wish you'd never told him?'

'That I knew – who it was.'

Wade uttered a sort of strangled grunt. Cass looked up from his notes and opened his mouth. Alleyn raised an eyebrow and stared thoughtfully at Valerie Gaynes.

'You knew – who it was who did *what?*'

'You know what. You've known all the time, haven't you? Why did you ask me what we talked about if you didn't know?'

'You mean that Mr Liversidge is responsible for this business tonight?'

'Tonight!' She almost screamed it at him. 'I didn't say that. You can't say I said that.'

'Good heavens,' said Alleyn. 'This is becoming altogether too difficult. We seem unable to understand each other, Miss Gaynes. Please let us tidy up this conversation. Will you tell us in so many words, what is this matter between you and Mr Liversidge? You suspect him of something, obviously. Apparently it is not murder. What is it?'

'I – I don't want to tell you.'

'Very well,' said Alleyn coldly. He stood up. 'We must leave it at that and go elsewhere for our information.'

She made no attempt to get up. She sat there staring at him, her fingers at her lips and her face disfigured with tears. She looked genuinely terrified.

'I'll have to tell you,' she whispered at last.

'I think it would be wiser,' said Alleyn, and sat down again.

'It's the money,' said Miss Gaynes. 'I think Frankie took my money. I didn't believe it at first when Mr Meyer spoke to me about it.'

'Lummy!' thought Alleyn. 'Now we're getting it.' He began to question her systematically and carefully, taking pains not to alarm her too much, so that gradually she became more composed, and out of her disjointed half-phrases an intelligible sequence of events began to appear. It seemed that on the last evening in the ship, when she paid her poker debts, Liversidge actually went into her cabin with her. She took the money from her suitcase while he was there, and gave him the ten pounds she owed him. At the same time she took out a ten-pound note which she subsequently changed at the first saloon bar and paid out in tips. Liversidge told her that she was a fool to leave her money in an unlocked suitcase. She told him she had lost the key of the suitcase and said she was not going to bother about it now, at the end of the voyage. He repeated his warning and left her. Next morning, when she returned from breakfast to pack her luggage, she prodded the leather notecase, felt the thick wad of paper, and fastened the suitcase without making any further investigation. It was not until she opened the notecase in the train that she knew she had been robbed. It was then that she paid her dramatic call on the Meyers and found Alleyn in their sleeper.

'And you suspected Mr Liversidge when you began to tell us about paying your debt to him?'

She said yes. The thought of Liversidge's possible complicity occurred to her at that moment. The next morning Meyer had taken her aside and questioned her closely about the money.

'He seemed to suspect Frankie – I don't know why – but he seemed to suspect him.'

It was then that Meyer had insisted on paying her the amount that had been stolen. He had not made any definite accusation against Liversidge but had warned her against forming any attachment that she might afterward regret.

'Did Miss Dacres speak to you about Mr Liversidge?'

But it appeared Carolyn had said nothing definite, though Miss Gaynes had received an impression that Carolyn, too, had something up her sleeve.

'And have you yourself said anything about this matter to Mr Liversidge?'

Here a renewed display of emotion threatened to appear. Alleyn steered her off it and got her back to the conversation that took place off-stage. She said that, guessing at Meyer's view of the theft, 'all sorts of dreadful thoughts' came into her mind when he was killed.

'Then you thought, at the outset, that it was a case of murder?'

Only, it seemed, because Gascoigne kept saying that there must have been some hanky-panky with the gear. After a great many tedious false starts she at last told Alleyn that, when they were all hustled away from the scene of the disaster, she had blurted out a single question to Liversidge: 'Has this got anything to do with my money?' and he had answered: 'For God's sake don't be a bloody little fool. Keep quiet about your money.' Then he had kept her back and had said hurriedly that for Courtney Broadhead's sake she had better not mention the theft. 'I'd never thought of Court until then,' said Miss Gaynes, 'but after that I got all muddled and of course I remembered how hard-up Court was and then I began to wonder. And now – now I – I simply don't know where I am, honestly I don't. If Frankie was trying to help Court and I've – I've betrayed him – '

'Nonsense,' said Alleyn very crisply. 'There's no question of betrayal. You have done the only possible thing. Tell me, please, Miss Gaynes, are you engaged to Mr Liversidge?'

She flushed at that and for the first time showed a little honest indignation.

'You've no business to ask me that.'

'I can assure you I am not prompted by idle curiosity,' said Alleyn equitably. 'The question is relevant. I still ask it.'

'Very well, then, I'm not actually engaged.'

'There is an understanding of some sort, perhaps?'

'I simply haven't made up my mind.' A trace of complacency crept into her voice. Alleyn thought: 'She is the type of young woman who always represents herself as a fugitive before the eager male. She would never admit lack of drawing-power in herself.'

'But now – ' she was saying, 'I wish we had never thought of it. I want to get away from all this. It's all so hateful – I want to get away from it. I'm going to cable to Daddy and ask him to send for me. I want to go home.'

'As a preliminary step,' said Alleyn cheerfully, 'I am going to send you off to your hotel. You are tired and distressed. Things won't seem so bad in the morning, you know. Goodnight.'

He shut the door after her and turned to the two New Zealanders.

'Silly young woman,' said Alleyn mildly.

But Wade was greatly excited.

'I reckon this changes the whole outfit,' he said loudly. 'I reckon it does. If Liversidge stole the cash, it changes the whole show. By crikey, sir, you caught them out nicely. By crikey, it was a corker! He tells you one story about this conversation with the girl Gaynes, and you get the other tale from her and then face her up with it. By gee, it was a beauty!'

'My dear Inspector,' said Alleyn uncomfortably, 'you are giving me far too much encouragement.'

'It wasn't so much the line taken,' continued Wade, explaining Alleyn to Cass, 'as the manner of taking it. I don't say I wouldn't have gone on the same lines myself. It was indicated, you might say, but I wouldn't have got in the fine work like the chief inspector. The girl Gaynes would have turned dumb on us very, very easy, but the chief just trotted her along quietly and got the whole tale. You seemed to guess there was something crook about this Liversidge from the kick-off, sir. What put you on to that, if I might ask?'

'In the first instance, Miss Gaynes herself. That night in the train she was full of the theft until she began to account for the money she had spent. She mentioned Francis Liversidge, suddenly looked

scared, and then shut up like an oyster. Tonight Mr Liversidge's gallantry in defending young Broadhead seemed to be as bogus as the
rest of his behaviour.'

'Including the queenie voice,' agreed Wade. 'Sounds as if he'd
swallowed the kitchen sink.'

'I fancy,' continued Alleyn, 'that Miss Dacres also doubts the
integrity of our Mr Liversidge. I fancy she does. She has made one
or two very cryptic remarks on the subject.'

'The girl Gaynes never said just *why* she reckoned he looked suspicious. Was it simply because he'd been in the cabin and seen
where she kept the money?'

'That, perhaps; and also, don't you think, because of whatever Mr
Alfred Meyer said to her on the subject?'

'*Cert-ain-ly*,' agreed Wade, with much emphasis. 'And if deceased
knew Liversidge pinched the money and let the Gaynes woman see he
knew, maybe she put in the good word to Liversidge and he thought:
"That's quite enough from you, Mr Meyer," and fixed it accordingly.'

'In which case,' said Alleyn, offering Wade a cigarette, 'we have
two murderous gentlemen instead of one?'

'Uh?'

'The first attempt on his life was made in the train before the theft
was discovered.'

'Aw, hell!' said Inspector Wade wearily. After a moment's thought
he brightened a little. 'Suppose Liversidge had found out by some
other means that the deceased knew he had taken the money?
Suppose he knew the deceased was on to his little game before they
left the ship?'

'By jove, yes,' said Alleyn, 'that'd do it, certainly. But look here,
Wade, does one man murder another simply because he's been
found out in a theft?'

'Well, sir, when you put it like that – '

'No,' interrupted Alleyn, 'you're quite right. It's possible. Meyer
would give him the sack, of course, and make the whole thing public. That would ruin Liversidge's career as an actor, no doubt. If he
could kill Meyer before he spoke – Yes, it's possible, but – but I don't
know. We'll have to see Miss Dacres and George Mason again, Wade.
If Meyer confided in anyone, it would be his wife or his partner. But
there's one catch in your theory.'

'What's that, sir?'

'It's rather nebulous perhaps, but when the little man told me about the assault in the train he was obviously at a complete loss to account for it. Now, if he'd already let Liversidge see he suspected the theft, he would have thought of him as a possible enemy. But he told me he was on terms of loving kindness and all the rest of it with his entire company, and I think he meant it.'

'It's a fair cow, that's what it is,' grunted Wade.

'Beg pardon, Inspector,' said the silent Cass after a pause, 'but if I might make a suggestion – it's just an idea, like.'

'Go ahead,' commanded Wade graciously.

'Well, sir, say this Mr Liversidge knew the deceased gentleman had seen him take the money, without deceased having let on that he saw, if you understand me, sir.'

'Well done, Sergeant,' said Alleyn quietly.

'Yes, but how?' objected Wade.

'Mr Liversidge might have overheard deceased say something to his wife or somebody, sir.' Cass took a deep breath and fixed his eyes on the opposite wall. 'What I mean to say,' he said doggedly, 'Mr Meyer saw Mr Liversidge take the money. Mr Liversidge knew Mr Meyer saw him. Mr Meyer thought Mr Liversidge didn't know he saw him.'

'And there,' concluded Alleyn, 'would be the motive without Mr Meyer realising it. He's quite right. You're fortunate, Inspector. An intelligent staff is not always given to us.'

Cass turned purple in the face, squared his enormous shoulders, and glared at the ceiling.

'There you are, Cass!' said Wade good-humouredly. 'Now buzz off and get us another of these actors.'

CHAPTER 14

Variation on a Police Whistle

Old Brandon Vernon looked a little the worse for wear. The hollows under his cheek bones and the lines round his eyes seemed to have made one of those grim encroachments to which middle-aged faces are so cruelly subject. A faint hint of a rimy stubble broke the smooth pallor of his chin; his eyes, in spite of their look of sardonic impertinence, were lacklustre and tired. Yet when he spoke one forgot his age, for his voice was quite beautiful; deep, and exquisitely modulated. He was one of that company of old actors that are only found in the West End of London. They still believe in using their voices as instruments, they speak without affectation, and they are indeed actors.

'Well, Inspector,' he said to Alleyn, you know how to delay an entrance. It was very effective business, coming out in your true colours like this.'

'I found it rather uncomfortable, Mr Vernon,' answered Alleyn. 'Do sit down, won't you, and have a smoke? Cigarette?'

'I'll have my comforter, if you don't mind.' And Vernon pulled out a pipe and pouch. 'Well,' he said, 'I'm not sorry to leave the wardrobe-room. That young cub's sulking and the other fellow has about as much conversation as a vegetable marrow. Dull.' He filled his pipe and gripped it between his teeth.

'We're sorry to have kept you waiting so long,' said Alleyn.

'Don't apologize. Used to it in this business. Half an actor's life is spent waiting. Bad show this. Was Alfred murdered?'

'It looks rather like it, I'm afraid.'

'Um,' rumbled old Vernon. 'I wonder why.'

'To be frank, so do we.'

'And I suppose we're all suspect. Lord, I've played in a good many mystery dramas but I never expected to appear in the genuine thing. Let me see, I suppose you're going to ask me what I was doing before and after the crime, eh?'

'That's the idea,' sighed Alleyn, smiling.

'Fire ahead, then,' said old Vernon.

Alleyn put the now familiar questions to him. He corroborated the account Liversidge and Broadhead had given of his movements. At the close of the play and after the catastrophe, he had gone straight to his dressing-room, where the other two afterwards joined him.

'I don't know if that constitutes an alibi,' he said, rolling his eyes round at Wade. 'If it doesn't I understand I am almost certain to be innocent.'

'So the detective books tell us,' said Alleyn, 'and they ought to know. As a matter of fact I think it does give you a pretty well cast-iron alibi.'

Vernon grimaced. 'Not so good. I must watch my step.'

'You've been with the firm of Incorporated Playhouses a good time, haven't you, Mr Vernon?'

'Let me see. I started with *Double Knock* at the old Curtain. Before that I was with Tree and afterwards with du Maurier.' He pondered. 'Ten years. Ten years with Inky-P. Long time to work with one management, ten years.'

'You must be the senior member of the club?'

'Pretty well. Susie runs me close, but she left us for *The Rat and the Beaver,* two years ago.'

'Ah, yes. You must have known Mr Meyer very well?'

'Yes, I did. As well as an actor ever knows his manager, and that's very thoroughly in some ways and not at all in others.'

'Did you like him?'

'Yes, I did. He was honest. Very fair with his actors. Never paid colossal salaries – not as they go nowadays – but you always got good money.'

'Mr Vernon, do you know of any incident in the past or present that could throw any light on this business?'

'I don't.'

'The Firm is all right, I suppose? Financially, I mean?'

'I believe so,' answered Vernon. There was an overtone in his voice that suggested a kind of guardedness.

'Any doubts at all about that?' asked Alleyn.

There are always rumours about managements like ours. I have heard a certain amount of gossip about some of the touring companies. They are supposed to have dropped money for the Firm. Then there was *Time Payment* That did a flop. Still, Inky-P has stood a flop or two in its time.'

'Were all Mr Meyer's interests bound up in the Firm, do you know?'

'I don't know anything about it. George Mason could tell you that, probably. Alfred was a very shrewd business man and he and Carolyn are not the social spotlight hunters that most of 'em are nowadays. They lived very quietly. The theatre before everything. I should say Alfred had saved money. Only a guess, you know.'

'I know. It'll all appear now, of course.'

'What puzzles me, Mr Alleyn, is who on earth would want to do in Alfred Meyer. None of us, you'd have thought. Shops aren't found so easily that we can afford to kill off the managers.' He paused and rolled his eyes round. 'I wonder,' he said, 'if that accident on Friday morning gave anybody the big idea.'

'What accident?' asked Alleyn sharply.

'The morning we got here. Didn't you hear about it? One of the staff was up in the flies fixing the weight for the mast. The head mechanist and Ted Gascoigne were down below on the stage, having an argument. Suddenly the gentleman in the flies got all careless and dropped the weight. It fell plum between the two men and crashed half through the stage. Ted Gascoigne raved at the poor swine for about ten minutes, and Fred – the head mechanist – nearly ate him. We all rushed out to see the fun. God, they were a sight! White as paper and making faces at each other.'

'Good lord!' said Alleyn.

'Yes. It would have laid him out for keeps if it had hit one of 'em. Great leaden thing like an enormous sash-weight and as heavy – '

'As heavy, very nearly, as a jeroboam of champagne,' finished Alleyn. 'It was used, afterwards, as a counterweight for the bottle.'

'Was it really!' exclaimed Vernon.

'Didn't you know how they fixed the gear for the bottle?'

'I heard poor old Alfred holding forth on the subject, of course, but I'm afraid I didn't pay much attention.'

'You all knew about the mishap with the counterweight?'

'Oh God, yes. Everyone came out helter-skelter. It shook the building. George ran along from the office, Val Gaynes flew out of her dressing-room in a pair of camiknicks. The two Australians nearly threw in their parts and returned to Sydney. It was a nine days' wonder.'

'I see,' said Alleyn. He turned to Wade. 'Anything else you'd like to ask Mr Vernon, Inspector?'

'Well now,' said Wade genially, 'I don't know that there's much left to ask, sir. I *was* wondering, Mr Vernon, you having been so long with the company, if you could give us a little idea about the domestic side of the picture, as you might say.'

Old Vernon swung round in his chair and looked at Wade without enthusiasm.

'Afraid I don't follow you,' he said.

'Well now, Mr Vernon, you'll understand we have to make certain inquiries in our line. You might say we have to get a bit curious. It's our job, you understand, and we may fancy it as little as other folk do, but we've got to do it. Now, Mr Vernon, would you describe Mr and Mrs Meyer as being a happy couple, if you know what I mean?'

'I can understand most common words of one or two syllables,' said Vernon, 'and I do know what you mean. Yes, I should.'

'No differences of any sort?'

'None.'

'Good-oh, sir. That's straight enough. So I suppose all this talk about her and Mr Hambledon is so much hot air?'

'All what talk? Who's been talking?'

'Now don't you worry about that, Mr Vernon. That'll be quite all right, sir.'

'What the hell d'you mean? What'll be quite all right? Who's been talking about Miss Dacres and Mr Hambledon?'

'Now never you mind about that, sir. We just want to hear – '

'If it's that damned little footpath comedian,' continued Vernon, glaring angrily at Wade, 'you can take it from me he's about as dependable as a cockroach. He's a very nasty little person, is Mr St John Ackroyd, *né* Albert Biggs, a thoroughly unpleasant piece of bluff and brass. And *what* a naughty actor!'

'*Né* Biggs?' murmured Alleyn.

'Certainly. And the sooner he goes back to his hairdresser's shop in St Helens the better for all concerned.'

'I gather,' said Alleyn mildly, 'that he has already spoken to you about the conversation he overheard in his dressing-room.'

'*Oh*, yes,' said old Vernon, with a particular air of elaborate irony that Alleyn had begun to associate with actors' conversation. '*Oh*, yes. I was told *all* about it as soon as he had a chance to speak his bit. Mr Ackroyd came in *well* on his cue with the old bit of dirt, you may be *quite* sure.'

Alleyn smiled: 'And it's as true as most gossip of that sort, I suppose?'

'I don't know what Ackroyd told you, but I'd swear till it snowed pink that Carolyn Dacres hasn't gone in for the funny business. Hailey *may* have talked a bit wildly. He may be very attracted. I don't say anything about that, but on her side – well, I can't believe it. She's one of the rare samples of the sort that stay put.'

And Vernon puffed out his cheeks and uttered a low growl.

'That's just what we wanted to know,' said Wade. 'Just wanted your opinion, you see, sir.'

'Well, you've got it. And the same opinion goes for anything Mr Ackroyd may have told you, including his little bit of dirt about George Mason. Anything else?'

'We'll get you to sign a statement about your own movements later on, if you don't mind,' said Wade.

'Ugh!'

'And that will be all.'

'Has the footpath comedian signed his pretty little rigmarole?'

'Not yet, Mr Vernon.'

'Not yet. No doubt he will,' said Vernon bitterly. He shook hands with Alleyn. 'Lucky you're here, Mr Alleyn. I shall now go to my home away from home. The bed is the undulating sort and I toboggan all night. The mattress appears to have been stuffed with the landlady's apple dumplings of which there are always plenty left over. Talk of counterweights! My God! Matthew, Mark, Luke and John, bless the bed that I lie on. Goodnight. Goodnight, Inspector Wade.'

'What is the name of your hotel, sir?'

'The Wenderby, Inspector. It is a perfect sample of the Jack's Come Home.'

'I've always heard it was very comfortable,' said Wade, with all the colonial's defensiveness. 'The landlady – '

'Oh, you must be a lover of your landlady's daughter,
  Or you don't get a second piece of pie,'

sang old Vernon surprisingly in a wheezy bass:

'Piece of pie, piece of pie, piece of pie, piece of pie,
  Or you don't get a second piece of pie.'

He cocked his eyebrow, turned up the collar of his overcoat, clapped his hat on one side of his head and marched out.

'Aw, he's mad,' said Wade disgustedly.

Alleyn lay back in his chair and laughed heartily.

'But he's perfect, Wade. The real old actor. Almost too good to be true.'

'Making out he's sorry deceased has gone and two minutes afterwards acting the fool. Our hotels are as good as you'd find anywhere,' grumbled Wade. 'What's he mean by a Jack's Come Home, anyway?'

'I fancy it's a professional term noting a slap-dash and carefree attitude on the part of the proprietress.'

'He's mad,' repeated Wade. 'Get the kid, Cass. Young Palmer.'

When Cass had gone, Wade got up and stamped about the office. 'It's chilly,' he said.

The room was both cold and stuffy. The fire had gone out and the small electric heater was quite unequal to the thin draughts of night air that came in under the door and through the ill-fitting window-frame. The place was rank with tobacco smoke and with an indefinable smell of dust and varnish. Somewhere outside in the sleeping town a clock struck two.

'Good lord!' said Alleyn involuntarily.

'Like to turn it up for tonight, sir?' asked Wade.

'No, no.'

'Good-oh, then. Look, sir. On what we've got, who do you reckon are the possibles? Just on the face of it?'

'I'm afraid it'd be quicker to tick off the unlikelies,' said Alleyn.

'Well, take it that way.'

Alleyn did not reply immediately and Wade answered himself.

'Well, sir, I've got their names here and I'll tick off the outsiders. Old Miss Max. No motive or opportunity. That old looney who's just wafted away, Brandon Vernon. Same for him. Gascoigne, the stage-manager. Same for him on the evidence we've got so far. The funny little bloke, St John Ackroyd, alias Biggs, according to Vernon. He may be a bit of a nosy but he doesn't look like a murderer. Besides, his movements are pretty well taped. The girl Gaynes. Well, I suppose you might say, if she's going with Liversidge and knew Meyer was in the position to finish his career for him, that there's a motive there, but I don't see that silly little tart fixing counterweights and working out the machinery for a job of this sort. Do you?'

'The imagination does rather boggle,' agreed Alleyn.

'Yes. Well, now we get into shaky country. Hambledon. Let's look at Mr Hailey Hambledon. He's after the wood. They none of them deny that. Seems as if he's been kind of keen for a long while. Now if Ackroyd's story is right, she said she'd marry him if Meyer was dead and not unless. There's the motive. Now for opportunity. Hambledon could have gone aloft the first time and taken away the weight. He says he went to his dressing-room and took the muck off his dial. Maybe, but he told the dresser he wasn't wanted, and he could have gone back on the stage, climbed aloft and done it. After the murder he went as far as her dressing-room with the Dacres woman – with deceased's wife. She said she wanted to be alone and then sent for him, some time later. During the interval he may have gone up and put the weight back. That right?'

'Yes,' said Alleyn.

'Then there's Carolyn Dacres. Same motive. Same opportunity. She was the last to appear for the party and she asked to be left alone after the fatality. I don't know whether she'd be up to thinking out the mechanics of the thing but – '

'One should also remember,' said Alleyn, 'that she was the one member of the party from whom the champagne stunt had been kept a secret.'

'By gum, yes. Unless she'd got wind of it somehow.

Ye-ers. Well, that's her. Now George Mason. Motive – he comes in for a fortune if the money's still there. Opportunity – not so good. Before the show he was in this room. The stage-doorkeeper remembers Mason running out and warning him about the guests and returning here. Te Pokiha saw him here. You remember him coming out when you arrived. To get behind, between those times, he'd have had to pass the doorkeeper and would have been seen by anybody who happened to be about.'

'Is there a pass-door through the proscenium from the stalls?'

'Eh? No. No, there's not. No, I don't see how he could have done it. After the murder he came back with Te Pokiha and I saw him in the office here as I passed the door. We'll check up just when Te Pokiha left him, but it doesn't look too likely.'

'It does not. It looks impossible, Wade.'

'I hate to say so,' admitted Wade. 'Next comes young Courtney Broadhead. If he stole the money and Meyer knew, that's motive. Or if he doped it out he'd say Meyer had lent it to him – that's another motive. There's that business on the train – '

'Always remembering,' said Alleyn, 'that the train attempt took place before Miss Gaynes discovered the theft of the money.'

'Aw, blast!' said Wade, 'It just won't make sense. Well – Liversidge. Motive. If he took the money and Meyer knew, and he knew Meyer knew – good enough. Opportunity. Each time he was the last to leave the stage. He could have done it. There you are, and where the bloody hell are you?'

'I weep with you,' said Alleyn. 'I deeply sympathize. Isn't Master Palmer taking rather a long time?'

He had scarcely asked his question before the most extraordinary rumpus broke out in the yard. There was a sudden scurry of running feet on asphalt, a startled bellow, and a crash, followed by a burst of lurid invective.

Alleyn, with Wade behind him, ran to the door, threw it open, and darted out into the yard. A full moon shone upon cold roofs and damp pavements, and upon the posterior view of Detective-Sergeant Cass. His head and shoulders were lost in shadow and he seemed, to their astonished eyes, to be attempting to batter his brains out against the wall of a bicycle shed. He was also kicking backwards with the brisk action of a terrier, this impression being enhanced by spurts of earth and gravel which shot out from beneath his flying boots.

'Here, 'ere, 'ere,' said Wade, 'what's all this?'

'Catch him!' implored a strangely muffled voice while Cass redoubled his activities. 'Go after the . . . little . . . Get me out of this! Gawd! Get me out of it.'

Alleyn and Wade flew to the demented creature. Wade produced a torch, and by its light they saw what ailed the sergeant. His head and his enormous shoulders were wedged between the wall of the bicycle shed and that of a closely adjoining building. His helmet had slipped over his face like a sort of extinguisher, his fat arms were clamped to his side. He could neither go forward nor back and he had already begun to swell.

'Get me out,' he ordered. 'Leave me alone. Go after 'im. Go after the . . . ! Gawd, get me out!'

'Go after who?' asked Wade. 'What sort of game do you think you're up to, Sergeant Cass?'

'Never mind what I'm up to, Mr Wade. That young bleeder's run orf behind this shed and it's that narrer I can't foller. Gawd knows where he is by this time!'

'By cripey, you're a corker, you are,' said Wade hotly. 'Here!'

He seized the sergeant's belt and turned to Alleyn.

'Do you mind giving a hand, sir?'

Alleyn was doubled up in ecstasy of silent laughter, but he managed to pull himself together and, after a closer look at the prisoner, he hunted in the wooden shed, unearthed a length of timber which they jammed between the two walls and thus eased the pressure a little. Cass was pried and hauled out, sweating vigorously. Alleyn slipped into the passage and round to the rear of the shed. Here he found another path running back towards the theatre. He darted along this alley between a ramshackle fence and the brick wall of the property-room. The path led to the rear of the theatre, past a closed door, and finally to a narrow back street. Here Alleyn paused. Back in the stage-door yard he could hear one of the distracted officials blowing a police whistle. The little street was quite deserted, but in a moment or two a police officer appeared from the far end. Alleyn shouted to him and he broke into a run.

'What's all this? Who's blowing that whistle?'

'Inspector Wade and Sergeant Cass,' said Alleyn. 'They're in the theatre yard. Has a young man in evening dress passed you during the last few minutes?'

'Yes. Up at the corner. What about him?'

'He's given us the slip. Which way?'

'Towards the Middleton Hotel. Here, you hold steady, sir. Where are you off to? You wait a bit.'

'Ask Wade,' said Alleyn. He sidestepped neatly and sprinted down the street.

It led him into a main thoroughfare. In the distance he recognized the familiar bulk of the Middleton Hotel. Three minutes later he was talking to the night porter.

'Has Mr Gordon Palmer returned yet?'

'Yes, sir. He came in a minute ago and went up to his room – No. 51. Anything wrong, sir?' asked the night porter, gazing at Alleyn's filthy shirtfront.

'Nothing in the wide world. I shall follow his example.'

He left the man gaping and ran upstairs. No. 51 was on the second landing. Alleyn tapped at the door. There was no answer, so he walked in and turned up the light.

Gordon Palmer sat on the edge of his bed. He was still dressed. In his hand was a tumbler.

'Drinking in the dark?' asked Alleyn.

Gordon opened his mouth once or twice but failed to speak.

'Really,' said Alleyn, 'you are altogether too much of a fool. Do you *want* to get yourself locked up?'

'You get to hell out of this.'

'I shall certainly go as quickly as I can. You reek of whisky, and you look revolting. Now listen to me. As you've heard already, I'm an officer of Scotland Yard. I shall be taking over certain matters in connection with this case. One of my duties will be to write to your father. Precisely what I put in my letters depends on our subsequent conversation. It's much too late and we're too busy to talk to you now. So I shall lock you in your room and leave you to think out a reasonable attitude. There's a fifty-foot drop from your window to the pavement. Good morning.'

CHAPTER 15

Six a.m. First Act Curtain

Alleyn longed for his bed. He was dirty and tired, and a dull lugging pain reminded him that he was supposed to be taking things easily after a big operation. He went into his room, washed, and changed quickly into grey flannels and a sweater. Then he went downstairs.

The night porter gazed reproachfully and suspiciously at him.

'Are you going out again, sir?'

'Oh yes, rather. It's my night to howl.'

'Beg pardon, sir?'

'You'll hear all about it,' said Alleyn, 'very shortly. There's something to keep out the cold.'

Back at the theatre he found Wade and Cass closeted with Mr Geoffrey Weston. There was an enormous tear in Cass's tunic and a grimy smudge across his face. He sat at the desk taking notes. Evidently his uncomfortable predicament had upset his digestion for he rumbled lamentably and at each uncontrollable gurgitation he assumed an air of huffy grandeur. Wade appeared to be irritable and Weston stolid. The office looked inexpressibly squalid and smelt beastly.

'I thought I'd better come back and report,' said Alleyn. 'I've locked up your darling little imp for what's left of the night, Mr Weston.'

'So he did go back to the pub,' grunted Weston disinterestedly. 'I told you he would, you know.'

'That's right, Mr Weston,' said Wade.

'I suppose the PC I met in the lane told you what I was up to,' said Alleyn.

'Yes, sir, he did, and very surprised he was when he heard who you were. I sent him after you, Mr Alleyn, and he saw you go into the Middleton so we left you to it. I've just been asking Mr Weston if he could give us an idea why Mr Palmer slipped up on us.' And Wade glanced uncomfortably at Weston, edged round behind him, and made an eloquent grimace at Alleyn.

Alleyn thought he had never seen any face that expressed as little as Geoffrey Weston's. It was an example of the dead norm in faces. It was neither good-looking nor plain, it had no distinguishing feature and no marked characteristic. It would be impossible to remember it with any degree of sharpness. It was simply a face.

'And why did he bolt, do you suppose?' asked Alleyn.

'Because he's a fool,' said Mr Weston.

'Oh, rather,' agreed Alleyn. 'No end of a fool; but even fools have motives. Why did he bolt? What was he afraid of?'

'He's run away from disagreeable duties,' said Weston, with unexpected emphasis, 'ever since he could toddle. He ran away from three schools. He's got no guts.'

'He displayed a good deal of mistaken effrontery in the wardrobe-room, when he as good as accused Courtney Broadhead of theft.'

'Egged on,' said Weston.

'By Liversidge?'

'Of course.'

'Do you believe the story about Broadhead, Mr Weston?'

'Not interested.'

'Did you speak of it to Mr Palmer?'

'Yes.'

'When?'

'In the wardrobe-room, after you'd gone.'

'You must have been very quiet about it.'

'I was.'

'What did you say?' pursued Alleyn, and to himself he murmured: 'Oyster, oyster, oyster; Open you *shall*.'

'Told him he'd be locked up for defamation of character.'

'Splendid. Did it frighten him?'

'Yes.'

'Do you think he bolted to avoid further questioning?'

'Yes.'

'It's all so simple,' said Alleyn pleasantly, 'when you understand.'
Weston merely stared at his boots.

'I suppose,' continued Alleyn, 'that you had heard all about the arrangements for the champagne business?'

'Knew nothing about it.'

'Mr Palmer?'

'No.'

'Can you help us about the missing tiki?'

'Afraid I can't.'

'Ah, well,' said Alleyn, that's about all, I fancy. Unless you've anything further, Inspector?'

'No, sir, I have not,' said Wade, with a certain amount of emphasis. 'We'll see the young gentleman in the morning.'

"That all?' asked Weston, getting to his feet.

'Yes, thank you, Mr Weston.'

'I'll push off. Goodnight.'

He walked out and they heard his footsteps die away before any of them spoke.

'He's a fair nark, that chap,' said Wade. 'Close! Gosh!'

'Not exactly come-toish,' agreed Alleyn.

'Blooming oyster! Well, that's the whole boiling of 'em now, sir.'

'Yes,' said Alleyn thankfully.

But they stayed on talking. A kind of perverseness kept them wedded to this discomfort. They grew more and more wakeful and their ideas seemed to grow sharper. Their thoughts cleared. Alleyn spoke for a long time and the other two listened to him eagerly. Quite suddenly he stopped and shivered. The virtue went out of them. They felt dirty, and dog-tired. Wade began to gather up his papers.

'I reckon that finishes us for tonight. We'll lock up this show and turn it up till tomorrow. There'll be the inquest next. Cripey, what a life!'

Alleyn had strolled over to the door in the back wall and was peering at a very murky framed drawing that hung beside it. He wiped the glass with his handkerchief.

'Plan of the theatre,' he said. 'All fine and handy. I think I'll just make a rough copy. It won't take a moment.'

He got a writing-pad from the desk and worked rapidly.

'Here we go,' he murmured. Stage-door. Footlights. Dressing-room passage here. Prompt-side ladder to the grid, about here. Back-stage one here. There's a back door there, you see. I noticed it when I was in full cry after Master Gordon. We'll have a look at it by the light of day. Now the front of the house. Stalls. Circle. No pass-door through the proscenium. Here's this office. Door into box-office. Door to yard. The bicycle shed isn't in their plan, but it begins just beyond this office. The shed comes forward like that. The yard widens out after you pass the sheds. Packing-cases. Then there's this affair – a garage, isn't it? – and the other shed here. And there's Master Gordon's getaway.'

'Need we mark that?' asked Wade, yawning horribly.

'I'm sure Cass thinks it worthy of record,' said Alleyn, smiling. 'How wide are you, Cass?'

'Twenty-four inches across the shoulders, sir,' said Cass, and was shaken by a stupendous belch. 'Pardon,' he added morosely.

'Then the space between the two buildings is certainly less,' murmured Alleyn. 'Of course, Master Gordon is a mere stripling. Tell me, Cass, how did it all happen?'

'He was coming along as quiet as you please, sir,' began Cass angrily, and instantly interrupted himself with a perfectly deafening rumble,' – as quiet as you please, when he suddenly lets out a sort of squeak and bolts down that gap like a bloody rabbit. I never stops to *think*, you see, sir. I tears into it good-oh, and I come at it that determined-like I swept all before me, as you might say, for the first six inches, and then it kind of shut down on me.'

'It did indeed,' said Alleyn.

'By gum, yes, sir, it did so. And I was doubled up like as I was saying to Mr Wade, sir, and I hadn't got no purchase.' He belched violently. 'Pardon. It's gone crook on my digestion. Being doubled up.'

'We can hear that for ourselves,' said Wade unsympathetically. 'You looked a big simp, Cass. Get your helmet. Gather up that stuff and bring it along to the station. I'll shut up here.'

'Yes, sir.'

'Finished your plan, Mr Alleyn?'

'Yes, thank you,' answered Alleyn.

He came out of the office and walked past the bicycle shed to the stage-door. Here he found Sergeant Packer.

'Hullo, Packer, are you here for the rest of the night?'

Packer came smartly to attention.

'Yessir. At least, I'll be relieved in half an hour, sir.'

'None too soon, I should imagine. It's cold.'

'It is too, sir,' agreed Packer. 'There's snow in the back-country.'

'Snow in the back-country!' exclaimed Alleyn, and suddenly he was aware of a new world. The experiences of the night slipped away and became insignificant. He was awake in a sleeping town and not far away there were mountains with snow on them and long tracts of hills with strange soft names.

'Are you a country-bred man?' he asked Packer.

'Yessir. I come from Omarama in the Mackenzie Country. That's in the South Island, sir. Very high sheep country, beyond Lake Pukaki.'

'I've heard of it. You go through a mountain pass, don't you?'

'That's right, sir. Burke's Pass in the north and the Lindis in the south. Still very cold at nights, this time of year, in the Mackenzie, but you get the sun all day.'

'I shall go there,' said Alleyn. Suddenly he felt a great distaste for the position in which he found himself. He had not crossed half a world of ocean to mess about over a squalid and tedious crime. He felt that he had been a fool, He was on a holiday in a new country and he knew that at the back of all his thoughts there lay a kind of delicious excitement which he would not savour until long after he had gone away again.

The office door banged and Wade and Cass stamped out into the yard, beyond the bicycle shed.

'Are you there, Chief Inspector?' called Cass.

'Here! Goodnight, Packer, or rather good morning, isn't it?'

'Yes, sir, it'll be getting light soon. Good morning, sir.'

Alleyn joined the other two, and together they left the theatre and turned into the main thoroughfare.

Their footsteps rang coldly on the asphalt pavement. Somewhere, a long way off, a dog barked. Then, still farther away, a cock crew and was echoed away into nothingness by other cocks. The moon had set but the darkness was thinning and the street lamps already looked wan.

At the second corner Wade and Cass stopped.

'We turn off here,' said Wade. 'It'll be light in half an hour. If I may, sir, I'll call in at the hotel sometime tomorrow.'

'Do,' said Alleyn cordially.

'It's been a great pleasure, sir, having you with us.'

'You've been damn' pleasant about it, Inspector. Hope you're none the worse, Cass.'

Cass saluted. Solemnly and rather ridiculously they both shook hands with Alleyn and tramped off.

The street ran uphill towards the hotel. At the far end there was a clean lightness of sky and, as Alleyn watched, it grew still lighter. Between the end of the street and the sky was the head of a faraway mountain. Its flowing margin was sharp against the dawn. Its base was drenched in a colder and more immaculate blue than Alleyn had ever before seen. And as Packer had told him, this mountain was crested white and the little cold wind that touched Alleyn's face came from those remote slopes. Alleyn paused outside his hotel, still looking up the street to the mountain and wondering at the line traced by its margin against the sky. He thought: 'It is like the outline of a lovely body. All beautiful edges are convex. Though the general sweep may be inward, to attain beauty, the line must be formed of outward curves.' Before he had completed this thought, the peak of the mountain was flooded with thin rose colour, too austere to be theatrical, but so vivid that its beauty was painful. He felt that kind of impatience and disquietude that sudden beauty brings. He could not stand and watch the flood of warmth flow down the flanks of the mountain nor the intolerable transfiguration of the sky. He rang the night bell and was admitted by the porter.

The clocks in the hotel, and the clocks outside in the town, all began to strike six as he got into bed, and when the last clock had struck, the vague rumour of innumerable cockcrows rang in his head. And as he fell asleep he heard the first chatter of waking birds.

CHAPTER 16

Entr'acte

Extract from a letter written by Chief Inspector Alleyn to Detective-Inspector Fox of the Criminal Investigation Department, New Scotland Yard:

– so you will agree, my dear Fox, it really is a bit of a teaser. I see you wag your head and I know you think what a fool I was not to make my statement and my exit as rapidly as possible. I confess I am surprised at myself and can only suppose that I must *like* teckery – an amazing discovery. You will have got my cable and I shall have received your answer long before this letter reaches you, even if I go a terrific bust and send it by Air Mail. Of course, unless Alfred Meyer made a later will, as far as money goes, George Mason has the strongest motive, but on the evidence before us he could never have got up into the flies to put back the weight. I've told you the whole story and I have outlined my tentative theory which, as you will see, hinges on this one incontrovertible point. Mason was with me on the stage after the murder, and he went with Te Pokiha to the office. I've rung Te Pokiha up and he says he stayed in the office with Mason until he heard the police arrive, and left Mason there when he, Te Pokiha, returned to the stage. To put the thing beyond all argument, it now appears that after the police had come, the doorkeeper went along the yard, saw Mason sitting in the office sipping his whisky, and stayed talking to him until Mason went to the

wardrobe-room. By that time the weight was back again.
I have laboured this point because I know Wade is going to try
and break Mason's alibi for this period and I am satisfied that
he cannot do it. Then there's this grim little tiki – I wish you
could see it – it's a tiny squint-eyed effigy with a lolling head
and curled-up rudimentary limbs. The resemblance to the
human embryo is obvious. It's leering at me now from the
blotting paper. They tried it for prints and it was smothered
with them. Well, it's reasonable to suppose that whoever put
the weight back, dropped the tiki on the floor of the grid
platform. Mason is ruled out. We have Hambledon, Carolyn
Dacres, Liversidge, Ackroyd and the girl, Valerie Gaynes. These
could, I believe, have gone aloft, unnoticed, at both the vital
times. At the risk of boring you to tears, my poor Fox, I now
append a timetable for the two visits to the grid. I include the
entire cast of characters, even our old friend Susan Max. Here
it is. You will notice that I have marked the names without
alibis. XA or XB stands for no alibi during the first or second
vital periods, and XX (Guinness is *good* for you) for no alibi at
either of these times. I've also noted the alleged motives.

As regards the attempt on the train (if it was an attempt and
not a playful gambol on the part of a homing rugger expert), I
regard any attempt to link it up with the theft – an attempt
which Wade longs to make – as a likely pitfall. At that time the
theft had not been discovered by Miss Gaynes. If Meyer had
seen the thief on the job and had tackled him about it, why
had he not forced him to return the money before the loss was
known? Or, conversely, why had he not made the business
public? As he did neither of these things, why should the thief
try to murder him? Sergeant Cass intelligently suggests that
perhaps the thief knew Meyer had twigged his little game, that
Meyer was unaware of this, and that the thief struck before
Meyer could take action, missed his pot on the train, and had
a more successful go at the theatre. This does not explain
Meyer's delay in tackling the matter in the first instance. The
force is now hunting up the train passengers, to try and let a
little more light into the affair. I still incline to the view that the
theft is a sideline, put in by the gods to make it more difficult.

But what god dropped the little green tiki into this puzzle? I have seen some of the Maori deities in the local museum. Wild grimacing abortions, with thrust-out tongues and glinting eyes. They seem to fascinate me. One seems to smell old New Zealand in them – a kind of dark wet smell like the native forest. Before this case came along I hired a car and make a trip into the country north of this town where a tract of native bush is preserved. On the way there are Maori villages – pas they call them – composed for the most part of horrid little modern cottages. The Maoris themselves wear European clothes with occasional native embellishments, among the older people. They have a talent for arranging themselves in pleasant groups and seem to be very lighthearted. The aristocrats among them are magnificent. Te Pokiha is an Oxford man. He is extremely good-looking, courteous, and most dignified. I am to dine with him and he is to tell me something of their folklore. When, as I have already described, the men handed the little tiki round and Meyer made merry, I felt that he was guilty of the grossest error in taste. Te Pokiha was very cool and well-bred about it. What an idea for a fantastic solution – he killed Meyer because of the insult to the tiki and left the tiki up there as a token of his vengeance. 'Cut it out,' as Inspector Wade would say. The local force is very polite to me. I am to meet the superintendent this morning. They might well have been a bit sticky over me and indeed, to begin with, I sensed a sort of defensiveness on Wade's part. It was a curious mixture of 'How about this for a genuine New Zealand (they say "New Zillund") welcome?' and 'Treat us fair and we'll treat you fair, but none of your bloody superiority stuff.' They are extremely nice fellows and good policemen, and I hope I shan't get on their nerves. One has to keep up a sort of strenuous heartiness, which I find a little fatiguing. The idiom is a bit puzzling but 'corker' seems to be the general adjective of approbation. 'Crook' means 'ill', 'angry', or 'unscrupulous' according to the context; and 'a fair nark', or, more emphatically, 'a fair cow', is anything inexpressibly tedious or baffling. The average working man – such as the railway porter and taxi driver (especially the older type) speaks much better English

	A	B	Motive
	After the show. Before the party. 1st visit to Grid. Weight removed. Pulley shifted. Approx. 10.30–11.	After the murder. 2nd visit to Grid. Weight replaced. Pulley replaced. Approx. 11.15–11.30	
Susan Max	In her dressing-room with Carolyn Dacres's maid.	Went with Carolyn Dacres to latter's dressing-room. Moved to her own room with maid. Returned later to Carolyn Dacres. Left on my arrival. Then to wardrobe-room.	None known.
Courtney Broadhead XB	Went to dressing-room with Brandon Vernon.	Went alone to dressing-room. Found Vernon there. Had a drink. Went to wardrobe-room.	Suggested by Palmer (prompted by Liversidge) that he stole Valerie Gaynes's money, said he'd been lent it by Meyer and killed latter to avoid discovery.
Brandon Vernon XB	In dressing-room with Courtney Broadhead.	Went alone to dressing-room where he was joined by Broadhead and Liversidge. Then went to wardrobe-room.	None known.
Francis Liversidge XX	Last to leave stage and go to dressing-room. Spoke on stage to Valerie Gaynes.	Last to leave stage. Spoke to Valerie Gaynes at entrance of passage. Then went to dressing-room, then wardrobe-room.	Suggested by Valerie Gaynes that he stole her money. If Meyer was aware of this and Liversidge knew it, he might kill Meyer to save his reputation and career.
George Mason ?XA	In office. Doorkeeper spoke to him and watched him go back. I met him in yard and went with him to stage.	On stage with us. Went to office with Pokiha. Remained in office talking to doorkeeper. Went to wardrobe-room.	Gets the money.
George Gascoigne ?	On stage. Working with staff.	On stage.	None known.

	A	B	Motive
Valerie Gaynes XX	Left stage after conversation with Liversidge. Went to dressing-room.	Left stage after second conversation with Liversidge. Went to dressing-room then to wardrobe-room.	None, unless to protect person who stole her money. If Liversidge is the thief, this is just possible.
St John Ackroyd ?X?X	Alone in dressing-room but says that he called out at intervals to the others.	Ditto, and then to wardrobe-room.	None known. NB Vernon says Carolyn Dacres snubbed his advances. Obviously bears Carolyn Dacres and Hambledon a grudge.
Hailey Hambledon XX	Alone in his dressing-room. Dismissed his dresser. Then on stage.	Says he took Carolyn Dacres to her dressing-room. Then went to his dressing-room. Returned to her. Fetched me from stage. Returned with me to her room. Fetched brandy. Went to wardrobe-room.	Rumoured to be in love with Carolyn Dacres. Ackroyd says he overheard Hambledon ask her if she'd marry him if Meyer was dead. She is reported to have said that she would.
Carolyn Dacres (Mrs Meyer) XX	Alone in dressing-room. Dismissed her dresser who went to Susan Max.	Hambledon took her to her dressing-room. She sent him away. Also sent dresser away. The latter went to Susan Max and later returned to Carolyn Dacres who sent for Susan. Hambledon returned and was sent for me.	Comes in for money but her salary must be enormous. Ackroyd says she refused to consider a divorce on account of being Roman Catholic. Seems hardly likely she would strain at divorce and swallow murder. (More possible that she would shield Hambledon if he did it).
Gordon Palmer	Came in among other guests. Joined party. Made a fuss about not being allowed to visit Carolyn Dacres's room.	Went with others to wardrobe-room.	None, unless calf-love.
Geoffrey Weston	With Palmer. Ditto throughout.		None.

than his English contemporary. One notices the accent in polite circles, but Lor' bless you, what of it? My poor Fox, I maunder at you. I hope you have enjoyed looking up the affairs of Mason and Meyer's Incorporated Playhouses, and of Mr Francis Liversidge. Such fun for you.

I am feeling much better, so you need not put on your scolding air over my police activities. It is so amusing to be unofficial and yet in the game. I feel I may give surmise and conjecture free rein.

Do write me a line when you've time.

Yours ever,
RODERICK ALLEYN

Alleyn sealed and addressed his letter and glanced at the lounge clock. Ten o'clock. Perhaps he had better take another look at Master Gordon Palmer who, at nine o'clock, appeared to be sunk in the very depths of sottish slumber. Alleyn took the lift to the second floor. The unwavering stare of the lift-boy told him that his identity was no longer a secret. He walked to Gordon's room, tapped on the door and walked in.

Gordon was awake but in bed. He looked very unattractive and rather ill.

'Good morning,' said Alleyn. 'Feeling poorly?'

'I feel like death,' said Gordon. He glanced nervously at the chief inspector, moistened his lips and then said rather sheepishly: 'I say, I'm sorry about last night. Can I have my key back? I want to get up.'

'I unlocked your door an hour ago,' said Alleyn. 'Haven't you noticed?'

'As a matter of fact my head is so frightful I haven't moved yet.'

'I suppose you drank yourself to sleep?'

Gordon was silent.

'How old are you?' asked Alleyn.

'Seventeen.'

'Good God!' exclaimed Alleyn involuntarily. 'What do you suppose you'll look like when you've grown up? An enfeebled old dotard. However, it's your affair.'

Gordon attempted to smile.

'And yet,' continued Alleyn, raising one eyebrow and screwing up his face, you don't look altogether vicious. You're pimply, of course, and your skin's a nauseating colour – that's late hours and alcohol – but if you gave your stomach and your lungs and your nerves a sporting change you might improve enormously.'

'Thanks very much.'

'Rude, you think? I'm twenty-five years older than you. Old gentlemen of forty-two are allowed to be impertinent. Especially when they are policemen. Do you want to get into trouble with the police, by the way?'

'I'm not longing to,' said Gordon, with a faint suggestion of humour.

'Then why, in heaven's name, did you bolt? You have permanently changed the silhouette of Detective-Sergeant Cass. He now presents the contour of a pouter-pigeon.'

'Oh no, does he? How superb!'

'How *superb!*' imitated Alleyn. 'The new inflexion. How *superb* for you, my lad, if you're clapped in durance vile.'

Gordon looked nervous.

'Come on,' continued Alleyn. Why did you bolt? Was it funk?'

'Oh, rather. I was terrified,' said Gordon lightly.

'Of what? Of your position in regard to Courtney Broadhead? Were you afraid the police would press you to restate your theory?'

'It's not my theory.'

'We came to that conclusion. Liversidge filled you up with that tarradiddle, didn't he? Yes, I thought so. Were you afraid we'd find that out?'

'Yes.'

'I see. So you postponed the evil hour by running away?'

'It was pretty bloody waiting in that room. Hour after hour. It was cold.'

His eyes dilated. Suddenly he looked like a frightened schoolboy.

'I've never seen anyone – dead – before,' said Gordon.

Alleyn looked at him thoughtfully.

'Yes,' he said at last, 'it was pretty foul, wasn't it? Give you the horrors?'

Gordon nodded. 'A bit.'

'That is bad luck,' said Alleyn. 'It'll wear off in time. I don't want to nag, you know, but alcohol's no good at all. Makes it worse. So you eluded Mr Cass because you'd got the jim-jams while you were waiting in the wardrobe-room?'

'It was so quiet. And outside there – on the stage – getting cold and stiff – '

'God bless my soul!' exclaimed Alleyn. 'They took him away long before that, you silly fellow. Now tell me, what did Liversidge say to you when you left the scene of the disaster?'

'Frankie?'

'Yes. In the dressing-room passage, before you went to the wardrobe-room?'

'He – he – I think he said something about – did I remember what we'd said.'

'What did he mean?'

'About Courtney and the money.'

'Now think carefully and answer me truthfully. It's important. Who made the suggestion that Broadhead might have taken that money – you or Mr Liversidge?'

'He did, of course,' said Gordon at once.

'Ah yes,' said Alleyn.

He sat down on the end of the bed and again he contemplated Gordon. It seemed to him that after all the boy was not so intolerably sophisticated. 'His sophistication is no more than a spurious glaze over his half-baked adolescence,' thought Alleyn. 'Under the stress of this affair it has already begun to crack. Perhaps he may even read detective stories.' And suddenly he asked Gordon:

'Are you at all interested in my sort of job?'

'I *was*, rather, in the abstract,' said Gordon.

'I'm puzzled by your reactions to this affair. Last night you know, you were so very alert and cock-a-hoop. Your attack on Broadhead! It was most determined.'

'I hadn't time to think. It didn't seem real then. None of it seemed real. Just rather exciting.'

'I know. Perhaps you are one of the people that ricochet from a shock, as a bullet does from an impenetrable surface. You fly off at an uncalculated angle, but do not at once lose speed.'

'Perhaps I am,' agreed Gordon, cheered by the delicious promise of self-analysis. 'Yes, I think I am like that. I – '

'It's a very common reaction,' said Alleyn. 'Let us see how the theory may be applied to your case. A man was murdered almost under your nose, and instead of screaming like Miss Gaynes, or being sick like Mr Mason, you found yourself sailing along in a sort of unreal state of stimulation. You felt rather intoxicated and into your mind, with startling insistence, came a little sequence of ideas about Courtney Broadhead. You thought of your discussion with Mr Liversidge and – an additional fillip – he actually reminded you of it in the passage. Still sailing along, you were seized with the idea of bringing off one of those startling coups, which, unfortunately for us, occur more often in fiction than in police investigations. You would confront Broadhead with his infamy and surprise him into betraying himself. It's a typical piece of adolescent behaviourism. Very interesting in its way. A projection of the king-of-the-castle phantasy – I forget the psychoanalytical description.'

He paused. Gordon, very red in the face, was silent.

'Well,' continued Alleyn, 'when that little affair was over you began to lose speed and come to earth. You had time to think. You tell me that as the others went out, one by one, until only you and Mr Weston were left under Packer's eye, you began to get the jim-jams. You got them so badly that when we sent for you, you bolted. I can't help wondering if there was some additional cause for this – if perhaps you had remembered something that seemed to throw a new light on this crime.'

Still watching the boy, Alleyn thought, 'Really, he changes colour like a chameleon. If he goes any whiter he'll faint.'

'What do you mean?' said Gordon.

'I see I am right. You *did* remember something. Will you tell me what it was?'

'I don't even know what you are talking about.'

'Don't you? It doesn't seem very difficult. Well, I had better leave it for the moment and ask a few routine questions. Let me see, you came round the front of the house to the stage as soon as the show was over?'

'Yes.'

'Did you walk straight on to the stage and remain there?'

'Yes.'

'You did not go to any of the dressing-rooms?'

'No. I wanted to go to Carolyn's room but Ted Gascoigne was stupid about it so I didn't.'

'Right. After the disaster, when I suggested that you should wait somewhere with your cousin until the police arrived, did you both keep together?'

'We went to the wardrobe-room. Geoff took me there.'

'Right. Now about this tiki. What were you going to say about that when I questioned Miss Dacres in the wardrobe-room?'

'Nothing.'

'Shall I make another guess? When I asked Miss Dacres where the tiki was, she put her hand up to her dress with that quick, almost involuntary gesture a woman uses when she has something hidden in what used to be called her bodice. You saw that gesture, and a moment afterwards you made an exclamation and then refused to explain it. That was because you remembered that during the supper-party you saw Miss Dacres slip the tiki under the bodice of her dress.'

'How do you know? I – I wasn't sure. I only thought – '

'A moment afterwards, she looked in her bag and then said she did not remember handling the tiki after she had put it down on the table.'

'There's nothing in that,' said Gordon hotly. 'She'd simply forgotten. That's not surprising after what happened. She wasn't trying to tell lies, if that's what you mean. She'd forgotten, I tell you. Why, I only happened to remember because of her hand – '

'I merely wanted to be sure that you'd seen her do it.'

'Well, if I did, what of it?'

'Nothing at all. And now I shall leave you to arise and greet the latter half of the morning. I suggest two aspirins, some black coffee and a brisk walk to the police station where Inspector Wade will be delighted to receive your apologies for your offensive behaviour. I forget what the penalty is for running away from the police in the execution of their duty. Something with a little boiling oil in it, perhaps. I suppose you loathe *The Mikado?*'

'Look here, sir, what'll they do to me?'

'If you tell them, nicely, what you've just told me, I shall try and stay their wrath. Otherwise – '

Alleyn made a portentous grimace and walked out of the room.

CHAPTER 17

Change of Scene

When Alleyn returned to the lounge he found Wade there, waiting for him. They retired to Alleyn's room where he related the gist of his conversation with Gordon.

'I've told him to give you the whole story himself.'

'I still don't see why he cleared out on us,' said Wade.

'I fancy it was partly because he'd worked himself up into a blue funk over the whole business. His nerves are in a lamentable state, silly little creature. And I do think, Wade, that he's in a devil of a twit over this business of the tiki.'

'Yee-es? And why's that, sir?'

Alleyn hesitated for a moment. A curious look of reluctance came into his face. When he spoke his voice was unusually harsh.

'Why? Because he caught Carolyn Dacres lying. Last night when I asked her about the tiki her hand went to her breast. She fingered her dress, expecting to feel the hard little tiki underneath. Then she said she had not handled it since it was left on the table. She looked in her bag. The only honest thing she did was involuntary – that movement of her hand. I've told you young Palmer started to speak, and stopped dead. This morning I trapped him into as good as admitting he'd seen her put the tiki into her dress.'

'But why did he stop? He couldn't have known where we found it, could he?'

'No. The young booby's head over ears in calf-love with her. He sensed the lie, as I did, and wouldn't give her away.'

'I reckon I'll talk to Miss Carolyn Dacres-Meyer before I do another thing. This looks like something, sir. And she could have gone up there. She could have done it all right.'

'Yes. Wade, at the risk of making an intolerable nuisance of myself, I'm going to ask a favour of you. Will you allow me to speak to her first? I – I've a perfectly legitimate reason for wanting to do this. At least,' said Alleyn with a wry smile, 'I think it's legitimate. It's just possible she may feel less on the defensive with me. You see – I know her.'

'You go to it, sir,' said Wade, with a violent heartiness that may possibly have concealed a feeling of chagrin. 'You do just as you please, and we'll be more than satisfied. That'll be quite OK. As you say, you'll get a lot more out of her than we would, seeing she looks on you as a friend.'

'Thank you,' said Alleyn. He looked rather sick.

'I'll get back to the station, sir. Let young Palmer come to me – better than seeing him here. The super will be calling in shortly, I fancy.'

'Have a drink before you go,' suggested Alleyn.

'Now, sir, I was just going to suggest, if you'd give me the pleasure – '

They went down to the bar and had drinks with each other.

Wade departed, and Alleyn, avoiding the unwavering stare with which everybody in the hotel followed his movements, buried himself behind a newspaper until the arrival of Superintendent Nixon. Nixon turned out to be a pleasant dignified officer with a nice sense of humour. He was cordial without finding any necessity to indulge in Wade's exuberant manifestations of friendliness. Alleyn liked him very much and saw that Nixon really welcomed his suggestions, and wished for his cooperation. They discussed the case fully and Nixon stayed until eleven-thirty when he exclaimed at the length of his visit, invited Alleyn to make full use of the local station and its officials, and accepted an invitation to dine the following evening.

When he had gone Alleyn, with the air of facing an unpleasant task, returned to the writing-desk. There were now nine people in the lounge, all ensconced behind newspapers. Six of them frankly folded their journals and turned their gaze on Alleyn. Two peered round the corners of their papers at him. The last, an old lady, lowered her paper until it masked the bottom part of her face like a yashmak, and glared at him unwinkingly over the top. Alleyn himself stared at a blank sheet of paper for minutes. At last he wrote quickly:

'Will you give me the pleasure of driving you into the country for an hour or so? It will be an improvement on the hotel, I think.' [He paused, frowning, and then added:] 'I hope my job will not make this suggestion intolerable.'

RODERICK ALLEYN

He was about to ring for someone to take this note to Carolyn's room, when he became aware of a sense of release. A rustling and stirring among the nine bold starers informed him of the arrival of a new attraction and, glancing through the glass partition, he saw Hambledon coming downstairs. He went to meet him.

'Hullo, Alleyn. Good morning. I suppose you've been up for hours.'

'Not so many hours.'

'Any of our people down yet?'

'I haven't seen them.'

'Gone to earth,' muttered Hambledon, 'like rabbits. But they'll have to come to light soon. Mason called us for noon at the theatre.'

'I don't think you'll get in there, do you know,' said Alleyn.

'Why? Oh – the police. I see. Well, I suppose it'll be somewhere in the hotel.'

The lift came down and Mason got out of it.

''Morning, Hailey. 'Morning, Mr Alleyn.'

'Hullo, George. Where are we meeting?'

'The people, here, have lent us the smoking-room. My God, Hailey, they're locking us out of our own theatre. Do you know that? Locking us out!'

They gazed palely at each other.

'First time in thirty years' experience it's ever happened to me,' said Mason. 'My God, what would Alf have thought! Locked out of our own house. It makes you feel awful, doesn't it?'

'It's all pretty awful, George.'

'Did you sleep?'

'Not remarkably well. Did you?'

'Damn' queer thing, but it's the first night for months that I
haven't been racked by dyspepsia – first time for months – and I lay
there without a gurgle, thinking about Alf all night.' Mason stared
solemnly at both of them. 'That's what you call irony,' he said.

'How will you let everybody know about the call for twelve?'
asked Hambledon.

'I've got hold of Ted and he's doing it.'

'Do you want Carolyn?'

'Have you seen her? How is she?'

'I haven't seen her.'

Mason looked surprised.

'Well, run up now, like a good fellow, Hailey, and tell her not to
bother about this call if she doesn't feel up to it.'

'All right,' said Hambledon.

'Would you mind giving her this note?' asked Alleyn, suddenly.
'It's just a suggestion that if she'd like to get away from the pub for
a bit of fresh air – she'll explain. Thank you so much.'

'Yes – certainly.' Hambledon looked sharply at Alleyn and then
made for the lift.

'This is a difficult situation for you, Mr Mason,' said Alleyn.

'Difficult! It's a bit more than difficult. We don't know what's to
happen. Here we are with the tour booked up – the advance is
down in Wellington and has put all the stuff out. We're due to open
there in six days and God knows if the police will let us go, and if
they do God knows if Carolyn will be able to play. And without
her – !'

'Who's her understudy?'

'Gaynes. I ask you! Flop! The Australian kid would have to take
Gaynes's bits. Of course if Carolyn does play – '

'But, after this! She's had a terrible shock.'

'It's different in the business,' said Mason. 'Always has been. The
show must go on. Doesn't mean we're callous but – well Alf would
have felt the same. The show must go on. It's always been like that.'

'I suppose it has. But surely – '

'I've seen people go on who would have been sent off to hospital
in any other business. Fact. I was born off-stage twenty minutes after
my mother took her last call. It was a costume piece, of course –
crinolines. It's a funny old game, ours.'

'Yes,' said Alleyn. Suddenly he was aware of a kind of nostalgia, a feeling of intense sympathy and kinship with the stage. 'A drab enough story to have aroused it,' he thought. 'A theme that has been thrashed to death in every back-stage plot from *Pagliacci* downwards. The show must go on!'

'Of course,' Mason was saying, 'Carolyn may feel differently. I'm not sure about it myself. The public might not like it. Besides suppose it's – one of us. Everybody would be wondering which of the cast is a bloody murderer. That's so, isn't it?'

'I suppose there would be a certain amount of conjecture.'

'Not the sort of advertisement the Firm wants,' said Mason moodily. 'Undignified.'

To this magnificent illustration of a meiosis, Alleyn could only reply: 'Quite so.'

Mason muttered on, unhappily: 'It's damn' difficult and expensive whichever way you look at it. And there's the funeral. I suppose that will be tomorrow. *And* the inquest. The papers will be full of us. Publicity! Poor old Alf! He was always a genius on the publicity side. My God, it's rum, isn't it? Oh well – see you later. You're going to give these fellows a hand, aren't you? Funny, you being a detective. I hear Alf knew all about it. My God, Alleyn, I hope you get him.'

'I hope we shall. Will you have a drink?'.

'Me? With my stomach it'd be dynamite. Thanks, all the same. See you later.'

He wandered off, disconsolately.

Alleyn remained in the hall. In a minute or two Hailey Hambledon came down in the lift and joined him.

'Carolyn says she would like to go out. I'm to thank you and say she will be down in ten minutes.'

'I'll order the car at once. She won't want to wait down here.'

'With all these rubbernecks? Heavens, no!'

Alleyn went into the telephone-box and rang up the garage. The car would be sent round at once. When he came out Hambledon was waiting for him.

'It's extraordinarily nice of you, Alleyn, to do this for her.'

'It is a very great pleasure.'

'She's so much upset,' contined Hambledon. He lowered his voice and glanced at the reception clerk who was leaning out of his window and affecting an anxious concern in the activities of the hall porter. The porter was engaged in a close inspection of the carpet within a six-foot radius from Alleyn and Hambledon. He had the air of a person who is looking for a lost jewel of great worth.

'Porter,' said Alleyn.

'Sir?'

'Here is half a crown. Will you be so good as to go out into the street and watch for a car which should arrive for me at any moment? You can continue your treasure hunt when I have gone.'

'Thank you, sir,' said the porter in some confusion, and retired through the revolving doors. Alleyn gazed placidly at the reception clerk who turned away with an abstracted air and picked his teeth.

'Come over here,' suggested Alleyn to Hambledon. 'The occupants of the lounge can gaze their fill but they can't hear you. You were saying – '

'I am sure the shock has been much greater than she realizes. As a matter of fact I can't help feeling she would be better to spend the day in bed.'

'Thinking?'

'She'll do that wherever she is. I'm very worried about her, Alleyn. She's altogether too bright and brave – it's not natural. Look here – you won't talk to her about Alf, will you? Keep right off this tragedy if you can. She's in no state to discuss it with anybody. Last night those damn' fellows kept her at it for God knows how long. I know that you, as a Yard man, are anxious to learn what you can, and I hope with all my heart that you get the swine; but – don't worry Carolyn again just yet. She gets quite hysterical at the mention of it. I know I can depend on you?'

'Oh,' said Alleyn vaguely, 'I'm very dependable. Here is Miss Dacres.'

Carolyn stepped out of the lift.

She wore a black dress that he had seen before and a black hat with a brim that came down over her face which, as usual, was beautifully made-up. But underneath the make-up he suspected she was very pale, and there was a darkness about her eyes. Carolyn looked a little older, and Alleyn felt a sudden stab of compassion. 'That won't do,' he thought, and started forward to greet her. He was aware that the old lady with the journalistic yashmak had boldly advanced to the plate-glass partition, and that three of the other occupants of the lounge were making hurriedly for the hall.

'Good morning,' said Carolyn. 'This is very nice of you.'

'Come out to the car,' said Alleyn. 'It is very nice of *you*.'

He and Hambledon walked out on either side of her. The porter, who had been deep in conversation with the mechanic from the garage, flew to open the door of the car. A number of people seemed to be hanging about on the footpath.

'Thank you,' said Alleyn to the mechanic. 'I'm driving myself. Come back at about three, will you? Here you are, Miss Dacres.'

'You're in a great hurry, both of you,' said Carolyn, as Hambledon slammed the door. Then she saw the little knot of loiterers on the footpath. 'I see,' she whispered.

'Goodbye, my dear,' said Hambledon. 'Have a lovely drive.'

'Goodbye, Hailey.'

The car shot forward.

'I suppose the paper is full of it,' said Carolyn.

'Not absolutely full. They don't seem to go in for the nauseating front-page stuff in this country.'

'Wait till the evening papers come out before you're sure of that.'

'Even they,' said Alleyn, 'will probably show a comparative sense of decency. I thought we might drive up to where those mountains begin. They say it's a good road and I got the people in the hotel to put some lunch in the car.'

'You felt sure I would come?' asked Carolyn.

'Oh, no,' said Alleyn lightly. 'I only hoped you would. I've been a fair distance along this road already. It's an uphill grade all the way, though you wouldn't think it, and when we get to the hills it's rather exciting.'

'You needn't bother to make conversation.'

'Needn't I? I rather fancy myself as a conversationalist. It's part of my job.'

'In that case,' said Carolyn loudly, 'you had better go on. You see, dear Mr Alleyn, I do realize this is just a rather expensive and delicate approach to an interrogation.'

'I thought you would.'

'And I must say I do think it's quite charming of you to take so much trouble over the setting. Those mountains *are* grand, aren't they? So very up-stage and magnificent.'

'You should have seen them at 6 a.m.'

'Now you are being a Ruth Draper. They couldn't have been any lovelier than they are at this moment, even with these depressing little bungalows in the foreground.'

'Yes, they were. They were so lovely I couldn't look at them for more than a minute.'

' "Mine eyes dazzle"?'

'Something like that. Why don't you do some of those old things? *The Maid's Tragedy?*'

'Too hopelessly frank and straightforward for the Lord Chamberlain, and not safe enough for the box-office. I did think once of *Millamant*, but Pooh said – ' She stopped for a second. 'Alfie thought it wouldn't go.'

'Pity,' said Alleyn.

They drove on in silence for a few minutes. The tram-line ended and the town began to thin out into scattered groups of houses.

'Here's the last of the suburbs,' said Alleyn. 'There are one or two small townships and then we are in the country.'

'And at what stage,' asked Carolyn, 'do we begin the real business of the day? Shall you break down my reserve with precipitous roads, and shake my composure with hairpin bends? And then draw up at the edge of a chasm and snap out a question, before I have time to recover my wits?'

'But why should I do any of these things? I can't believe that my few childish inquiries will prove at all embarrassing. Why should they?'

'I thought all detectives made it their business to dig up one's disreputable past and fling it in one's face.'

'Is your past so disreputable?'

'There you go, you see.'

Alleyn smiled, and again there was a long silence. Alleyn thought Hambledon had been right when he said that Carolyn was too brave to be true. There was a determined and painful brightness about her, her voice was pitched a tone too high, her conversation sounded brittle, and her silences were intensely uncomfortable. 'I'll have to wait,' thought Alleyn.

'Actually,' said Carolyn suddenly, 'my past is quite presentable. Not at all the sort of thing that most people imagine about the actress gay. It began in a parsonage, went on in a stock drama company, then repertory, then London. I went through the mill, you know. All sorts of queer little touring companies where one had to give a hand with the props, help on the stage, almost bring the curtain down on one's own lines.'

'Help on the stage? You don't mean you had to lug that scenery about?'

'Yes, I do. I could run up a box-set as well as most people. Flick the toggle-cords over the hooks, drop the back-cloth – everything. Oh, but how lovely that is! How lovely!'

They had now left all the houses behind them. The road wound upwards through round green hills whose firm margins cut across each other like the curves of a simple design. As Carolyn spoke, they turned a corner, and from behind this sequence of rounded greens rose the mountain, cold and intractable against a brilliant sky. They travelled fast, and the road turned continually, so that the hills and the mountain seemed to march solemnly about in a rhythm too large to be comprehensible. Presently Alleyn and Carolyn came to a narrow bridge and a pleasant little hinterland through which hurried a stream in a wide and stony bend.

'I thought we might stop here,' said Alleyn.

'I should like to do that.'

He drove along a rough track that led down to the river-bed, and stopped in the shadow of thick white flowering manuka shrubs, honey-scented.

They got out of the car and instead of the stuffiness of leather and petrol they found a smooth freshness of air with a tang of snow in it. Carolyn, an incongruous figure in her smart dress, stood with her face raised.

'It smells clean.'

The flat stones were hot in the sun, and a heat-haze wavered above the river-bed. The air was alive with the voice of the stream. They walked over the stones, over springy lichen, and patches of dry grass, to the border of the creek where the grass was greener. Here there were scattered prickly shrubs and sprawling bushes, that farther upstream led into a patch of dark trees.

'It must have been forested at one time,' said Alleyn. 'There are burnt tree stumps all over these hills.'

And from the trees came the voice of a solitary bird, a slow cadence, deeper than any they had ever heard, ringing, remote and cool, above the sound of water. Carolyn stopped to listen. Suddenly Alleyn realized that she was deeply moved and that her eyes had filled with tears.

'I'll go back for the luncheon basket,' he said, 'if you'll find a place for us to sit. Here's the rug.'

When he turned back he saw that she had gone farther up the river-bed and was sitting in shade, close to the stream. She sat very still and it was impossible to guess at her mood from her posture. As he walked towards her, he wondered of what she thought. He saw her hands move up and pull off the black London hat. In a moment she turned her head and waved to him. When he reached her side he saw that she had been crying.

'Well,' said Alleyn, 'how do you feel about lunch? They've given me a billy to make the authentic brew of tea – I thought you would insist on that, but if you're not tourist-minded, there's some sort of white wine. Anyway we'll make a fire because it smells pleasant. Will you unpack the lunch while I attempt to do my great open spaces stuff with sticks and at least three boxes of matches?'

She could not answer, and he knew that at last the sprightly, vague, delightfully artificial Carolyn had failed her, and that she was left alone with herself and with him.

He turned away, but her voice recalled him.

'You won't believe it,' she was saying. 'Nobody will believe it – but I was so fond of my Alfie-pooh.'

CHAPTER 18

Duologue

Alleyn did not at once reply. He ws thinking that by a sort of fluke he was about to reach a far deeper layer of Carolyn's personality than was usually revealed. It was as though the top layers of whimsicality and charm and gaiety had become transparent and through them appeared – not perhaps the whole innermost Carolyn but at least a part of her. 'And this because she is unhappy and I have jerked her away from her usual background and brought her to a place where the air is very clear and heady, and there is the sound of a mountain stream and the voice of a bird with a note like a little gong.'

Aloud he said:

'But I can believe it very easily. I thought you seemed fond of him.'

He began to break up a branch of dry driftwood.

'Not romantically in love with him,' continued Carolyn. 'My poor fat Alfie! He was not a romantic husband, but he was so kind and understanding. He never minded whether I was amusing or dull. He thought it impossible that I could be dull. I didn't have to bother about any of that.'

Alleyn laid his twigs between two flat stones and tucked a screw of paper under them.

'I know,' he said. 'There are people to whom one need not show off. It's a great comfort sometimes. I've got one of that kind.'

'Your wife! But I didn't know – '

Alleyn sat back on his heels and laughed. 'No, no. I'm talking about a certain Detective-Inspector Fox. He's large and slow and innocently straightforward. He works with me at the Yard. I never have to show off to old Fox, bless him. Now let's see if it will light. You try, while I fill the billy.'

He went down to the creek and, standing on a boulder, held the billy against the weight of the stream. The water was icy cold and swift-running, and the sound of it among the stones was so loud that it seemed to flow over his senses. Innumerable labials all sounding together with a deep undertone that muttered among the boulders. It was pleasant to lift the brimming billy out of the creek and to turn again towards the bank where Carolyn had lit the fire. A thin spiral of smoke rose from it, pungent and aromatic.

'It's alight – it's going!' cried Carolyn, 'and doesn't it smell good?'

She turned her face up to him. Her eyes were still dimmed with tears, her hair was not quite smooth, her lips parted tremulously. She looked beautiful.

'I would be so happy,' she said, 'if there was nothing but this.'

Alleyn set the can of water on the stones and built up the fire. They moved away from it and lit cigarettes.

'I am glad you do not go into ecstasies over nature,' said Alleyn. 'I was rather afraid you would.'

'I expect I should have – yesterday. Dear Mr Alleyn, will you ask me all your questions now? I would like to get it over, if you don't mind.'

But Alleyn would not ask his questions until they had lunched, saying that he was ravenous. They had white wine with their lunch, and he brewed his billy-tea to take the place of coffee. It was smoky but unexpectedly good. He wondered which of them was dreading most the business that was to come. She helped him to pack up their basket and then suddenly she turned to him:

'Now, please. The interview.'

For perhaps the first time in his life, Alleyn found himself unwilling to carry his case a step further. He had set the stage deliberately, hoping to bring about precisely this attitude in Carolyn. Here she was, taken away from her protective background, vulnerable, and not unfriendly and yet –

He thrust his hand into his pocket and pulled out a little box. He opened it and laid it on the rug between them.

'My first question is about that. You can touch it if you like. It has been "finger-printed".'

Inside the box lay the little green tiki.

'Oh! – ' It was an involuntary exclamation, he would have sworn. For a second she was simply surprised. Then she seemed to go very still. 'Why, it's my tiki – you've found it. I'm so glad.' The least fraction of a pause. 'Where was it?'

'Before I tell you where it was, I want to ask you if you remember what you did with it before we sat down at the table.'

'But I have already told you. I don't remember. I think I left it on the table.'

'And if I should tell you that I know you slipped it inside your dress?'

Another long pause. The fire crackled, and above the voice of the stream sounded the note of the solitary bird.

'It is possible. I don't remember.'

'I found it on the floor of the gallery above the stage.'

She was ready for that. Her look of astonishment was beautifully done. With her hands she made a gesture eloquent of bewilderment.

'But I don't understand. In the grid? How did it get there?'

'I suggest that it dropped out of your dress.'

How frightened she was! Cold nightmarish panic was drowning her before his eyes.

'I don't know – what – you – mean.'

'Indeed you do. You can refuse to answer me if you think it wise.' He waited a second. 'My next question is this: Did you go up into the grid before the catastrophe?'

'*Before!*' The relief was too much for her. The single word, with its damning emphasis, was spoken before she could command herself. When it was too late she said quietly: 'No. I did not go up there.'

'But afterwards? Ah, don't try!' cried Alleyn. 'Don't try to patch it up. Don't lie. It will only make matters worse for you and for him.'

'What do you mean? I don't understand.'

'You don't understand! Tell me this. Was that morning in your dressing-room the only time Hambledon asked you if you would marry him, supposing your husband to be dead?'

'Who told you this story? What morning?'

'The morning you arrived in Middleton. Your conversation was overheard. Now, please answer. Believe me I know altogether too much for there to be anything but disaster in your evasion. You will damage yourself and Hambledon, perhaps irrevocably, if you try to hold out.' He paused staring at his own thin hands clasped about his knees. 'You think, of course, that I am trying to trap you, to frighten you into a sort of confession. That may be true, but it is equally true that I am trying to help you. Can you believe that?'

'I don't know. I don't know.'

'The local police have heard the story of your conversation with Hambledon. They know where the tiki was found. They will learn, soon enough, that you had it on your person after the supper-party. And believe me, they will regard any further attempts at evasion with the very greatest suspicion.'

'What have I done!'

'Shall I tell you what I believe you to have done last night? After the catastrophe you went to your dressing-room. At first the shock was too great for you to think at all clearly, but after a minute or two you did begin to think. Hambledon had taken you to your dressing-room. In a minute I would like you to tell me what he said to you. Like everyone in the cast but yourself, he had been told about the champagne bottle, and knew how it was to be worked. Whatever he may have said, you sent him away saying that you wanted to be quite alone. I think that almost at once the suspicion came into your mind, the suspicion that Hambledon may have brought about the catastrophe. I know that as you left the stage you heard Gascoigne repeating that there had been foul play, that it could not have been an accident. You have told me that you are familiar with the mechanics of the stage, that very often you have actually helped with the scenery. I wonder if you thought you would go up to the grid and find out for yourself. Everyone else was in the dressing-rooms except Mason, Gascoigne, Dr Te Pokiha, and myself, and we were still on the stage, hidden behind the walls of the set. Perhaps you were still too shocked and agitated to think very coherently or wisely; but overwhelmed with this dreadful suspicion, scarcely aware of the risk you ran, you may have slipped round to the back of the stage and climbed the ladder to the gallery.'

He paused for a moment, watching her. Her head was bent down and inclined away from him. Her fingers plucked at the fringe of the rug.

'Stop me if I'm wrong,' said Alleyn. 'I fancy you climbed up to the grid and saw the end of the rope close to the pulley, and perhaps tripped over the weights which had been left on the gallery floor. With your knowledge of stage mechanics you at once realized what had been done. The counterweight had been removed and the bottle had fallen unchecked.'

A strand of the woollen fringe broke in her fingers.

'At this moment we had all moved off the stage into the wings. With some distracted notion of trying to make the whole thing look like an accident you hooked a weight to the ring. While you stooped to pick up the weight, the tiki fell from your dress on to the platform, and lodged between the slats where I found it soon afterwards. Am I right?'

'I – I – would rather not answer.'

'That is as you choose. I must tell you that I am bound to lay this theory before the local police. I have perhaps exceeded my duty in talking about it to you. You asked me last night if I was your friend. I told you that I would give you my help if in return you would give me your confidence. I assure you very solemnly that it is as your friend I urge you to tell me the truth and – really it is the only phrase that fits – the whole truth and nothing but the truth.'

'They can't prove any of this,' she said vehemently. 'Why shouldn't this weight have been there all the time? Why shouldn't it have been an accident? If it was too light – '

'But how did you know it was too light?'

She caught in her breath with a sort of sob.

'You see,' said Alleyn gently, 'you are not cut out for this sort of thing. So you knew it was much too light when you hooked it on? That was very quick and very intelligent. How did you know that? I wonder. The whole scheme had been kept a secret from you – '

Suddenly he stopped, resting his elbow on the ground beside her, and looked into her averted face.

'So you knew about the plan all the time?' he said softly.

She was trembling, now, as though she were very cold. He touched her hand lightly, impersonally.

'Poor you,' said Alleyn.

Then she was clinging to his hand and weeping very bitterly.

'I've been wicked – a fool – I ought never – now you'll suspect him more than before – more than if I had done nothing. You'll think I know. I don't know anything. He's innocent. It was only

because I was so shocked. I was mad even to dream of it. He could-
n't do that – to Alfie. You must believe me – he couldn't. I was mad.'
   'We don't suspect Hambledon more than anyone else.'
   'Is that true? Is it? *Is it?*'
   'Yes.'
   'If I hadn't blundered in, perhaps you would never have suspected
him? It's my fault – '
   'Not quite that. But you have made it a bit more complicated; you
and your fancy touches.'
   'If only you would believe me – if only I could put it right – '
   'If Hambledon is innocent you can put a number of things right
by answering my questions. There, that's better. Look here, I'm
going to give you ten minutes to dry your eyes and powder your
nose. Then I'll come back and finish what I've got to say.'
   He jumped lightly to his feet, and without another word strode off
towards the little gorge where the bush came down to the lip of the
stream. He turned uphill, and after a short climb, he entered into the
bush. It was all that remained of a tall forest. Boles of giant trees
stood like rooted columns among the heavy green underbrush, and
rose high above it into tessellated clusters of heavy green. Light and
dull green were the tree-ferns, light and dull green the ferns underfoot. There was something primal and earthy about this endless
interlacing of greens. It was dark in the bush, and cool, and the only
sound there was the sound of trickling water, finding its way down-
hill to the creek. There was a smell of wet moss, of cold wet earth,
and of the sticky sweet gum that sweated out of some of the tree
trunks. Alleyn thought it a good smell, clean and pungent. Suddenly,
close at hand, the bird called again – a solitary call, startlingly like a
bell. Then this unseen bird shook from its throat a phrase of notes in
a minor key, each note very round with something human in its
quality.
   The brief song ended in a comic splutter. There was a sound of
twigs. Then the call rang again and was answered from somewhere
deep in the bush, and back into the silence came the sound of running water.
   To Alleyn, standing there, it suddenly seemed absurd that he
should have withdrawn into such a place as this, to think of criminal investigation and to allow a woman time to recover from the

effects of her own falsehoods. It was an absurd juxtaposition of opposites. The sort of thing a very modern poet might fancy. 'The Man from the Yard in the Virgin Bush.' 'I should have worn a navy-blue suit, tan boots and a bowler, and I should complete the picture by blowing on a police whistle in answer to that intolerably lovely bird. Mr Rex Whistler would do the accompanying decorations. I'll give her another five minutes to think it over and, if the spell works, she'll come as clean as the week's wash.' He felt in his pocket for his pipe and his fingers encountered the box that held the tiki. He took the squat little monster out. 'This is the right setting for you, only you should hang on a flaxen cord against a thick brown skin like Te Pokiha's. No voluptuous whiteness for you, under black lace, against a jolting heart. That was all wrong. You little monstrosity! Sweaty dark breasts for you, dark fingers, dark savages in a heavy green forest. You've seen a thing or two in your day. Last night was not your first taste of blood, I'll be bound. And now you've got yourself mixed up in a *pakeha* killing. I wish to hell I knew how much you do mean.'

He lit his pipe and leant against the great column of a tree. The stillness of the place was like the expression of some large and simple personality. It seemed to say 'I am' with a kind of vast tranquillity. 'It is quite inhuman,' he thought, 'but it is not unfriendly.' He remembered hearing tales of bushmen who were brought far into the forest to mark trees for sawmills, and who were left to work there for a week but returned in three days, unable to endure the quiet of the forest.

It was easier to think of these things than of the murder of Alfred Meyer, and Alleyn was repopulating the bush with wandering Maoris, when he was startled by the sound of snapping twigs and hurried footsteps.

It was Carolyn, stumbling, in her thin shoes and fine black dress, through the tangled underbrush. She did not see him for several seconds and there was that in her face which made him feel that he must not watch her unseen.

'Hullo!' he called. 'Here I am.'

She turned, saw him, and stumbled towards him.

'I saw you come in here. I couldn't bear to be alone. It's quite true – everything you said. I'll tell you everything, but Hailey is innocent. I'll tell you everything.'

CHAPTER 19

Carolyn Moves Centre

Carolyn told her story as they sat by the sweet-smelling embers of the fire. The sun was bright on the river-bed, but it was still too early in the spring for the day to be unpleasantly hot. As she began to speak, a man came down the gully, followed by three panting sheep-dogs. The man's old felt hat was tilted over his nose. His jacket was slung across his shoulder and his shirt was open at the neck. He carried a long stick and moved with a sort of loose-jointed ease, as though he had been walking for a long time but was not particularly tired. Against the white glare of the shingle his face and arms were vermilion. He gave them 'good day' with a sideways wag of his head. The dogs trotted past with an air of preoccupation, saliva dripping from their quivering tongues.

'I suppose,' thought Alleyn, 'he imagines we are a courting pair and wonders if he has interrupted an amorous scene, instead of – '

'– so I was frightened,' Carolyn went on when the musterer was beyond earshot. 'You see there had been another scene that morning – yesterday morning. I can't believe it was only yesterday – my birthday. Hailey brought me my present. Something I said started him off again. We were alone in my sitting-room. Alfie had just gone out. He – he was all thrilled about his party and he kissed me before he went and was rather possessive. I think that upset Hailey. He was angry and then – violently demonstrative. He said he'd got to the end of his tether – all the old things over again only he was so – so vehement. I wish I was better at explaining myself – I am afraid to tell you exactly what he said because then you may not understand how I can be so certain, now, that Hailey is innocent. You will think I am only *saying* I know he is innocent because there is nothing else left for me to do.'

'Try me,' suggested Alleyn.

'I must try to explain myself first, my own thoughts from the time Hailey left me yesterday morning until after last night. The next thing to tell you is that, in a way, I knew about the champagne. My poor old boy!' Her voice shook for a moment and her lips parted in an uncertain smile. 'He tried so hard to keep it a secret but he was bursting with mysterious hints. I knew there was some plan, and yesterday morning I went down to the theatre and walked in at the stagedoor when they were in the middle of rehearsing the surprise. He and George, and Ted and Hailey, and some of the staff. That – that horrible thing – the champagne – you know – must have been hanging there, but out of sight, and they had the weights on the other end of the cord. There were two weights on it and Alfie said: "That's pounds too much. Take it off." I couldn't think what it was about and I just stood watching. They didn't see me. Ted Gascoigne took one weight off and the other shot up. They just grabbed it in time. It was very funny – seeing them all rush at it. Alfie swore frightfully and I stayed to see, thinking I'd rag him about it afterwards. At last they found the right weight – a single big one. We use three in the first act, you know. The masts and funnels of the yacht are let down with the small ones and the big one is used as a guide for the bridge. They are painted different colours to distinguish them. When they are not in use they are left up above. I heard them say this while I watched. It sounds as though it was a long time but it was only a few moments, I think, before he – my husband – turned and saw me. I said: "What do you funnies think you are up to?" and he became so mysterious, I guessed it was something to do with me. I didn't let them see that I guessed – he would have been so disappointed.'

She paused, compressing her lips. She raised her hand and pressed the palm against her mouth.

'Take it easy,' said Alleyn.

'Yes. When I saw the cord fastened to the table, I guessed it was something to do with all this business with the weights. Then after-wards – afterwards! Mr Alleyn, I think I went a little mad after it had happened. I could only see three things, and I saw them so horribly clearly, like the things one sees in nightmares. Hailey, angry and excited yesterday morning, Hailey, looking on while they fixed the weights, and – and what happened. That last picture. I sent him away from my dressing-room and then I got rid of Susie. I went out to the stage and I could hear Ted say over and over again: "There must have been some funny business." I think he was speaking to you. I thought I must see for myself there and then. In a way my mind was quite clear but it was a sort of delirious clarity. I went round to the back of the stage, took my shoes off, and climbed the ladder. When I reached the top platform I saw at once that the weight had been taken off the hook. I remembered how the smaller weight had shot up, and I thought: "If I put it on, it will look like an accident. It will look as if, in the hurry after the first act, they used the small weight instead of the large one." The stage down below was clear. I was just going to do it when I heard someone climbing the ladder on the prompt-side. That was just after Hailey had left the stage, and I thought it was Hailey. I stayed still but whoever it was – '

'Me,' said Alleyn.

'You? Oh, what a fool I was! I thought it was Hailey. You went away without getting off the ladder. Then I crept along the platform. I could see the stage. Ted had gone to meet the police – I heard him speak to them. No one was on the stage. I hooked on the small weight – I knew it would be ever so much lighter than even the empty bottle. Then I went down. Ted was still speaking to the detectives. They had gone on the stage and you were standing in the first entrance. I slipped round behind a flat into the dressing-room passage. When I got to my room, Hailey was there. He said he had been waiting there for me, and I told him I had been looking for him, and I sent him for Susie, and then for you.'

'Yes,' said Alleyn. 'That all fits. Now will you tell me, please, what made you change your mind. Why are you now so certain that he is innocent?'

'Because – this is what you will find so strange – because of what he said to me last night when we got back to the hotel. He said: "Carolyn, someone has killed Alfred. There's not a possibility of accident. Someoone has altered the weights." We were both quiet for a moment and then he said: "Yesterday – this morning – if I had known he was going to die I would have thought of you and – what

I might gain – and now – I can only think of him." As soon as he had spoken it was as though my brain cleared. I cannot describe how it was. I simply knew that he was quite innocent. I was so ashamed that I had ever thought he might be anything else. He stayed a little while, talking quietly about Alfie and our early days together. When he went away he said' – for a moment the deep voice faltered. Then she made an impatient movement with her head. 'He said: "You know I love you, Carolyn, but I am glad now that we did nothing to hurt him." '

There was a long pause. Carolyn seemed to be lost in her own thoughts. She had become much more composed, and Alleyn thought that while she was alone she must have deliberately set in order the events that she had made up her mind to relate. He realized that physically, as well as emotionally, she was exhausted.

'Shall we go back?' he asked gently.

'First tell me: Can you – do you understand how certain I am of Hailey's innocence? Does what I have said count at all?'

'Yes. It has impressed me very deeply. I am quite sure that you have told me what you believe to be the truth.'

'But you – what do you believe?'

'You must remember that I am a policeman. I attach a great deal of importance to what you have told me, but I would like very much to establish an alibi for the period before the supper-party.'

'For Hailey?'

'For Hambledon, certainly.'

He looked at her. 'Has she got no thought at all for herself?' he wondered. 'Can't she see? Or is she, after all, very, very clever?'

'Hailey was in his dressing-room,' said Carolyn. 'It is next to mine. I heard him send his dresser away. Wait! Wait! Let me think. Last night when that detective asked me questions I could only think about the other time. Wait! When he told Bob – that's his dresser – that he could go, I said to Minna, my maid, that I could manage without her. She helped me off with my dress and then she went out, and she and Bob were talking in the passage. I called out to her to hurry and get ready, and she went off, I think to Susie's room. Then – yes, I called out to Hailey through the wall and he answered. He answered.'

'What did you say?'

'Something about – what was it! – Yes. I said: "Hailey – I've just remembered. I've asked the Woods to the party and nobody knows. How awful!" And he called back: "Not Woods – Forrest." I always call people by their wrong names, you see. Then I asked him to go and tell someone about the Forrests and he said he would as soon as he had taken off his make-up. He said he had got grease-paint on his collar and would have to put on a clean one. We had to shout to hear each other. Someone else will have heard. Who is on the other side of Hailey?'

'We'll find out. Go on, please. After that?'

She held her head between her hands.

'After that? Wait. Bob was outside in the passage, whistling. I remember thinking: "It's in the passage so it doesn't matter." '

'But – what do you mean?'

'It's unlucky to whistle in the dressing-room. Bob stood there – he must have been just inside the doorway to the stage, because I heard him call out every now and then to the stage-hands. I remember thinking that he was evidently not going to bother about tidying himself for the party. He is a great "character" and has been with us for years.'

'Yes, yes,' said Alleyn quickly. 'Go on. Let me have the whole story – give me a clear picture of everything. You are all in your rooms, taking off the make-up. Bob is just outside your door, in the entrance from the stage to the passage. You hear him chaffing the stage-hands. How long was he there? Can you tell me that?'

She glanced at him in surprise.

'I don't know. Why – yes – yes – oh!' Suddenly her whole face was flooded with a kind of tragic thankfulness.

'Listen – listen. Bob was still there when Hailey went out. I heard Hailey say something about why wasn't he on the stage with the party. Bob said: "I don't like butting in, sir. Not my place," and I heard Hailey say: "Nonsense, you're all invited. Come along with me, and we'll make an entrance together." That was like Hailey – he's always considerate with the staff, and nice to them. But Bob was shy and hung back. I heard him say he would wait for Minna. He stayed there. So, don't you see, if Hailey had gone out before, and come back, Bob would have seen him, and when he *did* go he asked Bob to go with him? Don't you see it means Hailey could not have thought of going up to the grid? Why didn't I remember it before – oh, why didn't I!'

'I wish very much that you had. Never mind. How much longer did Bob stay there?'

'I heard the others speak to him as they went past. I don't know how many of them. That was before Hailey went out. But that does-n't matter. It's Hailey that matters – he would never have asked Bob to go with him if he meant to go up into the grid, and besides, I am sure it was too late then. If he had done it he would have gone out before, and Bob would have seen him.'

'Was Bob there when you went out?'

'I don't think so. Hailey and George and – and Alfie came for me. We met in the passage.'

'Tell me,' said Alleyn, 'why did you stay so long in your room?'

Something – the faintest shadow – of the old mischievous look, returned to Carolyn's face. He was reminded of that night in the train when she had looked out of one eye at him.

'I wanted to come on last,' she said. 'It was my party.'

'You deliberately delayed your entrance?'

'Of course I did. I remember wishing Bob *would* go. I heard Minna come along and they stood there talking. I wanted *everybody* – but *everybody* – to be on the stage.' She stared thoughtfully at Alleyn. 'It seems so incredible now, me waiting there to make a big entrance, but you see I *am* Carolyn Dacres. I don't suppose you understand.'

'Yes, yes, I do,' cried Alleyn with sudden exasperation, 'but can't you see, you divine donkey, that I want to get your alibi established!'

'Mine?' She caught her breath and then said softly: 'Yes, I do see. For a moment I had forgotten to be frightened about – me.'

'I hope that you will have no need to be frightened. I must see Bob, at once. Come on – get up. We're going back.'

He stood up and held out his hands.

She gave him hers and rose lightly to her feet. They stood for a moment facing each other, hand-fasted as though they were lovers. Her fingers tightened round his. He thought:

'Damn! She *is* attractive.'

She said: 'I hope for only one thing, Mr Alleyn – that you will soon believe us innocent and then I shall be able to be sorrowful.'

'I understand that.'

'It is so strange. I keep thinking "Pooh will tell me how to get out of this fix!" I only realize with my mind – not yet with my heart. Perhaps that sounds rather trite and affected but I can't find other words.'

'Indeed, I understand.' She still held his hands.

'Somehow at these sorts of times, after one has had a great shock, I mean, one speaks one's thoughts openly. I do feel, in the most strange way, that we are friends.'

'Yes,' said Alleyn.

She gave him a candid and gentle smile and withdrew her hands.

'Come along then. Let us return to – everything.'

He collected the rug and basket and they walked together to the car, the voice of the creek growing fainter as they drew away from it. The sun was near the edge of the warm hill and soon their little gully would slip in to the shade of afternoon. Carolyn paused and looked back.

'It is a lovely place,' she said. 'In spite of everything I shall think of it with pleasure. The painfulness of all this does not seem to have touched it at all.'

'No,' said Alleyn, 'it is very remote. We were interlopers but vaguely welcome, don't you think?'

'Yes. It is a friendly place, really.'

'Are you very tired?'

'I believe I am.'

'No sleep last night?'

'No.'

They got into the car which smelt of hot leather and petrol, and bumped over the rough up to the road.

On the way home they were both silent, Alleyn thinking to himself: 'I really believe her. I believe her story. I believe she feels just what she said – a kind of friendliness for me, no more. Was she quite unaware that she attracted me so vividly for those few moments, or was she using her charm deliberately? Is she in love with Hambledon? Probably.'

With an effort he screwed his thoughts round to the case. If this story about Bob was true, and if Bob turned out to be an intelligent fellow, they should be able to check the movements of the actors with much more accuracy than Alleyn had thought possible. As soon as he got back, he would look again at his plan of the theatre. He was practically certain that the passage was the only source of exit from the dressing-rooms to the stage, therefore anyone of the company who went from the dressing-rooms to the ladder, would have to go past Bob as he stood in the narrow entry. If Bob could only tell him exactly how long he had stood there!

They passed the musterer, riding a half-clipped, raky-looking horse at a lope along the rough grass at the roadside. The three panting sheep-dogs ran in the shade of the horse. The man again solemnly wagged his head at them and raised a hand as they passed. The folding hills marched about. A party of Maoris, grouped on a ramshackle veranda, grinned and waved. They overtook several cars and met several more. The settlements grew closer together, and at length they came over the brow of the last hill, and looked across the flat to Middleton.

'Last lap,' said Alleyn, breaking a long silence.

Carolyn did not answer. He turned to look at her. Her head was bent down and, as heavily as a mandarin's, nodded with the motion of the car. She was sound asleep. At the next bend she swayed towards him. With an equivocal grimace he raised his left hand and tipped her head against his shoulder. She did not wake until the car drew up outside the hotel.

CHAPTER 20

Exit Liversidge. Enter Bob Parsons
(whistling)

As soon as he had put Carolyn into the lift, Alleyn glanced into the writing-room. Should he try and get off a couple of letters for the English mail, or should he look up Wade and give him an account of the interview with Carolyn? He hovered uncertainly in the doorway, and then noticed George Mason, bent over one of the writing-tables, hard at work. Alleyn strolled across and seated himself at a neighbouring desk.

'Oh, hullo,' said Mason abstractedly. 'Have a nice day?'

Without waiting for an answer, he suddenly burst into a recital of his woes.

'I don't know what I'm doing, Alleyn. I'm all anyhow. I don't know what to tell our advance to do – whether to go on with the tour or cancel everything. And there's all the English end to attend to. I'm going crazy just with not knowing. How long do you think they'll keep us here, for God's sake?'

'Things are looking a bit clearer ahead now,' said Alleyn. 'The local men seem to be very efficient.'

'It's awful to be worrying about the business side of it with old Alf – Well, there it is. The whole thing's so damn' beastly. Everybody wondering about everybody else. No use mincing matters. Someone did it. It's this blasted *uncertainty*.'

'I know,' said Alleyn. 'I say, Mason, you know I've taken a hand in it, don't you?'

'Yes. Very glad to hear it.'

402

'Well, look here, I'm going to ask you a question in confidence.'
Mason looked alarmed. 'You needn't answer if you don't want to,
but it'd help matters a lot if you could tell me one thing.'

'Can but ask.'

'Right. Did Mr Meyer know who took Miss Gaynes's money?'

Mason stared at him like a dyspeptic owl.

'Matter of fact, he did,' he said at last.

'You know who it was?'

'Alfred told me,' said Mason uncomfortably. 'It was a question of
what we'd do. Damned awkward in the beginning of a tour like this.'

'Yes. Will you tell me who it was?'

Mason eyed him unhappily but shrewdly.

'What'll it lead to? Look here, Alleyn, you're not trying to link up
the theft and the murder, are you?'

'Personally, I long to disassociate them.'

'By jove!' said Mason slowly. 'I – wonder.'

'When did Mr Meyer guess who took the money?'

'Oh, Lor' – he saw it happen.'

'Did he, indeed! Come now, I'll put it to you, as our learned
friends say. I'll put one name to you, and one name only. If I'm
wrong, let it drop. I promise not to go on.'

'All right!' agreed Mason, looking rather relieved.

'Liversidge?'

There was a long silence.

'Oh, Lor',' repeated Mason, 'I thought you were going to say
Broadhead. After young Palmer's display, you know.'

'How did Mr Meyer come to see it?'

'It was on board – the last night. Alfred was going along the passage
to his state-room and passed Val's door. He'd just seen her in the
smoke-room. He heard someone moving about in her cabin and
thought it was a funny time for the stewardess to be in there. Then he
noticed that her light wasn't up – there's a thick glass fanlight, you
know. Alfred saw a sort of flicker as if someone had an electric torch
going. He was standing there, uncertain what to do, when the door
opened a crack. Opposite the door there was a man's lav. with curtains
in front of the entrance place. Alfred popped behind them and
watched. He thought perhaps one of the stewards was doing the odd

spot of pinching. Well, presently the door of Val Gaynes's room opened wider, and out came Mr Frankie Liversidge, very pussyfoot and cautious. Alf said it was just like a scene from one of the old French farces, and of course, he thought the explanation was the same.'

Mason pulled a face, and then rubbed his nose thoughtfully.

'Do go on,' said Alleyn.

'Well, here's the bit that'll sound rather peculiar, I dare say. You'd never have thought it after thirty years in the business, but Alfred was a bit straightlaced. Fact! He wouldn't stand for any funny business in any of his companies. I know it sounds queer,' said Mason apologetically, 'but that's how he was. Well, what did he do but come out through the curtains and fetch up, face-to-face, with Liversidge. He just stood there and stared at Liversidge reproachfully, and was cogitating what he'd say to him about the way nice young girls were to be held in respect or something, when Frankie said: "I've been making an apple-pie bed for Val." Frankie's face was as white as a sheet and he had his hands in his pockets. Alfie didn't say a word, and Frankie gave a kind of laugh and made an exit. What do you think old Alfred did next?'

'Had a look at the bed to see if it was in apple-pie order?'

'Got it in one,' said Mason, opening his eyes very wide. 'And it wasn't. I mean it was. All tidy and undisturbed. Nothing wrong with it. Well, Alfred toddled off to his own room and did a bit of hard thinking. He decided that Liversidge had been waiting there for Val and had changed his mind, for some reason. Alfred thought he'd watch the situation for a bit, and speak a few heavy-father lines to Val, if they seemed to be called for. That was that. Then came the discovery of the theft and Alf put two and two together and made a burglary.'

'When did he tell you about it?'

'The first evening we were here. He told me he'd tackled Liversidge and there was no doubt he'd done it. God knows why. He'd won a lot at poker. He's just a bad 'un. Well, Alfred said he'd pay it back to Val and stop it out of Liversidge's treasury. And of course Liversidge would go as soon as we could get a decent actor from Australia to play the parts. For the sake of the good name of Incorporated Playhouses he wouldn't make it public. I agreed and that was that. Now look, Alleyn, I've told you as much as I know myself but, if you can, keep it to yourself. The Firm – '

'I understand that. If it doesn't belong to the case we won't press it,' said Alleyn at once. He added a word or two to something he had written while Mason was talking.

'There's just one more thing,' he said. 'Did Mr Meyer get the impression that Liversidge knew he hadn't got away with the apple-pie bed story? At the same time, I mean?'

'I see what you mean. Alfred said Liversidge turned very white as soon as he saw him and seemed very uncomfortable. Alfred just stared at him, sort of more in sorrow than in anger. I don't think he made any pretence of believing the story. He said Frankie's face gave him away.'

'I see,' said Alleyn slowly. 'See here, Mr Mason, I'll have to hand this on to Wade, but I'll ask him not to make it public if he can avoid it. It may have no bearing on the case.'

'Damn' fair of you. Though now we've got murder in the Firm, my God, I suppose we can't be too fussy about an odd theft or so.' And Mason buried his face in his hands.

'I'm dead beat,' he said. 'I feel as if I'd got a red-hot cannon-ball in my chest and half a ton of sawdust in my stomach.'

'Can't you do anything about it?'

'I've seen half the men in Harley Street. I wonder if Te Pokiha would know anything? Some of these natives – Are you going?'

'I must get on. I promised I'd look in at the police station. Thank you so much, Mr Mason.'

Alleyn walked up the hill to the police station, where he found Wade and Superintendent Nixon. He gave them a full account of his interview with Carolyn and with Mason. Wade was inclined to be sceptical about Carolyn, until he heard the story of Liversidge.

'It looks the most promising thing we've got hold of up to date,' he said. 'If he thought Meyer suspected him he'd have the motive before they got on the train. I reckon it's almost good enough for a warrant, Super.'

'What do you think, Mr Alleyn?' asked Nixon.

'I think I'd hold off a bit,' said Alleyn. 'If you both agree I'll look up Liversidge and see if I can get the delicious creature to bare his nasty little soul for me. Perhaps, Mr Nixon, you would prefer to tackle this bit yourself?'

'No, no,' said Nixon quickly, 'we'll be only too pleased if you'll carry on with us, won't we, Wade?'

'Too right, sir. I want to look up old Singleton again. The stage-doorkeeper, Mr Alleyn. He's always boozy, but he's a bit less boozy at this time of day.'

'Why not ring up Liversidge and get him to come round now,' suggested Nixon, 'and we'll make a party of it?'

'Wouldn't that be fun!' said Alleyn grimly. 'All right. Let's.'

Nixon telephoned the hotel and spoke to Liversidge, who said he would 'toddle over' immediately. Alleyn and Nixon occupied the interval with a peaceful discussion on departmental shop. Liversidge arrived, looking too like a not-so-young actor to be credible.

'This is Mr Liversidge, Superintendent Nixon,' said Alleyn.

'Good afternoon,' said Liversidge grandly.

'Good afternoon, Mr Liversidge,' said Nixon. 'Will you take a seat? As you know, Mr Alleyn is very kindly working with us on this case. He has one or two questions he would like to ask you.'

'The indefatigable Mr Alleyn!' said Liversidge, seating himself gracefully. 'And what can I do for Mr Alleyn? Still worrying about what A said to B when the lights went out, Mr Alleyn?'

'Ah well,' answered Alleyn. 'It's my job, you know. As you make your apple-pie bed, so you must lie on it. Or about it, as the case may be.'

'I'm afraid that is too deep for me,' rejoined Mr Liversidge, turning an unlovely parchment colour.

'Haven't you ever made an apple-pie bed, Mr Liversidge?'

'Really!' said Liversidge. 'I didn't come here to discuss practical jokes.'

'You don't enjoy practical jokes?'

'No.'

'Did you take Miss Gaynes's money as a practical joke?'

'I simply don't know what you are talking about.'

'From information received, we learn that you took this money. Wait a moment, Mr Liversidge. I really should not bother to deny it if I were you. Denials of that sort are inclined to look rather the worse for wear in the face of the sort of evidence we have here. However – ' He took out his notebook and pen. 'Did you take this money or did you not?'

'I refuse to answer.'

'Right. On the whole the most sensible thing to do. Perhaps I should tell you that after your interview with Mr Meyer on the day you arrived in Middleton, Mr Meyer had another interview with Mr Mason. It was a matter that concerned the Firm, you see.'

'What has Mason – ?' Liversidge stopped short.

'What has he told us? Simply the gist of what Mr Meyer told him.'

'It was all a joke. Meyer took it the wrong way. Look here Mr – Mr Nixon – '

'You are speaking to Mr Alleyn, you know,' said Nixon, placidly.

'Yes, but – well then.' He turned, reluctantly, to Alleyn. 'It was this way. You must believe me, I swear I'm telling the truth. I'd been ragging Val about the way she left her money lying about. I said she'd have it pinched. She just laughed. It was when she'd got out some notes to pay her poker debts. I went back to the cabin and I – well, I took out the money and filled up the case with – er – with – er – toilet-paper. Just for a joke to make her more careful. That was all. Honestly. *Honestly!*'

'Why didn't you tell Mr Meyer this?'

'I tried to but he wouldn't listen,' said Liversidge, moistening his lips. 'He'd got no sense of humour.'

'Pity. Why did you prompt young Palmer to accuse Broadhead of the theft?'

'I didn't – I didn't mean it that way. I told you. He took me up all wrong. It was all a joke. Can't you see it was all a joke?'

'I've got no sense of humour, either,' said Alleyn, 'but I dare say a jury would laugh till they cried.'

'A jury! My God – '

'Now, Mr Liversidge,' continued Alleyn, composedly, 'the inquest on this case will be held tomorrow. Mr Mason will, of course, be one of the witnesses. As I expect you know – '

'I don't know anything about inquests,' interrupted Liversidge, in a hurry.

'Then it will be an interesting experience for you. If you like to give us a statement – a true statement – of this affair and we find it has no direct bearing on the murder – '

'The murder! My God, I swear – '

'We may possibly not think it necessary to bring it out in evidence. If, on the other hand, you prefer that the whole thing be left until the inquest – '

'I'll make a statement,' said Liversidge, and did so there and then, signing it, and taking himself off in extreme disorder.

'You gave him a nice thrashing,' said Nixon appreciatively when Liversidge had gone.

'I still think it looks good enough for a warrant,' said Wade. 'We've got everything, sir; motive, opportunity – everything. Meyer may even have threatened him with exposure.'

'He may,' agreed Alleyn. 'You're quite right, Wade, but all the same I *would* like to look up Hambledon's dresser, Bob Parsons. I can't help feeling his evidence may be very useful. I think we ought to have it before we crystallize on Liversidge.'

'If Liversidge prompted young Palmer to fake this charge against Broadhead,' said Nixon, 'it looks as if he's a more than usual thoroughgoing bad hat.'

'He's all that,' agreed Alleyn, 'but still – '

'Well, if you will, Mr Alleyn, do go and see Parsons,' said Nixon. 'Wade will give you his address.'

Wade produced the address.

Parsons was staying at a boarding-house close to the theatre. Alleyn went there at once, and in an atmosphere of bamboo and aspidistra he had his talk with Hambledon's dresser.

Bob Parsons was a wisp of a creature with a plaintive face that crinkled into a net of lines when he spoke. His forehead was so crossed with wrinkles that it looked as though it had been wrung out and left to dry and was badly in need of an iron. He had thin nondescript hair, a wide mouth, and a pair of very bright eyes. Alleyn liked the look of him and came directly to the point.

'I'm sorry to disturb you, Mr Parsons, but as I expect you will have heard, I am investigating this case in association with the local police. I want to ask you a few questions. I believe you may be able to help us very considerably.'

'Will you sit down, sir?'

'Thank you. Will you please tell me, as accurately as possible, what your movements were after Mr Hambledon told you to go and get ready for the supper-party last night?'

'*My* movements, sir?'

'Yes.'

'I went into the passage, sir, and watched other people working.'

'Just for a change, what? You mean the stage-hands?'

'Correct, sir. I stood in the doorway watching the boys work overtime.'

'You could see most of the stage from the doorway, I suppose?'

'I could, yes.'

'I suppose you've no idea what the time was?'

'Yes. I have so, sir. It was ten-twenty-five.'

'Good lord, how so accurate?'

'Always time the show, sir. I like to know how she runs. We rang down at ten-twenty-five, and I went straight to the dressing-room and Mr Hambledon came straight off and told me to clear out. "You'll want a clean swaller-and-sigh, sir," I said. "You've got No. 9 all over those." "Well, I can do that," he says, "and how about a clean collar and tie for yourself," he says. "What's the time?" So I told him the time – ten-twenty-six – and I went out.'

'How long were you in the passage?'

Bob screwed his face into a labyrinth of lines and thought for a moment.

'Well, sir, I rolled a fag and smoked it and I rolled another.'

'Whistling a bit, in between times?'

'That's the ticket, sir. I'm a great hand at whistling. My old Dad learnt me that forty years ago. He was a vordervil artist, "Pip Parsons, the 'Uman Hedgesparrer," and he trained me for a Child Wonder. Made me whistle for me tucker. All day he kept me at it. "Pipe up," he'd say, "there's only one place where you *can't* rehearse your stuff, and that's the dressing-room." It grew a habit and when I took on this business I had to unlearn it a good deal faster than I got it. Never do, you see, sir. Unlucky. Whistling people out of their jobs. When I first started whistling I was always being sent out to knock and come in again, to break the bad luck.'

'I see. Miss Dacres told me about this superstition.'

'Miss Carolyn's a fair terror on it, sir. Well I usually tunes up when I gets outside the door. Once through "A Bird in a Gilded Cage" while I roll me fag. That's what I did last night with the falsetto encore. Then I lights up.'

'How long does "A Bird in a Gilded Cage" take?'

'Well – can't say exactly, sir.'

'Look here – will you whistle it through now?'

'Pleased to oblige,' said Bob briskly.

Alleyn took out his stop-watch. Bob fixed his eyes on a picture of two horses being struck by lightning, assumed an expression of agonized intensity, moistened and pursed his lips. A singularly sweet roulade, in a high key, came through them.

'Just to tune up. Count it in, sir. Always do it.' His eyes glazed and he broke into the Victorian ballad, saccharine, long drawn out, and embellished with many stylish trills. The refrain was repeated an octave higher, ending on a top note that seemed to impinge on the outer rim of human hearing.

'Three minutes,' said Alleyn. 'Thank you Bob, it's a grand bit of whistling, that.'

'Used to go big in the old days, sir.'

'Yes, I can believe it did. By the time it was finished you had rolled your cigarette, and you lit it, I suppose?'

'Yes, sir.'

'Suppose you repeat the performance.'

Bob took a dilapidated tin from his pocket and from it produced a hand-made cigarette.

'Always keep some by me,' he said, and lit up. Alleyn glanced again at his watch.

'The next thing,' he said, 'is to remember who came past you from the dressing-room to the stage.'

Bob looked him straight in the eyes.

'I get the idea, sir. Watch me step here. If in doubt say so.'

'Exactly.'

'Well, when I first went out, some of them were still on the stage after the last curtain. Mr Hambledon always goes straight to his room. Mr Funny Ackroyd came along first and then old "I-Played-It-Well-Laddie," with young Broadhead.'

'Mr Vernon?'

'Yes, sir. The boys on the staff called him "I-Played-It-Well-Laddie" after his favourite remark. The last two were Mr Liversidge and Miss Gaynes. They stood talking on the stage – couldn't hear what they said – and then went past me to their rooms. I'd got to the falsetto repeat then, I remember.' Bob sucked his teeth meditatively. 'Well, sir, they was all stowed away by that time.'

'Parsons, you're a witness after my own heart. Now for when they came out.'

'Yes. Have to do a bit of thinking now. Take it easy, sir, it's on the way. Yes.' Bob shut his eyes and took a vigorous pull at his cigarette. 'The four gents was first. Mr Comedy Ackroyd, Mr Vernon, Mr Broadhead, Mr Liversidge, all come out together and they stands there chaffing me and asking why I wasn't wearing a tailcoat and a white tie. Ackroyd was that funny I nearly burst out crying. Footpath comedian!'

'You don't care for Mr Ackroyd?'

'Not so's you'd make a sky-sign of it. We're human, sir, even if we do earn our treasury dressing up the great "hactors". Mr Ackroyd doesn't seem to have thought that out for himself. I got Mr Ackroyd's number a long while back. So did my gentleman, and my gentleman *is* a gentleman, sir.'

'Mr Hambledon?'

'Ah! The genu-ine ticket. He knows all about Mr Saint John Ackroyd and so did the guv'nor.'

Bob re-lit his cigarette and looked significantly at Alleyn.

'Why?' asked Alleyn. 'How do you mean?'

'It's an old yarn now, sir. Ackroyd forgot 'imself one evening when we was at the Cri. He's very partial to 'is glass of whisky at times, and 'e don't break 'is heart if there's not much water with it. This night he'd just 'ad just that much too much, and he comes into Miss Carolyn's dressing-room without so much as knocking and 'e starts up on the funny business. 'Struth! What a scene! She tells 'im orf a snorter, and then the guv'nor 'e gets wind of it and 'e comes along and 'e tells 'im orf fit to suffercate. Laugh! I was outside the door when 'e comes out, and to see 'is face! Not so blooming comic and as red as a stick of carmine. Laugh! Next day 'e 'as to apologize. 'E'd 'ave got 'is notice if it hadn't been that piece, I do believe, but 'e was playing a big part and 'is understudy was not too classy. So the show went on, but since then Mr Funny Ackroyd 'as blooming well kept 'is place. Well now, where was we? Ah, I've got it. Mr Broadhead and Played-It-Well, and Mr Liversidge and Ackroyd, they all come out in a bunch. They 'as their spot of comedy with yours truly, and then I rather fancy Ackroyd goes orf to the stage-door. Not for long though. 'E comes back and joins the others, and then they

all goes on the stage, and froo the Prompt entrance to the set, see?
And they never comes orf again while I'm there.'

'Sure of that?'

'Yes, sir. Sure as s'welp me. Tell you for why. I could hear them
telling Mr Gascoigne what a lark they'd ad with me and how I was
too shy to come to the party. Very funny, they was.'

Bob paused, his face a painful crimson.

'They sound thoroughly objectionable,' said Alleyn.

'Oh, well, there you are,' said Bob, dismissing them. 'Well, sir.
After that lot, Miss Valerie Gaynes came out. She was on the look-
out for Mr Liversidge as per usual, and I think she heard his voice on
the stage. Anyway she made a bee-line for the door and went on. It
was about the time the visitors from the front began to come in. I see
you come with the guv'nor, sir, and that young Palmer and so forth.
Mr Gascoigne stood by the door looking out for them – the door on
the set I mean. Then Miss Max came out and stood talking to me for
a while. Always got a pleasant word for everybody. Then Minna
come along and starts telling me orf for not 'aving changed me
clobber. She's a one, old Minna. We chy-ikes a bit and I say I'll come
along in me own time, see, and Minna goes back to doll 'erself up.
Yes, that's right, that's 'ow she went.'

Bob paused.

'And then you joined the party, perhaps?'

'Nah! I felt kind of awkward, sir, and that's the truth. The boys – the
stage-staff, you know, sir – they was all on, be that time, see? They'd
been fixing the stage, see? Else I'd 'ave mucked in with them. Well,
blimey, sir, it was all posh-like. Wasn't as if there was a door over on the
OP. I could of slipped froo on the QT if there had of been, but there was
only the one door, see? So I kind of hung fire and made another fag.'

He glanced shyly at Alleyn.

'I know. It's a bit of a facer making an entrance, isn't it?'

'That is right, sir. Then, after a bit, my gentleman comes out – Mr
Hambledon – and he says, "Hullo Bob," he says, "waiting for something?" And 'e seems to tip I'm feeling silly-like and 'e says: "Come
on," 'e says, "and we'll make a big entrance, Bob," 'e says. Look, 'e's
all right, sir, my gentleman. 'E's very nice. But – 'struth, I couldn't go
on with 'im, sir. Wouldn't be the right thing would it, now? So
I says I'm waiting for Minna, and he smiles and cracks a joke,

pleasant-like, and 'e goes across to the door where Mr Gascoigne is still standing. I see him say something to Mr Gascoigne and look across at me, smiling, and then 'e goes in and Mr Gascoigne shuts the door and comes over to me and says: "We're waiting for you and Minna," and then Minna comes along, and I puts out me second fag and we all goes across together and nobody notices nothing. And in about two shakes Miss Carolyn comes in and after you give 'er that 'eathen image we all sits down to supper and – and my Gawd, sir, then we know what happened, don't we?'

'We do indeed. How long is two shakes, Bob?'

'Eh? Oh! See what you mean. Well now, sir. As we goes in everybody was just asking where was Miss Carolyn. So Mr Hambledon and the guv'nor and Mr Mason they went out to get 'er, passing Minna and me in the doorway. And they came back with her almost immediate.'

Alleyn made a sudden brusque movement, leaning forward in his chair.

'Then – Bob, this is important – it's very important. You can tell me how long it was between the time Miss Dacres came out of her dressing-room and the moment of her entrance with the three men.'

'No time at all, sir. Just a jiffy. They must of met 'er in the passage.'

'And Bob! Could you swear that she came straight off the stage and didn't leave her room till she went in to the party?'

'Yes, sir. 'Course I could. Didn't I tell you I was – '

'Yes, yes, I know. It's all perfectly splendid. Now for Mr Hambledon – '

'Same for 'im, sir. Look 'ere, sir, I'm fly to what you're after. You want to know who went up aloft after the guv'nor come down. That's a fact, now, isn't it, sir?'

'It is, Bob.'

'Well, sir, it wasn't Miss Carolyn or Mr Hambledon – physically imposs., sir. They both came straight orf after the curtain call. I *see* them. And they never come out of their rooms till they goes to the party, and they goes *straight* to the party. I'll take me Bible oaf on it, kiss the book, and face the judge. Can't say fairer than that now, can I, sir?'

'No. It's good enough. Is there any way out from the dressing-rooms except past the doorway where you were standing?'

'No fear, sir. Not bloody likely, if you'll excuse the expression, sir. Beats me they don't have the fire inspectors down on them. There's just the two rows of dressing-rooms downstairs, with the wardrobe-room at the end. The two star-rooms and Miss Max's room all open orf the passage. Then it goes round at right angles with the wardrobe-room on the right and the three other dressing-rooms on the left.'

'Yes, I know.'

'Yes. So that Mr Comedy Ackroyd's room runs behind the two star-rooms and Miss Max's. Suits 'im a fair treat; 'e can do 'is nosy-parkering nice with them wooden walls. I went to 'is room only the day we got 'ere, and there 'e was, standing on the table with 'is shell-like glued to the wall and 'is eyes shut, tuned in to Miss Carolyn and my gentleman what were 'aving a little pass-the-time-o'-day next door. Never saw me, 'e didn't, but when I goes back I call arht to Miss Carolyn they're getting near 'er entrance and she comes away, see? Mr Saint John Ackroyd!'

Alleyn remembered Ackroyd's version of this incident and chuck-led appreciatively.

'And there's no door at the far end of this back passage?'

'No, sir. Only a little window. All gummed up with dirt and cobwebs.'

'Big enough for someone to get through?'

''Ave to be very small, sir, and then it'd be a squeeze.'

'I'll have a look at it. Thank you very much, Bob. Nobody ever calls you Mr Parsons, do they?'

'Lord love you, sir, I sometimes forget I got another moniker. Might almost be an iggyliterate if you'll excuse the bit of fun. Going, sir?'

'Yes – I won't keep you any longer. It's after hours so we can't have a drink, but if you'll allow me – '

'Well, sir, that's very kind of you, but I'm sure I don't want any-thing. If it's a case of my gentleman, and looking after 'im, well I'm used to doing that and it's a pleasure.'

'I'm sure it is, but don't make me feel uncomfortable, Bob. Just to show you bear me no ill-will.'

'If you put it like that, sir – well, thank you very much, sir. Goodnight, sir, and I'm sure I hope you get the bloke. He was a very fair man, was the late guv'nor. Can't fancy 'ow anyone would want to bash 'is nut in, even if it was with liquor, which is a classy way of 'anding in your notice. I always says – '

Alleyn listened to a somewhat discursive reminiscence and at last got away. He had arranged to meet Wade at the theatre and found the inspector waiting for him.

'Well, Mr Alleyn. Any luck with the dresser?'

'Quite a purple patch.'

Alleyn related the gist of the information.

'By cripes!' said Wade. 'That's something to get our teeth into. How did the man strike you, sir? Reliable?'

'I think so. He's a type that will disappear before long, I'm afraid – the real undiluted Cockney. Undersized, sharp as they make them, loyal, independent, and violently opinionated. You should hear him on the subject of Ackroyd. We'll be able to check his statements, I think. I timed his cigarette – sixteen minutes – he had to keep re-lighting it. The whistled song took three minutes so that takes us to a quarter to eleven. He made and lit another cigarette, which he put out before joining the party – say three more minutes, which would mean twelve minutes to eleven when he left the passage. Now when everyone started asking for Miss Dacres, Mr Meyer looked at his watch and said: "It's ten to – time she was making an entrance," and about two minutes later she appeared. If Bob Parsons was in the passage all that time, she can't have done it.'

'Unless he's fixing an alibi for her, or for Hambledon.'

'We'll have to check his statement, of course. But if all these people remember talking to him, it'll be good enough. Personally, I was favourably impressed with him.'

Wade stared solemnly at Alleyn and then swore violently.

'Good heavens, Wade, what's the matter?'

'Here!' said Wade. 'If all he said is right, it – Look here, Mr Alleyn, don't you see what it means?'

'Oh, rather, yes. It washes out the whole bang lot of 'em at one fell swoop. Tiresome for you. Unless of course the little window – '

'We'll go right along and have a look at the little window. By gosh, talk about eliminating! This is a bit too sudden. What about Liversidge?'

'Bang he goes,' said Alleyn.

'Liversidge – with everything pointing that way! Not only that. Liversidge, Broadhead, the wife and Hambledon. Mason tied up with enough alibis to blow holes in a cast-iron case! Come on, sir. Come on. We'll have a damn' good look at this little window.'

CHAPTER 21

Business with Props

But the little window at the back of the dressing-room passage turned out to be exactly as Bob had described it – dirty and gummed up with cobwebs – and Wade turned to Alleyn with an air of disgruntled incredulity.

'It's a case of "where do we go for honey," isn't it, Wade?' asked Alleyn smiling.

'I'll see this Bob Parsons as soon as we get out of this,' said Wade. 'If anyone's squared him I'll shake it out of him if I have to go at it all night.'

'It's possible, of course,' agreed Alleyn, 'but look at it for a minute. Suppose Liversidge is the murderer. Liversidge plans to take off the weight. Instead of slipping round, unseen, to the back ladder after the last curtain, which would have been comparatively easy, he goes first to his dressing-room, knowing that he must come out again almost immediately into the brightly-lit narrow passage, where any of the others may be hanging about. Well, he risks that and comes out to find Parsons directly in his way. He knows that Parsons will see him go up to the back of the stage – knows, in short, that he is a man who can hang him. He decides to risk all this on the chance of bribing or corrupting the man. Do you think he'd do it? I don't. And the same argument applies to Miss Dacres. To all the rest of the cast for that matter. I think when you see Parsons you will agree that he is not a corruptible type. Check his statement by all means, my dear chap, but I feel certain he is speaking the truth. And now let us have a look at the back of the theatre.'

'The *back* of the theatre, sir?'

'Yes. When I chased round on the trail of Master Palmer, I thought of something that may be of interest. Come across the stage, will you?'

He led the way out of the dressing-room passage to the stage. They had turned on the working-lights, two desolate yellow bulbs up in the dusty proscenium, that cast a little dreary light on the tops of the box-set. Nothing had been moved. The door into the set stood open and through it they could see the white cloth, the chairs pushed back from the table, curiously eloquent, the huddle of broken glass and dead flowers, and the enormous bottle lying on the table.

'That can all be cleared away,' said Wade. 'We've gone over every inch of it today.'

'Come round behind the set,' said Alleyn.

They groped their way round. The stage smelt of old glue and dead paint. Alleyn switched on his torch and led Wade to the back wall.

'Here's the back ladder up to the grid. That, I feel sure, is the one that was used. Have you tried it for prints?'

'Yes. It's a fair muck of prints – so far, nothing that's any good to us. The stage-hands used it over and over again.'

'Of course. Well now, see here.'

In the back wall, a little to the left of the ladder, was a door.

'We noticed this on the plan,' said Alleyn, 'and discussed it as a possible entrance for – say Mason.'

'That's right, sir. But it won't wash as far as he is concerned. If Mason had gone through the audience, out at the front, and round the block, he'd have had to come in here. He would have to go aloft, do the job, come down, and sprint round the block again.'

'Ten minutes at the very least and the risk of being seen running like a madman by any number of people on the pavement outside,' said Alleyn. 'No. That cat won't jump. I saw the door last night when your PC was so suspicious of my movements. Have you got a torch? Let's have a good look at it.'

By the light of both their torches they inspected the door.

'Yale lock, with the key inside,' said Alleyn.

'We noted this door last night, Mr Alleyn. It wasn't overlooked.'

'My dear chap, I'm sure it wasn't. What did you make of it?'

'Well, seeing it was locked on the inside it doesn't look as though anyone could have used it for an entrance. And seeing that there's no exit from the dressing-rooms except to the stage, none of them could have used it for a getaway.'

'None of the cast, no.'

'You're still thinking of Mason. It's no go, sir. I wish to hell I could say otherwise, but it's no go. We've thrashed it over – every minute of it – every second of it. He was in the office at the end of the show, and was seen there by the men from the box-office. He ran along to the stage-door and gave old Singleton – the doorkeeper – the message about not letting in uninvited people. Singleton watched him go back to the office and a minute or two later joined him there. Then Dr Te Pokiha looked in. About two minutes later you overtook him yourself, on the way to the stage-door with the doctor.'

'Not with Dr Te Pokiha. He was at the party when Mr Mason and I got in.'

'Makes no odds, as far as Mason is concerned, sir.'

'That's true. Have you tried this key for prints?'

'Can't say we have.'

'It's early days yet,' murmured Alleyn, 'and you've had a lot of stuff to get through. I think if you don't mind – '

He produced an insufflator and a packet of chalk from his overcoat pocket, and by the light of their torches, tested the key for prints.

'None. It's as clean as a whistle.'

'That's funny,' said Wade, reluctantly. 'You'd have thought it would be used fairly frequently.'

'There's no dust,' said Alleyn, 'so presumably it has been wiped clean.'

Wade muttered something under his breath. Alleyn turned the key and opened the door. Outside was a dingy strip of yard, and a low tin fence with a rickety gate.

'This is where I came out on my chase after Master Palmer,' explained Alleyn. 'I met the PC in the street there. This door moves very sweetly.'

He flashed his torch on the hinges.

'Nicely oiled. Commendable attention to detail on the part of the staff – what?'

'Look here, Mr Alleyn, what *are* you getting at?'

'I think we should concentrate on this door, Wade. When we've done here, we'll go and have a look at the plan in the office and I shall propound my unlikely theory.'

He squatted on his heels and peered at the threshold.

'Not much chance here. Fine night and all that. I think it might be profitable to find out who oiled the hinges. Could you try? And the doorkeeper – Singleton is it? I suppose none of the guests went in twice? No, not Mason – anyone else.'

'*Went in twice?*'

'Yes. In at the stage-door. Out by this one. In again at the stage-door. Nothing in it, I dare say.'

'None of the guests has got a motive, though,' said Wade with a certain air of desperate reluctance.

'Not so far as we know. One might advance something rather fantastic. Young Palmer, mad for love, for instance. Far-fetched.'

'Well then – '

'And Gascoigne. He didn't go to the dressing-rooms. He was on the stage. Have you dwelt on Gascoigne, Wade?'

'Thrashed him to death. We can't get it down to what you might call a cast-iron alibi, sir, because he was mucking round on the stage here, but the hands say he never went off the set and we've found out he was there to welcome each of the guests as they came. No motive, far as we know.'

'And he would have no occasion to use this door.'

'This "in again, out again, gone again" stuff with the door. Is it probable do you think, Mr Alleyn? Is it possible?'

'Let's consider. Take any one of the guests – young Palmer or Dr Te Pokiha, for instance.'

'Go ahead, sir.'

'Young Palmer comes to the party, passes Singleton, gives his name, and instead of joining the party on the stage, slips round to the back and up the ladder. He takes off the weight, comes down, lets himself out by this door, shins round to the front, comes in again and joins the party.'

'I'm sure Singleton would have noticed it, Mr Alleyn. You see, Mason had warned him about gate-crashing. He was on the look-out. He had the list of guests and he ticked each one off.'

'Yes, that's the great objection,' agreed Alleyn. 'Still, I'd ask him.'

'Certainly, we'll ask him. The other objection is that the deceased was a stranger here, and most of the guests wouldn't have the ghost of a motive. What about Mason, now? Could he have done this door business, after he went in with you?'

'Unfortunately, I know he couldn't,' said Alleyn. 'He came on to the stage with me and we were together until he went to fetch Miss Dacres.'

'Anyway, sir. Think of the risk a man would run, tearing round the block in his evening duds. It'd look pretty crook if anyone saw him, now, wouldn't it?'

'I don't think he would tear round the block, Wade.'

'What's that?'

'Why not follow the Palmer route, in reverse, and come out in the yard?'

'By cripey, yes. Yes, that's so. But he'd have to know about the path behind the sheds, wouldn't he? Which young Palmer seems to have done, seeing the way he took to it afterwards. Is there anything in this business of young Palmer, do you reckon?'

'Not a damn' thing, I should say.'

'Aw, Geeze!' said Wade disgustedly. 'What a case! It's all cockeyed. Did you ever hear anything like this business of Miss Dacres! Owning up she fixed that weight to protect a man that, as far as we can see, couldn't have done it.'

'At least she's saved us the trouble of accounting for everybody's movements after the murder.'

'She's in a nasty hole. Messing about on the scene of the crime,' muttered Wade. 'She's going to find herself in a very, very uncomfortable little pozzy, is Miss Carolyn Dacres Meyer, widow of deceased.'

'I hope not,' said Alleyn. 'I may even try to corrupt the New Zealand force on her behalf. You never know.'

Wade looked doubtfully at him, decided he was attempting to amuse, and broke out into a guffaw.

'Aw, dikkon, Mr Alleyn!' said Wade.

'What did you say?'

'Haven't you heard that one, sir? I suppose it's NZ digger slang. "Dikkon." It's the same as if you'd say "Come off it." Used to hear it on the Peninsula. "Aw dikkon, dig." '

'On Gallipoli? You were in that show, were you, Wade?'

'Too right. Saw it through from the landing to the evacuation.'

'What ages ago it seems.'

Passing Sergeant Packer, who was on duty at the stage-door, they strolled back to the office, talking returned soldiers' shop.

'What do you think, Mr Alleyn? If there's another war will the young chaps come at it, same as we did, thinking it's great? Some party! And get the same jolt? What do you reckon?'

'I'm afraid to speculate,' said Alleyn.

'Same here. And yet you know I often think: well, it was bloody but it wasn't too bad. As long as you didn't think too much it wasn't too bad. There was a kind of feeling among the chaps that was all right. Know what I mean?'

'I do. One has to take that into account. The pacifists won't succeed until they do. You can't overstate the stupidity and squalid frightfulness, but equally you must recognize that there was a sort of – what? – a sort of emotional compensation; comradeship, I suppose, though it's an ill-used word.'

'I often wonder if crooks feel the same.'

'That's a thought.'

'Know what I mean?' continued Wade, encouraged. 'As if they kind of forgot they were crooks and anti-social, and got a kick out of being all together on the same old game.'

'I should think it was quite likely. All the same they're a hopeless lot – the rank and file. Not much honour among thieves in my experience. Don't you agree? That's why homicide cases are specialized work, Wade. We're not dealing with the class we've been trained to understand.'

'Too right. Look at this case, now.'

'Yes. Look at the damn' thing. We're wandering, Wade. We'll have to get back to business. Come into the office and look at this plan. Have a cigarette.'

'Thanks, I don't mind,' said Wade, taking one. They went into the office, more than ever subfusc in the late afternoon light, with dust already lying thick on Alfred Meyer's old desk, and last night's fire dead in the grate. Wade switched on the lamp and Alleyn walked over to the plan on the wall.

'Taking another look at the old lay-out, Mr Alleyn?'

'Yes. I've got together a sort of theory about the case,' said Alleyn, with his usual air of diffidence. 'If I may, I'll go over it with you. It's the result of this rather wholesale elimination of suspects. You'll probably find gaps in it as wide as a church door. I'd be not altogether sorry if you did.'

'Well, sir, let's have it.'

'Right you are. It begins about five minutes after the final curtain last night.'

Wade glanced up at Alleyn who still stood with his hands in his pockets contemplating the plan.

'How about taking the easy chair, sir?' asked Wade.

'You'll be seeing that thing in your sleep.'

'I dare say I shall. You see my whole theory is based on this plan. Come over here and I'll tell you why.'

Wade got up and joined him. Alleyn pointed a long finger at the plan and began to explain.

CHAPTER 22

Fourth Appearance of the Tiki

When Alleyn got back to the hotel he found Dr Te Pokiha waiting for him.

'Had you forgotten that you were to dine with me this evening, Mr Alleyn?'

'My dear Te Pokiha, no, I hadn't forgotten, but I had no idea it was so late. Please forgive me. I do hope you haven't been waiting very long.'

'I've only just arrived. Don't worry, we've plenty of time.'

'Then if I may rush up and change – ?'

'If you want to. Not a dinner jacket, please. We shall be alone.'

'Right. I shan't be five minutes.'

He was as good as his word. They had a cocktail together and then took the road in Te Pokiha's car.

'We take the north-east road towards Mount Ruapehu,' said Te Pokiha. 'I expect you are tired of hearing about our mountains and thermal districts. I am afraid New Zealanders are too eager to thrust these wonders at visitors, and to demand admiration.'

'I should like very much indeed to hear a Maori speak of them.'

'Really? You mean a real Maori – not a *pakeha*-Maori?'

'Yes.'

'We, too, are strangers in New Zealand, you know. We have only been here for about thirty generations. We brought our culture with us and applied it to the things we found here. Our religion too, and our science, if we may be allowed to call it science.'

Alleyn looked at the magnificent head. Te Pokiha was a pale Maori, straight-nosed, not very full-lipped. He might have been a

Greek or an Egyptian. There was an aristocratic flavour about him –
a complete absence of anything vulgar or tentative in his voice or his
movements. His speech, gravely formal, carefully phrased, suited
him and did not seem at all pedantic or affected.

'Where did you come from?' asked Alleyn.

'From Polynesia, and before that from Easter Island. The tohunga
and rangitira say that in the beginning it was from Assyria, but I
think the *pakeha* anthropologists do not follow us there. Our teaching was not given to everybody. Only the learned and noble classes
were permitted to know the history of their race. It was learnt oral-
ly and through the medium of the carvings and hieroglyphics. My
grandfather was a deeply-instructed rangitira and I learned much
from him. He was a survival of the old order and his kind will not be
seen much longer.'

'Do you regret the passing of the old order?'

'In some ways. I have a kind of pride of race – shall we say a savage pride? The *pakeha* has altered everything, of course. We have been
unable to survive the fierce white light of his civilisation. In trying to
follow his example we have forgotten many of our own customs and
have been unable wisely to assimilate his. Hygiene and eugenics for
example. We have become spiritually and physically obese. That is
only my own view. Most of my people are well content, but I see the
passing of the old things with a kind of nostalgia. The *pakeha* give their
children Maori Christian names because they sound pretty. They call
their ships and their houses by Maori names. It is perhaps a charming
compliment, but to me it seems a little strange. We have become a
side-show in the tourist bureau – our dances – our art – everything.'

'Such as the little green tiki? I understand what you mean.'

'Ah – the tiki.'

He paused and Alleyn had the impression that he had been going
to say more about the tiki but had stopped himself. It was growing
dark. Te Pokiha's head was silhouetted against a background of
green hills and very dark blue mountains.

'To the north are Ruapehu and Ngauruhoe,' he said. 'My grandfather would have told you that the volcanic fires of Ngauruhoe
were caused by the youngest son of the Earth Mother who lay deep
underground with her child at her breast. The fire was given him for
comfort by Rakahore, the rock-god.'

They drove on in silence until the mountains were black against the fading sky.

'My house is not very far off now,' said Te Pokiha quietly. And in a minute or two they crossed a clanking cattle-stop and plunged into a dark tunnel where the headlights shone on the stems of tree-ferns.

'I like the smell of the bush,' said Alleyn.

'Yes? Do you know I once did a very foolish thing. It was when I was at the House – my first year at Oxford, and my first year in England. I became very homesick and wrote in my letters of my homesickness. I said that I longed for the smell of burning bush-wood and begged them to send me some. So my father sent me a case of logs. It was a very expensive business as you may imagine, but I burnt them in my fireplace at the House and the smoke of Te-Ika-a-Maui hung over the famous Dreaming Spires.' He burst out laughing. 'Ridiculous, wasn't it?'

'Did you take your medical degree at home?'

'Yes, at Thomas's. I was a thorough *pakeha* by that time – almost. Here we are.'

They pulled up in a wide open space before the dark shape of a long one-storeyed house. From the centre of the front wall projected a porch with gable roof, and Alleyn saw that this porch was decorated with Maori carvings.

'An affectation on my part,' said Te Pokiha. 'You may question the taste of joining an old-time porch on to a modern building. At least the carving is genuine.'

'I like it.'

'You must see it by daylight. Come in.'

They dined in a pleasant room, waited on by an enormous and elderly Maori woman, who showed a tendency to join in the laughter when Alleyn cracked a modest joke. After dinner they moved into a comfortable living-room with an open fireplace where an aromatic log fire reminded Alleyn of Te Pokiha's story. The furniture was of the solid smoking-room type – very English and non-committal. A mezzotint of Christ Church, Oxford, an undergraduate group or two, and a magnificent feather cloak decorated the walls.

When, after some excellent brandy, they had lit their pipes, Alleyn asked Te Pokiha if his practice was a general one.

'Oh, yes. When I first came back I had some idea of specialising in gynaecology, but I think it is the one branch of my profession in which

my race would tell against me. And then, as I settled down, I began to
see the terrible inroads made by civilisation in the health of my own
people. Tuberculosis, syphilis, typhoid – none of them known in our savage days when ritual and health-giving dances, as well as strict hygien-
ic habits, were enforced. So I came down to earth – brown earth – and
decided that I would become a doctor to my own people.'

'I'm not sure you do not regret your choice.'

'No. Though it is depressing to see how quickly a healthy race can
degenerate. I am very busy – consulting-room hours in town, and a
wide country beat. I am re-learning some of my own race history.'

And he related several stories about his Maori patients, telling
them well, without too much emphasis. The time passed pleasantly
in this fashion.

At last Alleyn put his hand in his pocket and pulled out the tiki.
He put it on the arm of Te Pokiha's chair.

'May we talk about the tiki?' he asked.

Te Pokiha looked at it with surprise.

'Does Miss Dacres not wish to accept it? Has she returned it to you?'

'No. I hope she will still accept it, though she may not wish to do
so. At the moment it is by way of being used in evidence.'

'The tiki? What do you mean?'

'It was found in the gallery above the stage on the spot where the
murderer must have stood.'

Te Pokiha gazed at him with something like horror in his eyes.

'That is – is most extraordinary. Do you know how it got there?'

'Yes. I believe I do.'

'I see.'

There was relief and something else – could it be disappointment? –
in Te Pokiha's voice. Then, suddenly, he leant forward:

'But it's impossible – that lovely creature! No, there must be some
mistake. I cannot believe it of her.'

'Of Miss Dacres? Why should you suspect Miss Dacres?'

'Why, because I saw – but I do not suspect her.'

'Because you saw her slip it into her dress?'

'There is something very strange in this,' said Te Pokiha, staring at
the tiki. 'May I ask one question, Mr Alleyn. Do you suspect Miss
Dacres of murder?'

'No. I believe her to be innocent.'

'Then how did the tiki get there?'

'I'll tell you presently,' said Alleyn. 'It *was* strange, wasn't it? Almost as though the tiki itself had taken a hand, don't you think?'

'You ask a leading question,' said Te Pokiha, smiling. He had regained his poise completely, it seemed. 'Remember I am a materialistic general practitioner.'

'You are also a pure-blooded Maori aristocrat,' answered Alleyn. 'What would your grandfather have thought?'

Te Pokiha put out his thin dark hand as though to take up the tiki. Then he paused and drew back his hand.

'The demi-god Tiki was the father of mankind. These little symbols are named after him. They do not actually represent him but rather the human embryo and the fructifying force in mankind. The ornament and carving is purely phallic. I know something of the history of this tiki – it was *tapu*. Do you know what that means?'

'Sacred? Untouchable?'

'Yes. Long ago it was dropped from the breast of a woman in a very *tapu* place, a meeting-house, and remained there, unnoticed, for a long time. It therefore became *tapu* itself. The meeting-house was burned to the ground and a *pakeha* found and kept the tiki, afterwards telling where he had found it. My grandfather would have said that this in itself was a desecration, a pollution. The *pakeha*, not long afterwards, was drowned in attempting to ford a river. The tiki was found in his pocket and given, by his son, to the father of the man from whom you have bought it. Your man was once a very prosperous run-holder, but lost almost everything during the depression. Hence his desire to sell the tiki.'

'Miss Gaynes has repeatedly expressed her opinion that the tiki is unlucky,' said Alleyn dryly. 'It seems that she is right. What would your grandfather have thought of the reception they gave it last night? Poor little Meyer was very facetious, wasn't he, pretending to say his prayers to it?'

'Not only facetious but ill-bred,' said Te Pokiha quietly.

'I felt rather ashamed of my compatriots, Dr Te Pokiha, and, as I told you at the time, I regretted my impulse.'

'You need not regret it. The tiki is revenged.'

'Very much so. I shall ask Miss Dacres to return it to me, I think.'

Te Pokiha looked at him, hesitated a moment and then said: 'I do not think she need fear it.'

'Tell me,' said Alleyn, 'if it's not an impertinent question, do you yourself feel anything of – well, anything of what your ancestors would have felt in regard to this coincidence?'

There was a long pause.

'Naturally,' said Te Pokiha, at last, 'I do not feel exactly as a European would feel about the tiki. What do your gipsies say? "You have to dig deep to bury your daddy." '

'Yes,' murmured Alleyn, 'I suppose you do.'

'I hear you are working personally on the case,' said Te Pokiha after another silence. 'May one ask if you feel confident that the murderer will be found?'

'Yes, I am confident.'

'That is excellent,' said Te Pokiha, tranquilly.

'It is simply a question of eliminating the impossible. And, by the way, you can help us there.'

'Can I? In what way?'

'We are trying to establish alibis for all these people. Mr Mason's movements are a little more difficult to trace than those of the cast, because he was in his office before the supper-party. Wade says you saw him there.'

'Yes, I did. At the end of the play I made for the exit at the back of the stalls. I noticed that the office door into the box-office was open, and I thought I would look in on Mr Mason before going behind the scenes. He came in just as I did.'

'From the yard?'

'Yes. He had been out to speak to the stage-doorkeeper, he said.'

'That tallies with what we have. How long did you stay in the office? By the way I hope you don't mind me hauling in shop like this?'

'Not in the least. I hoped that we might discuss the case. Let me see. We stayed there for about ten minutes, I think. Mr Mason said that they would not be ready behind the scenes for some little time and suggested we should have a drink. We took off our overcoats and sat down by the fire. I refused the drink, but he had one, and we both smoked. The men from the box-office came in and Mason dealt with them. Someone came in from the bank to take the cash, and the stage-doorkeeper looked in too, I remember. Oh, yes, and Ackroyd, the little comic fellow, you know – he looked in.'

'Did he, now? What for?'

'As far as I remember it was to tell Mason the guests were beginning to arrive. It struck me he was looking for a free drink, but he didn't get it. Mason packed him off in no time.'

'Did you see him go?'

'How do you mean? I saw him go out into the yard. Then someone else looked in, I think. People were going in and out all the time.'

'Yes, I see.'

'I suppose that was a crucial time,' said Te Pokiha. 'I heard about the counterweight from Gascoigne and Mason, last night. They both insisted that there had been interference. Of course there must have been interference. That sort of thing couldn't happen accidentally.'

'Hardly, one would think. Yes, it's an important period that, when you were in the office. You left Mason there?'

'Yes. He was there when I returned, too; still in his chair by the fire.'

'You returned to the office? Why did you return?'

'Didn't I tell you? How stupid of me. When I got to the stage-door I found I had taken Mason's overcoat instead of my own. We had taken them off at the same time and put them down together. I took my own coat, said a word or two more, and left him locking things up in the office. I remember that I had only just gone on to the stage when you and Mason arrived.'

'I met him at the door of the office as I went down the yard.'

'Well, I suppose I have established Mason's alibi for him,' said Te Pokiha, with a smile, 'and my own too I hope, if I needed one.'

'It's always a handy little thing to have beside you.'

'I suppose so – still there's an absence of motive in my case.'

'Ah, yes,' murmured Alleyn, 'we must have motive, of course.'

He picked up the tiki, returned it to his pocket, and looked at his watch.

'Good lord, it's eleven o'clock and I haven't so much as rung up for a car.'

'There's no need. I shall drive you back and spend the night at my rooms. I often do that – it's all arranged. You must have a drink before you go.'

'No, really not, thanks. I promised Wade I'd ring him up before eleven-thirty, so if you don't mind – '

'You can telephone from here.'

'It may be rather a lengthy conversation, so perhaps I'd better leave it until I get to Middleton.'

'Come along, then,' rejoined Te Pokiha courteously. 'I mustn't try to keep you, I suppose.'

'It's been a delightful evening.'

'I hope it is not to be the last.'

They drove back in the starlight. To Alleyn it seemed strange that it was only that morning – a short eighteen hours ago – that he had stood in the deserted street to watch dawn break over the mountains. It seemed to be ages ago. So much had happened. Carolyn by the little stream, talking about her husband, the bush bird whistling. 'She was only a bird – ' with a wrinkled human face, Gordon Palmer drinking whisky that poured itself out of the neck of a gargantuan champagne bottle. 'Don't do that, it shouldn't be interfered with.' 'But my old dad taught me. It used to go big in vordevil.' And there was Wade running up and down a ladder like a performing monkey and saying: 'Eight minutes for refreshments at the central police station.' 'Don't do that, you'll muddle the prints.' 'It's all right if you sound your horn at the top. This horn is called a beep-beep. Listen – beep-beep – '

'This horn is called a "beep-beep," ' said Te Pokiha. 'It reminds me of the Paris streets.'

'Lord love us, I've been asleep,' said Alleyn.

'If you will allow me to say so, I think you're overtaxing your strength a little. You look tired. Aren't you supposed to be on a holiday?'

'I'll be able to sink back into sloth tomorrow.'

'As soon as that?'

'I hope so. Here we are at the hotel, I see. Well, thank you so much, Te Pokiha. It's been an extremely interesting evening.'

'I'm afraid I've been of little use as far as your case is concerned.'

'On the contrary,' said Alleyn, 'you have given me a piece of exceedingly valuable information.'

'Really? I mustn't ask questions, I suppose. Goodnight.'

'Goodnight.'

CHAPTER 23

Alleyn as Maskelyne

Alleyn slept heavily and dreamlessly until half past nine. He had arranged to meet Wade at ten, and the inspector was waiting for him when he came out of the breakfast-room. They walked down to the theatre together.

'I've fixed it with old Singleton, Mr Alleyn. He'll be there waiting for us. He's a funny old chap. Dismal Joe, the stage-hands call him; quite an old character in his way, he is, with a great gift of the gab. He says he's an old actor and I believe it's a fact, too.'

'Another actor! I remember giving him my name. He seemed rather a rum old article.'

'It's a theatre show this, isn't it, sir?'

They walked on in silence, and then Wade said:

'Well, Mr Alleyn, I hope you're quite satisfied with the work we've done for you.'

'My dear chap, more than satisfied. I've never had such a case. All the routine work done by you fellows, and damn' well done. All I had to do was to pick out the plums.'

'Well sir, as far as we're concerned it's been a pleasure. We very much appreciate the way you've worked with us, Mr Alleyn, taking us into your confidence all along. I must say when you rang up last night I got a bit of a surprise. I don't say we wouldn't have thrashed it out for ourselves and come to the right conclusion, but we would-n't have come there so quick.'

'I'm sure you'd have got there,' said Alleyn cordially. 'You fixed up the other business all right, I suppose?'

'Yes. I don't think there'll be any trouble. Packer and Cass are there.'

Packer and Cass met them in the theatre yard. Standing just behind them was the doorkeeper to whom Alleyn remembered giving his name on the night of the party. Old Singleton was an extraordinary figure. He was very tall, very bent, and remarkably dirty. His nose was enormous and gloomily purple, he suffered from asthma, and he smelt of whisky.

''Morning, Packer, 'morning, Cass,' said Alleyn.

'This is Mr Singleton, Chief Inspector,' said Wade.

'Chief Inspector who, Mr Wade?' asked Singleton earnestly, in a rumbling wheeze.

'Alleyn.'

'Of New Scotland Yard, London?'

'Yes, Mr Singleton,' said Alleyn good-humouredly.

'Shake, sir!' exclaimed Mr Singleton, extending a particularly filthy hand. Alleyn shook it.

'From the Dear Old Town!' continued Mr Singleton emotionally. 'The Dear Old Town!'

'You are a Londoner, Mr Singleton?'

'Holborn Empire! Ten years. I was first fiddle, sir.' Mr Singleton went through an elaborate pantomime of drawing a bow across the strings of an imaginary violin. 'You wouldn't think it to look at me now,' he added truthfully. 'I have fallen into the sere and yellow, Chief Inspector. I am declined into the vale of years. I am a fixed figure for the time of scorn to point his slow unmoving finger at. Yurrahumph!' He coughed unpleasantly and spat. 'You would not credit it, Superintendent Alleyn, if I were to tell you I played the Moor for six months to capacity business.'

As Alleyn really could not credit it, he contented himself with making a consolatory noise.

'Shakespeare!' ejaculated Mr Singleton, removing his hat. 'The Swan of Stratford-on-Sea! The Bard!'

'Nobody like him, is there?' said Alleyn cheerfully. 'Well, Mr Singleton, you're about to take the stage again. I want you to tell us all about last night.'

'Last night of all when that same star did entertain her guests. An improvisation, Chief Constable, based on the Bard. Last night. I could a tale unfold would harrow up thy soul, freeze thy young blood. As a matter of fact I am unable to do any such thing. Last night I merely discharged my degrading duties as a doorkeeper in the house of the ungodly, and repaired to my lonely attic'

He paused and blew his nose on an unspeakable handkerchief. Wade slipped behind him and gave a spirited imitation of someone draining a glass to the dregs.

'You kept a list of the guests, I understand, and checked off the names as they came in.'

Mr Singleton drew a piece of paper from his bosom and handed it to Alleyn with a slight bow.

'To witness if I lie,' he explained grandly.

It was the list. Alleyn glanced at it and returned to the job.

'Did Mr Ackroyd come out some time before the party?'

'Ackroyd, Ackroyd, Ackroyd. Let me see, let me see, let me see. Ackroyd. The comedian. Yes! Ackroyd came out.'

'You did not mention this to Mr Wade.'

'I take my stand on that document!' said Mr Singleton magnificently.

'Quite so. How long was Mr Ackroyd away.'

'He returned in the twinkling of an eye.'

'You're sure of that?'

'I am constant as the northern star,' said Mr Singleton, stifling a slight hiccough. 'Ackroyd eggzited and re-entered immediately. He went to the door of the office. He appeared to address those within. He returned.'

'You watched him?'

'With the very comment of my soul. Would it astonish you to learn that I played the Dane before – '

'Did you really? Mr George Mason came out of the office some time before that, I believe?'

'George Mason, George! The manager. He did. I have already made a statement to this effect, I believe, Mr Wade?'

'That's right, Joe, but Mr Alleyn just wants to check up.'

Mr Singleton inclined his head.

'Quite so. The manager, George Mason, came to the stage-door and repeated, gratuitously and un-nesh – uness-essraly, my instructions. I was to be sure to ask of each guest his local habitation and his name.'

'Mr Mason returned to the office?'

'I swear it.'

'You may have to,' said Alleyn. 'How long was Mr Mason away from the office?'

'Let me see. Let me see. While one with moderate haste might tell an hundred. I showed him my list. I convinced him of my incorruptible purpose. I called to mind, I recollect, the coincidence that I had played the part of the porter in *Macbeth*, and of the sentry, Bernardo, in the Dane – that was in my green and salad days, Commissioner. I had scarce embarked on this trifling reminiscence when Mason turned up the collar of his dinner jacket and observing that the air was chilly, turned and ran back to the office.'

Alleyn uttered a slight exclamation, glanced at Wade, and asked Singleton to repeat this statement, which he did at great length but to the same effect.

'Do you remember, now,' said Alleyn, 'if the office door was open on to the yard as it is now?'

'It was open.'

'Ah yes. You know Dr Te Pokiha by sight?'

'The native? Dark-visaged, like the Moor? The Moor was perhaps my greatest role. My favourite role. "Most potent grave – " '

'Wonderful play, that,' interrupted Alleyn. 'Dr Te Pokiha was among the last guests to arrive, I think?'

'True.'

'Did you notice him coming?'

'I marked him come, yes. He too emerged from the office, carrying his mantle. He darted back and reappeared. He approached me and I admitted him, striking out his name as I did so.'

'Now, Mr Singleton, I take it from what you have told me that you would be prepared to make a sworn statement that once Mr Ackroyd, or Mr Mason, or Dr Te Pokiha had gone in at the stage-door they did not return to the office, and once they had gone to the office, did not return to the stage without your knowledge?'

'I have sworn it, indeed. In common parlance, sir, you can bet your boots and put your shirt on it.'

'Well now, Mr Singleton, I'm going to ask you to help me in a little experiment. Will you do this?'

'Impart! Proceed!'

'I want you to stand here by the stage-door and treat me as though I was Mr Ackroyd, Dr Te Pokiha, or Mr Mason. As soon as I have gone, I want you to wait for five minutes and then walk along to the office. Will you do this?'

'Certainly.'

'Watch the office door,' said Alleyn, 'and Mr Wade will keep the time.' He glanced at Packer and Cass who had listened to the entire conversation with the liveliest interest. 'You look steadily down the alley, you two. Are you keen on conjuring tricks?'

'I remember – ' began Mr Singleton; but Alleyn interrupted him.

'Will any gentleman in the audience provide me with a handkerchief? Sergeant Packer? Thank you. You are perfectly certain this is your handkerchief? You see me place it in the right-hand pocket of my jacket? I thank you. Now, Mr Singleton, I am one of those three gentlemen aforesaid. You see me here in the yard. You are standing by the stage-door. I walk along the yard into the office. Got your watch out, Wade? Off we go.'

Singleton and the three officers stood in a group at the stage-door. Alleyn walked briskly down the yard and into the office, leaving the door open.

'What's the idea, Mr Wade?' asked Cass. 'He's a bit of a hard case, isn't he?'

'He'll do me,' said Packer. 'He's a corker.'

'Watch the door into the office,' snapped Wade. 'And the yard.'

The door remained open on the yard. Nobody spoke. The sound of traffic in the street, and footsteps on the pavement outside, broke the silence. One or two people walked past at the end of the yard.

'He hasn't come out, anyway,' said Cass.

'Time,' said Wade. 'Come on, Singleton. Come on, you two.'

They all walked down the yard and into the office. Alleyn was sitting at the desk.

'Well,' said Alleyn brightly. 'Still here, you see.'

'I thought, Superintendent,' said Mr Singleton, 'that you said we were to receive a surprise.'

'And you are disappointed?' He looked from one dubious face to the other. Wade was staring expectantly at him.

'I expect you'd like to know where the laugh and round of applause comes in,' said Alleyn. 'If Sergeant Packer will look at the bottom rung of the back-stage ladder into the grid he will learn something to his advantage.'

'Go on, Packer,' said Wade.

Packer hurried off through the stage-door. There was a short pause and then he came thundering back.

'By cripey, Mr Wade, it's a corker! By gosh, Mr Wade, it's a humdinger!'

He was waving the handkerchief. Cass's eyes opened very wide. Mr Singleton moistened his lips once or twice but, for a marvel, he had nothing to say.

'Tied to the bottom rung it was,' declared Packer. 'Tied to the bottom rung. By gum, it's a beaut!'

'You see it can be done, Wade,' said Alleyn.

'It's good enough,' said Wade delightedly, 'it's good enough.'

'Ah – um – very neat,' said Mr Singleton. He drew the palm of his hand across his mouth. 'I recollect seeing the Great Houdini – '

'Mr Singleton,' said Alleyn, 'I'm afraid I've taken up far too much of your time. We mustn't keep you any longer. Will you allow me to quote your favourite author? – "Spend this for me." '

Mr Singleton broke into a loud laugh as his fingers closed on the tip.

'Ah ha, sir, I can have at you again. "I'll be your purse-bearer and leave you for an hour." ' He removed his hat, bowed, said, 'Good morning gentlemen,' and hurried away.

'What a fabulous bit of wreckage,' said Alleyn. 'Poor old devil, I wonder if he – Oh, well! I suppose you'd like an explanation of all this.' He turned to Cass and Packer.

'Too right, sir,' said Packer. 'You've got us beat.'

'What I did was this. I came into this office, as you saw. I came out again as you apparently didn't see, and I went round to the back by what I feel should be called Cass's Alley.'

'But look here, sir, we were watching the yard.'

'I know. I left the door open and I sidled along to the street end keeping against the wall. I was hidden so far by the open door. If you go along to the stage-door you will see what I mean. I was just able to keep out of sight.'

'But the entrance at the end! You had to cross there, and I swear I never took my eyes off it,' burst out Cass.

'You saw me walk across, Cass.'

'I never! Pardon me, sir.'

'You didn't recognize your own overcoat and hat? You left them in here.'

Alleyn pointed to where they lay across the desk.

'I ventured to borrow them. As soon as I got in here I slipped them on, and, as I have said, sidled out under cover of the door, turned to the right when I got out to the pavement, and then walked briskly back across the open end of the yard. You did not recognize me. Now, as soon as I got across the entrance to the yard I was hidden by the projecting bicycle shed. I repeated the sidling game on the other side and came back to Cass's Alley. Once in there, I bolted round to the back door, having borrowed the key. All this took less than two minutes. Another half-minute going up the ladder. I allowed a minute to unhook the weight and came down in less than half. I put the key back in the door and returned by Cass's Alley, reversing the process. I just had time to get your hat and coat off, before you came along. D'you see?'

'I don't know that I do, sir, altogether,' confessed Cass, 'but you *did* it, so I reckon it's right.'

'Come and look at the plan here, and you'll see how it fits in.'

Wade, Packer and Cass all stared solemnly at the plan.

'It's a funny thing,' said Wade, 'how easy it is to miss the obvious thing. That alleyway now. You'd have thought we'd have picked it for something straight away.'

'You'd have thought *I* would,' grunted Cass, 'seeing I'm still sore from where I stuck.'

'It widens out as soon as you're round the corner,' said Alleyn.

'It'd need to,' said Cass.

Wade looked at his watch.

'It's time,' he said to Alleyn.

'Ah, yes,' said Alleyn.

They all stood listening. From the street outside came the irregular sound of mid-morning traffic, the whining clamour of trams, the roar of cars in low gear, punctured by intermittent horn notes, and behind it all the patter of feet on asphalt. One pair of feet seemed to separate and come closer.

Someone had turned into the yard.

CHAPTER 24

Dr Te Pokiha Plays to Type. Warn Curtain

But it was only Mr St John Ackroyd. Cass, who had moved into the yard, stopped him. The others could see him through the half-open door. Beside the gigantic Cass, Ackroyd looked a pygmy of a man. He stood there in his rather loud check overcoat and jaunty hat, staring cockily up at Cass.

'Excuse me, sir,' said Cass, 'but were you wanting to go into the theatre?'

'Yes, I was. I want to get to my wardrobe. Haven't a clean shirt to my back.'

'I'm afraid I can't let you in this morning, sir.'

'Oh, God! Why the devil not? Look here, you can come in with me and see I don't muck up the half-chewed cigar at the point marked X. Come on now, old boy, be a sport.'

'Very sorry, sir. I'm under orders and it can't be done.'

'Yes, but look, old boy. Here – '

Mr Ackroyd appeared to make an attempt to place his tiny hand confidingly in Cass's. Cass stepped back a pace.

'No, no, sir. We don't do things that way. Quite out of the question, thank you all the same.'

'Oh, blast! Well, what the hell am I supposed to do? Buy new shirts?'

'If you'll wait a little, sir, I'll inquire – '

'Here, Cass!' called Wade.

'Sir?'

'Just a minute. Come in, Mr Ackroyd, come in.'

The comic face was thrust round the door and distorted into a diverting grimace.

'Hullo, hullo! All the stars in one piece, including the Great Noise from the Yard. Any room for a little one?'

He came in, followed by Cass, and perched on the edge of Alfred Meyer's desk, cocking his hat jauntily over his left eye.

'Well. How's things?' he inquired.

'I'm glad you looked in, Mr Ackroyd,' said Wade. 'There's just one little matter I wanted to see you about.'

'Is there, by gum! Well, there's another little matter I'd like to see you about. I want to get at my wardrobe.'

'In the statement you gave us on the night of the fatality,' continued Wade in a monotonous chant, 'you said that you went from the dressing-rooms to the party.'

'That's right.'

'Remaining on the stage until after the fatality?'

'Yes. What's wrong with that?' demanded Ackroyd.

'You didn't come out into the yard, at all?'

'Eh? – I – how d'you mean?'

'Just that, Mr Ackroyd. You didn't leave the stage before the party and walk along to the office?'

'Oh, God! Look here, old boy, I – I believe I did.'

'You did?'

'Yes. It was only for a minute. Just to tell George people were beginning to come in.'

'Why didn't you tell us this before, Mr Ackroyd?'

'Damn it all, I'd forgotten all about it.'

'But now you state definitely that you did come here?'

'Yes,' said Ackroyd uncomfortably.

'We'll have to get a new statement to that effect,' said Wade. 'Will you tell us exactly what happened, Mr Ackroyd?'

'Just what I said. I came along and stood in the doorway there. I said: "The party's started, George," and George said: "Right you are. I've got a job here and then I'll be along," or something. The job he had seemed to be a perfectly good drink. Well, I passed a remark or two and went back to the party.'

'Was Mr Mason alone?'

'What? No, I rather fancy the black quack was there.'

'Pardon?' asked Wade, genteelly. 'Who did you say?'

'The black quack.'

'Can Mr Ackroyd possibly mean Dr Te Pokiha?' asked Alleyn of nobody in particular.

'You'd hardly think so, would you?' said Wade.

'Oh, no offence,' said Ackroyd. 'I forgot there was no colour bar in this country. The light-brown medico was on-stage. That better?'

'You want to be very careful when you make statements, Mr Ackroyd,' said Wade austerely. 'We'll have to get you to sign a new one. Seems funny, you forgetting you came along here.'

'Why the hell!' shouted Ackroyd hotly. 'What's funny about it? Why should I remember? Don't be silly.'

'Did you go straight back to the stage?'

'Yes, I did go straight back, I – hullo George!'

George Mason's unhappy face had appeared round the door.

'Hullo,' he mumbled. 'Can I come in?'

'Come in, Mr Mason,' said Wade. 'Take a seat. You're just the man we wanted to see. Do you remember Mr Ackroyd, here, coming along to the office before the party?'

Mr Mason passed his hand wearily over his forehead and slumped into a chair.

'Do I remember – Yes, I do. Didn't I tell you that? I'm sorry.'

'Quite all right. We just have to check up these little points. I don't think I asked you, definitely. Cass, take Mr Ackroyd along to his dressing-room and let him get anything he wants. Will you call in at the station between two and three this afternoon, Mr Ackroyd? Thank you. Good morning.'

'And that,' said Ackroyd bitterly, 'takes me *right* off. Good morning.'

When he had gone, Mason turned to Wade.

'Is there any mail here for me?' he asked.

'I think there is, Mr Mason. We'll let you have it.'

Mason groaned. 'I suppose you've nothing definite to tell me, Mr Wade? I've got our advance going nearly crazy in Wellington, not knowing whether he's representing a repertory company or a murder gang.'

'It won't be much longer.' Wade fell back on his stock opening gambit. 'I'm sorry to give you the trouble of coming down this morning but there's just one little matter I'd like to see you about,

Mr Mason. We've been talking to old Singleton, the doorkeeper, about the people that were outside, as you might say, before the party.'

'Boozy old devil. Was an actor once. Makes you think, doesn't it? There but for the wrath of God, or whatever it is!'

Alleyn chuckled.

'He's a bit too boozy for our liking,' continued Wade. He's given us one bit of information, and Dr Te Pokiha's given us another that contradicts it point-blank. It's only a silly little thing – '

'Don't talk to me about silly little things,' interjected Mason peevishly. 'I'm sick of the phrase. There's that Gaynes kid making a scene in fifteen different positions every five minutes, and demanding to be sent home to Daddy because she's "a silly little thing" and so, so upset. And I ate some of this native crayfish for dinner last night and it kept me awake till dawn – silly little thing! Ugh!'

'Mr Alleyn knows more about this than I do. He spoke about it to Dr Te Pokiha.'

'Te Pokiha's coming here, by the way. He looked in at the pub and said you wanted him.'

'If Mr Alleyn – ?' said Wade with a glance into the corner of the room where Alleyn sat peacefully smoking.

'It's just this,' said Alleyn. 'The old gentleman tells us that when you went out to the stage-door to warn him about asking the guests' names, you were bareheaded and in your dinner jacket.'

'Oh Lor',' groaned Mason, 'what of it? So I was.'

'And Dr Te Pokiha says that he came in here just as you returned from the stage-door and you were wearing an overcoat and hat.'

'It's a case of the drunk being right and the sober man wrong, as far as I can remember. I don't think I put on my coat to go out. No, I'm sure I didn't. I recollect old Singleton started one of his interminable reminiscences and I said it was too cold to stand about and made that the excuse to run away. I believe I did slip my coat on after I got back. Probably had it on when the doctor came in.'

'That explains that,' said Alleyn. 'It sounds idiotic, but we have to fiddle about with these things.'

'Well, if it's any help, that's what I think happened. Look here, Alleyn, *are* you any further on with this? I don't want to make a nuisance of myself but this game is literally costing the Firm hundreds.

It's driving me silly, honestly it is. What about the affair on the train, can't you get a lead from that?'

Alleyn got up and walked across to the fireplace.

'Wade,' he said, 'I don't know whether you'll approve of this, but I'm going to take Mr Mason into our confidence over the affair on the train.'

'Just as you please, Mr Alleyn,' said Wade, looking rather blank. 'You do just as you think best.'

'It's this,' said Alleyn, turning to Mason. 'You remember that before we got to Ohakune everyone in the carriage was asleep.'

'Well,' said Mason, 'I don't remember because I was asleep myself.'

'As Mr Singleton would say,' grinned Alleyn, 'a very palpable hit. I put it carelessly. Let me amend it. Each of us has admitted that he or she was asleep for some time before we got to Ohakune. I have asked all the others and they agree to this. They also agree that they were all awakened by a terrific jolt as we got on to the thing they call the spiral. Old Miss Max was decanted into my lap. You remember?'

'I do. Poor old Susie! She looked a scream, didn't she?'

'And Ackroyd let out a remarkably blue oath.'

'That's right. Foul-mouthed little devil – I don't like that sort of thing. Common. He will do it.'

'Well now, you remember all this – '

'Of course I do. I thought we'd run into a cow or something.'

'And Mr Meyer thought someone had given him a kick in the seat.'

'By George!' said Mason. 'Why didn't someone think of that?'

'That's what we're always saying to the chief, Mr Mason,' said Wade. 'The trouble is, we don't, and he does.'

There was a knock on the door.

'That'll be the doctor,' said Wade. 'Come in.' Dr Te Pokiha came in, smiling.

'I'm sorry I couldn't get here before. I had to go to the hospital – urgent case. You wanted to see me, Mr Alleyn?'

'We all want to see you, I think,' said Alleyn. 'It's in connection with our conversation last night.'

He repeated the story of Mason and his overcoat. Te Pokiha listened without a word. When Alleyn had finished, there was a pause.

'Well, Doctor, do you think you made a mistake?' said Wade.

'Certainly not. Mr Mason came in at the outside door wearing his coat and hat. He took them off afterwards, when I removed my own coat. I am not in the habit of making misstatements.'

'It's not that,' said Mason peaceably, it's just that I came in before you did and put on my coat because I was cold. I've got a weak tummy, Doctor,' he added with an air of giving the medical man a treat.

'You came in after I did,' said Te Pokiha with considerable emphasis. The whites of his eyes seemed to become more noticeable and his heavy brows came together.

'Well, I'm sorry, but I didn't,' said Mason.

'You mean to say I'm a liar.'

'Don't be silly, Doctor. You simply made a mistake.'

'I did not make any mistake. This is insufferable. You will please admit at once that I am right.'

'Why the deuce should I when you are obviously wrong,' said Mason irritably.

'Don't repeat that.' Te Pokiha's warm voice thickened. He lips coarsened into a sort of snarl. He showed his teeth like a dog. 'By Jove,' thought Alleyn, 'the odd twenty per cent of pure savage.'

'Oh, don't be a fool,' grunted Mason. 'You don't know what you're talking about.'

'You give me the lie!'

'Shut up. This isn't a Wild West show.'

'You give me the lie!'

'Oh, for God's sake don't go native,' said Mason – and laughed.

Te Pokiha made a sudden leap at him. Mason scuttled behind Packer. 'Keep off, you damn' Nigger!' he screamed.

The next five minutes were occupied in saving Mr Mason's life. Alleyn, Packer and Wade tackled Te Pokiha efficiently and scientifically, but even so it took their combined efforts to subdue him. He fought silently and savagely and only gave up when they had both his arms and one of his legs in chancery.

'Very well,' he said suddenly, and relaxed.

Cass appeared bulkily in the doorway. Ackroyd, clasping an armful of underwear, peered under his arm.

'Here, let me out,' said Mason.

'What's wrong, sir?' asked Cass, not moving.

'I apologize, Mr Alleyn,' said Te Pokiha quietly. 'You can loose your hand.'

'All right, Wade,' said Alleyn.

'Thank you.' He moved away from them, his brown hands at his tie. 'I am deeply ashamed,' he said. 'This man has spoken of my – my colour. It is true I am a "native". I come of a people who do not care for insults but I should not have forgotten that an *ariki*[1] does not lay hands on a *taurekareka.*'[2]

'What's all this?' asked Ackroyd greedily.

'You buzz off, sir,' advised Cass. Ackroyd disappeared.

'I will go now,' said Te Pokiha. 'If you wish to see me again, Mr Alleyn, I shall be at my rooms between one and two. I am very sorry indeed that I forgot myself. Good morning, gentlemen.'

'And with that he swep' off,' said Mason, coming out of cover. 'My God, what a savage. I think if you don't mind I'll go back to the pub. This has upset me. My God. Has he gone? Right, I'm off.'

He went down the yard. Te Pokiha was getting into his car.

'Follow him,' snapped Alleyn to Cass. 'Don't lose sight of him.'

'Who?' said Cass, startled. 'Te Pokiha?'

'No, Mason,' said Alleyn.

---

[1] Ariki – gentleman – (literally – first-born).
[2] Taurekareka – slave, low-class person.

CHAPTER 25

Alleyn Speaks the Tag

Extract from a letter written by Chief Detective-Inspector Alleyn to Detective-Inspector Fox, CID:

I've just returned from the arrest which took place immediately after the inquest. Mason gave no trouble. I think he was taken completely by surprise, though he must have felt things were getting dangerous as soon as the overcoat was mentioned. He said that he was innocent and that he would make no statement until he had consulted a lawyer. Psychologically he might be classed with Crippen, a drab everyday little man; but he's not got the excuse of the *crime passionel.* I suspect a stronger motive than the mere acquisition of money. Your cable seems to point to something fishy about the handling of his side of Incorporated Playhouses. I wouldn't mind betting that you find he's been gambling with the Firm's money and needed this bequest to get himself out of a hole. If the story of his leaving a company stranded in America is true, it looks as if we'll find a history of unscrupulousness over money matters.

He is a superb actor, of course. They told me so in the wardrobe-room and, by George, it's true. He got right into the skin of his part – the insignificant little dyspeptic, worrying about what would happen to the show. The dyspepsia is true enough; we've found half a pharmacopoeia of remedies in his room. Somebody ought to write a monograph on the effect of the stomach on the morals.

You will get a solemn letter of thanks from Nixon, I expect.
You've been remarkably nippy getting on to the trail, you cunning old devil. The case has interested me very much. It looked
so complicated and it was actually so simple, once Bob Parsons
had made his statement. Of course Mason had no idea Bob was
in a position to provide a cast-iron alibi for the entire company,
and no doubt thought that it would look as if any one of them
might have dodged out and popped up to the grid. We have
been very lucky. If Miss Dacres had not dropped the tiki I don't
believe we should have made an arrest. The stage-staff would
have sworn it was murder, but everyone else would have
thought they had made a mistake over the weights. I can't help
wondering if Mason meant, all along, to do just what Miss
Dacres did for him. He didn't get a chance, as it happened. I
packed him off to the office with Te Pokiha. Really, he planned
the thing quite well. His visit to the stage-door established his
alibi, and his remark about the cold air drew Singleton's attention to the fact that he was hatless and in his dinner-jacket. He
returned to the office, put on his overcoat and hat, slid along the
wall under cover of the open door – it's an ill-lit place at night –
walked boldly across the open end where there must have been
plenty of people coming away from the show, came back along
the yard, hidden from Singleton by the projecting bicycle shed,
and then doubled round to the back of the theatre, using the
back-door key and leaving it on the inside when he returned.

If Te Pokiha had not come in from the box-ofice, I fancy
Mason would have opened the door and shown himself, without his overcoat, to the clerks. That five minutes would never
have been accounted for. Of course, we are now going over
every inch of the path behind the sheds and hope to get something from it. The defence will have a little difficulty in
accounting for Mason's vivid recollection of an incident that
never took place. Susan Max was not projected into my lap in
the train, nor did Ackroyd utter any oaths.

Mason, of course, thought this little diversion must have
occurred when he was out on the platform taking a place kick at
Meyer's behind, and did not dare say he had not remembered it.
He couldn't say he had slept through it, as he's always talking

about being a light sleeper. Broadhead remembers someone coming back from the head of the carriage and sitting somewhere behind him. This, I believe, was Mason returning from his attempt. I fancy he got his idea for the second and successful attempt from the accident of the falling weight.

I've asked Nixon and Wade to give a miss to Carolyn Dacres's performance as a weight-lifter. They are willing enough as it would very much confuse the issue in the minds of a jury. I shall be called and shall give an account of the condition found on my first visit to the grid, when the weight was still missing. Ticklish and possibly rather hot, but quite honest in the last analysis.

I think the verdict will go against him, but there is a Labour Government in power here with anti-capital punishment leanings, so I fancy it will be a life-sentence. Miss Dacres insists on paying the cast a retaining salary for as long as they have to remain in this country. Hamledon and Gascoigne are trying to deal with affairs for her. I suppose she'll marry Hambledon one of these days. He's a nice fellow – Hambledon. I don't think he knows she ever suspected him and I hope she doesn't tell him. Liversidge is sweating blood and shaking in his fancy socks. He is a nasty bit of work and ought to be jugged. He's also rather a fool. I fancy his only idea in letting fall ambiguous remarks about Broadhead and the money was to try and divert suspicion of theft from himself, though, of course, he was terrified we'd find out about his conversation with Meyer and look upon it as a strong indication of motive to murder. He's such a skunk that I suppose he'd have used Broadhead or anyone else as a red herring. The parents of young Palmer and of Valerie Gaynes have cabled for their respective offspring but won't get 'em yet awhile. Young Palmer is not entirely porcine and may turn into a presentable citizen one day. Miss Gaynes is, beyond all hope, abominable, and I hope they don't give her the satisfaction of trying to be an actress in the witness-box. Ackroyd is chastened, old Brandon Vernon philosophical, and Gascoigne worried to death. Our old friend Miss Max shakes her head and keeps a friendly eye on Carolyn Dacres. Young Broadhead seems to be in a state of bewildered relief.

As you will see by this notepaper I am staying with Dr Te Pokiha. I am learning something of his people. He has apologized seven times, up to date, for losing his temper with Mason, and tells me all members of his family hate being called liars. I hope he doesn't fly into a rage with defending counsel, who is almost certain to question his veracity. He's an extraordinarily interesting fellow and, in spite of the temper, he has the most exquisite manners.

I've been asked to stay by several of the surrounding station-holders, so I shall see something of the North Island. They're an amazingly hospitable people, these New Zealanders, very anxious that one should admire their country, rather on the defensive about it, but once they accept you, extremely friendly. I am asked, embarrassingly and repeatedly, about 'the accent' and don't know how to answer. The intelligentsia, who seem to be a gentle distillation of the Press and the universities, speak a queerly careful language and tell funny stories with the most meticulous regard for the *mot juste*. Their views are blamelessly liberal. What a damn' superior ass I sound, talking like this about them. After this case is cleared up I go south to a high plateau encircled by mountains. I have fallen in love with the sound of this place, and indeed, with the country altogether. The air really *is* like wine, balmy and exciting. The colour is clear and everything is exquisitely defined – no pretty smudging.

Well, my old Fox, all this is a long cry from the case. There's no more to say except that I await your air-mail letter with composure and confidence. I shall end this letter by running my pen round the little greenstone tiki so that you have an idea of his shape and size. He will not appear in evidence, I hope, but you will see that in his own way he has played a not inconsiderable part in the affair. Carolyn Dacres tells me she still wants to have him. May he bring her better luck.

Goodbye, you old devil. It must be so exciting to be a detective.

Yours ever,

RODERICK ALLEYN

Epilogue

On an evening three months after the close of the case Alleyn, stretched luxuriously on a widely-spread tussock, looked across Lake Pukaki to where Aeorangi, the cloud-piercer, shone immaculate against the darkening sky. He would smoke one pipe before turning back to the little wooden hotel. With a sigh he put his hand in his pocket and took out three letters with English stamps on the envelopes. His holiday was nearly over, and here was old Fox saying how glad they would be at the Yard to see him again. The second was from his Assistant Commissioner – very cordial. He dropped them on the warm, lichen-surfaced earth, and once again he read the final paragraph in the third letter.

I felt I should like to tell you that Hailey and I think we shall be married in a year's time. Please give us your blessing, dear Mr Alleyn. One other thing. There will be a step-child for Hailey. So you see that the greenstone tiki has fulfilled its purpose and I shall have the best possible remembrance of my dear Alfie-Pooh.

September 16th, 1936.

Artists in Crime

For Phyllis and John

Contents

The Characters in the Tale

Chief Detective-Inspector
  Roderick Alleyn, CID

Miss Van Maes   *The success of the ship*

Agatha Troy, RA   *Of Tatler's End House, Bossicote, Bucks. Painter*

Katti Bostock   *Well-known painter of plumbers and Negro musicians*

Nigel Bathgate   *Journalist*

Lady Alleyn   *Of Danes Lodge, Bossicote, Bucks; mother of Chief Detective-Inspector Alleyn*

Cedric Malmsley   *A student with a beard*

Garcia   *A sculptor*

Sonia Gluck   *A model*

Francis Ormerin   *A student from Paris*

Phillida Lee   *A student from the Slade*

Watt Hatchett   *A student from Australia*

The Hon. Basil Pilgrim   *A student from the nobility*

Valmai Seacliff   *A student with sex-appeal*

Superintendent Blackman   *Of the Buckingham Constabulary*

Detective-Inspector Fox,
  CID

Detective-Sergeant Bailey,
  CID   *A fingerprint expert*

Detective-Sergeant
  Thompson, CID   *A photographic expert*

Dr Ampthill   *Police surgeon at Bossicote, Bucks.*

PC Sligo   *Of Bossicote Police Force*

A charlady

Bobbie O'Dawne   *A lady of the Ensemble*

An estate agent

Ted McCully   *Foreman at a car depot*

Dr Curtis   *Police surgeon, CID*

Captain Pascoe   *Of Boxover*

His servant

CHAPTER 1

Prologue at Sea

Alleyn leant over the deck-rail, looking at the wet brown wharf and the upturned faces of the people. In a minute or two now they would slide away, lose significance, and become a vague memory. 'We called at Suva.' He had a sudden desire to run a mental ring round the scene beneath him, to isolate it, and make it clear, for ever in his mind. Idly at first, and then with absurd concentration, he began to memorize, starting with a detail. The tall Fijian with dyed hair. The hair was vivid magenta against the arsenic green of a pile of fresh bananas. He trapped and held the pattern of it. Then the brown face beneath, with liquid blue half-tones reflected from the water, then the oily dark torso, fore-shortened, the white loincloth, and the sharp legs. The design made by the feet on wet planks. It became a race. How much of the scene could he fix in his memory before the ship sailed? The sound, too – he must get that – the firm slap of bare feet on wet boards, the languid murmur of voices and the snatches of song drifting from a group of native girls near those clumps of fierce magenta coral. Hie smell must not be forgotten – frangipanni, coconut oil, and sodden wood. He widened his circle, taking in more figures – the Indian woman in the shrill pink sari, sitting by the green bananas; wet roofs on the wharf and damp roads wandering aimlessly towards mangrove swamps and darkened hills. Those hills, sharply purple at their base, lost outline behind a sulky company of clouds, to jag out, fantastically peaked, against a motionless and sombre sky. The clouds themselves were indigo at the edges, heavy with the ominous depression of unshed rain. The darkness of everything and the violence of colour – it was a pattern of wet brown, acid green, magenta and indigo. The round voices of the Fijians, loud and deep, as though they spoke through resounding tubes, pierced the moist air and made it vibrant.

Everything shifted a little, stepped back a pace. The ship had parted from the wharf. Already the picture was remote, the sounds would soon fade out. Alleyn shut his eyes and found the whole impression vivid under the closed lids. When he opened them the space between vessel and land had widened. He no longer wanted to look at the wharf, and turned away.

'And am I *hart*?' the success of the ship was saying to a group of young men. 'Oh baby! 'I'll say I've left haff a stone back there in that one-eyed lil' burg. Hart! Phoo!'

The young men laughed adoringly.

'It's hotter than this in Honolulu!' teased one of the young men.

'Maybe. But it's not so enervating.'

'Very hot spot, Honolulu!'

'Oh boy!' chanted the success, rolling her eyes and sketching a Hawaiian movement with her hips. 'You wait a while till I show you round the lil' old home town. Gee, that label on my grips certainly looks good to me.' She saw Alleyn. 'Hello, hello, look who's here! Come right over and join the party.'

Alleyn strolled over. Ever since they sailed from Auckland he had been uneasily aware of a certain warmth in the technique of the success where he was concerned. He supposed it was rather one up to him with all these youngsters in hot pursuit. At this stage of speculation he invariably pulled a fastidious face and thought ruefully: 'Lord, Lord, the vanity of the male forties.' But he was very lonely, and the thought of her almost lent a little glamour to the possible expectation of the weary routine of a shipboard flirtation.

'Look at him!' cried the success. 'Isn't he the cutest thing! That quiet English stuff certainly makes one great big appeal with this baby. And does he flash the keep-clear signal! Boys, I'll take you right into my confidence. Listen! This Mr Alleyn is my big flop. I don't mean a thing to him.'

'She really is rather awful,' thought Alleyn, and he said: 'Ah, Miss Van Maes, you don't know a coward when you see one.'

'Meaning?'

'I – I really don't know,' mumbled Alleyn hurriedly. 'Hullo, we're going through the barrier,' said one of the youths.

They all turned to the deck-rail. The sea wrapped itself sluggishly about the thin rib of the reef and fell away on either side in an ener-vated pother of small breakers. Over Fiji the rain still hung in pon-derable clouds. The deep purple of the islands was lit by desultory patches of livid sunshine, banana-green, sultry, but without irides-cence. The ship passed through the fangs of the reef.

Alleyn slipped away, walked aft, and climbed the companion-way to the boat deck. Nobody about up there, the passengers in their shoregoing clothes were still collected on the main deck. He filled his pipe meditatively, staring back towards Fiji. It was pleasant up there. Peaceful.

'Damn!' said a female voice. 'Damn, damn, damn! Oh *blast*!'

Startled, Alleyn looked up. Sitting on the canvas cover of one of the boats was a woman. She seemed to be dabbing at something. She stood up and he saw that she wore a pair of exceedingly grub-by flannel trousers, and a short grey overall. In her hand was a long brush. Her face was disfigured by a smudge of green paint, and her short hair stood up in a worried shock, as though she had run her hands through it. She was very thin and dark. She scrambled to the bows of the boat and Alleyn was able to see what she had been at. A small canvas was propped up in the lid of an open paintbox. Alleyn drew in his breath sharply. It was as if his deliberately culti-vated memory of the wharf at Suva had been simplified and made articulate. The sketch was an almost painfully explicit statement of the feeling of that scene. It was painted very directly with crisp, nervous touches. The pattern of blue-pinks and sharp greens fell across it like the linked syllables of a perfect phrase. It was very sim-ply done, but to Alleyn it was profoundly satisfying – an expression of an emotion, rather than a record of a visual impression.

The painter, an unlit cigarette between her lips, stared dispassion-ately at her work. She rummaged in her trouser pockets, found nothing but a handkerchief that had been used as a paint-rag, and ran her fingers through her hair. 'Blast!' she repeated, and took the unlit cigarette from her lips.

'Match?' said Alleyn.

She started, lost her balance, and sat down abruptly.

'How long have you been there?' she demanded ungraciously.

'Only just come. I – I haven't been spying. May I give you a match?'

'Oh – thanks. Chuck up the box, would you?' She lit her cigarette, eyeing him over the top of her long thin hands, and then
turned to look again at her work.

'It is exceedingly good, isn't it?' said Alleyn.

She hunched up one shoulder as if his voice was a piercing
draught in her ear, muttered something, and crawled back to her
work. She picked up her palette and began mixing a streak of colour
with her knife.

'You're not going to do anything more to it?' said Alleyn involuntarily.

She turned her head and stared at him.

'Why not?'

'Because it's perfect – you'll hurt it. I say, please forgive me.
Frightful impertinence. I do apologize.'

'Oh, don't be ridiculous,' she said impatiently, and screwed up her
eyes to peer at the canvas.

'I merely thought – ' began Alleyn.

'I had an idea,' said the painter, 'that if I worked up here on this
hideously uncomfortable perch, I might possibly have the place to
myself for a bit.'

'You shall,' said Alleyn, and bowed to her profile. He tried to
remember if he had ever before been quite so pointedly snubbed by
a total stranger. Only, he reflected, by persons he was obliged to
interview in the execution of his duties as an officer of Scotland
Yard. On those occasions he persisted. On this an apologetic exit
seemed to be clearly indicated. He walked to the top of the companion-way, and then paused.

'But if you do anything more, you'll be a criminal. The thing's
perfect. Even I can see that, and I – '

' "Don't know anything about it, but I *do* know what I like," '
quoted the lady savagely.

'I was not about to produce that particular bromide,' said Alleyn
mildly.

For the first time since he had spoken to her, she gave him her
full attention. A rather charming grin lifted the corners of her
mouth.

'All right,' she said, I'm being objectionable. My turn to apologize. I thought at first you were one of the "don't put me in it" sort of onlookers.'

'Heaven forbid!'

'I wasn't going to do too much,' she went on, actually as if she had turned suddenly shy. It's just that figure in the foreground – I left it too late. Worked for an hour before we sailed. There should be a repetition of the bluish grey there, but I can't remember – ' She paused, worried.

'But there was!' exclaimed Alleyn. 'The reflection off the water up the inside of the thighs. Don't you remember?'

'Golly – you're right,' she said. 'Here – wait a bit.'

She picked up a thin brush, broke it through the colour, held it poised for a second, and then laid a delicate touch on the canvas. 'That?'

'Yes,' cried Alleyn excitedly. 'That's done it. Now you can stop.'

'All right, all right. I didn't realize you were a painting bloke.'

'I'm not. It's simply insufferable cheek.'

She began to pack up her box.

'Well, I must say you're very observant for a layman. Good memory.'

'Not really,' said Alleyn. 'It's synthetic'

'You mean you've trained your eye?'

'I've had to try to do so, certainly.'

'Why?'

'Part of my job. Let me take your box for you.'

'Oh – thank you. Mind the lid – it's a bit painty. Pity to spoil those lovely trousers. Will you take the sketch?'

'Do you want a hand down?' offered Alleyn.

'I can manage, thank you,' she said gruffly, and clambered down to the deck.

Alleyn had propped the canvas against the rail and now stood looking at it. She joined him, eyeing it with the disinterested stare of the painter.

'Why!' murmured Alleyn suddenly. 'Why, you must be Agatha Troy.'

'That's me.'

'Good Lord, what a self-sufficient fathead I've been.'

'Why?' said Agatha Troy. 'You were all right. Very useful.'

'Thank you,' said Alleyn humbly. 'I saw your one-man show a year ago in London.'

'Did you?' she said without interest.

'I should have guessed at once. Isn't there a sort of relationship between this painting and the "In the Stadium"?'

'Yes.' She moved her eyebrows quickly. 'That's quite true. The arrangement's much the same – radiating lines and a spotted pattern. Same feeling. Well, I'd better go down to my cabin and unpack.'

'You joined the ship at Suva?'

'Yes. I noticed this subject from the main deck. Things shove themselves at you like that sometimes. I dumped my luggage, changed, and came up.'

She slung her box over her shoulder and picked up the sketch.

'Can I – ?' said Alleyn diffidently.

'No, thanks.'

She stood for a moment staring back towards Fiji. Her hands gripped the shoulder-straps of her paintbox. The light breeze whipped back her short dark hair, revealing the contour of the skull and the delicate bones of the face. The temples were slightly hollow, the cheek-bones showed, the dark-blue eyes were deep-set under the thin ridge of the brows. The sun caught the olive skin with its smudge of green paint, and gave it warmth. There was a kind of spare gallantry about her. She turned quickly before he had time to look away and their gaze met.

Alleyn was immediately conscious of a clarification of his emotions. As she stood before him, her face slowly reddening under his gaze, she seemed oddly familiar. He felt that he already knew her next movement, and the next inflexion of her clear, rather cold voice. It was a little as though he had thought of her a great deal, but never met her before. These impressions held him transfixed, for how long he never knew, while he still kept his eyes on hers. Then something clicked in his mind, and he realized that he had stared her out of countenance. The blush had mounted painfully to the roots of her hair and she had turned away.

'I'm sorry,' said Alleyn steadily. 'I'm afraid I was looking at the green smudge on your cheek.'

She scrubbed at her face with the cuff of her smock.

'I'll go down,' she said, and picked up the sketch.

He stood aside, but she had to pass close to him, and again he was vividly aware of her, still with the same odd sense of surprised familiarity. She smelt of turpentine and paint, he noticed.

'Well – good evening,' she said vaguely.

Alleyn laughed a little.

'Good evening, madam.'

She started off down the ladder, moving sideways and holding the wet sketch out over the hand-rail. He turned away and lit a cigarette. Suddenly a terrific rumpus broke out on the deck below. The hot cheap reek of frangipanni blossoms drifted up, and with it the voice of the success of the ship.

'Oh, pardon me. Come right down. Gangway, fellows. Oh say, pardon me, but have you been making a picture? Can I have a keek? I'm just crazy about sketching. Look, boys – isn't that cute? The wharf? My, my, it's a shame you haven't been able to finish it, isn't it? It would have been swell! Look, boys, it's the wharf. Maybe a snapshot would help. We'll surely have to watch our step with an artist on board. Say, let's get acquainted. We've been celebrating and we feel fine. Meet the mob. I'm Virginia Van Maes.'

'My name's Troy,' said a voice that Alleyn could scarcely recognize. A series of elaborate introductions followed.

'Well, Miss Troy, I was going to tell you how Caley Burt painted my portrait in Noo York. You've heard of Caley Burt? I guess he's one of the most exclusive portraitists in America. Well, it seems he was just crazy to take my picture – '

The anecdote was a long one. Agatha Troy remained silent throughout.

'Well, when he was through – and say, did I get tired of that dress? – it certainly was one big success. Poppa bought it, and it's in our reception-hall at Honolulu. Some of the crowd say it doesn't just flatter, but it looks good to me. I don't pretend to know a whole lot about art, Miss Troy, but I know what I like.'

'Quite,' said Agatha Troy. 'Look here, I think I'd better get down to my cabin. I haven't unpacked yet. If you'll excuse me – '

'Why, certainly. We'll be seeing you. Say, have you seen that guy Alleyn around?'

'I'm afraid I don't know – '

'He's tall and thin, and I'll say he's good looking. And is he British? Gee! I'm crazy about him. I got a little gamble with these boys, I'll have him doing figure eights trying to dope out when the petting-party gets started.'

'I've kissed goodbye to my money,' one of the youths said.

'Listen to him, will you, Miss Troy? But we certainly saw Mr Alleyn around this way a while back.'

'He went up to the boat deck,' said a youth.

'Oh,' said Miss Troy clearly. 'That man! Yes, he's up there now.'

'Atta-boy!'

'Whooppee!'

'Oh damn!' said Alleyn softly.

And the next thing that happened was Miss Van Maes showing him how she'd made a real Honolulu *lei* out of Fijian frangipanni, and asking him to come down with the crowd for a drink.

'Has this party gone cuckoo or something? We're three rounds behind the clock. C'm on!'

'Virginia,' said a youth, 'you're tight.'

'What the hell! Is it my day to be sober? You coming, Mr Alleyn?'

'Thank you so much,' said Alleyn, 'but if you'll believe it, I'm a non-drinker at the moment. Doctor's orders.'

'Aw, be funny!'

'Fact. I assure you.'

'Mr Alleyn's thinking of the lady with the picture,' said a youth.

'What – her? With her face all mussed in green paint. Mr Alleyn's not screwy yet, is he? Gee, I'll say a woman's got no self-respect to go around that way in public. Did you get a look at that smock? And the picture! Well, I had to be polite and say it was cute, but it's nobody's big sorrow she didn't finish it. The wharf at Suva! Seems I struck it lucky, but what it's meant for's just anyone's guess. C'm on, Mr Strong-Silent Sleuth, put me out of my agony and say she don't mean one thing to you.'

'Miss Van Maes,' said Alleyn, 'do you know that you make me feel very middle-aged and inexpressibly foolish? I haven't got the smallest idea what the right answer is to any single one of your questions.'

'Maybe I could teach you. Maybe I could teach you a whole lot of fun, honey.'

'You're very kind, but, do you know, I'm afraid I'm past the receptive age.'

She widened her enormous eyes. The mascaraed lashes stuck out round them like black toothpicks. Her ash-fair hair was swept back from her very lovely face into a cluster of disciplined and shining curls. She had the un-human good looks of a film star. Undoubtedly she was rather tight.

'Well,' she said, 'my bet with the boys is still good. Twenty-five'll get anybody fifty you kiss me before we hit Honolulu. And I don't mean maybe.'

'I should be very much honoured – '

'Yeah? And I don't mean the get-by-the-censor stuff, either. No, sir!'

She stared at him, and upon her normally blank and beautiful face there dawned a look of doubt.

'Say,' she said, 'you're not going to tell me you got a yen for that woman?'

'I don't know what a yen is,' Alleyn said, 'but I've got nothing at all for Miss Troy, and I can assure you she has got even less than that for me.'

CHAPTER 2

Five Letters

From Miss Agatha Troy to her friend, Miss Katti Bostock, the well-known painter of plumbers, miners and Negro musicians:

S. S. *Niagara*,
August 1st.

Dear Katti,

I am breaking this journey at Quebec, so you'll get this letter about a fortnight before I get home. I'm glad everything is fixed up for next term. It's a bore in some ways having to teach, but now I've reached the giddy heights of picking and choosing I don't find it nearly so irksome. Damn good of you to do all the arranging for me. If you can, get the servants into the house by Sept. 1st – I get back on the 3rd – they ought to have everything fixed up by the 10th, when we start classes. Your air mail reached Suva the day we sailed. Yes, book Sonia Gluck for model. The little swine's beautiful and knows how to pose as long as she behaves herself. You yourself might do a big nude for the Group Show on the 16th or thereabouts. You paint well from the nude and I think you shouldn't remain wedded to your plumbers – your stuff will get static if you don't look out. I don't think I told you who is coming next term. Here is the list!

(1) Francis Ormerin. He's painting in Paris at the moment, but says the lot at Malaquin's has come all over surrealist and

he can't see it and doesn't want to. Says he's depressed about his work or something.

(2) Valmai Seacliff. That's the girl that did those dabby Rex Whistlerish posters for the Board of Trade. She says she wants to do some solid work from the model. Quite true, she does; but I rather fancy she's on the hunt.

(3) Basil Pilgrim. If I'm not mistaken, Basil is Valmai's quarry. He's an Hon., you know, and old Lord Pilgrim is doddering to the grave. He's the 'Peer that became a Primitive Methodist' a few years ago – you remember. The papers were full of it. He comes to light with the odd spot of hell-fire on the subject of birth-control, every now and then. Basil's got six elder sisters, and Lady Pilgrim died when he was born, so we don't know what she thought about it. I hardly think Valmai Seacliff will please the old gentleman. Basil's painting nearly drove him into the Salvation Army, I fancy.

(4) Watt Hatchett. This is new blood. He's an Australian youth I found working in Suva. Very promising stuff. Simplified form and swinging lines. He's as keen as mustard, and was practically living on bananas and cheek when I ran into him. His voice is like the crashing together of old tin cans, and he can talk of nothing but his work, his enthusiasms, and his dislikes. I'm afraid he'll get on their nerves and they may put him on the defensive. Still, his work is good.

(5) Cedric Malmsley. He's got a job illustrating some *de luxe* edition of medieval romances, and wants to get down to it with a model handy. It ought to work in all right. I told him to get in touch with you. I hear he's grown a blond beard that parts in the middle and wears sandals – Cedric, not the beard.

(6) Wolf Garcia, I had a letter from Garcia. No money, but a commission to do Comedy and Tragedy in marble for the new cinema in Westminster, so will I let him stay with me and do the clay model? No stamp on the envelope and written in conte chalk on lavatory paper. He will probably turn up long before you get this letter. Let him use the studio, will you, but look out, if you've got Sonia there. Garcia's got the use of someone's studio in London after the 20th, and hopes to have a cast ready by then, so it won't be for long. Now don't bully

me, Katti. You know the creature is really – Heaven save the mark – a genius; and the others all pay me through the nose, so I can afford to carry a couple of dead-heads. Yes, you're quite right. Hatchett *is* the other.

(7) One Phillida Lee. Just left the Slade, Rich father. She sent me some of her stuff and a rather gushing little request to work under me 'because she has always longed', etc., etc. I wrote back asking the earth in fees and she snapped at it.

(8) You, bless you. I've told them all to fix up with you. Malmsley, Ormerin and Pilgrim can have the dormitory; Garcia one attic, and Hatchett the other. You have the yellow room as usual, and put Valmai Seacliff and the Lee child in the blue. The great thing is to segregate Garcia. You know what he is, and I won't have that sort of thing – it's too muddly. On second thoughts it might be better to put him in the studio and the model in the attic. I rather think they were living together in London. By the way, I'm going to do a portrait of Valmai Seacliff. It'll do for Burlington House and the Salon, drat them. She'll be good enough to paint in the slap-up grand manner.

I'm scratching this off in the writing-room on my first night out from Suva. Did a small thing looking down on the wharf before we sailed. Came off rather well. I was interrupted by a man whom I thought was a fool, and who turned out to be intelligent, so I felt the fool. There's an American ex-cinema actress running about this ship half tight. She looks like one of their magazine covers and behaves like the wrath of God. The man seems to be her property, so perhaps he is a fool, after all.

If anything amusing happens, I'll add to this. It's been an interesting holiday, and I'm glad I did it. Your letters have been grand. Splendid the work goes on so well. I look forward to seeing it. Think about a nude for the Group. You don't want to be called the Plumber's Queen.

Later. We get into Vancouver tomorrow. It's been a peaceful trip since Honolulu, where the Ship's Belle left us. Before that it was rather hellish. Unfortunately someone had the number of *The Palette* that ran a special supplement of my show. The Belle got hold of it and decided I must be a real artist after all. When she saw the reproduction of the Royal portrait she laid her ears back and settled down to a steady pursuit. Wouldn't it be just wonderful if I did a portrait of her before we got to Honolulu? Her poppa would be tickled to death. She changed her clothes six times a day and struck a new attitude whenever she caught my eye. I had to pretend I'd got neuritis in my hand, which was a curse, as I rather wanted to do a head of one of the other passengers – a very paintable subject with plenty of good bone. However, I got down to it after Honolulu. The subject is a detective and looks like a grandee. Sounds like it, too – very old-world and chivalrous and so on. Damn! that looks like a cheap sneer, and it's not meant to. I'm rather on the defensive about this sleuth – I was so filthily rude to him, and he took it like a gent and made me feel like a bounder. Very awkward. The head is fairly successful.

Well, Katti, old lady, we meet on the 3rd. I'll come straight to Tatler's End. Best love.

Yours ever,
Troy

PS. – Perhaps you'd better give Garcia a shakedown in the studio and lock him in. We'll hope he'll have gone by the 20th.

Katti Bostock to Agatha Troy:

Tatler's End House,
Bossicote,
Bucks.
August 14th

Dear Troy,

You are a gump to collect these bloodsuckers. Yes, I know Garcia is damn good at sculping, but he's a nasty little animal, and thinks everyone else is born to keep him. God knows how much he's got out of you already. All right, I'll shut him up in the studio, but if he's after Sonia or anyone else, he'll crawl out by the ventilator. And if you imagine you'll get rid of him before the 20th, you're wandering. And who in the name of Bacchus is this Australian blight? You're paying his fare home, of course. Well, I suppose I can't talk, as you've given me the run of your house for twelve months. It's been a godsend, and I've done my

best work here. Been working on a thing of two Negro saxo-
phonists, worm's-eye view of, with cylindrical background. Not
bad, I fancy. It's finished now. I've started on a big thing, using
that little devil Sonia Gluck. It's a standing pose and she's behaving abominably, blast her! However, she agreed to come next
term for the usual exorbitant fee, as soon as she heard Garcia
and Pilgrim were to be in the class. Malmsley arrived today. The
beard is there all right, and looks like the Isle of Patmos gone
decadent. He's full of the book-illustration job, and showed me
some of the sketches – quite good. I've met Pilgrim several times,
and like him and his work. I hear he's always to be seen with the
Seacliff blight, so I suppose she's after the title. That girl's a
nymphomaniac, and a successful one at that. Funny this 'It'
stuff. I've never inspired a thought that wasn't respectable, and
yet I get on with men all right. You're different. They'd fall for
you if you'd let them, only you're so unprovocative they never
know where they are, and end by taking you at your own val-
uation. The Seacliff and Pilgrim arrive tomorrow. I've seen Miss
Phillida Lee. She's very would-be Slade. Wears hand-printed
clothes with high necks, and shudders and burbles alternately.
She comes on the 9th, and so does Ormerin, who writes from
Paris and sounds very depressed. Nice bloke. I don't know
whether it's struck you what a rum brew the class will be this
term. It's impossible to keep Sonia in her place, wherever a
model's place may be. Garcia, if he's here, will either be in full
cry after her, which will be unpleasant, or else sick of her, which
will be worse. Valmai Seacliff will naturally expect every male
on the premises to be hot on her trail, and if that comes off,
Sonia will get the pip. Perhaps with Basil Pilgrim on the tapis,
the Seacliff will be less catholic, but I doubt it. Oh, well, you
know your own business best, and I suppose will float through
on the good old recipe of not noticing. You are such a bloody
aristocrat. Your capacity for ignoring the unpleasant is a bit irritating to a plebeian like myself.

The servants are all right. The two Hipkins and Sadie Welsh
from the village. They only tolerate me and are thrilled over
your return. So am I, actually. I want your advice over the big
thing of Sonia, and I'm longing to see your own stuff. You say

don't forward any more letters, so I won't. Your allusions to a detective are quite incomprehensible, but if he interrupted you in your work, you had every right to bite his head off. What had you been up to, anyway? – Well, so long until the 3rd – *Katti*.

PS. – Garcia has just sent a case of clay and a lot of material – carriage forward, *of course* – so I suppose I may expect to be honoured with his company any time now. We'll probably get a bill for the clay.

PPS. – Plumber's Queen yourself.

PPPS. – The bill for Garcia's material has come.

Chief Detective-Inspector Roderick Alleyn, CID., to Mr Nigel Bathgate, journalist:

S.S. *Niagara* (At Sea).
August 6th

Dear Bathgate,

How is it with Benedict, the married man? I was extremely sorry to be away for the wedding, and thought of you both on my mountain fastness in New Zealand. What a perfect place that would have been for a honeymoon. A primitive but friendly back-country pub, a lovely lake, tall mountains and nothing else for fifty miles. But I suppose you and your Angela were fashionably on the Riviera or somewhere. You're a lucky young devil, and I wish you both all the happiness in the world, and send you my blessing. I'm glad my offering met with Mrs Angela's approval.

We get to Vancouver in no time now, and leave the same day on the C.P.R. Most of the passengers are going on. I am breaking my journey at Quebec, a place I have always wanted to see. That will still give me fifteen days in England before I climb back into the saddle. My mother expects me to spend a fortnight with her, and if I may, I'll come on to you about the 21st?

The passengers on this ship are much like all passengers on all ships. Sea voyages seem to act as rather searching re-agents on character. The essential components appear in alarming isolation. There is the usual ship's belle, this time a perfectly terrific American cinema lady who throws me into a fever of diffidence and alarm, but who exhibits the closeup type of loveliness to the nth degree of unreality. There is the usual sprinkling of pleasant globetrotters, bounders, and avid women. The most interesting person is Miss Agatha Troy, the painter. Do you remember her one-man show? She has done a miraculous painting of the wharf at Suva. I long to ask what the price will be, but am prevented by the circumstances of her not liking me very much. She bridles like a hedgehog (yes, they do) whenever I approach her, and as I don't believe I suffer from any of those things in the strip advertisements, I'm rather at a loss to know why. Natural antipathy, perhaps. I don't share it. Oddly enough, she suddenly asked me in a very gruff stand-offish voice if she might paint my head. I've never been took a likeness of before – it's a rum sensation when they get to the eyes; such a searching impersonal sort of glare they give you. She even comes close sometimes and peers into the pupils. Rather humiliating, it is. I try to return a stare every bit as impersonal, and find it tricky. The painting seems to me to be quite brilliant, but alarming.

Fox has written regularly. He seems to have done damn well over that arson case. I rather dread getting back into the groove, but suppose it won't be so bad when it comes. Hope I don't have to start off with anything big – if Mrs Angela thinks of putting rat's-bane in your Ovaltine, ask her to do it out of my division.

I look forward to seeing you both, my dear Bathgate, and send you my salutations the most distinguished.

Yours ever,

Roderick Alleyn

Chief Detective-Inspector Alleyn to Lady Alleyn, Danes Lodge, Bossicote, Bucks:

C.P.R.
August 15th.

My Dearest Mamma,

Your letter found me at Vancouver. Yes, please – I should like to come straight to you. We arrive at Liverpool on the 7th, and I'll make for Bucks as fast as may be. The garden sounds very attractive, but don't go doing too much yourself, bless you. No, darling, I did not lose my heart in the Antipodes. Would you have been delighted to welcome a strapping black Fijian lady? I might have got one to regard me with favour at Suva, perhaps, but they smell of coconut oil, which you would not have found particularly delicious. I expect if I ever do get it in the neck, she'll think me no end of a dull dog and turn icy. Talking of Suva, which I was not, do you know of a place called Tatler's End House, somewhere near Bossicote? Agatha Troy, who painted that picture we both liked so much, lives there. She joined this ship at Suva, and did a lovely thing of the wharf. Look here, Mamma, if ever a Virginia Van Maes writes and asks you to receive her, you must be away, or suffering from smallpox. She's an American beauty who looks people up in Kelly's and collects scalps. She looked me up and – Heaven knows why – she seemed inclined to collect ours. It's the title, I suppose. Talking of titles, how's the blasted Baronet? She was on to him like a shot. 'Gee, Mr Alleyn, I never knew your detective force was recruited from your aristocracy. I'm crazy to know if this Sir George Alleyn is your only brother.' You see? She threatens to come to England and has already said she's sure you must be the cutest old-world mother. She's quite capable of muscling in on the strength of being my dearest girlfriend. So you look out, darling, I've told her you're a horrid woman, but I don't think she cares. You'll be 65 on or about the day this arrives. In 30 years I shall be nearly 10 years older than you are now, and you'll still be trying to bully me. Do you remember how I found out your real age on your thirty-fifth birthday? My first really good bit of investigation, nasty little trick that I was. Well, little mum, don't flirt with the vicar, and be sure to have the red carpet out on the 7th.

Your dutiful and devoted son,

Roderick

PS. – Miss Troy has done a sketch of your son which he will purchase for your birthday if it's not too expensive.

From Lady Alleyn, Danes Lodge, Bossicote, to Chief Detective-Inspector Alleyn, Château Frontenac, Quebec:

Dear Roderick,

Your ingenuous little letter reached me on my birthday, and I was delighted to receive it. Thank you, my dear. It will be a great joy to have you for nearly a fortnight, greedily to myself. I trust I am *not* one of those avaricious mammas – clutch, clutch, clutch – which, after all, is only a form of cluck, cluck, cluck. It will be delightful to have a Troy version of you, and I hope it was not too expensive – if it was, perhaps you would let me join you, my dear. I should like to do that, but have no doubt you will ruin yourself and lie to your mother about the price. I shall call on Miss Troy, not only because you obviously wish me to do so, but because I have always liked her work, and should be pleased to meet her, as your Van Maes would say. George is with his family in Scotland. He talks of standing for Parliament, but I am afraid he will only make a fool of himself, poor dear. It's a pity he hasn't got your brains. I have brought a hand-loom and am also breeding Alsatians. I hope the bitch – Tunbridge Tessa – does not take a dislike to you. She is very sweet really. I always feel, darling, that you should not have left the Foreign Office, but at the same time, I am a great believer in everybody doing what he wants, and I *do* enjoy hearing about your cases.

Until the 7th, my dearest son.

Your loving
Mother

PS. – I have just discovered the whereabouts of Miss Troy's house, Tatler's End. It is only two miles out of Bossicote, and a nice old place. Apparently she takes students there. My spies tell me a Miss Bostock has been living in it during Miss Troy's absence. She returns on the 3rd. How old is she?

CHAPTER 3

Class Assembles

On the 10th of September at ten o'clock in the morning, Agatha Troy opened the door in the eastward wall of her house and stepped out into the garden. It was a sunny morning with a tang of autumn about it, a bland, mellow morning. Somewhere in the garden a fire had been lit, and an aromatic trace of smouldering brushwood threaded the air. There was not a breath of wind.

'Autumn!' muttered Troy. 'And back to work again. Damn! I'm getting older.' She paused for a moment to light a cigarette, and then she set off towards the studio, down on the old tennis court. Troy had built this studio when she inherited Tatler's End House from her father. It was a solid square of decent stone with top lighting, and a single window facing south on a narrow lane. It stood rather lower than the house, and about a minute's walk away from it. It was screened pleasantly with oaks and lilac bushes. Troy strode down the twisty path between the lilac bushes and pushed open the studio door. From beyond the heavy wooden screen inside the entrance she heard the voices of her class. She was out of patience with her class. 'I've been too long away,' she thought. She knew so exactly how each of them would look, how their work would take shape, how the studio would smell of oil colour, turpentine, and fixative, how Sonia, the model, would complain of the heat, the draught, the pose, the cold, and the heat again. Katti would stump backwards and forwards before her easel, probably with one shoe squeaking. Ormerin would sigh, Valmai Seacliff would attitudinize, and Garcia, wrestling with clay by the south window, would whistle between his teeth.

'Oh, well,' said Troy, and marched round the screen.

Yes, there it all was, just as she expected, the throne shoved against the left-hand wall, the easels with fresh white canvases, the roaring gas heater, and the class. They had all come down to the studio after breakfast and, with the exception of Garcia and Malmsley, waited for her to pose the model. Malmsley was already at work: the drawings were spread out on a table. He wore, she noticed with displeasure, a sea-green overall. 'To go with the beard, I suppose,' thought Troy. Garcia was in the south window, glooming at the clay sketch of Comedy and Tragedy. Sonia, the model wrapped in a white kimono, stood beside him. Katti Bostock, planted squarely in the centre of the room before a large black canvas, set her enormous palette. The rest of the class, Ormerin, Phillida Lee, Watt Hatchett, and Basil Pilgrim, were grouped round Valmai Seacliff.

Troy walked over to Malmsley's table and looked over his shoulder at the drawings.

'What's that?'

'That's the thing I was talking about,' explained Malmsley. His voice was high-pitched and rather querulous. 'It's the third tale in the series. The female has been murdered by her lover's wife. She's lying on a wooden bench, impaled on a dagger. The wife jammed the dagger through the bench from underneath, and when the lover pressed her down – you see? The knife is hidden by the drape. It seems a little far-fetched, I must say. Surely it would show. The wretched publisher man insists on having this one.'

'It needn't show if the drape is suspended a little,' said Troy. 'From the back of the bench, for instance. Then as she falls down she would carry the drape with her. Anyway, the probabilities are none of your business. You're not doing a "before and after", like a strip advertisement, are you?'

'I can't get the pose,' said Malmsley languidly. 'I want to treat it rather elaborately. Deliberately mannered.'

'Well, you can't go in for the fancy touches until you've got the flesh and blood to work from. That pose will do us as well as another, I dare say. I'll try it. You'd better make a separate drawing as a study.'

'Yes, I suppose I had,' drawled Malmsley. 'Thanks most frightfully.'

'Of course,' Valmai Seacliff was saying, 'I went down rather well in Italy. The Italians go mad when they see a good blonde. They used to murmur when I passed them in the streets. "Bella" and *"Bellissima"*. It was rather fun.'

'Is that Italian?' asked Katti morosely, of her flake-white.

'It means beautiful, darling,' answered Miss Seacliff.

'Oh hell!' said Sonia, the model.

'Well,' said Troy loudly. 'I'll set the pose.'

They all turned to watch her. She stepped on the throne, which was the usual dais on wheels, and began to arrange a seat for the model. She threw a cerise cushion down, and then from a chest by the wall she got a long blue length of silk. One end of this drape she threw across the cushion and pinned, the other she gathered carefully in her hands, drew round to one side, and then pinned the folds to the floor of the dais.

'Now, Sonia,' she said. 'Something like this.'

Keeping away from the drape, Troy knelt and then slid sideways into a twisted recumbent pose on the floor. The right hip was raised, the left took the weight of the pose. The torso was turned upwards from the waist so that both shoulders touched the boards. Sonia, noticing that twist, grimaced disagreeably.

'Get into it,' said Troy, and stood up. 'Only you lie across the drape with your head on the cushions. Lie on your left side, first.'

Sonia slid out of the white kimono. She was a most beautiful little creature, long-legged, delicately formed and sharp-breasted. Her black hair was drawn tightly back from the suave forehead. The bony structure of her face was sharply defined, and suggested a Slavonic mask.

'You little devil, you've been sunbathing,' said Troy. 'Look at those patches.'

'Well they don't like nudism, at Bournemouth,' said Sonia.

She lay across the drape on her left side, her head on the cerise cushion. Troy pushed her right shoulder over until it touched the floor. The drape was pressed down by the shoulders and broke into uneven blue folds about the body.

'That's your pose, Malmsley,' said Troy. 'Try it from where you are.'

She walked round the studio, eyeing the model.

'It's pretty good from everywhere,' she said. 'Right! Get going, everybody.' She glanced at her watch. 'You can hold that for forty minutes, Sonia.'

'It's a terrible pose, Miss Troy,' grumbled Sonia. 'All twisted like this.'

'Nonsense,' said Troy briskly.

The class began to settle itself.

Since each member of Troy's little community played a part in the tragedy that followed ten days later, it may be well to look a little more closely at them.

Katti Bostock's work is known to everyone who is at all interested in modern painting. At the time of which I am writing she was painting very solidly and smoothly, using a heavy outline and a simplified method of dealing with form. She painted large figure compositions, usually with artisans as subjects. Her 'Foreman Fitter' had been the picture of the year at the Royal Academy, and had set all the diehards by the ears. Katti herself was a short, stocky, dark-haired individual with an air of having no nonsense about her. She was devoted to Troy in a grumbling sort of way, lived at Tatler's End House most of the year, but was not actually a member of the class.

Valmai Seacliff was thin, blonde, and very, very pretty. She was the type that certain modern novelists write about with an enthusiasm which they attempt to disguise as satirical detachment. Her parents were well-to-do and her work was clever. You have heard Katti describe Valmai as a nymphomaniac and will be able to draw your own conclusions about the justness of this criticism.

Phillida Lee was 18, plump, and naturally gushing. Two years of Slade austerity had not altogether damped her enthusiasms, but when she remembered to shudder, she shuddered.

Watt Hatchett, Troy's Australian protégé, was a short and extremely swarthy youth, who looked like a dago in an American talking picture. He came from one of the less reputable streets of Sydney and was astoundingly simple, cocksure, egotistical and enthusiastic. He seemed to have no aesthetic perceptions of any description, so that his undoubted talent appeared to be a sort of parasite, flowering astonishingly on an unpromising and stunted stump.

Cedric Malmsley we have noticed already. Nothing further need be said about him at this stage of the narrative.

The Hon. Basil Pilgrim, son of the incredible Primitive Methodist peer, was a pleasant-looking young man of 23, whose work was sincere, able, but still rather tentative. His father, regarding all art schools as hot-beds of vice and depravity, had only consented to Basil becoming a pupil of Troy's because her parents had been landed gentry of Lord Pilgrim's acquaintance, and because Troy herself had once painted a picture of a revivalist meeting. Her somewhat ironical treatment of this subject had not struck Lord Pilgrim, who was, in many ways, a remarkably stupid old man.

Francis Ormerin was a slight and delicate-looking Frenchman who worked in charcoal and wash. His drawings of the nude were remarkable for their beauty of line, and for a certain emphatic use of accent. He was a nervous over-sensitive creature, subject to fits of profound depression, due said Troy, to his digestion.

And lastly Garcia, whose first name – Wolf – was remembered by nobody. Garcia, who preserved on his pale jaws a static ten days' growth of dark stubble which never developed into a beard, whose clothes consisted of a pair of dirty grey trousers, a limp shirt, and an unspeakable raincoat. Garcia, with his shock of unkempt brown hair, his dark impertinent eyes, his beautiful hands, and his complete unscrupulousness. Two years ago he had presented himself one morning at the door of Troy's studio in London. He had carried there a self-portrait in clay, wrapped about with wet and dirty clothes. He walked past her into the studio and unwrapped the clay head. Troy and Garcia stood looking at it in silence. Then she asked him his name and what he wanted. He told her – 'Garcia' – and he wanted to go on modelling, but had no money. Troy talked about the head, gave him twenty pounds, and never really got rid of him. He used to turn up, sometimes inconveniently, always with something to show her. In everything but clay he was quite inarticulate. It was as if he had been allowed only one medium of expression, but that an abnormally eloquent one. He was dirty, completely devoid of ordinary scruples, interested in nothing but his work. Troy helped him, and by and by people began to talk about his modelling. He began to work in stone. He was asked to exhibit with the New Phoenix Group, was given occasional commissions. He never had any money, and to most people he was entirely without charm, but to some women he was irresistible, and of this he took full advantage.

It was to Garcia that Troy went after she had set the pose. The others shifted their easels about, skirmishing for positions. Troy looked at Garcia's sketch in clay of the 'Comedy and Tragedy' for the

new cinema in Westminster. He had stood it on a high stool in the
south window. It was modelled on a little wooden platform with
four wheels, a substitute he had made for the usual turntable. The
two figures rose from a cylindrical base. Comedy was nude, but
Tragedy wore an angular robe. Above their heads they held the conventional masks. The general composition suggested flames. The
form was greatly simplified. The face of Comedy, beneath the grinning mask, was grave, but upon the face of Tragedy Garcia had
pressed a faint smile.

He stood scowling while Troy looked at his work.

'Well,' said Troy, 'it's all right.'

'I thought of – ' He stopped short, and with his thumb suggested
dragging the drape across the feet of Comedy.

'I wouldn't,' said Troy. 'Break the line up. But I've told you I
know nothing about this stuff. I'm a painter. Why did you come and
plant yourself here, may I ask?'

'Thought you wouldn't mind.' His voice was muffled and faintly
Cockney. 'I'll be clearing out in a fortnight. I wanted somewhere to
work.'

'So you said in your extraordinary note. Are you broke?'

'Yes.'

'Where are you going in a fortnight?'

'London. I've got a room to work in.'

'Where is it?'

'Somewhere in the East End, I think. It's an old warehouse. I
know a bloke who got them to let me use it. He's going to let me
have the address. I'll go for a week's holiday somewhere before I
begin work in London. I'll cast this thing there and then start on the
sculping.'

'Who's going to pay for the stone?'

'They'll advance me enough for that.'

'I see. It's coming along very well. Now attend to me, Garcia.'
Troy lowered her voice. 'While you're here you've got to behave
yourself. You know what I mean?'

'No.'

'Yes, you do. No nonsense with women. You and Sonia seem to
be sitting in each other's pockets. Have you been living together?'

'When you're hungry,' said Garcia, 'you eat.'

'Well, this isn't a restaurant and you'll please remember that. You understand? I noticed you making some sort of advance to Seacliff yesterday. That won't do, either. I won't have any bogus Bohemianism, or free love, or mere promiscuity at Tatler's End. It shocks the servants, and it's messy. All right?'

'OK,' said Garcia with a grin.

'The pose has altered,' said Katti Bostock from the middle of the studio.

'Yeah, that's right,' said Watt Hatchett. The others looked coldly at him. His Sydney accent was so broad as to be almost comic. One wondered if he could be doing it on purpose. It was not the custom at Troy's for new people to speak until they were spoken to. Watt was quite unaware of this and Troy, who hated rows, felt uneasy about him. He was so innocently impossible. She went to Katti's easel and looked from the bold drawing in black paint to the model. Then she went up to the throne and shoved Sonia's right shoulder down.

'Keep it on the floor.'

'It's a swine of a pose, Miss Troy.'

'Well, stick it a bit longer.'

Troy began to go round the work, beginning with Ormerin on the extreme left.

'Bit tied up, isn't it?' she said after a minute's silence.

'She is never for one moment still,' complained Ormerin. 'The foot moves, the shoulders are in a fidget continually. It is impossible for me to work – impossible.'

'Start again. The pose is right now. Get it down directly. You can do it.'

'My work has been abominable since three months or more. All this surrealism at Malaquin's. I cannot feel like that and yet I cannot prevent myself from attempting it when I am there. That is why I return to you. I am in a muddle.'

'Try a little ordinary study for a bit. Don't worry about style. It'll come. Take a new stretcher and make a simple statement.' She moved to Valmai Seacliff and looked at the flowing lines so easily laid down. Seacliff moved back, contriving to touch Ormerin's shoulder. He stopped working at once and whispered in her ear.

'I can understand French, Ormerin,' said Troy casually, still contemplating Seacliff's canvas. 'This is going quite well, Seacliff. I suppose the elongation of the legs is deliberate?'

'Yes, I see her like that. Long and slinky. They say people always paint like themselves, don't they?'

'Do they?' said Troy. 'I shouldn't let it become a habit.'

She moved on to Katti, who creaked back from her canvas. One of her shoes did squeak. Troy discussed the placing of the figure and then went on to Watt Hatchett. Hatchett had already begun to use solid paint, and was piling pure colour on his canvas.

'You don't usually start off like this, do you?'

'Naow, that's right, I don't, but I thought I'd give it a pop.'

'Was that, by any chance, because you could see Miss Bostock working in that manner?' asked Troy, not too unkindly. Hatchett grinned and shuffled his feet. 'You stick to your own ways for a bit,' advised Troy. 'You're a beginner still, you know. Don't try to acquire a manner till you've got a little more method. Is that foot too big or too small?'

'Too small.'

'Should that space there be wider or longer?'

'Longer.'

'Make it so.'

'Good oh, Miss Troy. Think that bit of colour there's all right?' asked Hatchett, regarding it complacently.

'It's perfectly good colour, but don't choke the pores of your canvas up with paint till you've got the big things settled. Correct your drawing and scrape it down.'

'Yeah, but she wriggles all the time. It's a fair nark. Look where the shoulder has shifted. See?'

'Has the pose altered?' inquired Troy at large.

'Naow!' said Sonia with vindictive mimicry.

'It's shifted a whole lot,' asserted Hatchett aggressively. 'I bet you anything you like – '

'Wait a moment,' said Troy.

'It's moved a little,' said Katti Bostock.

Troy sighed.

'Rest!' she said. 'No! Wait a minute.'

She took a stick of chalk from her overall pocket and ran it round the model wherever she touched the throne. The position of both legs, one flank, one hip, and one shoulder were thus traced on the boards. The blue drape was beneath the rest of the figure.

'Now you can get up.'

Sonia sat up with an ostentatious show of discomfort, reached out her hand for the kimono and shrugged herself into it. Troy pulled the drape out taut from the cushion to the floor.

'It'll have to go down each time with the figure,' she told the class.

'As it does in the little romance,' drawled Malmsley.

'Yes, it's quite feasible,' agreed Valmai Seacliff. 'We could try it. There's that Chinese knife in the lumber-room. May we get it, Miss Troy?'

'If you like,' said Troy.

'It doesn't really matter,' said Malmsley languidly getting to his feet.

'Where is it, Miss Seacliff?' asked Hatchett eagerly.

'On the top shelf in the lumber-room.'

Hatchett went into an enormous cupboard by the window, and after a minute or two returned with a long, thin-bladed knife. He went up to Malmsley's table and looked over his shoulder at the typescript. Malmsley moved away ostentatiously.

'Aw yeah, I get it,' said Hatchett. 'What a corker! Swell way of murdering somebody, wouldn't it be?' He licked his thumb and turned the page.

'I've taken a certain amount of trouble to keep those papers clean,' remarked Malmsley to no one in particular.

'Don't be so damned precious, Malmsley,' snapped Troy. 'Here, give me the knife, Hatchett, and don't touch other people's tools in the studio. It's not done.'

'Good oh, Miss Troy.'

Pilgrim, Ormerin, Hatchett and Valmai Seacliff began a discussion about the possibility of using the knife in the manner suggested by Malmsley's illustration. Phillida Lee joined in.

'Where would the knife enter the body?' asked Seacliff.

'Just here,' said Pilgrim, putting his hand on her back and keeping it there. 'Behind your heart. Valmai.'

She turned her head and looked at him through half-closed eyes. Hatchett stared at her. Malmsley smiled curiously. Pilgrim had turned rather white.

'Can you feel it beating?' asked Seacliff softly.

'If I move my hand – here.'

'Oh, come off it,' said the model violently. She walked over to Garcia. 'I don't believe you could kill anybody like that. Do you, Garcia?'

Garcia grunted unintelligibly. He, too, was staring at Valmai Seacliff.

'How would he know where to put the dagger?' demanded Katti Bostock suddenly. She drew a streak of background colour across her canvas.

'Can't we try it out?' asked Hatchett.

'If you like,' said Troy. 'Mark the throne before you move it.'

Basil Pilgrim chalked the position of the throne on the floor, and then he and Ormerin tipped it up. The rest of the class looked on with gathering interest. By following the chalked-out line on the throne they could see the spot where the heart would come, and after a little experiment found the plot of this spot on the underneath surface of the throne.

'Now, you see,' said Ormerin, 'the jealous wife would drive the knife through from underneath.'

'Incidentally taking the edge off,' said Basil Pilgrim.

'You could force it through the crack between the boards,' said Garcia suddenly, from the window.

'How? It'd fall out when she was shoved down.'

'No, it wouldn't. Look here.'

'Don't break the knife and don't damage the throne,' said Troy.

'I get you,' said Hatchett eagerly. 'The dagger's wider at the base. The boards would press on it. You'd have to hammer it through. Look, I'll bet you it could be done. There you are, I'll betcher.'

'Not interested, I'm afraid,' said Malmsley.

'Let's try,' said Pilgrim. 'May we, Troy?'

'Oh, do let's,' cried Phillida Lee. She caught up her enthusiasm with an apologetic glance at Malmsley. 'I adore bloodshed,' she added with a painstaking nonchalance.

'The underneath of the throne's absolutely filthy,' complained Malmsley.

'Pity if you spoiled your nice green pinny,' jeered Sonia.

Valmai Seacliff laughed.

'I don't propose to do so,' said Malmsley. 'Garcia can if he likes.'

'Go on,' said Hatchett. 'Give it a pop. I betcher five bob it'll work. Fair dinkum.'

'What does that mean?' asked Seacliff. 'You must teach me the language, Hatchett.'

'Too right I will,' said Hatchett with enthusiasm. 'I'll make a dinkum Aussie out of you.'

'God forbid,' said Malmsley. Sonia giggled.

'Don't you like Australians?' Hatchett asked her aggressively.

'Not particularly.'

'Well, I'll tell you one thing. Models at the school I went to in Sydney knew how to hold a pose for longer than ten minutes.'

'You don't seem to have taken advantage of it, judging by your drawing.'

'And they didn't get saucy with the students.'

'Perhaps they weren't all like you.'

'Sonia,' said Troy, 'that will do. If you boys are going to make your experiment, you'd better hurry up. We start again in five minutes.'

In the boards of the throne they found a crack that passed through the right spot. Hatchett slid the thin tip of the knife into it from underneath and shoved. By tapping the hilt of the dagger with an easel ledge, he forced the widening blade upwards through the crack. Then he let the throne back on to the floor. The blade projected wickedly through the blue chalk cross that marked the plot of Sonia's heart on the throne. Basil Pilgrim took the drape, laid it across the cushion, pulled it in taut folds down to the throne, and pinned it there.

'You see, the point of the knife is lower than the top of the cushion,' he said. It doesn't show under the drape.'

'What did I tell you?' said Hatchett.

Garcia strolled over and joined the group.

'Go into your pose, Sonia,' he said with a grin.

Sonia shuddered.

'Don't,' she said.

'I wonder if the tip should show under the left breast,' murmuring Malmsley. 'Rather amusing to have it in the drawing. With a cast shadow and a thin trickle of blood. Keep the whole thing black and white except for the little scarlet thread. After all, it is melodrama.'

'Evidently,' grunted Garcia.

'The point of suspension for the drape would have to be higher,' said Troy. 'It must be higher than the tip of the blade. You could do it. If your story was a modern detective novel, Malmsley, you could do a drawing of the knife as it is now.'

Malmsley smiled and began to sketch on the edge of his paper. Valmai Seacliff leant over him, her hands on his shoulders. Hatchett, Ormerin and Pilgrim stood round her, Pilgrim with his arm across her shoulder. Phillida Lee hovered on the outskirts of the little group. Troy, looking vaguely round the studio, said to herself that her worst forebodings were likely to be realized. Watt Hatchett was already at loggerheads with Malmsley and the model. Valmai was at her Cleopatra game, and there was Sonia in a corner with Garcia. Something in their faces caught Troy's attention. What the devil were they up to? Garcia's eyes were on the group round Malmsley. A curious smile lifted one corner of his mouth, and on Sonia's face, turned to him, the smile was reflected.

'You'll have to get that thing out now, Hatchett,' said Troy.

It took a lot of working and tugging to do this, but at last the knife was pulled out, the throne put back, and Sonia, with many complaints, took the pose again.

'Over more on the right shoulder,' said Katti Bostock.

Troy thrust the shoulder down. The drape fell into folds round the figure.

'Ow!' said Sonia.

'That is when the dagger goes in,' said Malmsley.

'Don't – you'll make me sick,' said Sonia.

Garcia gave a little chuckle.

'Right through the ribs and coming out under the left breast,' murmured Malmsley.

'Shut up!'

'Spitted like a little chicken.'

Sonia raised her head.

'I wouldn't be too damn funny, Mr Malmsley,' she said. 'Where do you get your ideas from, I wonder? Books? Or pictures?'

Malmsley's brush slipped from his fingers to the paper, leaving a trace of paint. He looked fixedly at Sonia, and then began to dab his drawing with a sponge. Sonia laughed.

'For God's sake,' said Katti Bostock, 'let's get the pose.'

'Quiet,' said Troy, and was obeyed. She set the pose, referring to the canvases. 'Now get down to it, all of you. The Phoenix Group Show opens on the 16th. I suppose most of us want to go up to London for it. Very well, I'll give the servants a holiday that week-end, and we'll start work again on the Monday.'

'If this thing goes decently,' said Katti, 'I want to put it in for the Group. If it's not done, it'll do for B. House next year.'

'I take it,' said Troy, 'you'll all want to go up for the Group's private view?'

'I don't,' said Garcia. 'I'll be pushing off for my holiday about then.'

'What about us?' asked Valmai Seacliff of Basil Pilgrim.

'What do you think, darling?'

' "Us"?' said Troy. ' "Darling"? What's all this?'

'We may as well tell them, Basil,' said Valmai sweetly. 'Don't faint, anybody. We got engaged last night.'

CHAPTER 4

Case for Mr Alleyn

Lady Alleyn knelt back on her gardening-mat and looked up at her son.

'I think we have done enough weeding for today, darling. You bustle off with that barrow-load and then we'll go indoors and have a glass of sherry and a chat. We've earned it.'

Chief Detective-Inspector Alleyn obediently trundled off down the path, tipped his barrow-load on the smudge fire, mopped his brow and went indoors for a bath. Half an hour later he joined his mother in the drawing-room.

'Come up to the fire, darling. There's the sherry. It's a bottle of the very precious for our last evening.'

'Ma'am,' said Alleyn, 'you are the perfect woman.'

'No, only the perfect mamma. I flatter myself I am a *very* good parent. You look charming in a dinner jacket, Roderick. I wish your brother had some of your finish. George always looks a little too hearty.'

'I like George,' said Alleyn.

'I quite like him, too,' agreed his mother.

'This is really a superlative wine. I wish it wasn't our last night, though. Three days with the Bathgates, and then my desk, my telephone, the smell of the yard, and old Fox beaming from ear to ear, bless him. Ah well, I expect I shall quite enjoy it once I'm there.'

'Roderick,' said Lady Alleyn, 'why wouldn't you come to Tatler's End House with me?'

'For the very good reason, little mum, that I should not have been welcomed.'

'How do you know?'

'Miss Troy doesn't like me.'

'Nonsense! She's a very intelligent young woman.'

'Darling!'

'The day I called I suggested she should dine with us while you were here. She accepted.'

'And put us off when the time came.'

'My dear man, she had a perfectly good excuse.'

'Naturally,' said Alleyn. 'She is, as you say, a very intelligent young woman.'

Lady Alleyn looked at the portrait head that hung over the mantelpiece.

'She can't dislike you very much, my dear. That picture gives the lie to your theory.'

'Aesthetic appreciation of a paintable object has nothing to do with personal preferences.'

'Bosh! Don't talk pretentious nonsense about things you don't understand.'

Alleyn grinned.

'I think you are being self-conscious and silly,' continued Lady Alleyn grandly.

'It's the lady that you should be cross about, not me.'

'I'm not cross, Roderick. Give yourself another glass of sherry. No, not for me.'

'Anyway,' said Alleyn, 'I'm glad you like the portrait.'

'Did you see much of her in Quebec?'

'Very little, darling. We bowed to each other at mealtimes and had a series of stilted conversations in the lounge. On the last evening she was there I took her to the play.'

'Was that a success?'

'No. We were very polite to each other.'

'Ha!' said Lady Alleyn.

'Mamma,' said Alleyn, 'you know I am a detective.' He paused, smiling at her. 'You look divine when you blush,' he added.

'Well, Roderick, I shan't deny that I would like to see you married.'

'She wouldn't dream of having me, you know. Put the idea out of your head, little mum. I very much doubt if I shall ever have another stilted conversation with Miss Agatha Troy.'

The head parlourmaid came in.

'A telephone call from London for Mr Roderick, m'lady.'

'From London?' asked Alleyn. 'Oh Lord, Clibborn, why didn't you say I was dead?'

Clibborn smiled the tolerant smile of a well-trained servant, and opened the door.

'Excuse me, please, Mamma,' said Alleyn, and went to the telephone.

As he unhooked the receiver, Alleyn experienced the little prick of foreboding that so often accompanies an unexpected long-distance call. It was the smallest anticipatory thrill and was succeeded at once by the unhappy reflection that probably Scotland Yard was already on his track. He was not at all surprised when a familiar voice said:

'Mr Alleyn?'

'That's me. Is it you, Watkins?'

'Yes, sir. Very pleasant to hear your voice again. The Assistant Commissioner would like to speak to you, Mr Alleyn.'

'Right!'

'Hullo, Mr Alleyn?' said a new voice.

'Hullo, sir.'

'You can go, Watkins.' A pause, and then: 'How are you, Rory?'

'Very fit, thanks, sir.'

'Ready for work?'

'Yes. Oh, rather!'

'Well now, look here. How do you feel about slipping into the saddle three days before you're due? There's a case cropped up a few miles from where you are, and the local people have called us in. It would save time and help the department if you could take over for us.'

'Certainly, sir,' said Alleyn, with a sinking heart. 'When?'

'Now. It's a homicide case. Take the details. Address, Tatler's End House.'

'*What!* I beg your pardon, sir. Yes?'

'A woman's been stabbed. Do you know the place, by any chance?'

'Yes, sir.'

'Thrrree minutes.'

'Extend the call, please. Are you there, Rory?'

'Yes,' said Alleyn. He noticed suddenly that the receiver was clammy.

'It belongs to the artist, Miss Agatha Troy.'

'I know.'

'You'll get the information from the local super – Blackman – who's there now. The model has been killed, and it looks like murder.'

'I – can't – hear.'

'The victim is an artist's model. I'll send Fox down with the other people and your usual kit. Much obliged. Sorry to drag you back before Monday.'

'That's all right, sir.'

'Splendid. I'll expect your report. Nice to see you again. Goodbye.'

'Goodbye, sir.'

Alleyn went back to the drawing-room.

'Well?' began his mother. She looked up at him, and in a moment was at his side. 'What's the matter, old man?'

'Nothing, ma'am. It was the Yard. They want me to take a case near here. It's at Tatler's End House.'

'But what is it?'

'Murder, it seems.'

'Roderick!'

'No, no. I thought that, too, for a moment. It's the model. I'll have to go at once. May I have the car?'

'Of course, darling.' She pressed a bell-push, and when Clibborn came, said: 'Mr Roderick's overcoat at once, Clibborn, and tell French to bring the car round quickly.' When Clibborn had gone she put her hand on Alleyn's. 'Please tell Miss Troy that if she would like to come to me – '

'Yes, darling. Thank you. But I must see what it's all about first. It's a case.'

'Well, you won't include Agatha Troy among your suspects, I hope?'

'If there's a question of that,' said Alleyn, 'I'll leave the service. Good night. Don't sit up. I may be late.'

Clibborn came in with his overcoat.

'Finish your sherry,' ordered his mother. He drank it obediently. 'And, Roderick, look in at my room, however late it is.'

He bowed, kissed her lightly, and went out to the car.

It was a cold evening with a hint of frost on the air. Alleyn dis-
missed the chauffeur and drove himself at breakneck speed towards
Tatler's End House. On the way, three vivid little pictures appeared,
one after another, in his mind. The wharf at Suva. Agatha Troy, in
her old smock and grey bags, staring out over the sea while the wind
whipped the short hair back from her face. Agatha Troy saying goodbye at night on the edge of the St Lawrence.

The headlights shone on rhododendrons and tree-trunks, and
then on a closed gate and the figure of a constable. A torch flashed
on Alleyn's face.

'Excuse me, sir – '

'All right. Chief Detective-Inspector Alleyn from the Yard.'

The man saluted.

'They're expecting you, sir.'

The gate swung open, and Alleyn slipped in his clutch. It was a
long winding drive, and it seemed an age before he pulled up before
a lighted door. A second constable met him and showed him into a
pleasant hall where a large fire burned.

'I'll tell the superintendent you've arrived, sir,' said the man, but
as he spoke, a door on Alleyn's left opened and a stout man with a
scarlet face came out.

'Hullo, hullo! This is very nice. Haven't seen you for ages.'

'Not for ages,' said Alleyn. They shook hands. Blackman had been
superintendent at Bossicote for six years, and he and Alleyn were
old acquaintances. 'I hope I haven't been too long.'

'You've been very quick indeed, Mr Alleyn. We only rang the
Yard half an hour ago. They told us you were staying with her ladyship. Come in here, will you?'

He led the way into a charming little drawing-room with pale-
grey walls and cerise-and-lemon-striped curtains.

'How much did they tell you from the Yard?'

'Only that a model had been knifed.'

'Yes. Very peculiar business. I don't mind telling you I'd have
liked to tackle it myself, but we've got our hands full with a big burglary case over at Ronald's Cross, and I'm short-staffed just now. So
the Chief Constable thought, all things considered, and you being so
handy, it'd better be the Yard. He's just gone. Sit down, and I'll give
you the story before we look at the body and so on. That suit you?'

'Admirably,' said Alleyn.

Blackman opened a fat pocketbook, settled his chins, and began.

'This property, Tatler's End House, is owned and occupied by Miss Agatha Troy, R.A., who returned here after a year's absence abroad, on September 3rd. During her absence the house was occupied by a Miss Katti Bostock, another painter. Miss Troy arranged by letter to take eight resident pupils from September to December, and all of these were already staying in the house when she arrived. There was also a Sonia Gluck, spinster aged 22, an artist's model, engaged by Miss Bostock for the coming term. The classes began officially on the 10th, but they had all been more or less working together since the 3rd. From the 10th to Friday the 16th they worked from the model every morning in the studio. On the 16th, three days ago, the class disbanded for the weekend, in order that members might attend a function in London. The servants were given Friday night off, and went to a cinema in Baxtonbridge. One student, Wolf Garcia, no permanent address, remained alone in the studio. The house was closed. Garcia is believed to have left on Saturday the 17th, the day before yesterday. Miss Troy returned on Saturday at midday and found Garcia had gone. The others came back on Sunday, yesterday, by car, and by the evening bus. This morning, September 19th, the class reassembled in the studio, which is a detached building situated about a hundred yards to the south-east of the rear eastward corner of the house. Here's the sketch plan of the house and studio,' said the superintendent in a more normal voice. 'And here's another of the studio interior.'

'Splendid,' said Alleyn, and spread them out before him on a small table. Mr Blackman coughed and took up the burden of his recital.

'At ten-thirty the class, with the exception of Garcia, who, as we have seen, had left, was ready to begin work. Miss Troy had given instructions that they were to start without her. This is her usual practice, except on the occasions when a new pose is to be set. The model lay down to resume the pose which she had been taking since September 10th. It was a recumbent position on her back. She lay half on a piece of silk material and half on the bare boards of the dais known as the model's "throne". The model was undraped. She lay first of all on her right side. One of the students, Miss Valmai Seacliff, of No. 8, Partington Mews, WC4, approached the model, placed her hands on Gluck's shoulders and thrust the left shoulder firmly over and down. This was the usual procedure. Gluck cried out "Don't!" as if in pain, but as she habitually objected to the pose, Miss Seacliff paid no attention, shifted her hands to the model's chest, and pressed down. Gluck made another sound, described by Miss Seacliff as a moan, and seemed to jerk and then relax. Miss Seacliff then said: "Oh, don't be such a fool, Sonia," and was about to rise from her stooping posture when she noticed that Gluck was in an abnormal condition. She called for the others to come. Miss Katti Bostock followed by two students, Mr Watt Hatchett, an Australian, and Mr Francis Ormerin, a Frenchman, approached the throne. Hatchett said: "She's taken a fit." Miss Bostock said: "Get out of the way." She examined the body. She states that the eyelids fluttered and the limbs jerked slightly. Miss Bostock attempted to raise Gluck. She placed her hand behind the shoulders and pulled. There was a certain amount of resistance, but after a few seconds the body came up suddenly. Miss Seacliff cried out loudly that there was blood on the blue silk drape. Mr Ormerin said: "Mong dew, the knife!" '

Mr Blackman cleared his throat and turned a page.

'It was then seen that a thin triangular blade protruded vertically through the drape. It appeared to be the blade of some sort of dagger that had been driven through a crack in the dais from underneath. It has not been moved. It seems that later on, when Miss Troy arrived, she stopped anybody from touching the dais as soon as she saw what had occurred. On examining Gluck a wound was discovered in the back somewhere about the position of the fourth rib and about three inches to the left of the spine. There was an effusion of blood. The blade was stained with blood. Miss Bostock attempted to staunch the wound with a rag. At this point Miss Troy arrived, and immediately sent Mr Basil Pilgrim, another student, to ring up the doctor. Dr Ampthill arrived ten minutes later and found life was extinct. Miss Troy states that Gluck died a few minutes after she – Miss Troy – arrived at the studio. Gluck made no statement before she died.'

Mr Blackman closed his notebook, and laid it on the table.

'That's just from notes,' he said modestly. 'I haven't got it down in a ship-shape report yet.'

'It is sufficiently clear,' said Alleyn. 'You might have been giving it to a jury.'

An expression of solemn complacency setded down among the superintendent's chins.

'Well,' he said, 'we haven't had a great deal of time. It's a curious business. We've taken statements from all this crowd, except, of course, the man called Garcia. He's gone, and we haven't got a line on him. That looks a bit funny on the face of it, but it seems he said he'd be leaving for a hiking trip on Saturday morning, and is due to turn up at some place in London in about a week's time. He left his luggage to be forwarded to this London address, and it had all gone when Miss Troy returned on Saturday about three o'clock. We're trying to get on to the carrier that called for it, but haven't got hold of anybody yet. It was all in the studio. It seems Garcia slept in the studio and had his gear there. I've got into touch with the police stations for fifty miles round and asked them to look out for this Garcia. Here's the description of him: Height – about five foot nine; sallow complexion, dark eyes, very thin. Thick dark hair, rather long. Usually dressed in old grey flannel trousers and a raincoat. Does not wear a hat. Probably carrying a rucksack containing painting materials. It seems he does a bit of sketching as well as sculping. We got that in the course of the statements made by the rest of this crowd. Will you look at the statements before you see anybody?'

Alleyn thought for moment.

'I'll see Miss Troy first,' he said. 'I have met her before.'

'Have you, really? I suppose with her ladyship being as you might say a neighbour – '

'The acquaintance is very slight,' said Alleyn. 'What about the doctors?'

'I said I'd let Ampthill know as soon as you came. He is the police surgeon. He heads the list in the directory, so Mr Pilgrim rang him first.'

'Very handy. Well, Mr Blackman, if you wouldn't mind getting hold of him while I see Miss Troy – '

'Right.'

'Fox and Co. ought to be here soon. We'll go and look at the scene of action when they arrive. Where is Miss Troy?'

'In the study. I'll take you there. It's across the hall.'

'Don't bother – I'll find my way.'

'Right you are – I'll ring the doctor and join you there. I've got the rest of the class penned up in the dining-room with a PC on duty. They're a rum lot and no mistake.' said Blackman, leading the way into the hall. 'Real artistic freaks. You know. There's the library door. See you in a minute.'

Alleyn crossed the hall, tapped on the door, and walked in.

It was a long room with a fireplace at the far end. The only light there was made by the flicker of flames on the book-lined walls. Coming out of the brightly lit hall, he was at first unable to see clearly and stood for a moment inside the door.

'Yes' said a quick voice from the shadows. 'Who is it? Do you want me?'

A slim, dark shape, outlined by a wavering halo of light, rose from a chair by the fire.

'It's me,' said Alleyn. 'Roderick Alleyn.'

'You!'

'I'm sorry to come in unannounced. I thought perhaps you would rather – '

'But – yes, please come in.'

The figure moved forward a little and held out a hand. Alleyn said apologetically.

'I'm coming as fast as I can. It's rather dark.'

'Oh!' There was a moment's pause, a movement, and then a shaded lamp came to life and he saw her clearly. She wore a long plain dress of a material that absorbed the light and gave off none. She looked taller than his remembrance of her. Her face was white under the short black hair. Alleyn took her hand, held it lightly for a second, and then moved to the fire.

'It was kind of you to come,' said Troy.

'No, it wasn't. I'm here on duty.'

She stiffened at once.

'I'm sorry. That was stupid of me.'

'If I was not a policeman,' Alleyn said, 'I think I should still have come. You could have brought about a repetition of our first meeting and sent me about my business.'

'Must you always remind me of my ill manners?'

'That was not the big idea. Your manners did not seem ill to me. May we sit down, please?'

'Do.'

They sat in front of the fire.

'Well,' said Troy, 'get out your notebook.'

Alleyn felt in the inside pocket of his dinner jacket.

'It's still there,' he said. 'The last time I used it was in New Zealand. Here we are. Have you had any dinner, by the way?'

'What's that got to do with it?'

'Come, come,' said Alleyn, 'you mustn't turn into a hostile witness before there's anything to be hostile about.'

'Don't be facetious. Oh damn! Rude again. Yes, thank you, I toyed with a chunk of athletic hen.'

'Good! A glass of port wouldn't do you any harm. Don't offer me any, please: I'm not supposed to drink on duty, unless it's with a sinister purpose. I suppose this affair has shaken you up a bit?'

Troy waited for a moment and then she said: 'I'm terrified of dead people.'

'I know,' said Alleyn. 'I was, at first. Before the war. Even now they are not quite a commonplace to me.'

'She was a silly little creature. More like a beautiful animal than a reasonable human. But to see her suddenly, like that – everything emptied away. She looked fairly astonished – that was all.'

'It's so often like that. Astonished, but sort of knowing. Are there any relatives to be informed?'

'I haven't the faintest idea. She lived alone – officially.'

'We'll have to try and find out.'

'What do you want me to do now?' asked Troy.

'I want you to bring this girl to life for me. I know the circumstances surrounding her death – the immediate circumstances – and as soon as my men get here from London, I'll look at the studio. In the meantime I'd like to know if any possible explanation for this business has occurred to you. I must thank you for having kept the place untouched. Not many people think like that on these occasions.'

'I've no explanation, reasonable or fantastic, but there's one thing you ought to know at once. I told the class they were not to speak of it to the police. I knew they'd all give exaggerated accounts of it, and thought it better that the first statement should come from me.'

'I see.'

'I'll make the statement now.'

'An official statement?' asked Alleyn lightly.

'If you like. When you move the throne you will find that a dagger has been driven through the boards from underneath.'

'Shall we?'

'Yes. You don't say 'How do you know?''

'Well, I expect you're going on to that, aren't you?'

'Yes. On the 10th, the first morning when I set this pose, I arranged it to look as if the figure had been murdered in exactly this way. Cedric Malmsley, one of my students, was doing a book illustration of a similar incident.' She paused for a moment, looking into the fire. 'During the rest they began arguing about the possibilities of committing a crime in this way. Hatchett, another student, got a knife that is in the junk-room, and shoved it through from underneath. Ormerin helped him. The throne was roughly knocked up for me in the village and the boards have warped apart. The blade is much narrower at the tip than at the hilt. The tip went through easily, but he hammered at the hilt to force it right up. The boards gripped the wider end. You will see all that when you look at it.'

'Yes.' Alleyn made a note in his book and waited.

'The drape was arranged to hide the knife and it all looked quite convincing. Sonia was – she was quite – frightened. Hatchett pulled the knife out – it needed some doing – and we put everything straight again.'

'What happened to the knife?'

'Let me see. I think Hatchett put it away.'

'From a practical point of view, how could you be sure that the knife would come through at exactly the right place to do what it has done?'

'The position of the figure is chalked on the floor. When she took the pose, Sonia fitted her right hip and leg into the chalk marks, and then slid down until the whole of her right side was on the floor. One of the students would move her until she was inside the marks. Then she let the torso go over until her left shoulder touched the floor. The left hip was off the ground. I could draw it for you.'

Alleyn opened his notebook at a clean page and handed it to her with his pencil. Troy swept a dozen lines down and gave it back to him.

'Wonderful!' said Alleyn, 'to be able to do that – so easily.'

'I'm not likely to forget that pose,' said Troy dryly.

'What about the drape? Didn't that cover the chalk-marks?'

'Only in places. It fell from a suspension-point on the cushion to the floor. As she went down, she carried it with her. The accidental folds that came that way were more interesting than any laboured arrangement. When the students made their experiment they found the place where the heart would be, quite easily, inside the trace on the floor. The crack passed through this point. Hatchett put a pencil through the crack and they marked the position on the underside of the throne.'

'Is there any possibility that they repeated this performance for some reason on Friday and forgot to withdraw the dagger?'

'I thought of that at once, naturally. I asked them. I begged them to tell me.' Troy moved her long hands restlessly. 'Anything,' she said, 'anything rather than the thought of one of them deliberately – there's no reason. I – I can't bear to think of it. As if a beastly unclean thing was in one of their minds, behind all of us. And then, suddenly, crawled out and did this.'

He heard her draw in her breath sharply. She turned her head away.

Alleyn swore softly.

'Oh, don't pay any attention to me,' said Troy impatiently. 'I'm all right. About Friday. We had the morning class as usual from ten o'clock to twelve-thirty, with that pose. We all lunched at one. Then we went up to London. The private view of the Phoenix Group Show was on Friday night, and several of us had things in it. Valmai Seacliff and Basil Pilgrim, who were engaged to be married, left in his two-seater immediately after lunch. Neither of them was going to the private view. They were going to his people's place, to break the engagement news, I imagine. Katti Bostock and I left in my car at about half-past two. Hatchett, Phillida Lee and Ormerin caught the three o'clock bus. Malmsley wanted to do some work, so he stayed behind until six, went up in the six-fifteen bus and joined us later at the show. I believe Phillida Lee and Hatchett had a meal together and went to a show. She took him to her aunt's house in London for the weekend, I fancy.'

'And the model?'

'Caught the three o'clock bus. I don't know where she went or what she did. She came back with Malmsley, Ormerin, Hatchett and Phillida Lee by yesterday evening's bus.'

'When Friday's class broke up, did you all leave the studio together and come up to the house?'

'I – let me think for a moment. No, I can't remember; but usually we come up in dribbles. Some of them go on working, and they have to clean up their palettes and so on. Wait a second. Katti and I came up together before the others. That's all I can tell you.'

'Would the studio be locked before you went to London'

'No.' Troy turned her head and looked squarely at him.

'Why not?' asked Alleyn.

'Because of Garcia.'

'Blackman told me about Garcia. He stayed behind, didn't he?'

'Yes.'

'Alone?'

'Yes,' said Troy unhappily. 'Quite alone.'

There was a tap at the door. It opened and Blackman appeared, silhouetted against the brightly lit hall.

'The doctor's here, Mr Alleyn, and I think the car from London is just arriving.'

'Right,' said Alleyn. 'I'll come.'

Blackman moved away. Alleyn rose and looked down at Troy in her armchair.

'Perhaps I may see you again before I go?'

'I'll be here or with the others in the dining-room. It's a bit grim sitting round there under the eye of the village constable.'

'I hope it won't be for very long,' said Alleyn.

Troy suddenly held out her hand.

'I'm glad it's you,' she said.

They shook hands.

'I'll try to be as inoffensive as possible,' Alleyn told her.

'Goodbye for the moment.'

CHAPTER 5

Routine

When Alleyn returned to the hall he found it full of men. The Scotland Yard officials had arrived, and with their appearance the case, for the first time, seemed to take on a familiar complexion. The year he had spent away from England clicked back into the past at the sight of those familiar overcoated and bowler-hatted figures with their cases and photographic impedimenta. There, beaming at him, solid, large, the epitome of horse-sense, was old Fox.

'Very nice indeed to have you with us again, sir.'

'Fox, you old devil, how are you?'

And there, looking three degrees less morose, was Detective-Sergeant Bailey, and behind him Detective-Sergeant Thompson. A gruff chorus began:

'Very nice indeed – '

A great shaking of hands, while Superintendent Blackman looked on amicably, and then a small, clean, bald man came forward. Blackman introduced him.

'Inspector Alleyn, this is Dr Ampthill, our divisional surgeon.'

'How d'you do, Mr Alleyn? Understand you want to see me. Sorry if I've kept you waiting.'

'I've not long arrived,' said Alleyn. 'Let's have a look at the scene of action, shall we?'

Blackman led the way down the hall to a side passage at the end of which there was a door. Blackman unlocked it and ushered them through. They were in the garden. The smell of box borders came up from their feet. It was very dark.

'Shall I lead the way?' suggested Blackman.

A long pencil of light from a torch picked up a section of flagged path. They tramped along in single file. Tree-trunks started up out of the darkness, leaves brushed Alleyn's cheek. Presently a rectangle of deeper dark loomed up.

Blackman said. 'You there, Sligo?'

'Yes, sir,' said a voice close by.

There was a jangle of keys, the sound of a door opening.

'Wait till I find the light switch,' said Blackman. 'Here we are.'

The lights went up. They walked round the wooden screen inside the door, and found themselves in the studio.

Alleyn's first impression was of a reek of paint and turpentine, and of a brilliant and localized glare. Troy had installed a high-powered lamp over the throne. This lamp was half shaded, so that it cast all its light on the throne, rather as the lamp above an operating-table is concentrated on the patient. Blackman had only turned on one switch, so the rest of the studio was in darkness. The effect at the moment could scarcely have been more theatrical. The blue drape, sprawled across the throne, was so brilliant that it hurt the eyes. The folds fell sharply from the cushion into a flattened mass. In the middle, stupidly irrelevant, was a spike. It cast a thin shadow irregularly across the folds of the drape. On the margin of this picture, disappearing abruptly into shadow, was a white mound.

'The drapery and the knife haven't been touched since the victim died,' explained Blackman. 'Of course, they disarranged the stuff a bit when they hauled her up.'

'Of course,' said Alleyn. He walked over to the throne and examined the blade of the knife. It was rather like an oversized packing-needle, sharp, three-edged, and greatly tapered towards the point. It was stained a rusty brown. At the base, where it pierced the drape, there was the same discoloration, and in one or two of the folds small puddles of blood had seeped through the material and dried. Alleyn glanced at Dr Ampthill.

'I suppose there would be an effusion of blood when they pulled her off the knife?'

'Oh yes, yes. The bleeding would probably continue until death. I understand that beyond lifting her away from the knife, they did not move her until she died. When I arrived the body was where it is now.'

He turned to the sheeted mound that lay half inside the circle of light.

'Shall I?'

'Yes, please,' said Alleyn.

Dr Ampthill drew away the white sheet.

Troy had folded Sonia's hands over her naked breast. The shadow cut sharply across the wrists so that the lower half of the torso was lost. The shoulders, hands and head were violently lit. The lips were parted rigidly, showing the teeth. The eyes were only half closed. The plucked brows were raised as if in astonishment.

'Rigor mortis is well established,' said the doctor. 'She was apparently a healthy woman, and this place was well heated. The gas fire was not turned off until some time after she died. She has been dead eleven hours.'

'Have you examined the wound, Dr Ampthill?'

'Superficially. The knife-blade was not absolutely vertical, evidently. It passed between the fourth and fifth ribs, and no doubt pierced the heart.'

'Let us have a look at the wound.'

Alleyn slid his long hands under the rigid body and turned it on its side. The patches of sunburn showed clearly on the back. About three inches to the left of the spine was a dark puncture. It looked very small and neat in spite of the traces of blood that surrounded it.

'Ah, yes,' said Alleyn. 'As you say. We had better have a photograph of this. Bailey, you go over the body for prints. You'd better tackle the drape, and the knife, and the top surface of the throne. Not likely to prove very useful, I'm afraid, but do your best.'

While Thompson set up his camera, Alleyn turned up the working-lamps and browsed about the studio. Fox joined him.

'Funny sort of case, sir,' said Fox. 'Romantic.'

'Good heavens, Fox, what a macabre idea of romance you've got.'

'Well, sensational,' amended Fox. 'The papers will make a big thing of it. We'll have them all down in hordes before the night's over.'

'That reminds me – I must send a wire to the Bathgates. I'm due there tomorrow. To business, Brer Fox. Here we have the studio as it was when the class assembled this morning. Paint set out on the palettes, you see. Canvases on all the easels. We've got seven versions of the pose.'

'Very useful, I dare say,' conceded Fox. 'Or, at any rate, the ones that look like something human may come in handy. That affair over on your left looks more like a set of worms than a naked female. I suppose it *is* meant for the deceased, isn't it?'

'I think so,' said Alleyn. 'The artist is probably a surrealist or a vorticalist or something.' He inspected the canvas and the paint-table in front of it.

'Here we are. The name's on the paintbox. Phillida Lee. It is a rum bit of work, Fox, no doubt of it. This big thing next door is more in our line. Very solid and simple.'

He pointed to Katti Bostock's enormous canvas.

'Bold,' said Fox. He put on his spectacles and stared blankly at the picture.

'You get the posture of the figure very well there,' said Alleyn.

They moved to Cedric Malmsley's table.

'This, I think, must be the illustrator,' continued Alleyn. 'Yes – here's the drawing for the story.'

'Good God!' exclaimed Fox, greatly scandalized. 'He's made a pic-ture of the girl after she was killed.'

'No, no. That was the original idea for the pose. He's merely added a dagger and the dead look. Here's the portfolio with all the drawings. H'm, very volup. and Beardsley, with a slap of modern thrown in. Hullo!' Alleyn had turned to a delicate watercolour in which three medieval figures mowed a charming field against a background of hayricks, pollard willows, and a turreted palace. 'That's rum!' muttered Alleyn.

'What's up, Mr Alleyn?'

'It looks oddly familiar. One half of the old brain functioning a fraction ahead of the other, perhaps. Or perhaps not. No matter. Look here, Brer Fox, I think before we go any further I'd better tell you as much as I know about the case.' And Alleyn repeated the gist of Blackman's report and of his conversations with Troy. 'This, you see,' he ended, 'is the illustration for the story. It was to prove the possibility of murdering someone in this manner that they made the experiment with the dagger, ten days ago.'

'I see,' said Fox. 'Well, somebody's proved it now all right, haven't they?'

'Yes,' agreed Alleyn. 'It is proved – literally, up to the hilt.'

'Cuh!' said Fox solemnly.

'Malmsley has represented the dagger as protruding under the left breast, you see. I suppose he thought he'd add the extra touch of what *you'd* call romance, Brer Fox. The scarlet thread of gore is rather effective in a meretricious sort of way. Good Lord, this is a queer show and no mistake.'

'Here's what I call a pretty picture, now,' said Fox approvingly. He had moved in front of Valmai Seacliff's canvas. Exaggeratedly slender, the colour scheme a light sequence of blues and pinks.

'Very elegant,' said Fox.

'A little too elegant,' said Alleyn. 'Hullo! Look at this.'

Across Francis Ormerin's watercolour drawing ran an ugly streak of dirty blue, ending in a blob that had run down the paper. The drawing was ruined.

'Had an accident, seemingly.'

'Perhaps. This student's stool is overturned, you'll notice, Fox. Some of the water in his paint-pot has slopped over and one of his brushes is on the floor.'

Alleyn picked up the brush and dabbed it on the china palette. A half-dry smudge of dirty blue showed.

'I see him or her preparing to flood a little of this colour on the drawing. He receives a shock, his hand jerks sideways and the brush streaks across the paper. He jumps up, overturning his stool and jolting the table. He drops the brush on the floor. Look, Fox. There are signs of the same sort of disturbance everywhere. Notice the handful of brushes on the table in front of the big canvas – I think that must be Katti Bostock's – I remember her work. Those brushes have been put down suddenly on the palette. The handles are messed in paint. Look at this very orderly array of tubes and brushes over here. The student has dropped a tube of blue paint and then trodden on it. Here are traces leading to the throne. It's a man's shoe, don't you think? He's tramped about all over the place, leaving a blue painty trail. The modern lady – Miss Lee – has overturned a bottle of turpentine, and it's run into her paintbox. There are even signs of disturbance on the illustrator's table. He has put a wet brush down on the very clean typescript. The place is like a first lesson in detection.'

'But beyond telling us they all got a start when the affair occurred, it doesn't appear to lead us anywhere,' said Fox. 'Not on the face of it.' He turned back to Seacliff's canvas and examined it with placid approval.

'You seem very taken with Miss Seacliff's effort,' said Alleyn.

'Eh?' Fox transferred his attention sharply to Alleyn. 'Now then, sir, how do you make out the name of this artist?'

'Rather prettily, Fox. This is the only outfit that is quite in order. Very neat everything is, you'll notice. Tidy box, clean brushes laid down carefully by the palette, fresh paint-rag all ready to use. I make a long guess that it belongs to Valmai Seacliff, because Miss Seacliff was with the model when she got her quietus. There is no reason why Miss Seacliff's paraphernalia should show signs of disturbance. In a sense, Miss Seacliff killed Sonia Gluck. She pressed her naked body down on the knife. Not a very pleasant reflection for Miss Seacliff now, unless she happens to be a murderess. Yes, I think this painting is hers.'

'Very neat bit of reasoning, chief. Lor', here's a mess.' Fox bent over Watt Hatchett's open box. It overflowed with half-used tubes of oil-colour, many of them without caps. A glutinous mess, to which all sorts of odds and ends adhered, spread over the trays and brushes. Cigarette butts, matches, bits of charcoal, were mixed up with fragments of leaves and twigs and filthy scraps of rag.

'This looks like chronic muck,' said Fox.

'It does indeed.' From the sticky depths of a tin tray Alleyn picked out a fragment of a dried leaf and smelt it.

'Blue gum,' he said. 'This will be the Australian, I suppose. Funny. He must have collected that leaf sketching in the bush, half the world away. I know this youth. He joined our ship with Miss Troy at Suva. Travelled second at her expense.'

'Fancy that,' said Fox placidly. 'Then you know this Miss Troy, sir?'

'Yes. Now you see, even he appears to have put his hand down on his palette. He'd hardly do that in normal moments.'

'We've finished, sir,' said the photographic expert.

'Right.'

Alleyn went over to the throne. The body lay as it was when he first saw it. He looked at it thoughtfully, remembering what Troy had said: 'I'm always frightened of dead people.'

'She was very lovely,' said Alleyn gently. He covered the body again. 'Carry her over to that couch. It's a divan-bed, I fancy. She can be taken away now. You'll do the post-mortem tomorrow, I suppose, Dr Ampthill?'

'First thing,' said the doctor briskly. 'The mortuary car is outside in the lane now. This studio is built into the brick wall that divides the garden from the lane. I thought it would save a lot of trouble and difficulty if we opened that window, backed the car up to it, and lifted the stretcher through.'

'Over there?'

Alleyn walked over to the window in the south wall. He stooped and inspected the floor.

'This is where the modelling fellow, Garcia, did his stuff. Bits of clay all over the place. His work must have stood on the tall stool here, well in the light. Wait a moment.'

He flashed his pocket-torch along the sill. It was scored by several cross-scratches.

'Someone else has had your idea, Dr Ampthill,' said Alleyn. He pulled a pair of gloves from his overcoat pocket, put them on, and opened the window. The light from the studio shone on the whole body of a mortuary van drawn up in the lane outside. The air smelt cold and dank. Alleyn shone his torch on the ground under the window-sill. He could see clearly the print of car tyres in the soft ground under the window.

'Look here, Mr Blackman.'

Blackman joined him.

'Yes,' he said. 'Someone's backed a car across the lane under the window. Miss Troy says the carrier must have called for this Mr Garcia's stuff on Saturday morning. The maids say nobody came to the house about it. Well now, suppose Garcia left instructions for them to come straight to this window? Eh? How about that? He'd help them put the stuff through the window on to the van and then push off himself to wherever he was going.'

'On his walking tour,' finished Alleyn. 'You're probably right. Look here, if you don't mind, I think we'll take the stretcher out through the door and along the path. Perhaps there's a door in the wall somewhere. Is there?'

'Well, the garage yard is not far off. We could take it through the yard into the lane, and the van could go along and meet them there.'

'I think it would be better.'

Blackman called through the window.

'Hullo there! Drive along to the back entrance and send the stretcher in from there. Keep over on the far side of the lane.'

'OK, super,' said a cheerful voice.

'Sligo, you go along and show the way.'

The constable at the door disappeared, and in a minute or two returned with two men and a stretcher. They carried Sonia's body out into the night.

'Well, I'll push off,' said Dr Ampthill.

'I'd like to get away, too, if you'll let me off, Mr Alleyn,' said Blackman. 'I'm expecting a report at the station on this other case. Two of my chaps are down with flu and I'm rushed off my feet. I needn't say we'll do everything we can. Use the station whenever you want to.'

'Thank you so much. I'll worry you as little as possible. Good night.'

The door slammed and the voices died away in the distance. Alleyn turned to Fox, Bailey and Thompson.

'The old team.'

'That's right, sir,' said Bailey. 'Suits us all right.'

'Well,' said Alleyn, 'it's always suited me. Let's get on with it. You've got your photographs and prints. Now we'll up-end the throne. Everything's marked, so we can get it back. Let me take a final look at the drape. Yes. You see, Fox, it fell taut from the cushion to the floor, above the point of the knife. Nobody would dream of disturbing it, I imagine. As soon as Miss Seacliff pressed the model over, the drape went with her, pulling away the drawing-pin that held it to the boards. That's all clear enough. Over with the throne.'

They turned the dais on its side. The light shone through the cracks in the roughly built platform. From the widest of these cracks projected the hilt of the dagger. It was a solid-looking round handle, bound with tarnished wire and protected by a crossbar guard. One side of the guard actually dug into the platform. The other just cleared it. The triangular blade had bitten into the edge of the planks. The end of the hilt was shiny.

'It's been hammered home at a slight angle, so that the blade would be at right-angles to the inclined plane of the body. It's an ingenious, dirty, deliberated bit of work, this. Prints, please, Bailey, and a photograph. Go over the whole of the under-surface. You won't get anything, I'm afraid.'

While Bailey and Thompson worked, Alleyn continued his tour of the room. He pulled back the cover of the divan and saw an unmade bed beneath it. 'Bad mark for Mr Garcia.' Numbers of stretched canvases stood with their faces to the wall. Alleyn began to inspect them. He thought he recognized a large picture of a trapeze artiste in pink tights and spangles as the work of Katti Bostock. That round, high-cheeked face was the one he had seen dead a few minutes ago. The head and shoulders had been scraped down with a knife. He turned another big canvas round and exclaimed softly.

'What's up, sir?' asked Fox.

'Look.'

It was a portrait of a girl in a green velvet dress. She stood, very erect, against a white wall. The dress fell in austere folds about the feet. It was most simply done. The hands looked as though they had been put down with twelve direct touches. The form of the girl shone through the heavy dress, in great beauty. It was painted with a kind of quiet thoughtfulness.

But across the head where the paint was wet, someone had scrubbed a rag, and scratched with red paint an idiotic semblance of a face with a moustache.

'Lor',' said Fox, 'is that a modern idea, too, sir?'

'I hardly think so,' murmured Alleyn. 'Good God, Fox, what a perfectly filthy thing to do. Don't you see, somebody's wiped away the face while the paint was wet, and then daubed this abortion on top of the smudge. Look at the lines of paint – you can see a kind of violence in them. The brush has been thrust savagely at the canvas so that the tip has spread. It's as if a nasty child had done it in a fit of temper. A stupid child.'

'I wonder who painted the picture, sir. If it's a portrait of this girl Sonia Gluck, it looks as if there's been a bit of spite at work. By gum, it'd be a rum go if the murderer did it.'

'I don't think this was Soma,' said Alleyn. 'There's a smudge of blonde hair left. Sonia Gluck was dark. As for the painter – ' He paused. 'I don't think there's much doubt about that. The painter was Agatha Troy.'

'You can pick the style, can you?'

'Yes.'

With a swift movement Alleyn turned the canvas to the wall. He lit a cigarette and squatted on his heels.

'Let us take what used to be called a "lunar" at the case. In a little while I must start interviewing people, but I'd like you fellows to get as clear an idea as possible of the case as we know it. At the moment we haven't got so much as a smell of motive. Very well. Eight students, the model, and Miss Troy have used this studio every morning from Saturday the 10th until last Friday, the 16th. On Friday they used it until twelve-thirty, came away in dribbles, lunched at the house, and then, at different intervals, all went away with the exception of Wolf Garcia, a bloke who models and sculps. He stayed behind, saying that he would be gone when they returned on Sunday. The studio was not locked at any time, unless by Garcia, who slept in it. They reopened this morning with this tragedy. Garcia and his belongings had gone. That's all. Any prints, Bailey?'

'There's a good many blue smears round the edge, sir, but it's unplaned wood underneath, and we can't do much with it. It looks a bit as if someone had mopped it up with a painty rag.'

'There's a chunk of paint-rag on the floor there. Is it dusty?'

'Yes, thick with it.'

'Possibly it was used for mopping up. Have a go at it.'

Alleyn began to prowl round the back of the throne.

'Hullo! More grist for the mill.' He pointed to a strip of wood lying in a corner of the studio. 'Covered with indentations. It's the ledge off an easel. That's what was used for hammering. Take it next, Bailey. Let's find an easel without a ledge. Detecting is so simple when you only know how. Mr Hatchett has no ledge on his easel – therefore Mr Hatchett is a murderer. Q.E.D. This man is clever. Oh, lawks-a-mussy me, I suppose I'd better start off on the statements. How goes it, Bailey?'

'This paint-rag's a mucky bit of stuff,' grumbled Bailey. 'It's been used for dusting all right. You can see the smudges on the platform. Same colour. I thought I might get a print off some of the smears of paint on the rag. They're still tacky in places. Yes, here's something. I'll take this rag back and have a go at it, sir.'

'Right. Now the ledge.'

Bailey used his insufflator on the strip of wood.

'No,' he said, after a minute or two. 'It's clean.'

'All right. We'll leave the studio to these two now, Fox. Try to get us as full a record of footprints as you can, Bailey. Go over the whole show. I can't tell you what to look out for. Just do your stuff. And, by the way, I want photographs of the area round the window and the tyre-prints outside. You'd better take a cast of them and look out for any other manifestations round about them. If you come across any keys, try them for prints. Lock the place up when you've done. Good sleuthing.'

Fox and Alleyn returned to the house.

'Well, Brer Fox,' said Alleyn on the way, 'how goes it with everybody?'

'The Yard's still in the same old place, sir. Pretty busy lately.'

'What a life! Fox, I think I'll see Miss Valmai Seacliff first. On the face of it she's a principal witness.'

'What about Miss Troy, sir?' asked Fox.

Alleyn's voice came quietly out of the darkness:

'I've seen her. Just before you came.'

'What sort of a lady is she?'

'I like her,' said Alleyn. 'Mind the step. Here's the side door. I suppose we can use it. Hullo! Look here. Fox.'

He paused, his hand on Fox's arm. They were close by a window. The curtains had been carelessly drawn and a wide band of light streamed through the gap. Alleyn stood a little to one side of this light and looked into the room. Fox joined him. They saw a long refectory table at which eight people sat. In the background, half in shadow, loomed the figure of a uniformed constable. Seven of the people round the table appeared to listen to the eighth, who was Agatha Troy. The lamplight was full on her face. Her lips moved rapidly and incisively; she looked from one attentive face to the other. No sound of her voice came to Alleyn and Fox, but it was easy to see that she spoke with urgency. She stopped abruptly and looked round the table as if she expected a reply. The focus of attention shifted. Seven faces were turned towards a thin, languid-looking young man with a blond beard. He seemed to utter a single sentence, and at once a stocky woman with black straight hair cut in a bang, sprang to her feet to answer him angrily. Troy spoke again. Then nobody moved. They all sat staring at the table.

'Come on,' whispered Alleyn.

He opened the side door and went along the passage to a door on the left. He tapped on this door. The policeman answered it.

'All right,' said Alleyn quietly, and walked straight in, followed by Fox and the constable. The eight faces round the table turned like automatons.

'Please forgive me for barging in like this,' said Alleyn to Troy.

'It's all right,' said Troy. 'This is the class. We were talking – about Sonia.' She looked round the table. 'This is Mr Roderick Alleyn,' she said.

'Good evening,' said Alleyn generally. 'Please don't move. If you don't mind, I think Inspector Fox and I will join you for a moment. I shall have to ask you all the usual sort of things, you know, and we may as well get it over. May we bring up a couple of chairs?'

Basil Pilgrim jumped up and brought a chair to the head of the table.

'Don't worry about me, sir,' said Fox. 'I'll just sit over here, thank you.'

He settled himself in a chair by the sideboard. Alleyn sat at the head of the table, and placed his notebook before him.

'The usual thing,' he said, looking pleasantly round the table, 'is to interview people severally. I think I shall depart from routine for once and see if we can't work together. I have got your names here, but I don't know which of you is which. I'll just read them through, and if you don't mind – '

He glanced at his notes.

'Reminiscent of a roll-call, I'm afraid, but here goes. Miss Bostock?'

'Here,' said Katti Bostock.

'Thank you. Mr Hatchett?'

'That's me.'

'Miss Phillida Lee?'

Miss Lee made a plaintive murmuring sound. Malmsley said: 'Yes.' Pilgrim said: 'Here.' Valmai Seacliff merely turned her head and smiled.

'That's that,' said Alleyn. 'Now then. Before we begin I must tell you that in my opinion there is very little doubt that Miss Sonia Gluck has been deliberately done to death. Murdered.'

They seemed to go very still.

'Now, as you all must realize, she was killed by precisely the means which you discussed and worked out among yourselves ten days ago. The first question I have to put to you is this. Has any one of you discussed the experiment with the dagger outside this class? I want you to think very carefully. You have been scattered during the weekend and it is possible, indeed very likely, that you may have talked about the pose, the model, and the experiment with the knife. This is extremely important, and I ask you to give me a deliberated answer.'

He waited for quite a minute.

'I take it that none of you have spoken of this matter, then,' said Alleyn.

Cedric Malmsley, leaning back in his chair, said: 'Just a moment.'

'Yes, Mr Malmsley?'

'I don't know, I'm sure, if it's of any interest,' drawled Malmsley, 'but Garcia and I talked about it on Friday afternoon.'

'After the others had gone up to London?'

'Oh, yes. I went down to the studio, you see, after lunch. I did some work there. Garcia was messing about with his stuff. He's usually rather sour when he's working, but on Friday he babbled away like the brook.'

'What about?'

'Oh,' said Malmsley vaguely, 'women and things. He's drearily keen on women, you know. Tediously oversexed.' He turned to the others. 'Did you know he and Sonia were living together in London?'

'I always said they were,' said Valmai Seacliff.

'Well, my sweet, it seems you were right.'

'I told you, Seacliff, didn't I?' began Phillida Lee excitedly. 'You remember?'

'Yes. But I thought so long before that.'

'Did you pursue this topic?' asked Alleyn.

'Oh, no, we talked about you, Seacliff.'

'About me?'

'Yes. We discussed your engagement, and your virtue and so on.'

'Very charming of you,' said Basil Pilgrim angrily.

'Oh, we agreed that you were damned lucky and so on. Garcia turned all knowing, and said – '

'Is this necessary – ' demanded Pilgrim, of Alleyn.

'Not at the moment, I think,' said Alleyn. 'How did you come to discuss the experiment with the dagger, Mr Malmsley?'

'Oh, that was when we talked about Sonia. Garcia looked at my drawing and asked me if I'd ever felt like killing my mistress just for the horror of doing it.'

CHAPTER 6

Sidelight on Sonia

'And was that all?' inquired Alleyn, after a rather deadly little pause.

'Oh, yes,' said Cedric Malmsley, and lit a cigarette. 'I just thought I'd better mention it.'

'Thank you. It was just as well. Did he say anything else that could possibly have a bearing on this affair?'

'I don't think so. Oh, he did say Sonia wanted him to marry her. Then he began talking about Seacliff, you know.'

'Couple of snotty little bounders,' grunted Katti Bostock unexpectedly.

'Oh, I don't think so,' said Malmsley, with an air of sweet reasonableness. 'Seacliff likes being discussed, don't you, my angel? She knows she's simply lousy with It.'

'Don't be offensive, please, Malmsley,' said Pilgrim dangerously.

'Good heavens! Why so sour? I thought you'd like to know we appreciated her.'

'That will do, Malmsley,' said Troy very quietly.

Alleyn said: 'When do you leave the studio on Friday afternoon, Mr Malmsley?'

'At five. I kept an eye on the time because I had to bath and change and catch the six o'clock bus.'

'You left Mr Garcia still working?'

'Yes. He said he wanted to pack up the clay miniature ready to send it up to London the next morning.'

'He didn't begin to pack it while you were there?'

'Well, he got me to help him carry in a zinc-lined case from the junk-room. He said it would do quite well.'

'He would,' said Troy grimly. 'I paid fifteen shillings for that case.'

'How would it be managed?' asked Alleyn. 'Surely a clay model is a ticklish thing to transport?'

'He'd wrap masses of damp cloths round it,' explained Troy.

'How about lifting it? Wouldn't it be very heavy?'

'Oh, he'd thought all that out,' said Malmsley, yawning horribly. 'We put the case on a tall stool in the window with the open end sideways, beside the tall stool he worked on. The thing was on a platform with wheels. He just had to wheel it into the case and fill the case with packing.'

'How about getting it into the van?'

'Dear me. Isn't this all rather tedious?'

'Extremely. A concise answer would enable us to move on to a more interesting narrative.'

Troy gave an odd little snort of laughter.

'Well, Mr Malmsley?' said Alleyn.

'Garcia said the lorry would back into the window from the lane outside. The sill is only a bit higher than the stool. He said they'd be able to drag the case on to the sill and get it in the lorry.'

'Did he say anything about arranging for the lorry?'

'He asked me if there was a man in the village,' said Troy. 'I told him Burridge would do it.'

The policeman at the door gave a deprecatory cough.

'Hullo?' said Alleyn, slewing round in his chair. 'Thought of something?'

'The super asked Burridges if they done it, sir, and they says no.'

'Right. Thank you. Now, Mr Malmsley, did you get any idea when Mr Garcia proposed to put the case on board the lorry?'

'He said early next morning – Saturday.'

'I see. There was no other mention of Miss Sonia Gluck, the pose, or Mr Garcia's subsequent plans?'

'No.'

'He didn't tell you where the clay model was to be delivered?'

'No. He just said he'd got the loan of a disused warehouse in London.'

'He told me he was going on a sketching-tramp for a week before he started work,' said Valmai Seacliff.

'To me also, he said this.' Francis Ormerin leant forward, glancing nervously at Alleyn. 'He said he wished to paint landscape for a little before beginning this big work.'

'He painted?' asked Alleyn.

'Oh, yes,' said Troy. 'Sculping was his long suit, but he painted and etched a bit as well.'

'Very interesting stuff,' said Katti Bostock.

'Drearily representational though, you must own,' murmured Malmsley.

'I don't agree,' said Ormerin.

'Good God!' exclaimed Basil Pilgrim, 'we're not here to discuss aesthetics.'

'Does anyone here,' Alleyn cut in firmly, 'know who lent this warehouse to Garcia, where it was, when he proposed to go there, or in what direction he has supposedly walked away.?'

'Silence.

'He is possibly the most uncommunicative young man in England,' said Troy suddenly.

'It would seem so, indeed,' agreed Alleyn.

'There's this, though,' added Troy. 'He told me the name of the man who commissioned the 'Comedy and Tragedy'. It's Charleston and I think he's secretary to the board of the New Palace Theatre, Westminster. Is that any help?'

'It may be a lot of help.'

'Do you think Garcia murdered Sonia?' asked Malmsley vaguely. 'I must say I don't.'

'The next point is this,' said Alleyn, exactly as though Malmsley had not spoken. 'I want to arrive at the order in which you all left the studio on Friday at midday. I believe Miss Troy and Miss Bostock came away together as soon as the model got down. Any objections to that?'

There was none apparently.

'Well, who came next?'

'I – I think I did,' said Phillida Lee, 'and I think I ought to tell you about an *extraordinary* thing that I heard Garcia say to Sonia one day – '

'Thank you so much, Miss Lee. I'll come to that later if I may. At the moment we're talking about the order in which you left the studio on Friday at noon. You followed Miss Troy and Miss Bostock?'

'Yes,' said Miss Lee restlessly.

'Good. Are you sure of that, Miss Lee?'

'Yes. I mean I know I did because I was absolutely *exhausted*. It always takes it out of me most *frightfully* when I paint. It simply drains every *ounce* of my energy. I even forget to *breathe*.'

'That must be most uncomfortable,' said Alleyn gravely. 'You came out to breathe, perhaps?'

'Yes. I mean I felt I must get away from it. So I simply put down my brushes and walked out. Miss Troy and Bostock were just ahead of me.'

'You went straight to the house?'

'Yes, I think so. Yes, I did.'

'Yeah, that's right,' said Watt Hatchett loudly. 'You came straight up here because I was just after you, see? I saw you through the dining-room window. This window here, Mr Alleyn. That's right, Miss Lee. You went up to the sideboard and began eating something.'

'I – I don't remember that,' said Miss Lee in a high voice. She darted an unfriendly glance at Hatchett.

'Well,' said Alleyn briskly, 'that leaves Miss Seacliff, Messrs Ormerin, Pilgrim, Malmsley and Garcia, and the model. Who came next?'

'We all did – except Garcia and Sonia,' said Valmai Seacliff. 'Sonia hadn't dressed. I remember I went into the junk-room and washed my brushes under the tap. Ormerin and Malmsley and Basil followed me there.'

She spoke with a slight hesitation, the merest shadow of a stutter, and with a markedly falling inflexion. She had a trick of uttering the last words of a phrase on an indrawn breath. Everything she looked and did, Alleyn felt, was the result of a carefully concealed deliberation. She managed now to convey the impression that men followed her inevitably, wherever she went.

'They were in the way,' she went on. 'I told them to go. Then I finished washing my brushes and came up to the house.'

'Garcia was in the junk-room, too, I think,' said Ormerin.

'Oh, yes,' agreed Seacliff softly. 'He came in, as soon as you'd gone. He would, you know. Sonia was glaring through the door –

furious, of course.' Her voice died away and was caught up on that small gasp. She looked through her eyelashes at Alleyn. 'I walked up to the house with the other three.'

'That is so,' agreed Ormerin.

'Leaving Mr Garcia and the model in the studio?' asked Alleyn.

'I suppose so.'

'Yes,' said Pilgrim.

'You say the model was furious, Miss Seacliff,' said Alleyn. 'Why was that?'

'Oh, because Garcia was making passes at me in the junk-room. Nothing much. He can't help himself – Garcia.'

'I see,' said Alleyn politely. 'Now, please. Did any of you revisit the studio before you went up to London?'

'I did,' said Ormerin.

'At what time?'

'Immediately after lunch. I wished to look again at my work. I was very troubled about my work. Everything was difficult. The model – ' He stopped short.

'Yes?'

'Never for a second was she still. It was impossible. Impossible! I believe that she did it deliberately.'

'She's dead now,' said Phillida Lee, on muted strings. 'Poor little Sonia.'

'Spare us the *nil nisi* touch, for God's sake,' begged Malmsley.

'Did you all notice the model's restlessness?'

'You bet!' said Watt Hatchett. 'She was saucy, that's what she was. Seemed to have got hold of the idea she amounted to something. She gave me a pain in the neck, dinkum, always slinging off about Aussie.'

' "Aussie," ' groaned Malmsley, ' "Aussie,", "Tassie," "a goodee," "a badee." Pray spare me those bloody abbreviations.'

'Look, Mr Malmsley, I'd sooner talk plain honest Australian than make a noise like I'd got a fish-bone stuck in me gullet. Aussie'll do me. And one other thing, too. If you walked down Bondi beach with that half-chewed mouthful of hay sprouting out of your dial, they'd phone the Zoo something was missing.'

'Hatchett,' said Troy. 'Pipe down.'

'Good oh, Miss Troy.'

'I gather,' said Alleyn mildly, 'that you didn't altogether like the model?'

'Who, me? Too right I didn't. I'm sorry the poor kid's coughed out. Gosh, I reckon it's a fair cow, but just the same she gave me a pain in the neck. I asked her one day had she got fleas or something, the way she was twitching. And did she go crook!' Hatchett uttered a raucous yelp of laughter. Malmsley shuddered.

'Thank you, Mr Hatchett,' said Alleyn firmly. 'The next point I want to raise is this. Have there been any definite quarrels with the model? Any scenes, any rows between Miss Gluck and somebody else?'

He looked round the table. Everyone seemed disconcerted. There was a sudden feeling of tension. Alleyn waited. After a silence of perhaps a minute, Katti Bostock said slowly:

'I suppose you might say there were a good many scenes.'

'You had one with her yourself, Bostock,' said Malmsley.

'I did.'

'What was that about, Miss Bostock?'

'Same thing. Wriggling. I'm doing – I was doing a big thing. I wanted to finish it in time for the Group show. It opened last Friday. She was to give me separate sittings – out of class, you know. She seemed to have the devil in her. Fidgeting, going out when I wanted her. Complaining. Drove me dotty. I didn't get the thing finished, of course.'

'Was that the trapeze artiste picture?' asked Alleyn.

Katti Bostock scowled.

'I dislike people looking at my things before they're finished.'

'I'm sorry; it is beastly, I know,' said Alleyn. 'But, you see, we've got to do our nosing around.'

'I suppose you have. Well' – she laughed shortly – 'it'll never be finished now.'

'It wouldn't have been finished anyway, though, would it?' asked Phillida Lee. 'I meant I heard you tell her you hated the sight of her, and she could go to the devil.'

'What d'you mean?' demanded Katti Bostock harshly. 'You were not there when I was working.'

'I happened to come in on Thursday afternoon. I only got inside the door, and you were having such a *frightful* row I beetled off again.'

'You'd no business to hang about and eavesdrop,' said Miss Bostock. Her broad face was full crimson; she leant forward, scowling.

'There's no need to lose your temper with me,' squeaked Miss Lee. 'I didn't eavesdrop. I simply walked in. You couldn't see me because of the screen inside the door, and anyway, you were in such a *seething* rage you wouldn't have noticed the Angel Gabriel himself.'

'For Heaven's sake, let's keep our sense of proportion,' said Troy. 'The poor little wretch was infuriating, and we've all lost our tempers with her again and again.' She looked at Alleyn. 'Really, you might say each of us has felt like murdering her at some time or another.'

'Yes, Miss Troy,' said Phillida Lee, still staring at Katti Bostock, 'but we haven't all said so, have we?'

'My God – '

'Katti,' said Troy. 'Please!'

'She's practically suggesting that – '

'No, no,' said Ormerin. 'Let us, as Troy says, keep our sense of proportion. If exasperation could have stabbed this girl, any one of us might be a murderer. But whichever one of us *did* – '

'I don't see why it need be one of us,' objected Valmai Seacliff placidly.

'Nor I,' drawled Malmsley. 'The cook may have taken a dislike to her and crawled down to the studio with murder in her heart.'

'Are we meant to laugh at that?' asked Hatchett.

'It is perfectly clearly to be seen,' Ormerin said loudly, 'what is the view of the police. This gentleman, Mr Alleyn, who is so quiet and so polite, who waits in silence for us to make fools of ourselves – he knows as each of us must know in his heart that the murderer of this girl was present in the studio on the morning we made the experiment with the dagger. That declares itself. There is no big motive that sticks out like a bundle in a haystack, so Mr Alleyn sits and says nothing and hears much. And we – we talk.'

'Mr Ormerin,' said Alleyn, 'you draw up the blinds on my technique, and leave it blinking foolishly in the light of day. I see that I may be silent no longer.'

'Ah-ah-ah! It is as I have said.' Ormerin wagged his head sideways, shrugged up his shoulders and threw himself back in his chair. 'But as for this murder – it is the *crime passionnel*, depend upon it. The girl was very highly sexed.'

'That doesn't necessarily lead to homicide,' Alleyn pointed out, with a smile.

'She was jealous,' said Ormerin; 'she was yellow with jealousy and chagrin. Every time Garcia looks at Seacliff she suffers as if she is ill. And when Pilgrim announces that he is affianced with Seacliff, again Sonia feels as if a knife is twisted inside her.'

'That's absolute bosh,' said Basil Pilgrim violently. 'You don't know what you are talking about, Ormerin.'

'Do I not? She was avid for men, that little one.'

'Dear me,' murmured Malmsley, 'this all sounds very Montmartre.'

'She certainly was a hot little dame,' said Hatchett.

'It was apparent,' added Ormerin. 'And when a more compelling – more *troublante* – woman arrived, she became quite frantic. Because Seacliff – '

'Will you keep Valmai's name out of this?' shouted Pilgrim.

'Basil, darling, how divinely county you are,' said Valmai Seacliff. 'I know she was jealous of me. We all know she was. And she obviously was very attracted to you, my sweet.'

'This conversation,' said Troy, 'seems slightly demented. All this, if it was true, might mean that Sonia would feel like killing Valmai or Pilgrim or Garcia, but why should anybody kill her?'

'Closely reasoned,' murmured Alleyn. Troy threw a suspicious glance at him.

'It is true, is it not,' insisted Ormerin, 'that you suspect one of us?'

'Or Garcia,' said Katti Bostock.

'Yes, there's always the little tripe-hound,' agreed Seacliff.

'And the servants,' added Malmsley.

'Very well,' amended Ormerin, still talking to Alleyn. 'You suspect one of this party, or Garcia, or – if you will – the servants.'

'An inside job,' said Hatchett, proud of the phrase.

'Oh, yes,' said Alleyn. 'I do rather suspect one of you – or Mr Garcia – or the servants. But it's early days yet. I am capable of almost limitless suspicion. At the moment I am going to tighten up this round-table conference.' He looked at Hatchett. 'How long have you been working without a tray on your easel?'

'Eh? What d'you mean?' Hatchett sounded startled.

'It's not very difficult. How long is it since you had a ledge on your easel?'

'Haven't I got one now?'

'No.'

'Oh yeah! That's right. I took it off to hammer the dagger into the throne.'

'What!' screamed Phillida Lee. 'Oh, I see.'

'On the day of the experiment?' asked Alleyn.

'That's right.'

'And it's been kicking about on the floor ever since?'

'I suppose so. Half a tick, though – has it? Naow – it hasn't, either. I've had a ledge all right. I stuck my dipper on it. Look, I had a ledge on me easel Fridee after lunch.'

'*After* lunch,' asked Alleyn.

'Yeah, I remember now. I ran down some time after lunch to have a look at the thing I'd been painting. I met you coming away, Ormerin, didn't I?'

'Yes. I only looked at my work and felt sick and came away.'

'Yeah. Well, when I got there I thought I'd play around with the wet paint, see? Well, I'd just had a smack at it when I heard Ormerin singing out the old bus went past the corner on the main road in ten minutes. Well, I remember now; I jammed my brush into my dipper so's it wouldn't go hard, and then beat it. But the dipper was on the ledge all right.'

'And was the ledge there this morning?'

'You're right. It wasn't. And it wasn't there Sundee night either.'

'Sunday night?' said Alleyn sharply.

'That's right. After we got back, see? I ran down to the studio just after tea.'

'After tea? But I thought you didn't come back until – ' Alleyn looked at his notes. 'Until six-thirty.'

'That's correct, Mr Alleyn. We finished tea at half-past eight, about.'

'The gentleman is talking of the evening meal, Inspector,' said Malmsley. 'They dine at noon in the Antipodes, I understand.'

'Aw go and chase yourself,' invited Hatchett. 'I went down to the studio at about eight-thirty, Inspector. "After dinnah" if you've got enlarged tonsils. "After tea" if you're normal.'

'Did you get in?'

'Too right. She was locked, but the key's left on a nail, and I opened her up and had a look-see at my picture. Gosh, it looked all right, too, Miss Troy, by artificial light. Have you seen it by lamplight, Miss Troy?'

'No,' said Troy. 'Don't wander.'

'Good oh, Miss Troy.'

'Well,' said Alleyn, 'you went into the studio, and put the lights up, and looked at your work. Did you look at the throne?'

'Er – yes. Yes, I did. I was wondering, if I'd paint a bit of the drape, and I had a look, and it was all straightened out. Like it always is before she gets down into the pose. Stretched tight from the cushion to the floor. If I had a pencil I could show you – '

'Thank you, I think I follow.'

'Good oh, then. Well, I wondered if I'd try and fix it like as if the model was laying on it. I'd an idea that I might get it right if I lay down myself in the pose. Cripes!' exclaimed Hatchett, turning paper-white. 'If I'd a-done that would I have got that knife in me slats? Cripey, Mr Alleyn, do you reckon that dagger was sticking up under the drape on Sundee evening?'

'Possibly.'

'What a cow!' whispered Hatchett.

'However, you didn't arrange yourself on the drape. Why not?'

'Well, because Miss Troy won't let anybody touch the throne without she says they can, and I thought she'd go crook if I did.'

'Correct?' asked Alleyn, with a smile at Troy.

'Certainly. It's the rule of the studio. Otherwise the drapes would get bundled about, and the chalked positions rubbed off.'

'Yeah, but listen, Miss Troy. Mr Alleyn, listen. I've just remembered something.'

'Come on, then,' said Alleyn.

'Gee, I reckon this is important,' continued Hatchett excitely. 'Look, when I went down to the studio just before we all went to catch the bus on Fridee, the drape was all squashed down, just as it had been when the model got up.'

'You're sure of that?'

'I'm certain. I'll swear to it.'

'Did you notice the drape on your brief visit to the studio after lunch, Mr Ormerin?'

'Yes,' said Ormerin excitedly. 'Now you ask I remember well. I looked at my work, and then automatically I looked at the throne as though the model was still there. And I got the small tiny shock one receives at the sight of that which one does not expect. Then I looked at my treatment of the drape and back to the drape itself. It was as Hatchett describes – crumpled and creased by the weight of her body, just as when she arose at midday.'

'Here!' exclaimed Hatchett. 'See, what that means? It means – '

'It is pregnant with signification, I'm sure, Mr Hatchett,' said Alleyn. Hatchett was silent. Alleyn looked at his notes and continued: 'I understand that Miss Troy and Miss Bostock left by car. So did Miss Seacliff and Mr Pilgrim. Then came the bus party at three o'clock. Miss Lee, Mr Ormerin, Mr Hatchett, and the model. It seems,' said Alleyn very deliberately, 'that at a few minutes before three when Mr Hatchett left to catch the bus, the drape was still flat and crushed on the floor.' He paused, contemplating Cedric Malmsley. 'What did you do after the others had gone?'

Malmsley lit a cigarette and took his time over it.

'Oh,' he said at last, 'I wandered down to the studio.'

'When?'

'Immediately after lunch.'

'Did you look at the drape on the throne?'

'I believe I did.'

'How was it then?'

'Quite well, I imagine. Just like a drape on a throne.'

'Mr Malmsley,' said Alleyn, 'I advise you not to be too amusing. I am investigating a murder. Was the drape still flat?'

'Yes.'

'How long did you stay in the studio?'

'I've told you. Until five.'

'Alone with Mr Garcia?'

'I've told you. Alone with Garcia.'

'Did either of you leave the studio during the afternoon?'

'Yes.'

'Who?'

'Garcia.'

'Do you know why?'

'I imagine it was to pay a visit to the usual offices.'

'How long was he away?'

'Dear me, I don't know. Perhaps eight or ten minutes.'

'When he worked, did he face the window?'

'I believe so.'

'With his back to the room?'

'Naturally.'

'Did you look at the drape before you left?'

'I don't think so.'

'Did you touch the drape, Mr Malmsley?'

'No.'

'Who scrawled that appalling defacement on Miss Troy's painting of a girl in green?'

There was an uneasy silence, broken at last by Troy.

'You mean my portrait of Miss Seacliff. Sonia did that.'

'The model?' exclaimed Alleyn.

'I believe so. I said we have all felt like murdering her. That was my motive, Mr Alleyn.'

CHAPTER 7

Alibi for Troy

Alleyn lifted a hand as if in protest. He checked himself and, after a moment's pause, went on with his customary air of polite diffidence.

'The model defaced your painting. Why did she do this?'

'Because she was livid with *me*,' said Valmai Seacliff. 'You see, it was rather a marvellous painting. Troy was going to exhibit it. Sonia hated that. Besides, Basil wanted to buy it.'

'When did she commit this – outrage?' asked Alleyn.

'A week ago,' said Troy. 'Miss Seacliff gave me the final sitting last Monday morning. The class came down to the studio to see the thing. Sonia came too. She'd been in a pretty foul frame of mind for some days. It's perfectly true what they all say. She was an extraordinary little animal and, as Ormerin has told you, extremely jealous. They all talked about the portrait. She was left outside the circle. Then Pilgrim asked me if he might buy it before it went away. Perhaps I should tell you that I have also done a portrait of Sonia which has not been sold. Sonia took that as a sort of personal slight on her beauty. It's hard to believe, but she did. She seemed to think I'd painted Miss Seacliff because I was dissatisfied with her own charms as a model. Then, when they all came down and looked at the thing and liked it, and Pilgrim said he wanted it, I suppose that upset her still more. Several of these people said in front of her, they thought the thing of Miss Seacliff was the best portrait I have done.'

'It was all worms and gallwood to her,' said Ormerin.

'Well,' Troy went on, 'we came away, and I suppose she stayed behind. When I went down to the studio later on that day, I found – ' she caught her breath – 'I found – what you saw.'

'Did you tackle her?'

'Not at first. I – felt sick. You see, once in a painter's lifetime he, or she, does something that's extra.'

'I know.'

'Something that they look at afterwards and say to themselves: 'How did the stumbling ninny that is me, do this?' It happened with the head in Valmai's portrait. So when I saw – I just felt sick.'

'Bloody little swine,' said Miss Bostock.

'Oh, well,' said Troy, 'I did tackle her that evening. She admitted she'd done it. She said all sorts of things about Valmai and Pilgrim, and indeed everybody in the class. She stormed and howled.'

'You didn't sack her?' asked Alleyn.

'I felt like it, of course. But I couldn't quite do that. You see, they'd all got going on these other things, and there was Katti's big thing, too. I think she was honestly sorry she'd done it. She really rather liked me. She simply went through life doing the first thing that came into her head. This business had been done in a blind fury with Valmai. She only thought of me afterwards. She fetched up by having hysterics and offering to pose for nothing for the rest of her life.' Troy smiled crookedly. 'The stable-door idea,' she said.

'Basil and I were frightfully upset,' said Valmai Seacliff. 'Weren't we, Basil?'

Alleyn looked to see how Pilgrim would take this remark. He thought that for a moment he saw a look of reluctant surprise.

'Darling!' said Pilgrim, 'of course we were.' And then in his eyes appeared the reflection of her beauty, and he stared at her with the solemn alarm of a man very deeply in love.

'Were there any more upheavals after this?' asked Alleyn after a pause.

'Not exactly,' answered Troy. 'She was chastened a bit. The others let her see that they thought she'd – she'd – '

'I went crook at her,' announced Hatchett. 'I told her I reckoned she was – '

'Pipe down, Hatchett.'

'Good oh, Miss Troy.'

'We were all livid,' said Katti Bostock hotly. 'I could have mur – '
She stopped short. 'Well, there you are, you see,' she said doggedly.
'I could have murdered her and I didn't. She knew how I felt, and
she took it out in the sittings she gave me.'

'It was sacrilege,' squeaked Phillida Lee. 'That exquisite thing. To
see it with that obscene – '

'Shut up, Lee, for God's sake,' said Katti Bostock.

'Oddly enough,' murmured Malmsley, 'Garcia seemed to take it
as heavily as anybody. Worse if anything. Do you know, he was
actually ill, Troy? I found him in the garden, a most distressing
sight.'

'How extraordinary!' said Valmai Seacliff vaguely. 'I always
thought he was entirely without emotion. Oh, but of course – '

'Of course – what?' asked Alleyn.

'Well, it *was* a portrait of me, wasn't it? I attracted him *tremendous-
ly* in the physical sense. I suppose that was why he was sick.'

'Oh, bilge and bosh!' said Katti Bostock.

'Think so?' said Seacliff quite amiably.

'Can any of you tell me on what sort of footing the model and Mr
Garcia were during the last week?' asked Alleyn.

'Well, I told you she'd been his mistress,' said Malmsley. 'He said
that himself during Friday afternoon.'

'Not while they were here, I hope,' said Troy. 'I told him I would-
n't have anything like that.'

'He said so. He was very pained and hurt at your attitude, I gathered.'

'Well, I *know* there was something going on, anyway,' said
Phillida Lee, with a triumphant squeak. 'I've been waiting to tell the
superintendent this, but you were all so busy talking, I didn't get a
chance. I know Sonia wanted him to marry her.'

'Why, Miss Lee?'

'Well, they were always whispering together, and I went to the
studio one day, about a week ago, I think, and there they were having a session – I mean, they were talking – nothing else.'

'You seem to have had a good many lucky dips in the studio, Lee,'
said Katti Bostock. 'What did you overhear this time?'

'You needn't be so acid. It may turn out a mercy I *did* hear them.
Mayn't it, Superintendent?' She appealed to Alleyn.

'I haven't risen to superintendent heights, Miss Lee. But please do tell me what you heard.'

'As a matter of fact, it wasn't *very* much, but it was exciting. Garcia said: "All right – on Friday night, then." And Sonia said: "Yes, if it's possible." Then there was quite a long pause and she said: "I won't stand for any funny business with *her*, you know," And Garcia said: "Who?" and she said – I'm sorry, Mr Alleyn – but she said: "The Seacliff bitch, of course." ' Miss Lee turned pink. 'I *am* sorry, Mr Alleyn.'

'Miss Seacliff will understand the exigencies of a verbatim report,' said Alleyn with the faintest possible twinkle.

'Oh, I've heard all about it. She knew what he was up to, of course,' said Valmai Seacliff. She produced a lipstick and mirror and, with absorbed attention, made up her lovely mouth.

'Why didn't you tell me the swine was pestering you?' Pilgrim asked her.

'My sweet – I could manage Garcia perfectly well,' said Seacliff with a little chuckle.

'Anything more, Miss Lee?' asked Alleyn.

'Well, yes. Sonia suddenly began to cry and say Garcia ought to marry her. He said nothing. She said something about Friday evening again, and she said if he let her down after that she'd go to Troy and tell her the whole story. Garcia just said – Mr Alleyn, he just sort of *grunted* it, but honestly it sounded *frightful*. Truly. And she didn't say another *thing*. I think she was *terrified* – really!'

'But you haven't told us what he did say, you know.'

'Well, he said: "If you don't shut up and leave me to get on with my work, I'll bloody well stop your mouth for keeps. Do what I tell you. Get out!" *There!*' ended Miss Lee triumphantly.

'Have you discussed this incident with anyone else?'

'I told Seacliff, in confidence.'

'I advised her to regard it as nobody's business but theirs,' said Seacliff.

'Well – I thought *somebody* ought to know.'

'I said,' added Seacliff, 'that if she still felt all repressed and congested, she could tell Troy.'

'Did you follow this excellent advice, Miss Lee?'

'No – I didn't – because – well, because I thought – I mean – '

'I have rather sharp views on gossip,' said Troy dryly. 'And even sharper views on listening-in. Possibly she realized this.' She stared coldly at Miss Lee, who turned very pink indeed.

'How did this incident terminate?' asked Alleyn.

'Well, I made a bangy sort of noise with the door to show I was there, and they stopped. And I *didn't* eavesdrop, Miss Troy, truly. I was just rooted to the ground with *horror*. It all sounded so *sinister*. And *now* see what's happened!'

Troy looked up at Alleyn. Suddenly she grinned, and Alleyn felt a sort of thump in his chest. 'Oh God,' he thought urgently, 'what am I going to do about this? I didn't *want* to lose my heart.' He looked away quickly.

'Are there any other incidents of any sort that might have some bearing on this tragedy?' he asked at large.

Nobody answered.

'Then I shall ask you all to stay in here for a little while longer. I want to see each of you separately, before we close down tonight. Miss Troy, will you allow us to use a separate room as a temporary office? I am sorry to give so much trouble.'

'Certainly,' said Troy. 'I'll show you – '

She led the way to the door and went into the hall without waiting for them. Alleyn and Fox followed, leaving the local man behind. When the door had shut behind them Alleyn said to Fox:

'Get through to the Yard, Fox. We'll have to warn all stations about Garcia. If he's tramping, he can't have walked so far in three days. If he's bolted, he may be anywhere by now. I'll try and get hold of a photograph. We'd better broadcast, I think. Make sure nobody's listening when you telephone. Tell them to get in touch with the city. We must find this warehouse. Then see the maids. Ask if they know anything at all about the studio on Friday night and Saturday morning. Come along to the drawing-room when you've finished, will you?'

'Right, sir. I'll just ask this PC where the telephone hangs out.'

Fox turned back, and Alleyn moved on to the end of the hall, where Troy waited in a pool of light that came from the library.

'In here,' she said.

'Thank you.'

She was turning away as Alleyn said:

'May I keep you a moment?'

He stood aside for her to go through the door. They returned to the fire. Troy got a couple of logs from the wood basket.

'Let me do that,' Alleyn said.

'It's all right.'

She pitched the logs on the fire and dusted her hands.

'There are cigarettes on that table, Mr Alleyn. Will you have one?'

He lit her cigarette and his own and they sat down.

'What now?' asked Troy.

'I want you to tell me exactly what you did from the time you left the studio on Friday at noon until the class assembled this morning.'

'An alibi?'

'Yes.'

'Do you think for a moment,' said Troy, in a level voice, 'that I might have killed this girl?'

'Not for a moment,' answered Alleyn.

'I suppose I shouldn't have asked you that. I'm sorry. Shall I begin with the time I got up to the house?'

'Yes, please,' said Alleyn.

He thought she was very stiff with him and supposed she resented the very sight of himself and everything he stood for. It did not occur to Alleyn that his refusal to answer that friendly grin had sent up all Troy's defences. Where women were concerned he was, perhaps, unusually intelligent and intuitive, but the whole of this case is coloured by his extraordinary wrong-headedness over Troy's attitude towards himself. He afterwards told Nigel Bathgate that he was quite unable to bring Troy into focus with the case. To Troy it seemed that he treated her with an official detachment that was a direct refusal to acknowledge any former friendliness. She told herself, with a sick feeling of shame, that he had probably thought she pursued him in the ship. He had consented to sit for her, with a secret conviction that she hoped it might lead to a flirtation. 'Or,' thought Troy, deliberately jabbing at the nerve, 'he probably decided I was fishing for a sale.'

Now, on this first evening at Tatler's End House, they treated each other to displays of frigid courtesy. Troy, summoning her wits, began an account of her weekend activities.

'I came up to the house, washed, changed and lunched. After lunch, as far as I remember, Katti and I sat in here and smoked. Then we went round to the garage, got the car, and drove up to our club in London. It's the United Arts. We got there about four o'clock, had tea with some people we ran into in the club, shopped for an hour afterwards, and got back to the club about six, I should think. I bathed, changed and met Katti in the lounge. We had a cocktail and then dined with the Arthur Jayneses. It was a party of six. He's president of the Phoenix Group. From there we all went to the private view. We supped at the Hungaria with the Jayneses. I got back to the club somewhere round two o'clock. On Saturday I had my hair done at Cattcherly's in Bond Street. Katti and I had another look at the show. I lunched early at the Ritz with a man called John Bellasca. Then I picked Katti up at the club and we got back here about three.'

'Did you go down to the studio?'

'Yes. I went there to collect my sketch-box. I wanted to see what materials I had and tidy it up. I was going to work out of doors on Sunday. I brought the box in here and spent the afternoon at different tidying jobs. After that Katti and I went for a walk to look for a subject. We dined out. I asked when we got here on Saturday if Garcia had gone, and the maids told me he hadn't been in to breakfast or lunch, so I supposed he had pushed off at daybreak. They had sent his dinner down to the studio the night before – Friday night. It was easier than having it up here. He sleeps in the studio, you know.'

'Why was that?'

'It was advisable. I didn't want him in the house. You've heard what he's like with women.'

'I see. On Saturday were you long in the studio?'

'No. I simply got my sketch-box. I was painting out of doors.'

'Anyone go in with you?'

'No.'

'Did you notice the drape?'

Troy leant forward, her cropped head between two clenched fists.

'That's what I've been trying to remember ever since Hatchett said it was stretched out when he saw it on Sunday.

'Give me a moment. I went straight to my cupboard behind the door and got out my sketching gear. I had a look in the box and found there was no turpentine in the bottle, so I took it to the junk-room and filled it up. Then I came back to the studio and – yes, yes!'

'You've remembered it?'

'Yes. I – I must tell you I hadn't screwed myself up to looking at
the portrait of Seacliff again. Not since I first saw what Sonia had
done to it. I just turned it face to the wall behind the throne. Well, I
saw it when I came out of the junk-room, and I thought: "I can't go
on cutting it dead. It can't stand there for ever, giving me queasy
horrors whenever I catch sight of it." So I began to walk towards it,
and I got as far as the edge of the throne, and I remember now quite
clearly I walked carefully round the drape, so as not to disturb it, and
I noticed, without noticing, don't you know, that the silk was in
position – stretched straight from the cushion and pinned to the
floor of the throne. You may have noticed that it was caught with a
safety-pin to the top of the cushion. That was to prevent it slipping
off when she lay down on it. It was fixed lightly to the floor with a
drawing-pin that flew out when the drape took her weight. The
whole idea was to get the accidental swill of the silk round the figure. It was stretched out like that when I saw it.'

'I needn't tell you the significance of this,' said Alleyn, slowly.
'You are absolutely certain the drape was in position?'

'Yes. I'd swear to it.'

'And did you look at the portrait of Miss Seacliff?'

Troy turned her face away from him.

'No,' she said gruffly, 'I funked it. Poor sort of business, wasn't it?'
She laughed shortly.

Alleyn made a quick movement, stopped himself, and said: 'I
don't think so. Did either of you go down to the studio at any time
during yesterday, do you know?'

'I don't know. I don't think so. I didn't, and Katti had an article to
do for *The Palette* and was writing in the library all day. She's got a
series of articles on the Italian primitives running in *The Palette*. You'd
better ask her about yesterday.'

'I will. To return to your own movements. You went out to paint
in the garden?'

'Yes. At eleven o'clock. The Bossicote church bell had just
stopped. I worked till about two o'clock and came in for a late lunch.
After lunch I cleaned up my brushes at the house. I hadn't gone to
the studio. Katti and I had a good glare at my sketch, and then she
read over her article and began to type it. I sat in here, working out
an idea for a decorative panel on odd bits of paper. Seacliff and

Pilgrim arrived in his car for tea at five, and the others came by the six o'clock bus.'

'Sonia Gluck with them?'

'Yes.'

'Did you all spend the evening together?'

'The class has a sort of common-room at the back of the house. In my grandfather's day it was really a kind of ballroom, but when my father lost most of his money, part of the house was shut up, including this place. I had a lot of odds and ends of furniture put into it and let them use it. It's behind the dining-room, at the end of an odd little passage. They all went in there after dinner on Sunday – yesterday – evening. I looked in for a little while.'

'They were all there?'

'I think so. Pilgrim and Seacliff wandered out through the french window into the garden. I suppose they wanted to enjoy the amenities of betrothal.'

Alleyn laughed unexpectedly. He had a very pleasant laugh.

'What's the matter?' asked Troy.

' "The amenities of betrothal," ' quoted Alleyn.

'Well, what's wrong with that?'

'Such a grand little phrase!'

For a moment there was no constraint between them. They looked at each other as if they were old friends.

'Well,' said Troy, 'they came back looking very smug and complacent and self-conscious, and all the others were rather funny about it. Except Sonia, who looked like thunder. It's quite true, what Seacliff says. Sonia, you see, was the main attraction last year, as far as the men-students were concerned. She used to hold a sort of court in the rest-times and fancied herself as a Bohemian siren, poor little idiot. Then Seacliff came and wiped her eye. She was beside herself with chagrin. You've seen what Seacliff is like. She doesn't exactly disguise the fact that she is attractive to men, does she? Katti says she's a successful nymphomaniac.'

'Pilgrim seems an honest-to-God sort of fellow.'

'He's a nice fellow, Pilgrim.'

'Do you approve of the engagement?'

'No, I don't. I think she's after his title.'

'You don't mean to say he's a son of the Methodist peer?'

'Yes, he is. And the Methodist peer may leave us for crowns and harps any moment now. The old gentleman's failing.'

'I see.'

'As a matter of fact – ' Troy hesitated.

'Yes?'

'I don't know that it matters.'

'Please, tell me anything you can think of.'

'You may attach too much importance to it.'

'We are warned against that at the Yard, you know.'

'I beg your pardon,' said Troy stiffly. 'I was merely going to say that I thought Basil Pilgrim had been worried about something since his engagement.'

'Have you any idea what it was?'

'I thought at first it might have been his father's illness, but somehow I don't think it was that.'

'Perhaps he has already regretted his choice. The trapped feeling.'

'I don't think so,' said Troy still more stiffly. 'I fancy it was something to do with Sonia.'

'With the model?'

'I simply meant that I thought he felt uncomfortable about Sonia. She was always uttering little jeers about engaged couples. I think they made Pilgrim feel uncomfortable.'

'Do you imagine there has ever been anything between Pilgrim and Sonia Gluck?'

'I have no idea,' said Troy.

There was a tap on the door, and Fox came in.

'I got through, sir. They'll get busy at once. The men have finished in the studio.'

'Ask them to wait. I'll see them in a minute.'

'Have you finished with me?' asked Troy, standing up.

'Yes, thank you, Miss Troy,' said Alleyn formally. 'If you wouldn't mind giving us the names and addresses of the people you met in London, I should be very grateful. You see, we are obliged to check all statements of this sort.'

'I quite understand,' answered Troy coldly.

She gave the names and addresses of her host and hostess, of the people she met in the club, and of the man who took her to lunch – John Bellasca, 44 Little Belgrave Street.

'The club porter may be useful,' she said, 'his name's Jackson. He may have noticed my goings out and comings in. I remember that I asked him the time, and got him to call taxis. The sort of things people do when they wish to establish alibis, I understand.'

'They occasionally do them at normal times, I believe,' said Alleyn. 'Thank you, Miss Troy. I won't bother you any more for the moment. Do you mind joining the others until we have finished this business.'

'Not at all,' answered Troy with extreme grandeur. 'Please use this room as much as you like. Good evening, good evening.'

'Good evening, miss,' said Fox.

Troy made an impressive exit.

CHAPTER 8

Sidelights on Garcia

'The lady seems a bit upset,' said Fox mildly, when Troy had gone.

'I irritate the lady,' answered Alleyn.

'*You* do, sir? I always think you've got a very pleasant way with female witnesses. Sort of informal and at the same time very polite.'

'Thank you, Fox,' said Alleyn wryly.

'Learn anything useful, sir?'

'She says the drape was in the second position on Saturday afternoon.'

'Stretched out straight?'

'Yes.'

'Well,' said Fox, 'if she's telling the truth, it looks as though the knife was fixed up between the time this Mr Malmsley walked out on Friday afternoon and the time Miss Troy looked in on Saturday. That's if Malmsley was telling the truth when he said the drape was crumpled and flat on Friday afternoon. It all points one way, chief, doesn't it.'

'It does, Brer Fox, it does.'

'The Yard's getting straight on to chasing up this Mr Garcia. I've rung all the stations round this district and asked them to make inquiries. I got a pretty fair description of him from the cook, and Bailey found a couple of photographs of the whole crowd in the studio. Here's one of them.'

He thrust a massive hand inside his pocket and produced a half-plate group of Troy and her class. It had been taken in the garden.

'There's the model, Fox. Look!'

Fox gravely put on his spectacles and contemplated the photograph.

'Yes, that's the girl,' he said. 'She looks merry, doesn't she, sir?'

'Yes,' said Alleyn slowly. 'Very merry.'

'That'll be this Garcia, then.' Fox continued. He pointed a stubby finger at a figure on the outside of the group. Alleyn took out a lens and held it over the photograph. Up leaped a thin, unshaven face, with an untidy lock of dark hair falling across the forehead. The eyes were set rather close and the brows met above the thin nose. The lips were unexpectedly full. Garcia had scowled straight into the camera. Alleyn gave Fox the lens.

'Yes,' said Fox, after a look through it, 'we'll have enlargements done at once. Bailey's got the other. He says it will enlarge very nicely.'

'He looks a pretty good specimen of a wild man,' said Alleyn.

'If Malmsley and Miss Troy are telling the truth,' said Fox, who had a way of making sure of his remarks, 'he's a murderer. Of course, the motive's not much of an affair as far as we've got.'

'Well, I don't know, Brer Fox. It looks as though the girl was badgering him to marry her. It's possible the P.M. may offer the usual explanation for that sort of thing.'

'In the family way?' Fox took off his spectacles and stared blandly at his chief. 'Yes. That's so. What did you make of that statement of Mr Malmsley's about Garcia being ill in the garden after he saw the defaced likeness? That seems a queer sort of thing to me. It wasn't as if he'd done the photo.'

'The painting, Fox,' corrected Alleyn. 'One doesn't call inspired works of art photographs, you know. Yes, that was rather a rum touch, wasn't it? You heard Miss Seacliff's theory. Garcia is infatuated with her and was all upheaved by the sight of her defeated loveliness.'

'Far-fetched,' said Fox.

'I'm inclined to agree with you. But it might be an explanation of his murdering Sonia Gluck when he realized she had done it. He might have thought to himself: "This looks like a more than usually hellish fury from the woman scorned – what am I in for?" and decided to get rid of her. There's a second possibility which will seem even more far-fetched to you, I expect. To me it seems conceivable that Garcia's aesthetic nerves were lacerated by the outrage on a lovely piece of painting. Miss Troy says the portrait of Valmai Seacliff was the best thing she has ever done.' Alleyn's voice deepened and was not quite steady. 'That means it was a really great work. I think, Fox, that if I had seen that painted head and known it for a superlatively beautiful thing, and then seen it again with that beastly deface-ment – I believe I might have sicked my immortal soul up into the nearest flower-bed. I also believe that I would have felt remarkably like murder.'

'Is that so, sir?' said Fox stolidly. 'But you wouldn't have done murder, though, however much you felt like it.'

'I'd have felt *damn* like it,' muttered Alleyn. He walked restlessly about the room. 'The secret of Garcia's reaction,' he said, 'lies behind this.' He wagged the photograph at Fox. 'Behind that very odd-look-ing head. I wish we knew more about Garcia. We'll have to go hunt-ing for his history, Brer Fox. Records of violence and so on. I wonder if there are any. Suppose he turns up quite innocently to do his "Comedy and Tragedy" in his London warehouse?'

'That'll look as if either Malmsley or Miss Troy was a liar, sir, won't it? I must say I wouldn't put Mr Malmsley down as a very dependable sort of gentleman. A bit cheeky in an arty sort of fashion.'

Alleyn smiled.

'Fox, what a neat description of him! Admirable! No, unless Malmsley is lying, the knife was hammered through and the drape stretched out after they had all gone on Friday. And if Miss Troy found it stretched out on Saturday afternoon, then the thing was done before then.'

'If,' said Fox. And after a moment's silence Alleyn replied:

' "If" – of course.'

'You might say Miss Troy had the strongest motive, sir, as far as the portrait is concerned.'

There was a longer pause.

'Do you think it at all likely that she is a murderess?' said Alleyn from the fireplace. 'A very deliberate murderess, Fox. The outrage to the portrait was committed a week before the murder.'

'I must say I don't think so, sir. Very unlikely indeed, I'd say. This Garcia seems the likeliest proposition on the face of it. What did you make of Miss Phillida Lee's statement, now? The conversation she overheard. Looks as though Garcia and the deceased were making

an assignation for Friday night, doesn't it? Suppose she came back to
the studio on Friday night in order that they should resume intimacy?'

'Yes, I know.'

'He seems to have actually threatened her, if the young lady can
be depended upon.'

'Miss Seacliff didn't contradict the account, and you must remember that extraordinary little party, Phillida Lee, confided the fruits of
her nosy-parkering to Miss Seacliff long before the tragedy. I think
we may take it that Garcia and Sonia Gluck had a pretty good dust-
up on the lines indicated by the gushing Lee. You took notes in the
dining-room, of course. Turn up her report of the quarrel, will you?'

Fox produced a very smug-looking notebook, put on his spectacles, and turned up a page.

'Garcia – ' he read slowly from his shorthand notes. ' "All right.
On Friday night then." Sonia Gluck: "Yes, if it's possible." Then later
Gluck said: "I won't stand for any funny business with her, you
know." Garcia said: "Who?" and Gluck answered: "The Seacliff bitch,
of course." Sonia Gluck said Garcia ought to marry her. He did not
reply. She threatened to go to Miss Troy with the whole story if he
let her down. He said; "If you don't shut up and leave me to get on
with my work, I'll bloody well stop your mouth for keeps." That's
the conversation, sir.'

'Yes. We'll have to get hold of something about Friday night.
Damn it all, the studio is built into the wall, and the window opens
on the lane. Surely to Heaven someone must have passed by that
evening and heard voices if Garcia had the girl in the place with
him.'

'And how did he get his stuff away on Friday night or Saturday
morning? They've tried all the carriers for miles around.'

'I know, Brer Fox, I know. Well, on we go. We've got to get all
these people's time-tables from Friday noon till Sunday evening.
What about Bailey? I'd better see him first, I suppose.'

Bailey came in with his usual air of mulish displeasure and
reported that they had finished in the studio. They had gone over
everything for prints, had photographed the scratched window-sill,
measured and photographed the car's prints and footprints in the
lane, and taken casts of them. They had found the key of the studio
hanging on a nail outside the door. It was smothered in prints. Under

the pillow was an empty whisky bottle. On the window-sill one set of prints occurred many times, and seemed to be superimposed on most of the others. He had found traces of clay with these prints, and with those on the bottle.

'Those will be Garcia's,' said Alleyn. 'He worked in the window.'

In the junk-room Bailey had found a mass of jars, brushes, bottles of turpentine and oil, costumes, lengths of materials, a spear, an old cutlass, and several shallow dishes that smelt of nitric acid. There was also what Bailey described as 'a sort of mangle affair with a whale of a heavy chunk of metal and a couple of rollers.'

'An etching press,' said Alleyn.

'There's a couple of stains on the floor of the junkroom,' continued Bailey. 'Look like nitric-acid stains. They're new. I can't find any nitric acid anywhere, though. I've looked in all the bottles and jars.'

'Um!' said Alleyn, and made a note of it.

'There's one other thing,' said Bailey. He opened a bag he had brought in with him, and out of it he took a small box which he handed to Alleyn.

'Hullo,' said Alleyn. 'This is the *bonne-bouche*, is it?'

He opened the little box and held it under the lamp. Inside was a flattened greenish-grey pellet.

'Clay,' said Alleyn. 'Where was it?'

'In the folds of that silk stuff that was rigged on the platform,' said Bailey, staring morosely at his boots.

'I see,' said Alleyn softly. 'Look here, Fox.'

Fox joined him. They could both see quite clearly that the flattened surface of the pellet was delicately scrolled by minute holes and swirling lines.

'A nice print,' said Fox, 'only half there, but very sharp what there is.'

'If the prints on the sill are Garcia's,' said Bailey, 'that's Garcia's too.'

There was a silence.

'Well,' said Alleyn at last, 'that's what you call a fat little treasure-trove, Bailey.'

'I reckon it must have dropped off his overall when he was stretching that stuff above the point of the knife, sir. That's what I reckon.'

'Yes. It's possible.'

'He must have used gloves for the job. There are one or two smudges about the show that look like glove-marks, and I think one of them's got a trace of the clay. We've photographed the whole outfit.'

'You've done rather well, Bailey.'

'Anything more, sir?'

'Yes, I'm afraid there is. I want you to find the deceased's room and go over it. I don't think we should let that wait any longer. One of the maids will show you where it is. Come and get me if anything startling crops up.'

'Very good, Mr Alleyn.'

'And when that's done, you can push off if you want to. You've left a man on guard, I suppose?'

'Yes, sir. One of these local chaps. Getting a great kick out of it.'

'Guileless fellow. Away you go, Bailey. I'll see you later on.'

'OK, sir.'

'Nitric acid?' ruminated Fox, when Bailey had gone.

'I think it's the acid they used for etching. I must ask Miss Troy about it.'

'Looks as if all we've got to do is to find Garcia, don't it, sir?'

'It do, Fox. But for the love of Mike don't let's be too sure of ourselves.'

'That bit of clay, you know, sir – how could it have got there by rights? He'd no business up on the model's throne now, had he?'

'No.'

'And according to Malmsley's story, the drape must have been fixed when the rest of them had gone up to London.'

'Yes. We'll have to trace 'em in London just the same. Have to get on to these others now. Go and take a dip in the dining-room, Fox, and see what the fairies will send us in the way of a witness.'

Fox went off sedately and returned with Katti Bostock. She came in looking very four-square and sensible. Her short and stocky person was clad in corduroy trousers, a red shirt and a brown jacket. Her straight black hair hung round her ears in a Cromwellian cut with a determined bang across her wide forehead. She was made up in a rather slap-dash sort of manner. Her face was principally remarkable for its exceedingly heavy eyebrows.

Alleyn pushed forward a chair and she slumped herself down on it. Fox went quietly to the desk and prepared to make a shorthand report. Alleyn sat opposite Katti.

'I'm sorry to bother you again, Miss Bostock,' he said. 'We've got a good deal of tidying up to do, as you may imagine. First of all, is nitric acid used in the studio for anything?'

'Etching,' said Katti. 'Why?'

'We've found stains in the junk-room that looked like it. Where is it kept?'

'In a bottle on the top shelf. It's marked with a red cross.'

'We couldn't find it.'

'It was filled up on Friday, and put on the top shelf. Must be there.'

'I see. Right. Now I just want to check everybody's movements from lunch-time on Friday. In your case it will be a simple matter. I believe you spent most of your time in London with Miss Troy?' He opened his notebook and put it on the arm of his chair.

'Yes,' he said. 'I see you both went to your club, changed and dined with Sir Arthur and Lady Jaynes at Eaton Square. From there you went to the private view of the Phoenix Group Show, and supped at the Hungaria. That right?'

'Yes. Quite correct.'

'You stayed at the club. What time did you get back from the Hungaria on Friday night?'

'Saturday morning,' corrected Katti. 'I left with the Jayneses at about twelve-thirty. They drove me to the club. Troy stayed on with John Bellasca and was swept out with the dust whenever they close.'

'You met again at breakfast?'

'Yes. We separated during the morning and met again at the show. I lunched with some people I ran into there – Graham Barnes and his wife – he's the watercolour bloke. Then Troy and I met at the club and came home. She lunched with John Bellasca.'

'Yes. That's all very straightforward. I'll have to ask Sir Arthur Jaynes or someone to confirm it. The usual game, you know.'

'That's all right,' said Katti. 'You want to find out whether either of us had time to sneak back here and set a death-trap for that little fool Sonia, don't you?'

'That's the sort of idea,' agreed Alleyn with a smile. 'I know Sir Arthur slightly. Would you like me to say you've lost a pearl neck-lace and want to trace it, or – '

'Good Lord, no. Tell him the facts of the business. Do I look like pearls? And John will fix up Troy's alibi for her. He'll probably come down at ninety miles an hour to say he did it himself if you're not careful.' Katti chuckled and lit a cigarette.

'I see,' said Alleyn. And into his thoughts came the picture of Troy as she had sat before the fire with her cropped head between her long hands. There had been no ring on those hands.

'When you got back to the club after you left the Hungaria, did anyone see you?'

'The night porter let me in. I don't remember anyone else.'

'Was your room near Miss Troy's?'

'Next door.'

'Did you hear her return?'

'No. She says she tapped on the door, but I must have been asleep. The maid came in at seven with my tea, but I'd have had time to go out, get Troy's car and drive down here and back, between twelve-thirty and seven, you know.'

'True,' said Alleyn. 'Did you?'

'No.'

'Well – we'll have to do our best with night porters, garage attendants, and petrol consumption.'

'Wish you luck,' said Katti.

'Thank you, Miss Bostock. You got back here for lunch, I understand. How did you spend the afternoon?'

'Dishing up bilge for *The Palette*. I was in here.'

'Did you at any time go to the studio?'

'No.'

'Was Miss Troy with you on Saturday afternoon?'

'She was in and out. Let's see. She spent a good time turning out that desk over there and burning old papers. Then she tidied her sketching-kit. We had tea in here. After tea we went out to look at a place across the fields where Troy thought of doing a sketch. We dined out with some people at Bossicote – the Haworths – and got home about eleven.'

'Thank you. Sunday?'

'I was at my article for *The Palette* all day. Troy painted in the morning and came in here in the afternoon. The others were all back for dinner.'

'Did you hear the model say anything about her own movements during the weekend?'

'No. Don't think so. I fancy she said she was going to London.'

'You engaged her for this term before Miss Troy returned, didn't you?'

'Yes.'

'How did you get hold of her?'

'Through Graham Barnes. He gave me her address.'

'Have you got it?'

'Oh Lord, where was it? Somewhere in Battersea, I think. Battersea Bridge Gardens. That's it. I've got it written down somewhere. I'll try and find it for you.'

'I wish you would. It would save us one item in a loathsome itinerary of dull jobs. Now, about this business with the model and your picture. The trapeze-artiste subject, I mean. Did she pose for you again after the day when there was the trouble described by Miss Phillida Lee?'

Again that dull crimson stained the broad face. Katti's thick eyebrows came together and her lips protruded in a sort of angry pout.

'That miserable little worm Lee! I told Troy she was a fool to take her, fees or no fees. The girl's bogus. She went to the Slade and was no doubt made to feel entirely extraneous. She tries to talk "Slade" when she remembers, but the original nice-girl gush oozes out all over the place. She sweats suburbia from every pore. She deliberately sneaked in and listened to what I had to say.'

'To the model?'

'Yes. Little drip!'

'It was true, then, that you did have a difference with Sonia?'

'If I did, that doesn't mean I killed her.'

'Of course it doesn't. But I should be glad of an answer, Miss Bostock.'

'She was playing up, and I ticked her off. She knew I wanted to finish the thing for the Group Show, and she deliberately set out to make work impossible. I scraped the head down four times, and now the canvas is unworkable – the tooth has gone completely. Troy is always too easy with the models. She spoils them. I gave the little brute hell because she needed it.'

'And did she pose again for you?'

'No. I've told you the thing was dead.'

'How did she misbehave? Just fidgeting?'

Katti leant forward, her square hands on her knees. Alleyn noticed that she was shaking a little, like an angry terrier.

'I'd got the head laid in broadly – I wanted to draw it together with a dry brush and then complete it. I wanted to keep it very simple and round, the drawing of the mouth was giving me trouble. I told her not to move – she had a damnable trick of biting her lip. Every time I looked at her she gave a sort of sneering smirk. As if she knew it wasn't going well. I mixed a touch of cadmium red for the under-lip. Just as I was going to lay it down she grimaced. I cursed her. She didn't say anything. I pulled myself together to put the brush on the canvas and looked at her. She stuck her foul little tongue out.'

'And that tore it to shreds, I imagine?'

'It did. I said everything I'd been trying not to say for the past fortnight. I let go.'

'Not surprising. It must have been unspeakably maddening. Why, do you suppose, was she so set on making things impossible?'

'She deliberately baited me,' said Katti, under her breath.

'But why?'

'Why? Because I'd treated her as if she was a model. Because I expected to get some return for the excessive wages Troy was giving her. I'd engaged her, and I managed things till Troy came back. Sonia resented that. Always hinting that I wasn't her boss and so on.'

'That was all?'

'Yes.'

'I see. You say her wages were excessively generous. What was she paid?'

'Four pounds a week and her keep. She's spun Troy some tale about doctor's bills, and Troy, as usual, believed the sad story and stumped up. She's anybody's mark for sponging. It's so damned immoral to let people get away with that sort of thing. It's no good talking to Troy. Streetbeggars see her coming a mile away. She's got two dead-heads here now.'

'Really? Which two?'

'Garcia, of course. She's been shelling out money to Garcia for ages. And now there's this Australian wild-man – Hatchett. She says she makes the others pay through the nose, but Lord knows if she ever gets the money. She's hopeless,' said Katti, with an air of exasperated affection.

'Would you call this a good photograph of Mr Garcia?' asked Alleyn suddenly. He held out the group. Katti took it and glowered at it.

'Yes, it's very like him,' she said. 'That thing was taken last year during the summer classes. Yes – that's Garcia all right.'

'He was here as Miss Troy's guest then, I suppose?'

'Oh Lord, yes. Garcia never pays for anything. He's got no sort of decency where money is concerned. No conscience at all.'

'No aesthetic conscience?'

'Um!' said Katti. 'I wouldn't say that. No – his work's the only thing he is honest about, and he's passionately sincere there.'

'I wish you'd give me a clear idea of him, Miss Bostock. Will you?'

'Not much of a hand at that sort of thing,' growled Katti, 'but I'll have a shot. He's a dark, dirty, weird-looking fellow. Very paintable head. Plenty of bone. You think he murdered the model, don't you?'

'I don't know who murdered the model.'

'Well, I think he did. It's just the sort of thing he would do. He's absolutely ruthless and as cold-blooded as a flatfish. He asked Malmsley if he ever felt like murdering his mistress, didn't he?'

'So Mr Malmsley told us.'

'I'll bet it's true. If Sonia interfered with his work and put him off his stride, and he couldn't get rid of her any other way, he'd get rid of her that way. She may have refused to give him any more money.'

'Did she give him money?'

'I think so. Ormerin says she was keeping him last year. He wouldn't have the slightest qualms about taking it. Garcia just looks upon money as something you've got to have to keep you going. He could have got a well-paid job with a monumental firm. Troy got on to it for him. When he saw the tombstones with angels and open Bibles he said something indecent and walked out. He was practically starving that time,' said Katti, half to herself, and with a sort of reluctant admiration, 'but he wouldn't haul his flag down.'

'You think the model was really attached to him?'

Katti took another cigarette and Alleyn lit it for her.

'I don't know,' she said. 'I'm not up in the tender passion. I've got an idea that she'd switched over to Basil Pilgrim, but whether it was to try and make Garcia jealous or because she'd fallen for Pilgrim is another matter. She was obviously livid with Seacliff. But then Garcia had begun to hang round Seacliff.'

'Dear me,' said Alleyn, 'what a labyrinth of untidy emotions.'

'You may say so,' agreed Katti. She hitched herself out of her chair. 'Have you finished with me, Mr Alleyn?'

'Yes, do you know, I think I have. We shall have a statement in longhand for you to look at and sign, if you will, later on.'

She glared at Fox. 'Is that what he's been up to?'

'Yes.'

'Pah!'

'It's only to establish your movements. Of course, if you don't want to sign it – '

'Who said I didn't? Let me wait till I see it.'

'That's the idea, miss,' said Fox, looking benignly at her over the top of his spectacles.

'Will you show Miss Bostock out, please, Fox?'

'Thank you, I know my way about this house,' said Katti with a prickly laugh. She stumped off to the door. Fox closed it gently behind her.

'Rather a tricky sort of lady, that,' he said.

'She is a bit. Never mind. She gave us some sidelights on Garcia.'

'She did that all right.'

There was a rap on the door and one of the local men looked in.

'Excuse me, sir, but there's a gentleman out here says he wants to see you very particular.'

'What's his name?'

'He just said you'd be very glad indeed to see him, sir. He never gave a name.'

'Is he a journalist?' asked Alleyn sharply. 'If he is, I shall be very glad indeed to kick him out. We're too busy for the Press just now.'

'Well, sir, he didn't say he was a reporter. He said – er – er – er – '

'What?'

'His words was, sir, that you'd scream the place down with loud cries of gladness when you clapped eyes on him.'

'That's no way to ask to see the chief,' said Fox. 'You ought to know that.'

'Go and ask him to give his name,' said Alleyn.

The policeman retired.

Fox eyed Alleyn excitedly.

'By gum, sir, you don't think it may be this Garcia? By all accounts he's eccentric enough to send in a message like that.'

'No,' said Alleyn, as the door opened. 'I rather fancy I recognize the style. I rather fancy, Fox, that an old and persistent friend of ours has got in first on the news.'

'Unerring as ever, Mr Alleyn,' said a voice from the hall, and Nigel Bathgate walked into the room.

CHAPTER 9

Phillida Lee and Watt Hatchett

'Where the devil did you spring from?' asked Alleyn. Nigel advanced with a shameless grin.

> ' "Where did I come from, 'Specky dear?
> The blue sky opened and I am here!'

'Hullo, Fox!'

'Good evening, Mr Bathgate,' said Fox.

'I suppose you've talked to my mamma on the telephone,' said Alleyn as they shook hands.

'There now,' returned Nigel, 'aren't you wonderful, Inspector? Yes, Lady Alleyn rang me up to say you'd been sooled on to the trail before your time, and she thought the odds were you'd forget to let us know you couldn't come and stay with us.'

'So you instantly motored twenty miles in not much more than as many minutes in order to tell me how sorry you were?'

'That's it,' said Nigel cheerfully. 'You read me like a book. Angela sends her fondest love. She'd have come too only she's not feeling quite up to long drives just now.'

He sat down in one of the largest chairs.

'Don't let me interrupt,' he said. 'You can give me the story later on. I've got enough to go on with from the local cop. I'll ring up the office presently and give them the headlines. Your mother – divine woman – has asked me to stay.'

'Has my mother gone out of her mind?' asked Alleyn of nobody in particular.

'Come, come Inspector,' reasoned Nigel, with a trace of nervousness in his eye, 'you know you're delighted to have me.'

'There's not the smallest excuse for your bluffing your way in, you know. I've a damn good mind to have you chucked out.'

'Don't do that. I'll take everything down in shorthand and nobody will see me if I turn the chair round. Fox will then be able to fix the stammering witness with a basilisk glare. All will go like clockwork. All right?'

'All right. It's quite irregular, but you occasionally have your uses. Go into the corner there.'

Nigel hurried into a shadowy corner, turned a high armchair with its back to the room and dived into it.

' "I am invisible," ' he said. ' "And I shall overhear their conference." The Bard.'

'I'll deal with you later,' said Alleyn grimly. 'Tell them to send another of these people along, Fox.'

When Fox had gone Nigel asked hoarsely from the armchair if Alleyn had enjoyed himself in New Zealand.

'Yes,' said Alleyn.

'Funny you getting a case there,' ventured Nigel. 'Rather a busman's holiday, wasn't it?'

'I enjoyed it. Nobody interfered and the reporters were very well-behaved.'

'Oh,' said Nigel.

There was a short silence broken by Nigel.

'Did you have a slap-and-tickle with the American lady on the boat deck?'

'I did not.'

'Oh! Funny coincidence about Agatha Troy. I mean she was in the same ship, wasn't she? Lady Alleyn tells me the portrait is quite miraculously like you.'

'Don't prattle,' said Alleyn. 'Have you turned into a gossip hound?'

'No. I say!'

'What!'

'Angela's started a baby.'

'So I gathered, and so no doubt Fox also gathered, from your opening remarks.'

'I'm so thrilled I could yell it in the teeth of the whole police force.'

Alleyn smiled to himself.

'Is she all right?' he asked.

'She's not sick in the mornings any more. We want you to be a godfather. Will you, Alleyn?'

'I should be charmed.'

'Alleyn!'

'What?'

'You might tell me a bit about this case. Somebody's murdered the model, haven't they?'

'Quite possibly.'

'How?'

'Stuck a knife through the throne so that when she took the pose – '

'She sat on it?'

'Don't be an ass. She lay on it and was stabbed to the heart, poor little fool!'

'Who's the prime suspect?'

'A bloke called Garcia, who has been her lover, was heard to threaten her, has possibly got tired of her, and has probably been living on her money.'

'Is he here?'

'No. He's gone on a walking tour to Lord knows where, and is expected to turn up at an unknown warehouse in London in the vaguely near future, to execute a marble statue of "Comedy and Tragedy" for a talkie house.'

'D'you think he's bolted?'

'I don't know. He seems to be one of those incredible and unpleasant people with strict aesthetic standards, and no moral ones. He appears to be a genius. Now shut up. Here comes another of his fellow-students.'

Fox came in with Phillida Lee.

Alleyn, who had only met her across the dining-room table, was rather surprised to see how small she was. She wore a dull red dress covered in a hand-painted design. It was, he realized, deliberately unfashionable and very deliberately interesting. Miss Lee's hair was parted down the centre and dragged back from her forehead with such passionate determination that the corners of her eyes had attempted to follow it. Her face, if left to itself, would have been round and eager, but the austerities of the Slade school had superimposed upon it a careful expression of detachment. When she spoke one heard a faint undercurrent of the Midlands. Alleyn asked her to sit down. She perched on the edge of a chair and stared fixedly at him.

'Well, Miss Lee,' Alleyn began in his best official manner, 'we shan't keep you very long. I just want to have an idea of your movements during the weekend.'

'How ghastly!' said Miss Lee.

'But why?'

'I don't know. It's all so terrible. I feel I'll never be quite the same again. The *shock*. Of course, I ought to try and sublimate it, I suppose, but it's so difficult.'

'I shouldn't try to do anything but be common-sensical if I were you,' said Alleyn.

'But I thought they used psycho methods in the police!'

'At all events we don't need to apply them to the matter in hand. You left Tatler's End House on Friday afternoon by the three o'clock bus?'

'Yes.'

'With Mr Ormerin and Mr Watt Hatchett?'

'Yes,' agreed Miss Lee, looking self-conscious and maidenly.

'What did you do when you got to London?'

'We all had tea at The Flat Hat in Vincent Square.'

'And then?'

'Ormerin suggested we should go to an exhibition of poster work at the Westminster. We did go, and met some people we knew.'

'Their names, please, Miss Lee.'

She gave him the names of half a dozen people and the addresses of two.

'When did you leave the Westminster Art School?'

'I don't know. About six, I should think. Ormerin had a date somewhere. Hatchett and I had dinner together at a Lyons. He took me. Then we went to the show at the Vortex Theatre.'

'That's in Maida Vale, isn't it?'

'Yes. I'm a subscriber and I had tickets. They were doing a play by Michael Sasha. It's called *Angle of Incidence*. It's *frightfully* thrilling and absolutely new. All about three County Council labourers in a sewer. Of course,' added Miss Lee, adopting a more mature manner, 'the Vortex is purely experimental.'

'So it would seem. Did you speak to anyone while you were there?'

'Oh yes. We talked to Sasha himself, and to Lionel Shand who did the décor. I know both of them.'

'Can you give me their addresses?'

Miss Lee was vague on this point, but said that care of the Vortex would always find them. Patiently led by Alleyn she gave a full account of her weekend. She had stayed with an aunt in the Fulham Road, and had spent most of her time in this aunt's company. She had also seen a great deal of Watt Hatchett, it seemed, and had gone to a picture with him on Saturday night.

'Only I *do* hope you won't have to ask Auntie anything, Inspector Alleyn, because you see she pays my fees with Miss Troy, and if she thought the *police* were after me she'd very likely turn sour, and then I wouldn't be able to go on painting. And that,' added Miss Lee with every appearance of sincerity, 'would be the most frightful tragedy.'

'It shall be averted if possible,' said Alleyn gravely, and got the name and address of the aunt.

'Now then, Miss Lee, about those two conversations you over-heard – '

'I don't want to be called as a witness,' began Miss Lee in a hurry.

'Possibly not. On the other hand you must realize that in a serious case – and this is a very serious case – personal objections of this sort cannot be allowed to stand in the way of police investigation.'

'But I didn't mean you to think that because Bostock flew into a blind rage with Sonia she was capable of *murdering* her.'

'Nor do I think so. It appears that half the class flew into rages at different times, and for much the same reason.'

'I didn't! I never had a row with her. Ask the others. I got on all right with her. I was sorry for her.'

'Why?'

'Because Garcia was so beastly to her. Oh, I do think he was *foul*! If you'd *heard* him that time!'

'I wish very much that I had.'

'When he said he'd shut her mouth for keeps – I mean it's the sort of thing you might think he'd say without meaning it, but he sounded

as if he did mean it. He spoke so softly in a kind of drawl. I thought
he was going to do it *then*. I was *terrified*. Truly! That's why I banged
the door and walked in.'

'About the scrap of conversation you overheard – did you get the
impression that they planned to meet on Friday night?'

'It sounded like that. Sonia said: "If it's possible." I think that's
what she meant. I think she meant to come back and bed down with
Garcia for the night while no one was here.'

'To *what*, Miss Lee?'

'Well – you know – to spend the night with him.'

'What did they do when you appeared?'

'Garcia just stared at me. He's got a beastly sort of way of looking
at you. As if you were an animal. I was awfully scared he'd guessed
I'd overheard them, but I saw in a minute that he hadn't. I said:
"Hullo, you two, what are you up to? Having a woo or something?"
I don't know how I managed it, but I did. And he said: "No, just a
little chat." He turned away and began working at his thing. Sonia
just walked out. She looked *ghastly*, Mr Alleyn, honestly. She always
made up pretty heavily except when we were painting the head, but
even under her make-up I could see she was absolutely *bleached*. Oh,
Mr Alleyn, I do believe he did it, I do, *actually*.

'You tell me you were on quite good terms with the model. Did
she ever say anything that had any bearing on her relationship with
Mr Garcia?'

Phillida Lee settled herself more comfortably in her chair. She was
beginning to enjoy herself.

'Well, of course, ever since this morning, I've been thinking of
everything I can remember. I didn't talk much to her until I'd been
here for a bit. As a matter of fact the others were so frightfully superior that I didn't get a chance to talk to *anybody* at first.'

Her round face turned pink, and suddenly Alleyn felt a little sorry
for her.

'It's always a bit difficult, settling down among new people,' he
said.

'Yes, I dare say it is, but if the new people just do their best to
make you feel they don't want you, it's worse than that. That was
why I left the Slade, really, Mr Alleyn. The instructors just used to
come round once in a blue moon and look at one's things and sigh.

And the students never even seemed to see one, and if they did they looked as if one smelt. And at first this place was just as bad, though of course Miss Troy's *marvellous*. Malmsley was at the Slade, and he's *typical*. Seacliff's worse. Anyway, Seacliff never *sees* another female, much less speaks to her. And all the men just beetle round Seacliff and never give anyone else a *thought*. It was a *bit* better after she said she was engaged to Pilgrim. Sonia felt like I did about Seacliff, and we talked about her a bit – and – well, we sort of sympathized about her.'
The thin voice with its faint echo of the Midlands went on and on.

Alleyn, listening, could see the two of them, Phillida Lee, sore and lonely; Sonia, God knew how angry and miserable, taking comfort in mutual abuse of Valmai Seacliff.

'So you made friends?' he asked.

'Sort of. Yes, we did. I'm not one to look down my nose at a girl because she's a model. I'm a communist, anyway. Sonia was furious about Seacliff. She called her awful names – all beginning with B, you know. She said somebody ought to tell Pilgrim what Seacliff really was like. She – she – said – '

Miss Lee stopped abruptly.

'Yes?'

'I don't know whether I ought to – I mean – I like Pilgrim awfully and – well, I *mean* – '

'Is it something that the model said about Miss Seacliff?' said Alleyn.

'About *her!* Ooo no! I wouldn't mind what anybody said about *her*. But I don't believe it was true about Pilgrim. I don't think he was *ever* attracted to Sonia. I think she just made it up.'

'Made what up, Miss Lee? Did she suggest there had been anything like a romance between herself and Mr Pilgrim?'

'Well, if you can call it romance. I mean she said – I mean, it was only *once* ages ago, after a party, and I mean I think men and women ought to be free to follow their sex-impulses anyway, and not repress them. But I mean I don't think Pilgrim *ever* did because he doesn't seem as if he would somehow, but anyway, I don't see why not, bcause as Garcia once said, if you're hungry – ' Miss Lee, scarlet with determination, shut her eyes and added: 'you eat.'

'Quite so,' said Alleyn, 'but you needn't guzzle, of course.'

'Oh well – no, I suppose you needn't. But I mean I should think Pilgrim never *did*.'

'The model suggested there had been a definite intimacy between herself and Pilgrim?'

'Yes. She said she could tell Seacliff a thing or two about him, and if he didn't look out she would.'

'I see.'

'But I don't think there ever was. Truly. It was because she was so furious with Pilgrim for not taking any notice of her.'

'You returned in the bus yesterday evening with the model, didn't you?'

'Yes. Watt – I mean Hatchett and me and Ormerin and Malmsley.'

'Did you notice anything out of the way about her?'

'No. She was doing a bit of a woo with Ormerin to begin with, but I think she was asleep for the last part of the trip.'

'Did she mention what she had done in London?'

'I think she said she'd gone to stay with a friend or something.'

'No idea where or with whom?'

'No, Mr Alleyn.'

'Nothing about Mr Garcia?'

'No.'

'Did she ever speak much of Garcia?'

'Not much. But she seemed as if – as if in a sort of way she was *sure* of Garcia. And yet he was tired of her. She'd lost her body-urge for him, if you ask me. But she seemed *sure* of him and yet furious with him. Of course, she wasn't very well.'

'Wasn't she?'

'No. I'm sure that was why she did that *terrible* thing to Troy's portrait of Seacliff. She was ill. Only she asked me not to say anything about it, because she said it didn't do a model any good for her to get a reputation of not being able to stand up to the work. I wouldn't have known except that I found her one morning looking absolutely *green*, and I asked her if anything was the matter. She said the pose made her feel sick – it was the twist that did it, she said. She was *honestly* sick, and she felt sort of giddy.'

Alleyn looked at Miss Lee's inquisitive, rather pretty, rather commonplace face and realized that her sophistication was more synthetic than even he had supposed. 'Bless my soul,' he thought, 'the creature's a complete baby – an infant that has been taught half a dozen indecorous phrases by older children.'

'Well, Miss Lee,' he said, 'I think that's all we need worry about for the moment. I've got your aunt's address – '

'Yes, but you *will* remember, won't you? I mean – '

'I shall be the very soul of tact. I shall say we are looking for a missing heiress believed to be suffering from loss of memory, and last heard of near Bossicote, and she will think me very stupid, and I shall learn that you spent the entire weekend in her company.'

'Yes. And Watt – Hatchett, I mean.'

'He was there too, was he?'

Again Miss Lee looked self-conscious and maidenly.

'Well, I mean, not *all* the time. I mean he didn't *stay* with us, but he came to lunch and tea – and dinner on Saturday and lunch on Sunday. Of course he *is* rough, and he does speak badly, but I told Auntie he can't help that because everybody's like that in Australia. Some of the others were pretty stinking to him too, you know. They made him feel dreadfully out of it. I was sorry for him, and I thought they were such snobs. And anyway, I think his work is frightfully exciting.'

'Where did he stay?'

'At a private hotel near us, in the Fulham Road. We went to the flicks on Saturday night. Oh, I told you that, didn't I?'

'Yes, thank you. When you go back to the dining-room, will you ask Mr Hatchett to come and see me in ten minutes' time?'

'Yes, I will.'

She got up and gazed at Alleyn. He saw a sort of corpse-side expression come into her face.

'Oh, Mr Alleyn,' she said, 'isn't it all *awful?*'

'Quite frightful,' responded Alleyn cheerfully. 'Good evening, Miss Lee.'

She walked away with an air of bereavement, and shut the door softly behind her.

'Oy!' said Nigel from the armchair.

'Hullo!'

'I'm moving over to the fire till the next one comes along. It's cold in this corner.'

'All right.'

Fox, who had remained silently at the writing-desk throughout the interview with Miss Lee, joined Alleyn and Nigel at the fire.

'That was a quaint little piece of Staffordshire,' said Nigel.

'Little simpleton! All that pseudo-modern nonsense! See here, Bathgate, you're one of the young intelligentsia, aren't you?'

'What do you mean? I'm a pressman.'

'That doesn't actually preclude you from the intelligentsia, does it?'

'Of course it doesn't.'

'Very well then. Can you tell me how much of this owlishness is based on experience, and how much on handbooks and hearsay?'

'You mean their ideas on sex?'

'I do.'

'Have they been shocking you, Inspector?'

'I find their conversation bewildering, I must confess.'

'Come off it,' said Nigel.

'What do you think, Fox?' asked Alleyn.

'Well, sir, I must say I thought they spoke very free round the dining-room table. All this talk about mistresses and appetites and so forth. Very free. Not much difference between their ways and the sort of folk we used to deal with down in the black divisions if you're to believe what you hear. Only the criminal classes are just promiscuous without being able to make it sound intellectual, if you know what I mean. Though I must say,' continued Fox thoughtfully, 'I don't fancy this crowd is as free-living as they'd like us to believe. This young lady, now. She seems like a nice little girl from a good home, making out she's something fierce.'

'I know,' agreed Alleyn. 'Little donkey.'

'And all the time she was talking about deceased and body-urges and so forth, she never seemed to realize what these sick, giddy turns might mean,' concluded Fox.

'Of course the girl was going to have a child,' said Nigel complacently.

'It doesn't follow as the night the day,' murmured Alleyn. 'She may have been liverish or run-down. Nevertheless, it's odd that the little thought never entered Miss Lee's head. You go back to your corner, Bathgate, here's Mr Watt Hatchett.'

Watt Hatchett came in with his hands thrust into his trousers pockets. Alleyn watched him curiously, thinking what a perfect type he was of the smart Sydney tough about to get on in the world. He was short, with the general appearance of a bad man in a South American movie. His hair resembled a patent-leather cap, his skin was swarthy, he walked with a sort of hard-boiled slouch, and his clothes fitted him rather too sleekly. A cigarette seemed to be perpetually gummed to his under-lip which projected. He had beautiful hands.

'Want me, Inspector?' he inquired. He never opened his lips more than was absolutely necessary, and he scarcely seemed to move his tongue, so that every vowel was strangled at birth, and for preference he spoke entirely through his nose. There was, however, something engaging about him; an aliveness, a raw virility.

'Sit down, Mr Hatchett,' said Alleyn. 'I shan't keep you long.'

Hatchett slumped into an armchair. He moved with the slovenly grace of an underbred bouncer, and this in its way was also attractive.

'Good oh,' he said.

'I'm sure you realize yourself the importance of the information we have from you as regards the drape.'

Too right. I reckon it shows that whoever did the dirty stuff with the knife did it after everyone except Garcia and Mr Highbrow Malmsley had cleared off to London.'

'Exactly. You will therefore not think it extraordinary if I ask you to repeat the gist of this information.'

Hatchett wanted nothing better. He went over the whole story again. He went down to the studio on Friday afternoon – he remembered now that it was half-past two by the hall clock when he left the house – and noticed the drape lying crumpled on the throne, as Sonia had left it when she got up at noon. It was still undisturbed when he went away to catch the bus.

'And yesterday evening it was stretched out tight. There you are.'

Alleyn said nothing about Troy's discovery of this condition on Saturday afternoon. He asked Hatchett to account for his own movements during the weekend. Hatchett described his Friday evening's entertainment with Phillida Lee and Ormerin.

'We had tea and then we went to a theatre they called the Vortex, and it was just about the lousiest show I've *ever* had to sit through. Gosh! it gave me a pain in the neck, dinkum it did. Three blokes in a sewer nagging each other for two bloody hours, and they called it a play. If that's a play give me the talkies in Aussie. They'll do me. We met the chap that runs the place. One of these die-away queens that likes to kid himself he amounts to something. You won't get me inside a theatre again.'

'Have you never seen a flesh-and-blood show before?'

'Naow, and I never will again. The talkies'll do me.'

'But I assure you the Vortex is no more like the genuine theatre than, shall we say Mr Malmsley's drawings are like Miss Troy's portraits.'

'Is that a fact?'

'Certainly. But we're straying a little from the matter in hand. You spent Friday night at the Vortex and returned with Miss Lee to the Fulham Road?'

'Yeah, that's right. I took her home and then I went to my own place close by.'

'Anyone see you come in?'

They plodded on. Hatchett could, if necessary, produce the sort of alibi that might hold together or might not. Alleyn gleaned enough material to enable him to verify the youth's account of himself.

'To return to Garcia,' he said at last. 'I want you to tell me if you have ever heard Garcia say anything about this warehouse he intends to use as a studio in London.'

'I never had much to do with that bloke. I reckon he's queer. If you talk to him, half the time he never seems to listen. I did say once I'd like to have a look when he started in on the marble. I reckon that statue'll be a corker. He's clever all right. D'you know what he said? He said he'd take care nobody knew where it was because he didn't want any of this crowd pushing in when he was working. He did let out that it belonged to a bloke that's gone abroad somewhere. I heard him tell the girl Sonia that much.'

'I see. That's no go, then. Now, on your bus trip to and from London, did you sit anywhere near Sonia Gluck?'

'Naow. After the way she mucked up Miss Troy's picture, I didn't want to have anything to do with her. It's just too bad she's got hers for keeps, but all the same I reckon she was a fair nark, that girl. Always slinging off about Aussie, she was. She'd been out there once with a Vordervill show, and I tipped it was a bum show because she was always shooting off her mouth about the way the Aussies don't know a good thing when they see it. These pommies! She gave me the jitters. Just because I couldn't talk big about my home and how swell my people were, and how we cut a lot of ice in Sydney, she treated me like dirt. I said to her one time, I said: "I reckon if Miss Troy thought I was good enough to come here, even if my old pop did keep a bottle store on Circular Quay, I reckon if she thought I was OK I'm good enough for you." I went very, very crook at her after she did that to the picture. Miss Troy's been all right to me. She's been swell. Did you know she paid my way in the ship?'

'Did she?'

'Too right she did. She saw me painting in Suva. I worked my way to Suva, you know, from Aussie, and I got a job there. It was a swell job, too, while it lasted. Travelling for Jackson's Confectionery. I bought this suit and some paints with my first cheque, and then I had a row with the boss and walked out on him. I used to paint all the time then. She saw me working and she reckoned I had talent, so she brought me home to England. The girl Sonia seemed to think I was living on charity.'

'That was a very unpleasant interpretation to put upon a gracious action.'

'Eh? Yeah! Yeah, that's what I told her.'

'Since you joined Miss Troy's classes, have you become especially friendly with any one of the other students?'

'Well, the little girl Lee's all right. She treats you as if you were human.'

'What about the men?'

'Malmsley makes me tired. He's nothing but a big sissie. The French bloke doesn't seem to know he's born, and Garcia's queer. They don't like me,' said Hatchett, with extraordinary aggression, 'and I don't like them.'

'What about Mr Pilgrim?'

'Aw, he's different. He's all right. I get on with him good oh, even if his old pot is one of these lords. Him and me's cobbers.'

'Was he on good terms with the model?'

Hatchett looked sulky and uncomfortable.

'I don't know anything about that,' he muttered.

'You have never heard either of them mention the other?'

'Naow.'

'Nor noticed them speaking to each other?'

'Naow.'

'So you can tell us nothing about the model except that you dis-liked her intensely?'

Hatchett's grey eyes narrowed in an extremely insolent smile.

'That doesn't exactly make me out a murderer though, does it?'

'Not precisely.'

'I'd be one big boob to go talking about how I couldn't stick her if I'd anything to do with it, wouldn't I?'

'Oh, I don't know. You might be sharp enough to suppose that you would convey just that impression.'

The olive face turned a little paler.

'Here! You got no call to talk that way to me. What d'you want to pick on me for? I've been straight enough with you. I've given you a square deal right enough, haven't I?'

'I sincerely hope so.'

'I reckon this country's crook. You've all got a down on the new chum. It's a blooming nark. Just because I said the girl Sonia made me tired you got to get leery and make me out a liar. I reckon the wonderful London police don't know they're alive yet. You've as good as called me a murderer.'

'My dear Mr Hatchett, may I suggest that if you go through life looking for insults, you may be comfortably assured of finding them. At no time during our conversation have I called you a murderer.'

'I gave you a square deal,' repeated Hatchett.

'I'm not absolutely assured of that. I think that a moment ago you deliberately withheld something. I mean, when I asked you if you could tell me anything about the model's relationship with Mr Pilgrim.'

Hatchett was silent. He moved his head slightly from side to side, and ostentatiously inhaled cigarette smoke.

'Very well,' said Alleyn. 'That will do, I think.'

But Hatchett did not get up.

'I don't know where you get that idea,' he said.

'Don't you? I need keep you no longer, Mr Hatchett. We shall probably check your alibi, and I shall ask you to sign a written account of our conversation. That is all at the moment.'

Hatchett rose, hunched his shoulders, and lit a fresh cigarette from the butt of the old one. He was still rather pale.

'I got nothing in for Pilgrim,' he said. 'I got no call to talk to dicks about my cobbers.'

'You prefer to surround them with a dubious atmosphere of uncertainty, and leave us to draw our own conclusions? You are doing Mr Pilgrim no service by these rather transparent evasions.'

'Aw, talk English, can't you!'

'Certainly. Good evening.'

'Pilgrim's a straight sort of a bloke. Him do anything like that! It's laughable.'

'Look here,' said Alleyn wearily. 'Are you going to tell me what you know, or are you going away, or am I going to remove you? Upon my word, if we have many more dark allusions to Mr Pilgrim's purity, I shall feel like clapping both of you in jug.'

'By cripey!' cried Hatchett violently. 'Aren't I telling you it was nothing at all! And to show you it was nothing at all, I'll bloody well tell you what it was. Now then.'

'Good! said Alleyn. 'Speak up!'

'It's only that the girl Sonia was going to have a kid, and Pilgrim's the father. So now what?'

CHAPTER 10

Weekend of an Engaged Couple

In the silence that followed Watt Hatchett's announcement Fox was heard to cough discreetly. Alleyn glanced quickly at him, and then contemplated Hatchett. Hatchett glared defiantly round the room rather as if he expected an instant arrest.

'How do you know this, Mr Hatchett?' asked Alleyn.

'I've seen it in writing.'

'Where?'

'It's like this. Me and Basil Pilgrim's got the same kind of paint-smocks, see? When I first come I saw his new one and I thought it was a goody. It's a sort of dark khaki stuff, made like a coat, with corking great pockets. He told me where he got it, and I sent for one. When I got it, I hung it up with the others in the junk-room. That was last Tuesdee. On Wensdee morning I put it on, and I noticed at the time that his smock wasn't there. He'd taken it up to the house for something, I suppose. Well, when we cleaned up at midday, I put me hand in one of me pockets and I felt a bit of paper. I took it out and had a look at it. Thought it might be the docket from the shop or something, see? When I got it opened up, I see it was a bit of a note scrawled on the back of a bill. It said, as near as I remember: "Congrats on the engagement, but what if I tell her she's going to have a step-child? I'll be in the studio tonight at ten. Advise you to come." Something like that it was. I may not have got it just the same as what it was, but that's near enough. It was signed "S".'

'What did you do with it?'

'Aw, cripey, I didn't know what to do. I didn't feel so good about reading it. Gee, it was a fair cow, me reading it by mistake like that. I just went into the junk-room and I saw he'd put his smock back by then, so I shoved the blooming paper into his pocket. That evening I could see he was feeling pretty crook himself, so I guessed he'd read it.'

'I see.'

'Look, Mr Alleyn, I'm sorry I went nasty just now. I'm like that. I go horribly crook, and the next minute I could knock me own block off for what I said. But look, you don't want to think too much about this. Honest! That girl Sonia was easy. Look, she went round asking for it, dinkum she did. Soon as I saw that note, I tipped she'd got hold of old Basil some time, and he'd just kind of thought, "Aw, what the hell" and there you were. Look, he's a decent old sport, dinkum he is. And now he's got a real corking girl like Valmai Seacliff, it'd be a nark if he got in wrong. His old pot's a wowser, too. That makes things worse. Look, Mr Alleyn, I'd hate him to think I – '

'All right, all right,' said Alleyn good-humouredly. 'We'll keep your name out of it if we can.'

'Good oh, Mr Alleyn. And, look, you won't – '

'I won't clap the handcuffs on Mr Pilgrim just yet.'

'Yeah, but – '

'You buzz off. And if you'll take a tip from an effete policeman, just think sometimes, before you label the people you meet: "No good" or "standoffish," or what is that splendid phrase? "fair cows." Have you ever heard of an inferiority complex?'

'Naow.'

'Thank the Lord for that. All the same I fancy you suffer from one. Go slow. Think a bit more. Wait for people to like you and they will. And forgive me if you can, for prosing away like a Victorian uncle. Now, off you go.'

'Good oh, Mr Alleyn.'

Hatchett walked to the door. He opened it and then swung round.

'Thanks a lot,' he said. 'Ta-ta for now.'

The door banged, and he was gone. Alleyn leant back in his chair and laughed very heartily.

'Cheeky young fellow, that,' said Fox. 'Australian. I've come across some of them. Always think you're looking down on them. Funny!'

'He's an appalling specimen,' said Nigel from the corner. 'Bumptious young larrikin. Even his beastly argot is bogus. Half-American, half-Cockney.'

'And pure Australian. The dialect is rapidly becoming Americanized.'

'A frightful youth. No wonder they sat on him. He ought to be told how revolting he is whenever he opens his mouth. Antipodean monster.'

'I don't agree with you,' said Alleyn. 'He's an awkward pup, but he might respond to reason in time. What do you make of this business of the note, Fox?'

'Hard to say,' said Fox. 'Looks like the beginnings of blackmail.'

'Very like, very like.'

'From all accounts it wouldn't be very surprising if we found Garcia had set her on to it, would it now?'

'Speculative, but attractive.'

'And then murdered her when he'd collared the money,' said Nigel.

'You're a fanciful fellow, Bathgate,' said Alleyn mildly.

'Well, isn't it possible?'

'Quite possible on what we've got.'

'Shall I get Mr Pilgrim, sir?'

'I think so, Fox. We'll see if he conforms to the Garcia theme or not.'

'I'll bet he does,' said Nigel. 'Is it the Basil Pilgrim who's the eldest son of the Methodist Peer?'

'That's the one. Do you know him?'

'No, but I know of him. I did a story for my paper on his old man. The son's rather a pleasant specimen. I fancy. Cricketer. He was a Blue and looked good enough for an M.C.C. star before he took to this painting.'

'And became a little odd?' finished Alleyn with a twinkle.

'I didn't say that, but it was rather a waste. Anyhow I fail to visualize him as a particularly revolting type of murderer. He'll conform to the Garcia theme, you may depend upon it.'

'That's because you want things to work out that way.'

'Don't you think Garcia's your man?'

'On what we've got I do, certainly, but it's much too early to become wedded to a theory. Back to your corner.'

Fox returned with Basil Pilgrim. As Nigel had remarked, Pilgrim was a very pleasant specimen. He was tall, with a small head, square shoulders and a narrow waist. His face was rather fine-drawn. He had a curious trick while he talked of turning his head first to one member of his audience and then to another. This habit suggested a nervous restlessness. He had a wide mouth, magnificent teeth and very good manners. Alleyn got him to sit down, gave him a cigarette and began at once to establish his movements after he drove away with Valmai Seacliff from Tatler's End House on Friday afternoon. Pilgrim said that they motored to some friends of Valmai Seacliff's who lived at Boxover, twelve miles away. They dined with these friends – a Captain and Mrs Pascoe – spent the evening playing bridge and stayed the night there. The next day they motored to Ankerton Manor, the Oxfordshire seat of Lord Pilgrim, where Basil introduced his fiancée to his father. They spent Saturday night at Ankerton and returned to Tatler's End House on Sunday afternoon.

'At what time did you break up your bridge party on Friday night?' asked Alleyn.

'Fairly early, I think, sir. About elevenish. Valmai had got a snorter of a headache and could hardly see the cards. I gave her some aspirin. She took three tablets, and turned in.'

'Did the aspirin do its job?'

'Oh, rather! She said she slept like the dead.' He looked from Alleyn to Fox and back again. 'She didn't wake till they brought in tea. Her head had quite cleared up.'

'Is she subject to these headaches?'

Pilgrim looked surprised.

'Yes, she is rather. At least, she's had one or two lately. I'm a bit worried about them. I want her to see an oculist, but she doesn't like the idea of wearing glasses.'

'It may not be the eyes.'

'Oh, I think it is. Painters often strain their eyes, you know.'

'Did you sleep comfortably?'

'Me?' Pilgrim turned to Alleyn with an air of bewilderment. 'Oh, I always sleep like a log.'

'How far is Ankerton Manor from here, Mr Pilgrim?'

'Eighty-five miles by my speedometer. I took a note of it.'

'So you had a run of seventy-three miles from Boxover on Saturday?'

'That's the idea, sir.'

'Right. Now about this unfortunate girl. Can you let any light in on the subject?'

'Afraid I can't. It's a damn bad show. I feel rotten about it.'

'Why?'

'Well, wouldn't anybody? It's a foul thing to happen, isn't it?'

'Oh, yes – perfectly abominable. I meant had you any personal reason for feeling rotten about it?'

'Not more than any of the others,' said Pilgrim, after a pause.

'Is that quite true, Mr Pilgrim?'

'What do you mean?' Again he looked from Alleyn to Fox. He had gone very white.

'I mean this. Had Sonia Gluck no closer link with you than with the rest of the class?'

If Pilgrim had been restless before, he was now very still. He stared straight in front of him, his lips parted, and his brows slightly raised.

'I see I shall have to make a clean breast of it,' he said at last.

'I think you would be wise to do so.'

'It's got nothing to do with this business,' he said. 'Unless Garcia knew and was furious about it. My God, I don't know what put you on to this, but I'm not sure it won't be a relief to talk about it. Ever since this morning when she was killed, I've been thinking of it. I'd have told you at once if I'd thought it had any bearing on the case, but I – I didn't want Valmai to know. It happened three months ago. Before I met Valmai. I was at a studio party in Bloomsbury and she – Sonia – was there. Everyone got pretty tight. She asked me to drive her back to her room and then she asked me if I wouldn't come in for a minute. Well – I did. It was the only time. I got a damned unpleasant surprise when I found she was the model here. I didn't say anything to her and she didn't say anything to me. That's all.'

'What about the child?' asked Alleyn.

'God! Then she *did* tell somebody?'

'She told you, at all events.'

'I don't believe it's true. I don't believe the child was mine. Everybody knows what sort of girl she was. Poor little devil! I don't want to blackguard her after this has happened, but I can see what you're driving at now, and it's a serious business for me. If I'd thought the child was my affair, I'd have looked after Sonia, but everybody knows she's been Garcia's mistress for months. She was poisonously jealous of Valmai, and after our engagement was announced she threatened this as a hit at Valmai.'

'How was the matter first broached?'

'She left a note in the pocket of my painting-coat. I don't know how long it had been there. I burnt it. She said she wanted me to meet her somewhere.'

'Did you do this?'

'Yes. I met her in the studio one evening. It was pretty ghastly.'

'What happened?'

'She said she was going to have a baby. She said I was the father. I said I didn't believe it. I knew she was lying, and I told her I knew. I said I'd tell Valmai the whole story myself and I said I'd go to Garcia and tell him. She seemed frightened. That's all that happened.'

'Are you sure of that?'

'Yes. What d'you mean? Of course I'm sure.'

'She didn't try blackmail? She didn't say she would go to Miss Seacliff with this story or, if that failed, she didn't threaten to appeal to your father?'

'She said all sorts of things. She was hysterical. I don't remember everything she said. She didn't know what she was talking about.'

'Surely you would remember if she threatened to go to your father?'

'I don't think she did say she'd do that. Anyway, if she had it wouldn't have made any difference. He couldn't force me to marry her. I know that sounds pretty low, but you see, I *knew* the whole thing was a bluff. It was all so foul and squalid. I was terrified some-one would hear her or something. I just walked away.'

'Did she carry out any of her threats?'

'No.'

'How do you know?'

'Well, I'd have heard pretty soon if she'd said anything to my father.'

'Then she *did* threaten to tell your father?'

'God damn you, I tell you I don't remember what she threat-ened.'

'Did you give her any money?'

Pilgrim moved his head restlessly.

'I advise you to answer me, Mr Pilgrim.'

'I needn't answer anything. I can get a lawyer.'

'Certainly. Do you wish to do that?'

Pilgrim opened his mouth and shut it again. He frowned to himself as if he thought very deeply, and at last he seemed to come to a
decision. He looked from Alleyn to Fox and suddenly he smiled.

'Look here,' he said, 'I didn't kill that girl. I couldn't have killed
her. The Parkers and Valmai will tell you I spent Friday night with
them. My father and everyone else at Ankerton knows I was there
on Saturday. I hadn't a chance to rig the knife. I suppose there's no
reason why I should shy off talking about this business with Sonia
except that – well, when there's a crime like this in the air one's apt
to get nervous.'

'Undoubtedly.'

'You know all about by father, I expect. He's been given a good
deal of publicity. Some bounder of a journalist wrote a lot of miserable gup in one of the papers the other day. The Methodist Peer and
all that. Everyone knows he's a bit fanatic on the subject of morals,
and if he ever got to hear of this business there'd be a row of simply
devastating magnitude. That's why I didn't want it to leak out. He'd
do some tremendous heavy-father stuff at me, and have a stroke on
top of it as likely as not. That's why I didn't want to say any more
about it than I could possibly help. I see now that I've been a fool
not to tell you the whole thing.'

'Good,' said Alleyn.

'As a matter of fact I did give Sonia a cheque for a hundred, and
she promised she'd make no more scenes. In the end she practically
admitted the child was not mine, but,' he smiled ruefully, 'as she
pointed out, she had a perfectly good story to tell my father or
Valmai if she felt inclined to do so.'

'Have you made a clean breast of this to Miss Seacliff?'

'No, I – I – couldn't do that. It seems so foul to go to her with a
squalid little story when we were just engaged. You see, I happen to
feel rather strongly about – well, about some things. I rather disliked
myself for what had happened. Valmai's so marvellous.' His face lit
up with a sudden intensity of emotion. He seemed translated. 'She's

so far beyond all that kind of thing. She's terribly, terribly attractive – you only had to see how the other men here fell for her – but she remains quite aloof from her own loveliness. Just accepts it as something she can't help and then ignores it. It's amazing that she should care – ' He stopped short. 'I don't know that we need discuss all this.'

'I don't think we need. I shall ask you later on to sign a statement of your own movements from Friday to Sunday.'

'Will the Sonia business have to come out, sir?'

'I can promise nothing about that. If it is irrelevant it will not be used. I think it advisable that you should tell Miss Seacliff, but that, of course, is entirely a matter for your own judgment.'

'You don't understand.'

'Possibly not. There's one other question. Did you return to the studio on Friday before you left for Boxover?'

'No. I packed my suitcase after lunch. Young Hatchett came in and talked to me while I was at it. Then I called Valmai and we set off in the car.'

'I see. Thank you. I won't keep you any longer, Mr Pilgrim.'

'Very well, sir. Thank you.'

Fox showed Pilgrim out and returned to the fire. He looked dubious. Nigel reappeared and sat on the wide fender.

'Well, Fox,' said Alleyn, raising an eyebrow, 'what did you think of that?'

'His ideas on the subject of his young lady seem a bit high-flown from what we've seen of her,' said Fox.

'What's she like?' asked Nigel.

'She's extremely beautiful,' Alleyn said. 'Beautiful enough to launch a thousand crimes, perhaps. But I should not have thought the Sonia episode would have caused her to so much as bat an eyelid. She has completely wiped the floor with all the other females, and that, I imagine, is all that matters to Miss Seacliff.'

'Of course, the poor fool's besotted on her. You can see that with half an eye,' said Nigel. He glanced at his shorthand notes. 'What about his alibi?'

'If this place Boxover is only twelve miles away,' grunted Fox, 'his alibi isn't of much account. Is it, Mr Alleyn? They went to bed early on Friday night. He could slip out, run over here, rig the knife and get back to Boxover almost within the hour.'

'You must remember that Garcia slept in the studio.'

'Yes, that's so. But he may not have been there on Friday night. He may have packed up by then and gone off on his tour.'

'Pilgrim must have known that, Fox, if he planned to come to the studio.'

'Yes. That's so. Mind, I still think Garcia's our man. This Mr Pilgrim doesn't strike me as the chap for a job of this sort.'

'He's a bit too obviously the clean young Englishman, though, isn't he?' said Nigel.

'Hullo,' remarked Alleyn, 'didn't Pilgrim come up to your high expectations, Bathgate?'

'Well, you were remarkably cold and snorty with him yourself.'

'Because throughout our conversation he so repeatedly shifted ground. That sort of behaviour is always exceedingly tedious. It was only because I was rough with him that we got the blackmail story at all.'

'He seemed quite an honest-to-God sort of fellow, really,' pronounced Nigel. 'I think it was that stuff about being ashamed of his affair with the model that put me off him. It sounded spurious. Anyway, it's the sort of thing one doesn't talk about to people one has just met.'

'Under rather unusual conditions,' Alleyn pointed out.

'Certainly. All the same, he talks too much.'

'The remark about bounding journalists and miserable gup was perhaps gratuitous.'

'I didn't mean that,' said Nigel in a hurry.

'I'm inclined to agree with you. Let us see Miss Valmai Seacliff, Brer Fox.'

'I wish you wouldn't make me coil up in that chair,' complained Nigel when Fox had gone. 'It's plaguily uncomfortable and right in a draught. Can't I just be here, openly? I'd like to have a look at this lovely.'

'Very well. I suppose you'll do no harm. The concealment was your own suggestion, if you remember. You may sit at the desk and make an attempt to look like the Yard.'

'You don't look much like it yourself in your smart gent's dinner jacket. Tell me, Alleyn, have you fallen in love with Miss Troy?'

'Don't be a fool, Bathgate,' said Alleyn, with such unusual warmth that Nigel's eyebrows went up.

'I'm sorry,' he said. 'Merely a pleasantry. No offence and so on.'

'I'm sorry, too. You must forgive me. I'm bothered about this case.'

'There, there,' said Nigel. 'Coom, coom, coom, it's early days yet.'

'True enough. But suppose Garcia walks in with a happy smile in answer to our broadcast? That bit of clay in the drape. Acid marks and no acid to make 'em. This legendary warehouse. Clay models of comedy and tragedy melted into the night. Damn, I've got the mumbles.'

The door was thrown open, and in came Valmai Seacliff, followed by Fox. Miss Seacliff managed to convey by her entrance that she never moved anywhere without a masculine satellite. That Inspector Fox in his double-breasted blue serge was not precisely in the right manner did nothing to unsettle her poise. She was dressed in a silk trousered garment. Her hair was swept off her forehead into a knot on the nape of her neck. Moving her hips voluptuously, she walked rather like a mannequin. When she reached the chair Alleyn had pushed forward, she turned, paused, and then sank into it with glorious certainly of a well trained show-girl. She stared languidly at Nigel, whose hand had gone automatically to his tie.

'Well, Mr Alleyn?' said Miss Seacliff.

The three men sat down. Alleyn turned a page of his tiny notebook, appeared to deliberate, and embarked upon the familiar opening.

'Miss Seacliff, my chief concern at the moment is to get a clear account of everybody's movements during the weekend. Mr Pilgrim has told us of your motor trip with him to Boxover, and then to Ankerton Manor. I should like you to corroborate his statement if you will. Did you return to the studio before you left?'

'No, I was packing. The housemaid helped me and carried my things down to the car.'

'You arrived at Captain and Mrs Pascoe's house in Boxover on Friday afternoon?'

'Yes.'

'And spent the afternoon together?'

'Yes. The Pascoes talked about tennis but I didn't feel inclined to play. I rather loathe tennis. So we talked.'

Alleyn noticed again her curious little stutter, and the trick she had of letting her voice die and then catching it up on an intake of breath.

'How did you spend the evening?'

'We played bridge for a bit. I had a frightful headache and went to bed early. I felt quite sick with it.'

'That was bad luck. Do you often have these headaches?'

'Never until lately. They started about a month ago. It's rather tiresome.'

'You should consult an oculist.'

'My eyes are perfectly all right. As a matter of fact a rather distinguished oculist once told me that intensely blue eyes like mine usually give no trouble. He said my eyes were the most vivid blue he had ever seen.'

'Indeed!' said Alleyn, without looking at them. 'How do you explain the headaches, then?'

'I'm perfectly certain the one on Friday night was due to champagne and port. The Pascoes had champagne at dinner to celebrate my engagement, and there was brandy afterwards. I loathe brandy, so Basil made me have a glass of port. I told him it would upset me but he went on and on. The coffee was filthy, too. Bitter and beastly. Sybil Pascoe is one of those plain women whom one expects to be good housekeepers, but I must say she doesn't appear to take the smallest trouble over the coffee. Basil says his was abominable, too.'

'When did you give up the bridge?'

'I've no idea, I'm afraid. I simply couldn't go on. Basil got me three aspirin and I went to bed. The others came up soon afterwards, I fancy. I heard Basil go into his room.'

'It was next to yours?'

'Yes.'

'Did you sleep?'

'Like the dead. I didn't wake till they brought my tea at nine o'clock.'

'And the headache had cleared up?'

'Yes, quite. I still felt a little unpleasant. It was a sort of carry-over from that damned port, I imagine.'

'Were your host and hostess anywhere near you upstairs?'

'Sybil and Ken? Not very. There was Basil and then me, and then I think two spare rooms and a bathroom. Then their room. Why?'

'It sounds rather absurd, I know,' said Alleyn, 'but you see we've got to find out as closely as possible what everyone did that night.'

'Basil didn't come into my room, if that's what you're hinting at,' said Miss Seacliff without heat. 'It wasn't that sort of party. And anyway, I'm not given to that kind of thing even when I haven't got a headache. I don't believe in it. Sooner or later you lose your glamour. Look at Sonia.'

'Quite so. Then as far as you know the household slept without stirring from Friday night to Saturday morning?'

'Yes,' said Miss Seacliff, looking at him as if he was slightly demented.

'And on Saturday you went on to Ankerton Manor. When did you start?'

'We had a glass of sherry at about ten, and then pushed off. Basil was in a great state lest we should be late for lunch, and wanted to get away earlier, but I saw no reason why we should go rushing about the countryside before it was necessary. We had plenty of time.'

'Why was he so anxious?'

'He kept saying that he was sure Sybil Pascoe wanted to get away. She was going up to London for a week and leaving Ken to look after himself. I pointed out that was no reason why we should bolt off. Then Basil said we mustn't be late at Ankerton. The truth was, the poor lamb wanted me to make a good impression on his extraordinary old father. I told him he needn't worry. Old men always go quite crazy about me. But Basil was absurdly nervous about the meeting and kept fidgeting me to start. We got there early as it was, and by luncheon-time the old person was talking about the family jewels. He's given me some emeralds that I'm going to have reset. They're rather spectacular.'

'You left Ankerton yesterday after luncheon, I suppose?'

'Yes. Basil was rather keen to stay on till Monday, but I'd had enough. The old person made me hack round the ancestral acres on a beastly little animal that nearly pulled my arms out. I saw you looking at my hand.'

With a slow and beautiful movement she extended her left arm, opened her hand, and held it close to Alleyn's face. It was warmly scented and the palm was rouged. At the base of the little finger were two or three scarlet marks.

'My hands are terribly soft, of course,' said Miss Seacliff, advancing it a little closer to his face.

'Yes,' said Alleyn. 'You are evidently not an experienced horse-woman.'

'What makes you say that?'

'Well, you know, these marks have not been made by a rein. I should say, Miss Seacliff, that your pony's mane had been called into service.'

She pulled her hand away and turned rather pink.

'I don't pretend to be a horsey woman, thank God! I simply loathe the brutes. I must say I got very bored with the old person. And besides, I didn't want to miss the pose this morning. I'd got a good deal to do to my thing of Sonia. I suppose I'll never get it done now.'

Fox coughed and Nigel glanced up at Valmai Seacliff in astonishment.

'I suppose not,' agreed Alleyn. 'Now, Miss Seacliff, we come to this morning's tragedy. Will you describe to us exactly what happened, please?'

'Have you got a cigarette?'

Alleyn sprang up and offered her his case.

'What are they? Oh, I see. Thank you.'

She took one and he lit it for her. She looked into his eyes deliberately but calmly, as if she followed a familiar routine. Alleyn returned her glance gravely and sat down again.

'This morning?' she said. 'You mean when Sonia was killed? It was rather ghastly. I felt wretched after it was all over. Ill. I suppose it was shock. I do think it was rather cruel that I should be the one to – to do it – to set the pose. They all knew I always pushed her shoulders down.' She caught her breath, and for the first time showed some signs of genuine distress. 'I believe Garcia deliberately planned it like that. He loathed the sight of Sonia, and at the same time he wanted to revenge himself on me because I didn't fall for him. It was just like Garcia to do that. He's a spiteful little beast. It was cruel. I – I can't get rid of the remembrance. I'll never be able to get rid of it.'

'I'm sorry that I am obliged to ask you to go over it again, but I'm sure you will understand – '

'Oh, yes. And the psycho people say one shouldn't repress things of this sort. I don't want to get nervy and lose my poise. After all, I didn't do it really. I keep telling myself that.'

'When did you go down to the studio?'

'Just before class time. Basil and I walked down together. Katti Bostock was there and – let me see -yes, the appalling Hatchett youth, Lee and Ormerin and Malmsley came down afterwards, I think.'

'Together?'

'I don't remember. They were not there when I got down.'

'I see. Will you go on, Miss Seacliff?'

'Well, we all put up our easels and set our palettes and so on. Sonia came in last and Katti said we'd begin. Sonia went into the junk-room and undressed. She came out in her white kimono and hung about trying to get the men to talk to her. Katti told her to go on to the throne. She got down into the chalk-marks. She always fitted her right thigh into its trace first, with the drape behind her. I don't know if you understand?'

'Yes, I think I do.'

And indeed Alleyn suddenly had a very vivid impression of what must have taken place. He saw the model, wrapped in the thin white garment, her warm and vital beauty shining through it. He saw her speak to the men, look at them perhaps with a pathetic attempt to draw their attention to herself. Then the white wrapper would slide to the floor and the nude figure sink gingerly into a half-recumbent posture on the throne.

'She grumbled as usual about the pose and said she was sick of it. I remember now that she asked if we knew where Garcia had gone on his hiking trip. I suppose he wouldn't tell her. Then she lay down on her side. The drape was still stretched taut behind her. There is generally a sort of key position among the different canvases. When we set the pose we always look at that particular canvas to get it right. My painting was in this position so it was always left to me to push her down into the right position. She could have done it all

herself but she always made such a scene. I'd got into the way of taking her shoulders and pressing them over. She wouldn't do it otherwise. So I leant over and gripped them. They felt smooth and alive.
She began to make a fuss. She said "Don't", and I said "Don't be such
a fool". Katti said: "Oh, for Heaven's sake, Sonia!" Something like
that. Sonia said: "Your hands are cold, you're hurting me". Then she
let herself go and I pushed down.' Valmai Seacliff raised her hands
and pressed them against her face.

'She didn't struggle but I felt her body leap under my hands and
then shudder. I can't tell you exactly what it was like. Everything
happened at the same moment. I saw her face. She opened her
eyes very wide, and wrinkled her forehead as if she was astonished. I think she said "Don't" again but I'm not sure. I thought –
you know how one's thoughts can travel – I thought how silly she
looked, and at the same moment I suddenly wondered if she was
going to have a baby and the pose really hurt her. I don't know
why I thought that. I knew s-something had happened. I didn't
know what it was. I just leant over her and looked into her face. I
think I said: "Sonia's ill". I think Katti or someone said "Rot". I still
touched her – leant on her. She quivered as if I tickled her and
then she was still. Phillida Lee said: "She's fainted". Then the others came up. Katti put her arms behind Sonia to raise her. She said:
"I can't move her – she seems stuck". Then she pulled. There was
a queer little n-noise and Sonia came up suddenly. Ormerin cried
out loudly: *"Mon Dieu, c'est le poignard"*. At least that's what he told
us he said. And the drape stuck to my fingers. It came out of the
hole in her back – the blood, I mean. Her back was wet. We moved
her a little, and Katti tried to stop the blood with a piece of rag.
Troy came. She sent Basil out to ring up the doctor. She looked at
Sonia and said she wasn't dead. Troy put her arms round Sonia. I
don't know how long it was before Sonia gave a sort of cough. She
opened her eyes very wide. Troy looked up and said: "She's gone".
Phillida Lee started to cry. Nobody said very much. Basil came back
and Troy said n-nobody was to leave the studio. She covered Sonia
with a drape. We began to talk about the knife. Lee and Hatchett
said G-Garcia had done it. We all thought Garcia had done it. Then
the doctor came and when he had seen Sonia he sent for the p-
police.'

Her voice died away. She had begun her recital calmly enough, but it was strange to see how the memory of the morning grew more vivid and more disquieting as she revived it. The slight hesitation in her speech became more noticeable. When she had finished her hands were trembling.

'I d-didn't know I was so upset,' she said. 'A doctor once told me my nerves were as sensitive as the strings of a violin.'

'It was a horrible experience for all of you,' said Alleyn. 'Tell me, Miss Seacliff, when did you yourself suspect that Garcia had laid this trap for the model?'

'I thought of Garcia at once. I remembered what Lee had told me about the conversation between Garcia and Sonia. I don't see who else could have done it, and somehow – '

'Yes?'

'Somehow it – it's the sort of thing he might do. There's something very cold-blooded about Garcia. He's quite mad about me, but I simply can't bear him to touch me. Lee says he's got masses of SA and he evidently had for Sonia – but I can't see it. I think he's rather repulsive. Women do fall for him, I'm told.'

'And the motive?'

'I imagine he was sick of her. She literally hurled herself at him. Always watching him. Men hate women to do that – ' She looked directly into Alleyn's eyes. 'Don't they, Mr Alleyn?'

'I'm afraid I don't know.'

'And of course he was livid when she defaced my portrait. She must have hated me to do that. In a way it was rather interesting, a directly sexual jealousy manifesting itself on the symbol of the hated person.'

Alleyn repressed a movement of impatience and said: 'No doubt.'

'My own idea is that she was going to have a baby and had threatened to sue him for maintenance. I suppose in a way I'm responsible.'

She looked grave enough as she made this statement, but Alleyn thought there was more than a hint of complacency in her voice.

'Surely not,' he said.

'Oh, yes. In a way. If he hadn't been besotted on me, I dare say he might not have done it.'

'I thought,' said Alleyn, 'that you were worrying about your actual hand in the business.'

'What do you mean?'

'I mean,' Alleyn's voice was grave, 'the circumstance of it being your hands, Miss Seacliff, that thrust her down upon the knife. Tell me, please, did you notice any resistance at first? I should have thought that there might even have been a slight sound as the point entered.'

'I – don't think – '

'We are considering the actual death throes of a murdered individual,' said Alleyn mildly. 'I should like a clear picture.'

She opened her eyes wide, a look of extreme horror came into her face. She looked wildly round the room, darted a furious glance at Alleyn, and said in a strangled voice; 'Let me out. I've got to go out.'

Fox rose in consternation, but she pushed him away and ran blindly to the door.

'Never mind, Fox,' said Alleyn.

The door banged.

'Here,' said Fox, 'what's she up to?'

'She's bolted,' exclaimed Nigel. 'Look out! She's doing a bolt.'

'Only as far as the cloak-room,' said Alleyn. 'The fatal woman is going to be very sick.'

CHAPTER 11

Ormerin's Nerves and Sonia's Correspondence

'Well, really, Alleyn,' said Nigel, 'I consider you were hard on that girl. You deliberately upset her lovely stomach.'

'How do you know her stomach's lovely?'

'By inference. What did you do it for?'

'I was sick of that Cleopatra nonsense. She and her catgut nerves!'

'Well, but she *is* terrifically attractive. A really magnificent creature.'

'She's as hard as nails. Still,' added Alleyn with satisfaction, 'I did make her sick. She went through the whole story the first time almost without batting an eyelid. Each time we came back to it she was a little less confident, and the last time when I mentioned the words 'death throes' she turned as green as asparagus.'

'Well, wasn't it natural?'

'Quite natural. Served her jolly well right. I dislike fatal women. They reek of mass production.'

'I don't think you can say she's as hard as nails. After all, she *did* feel ill. I mean she was upset by it all.'

'Only her lovely stomach. She's not in the least sorry for that unfortunate little animal who died under her hands. All that psychological clap-trap! She's probably nosed into a *Freud Without Tears* and picked out a few choice phrases.'

'I should say she was extremely intelligent.'

'And you'd be right. She's sharp enough. What she said about Garcia rang true, I thought. What d'you say, Brer Fox?'

'You mean when she talked about Garcia's cold-bloodedness, don't you, sir?'

'I do.'

'Yes. They all seem to agree about him. I think myself that it does-n't do to ignore other people's impressions. If you find a lot of sepa-rate individuals all saying so-and-so is a cold, unscrupulous sort of person, why then,' said Fox, 'it usually turns out that he is.'

'True for you.'

'They might all be in collusion,' said Nigel.

'Why?' asked Alleyn.

'I don't know.'

'More do I.'

'Well,' said Fox, 'if this Garcia chap doesn't turn up in answer to our broadcast and ads and so on, it'll look like a true bill.'

'He's probably the type that loathes radio and never opens a paper,' said Nigel.

'Highly probable,' agreed Alleyn.

'You'll have to arrest all hikers within a three-days' tramp from Tatler's End House. What a bevy of shorts and rucksacks.'

'He'll have his painting gear if he's innocent,' said Alleyn. 'If he's innocent, he's probably snoring in a pub not twenty miles away. The police stations have all been warned. We'll get him soon enough – if he's innocent.'

'And if he's guilty?'

'Then he's thought out the neatest method of murder that I've come across for a very long time,' said Fox, 'He knew that nobody would meddle with the throne, he knew he'd got two days' start before the event came off, and he very likely thought we'd have a tough job finding anything to pin on to him.'

'Those traces of modelling clay,' murmured Alleyn.

'He didn't think of that,' said Fox. 'If Bailey's right they dropped off his overall while he fixed the knife.'

'What's all this?' asked Nigel. Alleyn told him.

'We've got to remember,' said Alleyn, 'that he'd got the offer of a good job. Marble statues of Comedy and Tragedy are not commis-sioned for a few pounds. It is possible, Fox, that a guilty Garcia might be so sure of himself that he would turn up in his London ware-house at the end of a week or so's tramp and set to work. When we found him and hauled him up for a statement, he'd he all vague and surprised. When we asked how the traces of clay were to be accounted for, he'd say he didn't know, but that he'd often sat on the throne, or stood on it, or walked across it, and the clay might have dropped off him at any moment. We'll have to find out what sort of state his working smock was in. The bit of clay Bailey found is hardish. Modellers' clay is wettish and kept so. When faced with Phillida Lee's statement he'd say he'd had dozens of rows with Sonia, but hadn't plotted to kill her. If we find she was going to have a child he'd very likely ask what of it?'

'What about the appointment he made with her for Friday night?' asked Fox.

'Did he make an appointment with her for Friday night?'

'Well, sir, you've got it there. Miss Lee said – '

'Yes, I know, Fox. According to Miss Lee, Garcia said: "All right. On Friday night then." And Sonia answered: "Yes, if it's possible." But that may not have meant that they arranged to meet each other on Friday night. It might have meant a thousand and one things, damn it. Garcia may have talked about leaving on Friday night. Sonia may have said she'd do something for him in London on Friday night. It is true that the young Lee person got the impression that they arranged to meet here, but she may have been mistaken.'

'That's so,' said Fox heavily. 'We'll have to get on to deceased's movements from Friday afternoon till Sunday.'

'Did you get anything at all from the maids about Friday night?'

'Not a great deal, sir, and that's a fact. There's three servants living in the house, a Mr and Mrs Hipkin who do butler and cook, and a young girl called Sadie Welsh, who's housemaid. They all went to a cinema in Baxtonbridge on Friday night and returned by the front drive. There's another girl – Ethel Jones – who comes in as a daily from Bossicote. She leaves at five o'clock in the afternoon. I'll get on to her tomorrow, but it doesn't look promising. The Hipkins seem a very decent couple. Devoted to Miss Troy. They've not got much to say in favour of this crowd. To Mrs Hipkin's way of thinking they're all out of the same box. She said she wasn't surprised at the murder and expected worse.'

'What? Wholesale slaughter did she mean?'

'I don't think she knew. She's a Presbyterian – Auld Licht – maiden name McQumpha. She says painting from the figure is no better than living in open sin, and she gave it as her opinion that Sonia

Gluck was fair soused in wickedness. That kind of thing. Hipkin said
he always thought Garcia had bats in the belfy, and Sadie said he
once tried to assault her and she gave him a smack on the chops.
She's rather a lively girl, Sadie is. They say Miss Seacliff's no lady
because of the way she speaks to the servants. The only one they
seemed to have much time for was the Honourable Basil Pilgrim.'

'Good old snobs. What about Garcia's evening meal on Friday?'

'Well, I did get something there, in a way. Sadie took it on a tray
to the studio at seven-thirty. She tapped on the screen inside the
door and Mr Garcia called out to her to leave the tray there. Sadie
said she didn't know but what he had naked women exhibiting
themselves on the platform, so she put it down. When she went to
the studio on Saturday morning the tray was still there, untouched.
She looked into the studio but didn't do anything in the way of
housework. She's not allowed to touch anything on the throne and
didn't notice the drape. Garcia was supposed to make his own bed.
Sadie says it's her belief he just pulled the counterpane over it and
that's what we found, sir, isn't it?'

'Garcia wasn't there on Saturday morning?'

'No. Sadie says he'd gone and all his stuff as far as she could make
out. She said the room smelt funny, so she opened the window. She
noticed a queer smell there on Friday night, too. I wondered if it was
the acid Bailey found the marks of, but she said no. She's smelt the
acid before, when they've been using it for etching, and it wasn't the
same.'

'Look here, Fox, I think I'd like a word with your Sadie. Be a good
fellow and see if she's still up.'

Fox went off and was away some minutes.

'He must have broken into the virgin fastness of Sadie's bedroom,'
said Nigel.

Alleyn wandered round the room and looked at the books.

'What's the time?' he said.

'After ten. Ten-twenty-five.'

'Oh Lord! Here's Fox.'

Fox came in shepherding an extraordinary little apparition in
curling-pins and red flannel.

'Miss Sadie Welsh,' explained Fox, 'was a bit uncomfortable about
coming down, Mr Alleyn. She'd gone to bed.'

'I'm sorry to bring you out,' said Alleyn pleasantly. 'We shan't keep you here very long. Come over to the fire, won't you?'

He threw a couple of logs on the fire and persuaded Miss Welsh to perch on the extreme edge of a chair: with her feet on the fender. She was a girl of perhaps 22, with large brown eyes, a button nose and a mouth that looked as though she constantly said: 'Ooo.' She gazed at Alleyn as if he was a grand inquisitor.

'You're Miss Troy's housemaid, aren't you?' said Alleyn.

'Yes, sir.'

'Been with her long?'

'Ooo, yes, sir. I was a under-housemaid here when the old gentleman was alive; I was sixteen then, sir. And when Miss Troy was mistress I stayed on, sir. Of course, Miss Troy's bin away a lot, sir, but when the house was opened up again this year, Miss Bostock asked me to come with Mr and Mrs Hipkin to be housemaid. I never was a real housemaid like before, sir, but Mr Hipkin he's training me now for parlourmaid. He says I'll be called Welsh then, because Sadie isn't a name for a parlourmaid, Mr Hipkins says. So I'll be "Welsh".'

'Splendid. You like your job?'

'Well, sir,' said Sadie primly, 'I like Miss Troy very much, sir.'

'Not so sure about the rest of the party?'

'No, I am not, sir, and that's a fact. I was telling Mr Fox, sir, Queer! Well, I mean to say! That Mr Garcia, sir. Ooo! Well, I dare say Mr Fox has told you. I complained to Miss Troy, sir. I asked Mrs Hipkin what would I do and she said: "Go straight to Miss Troy," she said. "I would," she said, "I'd go straight to Miss Troy." Which I did. There was no trouble after that, sir, but I must say I didn't fancy taking his dinner down on Friday.'

'As it turned out, you didn't see Mr Garcia then, did you?'

'No, sir. He calls out in a sort of drawly voice: 'Is that you, Sadistic?' which was what he had the nerve to call me, and Mr Hipkin says he didn't ought to have because Mr Hipkin is very well educated, sir.'

'Astonishingly,' murmured Alleyn.

'And then I said: "Your dinner, Mr Garcia," and he called out – excuse me, sir – he called out: "Oh Gawd, eat it yourself." I said: "Pardon?" and he said "Put it down there and shove off." So I said: "Thank *you*," I said, "Mr Garcia," I said. And I put down the tray and as I told Mrs Hipkin, sir, I said: "There's something peculiar going on down there," I said, when I got back to the hall.'

'What made you think that?'

'Well, sir, he seemed that anxious I wouldn't go in, and what with the queer perfume and one thing and another – well!'

'You noticed an odd smell?'

'Yes, I did that, sir.'

'Ever smelt anything like it before?'

'Ooo well, sir, that's funny you should think of that because I said to myself: "Well, if that isn't what Mr Marzis's room smells like of a morning sometimes." '

'Mr Malmsley?'

'Yes, sir. It's a kind of – well, a kind of a bitterish sort of smell, only sort of thick and sour.'

'Not like whisky, for instance?'

'Oh no, sir. I didn't notice the perfume of whisky till I went down next morning.'

'Hullo!' said Fox genially, 'you never told me it was whisky you smelt on Saturday morning, young lady.'

'Didn't I, Mr Fox? Well, I must of forgotten, because there was the other smell, too, mixed up with it. Anyway, Mr Fox, it wasn't the first time I've noticed whisky in the studio since Mr Garcia's been there.'

'But you'd never noticed the other smell before?' asked Alleyn.

'Not in the studio, sir. Only in Mr Marzis's room.'

'Did you make the bed on Saturday morning?'

Sadie turned pink.

'Well, no, I didn't, sir. I opened the window to air the room, and thought I'd go back later. Mr Garcia's supposed to make his own bed. It looked fairly tidy so I left it.'

'And on Saturday morning Mr Garcia's clay model and all his things were gone?'

'That queer-looking mud thing like plasticine? Ooh yes, sir, it was gone on Saturday.'

'Right. I think that's all.'

'May I go, sir?'

'Yes, off you go. I'll ask you to sign your name to a statement later on. You'll do that, won't you? It will just be what you've told us here.'

'Very good, sir.'

'Good night, Welsh,' said Alleyn smiling. 'Thank you.'

'Good night, sir. I'm sure I'm sorry to come in, such a fright. I don't know what Mr Hipkin would say. It doesn't look very nice for "Welsh", the parlourmaid, does it, sir?'

'We think it was quite correct,' said Alleyn.

Fox, with a fatherly smile, shepherded Sadie to the door.

'Well, Fox,' said Alleyn, 'we'd better get on with it. Let's have Mr Francis Ormerin. How's the French, by the way?'

'I've mastered the radio course, and I'm on to *Hugo's Simplified* now. I shouldn't fancy an un-simplified, I must say. I can read it pretty steadily, Mr Alleyn, and Bob Thompson, the super at number three, has lent me one or two novels he picked up in Paris, on the understanding I translate the bits that would appeal to him. You know Bob.' Fox opened his eyes wide and an expression of mild naughtiness stole over his healthy countenance. 'I must say some of the passages are well up to expectation. Of course, you don't find all those words in the dictionary, do you?'

'You naughty old scoundrel,' said Alleyn. 'Go and get M. Ormerin.'

'Tout sweet,' said Fox. 'There you are.'

'And you'd better inquire after the Seacliff.' Fox went out. 'This case seems to be strewn with upheavals,' said Alleyn. 'Garcia was sick when he saw the defaced portrait. Sonia was sick in the mornings, and Miss Seacliff is heaving away merrily at this very moment, or I'm much mistaken.'

'I begin to get an idea of the case,' said Nigel, who had gone through his notes. 'You're pretty certain it's Garcia, aren't you?'

'Have I said so? All right, then, I do feel tolerably certain he laid the trap for this girl, but it's purely conjectural. I may be quite wrong. If we are to accept the statements of Miss Troy and Watt Hatchett, the knife was pushed through the boards some time after three o'clock on Friday afternoon, and before Saturday afternoon. Personally I am inclined to believe both these statements. That leaves us with Garcia and Malmsley as the most likely fancies.'

'There's – '

'Well?'

'Of course if you accept her statement it doesn't arise,' said Nigel nervously.

Alleyn did not answer immediately, and for some reason Nigel found that he could not look at him. Nigel ruffled the pages of his notes and heard Alleyn's voice: 'I only said I was inclined to believe Hatchett's statement – and hers. I shall not regard them as inviolable.'

Fox returned with Francis Ormerin and once again they settled down to routine. Ormerin had attended the private view of the Phoenix Group Show on Friday night, and had spent the weekend with a French family at Hampstead. They had sat up till about two o'clock on both nights and had been together during the day-time.

'I understand that during the bus drive back from London yesterday, the model sat beside you?' said Alleyn.

'Yes. That is so. This poor girl, she must always have her flirt in attendance.'

'And you filled the rôle on this occasion?'

Ormerin pulled a significant grimace.

'Why not? She makes an invitation with every gesture. It is a long and tedious drive. She is not unattractive. After a time I fell asleep.'

'Did she say anything about her movements in London?'

'Certainly. She told me that she stayed with another girl who is in the chorus of a vaudeville show at the Chelsea Theatre. It is called *Snappy*. Sonia shared this girl's room. She went to *Snappy* on Friday evening, and on Saturday she went to a studio party in Putney where she became exceedingly drunk, and was driven home by a young man, not so drunk, to the room of this girl whose name is – *tiens!* – ah yes – Bobbie is the name of the friend. Bobbie O'Dawne. All this was told me, and for a while I was complacent, and held her hand in the bus. Then after a time I fell asleep.'

'Did she say anything at all that could possibly be of any help to us?'

'Ah! Any help? I do not think so. Except one thing, perhaps. She said that I must not be surprised if I learn soon of another engagement.'

'What engagement was that?'

'She would not tell me. She became *retenue – espiègle* – in English, sly-boots. Sonia was very sly-boots on the subject of this engagement. I receive the impression, however, that it would be to Garcia.'

'I see. She did not talk about Garcia's movements on Friday?'

'But I think she did!' exclaimed Ormerin, after a moment's consideration. 'Yes, it is quite true, she did speak of him. It was after I had begun to get sleepy. She said Garcia would start for his promenade through this county on Saturday morning, and return to work in London in a week's time.'

'Did she say where his work-room was in London?'

'On the contrary, she asked me if I could tell her this. She said: "I do not know what his idea is, to make such a mystery of it." Then she laughed and said: "But that is Garcia – I shall have to put up with it, I suppose." She spoke with the air of a woman who has certain rights over a man. It may, of course, have been an assumption. One cannot tell. Very often I have noticed that it is when a woman begins to lose her power with a man that she assumes these little postures of the proprietress.'

'What did you think of Sonia Gluck, M. Ormerin?'

Ormerin's sharp black eyes flashed in his sallow face and his thin mouth widened.

'Of Sonia? She was a type, Mr Alleyn. That is all one can say of her. The *gamine* that so often drifts towards studio doors, and then imperceptibly, naturally, into the protection of some painter. She had beauty, as you have seen. She was very difficult. If she had lived, she would have had little work when her beauty faded. While she was still good for our purpose we endured her temperament, her caprice, for the sake of her lovely body, which we might paint when she was well-behaved.'

'Had you so much difficulty with her?'

'It was intolerable. Never for one minute would she remain in the same position. I myself began three separate drawings of the one pose. I cannot paint in such circumstances, my nerves are lacerated and my work is valueless. I had made my resolution that I would leave the studio.'

'Really! It was as bad as that?'

'Certainly. If this had not happened, I would have told Troy I must go. I should have been very sorry to do this, because I have a great admiration for Troy. She is most stimulating to my work. In her studio one is at home. But I am very greatly at the mercy of my nerves. I would have returned when Bostock and Pilgrim had completed their large canvases, and Troy had rid herself of Sonia.'

'And now, I suppose, you will stay?'

'I do not know.' Ormerin moved restlessly in his chair. Alleyn noticed that there was a slight tic in his upper-lip, a busy little cord that flicked under the dark skin. As if aware of Alleyn's scrutiny, Ormerin put a thin crooked hand up to his lip. His fingers were deeply stained by nicotine.

'I do not know,' he repeated. 'The memory of this morning is very painful. I am *bouleversé*. I do not know what I shall do. I like them all here at Troy's – even this clumsy, shouting Australian. I am *en rapport* with them well enough, but I shall never look towards the throne without seeing there the tableau of this morning. That little unfortunate with her glance of astonishment. And then when they move her – the knife – wet and red.'

'You were the first to notice the knife, I think?'

'Yes. As soon as they moved her I saw it.' He looked uneasily at Alleyn.

'I should have thought the body would still have hidden it.'

'But no. I knelt on the floor. I saw it. Let us not speak of it. It is enough that I saw it.'

'Did you expect to see the blade. Mr Ormerin?'

Ormerin was on his feet in a flash, his face ashen, his lips drawn back. He looked like a startled animal.

'What do you say? Expect! How should I expect to see the knife? Do you suspect me – *me* – of complicity in this detestable affair?' His violent agitation came upon him so swiftly that Nigel was amazed, and gaped at him, his notes forgotten.

'You are too sensitive,' Alleyn said quietly, 'and have read a meaning into my words that they were not intended to convey. I wondered if the memory of your experiment with the knife came into your mind before you saw it. I wondered if you guessed that the model had been stabbed.'

'Never!' exclaimed Ormerin, with a violent gesture of repudiation. 'Never! Why should I think of anything so horrible?'

'Since you helped in the experiment, it would not be so astonishing if you should remember it,' said Alleyn. But Ormerin continued to expostulate, his English growing more uncertain as his agitation mounted. At last Alleyn succeeded in calming him a little, and he sat down again.

'I must ask you to pardon my agitation,' he said, his stained fingers at his lips. 'I am much distressed by this crime.'

'That is very natural. I shall not keep you much longer. I spoke just now of the experiment with the dagger. I understand that you and Mr Hatchett did most of the work on the day you made this experiment?'

'They were all interested to see if it could be done. Each one as much as another.'

'Quite so,' agreed Alleyn patiently. 'Nevertheless you and Mr Hatchett actually tipped up the throne and drove the dagger through the crack.'

'And if we did! Does that prove us to be – '

'It proves nothing at all, M. Ormerin. I was about to ask if Mr Garcia had any hand in the experiment?'

'Garcia?' Ormerin looked hard at Alleyn, and then an expression of great relief came upon him and he relaxed. 'No,' he said thoughtfully, 'I do not believe that he came near us. He stood in the window with Sonia and watched. But I will tell you one more thing, Mr Alleyn. When it was all over and she went back to the pose, Malmsley began to mock her, pretending the dagger was still there. And Garcia laughed a little to himself. Very quietly. But I noticed him, and I thought to myself that was a very disagreeable little laugh. That is what I thought!' ended Ormerin with an air of great significance.

'You said in the dining-room that we might be sure this was a *crime passionel*. Why are you so sure of this?'

'But it is apparent – it protrudes a mile. This girl was a type. One had only to see her. It declared itself. She was avid for men.'

'Oh dear, oh dear,' murmured Alleyn.

'*Pardon?*'

'Nothing. Please go on, M. Ormerin.'

'She was not normal. You shall find, I have no doubt, that she was *enceinte*. I have been sure of it for some time. Even at the beginning women have an appearance, you understand? Her face was a little – ' he made an expressive movement with his hand down his own thin face – 'dragged down. And always she was looking at Garcia. Mr Alleyn, I have seen him return her look, and there was that in his eyes that made one shudder. It was not at all pretty to see him watching her. He is a cold young man. He must have women, but he is quite unable to feel any tenderness for them. It is a type.'

Ormerin's distress had apparently evaporated. He had become jauntily knowing.

'In a word,' said Alleyn, 'you consider he is responsible for this tragedy?'

'One draws one's own conclusions, of necessity, Mr Alleyn. Who else can it be?'

'She was on rather uncertain terms with most of you, it appears?'

'Ah yes, yes. But one does not perform murders from exasperation. Even Malmsley – '

Ormerin hesitated, grimaced, wagged his head sideways and was silent.

'What about Mr Malmsley?' asked Alleyn lightly.

'It is nothing.'

'By saying it is nothing, you know, you leave me with an impression of extreme significance. What was there between the model and Mr Malmsley?'

'I have not been able to discover,' said Ormerin rather huffily.

'But you think there was something?'

'She was laughing at him. On the morning of our experiment when Malmsley began to tease Sonia, pretending that the knife was still there, she entreated him to leave her alone, and when he would not she said: "I wouldn't be too damn funny. Where is it that you discover your ideas, is it in books or pictures?" He was very disconcerted and allowed his dirty brush to fall on his drawing. That is all. You see, I was right when I said it was nothing. Have you finished with me, Mr Alleyn?'

'I think so, thank you. There will be a statement later on,' said Alleyn vaguely. He looked at Ormerin, as though he wasn't there, seemed to recollect himself, and got to his feet.

'Yes, I think that's all,' he repeated.

'I shall wish you good night then, Mr Alleyn.'

'Good night,' said Alleyn, coming to himself. 'Good night, M. Ormerin.'

But when Ormerin had gone, Alleyn wandered about the room, whistled under his breath, and paid no attention at all to Fox or Nigel.

'Look here,' said Nigel at last, 'I want to use a telephone.'

'You?'

'Yes. Don't look at me as though I was a fabulous monster. I want to use the telephone, I say.'

'What for?'

'Ring up Angela.'

'It's eleven o'clock.'

'That's no matter. She'll be up and waiting.'

'You're burning to ring up your odious newspaper.'

'Well – I thought if I just said – '

'You may say that there has been a fatal accident at Tatler's End House, Bossicote, and that an artist's model has died as the result of this accident. You may add that the authorities are unable to trace the whereabouts of the victim's relatives and are anxious to communicate with Mr W. Garcia who is believed to be on a walking tour and may be able to give them some information about the model's family. Something on those lines.'

'And a fat lot of good – ' began Nigel angrily.

'If Garcia is not our man,' continued Alleyn to Fox, 'and sees that, he may do something about it.'

'That's so,' said Fox.

'And now we'll deal with the last of this collection, if you please, Fox. The languishing Malmsley.'

'I'll go to the telephone,' said Nigel.

'Very well. Don't exceed, now. You may tell them that there will be a further instalment tomorrow.'

'Too kind,' said Nigel haughtily.

'And Bathgate – you might ring my mamma up and say we won't be in until after midnight.'

'All right.'

Nigel and Fox collided in the doorway with Bailey, who looked cold and disgruntled.

'Hullo,' said Alleyn. 'Wait a moment, Fox. Let's hear what Bailey's been up to.'

'I've been over deceased's room,' said Bailey.

'Any good?'

'Nothing much, sir. It's an attic-room at the front of the house.'

He paused, and Alleyn waited, knowing that 'nothing much' from Bailey might mean anything from a vacuum to a phial of cyanide.

'There's deceased's prints,' continued Bailey, 'and one that looks
like this Garcia. It's inside the door where the maid's missed with the
duster, and there's another print close beside it that isn't either of
'em. Broad. Man's print, I'd say. And of course there are the maid's
all over the show. I've checked those. Nothing much about the
clothes. Note from Garcia in a pocket. She was in the family way all
right. Here it is.'

He opened his case, and from a labelled envelope drew out of a
piece of paper laid between two slips of glass.

'I've printed it and taken a photo.'

Alleyn took the slips delicately in his fingers and laid them on the
desk. The creases in the common paper had been smoothed out and
the scribbled black pencil lines were easy to read:

Dear S. – What do you expect me to do about it? I've got two
quid to last me till I get to Troy's. You asked for it, anyway.
Can't you get somebody to fix things? It's not exactly likely
that I should want to be saddled with a wife and a kid, is it?
I've got a commission for a big thing, and for God's sake don't
throw me off my stride. I'm sorry but I can't do anything. See
you at Troy's. *Garcia*

'A charming fellow,' said Alleyn.

'That was in a jacket pocket. Here's a letter that was just kicking
about at the back of the wardrobe. From somebody called Bobbie.
Seems as if this Bobbie's a girl.'

This letter was written in an enormous hand on dreadful pink
paper:

The Digs,
4 Batchelors Gardens,
Chelsea.
Monday.

Dear Sonia,

I'm sorry you're in for it dear I think it's just frightful and I
do think men are the limit but of course I never liked the
sound of that Garcia too far upstage if you ask me but they're
all alike when it comes to a girl. The same to you with bells on

and pleased to join in the fun at the start and sorry you've
been troubled this takes me off when they know you're growing melons. I've asked Dolores Duval for the address she went
to when she had a spot of trouble but she says the police found
out about that lady so it's no go. Anyway I think your idea is
better and if Mr Artistic Garcia is willing OK and why not dear
you might as well get it both ways and I suppose it's all right to
be married he sounds a lovely boy but you never know with
that sort did I ever tell you about my boy friend who was a
Lord he was a scream really but nothing ever came of it thank
God. It will be OK if you come here on Friday and I might ask
Leo Cohen for a brief but you know what managements are
like these days dear they sweat the socks off you for the basic
salary and when it comes to asking for a brief for a lady friend
it's just too bad but they've forgotten how the chorus goes in
that number. Thank you very much good morning. I laughed
till I sobbed over the story of the Seacliff woman's picture it
must have looked a scream when you'd done with it but all the
same dear your tempreement will land you well in the con-
sommy one of these days dear if you don't learn to kerb yourself which God knows you haven't done what with one thing
and another. What a yell about Marmelade's little bit of dirt.
Well so long dear and keep smiling see you Friday. Hoping this
finds you well as I am,

                            Cheerio. Ever so sincerely,
                                    Your old pal,
                                        Bobbie

PS. – You want to be sure B.P. won't turn nasty and say all right
go ahead I've told her the story of my life anyhow so now
what!

CHAPTER 12

Malmsley on Pleasure

Nigel returned while Alleyn was still chuckling over Miss O'Dawne's letter.

'What's up?' asked Nigel.

'Bailey has discovered a remarkably rich plum. Come and read it. I fancy it's the sort of thing your paper calls a human document. A gem in its own way.' Nigel read over Fox's shoulder.

'I like Dolores Duval and her spot of trouble,' he said.

'She got her pass from Leo Cohen for Sonia,' said Alleyn. 'Sonia told Ormerin she'd seen the show. Fox, what do you make of the passage where she says Sonia might as well get it both ways if Garcia is willing? Then she goes on to say she supposes it's all right to be married and he sounds a lovely boy.'

'The lovely boy seems to be the Hon. Pilgrim, judging by the next bit about her boy-friend that was a lord,' said Fox. 'Do you think Sonia Gluck had an idea she'd get Mr Pilgrim to marry her?'

'I hardly think so. No, I fancy blackmail was the idea there. Pilgrim confessed as much when he couldn't get out of it. If Mr Artistic Garcia was willing! Is she driving at the blackmail inspiration there, do you imagine? Her magnificent disregard for the convention that things that are thought of together should be spoken of together, is a bit baffling. I shall have to see Miss Bobbie O'Dawne. She may be the girl we all wait for. Anything else, Bailey?'

'Well,' said Bailey grudgingly, 'I don't know if there's anything in it but I found this.' He took out of his case a shabby blue book and handed it to Alleyn. 'It's been printed, Mr Alleyn. There's several of deceased's prints and a few of the broad one I got off the door. Some party had tried to get into the case where I found the book.'

'*The Consolations of a Critic,*' Alleyn muttered, turning the book over in his long hands. 'By C. Lewis Hind, 1911. Yes, I see. Gently select. Edwardian manner. Seems to be a mildly ecstatic excursion into aesthetics. Nice reproductions. Hullo! Hullo! Why stap me and sink me, there it is!'

He had turned the pages until he came upon a black and white reproduction of a picture in which three medieval figures mowed a charming field against a background of hayricks, pollard willows and turreted palaces.

'By gum and gosh, Bailey, you've found Mr Malmsley's secret. I knew I'd met those three nice little men before. Of course I had. Good Lord, what a fool! Yes, here it is. From *Les Très Riches Heures du Duc de Berry,* by Pol de Limbourge and his brothers. The book's in the Musée Condé at Chantilly. I had to blandish for half an hour before the librarian would let me touch it. It's the most exquisite thing. Well, I'll be jiggered, and I can't say fairer than that.'

'You can tell us what you're talking about, however,' suggested Nigel acidly.

'Fox knows,' said Alleyn. 'You remember, Fox, don't you?'

'I get you now, Mr Alleyn,' said Fox. 'That's what she meant when she sauced him on the day of the experiment.'

'Of course. This is the explanation of one of the more obscure passages in the O'Dawne's document. "What a yell about Marmelade's bit of dirt." What a yell indeed! Fetch him in, Fox – any nonsense from Master Cedric Malmsley and we have him on the hip.' He put the book on the floor beside his chair.

'You might tell me, Alleyn, why you are so maddeningly perky all of a sudden,' complained Nigel.

'Wait and see, my dear Bathgate. Bailey, you've done extremely well. Anything else for us in the room?'

'Not that I could make out, Mr Alleyn. Everything's put back as it was, but I thought there was nothing against taking these things.'

'Certainly not. Pack them into my case, please. I want you to wait until I've seen Mr Malmsley. Here's Fox.'

Malmsley drifted in ahead of Fox. Seen across the dining-room table he had looked sufficiently remarkable with his beard divided

into two. This beard was fine and straight and had the damp pallor
of an infant's crest. Malmsley wore a crimson shirt, a black tie and a
corduroy velvet jacket. Indeed he had the uncanny appearance of
a person who had come round, full circle, to the Victorian idea of a
Bohemian. He was almost an illustration for *Trilby*. 'Perhaps,'
thought Alleyn, 'there is nothing but that left for them to do.' He
wore jade rings on his, unfortunately, broad fingers.

'Ah, Mr Alleyn,' he said, 'you are painfully industrious.'

Alleyn smiled vaguely and invited Malmsley to sit down. Nigel
returned to the desk, Bailey walked over to the door, Fox stood in
massive silence by the dying fire.

'I want your movements from Friday noon to yesterday evening,
if you will be so obliging, Mr Malmsley,' said Alleyn.

'I am afraid that I am not fortunate enough to have a very obliging nature, Mr Alleyn. And as for my movements, I always move as
infrequently as possible, and never in the right direction.'

'London was, from your point of view, in the right direction on
Friday afternoon.'

'You mean that by going to London I avoided any question of
complicity in this unpleasant affair.'

'Not necessarily,' said Alleyn. Malmsley lit a cigarette. 'However,'
continued Alleyn, 'you have already told us that you went to
London by the six o'clock bus, at the end of an afternoon spent with
Mr Garcia in the studio.'

'I am absurdly communicative. It must be because I find my own
conversation less tedious, as a rule, than the conversation of other
people.'

'In that,' said Alleyn, 'you are singularly fortunate.'

Malmsley raised his eyebrows.

'What did Mr Garcia tell you about Mr Pilgrim during your conversation in the studio?' asked Alleyn.

'About Pilgrim? Oh, he said that he thought Valmai would find
Pilgrim a very boring companion. He was rather ridiculous and said
that she would soon grow tired of Pilgrim's good looks. I told him that
it was much more likely that she would tire of Pilgrim's virtue. Women
dislike virtue in a husband almost as much as they enjoy infidelity.'

'Good Lord!' thought Alleyn. 'He *is* late Victorian. This is Wilde
and Water.'

'And then?' he said aloud.

'And then he said that Basil Pilgrim was not as virtuous as I thought. I said that I had not thought about it at all. "The superficial observer," I told him, "is the only observer who ever lights upon a profound truth." Don't you agree with me, Mr Alleyn?'

'Being a policeman, I am afraid I don't. Did you pursue this topic?'

'No. I did not find it sufficiently entertaining. Garcia then invited me to speculate upon the chances of Seacliff's virtue saying that he could astonish me on that subject if he had a mind to. I assured him that I was unable to fall into an ecstasy of wonderment on the upshot of what was, as I believe racing enthusiasts would say, a fifty-fifty chance. I found Garcia quite, quite tedious and pedestrian on the subject of Seacliff. He is very much attracted by Seacliff, and men are always more amusing when they praise women they dislike than when they abuse the women to whom they are passionately attracted. I therefore changed the topic of conversation.'

'To Sonia Gluck?'

'That would be quite brilliant of you, Inspector, if I had not mentioned previously that we spoke of Sonia Gluck.'

'That is almost the only feature of our previous conversation that I do remember, Mr Malmsley. You told us that Garcia asked you if – ' Alleyn consulted his notebook – 'if you had ever felt like murdering your mistress just for the horror of doing it. How did you reply?'

'I replied that I had never been long enough attached to a woman for her to claim the title of my mistress. There is something dreadfully permanent in the sound of those two sibilants. However, the theme was a pleasant one and we embroidered it at our leisure. Garcia strolled across to my table and looked at my drawing. 'It wouldn't be worth it,' he said. I disagreed with him. One exquisite pang of horror! "One has not experienced the full gamut of nervous luxury," I said, "until one has taken a life." He began to laugh and returned to his work.'

'Is he at all insane, do you think?'

'Insane? My dear Inspector, who can define the borders of abnormality?'

'That is quite true,' said Alleyn patiently. 'Would you say that Mr Garcia is far from being abnormal?'

'Perhaps not.'

'Is he in the habit of taking drugs, do you know?'

Malmsley leant forward and dropped his cigarette on an ash-tray. He examined his jade rings and said:

'I really have no idea.'

'You have never noticed his eyes, for instance?' continued Alleyn, looking very fixedly into Malmsley's. 'One can usually tell, you know, by the eyes.'

'Really?'

'Yes. The pupils are contracted. Later on they occasionally become widely dilated. As you must have observed, Mr Malmsley, when you have looked in a mirror.'

'You are wonderfully learned, Mr Alleyn.'

'I ask you if, to your knowledge, Garcia has contracted this habit. I must warn you that a very thorough search will be made of all the rooms in this house. Whether I think it advisable to take further steps in following up evidence that is not relevant to this case, may depend largely upon your answer.'

Malmsley looked quickly from Fox to Nigel.

'These gentlemen are with me in this case,' said Alleyn. 'Come now, Mr Malmsley, unless you wish to indulge the – what was Mr Malmsley's remark about nervous enjoyment, Bathgate?'

Nigel looked at his notes.

'The full gamut of nervous luxury?' he said.

'That's it. Unless you feel like experiencing the full gamut of such nervous luxury as police investigations can provide, you will do well to answer my question.'

'He could not afford it,' said Malmsley. 'He is practically living on charity.'

'Have you ever treated him to – let us say – to a pipe of opium?'

'I decline to answer this question.'

'You are perfectly within your rights. I shall obtain a search warrant and examine your effects.'

Malmsley shrank a little in his chair.

'That would be singularly distasteful to me,' he said. 'I am fastidious in the matter of guests.'

'Was Garcia one of your guests?'

'And if he was? After all, why should I hesitate? Your methods are singularly transparent, Inspector. You wish to know if I have ever amused myself by exploring the pleasures of opium. I have done so. A friend has given me a very beautiful set in jade and ivory, and I have not been so churlish as to neglect its promise of enjoyment. On the other hand, I have not allowed myself to contract a habit. In point of fact, I have not used half the amount that was given to me. I am not a creature of habit.'

'Did you invite Garcia to smoke opium?'

'Yes.'

'When?'

'Last Friday afternoon.'

'At last,' said Alleyn. 'Where did you smoke your opium?'

'In the studio.'

'Where you were safe from interruption?'

'Where we were more comfortable.'

'You had the six o'clock bus to catch. Surely you felt disinclined to make the trip up to London?'

Malmsley moved restlessly.

'As a matter of fact,' he said, 'I did not smoke a full pipe. I did not wish to. I merely started one and gave it to Garcia.'

'How many pipes did you give him?'

'Only one.'

'Very well. You will now, if you please, give us an exact account of the manner in which you spent your afternoon. You went to the studio immediately after lunch. Was Garcia there?'

'Yes. He had just got there.'

'How long was it before you gave him opium?'

'My dear Inspector, how should I know? I should imagine it was round about four o'clock.'

'After your conversation about the model and so on?'

'It followed our conversation. We discussed pleasure. That led us to opium.'

'So you went to the house and fetched your jade and ivory paraphernalia?'

'Ah-yes.'

'In your first account you may remember that you told me you did not leave the studio until it was time to change and catch your bus?'

'Did I? Perhaps I did. I suppose I thought that the opium incident would over-excite you.'

'When you finally left the studio,' said Alleyn, 'what was Mr Garcia's condition?'

'He was very tranquil.'

'Did he speak after he had begun to smoke?'

'Oh, yes. A little.'

'What did he say?'

'He said he was happy.'

'Anything else?'

'He said that there was a way out of all one's difficulties if one only had the courage to take it. That, I think, was all.'

'Did you take your opium and the pipe back to the house?'

'No.'

'Why not?'

'The housemaid had said something about changing the sheets on my bed. I didn't particularly want to encounter her.'

'Where did you put the things then?'

'In a box under Garcia's bed.'

'And collected them?'

'This morning before class.'

'Had they been disturbed?'

'I have no idea.'

'Are you sure of that?'

Malmsley moved irritably.

'They were in the box. I simply collected them and took them up to the house.'

'How much opium should there be?'

'I don't know. I think the jar must be about half full.'

'Do you think Garcia may have smoked again, after you left?'

'Again I have no idea. I should not think so. I haven't thought of it.'

Alleyn looked curiously at Malmsley.

'I wonder,' he said, 'if you realize what you may have done?'

'I am afraid I do not understand.'

'I think you do. Everything you have told me about Mr Garcia points, almost too startlingly, to one conclusion.'

Malmsley made a sudden and violent gesture of repudiation.

'That is a horrible suggestion,' he said. 'I have told you the truth – you have no right to suggest that I have – that I had any other motive, but – but – '

'I think I appreciate your motives well enough, Mr Malmsley. For instance, you realized that I should discover the opium in any case if I searched your room. You realized that if Mr Garcia makes a statement about Friday, he will probably speak of the opium you gave him. You may even have known that a plea of irresponsibility due to the effect of opium might be made in the event of criminal proceedings.'

'Do you mean – if he was tried for murder, that I – *I* might be implicated? That is monstrous. I refuse to listen to such a suggestion. You must have a very pure mind, Inspector. Only the very pure are capable of such gross conceptions.'

'And only the very foolish attitudinize in the sort of circumstances that have risen round you and what you did on Friday afternoon. Come, Mr Malmsley, forget your prose for a moment. To my aged perceptions it seems a little as if you were mixing Dorian Grey with one of the second-rate intellectuals of the moment. The result is something that – you must forgive me – does not inspire a policeman with confidence. I tell you quite seriously that you are in a predicament.'

'You suspect Garcia?'

'We suspect everyone and no one at the moment. We note what you have told us and we believe that Garcia was alone in the studio in a semi-drugged condition on Friday evening when we suppose the knife was thrust through the throne. We learn that you drugged him.'

'At his own suggestion,' cried Malmsley.

'Really? Will he agree to that? Or will he say that you persuaded him to smoke opium?'

'He was perfectly ready to do it. He wanted to try. And he only had one pipe. A small amount. He would sleep it off in a few hours. I tell you he was already half asleep when I left.'

'When do you think he would wake?'

'I don't know. How should I know? The effect varies very much the first time. It is impossible to say. He would be well enough in five hours at all events.'

'Do you think,' said Alleyn very deliberately, 'that Garcia set this terrible trap for Sonia Gluck?'

Malmsley was white to the lips.

'I don't know. I know nothing about it. I thought he must have done it. You have forced me into an intolerable position. If I say I believe he did it – but not because of the opium – I refuse to accept – '

His voice was shrill, and his lips trembled. He seemed to be near to tears.

'Very well. We shall try to establish your own movements after you left the house. You caught the six o'clock bus?'

Malmsley eagerly gave an account of his weekend. He had attended the private view, had gone to the Savoy, and to a friend's flat. They had sat up till three o'clock. He had spent the whole of Saturday with this friend, and with him had gone to a theatre in the evening, and again they had not gone to bed until very late. Alleyn took him through the whole business up to his return on Sunday. Malmsley seemed to be very much shaken.

'Excellent, so far,' said Alleyn. 'We shall, of course, verify your statements. I have looked at your illustrations, Mr Malmsley. They are charming.'

'You shake my pleasure in them,' said Malmsley, rallying a little.

'I particularly liked the picture of the three little men with scythes.'

Malmsley looked sharply at Alleyn but said nothing.

'Have you ever visited Chantilly?' asked Alleyn.

'Never.'

'Then you have not seen *Les Très Riches Heures du Duc de Berry?*'

'Never.'

'You have seen reproductions of the illustrations, perhaps?'

'I – I may have.'

Nigel, staring at Malmsley, wondered how he could ever have thought him a pale young man.

'Do you remember a book *The Consolations of a Critic?*'

'I – don't remember – I – '

'Do you own a copy of this book?'

'No – I – I – '

Alleyn picked up the little blue volume from under his chair and laid it on Malmsley's knee.

'Isn't this book your property, Mr Malmsley?'

'I – I refuse to answer. This is intolerable.'

'It has your name on the fly-leaf.'

Nigel suddenly felt desperately sorry for Malmsley. He felt as if he himself had done something shameful. He wished ardently that Alleyn would let Malmsley go. Malmsley had embarked on a sort of explanation. Elaborate phrases faltered into lame protestations. The subconscious memory of beautiful things – all art was imitative – to refuse a model was to confess yourself without imagination. On and on he went, and ended in misery.

'All this,' said Alleyn, not too unkindly, 'is quite unnecessary. I am not here to inquire into the ethics of illustrative painting. The rightness or wrongness of what you have done is between yourself, your publisher, and your conscience, if such a thing exists. All I want to know is how this book came into the possession of Sonia Gluck.'

'I don't know. She was odiously inquisitive – I must have left it somewhere – I had it in the studio one afternoon when I – when I was alone. Someone came in and I – I put it aside. I am not in the least ashamed. I consider I had a perfect right. There are many dissimilarities.'

'That is what she was driving at when she asked you, on the morning of the experiment, where you got your ideas?'

'Yes. I suppose so. Yes.'

'Did you ask her for the book?'

'Yes.'

'And she refused to give it up?'

'It was abominable. It was not that I objected to anybody knowing.'

'Did you go to her room?'

'I had every right when she refused. It was my property.'

'I see. You tried to recover it while she was away. On Friday, perhaps, before you left?'

'If you must know, yes.'

'And you couldn't find your book?'

'No.'

'Where was this book, Bailey?'

'In a locked suitcase, sir, under deceased's bed. Someone had tried to pick the lock.'

'Was that you, Mr Malmsley?'

'I was entirely justified.'

'Was it you?'

'Yes.'

'Why did you not tell Miss Troy what had happened?'

'I – Troy might not look at it – Troy is rather British in such matters. She would confess with wonderful enthusiasm that her own work is rooted in the aesthetics of the primitives, but for someone who was courageous enough to use boldly such material from the past as seemed good to him, she would have nothing but abuse. Women – English women especially – are the most marvellous hypocrites.'

'That will do,' said Alleyn. 'What was Sonia's motive in taking this book?'

'She simply wanted to be disagreeable and infuriating.'

'Did you offer her anything if she returned it?'

'She was preposterous,' muttered Malmsley, 'preposterous.'

'How much did she ask?'

'I do not admit that she asked anything.'

'All right,' said Alleyn. 'It's your mess. Stay in it if you want to.'

'What am I to understand by that?'

'Think it out. I believe I need not keep you any longer, Mr Malmsley. I am afraid I cannot return your book just yet. I shall need a specimen of your fingerprints. We can take them from the cigarette-box you picked up when you came in, or from objects in your room which I am afraid I shall have to examine. It would help matters if you allowed Sergeant Bailey to take an official specimen now.'

Malmsley consented to this with a very ill grace, and made a great fuss over the printer's ink left on his thick white finger-tips.

'I fail to see,' he said, 'why I should have been forced to go through this disgusting performance.'

'Bailey will give you something to clean up the ink,' said Alleyn. 'Good evening, Mr Malmsley.'

'One more job for you, Bailey, I'm afraid,' said Alleyn, when Malmsley had gone. 'We'll have to look through these rooms before we let them go to bed. Are they still boxed up in the dining-room, Fox?'

'They are that,' said Fox, 'and if that young Australian talks much more, I fancy we'll have a second corpse on our hands.'

'I'll start off on Mr Malmsley's room, will I, sir?' asked Bailey.

'Yes. Then tackle the other men's. We'll be there in a jiffy. I don't expect to find much, but you never know in our game.'

'Very good, Mr Alleyn,' said Bailey. He went off with a resigned look.

'What do you make of this dope story, Mr Alleyn?' said Fox. 'We'll have to have a go at tracing the source, won't we?'

'Oh Lord, yes. I suppose so. Malmsley will say he got it from the friend who gave him the pretty little pipe and etceteras, and I don't suppose even Malmsley will give his dope merchant away. Not that I think he's far gone. I imagine he spoke the truth when he said he'd only experimented – he doesn't look like an advanced addict. I took a pot-shot on his eyes, his breath, and the colour of his beastly face. And I remembered Sadie noticing a smell. Luckily the shot went home.'

'Smoking,' ruminated Nigel. 'That's rather out of the usual in this country, isn't it?'

'Fortunately, yes,' agreed Alleyn. 'As a matter of fact it's less deadly than the other methods. Much less pernicious than injecting, of course.'

'Do you think Garcia may have done his stuff with the knife while he was still dopey?' asked Nigel.

'It would explain his careless ways,' said Fox, 'dropping clay about the place.'

'That's true, Brer Fox. I don't know,' said Alleyn, 'if, when he woke at, say, seven-thirty, when Sadie banged on the screen, he'd feel like doing the job. We'll have to have expert opinion on the carry-over from opium. I'm inclined to think he might wake feeling damned unpleasant and take a pull at his whisky botde. Had it been handled recently, Bailey?'

'Yes, sir, I'd say it had. It's very dusty in patches, but there's some prints that were left after the dust had settled. Only a very light film over the prints. Not more than a couple of days' deposit.'

'That's fairly conclusive,' said Alleyn. 'Taken with Sadie's statement it looks as if Garcia's Friday evening dinner was a jorum of whisky.'

'What beats me,' said Fox, 'is when he got his stuff away.'

'Some time on Friday night.'

'Yes, but *how?* Not by a local carrier. They've all been asked.'

'He must have got hold of a vehicle of some sort and driven himself,' said Nigel.

'Half doped and three-quarters tight, Mr Bathgate?'

'He may not have been as tight as all that,' said Alleyn. 'On the other hand – '

'Well?' asked Nigel impatiently.

'On the other hand he may have,' said Alleyn. 'Come on, we'll see how Bailey's got on, and then we'll go home.'

CHAPTER 13

Upstairs

When Fox had gone upstairs and Nigel had been left to write a very guarded story for his paper on one of Troy's scribbling-pads, Alleyn went down the hall and into the dining-room. He found the whole class in a state of extreme dejection. Phillida Lee, Ormerin and Watt Hatchett were seated at the table and had the look of people who have argued themselves to a standstill. Katti Bostock, hunched on the fender, stared into the fire. Malmsley was stretched out in the only armchair. Valmai Seacliff and Basil Pilgrim sat on the floor in a dark corner with their arms round each other. Curled up on a cushion against the wall was Troy – fast asleep. The local constable sat on an upright chair inside the door.

Katti looked up at Alleyn and then across to Troy.

'She's completely done up,' said Katti gruffly. 'Can't you let her go to bed?'

'Very soon now,' said Alleyn.

He walked swiftly across the room and paused, his head bent down, his eyes on Troy.

Her face looked thin. There were small shadows in the hollows of her temples and under her eyes. She frowned, her hands moved, and suddenly she was awake.

I'm so sorry,' said Alleyn.

'Oh, it's you,' said Troy. 'Do you want me?'

'Please. Only for a moment, and then I shan't bother you again tonight.'

Troy sat up, her hands at her hair, pushing it off her face. She rose but lost her balance. Alleyn put his arm out quickly. For a moment he supported her.

'My legs have gone to sleep,' said Troy. 'Damn!'

Her hand was on his shoulder. He held her firmly by the arms and wondered if it was Troy or he who trembled.

'I'm all right now,' she said, after an hour or a second. 'Thank you.' He let her go and spoke to the others.

'I am very sorry to keep you all up for so long. We have had a good deal to do. Before you go to your rooms we should like to have a glance at them. I hope nobody objects to this.'

'Anything, if we can only go to bed,' said Katti, and nobody contradicted her.

'Very well, then. If you – ' he turned to Troy – 'wouldn't mind coming with me – '

'Yes, of course.'

When they were in the hall she said: 'Do you want to search our rooms for something? Is that it?'

'Not for anything specific. I feel we should just – ' He stopped short. 'I detest my job,' he said; 'for the first time I despise and detest it.'

'Come on,' said Troy.

They went up to a half-landing where the stairs separated into two short flights going up to their left and right.

'Before I forget,' said Alleyn, 'do you know what has happened to the bottle of nitric acid that was on the top shelf in the junk-room?'

Troy stared at him.

'The acid? It's there. It was filled up on Friday.'

'Bailey must have missed it. Don't worry – we saw the stains and felt we ought to account for them. What about these rooms?'

'All the students' rooms are up there,' said Troy, and pointed to the upper landing on the right. 'The bathrooms, and mine, are on the other side. Through here' -she pointed to a door on the half-landing – 'are the servant's quarters, the back stairs and a little stair up to the attic-room where – where Sonia slept.'

Alleyn saw that there were lights under two of the doors on the student's landing.

'Fox and Bailey are up there,' he said. 'If you don't mind – '

'You'd better do my room,' said Troy. 'Here it is.'

They went into the second room on the left-hand landing. It was a large room, very spacious and well-proportioned. The walls, the carpet, and the narrow bed, were white. He saw only one picture and very few ornaments, but on the mantelpiece sparkled a little glass Christmas tree with fabulous glass flowers growing on it. Troy struck a match and lit the fire.

'I'll leave you to your job,' she said.

Alleyn did not answer.

'Is there anything else?' asked Troy.

'Only that I should like to say that if it was possible for me to make an exception – '

'Why should you make any exceptions?' interrupted Troy. 'There is no conceivable reason for such a suggestion.'

'If you will simply think of me as a ship's steward or – or some other sexless official – '

'How else should I think of you, Mr Alleyn? I can assure you there is no need for these scruples – if they are scruples.'

'They were attempts at an apology. I shall make a third and ask you to forgive me for my impertinence. I shan't keep you long.'

Troy turned at the door.

'I didn't meant to be beastly,' she said.

'Nor were you. I see now that I made an insufferable assumption.'

' – but you can hardly expect me to be genial when you are about to hunt through my under-garments for incriminating letters. The very fact that you suspect – '

Alleyn strode to the door and looked down at her. 'You little fool,' he said, 'haven't you the common-or-garden gumption to see that I no more suspect you than the girl in the moon?'

Troy stared at him as if he had taken leave of his senses. She opened her mouth to speak, said nothing, turned on her heel and left the room.

'Blast!' said Alleyn. 'Oh, blast and hell and bloody stink!'

He stood and looked at the door which Troy had only just not slammed. Then he turned to his job. There was a bow-fronted chest of drawers full of the sorts of garments that Alleyn often before had had to turn over. His thin fastidious hands touched them delicately, laid them in neat heaps on the bed and returned them carefully to their appointed places. There was a little drawer, rather untidy, where Troy kept her oddments. One or two letters. One that began 'Troy darling' and was signed 'Your foolishly devoted, John'. 'John,' thought Alleyn, 'John Bellasca?' He glanced through the letters quickly, was about to return them to the drawer, but on second thoughts laid them in a row on the top of the chest. 'An odious trade,' he muttered to himself. 'A filthy degrading job.' Then there were the dresses in the wardrobe, the slim jackets, Troy's smart evening dresses, and her shabby old slacks. All the pockets. Such odd things she kept in her pockets – bits of charcoal, india-rubbers, a handkerchief that had been disgracefully used as a paint-rag, and a sketchbook crammed into a pocket that was too small for it. There was a Harris tweed coat – blue. Suddenly he was back on the wharf at Quebec. The lights of Troy's ship were reflected in the black mirror of the river. Silver-tongued bells rang out from all the grey churches. The tug, with its five globes of yellow light, moved outwards into the night tide of the St Lawrence, and there on the deck was Troy, her hand raised in farewell, wearing blue Harris tweed. 'Goodbye. Thank you for my nice party. Goodbye.' He slipped his hand into a pocket of the blue coat and pulled out Katti Bostock's letter. He would have to read this.

. . . You are a gump to collect these bloodsuckers . . . he's a nasty little animal. . . that little devil Sonia Gluck . . . behaving abominably . . . funny this 'It' stuff . . . you're different. They'd fall for you if you'd let them, only you're so unprovocative . . . [Alleyn shook his head at Katti Bostock]. Your allusions to a detective are quite incomprehensible, but if he interrupted you in your work you had every right to bite his head off. What had you been up to anyway? Well, so long until the 3rd. *Katti*

The envelope was addressed to Troy at the Chateau Frontenac.

'Evidently,' thought Alleyn, 'I had begun to make a nuisance of myself on board. Interrupting her work. Oh Lord!'

In a minute or two he had finished. It would have been absolutely all right if he had never asked about her room. No need for that little scene. He hung up the last garment, glanced round the room and looked for the fourth or fifth time at the photograph of a man that stood on the top of the bow-fronted chest. A good-looking man who had signed himself 'John'. Alleyn, yielding to an unworthy impulse, made a hideous grimace at this photograph, turned to leave the room and saw Troy, amazed, in the doorway. He felt his face burning like a sky sign.

'Have you finished, Mr Alleyn?'

'Quite finished, thank you.'

He knew she had seen him. There was a singular expression in her eyes.

'I have just made a face at the photograph on your tallboy,' said Alleyn.

'So I observed.'

'I have gone through your clothes, fished in your pockets and read all your letters. You may go to bed. The house will be watched, of course. Good night, Miss Troy.'

'Good morning, Mr Alleyn.'

Alleyn went to Katti Bostock's room where he found nothing of note. It was a great deal untidier than Troy's room, and took longer. He found several pairs of paint-stained slacks huddled together on the floor of the wardrobe, an evening dress in close proximity to a painting-smock, and a row of stubborn-looking shoes with no trees in them. There were odds and ends in all the pockets. He plodded through a mass of receipts, colour-men's catalogues, drawings and books. The only personal letter he found was the one Troy had written and posted at Vancouver.* This had to be read. Troy's catalogue of the students was interesting. Then he came to the passages about himself. '. . . turned out to be intelligent, so I felt the fool. . . . Looks like a grandee . . . on the defensive about this sleuth. . . . Took it like a gent and made me feel like a bounder.' As he read, Alleyn's left eyebrow climbed up his forehead. He folded the letter very carefully, smoothed it out and returned it to its place among a box of half-used oil-colours. He began to whistle under his breath, polished off Katti Bostock's effects, and went in search of Fox and Bailey. They had finished the men's bedrooms.

Fox had found Malmsley's opium-smoking impedimenta and had impounded them. The amount of opium was small. There were signs that the jar had at one time been full.

*See page 467.

'Which does not altogether agree with Mr Malmsley's little story,' grunted Alleyn. 'Has Bailey tried the things for prints?'

'Yes. Two sets, Garcia and Malmsley's on the pipe, the lamp and the jar.'

'The jar. That's interesting. Well, let's get on with it.'

He sent Bailey into Phillida Lee's room, while he and Fox tackled Valmai Seacliff's. Miss Seacliff's walls were chiefly adorned with pictures of herself. Malmsley and Ormerin had each painted her, and Pilgrim had drawn her once and painted her twice.

'The successful nymphomaniac,' thought Alleyn, remembering Katti's letter.

A very clever pencil drawing of Pilgrim, signed 'Seacliff', stood on the bedside table. The room was extremely tidy and much more obviously feminine than Troy's or Katti's. Seacliff had at least three times as many clothes, and quantities of hats and berets. Alleyn noticed that her slacks were made in Savile Row, and her dresses in Paris. He was amused to find that even the Seacliff painting-bags and smock smelt of Worth. Her weekend case had not been completely unpacked. In it he found three evening dresses, a nightdress and bath-gown, shoes, three pairs of coloured gloves, two day dresses, two berets, and an evening bag containing among other things a half-full bottle of aspirin.

'Maybe Pilgrim's,' said Alleyn, and put them in his case. 'Now for the correspondence.'

They found more than enough of that. Two of her dressing-table drawers were filled with neatly tied-up packets of letters.

'Help!' said Alleyn. 'We'll have to glance at these, Fox. There might be something. Here, you take this lot. Very special. Red ribbon. Must be Pilgrim's, I imagine. Yes, they are.'

Fox put on his spectacles and began impassively to read Basil Pilgrim's love-letters.

'Very gentlemanly,' he said, after the first three.

'You're out of luck. I've struck a most impassioned series from a young man, who compares her bitterly and obscurely to a mirage. Golly, here's a sonnet.'

For some time there was no sound but the faint crackle of notepaper. Bailey came in and said he had drawn a blank in Phillida Lee's room. Alleyn threw a bundle of letters at him.

'There's something here you might like to see,' said Fox. 'The last one from the Honourable Mr Pilgrim.'

'What's he say?'

Fox cleared his throat.

' "Darling",' he began, 'I've got the usual sort of feelings about not being anything like good enough for you. Your last letter telling me you first liked me because I seemed a bit different from other men has made me feel rather bogus. I suppose, without being an insuffer-able prig, I might agree that I can at any rate bear comparison with the gang we've got to know – the studio lot – like Garcia and Malmsley and Co. But that's not a hell of a compliment to myself, is it? As a matter of fact, I simply loathe seeing you in that setting. Men like Garcia have no right to be in the same room as yourself, my lovely, terrifyingly remote Valmai. I know people scream with mirth at the sound of the word 'pure'. It's gone all *déclassé* like 'genteel'. But there is a strange sort of purity about you, Valmai, truly. If I've understood you, you've seen something of – God, this sounds fright-ful – something of the same sort of quality in me. Oh, darling, don't see *too* much of that in me. Just because I don't get tight and talk bawdy, I'm not a blooming Galahad, you know. This letter's going all the wrong way. Bless you a thousand, thousand – " I think that's the lot, sir,' concluded Fox.

'Yes. I see. Any letters in Pilgrim's room?'

'None. He may have taken them to Ankerton Manor, chief.'

'So he may. I'd like to see the one where Miss Seacliff praised his purity. By the Lord, Fox, she has without a doubt got a wonderful technique. She's got that not undesirable party, who'll be a perfect-ly good peer before very long, if it's true that old Pilgrim is failing; she's got him all besotted and wondering if he's good enough.' Alleyn paused and rubbed his nose. 'Men turn peculiar when they fall in love, Brer Fox. Sometimes they turn damned peculiar, and that's a fact.'

'These letters,' said Fox, tapping them with a stubby forefinger, 'were all written before they came down here. They've evidently been engaged in a manner of speaking for about a month.'

'Very possibly.'

'Well,' said Fox, 'there's nothing in these letters of Mr Pilgrim's to contradict any ideas we may have about Garcia, is there?'

'Nothing. What about Pilgrim's clothes?'

'Nothing there. Two overcoats, five suits, two pairs of odd trousers and an odd jacket. Nothing much in the pockets. His weekend suit-case hasn't been unpacked. He took a dinner suit, a tweed suit, pyjamas, dressing-gown, and toilet things.'

'Any aspirin?'

'No.'

'I fancy I found his bottle in one of Miss Seacliff's pockets. Come on. Let's get on with it.'

They got on with it. Presently Bailey said: 'Here's one from Garcia.'

'Let me see, will you?'

Like the note to Sonia, this was written in pencil on an odd scrap of paper. It was not dated or addressed, and the envelope was missing.

Dear Valmai,

I hear you're going to Troy's this term. So am I. I'm broke. I haven't got the price of the fare down, and I want one or two things – paints mostly. I'm going to paint for a bit. I took the liberty of going into Gibson's, and getting a few things on your account. I told old Gibson it would be all right, and he'd seen me in the shop with you, so it was. Do you think Basil Pilgrim would lend me a fiver? Or would you? I'll be OK when Troy gets back, and I've got a good commission, so the money's all right. If I don't hear from you, I'll ask Pilgrim. I can't think of anyone else. Is it true you're going to hitch up with Pilgrim? You'd much better try a spot of free love with me. – *G.*

'Cool,' said Fox.

'Does this bloke live on women?' asked Bailey.

'He lives on anyone that will provide the needful, I'd say,' grunted Fox.

'That's about it,' said Alleyn. 'We'll keep this and any other Garcia letters we find, Fox. Well, that's all, isn't it? Either of you got any more tender missives? All right then, we'll pack up. Fox, you might tell them all they may turn in now. My compliments and so on. Miss Troy has gone to her room. The others, I suppose, will still be in the dining-room. Come on, Bathgate.'

A few minutes later they all met in the hall. Tatler's End House was quiet at last. The fires had died down in all the grates, the rooms had grown cold. Up and down the passages the silence was broken only by the secret sounds made by an old house at night, small expanding noises, furtive little creaks, and an occasional slow whisper as though the house sighed at the iniquity of living men. Alleyn had a last look round and spoke to the local man who was to remain on duty in the hall. Bailey opened the door and Fox turned out the last of the lights. Nigel, huddled in an overcoat, stowed his copy away in a pocket and lit a cigarette. Alleyn stood at the foot of the stairs, his face raised, as if he listened for something.

'Right, sir?' asked Fox.

'Coming,' said Alleyn. 'Good night.'

'Good night, sir,' said the local man.

'By the way – where's the garage?'

'Round the house to the right, sir.'

'Thank you. Good night.'

The front door slammed behind them.

'Blast that fellow!' said Alleyn. 'Why the devil must he wake the entire household?'

It was a still, cold night, with no moon. The gravel crunched loudly under their feet.

'I'm just going to have a look at the garage,' said Alleyn. 'I've got the key from a nail in the lobby. I won't be long. Give me my case, Bailey. Bathgate – you drive on.'

He switched on his torch and followed the drive round the house to an old stables-yard. The four loose-boxes had been converted into garages, and his key fitted all of them. He found an Austin, and a smart supercharged sports car – 'Pilgrim's,' thought Alleyn – and in the last garage a small motor caravan. Alleyn muttered when he saw this. He examined the tyre-treads, measured the distance between the wheels and took the height from the ground to the rear doorstep. He opened the door and climbed in. He found a small lamp on a battery in the ceiling, and swtiched it on. It was not an elaborate interior, but it was well planned. There were two bunks, a folding table, a cupboard and plenty of lockers. He looked into the lockers and found painting gear and one or two canvases. He took one out. 'Troy's,' he said. He began to look very closely at the board floor.

On the doorstep he found two dark indentations. They were shiny and looked as though they had been made by small wheels carrying a heavy load. The door opened outwards. Its inner surface had been recently scored across. Alleyn looked through a lens at the scratches. The paint had frilled up a little and the marks were clean. The floor itself bore traces of the shiny tracks, but here they were much fainter. He looked at the petrol gauge and found it registered only two gallons. He returned to the floor and crawled over it with his torch. At last he came upon a few traces of a greenish-grey substance. These he scraped off delicately and put in a small tin. He went into the driver's cabin, taking an insufflator with him, and tested the wheel. It showed no clear prints. On the floor of the cabin Alleyn found several Player's cigarette-butts. These he collected and examined carefully. The ray from his torch showed him a tiny white object that had dropped into the gear-change slot. He fished it out with a pair of tweezers. It was the remains of yet another cigarette and had got jammed and stuck to the inside of the slot. A fragment of red paper was mixed with the flattened wad of tobacco strands. One of Troy's, perhaps. An old one. He had returned to the door with his insufflator, when a deep voice said:

'Have they remembered your hot-water bottle, sir, and what time would you wish to be called?'

'Fox!' said Alleyn, 'I am sorry. Have I been very long?'

'Oh no, sir. Bert Bailey's in his beauty sleep in the back of our car, and Mr Bathgate has gone off in his to her ladyship's. Mr Bathgate asked me to tell you, sir, that he proposed to make the telephone wires burn while the going was good.'

'I'd like to see him try. Fox, we'll seal up this caravan and then we really will go home. Look here, you send Bailey back to London and stay the night with us. My mother will be delighted. I'll lend you some pyjamas, and we'll snatch a few hours' sleep and start early in the morning. Do come.'

'Well, sir, that's very kind of you. I'd be very pleased.'

'Splendid!'

Alleyn sealed the caravan door with tape, and then the door of the garage. He put the key in his pocket.

'No little jaunts for them tomorrow,' he said coolly. 'Come along, Fox. Golly, it's cold.'

They saw Bailey, arranged to meet him at the Yard in the morning, and drove back to Danes Lodge.

'We'll have a drink before we turn in,' said Alleyn softly, when they were indoors. 'In here.'

Fox tiptoed after him towards Lady Alleyn's boudoir. At the door they paused and looked at each other. A low murmur of voices came from the room beyond.

'Well, I'll be damned,' said Alleyn, and walked in.

A large fire crackled in the open fireplace. Nigel sat before it crosslegged on the hearthrug. Curled up in a wing-backed chair was Lady Alleyn. She wore a blue dressing-gown and a lace cap and her feet were tucked under her.

'Ma'am!' said Alleyn.

'Hullo, darling! Mr Bathgate's been telling me all about your case. It's wonderfully interesting, and we have already solved it in three separate ways.'

She looked round the corner of her chair and saw Fox.

'This is disgraceful,' said Alleyn. 'A scene of license and depravity. May I introduce Mr Fox, and will you give him a bed?'

'Of course I will. This is perfectly delightful. How do you do, Mr Fox?'

Fox made his best bow and took the small, thin hand in his enormous fist.

'How d'you do, my lady?' he said gravely. 'It's very kind of you.'

'Roderick, bring up some chairs, darling, and get yourselves drinks. Mr Bathgate is drinking whisky, and I am drinking port. It's not a bit kind of me, Mr Fox. I have hoped so much that we might meet. Do you know, you look exactly as I have always thought you would look, and that is very flattering to me and to you. Roderick has told me so much about you. You've worked together on very many cases, haven't you?'

'A good many, my lady,' said Fox. He sat down and contemplated Lady Alleyn placidly. 'It's been a very pleasant association for me. Very pleasant. We're all glad to see Mr Alleyn back.'

'Whisky and soda, Fox?' said Alleyn. 'Mamma, what will happen to your bright eyes if you swill port at one a.m.? Bathgate?'

'I've got one, thank you. Alleyn, your mother is quite convinced that Garcia is not the murderer.'

'No,' said Lady Alleyn. 'I don't say he *isn't* the murderer, but I don't think he's the man you're after.'

'That's a bit baffling of you,' said Alleyn. 'How d'you mean?'

'I think he's been made a cat's-paw by somebody. Probably that very disagreeable young man with a beard. From what Mr Bathgate tells me – '

'I should be interested to know what Bathgate has told you.'

'Don't be acid, darling. He's given me a perfectly splendid account of the whole thing – as lucid as Lucy Lorrimer,' said Lady Alleyn.

'Who's Lucy Lorrimer?' asked Nigel.

'She's a prehistoric peep. Old Lord Banff's eldest girl she was, and never known to finish a sentence. She always got lost in the thickets of secondary thoughts that sprang up round her simplest remarks, so everybody used to say "as lucid as Lucy Lorrimer." No, but really, Roderick, Mr Bathgate was as clear as glass over the whole affair. I am absolutely *au fait*, and I feel convinced that Garcia has been a cat's-paw. He sounds so unattractive, poor fellow.'

'Homicides are inclined to be unattractive, darling,' said Alleyn.

'What about Mr Smith? George Joseph? You can't say that of *him* with all those wives. The thing that makes me so cross with Mr Smith,' continued Lady Alleyn, turning to Fox, 'is his monotony. Always in the bath and always a pound of tomatoes. In and out of season, one supposes.'

'If we consider Mr Malmsley, Lady Alleyn,' said Fox with perfect gravity, 'his only motive, as far as we know, would be vanity.'

'And a very good motive, too, Mr Fox. Mr Bathgate tells me Malmsley is an extremely affected and conceited young man. No doubt this poor murdered child threatened him with exposure. No doubt she said she would make a laughing-stock of him by telling everybody that he cribbed his illustration from Pol de Limbourge. I must say, Roderick, he showed exquisite taste. It is the most charming little picture imaginable. Do you remember we saw it at Chantilly?'

'I do, but I'm ashamed to say that I didn't at first spot it when I looked at his drawing.'

'That was rather slow of you, darling. Too gay and charming for words. Well, Mr Fox, suppose this young Malmsley deliberately stayed behind on Friday, deliberately gave Garcia opium, deliberately egged him on to set the trap, and then came away, hoping that Garcia would do it. How about that?'

'You put it very neatly indeed, my lady,' said Fox, looking at Lady Alleyn with serious approval. 'May I relieve you of your glass?'

'Thank you. Well now, Roderick, what about Basil Pilgrim?'

'What about him, little mum?'

'Of course, *he* might easily be unbalanced. Robert Pilgrim is as mad as a March Hare, and I think that unfortunate wife of his was a cousin of sorts, so there you are. And she simply set to work and had baby after baby after baby – all gels, poor thing – until she had this boy Basil, and died of exhaustion. Not a very good beginning. And Robert turned into a Primitive Methodist in the middle of it all, and used to ask everybody the most ill-judged questions about their private lives. I remember quite well when this boy was born, Roderick, your father said Robert's methods had been too primitive for Alberta. Her name was Alberta. Do you think the boy could have had anything to do with this affair?'

'Has Bathgate told you all about our interview with Pilgrim?' asked Alleyn.

'He was in the middle of it when you came in. What sort of boy has he grown into? Not like Robert, I hope?'

'Not very. He's most violently in love.'

'With this Seacliff gel. What kind of gel is she, Roderick? Modern and hard? Mr Bathgate says beautiful.'

'She's very good-looking and bit of a huntress.'

'At all murderish, do you imagine?'

'Darling, I don't know. Do you realize you ought to be in bed, and that you've led Bathgate into the father and mother of a row for talking out of school?'

'Mr Bathgate knows I'm as safe as the Roman Wall, don't you, Mr Bathgate?'

'I'm so much in love with you, Lady Alleyn,' said Nigel, 'that I wouldn't care if you were the soul of indiscretion. I should still open my heart to you.'

'There now, Roderick,' said his mother, '*isn't* that charming? I think perhaps I will go to bed.'

Ten minutes later, Alleyn tapped on his mother's door. The familiar, high-pitched voiced called: 'Come in, darling,' and he found Lady

Alleyn sitting bolt upright in her bed, a book in her hand, and spectacles on her nose.

'You look like a miniature owl,' said Alleyn, and sat on the bed.

'Are they tucked away comfortably?'

'They are. Both besotted with adoration of you.'

'Darling! Did I show off?'

'Shamelessly.'

'I do *like* your Mr Fox, Roderick.'

'Isn't he splendid? Mum – '

'Yes, darling?'

'This is a tricky business.'

'I suppose so. How is she?'

'Who?'

'Don't be affected, Roderick.'

'We had two minor rows and one major one. I forgot my manners.'

'You shouldn't do that. I don't know, though. Perhaps you should. Who do you think committed this horrible crime, my dear?'

'Garcia.'

'Because he was drugged?'

'I don't know. You won't say anything about – '

'Now, Roderick!'

'I know you won't.'

'Did you give her my invitation?'

'Unfortunately we were not on them terms. I'll be up betimes in the morning.'

'Give me a kiss, Rory. Bless you, dear. Good night.'

'Good night, little mum.'

CHAPTER 14

Evidence from a Twig

Alleyn and Fox were back at Tatler's End House at seven o'clock in the thin chilly light of dawn. A thread of smoke rose from one of the chimneys. The ground was hard and the naked trees, fast, fast asleep, stretched their lovely arms against an iron sky. The air was cold and smelt of rain. The two men went straight to the studio, where they found a local constable, wrapped in his overcoat, and very glad to see them.

'How long have you been here?' asked Alleyn.

'Since ten o'clock last night, sir. I'll be relieved fairly soon – eight o'clock with any luck.'

'You can go off now. We'll be here until then. Tell Superintendent Blackman I said it was all right.'

'Thank you very much, sir. I think I'll go straight home. Unless – '

'Yes?'

'Well, sir, if you're going to work here, I'd like to look on – if it's not a liberty, sir.'

'Stay, by all means. What's your name?'

'Sligo, sir.'

'Right. Keep your counsel about our business. No need to tell you that. Come along.'

Alleyn led them to the studio window. He released the blind and opened the window. The ledge outside was rimy with frost.

'Last night,' said Alleyn, 'we noticed certain marks on this window-sill. Look first of all at the top of the stool here. You see four marks – indentations in the surface?'

'Yes, sir.'

'We're going to measure them.'

Alleyn produced a thin steel tape and measured the distance between the indentations. Fox wrote the figure in his notebook.

'Now the window-sill. You see these marks?' He pointed to two lateral marks, shiny and well defined, like shallow grooves. Alleyn measured the distance between them and found that it corresponded exactly with the previous figure. The width of the marks, the depth, and the appearance were the same as those on the stool.

'Garcia had his model on a small wheeled platform,' said Alleyn. 'Now, Malmsley told us that Garcia proposed to wheel the model into the case and then put the whole thing on board whatever vehicle called to collect it. I think he changed his mind. I think he put the empty crate in the vehicle, drew the stool up to the sill, and wheeled the model over the sill into the crate, and aboard the caravan which was backed up to the window in the lane outside.'

'The caravan, sir?' asked Sligo. 'Was it a caravan?'

'Lock this place up and come along outside. You can get over the sill, but don't touch those two marks just yet. Jump well out to the side and away from the tyre-tracks.'

In the lane Alleyn showed them the traces left by the wheels. They had been frozen hard.

'Bailey has taken casts of these, but I want you to note them carefully. You see at once that the driver of the van or whatever it was did a good deal of skirmishing about. If there were any footprints within twelve feet of the window, they've been obliterated. Farther out are traces of the mortuary van, blast it. The caravan tracks overlap, and there are four sets of them. But if you look carefully, you can pick out the last impression on top of all the others. That's when the van was finally driven away. The next set, overlaid by these, represents the final effort to get in close to the window. Damn! It's beginning to rain. This will be our last chance in the lane, so let's make the most of it. Observe the tread, Sligo. There, you see, is the clear impression of a patch. I'll measure the distance between the wheels and the width of the tyres. There a little oil has dripped on the road. The van or whatever it is has been recently greased. It was backed in and the brakes jammed on suddenly, but not quite suddenly enough. The outer edge of the window-sill has had a knock.

The front wheels were turned after the vehicle had stopped. There are the marks. From them we get the approximate length of the wheel-base. Out in the middle lane they disappear under the tracks of more recent traffic. Now look at the branches of that elm. They reach across the lane almost to our side, and are very low. I wonder the county councillors have not lopped them down. Do you see that one or two twigs have been snapped off? There's been no wind, and the breaks are quite recent. See here!'

He stopped and picked up a broken twig.

'It is still sappy. There are several. One quite close to the studio wall, and there's another across the lane. If it should happen they were snapped off by the top of a vehicle, it must have moved from one side to the other. It is a fair chance, isn't it, that they were broken by our van, and, if this is so, they give an idea of its height. Right?'

'That's right, sir,' said Mr Sligo, breathing loudly through his nostrils.

'You know all this sort of stuff, of course,' said Alleyn, 'but it's a characteristic example of outside work. Now come along to the garage.'

They walked along the lane through a wide entrance into the garage yard. Alleyn unlocked the garage doors and broke the police tape. It had begun to rain steadily.

'I took some measurements here last night, but it would be as well to verify them. Suppose you have a stab at it, Sligo.'

Sligo, intensely gratified, measured the width of the tyres and the wheel-base.

'The tyres are the same, sir. Look here, sir, here's the patch on the rear tyre on the driving side. We found the trace on the left-hand as you faced the window, sir, so she was backed all right.'

'Good,' said Alleyn. 'That's the way, Sligo. Now take a look at the doorstep. Wait a moment. I'll just have a go at the handle for prints.'

He opened his bag and got out his insufflator. The grey powder showed no prints on the door or door-knob. Alleyn closely examined the three steps, which were worn and dirty.

'Don't touch these,' he said, and opened the door.

'Now then, Sligo – '

'There they are, sir, there they are. Same marks on the top step. That's the marks of them little wheels, sir, isn't it?'

'I think so. Check them to make sure. Here are the measurements of the scars on the window-sill.'

Out came Sligo's tape again.

'It's them for sure,' he said.

'Now have a look on the roof. If you climb on that bench, you'll do no harm. Go carefully, though. You never know if you won't spoil a perfectly good bit of evidence in the most unlikely spot.'

Sligo mounted the bench like a mammoth Agag, and peered over the roof of the caravan.

'Eh, there's a-plenty of scratches, sir, right enough, and Gor', Mr Alleyn, there's a bit of a twig jammed between the top roofing and the frame. Dug into the crack. Gor', that's a bit of all right, isn't it, sir?'

'It is indeed. Can you reach it?'

'Yes, sir.'

'Take these tweezers and draw it out carefully. That's right. Now you can come down. Let's have an envelope, Fox, may we? We'll put your twig in there, Sligo, and label it. How far is it from here to London?'

'Twenty miles exactly, sir, to the end of the drive from Shepherd's Bush,' answered Sligo promptly.

'Right!'

Alleyn packed his case and began with Fox and Sligo to examine the yard and the gateway into the lane.

'Here are the tracks clear enough in the lane,' said Fox. 'We've got enough here and more to show this caravan was driven into the lane, backed up to the studio window and loaded up through the window. Who does the caravan belong to?'

'Miss Troy, I think,' said Alleyn.

'Is that so?' responded Fox, without any particular emphasis.

'We'll find out presently. Seal the garage up again, will you, Fox? Blast this weather. We'd better have a look at Pilgrim's car.'

Basil Pilgrim's car was a very smart supercharged two-seater. The upholstery smelt definitely of Valmai Seacliff, and one of the side-pockets contained an elaborate set of cosmetics. 'For running repairs,' grunted Alleyn. They opened the dicky and found a man's rather shabby raincoat. Pilgrim's. 'Also for running repairs, I should think.' Alleyn examined it carefully, and sniffed at it. 'Very powerful scent that young woman uses. I fancy, Fox, that this is the pure young man's garment for changing wheels and delving in engines. Now then, Sligo, you have a look at this. It's ideal for demonstration purposes – the sort of thing Holmes and Thorndyke read like a book. Do you know Holmes and Thorndyke? You should. How about giving me a running commentary on an old raincoat?'

Sligo, breathing noisily, took the coat in his enormous hands.

'Go on,' said Alleyn; 'you're a Yard man, and I'm taking notes for you.'

'It's a man's mackintosh,' began Sligo. 'Made by Burberry. Marked "B. Pilgrim" inside collar. It's mucked up like and stained. Inside of collar a bit greasy, and it's got white marks, too, on it. Grease on one sleeve. That's car grease, I reckon, and there's marks down front. Pockets. Right-hand: A pair of old gloves used, likely, for changing tyres. There's other marks, too. Reckon he's done something to battery some time.'

'Well done,' said Alleyn. 'Go on.'

Sligo turned the gloves inside out.

'Left hand inside got small dark stain on edge of palm under base of little finger. Left-hand pocket: Piece of greasy rag. Box of matches.' Sligo turned the coat over and over. 'I can't see nothing more, sir, except a bit of a hole in right-hand cuff. Burnt by cigarette, likely. That's all, sir.'

Alleyn shut his notebook.

'That's the method,' he said. 'But – ' He glanced at his watch. 'Good Lord, it is eight o'clock. You'd better cut back to the studio or your relief will be giving you a bad mark.'

'Thank you very much, sir. I'm much obliged, sir. It's been a fair treat.'

'That's all right. Away you go.'

Sligo pounded off.

Leaving Fox at the garage, Alleyn walked round the house and rang the front-door bell. It was answered by a constable.

'Good morning. Do you know if Miss Troy is down yet?'

'She's in the library, sir.'

'Ask if I may see her for a moment.'

The man came back to say Troy would receive Alleyn, and he went into the library. By daylight it was a pleasant room, and already a fire blazed in the open grate. Troy, in slacks and a pullover, looked so much as she did on that first morning at Suva that Alleyn felt for a moment as if there had been nothing between them but the first little shock of meeting. Then he saw that she looked as if she had not slept.

'You are early at your job,' said Troy.

'I'm very sorry, indeed, to worry you at the crack of dawn. I want to ask you if the caravan in the garage belongs to you.'

'Yes. Why?'

'When did you last use it, please?'

'About a fortnight ago. We all went out in it to Kattswood for a picnic and a day's sketching.'

'Do you know how much petrol there was in the tank when you got back?'

'It must have been more than half full, I should think. I got it filled up when we started, and we only went about forty miles there and back.'

'What does she do to the gallon?'

'Twenty.'

'And the tank holds – ?'

'Eight gallons.'

'Yes. It's just over a quarter full this morning.'

Troy stared at him.

'There must be a leak in the petrol tank,' she said. 'I couldn't have used more than five that day – not possibly.'

'There isn't a leak,' said Alleyn. 'I looked.'

'Look here, what is all this?'

'You're sure no one else has used the caravan?'

'Of course I am. Not with my permission.' Troy seemed puzzled and worried. Then as her eyes widened, 'Garcia!' she cried out. 'You think Garcia took it, don't you?'

'What makes you so sure of that?'

'Why, because I've puzzled my own wits half the night to think how he got his stuff away. The superintendent here told me none of the local carriers knew anything about it. Of course Garcia took it! Just like him. Trust him not to pay a carrier if he could get his stuff there free.'

'Can he drive?'

'I really don't know. I shouldn't have thought so, certainly. I suppose he must be able to drive if he took the caravan.' She paused and looked steadily at Alleyn.

'I know you think he went in the caravan,' she said.

'Yes, I do.'

'He must have brought it back that night,' said Troy.

'Couldn't have been some time on Saturday before you came back?'

'He didn't know when I was coming back. He wouldn't have risked my arriving early and finding the caravan gone. Besides, anyone might have seen him.'

'That's perfectly true,' said Alleyn.

'If this warehouse place is somewhere in London, he could do the trip easily if it was late at night, couldn't he?' asked Troy.

'Yes. Dear me, I shall have to do a sum. Wait a moment. Your car does twenty to the gallon, and holds eight gallons. You went forty miles, starting with a full tank. Therefore there should be six gallons, and there are only about three. That leaves a discrepancy of sixty miles or so. How fast can she go?'

'I suppose forty to forty-five or fifty if pressed. She's elderly and not meant for Brooklands.'

'I know. I do wish he'd told one of you where this damned warehouse was.'

'But he did. At least, Seacliff said this morning she thought she remembered he said something about it being near Holloway.'

'Good Lord, why didn't she say so last night?'

'Why does she always behave in the most tiresome manner one could possibly conceive? I'm nearly as bad, not to have told you at once.'

'You're nothing like as bad. How did Miss Seacliff happen to remember Holloway?'

'It was at breakfast, which, I may tell you, was not a very sparkling event this morning. Phillida Lee would talk about every murder story she has ever read, and Hatchett was more bumptious than words can describe. At last the Lee child remarked that if a woman was convicted of murder, she was hanged at Holloway, and Seacliff suddenly exclaimed: "Holloway – that's it – that's where Garcia's warehouse is; he said something about it when he first came down." '

'Is she sure?'

'She seems to be fairly certain. Shall I send for her?'

'Would you?'

Troy rang the bell, which was answered by Hipkin, a large man with a small head and flat feet.

'Ask Miss Seacliff if she'll come and see me.'

Seacliff strolled in, dressed in black trousers and a magenta sweater. She looked very lovely.

'Good morning, Miss Seacliff,' said Alleyn cheerfully. 'Are you recovered?'

'Why, what was the matter with *you?*' Troy asked her.

Seacliff glared at Alleyn with positive hatred.

'Miss Seacliff was indisposed last night,' said Alleyn.

'What was the matter?'

'Nerves,' said Seacliff.

'Was it *you* who was sick in the downstairs bathroom?' demanded Troy with an air of sudden enlightenment. 'Sadie was furious at having to clear up. She said – '

'Need we discuss it, Troy? I'm really terribly upset.'

'You must have been,' agreed Troy, with a suspicion of a grin. 'I must say I think you might have cleared up after yourself. Sadie said she thought at least three men – '

'Troy!'

'All right. Do you want to be alone, Mr Alleyn?'

'No, no. I just wanted to ask Miss Seacliff about this Holloway business.'

'Oh,' said Seacliff. 'You mean the place where Garcia is going to sculp?'

'Yes. Did he tell you it was somewhere near Holloway?'

'Yes, he did. I'd forgotten. I suppose you are furious with me?' She smiled at Alleyn. Her glance said, very plainly: 'After all, you are rather good-looking.'

'I'd like to know exactly what he said, if you can remember the conversation.'

'I suppose I can remember a good deal of it if I try. It took place during one of his periodical attempts to make a pass or two at me. He asked me if I would come and see him while he was working. I forget what I said. Oh, I think I said I would if it wasn't too drearily far away or something. Then he said it was near Holloway, because I remember I asked him if he thought he'd be safe. I said I knew better than to spend an afternoon with him in a deserted studio, but I might get Basil to drive me there, and, of course, that made him quite livid with rage. However, he told me how to get there and drew a sort of map. I'm afraid I've lost it. As a matter of fact, I would rather like to see that thing, wouldn't you, Troy? Still, as long as he's not arrested or something, I suppose we shall see it in its proper setting. I told Garcia I thought it was a bit of a come-down to take a commission from a flick-shop. I said they'd probably ask him to put touches of gilt on the breasts and flood it with pink lights. He turned as acid as a lemon and said the surroundings were to be appropriate. He's got absolutely no sense of humour, of course.'

'Did he tell you exactly where it was?'

'Oh, yes. He drew up the map, but I can't remember anything but Holloway.'

'Not even the name of the street?' asked Alleyn resignedly.

'I don't think so. He must have mentioned it and marked it down, but I don't suppose I'd ever remember it,' said Seacliff, with maddening complacency.

'Then I think that's all, thank you, Miss Seacliff.'

She got up, frowned, and closed her eyes for a moment.

'What's the matter?' asked Troy.

'I've got another of these filthy headaches.'

'Carry-over, perhaps.'

'No, it's not. I've been getting them lately.'

'You're looking a bit white,' said Troy, more kindly. 'Why don't you lie down? Would you like some aspirin?'

'Basil gave me his last night, thanks.' She took out her mirror and looked at herself with intense concentration.

'I look bloody,' she said, and walked out of the room.

'Is she always like that?' asked Alleyn.

'Pretty much. She's spoilt. She'd have been comparatively easy to live with if she hadn't got that lovely face. She *is* beautiful, you know.'

'Oh! magnificent,' agreed Alleyn absently.

He was looking at Troy, at the delicate sparseness of her head, the straight line of her brows and the generous width between her grey-green eyes.

'Are you very tired?' he asked gently.

'Who, me? I'm all right.' She sat on the fender holding her thin hands to the fire. 'Only I can't get it out of my head.'

'Small wonder,' said Alleyn, and to himself he thought: 'She's treating me more like a friend this morning. Touch wood.'

'Oddly enough, it's not so much Sonia, poor little thing, but Garcia, that I can't get out of my head. You needn't bother to be mysterious and taciturn. I know you must suspect Garcia after what Phillida Lee and Malmsley said last night. But you see, in a way, Garcia's a sort of protégé of mine. He came to me when he was almost literally starving, and I've tried to look after him a bit. I know he's got no conscience at all in the usual sort of way. He's what they call un-moral. But he has got genius and I never use that word if I can get out of it. He couldn't *do* a shabby thing with clay. Wait a moment.'

She went out of the room for a few minutes. When she returned she carried a small bronze head, about half life-size, of an old woman. Troy put the head on a low table and pulled back the curtains. The cold light flooded the little bronze. It looked very tranquil and pure; its simple forms folded it into a great dignity. The lights shone austerely and the shadows seemed to breathe.

' "All passion spent," ' said Alleyn after a short pause.

'That's it,' agreed Troy. She touched it delicately with a long finger. 'Garcia gave me this,' she said.

'It wouldn't be too florid to say it looked as if it had been done by an inspired saint.'

'Well – it wasn't. It was done by a lecherous, thieving little guttersnipe who happens to be a superb craftsman. But – ' Troy's voice wavered. 'To catch and hang the man who made it – '

'God – yes, I know – I know.' He got up and moved restlessly about the room, returning to her.

'Oh, Troy, you mustn't cry,' he said.

'What the devil's it got to do with you?'

'Nothing, nothing, nothing, and don't I know it!'

'You'd better get on with your job,' said Troy. She looked like a boy with her head turned shamefacedly away. She groped in her trousers pocket and pulled out a handkerchief disgracefully stained with paint. 'Oh blast!' she said, and pitched it into the waste-paper basket.

'Have mine.'

'Thank you.'

Alleyn turned away from her and leant his arms on the mantel-piece. Troy blew her nose violently.

'My mother's so happy about my picture,' said Alleyn to the fire. 'She says it's the best present she's ever had. She said, if you'll for-give the implication, that you must know all about the subject. I sup-pose that's the sort of lay remark that is rather irritating to a crafts-man for whom the model must be a collection of forms rather than an individual.'

'Bosh!' said Troy down her nose and behind his handkerchief.

'Is it? I'm always terrified of being highfalutin about pictures. The sort of person, you know, who says: "The eyes follow you all round the room." It would be so remarkably rum if they didn't when the model has looked into the painter's eyes, wouldn't it? I told my mamma about the thing you did at Suva. She rather fancies her lit-tle self about pictures. I think her aesthetic taste is pretty sound. Do you know she remembered the Pol de Limbourge thing that Malmsley cribbed, for one of his illustrations.'

'What!' exclaimed Troy loudly.

'Didn't you spot it?' asked Alleyn, without turning. 'That's one up to the Alleyn family, isn't it? The drawing of the three little medieval reapers in front of the château; it's Sainte Chapelle, really, I think – do you remember?'

'Golly, I believe you're right,' said Troy. She gave a dry sob, blew her nose again, and said: 'Are there any cigarettes on the mantel-piece?'

Alleyn gave her a cigarette and lit it for her. When he saw her face, marred by tears, he wanted almost overwhelmingly to kiss it.

'Little serpent!' said Troy.

'Who – Malmsley?'

'Yes. Malmsley of all people, with his beard and his precicosity.'

'There's no such word as precicosity.'

'There may be.'

'It's preciosity if it's anything.'

'Well, don't be a scold,' said Troy. 'Did you face Malmsley with this?'

'Yes. He turned as red as a rose.'

Troy laughed.

'What a doody-flop for Cedric,' she said.

'I must get on with my odious job,' said Alleyn. 'May I use your telephone?'

'Yes, of course. There'll be an inquest, won't there?'

'Tomorrow, I think. It won't be so bad. Goodbye.'

'Goodbye.'

He turned at the doorway and said: 'Lady Alleyn's compliments to Miss Troy, and if Miss Troy would like to sample the amenities of Danes Lodge, Lady Alleyn will be very happy to offer them.'

'Your mother is very kind,' said Troy, 'but I think it would be better not. Will you thank her from me? Please say I am very grateful indeed.'

Alleyn bowed.

'I'm grateful to you too,' said Troy.

'Are you? That is rather dangerously nice of you. Goodbye.'

CHAPTER 15

Lady of the Ensemble

Before he left Tatler's End House Alleyn rang up Superintendent Blackman and asked if there was any news of Garcia. There was none. A discreetly-worded notice had appeared in the morning papers and the B.B.C. had instructions to send out a police message. The police, within a fifty-mile radius, had made intensive inquiries.

'It looks as if he didn't want to be found, Mr Alleyn. The weather's been fine and if he'd sketched as he said he intended to do, he wouldn't have gone far in two days. It looks to me as if the bird had flown.'

'It does a bit. Of course, he might have changed his plans and taken a train or bus. We'll have to get on to the railway stations. All that deadly game. Thanks so much, Mr Blackman. I'll let you know if there are any developments. Inquest tomorrow?'

'No, Thursday. Our gentleman's full up tomorrow. Bossicote Town Hall at eleven. He's a sensible sort of chap, our man.'

'Good. I'll call on the C.C. this morning, before I go up to London.

'Just as well. He likes to be consulted.'

'What about the post-mortem?'

'I wanted to let you know. She was going to have a child. About a month gone, the doctor says.'

'I thought as much. Look here, I think I'll get straight up to London. Make my apologies to the Chief Constable, will you? I want to catch a friend of Sonia Gluck's, and I can't risk missing her.'

'Right you are. He'll understand. So long. See you on Thursday.'

Alleyn found Fox, who had renewed his acquaintance with the Hipkins and Sadie, and drove him back through teeming rain to Danes Lodge for breakfast.

'I've had a bit of a yarn with Ethel Jones,' said Fox.

'Ethel? Oh yes, the help from the village. What had she got to say for herself?'

'Quite a bit,' said Fox. He opened his notebook and put on his spectacles.

'You're looking very bland, Brer Fox. What have you got on to?'

'Well, sir, it seems that Ethel and her boy took a walk on Friday night down the lane. They passed by the studio window on their way home from the pictures at about eleven-thirty, perhaps a bit later. There were lights going in the studio but the blind was down. They walked straight past, but when they'd gone a piece further down the lane they stopped in the shadow of the trees to have a bit of a cuddle as you might put it. Ethel doesn't know how long it lasted. She says you're apt to lose your idea of time on these occasions, but when they got back to earth and thought about moving on, she glanced down the lane and saw someone outside the studio window.'

'Did she, by gum! Go on, Fox!'

'Well, sir, she couldn't see him very distinctly.'

'Him?'

'Yes. She says she could just see it was a man, and he seemed to be wearing a raincoat, and a cap or beret of some sort. He was standing quite close to the window, Ethel reckons, and was caught by a streak of light coming through the blind. I asked her about the face, of course, but she says it was in shadow. She remembers that there was a small patch of light on the cap.'

'There's a hole in the blind,' said Alleyn.

'Is that so, sir? That might account for it, then. Ethel says the rest of the figure was in shadow. The collar of his raincoat was turned up and she thinks his hands were in his pockets.'

'What height?'

'About medium, Ethel thought, but you know how vague they are. She said to her boy: 'Look, there's someone down the lane. They must have seen us,' and I suppose she gave a bit of a giggle, like a girl would.'

'You ought to know.'

'Why not, sir? Then, she says, the man turned aside and disappeared into the darker shadow and they could just hear his footfall as he walked away. Well, I went into the lane to see if I could pick up his prints, but you've been there and you know there wasn't much to be seen near the window, except the tyre-tracks where the caravan had been manoeuvred about. When you get away from the window and out into the lane there are any number of them, but there's been people and cars up and down during the weekend, and there's not much hope of picking up anything definite.'

'No.'

'I've looked carefully and I can't find anything. It's different with the car traces under the window. They're off the beaten track, but this downpour about finishes the lane as far as we're concerned.'

'I know.'

'Well, we got a description of Garcia last night, of course, but to make sure, I asked the Hipkins and Sadie and Ethel to repeat it. They gave the same story. He always wears a very old mackintosh, whether it's wet or fine, and it's their belief he hasn't got a jacket. Miss Troy gave him a grey sweater and he wears that with a pair of old flannel trousers. Mrs Hipkin says Miss Troy had given him two shirts and Mr Pilgrim gave him some underclothes. He doesn't often wear anything on his head, but they have seen him in a black beret. Sadie says he looks as rough as bags. Ethel said straight out that she thought the figure outside the window was Garcia. She said so to her boy. She says it was the dead spit of Garcia, but then, we've got to remember it wasn't at all distinct, and she may think differently now that she knows Garcia has gone. You know how they make up all sorts of things without scarcely knowing what they're up to.'

'I do indeed. Had this figure by the window anything on its back – like a rucksack, for instance?'

'They say he hadn't, but of course, if it was Garcia, he might not have picked up his gear when they saw him.'

'No.'

'I look at it this way. He might have gone through the window to take a short cut to the garage by way of the lane, and he might have stood there, having a last look at the arrangement on the model's throne.'

'Through the hole in the blind? Rather a sinister picture, Fox. Wouldn't they have heard him open the window?'

'Um,' said Fox.

'It makes a fair amount of noise.'

'Yes. Yes, that's so.'

'Anything else?'

'No. They ambled off home. Hullo, sir, what's up?'

Alleyn had pulled up and now began to turn the car in the narrow lane.

'Sorry, Fox, but we're going back to have a look at the hole in the blind.'

And back to the studio they went. Alleyn measured the distance from the window-sill to the hole – a triangular tear, of which the flap had been turned back. He also measured the height of the lamps from the floor. He climbed on Fox's shoulders and tied a thread to the light nearest the window. He stretched the thread to the hole in the blind. Fox stood outside in the pouring rain. Alleyn threw the window up, passed the thread through the hole to Fox, who drew it tight and held it against his diaphragm.

'You see?' said Alleyn.

'Yes,' said Fox, 'I'm six foot two in my socks and it hits me somewhere – let's see – '

'About the end of the sternum.'

'That's right, sir.'

'Good enough, but we'll take a look at night. Let's go and have breakfast.'

And a few minutes later they joined Nigel Bathgate at breakfast.

'You might have told me you were going out,' complained Nigel.

'I wouldn't dream of interrupting your beauty sleep,' said Alleyn. 'Where's my mamma?'

'She finished her breakfast some minutes ago. She asked me to tell you she would be in her workshop. She's going to weave me some tweed for a shooting jacket.'

'Divine creature, isn't she? What have you written for your paper?'

'I'll show you. I've left Miss Troy's name out altogether, Alleyn. They simply appear as a group of artists in a charming old-world house in Buckinghamshire.'

'I'll try to be a good godfather,' said Alleyn gruffly.

'Good enough,' said Nigel. 'Can I publish a picture of the girl?'

'Sonia? Yes, if you can rake one up. I can give you one of Garcia. Just talk about him as a very brilliant young sculptor, mention the job for the cinema if you like, and if you can manage it, suggest that we suspect the thing to be the work of some criminal lunatic who had got wind of the way the model was posed. Far-fetched, but I understand the tallest, the most preposterous tarradiddle will be gulped down whole by your public. You may even suggest that we have fears for Garcia's safety. Do anything but cast suspicion on him. Is all this quite impossible, Bathgate?'

'I don't *think* so,' said Nigel thoughtfully. 'It can be brought out with what I have already written. There's nothing in this morning's paper. That's an almost miraculous bit of luck. Blackman and Co. must have been extraordinarily discreet.'

'The hunt will be up and the murder out, at any moment now. Show me your stuff. We're for London in twenty minutes.'

'May I come with you? I've telephoned the office. I'll make a bit of an entrance with this story.'

Alleyn vetted the story and Nigel made a great to-do at each alter-ation, but more as a matter of routine than anything else. He then went to the telephone to ring up his office, and his Angela. Alleyn left Fox with the morning paper and ran upstairs to his mother's work-shop. This was a large, sunny room, filled with what Lady Alleyn called her insurances against old age. An enormous hand-loom stood in the centre of the room. In the window was a bench for book-bind-ing. On one wall hung a charming piece of tapestry worked by Lady Alleyn in a bout of enthusiasm for embroidery and on another wall was an oak shrine executed during a wave of intense wood-carving. She had made the rugs on the floor, she had woven the curtains on the walls, she had created the petit-point on the backs of the chairs, and she had done all these things extremely and surprisingly well.

At the moment she was seated before her hand-loom, sorting coloured wools. She looked solemn. Turnbridge Tessa, an Alsatian bitch, lay at her feet.

'Hullo, darling,' said Lady Alleyn. 'Do you think Mr Bathgate could wear green and red? His eyes are grey, of course. Perhaps grey and purple.'

'His eyes!'

'Don't be silly, Roderick. I've promised him some tweed. Yours is finished. It's in the chest over there. Go and look at it.'

'But – your dog!'

'What about her? She's obviously taken a fancy to you.'

'Do you think so? She certainly has had her eye on me.'

Alleyn went to the hand-carved chest, closely followed by Tunbridge Tessa. He found his tweed.

'But, darling, it really is quite amazingly good,' he said. 'I'm delighted with it.'

'Are you?' asked his mother a little anxiously.

'Indeed I am.'

'Well, your eyes are so blue it was easy for me. Mr Bathgate has told me all about the baby coming. We've had a lovely talk. How did you get on at Tatler's End House, Roderick?'

'Better, thank you. We're off now, darling. I hope I'm going to spend the rest of the morning in a chorus lady's bed-sit in Chelsea.'

'Are you?' said his mother vaguely. 'Why?'

'Routine.'

'It seems to lead you into strange places. I'll come downstairs and see you off. You may take the car, Roderick.'

'I wouldn't dream of it.'

'I've already told Finch to drive you in. I've a job for him in Sloane Street.'

When they were half-way downstairs she said:

'Roderick, shall I ring her up? Would you like me to ring her up?'

'Very much,' said Alleyn.

He collected Fox and Nigel. They wrote their names in Lady Alleyn's book.

'And you will come again whenever you like?' she said.

'That will be very soon, I'm afraid,' Nigel told her.

'Not too soon. What about Mr Fox?'

'It has been very pleasant indeed, my lady,' said Fox. He straightened up, pen in hand, and gravely unhooked his spectacles. 'I shall like to think about it. It's been quite different, you see, from my usual run of things. Quite an experience, you might say, and a very enjoyable one. If I may say so, you have a wonderful way with you, my lady. I felt at home.'

Alleyn abruptly took his arm.

'You see, ma'am,' he said, 'we have courtiers at the Yard.'

'Something a little better than that. Goodbye, my dear.'

In the car Alleyn and Fox thumbed over their notebooks and occasionally exchanged remarks. Nigel, next the chauffeur, spent the time in pleasurable anticipation of his reception at the office. They cut through from Shepherd's Bush to Holland Road and thence into Chelsea. Alleyn gave the man directions which finally brought them into a narrow and not very smart cul-de-sac behind Smith Street.

'This is Batchelors Gardens,' said Alleyn. 'And there's No. 4. You can put me down here. If I don't come out in five minutes take Mr Fox to the Yard and Mr Bathgate to his office, will you, French? Goodbye, Bathgate. Meet you at the Yard somewhere round noon, Fox.'

He waved his hand and crossed the street to No. 4, a set of flats that only just escaped the appearance of a lodging-house. Alleyn inspected the row of yellowing cards inside the front door. Miss Bobbie O'Dawne's room was up two flights. He passed the inevitable charwoman with her bucket of oil and soot, and her obscene grey wiper so like a drowned rat.

'Good morning,' said Alleyn, 'is Miss O'Dawne at home, can you tell me?'

'At 'ome,' said the charlady, viciously wringing the neck of the rat. ''Er! She won't be out of 'er bed!'

'Thank you,' said Alleyn and tapped at Miss O'Dawne's door. He tapped three times, closely watched by the charlady, before a submerged voice called out: 'All *right*.' There were bumping noises, followed by the sound of bare feet on thin carpet. The voice, now much nearer, asked: 'Who is it?'

'May I speak to Miss O'Dawne?' called Alleyn. 'I've an important message for her.'

'For me?' said the voice in more refined accents. 'Wait a moment, please.'

He waited while the charlady absently swilled the rat round and round in the oil and soot before slopping it over the top stair. The door opened a few inches and then widely enough to admit the passage of a mop of sulphur-coloured curls and a not unattractive face.

'Oh,' said the face, 'pardon me, I'm afraid – '

'I'm sorry to disturb you so early,' said Alleyn, 'but I would be most grateful if you could see me for a moment.'

'I don't want anything,' said Miss O'Dawne dangerously.

'And I'm not selling anything,' smiled Alleyn.

'Sorry, I'm sure, but you never know, these days, do you, with 'varsity boys travelling in anything from vacuums to foundation garments.'

'It's about Sonia Gluck,' said Alleyn.

'Sonia? Are you a pal of hers? Why didn't you say so at first? Half a tick, and I'll get dressed. Pardon the stage-wait, but the lonely west wing's closed on account of the ghost, and the rest of the castle's a ruin.'

'Don't hurry,' said Alleyn, 'the morning's before us.'

'I'll say! Tell yourself stories and be good!'

The door slammed. Alleyn lit a cigarette. The charlady descended three steps backwards with a toad-like posture.

'Cold morning,' she said suddenly.

'Very cold,' agreed Alleyn, noticing with a pang that her old hands were purple.

'You a theatrical?'

'No, no. Nothing so interesting, I'm afraid.'

'Not a traveller neither?'

'No – not even a traveller.'

'You look too classy now I come to look atcher. I was in service for ten years.'

'Were you?'

'Yers. In service. Lidy by the name of Wells. Then she died of dibeets and I 'adter come down to daily. It's all right in service, you know. Comferble. Meals and that. Warm.'

'It's beastly to be cold,' said Alleyn.

'That's right,' she said dimly.

Alleyn felt unhappily in his pocket and she watched him. Inside the room Miss O'Dawne began to whistle. On the next landing a door banged, and a young man in a tight fitting royal blue suit tripped lightly downstairs, singing professionally. He had a good stare at Alleyn and said: "Morning, ma! How's tricks?"

"Mornin', Mr Chumley.'

'Look out, now, I don't want to kick the bucket just yet.' He vaulted over the wet steps and disappeared in full voice.

"'E's in the choreus,' said the charlady. 'They get a lot of money in the choreus.'

She had left her dustpan on the landing. Alleyn dropped his gloves, and as he stooped he put two half-crowns under the dustpan. He did it very neatly and quickly but not neatly enough, it seemed.

'Yer dropped some money, sir,' said the charlady avidly.

'That's – that's for you,' said Alleyn, and to his relief the door opened.

'Take your place in the queue and don't rush the ushers,' said Miss O'Dawne. Alleyn walked in.

Miss O'Dawne's bed-sitting room looked a little as if it had been suddenly slapped up and bounced into a semblance of tidiness. The cupboard doors had an air of pressure from within, the drawers looked as if they had been rammed home under protest, the divan-bed hunched its shoulders under a magenta artificial-silk counterpane. Two jade green cushions cowered against the wall at the head of the bed, the corner of a suit-case peeped out furtively from underneath. Miss O'Dawne herself was surprisingly neat. Her make-up suggested that she was a quick-change artist.

'Sit down,' she said, 'and make yourself at our place. It's not Buckingham Palace with knobs on, but you can't do much on chorus work and "Hullo, girls, have you heard the news?" Seen our show?'

'Not yet,' said Alleyn.

'I've got three lines in the last act and a kiss from Mr Henry Molyneux. His breath smells of whisky, carbide and onions, but it's great to be an actress. Well, how's tricks?'

'Not so wonderful,' said Alleyn, feeling for the right language.

'Cheer up, you'll soon be dead. I was going to make a cup of coffee. How does that strike you?'

'It sounds delightful,' said Alleyn.

'Well, we strive to please. Service with a smile. No charge and all questions answered by return in plain envelopes.'

She lit her gas-ring and clapped a saucepan over it.

'By the way, you haven't told me who you are.'

'My name's Roderick Alleyn, I'm afraid – '

'Roderick Alleyn? Sounds pretty good. You're not in the business, are you?'

'No, I'm – '

'Well, if you'll excuse my freshness you look a bit more Eton and Oxford than most of Sonia's boyfriends. Are you an artist?'

'No. I'm a policeman.'

'And then he came to. Is this where the big laugh comes, Roddy?'

'Honestly.'

'A policeman? Where's your make-up? Pass along there, please, pass along there. Go on, you're kidding.'

'Miss O'Dawne, I'm an official of Scotland Yard.'

She looked sharply at him.

'Here, what's wrong?' she said.

'Was Miss Gluck a very close friend of yours?' asked Alleyn gently.

'*Was!* What d'you mean? Here, has anything happened to Sonia?'

'I'm afraid so.'

'What, God, she's not – !'

'Yes.'

The coffee-pot bubbled and she automatically turned down the gas. Her pert little face had gone white under the make-up.

'What had she done?' she said.

'She hadn't done anything. I think I know what you mean. She was going to have a child.'

'Yes. I know that, all right. Well – what happened?'

Alleyn told her as kindly as possible. She made the coffee as she listened to him, and her distress was so unaffected that he felt himself warm to her.

'You know, I can't sort of believe it,' she said. 'Murder. That seems kind of not real, doesn't it? Know what I mean? Why, it was only Saturday she was sitting where you are now and telling me all her bits and pieces.'

'Were you great friends?'

'Well, *you* know. We'd sort of teamed up, in a way. Mind, she's not my real pal like Maudie Lavine or Dolores Duval, but I was quite matey with her. Here's your coffee. Help yourself to shoog. God, I can't believe it. Murdered!'

She stirred her coffee and stared at Alleyn. Suddenly she made a jab at him with her spoon.

'Garcia!' she said.

Alleyn waited.

'Garcia's done it,' said Miss O'Dawne, 'you take it from me. I never liked that boy. She brought him up here once or twice and I said to her: 'You watch your business with that gentleman,' I said. 'In my opinion he's a very dirty bit of work and I don't mind who hears me.' Well, I mean to say! Letting a girl as good as keep him. And when the spot of trouble comes along it's "Thanks for the buggy ride, it was OK while it lasted." Had she tried the funny business with the kid? You know.'

'I don't think so.' Alleyn took Miss O'Dawne's letter from his pocket and handed it to her.

'We found this in her room. That's what made me come to you.'

She looked sharply at him.

'What about it?'

'You can understand that we want to collect any information that is at all likely to lead us to an arrest.'

'I can understand that all right, all right.'

'Well, Miss O'Dawne, this letter suggests that you may be able to give us this information. It suggests, at all events, that you may know more about the Sonia-Garcia situation than we do.'

'I know all there was to know. She was going to have his kid, and he'd got sick of her. Pause for laugh. Laugh over.'

'Isn't there a bit more to it than that?'

'How d'you mean?'

'I think I may as well tell you that we know she got a hundred pounds from Mr Basil Pilgrim.'

'Did he tell you?'

'Yes. Was that the plan you refer to in this letter?'

'Since you're asking, Mr Clever, it was. Pilgrim's had his fun and Sonia didn't see why he shouldn't pay for it.'

'But the child was not Pilgrim's?'

'Oh no, dear, but for all he knew – '

'Yes, I see. She said she'd go to his father if he didn't pay up. Was that it?'

'That was the big idea. Or to his girl. Sonia told me this boy Basil is a bit silly. You know – one of the purity song and dance experts. He must be a bit soft, from what she told me. Said his feeongsay thought he was as pure as her. Soft music and tears in the voice. Sonia said it was a big laugh, anyway, because the girl's not so very very ongenoo either. Anyway, Basil was all worked up and gave Sonia the cheque.'

'What did she do with his cheque?'

'Oh, she cashed it and gave the money to Garcia, dear. What do you know about that? Could you beat it? I told her she was crazy. On Saturday when she was here I said: 'Well, did it all go big?' and she said this boy Basil came in on his cue all right, but she'd handed the money to Garcia and asked him if they couldn't get married straight away. And Garcia started his funny business. He said a hundred quid wasn't enough to marry with.'

'Hadn't she got anything out of Malmsley?'

'Listen, Mr Blake, aren't you wonderful? How did you get on to the Marmalade stuff?'

Alleyn folded his arms and raised his eyebrows.

' "I have my methods," said the great sleuth.'

'Well, of course!' exclaimed Miss O'Dawne, greatly diverted. 'Aren't you a yell!'

'Please tell me,' said Alleyn. 'What happened when she offered to sell Malmsley his own book?'

'He wouldn't give more than five pounds, dear, and Sonia stuck out for twenty. Well, I mean to say, what's five pounds to a girl in her condition? So she said she'd give him the weekend to think it over. She didn't mind waiting. It wasn't as if she hadn't got – ' Miss O'Dawne stopped short, gave Alleyn another of her sharp glances, and lit a cigarette.

'Hadn't got what?' asked Alleyn.

'Look here – you're asking a lot of questions, aren't you, dear? Keep forgetting you're a booby with all this upstage-and-county manners of yours. What's wrong with a girl getting her own back like Sonia did?'

'Well, it was blackmail, you know.'

'Was it? Isn't that a pity, I don't suppose. Have some more coffee?'

'Thank you, it's extremely good.'

'That's right. I say, it's all very funny us talking away sort of cosy like this, but when I think of Sonia – honest, I *am* upset, you know. You have to keep on cracking hardy, but just the same it's a swine, isn't it? You know what I mean. Help yourself to shoog. No, reely, I *am* upset.'

'I'm quite sure you are.'

'Look, Roddy. You don't mind me calling you Roddy, do you?'

'I'm delighted,' said Alleyn.

'Well, look, if what Sonia did was blackmail, I don't want to let everybody know the dirt about her after she's gone. Don't sling off at the dead's what I've always said, because they can't come in on the cross-talk and score the laughs where they are. See? You've got on to the Garcia-Pilgrim-Malmsley tale. All right! That's your luck or your great big talent. But I'm not in on this scene. See?'

'Yes, I do see. But you don't want her murderer to get off, do you?'

'Do I look funny?'

'Very well, then. I'm afraid the blackmail is bound to come out in evidence. You can't stop that, and won't you help us? Won't you tell me anything you know that may throw a little light on the tragedy of her death? There is something more, I'm sure. Isn't there?'

'Do you mean the joke with the picture of Basil's girl?'

'No,' said Alleyn.

'Do you know about that?'

'Yes.'

'Well, then!'

'Is there anything else about the Pilgrim stunt? Did she threaten to take any further steps?'

'With Pilgrim?' Miss O'Dawne's eyes looked thoughtfully at Alleyn. 'No. She didn't. She'd done her stuff with the Hon. Bas. Mine's a Bass, I *don't* suppose.'

'Well then, had Garcia any more tricks up his sleeve?'

Miss O'Dawne twisted her fingers together. 'She's frightened about something,' thought Alleyn.

'If you know anything more about Garcia,' he said, 'I do beg of you to tell me what it is.'

'Yeah? And get a permanent shop where Sonia's gone? It's no good? It's no good, dear, I'm not in on this act.'

'I promise you that no harm – '

'No, dear, there's nothing doing. I don't know anything that you haven't found out.'

'Was Garcia off on a separate line?'

'You go for Garcia,' said Miss O'Dawne. 'That's all I'm going to say. Go for Garcia. Have you arrested him?'

'No. He's gone on a walking tour.'

'Well, that's a scream – I bloody well don't think. Pardon my refinement,' said Miss O'Dawne.

CHAPTER 16

Back to the Yard

Alleyn cursed himself secretly and heartily for that unlucky word 'Blackmail'. Miss Bobbie O'Dawne refused, point-blank, to give him any further information that might possibly come under that heading. He seemed to have come up against a tenet. If Sonia had committed blackmail and Sonia was dead, Bobbie O'Dawne wasn't going to give her away. However, she told him quite willingly how Sonia had spent the weekend, and pretty well proved that Sonia could not possibly have gone down to Tatler's End House between Friday and Monday. With this Alleyn had to be content. He thanked his hostess and promised to go and see her show.

'That's right, dear, you come along. It's a bright show. I don't have much to do, you know. I hope you don't think any the worse of me for minding my own business about Sonia?'

'No. But if it comes to – well – if it comes to the arrest of an innocent person and you know you could save them, what would you do then?'

'Garcia's not innocent, dear, not so's you'd notice it.'

'It might not be Garcia.'

'Come off it. Listen. Do you know Garcia told the poor kid that if she let on to anybody that the child was his, he'd do for her? Now! She told me that herself. She was dead scared I'd forget and let something out. She made me swear I wouldn't. She said he'd do for both of us if we talked. Isn't that good enough?'

'It's sufficiently startling,' said Alleyn. 'Well, I suppose I'd better be off. I do ask you, very seriously, Miss O'Dawne, to think over what I have said. There is more than one kind of loyalty, you know.'

'I wouldn't have said a thing about the kid if I didn't know you'd find out. Anyway, that's the sort of thing that might happen to any girl. But I'm not going to do the dirty and have them calling her criminal names, and it's no good asking me to. Are you going, dear? Well, so long. See you some more.'

'Suppose I sent a man along from one of the evening papers, would you care to give him an interview?'

'Who, me? Well, I don't pretend a bit of publicity doesn't help you in the business,' said Miss O'Dawne honestly. 'D'you mean the "Sonia Gluck as I knew her" gag?'

'Something like that.'

'With perhaps my picture along of hers? I've got a nice picture of Sonia. You know – wound up in georgette with the light behind her. Very nice. Well, as long as they don't want the dirt about her, I wouldn't mind the ad, dear. You know. It sounds hard, but it's a hard old world.'

'I'll come again, if I may.'

'Welcome, I'm sure. Be good.'

Alleyn went thoughtfully to Scotland Yard. He saw his Assistant Commissioner and went over the case with him. Then he went to his office. He had been for a year in the south of the world and the room looked at once strange and familiar. The respectably worn leather chairs, his desk, the untidy groove where he had once let a cigarette burn itself out, the little dark print of a medieval town above the mantelpiece – there they all were, as it seemed, waiting for him after a period of suspension. He sat at his desk and began to work on the report of this case. Presently Fox came in. Alleyn realized that he had clicked right back into his socket in the vast piece of machinery that was Scotland Yard. New Zealand, the wharf at Suva, the night tide of the St Lawrence – all had receded into the past. He was back on his job.

He related to Fox the gist of his interview with Miss O'Dawne.

'What about yourself?' he asked when he had finished. 'Any news, Brer Fox?'

'The city's been set going on the warehouse business. It's a bit of a job and no mistake. According to Miss Troy's reckoning, we've got sixty miles to account for. That correct, sir?'

'Yes.'

'Yes. Well, supposing Garcia didn't tell lies about his warehouse, it's somewhere in London. It's twenty miles to Shepherd's Bush from the house. There and back, forty. Of course, he might not have come in by the Uxbridge Road, but it's by far the most direct route and it would be the one he was familiar with. For the sake of argument say he took it. That leaves us a radius of ten miles, roughly, from Shepherd's Bush to wherever the warehouse is. Twenty, there and back.'

'Total, sixty.'

'Yes. Of course, if this warehouse is somewhere west, north-west, or south-west, he might have branched off before he got to Shepherd's Bush, but he said Holloway to Miss Seacliff and if he went to Holloway he'd go by Shepherd's Bush. Then on by way of, say Albany Street and the Camden Road. As the crow flies, Holloway Prison is only about five miles from Shepherd's Bush, but the shortest way by road would be nearer to nine. Holloway fits in all right as far as the petrol consumption goes. Of course, it's all very loose,' added Fox, looking over his spectacles at Alleyn, 'but so's our information.'

'Very loose. Holloway's a large district.'

'Yes. Still, it squares up, more or less, with what we've got.'

'True enough.'

'Well, sir, following out your suggestion we've concentrated on Holloway and we're raking it for warehouses.'

'Yes, it's got to be done.'

'On the other hand,' continued Fox stolidly, 'as you pointed out on the trip up, it may not be in Holloway at all. Suppose Garcia lied about the position of the warehouse, having already planned the job when he spoke to Miss Seacliff. Suppose he deliberately misled her, meaning to use this warehouse as a hide-out after the job was done?'

'It doesn't look like that, Fox. She says Garcia tried to persuade her to visit him there alone. He actually gave her a sketch-map of how to get to the studio. She's lost it, of course.'

'Look here,' said Fox. 'The idea was that Pilgrim should drive her up. I wonder if there's a chance she handed the sketch-map to Pilgrim and he knows where the place is?'

'Yes. If he does know he didn't bother to mention it when I asked them all about the warehouse. Of course, that might have been bluff, but the whole warehouse story is rather tricky. Suppose Garcia planned this murder in cold blood. He would have to give up all idea of carrying out his commission for the marble group unless he meant to brazen it out, go for his walk, and turn up at the warehouse to get on with his work. If he meant to do this it would be no good to tell preliminary lies about the site, would it? Suppose, on the other hand, he meant to disappear. He wouldn't have mentioned a warehouse at all if he meant to lie doggo in it.'

'That's right enough. Well, sir, what if he planned the murder while he was still dopey after the opium?'

'That, to me, seems more probable. Malmsley left the pipe, the jar and the lamp in a box under Garcia's bed because he was afraid of your friend Sadie catching him if he returned them to his bedroom. Bailey found Garcia's as well as Malmsley's prints on the jar. There's less opium than Malmsley said there would be. It's at least possible that Garcia had another go at it after Malmsley had gone. He may have woken up, felt very dreary, and sought to recapture the bliss. He may have smoked another pipe or taken a pull at his whisky. He may have done both. He may even have laid the trap with the dagger while still under the influence of the opium and – or – whisky. This is shamefully conjectural, Fox, but it seems to me that it is not too fantastic. The macabre character of the crime is not inconsistent, I fancy, with the sort of thing one might expect from a man in Garcia's condition. So far – all right. Possible, at any rate. But would he be sensible enough to get Miss Troy's caravan, back it, however clumsily, up to the window, put the empty case on board and wheel the model through the window and into the case? And what's more, my old Foxkin, would he have the gumption to drive to this damnable warehouse, dump his stuff, return the caravan to Tatler's End House, and set out on his walking tour? Would he not rather sink into a drugged and disgusting slumber lasting well into Saturday morning? And having come to himself would he not undo his foul trap for Sonia?'

'But if he *wanted* her out of the way,' persisted Fox.

'I know, I know. But if he was going to bolt he had so much to lose. His first big commission?'

'Well, perhaps he'll turn up and brazen it out. He doesn't know he dropped the pellet of clay with his thumb-print. He doesn't know

Miss Lee overheard his conversations with Sonia. He doesn't know
Sonia told anyone she was going to have his child. He'll think the
motive won't appear.'

'He'll know what will appear at the post-mortem. What's worrying me is the double aspect of the crime, if Garcia's the criminal.
There's no reason to suppose Malmsley lied about giving Garcia the
opium. It's the sort of thing he'd suppress if he could. Very well. The
planning of the murder and the laying of the trap might have been
done under the influence of a pipe or more of opium. The subsequent business with the caravan has every appearance of the work
of a cool and clear-headed individual.'

'Someone else in it?'

'Who?'

'Gawd knows,' said Fox.

'Meanwhile Garcia does not appear.'

'Do you think he may have got out of the country?'

'I don't know. He had a hundred pounds.'

'Where d'you get that, chief?'

'From Miss Bobbie O'Dawne. Sonia gave him the hundred
pounds she got from Basil Pilgrim.'

'I've fixed up with the people at the ports,' said Fox. 'He won't get
by, now. But has he already slipped through? That's what's worrying
me.'

'If he left Tatler's End House on his flat feet in the early hours of
Saturday morning,' said Alleyn, 'we'll pick up his track.'

'If?'

'It's the blasted psychology of the brute that's got me down,' said
Alleyn with unusual violence. 'We've got a very fair picture of
Garcia from all these people. They all agree that he lives entirely for
his work, that he will sacrifice himself and everyone else to his work,
that his work is quite remarkably good. I can't see a man of this type
deliberately committing a crime that would force him to give up the
biggest job he has ever undertaken.'

'But if the opium's to blame? Not to mention the whisky?'

'If they're to blame I don't think he's responsible for the rest of
the business with the caravan. He'd either sleep it off there in the
studio or wander away without taking any particular pains to cover
his tracks. In that case we'd have found him by now.'

'Then do you think there's any likelihood of someone else driving him up to London and hiding him in this blasted warehouse? What about the man Ethel and her boy saw in the lane? Say it wasn't Garcia, but someone else. Could he have found Garcia under the weather and offered to drive him up to London with the stuff and return the caravan?'

'Leaving the knife where it was?' said Alleyn. 'Yes, that's possible, of course. He may not have noticed the knife, this lurker in the lane. On the other hand – '

Alleyn and Fox stared thoughtfully at each other.

'As soon as I got here this morning,' said Fox at last, 'I looked up this Mr Charleson, the secretary to the board of the New Palace Theatre in Westminster. Had a bit of luck, he was on the premises and answered the telephone. He's coming in at eleven-thirty, but beyond confirming the business about this statue he can't help us. Garcia was to order the marble and start work on next Monday. They offered him two hundred pounds and they were going to pay for the marble after he'd chosen it. Mr Charleson says they'd never met anyone else at that price whose work is as good as Garcia's.'

'Bloodsucker,' grunted Alleyn.

'But he's no idea where the work was to be done.'

'Helpful fellow. Well, Fox, we'd better get a move on. We're going to spend a jolly day checking up alibis. I'll take Miss Troy's and Miss Bostock's to begin with. You start off with young Hatchett and Phillida Lee. To your lot will fall the bearded intelligentsia of the Vortex Experimental Studio theatre, the Lee aunt, and the Hatchett boarding-house keeper. To mine Sir Arthur Jaynes, Cattcherley's hairdressing establishment, Mr Graham Barnes, and the staff of the United Arts Club.'

'And this Mr John Bellasca, sir, Miss Troy's friend.'

'Yes,' said Alleyn. 'Me too.'

'And then what?'

'If we get done today we'll run down to Boxover in the morning and see the people with whom Pilgrim and Miss Seacliff stayed on Friday night.'

He opened a drawer in his desk and took out the photograph of the group at Tatler's End House.

'How tall is Garcia?' he asked. 'Five foot nine according to the statement Blackman gave us. Yes. Pilgrim looks about two and a half inches taller in this photograph, doesn't he? You get a very good idea of the comparative heights. Ormerin, Hatchett and Garcia are all within an inch of each other. Miss Bostock, Miss Seacliff and Miss Lee are much shorter. The model is a little taller than Miss Bostock, but not so tall as the others. Miss Troy is taller than the first batch, but about two inches shorter than Pilgrim. Pilgrim is the tallest of the lot. Alas, alas, Fox, how little we know about these people! We interview them under extraordinary circumstances and hope to get a normal view of their characters. We ask them alarming questions and try to draw conclusions from their answers. How can we expect to discover them when each must be secretly afraid that his most innocent remark may cast suspicion upon himself? How would you or I behave if we came within the range of conjecture in a murder case? Well, damn it, let's get on with the job.'

The desk telephone rang and he answered it.

'It's me,' said Nigel's voice winningly.

'What do you want?'

'I'd like to come and see you, Alleyn.'

'Where are you?'

'In a call-box about five minutes away.'

'Very well, come up. I've got a job for you.'

'I'll be there.'

Alleyn hung up the receiver.

'It's Bathgate. I'll send him round to get an exclusive story from Miss Bobbie O'Dawne. There's just a remote hope she may become less discreet under the influence of free publicity. I'm damn well positive she's keeping something up her sleeve about the blackmailing activities. She's rather an attractive little creature, Fox. Hard as nails and used to the seamy side of life, but a curious mixture of simplicity and astuteness. She knew we'd find out about the child and had no qualms in talking about it, but as soon as the word blackmail cropped up she doubled up like a hedgehog. I don't think it had occurred to her that Sonia's gentle art of extracting money was in any sense criminal. And I – blundering booby that I was – must needs enlighten her. She's terrified of Garcia. She's convinced he murdered Sonia and I honestly think she believes he'd go for her if she informed against him.'

He moved restlessly about the room.

'There's something missing,' he said. 'I'm positive there's something missing.'

'Garcia,' said Fox. 'He's missing all right.'

'No, blast you, not Garcia. Though Lord knows, we'll have to get him. No, there was something else that the O'Dawne had on the tip of her tongue. By gum, Fox, I wonder – Look here.'

Alleyn was still talking when the telephone rang to say Nigel Bathgate had arrived.

'Send him up,' said Alleyn. And when Nigel appeared Alleyn talked about Bobbie O'Dawne and suggested that Nigel should get a special interview.

'This is extraordinarily decent of you, Alleyn,' said Nigel.

'It's nothing of the sort. You're the tool of the Yard, my boy, and don't you forget it. Now listen carefully and I'll tell you what line you're to take. You must impress upon her that you are to be trusted. If she thinks you'll publish every word she utters, she'll say nothing to the point. If you can, write the interview there and then and read it to her. Assure her that you will print nothing without her permission. Photograph the lady in every conceivable position. Then get friendly. Let her think you are becoming indiscreet. You may say that you have had instructions from the Yard to publish a story about Sonia's blackmailing activities unless we can hear, privately, exactly what they were. You may say that we think of publishing an appeal through the paper to any of her victims, asking them to come forward and tell us without prejudice what they paid her. We hope that this will lead to the arrest of Garcia. Emphasize this. It's Garcia we're after, but we can't lay it home to him without the evidence of the people Sonia blackmailed. We think Sonia refused to give him any more of the proceeds and he killed her to get them. It's a ridiculous tarradiddle, but I think if you are low and cunning she may believe you. She'll tell you about Pilgrim and Malmsley, I fancy, because she knows we have already got hold of that end of the stick. If, however, she thinks she may save Sonia's name by going a bit farther, there's just a chance she may do it. Do you understand?'

'I think so.'

'If you fail, we'll be no worse off than we were before. Off you go.'

'Very well.' Nigel hesitated, his hand in his coat pocket.

'What is it?' asked Alleyn.

'Do you remember that I made a sort of betting list on the case last time you allowed me to Watson for you?'

'I do.'

'Well – I've done it again,' said Nigel modestly.

'Let me have a look.'

Nigel took a sheet of foolscap from his pocket and laid it before Alleyn with an anxious smile.

'Away you go,' said Alleyn. 'Collect your cameraman and use your wits.'

Nigel went out and Alleyn looked at his analysis of the case.

'I'd half a mind to do something of the sort myself, Fox,' he said. 'Let us see what he makes out.'

Fox looked over his shoulder. Nigel had headed his paper: 'Murder of an Artist's Model. Possible Suspects.'

(1) Garcia

Opportunity. Was in the studio on Friday after all the others had gone. Knew the throne would not be touched (rule of studio).

Motive. Sonia was going to have a baby. Probably his. He had tired of her and was after Valmai Seacliff (V.S.'s statement). They had quarrelled (Phillida Lee's statement), and he had said he'd kill her if she pestered him. Possibly she threatened to sue him for maintenance. He may have egged her on to blackmail Pilgrim and taken the money. If so, she may have threatened to give him away to Troy. He had taken opium at about four o'clock in the afternoon. How long would he take to get sufficiently over the effect to drive a car to London and back?

(2) Agatha Troy

Opportunity. Could have done it on Saturday after she returned from London, or on Sunday. We have only her word for it that the drape was already arranged when she visited the studio on Saturday afternoon.

Motive. Sonia had hopelessly defaced the portrait of Valmai Seacliff – on Troy's own admission the best picture she had painted.

(3) Katti Bostock

Same opportunities as Troy.

Motive. Sonia had driven her to breaking-point over the sittings for her large picture.

(4) Valmai Seacliff

Opportunity. Doubtful, but possibly she could have returned from Boxover after they had all gone to bed. The headache might have been an excuse.

Motive. Unless you count Sonia's defacement of her portrait by Troy, there is no motive. If she had heard of Pilgrim's affair with Sonia, she might be furious, but hardly murderous. Anyway, she had cut Sonia out.

(5) Basil Pilgrim

Opportunity. Same as Seacliff. Perhaps more favourable. If she had taken aspirin, she would sleep soundly, and the others were nowhere near his room. He would have slipped out after they had all gone to bed, taken his car, gone to the studio and fixed the knife.

Motive. Sonia had blackmailed him, threatening to tell Seacliff and Lord Pilgrim that the child was Basil's. He seems to have a kink about purity and Seacliff. On the whole, plenty of motive.

N.B. If Seacliff or Pilgrim did it, either Garcia was not at the studio or else he is a confederate. If he was not at the studio, who took the caravan and removed his stuff? Could he have done this before Pilgrim arrived, leaving the coast clear?

(6) Cedric Malmsley

Opportunity. He could have fixed the knife after he had knocked Garcia out with opium.

Motive. Sonia was blackmailing him about his illustration. He is the type that would detest an exposure of this sort.

(7) Francis Ormerin

Opportunity. If Hatchett and Malmsley are correct in saying the drape was still crumpled on Friday afternoon after Ormerin had left, and if Troy is correct in saying it was stretched out on Saturday before he returned, there seems to be no opportunity.

Motive. Only the model's persistent refusal to keep still (v unlikely).

(8) Phillida Lee
Opportunity. Accepting above statements – none.
Motive. None.

(9) Watt Hatchett
Opportunity. On Malmsley's and Troy's statements – none.
Motive. Appears to have disliked her intensely and quarrelled over the pose. Sonia gibed about Australia (poor motive).

Remarks. It seems to me there is little doubt that Garcia did it. Probably gingered up by his pipe of opium. If he fails to answer advertisements, it will look still more suspicious.
Suggestion. Find warehouse.

Alleyn pointed a long finger at Nigel's final sentence.

'Mr Bathgate's bright idea for the day,' he said.

'Yes,' said Fox. 'It looks nice and simple just jotted down like that.'

'The thing's quite neat in its way, Fox.'

'Yes, sir. And I think he's got the right idea, you know.'

'Garcia?'

'Yes. Don't you?'

'Oh Lord, Fox, you've heard my trouble. I don't see how we can be too sure.'

'There's that bit of clay with his print on it,' said Fox. 'On the drape, where it had no business.'

'Suppose it was planted? There'd be any number of bits like that lying on the floor by the window. We found some. Let's get Bailey's further report on the prints, shall we?'

Alleyn rang through to Bailey's department and found that Bailey had finished his work and was ready to make a report. In a minute or two he appeared with a quantity of photographs.

'Anything fresh?' asked Alleyn.

'Yes, sir, in a sort of way there is,' said Bailey, with the air of making a reluctant admission.

'Let's have it.'

Bailey laid a set of photographs on Alleyn's desk.

'These are from the empty whisky bottle under Garcia's bed. We got them again from different parts of the bed-frame, the box underneath and the stool he used for his work. Some of them cropped up on the window-sill and there's a good thumb and forefinger off the light switch above his bed. These – ' he pointed to a second group – 'come from bits of clay that were lying about the floor. Some of them were no good, but there's a couple of clear ones. They're made by the same fingers as the first lot. I've marked them "Garcia".'

'I think we may take it they are his,' said Alleyn.

'Yes. Well then, sir, here's the ones off the opium-box and the pipe. Four of those I've identified as Mr Malmsley's. The others are Garcia's. Here's a photo of the clay pellet I found in the drape. Garcia again. This set's off the edge of the throne. There were lots of prints there, some of them Mr Hatchett's, some of Mr Pilgrim's and some the French bloke's – this Mr Ormerin. They seem to have had blue paint on their fingers, which was useful. But this set is Garcia's again and I found it on top of the others. There were traces of clay in this lot, which helped us a bit.'

Alleyn and Fox examined the prints without comment. Bailey produced another photograph and laid it on the desk.

'I got that from the drape. Took a bit of doing. Here's the enlargement.'

'Garcia,' said Alleyn and Fox together.

'I reckon it is,' said Bailey. 'We'd never have got it if it hadn't been for the clay. It looks to me, Mr Alleyn, as if he'd only half done the job. There's no prints on the knife, so I suppose he held that with a cloth or wiped it after he'd finished. It must have been a paint-rag, because there's a smudge of blue on the knife. You may remember there were the same blue smudges on the throne and the easel-ledge that was used to hammer in the dagger. Now, this print we got from the bit of paint-rag that you suggested was used to wipe off the prints. Some of the paint on the rag was only half dry, and took a good impression. It matches the paint smudges on the knife. Blue.'

'Garcia's?'

'That's correct, sir.'

'This about settles it, Mr Alleyn,' said Fox.

'That Garcia laid the trap? I agree with you.'

'We'll have to ask for more men. It's going to be a job getting him, sir. He had such a big start. How about letting these alibis wait for today, Mr Alleyn?'

'I think we'd better get through them, but I tell you what, Fox. I'll ask for another man and leave the alibi game to the pair of you. I'm not pulling out the plums for myself, Foxkin.'

'I've never known you do that, Mr Alleyn, don't you worry. We'll get through these alibis,' said Fox. 'I'd like to see what our chaps are doing round the Holloway district.'

'And I,' said Alleyn, 'think of going down to Brixton.'

'Is that a joke?' asked Fox suspiciously, after a blank pause.

'No, Fox.'

'Brixton? Why Brixton?'

'Sit down for a minute,' said Alleyn, 'and I'll tell you.'

CHAPTER 17

The Man at the Table

At four o'clock on the following afternoon, Wednesday, September 21st, Alleyn turned wearily into the last land and estate agents' office in Brixton. A blond young man advanced upon him.

'Yes, sir? What can I have the pleasure of doing for you?'

'It's not much of a pleasure, I'm afraid. If you will, *and* if you can, tell me of any vacant warehouses in this district, or of any warehouses that have let part of themselves to artists, or of any artists who, having rented such premises, have taken themselves off to foreign parts and lent the premises to a young man who sculps. As you will probably have guessed, I am an officer of Scotland Yard. Here's my card. Do you mind awfully if I sit down?'

'Er – yes. Of course not. Do,' said the young man in some surprise.

'It's a weary world,' said Alleyn. 'The room would be well lit. I'd better show you my list of all the places I have already inspected.'

The list was a long one. Alleyn had continued his search at eleven o'clock that morning.

The blond young man ran through it, muttering to himself. Occasionally he cast a glance at his immaculately-dressed visitor.

'I suppose,' he said at last, with an avid look towards an evening paper on the corner of his desk, 'I suppose this wouldn't happen to have any connection with the missing gentleman from Bucks?'

'It would,' said Alleyn.

'By the name of Garcia?'

'Yes. We believe him to be ill and suffering from loss of memory. It is thought he may have wandered in this direction, poor fellow.'

'What an extraordinary thing!' exclaimed the young man.

'Too odd for words,' murmured Alleyn. 'He's a little bit ga-ga, we understood. Clever, but dottyish. Do you think you can help us?'

'Well now, let me see. This list is pretty comprehensive. I don't know if – '

He bit his finger and opened a large book. Alleyn closed his eyes.

'What an extraordinary thing!' exclaimed the young man. 'I mean to say, any of the warehouses round here might have a room to let and we'd never hear of it. See what I mean?'

'Alas, yes,' said Alleyn.

'Now there's Solly and Perkins. Big place. Business not too good, they tell me. And there's Anderson's shirt factory, and Lacker and Lampton's used-car depot. That's in Gulper Row, off Cornwall Street. Just by the waterworks. Opposite the prison. Quite in your line, Inspector.'

He laughed shrilly.

'Damn funny,' agreed Alleyn.

'Lacker and Lampton's foreman was in here the other day. He's taken a house from us. Now, he did say something about there being a lot of room round at their place. He said something about being able to store his furniture there if they went into furnished rooms. Yes. Now, I wonder. How about Lacker and Lampton's?'

'I'll try it. Could you give me the foreman's name?'

'McCully's the name. Ted McCully. He's quite a pal of mine. Tell him I sent you. James is my name. Look here, I'll come round with you, if you like.'

'I wouldn't dream of troubling you,' said Alleyn firmly. 'Thank you very much indeed. Goodbye.'

He departed hurriedly, before Mr James could press his offer home. A fine drizzle had set in, the sky was leaden, and already the light had begun to fade. Alleyn turned up the collar of his raincoat, pulled down the brim of his hat and strode off in the direction of Brixton Prison. Cornwall Street ran along one side of the waterworks and Gulper Row was a grim and deadly little alley off Cornwall Street. Lacker and Lampton's was at the far end. It was a barn of a place and evidently combined wrecking activities with the trade in used cars. The ground floor was half full of spare parts, chassis without wheels, engines without chassis, and bodies without either.

Alleyn asked for Mr Ted McCully, and in a minute or two a giant in oil-soaked dungarees came out of a smaller workshop, wiping his hands on a piece of waste.

'Yes, sir?' he asked cheerfully.

'I'm looking for an empty room with a good light to use as a painting-studio,' Alleyn began. 'I called in at the estate agents, behind the prison, and Mr James there said he thought you might have something.'

'Bert James?' said Mr McCully with a wide grin. 'What's he know about it? Looking for a commission as per usual, I'll bet.'

'Have a cigarette. Will that thing stand my weight?'

'Thank you, sir. I wouldn't sit there; it's a bit greasy. Take the box.'

Alleyn sat on a packing-case.

'Have you any vacant rooms that would do to paint in?'

'Not here, we haven't, but it's a funny thing you should ask.'

'Why's that?'

'Well, it's a bit of a coincidence,' said Mr McCully maddeningly.

'Oh?'

'Yes. The world's a small place, you know, sir. Isn't it, now?'

'No bigger than a button,' agreed Alleyn.

'That's right. Look at this little coincidence, now. I dare say you've had quite a ramble looking for this room you want?'

'I have rambled since eleven o'clock this morning.'

'Is that a fact? And then you look in on Bert James and he sends you round here. And I'll swear Bert knows nothing about it, either. Which makes it all the more of a coincidence.'

'Makes what, though?' asked Alleyn, breathing through his nostrils.

'I was just going to tell you,' said Mr McCully. 'You see, although we haven't got the sort of thing you'd be wanting, on the premises, there's a bit of a storehouse round the corner that would do you down to the ground. Skylight. Paraffin heater. Electric light. Plenty of room. Just the thing.'

'May I – '

'Ah! Wait a bit, though. It's taken. It's in use in a sort of way.'

'What sort of way?'

'That's the funny thing. It was taken by an artist like yourself.'

Alleyn flicked the ash off his cigarette.

'Really?' he said.

'Yes. Gentleman by the name of Gregory. He used to look in here pretty often. He once took a picture of this show. What a thing to want to take a photo of, I said, but he seemed to enjoy it. I wouldn't have the patience myself.'

'Is he in his studio this afternoon?'

'Hasn't been there for three months. He's in Hong Kong.'

'Indeed,' murmured Alleyn, and he thought: 'Easy now. Don't flutter the brute.'

'Yes. In Hong Kong taking pictures of the Chinks.'

'Would he sublet, do you know?'

'I don't know whether he *would* but he *can't*.'

'Why not?'

'Because he promised the loan of it to someone else.'

'I see. Then somebody else is using it?'

'That's where the funny part comes in. He isn't. Never turned up.'

'Gosh!' thought Alleyn.

'Never turned up,' repeated Mr McCully. 'As a matter of fact I asked the boss only yesterday if I might store some bits of furniture there during Christmas because the wife and I are moving and it's a bit awkward what with this and that and the other thing – '

He rambled on. Alleyn listened with an air of sympathetic attention.

'. . . so the boss said it would be all right if this other chap didn't turn up, but all Mr Gregory said was that he'd offered the room to this other chap and given him the key, and he'd just come in when he wanted it. So that's how it stands.'

'What was this other man's name, do you know?'

'Have I heard it now?' ruminated Mr McCully, absently accepting another of Alleyn's cigarettes. 'Wait a bit now. It was a funny sort of name. Reminded me of something. What was it? By crikey, I remember. It reminded me of the rubbish van – you know – the chaps that come round for the garbage tins.'

'Garbage?'

'Garbage – that's the name. Or nearly.'

'Something like Garcia, perhaps.' And Alleyn thought: 'Has he read the evening paper or hasn't he?'

'That's it! Garcia! Well, fancy you getting it. Garcia! That's the chap. Garcia.' Mr McCully laughed delightedly.

Alleyn stood up.

'Look here,' he said, 'I wish you'd just let me have a look at this place, will you? In case there is a chance of my getting it.'

'Well, I suppose there's nothing against that. The boss is away just now, but I don't see how he could object. Not that there's anything to see. We don't go near it from one week to another. I'll just get our key and take you along. Fred!'

'Hooray?' said a voice in the workshop.

'I'm going round to the shed. Back before knock-off.'

'Right-oh.'

Mr McCully got a key from behind a door, hooked an old tarpaulin over his shoulders and, talking incessantly, led the way out of the garage by a side door into a narrow alley.

It was now raining heavily. The alley smelt of soot, grease, and stagnant drainage. Water streamed down from defective gutters and splashed about their feet. The deadliness and squalor of the place seemed to close about them. Their footsteps echoed at the far end of the alley.

'Nasty weather,' said Mr McCully. 'It's only a step.'

They turned to the left into a wider lane that led back towards Cornwall Street, McCully stopped in front of a pair of rickety double-doors fastened with a padlock and chain.

'Here we are, sir. Just half a tick and I'll have her opened. She's a bit stiff.'

While he fitted the key in the padlock Alleyn looked up the lane. He thought how like this was to a scene in a modern talking-picture of the realistic school. The sound of the rain, the grime streaked with running trickles, the distant mutter of traffic, and their own figures, black against grey – it was almost a Dostoievsky setting. The key grated in the lock, the chain rattled and McCully dragged the reluctant doors back in their grooves.

'Darkish,' he said. I'll turn up the light.'

It was very dark inside the place they had come to. A greyness filtered through dirty skylights. The open doors left a patch of light on a wooden floor, but the far end was quite lost in shadow. McCully's boots clumped over the boards.

'I don't just remember where the switch is,' he said, and his voice echoed away into the shadows. Alleyn stood like a figure of stone in the entrance, waiting for the light. McCully's hand fumbled along the wall. There was a click and a dull yellow globe, thick with dust, came to life just inside the door.

'There we are, sir.'

Alleyn walked in.

The place at first looked almost empty. A few canvases stood at intervals with their faces to the wall. Half-way down there was a large studio easel, and beyond it, far away from the light, stood a packing-case with a few odd chairs and some shadowy bundles. Beyond that again, deep in shadow, Alleyn could distinguish the corner of a table. An acrid smell hung on the air. McCully walked on towards the dark.

'Kind of lonesome, isn't it?' he said. 'Not much comfort about it. Bit of a smell, too. There was some storage batteries in here. Wonder if he broke one of them.'

'Wait a moment,' said Alleyn, but McCully did not hear him.

'There's another light at this end. I'll find the switch in a minute,' he said. 'It's very dark, isn't it? Cripes, what a stink. You'd think he'd – '

His voice stopped as if someone had gagged him. He stood still. The place was filled with the sound of rain and with an appalling stench.

'What's the matter?' asked Alleyn sharply.

There was no answer.

'McCully! Don't move.'

'Who's that!' said McCully violently.

'Where? Where are you?'

'Here – who – *Christ*!'

Alleyn strode swiftly down the room.

'Stay where you are,' he said.

'There's someone sitting at the table,' McCully whispered.

Alleyn came up with him and caught him by the arm. McCully was trembling like a dog.

'Look! Look there!'

In the shadow cast by the packing-case Alleyn saw the table. The man who sat at it leant across the top and stared at them. His chin seemed to be on the surface of the table. His arms were stretched so far that his hands reached the opposite edge. It was an uncouth posture, the attitude of a scarecrow. They could see the lighter disc that

was his face and the faint glint of his eyeballs. Alleyn had a torch in
his pocket. He groped for it with one hand and held McCully's arm
with the other. McCully swore endlessly in a whisper.

The sharp beam of light ran from the torch to the table. It ended
in the man's face. It was the face of a gargoyle. The eyeballs started
from their sockets, the protruding tongue was sulphur yellow. The
face was yellow and blue. McCully wrenched his arm from Alleyn's
grasp and flung it across his eyes.

Alleyn walked slowly towards the table. The area of light widened
to take in an overturned cup and a bottle. There was a silence of a
minute broken by McCully.

'Oh, God!' said McCully. 'Oh, God, help me! Oh, God!'

'Go back to your office,' said Alleyn. 'Telephone Scotland Yard.
Give this address. Say the message is from Inspector Alleyn. Ask
them to send Fox, Bailey, and the divisional surgeon. Here!'

He turned McCully round, marched him towards the door and
propped him against the wall.

'I'll write it down.' He took out his notebook, wrote rapidly and
then looked at McCully. The large common face was sheet-white
and the lips were trembling.

'Can you pull yourself together?' asked Alleyn. 'Or had I better
come with you? It would help if you could do it. I'm a CID officer.
We're looking for this man. Come now, can you help me?'

McCully drew the back of his hand across his mouth.

'He's dead,' he said.

'Bless my soul, of course he is. Will you take this message? I don't
want to bully you. I just want you to tell me if you can do it.'

'Give us a moment, will you?'

'Of course.'

Alleyn looked up and down the alley.

'Wait here a minute,' he said.

He ran through the pelting rain to the top of the alley and looked
into Cornwall Street. About two hundred yards away he saw a constable, walking along the pavement towards him. Alleyn waited for
him, made himself known, and sent the man off to the nearest telephone. Then he returned to McCully.

'It's all right, McCully, I've found a PC. Sit down on this box.
Here.' He pulled a flask from his pocket and made McCully drink.

'Sorry I let you in for this,' he said. 'Now wait here and don't admit anyone. When I've turned up the light at the back of this place, close the doors. You needn't look round.'

'If it's all the same to you, sir, I'll wait outside.'

'All right. Don't speak to anyone unless they say they're from the Yard.'

Using his torch, Alleyn went back to the far end of the room. He found the light switch, turned it on, and heard McCully drag the doors together.

The lamp at this end of the room was much more brilliant. By its light Alleyn examined the man at the table. The body was flaccid. Alleyn touched it, once. The man was dressed in an old mackintosh and a pair of shabby grey trousers. The hands were relaxed, but their position suggested that they had clutched the edge of the table. They were long, the square finger-tips were lightly crusted with dry clay and the right thumb and forefinger were streaked with blue. On the backs of the hands Alleyn saw sulphur-coloured patches. Not without an effort he examined the terrible face. There were yellow spots on the jaw amongst the half-grown beard. The mouth was torn, and a glance at the finger-nails showed by what means. On the chin, the table and the floor Alleyn found further ghastly evidence of what had happened before the man died.

Alleyn dropped his silk handkerchief over the head.

He looked at the overturned bottle and cup. The bottle was marked clearly with a label bearing a scarlet cross. It was almost empty and from its neck a corroded patch spread over the table. The same marks appeared on the table round the cup. The table had been heavily coated with dust when the man sat at it. His arms had swept violently across the surface. The floor was littered with broken china and with curiously shaped wooden tools, rather like enormous orange-sticks. Alleyn looked at the feet. The shoes, though shabby and unpolished, had no mud on them. One foot was twisted round the chair-leg, the other had been jammed against the leg of the table. The whole posture suggested unspeakable torture.

Alleyn turned to the packing-case. It was five feet square and well made. One side was hinged and fastened with a bolt. It was not locked. He pulled on his gloves and, touching it very delicately, drew the bolt. The door opened smoothly. Inside the case, on a wheeled platform, was an irregularly shaped object that seemed to be swathed in cloths. Alleyn touched it. The cloths were still damp. 'Comedy and Tragedy,' he murmured. He began to go over the floor. McCully's and his own wet prints were clear enough, but as far as he could see, with the exception of the area round the table, the wooden boards held no other evidence. He turned his torch on the border where the floor met the wall. There he found a thick deposit of dust down the entire length of the room. In a corner there was a large soft broom. Alleyn looked at this closely, shook the dust from the bristles on to a sheet of paper and then emptied it into an envelope. He returned to the area of floor round the table and inspected every inch of it. He did not disturb the pieces of broken china there, nor the wooden tools, but he found at last one or two strands of dark-brown hair and these he put in an envelope. Then he looked again at the head of the dead man.

Voices sounded, the doors rattled open. Outside in the pouring rain was a police car and a mortuary van. Fox and Bailey stood in the doorway with McCully. Alleyn walked quickly towards them.

'Hullo, Fox.'

'Hullo, sir. What's up?'

'Come in. Is Curtis there?'

'Yes. Ready, doctor?'

Dr Curtis, Alleyn's divisional surgeon, dived out of the car into shelter.

'What the devil have you found, Alleyn?'

'Garcia,' said Alleyn.

'Here!' ejaculated Fox.

'Dead?' asked Curtis.

'Very.' Alleyn laid his hand on Fox's arm. 'Wait a moment. McCully, you can sit in the police car if you like. We shan't be long.'

McCully, who still looked very shaken, got into the car. A constable and the man off the local beat joined the group in the doorway.

'I think,' said Alleyn, 'that before you see the body I had better warn you that it is not a pleasant sight.'

'Us?' asked Fox, surprised. 'Warn us?'

'Yes, I know. We're pretty well seasoned, aren't we? I've never seen anything quite so beastly as this – not even in Flanders. I think he's taken nitric acid.'

'Good God!' said Curtis.

'Come along,' said Alleyn.

He led them to the far end of the room, where the man at the table still sat with a coloured handkerchief over his face. Fox, Bailey and Curtis stood and looked at the body.

'What's the stench?' asked Fox. 'It's bad, isn't it?'

'Nitric acid?' suggested Bailey.

'And other vomited matter,' said Curtis.

'You may smoke, all of you,' said Alleyn, and they lit cigarettes.

'Well,' said Curtis, 'I'd better look at him.'

He put out his well-kept doctor's hand and drew away the hand-kerchief from the face.

'Christ!' said Bailey.

'Get on with it,' said Alleyn harshly. 'Bailey, I want you to take his prints first. It's Garcia all right. Then compare them with anything you can get from the bottle and cup. Before you touch the bottle we'll take a photograph. Where's Thompson?'

Thompson came in from the car with his camera and flashlight. The usual routine began. Alleyn, looking on, was filled with a violent loathing of the whole scene. Thompson took six photographs of the body and then they covered it. Alleyn began to talk.

'You'd better hear what I make of all this on the face of the information we've already got. Bailey, you carry on while I'm talking. Go over every inch of the table and surrounding area. You've got my case? Good. We'll want specimens of this unspeakable muck on the floor. I'll do that.'

'Let me fix it, sir,' said Fox. 'I'm out of a job, and we'd like to hear your reconstruction of this business.'

'You'd better rig something over your nose and mouth. Nitric acid fumes are no more wholesome than they are pleasant, are they, Curtis?'

'Not too good,' grunted Curtis. 'May as well be careful.'

The doors at the end opened to admit the PC whom Alleyn had left on guard.

'What is it?' asked Alleyn.

'Gentleman to see you, sir.'

'Is his name Bathgate?'

'Yes, sir.'

'Miserable young perisher,' muttered Alleyn. 'Tell him to wait. No. Half a minute. Send him in.'

When Nigel appeared Alleyn asked fiercely: 'How did you get wind of this?'

'I was down at the Yard. They'd told me you were out. I saw Fox and the old gang tootle away in a car, then the mortuary van popped out. I followed in a taxi. What's up? There's a hell of a stink in here.'

'The only reason I've let you in is to stop you pitching some cock-and-bull story to your filthy paper. Sit down in a far corner and be silent.'

'All right, all right.'

Alleyn turned to the others.

'We'll get on. Don't move the body just yet, Curtis.'

'Very good,' said Dr Curtis, who was cleaning his hands with ether. 'Speak up, Alleyn. Are you going to tell us this fellow's swallowed nitric acid?'

'I think so.'

'Bloody loathsome way of committing suicide.'

'He didn't know it was nitric acid.'

'Accident?'

'No. Murder.'

CHAPTER 18

One of Five

'I think,' said Alleyn, 'that we'll start off with the packing case.'

He walked over to it and flashed his torch on the swathed shape inside.

'That, I believe, is Garcia's clay model of the Comedy and Tragedy for the cinemas at Westminster. We'll have a look at it when Bailey has dealt with the case and the wet clothes. The point with which I think we should concern ourselves now is this. How did it get here?'

He lit a cigarette from the stump of his old one.

'In the caravan we looked at this morning?' suggested Fox from behind a white handkerchief he had tied across the lower half of his face. He was doing hideous things on the floor with a small trowel and a glass bottle.

'It would seem so, Brer Fox. We found pretty sound evidence that the caravan had been backed up to the window. Twig on the roof, tyre-tracks under the sill, traces of the little wheeled platform on the ledge and the step and floor of the caravan. The discrepancy in the petrol fits in with this place quite comfortably, I think. Very well. That was all fine and dandy as long as Garcia was supposed to have driven himself and his gear up to London, and himself back to Tatler's End House. Now we've got a different story. Someone returned the caravan to Tatler's End House, and that person has kept quiet about it.'

'Is it possible,' asked Fox, 'that Garcia drove the car back and returned here by some other means?'

'Hardly, Fox, I think. On Friday night Garcia was recovering from a pipe or more of opium, and possibly a jorum of whisky. He was in no condition to get his stuff aboard a caravan, drive it thirty miles, open this place up, manoeuvre the caravan inside, unload it, drive it back, and then start off again to tramp back to London or catch a train or bus. But suppose somebody arrived at the studio on Friday night and found Garcia in a state of semi-recovery. Suppose this person offered to drive Garcia up to London and return the caravan. Does that quarrel with anything we have found? I don't think it does. Can we find anything here to support such a theory? I think we can. The front part of the floor has been swept. Why the devil should Garcia sweep the floor of this place at midnight while he was in the condition we suppose him to have been in? Bailey, have you dealt with the bottle on the table?'

'Yes, sir. We've got a fairly good impression of the deceased's left thumb, forefinger and second finger.'

'Very good. Will you all look now at the hands?'

Alleyn turned to the shrouded figure. The arms projected from under the sheets. The hands at the far edge of the table were uncovered.

'Rigor mortis,' said Alleyn, 'has disappeared. The body is flaccid. But notice the difference between the right hand and the left. The fingers of the right are still curved slightly. If I flash this light on the under-surface of the table, you can see the prints left by the fingers when they clutched it. Bailey had brought them up with powder. You took a shot of these, Thompson, didn't you? Good. As rigor wore off, you see, the fingers slackened. Now look at the left hand. It is completely relaxed and the fingers are straight. On the under-surface of the table-edge, about three inches to the right of the left hand, are four marks made by the fingers. They are blurred, but the impression was originally a strong one, made with considerably pressure. Notice that the blurs do not seem to have been caused by any relaxation of the fingers. It looks rather as if the pressure had not been relaxed at all, but the fingers dragged up the edge while they still clutched it. Notice that the present position of the hand bears no sort of relation to the points – it is three inches away from them. Did you find any left-hand prints on the top of the table, Bailey?'

'No, sir.'

'No. Now, taking into consideration the nature and direction of the blurs and all the rest of it, in my opinion there is a strong assumption that this hand was forcibly dragged from the edge of the table, possibly while in a condition of cadaveric spasm. At all events, there is nothing here to contradict such an assumption. Now have a look at this cup. It contains dregs of what we believe to be nitric acid and is standing in a stain made, presumably, by nitric acid. It is on the extreme right hand of the body. You've tried it for prints, Thompson, and found – ?'

'Four left-hand fingerprints and the thumb.'

'Yes, by Jove!' Alleyn bent over the cup. 'There's a good impression of the left hand. Now see here. You notice these marks across the table. It was thickly covered in dust when this man sat down at it. Dust on the under-surface of his sleeves – lots of it. If we measure these areas where the dust has been removed and compare it with the length of the sleeve, we find pretty good evidence that he must have swept his arms across the surface of the table. Something like this.'

Alleyn took the dead arms and moved them across the table. 'You see, they follow the marks exactly. Here on the floor are the things he knocked off. Modeller's tools. A plate – smashed in four pieces. Two dishes that were probably intended for use as etching baths. There's almost as much dust under them as there is on the rest of the floor, so they haven't been there more than a day or two. They themselves are not very dusty – he brushed them with his sleeves. Agreed that there's a strong likelihood he swept them off?'

'Certainly,' said Fox.

'All right. Now look again at the table. This bottle which held the nitric acid and this cup into which it was poured – these two objects we find bang in the middle of the area he swept with his arms in the violent spasm that followed the moment when he drank. Why were they not hurled to the floor with the plate and the modeller's tools?'

'By God, because they were put there afterwards,' said Curtis.

'Yes, and why was that cup which he held with his left hand put down on the right of the table with the print on the far side? To put the cup down where we found it he must have stood where I am now – or here – or perhaps here. Well, say he drank the stuff while he was in such a position. After taking it he put the cup at this end of the table and the bottle, which has a left-hand print, beside it. He then moved to the chair, swept away the other stuff in his death throes, but replaced the bottle and the cup.'

'Which is absurd,' said Thompson solemnly.

'Ugh,'said Bailey.

'I think it is,' said Alleyn. He glanced at Curtis. 'What would happen when he drank nitric acid?'

'Undiluted?'

'I think so.'

'Very quick and remarkably horrible.' Curtis gave a rapid description of what would happen. 'He wouldn't perform any intelligent action. The initial shock would be terrific, and intense spasms would follow immediately. It's quite beyond the bounds of possibility that he would replace the cup, seat himself, or do anything but make some uncontrolled and violent movement such as you've described in reference to the arms. But I cannot believe, Alleyn, that anybody in his senses could ever take nitric acid without knowing what he was doing.'

'If he was not in his senses, but half doped with opium, and very thirsty? If he asked for a drink and it was put beside him?'

'That's more likely, certainly, but still – '

'If he was asleep in his chair with his mouth open, and it was poured into his mouth,' said Alleyn. 'What about that?'

'Well then – of course' – Curtis shrugged – 'that would explain everything.'

'It may be the explanation,' said Alleyn. 'The stuff had spilled over the face very freely. I want you now to look at the back of the head.' With his long, fastidious fingers he uncovered the hair, leaving the face veiled.

'He wore his hair long, you see. Now look here. Look. Do you see these tufts of hair that are shorter? They seem to have been broken, don't they? And see this. Hold your torch down and use a lens. The scalp is slightly torn as though a strand of hair has actually been wrenched away. On the floor behind this chair I found several hairs, and some of them have little flakes of scalp on the ends. Notice how the hair round the torn scalp is tangled. What's the explanation? Doesn't it suggest that a hand has been twisted in his hair? Now see the back of the chair. I think we shall find that these stains were made by nitric acid, and the floor beneath is stained in the same way. These are nitric stains – I'm afraid I'll have to uncover the face – yes – you see, running from the corners of the mouth down the line of the jaw to the ears and the neck. Notice the direction. It's important. It suggests strongly that the head was leaning back, far back, when the stuff was taken. Now if we lean him back in the chair – God, this is a filthy business! All right, Bathgate, damn you, get out. Now, Curtis, and you, Fox. Look how the hair fits between the acid stains on the back of the chair, and how the stains carry on from the jaw to the chair as if the stuff had run down. Would a man ever drink in this attitude with his face to the ceiling? Don't you get a picture of someone standing behind him and pouring something into his mouth? He gasps and makes a violent spasmodic movement. A hand is wound in his hair and holds back his head. And still nitric acid is poured between his lips. God! Cover it up again. Now, let's go to the door.'

They walked in silence down the place, opened the door, and were joined by a very green Nigel. Alleyn filled his pipe and lit it. 'To sum up,' he said, 'and for Heaven's sake, all of you, check me if I go too far – we have difficulty in fitting the evidence of the hands, the table, the position of the body, the cup and the bottle, with any theory of suicide. On the other hand, we find nothing to contradict the suggestion that this man sat at this table, was given a dose of nitric acid, made a series of violent and convulsive movements, vomited, clutched the edge of the table and died. We find nothing to contradict the theory that his murderer dragged the left hand away from the ledge of the table and used it to print the bottle and the cup, and then left them on the table. I don't for a moment suggest there is a good case for us here, but at least there is a better case for murder than for suicide.' He looked from one dubious face to another.

'I know it's tricky,' he said. 'Curtis – how long would he take to die?'

'Difficult to say. Fourteen hours. Might be more, might be less.'

'Fourteen hours! Damn and blast! That blows the whole thing sky-high.'

'Wait a moment, Alleyn. Have we any idea how much of the stuff he took?'

'The bottle was full. Miss Troy and Miss Bostock said it was full on Friday morning. Allowing for the amount that splashed over, it might have been quite a cupful.'

'This is the most shocking affair,' said little Curtis. 'I – never in the whole course of my experience have I – however. My dear chap, if a stream of the stuff was poured into his mouth while his head was held back, he may have died in a few minutes of a particularly unspeakable form of asphixiation. Actually, we may find he got some of it down his larynx, in which case death would be essentially from obstruction to breathing and would take place very quickly unless relieved by tracheotomy. You notice that the portions of the face that are not dicoloured by acid are bluish. That bears out this theory. If you are right, I suppose that's what we shall find. We'd better clear up here and get the body away. We'll have the autopsy as soon as possible.'

It was almost dark when they got back to the Yard. Alleyn went straight to his room, followed by Fox and by a completely silent Nigel. Alleyn dropped into an armchair. Fox switched on the light.

'You want a drink, sir,' he said, with a look at Alleyn.

'We all do. Bathgate, I don't know what the hell you're doing here, but if you are going to be ill, you can get out. We've had enough of that sort of thing.'

'I'm all right now,' said Nigel. 'What shall I do about this? The late edition – '

'A hideous curse on the late edition! All right. Tell them we've found him and where, and suggest suicide. That's all. Go away, there's a good chap.'

Nigel went.

'For pity's sake, Fox,' said Alleyn violently, 'why do you stand there staring at me like a benevolent bullock? Is my face dirty?'

'No, sir, but it's a bit white. Now, you have that drink, Mr Alleyn, before we go any further. I've got my emergency flask here.'

'I poured most of mine down McCully's gullet,' said Alleyn. 'Very well, Fox. Thank you. Have one yourself and let's be little devils together. Now then, where do we stand? You were very silent in that place of horror. Do you agree with my theory?'

'Yes, sir, I do. I've been turning it over in my mind and I don't see how any other theory will fit all the facts, more especially the tuft of hair torn from the scalp and found, as you might say, for the greater part on the floor.'

Fox briefly sucked in his short moustache and wiped his hand across his mouth.

'He must have jerked about very considerably,' he said, 'and have been held on to very determinedly.'

'Very.'

'Yes. Now sir, as we know only too well, it's one thing to have a lot of circumstantial evidence and another to tie somebody up in it. As far as times go, we're all over the shop here, aren't we? Some time late Friday night or early Saturday morning's the nearest we can get to when Garcia left Tatler's End House. All we can say about the time the caravan was returned is that it was probably before it was light on Saturday morning. Now, which of this crowd could have got away for at least two hours?'

'At the very least.'

'Yes. Two hours between seven-thirty on Friday evening, when Sadie Welsh heard Garcia speak, and before anybody was about – say, five o'clock – on Saturday morning. Do you reckon any of the lot that were up in London may have met him here?'

'Murdered him, taken the caravan to Tatler's End House and returned here – how?'

'That's true.'

'And I repeat, Fox, that I cannot believe a man in Garcia's condition could have gone through all the game with the caravan and the transport. We don't even know if he could drive and I should not be at all surprised if we find he couldn't. It would take a tolerably good driver to do all this. If it was one of the London lot, he went to Tatler's End House by means unknown, brought Garcia here and murdered him, returned the caravan and came back here, again by means unknown. You've seen the alibis. Pretty hopeless to fit anything on to any single one of them, isn't it?'

'I suppose so.'

'Except, perhaps, Malmsley. Could Malmsley have stayed behind and not caught the six o'clock bus? Where's the stuff about Malmsley?'

Fox got a file from the desk and thumbed it over.

'Here we are, sir. I saw the conductor of the six o'clock this morning. He says four people got on at Bossicote corner on Friday evening.

One woman and three men. He's a dull sort of chap. I asked him if any of the men had beards and he said he couldn't rightly remember, but he thinks one had a very wide-brimmed hat and wore a muffler, so he might have had a beard. Silly sort of chap. We did see a wide-brimmed affair in Malmsley's wardrobe, too, but we'll have to try and get closer to it than that.'

'Yes. If Malmsley did it, what about his dinner at the Savoy and his late night with his friend? I suppose he could have driven the caravan, killed Garcia and left the body here at about seven to eight-thirty, come back after he'd seen his friend to bed, and done all the rest of it. But how the devil did he get back from the studio to London after returning the caravan?'

'That's right.' Fox licked his thumb and turned a page. 'Now, here's Miss Troy and Miss Bostock. Their alibis are the only ones we seem to have a chance of breaking among the London push. They've been checked up all right and were both seen by the club night porter when they came in, Miss Bostock at about one o'clock and Miss Troy at two-twenty. I've seen Miss Troy's friend, Mr Bellasca, and he says he took her back to the club at two-twenty, or there-abouts. So that fits.'

'Is he a reliable sort of fellow?'

'I think so, sir. He's very concerned on Miss Troy's behalf. He's been ringing her up, but apparently she didn't exactly encourage him to go down there. He's a very open sort of young gentleman and said she always treated him as if he was a schoolboy. However, the time at the club's all right. The porter says definitely he let Miss Troy in at two-twenty. She exclaimed at the time, he says, so he remembered that. He says neither she nor Miss Bostock came out again, but he sits in a little cubby-hole by the lift, and may have dozed off. The garage is open all night. Their car was by the door. The chap there admits he slipped out to the coffee stall at about three o'clock.' Fox glanced up from the notes, looked fixedly at Alleyn's white face, and then cleared his throat. 'Not that I'm suggesting there's anything in that,' he said.

'Go on,' said Alleyn.

'Well, sir, we may still admit there's a possibility in the cases of these two ladies and Malmsley. On the evidence in this file I'd say all the others are wash-outs. That leaves us with what you might call a narrowed field. The Hon. Basil Pilgrim, Miss Seacliff, Miss Troy, Miss Bostock, and Mr Malmsley.'

'Yes. Oh Lord, Fox, I forgot to ask Bathgate if he had any success with Miss Bobbie O'Dawne. I must be sinking into a detective's dotage. I'd better go along and tell the AC about this afternoon. Then I'll write up my report and I think this evening we'd better go broody on the case.'

Alleyn had a long interview with his Assistant Commissioner, a dry man with whom he got on very well. He then wrote up his report and took Fox off to dine at his own flat in a cul-de-sac off Coventry Street. After dinner they settled down over the fire to a systematic review of the whole case.

At eleven o'clock, while they were still at it, Nigel turned up.

'Hullo,' said Alleyn, 'I rather wanted to see you.'

'I guessed as much,' said Nigel complacently.

'Get yourself a drink. How did you hit it off with Bobbie O'Dawne? I see your extraordinary paper has come out strong with a simpering portrait.'

'Good, isn't it? She liked me awfully. We clicked.'

'Anything to the purpose?'

'Ah, ah, ah! *Wouldn't* you like to know!'

'We are not in the mood,' said Alleyn, 'for comedy.'

'All right. As a matter of fact, I'm afraid from your point of view the visit was not a howling success. She said she wouldn't have Sonia's name blackened in print and gave me a lot of stuff about how Sonia was the greatest little pal and a real sport. I took her out to lunch and gave her champagne, for which I expect the Yard to reimburse me. She got fairly chatty, but nothing much to the purpose. I told her I knew all about Sonia's little blackmailing games with Pilgrim and Malmsley, and she said that was just a bit of fun. I asked her if Sonia had the same kind of fun with anyone else, and she told me, with a jolly laugh, to mind my own business. I filled up her glass and she did get a bit unreserved. She said Garcia found out Sonia had told her about the Pilgrim game. Garcia was absolutely livid and said he'd do Sonia in if she couldn't hold her tongue. Of course, Sonia told Bobbie all this and made her swear on a Bible and a rosary that she wouldn't split to anyone. It was at this stage, Alleyn, that Bobbie took another pull at her champagne and then said – I memorized her actual words – 'So you see, dear, with an oath like that on my conscience I couldn't say anything about Friday night, could I?' I said: 'How d'you mean?' and she said: 'Never mind, dear. She oughn't to have told me. Now I'm scared. If he knows she told me, as sure as God's above he'll do for me, too.' And then, as there was no more champagne, the party broke up.'

'Well – I'll pay for the champagne,' said Alleyn. 'Damn this girl, Fox, she's tiresome. Sink me if I don't believe she knows who had the date with Garcia on Friday night. She's proved that it wasn't Sonia. Sonia spent the weekend with her. Well – who was it?'

The telephone rang. Alleyn picked up the receiver. 'Hullo. Yes, Bailey? I see. He's sure of that? Yes. Yes, I see. Thank you.'

He put down the receiver and looked at Fox.

'The hole on the cuff of Pilgrim's coat was made by an acid. Probably nitric acid.'

'Is that so?' said Fox. He rose slowly to his feet.

'There's your answer!' cried Nigel. 'I don't see how you can get away from it, Alleyn. You've got motive and opportunity. You've got evidence of a man who stood in the lane and looked in at the studio window. It might just have been Malmsley, but by God, I think it was Pilgrim.'

'In that case,' said Alleyn, 'we'll call on Captain and Mrs Pascoe at Boxover, where Pilgrim and Miss Seacliff spent the night. Run along, Bathgate. I want to talk to Inspector Fox. I'm most grateful for your work with Bobbie O'Dawne and I won't tell your wife you spend your days with ladies of the chorus. Good evening.'

CHAPTER 19

Alleyn Makes a Pilgrimage

The inquest on the body of Sonia Gluck was held at Bossicote on the morning of Thursday, September 22nd. The court, as might have been expected, was jammed to the doors; otherwise the proceedings were as colourless as the coroner, a gentleman with an air of irritated incredulity, could make them. He dealt roundly with the witnesses and with the evidence, reducing everything by a sort of sleight-of-hand to a dead norm. One would have thought that models impaled on the points of poignards were a commonplace of police investigation. Only once did he appear to be at all startled and that was when Cedric Malmsley gave evidence. The coroner eyed Malmsley's beard as if he thought it must be detachable, abruptly changed his own glasses, and never removed his outraged gaze from the witness throughout his evidence. The barest outline of the tragedy was brought out. Alleyn gave formal evidence on the finding of Garcia's body, and the court was fraught with an unspoken inference that it was a case of murder and suicide. Alleyn asked for an adjournment, and the whole thing was over by eleven o'clock.

In the corridor Alleyn caught Fox by the arm.

'Come on, Brer Fox. We're for Boxover. The first stop in the pilgrimage. I've got my mother's car – looks less official. It's over there – wait for me, will you?'

He watched Fox walk away and then turned quickly into a side lane where Troy sat in her three-seater. Alleyn came up to her from behind, and she did not see him. She was staring straight in front of her. He stood there with his hat in his hands, waiting for her to turn her head. When at last she woke from her meditation and saw him, her eyes widened. She looked at him gravely and then smiled.

'Hullo. It's you,' said Troy, 'I'm waiting for Katti.'

'I have to say a word to you,' said Alleyn.

'What is it?'

'I don't know. Any word. Are you all right?'

'Yes, thank you.'

'I'm afraid it's difficult for you,' said Alleyn, 'having all these people still in the house. This second case made it necessary. We can't let them go.'

'It's all right. We're doing some work out of doors when it's fine, and I've moved everything round in the studio and got a man from the village to sit. Katti's doing a life-size thing of the policeman at the front gate. It's a bit – difficult – at times, but they seem to have made up their minds Garcia did it.'

'This last thing – about Garcia. It's been a pretty bad shock to you.'

'In a way – yes,' said Troy. 'It was kind of you to send me a telegram.'

'Kind! Oh, well, if it broke the news a bit, that's something. You had no particular feeling about him, had you? It was his work, wasn't it?'

'True enough. His work. That clay group was really good, you know. I think it would have been the best thing he ever did. Somebody will do the marble from the model, I suppose.' She looked directly in Alleyn's eyes. 'I'm – I'm horrified,' she whispered.

'I know.'

'Nitric acid! It's so beyond the bounds of one's imagination that anyone could possibly – Please tell me – they seemed to suggest that Garcia himself – I *must* know. Did he kill her and then himself? I can't believe he did. He would never do that. The first – all that business with the knife – I *can* imagine his suddenly deciding to kill Sonia like that. In a ghastly sort of way it might appeal to his imagination, but it's just because his imagination was so vivid that I am sure he wouldn't kill himself so horribly. Why – why, Ormerin once spilt acid from that bottle on his hand – Garcia was there. He knew. He saw the burn.'

'He was drugged at the time he died. He'd been smoking opium.'

'Garcia! But – All right. It's not fair to ask you questions.'

'I'm so sorry. I think we're nearly at an end. Tomorrow, perhaps, we shall know.'

'Don't look so – worried,' said Troy suddenly.

'I wonder if it has ever entered your head,' said Alleyn, 'that it is only by wrenching my thoughts round with a remarkable effort that I can keep them on my job and not on you.'

She looked at him without speaking.

'Well,' he said. 'What have you got to say to that, Troy?'

'Nothing. I'm sorry. I'd better go.'

'A woman never actually objects to a man getting into this state of mind about her, does she? I mean – as long as he behaves himself?'

'No. I don't think she does.'

'Unless she happens to associate him with something particularly unpleasant. As you must me. Good God, I'm a pretty sort of fellow to shove my damned attentions on a lady in the middle of a job like this.'

'You're saying too much,' said Troy. 'You must stop. Please.'

'I'm extremely sorry. You're perfectly right – it was unpardonable. Goodbye.'

He stood back. Troy made a swift movement with her hands and leant towards him.

'Don't be so "pukka sahib",' she said. 'It is quite true – a woman doesn't mind.'

'Troy!'

'Now I'm saying too much. It's her vanity. Even mixed up with horrors like these she rather likes it.'

'We seem to be an odd pair,' said Alleyn. 'I haven't the smallest idea of what you think of me. No, truly, not the smallest idea. But even in the middle of police investigations we appear to finish our thoughts. Troy, have you ever thought of me when you were alone?'

'Naturally.'

'Do you dislike me?'

'No.'

'That will do to go on with,' said Alleyn. 'Good morning.'

With his hat still in his hand he turned and walked away quickly to his mother's car.

'Off we go, Fox,' he said. 'Alley houp. The day is ours.'

He slipped in the clutch and in a very few minutes they were travelling down a fortunately deserted road at fifty miles an hour. Fox cleared his throat.

'What's that, Brer Fox?' asked Alleyn cheerfully.

'I didn't speak, Mr Alleyn. Are we in a hurry?'

'Not particularly. I have a disposition of speed come upon me.'

'I see,' said Fox dryly.

Alleyn began to sing.

> 'Au clair de la lune
> Mon ami, Pierrot.'

Trees and hedges flew past in a grey blur. From the back of the car a muffled voice suddenly chanted:

'I thought I saw Inspector Alleyn hunting for a clue.

I looked again and saw it was an inmate at the Zoo.

"Good God," I said, "It's very hard to judge between these two." '

Alleyn took his foot off the accelerator. Fox slewed round and stared into the back of the car. From an upheaval of rugs Nigel's head emerged.

'I thought,' he continued, 'I saw Gargantua in fancy worsted socks.

I looked again and saw it was a mammoth picking locks.

"Good God," I said, "it might have been my friend Inspector Fox." '

'Rude is never funny,' said Alleyn. 'When did you hide in my mother's car?'

'Immediately after the old gentleman pronounced the word "adjournment." Where are we bound for?'

'I shan't tell you. Alley houp! Away we go again.'

'Mr Fox,' said Nigel, 'what has overtaken your chief? Is he mad, drunk, or in love?'

'Don't answer the fellow, Brer Fox,' said Alleyn. 'Let him burst in ignorance. Sit down, behind, there.'

They arrived at Boxover and drew up outside a rather charming Georgian house on the outskirts of the village.

'Twenty minutes,' said Alleyn, looking from his watch to the speedometer. 'Twenty minutes from Bossicote and twelve miles. It's two miles from the studio to Bossicote. Fourteen miles and a straightish road. We slowed down once on Bathgate's account and once to ask the way. At night you could do the whole trip in a quarter of an hour or less. Now then. A certain amount and yet not too much finesse is indicated. Come on, Fox.'

'May I come?' asked Nigel.

'You? You have got the most colossal, the most incredible, the most appalling cheek. Your hide! Your effrontery! Well, well, well. Come along. You are a Yard typist. Wait by the car until I give you a leery nod, both of you.'

He rang the front door bell and whistled very sweetly and shrilly.

'What *is* the matter with him, Fox?' asked Nigel.

'Search me, Mr Bathgate. He's been that worried over this case ever since we found Garcia, you'd think he'd never crack a joke again, and then he comes out from this inquest, crosses the road to have a word with Miss Troy and comes back, as you might say, with bells on.'

'Oh ho!' said Nigel. 'Say you so, Fox. By gum, Fox, do you suppose – '

The door was opened by a manservant. Alleyn spoke to him and gave him a card. The man stood back and Alleyn with a grimace at them over his shoulder, stepped inside, leaving the door open.

'Come on, Mr Bathgate,' said Fox. 'That means us.'

They joined Alleyn in a little hall that was rather overwhelmed with the horns, masks, and hides of dead animals.

'Mrs Pascoe is away,' whispered Alleyn, 'but the gallant captain is within. Here he comes.'

Captain Pascoe was short, plump and vague-looking. He had prominent light blue eyes and a red face. He smelt of whisky. He looked doubtfully from Alleyn to Fox.

'I'm sorry to bother you, Captain Pascoe,' said Alleyn.

'That's all right. You're from Scotland Yard, aren't you? This business over at Bossicote, what?'

'That's it. We're checking up everybody's movements on the night in question – you'll understand it has to be done.'

'Oh quite. Routine, what?'

'Exactly. Inspector Fox and Mr Bathgate are with me.'

'Oh ya',' said Captain Pascoe. ''H' are y'. H' are y'. Have a drink.'

'Thank you so much, hut I think we'll get on with the job.'

'Oh. Right-ho. I suppose it's about Valmai – Miss Seacliff – and Pilgrim, isn't it? I've been followin' the case. Damn funny, isn't it?

They're all right. Spent Friday here with us. Slept here and went on to old Pilgrim's place next day.'

'So they told us. I'm just going to ask you to check up the times. It won't take a moment.'

'Oh, quite. Right-ho. Sit down.'

Alleyn led him through the weekend from the moment when Valmai Seacliff and Pilgrim arrived, up to the time they all sat down to dinner. Captain Pascoe said nothing to contradict the information given by the other two. Alleyn complimented him on his memory and on the crispness of his recital, which was anything but crisp. The little man expanded gratefully.

'And now,' said Alleyn, 'we come to the important period between ten o'clock on Friday night and five the following morning. You are a soldier, sir, and you understand the difficulties of this sort of thing. One has to be very discreet – ' Alleyn waved his hands and looked respectfully at Captain Pascoe.

'By Jove, ya'. I 'member there was feller in my reg'ment' – the anecdote wound itself up into an impenetrable tangle – 'and, by Jove, we nearly had a court martial over it.'

'Exactly. Just the sort of thing we want to avoid. So you see, if we can account, now, for every second of their time during Friday evening they will be saved a lot of unpleasantness later on. You know yourself, sir – '

'Oh, quite. All for it. Damned unpleasant. Always flatter myself I've got the faculty of observing detail.'

'Yes. Now I understand that during dinner Miss Seacliff complained of a headache?'

'No, no. Not till after dinner. Minor point, but we may's well be accurate, Inspector.'

'Certainly, sir. Stupid of me. Was it about the time you had coffee that she first spoke of it?'

'No. Wait a bit, though. Tell you what – just to show you – what I was saying about my faculty for tabulatin' detail – '

'Yes.'

'I 'member Valmai made a face over her coffee. Took a swig at it and then did a sort of shudder and m'wife said: "What's up?" or words to the same effect, and Val said the coffee was bitter, and then Pilgrim looked a bit sheepish and I said: "Was yours bitter?" and he said:

"Matter of fact it was!" Funny – mine was all right. But my idea is that Val was feeling a bit off colour then, and he just agreed the coffee was bitter to keep her in countenance. In my opinion the girl had a liver. Pilgrim persuaded her to have a glass of port after champagne, and she said at the time it would upset her. Damn bad show. She's a lovely thing. Damn good rider to hounds. Lovely hands. Goes as straight and as well as the best of 'em. Look at that.' He fumbled in a drawer of his writing-desk and produced a press photograph of Valmai Seacliff looking magnificent on a hunter. Captain Pascoe gloated over it, handed it to Alleyn, and flung himself back in his chair. He appeared to collect his thoughts. 'But to show you how one notices little things,' he resumed. 'Not till after dinner that she talked about feeling under the weather. Matter of fact, it was when I took her empty cup. Precise moment. There you are.' And he laughed triumphantly.

'Splendid, sir. I wish everyone was as clear-minded. I remember a case where the whole thing hinged on just such an incident. It was a question of who put sugar in a cup of tea, and do you think we could get anyone who remembered? Not a bit of it. It's only one witness in a hundred who can give us that sort of thing.'

'Really? Well, I'll lay you a tenner, Inspector, I can tell you about the coffee on Friday night. Just for the sake of argument.'

'I'm not betting, sir.'

'Ha, ha, ha. Now then. M'wife poured out our coffee at that table over there. Pilgrim handed it round for her. He put Val's down beside her with his own, told her he'd put sugar in it, and went back to the table for mine. There you are, Inspector. Val complained her coffee was bitter. She asked Pilgrim if his tasted funny and he said it did, and – ' He stopped short and his eyes bulged. 'Look here,' he said, 'way I'm talking anybody might think this was a case of hanky-panky with the coffee. Good Lord, Inspector. Here! I say, I hope you don't – '

'Don't let that bother you, sir. We're only taking a sample case and I congratulate you. We don't get our information as lucidly as that very often, do we, Fox?'

'Very nice, indeed, sir,' agreed Fox, wagging his head.

'And then,' said Alleyn. 'I believe you played bridge?'

'Yes. That's right. But by that time Val was looking very seedy and said her head was splitting, so after two or three hands we chucked it up and m'wife took Val up to her room.'

'Gave her some aspirin perhaps?'

'No. Pilgrim rushed off and got some aspirin for her. Anxious about her as an old man. Engaged couples, what? Ha! She took the bottle up with her. M'wife tucked her up and went to her own room. Pilgrim said he was sleepy – I must say he's a dreary young blighter. Not nearly good enough for Val. Said he felt like bed and a long sleep. Dull chap. So we had a whisky and soda and turned in. That was at half-past ten. I wound up the clocks, and we went and had a look at Val and found she was in bed. Very attractive creature, Val. Naughty little thing hadn't taken the aspirin. Said it made her sick trying to swallow. So Pilgrim dissolved three in water and she promised she'd take 'em. M'wife looked in later and found her sound alseep. We were all tucked up and snoozing by eleven, I should think. And now let's see. Following morning – '

Captain Pascoe described the following morning with a wealth of detail to which Alleyn listened with every sign of respect and appreciation. Drinks were again suggested. 'Well, if you won't, I will,' said Captain Pascoe, and did, twice. Alleyn asked to see the bedrooms. Captain Pascoe mixed himself a third drink, and somewhat noisily escorted them over the house. The guest-rooms were at the top of the stairs.

'Val had this one, and that fellow was next door. What! Felt like a good long sleep! My God.' Here the captain laughed uproariously and pulled himself together. 'Not that Val'd stand any nonsense. Thoroughly nice girl. Looks very cometoish, but b'lieve me – na poo. I know. Too much other way 'fanything. I mean, give you 'ninstance. Following morning took her round rose garden. Looking lovely. Little purple cap and little purple gloves. Lovely. Just in friendly spirit I said, ''ffected little thing, wearing little purple gloves,' and gave little left-hand purple glove little squeeze. Just like that. Purely platonalistic. Jumped as if I'd bitten her and snatched away. Pooff!'

Captain Pascoe sat on the edge of Valmai's bed and finished his drink. He glared round the room, sucking his upper lip.

'Tchah!' he said suddenly. 'Look 't that. Disgraceful. Staff work in this house is 'bominable. M'wife's away. Maid's away. Only that feller to look after me. Meals at club. Nothing to do, and look at that.'

He pointed unsteadily to the mantelpiece.

''Bominable. Never been touched. Look at this!'

He turned his eye on the bedside table. Upon it stood a row of books. A dirty table-napkin lay on top of the books. Captain Pascoe snatched it up. Underneath it was a tumbler holding three fingers of murky fluid.

'D'yer know what that is? That's been there since Friday night. I mean!' He lurched again towards the bedside table. Alleyn slipped in front of him.

'Maddening that sort of thing. I wonder if we might see Mr Pilgrim's room, sir.'

'By George, we'll see every room in this house,' shouted Captain Pascoe. 'By God, we'll catch them red-handed.'

With this remarkable pronouncement he turned about and made for the door. Alleyn followed him, looked over his shoulder at Fox, raised his left eyebrow, and disappeared.

To Nigel's surprise, Fox said: 'Wait here, Mr Bathgate, please,' darted out of the room and reappeared in about a minute.

'Stand by that door if you please, Mr Bathgate,' whispered Fox. 'Keep the room clear.'

Nigel stood by the door and Fox, with surprising dexterity and speed, whipped a small wide-necked bottle from his pocket, poured the contents of the tumbler into it, corked it, and wrapped the tumbler up in his handkerchief.

'Now, sir. If you'll take those down to the car and put them in the chief's case – thank you very much. Quickly does it.'

When Nigel got back he found that Captain Pascoe, accompanied by Alleyn, had returned to the hall and was yelling for his servant. The servant arrived and was damned to heaps. Fox came down. Captain Pascoe suddenly collapsed into an armchair, showed signs of drowsiness, and appeared to lose all interest in his visitors. Alleyn spoke to the servant.

'We are police officers and are making a few inquiries about the affair at Bossicote. Will you show us the garage, please?'

'Very good, sir,' said the man stolidly.

'It's nothing whatever to do with your employer, personally, by the way.'

Captain Pascoe's servant bestowed a disappointed glance upon his master and led his visitors out by the front door.

'The garage is a step or two down the lane, sir. The house, being old and what they call restored, hasn't many conveniences.'

'Do you keep early hours here? What time do you get up in the mornings?'

'Breakfast is not till ten, sir. The maids are supposed to get up at seven. It's more like half-past. The Captain and Mrs Pascoe breakfast in their rooms, you see, and so do most guests.'

'Did Mr Pilgrim and Miss Seacliff breakfast in their rooms?'

'Oh yes, sir. There's the garage, sir.'

He showed them a double garage about 200 yards down the lane. Captain Pascoe's Morris Cowley occupied less than half the floor space.

'Ah yes,' said Alleyn. 'Plenty of room here. I suppose, now, that Mr Pilgrim's car fitted in very comfortably?'

'Oh yes, sir.'

'Nice car, isn't it?'

'Very nice job, sir. Tiger on petrol, sir.'

'Really? What makes you think that?'

'Well, sir, I asked the gentleman on Saturday morning was she all right for petrol – I'm butler-chauffeur, sir – and he said yes, she was filled up as full as she'd go in Bossicote. Well, sir, I looked at the gauge and she'd eaten up two gallons coming over here. Twelve miles, sir, no more. I looked to see if she was leaking but she wasn't. Something wrong there, sir, isn't there?'

'I agree with you,' said Alleyn. 'Thank you very much, I think that's all.'

'Thank you very much indeed, sir,' said the butler-chauffeur, closing his hand gratefully.

Alleyn, Fox and Nigel returned to their car and drove away.

'Get that tumbler, Fox?' asked Alleyn.

'Yes, sir. And the liquid. Had to go down to the car for a bottle.'

'Good enough. What a bit of luck, Fox! You remember the Seacliff told us Mrs Pascoe was leaving on Saturday and giving the maids a holiday? My golly, *what* a bit of luck.'

'Do you think the stuff was the melted aspirin Pilgrim doled out for her on Friday night?' asked Nigel.

'That's my clever little man,' said Alleyn. 'I do think so. And if the tumbler has Pilgrim's prints, and only his, we'll know.'

'Are you going to have the stuff analyzed?'

'Yes. Damn quick about it, too, if possible.'

'And what then?'

'Why then,' said Alleyn, 'we'll be within sight of an arrest.'

CHAPTER 20

Arrest

The analyst's report on the contents of the tumbler came through at nine-thirty that evening. The fluid contained a solution of Bayer's Aspirin – approximately three tablets. The glass bore a clear imprint of Basil Pilgrim's fingers and thumb. When Alleyn had read the analyst's report he rang up his Assistant Commissioner, had a long talk with him, and then sent for Fox.

'There's one thing we must make sure of,' he said wearily, 'and that's the position of the light on the figure outside the studio window. Our game with the string wasn't good enough. We'll have to get something a bit more positive, Brer Fox.'

'Meaning, sir?'

'Meaning, alas, a trip to Tatler's End.'

'Now?'

'I'm afraid so. We'll have a Yard car. It'll be needed in the morning. Come on.'

So for the last time Alleyn and Fox drove through the night to Tatler's End House. The Bossicote church clock struck midnight as Fox took up his old position outside the studio window. A fine drizzle was falling, and the lane smelt of leaf-mould and wet grass. The studio lights were on and the blind was drawn down.

'I shall now retire to the shady spot where Ethel and her boy lost themselves in an interlude of modified rapture,' said Alleyn.

He walked down the lane and returned in a few minutes.

'Fox,' he said, 'the ray of light that comes through the hole in the blind alights upon your bosom. I think we are on the right track.'

'Looks like it,' Fox agreed. 'What do we do now?'

'We spend the rest of the night with my mamma. I'll ring up the Yard and get the official party to pick us up at Danes Lodge in the morning. Come on.'

'Very good, Mr Alleyn. Er – '

'What's the matter?'

'Well, sir. I was thinking of Miss Troy. It's going to be a bit unpleasant for her, isn't it? I was wondering if we couldn't do something to make it a bit easier.'

'Yes, Fox. That's rather my idea, too. I think – damn it all, it's too late to bother her now. Or is it? I'll ring up from Danes Lodge. Come on.'

They got to Danes Lodge at twelve-thirty, and found Lady Alleyn reading D. H. Lawrence before a roaring fire in her little sitting-room.

'Good evening,' said Lady Alleyn. 'I got your message, Roderick. How nice to see you again, Mr Fox. Come and sit down.'

'I'm just going to telephone,' said Alleyn. 'Won't be long.'

'All right, darling. Mr Fox, help yourself to a drink and come and tell me if you have read any of this unhappy fellow's books.'

Fox put on his spectacles and gravely inspected the outside of *The Letters of D. H. Lawrence*.

'I can't say I have, my lady,' he said, 'but I seem to remember we cleaned up an exhibition of this Mr Lawrence's pictures a year or two ago. Very fashionable show it was.'

'Ah yes. Those pictures. What did you think of them?'

'I don't exactly know,' said Fox. 'They seemed well within the meaning of the act, I must say, but the colours were pretty. You wouldn't have cared for the subjects, my lady.'

'Shouldn't I? He seems never to have found his own centre of gravity, poor fellow. Some of these letters are wise and some are charming, and some are really rather tedious. All these negroid deities growling in his interior! One feels sorry for his wife, but she seems to have had the right touch with him. Have you got your drink? That's right. Are you pleased with your progress in this case?'

'Yes, thank you. It's coming on nicely.'

'And so you are going to arrest somebody tomorrow morning? I thought as much. One can always tell by my son's manner when he is going to make an arrest. He gets a pinched look.'

'So does his prisoner, my lady,' said Fox, and was so enraptured with his own pun that he shook from head to foot with amazed chuckles.

'Roderick!' cried Lady Alleyn as her son came in, 'Mr Fox is making nonsense of your mother.'

'He's a wise old bird if he can do that,' said Alleyn. 'Mamma, I've asked Miss Agatha Troy if she will lunch here with you tomorrow. She says she will. Do you mind? I shan't be here.'

'But I'm delighted, darling. She will be charming company for me and for Mr Bathgate.'

'What the devil – !'

'Mr Bathgate is motoring down tomorrow to their cottage to see his wife. He asked if he might call in.'

'It's forty miles off his course, the little tripe-hound.'

'Is it, darling? When I told him you would be here he said he'd arrive soon after breakfast.'

'Really, Mum! Oh well, I suppose it's all right. He's well trained. But I'm afraid he's diddled you.'

'He thinks he has, at all events,' said Lady Alleyn. 'And now, darling, as you are going to make an arrest in the morning, don't you think you ought to get a good night's sleep?'

'Fox?'

'Mr Fox has been fabulously discreet, Roderick.'

'Then how did you know we were going to arrest anybody?'

'You have just told me, my poor baby. Now run along to bed.'

At ten o'clock the next morning two police cars drove up to Tatler's End House. They were followed by Nigel in a baby Austin. He noted, with unworthy satisfaction, that one or two young men in flannel trousers and tweed coats hung about the gate and had evidently been refused admittance by the constable on duty. Nigel himself had been given a card by Alleyn on the strict understanding that he behaved himself and brought no camera with him. He was not allowed to enter the house. He had, he considered, only a minor advantage over his brother journalists.

The three cars drew up in the drive. Alleyn, Fox, and two plain-clothes men went up the steps to the front door. Nigel manoeuvred his baby Austin into a position of vantage. Alleyn glanced down at him and then turned away as Troy's butler opened the front door.

'Will you come in, please?' said the butler nervously. He showed them into Troy's library. A fire had been lit and the room would now have seemed pleasantly familiar to Alleyn if he had been there on any other errand.

'Will you tell Miss Troy of our arrival, please?'

The butler went out.

'I think, Fox, if you don't mind – ' said Alleyn.

'Certainly, sir. We'll wait in the hall.'

Troy came in.

'Good morning,' said Alleyn, and his smile contradicted the formality of his words. 'I thought you might prefer to see us before we go any further.'

'Yes.'

'You've realized from what I said last night on the telephone that as far as the police are concerned the first stage of this business may come to an end this morning?'

'Yes. You are going to make an arrest, aren't you?'

'I think we shall probably do so. It depends a little on the interview we hope to have in a minute or two. This has been an abominable week for you. I'm sorry I had to keep all these people together here and station bluebottles at your doors and before your gates and so on. It was partly in your own interest. You would have been overrun with pressmen.'

'I know.'

'Do you want me to tell you – ?'

'I think I know.'

'You *know*?'

'I think I do. Last night I said to myself: "Which of these people do I feel in my own bones is capable of this crime?" There was only one – only one of whom it did not seem quite preposterous to think: "It might – it just *might* be you!" I don't know why – there seems to be no motive, but I believe I am right. I suppose woman's instinct is the sort of phrase you particularly abominate.'

'That depends a little on the woman,' said Alleyn gravely.

'I suppose it does,' said Troy and flushed unexpectedly.

'I'll tell you who it is,' he said after a moment. And he told her. 'I can see that this time the woman's instinct was not at fault.'

'It's – so awful,' whispered Troy.

'I'm glad you decided to lunch with my mother,' said Alleyn. 'It will be easier for you to get right away from everything. She asked me to say that she would be delighted if you would come early. I suggest that you drive over there now.'

Troy's chin went up.

'Thank you,' she said, 'but I'm not going to rat.'

'There's no question of ratting – '

'After all, this is *my* ship.'

'Of course it is. But it's not sinking and, unfortunately, you can't do anything about this miserable business. It may be rather particularly unpleasant. I should take a trip ashore.'

'It's very kind of you to think of me, but, however illogically, I would feel as if I was funking something if I went away before – before you did. I've got my students to think of. You must see that. And even – even Pilgrim – '

'You can do nothing about him – '

'Very well,' said Troy angrily, 'I shall stay and do nothing.'

'Don't, please, be furious with me. Stay, then, but stay with your students.'

'I shan't make a nuisance of myself.'

'You know perfectly well that ever since I met you, you have made a nuisance of yourself. You've made my job one hundred per cent more difficult, because you've taken possession of my thoughts as well as my heart. And now, you go off to your students and think that over. I want to speak to Pilgrim, if you please.'

Troy gazed bleakly at him. Then she bit her lips and Alleyn saw that her eyes were full of tears.

'Oh, hell and damnation, darling,' he said.

'It's all right. I'm going. Shut up,' mumbled Troy, and went.

Fox came in.

'All right,' said Alleyn. 'Tell them to get Pilgrim, and come in.'

Fox spoke to someone outside and joined Alleyn at the fire.

'We'll have to go warily, Fox. He may give a bit of trouble.'

'That's so, sir.'

They waited in silence until Basil Pilgrim came in with one of the Yard men. The second man walked in after them and stood inside the door.

'Good morning,' said Pilgrim.

'Good morning, Mr Pilgrim. We would like to clear up one or two points relating to your former statement and to our subsequent investigations.'

'Certainly.'

Alleyn consulted his notebook.

'What does your car do to the gallon?' he asked.

'Sixteen.'

'Sure of that?'

'Yes. She may do a bit more on long runs.'

'Right. Now, if you please, we'll go back to Friday evening during your visit to Captain and Mrs Pascoe. Do you remember the procedure when coffee was brought in?'

'I suppose so. It was in the hall.'

He looked, with that curiously restless turn of his head, from Alleyn to Fox and back again.

'Can you tell us who poured out and who handed round the coffee?'

'I suppose so. Though what it can have to do with Sonia – or Garcia – Do you mean about Val's coffee being bitter? Mine was bitter, too. Beastly.'

'We should like to know who poured the coffee out.'

'Mrs Pascoe.'

'And who handed it round?'

'Well – I did.'

'Splendid. Can you remember the order in which you took it round?'

'I'm not sure. Yes, I think so. I took mine over with Val's to where she was sitting, and then I saw Pascoe hadn't got his, and I got it for him. Mrs Pascoe had poured out her own. Then I went back and sat with Val and I had my coffee.'

'You both took black coffee?'

'Yes.'

'And sugar?'

'And sugar.'

'Who put the sugar in the coffee?'

'Good Lord! I don't know. I believe I did.'

'You didn't say anything about your coffee being bitter?'

'I didn't like to. I gave Val a look and made a face and she nodded. She said: "Sybil, darling, your coffee is perfectly frightful."'

Mrs Pascoe was – ' he laughed – 'well, she was a bit huffy, I think. Val is always terribly direct. They both appealed to me and I – well, I just said I thought the coffee wasn't quite what one usually expects of coffee, or something. It was dashed awkward.'

'It must have been. Later on, when Miss Seacliff complained of feeling unwell, you gave her some aspirin, didn't you?'

'Yes. Why?' asked Pilgrim, looking surprised.

'Was the bottle of aspirins in your pocket?'

'What do you mean? I went upstairs and got it out of my suitcase. Look here, what are you driving at?'

'Please, Mr Pilgrim, let us get this tidied up. When did you actually give Miss Seacliff the aspirins?'

'When she went to bed. I tell you I got them from my suitcase and took them downstairs and gave her three.'

'Did she take them?'

'Not then. We looked in after she was in bed and she said she could never swallow aspirins, and so I dissolved three in water and left the tumbler by her bedside.'

'Did you see her drink this solution?'

'No. I think I said, Inspector, that I left it at her bedside.'

'Yes,' said Alleyn, 'I've got that. Where's the bottle?'

'What bottle? Oh, the aspirin. I don't know. I suppose it's in my room upstairs.'

'After you left Miss Seacliff's room on Friday night where did you go?'

'I had a drink with Pascoe and went to bed.'

'Did you get up at all during the night?'

'No.'

'You slept straight through the night?'

'Like the dead,' said Pilgrim. He was no longer restless. He looked steadily at Alleyn and he was extremely pale.

'It is strange you should have slept so soundly. There was a very severe thunderstorm that night,' lied Alleyn. 'Lightning. Doors banging. Maids bustling about. Didn't you hear it?'

'As a matter of fact,' said Pilgrim, after a pause, 'it's a funny thing, but I slept extraordinarily soundly that night. I'm always pretty good, but that night I seemed to be fathoms deep. I suppose I'd had a bit too much of Pascoe's 1875 Courvoisier.'

'I see. Now, Mr Pilgrim, I want you to look at this, if you please.'

He nodded to one of his men, who came forward with a brown-paper parcel. He opened it and took out a most disreputable garment.

'Why,' said Pilgrim, 'that's my old car coat.'

'Yes.'

'What on earth do you want with that, Mr Alleyn?'

'I want you to tell me when you burnt this little hole in the cuff. There, do you see.'

'I don't know. How the devil should I know! I've had the thing for donkey's years. It never comes out of the car. I've crawled under the car in it. It's obviously a cigarette burn.'

'It's an acid burn.'

'Acid? Rot! I mean, how could it be acid?'

'That is what we would like you to tell us.'

'Well, I'm afraid I can't tell you. Considering the use the thing's had, I suppose it might have come in contact with acid some time or another.'

'This is a recent stain.'

'Is it? Well then, it is. So what?'

'Might it be nitric acid?'

'Why?'

'Do you do any etching, Mr Pilgrim?'

'Yes. But not in my garage coat. Look here, Mr Alleyn – '

'Will you feel in the pockets?'

Pilgrim thrust a hand into one of the pockets and pulled out a pair of gloves.

'If you look on the back of the right-hand glove,' said Alleyn, 'you will see among all the greasy stains and worn patches another very small mark. Look at it, please. There. It is exceedingly small, but it, too, was made by an acid. Can you account for it?'

'Quite frankly, I can't. The gloves are always left in the pocket. Anything might happen to them.'

'I see. Have you ever lent this coat to anyone else? Has anyone else ever worn the gloves?'

'I don't know. They may have.' He looked up quickly and his eyes were suddenly bright with terror. 'I think it's quite likely I've lent it,' he said. 'Or a garage hand might have put it on some time – easily. It may be acid from a battery.'

'Have you ever lent it to Miss Seacliff, for instance?'

'Never.'

'It's an old riding Burberry, isn't it?'

'Yes.'

'You didn't lend it to her to hack in at your father's house – Ankerton – during the weekend?'

'Good Lord, no! Valmai has got very smart riding clothes of her own.'

'Not even the gloves?'

Pilgrim achieved a laugh. 'Those gloves! I had just given Valmai six pairs of coloured gloves which she tells me are fashionable. She was so thrilled she even lunched in purple gloves and dined in scarlet ones.'

'I mean to ride in?'

'She had her own hunting gloves. What *is* all this?'

'She goes well to hounds, doesn't she?'

'Straight as the best.'

'Yes. What sort of horse did you mount her on?'

'A hunter – one of mine.'

'Clubbed mane and tail?'

'Yes.'

'Look inside the right-hand glove – at the base of the little finger. Do you see that bloodstain?'

'I see a small stain.'

'It has been analysed. It is a bloodstain. Do you remember recently cutting or scratching the base of your little finger?'

'I – yes – I think I do.'

'How did it happen?'

'I forget. I think it was at Ankerton – on a bramble or something.'

'And you had these gloves with you at the time?'

'I suppose so. Yes.'

'I thought you said the gloves and coat always lived in the car?'

'It is rather absurd to go on with this,' Pilgrim said. 'I'm afraid I must refuse to answer any more questions.'

'You are perfectly within your rights. Fox, ask Miss Seacliff if she will be good enough to come in. Thank you, Mr Pilgrim; will you wait outside?'

'No,' said Pilgrim. 'I'm going to hear what you say to her.'

Alleyn hesitated.

'Very well,' he said at last. He dropped the coat and gloves behind the desk.

Valmai Seacliff arrived in her black slacks and magenta pullover. She made, as usual, a good entrance, shutting the door behind her and leaning against it for a moment to survey the men.

'Hallo,' she said. 'More investigations? What's the matter with you, Basil, you look as if you'd murdered somebody?'

Pilgrim didn't answer.

Alleyn said: 'I have sent for you, Miss Seacliff, to know if you can help us.'

'But I should adore to help you, Mr Alleyn.'

'Did you drink the solution of aspirin that Mr Pilgrim prepared for you on Friday night?'

'Not all of it. It was too bitter.'

'But you said, before, that you drank it.'

'Well, I did have a sip. I slept all right without it.'

'How is your cut hand?'

'My – ? Oh, it's quite recovered.'

'May I see it, please?'

She held it out with the same gesture that she had used on Monday night, but this time the fingers trembled. Below the base of the little finger there was still a very thin reddish scar.

'What's this?' said Pilgrim violently. 'Valmai – don't answer any of his questions. Don't answer!'

'But, why not, Basil!'

'You told me that you cut your hand on your horse's mane,' said Alleyn.

'No. You told me that, Mr Alleyn.'

'You accepted the explanation.'

'Did I?'

'How do you say, now, that you cut your hand?'

'I did it on the reins.'

'Mr Pilgrim, did you see this cut on Saturday evening? It must have been quite sore then. A sharp, thin cut.'

'I didn't see her hand. She wore gloves.'

'All through dinner?'

'Scarlet gloves. They looked lovely,' she said, 'didn't they, Basil?'

'Do you remember that on Monday night you told me you had no pretensions to being a good horsewoman?'

'Modesty, Mr Alleyn.'

Alleyn turned aside. He moved behind the desk, stooped, and in a second the old raincoat and the gloves were lying on the top of the desk.

'Have you ever seen those before?' asked Alleyn.

'I – don't know. Oh yes. It's Basil's, isn't it?'

'Come and look at it.'

She walked slowly across to the desk and looked at the coat and gloves. Alleyn picked up the sleeve and without speaking pointed a long forefinger to the acid hole in the cuff. He lifted the collar, and turned it back, and pointed to a whitish stain. He dropped the coat, took up the left-hand glove and turned it inside out. He pointed to a small stain under the base of the little finger. And still he did not speak. It was Basil Pilgrim who broke the silence.

'I don't know what he's driving at, Val, but you've never worn the things. I know you haven't. I've told him so. I'll swear it – I'll swear you've never worn them. I *know* you haven't.'

'You bloody fool,' she screamed. 'You bloody fool!'

'Valmai Seacliff,' began Alleyn, 'I arrest you for the murder of Wolf Garcia on – '

CHAPTER 21

Epilogue in a Garden

Troy sat on a rug in the central grass plot of Lady Alleyn's rose garden. Alleyn stood and looked down at her.

'You see,' he said, 'it was a very clumsy, messy, and ill-planned murder. It seemed the most awful muddle, but it boils down to a fairly simple narrative. We hadn't much doubt after Monday night that Garcia had set the trap for Sonia. He left his prints on the opium jar and, as Malmsley had prepared the first pipe, Garcia evidently gave himself another. He must have been in a state of partial recovery with a sort of exalted carry-over, when he got the idea of jamming the knife through the floor of the throne. Motive – Sonia had been badgering him to marry her. She was going to have his child and wouldn't let him alone. He had exhausted her charms and her possibilities as a blackmailing off-sider, and he was nauseated by her persistence. She came between him and his work. She probably threatened to sue him for maintenance, to make a full-sized scandal, to raise hell with a big stick in a bucket. The opium suggested a beautifully simple and macabre way out of it all. I saw Sonia's friend in the chorus – Miss O'Dawne – again this morning after the arrest. I got a rather fuller account of the blackmailing game. Sonia and Garcia were both in it. Sonia had tackled Pilgrim and threatened to tell the Methodist peer that Basil was the father of her child. He wasn't, but that made no odds. Basil stumped up and Sonia handed the cash to Garcia. We found a note from Garcia to Valmai Seacliff in which he coolly said he'd bought painting-materials at her shop and put them down to her. The wording of the letter suggested that he had some sort of upper hand over her, and when I first saw Bobbie O'Dawne she obviously had information up her sleeve and admitted as much. She told Bathgate that Sonia had said Garcia would kill both of them if they babbled. When Sonia died Bobbie O'Dawne was certain Garcia had done it, and that she'd be the next victim if she didn't keep quiet. Now he's dead, and we've got Valmai Seacliff, Miss O'Dawne is all for a bit of front-page publicity, and told me this morning that Sonia had kept her *au fait* with the whole story. Garcia blackmailed Valmai Seacliff. He said he'd tell Basil Pilgrim that she'd been his – Garcia's – mistress. He said he'd go to the Methodist peer with a story of studio parties that would throw the old boy into a righteous fury, and completely cook Seacliff's goose. Garcia worked the whole thing out with Sonia. She was to tackle Pilgrim while he went for Valmai Seacliff. Garcia had started to work with Seacliff, who at first wouldn't rise. But he'd done some drawings of Seacliff in the nude which he said he'd sent to old Pilgrim with a suitable letter, and he told her that Sonia was also prepared to do her bit of blackmail as well. At last, Valmai Seacliff – terrified of losing Pilgrim – said she'd meet Garcia on Friday night in the studio, when they were all safely away, and discuss payment. All this Garcia told Sonia, and Sonia told Bobbie O'Dawne, swearing her to secrecy. O'Dawne was too frightened of Garcia to tell me the Seacliff side, and I also think she honestly felt she couldn't break her word. She's got a sort of code, that funny hard little baggage, and she's stuck to it. But, of course, without her evidence we'd got no motive as far as Seacliff was concerned.'

'When did you suspect Valmai?'

'I wasn't very certain until I saw that the person who murdered Garcia had held his head back by the hair, and that he had struggled so hard that – well, that he had struggled. I then remembered the cut on Seacliff's hand, and how she had showed it to me only when she saw me looking at it, and how she had said it had been made by her horse's reins, when it had obviously been made by some thing much finer. I remembered how, when I suggested it was not the reins, but the horse's mane, she had agreed. But to go back a bit. From the moment we learned that it was Seacliff who posed the model I felt that we must watch her pretty closely.'

'I don't understand that. You say Garcia set the trap with the knife.'

'Yes, but I believe Seacliff watched him through a hole in the studio window-blind.'

'Seacliff!'

'Yes. She had put three aspirins in Pilgrim's coffee to ensure his sleeping soundly. When she realized he had noticed the coffee tasted odd – he made a face at her – she quickly raised an outcry about her own. She pretended to have a headache in order to get them all to bed early. She slipped out to the garage, wearing slacks and a sweater, put on Pilgrim's old coat and gloves, and drove back to the studio, getting there about midnight, with the intention of arguing about blackmail with Garcia. This was the meeting Miss Phillida Lee overheard Sonia discussing with Garcia. Sonia told Miss Bobbie O'Dawne all about it, and Miss O'Dawne told me, this morning. But you should remember that until this morning Miss O'Dawne had only elaborated what we already knew – the Pilgrim-Sonia side. However, I give you the whole thing as completely as I can. Valmai Seacliff arrived at the studio in a desperate attempt to placate Garcia. She must have left the car somewhere in the lane and walked down, meaning to come in at the side gate. Your maid Ethel and her boy, returning from the flicks, saw the figure of a shortish man standing outside the studio window, apparently looking through the hole in the blind. He wore a mackintosh with the collar turned up. The ray of light caught his beret, which was pulled down on one side, hiding his face. Both Garcia and Pilgrim were too tall for the light to get them anywhere above the chest. So was Malmsley. Seacliff seemed to be the only one about the right height. When we saw Pilgrim's old coat in his car we noticed whitish marks on the collar that suggested face-or neck-powder, and they smelt of Seacliff. It was so dirty it didn't seem likely she would let him embrace her while he was wearing it. When we looked inside the left-hand glove we noticed a bloodstain that corresponded with the cut on her hand. That, of course, came into the picture after the Garcia affair. I believe that she actually watched Garcia set his trap for Sonia and decided to say nothing about it. I believe she went in, probably got him to drink a good deal more whisky, and offered to drive him up to London. You told me he did a little etching.'

'Yes. He'd prepared a plate a few days before he went.'

'Then perhaps he said he'd take the acid to bite it. Is that the right word? Anyway, she got out your caravan and backed it up to the window. There's a slope down from the garage – enough to free-wheel into the lane and start on compression. The servants would-n't think anything odd if they heard a car in the lane. Malmsley had helped Garcia get everything ready. All she had to do was open the window, wheel the clay model over the sill into the caravan, get Garcia aboard and start off. The packing-case had already been addressed by Garcia. So she knew the address, even if he was inca-pable of directing her. I think myself that he had told her exactly where the warehouse was when he asked her to go there to see him, and she has admitted that he gave her a sketch-map. Probably his idea was that she should pay blackmail to him while he was there. She made another rather interesting slip over that. Do you remem-ber how she said she was reminded of the warehouse address by a remark someone made at breakfast about Holloway? She told me – and, I think, you – that as soon as she heard the word Holloway she remembered that Garcia had said his warehouse was near the prison, and she had told him to be careful he didn't get locked up. Holloway is a woman's prison. Her very feeble joke would have been a little less feeble if he was blackmailing her, and the place of assig-nation was not Holloway, but Brixton. By giving us Holloway as the district, she was sending us off in exactly the opposite direction to the right one. We might have hunted round Holloway for weeks. I wondered if she had been the victim of a sort of word-association and I decided to go for Brixton. Luckily enough, as it turned out. As a matter of fact, she had twice fallen into the trap of substituting for the truth something that is linked with it in her mind. The first time was over the cut on her hand. It had been made when she was standing above Garcia with her hand wound in his hair. She saw me looking at the scar, decided to speak of it before I did, was perhaps, reminded subconsciously of horses' hair, a mane gripped in the hand, rejected the idea of hair altogether and substituted reins. Have you had enough of this, Troy?'

'No. I want to know all about it.'

'There's not much more. She drove Garcia to his warehouse. He'd got the keys. She murdered him there, because she was hell-bent on marrying Pilgrim, and becoming a very rich peeress, and because it was in Garcia's power to stop her. She's an egomaniac. She drove the caravan back to your garage and drove herself back to the Pascoes' house in Pilgrim's car. The distance to the warehouse is thirty miles. At that time of night she'd do it easily in an hour and a half. She must have been back at the studio by three and probably got to the Pascoes' by half-past. Even supposing she lost her way – and I don't think she would, because there's a good map in the caravan – she'd a margin of two hours before there was a chance of the servants being about.'

'Why didn't you think it was Pilgrim?'

'I wondered if it was Pilgrim, of course. After we had checked all the alibis, it seemed to me that Pilgrim and Valmai Seacliff were by far the most likely. I even wondered if Pilgrim had drugged Seacliff with aspirin instead of Seacliff drugging Pilgrim – until she lied about her cut hand, her horsemanship and the address of the warehouse. On top of that there was the glove and the smell of the raincoat. She said she had taken the aspirins Pilgrim gave her. We found that she hadn't. We found that she had aspirins of her own in the evening bag she had taken to Boxover. Why should she pretend she had none? And why, after all, should Pilgrim kill Garcia? He had paid Sonia off, but as far as we know, Garcia had kept out of the picture where Pilgrim was concerned. Garcia was tackling Valmai Seacliff, not Pilgrim. No, the weight of evidence was against her. She lied where an innocent woman would not have lied. And – I'm finishing up where I began – I think that an innocent person would not have pressed Sonia down upon the point of that knife after she had cried out. She would not have disregarded that first convulsive start. She murdered Sonia, knowing the knife was there, as deliberately as she murdered Garcia.'

'Will they find her guilty?'

'I don't know, Troy. Her behaviour when we arrested her was pretty damning. She turned on Pilgrim like a wild cat because he kept saying he'd swear she'd never worn the coat. If he'd said she had often worn it, half our case would have gone up in smoke.'

Alleyn was silent for a moment, and then knelt down on the rug beside Troy.

'Has this all made a great difference to you?' he said. 'Is it going to take you a long time to put it behind you?'

'I don't know. It's been a bit of a shock for all of us.'

'For Pilgrim – yes. The others will be dining out on it in no time. Not you.'

'I think I'm sort of stunned. It's not that I liked any of them much. It's just the feeling of all the vindictiveness in the house. It's so disquieting to remember what Seacliff's thoughts must have been during the last week. I almost feel I ought to have a priest in with bell and book to purify the house. And now – the thought of the trial is unspeakably shocking. I don't know where – I am – '

She turned helplessly towards Alleyn and in a moment she was in his arms.

'No, no,' said Troy. 'I mustn't. You mustn't think – '

'I know.' Alleyn held her strongly. He could feel her heart beating secretly against his own. Everything about him, the trees, the ground beneath him, and the clouds in the still autumn sky, rose like bright images in his mind and vanished in a wave of exultation. He was alone in the world with her. And with that moment of supremacy before him came the full assurance that he must not take it. He knew quite certainly that he must not take it. He knew quite certainly that he must let his moment go by. He heard Troy's voice and bent his head down.

' – you mustn't think because I turn to you – '

'It's all right,' said Alleyn. 'I love you, and I know. Don't worry.'

They were both silent for a little while.

'Shall I tell you,' said Alleyn at last, 'what I think? I think that if we had met again in a different way you might have loved me. But because of all that has happened your thoughts of me are spoiled. There's an association of cold and rather horrible officiousness. Well, perhaps it's not quite as bad as all that, but my job has come between us. You know, at first I thought you disliked me very much. You were so prickly. Then I began to hope a little. Don't cry, dear Troy. It's a great moment for me, this. Don't think I misunderstand. You so nearly love me, don't you?' For the first time his voice shook.

'So nearly.'

'Then,' said Alleyn, 'I shall still allow myself to hope a little.'

Death on the Air

Death on the Air was first published in
Grand Magazine in 1936.

On the 25th of December at 7.30 a.m. Mr Septimus Tonks was found dead beside his wireless set.

It was Emily Parks, an under-housemaid, who discovered him. She butted open the door and entered, carrying mop, duster, and carpet-sweeper. At that precise moment she was greatly startled by a voice that spoke out of the darkness.

'Good morning, everybody,' said the voice in superbly inflected syllables, 'and a Merry Christmas!'

Emily yelped, but not loudly, as she immediately realized what had happened. Mr Tonks had omitted to turn off his wireless before going to bed. She drew back the curtains, revealing a kind of pale murk which was a London Christmas dawn, switched on the light, and saw Septimus.

He was seated in front of the radio. It was a small but expensive set, specially built for him. Septimus sat in an armchair, his back to Emily and his body tilted towards the wireless.

His hands, the fingers curiously bunched, were on the ledge of the cabinet under the tuning and volume knobs. His chest rested against the shelf below and his head leaned on the front panel.

He looked rather as though he was listening intently to the interior secrets of the wireless. His head was bent so that Emily could see the bald top with its trail of oiled hairs. He did not move.

'Beg pardon, sir,' gasped Emily. She was again greatly startled. Mr Tonks' enthusiasm for radio had never before induced him to tune in at seven thirty in the morning.

'Special Christmas service,' the cultured voice was saying. Mr Tonks sat very still. Emily, in common with the other servants, was terrified of her master. She did not know whether to go or to stay. She gazed wildly at Septimus and realized that he wore a dinner-jacket. The room was now filled with the clamour of pealing bells.

Emily opened her mouth as wide as it would go and screamed and screamed and screamed . . .

Chase, the butler, was the first to arrive. He was a pale, flabby man but authoritative. He said: 'What's the meaning of this outrage?' and then saw Septimus. He went to the armchair, bent down, and looked into his master's face.

He did not lose his head, but said in a loud voice: 'My Gawd!' And then to Emily: 'Shut your face.' By this vulgarism he betrayed his agitation. He seized Emily by the shoulders and thrust her towards the door, where they were met by Mr Hislop, the secretary, in his dressing-gown.

Mr Hislop said: 'Good heavens, Chase, what is the meaning – ' and then his voice too was drowned in the clamour of bells and renewed screams.

Chase put his fat white hand over Emily's mouth.

'In the study if you please, sir. An accident. Go to your room, will you, and stop that noise or I'll give you something to make you.' This to Emily, who bolted down the hall, where she was received by the rest of the staff who had congregated there.

Chase returned to the study with Mr Hislop and locked the door. They both looked down at the body of Septimus Tonks. The secretary was the first to speak.

'But – but – he's dead,' said little Mr Hislop.

'I suppose there can't be any doubt,' whispered Chase.

'Look at the face. Any doubt! My God!'

Mr Hislop put out a delicate hand towards the bent head and then drew it back. Chase, less fastidious, touched one of the hard wrists, gripped, and then lifted it. The body at once tipped backwards as if it was made of wood. One of the hands knocked against the butler's face. He sprang back with an oath.

There lay Septimus, his knees and his hands in the air, his terrible face turned up to the light. Chase pointed to the right hand. Two fingers and the thumb were slightly blackened.

Ding, dong, dang, ding.

'For God's sake stop those bells,' cried Mr Hislop. Chase turned off the wall switch. Into the sudden silence came the sound of the door handle being rattled and Guy Tonks' voice on the other side.

'Hislop! Mr Hislop! Chase! What's the matter?'

'Just a moment, Mr Guy.' Chase looked at the secretary. 'You go, sir.'

So it was left to Mr Hislop to break the news to the family. They listened to his stammering revelation in stupefied silence. It was not until Guy, the eldest of the three children, stood in the study that any practical suggestion was made.

'What has killed him?' asked Guy.

'It's extraordinary,' burbled Hislop. 'Extraordinary. He looks as if he'd been – '

'Galvanized,' said Guy.

'We ought to send for a doctor,' suggested Hislop timidly.

'Of course. Will you, Mr Hislop? Dr Meadows.'

Hislop went to the telephone and Guy returned to his family. Dr Meadows lived on the other side of the square and arrived in five minutes. He examined the body without moving it. He questioned Chase and Hislop. Chase was very voluble about the burns on the hand. He uttered the word 'electrocution' over and over again.

'I had a cousin, sir, that was struck by lightning. As soon as I saw the hand – '

'Yes, yes,' said Dr Meadows. 'So you said. I can see the burns for myself.'

'Electrocution,' repeated Chase. 'There'll have to be an inquest.'

Dr Meadows snapped at him, summoned Emily, and then saw the rest of the family – Guy, Arthur, Phillipa, and their mother. They were clustered round a cold grate in the drawing room. Phillipa was on her knees, trying to light the fire.

'What was it?' asked Arthur as soon as the doctor came in.

'Looks like electric shock. Guy, I'll have a word with you if you please. Phillipa, look after your mother, there's a good child. Coffee with a dash of brandy. Where are those damn maids? Come on, Guy.'

Alone with Guy, he said they'd have to send for the police.

'The police!' Guy's dark face turned very pale. 'Why? What's it got to do with them?'

'Nothing, as like as not, but they'll have to be notified. I can't give a certificate as things are. If it's electrocution, how did it happen?'

'But the police!' said Guy. 'That's simply ghastly. Dr Meadows, for God's sake couldn't you –?'

'No,' said Dr Meadows, 'I couldn't. Sorry, Guy, but there it is.'

'But can't we wait a moment? Look at him again. You haven't examined him properly.'

'I don't want to move him, that's why. Pull yourself together, boy. Look here. I've got a pal in the CID – Alleyn. He's a gentleman and all that. He'll curse me like a fury, but he'll come if he's in London, and he'll make things easier for you. Go back to your mother. I'll ring Alleyn up.'

That was how it came about that Chief Detective-Inspector Roderick Alleyn spent his Christmas Day in harness. As a matter of fact he was on duty, and as he pointed out to Dr Meadows, would have had to turn out and visit his miserable Tonkses in any case. When he did arrive it was with his usual air of remote courtesy. He was accompanied by a tall, thickset officer – Inspector Fox – and by the divisional police surgeon. Dr Meadows took them into the study. Alleyn, in his turn, looked at the horror that had been Septimus.

'Was he like this when he was found?'

'No. I understand he was leaning forward with his hands on the ledge of the cabinet. He must have slumped forward and been propped up by the chair arms and the cabinet.'

'Who moved him?'

'Chase, the butler. He said he only meant to raise the arm. *Rigor* is well established.'

Alleyn put his hand behind the rigid neck and pushed. The body fell forward into its original position.

'There you are, Curtis,' said Alleyn to the divisional surgeon. He turned to Fox. 'Get the camera man, will you, Fox?'

The photographer took four shots and departed. Alleyn marked the position of the hands and feet with chalk, made a careful plan of the room and then turned to the doctors.

'Is it electrocution, do you think?'

'Looks like it,' said Curtis. 'Have to be a p.m. of course.'

'Of course. Still, look at the hands. Burns. Thumb and two fingers bunched together and exactly the distance between the two knobs apart. He'd been tuning his hurdy-gurdy.'

'By gum,' said Inspector Fox, speaking for the first time.

'D'you mean he got a lethal shock from his radio?' asked Dr Meadows.

'I don't know. I merely conclude he had his hands on the knobs when he died.'

'It was still going when the housemaid found him. Chase turned it off and got no shock.'

'Yours, partner,' said Alleyn, turning to Fox. Fox stooped down to the wall switch. 'Careful,' said Alleyn.

'I've got rubber soles,' said Fox, and switched it on. The radio hummed, gathered volume, and found itself.

'No-oel, No-o-el,' it roared. Fox cut it off and pulled out the wall plug.

'I'd like to have a look inside this set,' he said.

'So you shall, old boy, so you shall,' rejoined Alleyn. 'Before you begin, I think we'd better move the body. Will you see to that, Meadows? Fox, get Bailey, will you? He's out in the car.'

Curtis, Hislop, and Meadows carried Septimus Tonks into a spare downstairs room. It was a difficult and horrible business with that contorted body. Dr Meadows came back alone, mopping his brow, to find Detective-Sergeant Bailey, a fingerprint expert, at work on the wireless cabinet.

'What's all this?' asked Dr Meadows. 'Do you want to find out if he'd been fooling round with the innards?'

'He,' said Alleyn, 'or – somebody else.'

'Umph!' Dr Meadows looked at the Inspector. 'You agree with me, it seems. Do you suspect –?'

'Suspect? I'm the least suspicious man alive. I'm merely being tidy. Well, Bailey?'

'I've got a good one off the chair arm. That'll be the deceased's, won't it, sir?'

'No doubt. We'll check up later. What about the wireless?'

Fox, wearing a glove, pulled off the knob of the volume control.

'Seems to be OK,' said Bailey. 'It's a sweet bit of work. Not too bad at all, sir.' He turned his torch into the back of the radio, undid a couple of screws underneath the set, and lifted out the works.

'What's the little hole for?' asked Alleyn.

'What's that, sir?' said Fox.

'There's a hole bored through the panel above the knob. About an eighth of an inch in diameter. The rim of the knob hides it. One might easily miss it. Move your torch, Bailey. Yes. There, do you see?'

Fox bent down and uttered a bass growl. A fine needle of light came through the front of the radio.

'That's peculiar, sir,' said Bailey from the other side. 'I don't get the idea at all.'

Alleyn pulled out the tuning knob.

'There's another one there,' he murmured. 'Yes. Nice clean little holes. Newly bored. Unusual, I take it?'

'Unusual's the word, sir,' said Fox.

'Run away, Meadows,' said Alleyn.

'Why the devil?' asked Dr Meadows indignantly. 'What are you driving at? Why shouldn't I be here?'

'You ought to be with the sorrowing relatives. Where's your corpse-side manner?'

'I've settled them. What are you up to?'

'Who's being suspicious now?' asked Alleyn mildly. 'You may stay for a moment. Tell me about the Tonkses. Who are they? What are they? What sort of a man was Septimus?'

'If you must know, he was a damned unpleasant sort of a man.'

'Tell me about him.'

Dr Meadows sat down and lit a cigarette.

'He was a self-made bloke,' he said, 'as hard as nails and – well, coarse rather than vulgar.'

'Like Dr Johnson perhaps?'

'Not in the least. Don't interrupt. I've known him for twenty five years. His wife was a neighbour of ours in Dorset. Isabel Foreston. I brought the children into this vale of tears and, by jove, in many ways it's been one for them. It's an extraordinary household. For the last ten years Isabel's condition has been the sort that sends these psycho jokers dizzy with rapture. I'm only an out of date GP, and I'd just say she is in an advanced stage of hysterical neurosis. Frightened into fits of her husband.'

'I can't understand these holes,' grumbled Fox to Bailey.

'Go on, Meadows,' said Alleyn.

'I tackled Sep about her eighteen months ago. Told him the trouble was in her mind. He eyed me with a sort of grin on his face and said: "I'm surprised to learn that my wife has enough mentality to –"'

But look here, Alleyn, I can't talk about my patients like this. What the devil am I thinking about.'

'You know perfectly well it'll go no further unless – '

'Unless what?'

'Unless it has to. Do go on.'

But Dr Meadows hurriedly withdrew behind his professional rectitude. All he would say was that Mr Tonks had suffered from high blood pressure and a weak heart, that Guy was in his father's city office, that Arthur had wanted to study art and had been told to read for law, and that Phillipa wanted to go on the stage and had been told to do nothing of the sort.

'Bullied his children,' commented Alleyn.

'Find out for yourself. I'm off.' Dr Meadows got as far as the door and came back.

'Look here,' he said, 'I'll tell you one thing. There was a row here last night. I'd asked Hislop, who's a sensible little beggar, to let me know if anything happened to upset Mrs Sep. Upset her badly, you know. To be indiscreet again, I said he'd better let me know if Sep cut up rough because Isabel and the young had had about as much of that as they could stand. He was drinking pretty heavily. Hislop rang me up at ten twenty last night to say there'd been a hell of a row; Sep bullying Phips – Phillipa, you know; always call her Phips – in her room. He said Isabel – Mrs Sep – had gone to bed. I'd had a big day and I didn't want to turn out. I told him to ring again in half an hour if things hadn't quieted down. I told him to keep out of Sep's way and stay in his own room, which is next to Phips', and see if she was all right when Sep cleared out. Hislop was involved. I won't tell you how. The servants were all out. I said that if I didn't hear from him in half an hour I'd ring again and if there was no answer I'd know they were all in bed and quiet. I did ring, got no answer, and went to bed myself. That's all. I'm off. Curtis knows where to find me. You'll want me for the inquest, I suppose. Goodbye.'

When he had gone Alleyn embarked on a systematic prowl round the room. Fox and Bailey were still deeply engrossed with the wireless.

'I don't see how the gentleman could have got a bump-off from the instrument,' grumbled Fox. 'These control knobs are quite in order. Everything's as it should be. Look here, sir.'

He turned on the wall switch and tuned in. There was a pro-
longed humming.

' . . . concludes the programme of Christmas carols,' said the
radio.

'A very nice tone,' said Fox approvingly.

'Here's something, sir,' announced Bailey suddenly.

'Found the sawdust, have you?' said Alleyn.

'Got it in one,' said the startled Bailey.

Alleyn peered into the instrument, using the torch. He scooped
up two tiny traces of sawdust from under the holes.

'Vantage number one,' said Alleyn. He bent down to the wall
plug. 'Hullo! A two-way adapter. Serves the radio and the radiator.
Thought they were illegal. This is a rum business. Let's have another look at those knobs.'

He had his look. They were the usual wireless fitments, bakelite
knobs fitting snugly to the steel shafts that projected from the front
panel.

'As you say,' he murmured, 'quite in order. Wait a bit.' He produced a pocket lens and squinted at one of the shafts. 'Ye-es. Do they
ever wrap blotting paper round these objects, Fox?'

'Blotting paper!' ejaculated Fox. 'They do not.'

Alleyn scraped at both the shafts with his penknife, holding an
envelope underneath. He rose, groaning, and crossed to the desk. 'A
corner torn off the bottom bit of blotch,' he said presently. 'No prints
on the wireless, I think you said, Bailey?'

'That's right,' agreed Bailey morosely.

'There'll be none, or too many, on the blotter, but try, Bailey, try,'
said Alleyn. He wandered about the room, his eyes on the floor; got
as far as the window and stopped.

'Fox!' he said. 'A clue. A very palpable clue.'

'What is it?' asked Fox.

'The odd wisp of blotting paper, no less.' Alleyn's gaze travelled
up the side of the window curtain. 'Can I believe my eyes?'

He got a chair, stood on the seat, and with his gloved hand pulled
the buttons from the ends of the curtain rod.

'Look at this.' He turned to the radio, detached the control
knobs, and laid them beside the ones he had removed from the curtain rod.

Ten minutes later Inspector Fox knocked on the drawing-room door and was admitted by Guy Tonks. Phillipa had got the fire going and the family was gathered round it. They looked as though they had not moved or spoken to one another for a long time.

It was Phillipa who spoke first to Fox. 'Do you want one of us?' she asked.

'If you please, miss,' said Fox. 'Inspector Alleyn would like to see Mr Guy Tonks for a moment, if convenient.'

'I'll come,' said Guy, and led the way to the study. At the door he paused. 'Is he – my father – still –?'

'No, no, sir,' said Fox comfortably. 'It's all ship-shape in there again.'

With a lift of his chin Guy opened the door and went in, followed by Fox. Alleyn was alone, seated at the desk. He rose to his feet.

'You want to speak to me?' asked Guy.

'Yes, if I may. This has all been a great shock to you, of course. Won't you sit down?'

Guy sat in the chair farthest away from the radio.

'What killed my father? Was it a stroke?'

'The doctors are not quite certain. There will have to be a post-mortem.'

'Good God! And an inquest?'

'I'm afraid so.'

'Horrible!' said Guy violently. 'What do they think was the matter? Why the devil do these quacks have to be so mysterious? What killed him?'

'They think an electric shock.'

'How did it happen?'

'We don't know. It looks as if he got it from the wireless.'

'Surely that's impossible. I thought they were foolproof.'

'I believe they are, if left to themselves.'

For a second undoubtedly Guy was startled. Then a look of relief came into his eyes. He seemed to relax all over.

'Of course,' he said, 'he was always monkeying about with it. What had he done?'

'Nothing.'

'But you said – if it killed him he must have done something to it.'

'If anyone interfered with the set it was put right afterwards.'

Guy's lips parted but he did not speak. He had gone very white.

'So you see,' said Alleyn, 'that your father could not have done anything.'

'Then it was not the radio that killed him.'

'That we hope will be determined by the postmortem.'

'I don't know anything about wireless,' said Guy suddenly. 'I don't understand. This doesn't seem to make sense. Nobody ever touched the thing except my father. He was most particular about it. Nobody went near the wireless.'

'I see. He was an enthusiast?'

'Yes, it was his only enthusiasm except – except his business.'

'One of my men is a bit of an expert,' Alleyn said. 'He says this is a remarkably good set. You are not an expert, you say. Is there anyone in the house who is?'

'My young brother was interested at one time. He's given it up. My father wouldn't allow another radio in the house.'

'Perhaps he may be able to suggest something.'

'But if the thing's all right now – '

'We've got to explore every possibility.'

'You speak as if – as – if – '

'I speak as I am bound to speak before there has been an inquest,' said Alleyn. 'Had anyone a grudge against your father, Mr Tonks?'

Up went Guy's chin again. He looked Alleyn squarely in the eyes.

'Almost everyone who knew him,' said Guy.

'Is that an exaggeration?'

'No. You think he was murdered, don't you?'

Alleyn suddenly pointed to the desk beside him.

'Have you ever seen those before?' he asked abruptly. Guy stared at two black knobs that lay side by side on an ashtray.

'Those?' he said. 'No. What are they?'

'I believe they are the agents of your father's death.'

The study door opened and Arthur Tonks came in.

'Guy,' he said, 'what's happening? We can't stay cooped up together all day. I can't stand it. For God's sake, what happened to him?'

'They think those things killed him,' said Guy.

'Those?' For a split second Arthur's glance slewed to the curtain rods. Then, with a characteristic flicker of his eyelids, he looked away again.

'What do you mean?' he asked Alleyn.

'Will you try one of those knobs on the shaft of the volume control?'

'But,' said Arthur, 'they're metal.'

'It's disconnected,' said Alleyn.

Arthur picked one of the knobs from the tray, turned to the radio, and fitted the knob over one of the exposed shafts.

'It's too loose,' he said quickly, 'it would fall off.'

'Not if it was packed – with blotting paper, for instance.'

'Where did you find these things?' demanded Arthur.

'I think you recognized them, didn't you? I saw you glance at the curtain rod.'

'Of course I recognized them. I did a portrait of Phillipa against those curtains when – he – was away last year. I've painted the damn things.'

'Look here,' interrupted Guy, 'exactly what are you driving at, Mr Alleyn? If you mean to suggest that my brother – '

'I!' cried Arthur. 'What's it got to do with me? Why should you suppose – '

'I found traces of blotting paper on the shafts and inside the metal knobs,' said Alleyn. 'It suggested a substitution of the metal knobs for the bakelite ones. It is remarkable, don't you think, that they should so closely resemble one another? If you examine them, of course, you find they are not identical. Still, the difference is scarcely perceptible.'

Arthur did not answer this. He was still looking at the wireless.

'I've always wanted to have a look at this set,' he said surprisingly.

'You are free to do so now,' said Alleyn politely. 'We have finished with it for the time being.'

'Look here,' said Arthur suddenly, 'suppose metal knobs were substituted for bakelite ones, it couldn't kill him. He wouldn't get a shock at all. Both the controls are grounded.'

'Have you noticed those very small holes drilled through the panel?' asked Alleyn. 'Should they be there, do you think?'

Arthur peered at the little steel shafts. 'By God, he's right, Guy,' he said. 'That's how it was done.'

'Inspector Fox,' said Alleyn, 'tells me those holes could be used for conducting wires and that a lead could be taken from the – the transformer, is it? – to one of the knobs.'

'And the other connected to earth,' said Fox. 'It's a job for an expert. He could get three hundred volts or so that way.'

'That's not good enough,' said Arthur quickly; 'there wouldn't be enough current to do any damage – only a few hundredths of an amp.'

'I'm not an expert,' said Alleyn, 'but I'm sure you're right. Why were the holes drilled then? Do you imagine someone wanted to play a practical joke on your father?'

'A practical joke? On *him*?' Arthur gave an unpleasant screech of laughter. 'Do you hear that, Guy?'

'Shut up,' said Guy. 'After all, he is dead.'

'It seems almost too good to be true, doesn't it?'

'Don't be a bloody fool, Arthur. Pull yourself together. Can't you see what this means? They think he's been murdered.'

'Murdered! They're wrong. None of us had the nerve for that, Mr Inspector. Look at me. My hands are so shaky they told me I'd never be able to paint. That dates from when I was a kid and he shut me up in the cellars for a night. Look at me. Look at Guy. He's not so vulnerable, but he caved in like the rest of us. We were conditioned to surrender. Do you know – '

'Wait a moment,' said Alleyn quietly. 'Your brother is quite right, you know. You'd better think before you speak. This may be a case of homicide.'

'Thank you, sir,' said Guy quickly. 'That's extraordinarily decent of you. Arthur's a bit above himself. It's a shock.'

'The relief, you mean,' said Arthur. 'Don't be such an ass. I didn't kill him and they'll find it out soon enough. Nobody killed him. There must be some explanation.'

'I suggest that you listen to me,' said Alleyn. 'I'm going to put several questions to both of you. You need not answer them, but it will be more sensible to do so. I understand no one but your father touched this radio. Did any of you ever come into this room while it was in use?'

'Not unless he wanted to vary the programme with a little bullying,' said Arthur.

Alleyn turned to Guy, who was glaring at his brother.

'I want to know exactly what happened in this house last night. As far as the doctors can tell us, your father died not less than three and not more than eight hours before he was found. We must try to fix the time as accurately as possible.'

'I saw him at about a quarter to nine,' began Guy slowly. 'I was going out to a supper party at the Savoy and had come downstairs. He was crossing the hall from the drawing room to his room.'

'Did you see him after a quarter to nine, Mr Arthur?'

'No. I heard him, though. He was working in here with Hislop. Hislop had asked to go away for Christmas. Quite enough. My father discovered some urgent correspondence. Really, Guy, you know, he was pathological. I'm sure Dr Meadows thinks so.'

'When did you hear him?' asked Alleyn.

'Some time after Guy had gone. I was working on a drawing in my room upstairs. It's above his. I heard him bawling at little Hislop. It must have been before ten o'clock, because I went out to a studio party at ten. I heard him bawling as I crossed the hall.'

'And when,' said Alleyn, 'did you both return?'

'I came home at about twenty past twelve,' said Guy immediately. 'I can fix the time because we had gone on to Chez Carlo, and they had a midnight stunt there. We left immediately afterwards. I came home in a taxi. The radio was on full blast.'

'You heard no voices?'

'None. Just the wireless.'

'And you, Mr Arthur?'

'Lord knows when I got in. After one. The house was in darkness. Not a sound.'

'You had your own key?'

'Yes,' said Guy. 'Each of us has one. They're always left on a hook in the lobby. When I came in I noticed Arthur's was gone.'

'What about the others? How did you know it was his?'

'Mother hasn't got one and Phips lost hers weeks ago. Anyway, I knew they were staying in and that it must be Arthur who was out.'

'Thank you,' said Arthur ironically.

'You didn't look in the study when you came in,' Alleyn asked him.

'Good Lord, no,' said Arthur as if the suggestion was fantastic. 'I say,' he said suddenly, 'I suppose he was sitting here – dead. That's a queer thought.' He laughed nervously. 'Just sitting here, behind the door in the dark.'

'How do you know it was in the dark?'

'What d'you mean? Of course it was. There was no light under the door.'

'I see. Now do you two mind joining your mother again? Perhaps your sister will be kind enough to come in here for a moment. Fox ask her, will you?'

Fox returned to the drawing room with Guy and Arthur and remained there, blandly unconscious of any embarrassment his presence might cause the Tonkses. Bailey was already there, ostensibly examining the electric points.

Phillipa went to the study at once. Her first remark was characteristic. 'Can I be of any help?' asked Phillipa.

'It's extremely nice of you to put it like that,' said Alleyn. 'I don't want to worry you for long. I'm sure this discovery has been a shock to you.'

'Probably,' said Phillipa. Alleyn glanced quickly at her. 'I mean,' she explained, 'that I suppose I must be shocked but I can't feel anything much. I just want to get it all over as soon as possible. And then think. Please tell me what has happened.'

Alleyn told her they believed her father had been electrocuted and that the circumstances were unusual and puzzling. He said nothing to suggest that the police suspected murder.

'I don't think I'll be much help,' said Phillipa, 'but go ahead.'

'I want to try to discover who was the last person to see your father or speak to him.'

'I should think very likely I was,' said Phillipa composedly. 'I had a row with him before I went to bed.'

'What about?'

'I don't see that it matters.'

Alleyn considered this. When he spoke again it was with deliberation.

'Look here,' he said, 'I think there is very little doubt that your father was killed by an electric shock from his wireless set. As far as I know the circumstances are unique. Radios are normally incapable of giving a lethal shock to anyone. We have examined the cabinet and are inclined to think that its internal arrangements were disturbed last night. Very radically disturbed. Your father may have experimented with it. If anything happened to interrupt or upset him, it is possible that in the excitement of the moment he made some dangerous readjustment.'

'You don't believe that, do you?' asked Phillipa calmly.

'Since you ask me,' said Alleyn, 'no.'

'I see,' said Phillipa; 'you think he was murdered, but you're not sure.' She had gone very white, but she spoke crisply. 'Naturally you want to find out about my row.'

'About everything that happened last evening,' amended Alleyn.

'What happened was this,' said Phillipa; 'I came into the hall some time after ten. I'd heard Arthur go out and had looked at the clock at five past. I ran into my father's secretary, Richard Hislop. He turned aside, but not before I saw . . . not quickly enough. I blurted out: "You're crying." We looked at each other. I asked him why he stood it. None of the other secretaries could. He said he had to. He's a widower with two children. There have been doctor's bills and things. I needn't tell you about his . . . about his damnable servitude to my father nor about the refinements of cruelty he'd had to put up with. I think my father was mad, really mad, I mean. Richard gabbled it all out to me higgledy-piggledy in a sort of horrified whisper. He's been here two years, but I'd never realized until that moment that we . . . that . . .' A faint flush came into her cheeks. 'He's such a funny little man. Not at all the sort I've always thought . . . not good-looking or exciting or anything.'

She stopped, looking bewildered.

'Yes?' said Alleyn.

'Well, you see – I suddenly realized I was in love with him. He realized it too. He said: "Of course, it's quite hopeless, you know. Us, I mean. Laughable, almost." Then I put my arms round his neck and kissed him. It was very odd, but it seemed quite natural. The point is my father came out of this room into the hall and saw us.'

'That was bad luck,' said Alleyn.

'Yes, it was. My father really seemed delighted. He almost licked his lips. Richard's efficiency had irritated my father for a long time. It was difficult to find excuses for being beastly to him. Now, of course . . . He ordered Richard to the study and me to my room. He followed me upstairs. Richard tried to come too, but I asked him not to. My father . . . I needn't tell you what he said. He put the worst possible construction on what he'd seen. He was absolutely foul, screaming at me like a madman. He was insane. Perhaps it was DTs. He drank terribly, you know. I dare say it's silly of me to tell you all this.'

'No,' said Alleyn.

'I can't feel anything at all. Not even relief. The boys are frankly relieved. I can't feel afraid either.' She stared meditatively at Alleyn. 'Innocent people needn't feel afraid, need they?'

'It's an axiom of police investigation,' said Alleyn and wondered if indeed she was innocent.

'It just *can't* be murder,' said Phillipa. 'We were all too much afraid to kill him. I believe he'd win even if you murdered him. He'd hit back somehow.' She put her hands to her eyes. 'I'm all muddled,' she said.

'I think you are more upset than you realize. I'll be as quick as I can. Your father made this scene in your room. You say he screamed. Did anyone hear him?'

'Yes. Mummy did. She came in.'

'What happened?'

'I said: "Go away, darling, it's all right." I didn't want her to be involved. He nearly killed her with the things he did. Sometimes he'd . . . we never knew what happened between them. It was all secret, like a door shutting quietly as you walk along a passage.'

'Did she go away?'

'Not at once. He told her he'd found out that Richard and I were lovers. He said . . . it doesn't matter. I don't want to tell you. She was terrified. He was stabbing at her in some way I couldn't understand. Then, quite suddenly, he told her to go to her own room. She went at once and he followed her. He locked me in. That's the last I saw of him, but I heard him go downstairs later.'

'Were you locked in all night?'

'No. Richard Hislop's room is next to mine. He came up and spoke through the wall to me. He wanted to unlock the door, but I said better not in case – he – came back. Then, much later, Guy came home. As he passed my door I tapped on it. The key was in the lock and he turned it.'

'Did you tell him what had happened?'

'Just that there'd been a row. He only stayed a moment.'

'Can you hear the radio from your room?'

DEATH ON THE AIR

She seemed surprised.

'The wireless? Why, yes. Faintly.'

'Did you hear it after your father returned to the study?'

'I don't remember.'

'Think. While you lay awake all that long time until your brother came home?'

'I'll try. When he came out and found Richard and me, it was not going. They had been working, you see. No, I can't remember hearing it at all unless – wait a moment. Yes. After he had gone back to the study from mother's room I remember there was a loud crash of static. Very loud. Then I think it was quiet for some time. I fancy I heard it again later. Oh, I've remembered something else. After the static my bedside radiator went out. I suppose there was something wrong with the electric supply. That would account for both, wouldn't it? The heater went on again about ten minutes later.'

'And did the radio begin again then, do you think?'

'I don't know. I'm very vague about that. It started again sometime before I went to sleep.'

'Thank you very much indeed. I won't bother you any longer now.'

'All right,' said Phillipa calmly, and went away.

Alleyn sent for Chase and questioned him about the rest of the staff and about the discovery of the body. Emily was summoned and dealt with. When she departed, awe-struck but complacent, Alleyn turned to the butler.

'Chase,' he said, 'had your master any peculiar habits?'

'Yes, sir.'

'In regard to his use of the wireless?'

'I beg your pardon, sir. I thought you meant generally speaking.'

'Well, then, generally speaking.'

'If I may say so, sir, he was a mass of them.'

'How long have you been with him?'

'Two months, sir, and due to leave at the end of this week.'

'Oh. Why are you leaving?'

Chase produced the classic remark of his kind.

'There are some things,' he said, 'that flesh and blood will not stand, sir. One of them's being spoke to like Mr Tonks spoke to his staff.'

'Ah. His peculiar habits, in fact?'

'It's my opinion, sir, he was mad. Stark, staring.'

'With regard to the radio. Did he tinker with it?'

'I can't say I've ever noticed, sir. I believe he knew quite a lot about wireless.'

'When he tuned the thing, had he any particular method? Any characteristic attitude or gesture?'

'I don't think so, sir. I never noticed, and yet I've often come into the room when he was at it. I can seem to see him now, sir.'

'Yes, yes,' said Alleyn swiftly. 'That's what we want. A clear mental picture. How was it now? Like this?'

In a moment he was across the room and seated in Septimus's chair. He swung round to the cabinet and raised his right hand to the tuning control.

'Like this?'

'No, sir,' said Chase promptly, 'that's not him at all. Both hands it should be.'

'Ah.' Up went Alleyn's left hand to the volume control. 'More like this?'

'Yes, sir,' said Chase slowly. 'But there's something else and I can't recollect what it was. Something he was always doing. It's in the back of my head. You know, sir. Just on the edge of my memory, as you might say.'

'I know.'

'It's a kind – something – to do with irritation,' said Chase slowly.

'Irritation? His?'

'No. It's no good, sir. I can't get it.'

'Perhaps later. Now look here, Chase, what happened to all of you last night? All the servants, I mean.'

'We were all out, sir. It being Christmas Eve. The mistress sent for me yesterday morning. She said we could take the evening off as soon as I had taken in Mr Tonks' grog-tray at nine o'clock. So we went,' ended Chase simply.

'When?'

'The rest of the staff got away about nine. I left at ten past, sir, and returned about eleven twenty. The others were back then, and all in bed. I went straight to bed myself, sir.'

'You came in by a back door, I suppose?'

'Yes, sir. We've been talking it over. None of us noticed anything unusual.'

'Can you hear the wireless in your part of the house?'

'No, sir.'

'Well,' said Alleyn, looking up from his notes, 'that'll do, thank you.'

Before Chase reached the door Fox came in.

'Beg pardon, sir,' said Fox, 'I just want to take a look at the *Radio Times* on the desk.'

He bent over the paper, wetted a gigantic thumb, and turned a page.

'That's it, sir,' shouted Chase suddenly. 'That's what I tried to think of. That's what he was always doing.'

'But what?'

'Licking his fingers, sir. It was a habit,' said Chase. 'That's what he always did when he sat down to the radio. I heard Mr Hislop tell the doctor it nearly drove him demented, the way the master couldn't touch a thing without first licking his fingers.'

'Quite so,' said Alleyn. 'In about ten minutes, ask Mr Hislop if he will be good enough to come in for a moment. That will be all, thank you, Chase.'

'Well, sir,' remarked Fox when Chase had gone, 'if that's the case and what I think's right, it'd certainly make matters worse.'

'Good heavens, Fox, what an elaborate remark. What does it mean?'

'If metal knobs were substituted for bakelite ones and fine wires brought through those holes to make contact, then he'd get a bigger bump if he tuned in with *damp* fingers.'

'Yes. And he always used both hands. Fox!'

'Sir.'

'Approach the Tonkses again. You haven't left them alone, of course?'

'Bailey's in there making out he's interested in the light switches. He's found the main switchboard under the stairs. There's signs of a blown fuse having been fixed recently. In a cupboard underneath there are odd lengths of flex and so on. Same brand as this on the wireless and the heater.'

'Ah, yes. Could the cord from the adapter to the radiator be brought into play?'

'By gum,' said Fox, 'you're right! That's how it was done, Chief. The heavier flex was cut away from the radiator and shoved through. There was a fire, so he wouldn't want the radiator and wouldn't notice.'

'It might have been done that way, certainly, but there's little to prove it. Return to the bereaved Tonkses, my Fox, and ask prettily if any of them remember Septimus's peculiarities when tuning his wireless.'

Fox met little Mr Hislop at the door and left him alone with Alleyn. Phillipa had been right, reflected the Inspector, when she said Richard Hislop was not a noticeable man. He was nondescript. Grey eyes, drab hair; rather pale, rather short, rather insignificant; and yet last night there had flashed up between those two the realization of love. Romantic but rum, thought Alleyn.

'Do sit down,' he said. 'I want you, if you will, to tell me what happened between you and Mr Tonks last evening.'

'What happened?'

'Yes. You all dined at eight, I understand. Then you and Mr Tonks came in here?'

'Yes.'

'What did you do?'

'He dictated several letters.'

'Anything unusual take place?'

'Oh, no.'

'Why did you quarrel?'

'Quarrel!' The quiet voice jumped a tone. 'We did not quarrel, Mr Alleyn.'

'Perhaps that was the wrong word. What upset you?'

'Phillipa has told you?'

'Yes. She was wise to do so. What was the matter, Mr Hislop?'

'Apart from the . . . what she told you . . . Mr Tonks was a difficult man to please. I often irritated him. I did so last night.'

'In what way?'

'In almost every way. He shouted at me. I was startled and nervous, clumsy with papers, and making mistakes. I wasn't well. I blundered and then . . . I . . . I broke down. I have always irritated him. My very mannerisms – '

'Had he no irritating mannerisms, himself?'

'He! My God!'

'What were they?'

'I can't think of anything in particular. It doesn't matter does it?'

'Anything to do with the wireless, for instance?'

There was a short silence.

'No,' said Hislop.

'Was the radio on in here last night, after dinner?'

'For a little while. Not after – after the incident in the hall. At least, I don't think so. I don't remember.'

'What did you do after Miss Phillipa and her father had gone upstairs?'

'I followed and listened outside the door for a moment.' He had gone very white and had backed away from the desk.

'And then?'

'I heard someone coming. I remembered Dr Meadows had told me to ring him up if there was one of the scenes. I returned here and rang him up. He told me to go to my room and listen. If things got any worse I was to telephone again. Otherwise I was to stay in my room. It is next to hers.'

'And you did this?' He nodded. 'Could you hear what Mr Tonks said to her?'

'A – a good deal of it.'

'What did you hear?'

'He insulted her. Mrs Tonks was there. I was just thinking of ringing Dr Meadows up again when she and Mr Tonks came out and went along the passage. I stayed in my room.'

'You did not try to speak to Miss Phillipa?'

'We spoke through the wall. She asked me not to ring Dr Meadows, but to stay in my room. In a little while, perhaps it was as much as twenty minutes – I really don't know – I heard him come back and go downstairs. I again spoke to Phillipa. She implored me not to do anything and said that she herself would speak to Dr Meadows in the morning. So I waited a little longer and then went to bed.'

'And to sleep?'

'My God, no!'

'Did you hear the wireless again?'

'Yes. At least I heard static.'

'Are you an expert on wireless?'

'No. I know the ordinary things. Nothing much.'

'How did you come to take this job, Mr Hislop?'

'I answered an advertisement.'

'You are sure you don't remember any particular mannerism of Mr Tonks's in connection with the radio?'

'No.'

'Will you please ask Mrs Tonks if she will be kind enough to speak to me for a moment?'

'Certainly,' said Hislop, and went away.

Septimus's wife came in looking like death. Alleyn got her to sit down and asked her about her movements on the preceding evening. She said she was feeling unwell and dined in her room. She went to bed immediately afterwards. She heard Septimus yelling at Phillipa and went to Phillipa's room. Septimus accused Mr Hislop and her daughter of 'terrible things'. She got as far as this and then broke down quietly. Alleyn was very gentle with her. After a little while he learned that Septimus had gone to her room with her and had continued to speak of 'terrible things'.

'What sort of things?' asked Alleyn.

'He was not responsible,' said Isabel. 'He did not know what he was saying. I think he had been drinking.'

She thought he had remained with her for perhaps a quarter of an hour. Possibly longer. He left her abruptly and she heard him go along the passage, past Phillipa's door, and presumably downstairs. She had stayed awake for a long time. The wireless could not be heard from her room. Alleyn showed her the curtain knobs, but she seemed quite unable to take in their significance. He let her go, summoned Fox, and went over the whole case.

'What's your idea on the show?' he asked when he had finished.

'Well sir,' said Fox, in his stolid way, 'on the face of it the young gentlemen have got alibis. We'll have to check them up, of course, and I don't see we can go much further until we have done so.'

'For the moment,' said Alleyn, 'let us suppose Masters Guy and Arthur to be safely established behind cast-iron alibis. What then?'

'Then we've got the young lady, the old lady, the secretary, and the servants.'

'Let us parade them. But first let us go over the wireless game. You'll have to watch me here. I gather that the only way in which the radio could be fixed to give Mr Tonks his quietus is like this: Control knobs removed. Holes bored in front panel with fine drill. Metal knobs substituted and packed with blotting paper to insulate them from metal shafts and make them stay put. Heavier flex from adapter to radiator cut and the ends of the wires pushed through the drilled holes to make contact with the new knobs. Thus we have a positive and negative pole. Mr Tonks bridges the gap, gets a mighty wallop as the current passes through him to the earth. The switchboard fuse is blown almost immediately. All this is rigged by murderer while Sep was upstairs bullying wife and daughter. Sep revisited study some time after ten twenty. Whole thing was made ready between ten, when Arthur went out, and the time Sep returned – say, about ten forty five. The murderer reappeared, connected radiator with flex, removed wires, changed back knobs, and left the thing tuned in. Now I take it that the burst of static described by Phillipa and Hislop would be caused by the short-circuit that killed our Septimus?'

'That's right.'

'It also affected all the heaters in the house. *Vide* Miss Tonks's radiator.'

'Yes. He put all that right again. It would be a simple enough matter for anyone who knew how. He'd just have to fix the fuse on the main switchboard.'

'How long do you say it would take to – what's the horrible word? – to recondition the whole show?'

'M'm,' said Fox deeply. 'At a guess, sir, fifteen minutes. He'd have to be nippy.'

'Yes,' agreed Alleyn. 'He or she.'

'I don't see a female making a success of it,' grunted Fox. 'Look here, Chief, you know what I'm thinking. Why did Mr Hislop lie about deceased's habit of licking his thumbs? You say Hislop told you he remembered nothing and Chase says he overheard him saying the trick nearly drove him dippy.'

'Exactly,' said Alleyn. He was silent for so long that Fox felt moved to utter a discreet cough.

'Eh?' said Alleyn. 'Yes, Fox, yes. It'll have to be done.' He consulted the telephone directory and dialled a number.

'May I speak to Dr Meadows? Oh, it's you, is it? Do you remember Mr Hislop telling you that Septimus Tonks's trick of wetting his fingers nearly drove Hislop demented. Are you there? You don't? Sure? All right. All right. Hislop rang you up at ten twenty, you said? And you telephoned him? At eleven. Sure of the times? I see. I'd be glad if you'd come round. Can you? Well, do if you can.'

He hung up the receiver.

'Get Chase again, will you, Fox?'

Chase, recalled, was most insistent that Mr Hislop had spoken about it to Dr Meadows.

'It was when Mr Hislop had flu, sir. I went up with the doctor. Mr Hislop had a high temperature and was talking very excited. He kept on and on, saying the master had guessed his ways had driven him crazy and that the master kept on purposely to aggravate. He said if it went on much longer he'd . . . he didn't know what he was talking about, sir, really.'

'What did he say he'd do?'

'Well, sir, he said he'd – he'd do something desperate to the master. But it was only his rambling, sir. I daresay he wouldn't remember anything about it.'

'No,' said Alleyn, 'I daresay he wouldn't.' When Chase had gone he said to Fox: 'Go and find out about those boys and their alibis. See if they can put you on to a quick means of checking up. Get Master Guy to corroborate Miss Phillipa's statement that she was locked in her room.'

Fox had been gone for some time and Alleyn was still busy with his notes when the study door burst open and in came Dr Meadows.

'Look here, my giddy sleuth-hound,' he shouted, 'what's all this about Hislop? Who says he disliked Sep's abominable habits?'

'Chase does. And don't bawl at me like that. I'm worried.'

'So am I, blast you. What are you driving at? You can't imagine that . . . that poor little broken-down hack is capable of electrocuting anybody, let alone Sep?'

'I have no imagination,' said Alleyn wearily.

'I wish to God I hadn't called you in. If the wireless killed Sep, it was because he'd monkeyed with it.'

'And put it right after it had killed him?'

Dr Meadows stared at Alleyn in silence.

'Now,' said Alleyn, 'you've got to give me a straight answer, Meadows. Did Hislop, while he was semi-delirious, say that this habit of Tonks's made him feel like murdering him?'

'I'd forgotten Chase was there,' said Dr Meadows.

'Yes, you'd forgotten that.'

'But even if he did talk wildly, Alleyn, what of it? Damn it, you can't arrest a man on the strength of a remark made in delirium.'

'I don't propose to do so. Another motive has come to light.'

'You mean – Phips – last night?'

'Did he tell you about that?'

'She whispered something to me this morning. I'm very fond of Phips. My God, are you sure of your grounds?'

'Yes,' said Alleyn. 'I'm sorry. I think you'd better go, Meadows.'

'Are you going to arrest him?'

'I have to do my job.'

There was a long silence.

'Yes,' said Dr Meadows at last. 'You have to do your job. Goodbye, Alleyn.'

Fox returned to say that Guy and Arthur had never left their parties. He had got hold of two of their friends. Guy and Mrs Tonks confirmed the story of the locked door.

'It's a process of elimination,' said Fox. 'It must be the secretary. He fixed the radio while deceased was upstairs. He must have dodged back to whisper through the door to Miss Tonks. I suppose he waited somewhere down here until he heard deceased blow himself to blazes and then put everything straight again, leaving the radio turned on.' Alleyn was silent.

'What do we do now, sir?' asked Fox.

'I want to see the hook inside the front door where they hang their keys.'

Fox, looking dazed, followed his superior to the little entrance hall. 'Yes, there they are,' said Alleyn. He pointed to a hook with two latchkeys hanging from it. 'You could scarcely miss them. Come on, Fox.'

Back in the study they found Hislop with Bailey in attendance.

Hislop looked from one Yard man to another. 'I want to know if it's murder.'

'We think so,' said Alleyn.

'I want you to realize that Phillipa – Miss Tonks – was locked in her room all last night.'

'Until her brother came home and unlocked the door,' said Alleyn. 'That was too late. He was dead by then.'

'How do you know when he died?'

'It must have been when there was that crash of static'

'Mr Hislop,' said Alleyn, 'why would you not tell me how much that trick of licking his fingers exasperated you?'

'But – how do you know! I never told anyone.'

'You told Dr Meadows when you were ill.'

'I don't remember.' He stopped short. His lips trembled. Then, suddenly he began to speak.

'Very well. It's true. For two years he's tortured me. You see, he knew something about me. Two years ago when my wife was dying, I took money from the cash-box in that desk. I paid it back and thought he hadn't noticed. He knew all the time. From then on he had me where he wanted me. He used to sit there like a spider. I'd hand him a paper. He'd wet his thumbs with a clicking noise and a sort of complacent grimace. Click, click. Then he'd thumb the papers. He knew it drove me crazy. He'd look at me and then . . . click, click. And then he'd say something about the cash. He never quite accused me, just hinted. And I was impotent. You think I'm insane. I'm not. I could have murdered him. Often and often I've thought how I'd do it. Now you think I've done it. I haven't. There's the joke of it. I hadn't the pluck. And last night when Phillipa showed me she cared, it was like Heaven – unbelievable. For the first time since I've been here I *didn't* feel like killing him. And last night someone else *did*!'

He stood there trembling and vehement. Fox and Bailey, who had watched him with bewildered concern, turned to Alleyn. He was about to speak when Chase came in. 'A note for you, sir,' he said to Alleyn. 'It came by hand.'

Alleyn opened it and glanced at the first few words. He looked up.

'You may go, Mr Hislop. Now I've got what I expected – what I fished for.'

When Hislop had gone they read the letter.

Dear Alleyn,

Don't arrest Hislop. I did it. Let him go at once if you've arrested him and don't tell Phips you ever suspected him. I was in love with Isabel before she met Sep. I've tried to get her to divorce him, but she wouldn't because of the kids. Damned nonsense, but there's no time to discuss it now. I've got to be quick. He suspected us. He reduced her to a nervous wreck. I was afraid she'd go under altogether. I thought it all out. Some weeks ago I took Phips's key from the hook inside the front door. I had the tools and the flex and wire all ready. I knew where the main switchboard was and the cupboard. I meant to wait until they all went away at the New Year, but last night when Hislop rang me I made up my mind to act at once. He said the boys and servants were out and Phips locked in her room. I told him to stay in his room and to ring me up in half an hour if things hadn't quieted down. He didn't ring up. I did. No answer, so I knew Sep wasn't in his study.

I came round, let myself in, and listened. All quiet upstairs, but the lamp still on in the study, so I knew he would come down again. He'd said he wanted to get the midnight broadcast from somewhere.

I locked myself in and got to work. When Sep was away last year, Arthur did one of his modern monstrosities of paintings in the study. He talked about the knobs making good pattern. I noticed then that they were very like the ones on the radio and later on I tried one and saw that it would fit if I packed it up a bit. Well, I did the job just as you worked it out, and it only took twelve minutes. Then I went into the drawing room and waited.

He came down from Isabel's room and evidently went straight to the radio. I hadn't thought it would make such a row, and half expected someone would come down. No one came. I went back, switched off the wireless, mended the fuse in the main switchboard, using my torch. Then I put everything right in the study.

There was no particular hurry. No one would come in while he was there, and I got the radio going as soon as possible to suggest he was at it. I knew I'd be called in when they found him. My idea was to tell them he had died of a stroke. I'd been warning Isabel it might happen at any time. As soon as I saw the burned hand I knew that cat wouldn't jump. I'd have tried to get away with it if Chase hadn't gone round bleating about electrocution and burned fingers. Hislop saw the hand. I daren't do anything but report the case to the police, but I thought you'd never twig the knobs. One up to you.

I might have bluffed through if you hadn't suspected Hislop. Can't let you hang the blighter. I'm enclosing a note to Isabel, who won't forgive me, and an official one for you to use. You'll find me in my bedroom upstairs. I'm using cyanide. It's quick.

I'm sorry, Alleyn. I think you knew, didn't you? I've bungled the whole game, but if you will be a super-sleuth . . . Goodbye.

Henry Meadows